P9-DMA-616

ANNA
KARENINA

Leo Tolstoy

Anna Karenina

Introduction by Mona Simpson

Edited by Leonard J. Kent and Nina Berberova

THE CONSTANCE GARNETT TRANSLATION HAS BEEN
REVISED THROUGHOUT BY THE EDITORS

THE MODERN LIBRARY

NEW YORK

2000 Modern Library Paperback Edition

Biographical note copyright © 1994 by Random House, Inc.
Copyright © 1965, 1993 by Random House, Inc.
Introduction copyright © 2000 by Mona Simpson

All rights reserved under International and Pan-American Copyright Conventions.
Published in the United States by Random House, Inc., New York, and simultaneously
in Canada by Random House of Canada Limited, Toronto.

MODERN LIBRARY and colophon are registered trademarks of Random House, Inc.

LIBRARY OF CONGRESS CATALOGING-IN-PUBLICATION DATA
Tolstoy, Leo, graf, 1828–1910.
[Anna Karenina. English]
Anna Karenina/Leo Tolstoy; with an introduction by Mona Simpson; edited by
Leonard J. Kent and Nina Berberova.
p.   cm.
"The Constance Garnett translation has been revised throughout by the editors."
ISBN 0-679-78330-X (pbk.)
1. Russia—Social life and customs—1533–1917—Fiction. 2. Adultery—Russia—Fiction.
I. Kent, Leonard J., 1930–   II. Berberova, Nina Nikolaevna. III. Garnett, Constance
Black, 1862–1946. IV. Title.
PG3366.A6   2000
891.73´3—dc21   00-56640

Modern Library website address: www.modernlibrary.com

Printed in the United States of America

9

LEO TOLSTOY

Count Lev (Leo) Nikolayevich Tolstoy was born on August 28, 1828, at Yasnaya Polyana (Bright Glade), his family's estate located 130 miles southwest of Moscow. He was the fourth of five children born to Count Nikolay Ilyich Tolstoy and Marya Nikolayevna Tolstoya (née Princess Volkonskaya, who died when Tolstoy was barely two). He enjoyed a privileged childhood typical of his elevated social class (his patrician family was older and prouder than the tsar's). Early on, the boy showed a gift for languages as well as a fondness for literature—including fairy tales, the poems of Pushkin, and the Bible, especially the Old Testament story of Joseph. Orphaned at the age of nine by the death of his father, Tolstoy and his brothers and sister were first cared for by a devoutly religious aunt. When she died in 1841 the family went to live with their father's only surviving sister in the provincial city of Kazan. Tolstoy was educated by French and German tutors until he enrolled at Kazan University in 1844. There he studied law and Oriental languages and developed a keen interest in moral philosophy and the writings of Rousseau. A notably unsuccessful student who led a dissolute life, Tolstoy abandoned his studies in 1847 without earning a degree and returned to Yasnaya Polyana to claim the property (along with 350 serfs and their families) that was his birthright.

After several aimless years of debauchery and gambling in Moscow and St. Petersburg, Tolstoy journeyed to the Caucasus in 1851 to join his older brother Nikolay, an army lieutenant participating in the Caucasian campaign. The following year Tolstoy officially enlisted in the military, and in 1854 he became a commissioned officer in the artillery, serving first on the Danube and later in the Crimean War. Although his sexual escapades and profligate gambling during this period shocked even his fellow soldiers, it was while in the army that Tolstoy began his literary apprenticeship. Greatly influenced by the works of Charles Dickens, Tolstoy wrote *Childhood*, his first novel. Published pseudonymously in September 1852 in the *Contemporary*, a St. Petersburg journal, the book received highly favorable reviews—earning the praise of Turgenev—and overnight established Tolstoy as a major writer. Over the next years he contributed several novels and short stories (about military life) to the *Contemporary*—including *Boyhood* (1854), three *Sevastopol* stories (1855–1856), *Two Hussars* (1856), and *Youth* (1857).

In 1856 Tolstoy left the army and went to live in St. Petersburg, where he was much in demand in fashionable salons. He quickly discovered, however, that he disliked the life of a literary celebrity (he often quarreled with fellow writers, especially Turgenev) and soon departed on his first trip to western Europe. Upon returning to Russia, he produced the story "Three Deaths" and a short novel, *Family Happiness*, both published in 1859. Afterward, Tolstoy decided to abandon literature in favor of more "useful" pursuits. He retired to Yasnaya Polyana to manage his estate and established a school there for the education of children of his serfs. In 1860 he again traveled abroad in order to observe European (especially German) educational systems; he later published *Yasnaya Polyana*, a journal expounding his theories on pedagogy. The following year he was appointed an arbiter of the peace to settle disputes between newly emancipated serfs and their former masters. But in July 1862 the police raided the school at Yasnaya Polyana for evidence of subversive activity. The search elicited an indignant protest from Tolstoy directly to Alexander II, who officially exonerated him.

That same summer, at the age of thirty-four, Tolstoy fell in love with eighteen-year-old Sofya Andreyevna Bers, who was living with her parents on a nearby estate. (As a girl she had reverently memorized whole passages of *Childhood*.) The two were married on September 23, 1862, in a church inside the Kremlin walls. The early years of the marriage were largely joyful (thirteen children were born of the union) and coincided with the period of Tolstoy's great novels. In 1863 he not only published *The Cossacks*, but began work on *War and Peace*, his great epic novel that came out in 1869.

Then, on March 18, 1873, inspired by the opening of a fragmentary tale by Pushkin, Tolstoy started writing *Anna Karenina*. Originally titled *Two Marriages*, the book underwent multiple revisions and was serialized to great popular and critical acclaim between 1875 and 1877.

It was during the torment of writing *Anna Karenina* that Tolstoy experienced the spiritual crisis that recast the rest of his life. Haunted by the inevitability of death, he underwent a "conversion" to the ideals of human life and conduct that he found in the teachings of Christ. *A Confession* (1882), which was banned in Russia, marked this change in his life and works. Afterward, he became an extreme rationalist and moralist, and in a series of pamphlets published during his remaining years Tolstoy rejected both church and state, denounced private ownership of property, and advocated celibacy, even in marriage. In 1897 he even went so far as to renounce his own novels, as well as many other classics, including Shakespeare's *Hamlet* and Beethoven's Ninth Symphony, for being morally irresponsible, elitist, and corrupting. His teachings earned him numerous followers in Russia ("We have two tsars, Nicholas II and Leo Tolstoy," a journalist wrote) and abroad (most notably, Mahatma Gandhi) but also many opponents, and in 1902 he was excommunicated by the Russian holy synod. Prompted by Turgenev's deathbed entreaty ("My friend, return to literature!"), Tolstoy did produce several more short stories and novels—including the ongoing series *Stories for the People*, "The Death of Ivan Ilyich" (1886), *The Kreutzer Sonata* (1889), "Master and Man" (1895), *Resurrection* (1899), and *Hadji Murat* (published posthumously)—as well as a play, *The Power of Darkness* (1886).

Tolstoy's controversial views produced a great strain on his marriage, and his relationship with his wife deteriorated. "Until the day I die she will be a stone around my neck," he wrote. "I must learn not to drown with this stone around my neck." Finally, on the morning of October 28, 1910, Tolstoy fled by railroad from Yasnaya Polyana headed for a monastery in search of peace and solitude. However, illness forced Tolstoy off the train at Astapovo; he was given refuge in the stationmaster's house and died there on November 7. His body was buried two days later in a forest at Yasnaya Polyana.

CONTENTS

INTRODUCTION
MONA SIMPSON

Since *Anna Karenina* was published in 1877, almost everyone who matters in the history of literature has put in his two cents (and a few who stand out in other realms—from Matthew Arnold, who wrote a cogent essay in 1887 about "Count Tolstoy's" novel, to Lenin, who, while acknowledging his "first class works of world literature," refers to him as "a worn out sniveller who beat his breast and boasted to the world that he now lived on rice patties").

Dostoyevsky, a contemporary, declared *Anna Karenina* perfect "as an artistic production." Proust calls Tolstoy "a serene god." Comparing his work to that of Balzac, he said, "In Tolstoi everything is great by nature—the droppings of an elephant beside those of a goat. Those great harvest scenes in *Anna K.*, the hunting scenes, the skating scenes . . ." Flaubert just exclaims, "What an artist and what a psychologist!" Virginia Woolf declares him "greatest of all novelists. . . . He notices the blue or red of a child's frock . . . every twig, every feather sticks to his magnet."

A few cranks, of course, weigh in on the other side. Joseph Conrad wrote a complimentary letter to Constance Garnett's husband and mentioned, "of the thing itself I think but little," a crack Nabokov never forgave him. Turgenev said, "I don't like *Anna Karenina*, although there are some truly great pages in it (the races, the mowing, the hunting). But it's all sour, it reeks of Moscow, incense, old maids, Slavophilism, the nobility, etc. . . . The second part is trivial and boring." But Turgenev was by then an ex-friend and Tolstoy had once challenged him to a duel.

E. M. Forster said, "Great chords begin to sound, and we cannot say exactly what struck them. They do not arise from the story. . . . They do not come from the episodes nor yet from the characters. They come from the immense area of Russia. . . . Many novelists have the feeling for place . . . very few have the sense of space, and the possession of it ranks high in Tolstoy's divine equipment."

After finishing *Anna Karenina*, Tolstoy himself said (*to* himself, in his journal), "Very well, you will be more famous than Gogol or Pushkin or Shakespeare or Molière, or than all the writers of the world—and what of it?"

More great essays than I can recount here have been written about the book, especially those by George Steiner, Gary Saul Morson, Eduard Babev, and Raymond Williams.

Tolstoy criticism continues to thrive, and now includes its own home called the *Tolstoy Studies Journal*. Resorting to any library today, one can page through recent articles with titles like "Tolstoy on the Couch: Misogyny, Masochism, the Absent Mother," by Daniel Rancour-Lafarriere; "Passion in Competition: The Sporting Motif in *Anna Karenina*," by Howard Schwartz; "Food and the Adulterous Woman: Sexual and Social Morality in *Anna Karenina*," by Karin Horwatt; and even "Anna Karenina's Peter Pan Syndrome," by Vladimir Goldstein.

What's left, in the year 2000, for me to say?

Once, when I was a girl of eleven or twelve, sprawled on a sofa reading, an adult friend of the family noticed that I went through books quickly and suggested that every time I finished one, I enter the name of the author and title, publisher, the dates during which I read it, and what my impressions were on a three-by-five index card.

That kind of excellent habit is one we can easily imagine cultivated by the young Shcherbatsky princesses, when we first meet them "wrapped in a mysterious poetical veil." Levin wonders from afar, "Why it was the three young ladies had to speak French and English on alternate days; why it was that at certain hours they took turns playing the piano, the sounds of which were audible in their brother's room . . . why they were visited by those professors of French literature, of music, of drawing, of dancing; why at certain hours all three young ladies, and Mademoiselle Linon, drove in the coach to Tverskoy Boulevard, dressed in their satin cloaks, Dolly in a long one, Natalie in a shorter one, and Kitty in one so short that her shapely little legs in tight red stockings were exposed."

Of course, I was an American girl, not a Russian princess, and instead of foreign languages and piano tutors what I had was outside. From dawn to dusk, all summer, we ran to the woods, scavenging lumber, hauling boards, digging holes to build forts that were rarely completed; but we became muddy and tired.

I never followed the family friend's good advice.

Now I wish I had. A reason to keep a reading journal would be to compare the experience of the same book met at different ages. It could provide the deepest kind of diary. *Anna Karenina, War and Peace, In Search of Lost Time* and *Middlemarch* hold sway over a reader for weeks, months, a whole summer, and so we tend to remember our lives along with them, the way we would someone we'd roomed with for a period of months and then not seen again. I remember Tolstoy's novels personally—where I was when I first read them, for whom I was pining or from whom I was recovering. (For me, the novels were a bit long to read *in the throes*.)

Tolstoy himself kept just such a diary, his biographers tell us, a journal of "girls and reading. And remorse." He presented these journals, with all their literary impressions and squalid confessions, to his young fiancé, Sofia Behrs, as Levin does to Kitty in *Anna Karenina*.

In the novel, as in Tolstoy's life, the squalor got all the attention from the young bride to be. But for history, as it might have been for Tolstoy later in his life, his youthful writing about books proves to be not only more important but more *personal*.

Though I didn't keep a journal of reading, I did keep journals of "feelings," largely of boys whose names the black-bound volumes record. A list of those names no longer conjures the faces or characteristic gestures.

But I remember where I was the first time I read *Anna Karenina*. I was at Yaddo, a writers' colony in upstate New York, during the high season, and I felt distinctly outside the community's social world. Another young female writer arrived with, it seemed to me, a better wardrobe. I found myself checking what she was wearing at every meal. I hadn't considered that I was visiting a town that for more than 150 years had been a summer "watering hole." A small backpack held all my clothes for the summer. A pretty orchestra conductor with whom I jogged examined a pin-sized stain on my best white blouse. "I wouldn't wear it," she said.

I was twenty-four years old and, I'll admit it, I read the novel to learn about love. I was at the beginning of my life and I'd come from one of the unhappy families Tolstoy mentions. I was, in my own oblique way, writing about that circus in all its distinction. But I wanted my own life to be one of the happy ones and I felt at peace there, in my studio on the second story of an old wooden, formal house. I had the time to lie on my white bed with the pine fronds ticking the window and learn how.

I felt enchanted, as any girl might be, with the balls, the ice-skating parties, most especially with Kitty's European tour to recover from heartbreak. I identified with Anna and with Kitty, never for a second with Varenka, whose position might have actually been closest to my own.

In fact, I was young enough to remember a particular magazine I'd read while in a toy store as a child, no doubt published by the Mattel Corporation, that chronicled a holiday week in the life of a doll called Barbie. Like the characters in *Anna Karenina*, Barbie also went to an ice-skating party and wore a muff. Barbie also owned formal gowns. Barbie, too, sat to have her portrait painted.

I mention this not to call attention to the rather girlish and unsophisticated imagination I still had but rather to show how far into a child's fantasy Tolstoy ventures before then shocking us by rendering our heroine's aversion to touching her husband. And here I'm not talking only about Anna. He makes mention of Kitty's "revulsion" toward Levin as well.

I read—that first time—for the central characters, to see whom they married; to decide what was dangerous in a man, what fulfilling; what kind of love to hope for, to fear.

—

I didn't like Vronsky. Or I did, but I was afraid of him.

Vronsky says something at the beginning of the novel that the repeat reader will never forget. We meet him, in his first appearance, as Kitty's suitor, and already fear—as her mother will not quite let herself—that he will turn out to be a cad. The conversation in the parlor turns to table-rapping and spirits, and Countess Nordston, who believed in spiritualism, begins to describe the marvels she has seen.

Vronsky says, " '. . . for pity's sake, do take me to see them! I have never seen anything extraordinary, though I am always on the lookout for it everywhere.' " He says this in Kitty's living room, in her presence. Of course, he has not yet seen Anna.

That night, after flirting with Kitty, he goes straight home to his rented room and falls asleep early, musing, "That's why I like the Shcherbatskys', because I become better there."

His yearning for the extraordinary, the small account he gives to the peace-giving quality of the Shcherbatskys, tells his whole story, the way a prologue often announces the great Shakespearean themes. Kitty's father has never liked or trusted Vronsky, while her mother favors him, considering Levin only a "good" match, but Vronsky a "brilliant" one.

The dangers and glory of that kind of exceptionalism—in love—were for me, that first time, the subject of the novel.

That question of the viability of extraordinary and ordinary loves was even more riveting for me, at twenty-four, than the differences between happy and unhappy families. This dilemma, in fact—along with work and how to get by on little money in New York City—was the main thing my friends and I talked about. How X loves Y, but Y loves Z, but Z loves . . . all coming down to whether we would have great loves or have to "settle," as we put it.

Of course, we all want to have something extraordinary, in love. None of us, at twenty-four anyway, wants to settle or be settled for.

—

Part of what is touching, on a second reading, is Vronsky's first meeting with Anna. If you had asked me about that scene before I reread the book, I would have relied on convention and said that Vronsky met a beautiful woman at the train station. But on first seeing Anna—who will be for Vronsky *the* great love—Vronsky sees her full of life, but not necessarily exceptional. He glances at her once more "not because she was very beautiful" but because of an expression on her face of "something peculiarly . . . soft." Vronsky has not had an ordinary family life. He doesn't much remember his father, and his mother, now "a dried-up old lady," had been "a brilliant society woman, who had had during her married life, and especially afterward, many love affairs notorious in all society." Tolstoy makes it clear that Vronsky does not love or respect his mother.

Anna says, " 'The countess and I have been talking all the time, I of my son and she of hers.' "

Vronsky recognizes Anna first as a mother, a mother miserable to be away—for only a few days—from her beloved son. We might say that what seemed extraordinary for him was just the quality of ordinary maternal devotion his own mother never had.

And here we feel the tragic parallel. Anna is bound to become a woman like Vronsky's mother, notorious for her affair. Later on, her great concern will be that her son may lose respect for her.

Vronsky will wish for nothing more than to make his daughter legitimate and to marry Anna, in the usual way.

" 'My love keeps growing more passionate and selfish, while his is dying, and that's why we're drifting apart,' " Anna says, near the end. " 'He is everything to me, and I want him more and more to give himself up to me entirely. And he wants more and more to get away from me. . . . If I could be anything but a mistress, passionately caring for nothing but his caresses; but I can't and I don't care to be anything else. And by that desire I rouse aversion in him, and he rouses fury in me, and it cannot be different.' "

There, Anna is, I believe, talking about sex. But by then, Vronsky wants the precious ordinary: a marriage, a family—which is as unattainable for him as his heightened passion is for Kitty or Levin or Dolly or even Stiva.

———

During my first reading I was rooting for Vronsky to get Anna—even though, like her father, I didn't entirely trust him.

In the way that soldiers and sailors ashore roaming the streets look menacing when you are a child and innocent when you are older than they are, nothing now seems to me so unsympathetic about Vronsky's hope for a great, exceptional love. He's not a cad in the simple sense of the word. Or perhaps at a certain age one outgrows one's fear of cads. There seem to be worse things. And certainly, Tolstoy shows us Vronsky's attempts at honor. He first tells us that Vronsky never cried and then twice lets us see him weeping. First we hear the sound of tears in his voice, and then feel them on Anna's hands. There may be nothing so appealing to a young woman as a handsome man crying.

When he says "I didn't know" to Anna, after breaking her life, as he broke the back of his beloved horse Frou-Frou, I now believe him.

I rooted for Vronsky because, like Kitty, I preferred him to Levin, and wanted him to turn out to be good. I must have realized even then that, as much as Tolstoy split himself up among his characters the way fiction writers do, he gave a larger portion of himself to Levin, so I was, in effect, reading the book written by Levin.

Even Dolly and Levin, the characters in the book most entrenched and committed to stability, with all its dowdiness, have moments when they look to the sky and wonder if their lives could have been different. They are not immune to Vronsky's spell, either. Levin, meeting Anna living with Vronsky, finds her captivating; and Dolly, on her carriage ride to see Anna, thinks to herself, " 'Even to this day I don't feel sure I did right in listening to her at that terrible time when she came to me in Moscow. I ought then to have cast off my husband and have been loved the real way.' "

Part of what is so moving in this brief inner monologue is that we know just what Dolly's chances are for finding a different, greater love. But Tolstoy allows his characters' vanities, with the utmost respect and tact. His irony has the lightest possible touch. One never feels he is making fun of their most preposterous tender wishes. He allows Dolly to be the one to tell us that Kitty has lost her looks.

Kitty herself, when she believed she had the choice, picked Vronsky. But in her feelings toward him ". . . there always entered a certain element of awkwardness, though he was in the highest degree well bred and poised, as though there was some false note—not in Vronsky, he was very simple and nice, but in herself, while with Levin she felt perfectly at ease."

At twenty-four, I understood exactly what Kitty meant. There was a letter which had arrived on Yaddo's mail table for me, from a certain young man in New York. I'd rewritten my unsent reply five or six times already, convinced that it could not be me, regular me, first-draft me he would fall in love with.

Not everyone can *be* Vronsky. Levin also found Anna fascinating. But he could never have gotten her. Tolstoy all but tells us that anyone, given the choice, would elect to be Anna or Vronsky, rather than Kitty or Levin, but, thank god, luckily we couldn't (and neither could he). But we all tend to root, with a combination of thrill and dread, for Vronsky.

D. H. Lawrence said, "No one in the world is anything but delighted when Vronsky gets Anna Karenina." It is part of the strategy of the novel to engage the reader in the momentum and suspense of a chase. We see Anna at first resisting Vronsky and taking solace in the safety of virtue, spending the night at home with her son.

But as in *Lolita*, the story of resisting temptation is hardly a novel. We watch the magnetic attraction work its force on the characters, like the spectators at Vronsky's horse race, and then, already complicit for urging them on in order to fulfill our craving for narrative spectacle and romance, once the seduction is accomplished, we are left to live with them through the muck.

As the reviews of Tolstoy's time point out—several of them expressing gratitude that Tolstoy was not as prurient as Flaubert—the seduction happens between chapters. We see Anna after the event, described as a murdered corpse.

We are now far from the enchantment of balls and portraits. It happens suddenly, as it does in *Lolita*. We are jarred from our own sweet daydreams into the harshness of reality.

By the time Anna almost dies in childbirth and finds herself grateful to her husband again, I'd had enough of Vronsky and was ready to settle her back into her marriage. As a reader, I felt oddly as if *we* had been given a second chance. And, of course, Karenin had one of those Whartonesque rises in emotional stature. Now I was cheering for the marriage.

It is a rather chilling moment, then—I find myself shocked each time I read the scene—when Anna doesn't want to touch her husband's hand. One feels then what she has felt for some time—that there really is no viable choice.

———

I remember the grinding frustration of the book, the way the solution of the novel's two strands—the Anna-Vronsky thread and the

Kitty-Levin one—seemed to leave me—and not only Anna—with no viable romantic future.

My friend Allan Gurganus became impatient with my nagging question, "What's one to do?"

"It's not a self-help manual," he said.

And so what is left for those of us (including Tolstoy) who can't be Vronsky and Anna?

To a twenty-four-year-old, and even to someone now a generation older, the satisfactions of Kitty and Levin's life are decidedly "mixed." Tolstoy's description of Kitty and Levin's connection is hardly the Barbie version, leaving my twenty-four-year-old self wondering whether husbands always elicited a bit of revulsion. (Kitty was "bound" to Levin, we are told, with "a feeling of alternate attraction and repulsion, even less comprehended than the man himself. . . .")

Not a train I wanted to catch anytime soon.

Levin, like Gabriel in Joyce's *The Dead*, has his highest romantic moment not as the leading man but rather as the understudy, who understands and pities Kitty.

After she rejects him the first time, Levin sees her happy face gazing at Vronsky and hurries back to the country, where he lifts two thirty-six-pound dumbells "trying to restore his self-confidence."

Much later—after Kitty's restorative European tour—he tells himself, " 'I can't ask her to be my wife merely because she can't be the wife of the man she wanted to marry.' "

Then, during a dinner table conversation about the place and position of women in society, he senses Kitty's terror of becoming an old maid. He sees how humiliating that would be to her and he pities her. Rather than feeling insulted at being "settled for"—as my young friends and I would have put it—he, too, feels her terror and humiliation.

Tolstoy is a genius at rendering the feelings of new love—even the second time around, with Levin knowing that Kitty is marrying him partly just to be married—and page 460 is beautiful, reminiscent of the luminous writing in his novella whose title is alternately translated as "Family Happiness" and "A Happy Married Life."

Levin is in a state. But that kind of exalted happiness is always over just as it begins. "And what he saw then, he never saw again."

Soon they are bogged down with a conventional mother-in-law and details of linens, and Levin finds himself in the perennial position of the new husband, amazed that his Kitty could actually be interested in tablecloths.

Their married happiness seemed to be years ago and still seems both claustrophobic and childish. The scene in which they are both in the same room—her with her needlework, him trying to write the book about agriculture—is still enough to make my skin crawl. Only the servant announcing tea provides any sense of structure in their lives.

Tolstoy sees Kitty's vacancy of purpose as a kind of latency period, waiting for motherhood, which will be her life's work, but he repeatedly sounds the note of Levin's idleness. Levin says, " 'I do nothing, and I fret about it' " enough times that one feels there's some truth to it.

And Tolstoy describes the "revolution" taking place in Kitty's life, now that she's a married woman living with her husband rather than a girl living with her mother and father, as having more to do with her being able to order as many sweets as she likes and instruct the servants to make all manner of puddings than it does with sexuality.

We remember Anna's awakening and her craving for more and more caresses. What she wants is sex and what Kitty seems to be given instead is pudding.

But Tolstoy sees to it that Kitty and Levin get their moments of the extraordinary, in life's other passions, death and birth. ". . . that grief and this joy were alike beyond the ordinary conditions of life; they were openings, as it were, in that ordinary life through which there came glimpses of something sublime."

Even this time around, reading as a middle-aged married woman who has herself experienced the heightened hours of birth, looking out a hospital window and feeling the aggregate small cares of life fall away, I still think Kitty is a bit of a drip. Her obsession with sheets is too much, even for me. I can't help blaming her for how she speaks to her baby's nurse. The way she tells her husband about her sister Dolly's money troubles, practically forgetting, then remembering and pulling together a somber face, reveals a tacit, smug delight in her own security.

And of course, at twenty-four, reading about the raptures Kitty attained during the death of Levin's brother and the birth of Levin's child, I thought, yes, yes, but couldn't one achieve those same heights nursing Vronsky's brother or giving birth to Vronsky's child?

———

But apparently, according to Tolstoy, one could not.

Anna is not presented as a mother. The impression of maternity she gave Vronsky during their first meeting comes to feel, later on, like a false impression. Her maternity feels most stable during our first glimpse of her, when she is parted from Seryozha and longing for him, carrying his picture with her. That position—of distant, devoted longing—is her relation to her son throughout the book.

The only dramatized scene we are ever given between them is when she sneaks back into his bed one morning after she has been long gone. It's a wonderful scene. He has been told she died, but he never quite believed his father and Lydia Ivanovna. So his mother's return for him is a rising from the dead. (This is only one of the moments we see of Tolstoy using his work to give himself what life never could. His own mother died when he was barely two and no portrait of her survived. His father died when he was nine, and our biographers tell us that he, like Seryozha, wandered the streets afterward, seeing his father in every face. Incidentally, Tolstoy, like Anna, had a son named Seryozha.)

Tolstoy alludes to one other private scene between Anna and her son. This is the night when she feels virtuous staying home with Seryozha, after she returns from Moscow, having met Vronsky. (Vronsky had such a night when he went to bed early after the improving effect of visiting the Shcherbatskys.) But we're told, Anna did not go out "principally because the dress she had counted on was not ready."

Numerous times, Tolstoy refers not only to the Italian wet nurse of Annie, Anna's baby with Vronsky, but also to Seryozha's old wet nurse, and her continuing closeness to the boy. We are told Anna wanted to nurse Annie but wasn't able to (we presume she was too ill), and we surmise she didn't nurse Seryozha either. This is in contrast to the Shcherbatsky women, for whom nursing forms a central part of life and conversation. When Anna visits, late in the novel, the two sisters are "talking about nursing."

Anna is first unable to nurse, then unable to love Vronsky's child.

The sense of Anna as inadequately maternal accrues. When she is off in the country with Vronsky, we are told more than once that she is jealous of the pretty wet nurse, and we sense in her edginess that she is not only jealous over the woman's allure for Vronsky but also because of the baby's attachment to her.

" 'We had a great deal of trouble,' " she began telling Dolly, in a nervousness I now recognize, " 'over nurses. We had an Italian wet nurse. A good creature, but so stupid! We wanted to get rid of her, but the baby is so used to her that we've gone on keeping her on.' "

As a working mother, I sympathize with her, knowing, as she must, how a mother like Dolly will receive such a confession.

It is during this same visit that Anna confides in Dolly that she is willing and able to prevent pregnancy.

" 'I shall have no more children,' " Anna announces.

" 'How can you tell that you won't?' "

" 'I shall not because I don't wish it,' " Anna says. Anna rather enjoys shocking Dolly. But the reader doesn't hear the explanation she gives Dolly. She begins " 'The doctor told me after my illness . . .' " and Tolstoy leaves us, in the ellipsis, wondering if Anna is referring to birth control devices or of something more drastic.

The central idea, that Anna has opted out of maternity by not wishing for it—while for other women it is a part of nature, mysterious and unstoppable—makes Dolly all of a sudden understand all those families of one or two children. She, naturally, feels it is immoral.

This was a time when one was a mother to children dead and alive. Dolly is given one paragraph in the 923-page novel to remember her last little baby, who died of croup. How different the fact of losing a baby would be in a contemporary novel, now that infant mortality is so much rarer in the developed world?

Anna then goes on to equate pregnancy with being an invalid and makes a joke. " 'How am I to keep his love? Not like this?' " she says, pantomiming a large belly.

By this point in the book, Anna is openly vain, bragging to Dolly, of all people, that she inspires passion. She is often changing clothes, from one French import to another. She has also, incidentally, given over the running of the household to Vronsky. He is the one to glance at the butler to see that the dinner is served properly, to make his guests feel "that all that is well ordered in his house has cost him, the host, no trouble whatever. . . . Darya Aleksandrovna was well aware that even porridge for the children's breakfast does not come automatically. . . ."

Being at the stage of life at which I am acutely aware that even children's breakfasts do not come automatically, I definitely decided, at this point in the book, this reading, that Vronsky was not, whatever they say about him, my idea of a cad.

Anna's brother Stepan Arkadyevich, says of her that she is not " '*une couveuse*,' " a simple brooding hen. " 'No, she brings her [Annie] up very well, I believe, but one doesn't hear about her. She's busy, in the first place, with what she writes. I see you're smiling ironically, but you're wrong. She's writing a children's book, and doesn't talk about it to anyone, but she read it to me and I gave the manuscript to Vorkuyev . . . you know the publisher. . . . ' "

This time around, I had a greater sense of Anna as a maverick. In the country "Anna devoted just as much care to her appearance when they had no visitors," but she also "did a great deal of reading, both of novels and of what serious literature was in fashion."

—

With Tolstoy so focused on what these two very different loves produce, in terms of families, it is interesting to see what becomes of the children. We watch Dolly, despite her husband's profligacy, doing a good job rearing her children, and we have little doubt that they will become, as she hopes, " 'decent people.' "

We also watch Seryozha's settlement in life, his acceptance of Lydia Ivanovna, the closest thing the novel offers to a contemporary stepmother. Seryozha is a far cry from Emma Bovary's daughter. His end will not be tragic but interesting. Even motherless, he is still the rich young master. We see him reared, not only by a limited but concerned father but also by a number of people in the household, including his old wet nurse.

Children bridge the gap between the nobility and the servants in this world. They are part of the daily life of the house. Seryozha knows the porter's daughter is a ballet dancer.

One can't help but feel relieved, in the end, to learn that Karenin has adopted Annie. Despite Vronsky's vast wealth and luxuries, which include not only the charming Italian nurse but an imported wash machine, one feels she will be better off in Karenin's house.

Karenin and Levin, both orphans, as was Tolstoy himself, prove to be the novel's most viable fathers.

———

Reading *Anna Karenina* from the and-what-can-I-learn-to-improve-myself angle from which I approached most serious reading at twenty-four, I felt the women had a raw deal. While Tolstoy clearly pressed hard on the idea that a woman's work and fulfillment lay in motherhood, he clearly saw, as I did, the glamour of Anna in her Parisian dresses, reading international books and papers, or sitting on her horse. I somehow imagined her with a gun, riding along on one of those epic hunts. Reading the book over again, I see that the men have a rough time too. Levin and Vronsky—who don't exactly work—are constantly feeling they do nothing. Levin is fulfilled only when he's out mowing with his peasants, and even then he is haunted by the idea that he's unnecessary. Vronsky, once he's given up his army career and is living in the country, has a sense of long empty hours, which he tries to fill with local politics. He's using his wealth to build Russia's first (if we believe him) state-of-the-art hospital. "Sixteen hours of the day must be occupied in some way," we are told. The only character we're close to who really works is Karenin, and he needs work to escape life.

Anna Karenina was written as a contemporary novel, unlike *War and Peace*, and is generous with details, tossed about with the aplomb of a writer who knows he will be read a hundred years into the future. We hear that electric light is already everywhere in the cities, though new enough to be mentioned by the characters, while in the country, we see Levin's study slowly be lit by a candle. Railroads, far from being a nostalgic note, are new and controversial. (Levin is against them.) In Moscow, sleighs were more or less like taxis. (" 'A 'sleigh, sir?' 'Yes, a sleigh.' ")

As in Proust, we get a sense of the fashions. Kitty's mesh stockings and pink slippers with high curved heels would be familiar to any debutante today. Married couples bicker wearing squirrel-fur-lined robes. Vronsky wears a beaver coat and white cravat.

It's as if the characters look out through the bars and cages of history and talk to us.

———

One element of the book I glided right over the first time was the literal nobility of the characters. I suppose I must have noticed people addressing each other as Princess This or Count That, but I think I attributed it all to the quaint anachronism of an era before Ms. and the wide use of first names.

I was more aware of class in this reading. We can forget what nobility means until we see all the oglers even at the wedding of plain Levin. There is a *People* magazine element to the book. They're all royals, more or less like Diana and Prince William—or, for that matter, like movie stars.

One reads along for the particularity of the characters, and then, all of a sudden at Kitty and Levin's wedding, the church is filled with paparazzi, whose commentary Tolstoy shares with us.

A wedding, being essentially a party, affords Tolstoy an opportunity to use his agile omniscience, to skip around to various characters of different ages and classes, women of all stations remembering "the one day of their triumph." The marriage of Kitty and Levin, which I had considered so personally, so privately—whether Kitty would be able to love him, whether I would be, if he'd manage to propose—has a political dimension, too.

It is a shock to read that "In the church there was all Moscow." Imagine if that line, or the geographic equivalent, were written about the wedding of Dorothea Brooke and Mr. Casaubon or of Elizabeth Bennet and Mr. Darcy. A wedding that felt to us like a wedding inside our own family suddenly turns out to have the world watching.

(Tolstoy's family traced their descent to Prince Rurik and considered themselves grander than the Romanovs. The fact that Tolstoy got invitations to court functions did not go unnoticed among his literary friends. His biographer A. N. Wilson tells us that Turgenev yelled at a literary dinner, "Why bother to come here? Go off and see your princesses.")

It is in the details of class that we feel the deep reverberations of Tolstoy's characterizations, his tendency to split himself up between his characters. To Mikhailov, a self-educated Russian artist in Italy, Vronsky and Anna are people of "consequence." To them, he is the talented son of a butler. Though Tolstoy is of the class and background and cultural education of Vronsky, we have no doubt that to him it is the artist who is of consequence.

The interlude with Mikhailov ends in Vronsky's buying a beautiful painting. He must possess the exquisite. He can't make it. Early on in the novel, we're told "He looked at people as if they were things."

A close reading reveals many nuances of class. Apparently, many people reading the book wonder why it is that Anna married Karenin. (Several twentieth-century critics object to the omission of an explanation.) But the marriage is no real mystery. Anna was raised by a wealthy, provincial aunt. We can surmise that she herself had no family wealth from the fact that her brother Stepan, Dolly's husband, is always scrambling for positions and selling off his wife's inherited forests.

Karenin, though an orphan, was already a middle-aged governor at the time that Anna's aunt pushed her young niece on him. Anna married an older man of position, as young women had done for centuries before and continue to do now. When we meet her as Karenin's wife, she has the stature of a grande dame. We're also told that as a young bride she was awestruck by her husband's important friends.

———

In the early sections of the book, everyone seems rich. The young men seem to move freely in and out of the opulent Moscow and Petersburg restaurants and clubs. But later—it is sometimes hard to remember only four years pass in the book—they seem more middle-aged, middle class, scrambling for money. It's touching to see Levin's spending much more than he can on rented sleighs in the city during Kitty's confinement.

Read another way, Vronsky and Anna are living according to the values of youth well into middle age. While all of our characters cared a bit more about dresses at the outset, by the end of the book, most of them are living more frugal family lives.

The only one who turns out to be really rich is Vronsky. When we see him living in his conspicuously international dacha in the country with Anna and his illegitimate daughter, we understand the full force of meaning behind Princess Shcherbatsky's idea that he would have been a "brilliant" match for her daughter.

Vronsky re-creates Petersburg court life out in the sticks, but with no court. And their world—with its formal, perfect dinners and their ragtag collection of guests—has a feeling of all dressed up and nowhere to go, despite the European luxury Dolly "had read about in English novels, but had never seen in Russia. . . ."

Though we get a more nuanced sense of the real story that money plays in the main characters' lives as the novel goes on, we get very little detail about their support staff.

We see a household of "old house serfs who had stuck to their master" in the country, but we don't get any closer to them than that line. We somehow feel Seryozha's intimacy with servants in his own house, but we assume that will change as he becomes older. We're told that Levin talks a great deal to Agafya Mikhailovna, his housekeeper in the country (which was the name of Tolstoy's actual maid of Yasnaya Polyana), but we don't see her in anything near the same detail we see the noblewomen.

But Tolstoy doesn't hide all that is done for the characters by others. Even on their rustic hunt, when Levin and Stepan and their friend sleep in a barn, "coachmen" make up beds for them there.

" 'Why is it we spend our time riding, drinking, shooting, doing nothing,' " Levin's friend asks rather more rhetorically than not, " 'while they are forever at work?' "

It's only the Shcherbatsky women who make their own baby clothes and their own jam.

Yaddo, the artists colony where I was that summer, with all my leisure, reading Tolstoy, seemed to me to be run very much like a Russian dacha. Meals were served at set times; there was a huge, old-fashioned kitchen behind swinging doors. But of course there was a sloped gravel parking lot where the cooks and people who cleaned up parked their cars, during the days driving home at eight or eight-thirty, while it was still light.

I'm left to wonder, when Vronsky calls for his servant when he wants to get dressed, does the man simply bring freshly laundered and pressed clothes, as a valet would in a good hotel, or does he help his master step into his trousers? Is there a ritual of buttoning and fastening?

———

Raymond Williams—one of the better critics I found, reading about Tolstoy—complains that what most people remember of the book is the Anna-Vronsky-Karenin story, though it takes up less than half of the actual narrative. This may be more or less natural, but this time around, I found myself as or more riveted by the minor characters and their loves, attempts at family, and disappointments.

If we consider the famous opening line of the novel—probably as famous as "To be or not to be" and quoted by hundreds who haven't read the book—it applies to many more people than Dolly and Stepan or Vronsky and Anna.

We have the tiny set piece of Lydia Ivanovna's failed marriage and her later crush on Karenin. Lydia sends Karenin two to three letters a day. (Karenin, post Anna, is touching in his essential insecurity, as he notices a young man's strong calves and wonders if others love and marry differently.)

———

The novel opens with the disarray of the Oblonsky household when Dolly discovers her husband's affair with the governess. Stepan is in some ways the master of ceremonies, the reader's host in the novel, because he lives so easily in the world. Despite the shambles, he wakes, on his Morocco leather couch, in radiant health. His world is still intact and running (though we're not sure on what—the bills are mounting).

Through Stephen's vantage Tolstoy can easily assert his omniscience in conventional wisdom. "As is so often the case . . ." he says, or "like all fathers indeed . . ." and "characteristic of every secretary . . ." " 'Every girl's proud of a proposal.' "

" 'What can one do?' " Stepan Oblonsky says early on in the book. " 'The world's made like that.' "

Part of the way this world was made is that wives get older faster than their husbands. Stepan seems, by any measure, at the prime of life, whereas Dolly, at age thirty-three, is the mother of five living children (two have died), and her hair, once luxuriant and beautiful, is already scant.

If Stepan is ever serious about anything, it is about food. His job is never real to us. We are told his brother-in-law obtained the position for him, but he could have got his job "through a hundred other people—brothers, sisters, cousins, uncles, and aunts."

Stepan was good at what he did because of "his complete indifference to the business in which he was engaged, in consequence of which he was never carried away, and never made mistakes."

His view of marriage is as liberal as ours. Talking of his sister Anna, he says, " 'As soon as the divorce is over, she will marry Vronsky. How stupid that old ceremony is, walking round and round and singing *Rejoice, O Isaiah*! that no one believes in and that stands in the way of the happiness of people. . . . Well, then their situation will be as regular as mine, as yours.' "

Stepan, not Vronsky, ends up being the book's real villain.

Throughout, we never know quite how to read Stepan. Worldly, yet seemingly kind, his sins are always usually of omission. We watch him perform small acts of kindness, social decencies (here Tolstoy has learned his Dickens), while we see, as if unconnected, his wife and children in their broken-down country house—without milk, the cows hard uddered, and no place to bathe—or staying with Levin, who will support them. We see Stepan in town standing next to a snowy carriage with his wife and children. It's a bouyant scene until, just as he is leaving, she has to call him to beg for money for the children's coats. In the next scene he is bringing a ballet girl a coral necklace.

Our last vision of him is chilling. Profligate to the end, at a train station, perennially broke Stepan puts money in a collection box for the men leaving to fight in the Russo-Turkish war. " 'You don't say so!' he cried when the princess told him that Vronsky was going by this train. For an instant Stepan Arkadyevich's face looked sad, but a minute later, when smoothing his whiskers and with a spring in his walk, he went into the hall where Vronsky was, he had completely forgotten his own despairing sobs over his sister's corpse, and he saw in Vronsky only a hero and an old friend."

I've thought one of the scenes Tolstoy gave to Levin from his own life (the young bride to be reading his confessional diaries) should have been attributed to Stepan rather than Levin. It's hard to imagine Levin having had such a florid, promiscuous life. (Tolstoy himself had long affair with a married peasant on his property. He had a son with her, who grew up to be the coachman for one of his legitimate sons. This would have been unthinkable for Levin. One of his biographers pointed out that when Tolstoy fictionalized his own life, he often made himself not only better [morally] but also richer.)

—

The character whose story seemed most tragic to me that long summer ago was not even Anna. It was Varenka, the virtuous impoverished spinster.

I was struck and stunned by the fragility of her fate, the proposal that almost could have but did not happen.

This time the scene of the mushroom hunt read to me more lightly. Tolstoy's psychological acuity is everywhere felt. How it would have been better if she had been silent; his feeling annoyed at her small talk about the mushrooms and wanting to bring her back to the first words she'd uttered about her childhood; how, when they both felt the moment drain away without the words being said, Varenka felt both hurt and ashamed but also relieved.

This time I felt the tentative nature of their attraction. How he was pleased by her loneliness and potential dependency. How absurd it was that one nervous comment about mushrooms could throw him off, make him change course and not propose. The first time through I panicked: sure that I would make a similar blunder and cost myself my whole future.

The sad truth was, in the 1980s in America, I was, like Kitty, worried about becoming an old maid. Not yet, of course, not then. But I was already aware that in the distance there was a faint rumble that would materialize into a train: I would either be given a hand to step on board or not.

But, of course, a large part of what makes Varenka's story poignant is contained in her thought that "to be the wife of a man like Koznyshev, after her position with Madame Stahl, was to her imagination the height of happiness." Varenka needed Koznyshev to have a decent life, free of her patron. She did not inherit a sufficient fortune for independence and she didn't have the option, as I would, of working.

In the pages immediately following Anna's death, Tolstoy turns to another tragedy, though a smaller, quieter one, the death of Koznyshev's book, the fruit of six years work. So after turning his face away from love, in middle age, Koznyshev has another great disappointment.

Oddly, I still know a few "Varenkas" whom I met that summer at Yaddo, women artists who live in lofts in New York City, having never married, never had children.

That was what I was most afraid of becoming then. Now, those lives shimmer to me with a burnished beauty, because I've seen their work grow.

Anything loved so much, with a daily effort, grows.

———

While I was asking, "So what is there for those of us who can't be Vronsky and Anna?" and worrying about a young man back in New York City, I was answering the question myself, every day for six or seven hours.

Tolstoy himself, in contrast to the men he created who fretted so much about doing nothing, worked on *Anna Karenina* for five years.

What is there for those of us who can't be Vronsky and Anna?

The muck of life into old age and the book, the writing of the book.

EDITORS' NOTE

Some sixty years after Constance Garnett put *Anna Karenina* into English, her work remains, on balance, a singularly successful achievement; and for this reason the decision was made to use her translation as the basic text of this new edition. That she made errors and that her heritage dictated pruderies which occasionally mute some of Tolstoy is certain, but that her language and syntax almost always faithfully reproduce both the letter *and* the tone of the original is no less true; indeed, we remain as unconvinced as many others that her translation has ever been superseded. Some more recent translators sometimes alter the text to make it "clearer," omit what they feel is superfluous or redundant, "freshen up" the text to the point where nineteenth-century Russia becomes quite contemporary, and so on. In a sentence, too often, it seems to us, do they leave their own signatures behind.

The thousands of revisions made (some of which are extensive) are primarily concerned with correcting errors of translation, tightening the prose, converting Britishisms, and casting light on areas Mrs. Garnett did not explore.

To preserve the tone of the original, Russian names are given in full, and, as far as feasible, the transliterations have not involved American-English equivalents. Aleksey Aleksandrovich Karenin, for example, has therefore become neither "Alex" nor "Mr. Karenin," Matvey has not become "Matthew," and Agafya Mikhailovna has absolutely refused to become "Agatha." Money is referred to only in kopeks and rubles; where French and German expressions are used by Tolstoy, they are unaltered and translated in footnotes; and the author's inconsistencies and occasional "heavy-handedness" have been neither corrected nor "improved." Annotation designed primarily to meet the needs of the reader not intimately acquainted with Russia and things Russian, is provided, as is a chart of civil, military, and court ranks (see page xxviii).

It is our hope that this edition adds something to the pleasure of reading a great book.

L. J. K
N. B.

Nineteenth-Century Russian Civil, Military, and Court Ranks*

CIVIL RANKS	CORRESPONDING RANKS		
	ARMY	NAVY	COURT
1 Chancellor (of the Empire)	Commander in Chief	Admiral in Chief	. . . .
2 Actual Privy Councilor	General of Cavalry General of Infantry General of Artillery	Admiral	Chief Chamberlain Chief Marshal Chief Equerry Chief Huntsman Chief Steward Chief Cup-bearer Chief Master of Ceremonies** Chief Carver**
3 Privy Councilor	Lieutenant General	Vice Admiral	Marshal Equerry Huntsman Steward Chief Master of Ceremonies** Chief Carver**
4 Actual Councilor of State Attorney-general Master of Heraldry	Major General	Rear Admiral	Chamberlain (ranks 3, 4)
5 Councilor of State	. . . .	. . . .	Master of Ceremonies
6 Collegiate Councilor Military Councilor	Colonel	Captain (1st class)	Gentleman of the Bedchamber (ranks 5–8)
7 Court Councilor	Lieutenant Colonel	Captain (2nd class)	
8 Collegiate Assessor	Major (Captain or Cavalry Captain)	. . . .	
9 Titular Councilor	Staff Captain Staff Cavalry Captain	Lieutenant	. . . .
10 Collegiate Secretary	Lieutenant	Midshipman	
11 Naval Secretary	. . . .	. . . .	. . . .
12 County Secretary	2nd Lieutenant Cornet	. . . .	. . . .
13 Provincial Secretary Senate, Synod, & Cabinet Registrar	Ensign	. . . .	. . . .
14 Collegiate Registrar	. . . .	. . . .	

* According to Peter the Great's Table of Ranks, civilians held military titles which corresponded with the grade they had achieved in the civil service. Such titles were rarely used, except by those in the upper grades, the "generals."

** The titles of Chief Master of Ceremonies and Chief Carver could belong to persons of either the second or third class.

ANNA
KARENINA

"Vengeance is mine, I will repay."[1]

PART ONE

CHAPTER ONE

Happy families are all alike; every unhappy family is unhappy in its own way.[1]

Everything was in confusion in the Oblonsky household. The wife had discovered that the husband was carrying on an affair with their former French governess, and she had announced to her husband that she could not go on living in the same house with him. This situation had now lasted three days, and not only the husband and wife, but also all the members of their family and household, were painfully conscious of it. Every person in the house felt that there was no sense in their living together, and that people who met by chance in any inn had more in common with one another than they, the members of the Oblonsky family and household. The wife did not leave her own room; the husband had not been home for three days. The children ran wild all over the house; the English governess quarreled with the housekeeper, and wrote to a friend asking her to look out for a new position for her; the chef had walked out the day before just at dinnertime; the servant's cook and the coachman had given notice.

Three days after the quarrel, Prince Stepan Arkadyevich Oblonsky[2]—Stiva, as he was called in society—woke up at his usual hour,

---

[1] Romans 12:19. Variously interpreted, Tolstoy's words on this epigraph offer some light. He told Vikenty Smidovich (Russian novelist who wrote under the pseudonym Veresaev) that "I selected [it] simply to express the idea that the evil committed by man results in all bitter things that come from God and not from men, as Anna Karenina also experienced it . . ."

[2] The second of a Russian's three names is the patronymic, e.g., Stepan Arkadyevich Oblonsky and Anna Arkadyevna Karenina, brother and sister, carry the given name of their father, Arkady. The a ending is almost always feminine, except for masculine nicknames. Further, the profusion of titles in evidence has nothing to do with royalty, nor, indeed, anything necessarily to do with wealth. Russian nobility consisted primarily of landowners, some of whom inherited titles.

that is, at eight o'clock in the morning, not in his wife's bedroom, but on the morocco leather sofa in his study. He turned his plump, pampered body on the springy sofa, as though he would sink into a long sleep again; he vigorously embraced the pillow on the other side and buried his face in it; but all at once he jumped up, sat up on the sofa, and opened his eyes.

"Yes, yes, how was it, now?" he thought, going over his dream. "Now, how was it? To be sure! Alabin was giving a dinner at Darmstadt; no, not Darmstadt, but something American. Yes, but then, Darmstadt was in America. Yes, Alabin was giving a dinner on glass tables, and the tables sang *Il mio tesoro*—not *Il mio tesoro*, though, but something better, and there were some sort of little decanters on the table, and they were women, too," he remembered.

Stepan Arkadyevich's eyes twinkled gaily, and he pondered with a smile. "Yes, it was nice, very nice. There was a great deal more that was delightful, only there's no putting it into words, or even expressing it in one's thoughts once awake." And noticing a gleam of light peeping in beside one of the wool curtains, he cheerfully dropped his feet over the edge of the sofa and felt about for his slippers, a present on his last birthday, embroidered for him by his wife on goldcolored morocco. And, as he had done every day for the last nine years, he stretched out his hand, without getting up, toward the place where his dressing gown always hung in his bedroom. And thereupon he suddenly remembered that he was not sleeping in his wife's room but in his study, and why: the smile vanished from his face; he knitted his brows.

"Ah, ah, ah! Oo! . . ." he groaned, recalling everything that had happened. And as he recalled every detail of his quarrel with his wife, he realized the hopelessness of his situation, and, most tormenting thought of all, that it was his own fault.

"Yes, she won't forgive me; she can't forgive me. And the most awful thing about it is that it's all my fault—all my fault, though I'm not to blame. That's the point of the whole situation," he reflected. "Oh, oh, oh!" he kept repeating in despair, as he remembered the acutely painful sensations caused him by this quarrel.

Most unpleasant of all was the first minute when, on coming, happy and good-humored, from the theater, with a huge pear in his hand for his wife, he had not found his wife in the drawing room, to his surprise had not found her in the study either, and saw her at last in her bedroom, holding the unfortunate letter that revealed everything.

She, his Dolly, forever fussing and worrying, whom he considered rather simple, was sitting perfectly still with the letter in her hand, looking at him with an expression of horror, despair, and indignation.

"What's this? This?" she asked, pointing to the letter.

And at this recollection, Stepan Arkadyevich, as is so often the case, was not so much annoyed at the fact itself as at the way in which he had reacted to his wife's words.

There happened to him at that instant what happens to people when they are unexpectedly caught in something very disgraceful. He did not succeed in assuming an expression suitable to the position in which he was placed by his wife's discovery of his guilt. Instead of acting hurt, denying, defending himself, begging forgiveness, instead of remaining indifferent, (anything would have been better than what he did do), his face utterly involuntarily (reflex action of the brain, reflected Stepan Arkadyevich, who was fond of physiology) —utterly involuntarily assumed its habitual, good-humored, and therefore foolish smile.

This foolish smile he could not forgive himself. Catching sight of that smile, Dolly shuddered as though in physical pain, broke out with her characteristic passion into a flood of cruel words, and rushed out of the room. Since then she had refused to see her husband.

"It's that idiotic smile that's to blame for it all," thought Stepan Arkadyevich.

"But what's to be done? What's to be done?" he said to himself in despair, and found no answer.

CHAPTER TWO

Stepan Arkadyevich was a truthful man with himself. He was incapable of deceiving himself and persuading himself that he repented of his conduct. He could not at this date feel repentant that he, a handsome, women-prone man of thirty-four, was not in love with his wife, the mother of five living and two dead children, and only a year younger than himself. All he was sorry about was that he had not succeeded better in hiding it from his wife. But he felt the seriousness of his position and was sorry for his wife, his children, and himself. Possibly he might have managed to conceal his sins better from his wife if he had anticipated the effect on her should she discover them. He had never clearly thought out the subject, but he had vaguely conceived that his wife must long ago have suspected him of being unfaithful to her, and shut her eyes to the fact. He had even supposed that she, a worn-out woman no longer young or good-looking, and in no way remarkable or interesting, merely a good mother, ought from a sense of fairness to take an indulgent view. It had turned out quite the other way.

"Oh, it's awful! Oh dear, oh dear! Awful!" Stepan Arkadyevich kept repeating to himself, and he could think of no way out. "And how well things were going up till now! How well we got along! She was contented and happy in her children; I never interfered with her in anything; I let her manage the children and the house just as she liked. It's true it's bad *her* having been a governess in our house. That's bad! There's something common, vulgar, in making love to one's governess. But what a governess!" (He vividly recalled Mlle Roland's mischievous black eyes, and her smile.) "But after all, while she was in the house I never took liberties. And the worst of it all is that she's already . . . it seems as if it all happened for spite! Oh, oh! But what, what is to be done?"

There was no solution but that usual solution which life gives to all questions, even the most complex and insoluble. That answer is: one must live in the needs of the day—that is, forget oneself. To forget himself in sleep was impossible now, at least till nighttime; he could not go back now to the music sung by the decanter women; so he must forget himself in the dream of daily life.

"Then we shall see," Stepan Arkadyevich said to himself, and getting up, he put on a gray dressing gown lined with blue silk, tied the tassels in a knot, and, drawing a deep breath of air into his broad chest, walked to the window with his usual confident step, his feet turned out slightly. He pulled up the blind and rang the bell loudly.

It was at once answered by the appearance of an old friend, his valet, Matvey, carrying his clothes, his boots, and a telegram. Matvey was followed by the barber with all the tools for shaving.

"Are there any papers from the office?" asked Stepan Arkadyevich, taking the telegram and seating himself at the mirror.

"On the table," replied Matvey, glancing sympathetically at his master; and, after a short pause, he added with a sly smile, "They've sent from the livery stable."

Stepan Arkadyevich made no reply; he merely glanced at Matvey in the mirror. In the glance, in which their eyes met in the mirror, it was clear that they understood one another. Stepan Arkadyevich's eyes asked: "Why do you tell me that? Don't you know?"

Matvey put his hands in his jacket pockets, kicked out one leg, and gazed silently, good-humoredly, with a faint smile, at his master.

"I told them to come on Sunday, and till then not to trouble you or themselves for nothing," he said. He had obviously prepared the sentence beforehand.

Stepan Arkadyevich saw that Matvey intended to make a joke and attract attention to himself. Tearing open the telegram, he read it through, guessing at the words, misspelled as they always are in telegrams, and his face brightened.

"Matvey, my sister Anna Arkadyevna will be here tomorrow," he said, checking for a minute the sleek, plump hand of the barber cutting a pink path through his long, curly whiskers.

"Thank God!" said Matvey, showing by this response that he, like his master, realized the significance of this arrival—that is, that Anna Arkadyevna, the sister he was so fond of, might bring about a reconciliation between husband and wife.

"Alone, or with her husband?" inquired Matvey.

Stepan Arkadyevich could not answer, as the barber was at work on his upper lip, and he raised one finger. Matvey nodded at the mirror.

"Alone. Is the room to be made ready upstairs?"

"Inform Darya Aleksandrovna; let her decide."

"Darya Aleksandrovna?" Matvey repeated, as though in doubt.

"Yes, inform her. Here, take the telegram; give it to her, and then do what she tells you."

"You want to see what happens," Matvey thought, but he only said, "Yes, sir."

Stepan Arkadyevich was already washed and combed and ready to be dressed, when Matvey, stepping deliberately in his creaky boots, came back into the room with the telegram in his hand. The barber had gone.

"Darya Aleksandrovna told me to inform you that she is going away. Let him do—that is, you—as he likes," he said, laughing only with his eyes, and putting his hands in his pockets, he watched his master with his head on one side. Stepan Arkadyevich was silent a minute. Then a kind and rather pathetic smile showed itself on his handsome face.

"Eh, Matvey?" he said, shaking his head.

"It's all right, sir; it will work out," said Matvey.

"Work out?"

"Yes, sir."

"Do you think so? Who's there?" asked Stepan Arkadyevich, hearing the rustle of a woman's dress at the door.

"It's me," said a woman's firm, pleasant voice, and the stern, pock-marked face of Matryona Filimonovna, the nurse, was thrust in at the doorway.

"Well, what is it, Matryona?" asked Stepan Arkadyevich, walking up to her.

Although Stepan Arkadyevich was completely in the wrong as regards his wife, and was conscious of this himself, almost everyone in the house (even the nurse, Darya Aleksandrovna's chief ally) was on his side.

"Well, what now?" he asked dejectedly.

"Go to her, sir; admit your guilt again. Maybe God will aid you. She is suffering so, it is sad to see her; and besides, everything in the house is topsy-turvy. You must have pity, sir, on the children. Beg her forgiveness, sir. There's no other way! One must take the consequences . . ."

"But she won't see me."

"You do your part. God is merciful; pray to God, sir, pray to God."

"Come, that'll do, you can go," said Stepan Arkadyevich, blushing suddenly. "Well now, dress me." He turned to Matvey and threw off his dressing gown decisively.

Matvey was already holding up the shirt like a horse's collar, and, blowing off some invisible speck, he slipped it with obvious pleasure over the well-groomed body of his master.

CHAPTER THREE

When he was dressed, Stepan Arkadyevich sprayed some eau de Cologne on himself, pulled down his cuffs, distributed into his pockets his cigarettes, wallet, matches, and watch with its double chain and seals, and shaking out his handkerchief, feeling himself clean, fragrant, healthy, and physically at ease, in spite of his unhappiness, he walked with a slight spring in each step into the dining room, where coffee was already waiting for him, and letters and papers from the office too.

He read the letters. One was very unpleasant, from a merchant who was buying a forest on his wife's property. To sell this forest was absolutely essential; but at present, until he was reconciled with his wife, the subject could not be discussed. The most unpleasant thing of all was that his pecuniary interests should in this way enter into the question of his reconciliation with his wife. And the idea that he might be influenced by self-interest, that he might seek a reconciliation with his wife on account of the sale of the forest—that idea hurt him.

When he had finished his letters, Stepan Arkadyevich took his office papers, rapidly looked through two pieces of business, made a few notes with a big pencil, and, pushing away the papers, turned to his coffee. As he sipped his coffee, he opened a still damp morning paper[1] and began reading it.

Stepan Arkadyevich took and read a liberal paper, not an extreme one, but one advocating the views held by the majority. And in spite of the fact that science, art, and politics had no special interest for him, he firmly held those views on all these subjects which were held by the majority and by his paper, and changed them only when the

---

[1] I.e., a paper on which the ink had not yet dried.

majority changed them—or, more strictly speaking, they seemed to change of themselves within him.

Stepan Arkadyevich had not chosen his political opinions or his views; these political opinions and views had come to him of themselves, just as he did not choose the shapes of his hat and coat, but simply took those that were in style. And for him, living in a certain social environment, where a desire for some sort of mental activity was part of maturity, to hold views was just as indispensable as to have a hat. If there was a reason for his preferring liberal to conservative views, which were held also by many of his circle, it arose not from his considering liberalism more rational, but from its being in closer accordance with his manner of life. The liberal party said that in Russia everything is wrong, and certainly Stepan Arkadyevich had many debts and was decidedly short of money. The liberal party said that marriage is an institution quite out of date, and that it needs reconstruction; and family life certainly afforded Stepan Arkadyevich little gratification, and forced him into lying and hypocrisy, which were so repulsive to his nature. The liberal party said, or rather allowed it to be understood, that religion is only a curb to keep in check the barbarous classes of the people; and Stepan Arkadyevich could not get through even a short service without his legs aching from standing up, and could never make out what was the object of all the terrible and high-flown language about another world when life might be so very amusing in this world. And with all this, Stepan Arkadyevich, who liked a joke, was fond of perplexing a simple man by saying that if he prided himself on his origin, he ought not to stop at Rurik[2] and disown the first founder of his family—the monkey. And so liberalism had become a habit of Stepan Arkadyevich's, and he liked his newspaper, as he did his cigar after dinner, for the slight fog it diffused in his brain. He read the leading article, in which it was maintained that it was quite senseless in our day to raise an outcry that radicalism was threatening to swallow up all conservative elements, and that the government ought to take measures to crush the revolutionary hydra;

---

[2] (d. 879), the reputed founder of Russia. Allegedly he led a band of Varangians (Scandinavian merchant-warriors who penetrated Russia in the ninth century) who settled in Novgorod in 862. His heirs ruled till 1598.

that, on the contrary, "in our opinion the danger lies not in that fantastic revolutionary hydra, but in the obstinacy of traditionalism clogging progress," etc., etc. He read another article, too, a financial one, which alluded to Bentham and Mill[3] and dropped some innuendoes reflecting on the government. With his characteristic quick-wittedness he caught the drift of each innuendo, divined whence it came, at whom, and on what ground it was aimed, and that afforded him, as it always did, a certain satisfaction. But today that satisfaction was embittered by Matryona Filimonovna's advice and the unsatisfactory state of the household. He read, too, that Count Beist was rumored to have left for Wiesbaden, and that one need have no more gray hair, and of the sale of a light carriage, and of a young person seeking a situation; but these items of information did not give him, as usual, a quiet, ironical gratification. Having finished the paper, a second cup of coffee, and a roll and butter, he got up, shaking the crumbs of the roll off his waistcoat, and, squaring his broad chest, he smiled joyously: not because he was thinking of anything particularly agreeable; the joyous smile was evoked by good digestion.

But this joyous smile at once reminded him of everything, and he grew thoughtful.

Two childish voices (Stepan Arkadyevich recognized the voices of Grisha, his youngest boy, and Tanya, his eldest daughter) were heard outside the door. They were carrying something, and dropped it.

"I told you not to put passengers on the roof," said the little girl in English. "Now pick them up!"

"Everything's in confusion," thought Stepan Arkadyevich. "Here the children are, running wild." And going to the door, he called them. They threw down the box, which served as a train, and came to their father.

The little girl, her father's favorite, ran up boldly, embraced him, and hung laughingly on his neck, enjoying as she always did the scent that came from his whiskers. At last the little girl kissed his face, which was flushed from his stooping posture and beaming with ten-

---

[3] Jeremy Bentham (1748-1832), English writer on law and utilitarian ethics; and John Stuart Mill (1806-73), English philosopher and radical reformer who became leader of Benthamite movement and a foremost proponent of utilitarian thought.

derness, loosened her hands, and was about to run away again; but her father held her back.

"How is Mama?" he asked, passing his hand over his daughter's smooth, soft little neck. "Good morning," he said, smiling to the boy, who had come up to greet him. He was conscious that he loved the boy less, and always tried to be fair; but the boy felt it, and did not respond with a smile to his father's cold smile.

"Mama? She is up," answered the girl.

Stepan Arkadyevich sighed, "That means that she hasn't slept again all night," he thought.

"Well, is she cheerful?"

The little girl knew that there was a quarrel between her father and mother, and that her mother could not be cheerful, and that her father must be aware of this, and that he was pretending when he asked about it so lightly. And she blushed for her father. He at once perceived it, and blushed too.

"I don't know," she said. "She did not say we must do our lessons, but she said we were to go for a walk with Miss Hull to Grandmama's."

"Well, go, Tanya, my darling. Oh, wait a minute," he said, detaining her and stroking her soft little hand.

He took a little box of candy from the mantelpiece, where he had put it yesterday, and gave her two, picking out her favorites, a chocolate and a fondant.

"For Grisha?" said the little girl, pointing to the chocolate.

"Yes, yes." And still stroking her little shoulder, he kissed her at the roots of her hair and the nape of her neck and let her go.

"The carriage is ready," said Matvey; "but there's some woman to see you with a petition."

"Been here long?" asked Stepan Arkadyevich.

"Half an hour."

"How many times have I told you to tell me at once?"

"One must let you drink your coffee in peace, at least," said Matvey, in the affectionately gruff tone with which it was impossible to be angry.

"Well, show the person up at once," said Oblonsky, frowning with vexation.

The petitioner, the widow of a staff captain named Kalinin, came with a request impossible and unreasonable; but Stepan Arkadyevich, as he generally did, made her sit down, heard her to the end attentively without interrupting her, and gave her detailed advice as to how and to whom to apply, and even wrote her, in his large, sprawling, attractive, and legible hand, a confident and fluent little note to a person who might be of use to her. Having got rid of the staff captain's widow, Stepan Arkadyevich took his hat and stopped to recollect whether he had forgotten anything. It appeared that he had forgotten nothing except what he wanted to forget—his wife.

"Ah, yes!" He bowed his head, and his handsome face assumed a harassed expression. "To go, or not to go!" he said to himself; and an inner voice told him he must not go, that nothing could come of it but hypocrisy; that to amend, to set right their relations was impossible, because it was impossible to make her attractive again and able to inspire love, or to make him an old man, not susceptible to love. Only deceit and lying could come of it now; and deceit and lying were contrary to his nature.

"It must be done sooner or later; it can't go on like this," he said, trying to give himself courage. He squared his chest, took out a cigarette, took a few puffs, flung it into a mother-of-pearl ash tray, and, with rapid steps, walked through the gloomy drawing room and opened the other door into his wife's bedroom.

CHAPTER FOUR

Darya Aleksandrovna, in a bed jacket, and with her now scanty, once luxuriant and beautiful hair fastened up with hairpins on the nape of her neck, with a sunken, thin face and large, startled eyes, which looked prominent because of the thinness of her face, was standing amidst litter of all sorts of things scattered all over the room, before an open bureau, from which she was taking something. Hearing her husband's steps, she stopped, looking toward the door, and trying, in vain, to give her features a severe and contemptuous expression. She felt that she was afraid of him, and dreaded the coming interview. She was just trying to do what she had tried to do ten times already in these last three days—to sort out the children's things and her own so as to take them to her mother's—and again she could not bring herself to do it; for, as each time before, she kept saying to herself that things could not go on like this, that she must take some step to punish him, put him to shame, pay him back at least for some little part of the suffering he had caused her. She still continued to tell herself that she should leave him, but she was conscious that this was impossible; it was impossible because she could not get out of the habit of regarding him as her husband and loving him. Besides this, she realized that if even here in her own house she could hardly manage to look after her five children properly, they would be still worse off where she was going with them all. As it was, even in the course of these three days, the youngest was sick from being given spoiled soup, and the others had almost gone without their dinner the day before. She was conscious that it was impossible to go away; but, deceiving herself, she went on all the same, sorting her things and pretending she was going.

Seeing her husband, she reached her hands into the bureau drawer as though looking for something, and looked around at him only when he had come close to her. But her face, to which she tried to give a severe and determined expression, betrayed bewilderment and suffering.

"Dolly!" he said in a subdued and timid voice. He drew his head into his shoulders and tried to look pitiful and humble, but he was radiant with freshness and health. In a rapid glance she scanned his figure that glowed with health and freshness. "Yes, he is happy and content!" she thought, "while I . . . And that disgusting good nature, which everyone likes him for and praises—I hate that good nature of his." Her mouth stiffened, the muscles of the cheek contracted on the right side of her pale, nervous face.

"What do you want?" she said in a rapid, deep, unnatural voice.

"Dolly!" he repeated, with a quiver in his voice. "Anna is coming today."

"Well, what is that to me? I can't see her!" she cried.

"But you must, really, Dolly . . ."

"Go away, go away, go away!" she shrieked, not looking at him, as though this shriek were called up by physical pain.

Stepan Arkadyevich could be calm when he thought of his wife, he could hope that things would *work out*, as Matvey expressed it, and he could quietly go on reading his paper and drinking his coffee; but when he saw her tortured, suffering face, heard the tone of her voice, submissive to fate and full of despair, there was a catch in his breath and a lump in his throat, and his eyes began to glisten with tears.

"My God! What have I done? Dolly! For God's sake! . . . You know . . ." He could not go on; there was a sob in his throat.

She shut the bureau with a slam, and glanced at him.

"Dolly, what can I say? . . . One thing: forgive . . . Remember, cannot nine years of my life atone for an instant . . ."

She lowered her eyes and listened, expecting what he would say, as though beseeching him in some way or other to make her believe differently.

"—instant of passion? . . ." he said, and would have gone on, but at that word, as at a pang of physical pain, her lips stiffened again, and again the muscles of her right cheek worked.

"Go away, get out of this room!" she shrieked, still more shrilly, "and don't talk to me of your passion and your loathsomeness."

She tried to go out, but tottered, and clung to the back of a chair to support herself. His face relaxed, his lips swelled, his eyes were swimming with tears.

"Dolly!" he said, sobbing now, "for mercy's sake, think of the children; they are not to blame! I am to blame, and punish me, make me expiate my guilt. Anything I can do, I am ready to do anything! I am to blame, no words can express how much I am to blame! But, Dolly, forgive me!"

She sat down. He listened to her hard, heavy breathing, and he was unutterably sorry for her. She tried several times to begin to speak, but could not. He waited.

"You remember the children, Stiva, to play with them; but I remember them, and know that this means their ruin," she said— obviously one of the phrases she had more than once repeated to herself in the course of the last few days.

She had called him "Stiva," and he glanced at her with gratitude, and moved to take her hand, but she drew back from him with disgust.

"I think of the children, and for that reason I would do anything in the world to save them; but I don't myself know how to save them—by taking them away from their father, or by leaving them with a depraved father . . . yes, a vicious father . . . Tell me, after what . . . has happened, can we live together? Is that possible? Tell me, eh, is it possible," she repeated, raising her voice, "after my husband, the father of my children, has had an affair with his own children's governess?"

"But what could I do? What could I do?" he kept saying in a pitiful voice, not knowing what he was saying, as his head sank lower and lower.

"You are loathsome to me, repulsive!" she shrieked, getting more and more excited. "Your tears mean nothing! You have never loved me; you have neither heart nor honorable feeling! You are hateful to me, disgusting, a stranger—yes, a complete stranger!" With pain and hatred she uttered the word so terrible to her—"*stranger.*"

He looked at her, and the fury expressed in her face alarmed and amazed him. He did not understand that his pity for her exasperated her. She saw in him sympathy for her, but not love. "No, she hates me. She will not forgive me," he thought.

"It is terrible! Terrible!" he said.

At that moment in the next room a child began to cry; probably it had fallen down. Darya Aleksandrovna listened, and her face suddenly softened.

She seemed to pull herself together for a few seconds, as though she did not know where she was and what she was doing, and getting up rapidly, she moved toward the door.

"Well, she loves my child," he thought, noticing the change of her face at the child's cry, "my child. How can she hate me?"

"Dolly, one word more," he said, following her.

"If you come near me, I will call in the servants, the children! They may all know you are a scoundrel! I am going away at once, and you may live here with your mistress!"

And she went out, slamming the door.

Stepan Arkadyevich sighed, wiped his face, and, with a subdued step, walked out of the room. "Matvey says things will work out; but how? I don't see the least chance of it. Ah, oh, how horrible it is! And how vulgarly she shouted," he said to himself, remembering her shriek and the words, "scoundrel" and "mistress." "And very likely the maids were listening! Horribly vulgar! Horrible!" And, squaring his chest again, he went downstairs.

It was Friday, and in the dining room the German clockmaker was winding the clock. Stepan Arkadyevich remembered his joke about this punctual, bald clockmaker, "that the German was wound up for a whole lifetime himself, to wind up clocks," and he smiled. "Maybe things will work out! That's a good expression, work out," he thought. "I must repeat that."

"Matvey!" he shouted. "Arrange everything with Marya in the sitting room for Anna Arkadyevna," he said to Matvey when he came in.

"Yes, sir."

Stepan Arkadyevich put on his fur coat and went out onto the steps.

"You won't dine at home?" said Matvey, seeing him off.

"That depends. But here's for the housekeeping," he said, taking ten rubles from his wallet. "That'll be enough."

"Enough or not enough, we must make it do," said Matvey, slamming the carriage door and stepping back onto the steps.

Meanwhile, Darya Aleksandrovna, having pacified the child, and knowing from the sound of the carriage that he had gone off, went back to her bedroom again. It was her only refuge from the household cares that crowded upon her as soon as she left it. Even now, in the short time she had been in the nursery, the English governess and Matryona Filimonovna had succeeded in putting several questions to her which did not brook delay, and which only she could answer: "What were the children to put on for their walk? Should they have any milk? Shouldn't a new cook be sent for?"

"Ah, let me alone, let me alone!" she said, and going back to her bedroom, she sat down in the same place she had sat in when talking to her husband, clasping tightly her thin hands with the rings that slipped down on her bony fingers, and began going over in her memory the entire conversation. "He has gone! But has he broken it off with her?" she thought. "Can it be he sees her? Why didn't I ask him! No, no, reconciliation is impossible. Even if we remain in the same house, we are strangers—strangers forever!" She repeated again with special significance the word so dreadful to her. "And how I loved him! My God, how I loved him! . . . How I loved him! And now don't I love him? Don't I love him more than before? The most horrible thing . . ." she began, but did not finish her thought, because Matryona Filimonovna put her head in at the door.

"Let us send for my brother," she said; "he can get a dinner prepared anyway, or we shall have the children getting nothing to eat till six again, like yesterday."

"Very well, I will come right away and see about it. But did you send for some fresh milk?"

And Darya Aleksandrovna plunged into the duties of the day, and drowned her grief in them for a time.

CHAPTER FIVE

Stepan Arkadyevich had learned easily at school, thanks to his excellent natural abilities, but he had been lazy and mischievous, and therefore was one of the lowest in his class. But in spite of his habitually dissipated mode of life, his inferior grade in the service,[1] and his comparative youth, he occupied the honorable and lucrative position of head of one of the government boards at Moscow. This post he had received through his sister Anna's husband, Aleksey Aleksandrovich Karenin, who held one of the most important positions in the ministry to whose department the Moscow office belonged. But even if Karenin had not got his brother-in-law this position, then through a hundred other people—brothers, sisters, cousins, uncles, and aunts—Stiva Oblonsky would have obtained it, or some similar one, with the salary of six thousand[2] which he found necessary, as his affairs, in spite of his wife's considerable property, were in sad shape.

Half of Moscow and Petersburg were friends and relations of Stepan Arkadyevich. He was born in the midst of those who had been and are the great ones of this world. One third of the men in the

[1] I.e., the civil service. See chart on page xxv.
[2] In nineteenth-century Russia the ruble was worth about fifty-one cents.

government, the older men, had been friends of his father's, and had known him in diapers; another third were his intimate chums; and the remainder were friendly acquaintances. Consequently, the distributors of earthly blessings in the shape of places, rents, shares, and such were all his friends, and could not overlook one of their own set; and Oblonsky had no need to make any special exertion to get a lucrative post. He had only not to refuse things, not to show jealousy, not to be quarrelsome or take offense, all of which from his characteristic good nature he never did. It would have struck him as absurd if he had been told that he would not get a position with the salary he required, especially as he expected nothing extraordinary; he wanted only what the men of his own age and standing got, and he was no worse qualified for performing these duties than any other man.

Stepan Arkadyevich was liked by all who knew him, not merely for his humor, but also for his bright disposition and his unquestionable honesty. In him, in his handsome, radiant figure, his sparkling eyes, black hair and eyebrows, and the white and red of his face, there was something that produced a physical effect of kindliness and cheerfulness on the people who met him. "Aha! Stiva! Oblonsky! Here he is!" was almost always said with a smile of delight on meeting him. Even though it happened at times that after a conversation with him it seemed that nothing particularly delightful had happened, the next day, and the next, everyone was just as delighted at meeting him again.

After filling, for three years, the post of president of one of the government boards at Moscow, Stepan Arkadyevich had won the respect, as well as the affection, of his fellow officials, subordinates, and superiors, and all who had done business with him. The principal qualities in Stepan Arkadyevich which had gained him this universal respect in the service consisted, first, of his extreme indulgence for others, founded on a consciousness of his own shortcomings; second, of his perfect liberalism—not the liberalism he read of in the papers, but the liberalism that was in his blood, in virtue of which he treated all men perfectly equally and exactly the same, whatever their fortune or calling might be; and third—the most important point—his complete indifference to the business in which he was engaged, in consequence of which he was never carried away, and never made mistakes.

On reaching the offices of the board, Stepan Arkadyevich, escorted by a deferential porter with his portfolio, went into his little private room, put on his uniform,[3] and went into the board room. The clerks and copyists all rose, greeting him with cheerful deference. Stepan Arkadyevich moved quickly, as always, to his place, shook hands with his colleagues, and sat down. He made a joke or two, and talked just as much as was consistent with due decorum, and began work. No one knew better than Stepan Arkadyevich how to hit on the exact line between freedom, simplicity, and official stiffness necessary for the agreeable conduct of business. A secretary, with good-humored deference common to everyone in Stepan Arkadyevich's office, came up with papers, and began to speak in the familiarly liberal tone which had been introduced by Stepan Arkadyevich.

"We have succeeded in getting the information from the government department of Penza. Here, would you care? . . ."

"You've got them at last?" said Stepan Arkadyevich, laying his finger on the paper. "Now, gentlemen . . ."

And the meeting of the board began.

"If they knew," he thought, bending his head with a significant air as he listened to the report, "what a guilty little boy their president was half an hour ago." And his eyes twinkled during the reading of the report. Till two o'clock the meeting went on without a break; at two o'clock there would be an interval and lunch.

It was not yet two when the large glass doors of the board room suddenly opened and someone came in.

All the officials sitting on the further side under the portrait of the Tsar and the Mirror of Justice,[4] delighted at any distraction, looked round at the door; but the doorkeeper standing at the door at once drove out the intruder, and closed the glass door after him.

When the case had been read through, Stepan Arkadyevich got up and stretched, and by way of tribute to the liberalism of the times,

---

[3] Civil servants wore a uniform.
[4] A three-sided prism on which the edicts of Peter the Great were engraved.

he took out a cigarette in the board room and went into his office. Two of the members of the board, the old veteran in the service, Nikitin, and a court chamberlain, Grinevich, went in with him.

"We will have time to finish after lunch," said Stepan Arkadyevich.

"Certainly we will!" said Nikitin.

"A pretty sharp fellow this Fomin must be," said Grinevich of one of the persons taking part in the case they were examining.

Stepan Arkadyevich frowned at Grinevich's words, indicating thereby that it was improper to pass judgment prematurely, and made no reply.

"Who was it that came in?" he asked the doorkeeper.

"Someone, Your Excellency, crept in without permission as soon as my back was turned. He was asking for you. I told him, when the members come out, then . . ."

"Where is he?"

"Maybe he's gone into the passage, but here he comes anyway. That's him," said the doorkeeper, pointing to a strongly built, broad-shouldered man with a curly beard, who, without taking off his sheepskin cap, was running lightly and rapidly up the worn steps of the stone staircase. One of the members going down—a lean official with a portfolio—stood out of his way and looked disapprovingly at the feet of the stranger, then glanced inquiringly at Oblonsky.

Stepan Arkadyevich was standing at the top of the stairs. His good-naturedly beaming face above the embroidered collar of his uniform beamed more than ever when he recognized the man coming up.

"Why, it's actually you, Levin, at last!" he said with a friendly, mocking smile, scanning Levin as he approached. "How is it you have deigned to look me up in this den of thieves?" said Stepan Arkadyevich, and not content with shaking hands, he kissed his friend. "Have you been here long?"

"I have just come, and very much wanted to see you," said Levin, looking shyly and at the same time resentfully and uneasily around.

"Well, let's go into my office," said Stepan Arkadyevich, who knew his friend's sensitive and irritable shyness, and taking his arm, he drew him along as though guiding him through dangers.

Stepan Arkadyevich was on familiar terms with almost all his acquaintances, and called almost all of them by their Christian names: old men of sixty, boys of twenty, actors, ministers, merchants, and adjutant generals, so that many of his intimate chums were to be found at the extreme ends of the social ladder, and would have been very much surprised to learn that they had, through the medium of Oblonsky, something in common. He was the familiar friend of everyone with whom he took a glass of champagne, and he took a glass of champagne with everyone, and when in consequence he met any of his *disreputable* chums (as he used to call many of his friends in jest) in the presence of his subordinates, he well knew how, with his characteristic tact, to diminish the disagreeable impression made on them. Levin was not a disreputable chum, but Oblonsky, with his ready tact, felt that Levin thought he might not care to show his intimacy with him before his subordinates, and so he made haste to take him off into his office.

Levin was almost of the same age as Oblonsky; their intimacy was not based merely on champagne. Levin had been the friend and companion of his early youth. They were fond of one another in spite of the difference of their characters and tastes, as friends who have been together in early youth are fond of one another. But in spite of this, each of them—as is often the way with men who have selected careers of different kinds—though in discussion would even justify the other's career, in his heart despised it. It seemed to each of them that the life he led himself was the only real life, and the life led by his friend was a mere illusion. Oblonsky could not restrain a slight sarcastic smile at the sight of Levin. How often he had seen him come up to Moscow from the country where he was doing something, but precisely what Stepan Arkadyevich could never quite make out, and indeed he took no interest in the matter. Levin arrived in Moscow always excited and in a hurry, rather ill at ease and irritated by his own lack of ease, and for the most part with a perfectly new unexpected view of things. Stepan Arkadyevich laughed at this, and liked it. In the same way, Levin in his heart despised the town mode of life of his friend and his official duties, which he laughed at and regarded as trifling. But the difference was that Oblonsky, as he was doing the same as everyone did, laughed complacently and good-humoredly, while Levin laughed without complacency and sometimes angrily.

"We have long been expecting you," said Stepan Arkadyevich, going into his room and letting Levin's hand go as though to show that here all danger was over. "I am very, very glad to see you," he went on. "Well, how are you? Eh? When did you come?"

Levin was silent, looking at the unknown faces of Oblonsky's two companions, and especially at the hand of the elegant Grinevich, which had such long white fingers, such long yellow nails curving at the ends, and such huge shining cuff links that apparently they absorbed his attention completely, leaving him no freedom of thought. Oblonsky noticed this at once, and smiled.

"Ah, to be sure, let me introduce you," he said. "My colleagues: Filipp Ivanych Nikitin, Mikhail Stanislavich Grinevich"—and turning to Levin—"an active member of the district council and a man with fresh ideas, and a gymnast who can lift a hundred-and-eighty-pound weight with one hand, a cattle breeder and sportsman, and my friend, Konstantin Dimitrievich Levin, the brother of Sergey Ivanovich Koznyshev."

"Delighted," said the veteran.

"I have the honor of knowing your brother, Sergey Ivanovich," said Grinevich, holding out his slender hand with its long nails.

Levin frowned, shook hands coldly, and at once turned to Oblonsky. Though he had great respect for his half-brother, an author well known to all Russia, he could not endure it when people treated him not as Konstantin Levin but as the brother of the celebrated Koznyshev.

"No, I am no longer a district councilor. I have quarreled with them all, and don't go to the meetings any more," he said, turning to Oblonsky.

"Didn't take you long!" said Oblonsky with a smile. "But how? Why?"

"It's a long story. I will tell you sometime," said Levin, but he began telling him at once. "Well, to make it short, I was convinced that nothing was really done by the district councils, or ever could be," he began, as though someone had just insulted him. "On one side it's a plaything; they play at being a parliament, and I'm neither young enough nor old enough to find amusement in playthings; and on the other hand" (he stammered) "it's a means for the coterie of the district to make money. Formerly they had wardships, courts of justice, now they have the district council—not in the form of bribes, but in the form of unearned salary," he said, as hotly as though some of those present had opposed his opinion.

"Aha! You're in a new phase again, I see—a conservative," said Stepan Arkadyevich. "However, we can go into that later."

"Yes, later. But I wanted to see you," said Levin, looking with hatred at Grinevich's hand.

Stepan Arkadyevich gave a scarcely perceptible smile.

"Didn't you used to say you would never wear European clothes again?" he said, scanning his new suit, obviously cut by a French tailor. "Ah! I see: a new phase."

Levin suddenly blushed, not as grown men blush, slightly, without being themselves aware of it, but as boys blush, feeling that they are ridiculous in their shyness, and consequently ashamed of it and blushing still more, almost to the point of tears. And it was so strange to see this sensible, manly face in such a childish plight that Oblonsky stopped looking at him.

"Oh, where shall we meet? You know I want very much to talk to you," said Levin.

Oblonsky seemed to ponder.

"I'll tell you what: let's go to Gurin's for lunch, and there we can talk. I am free till three."

"No," answered Levin, after an instant's thought, "I have got to go on somewhere else."

"All right, then, let's dine together."

"Dine together? But I have nothing very particular, only a few words to say, and a question I want to ask you, and we can have a talk afterwards."

"Well, say the few words, then, at once, and we'll gossip after dinner."

"Well, it's this," said Levin: "but it's of no importance, though."

His face all at once took on an expression of anger from the effort he was making to surmount his shyness.

"What are the Shcherbatskys doing? Everything as it used to be?" he said.

Stepan Arkadyevich, who had long known that Levin was in love with his sister-in-law, Kitty, gave a hardly perceptible smile, and his eyes sparkled merrily.

"You said a few words, but I can't answer in a few words, because . . . Excuse me a minute . . ."

A secretary came in, with respectful familiarity and the modest consciousness, characteristic of every secretary, of superiority to his chief in the knowledge of their business; he went up to Oblonsky with some papers and began, under pretense of asking a question, to explain some objection. Stepan Arkadyevich, without hearing him out, laid his hand genially on the secretary's sleeve.

"No, you do as I told you," he said, softening his words with a smile, and with a brief explanation of his view of the matter, he turned away from the papers and said: "So do it in that way, if you please, Zakhar Nikitich."

The secretary retired in confusion. During the consultation with the secretary Levin had completely recovered from his embarrassment. He was standing with his elbows on the back of a chair, and on his face was a look of sarcastic attention.

"I don't understand it, I don't understand it," he said.

"What don't you understand?" said Oblonsky, smiling as brightly as ever, and picking up a cigarette. He expected some strange outburst from Levin.

"I don't understand what you are doing," said Levin, shrugging his shoulders. "How can you do it seriously?"

"Why not?"

"Why, because there's nothing in it."

"You think so, but we're overwhelmed with work."

"Paper work. But, there, you've a gift for it," added Levin.

"That is to say, you think there's something lacking in me?"

"Perhaps so," said Levin. "But all the same I admire your grandeur, and am proud that I've a friend who is such a great person. You've not answered my question, though," he went on, with a desperate effort looking Oblonsky straight in the face.

"Oh, that's all very well. You wait a while, and you'll come to it yourself. It's very nice for you to have over eight thousand acres in

the Karazinsky county, and such muscles, and the freshness of a girl
of twelve; still you'll be one of us one day. Yes, as to your question,
there is no change, but it's a pity you've been away so long."

"Oh, why so?" Levin queried, panic-stricken.

"Oh, nothing," responded Oblonsky. "We'll talk it over. But
what's brought you to town?"

"Oh, we'll talk about that, too, later on," said Levin, reddening
again up to his ears.

"All right, I see," said Stepan Arkadyevich, "I should ask you to
come see us, you know, but my wife's not quite well. But I tell you
what; if you want to see them, they're sure to be at the Zoological
Gardens from four to five. Kitty skates. You drive along there, and
I'll come and fetch you, and we'll go and dine somewhere together."

"Wonderful. So good-by till then."

"Careful you don't forget. I know you, you might rush off home to
the country!" Stepan Arkadyevich called out, laughing.

"No, I won't!"

And Levin went out of the room. Only when he was in the doorway did he remember that he had forgotten to say good-by to
Oblonsky's colleagues.

"That gentleman must be a man of great energy," said Grinevich,
when Levin had gone.

"Yes, my dear boy," said Stepan Arkadyevich, nodding his head.
"He's a lucky fellow! Over eight thousand acres in the Karazinsky
district; everything before him; and what youth and vigor! Not like
some of us."

"You have a great deal to complain of, haven't you, Stepan
Arkadyevich?"

"Ah, yes, I'm in a bad way," said Stepan Arkadyevich with a heavy
sigh.

CHAPTER SIX

When Oblonsky asked Levin what had brought him to town, Levin
blushed, and was furious with himself for blushing, because he could

not answer, "I have come to propose to your sister-in-law," though that was precisely what he had come for.

The families of the Levins and the Shcherbatskys were old, noble Moscow families, and had always been on intimate and friendly terms. This intimacy had grown still closer during Levin's student days. He had both prepared for the university with the young Prince Shcherbatsky, the brother of Kitty and Dolly, and had entered at the same time with him. In those days Levin used to be in the Shcherbatskys' house frequently and he was in love with the Shcherbatsky family. Strange as it may appear, it was the entire family with which Konstantin Levin was in love, especially with the feminine half of it. Levin did not remember his own mother, and his only sister was older than he was, so that it was in the Shcherbatskys' house that he saw for the first time that inner life of an old, noble, cultivated, and honorable family of which he had been deprived by the death of his father and mother. All the members of that family, especially the feminine half, were pictured by him, as it were, wrapped in a mysterious poetical veil, and he not only perceived no defects whatever in them, but behind the poetical veil that shrouded them he assumed the existence of the loftiest sentiments and every possible perfection. Why it was the three young ladies had to speak French and English on alternate days; why it was that at certain hours they took turns playing the piano, the sounds of which were audible in their brother's room above, where the students used to work; why they were visited by those professors of French literature, of music, of drawing, of dancing; why at certain hours all three young ladies, and Mademoiselle Linon, drove in the coach to Tverskoy Boulevard, dressed in their satin cloaks, Dolly in a long one, Natalie in a shorter one, and Kitty in one so short that her shapely little legs in tight red stockings were exposed; why it was they had to walk about Tverskoy Boulevard escorted by a footman with a gilt cockade in his hat—all this and much more that was done in their mysterious world he did not understand, but he was sure that everything that was done there was very good, and he was in love precisely with the mystery of the proceedings.

In his student days he had all but been in love with the eldest,

Dolly, but she was soon married to Oblonsky. Then he began being in love with the second. He felt, as it were, that he had to be in love with one of the sisters, only he could not quite make out which. But Natalie, too, had hardly made her appearance in the world when she married the diplomat Lvov. Kitty was still a child when Levin left the university. Young Shcherbatsky went into the navy, was drowned in the Baltic, and Levin's relations with the Shcherbatskys, in spite of his friendship with Oblonsky, became less intimate. But when, early in the winter of this year, Levin came to Moscow after a year in the country, and saw the Shcherbatskys, he realized which of the three sisters he was indeed destined to love.

One would have thought that nothing could be simpler than for him, a man of good family, more rich than poor, and thirty-two years old, to make the young Princess Shcherbatsky an offer of marriage; in all likelihood he would at once have been looked upon as a good match. But Levin was in love, and so it seemed to him that Kitty was so perfect in every respect that she was a creature far above everything earthly; and that he was a creature so low and so earthly that it could not even be conceived that other people and she herself could regard him as worthy of her.

After spending two months in Moscow in a daze, seeing Kitty almost every day in society, into which he went so as to meet her, he abruptly decided that it could not be, and went back to the country.

Levin's conviction that it could not be was founded on the idea that in the eyes of her family he was a disadvantageous and worthless match for the charming Kitty, and that Kitty herself could not love him. In her family's eyes he had no ordinary, definite career and position in society, while his contemporaries by this time, when he was thirty-two, were already, one a colonel, and another a professor, another director of a bank and railways, or president of a board, like Oblonsky. But (he knew very well how he must appear to others) he was a country gentleman, occupied in breeding cattle, shooting snipe, and building barns; in other words, a fellow of no ability, who had not turned out well, and who was doing just what, according to the ideas of the world, is done by people fit for nothing else.

The mysterious, enchanting Kitty herself could not love such an ugly person as he conceived himself to be, and, above all, such an ordinary, in no way striking person. Moreover, his attitude toward Kitty in the past—the attitude of a grown-up person toward a child, arising from his friendship with her brother—seemed to him yet another obstacle to love. An ugly, pleasant man, as he considered himself, might, he supposed, be liked as a friend; but to be loved with such a love as that with which he loved Kitty, one would need to be a handsome and, still more, a distinguished man.

He had heard that women often did care for ugly and ordinary men, but he did not believe it, for he judged by himself, and he could not himself have loved any but beautiful, mysterious, and exceptional women.

But after spending two months alone in the country, he was convinced that this was not one of those passions of which he had had experience in his early youth; that this feeling gave him not an instant's rest; that he could not live without deciding the question, would she or would she not be his wife, and that his despair had arisen only from his own imaginings, that he had no proof that he would be rejected. And he had now come to Moscow with a firm determination to make an offer, and get married if he was accepted. Or . . . he could not conceive what would become of him if he were rejected.

CHAPTER SEVEN

On arriving in Moscow by a morning train, Levin had gone directly to the house of his elder half-brother, Koznyshev. After changing his clothes, he went down to his brother's study, intending to talk to him at once about the object of his visit, and to ask his advice; but his brother was not alone. With him there was a famous professor of philosophy, who had come from Kharkov expressly to clear up a difference that had arisen between them on a very important philosophical question. The professor was carrying on a hot crusade against materialists. Sergey Koznyshev had been following this crusade with interest, and after reading the professor's last article, he had written him a letter stating his objections. He accused the professor of making too great concessions to the materialists. And the professor had promptly appeared to argue the matter out. The point in dis-

cussion was the question then in vogue: Is there a line to be drawn
between psychological and physiological phenomena in man, and if
so, where?   •

Sergey Ivanovich met his brother with the smile of chilly friendliness he always had for everyone, and introducing him to the professor, he went on with the conversation.

A little man in spectacles, with a narrow forehead, tore himself
from the discussion for an instant to greet Levin, and then went on
talking without paying any further attention to him. Levin sat down
to wait for the professor to finish and go but he soon began to get
interested in the subject under discussion.

He had come across the magazine articles about which they were
disputing, and had read them, interested in them as a development of
the first principles of science, familiar to him as a natural science student at the university. But he had never connected these scientific
deductions as to the origin of man as an animal, as to reflex action,
biology, and sociology, with those questions concerning the meaning
of life and death to himself, which had of late been more and more in
his mind.

As he listened to his brother's argument with the professor, he
noticed that they connected these scientific questions with the spiritual, that at times they almost touched on the latter; but every time
they came near what seemed to him the chief point, they promptly
beat a hasty retreat, and plunged again into a sea of subtle distinctions,
reservations, quotations, allusions, and appeals to authorities, and it
was with difficulty that he understood what they were talking about.

"I cannot admit it," said Sergey Ivanovich, with his habitual clarity, precision of expression, and elegance of phrase. "I cannot in any
case agree with Keiss that my whole conception of the external world
has been derived from perceptions. The most fundamental idea, the
idea of existence, has not been received by me through sensation;
indeed, there is no special sense organ for the transmission of such an
idea."

"Yes, but they—Wurst, and Knaust,[1] and Pripasov—would answer

---

[1]Comic German names. *Wurst* is "sausage," and Knaust strongly suggests *Knauser*,
"miser."

that your consciousness of existence is derived from the conjunction of all your sensations, that that consciousness of existence is the result of your sensations. Wurst, indeed, says plainly that, assuming there are no sensations, it follows that there is no idea of existence."

"I maintain the contrary," said Sergey Ivanovich.

But here again it seemed to Levin that just as they were close to the real point of the matter, they were retreating, and he made up his mind to put a question to the professor.

"According to that, if my senses are annihilated, if my body is dead, I can have no existence of any sort?" he queried.

The professor, in annoyance, looking as though the interruption had caused him great suffering, glanced at the strange inquirer, more like a bargeman than a philosopher, and turned his eyes upon Sergey Ivanovich, as though to ask: What's one to say to him? But Sergey Ivanovich, who had been talking with far less heat and one-sidedness than the professor, and who had sufficient breadth of mind to answer the professor, and at the same time to comprehend the simple and natural point of view from which the question was put, smiled and said:

"That question we have no right to answer as yet."

"We have not the requisite data," chimed in the professor, and he went back to his argument. "No," he said; "I would point out the fact that if, as Pripasov directly asserts, perception is based on sensation, then we are bound to distinguish sharply between these two conceptions."

Levin listened no more, and simply waited for the professor to go.

CHAPTER EIGHT

When the professor had gone, Sergey Ivanovich turned to his brother.

"Delighted that you've come. For some time, is it? How's your farming getting on?"

Levin knew that his elder brother took little interest in farming, and only put the question in deference to him, and so he told him only about the sale of his wheat, and money matters.

Levin had meant to tell his brother of his determination to get married, and to ask his advice; he had indeed firmly resolved to do so. But after seeing his brother, listening to his conversation with the professor, hearing afterward the unconsciously patronizing tone in which his brother questioned him about agricultural matters (their mother's property had not been divided, and Levin took charge of both their shares), Levin felt that for some reason he could not begin to talk to him of his intention of marrying. He felt that his brother would not look at it as he would have wished him to.

"Well, how is your district council doing?" asked Sergey Ivanovich, who was greatly interested in these local boards and attached great importance to them.

"I really don't know."

"What! Why, surely you're a member of the board?"

"No, I'm not a member now; I've resigned," answered Levin, "and I no longer attend the meetings."

"What a pity!" commented Sergey Ivanovich, frowning.

Levin, defensively, began to describe what took place in the meetings in his district.

"That's how it always is!" Sergey Ivanovich interrupted him. "We Russians are always like that. Perhaps it's our strong point, really, the faculty of seeing our own shortcomings; but we overdo it, we comfort ourselves with irony which we always have on the tip of our tongues. All I say is, give such rights as our local self-government to any other European people—why, the Germans or the English would have worked their way to freedom from them, while we simply turn them into ridicule."

"But how can it be helped?" said Levin penitently. "It was my last effort. And I did try with all my soul. I can't. I'm no good at it."

"It's not that you're no good at it," said Sergey Ivanovich, "it is that you don't look at it as you should."

"Perhaps not," Levin answered dejectedly.

"Oh! Do you know brother Nikolai's turned up again?"

This brother Nikolai was the elder brother of Konstantin Levin, and half-brother of Sergey Ivanovich; a man utterly ruined, who had dissipated the greater part of his fortune, was living in the strangest and lowest company, and had quarreled with his brothers.

"What did you say?" Levin cried with horror. "How do you know?"

"Prokofy saw him in the street."

"Here in Moscow? Where is he? Do you know?" Levin got up from his chair, as though on the point of starting off at once.

"I am sorry I told you," said Sergey Ivanovich, shaking his head at his younger brother's excitement. "I sent to find out where he is living, and sent him his IOU to Trubin, which I paid. This is the answer he sent me."

And Sergey Ivanovich took a note from under a paperweight and handed it to his brother.

Levin read in the strange, familiar handwriting:

I humbly beg you to leave me in peace. That's the only favor I ask of my gracious brothers.—Nikolai Levin.

Levin read it, and, without raising his head, stood with the note in his hands opposite Sergey Ivanovich.

There was a struggle in his heart between the desire to forget his unhappy brother for the time, and the awareness that it would be base to do so.

"He obviously wants to offend me," pursued Sergey Ivanovich; "but he cannot offend me. I would have wished with all my heart to assist him, but I know it's impossible to do that."

"Yes, yes," repeated Levin. "I understand and appreciate your attitude toward him; but I shall go and see him."

"If you want to, do; but I wouldn't advise it," said Sergey Ivanovich. "As regards myself, I have no fear of your doing so; he will not make you quarrel with me; but for your sake, I think you would do better not to go. You can't do him any good; still, do as you please."

"Very likely I can't do any good, but I feel, especially at such a moment—but that's another thing—I feel I could not be at peace."

"Well, that I don't understand," said Sergey Ivanovich. "One thing I do understand," he added, "it's a lesson in humility. I have come to look very differently and more charitably on what is called infamy since brother Nikolai has become what he is . . . you know what he did . . ."

"Oh, it's awful, awful!" Levin said.

After obtaining his brother's address from Sergey Ivanovich's footman, Levin was on the point of setting off at once to see him, but on second thought he decided to put off his visit till the evening. The first thing to do to set his heart at rest was to accomplish what he had come to Moscow for. From his brother's, Levin went to Oblonsky's office, and on getting news of the Shcherbatskys from him, he drove to the place where he had been told he might find Kitty.

CHAPTER NINE

At four o'clock, conscious of his throbbing heart, Levin stepped out of a hired sleigh at the Zoological Gardens, and turned along the path to the frozen mounds and the skating rink, knowing that he would certainly find her there, as he had seen the Shcherbatskys' carriage at the entrance.

It was a bright, frosty day. Rows of carriages, sleighs, cabmen, and policemen were standing in the approach. Crowds of well-dressed people, with hats bright in the sun, swarmed about the entrance and along the well-swept little paths between the little houses adorned with carving in the Russian style. The old curly birches of the gardens, all their twigs laden with snow, looked freshly decked in festive vestments.

He walked along the path toward the skating rink, and kept saying to himself: "You mustn't be excited, you must be calm. What's the matter with you? What do you want? Be quiet, stupid," he conjured his heart. And the more he tried to compose himself, the more breathless he found himself. An acquaintance met him and called him by his name, but Levin did not even recognize him. He went toward the mounds, whence came the clank of the chains, of sleighs as they slipped down or were dragged up, the rumble of sliding sleighs, and the sounds of merry voices. He walked on a few steps, and the skating rink lay open before his eyes, and at once, amidst all the skaters, he knew her.

He knew she was there by the rapture and the terror that seized his heart. She was standing talking to a lady at the opposite end of the rink. There was apparently nothing striking either in her dress or her attitude. But for Levin she was as easy to find in that crowd as a rose among nettles. Everything was made bright by her. She was the smile that shed light on all around her. "Is it possible I can go over there on the ice, go up to her?" he thought. The place where she stood seemed to him a holy shrine, unapproachable, and there was one moment when he was almost retreating, so overwhelmed was he with terror. He had to make an effort to master himself, and to remind himself that people of all sorts were moving about her, and that he too might come there to skate. He walked down, for a long while avoiding looking at her as at the sun, but seeing her, as one does the sun, without looking.

On that day of the week and at that time of day people of the same set, all acquainted with one another, used to meet on the ice. There were crack skaters there, showing off their skill, and learners clinging to chairs with timid, awkward movements, boys, and elderly people skating for their health. They seemed to Levin an elect band of blissful beings because they were here, near her. All the skaters, it seemed, with perfect self-possession, skated toward her, skated by her, even spoke to her, and were happy, quite apart from her, enjoying the wonderful ice and the fine weather.

Nikolai Shcherbatsky, Kitty's cousin, in a short jacket and tight trousers, was sitting on a garden seat with his skates on. Seeing Levin, he shouted to him:

"Ah, the best skater in Russia! Been here long? Marvelous ice. Put your skates on."

"I haven't got my skates," Levin answered, marveling at this boldness and ease in her presence, and not for one second losing sight of her, though he did not look at her. He felt as though the sun were coming near him. She was in a corner, and turning out her slender feet in their high boots with obvious timidity, she skated toward him. A boy in Russian dress, desperately waving his arms and bowed down to the ground, overtook her. She skated a little uncertainly; taking her hands out of the little muff that hung on a cord, she held them ready for emergency, and looking toward Levin, whom she had recognized, she smiled at him, and at her own fears. When she had turned the corner, she gave herself a push off with one foot, and skated straight up to Shcherbatsky. Clutching at his arm, she nodded smilingly to Levin. She was more lovely than he had imagined her.

When he thought of her, he could call up a vivid picture of her to himself, especially the charm of that little fair head, so lightly set on the shapely girlish shoulders, and so full of childish brightness and kindness. The childishness of her expression, together with the delicate beauty of her figure, made up her special charm, and that he fully realized. But what always struck him in her as something unlooked for was the expression of her eyes, soft, serene, and truthful, and above all, her smile, which always transported Levin to an enchanted world, where he felt himself softened and filled with tenderness, as he remembered himself in some days of his early childhood.

"Have you been here long?" she said, giving him her hand. "Thank you," she added, as he picked up the handkerchief that had fallen out of her muff.

"I? I've not long . . . Yesterday . . . I mean today . . . I arrived," answered Levin, in his excitement not at once understanding her question. "I was meaning to come and see you," he said; and then, recollecting with what intention he was trying to see her, he was promptly overcome with confusion and blushed.

"I didn't know you could skate, and skate so well."

She looked at him earnestly, as though wishing to understand the cause of his confusion.

"Your praise is worth having. The tradition here is that you are the best of skaters," she said, with her little black-gloved hand brushing a grain of hoarfrost off her muff.

"Yes, once I used to skate with passion; I wanted to reach perfection."

"You do everything with passion, I think," she said, smiling. "I would so like to see how you skate. Put on skates, and let us skate together."

"Skate together! Can that be possible?" thought Levin, gazing at her.

"I'll put them on at once," he said.

And he went off to get skates.

"It's a long while since we've seen you here, sir," said the attendant, supporting his foot and screwing on the heel of the skate. "Since you, we've had no gentleman who is so masterful. Will that be all right?" he said, tightening the strap.

"Oh, yes, yes; quickly, please," answered Levin, with difficulty restraining the smile of rapture that would overspread his face. "Yes," he thought, "now this is happiness! Together, she said let us skate together! Speak to her now? But that's just why I'm afraid to speak— because I'm happy now, happy in hope, anyway . . . And then? . . . But I must! I must! I must! Away with weakness!"

Levin rose to his feet, took off his overcoat, and, scurrying over the rough ice around the hut, came out on the smooth ice and skated without effort, sheer will power, as it were, increasing and slackening speed and turning his course. He approached with timidity, but again her smile reassured him.

She gave him her hand, and they set off side by side, going faster and faster, and the more rapidly they moved, the more tightly she grasped his hand.

"With you I would soon learn; I somehow feel confidence in you," she said to him.

"And I have confidence in myself when you are leaning on me," he said, but was at once panic-stricken at what he had said, and blushed. And indeed, no sooner had he uttered these words than all at once, like the sun going behind a cloud, her face lost all its friendliness, and Levin detected the familiar change in her expression that denoted the working of thought; a crease showed on her smooth brow.

"Is there anything troubling you?—though I've no right to ask such a question," he said hurriedly.

"Oh, why so? . . . No, I have nothing to trouble me," she responded coldly; and she added immediately: "You haven't seen Mlle Linon, have you?"

"Not yet."

"Go and speak to her, she likes you so much."

"What's wrong? I have offended her. Lord help me!" thought Levin, and he flew toward the old Frenchwoman with the gray ringlets, who was sitting on a bench. Smiling and showing her false teeth, she greeted him as an old friend.

"Yes, you see we're growing up," she said to him, glancing toward

Kitty, "and growing old. Tiny bear has grown big now!" pursued the Frenchwoman, laughing, and she reminded him of his joke about the three young ladies whom he had compared to the three bears in the English nursery tale. "Do you remember that's what you used to call them?"

He remembered absolutely nothing, but she had been laughing at the joke for ten years now, and was fond of it.

"Now, go and skate, go and skate. Our Kitty has learned to skate nicely, hasn't she?"

When Levin darted up to Kitty, her face was no longer stern; her eyes looked at him with the same sincerity and friendliness, but Levin imagined that in her friendliness there was a certain note of deliberate composure. And he felt depressed. After talking a little of her old governess and her peculiarities, she questioned him about his life.

"Surely you must be bored in the country in the winter, aren't you?" she said.

"No, I'm not bored, I am very busy," he said, feeling that she was holding him in check by her composed tone, which he would not have the force to break through, just as it had been at the beginning of the winter.

"Are you going to stay in town long?" Kitty questioned him.

"I don't know," he answered, not thinking of what he was saying. He believed that if he was held in check by her tone of quiet friendliness, he would end by going back again without deciding anything, and he resolved to make a struggle against it.

"How is it you don't know?"

"I don't know. It depends upon you," he said, and was immediately horror-stricken at his own words.

Whether it was that she had heard his words, or that she did not want to hear them, she made a sort of stumble, twice struck out, and hurriedly skated away from him. She skated up to Mlle Linon, said something to her, and went toward the pavilion where the ladies took off their skates.

"My God! What have I done! Merciful God! Help me, guide me," said Levin, praying inwardly, and at the same time, feeling a need of violent exercise, he skated about, describing inner and outer circles.

At that moment one of the young men, the best of the skaters of the day, came out of the coffeehouse in his skates, with a cigarette in his mouth. Taking a run, he dashed down the steps in his skates, crashing and bounding up and down. He flew down, and without even changing the position of his hands, he skated away over the ice.

"Ah, that's a new trick!" said Levin, and he promptly ran up to the top to do this new trick.

"Don't break your neck! It takes practice!" Nikolai Shcherbatsky shouted after him.

Levin went to the steps, took a run from above as best he could, and dashed down, preserving his balance in this unaccustomed movement with his hands. On the last step he stumbled, but barely touching the ice with his hand, with a violent effort he recovered himself and skated off, laughing.

"How wonderful, how nice he is!" Kitty was thinking at that moment, as she came out of the pavilion with Mlle Linon, and looked toward him with a smile of quiet affection, as though he was a favourite brother. "And can it be my fault, can I have done anything wrong? They talk of flirtation. I know it's not he that I love; but still I am happy with him, and he's so nice. Only, why did he say that? . . ." she mused.

Catching sight of Kitty going away, and her mother meeting her at the steps, Levin, flushed from his rapid exercise, stood still and pondered a minute. He took off his skates, and overtook the mother and daughter at the entrance of the gardens.

"Delighted to see you," said Princess Shcherbatskaya. "On Thursdays we are home, as always."

"Today, then?"

"We shall be pleased to see you," the princess said stiffly.

This stiffness hurt Kitty, and she could not resist the desire to smooth over her mother's coldness. She turned her head and, with a smile, said:

"Good-by till this evening."

At that moment Stepan Arkadyevich, his hat cocked on one side, with beaming face and eyes, strode into the garden like a conquering hero. But as he approached his mother-in-law, he responded in a mournful and crestfallen tone to her inquires about Dolly's health.

After a little subdued and dejected conversation with his mother-in-law, he threw out his chest again, and put his arm in Levin's.

"Well, shall we set off?" he asked. "I've been thinking about you all this time, and I'm very, very glad you've come," he said, looking him in the face with a significant air.

"Yes, come along," answered Levin in ecstasy, hearing unceasingly the sound of that voice saying, "Good-by till this evening," and seeing the smile with which it was said.

"To the Anglia or the Hermitage?"

"I don't mind which."

"All right, then, the Anglia," said Stepan Arkadyevich, selecting that restaurant because he owed more there than at the Hermitage, and consequently considered it wrong to avoid it. "Have you got a sleigh? That's very good, for I sent my carriage home."

The friends hardly spoke all the way. Levin was wondering what that change in Kitty's expression had meant, and alternately assuring himself that there was hope, and falling into despair seeing clearly that his hopes were insane, and yet all the while he felt himself quite another man, utterly unlike what he had been before her smile and those words, "Good-by till this evening."

Stepan Arkadyevich was absorbed during the drive in composing the menu of the dinner.

"You like turbot, don't you?" he said to Levin as they were arriving.

"Eh?" responded Levin. "Turbot? Yes, I'm awfully fond of turbot."

CHAPTER TEN

When Levin went into the restaurant with Oblonsky, he could not help noticing a certain peculiarity of expression, as it were, a restrained radiance, about the face and whole figure of Stepan Arkadyevich. Oblonsky took off his overcoat, and, with his hat over one ear, walked into the dining room, giving directions to the Tartar waiters, who were clustered about him in evening coats, bearing napkins. Bowing to right and left to the people he met, and here as everywhere joyously greeting acquaintances, he went up to the buffet for a preliminary appetizer of fish and vodka, and said to the painted Frenchwoman decked in ribbons, lace, and ringlets behind the counter something so amusing that even she was moved to genuine laughter. Levin for his part refrained from taking any vodka simply because he felt such a loathing of that Frenchwoman, all made up, it seemed, of false hair, *poudre de riz*, and *vinaigre de toilette*.[1] He made haste to move away from her, as from a dirty place. His whole soul was filled with memories of Kitty, and there was a smile of triumph and happiness shining in his eyes.

"This way, Your Excellency, please. Your Excellency won't be disturbed here," said a particularly pertinacious, white-headed old Tartar with immense hips and coattails gaping widely behind. "Walk in, Your Excellency," he said to Levin, by way of showing his respect to Stepan Arkadyevich, being attentive to his guest as well.

Instantly flinging a fresh cloth over the round table under the bronze chandelier, though it already had a tablecloth on it, he pushed up velvet chairs, and came to a standstill before Stepan Arkadyevich with a napkin and a menu in his hands, awaiting his orders.

"If you prefer it, Your Excellency, a private room will be free very soon; Prince Golitsyn with a lady. Fresh oysters have come in."

"Ah, oysters."

Stepan Arkadyevich became thoughtful.

"What if we were to change our plans, Levin?" he said, keeping his finger on the menu, and his face expressed serious hesitation. "Are the oysters good? Absolutely?"

"They're Flensburg, Your Excellency. We've no Ostend."

"Flensburg will do, but are they fresh?"

"Only arrived yesterday."

"Well, then, what if we were to begin with oysters, and so change the whole menu? Eh?"

"It's all the same to me. I would like cabbage soup and *kasha*[2] better than anything; but of course there's nothing like that here."

"*Kasha à la Russe*, Your Honor would like?" said the Tartar, bending down to Levin like a nurse speaking to a child.

---

[1] "Rice powder and toilet water."
[2] I.e., buckwheat porridge.

"No, joking aside, whatever you choose is sure to be good. I've been skating, and I'm hungry. And don't imagine," he added, detecting a look of dissatisfaction on Oblonsky's face, "that I won't appreciate your choice. I am fond of good things."

"I should hope so! After all, it's one of the pleasures of life," said Stepan Arkadyevich. "Well. then, my friend, you give us two—better say three—dozen oysters, clear soup with vegetables . . ."

"*Printanière*," prompted the Tartar. But Stepan Arkadyevich apparently did not care to allow him the satisfaction of giving the French names of the dishes.

"With vegetables in it, you know. Then turbot with thick sauce, then . . . roast beef; and be sure it's good. Yes, and capons, perhaps, and then preserved fruit."

The Tartar, recollecting that it was Stepan Arkadyevich's way not to call the dishes by the names in the French menu, did not repeat them after him, but could not resist rehearsing the whole menu to himself according to the bill: "*Soupe printanière, turbot, sauce Beaumarchais, poulard à l'estragon, macédoine de fruits* . . . etc.," and then instantly, as though worked by springs, laying down one bound menu, he took up another, the list of wines, and submitted it to Stepan Arkadyevich.

"What shall we drink?"

"What you like, only not too much. Champagne," said Levin.

"What! To start with? You're right, though, why not? Do you like the white seal?"

"*Cachet blanc*," prompted the Tartar.

"Very well, then, give us that brand with the oysters, and then we'll see."

"Yes, sir. And what table wine?"

"You can give us Nuits. Oh, no, better the classic Chablis."

"Yes, sir. And *your* cheese, Your Excellency?"

"Oh, yes, Parmesan. Or would you like another?"

"No, it's all the same to me," said Levin, unable to suppress a smile.

And the Tartar ran off with flying coattails, five minutes later darting back with a dish of opened oysters on mother-of-pearl shells, and a bottle between his fingers.

Stepan Arkadyevich crushed the starchy napkin, tucked it into his vest, and, settling his arms comfortably, started on the oysters.

"Not bad," he said, stripping the oysters from the pearly shells with a silver fork, and swallowing them one after another. "Not bad," he repeated, turning his dewy, brilliant eyes from Levin to the Tartar.

Levin ate the oysters, though white bread and cheese would have pleased him better. But he was admiring Oblonsky. Even the Tartar, uncorking the bottle and pouring the sparkling wine into the thin, wide glasses, glanced at Stepan Arkadyevich, and settled his white cravat with a perceptible smile of satisfaction.

"You don't care much for oysters, do you?" said Stepan Arkadyevich, emptying his wine glass. "Or you're worried about something. Eh?"

He wanted Levin to be in good spirits. But it was not that Levin was not in good spirits; he was ill at ease. With what he had in his soul, he felt sore and uncomfortable in the restaurant, in the midst of private rooms where men were dining with ladies, in all this fuss and bustle; the surroundings of bronzes, mirrors, gaslights, and waiters— all of it was offensive to him. He was afraid of sullying what his soul was imbued with.

"I? Yes, I am; but besides, all this bothers me," he said. "You can't conceive how strange it all seems to a country person like me, as strange as that gentleman's nails I saw at your place . . ."

"Yes, I saw how much interested you were in poor Grinevich's nails," said Stepan Arkadyevich, laughing.

"It's too much for me," responded Levin. "Do try and put yourself in my place, take the point of view of a country person. We in the country try to have our hands in such condition as will be most convenient for working with. So we cut our nails; sometimes we turn up our sleeves. And here people let their nails grow as long as they will, and put on small saucers for cuffs links, so that they can do nothing with their hands."

Stepan Arkadyevich smiled gaily.

"Oh, yes, that's just a sign that he has no need to do coarse work. His work is with the mind . . ."

"Maybe. But still it's strange to me, just as at this moment it seems strange to me that we country folks try to get our meals over with as soon as we can so as to be ready for our work, while here we are trying to drag out our meals as long as possible, and with that object eating oysters . . ."

"Why, of course," objected Stepan Arkadyevich. "But that's just the aim of civilization—to make everything a source of enjoyment."

"Well, if that's its aim, I'd rather be a savage."

"And so you are a savage. All you Levins are savages."

Levin sighed. He remembered his brother Nikolai, and felt ashamed and distressed, and he scowled; but Oblonsky began speaking of a subject that at once drew his attention.

"Oh, are you going tonight to our people—the Shcherbatskys', I mean?" he said, his eyes sparkling significantly as he pushed away the empty rough shells, and drew the cheese toward him.

"Yes, I shall certainly go," replied Levin; "though I thought the princess was not very warm in her invitation."

"What nonsense! That's her manner . . . Come, boy, the soup! . . . That's her manner—*grande dame*," said Stepan Arkadyevich. "I'm coming, too, but I have to go to the Countess Banina's rehearsal. Come, isn't it true you're a savage? How do you explain the sudden way in which you vanished from Moscow? The Shcherbatskys were continually asking me about you, as though I ought to know. The only thing I know is that you always do what no one else does."

"Yes," said Levin, slowly and with emotion, "you're right. I am a savage. Only, my savageness is not in having gone away but in coming now. Now I have come—"

"Oh, what a lucky fellow you are!" Stepan Arkadyevich broke in, looking into Levin's eyes.

"Why?"

"I recognize the lively steeds by their brands, and I recognize young lovers by their eyes,"[3] he declaimed. "Everything is before you."

"Why, is it over for you already?"

"No; not over exactly, but the future is yours, and the present is mine, and the present—well, it's not all that it might be."

[3] From Pushkin's translation of the Greek poet Anacreon's "Ode 55."

"How so?"

"Oh, things go wrong. But I don't want to talk of myself, and besides, I can't explain it all," said Stepan Arkadyevich. "Well, why have you come to Moscow, then? . . . Take this away!" he called to the Tartar.

"You guess?" Levin asked, his eyes like deep wells of light fixed on Stepan Arkadyevich.

"I guess, but I can't be the first to talk about it. You can see by that whether I guess right or wrong," said Stepan Arkadyevich, gazing at Levin with a subtle smile.

"Well, and what have you to say to me?" said Levin in a quivering voice, feeling that all the muscles of his face were quivering too. "How do you look at the question?"

Stepan Arkadyevich slowly emptied his glass of Chablis, never taking his eyes off Levin.

"I?" said Stepan Arkadyevich. "There's nothing I desire so much as that— nothing! It would be the best thing that could be."

"But you're not making a mistake? You know what we're speaking of?" said Levin, piercing him with his eyes. "You think it's possible?"

"I think it's possible. Why not possible?"

"No! Do you really think it's possible? No, tell me all you think! Oh, but if . . . if refusal's in store for me! . . . Indeed I feel sure . . ."

"Why should you think that?" said Stepan Arkadyevich, smiling at his excitement.

"It seems so to me sometimes. That will be awful for me, and for her too."

"Oh, well, anyway there's nothing awful in it for a girl. Every girl's proud of a proposal."

"Yes, every girl, but not she."

Stepan Arkadyevich smiled. He so well knew that feeling of Levin's that for him all the girls in the world were divided into two classes: one class—all the girls in the world except her, those with all sorts of human weaknesses, ordinary: the other class—she alone, having no weakness of any sort and higher than all humanity.

"Wait, take some sauce," he said, holding back Levin's hand as it pushed away the sauce.

Levin obediently helped himself to sauce, but would not let Stepan Arkadyevich go on with his dinner.

"No, stop a minute, stop a minute," he said. "You must understand that it's a question of life and death for me. I have never spoken to anyone of this. And there's no one I could speak of it to, except you. You know we're utterly unlike each other, different tastes and views and everything; but I know you're fond of me and understand me, and that's why I like you so much. But for God's sake, be quite straightforward with me."

"I tell you what I think," said Stepan Arkadyevich, smiling. "But I will say more: my wife is a wonderful woman . . ." Stepan Arkadyevich sighed, remembering his position with his wife and after a moment's silence, resumed: "She has a gift of foreseeing things. She sees right through people; but that's not all; she knows what will come to pass, especially in the way of marriages. She foretold, for instance, that Princess Shakhovskaya would marry Brenteln. No one would believe it, but it came to pass. And she's on your side."

"How do you mean?"

"It's not only that she likes you—she says that Kitty is certain to be your wife."

At these words Levin's face suddenly lighted up with a smile, a smile not far from tears of emotion.

"She says that!" cried Levin. "I always said she was exquisite, your wife. There, that's enough, enough said about it," he said, getting up from his seat.

"All right, but do sit down."

But Levin could not sit down. He strode up and down the little cage of a room, blinked his eyelids that his tears might not fall, and only then sat down at the table.

"You must understand," said he, "it's not love. I've been in love, but it's not that. It's not my feeling, but a sort of force outside me has taken possession of me. I went away, you see, because I made up my mind that it could never be, you understand, as a happiness that does not come on earth; but I've struggled with myself, I see there's no living without it. And it must be settled."

"What did you go away for?"

"Ah, stop a minute! Ah, the thoughts that came crowding on one!

The questions one must ask oneself! Listen. You can't imagine what you've done for me by what you said. I'm so happy that I've become positively disgusting; I've forgotten everything. I heard today that my brother Nikolai . . . you know, he's here . . . I had even forgotten him. It seems to me that he's happy too. It's a sort of madness. But one thing's awful. . . . Here, you've been married, you know the feeling . . . it's awful that we—old—with past . . . not of love, but of sins . . . and are brought all at once so near to a creature pure and innocent; it's loathsome, and that's why one can't help feeling oneself unworthy."

"Oh, well, you've not many sins on your conscience."

" 'Alas! all the same,' " said Levin, " 'when with loathing I go over my life, I shudder and curse and bitterly complain . . .'[4] Yes."

"What can one do? The world's made like that," said Stepan Arkadyevich.

"The one comfort is like that prayer which I always liked: 'Forgive me not according to my unworthiness, but according to Thy loving kindness.' That's the only way she can forgive me."

CHAPTER ELEVEN

Levin emptied his glass, and they were silent for a while.

"There's one other thing I ought to tell you. Do you know Vronsky?" Stepan Arkadyevich asked Levin.

"No, I don't. Why do you ask?"

"Give us another bottle," Stepan Arkadyevich directed the Tartar, who was filling up their glasses and fidgeting around them just when he was not wanted.

"Why, you ought to know Vronsky because he's one of your rivals."

"Who's Vronsky?" said Levin, and his face was suddenly transformed from the look of childlike ecstasy which Oblonsky had just been admiring to an angry and unpleasant expression.

"Vronsky is one of the sons of Count Kirill Ivanovich Vronsky, and one of the finest specimens of the gilded youth of Petersburg. I

[4] From Pushkin's "Remembrance."

made his acquaintance in Tver when I was there an official business, and he came there for the levy of recruits. Very rich, handsome, great connections, an aide-de-camp, and with all that a very nice, good-natured fellow. But he's more than simply a good-natured fellow, as I've found out here—he's a cultivated man, too, and very intelligent; he's a man who'll make his mark."

Levin scowled and was silent.

"Well, he turned up here soon after you'd gone, and as far as I can see, he's head over ears in love with Kitty, and you know that her mother—"

"Excuse me, but I know nothing," said Levin, frowning gloomily. And immediately he recollected his brother Nikolai and how loathsome he was to have been able to forget him.

"But wait a minute, wait a minute," said Stepan Arkadyevich, smiling and touching his hand. "I've told you what I know, and I repeat that in this delicate and tender matter, as far as one can judge, I believe the chances are in your favor."

Levin dropped back in his chair; his face was pale.

"But I would advise you to settle the thing as soon as possible," Oblonsky went on, filling up his glass.

"No, thanks, I can't drink any more," said Levin, pushing away his glass. "I shall be drunk . . . Come, tell me, how are you getting on?" he said, obviously anxious to change the conversation.

"One word more: in any case I advise you to settle the question soon. Tonight I don't advise you to speak," said Stepan Arkadyevich. "Go round tomorrow morning, make an offer in due form, and God bless you . . ."

"Oh, are you still thinking of coming down for some shooting? Come next spring," said Levin.

Now his whole soul was full of remorse that he had begun this conversation with Stepan Arkadyevich. A feeling such as his was profaned by talk of the rivalry of some Petersburg officer, of the suppositions and the counsels of Stepan Arkadyevich.

Stepan Arkadyevich smiled. He knew what was going on in Levin's soul.

"I'll come someday," he said. "But women, my boy, they're the pivot everything turns upon. Things are in a bad way with me, very bad. And it's all through women. Tell me frankly, now," he pursued, picking up a cigar and keeping one hand on his glass; "give me your advice."

"Why, what is it?"

"I'll tell you. Suppose you're married, you love your wife, but you're fascinated by another woman . . ."

"Excuse me, but I'm absolutely unable to comprehend how . . . just as I can't comprehend how I could now, after my dinner, go straight to a baker's shop and steal a roll."

Stepan Arkadyevich's eyes sparkled more than usual.

"Why not? Rolls will sometimes smell so good one can't resist them!

> *'Himmlisch ist's, wenn ich bezwungen*
> *Meine irdische Begier;*
> *Aber doch wenn's nicht gelungen*
> *Hatt' ich auch recht hübsch Plaisir!'* "[1]

As he said this, Stepan Arkadyevich smiled subtly. Levin, too, could not help smiling.

"Yes, but joking aside," Stepan Arkadyevich resumed, "you must understand that the woman is a sweet, gentle, loving creature, poor and lonely, and has sacrificed everything. Now, when the thing's done, don't you see, can one possibly cast her off? Even supposing one parts from her so as not to break up one's family life, still, can one help feeling for her, setting her on her feet, softening her position?"

"Well, you must excuse me there. You know, to me all women are divided into two classes . . . at least no . . . truer to say: there are women and there are . . . I've never seen exquisite fallen beings, and I never shall see them, but such creatures as that painted French-woman at the counter with the ringlets are vermin to my mind, and all fallen women are the same."

[1] It is heavenly whenever I mastered
My earthly desire;
But whenever I did not succeed
I still took my pleasure.
[Heine's *Nachlese Zur "Heimkehr,"* 9.]

"But the Magdalen?"

"Ah, drop that! Christ never would have said those words if He had known how they would be abused. Of all the Gospel those words are the only ones remembered. However, I'm not saying so much what I think as what I feel. I have a loathing for fallen women. You're afraid of spiders, and I of these vermin. Most likely you've not made a study of spiders and don't know their character; and so it is with me."

"It's very well for you to talk like that; it's very much like that gentleman in Dickens who used to fling all difficult questions over his right shoulder with his left hand.[2] But to deny the facts is no answer. What's to be done—you tell me that, what's to be done? Your wife gets older, while you're full of life. Before you've time to look around, you feel that you can't love your wife with love, however much you may esteem her. And then all at once love turns up, and you're done for, done for," Stepan Arkadyevich said with weary despair.

Levin half smiled.

"Yes, you're done for," Oblonsky repeated. "But what's to be done?"

"Don't steal rolls."

Stepan Arkadyevich laughed outright.

"Oh, moralist! But you must understand, there are two women; one insists only on her rights and those rights are your love, which you can't give her; and the other sacrifices everything for you and asks for nothing. What are you to do? How are you to act? There's a fearful tragedy in it."

"If you care for my profession of faith as regards that, I'll tell you that I don't believe there was any tragedy about it. And this is why. To my mind, love . . . both kinds of love, which you remember Plato defines in his *Symposium*, serve as the test of men. Some men understand only one kind and some only the other. And those who know

---

[2]Tolstoy may have had in mind either Harold Skimpol in *Bleak House* (especially his attitude in chapters 6 and 8) or, more likely, Podsnap in *Our Mutual Friend*, chapter 11: "Mr. Podsnap had even acquired a peculiar flourish of his right arm in often clearing the world of its most difficult problems, by sweeping them behind him."

only the nonplatonic love have no need to talk of tragedy. In such love there can be no tragedy. 'I'm much obliged for the gratification, my humble respects'—that's the whole tragedy. And in platonic love there can be no tragedy, because in that love all is clear and pure, because . . ."

At that instant Levin recollected his own sins and the inner conflict he had lived through. And he added unexpectedly:

"But perhaps you are right. Very likely . . . I don't know, I don't know."

"It's this, don't you see," said Stepan Arkadyevich: "you're very much all of a piece. That's your strong point and your failing. You have a character that's all of a piece and you want the whole of life to be a piece too—but that's not how it is. You despise public official work because you want the reality to be invariably corresponding all the while with the aim— and that's not how it is. You want a man's work, too, always to have a defined aim, and love and family life always to be undivided—and that's not how it is. All the variety, all the charm, all the beauty of life is made up of light and shadow."

Levin sighed and made no reply. He was thinking of his own affairs, and did not hear Oblonsky.

And suddenly both of them felt that though they were friends, though they had been dining and drinking together, which should have drawn them closer, each was thinking only of his own affairs, and they had nothing to do with one another. Oblonsky had more than once experienced this extreme sense of aloofness, instead of intimacy, coming on after dinner, and he knew what to do in such cases.

"Bill!" he called, and went into the next room, where he promptly came across an aide-de-camp of his acquaintance, and fell into conversation with him about an actress and her protector. And at once, in the conversation with the aide-de-camp, Oblonsky had a sense of relaxation and relief after the conversation with Levin, which always put him to too great a mental and spiritual strain.

When the Tartar appeared with a bill for twenty-six rubles and odd kopeks, besides a tip for himself, Levin, who, like anyone from the country, would another time have been horrified at his share of fourteen rubles, did not notice it, paid, and set off homeward to dress and go to the Shcherbatskys', there to decide his fate.

CHAPTER TWELVE

The young Princess Kitty Shcherbatskaya was eighteen. It was the first winter that she had been out in the world. Her success in society had been greater than that of either of her elder sisters, and greater even than her mother had anticipated. To say nothing of the young men who danced at the Moscow balls almost all being in love with Kitty, two serious suitors had already this first winter made their appearance: Levin, and immediately after his departure, Count Vronsky.

Levin's appearance at the beginning of the winter, his frequent visits and evident love for Kitty, had led to the first serious conversation between Kitty's parents as to her future, and to disputes between them. The prince was on Levin's side; he said he wished for nothing better for Kitty. The princess, for her part, approaching the question in the manner peculiar to women, maintained that Kitty was too young, that Levin had done nothing to prove that he had serious intentions, that Kitty felt no great attraction to him, and other side issues; but she did not state the principal point, which was that she looked for a better match for her daughter, and that Levin was not to her liking, and she did not understand him. When Levin had abruptly departed, the princess was delighted, and said to her husband triumphantly: "You see I was right." When Vronsky appeared on the scene, she was still more delighted, confirmed in her opinion that Kitty was to make not simply a good but a brilliant match.

In the mother's eyes there could be no comparison between Vronsky and Levin. She disliked in Levin his strange and uncompromising opinions and his shyness in society, founded, as she supposed, on his pride and his peculiar sort of life, as she considered it, absorbed in cattle and peasants. She did not very much like it that he, who was in love with her daughter, had kept coming to the house for six weeks, as though he were waiting for something, inspecting, as though he were afraid he might be doing them too great an honor by making an offer, and did not realize that a man who continually visits at a house where there is a young unmarried girl is bound to make his intentions clear. And suddenly without doing so, he disappeared. "It's good that he's not attractive enough for Kitty to have fallen in love with him," thought the mother.

Vronsky satisfied all the mother's desires, very wealthy, clever, of aristocratic family, on the highroad to a brilliant career in the army and at court, and a fascinating man. Nothing better could be wished for.

Vronsky openly flirted with Kitty at balls, danced with her, and came continually to the house; consequently there could be no doubt of the seriousness of his intentions. But in spite of that, the mother had spent the whole of that winter in a state of terrible anxiety and agitation.

Princess Shcherbatskaya herself had been married thirty years ago, her aunt arranging the match. Her husband, about whom everything was well known beforehand, had come, looked at his future bride, and been looked at. The matchmaking aunt had ascertained and communicated their mutual impression. That impression had been favorable. Afterward, on a day fixed beforehand, the expected offer was made to her parents, and accepted. All had passed very simply and easily. So it seemed, at least, to the princess. But over her own daughters she had felt how far from simple and easy is the business, apparently so commonplace, of marrying off one's daughters. The panics that had been lived through, the thoughts that had been brooded over, the money that had been wasted, and the disputes with her husband over marrying the two elder girls, Darya and Natalie! Now, since the youngest had come out, she was going through the same terrors, the same doubts, and quarrels with her husband still more violent than those over the older girls. The old prince, like all fathers indeed, was exceedingly punctilious on the score of the honor and reputation of his daughters. He was irrationally jealous over his daughters, especially over Kitty, who was his favorite. At every turn he had scenes with the princess for compromising her daughter. The princess had grown accustomed to this already with her other daughters, but now she felt that there was more ground for the prince's touchiness. She saw that of late years much was changed in the manners of society, that a mother's duties had become still more difficult. She saw that girls of Kitty's age formed some sort of clubs, went to some sort of lectures, mixed freely in men's society, drove about the streets alone, many of them did not curtsey, and, what was the most important thing, all the people were firmly convinced that to choose their husband was their own affair and not their parents'. "Marriages aren't made nowadays as they used to be," was thought and said by all these young girls, and even by their elders. But how marriages were made now, the princess could not learn from anyone. The French fashion— of the parents arranging their children's future—was not accepted; it was condemned. The English fashion of the complete independence of girls was also not accepted, and not possible in Russian society. The Russian fashion of matchmaking by the officer of intermediate persons was for some reason considered disgraceful; it was ridiculed by everyone, and by the princess herself. But how girls were to be married, and how parents were to marry them, no one knew. Everyone with whom the princess had chanced to discuss the matter said the same thing: "It's high time in our day to cast off all that old-fashioned business. It's the young people who have to marry, and not their parents; and so we ought to leave the young people to arrange it as they choose." It was very easy for anyone to say that who had no daughters, but the princess realized that in the process of getting to know various men her daughter might fall in love, and fall in love with someone who did not care to marry her, or who was quite unfit to be her husband. And, however much it was instilled into the princess that in our times young people ought to arrange their lives for themselves, she was unable to believe it, just as she would have been unable to believe that, at any time whatever, the most suitable playthings for children five years old ought to be loaded pistols. And so the princess was more uneasy over Kitty than she had been over her elder daughters.

Now she was afraid that Vronsky might confine himself to simply flirting with her daughter. She saw that her daughter was in love with him, but tried to comfort herself with the thought that he was an honorable man, and would not do this. But at the same time she knew how easy it is, with the freedom of manners of today, to turn a girl's head, and how lightly men generally regard such a crime. The week before, Kitty had told her mother of a conversation she had had with Vronsky during a mazurka. This conversation had partly reassured the princess; but perfectly at ease she could not be. Vronsky had told Kitty that both he and his brother were so used to obeying their mother that they never made up their minds to any important undertaking without consulting her. "And just now I am awaiting my mother's arrival from Petersburg, as a supreme blessing," he told her.

Kitty had repeated this without attaching any significance to the words. But her mother saw them in a different light. She knew that the old lady was expected from day to day, that she would be pleased at her son's choice, and she felt it strange that he should not make his offer through fear of vexing his mother. However, she was so anxious for the marriage itself, and still more for relief from her fears, that she believed it was so. Bitter as it was for the princess to see the unhappiness of her eldest daughter, Dolly, on the point of leaving her husband, her anxiety over the decision of her youngest daughter's fate engaged all her feelings. Today, with Levin's reappearance, a fresh source of anxiety arose. She was afraid that her daughter, who had at one time, she thought, a feeling for Levin, might, from extreme sense of honor, refuse Vronsky, and that Levin's arrival might generally complicate and delay the affair so near being concluded.

"Why, has he been here long?" the princess asked about Levin, as they returned home.

"He came today, Mama."

"There's one thing I want to say . . ." the princess began, and from her serious and alert face, Kitty guessed what it would be.

"Mama," she said, flushing hotly and turning quickly to her, "please, please don't say anything about that. I know, I know all about it."

She wished for what her mother wished for, but the motives of her mother's wishes wounded her.

"I only want to say that to raise hopes—"

"Mama, darling, for goodness' sake, don't talk about it. It's so horrible to talk about it."

"I won't," said her mother, seeing the tears in her daughter's eyes; "but one thing, my love, you promised me you would have no secrets from me. You won't?"

"Never, Mama, none," answered Kitty, flushing a little, and looking her mother straight in the face; "but there's no use in my telling you anything, and I . . . I . . . if I wanted to, I don't know what to say or how . . . I don't know . . ."

"No, she could not tell an untruth with those eyes," thought the mother, smiling at her agitation and happiness—smiling, because what was taking place just now in her daughter's soul seemed to the poor child so immense and so important.

CHAPTER THIRTEEN

After dinner, and till the beginning of the evening, Kitty was feeling a sensation akin to that of a young man before a battle. Her heart throbbed violently, and she could not fix her thoughts on anything.

She felt that this evening, when they would meet each other for the first time, would be a turning point in her life. And she was continually picturing them to herself, at one moment each separately, and then both together. When she mused on the past, she dwelled with pleasure, with tenderness, on the memories of her relations with Levin. The memories of childhood and of Levin's friendship with her dead brother gave a special poetic charm to her relations with him. His love for her, of which she felt certain, was flattering and delightful to her; and it was pleasant for her to think of Levin. In her memories of Vronsky there always entered a certain element of awkwardness, though he was in the highest degree well bred and poised, as though there was some false note—not in Vronsky, he was very simple and nice, but in herself, while with Levin she felt perfectly at ease. But, on the other hand, as soon as she thought of the future with Vronsky, there arose before her a perspective of brilliant happiness; with Levin the future seemed misty.

When she went upstairs to dress, and looked into the mirrors, she noticed with joy that it was one of her good days, and that she was in complete possession of all her powers— she needed this so for what lay before her: she was conscious of external composure and free grace in her movements.

At half-past seven she had just gone down into the drawing room, when the footman announced, "Konstantin Dmitrievich Levin." The princess was still in her room, and the prince had not come in. "So it is to be," thought Kitty, and all the blood seemed to rush to her heart. She was horrified at her paleness as she glanced into the mirror. At that moment she knew beyond doubt that he had come early on purpose to find her alone and to propose to her. And then for the first time the whole thing presented itself in a new, different aspect; only then did she realize that the question did not affect her only—with whom she would be happy, and whom she loved—but that she would that moment have to wound a man whom she liked. And to wound him cruelly. What for? Because he, dear fellow, loved her, was in love with her. But there was no help for it, so it must be, so it would have to be.

"My God! Must I really have to say it to him?" she thought. "Can I tell him I don't love him? That will be a lie. What am I to say to him? That I love someone else? No, that's impossible. I'm going away, I'm going away."

She had reached the door when she heard his step. "No! it's not fair. What have I to be afraid of? I have done nothing wrong. What is to be, will be! I'll tell the truth. And with him one can't be ill at ease. Here he is," she said to herself, seeing his powerful, shy figure, with his shining eyes fixed on her. She looked straight into his face, as though imploring him to spare her, and gave him her hand.

"It's not time yet; I think I'm too early," he said, glancing around the empty drawing room. When he saw that his expectations were realized, that there was nothing to prevent him from speaking, his face became gloomy.

"Oh, no," said Kitty, and sat down at the table.

"But this was just what I wanted, to find you alone," he began, not sitting down, and not looking at her, so as to keep up his courage.

"Mama will be down right away. She was very tired . . . Yesterday . . ."

She talked on, not knowing what her lips were uttering, and not taking her supplicating and caressing eyes off him.

He glanced at her; she blushed, and ceased speaking.

"I told you I did not know whether I would be here long . . . that it depended on you . . ."

She bent her head lower and lower, not knowing herself what answer she would make to what was coming.

"That it depended on you," he repeated. "I meant to say . . . I meant to say . . . I came for this . . . to be my wife!" he brought out, not knowing what he was saying; but feeling that the most terrible thing was said, he stopped short and looked at her. . . .

She was breathing heavily, not looking at him. She was feeling ecstasy. Her soul was flooded with happiness. She had never anticipated that the utterance of love would produce such a powerful effect on her. But it lasted only an instant. She remembered Vronsky. She lifted her clear, truthful eyes, and seeing his desperate face, she answered hastily:

"That cannot be . . . forgive me."

A moment ago, and how close she had been to him, of what importance in his life! And how aloof and remote from him she had become now!

"It was bound to be so," he said, not looking at her.

And, bowing, he prepared to leave.

CHAPTER FOURTEEN

But at that very moment the princess came in. There was a look of horror on her face when she saw them alone, and their disturbed faces. Levin bowed to her and said nothing. Kitty did not speak or lift her eyes. "Thank God, she has refused him," thought the mother, and her face lighted up with the habitual smile with which she greeted her guests on her Thursdays. She sat down and began questioning Levin about his life in the country. He sat down again, waiting for other visitors to arrive, in order to retreat unnoticed.

Five minutes later there arrived a friend of Kitty's, married the preceding winter, Countess Nordston.

She was a thin, sallow, sickly, and nervous woman, with brilliant black eyes. She was fond of Kitty, and her affection for her showed itself, as the affection of married women for girls always does, in the desire to make a match for Kitty after her own ideal of married happiness; she wanted her to marry Vronsky. She had often met Levin at the Shcherbatskys' early in the winter, and she had always disliked him. Her invariable and favorite pursuit, went they met, consisted of making fun of him.

"I do like it when he looks down at me from the height of his grandeur, or breaks off his learned conversation with me because I'm a fool, or is condescending to me. I like that so; to see him condescending! I am so glad he can't bear me," she used to say of him.

She was right, for Levin actually could not bear her, and despised her for what she was proud of and regarded as a fine characteristic— her nervousness, her delicate contempt and indifference for everything coarse and earthly.

The Countess Nordston and Levin had got into that relation with one another not seldom seen in society, when two persons, who remain externally on friendly terms, despise each other to such a degree that they cannot even take each other seriously, and cannot even be offended by each other.

The Countess Nordston pounced upon Levin at once.

"Ah, Konstantin Dmitrievich! So you've come back to our corrupt Babylon," she said, giving him her tiny yellow hand, and recalling what he had chanced to say early in the winter, that Moscow was a Babylon. "Come, is Babylon reformed, or have you degenerated?" she added, glancing with a simper at Kitty.

"It's very flattering for me, Countess, that you remember my words so well," responded Levin, who had succeeded in recovering his composure, and at once from habit dropped into his tone of joking hostility to the Countess Nordston. "They must certainly make a great impression on you."

"Oh, I should think so! I always note it all down. Well, Kitty, have you been skating again? . . ."

And she began talking to Kitty. Awkward as it was for Levin to withdraw now, it would still have been easier for him to suffer this awkwardness than to remain all evening and see Kitty, who glanced at him now and then and avoided his eyes. He was on the point of getting up, when the princess, noticing that he was silent, addressed him.

"Will you be long in Moscow? You're busy with the district council, though, aren't you, and can't be away for long?"

"No, Princess, I'm no longer a member of the council," he said. "I have come up for a few days."

"There's something the matter with him," thought Countess Nordston, glancing at his stern, serious face. "He isn't in his old argumentative mood. But I'll draw him out. I do love making a fool of him before Kitty, and I'll do it."

"Konstantin Dmitrievich," she said to him, "do explain something to me, please: you know all about such things. At home in our village of Kaluga all the peasants and all the women have drunk up all they possessed, and now they can't pay us any rent. What's the meaning of that? You always praise the peasants so."

At that instant another lady came into the room, and Levin got up.

"Excuse me, Countess, but I really know nothing about it, and can't tell you anything," he said, and looked around at the officer who came in behind the lady.

"That must be Vronsky," thought Levin, and, to be sure of it, glanced at Kitty. She had already had time to look at Vronsky, and looked back at Levin. And simply from the look in her eyes, which grew unconsciously brighter, Levin knew that she loved that man, knew it as surely as if she had told him so in words. But what sort of a man was he? Now, whether for good or for ill, Levin could not choose but remain; he must find out what the man was like whom she loved.

There are people who, on meeting a successful rival, no matter in what, are at once disposed to turn their backs on everything good in him, and to see only what is bad. There are people, on the other hand, who desire above all to find in that lucky rival the qualities by which he has outstripped them, and seek with a throbbing ache at heart only what is good. Levin belonged to the second class. But he had no difficulty in finding what was good and attractive in Vronsky. It was apparent at the first glance. Vronsky was a squarely built, dark man, not very tall, with a good-humored, handsome, and exceedingly calm and resolute face. Everything about his face and figure, from his short-cropped black hair and freshly shaven chin down to his loosely fitting, brand-new uniform, was simple and at the same time elegant. Making way for the lady who had come in, Vronsky went up to the princess and then to Kitty.

As he approached her, his beautiful eyes shone with a specially tender light, and with a faint, happy, and modestly triumphant smile (so it seemed to Levin), bowing carefully and respectfully over her, he held out his small, broad hand to her.

Greeting and saying a few words to everyone, he sat down without once glancing at Levin, who had never taken his eyes off him.

"Let me introduce you," said the princess, indicating Levin. "Konstantin Dmitrievich Levin, Count Aleksey Kirillovich Vronsky."

Vronsky got up and, looking cordially at Levin, shook hands with him.

"I believe I was to have dined with you this winter," he said, smiling his simple and open smile; "but you had unexpectedly left for the country."

"Konstantin Dmitrievich despises and hates town and us townspeople," said Countess Nordston.

"My words must make a deep impression on you, since you remember them so well," said Levin, and suddenly conscious that he had said just the same thing before, he reddened.

Vronsky looked at Levin and Countess Nordston, and smiled.

"Are you always in the country?" he inquired. "I should think it must be dull in the winter."

"It's not dull if one has work to do; besides, one's not bored by oneself," Levin replied curtly.

"I am fond of the country," said Vronsky, noticing, and affecting not to notice, Levin's tone.

"But I hope, Count, you would not consent to live in the country always," said Countess Nordston.

"I don't know; I have never tried for long. I experienced a strange feeling once," he went on. "I never longed so for the country, Russian country, with bast shoes and peasants, as when I was spending a winter with my mother in Nice. Nice itself is dull enough, you know. And indeed, Naples and Sorrento are pleasant only for a short time. And it's there that Russia comes back to me most vividly, and especially the country. It's as though . . ."

He talked on, addressing both Kitty and Levin, turning his serene, friendly eyes from one to the other, and obviously saying just what came into his head.

Noticing that Countess Nordston wanted to say something, he

stopped short without finishing what he had begun, and listened attentively to her.

The conversation did not flag for an instant, so that the princess, who always kept in reserve, in case a subject should be lacking, two heavy guns—the relative advantages of classical and of scientific education, and universal military service—had not to move out either of them, while Countess Nordston had a chance of teasing Levin.

Levin wanted to, and could not, take part in the general conversation; saying to himself every instant, "Now go," he still did not go, as though waiting for something.

The conversation fell upon table-rapping and spirits, and Countess Nordston, who believed in spiritualism, began to describe the marvels she had seen.

"Ah, Countess, you really must take me, for pity's sake do take me to see them! I have never seen anything extraordinary, though I am always on the lookout for it everywhere," said Vronsky, smiling.

"Very well, next Saturday," answered Countess Nordston. "But you, Konstantin Dmitrievich, do you believe in it?" she asked Levin.

"Why do you ask me? You know what I shall say."

"But I want to hear your opinion."

"My opinion," answered Levin, "is only that this table-rapping simply proves that educated society—so-called—is no higher than the peasants. They believe in the evil eye, and in witchcraft and omens, while we—"

"Oh, then you don't believe in it?"

"I can't believe in it, Countess."

"But if I've seen it myself?"

"The peasant women too tell us they have seen goblins."

"Then you think I tell a lie?"

And she laughed a mirthless laugh.

"Oh, no, Masha, Konstantin Dmitrievich said he could not believe in it," said Kitty, blushing for Levin, and Levin saw this, and, still more exasperated, would have answered, but Vronsky, with his bright, frank smile, rushed to the support of the conversation, which was threatening to become disagreeable.

"You do not admit the conceivability at all?" he queried. "But why not? We admit the existence of electricity, of which we know nothing. Why should there not be some new force, still unknown to us, which—"

"When electricity was discovered," Levin interrupted hurriedly, "it was only the phenomenon that was discovered, and it was unknown from what it proceeded and what were its effects, and ages passed before its applications were conceived. But the spiritualists have begun with tables writing for them, and spirits appearing to them, and have only later started saying that it is an unknown force."

Vronsky listened attentively to Levin, as he always did listen, obviously interested in his words.

"Yes, but the spiritualists say we don't know at present what this force is, but there is a force, and these are the conditions in which it acts. Let the scientific men find out what the force consists of. No, I don't see why there shouldn't be a new force, if it—"

"Why, because with electricity," Levin interrupted again, "every time you rub resin against wool, a recognized phenomenon is manifested, but in this case it does not happen every time, and so it follows it is not a natural phenomenon."

Feeling probably that the conversation was taking a tone too serious for a drawing room, Vronsky made no rejoinder, but by way of trying to change the conversation, he smiled brightly and turned to the ladies.

"Do let us try at once, Countess," he said. But Levin wanted to finish saying what he thought.

"I think," he went on, "that this attempt of the spiritualists to explain their marvels as some sort of new natural force is most futile. They boldly talk of spiritual force, and then try to subject it to material experiment."

Everyone was waiting for him to finish, and he felt it.

"And I think you would be a first-rate medium," said Countess Nordston; "there's something enthusiastic in you."

Levin opened his mouth, was about to say something, reddened, and said nothing.

"Do let us try table-rapping at once, please," said Vronsky. "Princess, will you allow it?"

And Vronsky stood up, looking about for a little table.

Kitty got up to fetch a table, and as she passed, her eyes met

Levin's. She felt for him with her whole heart, the more because she was pitying him for suffering from the pain she had caused. "If you can, forgive me," said her eyes, "I am so happy."

"I hate them all, and you, and myself," his eyes responded, and he picked up his hat. But he was not destined to escape. Just as they were arranging themselves around the table, and Levin was on the point of leaving, the old prince came in, and after greeting the ladies, addressed Levin.

"Ah!" he began joyously. "Been here long, my boy? I didn't even know you were in town. Very glad to see you."

In addressing Levin, the prince sometimes used "thou," sometimes "you."[1] The old prince embraced Levin, and, talking to him, did not observe Vronsky, who had risen and was quietly waiting till the prince should turn to him.

Kitty felt how distasteful her father's warmth was to Levin after what had happened. She saw, too, how coldly her father responded at last to Vronsky's bow, and how Vronsky looked with amiable bewilderment at her father, as though trying and failing to understand how and why anyone could be hostilely disposed toward him, and she flushed.

"Prince, let us have Konstantin Dmitrievich," said Countess Nordston; "we want to try an experiment."

"What experiment? Table-rapping? Well, you must excuse me, ladies and gentlemen, but to my mind it is better fun to play the ring game,"[2] said the old prince, looking at Vronsky and guessing that it had been his suggestion. "There's some sense in that, anyway."

Vronsky looked wonderingly at the prince with his resolute eyes, and, with a faint smile, began immediately talking to Countess Nordston of the great ball that was to come off next week.

"I hope you will be there?" he said to Kitty. As soon as the old prince turned away from him, Levin went out unnoticed, and the last impression he carried away with him of that evening was the smiling, happy face of Kitty answering Vronsky's inquiry about the ball.

---

[1] I.e., the familiar *ty*, the more formal *vy*. *Ty* was reserved for conversations between intimates and when speaking to social inferiors.
[2] A variation of blindman's buff.

CHAPTER FIFTEEN

At the end of the evening Kitty told her mother of her conversation with Levin, and in spite of all the pity she felt for Levin, she was glad at the thought that she had received a *proposal*. She had no doubt that she had acted properly. But after she had gone to bed, for a long while she could not sleep. One impression pursued her relentlessly. It was Levin's face, with his scowling brows, and his kind eyes looking out in dark dejection below them, as he stood listening to her father, and glancing at her and at Vronsky. And she felt so sorry for him that tears came into her eyes. But immediately she thought of the man for whom she had given him up. She vividly recalled his manly, resolute face, his noble self-possession, and the good nature conspicuous in everything he did toward everyone. She remembered the love for her of the man she loved, and once more all was gladness in her soul, and she lay on the pillow smiling with happiness. "I'm sorry, I'm sorry; but what could I do? It's not my fault," she said to herself; but an inner voice told her something else. Whether she felt remorse at having won Levin's love, or at having refused him, she did not know. But her happiness was poisoned by doubts. "Lord, have mercy on us; Lord, have mercy on us; Lord, have mercy on us!" she repeated to herself, till she fell asleep.

Meanwhile, below, in the prince's little library, there occurred one of the scenes so often repeated between the parents on account of their favorite daughter.

"But, really, for mercy's sake, Prince, what have I done?" said the princess, almost crying.

"What? I'll tell you what!" shouted the prince, waving his arms. and wrapping his squirrel-lined dressing gown around him again. "You've no pride, no dignity; you're disgracing, ruining your daughter by this vulgar, stupid matchmaking!"

She, pleased and happy after her conversation with her daughter, had gone to the prince to say good night as usual, and though she had no intention of telling him of Levin's offer and Kitty's refusal, still she hinted to her husband that she thought things were practically settled with Vronsky, and that he would declare himself as soon as his mother arrived. And thereupon, at those words, the prince had all at once flown into a passion, and begun to use unpleasant language.

"What have you done? I'll tell you what. First of all, you're trying to catch an eligible gentlemen, and all Moscow will be talking of it, and with good reason. If you have evening parties, invite everyone, don't pick out just the possible suitors. Invite all the young bucks," (which is what the prince called Moscow's young men). "Engage a piano player and let them dance, and not as you've been doing things, hunting up good matches. It makes me sick, sick to see it, and you've gone on till you've turned the poor girl's head. Levin's a thousand times the better man. As for this little Petersburg dandy, they're turned out by machinery, all on one pattern, and all precious rubbish. But even if he were a prince of the blood, my daughter need not run after anyone."

"But what have I done?"

"Why, you've—" the prince cried wrathfully.

"I know if one were to listen to you," the princess interrupted, "we would never marry our daughter. If it's to be so, we'd better go into the country."

"Well, we had better."

"But do wait a minute. Do I try and catch them? I don't try to catch them in the least. A young man, and a very nice one, has fallen in love with her, and she, I imagine—"

"Oh, yes, you imagine! And what if she really is in love, and he's no more thinking of marriage than I am! . . . Oh, that I should live to see it! . . . Ah! Spiritualism! Ah! Nice! Ah! The ball!"— and the prince, imagining that he was mimicking his wife, made a mincing curtsey at each word. "And this is how we're preparing wretchedness for Katya; and she's really got the notion into her head—"

"But what makes you suppose so?"

"I don't suppose, I know. We have eyes for such things, though women haven't. I see a man who has serious intentions, that's Levin; and I see a peacock, like this featherhead, who's only amusing himself."

"Oh, well, when once you get an idea into your head!"

"Well, you'll remember my words, but too late, just as with Dolly."

"Well, well, we won't talk of it," the princess said quickly, recollecting her unlucky Dolly.

"By all means, and good night!"

And making the sign of the cross over each other, the husband and wife parted with a kiss, feeling that they each remained of their own opinion.

The princess had at first been quite certain that that evening had settled Kitty's future, and that there could be no doubt of Vronsky's intentions, but her husband's words had disturbed her. And returning to her own room in terror before the unknown future, she too, like Kitty, repeated several times in her heart, "Lord, have mercy on us; Lord, have mercy on us; Lord, have mercy on us."

CHAPTER SIXTEEN

Vronsky had never had a real family life. His mother had been in her youth a brilliant society woman, who had had during her married life, and especially afterward, many love affairs notorious in all society. His father he scarcely remembered, and he had been educated in the Corps of Pages.[1]

Leaving the school very young as a brilliant officer, he had at once got into the circle of wealthy Petersburg military men. Although he did go more or less into Petersburg society, his love affairs had always hitherto been outside it.

In Moscow he had for the first time felt, after his luxurious and coarse life at Petersburg, all the charm of intimacy with a sweet and innocent girl of his own rank, who cared for him. It never even entered his head that there could be any harm in his relations with Kitty. At balls he danced mostly with her. He was a constant visitor at their house. He talked to her as people commonly do talk in society—all sorts of nonsense, but nonsense to which he could not help attaching a special meaning in her case. Although he said nothing to her that he could not have said before everybody, he felt that she was becoming more and more dependent upon him, and the more he felt this, the better he liked it, and the tenderer was his feeling for her. He did not know that this mode of behavior in relation to Kitty had

[1] Military school for aristocrats.

a definite character, that it is courting young girls with no intentions of marriage, and that such courting is one of the evil actions common among brilliant young men such as he was. It seemed to him that he was the first who had discovered this pleasure, and he was enjoying his discovery.

If he could have heard what her parents were saying that evening, if he could have put himself in the position of her family and have heard that Kitty would be unhappy if he did not marry her, he would have been greatly astonished, and would not have believed it. He could not believe that what gave such great and delicate pleasure to him, and above all to her, could be wrong. Still less could he have believed that he ought to marry.

Marriage had never presented itself to him as a possibility. He disliked not only family life, but a family—and especially to be a husband was, in accordance with the views general in the bachelor world in which he lived, conceived as something alien, repellent, and, above all, absurd.

But though Vronsky had not the least suspicion what the parents were saying, he felt, on coming away from the Shcherbatskys', that the secret spiritual bond which existed between him and Kitty had grown so much stronger that evening that some step must be taken. But what step could and ought to be taken he could not imagine.

"What is so exquisite," he thought, as he returned from the Shcherbatskys', carrying away with him, as he always did, a delicious feeling of purity and freshness, arising partly from the fact that he had not smoked for a whole evening, and with it a new feeling of tenderness at her love for him—"what is so exquisite is that not a word has been said by me or by her, but we understand each other so well in this unseen language of looks and tones that this evening more clearly than ever she told me she loves me. And how secretly, simply, and most of all, how trustfully! I feel myself better, purer. I feel that I have a heart, and that there is a great deal of good in me. Those sweet, loving eyes! When she said, 'Indeed I do . . .'

"Well, what then? Oh, nothing. It's good for me, and good for her." And he began wondering where to finish the evening.

He thought of the places he might go. "The club? A game of bezique, champagne with Ignatov? No, I'm not going. Château des

Fleurs, where I'll find Oblonsky, songs, the cancan? No, I'm sick of it. That's why I like the Shcherbatskys', because I become better there. I'll go home." He went straight to his room at Dussot's, ordered supper, and then undressed, and as soon as his head touched the pillow, he fell into a sound sleep.

CHAPTER SEVENTEEN

The next day at eleven o'clock in the morning Vronsky drove to the station of the Petersburg railway to meet his mother, and the first person he came across on the great flight of steps was Oblonsky, who was expecting his sister by the same train.

"Ah! Your Excellency!" cried Oblonsky, "whom are you meeting?"

"My mother," Vronsky responded, smiling, as everyone did who met Oblonsky. He shook hands with him, and together they ascended the steps. "She is coming here from Petersburg today."

"I was looking for you till two o'clock last night. Where did you go after the Shcherbatskys'?"

"Home," answered Vronsky. "I must admit I felt so very content yesterday after the Shcherbatskys' that I didn't care to go anywhere."

"I recognize the lively steeds by their brands, and I recognize young lovers by their eyes," declaimed Stepan Arkadyevich, just as he had done before to Levin.

Vronsky smiled with a look that seemed to say that he did not deny it, but he promptly changed the subject.

"And whom are you meeting?" he asked.

"I? I've come to meet a pretty woman," said Oblonsky.

"You don't say so!"

"*Honi soit qui mal y pense!* [1] My sister Anna."

"Ah! That's Madame Karenina," said Vronsky.

"You know her, no doubt?"

"I think I do. Or perhaps not . . . I really am not sure," Vronsky answered absent-mindedly, with a vague recollection of something stiff and tedious evoked by the name Karenina.

---

[1] "Evil to him who evil thinks": the motto of the Order of the Garter.

"But Aleksey Aleksandrovich, my celebrated brother-in-law, you surely must know. All the world knows him."

"I know him by reputation and by sight. I know that he's clever, learned, mystical somewhat . . . But you know that's not . . . *not in my line*," said Vronsky in English.

"Yes, he's a very remarkable man; rather a conservative, but a splendid man," Stepan Arkadyevich observed, "a splendid man."

"Oh, well, so much the better for him," said Vronsky smiling. "Oh, you've come," he said, addressing a tall old footman of his mother's standing at the door; "come here."

Besides the charm Oblonsky had in general for everyone, Vronsky had felt of late specially drawn to him by the fact that in his imagination he was associated with Kitty.

"Well, what do you say? Shall we give a supper on Sunday for the *diva*?" he said to him with a smile, taking his arm.

"Of course. I'm making a collection. Oh, did you make the acquaintance of my friend Levin?" asked Stepan Arkadyevich.

"Yes; but he left rather early."

"He's a fine fellow," Oblonsky said. "Isn't he?"

"I don't know why it is," Vronsky responded, "in all Moscow people—present company of course excepted," he put in jestingly, "there's something uncompromising. They are all on the defensive, lose their tempers, as though they all want to make one feel something . . ."

"Yes, that's true, it is so," said Stepan Arkadyevich, laughing good-humoredly.

"Will the train be in soon?" Vronsky asked a railway official.

"The train's signaled," answered the man.

The approach of the train was more and more evident by the preparatory bustle in the station, the rush of porters, the movement of policemen and attendants, and people meeting the train. Through the frosty vapor could be seen workmen in short sheepskins and soft felt boots crossing the rails of the curving line. The hiss of the boiler could be heard on the distant rails, and the rumble of something heavy.

"No," said Stepan Arkadyevich, who felt a great inclination to tell Vronsky of Levin's intentions in regard to Kitty. "No, you've not got a true impression of Levin. He's a very nervous man, and is some-times out of humor, it's true, but then he is often very nice. He has such a true, honest nature, and a heart of gold. But yesterday there were special reasons," Stepan Arkadyevich said, with a meaningful smile, totally oblivious of the genuine sympathy he had felt the day before for his friend, and feeling the same sympathy now, only for Vronsky. "Yes, there were reasons why he could not help being either particularly happy or particularly unhappy."

Vronsky stood still and asked directly: "How so? Do you mean he made your *belle-soeur*[2] a proposal yesterday?"

"Maybe," said Stepan Arkadyevich. "I thought something of the sort yesterday. Yes, if he went away early, and was out of humor too, it must mean it . . . He's been in love so long, and I'm very sorry for him."

"So that's it! . . . I should imagine, though, that she could expect a better match," said Vronsky, drawing himself up and walking about again, "though I don't know him, of course," he added. "Yes, that is a painful position! That's why most fellows prefer our Claras.[3] If you don't succeed with them, it only proves that you've not enough cash, but in this case one's dignity's at stake. But here's the train."

The engine had already whistled in the distance. A few instants later the platform was quivering, and with puffs of steam hanging low in the air from the frost, the engine rolled up, with the lever of the middle wheel rhythmically moving up and down, and the stooped, muffled figure of the engine driver covered with frost. Behind the tender, setting the platform more and more slowly swaying, came the luggage van with a dog whining in it. At last the passenger cars rolled in, jolting as they came to a standstill.

A dashing guard jumped out, giving a whistle, and after him one by one the important passengers began to get down: an officer of the guards, holding himself erect and looking severely about him; a nim-ble little merchant with a satchel, smiling gaily; a peasant with a sack over his shoulder.

Vronsky, standing beside Oblonsky, watched the carriages and the

[2] "Sister-in-law."
[3] I.e., tarts.

passengers, totally oblivious of his mother. What he had just heard about Kitty excited and delighted him. Unconsciously he squared his shoulders, and his eyes flashed. He felt himself a conqueror.

"Countess Vronsky is in that compartment," said the dashing guard, going up to Vronsky.

The guard's words roused him, and forced him to think of his mother and his approaching meeting with her. He did not in his heart respect his mother, and without acknowledging it to himself, he did not love her, though in accordance with the ideas of the set in which he lived, and with his own education, he could not have conceived of any behavior to his mother not in the highest degree respectful and obedient, and the more externally obedient and respectful his behavior, the less in his heart he respected and loved her.

CHAPTER EIGHTEEN

Vronsky followed the guard to the carriage, and at the door of the compartment he stopped short to make room for a lady who was getting out.

With the insight of a man of the world, from one glance at this lady's appearance Vronsky classified her as belonging to the best society. He excused himself, and was about to get into the carriage, but felt he must glance at her once more; not because she was very beautiful, not because of the elegance and modest grace that were apparent in her whole figure, but because in the expression of her charming face, as she passed close by him, there was something peculiarly caressing and soft. As he looked around, she too turned her head. Her shining gray eyes, which looked dark from the thick lashes, rested with friendly attention on his face, as though she recognized him, and then promptly turned away to the passing crowd, as though seeking someone. In that brief look Vronsky had time to notice the suppressed eagerness which played over her face, and flitted between the brilliant eyes and the faint smile that curved her red lips. It was as though her nature was so brimming over with something that against her will it showed itself now in the flash of her eyes, and now in her smile. Deliberately she shrouded the light in her eyes, but it shone against her will in the faintly perceptible smile.

Vronsky stepped into the carriage. His mother, a dried-up old lady with black eyes and ringlets, screwed up her eyes, scanning her son, and smiled slightly with her thin lips. Getting up from the seat and handing her maid a bag, she gave her little wrinkled hand to her son to kiss, and, lifting his head from her hand, kissed him on the cheek.

"You got my telegram? Quite well? Thank God."

"You had a good journey?" said her son, sitting down beside her, and involuntarily listening to a woman's voice outside the door. He knew it was the voice of the lady he had met at the door.

"All the same I don't agree with you," said the lady's voice.

"It's the Petersburg view, madame."

"Not Petersburg, but simply feminine," she responded.

"Well, well, allow me to kiss your hand."

"Good-by, Ivan Petrovich. And would you see if my brother is here, and send him to me?" said the lady in the doorway, and stepped back again into the compartment.

"Well, have you found your brother?" asked Countess Vronsky, addressing the lady.

Vronsky understood now that this was Madame Karenina.

"Your brother is here," he said, standing up. "Excuse me, I did not know you, and, indeed, our acquaintance was so slight," said Vronsky, bowing, "that no doubt you do not remember me."

"Oh, no," said she, "I would have known you because your mother and I have been talking, I think, of nothing but you all the way." As she spoke she let the eagerness that would insist on coming out show itself in her smile. "And still no sign of my brother."

"Do call him, Alyosha," said the old countess. Vronsky stepped out onto the platform and shouted:

"Oblonsky! Here!"

Madame Karenina, however, did not wait for her brother, but, catching sight of him, stepped out with her light, determined step. And as soon as her brother had reached her, she flung her left arm around his neck, drew him rapidly to her, and kissed him warmly, with a gesture that struck Vronsky by its decision and its grace. Vronsky gazed, never taking his eyes from her, and smiled, he could not have said why. But recollecting that his mother was waiting for him, he went back again into the carriage.

"She's very sweet, isn't she?" said the countess of Madame Karenina. "Her husband put her with me, and I was delighted to have her. We've been talking all the way. And so you, I hear . . . *vous filez le parfait amour. Tant mieux, mon cher, tant mieux*".[1]

"I don't know what you are referring to, *Maman*," he answered coldly. "Come, *Maman*, let us go."

Madame Karenina entered the carriage again to say good-by to the countess.

"Well, Countess, you have met your son, and I my brother," she said. "And all my gossip is exhausted. I would have nothing more to tell you."

"Oh, no," said the countess, taking her hand. "I could go all around the world with you and never be bored. You are one of those delightful women in whose company it's sweet to be silent as well as to talk. Now please don't fret over your son; you can't expect never to be parted."

Madame Karenina stood quite still, holding herself very erect, and her eyes were smiling.

"Anna Arkadyevna," the countess said in explanation to her son, "has a little son eight years old, I believe, and she has never been parted from him before, and she keeps worrying over leaving him."

"Yes, the countess and I have been talking all the time, I of my son and she of hers," said Madame Karenina, and again a smile lighted up her face, a caressing smile intended for him.

"I am afraid that you must have been dreadfully bored," he said, promptly catching the ball of coquetry she had flung him. But apparently she did not care to pursue the conversation in that strain, and she turned to the old countess.

"Thank you so much. The time has passed so quickly. Good-by, Countess."

"Good-by, darling," answered the countess. "Let me have a kiss of your pretty face. I speak plainly at my age, and I tell you simply that I've lost my heart to you."

---

[1] " You are head over heels in love. So much the better, my dear, so much the better."

Stereotyped as the phrase was, Madame Karenina obviously believed it and was delighted by it. She flushed, bent down slightly, and put her cheek to the countess's lips, drew herself up again, and with the same smile fluttering between her lips and her eyes, she gave her hand to Vronsky. He pressed the little hand she gave him, and was delighted, as though at something special, by the energetic squeeze with which she freely and vigorously shook his hand. She went out with the rapid step that bore her rather fully developed figure with such strange lightness.

"Very charming," said the countess.

That was just what her son was thinking. His eyes followed her till her graceful figure was out of sight, and then the smile remained on his face. He saw out of the window how she went up to her brother, put her arm in his, and began telling him something eagerly, obviously something that had nothing to do with him, Vronsky, and at that he felt annoyed.

"Well, *Maman*, are you perfectly well?" he repeated, turning to his mother.

"Everything has been delightful. Aleksander has been very good, and Marie has grown very pretty. She's very interesting."

And she began telling him again of what interested her most—the christening of her grandson, for which she had been staying in Petersburg, and the special favor shown her elder son by the Tsar.

"Here's Lavrenty," said Vronsky, looking out of the window; "now we can go, if you like."

The old butler who had traveled with the countess came to the carriage to announce that everything was ready, and the countess got up to go.

"Come; there's not such a crowd now," said Vronsky.

The maid took a bag and the lap dog; the butler and a porter the other luggage. Vronsky gave his mother his arm; but just as they were getting out of the carriage, several men suddenly ran by with panic-stricken faces. The stationmaster, too, ran by in his extraordinary colored cap. Obviously something unusual had happened. The crowd who had left the train was running back again.

"What? . . . What? . . . Where? . . . Flung himself! . . . Crushed! . . ." was heard among the crowd. Stepan Arkadyevich, with his sister on his arm, turned back. They too looked scared, and stopped at the carriage door to avoid the crowd.

The ladies got in, while Vronsky and Stepan Arkadyevich followed the crowd to find out details of the disaster.

A guard, either drunk or too much muffled up in the bitter frost, had not heard the train moving back, and had been crushed.

Before Vronsky and Oblonsky came back, the ladies heard the facts from the butler.

Oblonsky and Vronsky had both seen the mutilated corpse. Oblonsky was evidently upset. He frowned and seemed ready to cry.

"Ah, how awful! Ah, Anna, if you had seen it! Ah, how awful!" he said.

Vronsky did not speak; his handsome face was serious, but perfectly composed.

"Oh, if you had seen it, Countess," said Stepan Arkadyevich. "And his wife was there. . . . It was awful to see her! . . . She flung herself on the body. They say he was the only support of an immense family. How awful!"

"Couldn't one do anything for her?" said Madame Karenina in an agitated whisper.

Vronsky glanced at her, and immediately got out of the carriage.

"I'll be back directly, *Maman*," he remarked, turning round in the doorway.

When he came back a few minutes later, Stepan Arkadyevich was already in conversation with the countess about the new singer, while the countess was impatiently looking toward the door, waiting for her son.

"Now let us be off," said Vronsky, coming in. They went out together. Vronsky was in front with his mother. Behind walked Madame Karenina with her brother. Just as they were going out of the station the stationmaster overtook Vronsky.

"You gave my assistant two hundred rubles. Would you kindly explain for whose benefit you intend them?"

"For the widow," said Vronsky, shrugging his shoulder. "I should have thought there was no need to ask."

"You gave that?" cried Oblonsky from behind, and, pressing his sister's hand, he added: "Very nice, very nice! Isn't he a splendid fellow? Good-by, Countess."

And he and his sister stood still, looking for her maid.

When they went out, the Vronskys' carriage had already driven away. People coming in were still talking of what had happened.

"What a horrible death!" said a gentleman passing by. "They say he was cut in two pieces."

"On the contrary, I think it's the easiest—instantaneous," observed another.

"How is it they don't take proper precautions?" said a third.

Madame Karenina seated herself in the carriage, and Stepan Arkadyevich saw with surprise that her lips were quivering, and she was with difficulty restraining her tears.

"What is it, Anna?" he asked, when they had driven several hundred yards.

"It's an evil omen," she said.

"What nonsense!" said Stepan Arkadyevich. "You've come, that's the main thing. You can't conceive how I'm resting my hopes on you."

"Have you known Vronsky long?" she asked.

"Yes. You know we're hoping he will marry Kitty."

"Yes?" said Anna softly. "Come now, let us talk of you," she added, tossing her head, as though she would physically shake off something superfluous oppressing her. "Let us talk of your affairs. I got your letter, and here I am."

"Yes, all my hopes are in you," said Stepan Arkadyevich.

"Well, tell me all about it."

And Stepan Arkadyevich began to tell his story.

On reaching home, Oblonsky helped his sister out, sighed, pressed her hand, and went off to his office.

CHAPTER NINETEEN

When Anna went into the room, Dolly was sitting in the little drawing room with a light-haired chubby little boy, who already resembled his father, giving him a lesson in French reading. As the boy read, he kept twisting and trying to tear off a button that was nearly off his jacket. His mother had several times taken his hand from it, but the fat little hand went back to the button again. His mother pulled the button off and put it in her pocket.

"Keep your hands still, Grisha," she said, and she took up her work, a blanket she had long been making. She always began to work on it at depressed moments, and now she knitted at it nervously, twitching her fingers and counting the stitches. Though she had sent word the day before to her husband that it was nothing to her whether his sister came or not, she had made everything ready for her arrival, and was expecting her sister-in-law anxiously.

Dolly was crushed by her sorrow, utterly swallowed up by it. Still she did not forget that Anna, her sister-in-law, was the wife of one of the most important personages in Petersburg, and was a Petersburg *grande dame*. And, thanks to this circumstance, she did not carry out her threat to her husband—that is to say, she remembered that her sister-in-law was coming. "And, after all, Anna is in no way to blame," thought Dolly. "I know nothing of her except the very best, and I have seen nothing but kindness and affection from her toward myself." It was true that as far as she could recall her impressions in Petersburg at the Karenins', she did not like their household itself; there was something artificial in the whole framework of their family life. "But why should I not receive her? If only she doesn't take it into her head to console me!" thought Dolly. "All consolation and counsel and Christian forgiveness, all that I have thought over a thousand times, and it's all no use."

All these days Dolly had been alone with her children. She did not want to talk of her sorrow, but with that sorrow in her heart she could not talk of outside matters. She knew that in one way or another she would tell Anna everything, and she was alternately glad at the thought of speaking freely, and angry at the necessity of speaking of her humiliation with her, his sister, and of hearing her ready-made phrases of good advice and comfort. She had been on the lookout for her, glancing at her watch every minute, and, as often happens, let slip just that minute when her visitor arrived, so that she did not hear the bell.

Catching a sound of skirts and light steps at the door, she looked around, and her careworn face unconsciously expressed not gladness but wonder. She got up and embraced her sister-in-law.

"What, here already!" she said as she kissed her.

"Dolly, how glad I am to see you!"

"I am glad too," said Dolly, faintly smiling, and trying by the expression of Anna's face to find out whether she knew. "Most likely she knows," she thought, noticing the sympathy in Anna's face. "Well, come along, I'll take you to your room," she went on, trying to defer as long as possible the moment of confidences.

"Is this Grisha? Heavens, how he's grown!" said Anna; and kissing him, never taking her eyes off Dolly, she stood still and flushed a little. "No, please, let us stay here."

She took off her kerchief and her hat, and catching it in a lock of her black hair, which was a mass of curls, she tossed her head and shook her hair down.

"You are radiant with health and happiness!" said Dolly, almost with envy.

"I? . . . Yes," said Anna. "Merciful Heavens, Tanya! You're the same age as my Seryozha," she added, addressing the little girl as she ran in. She took her in her arms and kissed her. "Delightful child, delightful! Show me them all."

She mentioned them, remembering not only the names but also the years, months, characters, and illnesses of all the children, and Dolly could not but appreciate that.

"Very well, we will go to them," she said. "It's a pity Vasya's asleep."

After seeing the children, they sat down, alone now, in the drawing room, to coffee. Anna took the tray, and then pushed it away from her.

"Dolly," she said, "he has told me."

Dolly looked coldly at Anna; she was waiting now for phrases of conventional sympathy, but Anna said nothing of the sort.

"Dolly, dear," she said, "I don't want to speak for him, or try to comfort you; that's impossible. But, darling, I'm simply sorry, sorry from my heart for you!"

Under the thick lashes of her shining eyes tears suddenly glittered. She moved nearer to her sister-in-law and took her hand in her vigorous little hand. Dolly did not shrink away, but her face did not lose its frigid expression. She said:

"To comfort me's impossible. Everything's lost after what has happened, everything's over!"

And as soon as she had said this, her face suddenly softened. Anna lifted the wasted, thin hand of Dolly, kissed it, and said:

"But, Dolly, what's to be done, what's to be done? How is it best to act in this awful situation—that's what you must think of."

"All's over, and there's nothing more," said Dolly. "And the worst of it all is, you see, that I can't cast him off: there are the children, I am tied. And I can't live with him! It's torture to see him."

"Dolly, darling, he has spoken to me, but I want to hear it from you: tell me all about it."

Dolly looked at her inquiringly. Sympathy and sincere love were visible on Anna's face.

"Very well," she said at once. "But I will tell it from the beginning. You know how I was married. With the education Mama gave us I was more than innocent; I was stupid. I knew nothing. I know they say men tell their wives of their former lives, but Stiva"—she corrected herself—"Stepan Arkadyevich told me nothing. You'll hardly believe it, but till now I imagined that I was the only woman he had known. So I lived eight years. You must understand that I was so far from suspecting infidelity, I regarded it as impossible, and then—try to imagine it—with such ideas to find out suddenly all the horror, all the loathsomeness . . . You must try and understand me. To be fully convinced of one's happiness, and all at once . . ." continued Dolly, holding back her sobs, "to get a letter . . . his letter to his mistress, my governess. No, it's too awful!" She hastily pulled out her handkerchief and hid her face in it. "I can understand being carried away by feeling," she went on after a brief silence, "but deliberately, slyly deceiving me . . . and with whom? . . . To go on being my husband together with her . . . it's awful! You can't understand . . ."

"Oh, yes, I understand! I understand! Dolly, dearest, I do understand," said Anna, pressing her hand.

"And do you think he realizes the horror of my position?" Dolly resumed. "Not the slightest! He's happy and contented."

"Oh, no!" Anna interposed quickly. "He's to be pitied, he's weighed down by remorse—"

"Is he capable of remorse?" Dolly interrupted, gazing intently into her sister-in-law's face.

"Yes. I know him. I could not look at him without feeling sorry for him. We both know him. He's good-hearted, but he's proud, and now he's so humiliated. What touched me most . . ." (and here Anna guessed what would touch Dolly most) "he's tortured by two things: that he's ashamed for the children's sake, and that, loving you—yes, yes, loving you beyond everything on earth," she hurriedly interrupted Dolly, who would have answered—"he has hurt you, pierced you to the heart. 'No, no, she cannot forgive me,' he keeps saying."

Dolly looked dreamily away beyond her sister-in-law as she listened to her words.

"Yes, I can see that his position is awful; it's worse for the guilty than the innocent," she said, "if he feels that all the misery is his fault. But how am I to forgive him, how am I to be his wife again after her? For me to live with him now would be torture, just because I love my past love for him . . ."

And sobs cut short her words. But as though intentionally, each time she was softened she began to speak again of what exasperated her.

"She's young, you see, she's pretty," she went on. "Do you know, Anna, my youth and my beauty are gone, taken by whom? By him and his children. I have worked for him, and all I had has gone in his service, and now of course any fresh, vulgar creature has more charm for him. No doubt they talked of me together, or, worse still, they were silent. Do you understand?"

Again her eyes glowed with hatred.

"And after that he will tell me . . . What! Can I believe him? Never! No, everything is over, everything that once made my comfort, the reward of my work, and my sufferings . . . Would you believe it, I was teaching Grisha just now: once this was a joy to me, now it is a torture. What have I to strive and toil for? Why are the children here? What's so dreadful is that all at once my heart's revolted, and instead of love and tenderness, I have nothing but hatred for him; yes, hatred. I could kill him."

"Darling Dolly, I understand, but don't torture yourself. You are so distressed, so overwrought, that you look at many things mistakenly."

Dolly grew calmer, and for two minutes both were silent.

"What's to be done? Think for me, Anna, help me. I have thought over everything, and I see nothing."

Anna could think of nothing, but her heart responded instantly to each word, to each change of expression of her sister-in-law.

"One thing I would say," began Anna. "I am his sister, I know his character, that faculty of forgetting everything, everything" (she waved her hand before her forehead), "that faculty for being completely carried away, but for completely repenting too. He cannot believe it, he cannot comprehend now how he can have acted as he did."

"No; he understands, he understood!" Dolly broke in. "But I . . . you are forgetting me . . . does it make it easier for me?"

"Wait a minute. When he told me, I will admit I did not realize the full horror of your position. I saw nothing but him, and that the family was broken up. I felt sorry for him, but after talking to you, I see it as a woman, quite differently. I see your agony, and I can't tell you how sorry I am for you! But, Dolly, darling, I fully realize your sufferings, only there is one thing I don't know; I don't know . . . I don't know how much love there is still in your heart for him. That you know—whether there is enough for you to be able to forgive him. If there is, forgive him!"

"No," Dolly was beginning, but Anna cut her short, kissing her hand once more.

"I know more of the world than you do," she said. "I know how men like Stiva look at it. You speak of his talking of you with her. That never happened. Such men are unfaithful, but their own home and wife are sacred to them. Somehow or other these women are still looked on with contempt by them, and do not touch on their feeling for their family. They draw a sort of line that can't be crossed between them and their families. I don't understand it, but it is so."

"Yes, but he has kissed her . . ."

"Dolly, hush, darling. I saw Stiva when he was in love with you. I remember the time when he came to me and cried, talking of you, and all the poetry and loftiness of his feeling for you, and I know that the longer he has lived with you, the loftier you have been in his eyes. You know we have sometimes laughed at him for putting in at every word, 'Dolly's a marvelous woman.' You have always been a divinity

for him, and you are that still, and this has not been an infidelity of
the heart . . ."

"But if it is repeated?"

"It cannot be, as I understand it . . ."

"Yes, but could you forgive it?"

"I don't know, I can't judge . . . Yes, I can," said Anna, thinking a
moment; and grasping the position in her thought and weighing it in
her mind, she added: "Yes, I can, I can, I can. Yes, I could forgive it.
I could not be the same, no; but I could forgive it, and forgive it as
though it had never been, never been at all . . ."

"Oh, of course," Dolly interposed quickly, as though saying what
she had more than once thought, "else it would not be forgiveness. If
one forgives, it must be completely, completely. Come, let us go; I'll
take you to your room," she said, getting up, and on the way she
embraced Anna. "My dear, how glad I am you came. It has made
things better, so very much better."

CHAPTER TWENTY

The whole of that day Anna spent at home, that is to say at the
Oblonskys', and received no one, though some of her acquaintances
had already heard of her arrival, and came to see her. Anna spent the
whole morning with Dolly and the children. She merely sent a brief
note to her brother to tell him that he must not fail to dine at home.
"Come, God is merciful," she wrote.

Oblonsky did dine at home: the conversation was general, and his
wife, speaking to him, addressed him as "Stiva," as she had not done
before. In the relations of the husband and wife the same estrangement still remained, but there was no talk now of separation, and
Stepan Arkadyevich saw the possibility of explanation and reconciliation.

Immediately after dinner Kitty came in. She knew Anna, but only
very slightly, and she came now to her sister's with some trepida-
tion at the prospect of meeting this fashionable Petersburg lady,
whom everyone spoke so highly of. But she made a favorable
impression on Anna—she saw that at once. Anna was unmistakably

struck by her loveliness and her youth, and before Kitty knew where she was she found herself not merely under Anna's influence, but in love with her, as young girls do fall in love with older and married women. Anna was not like a fashionable lady, nor the mother of a boy eight years old. In the elasticity of her movements, the freshness and the unflagging eagerness which persisted in her face, and broke out in her smile and her glance, she would have passed for a girl of twenty, had it not been for a serious and at times mournful look in her eyes, which struck and attracted Kitty. Kitty felt that Anna was perfectly natural and was concealing nothing, but that she had another higher world of interests inaccessible to her, complex and poetic.

After dinner, when Dolly went away to her own room, Anna rose quickly and went up to her brother, who was just lighting a cigar.

"Stiva," she said to him, winking gaily, making the sign of the cross over him, and glancing toward the door, "go, and God help you."

He threw down the cigar, understanding her, and departed through the doorway.

When Stepan Arkadyevich had disappeared, she went back to the sofa where she was sitting, surrounded by the children. Either because the children saw that their mother was fond of this aunt, or that they felt a special charm in her themselves, the two elder ones, and the younger following their lead, as children so often do, had clung about their new aunt since before dinner, and would not leave her side. And it had become a sort of game among them to sit as close as possible to her, to touch her, hold her little hand, kiss it, play with her ring, or at least touch the ruffles of her skirt.

"Come, come, as we were sitting before," said Anna, sitting down in her place.

And again Grisha poked his little face under her arm, and nestled with his head on her gown, beaming with pride and happiness.

"And when is your next ball?" she asked Kitty.

"Next week, and a splendid ball. One of those balls where one always enjoys oneself."

"Why, are there balls where one always enjoys oneself?" Anna said, with tender irony.

"It's strange, but there are. At the Bobrishchevs' one always enjoys oneself, and at the Nikitins' too, while at the Mezhkovs' it's always dull. Haven't you noticed it?"

"No, my dear, for me there are no balls now where one enjoys oneself," said Anna, and Kitty detected in her eyes that mysterious world which was not open to her. "For me there are some less boring and tiresome."

"How can *you* be bored at a ball?"

"Why should I not be bored at a ball?" inquired Anna.

Kitty perceived that Anna knew what answer would follow.

"Because you always look better than anyone."

Anna had the faculty of blushing. She blushed a little, and said:

"In the first place it's never so; and secondly, if it were, what difference would it make to me?"

"Are you coming to this ball?" asked Kitty.

"I imagine it won't be possible to avoid going. Here, take it," she said to Tanya, who was pulling the loose-fitting ring off her white, slender-tipped finger.

"I shall be so glad if you go. I should so like to see you at a ball."

"Anyway, if I do go, I shall comfort myself with the thought that it's a pleasure to you . . . Grisha, don't pull my hair. It's untidy enough without that," she said, putting up a straying lock that Grisha had been playing with.

"I imagine you at the ball in lilac."

"And why in lilac precisely?" asked Anna, smiling. "Now, children, run along, run along. Do you hear? Miss Hull is calling you to tea," she said, tearing the children from her and sending them off to the dining room.

"I know why you are eager for me to come to the ball. You expect a great deal of this ball, and you want everyone to be there to take part in it."

"How do you know? Yes."

"Oh! How good it is to be your age!" pursued Anna. "I remember, and I know that blue haze like the mist on the mountains in Switzerland. That mist which covers everything in that blissful time when childhood is just ending, and out of that vast circle, happy and gay, there is a path growing narrower and narrower, and it is delightful and alarming to enter the ballroom, bright and splendid as it is . . . Who has not been through it?"

Kitty smiled without speaking. "But how did she go through it? How I'd like to know the whole romance of her life!" thought Kitty, recalling the unromantic appearance of Aleksey Aleksandrovich, her husband.

"I know something. Stiva told me, and I congratulate you. I liked him very much," Anna continued. "I met Vronsky at the railway station."

"Oh, was he there?" asked Kitty, blushing. "What was it Stiva told you?"

"Stiva gossiped about it all. And I should be so glad . . . I traveled yesterday with Vronsky's mother," she went on, "and she talked without pause of him, he's her favorite. I know mothers are partial, but . . ."

"What did his mother tell you?"

"Oh, a great deal! And I know that he's her favorite; still, one can see how chivalrous he is . . .Well, for instance, she told me that he had wanted to give up all his property to his brother, that he had done something extraordinary when he was a boy, saved a woman out of the water. He's a hero, in fact," said Anna, smiling and recollecting the two hundred rubles he had given at the station.

But she did not tell about the two hundred rubles. For some reason it was unpleasant for her to think of it. She felt that there was something in it that had to do with her, something that ought not to have been.

"She was very eager for me to go and see her," Anna went on; "and I'll be glad to go see her tomorrow. Stiva is staying a long while in Dolly's room, thank God," Anna added, changing the subject and getting up, Kitty thought, displeased with something.

"No, I'm first! No, me!" screamed the children, who had finished tea, running up to their Aunt Anna.

"All together," said Anna, and she ran laughing to meet them, and embraced and swung round the whole heap of children, shrieking with delight and struggling on the floor.

CHAPTER TWENTY-ONE

Dolly came out of her room to the tea for the grownups. Stepan Arkadyevich did not come out. He must have left his wife's room by the other door. "I am afraid you'll be cold upstairs," observed Dolly, addressing Anna; "I want to move you downstairs, and we shall be nearer."

"Oh, please, don't trouble about me," answered Anna, looking intently into Dolly's face, trying to make out whether there had been reconciliation or not.

"It will be lighter for you here," answered her sister-in-law.

"I assure you that I sleep anywhere, and always like a dormouse."

"What's it about?" inquired Stepan Arkadyevich, coming out of his room and addressing his wife.

From his tone, both Kitty and Anna knew that a reconciliation had taken place.

"I want to move Anna downstairs, but we must change the curtains. No one knows how to do it; I must see to it myself," answered Dolly, addressing him.

"God knows whether they are fully reconciled," thought Anna, hearing her tone, cold and composed.

"Oh, nonsense, Dolly, always making difficulties," answered her husband. "Come, I'll do it all, if you like . . ."

"Yes, they must be reconciled," thought Anna.

"I know how you do everything," answered Dolly. "You tell Matvey to do what can't be done, and go away yourself, leaving him to make a mess of everything," and her habitual, mocking smile curved the corners of Dolly's lips as she spoke.

"Full, full reconciliation, full," thought Anna; "thank God!" and rejoicing that she was the cause of it, she went up to Dolly and kissed her.

"Not at all. Why do you always look down on me and Matvey?" said Stepan Arkadyevich, smiling perceptibly, and addressing his wife.

The whole evening Dolly was, as always, a little ironical in her tone toward her husband, while Stepan Arkadyevich was happy and cheerful, but not so as to seem as though, having been forgiven, he had forgotten his offense.

At half-past nine a particularly joyful and pleasant family conversation over the tea table at the Oblonskys' was broken up by an apparently simple incident. But this simple incident for some reason struck everyone as strange. Talking about common acquaintances in Petersburg, Anna got up quickly.

"She is in my album," she said; "and, by the way, I'll show you my Seryozha," she added, with a mother's smile of pride.

Toward ten o'clock, when she usually said good night to her son, and often before going to a ball put him to bed herself, she felt depressed at being so far from him; and whatever she was talking about, she kept returning to thoughts of her curly-headed Seryozha. She longed to look at his photograph and talk of him. Seizing the first pretext, she got up and, with her light, resolute step, went for her album. The stairs up to her room came out on the landing of the large heated main staircase.

Just as she was leaving the drawing room, a ring was heard in the hall.

"Who can that be?" said Dolly.

"It's early for me to be fetched, and for anyone else it's late," observed Kitty.

"Sure to be someone with papers for me," put in Stepan Arkadyevich. When Anna was rounding the top of the staircase, a servant was running up to announce the visitor, while the visitor himself was standing under a lamp. Anna, glancing down, at once recognized Vronsky, and a strange feeling of pleasure, and at the same time of dread of something, stirred in her heart. He was standing still, not taking off his coat, pulling something out of his pocket. At the instant when she was just facing the stairs, he raised his eyes, catching sight of her, and into the expression of his face there passed a shade of embarrassment and fear. With a slight inclination of her head she passed, hearing behind her Stepan Arkadyevich's loud voice calling him to come up, and the quiet, soft, and composed voice of Vronsky refusing.

When Anna returned with the album, he was already gone, and Stepan Arkadyevich was telling them that he had called to inquire about the dinner they were giving next day for a celebrity who had just arrived. "And nothing would induce him to come up. What a strange fellow he is!" added Stepan Arkadyevich.

Kitty blushed. She thought that she was the only person who knew why he had come, and why he would not come up. "He has been at home," she thought, "and didn't find me, and thought I should be here, but he did not come up because he thought it late, and Anna's here."

All of them looked at each other, saying nothing, and began to look at Anna's album.

There was nothing either exceptional or strange in a man's calling at half-past nine on a friend to inquire details of a proposed dinner party and not coming in, yet it seemed strange to all of them. Above all, it seemed strange and wrong to Anna.

CHAPTER TWENTY-TWO

The ball was only just beginning as Kitty and her mother walked up the grand staircase, flooded with light and lined with flowers and footmen in powder and red livery. From the rooms came a constant, steady hum, as from a beehive, and the rustle of movement; and while on the landing, between the plants, they gave last touches to their hair and dresses before the mirror, they heard from the ball-room the careful, distinct notes of the fiddles of the orchestra beginning the first waltz. A little old man in civilian clothes, arranging his gray curls before another mirror, and smelling of perfume, stumbled against them on the stairs and stood aside, evidently admiring Kitty, whom he did not know. A beardless youth, one of those society youths whom the old Prince Shcherbatsky called "young bucks," in an exceedingly open vest, straightening his white tie as he went, bowed to them and, after running by, came back to ask Kitty for a quadrille. As the first quadrille had already been given to Vronsky, she had to promise this youth the second. An officer, buttoning his glove, stood aside in the doorway and, stroking his mustache, admired the rosy Kitty.

Although her dress, her coiffure, and all the preparations for the ball had cost Kitty great trouble and consideration, at this moment she walked into the ballroom in her elaborate tulle dress over a pink slip as easily and naturally as though all the rosettes and lace, all the minute details of her attire, had not cost her or her family a moment's attention, as though she had been born in that tulle and lace, with her hair done up high on her head and a rose and two leaves on the top of it.

When, just before entering the ballroom, the princess, her mother, tried to straighten the ribbon of her sash, Kitty had drawn back a little. She felt that everything must be naturally right and graceful, and nothing could need adjusting.

It was one of Kitty's best days. Her dress was not uncomfortable anywhere; her lace berthe did not droop anywhere; her rosettes were not crushed or torn off; her pink slippers with high, curved heels did not pinch but delighted her feet; and the thick rolls of fair chignon stayed up on her head as if they were her own hair. All three buttons fastened without tearing on the long glove that covered her hand without concealing its lines. The black velvet of her locket nestled with special softness around her neck. That velvet ribbon was delicious; at home, looking at her neck in the mirror, Kitty had felt that it was eloquent. About everything else there might be a doubt, but the velvet was delicious. Kitty smiled here too, at the ball, when she glanced at it in the mirror. Her bare shoulders and arms gave her a sense of chill marble, a feeling she particularly liked. Her eyes sparkled, and her rosy lips could not keep from smiling from her awareness of her own attractiveness. She had scarcely entered the ballroom and reached the throng of ladies, all tulle, ribbons, lace, and flowers waiting to be asked to dance—Kitty was never one of that throng—when she was asked for a waltz, and asked by the best partner, the first star in the hierarchy of the ballroom, a renowned dancing instructor, a married man, handsome and well-built, Yegorushka Korsunsky. He had just left the Countess Banina, with whom he had danced the first half of the waltz, and, scanning his kingdom—that is to say, a few couples who had started dancing—he caught sight of Kitty entering, and glided up to her with that peculiar, easy gait which is confined to directors of balls. Without even asking her if she cared to dance, he put out his arm to encircle her slender waist. She looked around for someone to give her fan to, and their hostess, smiling at her, took it.

"How nice you've come at the right time," he said to her, embracing her waist; "such a bad habit to be late." Bending her left hand, she laid it on his shoulder, and her little feet in their pink slippers began swiftly, lightly, and rhythmically moving over the slippery floor in time to the music.

"It's a rest to waltz with you," he said to her, as they fell into the first slow steps of the waltz. "It's exquisite—such lightness, precision." He said to her the same thing he said to almost all his partners whom he knew well.

She smiled at his praise, and continued to look about the room over his shoulder. She was not like a girl at her first ball, for whom all faces in the ballroom melt into one vision of fairyland. And she was not a girl who had gone the stale round of balls till every face in the ballroom was familiar and tiresome. But she was in the middle stage between these two; she was excited, and at the same time she had sufficient self-possession to be able to observe. In the left corner of the ballroom she saw the cream of society gathered together. There—incredibly naked—was the beauty Lydie, Korsunsky's wife; there was the hostess; there shone the bald head of Krivin, always to be found where the best people were. In that direction gazed the young men, not venturing to approach. There, too, her eyes found Stiva, and there she saw the exquisite figure and head of Anna in a black velvet gown. And *he* was there. Kitty had not seen him since the evening she refused Levin. With her far-sighted eyes, she knew him at once, and was even aware that he was looking at her.

"Another turn, eh? You're not tired?" said Korsunsky, a little out of breath.

"No, thank you!"

"Where shall I take you?"

"Madame Karenina's here, I think . . . take me to her."

"Wherever you command."

And Korsunsky began waltzing, gradually slowing down, straight toward the group in the left corner, continually saying, "*Pardon, mesdames, pardon, pardon, mesdames*"; and steering his course through the sea of lace, tulle, and ribbon, and not disarranging a feather, he turned his partner sharply round, so that her slim ankles, in their mesh stockings, were exposed to view, and her train floated out in fan shape and covered Krivin's knees. Korsunsky bowed, set straight his broad shirt-front, and gave her his arm to conduct her to Anna Arkadyevna. Kitty, flushed, took her train from Krivin's knees and, a little giddy, looked around, seeking Anna. Anna was not in lilac, as Kitty had so urgently wished, but in a black, low-cut, velvet gown, showing her full shoulders and bosom that looked as though carved of old ivory, and her rounded arms, with tiny, slender wrists. The whole gown was trimmed with Venetian lace. In her black hair, all her own, was a little wreath of pansies, and there were more of the same in the black ribbon winding through the white lace encircling her waist. Her coiffure was not striking. All that was noticeable was the little wilful tendrils of her curly hair that would always break free about her neck and temples. Around her finely chiseled, strong neck was a thread of pearls.

Kitty had been seeing Anna every day; she adored her, and had pictured her invariably in lilac. But now, seeing her in black, she felt that she had not fully seen her charm. She saw her now as someone quite new and surprising to her. Now she understood that Anna could not have been in lilac, and that her charm was just that she always stood out from her attire, that her dress could never be conspicuous on her. And her black dress, with its sumptuous lace, was not conspicuous on her; it was only the frame, and all that was seen was she—simple, natural, elegant, and at the same time gay and animated.

She was standing holding herself, as always, very erect, and when Kitty drew near the group, she was speaking to the host, her head slightly turned toward him.

"No, I don't throw stones," she was saying, in answer to something, "though I can't understand it," she went on, shrugging her shoulders, and she turned at once with a soft smile of protection toward Kitty. With a rapid, feminine glance she scanned her attire, and made a movement of her head, hardly perceptible, but understood by Kitty, signifying approval of her dress and her looks. "You came into the room dancing," she added.

"This is one of my most faithful supporters," said Korsunsky, bowing to Anna Arkadyevna, whom he had not yet seen. "The princess helps to make balls happy and successful. Anna Arkadyevna, a waltz?" he said, bending down to her.

"Why, have you met?" inquired their host.

"Is there anyone we have not met? My wife and I are like white wolves—everyone knows us," answered Korsunsky. "A waltz, Anna Arkadyevna?"

"I don't dance when it's possible not to dance," she said.

"But tonight it's impossible," answered Korsunsky.

At that instant Vronsky came up.

"Well, since it's impossible tonight, let us start," she said, ignoring Vronsky's bow, and she hastily put her hand on Korsunsky's shoulder.

"Why is she vexed with him?" thought Kitty, discerning that Anna had intentionally not responded to Vronsky's bow. Vronsky went up to Kitty, reminding her of the first quadrille, and expressing his regret that he had not seen her all this time. Kitty gazed in admiration at Anna waltzing, and listened to him. She expected him to ask her for a waltz, but he did not, and she glanced at him with surprise. He flushed slightly, and hurriedly asked her to waltz, but he had just put his arm around her waist and taken the first step when the music suddenly stopped. Kitty looked into his face, which was so close to her own, and long afterward—for several years after—that look, full of love she gave him, to which he made no response, cut her to the heart with an agony of shame.

"*Pardon! Pardon!* Waltz! Waltz!" shouted Korsunsky from the other side of the room, and seizing the first young lady he came across, he himself began dancing.

CHAPTER TWENTY-THREE

Vronsky and Litty waltzed several times around the room. After the first waltz Kitty went to her mother, and she had hardly time to say a few words to Countess Nordston when Vronsky came up again for the first quadrille. During the quadrille nothing special was said: there was disjointed talk between them of the Korsunskys, husband and wife, whom he described very amusingly as delightful children at forty, and of the future town theater; and only once did the conversation touch her to the quick, when he asked her about Levin, whether he was here, and added that he like him very much. But Kitty did not expect much from the quadrille. Her heart thrilled in anticipation of the mazurka. It seemed to her that in the mazurka everything must be decided. The fact that he did not during the quadrille ask for the mazurka did not trouble her. She felt sure she would dance the mazurka with him as she had done at former balls, and refused five young men, saying she was engaged for the mazurka. The whole ball up to the last quadrille was for Kitty an enchanted vision of delightful colors, sounds, and motions. She sat down only when she felt too tired and begged for a rest. But as she was dancing the last quadrille with one of the tiresome young men whom she could not refuse, she chanced to be *vis-à-vis* with Vronsky and Anna. She had not been near Anna since the beginning of the evening, and now again she saw her suddenly quite new and surprising. She saw in her the signs of that thrill she knew so well in herself; she saw that she was intoxicated with the delighted admiration she was exciting. She knew that feeling and knew its signs, and saw them in Anna; saw the quivering, flashing light in her eyes, and the smile of happiness and excitement unconsciously playing on her lips, and the deliberate grace, precision, and lightness of her movements.

"Who?" she asked herself. "All or one?" And not assisting the harassed young man she was dancing with in the conversation, the thread of which he had lost and could not pick up again, she obeyed with external liveliness the peremptory shouts of Korsunsky starting them all into the *grand rond*, and then into the *chaîne*, and at the same time she kept watch with a growing pang at her heart. "No, it's not the admiration of the crowd that has intoxicated her, but the adoration of one. And that one? Can it be *he*?" Every time he spoke to Anna the joyous light flashed into her eyes, and the smile of happiness curved her red lips. She seemed to make an effort to control herself, not to show these signs of delight, but they came out on her face by themselves. "But what of him?" Kitty looked at him and was filled with terror. What was pictured so clearly to Kitty in the mirror of Anna's face she saw in him. What had become of his always self-possessed resolute manner, and the carelessly serene expression of his face? Now every time he turned to her, he bent his head, as though he would have fallen at her feet, and in his eyes there was nothing but humble submission and dread. "I would not offend you," his eyes seemed every time to be saying, "but I want to save myself, and I don't know how." On his face was a look such as Kitty had never seen before.

They were speaking of common acquaintances, keeping up the most trivial conversation, but to Kitty it seemed that every word they said was determining their fate and hers. And strange it was that they were actually talking of how absurd Ivan Ivanovich was with his French, and how the Eletsky girl might have made a better match, yet these words were important for them, and they felt just as Kitty did. The whole ball, the whole world, everything seemed lost in a mist in Kitty's soul. Nothing but the stern discipline of her upbringing supported her and forced her to do what was expected of her, that is, to dance, to answer questions, to talk, even to smile. But before the mazurka, when they were beginning to rearrange the chairs and a few couples moved out of the smaller rooms into the big room, a moment of despair and horror came for Kitty. She had refused five partners, and now she was not dancing the mazurka. She had not even a hope of being asked for it, because she was so successful in society that the idea would never occur to anyone that she had no partner. She would have to tell her mother she felt ill and go home, but she had not the strength to do this. She felt crushed.

She went to the furthest end of the little drawing room and sank into a low chair. Her airy skirts rose like a cloud about her slender waist; one bare, thin, soft, girlish arm, hanging listlessly, was lost in the folds of her pink tunic; in the other she held her fan, and with rapid, short strokes fanned her burning face. But while she looked like a butterfly clinging to a blade of grass, and just about to open its rainbow wings for fresh flight, her heart ached with horrible despair.

"But perhaps I am wrong, perhaps it was not so?" And again she recalled all she had seen.

"Kitty, what is it?" said Countess Nordston, stepping noiselessly over the carpet toward her. "I don't understand it."

Kitty's lower lip began to quiver; she got up quickly.

"Kitty, you're not dancing the mazurka?"

"No, no," said Kitty in a voice shaking with tears.

"He asked her for the mazurka before me," said Countess Nordston, knowing Kitty would understand who "he" and "her" were.

"She said: 'Why, aren't you going to dance it with Princess Shcherbatskaya?'"

"Oh, I don't care!" answered Kitty.

No one but herself understood her position; no one knew that she had just refused the man whom perhaps she loved, and refused him because she had put her faith in another.

Countess Nordston found Korsunsky, with whom she was to dance the mazurka, and told him to ask Kitty.

Kitty danced in the first pair, and luckily for her she did not have to talk, because Korsunsky ran about directing the dancers. Vronsky and Anna sat almost opposite her. She saw them with her far-sighted eyes, and saw them too, close by, when they met in couples, and the more she saw of them, the more convinced was she that her unhappiness was complete. She saw that they felt themselves alone in that crowded room. And Vronsky's face, always so firm and independent, held that look that had struck her, of bewilderment and humble submissiveness, like the expression of an intelligent dog when it has done wrong.

Anna smiled, and her smile was reflected by him. She grew thoughtful, and he became serious. Some supernatural force drew Kitty's eyes to Anna's face. She was enchanting in her simple black dress, enchanting were her round arms with their bracelets, enchanting was her firm neck with its thread of pearls, fascinating the straying curls of her loose hair, enchanting the graceful, light movements of her little feet and hands, enchanting was that lovely face in its animation, but there was something terrible and cruel about her charm.

Kitty admired her more than ever, and more and more acute was her suffering. Kitty felt overwhelmed, and her face showed it. When Vronsky saw her during the mazurka, he did not at once recognize her, so changed was she.

"Delightful ball!" he said to her, for the sake of saying something.

"Yes," she answered.

In the middle of the mazurka, repeating a complicated figure newly invented by Korsunsky, Anna came forward into the center of the circle, chose two gentlemen, and summoned a lady and Kitty. Kitty gazed at her in dismay as she went up. Anna looked at her with drooping eyelids, and smiled, pressing her hand. But noticing that Kitty responded to her smile only with a look of despair and amazement, she turned away from her, and began gaily talking to the other lady.

"Yes, there is something uncanny, demonic and fascinating in her," Kitty said to herself.

Anna did not mean to stay for supper, but the host began to insist that she stay.

"Nonsense, Anna Arkadyevna," said Korsunsky, drawing her bare arm under the sleeve of his dress coat, "I've a marvelous idea for a *cotillon! Un bijou!*" [1]

And he moved gradually on, trying to draw her along with him. Their host smiled approvingly.

"No, I am not going to stay," answered Anna, smiling, but in spite of her smile, both Korsunsky and the host saw from her resolute tone that she would not stay.

"No; why, as it is, I have danced more at your ball in Moscow than I have all winter in Petersburg," said Anna, looking round at Vronsky, who stood near her. "I must rest a little before my journey."

"Are you really going tomorrow, then?" asked Vronsky.

"Yes, I suppose so," answered Anna, wondering at the boldness of his question; but the irrepressible, flashing brilliance of her eyes and her smile set him on fire as she said it.

Anna Arkadyevna did not stay to supper, but went home.

CHAPTER TWENTY-FOUR

"Yes, there is something in me repulsive and repellent," thought Levin, as he came away from the Shcherbatskys' and walked in the direction of his brother's lodgings. "And I don't get on with other people. Pride, they say. No, I have no pride. If I had any pride, I would not have put myself in such a position." And he pictured to himself Vronsky, happy, good-natured, clever, and self-possessed, certainly never placed in the awful position in which he had been that evening. "Yes, she was bound to choose him. So it had to be, and I cannot complain of anyone or anything. I am myself to blame. What

[1] "A jewel."

right had I to imagine she would care to join her life to mine? Who am I and what am I? A nobody, not wanted by anyone, or of use to anybody." And he recalled his brother Nikolai, and dwelt with pleasure on the thought of him. "Isn't he right that everything in the world is base and loathsome? And are we fair in our judgment of brother Nikolai? Of course, from Prokofy's point of view, seeing him in a torn cloak and tipsy, he's a despicable person. But I know him differently. I know his soul, and know that we are like him. And I, instead of going to seek him out, went out to dinner and came here." Levin walked up to a lamppost, read his brother's address, which was in his notebook, and called a sleigh. During the long ride to his brother's, Levin vividly recalled all the facts familiar to him of Nikolai's life. He remembered how his brother, while at the university, and for a year afterward, had, in spite of the jeers of his companions, lived like a monk, strictly observing all religious rites, services, and fasts, and avoiding every sort of pleasure, especially women. And afterward, how he had all at once broken loose: he had associated with the most horrible people, and rushed into the most senseless debauchery. He remembered later the scandal over a boy whom he had taken from the country to bring up and, in a fit of rage, had so violently beaten that proceedings were brought against him for causing bodily damage. Then he recalled the scandal with a card shark to whom he had lost money and given a promissory note, and against whom he had himself lodged a complaint, asserting that he had cheated him. (This was the money Sergey Ivanovich had paid.) Then he remembered how he had spent a night in the police station for disorderly conduct in the street. He remembered the shameful proceedings he had tried to instigate against his brother Sergey Ivanovich, accusing him of not having paid him his share of his mother's fortune, and the last scandal, when he had gone to a western province in an official capacity, and there had got into trouble for assaulting a village elder . . . It was all horribly disgusting, yet to Levin it appeared not at all in the same disgusting light as it inevitably would to those who did not know Nikolai, did not know his whole story, did not know his heart.

Levin remembered that when Nikolai had been in the devout stage, the period of fasts and monks and church services, when he was seeking in religion a support and a curb for his passionate temperament, everyone, far from encouraging him, had jeered at him, and he, too, with the others. They had teased him, called him Noah and Monk; and, when he had broken loose, no one had helped him, everyone had turned away from him in horror and disgust.

Levin felt that in spite of all the ugliness of his life, his brother Nikolai, in his soul, in the very depths of his soul, was no more in the wrong than the people who despised him. He was not to blame for having been born with his unbridled temperament and his somehow constrained intelligence. He had always wanted to be good. "I will talk frankly, without reserve, and I will make him speak without reserve, too, and I'll show him that I love him, and so understand him," Levin resolved to himself, as, toward eleven o'clock, he reached the hotel.

"At the top, twelve and thirteen," the porter said, in answer to Levin's inquiry.

"At home?"

"Sure to be at home."

The door of No. 12 was half open, and into the streak of light, came thick fumes of cheap, foul tobacco and the sound of a voice unknown to Levin; but he knew at once that his brother was there: he heard his cough.

As he went up to the door, the unknown voice was saying:

"It all depends with how much judgment and knowledge the thing's done."

Konstantin Levin looked in at the door, and saw that the speaker was a young man with an immense shock of hair, wearing a Russian coat, and that a pockmarked woman in a wool gown without collar or cuffs[1] was sitting on the sofa. His brother was not to be seen. Konstantin felt a sharp pang at his heart at the thought of the strange company in which his brother spent his life. No one had heard him, and Konstantin, taking off his galoshes, listened to what the man in the coat was saying. He was speaking of some enterprise.

"To hell with the privileged classes," his brother's voice responded, with a cough. "Masha! Get us some supper and some wine if there's any left; or else go and get some."

---

[1] Women of a better class wore lace collars and cuffs.

The woman rose, came out from behind the screen, and saw Konstantin.

"There's some gentleman, Nikolai Dmitrievich," she said.

"Whom do you want?" said the voice of Nikolai Levin, angrily.

"It's me," answered Konstantin Levin, coming forward into the light.

"Who's *me*?" Nikolai's voice said again, still more angrily. He could be heard getting up hurriedly, stumbling against something, and Levin saw, facing him in the doorway, the big scared eyes and the huge, thin, stooping figure of his brother, so familiar and yet astonishing in its weirdness and sickliness.

He was even thinner than three years before, when Konstantin had seen him last. He was wearing a short coat, and his arms and his large hands seemed bigger than ever. His hair had grown thinner, the same walrus mustaches hid his lips, the same eyes gazed strangely and naïvely at his visitor:

"Ah, Kostya!" he exclaimed suddenly, recognizing his brother, and his eyes lighted up with joy. But the same second he looked around at the young man, and gave the nervous jerk of his head and neck that Konstantin knew so well, as if his neck band hurt him; and a quite different expression, wild, suffering, and cruel, settled on his emaciated face.

"I wrote to you and Sergey Ivanovich both that I don't know you and don't want to know you. What is it you want?"

He was not at all the same as Konstantin had imagined him. The worst and most tiresome part of his character, that which made all relations with him so difficult, had been forgotten by Konstantin Levin when he thought of him, but now when he saw his face, and especially that nervous twitching of his head, he remembered it all.

"I don't want anything," he answered timidly. "I've simply come to see you."

His brother's timidity obviously softened Nikolai. His lips twitched.

"Oh, so that's it?" he said. "Well, come in; sit down. Like some supper? Masha, bring supper for three. No, wait a minute. Do you know who this is?" he said, addressing his brother and indicating the gentleman in the coat: "This is Kritsky, my friend from Kiev, a very remarkable man. He's persecuted by the police, of course, because he's not a scoundrel!"

And he looked around in the way he always did at everyone in the room. Seeing that the woman standing in the doorway was starting to leave, he shouted to her, "Wait a minute, I said!" And with the inability to express himself, the incoherence that Konstantin knew so well, he began, with another look around at everyone, to tell his brother Kritsky's story: how he had been expelled from the university for starting a benefit society for the poor students and Sunday schools; and how he had afterward been a teacher in a peasant school, and how he had been driven out of that, too, and had afterward been condemned for something or other.

"You're of the Kiev university?" said Konstantin Levin to Kritsky, to break the awkward silence that followed.

"Yes, I was of Kiev," Kritsky replied angrily, his face darkening.

"And this woman," Nikolai Levin interrupted him, pointing to her, "is my life's companion, Marya Nikolaevna. I took her out of a whorehouse," and he jerked his neck saying this; "but I love her and respect her, and anyone who wants to know me," he added, raising his voice and knitting his brows, "I beg to love her and respect her. She's just the same as my wife, just the same. So now you know whom you're dealing with. And if you think you're lowering yourself—well, here's the floor and there's the door."

And again his eyes traveled inquiringly over all of them.

"Why I should be lowering myself I don't understand."

"Then, Masha, tell them to bring supper; three portions, vodka and wine . . . No, wait a minute . . . No, it doesn't matter . . . Run along."

CHAPTER TWENTY-FIVE

"So you see," pursued Nikolai Levin, painfully wrinkling his forehead and twitching.

It was obviously difficult for him to think of what to say and do.

"Here, do you see?". . . He pointed to some iron bars tied together with string, lying in a corner of the room. "Do you see that? That's

the beginning of a new thing we're going into. It's a productive association . . ."

Konstantin scarcely heard him. He looked into his sickly, consumptive face, and he was more and more sorry for him, and he
could not force himself to listen to what his brother was telling him
about the association. He saw that this association was a mere anchor
to save him from self-contempt. Nikolai Levin went on talking:

"You know that capital oppresses the laborer. Our laborers, the
peasants, bear all the burden of labor, and are so placed that however much they work they can't escape from their position of beasts
of burden. All the profits of labor, on which they might improve their
position and gain leisure for themselves, and after that education, all
the surplus values are taken from them by the capitalists. And society's so constituted that the harder they work, the greater the profit
of the merchants and landowners, while they stay beasts of burden to
the end. And that state of things must be changed," he finished up,
and he looked questioningly at his brother.

"Yes, of course," said Konstantin, looking at the patch of red that
had come out on his brother's projecting cheekbones.

"And so we're forming a locksmiths' association, where all the
production and profit and the chief instruments of production will be
in common."

"Where is the association to be?" asked Konstantin Levin.

"In the village of Vozdrem, Kazansky province."

"But why in a village? I should think that in the villages there is
plenty of work as it is. Why a locksmiths' association in a village?"

"Why? Because the peasants are just as much slaves as they ever
were, and that's why you and Sergey Ivanovich don't like people to
try and get them out of their slavery," said Nikolai Levin, exasperated
by the objection.

Konstantin Levin sighed, looking meanwhile about the cheerless
and dirty room. This sigh seemed to exasperate Nikolai still more.

"I know your and Sergey Ivanovich's aristocratic views. I know
that he applies all the power of his intellect to justify existing evils."

"No; and why do you talk of Sergey Ivanovich?" said Levin, smiling.

"Sergey Ivanovich? I'll tell you why!" Nikolai Levin shrieked suddenly at the name of Sergey Ivanovich. "I'll tell you why. . ." But what's the use of talking? There's only one thing. . . What did you come here for? You despise this, and that's right—then go away, in God's name go away!" he shrieked, getting up from his chair. "Go away, go away!"

"I don't look down on it at all," said Konstantin Levin timidly. "I don't even dispute it."

At that instant Marya Nikolaevna came back. Nikolai Levin looked around angrily at her. She went quickly to him, and whispered something.

"I'm not well; I've grown irritable," said Nikolai Levin, getting calmer and breathing painfully; "and then you talk to me of Sergey Ivanovich and his article. It's such rubbish, such lying, such self-deception. What can a man write of justice who knows nothing of it? Have you read his article?" he asked Kritsky, sitting down again at the table and brushing from it a pile of half-filled cigarettes so as to provide space.

"I've not read it," Kritsky responded gloomily, obviously not desiring to enter into the conversation.

"Why not?" said Nikolai Levin, now turning with exasperation upon Kritsky.

"Because I didn't see the use of wasting my time over it."

"Oh, but excuse me, how did you know it would be wasting your time? That article's too profound for many people—that is to say, it's over their heads. But with me, it's another thing; I see through his ideas, and I know where its weakness lies."

Everyone was mute. Kritsky got up deliberately and reached for his cap.

"Won't you have supper? All right, good-by! Come around tomorrow with the locksmith."

Kritsky had hardly gone out when Nikolai Levin smiled and winked.

"He's no good, either," he said. "I see, of course . . ."

But at that instant Kritsky, at the door, called him.

"What do you want now?" he said, and went out to him in the passage. Left alone with Marya Nikolaevna, Levin turned to her.

"Have you been with my brother long?" he said to her.

"Yes, more than a year. Nikolai Dmitrievich's health has become very poor. Nikolai Dmitrievich drinks a great deal," she said.

"That is . . . what does he drink?"

"Vodka, and it's bad for him."

"And a great deal?" whispered Levin.

"Yes," she said, looking timidly toward the doorway, where Nikolai Levin had reappeared.

"What were you talking about?" he said, knitting his brows and turning from one to the other with frightened eyes. "What was it?"

"Oh, nothing," Konstantin answered in confusion.

"Oh, if you don't want to say, don't. Only it's no good your talking to her. She's a whore, and you're a gentleman," he said with a jerk of the neck. "You understand everything, I see, and have taken stock of everything, and look with commiseration on my shortcomings," he began again, raising his voice.

"Nikolai Dmitrievich, Nikolai Dmitrievich," whispered Marya Nikolaevna, again going up to him.

"Oh, very well, very well! . . . But where's the supper? Ah, here it is," he said, seeing a waiter with a tray. "Here, set it here," he added angrily, and promptly seizing the vodka, he poured out a glassful and drank it greedily. "Like a drink?" He turned to his brother, and at once became better humored.

"Well, enough of Sergey Ivanovich. I'm glad to see you, anyway. After all's said and done, we're not strangers. Come, have a drink. Tell me what you're doing," he went on, greedily munching a piece of bread and pouring out another glassful. "How are you living?"

"I live alone in the country, as I used to. I'm busy looking after the land," answered Konstantin, watching with horror the greediness with which his brother ate and drank, and trying to conceal the fact that he noticed it.

"Why don't you get married?"

"It just hasn't happened," Konstantin answered, reddening a little.

"Why not? For me now. . . everything's at an end! I've made a mess of my life. But this I've said, and I say still, that if my share had been given me when I needed it, my whole life would have been different."

Konstantin made haste to change the conversation.

"Do you know your little Vanyushka's[1] with me, a clerk in my office at Pokrovskoe?"

Nikolai jerked his neck, and sank into thought.

"Yes, tell me what's going on at Pokrovskoe. Is the house still standing, and the birch trees, and our schoolroom? And Filipp the gardener, is he living? How I remember the arbor and the seat! Now, see that you don't alter anything in the house, but hurry up and get married, and make everything as it used to be again. Then I'll come and see you, if your wife is nice."

"But come to me now," said Levin. "How nicely we would arrange it!"

"I'd come and see you if I were sure I would not find Sergey Ivanovich."

"You wouldn't find him there. I live quite independently of him."

"Yes, but say what you like, you will have to choose between me and him," he said, looking timidly into his brother's face.

This timidity touched Konstantin.

"If you want to hear my confession of faith on the subject, I tell you that in your quarrel with Sergey Ivanovich I take neither side. You're both wrong. You're more wrong externally, and he inwardly."

"Ah, ah! You see that, you see that!" Nikolai shouted joyfully.

"But I personally value friendly relations with you more because . . ."

"Why, why?"

Konstantin could not say that he valued it more because Nikolai was unhappy and needed affection. But Nikolai knew that this was just what he meant to say, and, scowling, he took up the vodka again.

"Enough, Nikolai Dmitrievich," said Marya Nikolaevna, stretching out her plump, bare arm toward the decanter.

"Let it be! Don't insist! I'll beat you!" he shouted.

Marya Nikolaevna smiled a sweet, and good-natured smile, which was at once reflected on Nikolai's face, and she took the bottle.

"And do you suppose she understands nothing?" said Nikolai. "She understands it all better than any of us. Isn't it true there's something good and sweet in her?"

[1]Diminutive of Ivan.

"Were you never before in Moscow?" Konstantin said to her, for the sake of saying something.

"Don't say '*vy*' to her.[2] It frightens her. No one ever said '*vy*' to her like that but the magistrate who tried her for trying to get out of a brothel. Heaven help us, the senselessness in the world!" he cried suddenly. "These new institutions, these magistrate courts, rural council, how monstrous it all is!"

And he began to enlarge on his encounters with the new institutions.

Konstantin Levin heard him, and the disbelief in the sense of all public institutions, which he shared with him and often expressed, was distasteful to him now from his brother's lips.

"In another world we shall understand it all," he said lightly.

"In another world! Ah, I don't like that other world! I don't like it," he said, letting his frightened eyes rest on his brother's. "Here one would think that to get out of all the baseness and the mess, one's own and other people's, would be a good thing, and yet I'm afraid of death, terribly afraid of death." He shuddered. "But drink something. Would you like some champagne? Or shall we go somewhere? Let's go to the Gypsies! Do you know, I've grown fond of the Gypsies and Russian songs."

His speech had begun to falter, and he passed abruptly from one subject to another. Konstantin, with Masha's help, persuaded him not to go out anywhere, and got him to bed hopelessly drunk.

Masha promised to write to Konstantin in case of need, and to persuade Nikolai Levin to go and stay with his brother.

CHAPTER TWENTY-SIX

In the morning Konstantin Levin left Moscow, and toward evening he reached home. On the journey in the train he talked to his neighbors about politics and the new railways, and, just as in Moscow, he was overcome by a sense of confusion of ideas, dissatisfaction with himself, shame about something or other. But when he got out at

[2] See note on page 64.

his own station, when he saw his one-eyed coachman, Ignat, with the collar of his coat turned up; when, in the dim light reflected by the station lights, he saw his own sleigh, his own horses with their tails tied up, in their harness trimmed with rings and tassels; when Ignat, as he put in his luggage, told him the village news, that the contractor had arrived, and that Pava had calved—he felt that little by little the confusion was clearing up, and the shame and self-dissatisfaction were passing away. He felt this at the mere sight of Ignat and the horses; but when he had put on the sheepskin brought to him, had sat down wrapped up in the sleigh, and had driven off pondering on the work that lay before him in the village, and staring at the side horse (once a saddle horse, worn out now, but a spirited beast from the Don), he began to see what had happened to him in quite a different light. He felt that he was himself, and did not want to be anyone else. All he wanted now was to be better than before. First, he resolved that from that day he would give up hoping for any extraordinary happiness, such as marriage might have given him, and consequently would not so disparage what he really had. Second, he would never again let himself give way to disgusting passion, the memory of which had so tortured him when he had been making up his mind to make a proposal. Then, remembering his brother Nikolai, he resolved that he would never allow himself to forget him, that he would follow him up and not lose sight of him, so as to be ready to help should things go badly with him. And that would be soon, he felt. Then, too, his brother's talk of communism, which he had treated so lightly at the time, now made him think. He considered a revolution in economic conditions nonsense. But he always felt the injustice of his own abundance in comparison with the poverty of the peasants, and now he determined that so as to feel completely in the right, though he had worked hard and lived by no means luxuriously before, he would now work still harder, and would allow himself even less luxury. And all this seemed to him so easy a conquest over himself that he spent the whole drive in the pleasantest daydreams. With a resolute feeling of hope in a new, better life, he reached home before nine o'clock at night.

The snow of the little quadrangle before the house was lit up by a light in the bedroom windows of his old nurse, Agafya

Mikhailovna, who performed the duties of housekeeper in his house. She was not yet asleep. Kuzma, wakened by her, came sidling sleepily out onto the steps. A setter bitch, Laska, ran out too, almost upsetting Kuzma, and whining, the dog circled Levin's knees, jumping up and longing but not daring to put her forepaws on his chest.

"You're back early, sir," said Agafya Mikhailovna.

"I got tired of it, Agafya Mikhailovna. Visiting friends is all very well, but there is no place like home," he answered, and went into his study.

The study was gradually lit up as the candle was brought in. The familiar details came out: the stag's horns, the book shelves, the mirror, the stove with its ventilator, which had long been in need of fixing, his father's sofa, a large table, on the table an open book, a broken ash tray, a notebook with his writing. As he saw all this, there came over him for an instant a doubt of the possibility of starting a new life, of which he had been dreaming on the road. All these traces of his life seemed to clutch him and say to him: "No, you're not going to get away from us, and you're not going to be different, you're going to be the same as you've always been; with doubts, everlasting dissatisfaction with yourself, vain efforts to improve, and failures, and continual expectation of a happiness that has eluded you and that isn't possible for you."

This the things said to him, but another voice in his heart was telling him that he must not fall under the sway of the past, and that one can do anything with oneself. And hearing that voice, he went into the corner where his two thirty-six-pound dumbbells were and began exercising with them like a gymnast, trying to restore his self-confidence. There was a creak of steps at the door. He hastily put down the dumbbells.

The bailiff came in and said that everything, thank God, was doing well; but informed him that the buckwheat in the new drying kiln had been a little scorched. This piece of news irritated Levin. The new kiln had been constructed and partly invented by Levin. The bailiff had always been against the kiln, and now it was with suppressed triumph that he announced that the buckwheat had been scorched. Levin was firmly convinced that if the buckwheat had been scorched, it was only because the precautions had not been taken, for which he had hundreds of times given orders. He was annoyed, and reprimanded the bailiff. But there had been an important and joyful event: Pava, his best cow, an expensive animal bought at a cattle show, had calved.

"Kuzma, give me my sheepskin. And you tell them to take a lantern. I'll come and look at her," he said to the bailiff.

The sheds for the more valuable cows were just behind the house. Walking across the yard, passing a snow drift by the lilac bush, he went into the shed. There was the warm, steamy smell of dung when the frozen door was opened, and the cows, startled at the unfamiliar light of the lantern, stirred on the fresh straw. He caught a glimpse of the broad, smooth, black-and-white back of a Dutch cow. Berkut, the bull, was lying down with his ring in his nose, and seemed about to get up, but thought better of it, and only gave two snorts as they passed by him. Pava, a perfect beauty, as huge as a hippopotamus, with her back turned to them, prevented their seeing the calf as she sniffed her all over.

Levin went into the pen, looked Pava over, and lifted the red and spotted calf onto her long, tottering legs. Pava, uneasy, began lowing, but when Levin put the calf close to her she was soothed, and, sighing heavily, began licking her with her rough tongue. The calf, fumbling, poked her nose under her mother's udder, and stiffened her tail out straight.

"Here, bring the light, Fyodor, this way," said Levin, examining the calf. "Like the mother, though the color is like the father's; but that's nothing. Very good. Long and broad in the haunch. Vasily Fydorovich, isn't she marvelous?" he said to the bailiff, quite forgiving him for the buckwheat under the influence of his delight in the calf.

"How could she fail to be? Oh, Semyon the contractor came the day after you left. You must settle with him, Konstantin Dmitrievich," said the bailiff. "I did inform you about the machine."

This question was enough to take Levin back to all the details of his work on the estate, which was on a large scale and complicated. He went straight from the cowshed to the office, and after a little conversation with the bailiff and Semyon the contractor, he went back to the house and straight upstairs to the drawing room.

CHAPTER TWENTY-SEVEN

The house was big and old-fashioned, and Levin, though he lived alone, had the whole house heated and used all of it. He knew that this was stupid, he knew that it was positively wrong and contrary to his present new plans, but this house was a whole world to Levin. It was the world in which his father and mother had lived and died. They had lived just the life that to Levin seemed the ideal of perfection, and that he had dreamed of renewing with his wife, with his own family.

Levin scarcely remembered his mother. His conception of her was for him a sacred memory, and his future wife was bound to be in his imagination a repetition of that exquisite, holy ideal of a woman that his mother had been.

He was so far from conceiving of love for woman apart from marriage that he actually pictured to himself first the family, and only secondarily the woman who would give him a family. His ideas of marriage were, consequently, very unlike those of the great majority of his acquaintances, for whom getting married was one of the numerous facts of social life. For Levin it was the chief affair of life, on which its whole happiness turned. And now he had to give that up.

When he had gone into the little drawing room, where he always had tea, and had settled himself in his armchair with a book, and Agafya Mikhailovna had brought him tea, and with her usual, "Well, I'll stay a while, sir," had seated herself at the window, he felt that, however strange it might be, he had not parted from his daydreams, and that he could not live without them. Whether with her or with another, still it would be. He was reading a book, and thinking of what he was reading, and stopping to listen to Agafya Mikhailovna, who gossiped away without stopping, and yet with all that, all sorts of pictures of family life and work in the future rose disconnectedly before his imagination. He felt that in the depth of his soul something had been put in its place, settled down, and laid to rest.

He heard Agafya Mikhailovna talking of how Prokhor had forgotten his duty to God, and, with the money Levin had given him to buy a horse, had been drinking without stopping, and had beaten his wife till he'd half killed her. He listened, and read his book, and recalled the whole train of his ideas suggested by his reading. It was Tyndall's[1] *Treatise on Heat*. He recalled his own criticisms of Tyndall for his complacent satisfaction in the cleverness of his experiments, and for his lack of philosophic insight. And suddenly there floated into his mind the joyful thought: "In two years' time I shall have two Dutch cows; Pava herself will perhaps still be alive, a dozen young daughters of Berkut, and, to top it off, these three—how wonderful!"

He took up his book again. "Very good, electricity and heat are the same thing; but is it possible to substitute the one quantity for the other in the equation for the solution of any problem? No. Well, then, what of it? The connection between all the forces of nature is felt instinctively . . . It's particularly nice if Pava's daughter should be a red-spotted cow, and all the herd will take after her, and the other three, too! Splendid! To go out with my wife and visitors to meet the herd . . . My wife will say, 'Kostya and I looked after the calf like a child.' 'How can it interest you so much?' says a visitor. 'Everything that interests him, interests me.' But who will she be?" And he remembered what had happened in Moscow . . . "Well, there's nothing to be done . . . It's not my fault. But now everything shall go on in a new way. It's nonsense to pretend that life won't allow it, that the past won't allow it. One must struggle to live better, much better." He raised his head, and sank into thought. Old Laska, who had not yet fully digested her delight at his return and had run out into the yard to bark, came back wagging her tail and crept up to him, bringing in the scent of the fresh air, put her head under his hand, and whined plaintively, asking to be petted.

"There, who'd have thought it?" said Agafya Mikhailovna. "The dog now . . . why, she understands that her master's come home and that he's depressed."

"Why depressed?"

"Do you suppose I don't see it, sir? It's high time I should know the gentry. Why, I've grown up from a little thing with them. It's nothing, sir, so long as there's health and a clear conscience."

Levin looked intently at her, surprised at how well she knew his thought.

[1] John Tyndall (1820-93), Irish physicist.

"Shall I fetch you another cup?" she said, and taking his cup, she went out.

Laska kept poking her head under his hand. He petted her, and she promptly curled up at his feet, laying her head on a hind paw. And in token of everything now being satisfactory, she opened her mouth a little, smacked her lips, and, settling her sticky lips more comfortably about her old teeth, sank into blissful repose. Levin watched all of her movements attentively.

"That's what I'll do," he said to himself; "that's what I'll do! Nothing's wrong . . . All's well."

CHAPTER TWENTY-EIGHT

After the ball, early next morning, Anna Arkadyevna sent her husband a telegram saying that she was leaving Moscow the same day.

"No, I must go, I must go." She explained to her sister-in-law her change of plans in a tone that suggested that she had to remember so many things that there was no enumerating them. "No, it had really better be today!"

Stepan Arkadyevich was not dining at home, but he promised to come see his sister off at seven o'clock.

Kitty, too, did not come, sending a note that she had a headache. Dolly and Anna dined alone with the children and the English governess. Whether it was that the children were fickle, or that they were very sensitive, and felt that Anna was quite different that day from what she had been when they had taken such a liking to her, that she was now uninterested in them—they abruptly dropped their play with their aunt, and their love for her, and were quite indifferent that she was going away. Anna was absorbed the whole morning in preparations for her departure. She wrote notes to her Moscow acquaintances, did her accounts, and packed. Altogether, Dolly thought she was not in a placid state of mind but in that worried mood which Dolly knew well with herself, and which does not come without cause, and for the most part covers dissatisfaction with self. After dinner, Anna went up to her room to dress, and Dolly followed her.

"How strange you are today!" Dolly said to her.

"I? Do you think so? I'm not strange, but I'm depressed. I am like that sometimes. I keep feeling as if I could cry. It's very stupid, but it will pass," said Anna quickly, and she bent her flushed face over a tiny bag in which she was packing a night cap and some batiste handkerchiefs. Her eyes were particularly bright, and were continually swimming with tears. "In the same way I didn't want to leave Petersburg, and now I don't want to go away from here."

"You came here and did a good deed," said Dolly, looking intently at her.

Anna looked at her with eyes wet with tears.

"Don't say that, Dolly. I've done nothing, and could do nothing. I often wonder why people are all conspiring to spoil me. What have I done, and what could I do? In your heart you found love enough to forgive . . ."

"If it had not been for you, God knows what would have happened! How happy you are, Anna!" said Dolly. "Everything is clear and good in your heart."

"Everyone has a skeleton in his closet, as the English say."

"You have no skeleton, have you? Everything is so serene in you."

"I have!" said Anna suddenly, and, unexpectedly after her tears, a sly, ironical smile curved her lips.

"Well, he's amusing, anyway, your skeleton, and not depressing," said Dolly, smiling.

"No, he's depressing. Do you know why I'm going today instead of tomorrow? It's a confession that weighs on me; I want to make it to you," said Anna, letting herself drop resolutely into an armchair, and looking straight into Dolly's face.

And to her surprise, Dolly saw that Anna was blushing up to her ears, up to the curly black ringlets on her neck.

"Yes," Anna went on. "Do you know why Kitty didn't come to dinner? She's jealous of me. I have spoiled . . . I've been the cause of that ball being a torture to her instead of a pleasure. But truly, truly, it's not my fault, or only my fault a little bit," she said, daintily drawling the words "a little bit."

"Oh, how like Stiva you said that!" said Dolly, laughing.

Anna was hurt.

"Oh no, oh no! I'm not Stiva," she said, knitting her brows.

"That's why I'm telling you, just because I could never let myself doubt myself for an instant," said Anna.

But at the very moment she was uttering the words, she felt that they were not true. She was not merely doubting herself, she felt emotion at the thought of Vronsky, and was going away sooner than she had meant simply to avoid meeting him.

"Yes, Stiva told me you danced the mazurka with him, and that he—"

"You can't imagine how absurdly it all came about. I only meant to be matchmaking, and all at once it turned out quite differently. Possibly against my own will . . ."

She crimsoned and stopped.

"Oh, they feel it directly!" said Dolly.

"But I should be in despair if there were anything serious in it on his side," Anna interrupted her. "And I am certain it will all be forgotten, and Kitty will stop hating me."

"All the same, Anna, to tell you the truth, I'm not very anxious for this marriage for Kitty. And it's better it should come to nothing if he, Vronsky, is capable of falling in love with you in a single day."

"Oh, heavens, that would be too silly!" said Anna, and again a deep flush of pleasure came out on her face when she heard the idea, which absorbed her, put into words. "And so here I am going away, having made an enemy of Kitty, whom I liked so much! Ah, how sweet she is! But you'll make it right, Dolly? Eh?"

Dolly could scarcely suppress a smile. She loved Anna, but she enjoyed seeing that she too had her weaknesses.

"An enemy? That can't be."

"I did so want you all to care for me, as I do for you, and now I care for you more than ever," said Anna, with tears in her eyes. "Ah, how silly I am today!"

She passed her handkerchief over her face and began dressing.

At the very moment of departure, Stepan Arkadyevich arrived, late, rosy, and happy, smelling of wine and cigars.

Anna's emotionalism had infected Dolly, and when she embraced her sister-in-law for the last time, she whispered: "Remember, Anna, what you've done for me—I shall never forget. And remember that I love you, and shall always love you as my dearest friend!"

"I don't know why," said Anna, kissing her and hiding her tears. "You understood me, and you understand. Good-by, my darling!"

CHAPTER TWENTY-NINE

"Well, it's all over, and thank God!" was the first thought that came to Anna Arkadyevna when she had said good-by for the last time to her brother, who had stood blocking up the entrance to the carriage till the third bell rang. She sat down on her lounge beside Annushka, and looked about her in the twilight of the sleeping car. "Thank God! Tomorrow I shall see Seryozha and Aleksey Aleksandrovich, and my life will go on in the old way, all nice and as usual."

Still in the same anxious frame of mind as she had been all that day, Anna took pleasure in arranging herself for the journey with great care. With her deft little hands she opened and shut her little red bag, took out a cushion, laid it on her knees, and, carefully wrapping up her feet, settled herself comfortably. An invalid lady had already laid down to sleep. Two other ladies began talking to Anna, and a stout elderly lady tucked up her feet, and made observations about the heating of the train. Anna answered a few words, but not foreseeing any entertainment from the conversation, she asked Annushka to get her lamp, hooked it onto the arm of her seat, and took from her bag a paper knife and an English novel. At first her reading made no progress. The fuss and bustle were disturbing; then when the train had started, she could not help listening to the noises; then the snow beating on the left window and sticking to the pane, and the sight of the muffled conductor passing by, covered with snow on one side, and the conversations about the terrible snowstorm raging outside, distracted her attention. Further on, it was continually the same again and again: the same shaking and rattling, the same snow on the window, the same rapid transitions from steaming heat to cold, and back again to heat, the same passing glimpses of the same figures in the twilight, and the same voices, and Anna began to read and to understand what she read. Annushka was already dozing, the red bag on her lap clutched by her broad hands, in gloves, one of which was torn. Anna Arkadyevna read and understood; but it was distasteful to her to read, that is, to follow the reflection of other people's lives. She had too great a desire to live herself. If she read that the heroine of the novel was nursing a sick man, she longed to move with noiseless steps about the room of a sick man; if she read of a member of Parliament making a speech, she longed to be delivering the speech; if she read of how Lady Mary had ridden after the hounds, and had provoked her sister-in-law, and had surprised everyone by her boldness, she too wished to be doing the same. But there was no chance of doing anything; and twisting the smooth paper knife in her little hands, she forced herself to read.

The hero of the novel had almost attained his English happiness, a baronetcy and an estate, and Anna was feeling a desire to go with him to the estate, when she suddenly felt that *he* ought to feel ashamed, and that she was ashamed of the same thing. But what had he to be ashamed of? "What have I to be ashamed of?" she asked herself in injured surprise. She laid down the book and sank against the back of the chair, tightly gripping the paper cutter in both hands. There was nothing. She went over all her Moscow recollections. All were good, pleasant. She remembered the ball, remembered Vronsky and his face of slavish adoration, remembered her conduct with him: there was nothing shameful. And for all that, at the same point in her memories, the feeling of shame was intensified, as though some inner voice, just at the point when she thought of Vronsky, were saying to her, "Warm, very warm, hot." "Well, what is it?" she said to herself resolutely, shifting her seat in the lounge. "What does it mean? Am I afraid to look it straight in the face? Why, what is it? Can it be that between me and this officer boy there exist, or can exist, any other relations than such as are common with every acquaintance?" She laughed contemptuously and took up her book again; but now she was definitely unable to follow what she read. She passed the paper knife over the windowpane, then laid its smooth, cool surface to her cheek, and almost laughed aloud at the feeling of delight that all at once without cause came over her. She felt as though her nerves were strings being strained tighter and tighter on some sort of peg. She felt her eyes opening wider and wider, her fingers and toes twitching nervously, something within oppressing her breathing, while all shapes and sounds seemed in the uncertain half-light to strike her with unaccustomed vividness. Moments of doubt were continually coming upon her, when she was uncertain whether the train was going forward or backward or standing still altogether; whether it was Annushka at her side or a stranger. "What's that on the arm of the chair, a fur cloak or some beast? And what am I myself? Myself or some other woman?" She was afraid of giving way to this delirium. But something drew her toward it, and she could yield to it or resist it at will. She got up to rouse herself, and discarded her blanket and the cape of her warm dress. For a moment she regained her self-possession, and realized that the thin peasant who had come in wearing a long overcoat, with buttons missing from it, was the stoveheater, that he was looking at the thermometer, that it was the wind and snow bursting in after him at the door; but then everything grew blurred again . . .That peasant with the long waist seemed to be gnawing at something on the wall, the old lady began stretching her legs the whole length of the carriage and filling it with a black cloud; then there was a fearful shrieking and banging, as though someone was being torn to pieces; then there was a blinding dazzle of red fire before her eyes and a wall seemed to rise up and hide everything. Anna felt as though she was sinking down. But it was not terrible, but delightful. The voice of a man muffled up and covered with snow shouted something in her ear. She got up and pulled herself together; she realized that they had reached a station and that this was the conductor. She asked Annushka to hand her the cape she had taken off and her shawl, put them on, and moved toward the door.

"Do you wish to get out?" asked Annushka.

"Yes, I want a little air. It's very hot in here." And she opened the door. The driving snow and the wind rushed to meet her and struggled with her over the door. But she enjoyed the struggle.

She opened the door and went out. The wind seemed as though lying in wait for her; with gleeful whistle it tried to snatch her up and bear her off, but she clung to the cold handrail and, holding her skirt, got down onto the platform and under the shelter of the carriages. The wind had been powerful on the steps, but on the platform, under the lee of the carriages, there was a lull. With enjoyment she drew deep breaths of the frozen, snowy air and, standing near the carriage, looked about the platform and the lighted station.

CHAPTER THIRTY

The raging tempest rushed whistling between the wheels of the carriages, about the scaffolding, and around the corner of the station. The carriages, posts, people, everything that was to be seen was covered with snow on one side and was getting more and more thickly covered. For a moment there would come a lull in the storm, but then it would swoop down again with such onslaughts that it seemed impossible to stand against it. Meanwhile men ran to and fro, talking merrily together, their steps crackling on the platform as they continually opened and closed the big doors. The bent shadow of a man glided by at her feet, and she heard sounds of a hammer upon iron. "Hand over that telegram!" came an angry voice out of the stormy darkness on the other side. "This way! Number 28!" several different voices shouted again, and muffled figures ran by covered with snow. Two gentlemen with lighted cigarettes passed by her. She drew one more deep breath of the fresh air, and had just put her hand out of her muff to take hold of the handrail and get back into the carriage, when another man in a military overcoat, quite close beside her, stepped between her and the flickering light of the lamppost. She looked around, and the same instant recognized Vronsky's face. Putting his hand to the peak of his cap, he bowed to her and asked, Was there anything she wanted? Could he be of any service to her? She gazed a long while at him without answering, and in spite of the shadow in which he was standing, she saw, or thought she saw, the expression of both his face and his eyes. It was again that expression of reverential ecstasy which had so affected her the day before. More than once she had told herself during the past few days, and again only a few moments before, that Vronsky was for her only one of the hundreds of young men, forever exactly the same, that are met everywhere, that she would never allow herself to bestow a thought upon him. But now at the first instant of meeting him, she was seized by a feeling of joyful pride. She had no need to ask why he had come. She knew as certainly as if he had told her that he was here to be where she was.

"I didn't know you were going. What are you coming for?" she said, letting fall the hand with which she had grasped the handrail. And irrepressible delight and eagerness shone in her face.

"What am I coming for?" he repeated, looking straight into her eyes. "You know that I have come to be where you are," he said; "I can't help it."

At that moment the wind, as if surmounting all obstacles, sent the snow flying from the carriage roofs, and clanked some sheet of iron it had torn off, while the hoarse whistle of the engine roared in front, plaintively and gloomily. All the awfulness of the storm seemed to her more splendid now. He had said what her soul longed to hear, though she feared it with her reason. She made no answer, and in her face he saw conflict.

"Forgive me, if you dislike what I said," he said humbly.

He had spoken courteously, deferentially, yet so firmly, so stubbornly, that for a long while she could make no answer.

"It's wrong, what you say, and I beg you, if you're a good man, to forget what you've said, as I forget it," she said at last.

"Not one word, not one gesture of yours shall I, could I, ever forget . . ."

"Enough, enough!" she cried, vainly trying to give a stern expression to her face, into which he was gazing greedily. And clutching at the cold handrail, she clambered up the steps and got rapidly into the corridor of the carriage. But in the little corridor she paused, going over in her imagination what had happened. Though she could not recall her own words or his, she realized instinctively that that momentary conversation had brought them fearfully closer; and she was panic-stricken and blissful at it. After standing still a few seconds, she went into the carriage and sat down in her place. The overwrought condition which had tormented her before did not only come back, but was intensified, and reached such a pitch that she was afraid every minute that something would snap within her from the excessive tension. She did not sleep all night. But in that nervous tension, and in the visions that filled her imagination, there was nothing disagreeable or gloomy: on the contrary, there was something blissful, glowing, and exhilarating. Toward morning Anna sank into a doze, sitting in her place, and when she wakened, it was daylight and the train was near Petersburg. At once thoughts of home, of husband and of son, and the details of that day and the following came upon her.

At Petersburg, as soon as the train stopped and she got out, the first person who attracted her attention was her husband. "Oh, my God! Why do his ears look like that?" she thought, looking at his frigid and distinguished figure, and especially the ears that struck her at the moment as propping up the brim of his round hat. Catching sight of her, he came to meet her, his lips falling into their habitual sarcastic smile, and his big, tired eyes, looking straight at her. An unpleasant sensation gripped at her heart when she met his obstinate and weary glance, as though she had expected to see him different. She was especially struck by the feeling of dissatisfaction with herself that she experienced on meeting him. That feeling was an intimate, familiar feeling, like a consciousness of hypocrisy, which she experienced in her relations with her husband. But hitherto she had not taken note of the feeling, now she was clearly and painfully aware of it.

"Yes, as you see, your tender spouse, as devoted as the first year after marriage, burned with impatience to see you," he said in his deliberate, high-pitched voice, and in that tone which he almost always took with her, a tone of jeering at anyone who should say in earnest what he said.

"Is Seryozha well?" she asked.

"And is this all the reward," said he, "for my ardor? He's well, very well . . ."

CHAPTER THIRTY-ONE

Vronsky had not even tried to sleep all that night. He sat in his seat, looking straight before him or scanning the people who got in and out. If he had indeed on previous occasions struck and impressed people who did not know him by his air of unhesitating composure, he seemed now more haughty and self-possessed than ever. He looked at people as if they were things. A nervous young man, a clerk in a district court, sitting opposite him, hated him for that look. The young man asked him for a light, and entered into conversation with him, and even pushed against him, to make him feel that he was not a thing but a person. But Vronsky gazed at him exactly as he did at the lamp, and the young man made a wry face, feeling that he was losing his self-possession under the oppression of this refusal to recognize him as a person.

Vronsky saw nothing and no one. He felt himself a king, not because he believed that he had made an impression on Anna—he did not yet believe that—but because the impression she had made on him gave him happiness and pride.

What would come of it all he did not know, he did not even think. He felt that all his forces, hitherto dissipated, wasted, were concentrated on one thing, and bent with fearful energy on one blissful goal. And he was happy at it. He knew only that he had told her the truth, that he had come where she was, that all the happiness of his life, the only meaning in life for him, now lay in seeing and hearing her. And when he got out of the carriage at Bologoe to get some water, and caught sight of Anna, involuntarily his first word had told her just what he thought. And he was glad he had told her it, that she knew it now and was thinking of it. He did not sleep all night. When he was back in the carriage, he kept unceasingly going over every position in which he had seen her, every word she had uttered, and before his imagination, making his heart faint with emotion, floated pictures of a possible future.

When he got out of the train at Petersburg, he felt after his sleepless night as keen and fresh as after a cold bath. He paused near his compartment, waiting for her to get out. "Once more," he said to himself, smiling unconsciously, "once more I shall see her walk, her face; she will say something, turn her head, glance, smile, maybe." But before he caught sight of her, he saw her husband, whom the stationmaster was deferentially escorting through the crowd. "Ah, yes! The husband." Only now for the first time did Vronsky realize clearly the fact that there was a person attached to her, a husband. He knew that she had a husband, but had hardly believed in his existence, and only now fully believed in him, with his head and shoulders, and legs clad in black trousers; especially when he saw this husband calmly take her arm with an air of ownership.

Seeing Aleksey Aleksandrovich with his Petersburg face and

severely self-confident figure, in his round hat, with his rather prominent spine, he believed in him, and was aware of a disagreeable sensation, such as a man might feel tortured by thirst, who, on reaching a spring, should find a dog, a sheep, or a pig who has drunk of it and muddied the water. Aleksey Aleksandrovich's manner of walking, with a swing of the hips and flat feet, particularly annoyed Vronsky. He could recognize in no one but himself an indubitable right to love her. But she was still the same, and the sight of her affected him the same way, physically reviving him, stirring him, and filling his soul with rapture. He told his German valet, who ran up to him from the second class, to take his things and go on, and he himself went up to her. He saw the first meeting between the husband and wife, and noted with a lover's insight the signs of slight reserve with which she spoke to her husband. "No, she does not love him and cannot love him," he decided to himself.

At the moment when he was approaching Anna Arkadyevna he noticed too with joy that she was conscious of his being near and looked around, and, seeing him, turned again to her husband.

"Have you had a good night?" he said, bowing to her and her husband together, and leaving it to Aleksey Aleksandrovich to accept the bow on his own account, and to recognize it or not, as he might see fit.

"Thank you, very good," she answered.

Her face looked weary, and there was not that play of eagerness in it, peeping out in her smile and her eyes; but for a single instant, as she glanced at him, there was a flash of something in her eyes, and although the flash died away at once, he was happy for that moment. She glanced at her husband to find out whether he knew Vronsky. Aleksey Aleksandrovich looked at Vronsky with displeasure, vaguely recalling who this was. Vronsky's composure and self-confidence here struck, like a scythe against a stone, upon the cold self-confidence of Aleksey Aleksandrovich.

"Count Vronsky," said Anna.

"Ah! We are acquainted, I believe," said Aleksey Aleksandrovich indifferently, giving his hand.

"You go with the mother and you return with the son," he said, articulating each word as though they were worth a ruble apiece.

"You're back from leave, I suppose?" he said, and without waiting for a reply, he turned to his wife in his jesting tone: "Well, were a great many tears shed at Moscow at parting?"

By addressing his wife like this, he made Vronsky understand that he wished to be left alone, and, turning slightly toward him, he touched his hat; but Vronsky turned to Anna Arkadyevna.

"I hope I may have the honor of calling on you," he said.

Aleksey Aleksandrovich glanced with his weary eyes at Vronsky.

"Delighted," he said coldly. "On Mondays we're at home. Most fortunate," he said to his wife, dismissing Vronsky altogether, "that I should just have half an hour to meet you, so that I can prove my devotion," he went on in his usual bantering tone.

"You lay too much stress on your devotion for me to value it much," she responded in the same playful tone, involuntarily listening to the sound of Vronsky's steps behind them. "But what has it to do with me?" she said to herself, and she began asking her husband how Seryozha had got on without her.

"Oh, splendidly! Mariette says he has been very good, and . . . I must disappoint you . . . but he has not missed you as your husband has. But once more *merci*, my dear, for giving me a day. Our dear *Samovar* will be delighted." (He called the celebrated Countess Lydia Ivanovna a samovar, because she was always bubbling over with excitement.) "She has been continually asking after you. And, do you know, if I may venture to advise you, you should go and see her today. You know how she takes everything to heart. Just now, with all her own cares, she's anxious about the Oblonskys being brought together."

The Countess Lydia Ivanovna was a friend of her husband's, and the center of that one of the coteries of the Petersburg world with which Anna was, through her husband, in the closest relations.

"But you know I wrote to her?"

"Still she'll want to hear details. Go and see her, if you're not too tired, my dear. Well, Kondraty will take you in the carriage while I go to my committee. I shall not be alone at dinner again," Aleksey Aleksandrovich went on, no longer in a sarcastic tone. "You wouldn't believe how I've missed . . ." And with a long pressure of her hand and a meaningful smile, he put her in her carriage.

CHAPTER THIRTY-TWO

The first person to meet Anna at home was her son. He dashed down the stairs to her, in spite of the governess's call, and with desperate joy shrieked: "Mother! Mother!" Running up to her, he hung on her neck.

"I told you it was Mother!" he shouted to the governess. "I knew!"

And her son, like her husband, aroused in Anna a feeling akin to disappointment. She had imagined him better than he was in reality. She had to let herself descend to reality to enjoy him as he really was. But even as he was, he was charming, with his fair curls, his blue eyes, and his plump, graceful little legs in tight-fitting stockings. Anna experienced almost physical pleasure in the sensation of his nearness, and his caresses, and moral soothing when she met his simple, confiding, and loving glances, and heard his naïve questions. Anna took out the presents Dolly's children had sent him, and told her son about a little girl in Moscow named Tanya, and how Tanya could read and even taught the other children.

"Why, am I not as nice as she?" asked Seryozha.

"To me you're nicer than anyone in the world."

"I know that," said Seryozha, smiling.

Anna had not had time to drink her coffee when the Countess Lydia Ivanovna was announced. The countess was a tall, stout woman, with an unhealthily sallow face and splendid, pensive black eyes. Anna liked her, but today she seemed to be seeing her for the first time with all her defects.

"Well, my dear, so you took the olive branch?" inquired Countess Lydia Ivanovna, as soon as she came into the room.

"Yes, it's all over, but it was all much less serious than we had supposed," answered Anna. "My *belle-soeur* is in general too impulsive."

But Countess Lydia Ivanovna, though she was interested in everything that did not concern her, had a habit of never listening to what interested her; she interrupted Anna:

"Yes, there's plenty of sorrow and evil in the world. I am so worried today."

"Oh, why?" asked Anna, trying to suppress a smile.

"I'm beginning to be weary of fruitlessly championing the truth, and sometimes I'm quite unhinged by it. The society of the Little Sisters" (this was a religious, patriotic, philanthropic institution) "was going splendidly, but with these gentlemen it's impossible to do anything," added the countess in a tone of ironical submission to destiny. "They pounce on the idea, and distort it, and then work it out so pettily and unworthily. Two or three people, your husband among them, understand the importance of the thing, but the others simply drag it down. Yesterday Pravdin wrote to me . . ."

Pravdin was a well-known Panslavist[1] abroad, and Countess Lydia Ivanovna described the purport of his letter.

Then the countess told her of more disagreements and intrigues against the work of the unification of the churches, and departed in haste, as she had that day to be at the meeting of some society and also at the Slavic committee.

"It was all the same before, of course; but why was it I didn't notice it before?" Anna asked herself. "Or had she been very much irritated today? It's really ludicrous; her object is doing good; she's a Christian, yet she's always angry; and she always has enemies, and always enemies in the name of Christianity and doing good."

After Countess Lydia Ivanovna, another friend came, the wife of a chief secretary, who told her all the news of the town. At three o'clock she too went away, promising to come to dinner. Aleksey Aleksandrovich was at the ministry. Anna, left alone, spent the time till dinner in assisting with her son's dinner (he dined apart from his parents) and in putting her things in order, and in reading and answering the notes and letters which had accumulated on her table.

That unreasonable shame which she had felt on the journey, and her excitement, too, had completely vanished. In the habitual condition of her life she felt again resolute and irreproachable.

She recalled with wonder her state of mind on the previous day. "What was it? Nothing. Vronsky said something silly, which it was easy to put a stop to, and I answered as I should have. To speak of it to my husband would be unnecessary and out of the question. To speak of it would be to attach importance to what has no impor-

---

[1]Panslavism, a movement to unite all Slavic-speaking peoples, gained strength in nineteenth-century Russia, especially among nationalist intellectuals who saw it as a means of enhancing Russia's position in Europe.

tance." She remembered how she had told her husband of what was almost a declaration made her at Petersburg by a young man, one of her husband's subordinates, and how Aleksey Aleksandrovich had answered that every woman living in the world was exposed to such incidents, but that he had the fullest confidence in her tact, and could never lower her and himself by jealousy. "So then there's nothing to speak of," she told herself.

CHAPTER THIRTY-THREE

Aleksey Aleksandrovich came back from the meeting of the ministers at four o'clock, but as often happened, he had not time to come in to her. He went into his study to see the people waiting for him with petitions, and to sign some papers brought him by his chief secretary. At dinnertime (there were always a few people dining with the Karenins) there arrived an old lady, a cousin of Aleksey Aleksandrovich, the chief secretary of the department and his wife, and a young man who had been recommended to Karenin for the service. Anna went into the drawing room to receive these guests. Precisely at five o'clock, before the bronze Peter the First clock had struck the fifth stroke, Aleksey Aleksandrovich came in, wearing a white tie and evening coat with two stars, as he had to go out directly after dinner. Every minute of Karenin's life was portioned out and filled. And to make time to get through all that lay before him every day, he adhered to the strictest punctuality. "Without haste, without rest"[1] was his motto. He came into the dining hall, greeted everyone, and hurriedly sat down, smiling to his wife.

"Yes, my solitude is over. You wouldn't believe how embarrassing" (he laid stress on the word "embarrassing") "it is to dine alone."

At dinner he talked a little to his wife about Moscow matters, and, with a sarcastic smile, asked her after Stepan Arkadyevich; but the conversation was for the most part general, dealing with Petersburg official and public news. After dinner he spent half an hour with his guests, and again, with a smile, pressed his wife's hand, withdrew, and

---

[1] Goethe: "*Ohne Hast, ohne Rast.*"

drove off to the council. Anna did not go out that evening either to the Princess Betsy Tverskaya, who, hearing of her return, had invited her, or to the theater, where she had a box for that evening. She did not go out principally because the dress she had counted on was not ready. On the whole, Anna, on turning, after the departure of her guests, to the consideration of her wardrobe, was very much annoyed. She was generally a mistress of the art of dressing well without great expense, and before leaving Moscow she had given her dressmaker three dresses to alter. The dresses had to be altered so that they could not be recognized, and they ought to have been ready three days before. It appeared that two dresses had not been done at all, while the other one had not been altered as Anna had intended. The dressmaker came to explain, declaring that it would be better as she had done it, and Anna was so furious that she felt ashamed when she thought of it afterward. To regain her serenity completely she went into the nursery and spent the whole evening with her son, put him to bed herself, made the sign of the cross over him, and tucked him in. She was glad she had not gone out anywhere, and had spent the evening so well. She felt so light-hearted and serene, she saw clearly that all that had seemed to her so important on her railway journey was only one of the common trivial incidents of fashionable life, and that she had no reason to feel ashamed before anyone else or before herself. Anna sat down at the fireplace with an English novel and waited for her husband. Exactly at half-past nine she heard his ring, and he came into the room.

"Here you are at last!" she observed, holding out her hand to him. He kissed her hand and sat down beside her.

"Altogether, then, I see your visit was a success," he said to her.

"Oh, yes," she said, and she began telling him about everything from the beginning: her journey with Countess Vronsky, her arrival, the accident at the station. Then she described the pity she had felt, first for her brother, and afterward for Dolly.

"I imagine one cannot exonerate such a man from blame, though he is your brother," said Aleksey Aleksandrovich severely.

Anna smiled. She knew that he said that simply to show that family considerations could not prevent him from expressing his genuine opinion. She knew that characteristic in her husband, and liked it.

"I am glad it has all ended so satisfactorily, and that you are back again," he went on. "Come, what do they say about the new act I got passed in the council?"

Anna had heard nothing of this act, and she felt conscience-stricken at having been able so readily to forget what was to him of such importance.

"Here, on the other hand, it has made a great sensation," he said, with a complacent smile.

She saw that Aleksey Aleksandrovich wanted to tell her something agreeable to himself about it, and she encouraged him by asking appropriate questions. With the same complacent smile he told her of the ovations he had received in consequence of the act he had passed.

"I was very, very glad. It shows that at last a reasonable and steady view of the matter is becoming prevalent among us."

Having drunk his second cup of tea with cream, and bread, Aleksey Aleksandrovich got up and started toward his study.

"And you've not been anywhere this evening? You've been bored, I imagine?" he said.

"Oh, no!" she answered, getting up after him and accompanying him across the room to his study. "What are you reading now?" she asked.

"Just now I'm reading Duc de Lille,[2] *Poésie des Enfers*," he answered. "A very remarkable book."

Anna smiled as people smile at the weakness of those they love, and putting her hand under his, she escorted him to the door of the study. She knew his habit, which had grown into a necessity, of reading in the evening. She knew, too, that in spite of his official duties, which swallowed up almost all his time, he considered it his duty to keep up with everything of note that appeared in the intellectual world. She knew, too, that he was really interested in books dealing with politics, philosophy, and theology, that art was utterly foreign to his nature; but, in spite of this, or rather, in consequence of it, Aleksey Aleksandrovich never missed anything in the world of art, but made it

[2] Duc de Lille probably never existed. Tolstoy may be alluding to Leconte de Lisle (1818-94), French poet and translator; or he may be satirizing Comte de Villiers de l'Isle-Adam (1838-89), French pioneer symbolist.

his duty to read everything. She knew that in politics, in philosophy, in theology he often had doubts, and made investigations; but in questions of art and poetry, and, above all, of music, of which he was totally devoid of understanding, he had the most distinct and decided opinions. He was fond of talking about Shakespeare, Raphael, Beethoven, of the significance of new schools of poetry and music, all of which were classified by him with very logical consistency.

"Well, God be with you," she said at the door of the study, where a shaded candle and a decanter of water were already put by his armchair. "And I'll write to Moscow."

He pressed her hand, and again kissed it.

"All the same, he's a good man; truthful, good-hearted, and remarkable in his own line," Anna said to herself, going back to her room, as though she were defending him to someone who had attacked him and said that one could not love him. "But why is it his ears stick out so strangely? Or has he had his hair cut?"

Precisely at twelve o'clock, when Anna was still sitting at her writing desk, finishing a letter to Dolly, she heard the sound of measured steps in slippers, and Aleksey Aleksandrovich, freshly washed and combed, with a book under his arm, came in to her.

"It's time, it's time," said he, with a meaningful smile, and he went into their bedroom.

"And what right had he to look at him like that?" thought Anna, recalling Vronsky's glance at Aleksey Aleksandrovich.

Undressing, she went into the bedroom; but her face had none of the eagerness which, during her stay at Moscow, had fairly flashed from her eyes and her smile; on the contrary, now the fire seemed quenched in her, hidden somewhere far away.

CHAPTER THIRTY-FOUR

When Vronsky went to Moscow from Petersburg, he had left his large set of rooms in Morskaya to his friend and favorite comrade Petritsky.

Petritsky was a young lieutenant, not of a particularly aristocratic family, and not merely not wealthy, but always hopelessly in debt.

Toward evening he was always drunk, and he had often been locked up after all sorts of ludicrous and disgraceful scandals, but he was a favorite both of his comrades and his superior officers. On arriving at twelve o'clock from the station at his apartment, Vronsky saw, at the outer door, a hired carriage familiar to him. While still outside his own door, as he rang, he heard masculine laughter, the lisp of a feminine voice, and Petritsky's voice. "If that's one of the villains, don't let him in!" Vronsky told the servant not to announce him, and slipped quietly into the first room. Baroness Shilton, a friend of Petritsky's with a rosy little face and flaxen hair, resplendent in a lilac satin gown, and filling the whole room, like a canary, with her Parisian chatter, sat at the round table making coffee. Petritsky, in his overcoat, and the cavalry captain Kamerovsky, in full uniform, probably just come from duty, were sitting on each side of her.

"Bravo! Vronsky!" shouted Petritsky, jumping up, scraping his chair. "Our host himself! Baroness, some coffee for him out of the new coffeepot. Why, we didn't expect you! Hope you're satisfied with this ornament to your study," he said, indicating the baroness. "You know each other, of course?"

"I should think so," said Vronsky, with a bright smile, pressing the baroness's little hand. "Of course! I'm an old friend."

"You're home after a journey," said the baroness, "so I'm flying. Oh, I'll be off this minute, if I'm in the way."

"You're home wherever you are, Baroness," said Vronsky. "How do you do, Kamerovsky?" he added, coldly shaking hands with Kamerovsky.

"There, you never know how to say such pretty things," said the baroness, turning to Petritsky.

"No; what's that for? After dinner I'll say things just as good."

"After dinner there's no merit in it! Well, then, I'll make you some coffee, so wash and clear out," said the baroness, sitting down again and anxiously turning the screw in the new coffeepot. "Pierre, give me the coffee," she said, addressing Petritsky, whom she called Pierre as a contraction of his surname, making no secret of her relations with him. "I'll put it in."

"You'll spoil it!"

"No, I won't spoil it! Well, and your wife?" said the baroness suddenly, interrupting Vronsky's conversation with his comrade. "We've been marrying you here. Have you brought your wife?"

"No, Baroness. I was born a gypsy, and a gypsy I shall die."

"So much the better, so much the better. Shake hands on it."

And the baroness, detaining Vronsky, began telling him, with many jokes, about her most recent plans, asking his advice.

"He persists in refusing to give me a divorce! Well, what am I to do?" (*He* was her husband.) "Now I want to begin a suit against him. What do you advise? Kamerovsky, look after the coffee; it's boiling over. You see, I'm engrossed with business! I want a lawsuit, because I must have my property. Do you understand the folly of it, that on the pretext of my being unfaithful to him," she said contemptuously, "he wants to get the benefit of my fortune."

Vronsky heard with pleasure this light-hearted prattle of a pretty woman, agreed with her, gave her half-joking counsel, and altogether dropped at once into the tone habitual to him in talking to such women. In his Petersburg world all people were divided into utterly opposed classes. One, the lower class, vulgar, stupid, and, above all, ridiculous people, who believe that one husband ought to live with the one wife to whom he is lawfully married; that a girl should be innocent, a woman modest, and a man manly, self-controlled, and strong; that one ought to bring up one's children, earn one's bread, and pay one's debts; and various similar absurdities. This was the class of old-fashioned and ridiculous people. But there was another class of people, the real people. To this class they all belonged, and in it the great thing was to be elegant, generous, plucky, gay, to abandon oneself without a blush to every passion, and to laugh at everything else.

For the first moment only, Vronsky was startled after the impression of a quite different world that he had brought with him from Moscow. But immediately, as though slipping his feet into old slippers, he dropped back into the light-hearted, pleasant world he had always lived in.

The coffee was never really made, but splashed over everyone, and boiled away, doing just what was required of it—that is, providing cause for much noise and laughter, and spoiling a costly rug and the baroness's gown.

"Well now, good-by, or you'll never get washed, and I shall have on my conscience the worst sin a gentleman can commit. So you would advise a knife to his throat?"

"To be sure, and manage it so that your hand will not be far from his lips. He'll kiss your hand, and all will end satisfactorily," answered Vronsky.

"So at the Français!"[1] and, with a rustle of her skirts, she vanished.

Kamerovsky got up too, and Vronsky, not waiting for him to go, shook hands and went off to his dressing room.

While he was washing, Petritsky described to him in brief outlines his situations as far as it had changed since Vronsky had left Petersburg. No money at all. His father said he wouldn't give him any or pay his debts. His tailor was trying to get him locked up, and another fellow, too, was threatening to get him locked up. The colonel of the regiment had announced that if these scandals did not cease he would have to leave. As for the baroness, he was sick to death of her, especially since she'd taken to offering continually to lend him money. But he had found a girl—he'd show her to Vronsky—a marvel, exquisite, in the purest Oriental style, "genre of the slave Rebecca,[2] you know." He'd had a row, too, with Berkoshov, and was going to send seconds to him, but of course it would come to nothing. On the whole, everything was supremely amusing and jolly. And, not letting his comrade enter into further details of his position, Petritsky's familiar stories in the familiar setting of the rooms he had spent the last three years in, Vronsky felt a delightful sense of coming back to the carefree life that he was used to.

"Impossible!" he cried, releasing the pedal of the wash basin in which he had been washing his healthy, ruddy neck.

"Impossible!" he cried, at the news that Laura had thrown over Fertinhof and had made up with Mileyev. "And is he as stupid and pleased as ever? Well, and how's Buzulukov?"

"Oh, there is a tale about Buzulukov—simply lovely!" cried Petritsky. "You know his weakness for balls, and he never misses a single court ball. He went to a big ball in a new helmet. Have you

---

[1] French theater in St. Petersburg.
[2] The beautiful and dutiful daughter of Isaac in Scott's *Ivanhoe*.

seen the new helmets? Very nice, lighter. Well, so he's standing . . . No, please listen."

"I am listening," answered Vronsky, rubbing himself with a rough towel.

"Up comes the grand duchess with some ambassador or other, and, as ill luck would have it, she begins talking to him about the new helmets. She positively wanted to show the new helmet to the ambassador. They see our friend standing there." (Petritsky mimicked how he was standing with the helmet.) "The grand duchess asks him to give her the helmet; he doesn't give it to her. What do you think of that? Well, everyone's winking at him, nodding, frowning—give it to her! He doesn't give it to her. He's as mute as a fish. Just picture it! . . . Well, the—what's his name, whatever he was—tries to take the helmet from him . . . he won't give it up! . . . He pulls it from him and hands it to the grand duchess. 'Here, Your Highness,' says he, 'is the new helmet.' She turns the helmet the other side up, and—just picture it!—plop goes a pear and sweets out of it, two pounds of sweets! . . . He'd been storing them up, the dear fellow!"

Vronsky burst into roars of laughter. And long afterward, when he was talking of other things, he broke out into his healthy laugh, showing his strong, even teeth, when he thought of the helmet.

Having heard all the news, Vronsky, with the assistance of his valet, got into his uniform and went off to report himself. He intended, when he had done that, to drive to his brother's, and to Betsy's, and to pay several visits with a view to entering that society where he might meet Madame Karenina. As he always did in Petersburg, he left home not meaning to return till late at night.

PART TWO

CHAPTER ONE

Toward the end of the winter, in the Shcherbatskys' house, a consultation was being held, which was to decide the state of Kitty's health and the measures to be taken to restore her failing strength. She had been ill, and as spring approached she grew worse. The family doctor gave her cod-liver oil, then iron, then nitrate of silver, but as the first and the second and the third were alike in doing no good, and as his advice when spring came was to go abroad, a celebrated physician was called in. The celebrated physician, a very handsome man, still youngish, asked to examine the patient. He maintained, with peculiar satisfaction, it seemed, that maiden modesty is a mere relic of barbarism, and that nothing could be more natural than for a man still youngish to touch a young naked girl. He thought it natural because he did it every day, and felt and thought, as it seemed to him, no harm as he did it, and consequently he considered modesty in the girl not merely as a relic of barbarism but also as an insult to himself.

There was nothing to do but to submit, since, although all the doctors had studied in the same school, had read the same books, and learned the same science, and though some people said this celebrated doctor was a bad doctor, in the princess's household and circle it was for some reason accepted that this celebrated doctor alone had some special knowledge, and that he alone could save Kitty. After a careful examination and sounding of the embarrassed patient, overcome with shame, the celebrated doctor, having scrupulously washed his hands, was standing in the drawing room talking to the prince. The prince frowned and coughed, listening to the doctor. As a man who had seen something of life, and neither a fool nor an invalid, he had no faith in medicine, and in his heart was furious at the whole farce, specially as he was perhaps the only one who fully comprehended the cause of Kitty's illness. "Jabbering windbag!" he thought, as he listened to the celebrated doctor's chatter about his daughter's symptoms. The doctor was meantime with difficulty restraining the expression of his contempt for this old gentleman, and with difficulty condescending to the level of his intelligence. He perceived that it was no good talking to the old man, and that the head of the house was the mother. Before her he decided to scatter his pearls. At that instant the princess came into the drawing room with the family doctor. The prince withdrew, trying not to show how ridiculous he thought the whole performance. The princess was confused, and did not know what to do. She felt guilty about Kitty.

"Well, Doctor, decide our fate," said the princess. "Tell me everything."

"Is there hope?" she meant to say, but her lips quivered, and she could not utter the question. "Well, Doctor?"

"Immediately, Princess. I will talk it over with my colleague, and then I will have the honor of laying my opinion before you."

"So we had better leave you?"

"As you please."

The princess went out with a sigh.

When the doctors were left alone, the family doctor began timidly explaining his opinion, that there was a commencement of tuberculous trouble, but . . . and so on. The celebrated doctor listened to him, and in the middle of his sentence looked at his big gold watch.

"Yes," said he. "But. . ."

The family doctor respectfully ceased in the middle of his observations.

"The commencement of the tuberculous process we are not, as you are aware, able to define; till there are cavities, there is nothing definite. But we may suspect it. And there are indications; malnutrition, nervous excitability, and so on. The question stands thus: in presence of indications of tuberculous process, what is to be done to maintain nutrition?"

"But, you know, there are always moral, spiritual causes at the back in these cases," the family doctor permitted himself to interpolate with a subtle smile.

"Yes, that's an understood thing," responded the celebrated physician, again glancing at his watch. "Beg pardon, is the Yauzky Bridge done yet, or shall I have to drive around?" he asked. "Ah, it is! Oh, well, then I can do it in twenty minutes. So we were saying the problem may be put thus: to maintain nutrition and to give tone to the nerves. The one is in close connection with the other, one must attack both sides at once."

"And how about a tour abroad" asked the family doctor.

"I don't like foreign tours. And take note: if there is an early stage of tuberculous process, of which we cannot be certain, a foreign tour will be of no use. What is wanted is means of improving nutrition, and not for lowering it." And the celebrated doctor expounded his plan of treatment with Soden waters, a remedy obviously prescribed primarily on the ground that they could do no harm.

The family doctor listened attentively and respectfully.

"But in favor of foreign travel I would urge the change of habits, the removal from conditions calling up reminiscences. And then the mother wishes it," he added.

"Ah! Well, in that case, to be sure, let them go. Only, those German quacks are dangerous . . . They ought to be persuaded . . . Well, let them go, then."

He glanced once more at his watch.

"Oh! Time's up already," and he went to the door. The celebrated doctor announced to the princess (a feeling of what was due from him dictated his doing so) that he ought to see the patient once more.

"What! Another examination!" cried the mother with horror.

"Oh, no, only a few details, Princess."

"Come this way."

And the mother, accompanied by the doctor, went into the drawing room to Kitty. Thin and flushed, with a peculiar glitter in her eyes, left there by the agony of shame she had been put through, Kitty stood in the middle of the room. When the doctor came in she flushed crimson, and her eyes filled with tears. Her illness and treatment struck her as a thing so stupid, even ludicrous! Doctoring her seemed to her as absurd as putting together the pieces of a broken vase. Her heart was broken. Why would they try to cure her with pills and powders? But she could not grieve her mother, especially as her mother considered herself to blame.

"May I trouble you to sit down, Princess?" the celebrated doctor said to her.

He sat down with a smile, facing her, felt her pulse, and again began asking her tiresome questions. She answered him, and all at once got up furious.

"Excuse me, Doctor, but there is really no point in this. This is the third time you've asked me the same thing."

The celebrated doctor did not take offense.

"Nervous irritability," he said to the princess, when Kitty had left the room. "However, I had finished . . ."

And the doctor began scientifically explaining to the princess, as an exceptionally intelligent woman, the condition of the young princess, and concluded by insisting on the drinking of the waters, which were certainly harmless. At the question: Should they go abroad? the doctor plunged into deep meditation, as though resolving a weighty problem. Finally his decision was pronounced: they were to go abroad, but to put no faith in foreign quacks, and to apply to him in any need.

It seemed as though some piece of good fortune had come to pass after the doctor had gone. The mother was much more cheerful when she went back to her daughter, and Kitty pretended to be more cheerful. She had often, almost always, to be pretending now.

"Really, I'm quite well, Mama. But if you want to go abroad, let's go!" she said, and trying to appear interested in the proposed tour, she began talking of the preparations for the journey.

CHAPTER TWO

Soon after the doctor left, Dolly arrived. She knew that there was to be a consultation that day, and though she was just up after her confinement (she had another baby, a little girl, born at the end of the winter), though she had trouble and anxiety enough of her own, she had left her tiny baby and a sick child to come and hear Kitty's fate, which was to be decided that day.

"Well, well?" she said, coming into the drawing room without taking off her hat. "You're all in good spirits. Good news, then?"

They tried to tell her what the doctor had said, but it appeared that though the doctor had talked distinctly enough and at great length, it was utterly impossible to report what he had said. The only point of interest was that it was settled that they should go abroad.

Dolly could not help sighing. Her dearest friend, her sister, was going away. And her life was not a cheerful one. Her relations with Stepan Arkadyevich after their reconciliation had become humiliating. The union Anna had cemented turned out to be less than solid, and family harmony was breaking down again at the same point. There had been nothing definite, but Stepan Arkadyevich was hardly ever at home; money, too, was hardly ever forthcoming, and Dolly was continually tortured by suspicions of infidelity, which she tried to dismiss, dreading the agonies of jealousy she had already been through. The first onslaught of jealousy, once lived through, could never come back again, and even the discovery of infidelities could never now affect her as it had the first time. Such a discovery now would only mean breaking up family habits, and she let herself be deceived, despising him and still more herself for the weakness. Besides this, the care of her large family was a constant worry to her: first, the nursing of her young baby did not go well, then the nurse had gone away, now one of the children had fallen ill.

"Well, how are all of you?" asked her mother.

"Ah, Mama, we have plenty of troubles of our own. Lily is ill, and I'm afraid it's scarlet fever. I have come here now to hear about Kitty, and then I shall shut myself up entirely, if—God forbid—it should be scarlet fever."

The old prince too had come in from his study after the doctor's departure, and after presenting his cheek to Dolly and saying a few words to her, he turned to his wife:

"How have you settled it? You're going? Well, and what do you mean to do with me?"

"I suppose you had better stay here, Aleksander," said his wife.

"Just as you like."

"Mama, why shouldn't Father come with us?" said Kitty. "It'll be nicer for him and for us too."

The old prince got up and stroked Kitty's hair. She lifted her head and looked at him with a forced smile. It always seemed to her that he understood her better than anyone in the family, though he did not say much about her. Being the youngest, she was her father's favorite, and she imagined that his love gave him insight. When now her glance met his blue kindly eyes looking intently at her, it seemed to her that he saw right through her, and understood all that was not good that was going on within her. Reddening, she stretched out toward him, expecting a kiss, but he only patted her hair and said:

"These stupid chignons! There's no getting at the real daughter, one simply strokes the bristles of dead women. Well, Dolinka," he said, turning to his elder daughter, "what's your young buck doing, hey?"

"Nothing, Father," answered Dolly, understanding that he meant her husband. "He's always out; I scarcely ever see him," she could not resist adding with a sarcastic smile.

"Why, hasn't he gone into the country yet—to see about selling that forest?"

"No, he's still getting ready for the journey."

"Oh, that's it!" said the prince. "And so am I to be getting ready for a journey too? At your service," he said to his wife, sitting down. "And I tell you what, Katya," he went on to his younger daughter, "you must wake up one fine day and say to yourself: 'Why, I'm very well, and happy, and going out again with Father for an early morning walk in the frost.' Hey?"

What her father said seemed simple enough, yet at these words Kitty became confused and overcome like a detected criminal. "Yes, he sees it all, he understands it all, and in these words he's telling me that though I'm ashamed, I must get over my shame." She could not pluck up spirit to make any answer. She tried to begin, and all at once burst into tears, and rushed out of the room.

"See what comes of your jokes!" the princess pounced down on her husband. "You're always . . . " she began a string of reproaches.

The prince listened to the princess's scolding rather a long while without speaking, but he frowned more and more.

"She's so much to be pitied, poor child, so much to be pitied, and you don't feel how it hurts her to hear the slightest reference to the cause of it. Ah! To be so mistaken in people!" said the princess, and by the change in her tone both Dolly and the prince, knew she was speaking of Vronsky. "I don't know why there aren't laws against such base, dishonorable people."

"Ah, I can't bear to hear you!" said the prince gloomily, getting up from his low chair, and seeming anxious to get away, yet stopping in the doorway. "There are laws, madam, and since you've challenged me to it, I'll tell you who's to blame for it all: you, you, you and nobody else. Laws against such young gallants there have always been, and there still are! Yes, if there has been nothing that ought not to have been, old as I am, I'd have challenged him, the young fop. Yes, and now you dose her and call in these quacks."

The prince apparently had plenty more to say, but as soon as the princess heard his tone she subsided at once, and became penitent, as she always did on serious occasions.

"Aleksandr, Aleksandr," she whispered, moving toward him and beginning to weep.

As soon as she began to cry the prince too calmed down. He went up to her.

"There, that's enough, that's enough! You're wretched too, I know. It can't be helped. There's no great harm done. God is merciful . . . thanks . . ." he said, not knowing what he was saying, as he responded to the tearful kiss of the princess that he felt on his hand. And the prince went out of the room.

Before this, as soon as Kitty went out of the room in tears, Dolly, with her motherly, family instincts, had promptly perceived that here a woman's work lay before her, and she prepared to do it. She took off her hat, and, mentally, rolled up her sleeves and prepared for action. While her mother was attacking her father, she tried to restrain her mother, so far as filial reverence would allow. During the prince's outburst she was silent; she felt ashamed for her mother, and tender toward her father for so quickly being kind again. But when her father left them she prepared for what was most needed—to go to Kitty and console her.

"I'd been meaning to tell you something for a long while, Mama: did you know that Levin meant to propose to Kitty when he was here the last time? He told Stiva so."

"Well, so what? I don't understand. . ."

"So did Kitty perhaps refuse him? . . . She didn't tell you?"

"No, she has said nothing to me either of one or the other; she's too proud. But I know it's all on account of the other."

"Yes, but suppose she had refused Levin, and she wouldn't have refused him if it hadn't been for the other, I know. And then, he had deceived her so horribly."

It was too terrible for the princess to think of how she had sinned against her daughter, and she broke our angrily:

"Oh, I really don't understand! Nowadays they all go their own way, and mothers haven't a word to say in anything, and then—"

"Mama, I'll go to her."

"Well, do. Did I tell you not to?" said her mother.

CHAPTER THREE

When she went into Kitty's room, a pretty, pink little room, full of knickknacks made of *vieux saxe*,[1] as fresh and pink and white and gay as Kitty herself had been two months ago, Dolly remembered how they had decorated the room the year before together, with what love and gaiety. Her heart turned cold when she saw Kitty sitting on a low chair near the door, her eyes fixed immovably on a corner of the rug. Kitty glanced at her sister, and the cold, rather severe expression of her face did not change.

"I'm going now, and I shall have to stay in and you won't be able to come to see me," said Dolly, sitting down beside her. "I want to talk to you."

"What about?" Kitty asked swiftly, lifting her head in dismay.

"What should it be but your trouble?"

"I have no trouble."

"Nonsense, Kitty. Do you suppose I could help knowing? I know all about it. And believe me, it's of so little consequence . . . We've all been through it."

Kitty did not speak, and her face had a stern expression.

"He's not worth your grieving over him," pursued Darya Aleksandrovna, coming straight to the point.

---

[1] "Old Saxony," i.e., porcelain.

"No, because he has treated me with contempt," said Kitty, in a breaking voice. "Don't talk of it! Please, don't talk of it!"

"But who can have told you so? No one had said that. I'm certain he was in love with you, and would still be in love with you, if it hadn't—"

"Oh, the most awful thing of all for me is the sympathizing!" shrieked Kitty, suddenly flying into a passion. She turned around on her chair, flushed crimson, and, rapidly moving her fingers, pinched the buckle of her belt first with one hand and then with the other. Dolly knew this habit her sister had of clenching her hands when she was very excited; she knew, too, that in moments of excitement Kitty was capable of forgetting herself and saying a great deal too much, and Dolly would have soothed her, but it was too late.

"What, what is it you want to make me feel, eh?" said Kitty quickly. "That I've been in love with a man who didn't care a straw for me, and that I'm dying of love for him? And this is said to me by my own sister, who imagines that . . . that . . . that she's sympathizing with me! . . . I don't want this commiseration and this hypocrisy!"

"Kitty, you're unfair."

"Why are you tormenting me?"

"But I . . . quite the contrary . . . I see you're unhappy . . ."

But Kitty in her fury did not hear her.

"I've nothing to grieve over and be comforted about. I am too proud ever to allow myself to care for a man who does not love me."

"Yes, I don't say so, either . . . Only one thing. Tell me the truth," said Darya Aleksandrovna, taking her by the hand: "tell me, did Levin speak to you? . . ."

The mention of Levin's name seemed to deprive Kitty of the last vestige of self-control. She leaped up from her chair, and flinging her buckle on the ground, she gesticulated rapidly with her hands and said:

"Why bring Levin in too? I can't understand why you want to torment me. I've told you, and I say it again, that I have some pride, and never, *never* would I do as you're doing—go back to a man who's deceived you, who has cared for another woman. I can't understand it. You may, but I can't!"

And saying these words, she glanced at her sister, and seeing that Dolly sat silent, her head mournfully bowed, Kitty, instead of running out of the room, as she had meant to do, sat down near the door and hid her face in her handkerchief.

The silence lasted for a minute or two. Dolly was thinking of herself. That humiliation of which she was always conscious came back to her with a peculiar bitterness when her sister reminded her of it. She had not expected such cruelty from her sister, and she was angry with her. But suddenly she heard the rustle of a skirt, and with it the sound of heart-rending, smothered sobbing, and felt arms about her neck. Kitty was on her knees before her.

"Dolinka, I am so, so wretched!" she whispered penitently. And the sweet face covered with tears hid itself in Darya Aleksandrovna's skirt.

As though tears were the indispensable oil without which the machinery of mutual confidence could not run smoothly between the two sisters, the sisters after their tears talked, not of what was uppermost in their minds, but, though they talked of outside matters, they understood each other. Kitty knew that the words she had uttered in anger about her husband's infidelity and her humiliating position had cut her poor sister to the heart, but that she had forgiven her. Dolly for her part knew all she had wanted to find out. She felt certain that her surmises were correct; that Kitty's misery, her inconsolable misery, was due precisely to the fact that Levin had made her a proposal and she had refused him, and Vronsky had deceived her, and that she was fully prepared to love Levin and to detest Vronsky. Kitty said not a word of that; she talked of nothing but her state of mind.

"I have nothing to make me miserable," she said, getting calmer; "but can you understand that everything has become hateful, loathsome, coarse to me, and I myself most of all? You can't imagine what loathsome thoughts I have about everything."

"Why, whatever loathsome thoughts can you have?" asked Dolly, smiling.

"The most utterly loathsome and coarse: I can't tell you. It's not unhappiness, or low spirits, but much worse. As though everything that was good in me was all hidden away, and nothing was left but the most loathsome. Come, how am I to tell you?" she went on, seeing the puzzled look in her sister's eyes. "Father began saying something to me just now . . . It seems to me he thinks all I want is to be married. Mother takes me to a ball: it seems to me she only takes me to get me married off as soon as possible, and be rid of me. I know it's not the truth, but I can't drive away such thoughts. Eligible suitors, as they call them—I can't bear to see them. It seems to me they're taking stock of me and summing me up. In old days to go anywhere in a ball dress was a simple joy to me, I admired myself; now I feel ashamed and awkward. And then! The doctor . . . Then . . ." Kitty hesitated; she wanted to say further that ever since this change had taken place in her, Stepan Arkadyevich had become insufferably repulsive to her, and that she could not see him without the grossest and most hideous conceptions rising before her imagination.

"Oh, well, everything presents itself to me in the coarsest, most loathsome light," she went on. "That's my illness. Perhaps it will pass."

"But you mustn't think about it."

"I can't help it. I'm never happy except with the children at your house."

"What a pity you can't be with me!"

"Oh, yes. I'm coming. I've had scarlet fever, and I'll persuade Mama to let me."

Kitty insisted on having her way, and went to stay at her sister's and nursed the children all through the scarlet fever, for that is what it turned out to be. The two sisters brought all six children successfully through it, but Kitty was no better in health, and in Lent the Shcherbatskys went abroad.

CHAPTER FOUR

The highest Petersburg society is essentially one: in it everyone knows everyone else, everyone even visits everyone else. But this great set had its subdivisions. Anna Arkadyevna Karenina had friends and close ties in three different circles of this highest society. One circle was her husband's government official set, consisting of his colleagues and subordinates, brought together in the most various and capricious manner, and belonging to different social strata. Anna found it difficult now to recall the feeling of almost awe-stricken reverence which she had at first entertained for these persons. Now she knew all of them as people know one another in a country town; she knew their habits and weaknesses, and where a shoe pinched each one of them. She knew their relations with one another and with the top authorities, knew who was for whom, and how each one maintained his position, and where they agreed and disagreed. But that circle of political, masculine interests had never interested her, in spite of Countess Lydia Ivanovna's influence, and she avoided it.

Another little set with which Anna was in close contact was the one by means of which Aleksey Aleksandrovich had made his career. The center of this circle was the Countess Lydia Ivanovna. It was a set made up of elderly, ugly, benevolent, and godly women, and clever, learned, and ambitious men. One of the clever people belonging to the set had called it "the conscience of Petersburg society." Aleksey Aleksandrovich had the highest esteem for this circle; and Anna, with her special gift for getting on with everyone, had in the early days of her life in Petersburg made friends in this circle also. Now, since her return from Moscow, she had come to feel this set insufferable. It seemed to her that both she and they were insincere, and she felt so bored and ill at ease in that world that she went to see the countess as little as possible.

The third circle with which Anna had ties was the world of high society—the world of balls, of dinners, of sumptuous dresses, the world that hung on to the court with one hand so as to avoid sinking to the level of the *demi-monde*. For the *demi-monde* the members of that fashionable world believed that they despised, though their tastes were not merely similar but in fact identical. Her connection with this circle was kept up through Princess Betsy Tverskaya, her cousin's wife, who had an income of a hundred and twenty thousand rubles, and who had taken a great fancy to Anna ever since she first came out, showed her much attention, and drew her into her set, making fun of Countess Lydia Ivanovna's set.

"When I'm old and ugly I'll be the same," Betsy used to say; "but for a pretty young woman like you, it's too early for that house of charity."

Anna had at first avoided as far as she could Princess Tverskaya's world, because it necessitated an expenditure beyond her means, and besides, in her heart she preferred the first circle. But since her visit to Moscow she had done quite the contrary. She avoided her serious-minded friends, and went out into the fashionable world. There she met Vronsky, and experienced a tremulous joy at those meetings. She met Vronsky most often at Betsy's, for Betsy was a Vronsky by birth, and his cousin. Vronsky was everywhere where he had any chance of meeting Anna, and speaking to her, when he could, of his love. She gave him no encouragement, but every time she met him, there surged up in her heart that same feeling of quickened life that had come upon her that day in the railway carriage when she was with him for the first time. She was conscious herself that her delight sparkled in her eyes and curved her lips into a smile, and she could not quench the expression of this delight.

At first Anna sincerely believed that she was displeased with him for daring to pursue her. Soon after her return from Moscow, on arriving at a party where she had expected to meet him, and not finding him there, she realized distinctly from the rush of disappointment that she had been deceiving herself, and that this pursuit was not merely not distasteful to her, but that it was the whole interest of her life.

The celebrated prima donna was singing for the second time, and the whole fashionable world was in the theater. Vronsky, seeing his cousin from his stall in the front row, did not wait till the intermission but went straight to her box.

"Why didn't you come to dinner?" she said to him. "I marvel at the clairvoyance of lovers," she added with a smile, so that no one but he could hear. "*She wasn't there.* But come after the opera."

Vronsky looked inquiringly at her. She nodded. He thanked her by a smile, and sat down beside her.

"But how I remember your jeers!" Princess Betsy continued, taking a peculiar pleasure in following up this passion to a successful issue. "What's become of all that? You're caught, my dear boy."

"That's my one desire, to be caught," Vronsky answered, with his serene, good-humored smile. "If I complain of anything it's only that I'm not caught enough, to tell the truth. I begin to lose hope."

"Why, what hope can you have?" said Betsy, offended on behalf of her friend. "*Entendons nous*[1] . . ." But in her eyes there were gleams of light that betrayed that she understood perfectly and precisely what hope he might have.

"None whatever," said Vronsky, laughing and showing his even rows of teeth. "Excuse me," he added, taking the opera glasses out of her hand and proceeding to scrutinize, over her bare shoulder, the row of boxes facing them. "I'm afraid I'm becoming ridiculous."

He was very well aware that he ran no risk of being ridiculous in the eyes of Betsy or of any other fashionable people. He was very well aware that in their eyes the position of an unsuccessful lover of a girl, or of any woman free to marry, might be ridiculous. But the position of a man pursuing a married woman, and, regardless of everything, staking his life on drawing her into adultery, has something fine and grand about it, and can never be ridiculous; and so it was with a proud and gay smile under his mustaches that he lowered the opera glasses and looked at his cousin.

"But why was it you didn't come to dinner?" she said, admiring him.

"I must tell you about that. I was busily employed, and doing what, do you suppose? I'll give you a hundred guesses, a thousand . . . you'd never guess. I've been reconciling a husband with a man who'd insulted his wife. Yes, really!"

"Well, did you succeed?"

"Almost."

"You really must tell me about it," she said, getting up. "Come to me in the next intermission."

"I can't; I'm going to the French theater."

"From Nilsson?" Betsy queried in horror, though she could not herself have distinguished Nilsson's voice from any chorus girl's.

"Can't help it. I've an appointment there, all to do with my mission of peace."

" 'Blessed are the peacemakers; theirs is the kingdom of heaven,' "

---

[1] "Let us understand each other."

said Betsy, vaguely recollecting she had heard some similar saying from someone. "Very well, then, sit down and tell me what it's all about."

And she sat down again.

CHAPTER FIVE

"This is rather indiscreet, but it's so good, it's an awful temptation to tell the story," said Vronsky, looking at her with his laughing eyes. "I'm not going to mention any names."

"But I shall guess, so much the better."

"Well, listen, two gay young men were driving—"

"Officers of your regiment, of course?"

"I didn't say they were officers—two young men who had been eating lunch."

"In other words, drinking."

"Possibly. They were driving on their way to dinner with a friend in the best of spirits. And they beheld a pretty woman in a hired sleigh; she overtakes them, looks around at them, and, so they think anyway, nods to them and laughs. They, of course, follow her. They gallop at full speed. To their amazement, the beauty alights at the entrance of the very house to which they were going. The beauty darts upstairs to the top floor. They get a glimpse of red lips under a short veil, and exquisite little feet."

"You describe it with such feeling that I think you must be one of the two."

"And after what you said, just now! Well, the young men go into their comrade's; he was giving a farewell dinner. There they certainly did drink a little too much, as one always does at farewell dinners. And at dinner they inquire who lives at the top in that house. No one knows; only their host's valet, in answer to their inquiry whether any 'young ladies' are living on the top floor, answered that there were a great many of them all over the place. After dinner the two young men go into their host's study, and write a letter to the unknown beauty. They compose an ardent epistle, a declaration, in fact, and they carry the letter upstairs themselves, so as to elucidate whatever might appear not perfectly intelligible in the letter."

"Why are you telling me these horrible stories? Well?"

"They ring. A maid opens the door; they hand her the letter, and assure her that they're both so in love that they'll die on the spot at the door. The maid, stupefied, carries in their message. All at once a gentleman appears with whiskers like sausages, as red as a lobster, announces that there is no one living in that flat except his wife, and sends them both about their business."

"How do you know he had whiskers like sausages, as you say?"

"Ah, you shall hear. I've just been to make peace between them."

"Well, and what then?"

"That's the most interesting part of the story. It appears that it's a happy couple, a government clerk, a titular councilor, and his lady. The government clerk lodges a complaint, and I became a meditator, and such a mediator! . . . I assure you Talleyrand couldn't hold a candle to me."

"Why, where was the difficulty?"

"Ah, you shall hear . . . We apologize in due form: we are in despair, we entreat forgiveness for the unfortunate misunderstanding. The government clerk with the sausages begins to melt, but he, too, desires to express his sentiments, and as soon as he begins to express them, he begins to get hot and say nasty things, and again I'm obliged to trot out all my diplomatic talents. I allowed that their conduct was bad, but I urged him to take into consideration their heedlessness, their youth; then, too, the young men had only just been dining together. 'You understand. They regret it deeply, and beg you to overlook their misbehavior.' The government clerk was softened once more. 'I consent, Count, and am ready to overlook it; but you perceive that my wife—my wife's a respectable woman—has been exposed to the persecution, and insults, and effrontery of young upstarts, scoundrels . . .' And you must understand, the young upstarts are present all the while, and I have to keep peace between them. Again I call out all my diplomacy, and again as soon as the thing was about at an end, our friend the government clerk gets hot and red, and his sausages stand on end with wrath, and once more I launch out into diplomatic wiles."

"Ah, he must tell you this story!" said Betsy, laughing, to a lady who came into her box. "He has been making me laugh so."

"Well, *bonne chance!*"[1] she added, giving Vronsky one finger of the hand in which she held her fan, and with a shrug of her shoulders, she lowered the bodice of her gown, which had worked its way up, so as to be properly naked as she moved forward toward the front of the box into the glare of the gaslight and the gaze of all eyes.

Vronsky drove to the French theater, where he really had to see the colonel of his regiment, who never missed a single performance there. He wanted to see him to report on the result of his mediation, which had occupied and amused him for the last three days. Petritsky, whom he liked, was implicated in the affair, and the other culprit was a wonderful fellow and first-rate comrade who had lately joined the regiment, the young Prince Kedrov. And what was most important, the interests of the regiment were involved in it too.

Both the young men were in Vronsky's company. The colonel of the regiment was visited by the titular councilor, Wenden, with a complaint against his officers, who had insulted his wife. His young wife, so Wenden told the story—he had been married half a year— was at church with her mother, and suddenly overcome by indisposition, arising from her interesting condition, she could not remain standing; she drove home in the first sleigh she came across. Then the officers started in pursuit of her; she was alarmed, and feeling still worse, ran up the staircase home. Wenden himself, on returning from his office, heard a ring at their bell and voices, went out, and seeing the intoxicated officers with a letter, he showed them out. He asked that they be severely punished.

"No, say what you will," said the colonel to Vronsky, whom he had invited to come and see him. "Petritsky's becoming impossible. Not a week goes by without some scandal. This government clerk won't let it drop, he'll go on with the thing."

Vronsky saw all the thanklessness of the business, and that there could be no question of a duel in it, that everything must be done to soften the government clerk, and hush the matter up. The colonel had called in Vronsky just because he knew him to be an honorable and intelligent man, and above all, a man who cared for the honor

[1] "Good luck."

of the regiment. They talked it over, and decided that Petritsky and Kedrov must go with Vronsky to Wenden's to apologize. The colonel and Vronsky were both fully aware that Vronsky's name and rank would be sure to contribute greatly to the softening of the injured husband's feelings.

And these two influences were not in fact without effect, though the result remained, as Vronsky had explained, uncertain.

On reaching the French theater, Vronsky retired to the foyer with the colonel, and reported to him his success, or non-success. The colonel, thinking it all over, made up his mind not to pursue the matter further, but then for his own satisfaction proceeded to cross-examine Vronsky about his interview; and it was a long while before he could restrain his laughter, as Vronsky described how the government clerk, after subsiding for a while, would suddenly flare up again as he recalled the details, and how Vronsky, at the last half-word of conciliation, skillfully maneuvered a retreat, shoving Petritsky out before him.

"It's a disgraceful story, but terribly funny. Kedrov really can't fight the gentleman! Was he so very excited?" he commented, laughing. "But what do you say to Claire today? She's marvelous," he went on, speaking of a new French actress. "However often you see her, every day she's different. It's only the French who can do that."

CHAPTER SIX

Princess Betsy drove home from the theater without waiting for the end of the last act. She had hardly time to go into her dressing room, sprinkle her long, pale face with powder, rub it, arrange her dress, and order tea in the big drawing room, when one after another carriages drove up to her huge house in Bolshaya Morskaya. Her guests stepped out at the wide entrance, and the stout porter, who used to read the newspapers in the morning behind the glass door, to the edification of the passers-by, noiselessly opened the immense door, letting the visitors pass by him into the house.

Almost at the same instant the hostess, with freshly arranged coif-

fure and freshened face, walked in at one door and her guests at the
other door of the drawing room, a large room with dark walls, thick
rugs, and a brightly lighted table, gleaming with the light of candles,
white cloth, silver samovar, and transparent china tea service.

The hostess sat down at the table and took off her gloves. Chairs
were set with the aid of footmen, moving almost imperceptibly about
the room; the party settled itself, divided into two groups: one
around the samovar near the hostess, the other at the opposite end of
the drawing room, around an ambassador's handsome wife, in black
velvet, with sharply defined black eyebrows. In both groups conversation wavered, as it always does, for the first few minutes, broken up
by meetings, greetings, offers of tea, and, as it were, feeling about for
something to rest upon.

"She's exceptionally good as an actress; one can see she's studied
Kaulbach,"[1] said a diplomatic attaché in the group around the ambassador's wife. "Did you notice how she fell down? . . ."

"Oh, please, don't let us talk about Nilsson! No one can possibly
say anything new about her," said a fat, red-faced, flaxen-haired lady,
without eyebrows and chignon, wearing on old silk dress. This was
Princess Myahkaya, noted for her simplicity and the harshness of her
manner, and nicknamed *enfant terrible*. Princess Myahkaya, sitting
in the middle between the two groups, and listening to both, took
part in the conversation first of one and then of the other. "Three
people have used that very phrase about Kaulbach to me today
already, just as though they had conspired about it. And I can't see
why they liked that remark so."

The conversation was cut short by this observation, and a new
subject had to be thought of again.

"Do tell me something amusing but not spiteful," said the ambassador's wife, a great proficient in the art of that elegant conversation
called by the English "small talk." She addressed the attaché, who
was at a loss now what to begin upon.

"They say that that's a difficult task, that nothing's amusing that
isn't spiteful," he began with a smile. "But I'll try. Get me a subject.

[1] Wilhelm Kaulbach (1805-74), famous German painter.

It all lies in the subject. If a subject's given me, it's easy to spin something around it. I often think that the celebrated talkers of the last
century would have found it difficult to talk cleverly now. Everything
clever is so stale . . ."

"That has been said long ago," the ambassador's wife interrupted
him, laughing.

The conversation began amiably, but just because it was too amiable, it came to a stop again. They had to have recourse to the sure,
never-failing topic—slander.

"Don't you think there's something Louis XV about Tushkevich?"
he said, glancing toward a handsome, fair-haired young man standing at the table.

"Oh, yes! He matches the drawing room, and that's why he's here
so often."

This conversation was maintained, since it rested on allusions to
what could not be talked of in that room—that is to say, of the relations of Tuskevich with their hostess.

Round the samovar and the hostess, the conversation, after flickering for some time between three inevitable topics—the latest
pieces of public news, the theater, and malicious gossip—finally
caught on when it got to the last subject, that is, scandal.

"Have you heard, the Maltishcheva woman—the mother, not the
daughter—has ordered a costume in *diable rose*?"

"Nonsense! No, that's delicious!"

"I wonder that with her sense—for she's not a fool, you know—
she doesn't see how funny she is."

Everyone had something to say in censure and ridicule of the
luckless Madame Maltishcheva, and the conversation crackled merrily, like a burning bonfire.

Princess Betsy's husband, a good-natured fat man, an ardent col-
lector of prints, hearing that his wife had visitors, came into the
drawing room before going to his club. Stepping noiselessly over the
thick rugs, he went up to Princess Myahkaya.

"How did you like Nilsson?" he asked.

"Oh, how can you sneak up on anyone like that! How you startled me!" she responded. "Please don't talk to me about the opera;

you know nothing about music. I'd better meet you on your own ground, and talk about your majolica and prints. Come now, what treasure have you been buying lately at the old flea market?"

"Would you like me to show you? But you don't understand such things."

"Oh, show me! I've been learning about them at those—what's their names?—the bankers . . . they've some splendid prints. They showed them to us."

"Why, have you been at the Schützburgs?" asked the hostess from her place by the samovar.

"Yes, *ma chère*. They asked my husband and me to dinner, and told us the sauce at that dinner cost a thousand rubles," Princess Myahkaya said, speaking loudly, and conscious that everyone was listening; "and very disgusting sauce it was, some green mess. We had to ask them, and I made them sauce that cost eighty-five kopeks, and everybody was very pleased with it. I can't afford thousand-ruble sauces."

"She's unique!" said the lady of the house.

"Marvelous!" said someone.

The sensation produced by Princess Myahkaya's speeches was always unique, and the secret of the sensation she produced lay in the fact that though she spoke not always appropriately, as now, she said simple things with some sense in them. In the society in which she lived, such statements produced the effect of the wittiest epigram. Princess Myahkaya could never see why it had that effect, but she knew it had, and took advantage of it.

As everyone had been listening while Princess Myahkaya spoke, and so the conversation around the ambassador's wife had dropped, Princess Betsy tried to bring the whole party together, and she turned to the ambassador's wife.

"Will you really not have tea? You should come over here by us."

"No, we're very happy here," the ambassador's wife responded with a smile, and she went on with the conversation that had been begun.

It was a very agreeable conversation. They were criticizing the Karenins, husband and wife.

"Anna is quite changed since her stay in Moscow. There's something strange about her," said her friend.

"The great change is that she brought back with her the shadow of Aleksey Vronsky," said the ambassador's wife.

"Well, what of it? There's a tale by Grimm, 'The Man without a Shadow,' about a man who loses his shadow.[2] That's his punishment for something. I never could understand how it was a punishment. But a woman would dislike being with a shadow."

"Yes, but women with a shadow usually come to a bad end," said Anna's friend.

"A plague on your tongue!" said Princess Myahkaya suddenly. "Madame Karenina's a splendid woman. I don't like her husband, but I like her very much."

"Why don't you like her husband? He's such a remarkable man," said the ambassador's wife. "My husband says there are few statesmen like him in Europe."

"And my husband tells me just the same, but I don't believe it," said Princess Myahkaya. "If our husbands didn't talk to us, we would see the facts as they are. Aleksey Aleksandrovich, to my thinking, is simply a fool. I say it in a whisper . . . but doesn't it really make everything clear? Before, when I was told to consider him clever, I kept looking for his ability, and thought myself a fool for not seeing it; but as soon as I said *he's a fool*, though only in a whisper, everything became clear, don't you think so?"

"How nasty you are today!"

"Not a bit. I'd no other way out of it. One of the two had to be a fool. And, well, you know one can't say that of oneself."

" 'No one is satisfied with his fortune, and everyone is satisfied with his wit.' " The attaché repeated the French saying.

"That's just it, just it." Princess Myahkaya turned to him. "But the point is that I won't abandon Anna to your mercies. She's so nice, so charming. How can she help it if they're all in love with her, and follow her about like shadows?"

"Oh, I had no thought of blaming her for it," Anna's friend said in self-defense.

"If no one follows us about like a shadow, that's no proof that we've any right to blame her."

[2] An error. The man who lost his shadow is in *Peter Schlemihl*, a story by Chamisso (1781-1838), German writer.

And having duly disposed of Anna's friend, the Princess Myahkaya got up and, together with the ambassador's wife, joined the group at the table, where the conversation was dealing with the king of Prussia.

"What wicked gossip were you talking over there?" asked Betsy.

"About the Karenins. The princess gave us a sketch of Aleksey Aleksandrovich," said the ambassador's wife with a smile as she sat down at the table.

"Pity we didn't hear it!" said Princess Betsy, glancing toward the door. "Ah, here you are at last!" she said, turning with a smile to Vronsky as he came in.

Vronsky was not merely acquainted with all the persons whom he was meeting here; he saw them all every day; and so he came in with the quiet manner with which one enters a room full of people from whom one has only just parted.

"Where do I come from?" he said, in answer to a question from the ambassador's wife. "Well, there's no way out, I must confess. From the *opéra bouffe*. I believe I've seen it a hundred times, and always with fresh enjoyment. It's exquisite! I know it's disgraceful, but I go to sleep at the opera, while I sit out the *opéra bouffe* to the last minute, and enjoy it. This evening . . ."

He mentioned a French actress, and was going to tell something about her; but the ambassador's wife, with playful horror, cut him short.

"Please don't tell us about those horrors."

"All right, I won't, especially as everyone knows those horrors."

"And we would all go to see them if it were accepted as the correct thing, like the opera," chimed in Princess Myahkaya.

CHAPTER SEVEN

Steps were heard at the door, and Princess Betsy, knowing it was Madame Karenina, glanced at Vronsky. He was looking toward the door, and his face wore a strange new expression. Joyfully, intently, and at the same time timidly, he gazed at the approaching figure, and slowly he rose to his feet. Anna walked into the drawing room.

Holding herself extremely erect, as always, looking straight before her, and moving with her swift, resolute, and light step, which distinguished her from all other society women, she crossed the short space to her hostess, shook hands with her, smiled, and with the same smile looked around at Vronsky. Vronsky bowed low and pushed a chair up for her.

She acknowledged this only by a slight nod, flushed a little, and frowned. But immediately, while rapidly greeting her acquaintances and shaking the hands proffered to her, she addressed Princess Betsy:

"I have been at Countess Lydia's, and meant to have come here earlier, but I stayed on. Sir John was there. He's very interesting."

"Oh, that's this missionary?"

"Yes; he told us about the life of Indians; most interesting."

The conversation, interrupted by her coming in, flickered like the light of a lamp being blown out.

"Sir John! Yes, Sir John; I've seen him. He speaks well. The Vlasieva girl's madly in love with him."

"And is it true the younger Vlasieva girl's to marry Topov?"

"Yes, they say it's settled."

"I am surprised at the parents! They say it's a marriage of love."

"Of love? What antediluvian notions you have! Can one talk of love these days?" said the ambassador's wife.

"What's to be done? It's a foolish old fashion that's still popular," said Vronsky.

"So much the worse for those who follow the fashion. The only happy marriages I know are marriages of convenience."

"Yes, but then how often the happiness of the convenient marriages flies away like dust just because that passion turns up that they have refused to recognize," said Vronsky.

"But by marriages of convenience we mean those in which both parties have sown their wild oats already. That's like scarlet fever—one has to go through it and get over it."

"Then they ought to find out how to vaccinate for love, like smallpox."

"I was in love in my young days with a deacon," said the Princess Myahkaya. "I don't know that it did me any good."

"No; I imagine, joking aside, that to know love, one must make mistakes and then correct them," said Princess Betsy.

"Even after marriage?" said the ambassador's wife playfully.

" 'It's never too late to mend.' " The attaché quoted the English proverb.

"Exactly," Betsy agreed; "one must make mistakes and correct them. What do you think about it?" She turned to Anna, who, with a faintly perceptible resolute smile on her lips, was listening in silence to the conversation.

"I think," said Anna, playing with the glove she had taken off, "I think . . . if so many men, so many minds, certainly so many hearts, so many kinds of love."

Vronsky was gazing at Anna and, with a sinking heart, waiting for what she would say. He sighed as if the danger he anticipated had passed when she uttered these words.

Anna suddenly turned to him.

"Oh, I have had a letter from Moscow. They write me that Kitty Shcherbatskaya's very ill."

"Really?" said Vronsky, frowning.

Anna looked sternly at him.

"That doesn't interest you?"

"On the contrary, it does, very much. What was it exactly they told you, if I may know?" he questioned.

Anna got up and went to Betsy.

"Give me a cup of tea," she said, standing at her table.

While Betsy was pouring the tea, Vronsky went up to Anna.

"What is it they write to you?" he repeated.

"I often think men have no understanding of what's not honorable though they're always talking of it," said Anna, without answering him. "I've wanted to tell you so a long while," she added, and moving a few steps away, she sat down at a table in a corner covered with albums.

"I don't quite understand the meaning of your words," he said, handing her the cup.

She glanced toward the sofa beside her, and he instantly sat down.

"Yes, I have been wanting to tell you," she said, not looking at him. "You behaved badly, very badly."

"Do you suppose I don't know that I've acted badly? But who was the cause of it?"

"What do you say that to me for?" she said, glancing severely at him.

"You know why," he answered boldly and joyfully, meeting her glance and not dropping his eyes.

Not he, but she, was confused.

"That only shows you have no heart," she said. But her eyes said that she knew he had a heart, and that was why she was afraid of him.

"What you spoke of just now was a mistake, and not love."

"Remember that I have forbidden you to utter that word, that hateful word," said Anna, with a shudder. But at once she felt that by the very word "forbidden" she had shown that she acknowledged certain rights over him, and by that very fact was encouraging him to speak of love. "I have long meant to tell you this," she went on, looking resolutely into his eyes, and hot all over from the burning flush on her cheeks. "I've come on purpose this evening knowing I should meet you. I have come to tell you that this must end. I have never blushed before anyone, and you force me to feel guilty for something."

He looked at her and was struck by a new spiritual beauty in her face.

"What do you wish of me?" he said simply and seriously.

"I want you to go to Moscow and ask for Kitty's forgiveness," she said.

"You don't wish that?" he said.

He saw she was saying what she forced herself to say, and not what she wanted to say.

"If you love me, as you say," she whispered, "do so that I may be at peace."

His face grew radiant.

"Don't you know that you're my whole life? But I know no peace, and I can't give it to you; all of myself—and love . . . yes. I can't think of you and myself apart. You and I are one to me. And I see no chance before us of peace for me or for you. I see a chance of despair, of wretchedness . . . or I see a chance of bliss, what bliss! . . . Can it be there's no chance of it?" he murmured with his lips only; but she heard.

She strained every effort of her mind to say what ought to be said. But instead of that she let her eyes rest on him, full of love, and made no answer.

"It's come!" he thought in ecstasy. "When I was beginning to despair, and it seemed there would be no end—it's come! She loves me! She admits it!"

"Then do this for me: never say such things to me, and let us be friends," she said in words; but her eyes spoke quite differently.

"Friends we shall never be, you know that yourself. Whether we shall be the happiest or the wretchedest of people—that's in your hands."

She would have said something, but he interrupted her.

"I ask one thing only: I ask for the right to hope, to suffer as I do. But if even that cannot be, command me to disappear, and I disappear. You shall not see me if my presence is distasteful to you."

"I don't want to drive you away."

"But don't change anything, leave everything as it is," he said in a shaky voice. "Here's your husband."

At that instant Aleksey Aleksandrovich did in fact walk into the room with his calm, awkward gait.

Glancing at his wife and Vronsky, he went up to the lady of the house, and sitting down for a cup of tea, he began talking in his deliberate, always audible voice, in his habitual tone of banter, ridiculing someone.

"Your Rambouillet[1] is in full conclave," he said, looking round at the entire party; "the Graces and the Muses."

But Princess Betsy could not endure that tone of his—"sneering," she called it, using the English word—and like a skillful hostess, she at once drew him into a serious conversation on the subject of universal conscription. Aleksey Aleksandrovich was immediately interested in the subject, and began seriously defending the new Imperial decree against Princess Betsy, who had attacked it.

---

[1] I.e., "Your literary salon is in full conclave." The Marquise de Rambouillet (1588-1665) gathered together the talent and wit of the literary world for fifty years.

Vronsky and Anna still sat at the little table.

"This is getting indecent," whispered one lady, with an expressive glance at Madame Karenina, Vronsky, and her husband.

"What did I tell you?" said Anna's friend.

But not only those ladies, almost everyone in the room, even the Princess Myahkaya and Betsy herself, looked several times in the direction of the two who had withdrawn from the general circle, as though that were a disturbing fact. Aleksey Aleksandrovich was the only person who did not once look in that direction, and was not diverted from the interesting discussion he had entered upon.

Noticing the disagreeable impression that was being made on everyone, Princess Betsy slipped someone else into her place to listen to Aleksey Aleksandrovich, and went up to Anna.

"I'm always amazed at the clearness and precision of your husband's language," she said. "The most transcendental ideas seem to be within my grasp when he's speaking."

"Oh, yes!" said Anna, radiant with a smile of happiness, and not understanding a word of what Betsy had said. She crossed over to the big table and took part in the general conversation.

Aleksey Aleksandrovich, after staying half an hour, went up to his wife and suggested that they should go home together. But she answered, not looking at him, that she was staying to supper. Aleksey Aleksandrovich made his bows and withdrew.

The fat old Tartar, Madame Karenina's coachman, in his shining leather coat, was with difficulty holding one of her pair of grays, chilled with the cold and rearing at the entrance. A footman stood opening the carriage door. The hall porter stood holding open the great door of the house. Anna Arkadyevna, with her quick little hand, was unfastening the lace of her sleeve, caught in the hook of her fur cloak, and, with bent head, listening with rapture to the words Vronsky murmured as he escorted her down.

"You've said nothing, of course, and I ask nothing," he was saying; "but you know that friendship's not what I want: that there's only one happiness in life for me, that word that you dislike so . . . yes, love! . . ."

"Love," she repeated slowly, to herself, and suddenly, at the very instant she unhooked the lace, she added, "Why I don't like the word is that it means too much to me, far more than you can under-stand," and she glanced into his face. "Good-by!"

She gave him her hand, and with her rapid, springy step she passed by the porter and vanished into the carriage.

Her glance, the touch of her hand, set him aflame. He kissed the palm of his hand where she had touched it, and went home, happy in the sense that he had got nearer to the attainment of his aims that evening than during the last two months.

CHAPTER EIGHT

Aleksey Aleksandrovich had seen nothing striking or improper in the fact that his wife was sitting with Vronsky at a separate table, in eager conversation with him about something. But he noticed that to the rest of the party this appeared to be something striking and improper, and for that reason it seemed to him too to be improper. He made up his mind that he must speak of it to his wife.

On reaching home, Aleksey Aleksandrovich went to his study, as he usually did, seated himself in his low chair, opened a book on the Papacy at the place where he had inserted the paper knife, and read till one o'clock, just as he usually did. But from time to time he rubbed his high forehead and shook his head, as though to drive away something. At his usual time he got up and prepared for bed. Anna Arkadyevna had not yet come in. With a book under his arm he went upstairs. But this evening, instead of his usual thoughts and meditations upon official details, his thoughts were absorbed by his wife and something disagreeable connected with her. Contrary to his usual habit, he did not get into bed, but started walking up and down the rooms with his hands clasped behind his back. He could not go to bed, feeling that it was absolutely necessary for him first to think thoroughly over the situation that had just arisen.

When Aleksey Aleksandrovich had made up his mind that he must talk to his wife about it, it had seemed a very easy and simple mat-ter. But now, when he began to think over the question that had just presented itself, it seemed to him very complicated and difficult.

Aleksey Aleksandrovich was not jealous. Jealousy, according to his notions, was an insult to one's wife, and one ought to have confidence in one's wife. Why one ought to have confidence—that is to say, complete conviction that his young wife would always love him—he did not ask himself. But he had had no experience of lack of confidence, because he had confidence in her, and told himself that he ought to have it. Now, though his conviction that jealousy was a shameful feeling and that one ought to feel confidence had not broken down, he felt that he was standing face to face with something illogical and irrational, and did not know what was to be done. Aleksey Aleksandrovich was standing face to face with life, with the possibility of his wife's loving someone other than himself, and this seemed to him very irrational and incomprehensible because it was life itself. All his life Aleksey Aleksandrovich had lived and worked in official spheres, dealing with the reflection of life. And every time he had stumbled against life itself he had shrunk away from it. Now he experienced a feeling akin to that of a man who, while calmly crossing a bridge over a precipice, should suddenly discover that the bridge is broken, and that there is a chasm below. That chasm was life itself, the bridge that artificial life in which Aleksey Aleksandrovich had lived. For the first time the question presented itself to him of the possibility of his wife's loving someone else, and he was horrified at it.

He did not undress, but walked up and down with his even steps over the resounding parquet of the dining room, where one lamp was burning, over the carpet of the dark drawing room, in which the light was reflected on the big new portrait of himself hanging over the sofa, and across her boudoir, where two candles burned, lighting up the portraits of her parents and woman friends, and the pretty knick-knacks of her writing table which he knew so well. He walked across her boudoir to the bedroom door, and turned back again. At each turn in his walk, especially at the parquet of the lighted dining room, he halted and said to himself, "Yes, this I must decide and put a stop to; I must express my view of it and my decision." And he turned back again. "But express what—what decision?" he said to himself in the drawing room, and he found no reply. "But after all," he asked himself before turning into the boudoir, "what has occurred? Nothing. She was talking a long while with him. But what of that? Surely women in society can talk to whom they please. And then, jealousy

means lowering both myself and her," he told himself as he went into
her boudoir; but this dictum, which had always carried such weight
with him before, now carried no weight and had no meaning at all.
And from the bedroom door he turned back again; but as he entered
the dark drawing room some inner voice told him that it was not so,
and that if others noticed it, there was something in it. And he said to
himself again in the dining room, "Yes, I must decide and put a stop
to it, and express my view of it . . ." And again at the turn in the drawing room he asked himself, "Decide how?" And again he asked himself, "What had occurred?" and answered, "Nothing," and
recollected that jealousy was a feeling insulting to his wife; but again
in the drawing room he was convinced that something had happened. His thoughts, like his body, went round a complete circle,
without coming upon anything new. He noticed this, rubbed his
forehead, and sat down in her boudoir.

There, looking at her table, with the malachite blotting pad lying
on the top and an unfinished letter, his thoughts suddenly changed.
He began to think of her, of what she was thinking and feeling. For
the first time he pictured vividly to himself her personal life, her ideas,
her desires, and the idea that she could and should have a separate life
of her own seemed to him so alarming that he made haste to dispel
it. It was the chasm which he was afraid to peep into. To put himself in
thought and feeling in another person's place was a spiritual exercise
not natural to Aleksey Aleksandrovich. He looked on this spiritual
exercise as a harmful and dangerous abuse of the imagination.

"And the worst of it all," thought he, "is that just now, at the very
moment when my great work is approaching completion" (he was
thinking of the project he was bringing forward at the time), "when
I stand in need of all my mental peace and all my energies, just now
this stupid worry should fall on me. But what's to be done? I'm not
one of those men who submit to uneasiness and worry without having the force of character to face them."

"I must think it over, come to a decision, and put it out of my
mind," he said aloud.

"The question of her feelings, of what has passed and may be passing in her soul, that's not my affair; that's the affair of her conscience,
and falls under the head of religion," he said to himself, feeling con-

solation in the sense that he had found to which division of regulating principles this new circumstance could be properly referred.

"And so," Aleksey Aleksandrovich said to himself, "questions as to her feelings, and so on, are questions for her conscience, with which I can have nothing to do. My duty is clearly defined. As the head of the family, I am a person bound in duty to guide her, and consequently, in part the person responsible; I am bound to point out the danger I perceive, to warn her, even to use my authority. I ought to speak frankly to her." And everything that he would say tonight to his wife took clear shape in Aleksey Aleksandrovich's head. Thinking over what he would say, he somewhat regretted that he should have to use his time and mental powers for domestic consumption with so little to show for it, but in spite of that, the form and contents of the speech before him shaped itself as clearly and distinctly in his head as a ministerial report.

"I must say and express fully the following points: first, exposition of the value to be attached to public opinion and to decorum; second, exposition of religious significance of marriage; third, if need be, reference to the calamity possible ensuing to our son; fourth, reference to the unhappiness likely to result to herself." And, interlacing his fingers, Aleksey Aleksandrovich stretched them, and the joints of the fingers cracked. This trick, a bad habit, always soothed him, and gave precision to his thoughts, so needful to him at this juncture.

There was a sound of a carriage driving up to the front door. Aleksey Aleksandrovich halted in the middle of the room.

A woman's step was heard mounting the stairs. Aleksey Aleksandrovich, ready for his speech, stood compressing his crossed fingers, waiting to see if the crack would come again. One joint cracked.

Already, from the sound of light steps on the stairs, he was aware that she was close, and though he was satisfied with his speech, he felt frightened of the explanation confronting him . . .

CHAPTER NINE

Anna came in with bowed head, playing with the tassels of her hood. Her face was brilliant and glowing; but this glow was not one of brightness; it suggested the fearful glow of a conflagration in the midst of a dark night. On seeing her husband, Anna raised her head and smiled, as though she had just waked up.

"You're not in bed? What a surprise!" she said, letting her hood fall, and without stopping, she went on into the dressing room. "It's late, Aleksey Aleksandrovich," she said, when she had gone through the doorway.

"Anna, it's necessary for me to have a talk with you."

"With me?" she said, with surprise. She came out from behind the door of the dressing room and looked at him. "Why, what is it? What about?" she asked, sitting down. "Well, let's talk, if it's so necessary. But it would be better to get to sleep."

Anna said what came to her lips, and marveled, hearing herself, at her own capacity for lying. How simple and natural were her words, and how likely that she was simply sleepy! She felt herself clad in an impenetrable armor of falsehood. She felt that some unseen force had come to her aid and was supporting her.

"Anna, I must warn you," he began.

"Warn me?" she said. "Of what?"

She looked at him so simply, so brightly, that anyone who did not know her as her husband knew her could not have noticed anything unnatural, either in the sound or the sense of her words. But to him, knowing her, knowing that whenever he went to bed five minutes later than usual she noticed it and asked him the reason; to him, knowing that every joy, every pleasure and pain that she felt she communicated to him at once; to him, now to see that she did not care to notice his state of mind, that she did not care to say a word about herself, meant a great deal. He saw that the inmost recesses of her soul, which had always hitherto lain open before him, were closed against him. More than that, he saw from her tone that she was not even perturbed at that, but seemed to say openly to him: "Yes, it's shut up, and so it must be, and will be in the future." Now he experienced a feeling such as a man might have on returning home and finding his own house locked up. "But perhaps the key may yet be found," thought Aleksey Aleksandrovich.

"I want to warn you," he said in a low voice, "that through thoughtlessness and lack of caution you may cause yourself to be talked about in society. Your too animated conversation this evening with Count Vronsky" (he enunciated the name firmly and with deliberate emphasis) "attracted attention."

He talked and looked at her laughing eyes, which frightened him now with their impenetrable look, and as he talked, he felt the utter uselessness and futility of his words.

"You're always like that," she answered, as though completely misunderstanding him, and of all he had said only taking in the last phrase. "One time you don't like my being bored, and another time you don't like my being lively. I wasn't bored. Does that offend you?"

Aleksey Aleksandrovich shivered, and bent his hands to make the joints crack.

"Oh, please, don't do that, I do so dislike it," she said.

"Anna, is this you?" said Aleksey Aleksandrovich, quietly making an effort over himself, and restraining the motion of his fingers.

"But what is it all about?" she said, with such genuine and comic wonder. "What do you want of me?"

Aleksey Aleksandrovich paused, and rubbed his forehead and his eyes. He saw that instead of doing as he had intended—that is to say, warning his wife against a mistake in the eyes of the world—he had unconsciously become agitated over what was the affair of her conscience, and was struggling against the barrier he thought between them.

"This is what I meant to say to you," he went on coldly and composedly, "and I beg you to listen to it. I consider jealousy, as you know, a humiliating and degrading feeling, and I shall never allow myself to be influenced by it; but there are certain rules of decorum which cannot be disregarded with impunity. This evening it was not I who observed it, but judging by the impression made on the company, everyone observed that your conduct and deportment were not altogether what could be desired."

"I positively don't understand," said Anna, shrugging her shoulders.—"He doesn't care," she thought. "But other people noticed it, and that's what upsets him."—"You're not well, Aleksey Aleksandrovich," she added, getting up and moving toward the door; but he moved forward as if to stop her.

His face was ugly and forbidding, as Anna had never seen him. She stopped, and bending her head back and to one side, she began rapidly taking out her hairpins.

"Well, I'm listening to what's to come," she said, calmly and ironically; "and indeed I listen with interest, for I should like to understand what's the matter."

She spoke, and marveled at the confident, calm, and natural tone in which she was speaking, and the choice of the words she used.

"To enter into all the details of your feelings I have no right, and besides, I regard that as useless and even harmful," began Aleksey Aleksandrovich. "Ferreting in one's soul, one often ferrets out something that might have lain there unnoticed. Your feelings are an affair of your own conscience; but I am in duty bound to you, to myself, and to God to point out to you your duties. Our life has been joined, not by man, but by God. That union can be severed only by a crime, and a crime of that nature brings its own chastisement."

"I don't understand a word. And, oh dear! How sleepy I am, unfortunately," she said, rapidly passing her hand through her hair, feeling for the remaining hairpins.

"Anna, for God's sake don't speak like that," he said gently. "Perhaps I am mistaken, but believe me, what I say, I say as much for myself as for you. I am your husband, and I love you."

For an instant her face fell, and the sardonic gleam in her eyes died away; but the word "love" threw her into revolt again. She thought: "Love? Can he love? If he hadn't heard there was such a thing as love, he would never have used the word. He doesn't even know what love is."

"Aleksey Aleksandrovich, really I don't understand," she said. "Define what it is you find—"

"Excuse me, let me say all I have to say. I love you. But I am not speaking of myself; the most important persons in this matter are our son and yourself. It may very well be, I repeat, that my words seem to you utterly unnecessary and out of place; it may be that they are called forth by my mistaken impression. In that case, I beg you to forgive me. But if you are conscious yourself of even the smallest foundation for them, then I beg you to think a little, and if your heart prompts you to speak out to me . . ."

Aleksey Aleksandrovich was unconsciously saying something utterly unlike what he had prepared.

"I have nothing to say. And besides," she said hurriedly, with difficulty repressing a smile, "it's really time to be in bed."

Aleksey Aleksandrovich sighed, and, without saying more, went into the bedroom.

When she came into the bedroom, he was already in bed. His lips were sternly compressed, and his eyes looked away from her. Anna got into her bed, expecting every minute that he would begin to speak to her again. She both feared his speaking and wished for it. But he was silent. She waited for a long while without moving, and had forgotten about him. She thought of that other; she pictured him, and felt how her heart was flooded with emotion and guilty delight at the thought of him. Suddenly she heard an even, tranquil snore. For the first instant Aleksey Aleksandrovich seemed appalled at his own snoring, and ceased; but after an interval during which he breathed twice, the snore sounded again, with a new tranquil regularity.

"It's late, it's late," she whispered with a smile. She lay a long while, not moving, with open eyes, whose brilliance it almost seemed she herself could see in the darkness.

CHAPTER TEN

From that time on, a new life began for Aleksey Aleksandrovich and for his wife. Nothing special happened. Anna went out into society, as she had always done, was particularly often at Princess Betsy's, and met Vronsky everywhere. Aleksey Aleksandrovich saw this but could do nothing. All his efforts to draw her into open discussion she confronted with a barrier that he could not penetrate, made up of a sort of amused perplexity. Outwardly everything was the same, but their inner relations were completely changed. Aleksey Aleksandrovich, a man of great power in the world of politics, felt himself helpless in this. Like an ox with head bent, submissively, he awaited the blow of the ax which he felt was raised over him. Every time he began to think about it, he felt that he must try once more, that by kindness, tenderness, and persuasion there was still hope of saving her, of bringing her back to herself, and every day he prepared to talk to her. But every time he began talking to her, he felt that the spirit of evil and deceit which had taken possession of her had possession of him too, and he talked to her in a tone quite unlike that in which he had meant to. Involuntary he talked to her in his habitual tone of jeering, as if he were ridiculing anyone who would say what he was saying. And in that tone it was impossible to say what needed to be said to her.

CHAPTER ELEVEN

That which had been for almost a whole year the one absorbing desire of Vronsky's life, replacing all his old desires; that which for Anna had been an impossible, terrible, and even for that reason more entrancing dream of bliss, that desire had been fulfilled. He stood before her, pale, his lower jaw quivering, and besought her to be calm, not knowing how or why.

"Anna! Anna!" he said with a choking voice, "Anna, for God's sake! . . ."

But the louder he spoke, the lower she dropped her once proud and gay, now shame-stricken head, and she bowed down and sank from the sofa where she was sitting, down on the floor, at his feet; she would have fallen on the carpet if he had not held her.

"My God! Forgive me!" she said, sobbing, pressing his hands to her bosom.

She felt so sinful, so guilty, that nothing was left her but to humiliate herself and beg forgiveness; and as now there was no one in her life but him, to him she addressed her prayer for forgiveness. Looking at him, she had a physical sense of her humiliation, and she could say nothing more. He felt what a murderer must feel when he sees the body he has robbed of life. That body, robbed by him of life, was their love, the first stage of their love. There was something awful and revolting in the memory of what had been bought at this fearful price of shame. Shame at their spiritual nakedness crushed her and infected him. But in spite of all the murderer's horror before the body of his victim, he must hack it to pieces, hide the body, must use what he has gained by his murder.

And with fury, as it were with passion, the murderer falls on the body and drags it and hacks at it; so he covered her face and shoulders with kisses. She held his hand, and did not stir. "Yes, these kisses—that is what has been bought by this shame. Yes, and one hand, which will always be mine—the hand of my accomplice." She lifted up that hand and kissed it. He sank on his knees and tried to see her face; but she hid it, and said nothing. At last, as though making an effort over herself, she got up and pushed him away. Her face was still as beautiful, but it was only more pitiful because of that.

"All is over," she said; "I have nothing but you. Remember that."

"I can never forget what is my whole life. For one instant of this happiness—"

"Happiness!" she said with terror and loathing, and her terror unconsciously infected him. "For God's sake, not a word, not a word more."

She rose quickly and moved away from him.

"Not a word more," she repeated, and with a look of chill despair, incomprehensible to him, she parted from him. She felt that at that moment she could not put into words the sense of shame, of rapture, and of horror at this stepping into a new life, and she did not want to speak of it, to vulgarize this feeling by inappropriate words. But later too, and the next day and the third day, she still found no words in which she could express the complexity of her feelings; indeed, she could not even find thoughts in which she could clearly think out all that was in her soul.

She said to herself: "No, now I can't think of it, later on, when I am calmer." But this calm for thought never came; every time the thought rose of what she had done and what would happen to her, and what she ought to do, a horror came over her and she drove those thoughts away.

"Later, later," she said—"when I am calmer."

But in dreams, when she had no control over her thoughts, her situation presented itself to her in all its hideous nakedness. One dream haunted her almost every night. She dreamed that both were her husbands at once, that both were lavishing caresses on her. Aleksey Aleksandrovich was weeping, kissing her hands, and saying, "How good it is now!" And Aleksey Vronsky was there too, and he too was her husband. And she was amazed that it had once seemed impossible to her, was explaining to them, laughing, that this was so much simpler, and that now both of them were happy and contented. But this dream weighed on her like a nightmare, and she awoke from it in terror.

CHAPTER TWELVE

In the early days after his return from Moscow, whenever Levin shuddered and grew red, remembering the disgrace of his rejection, he said to himself: "This was just how I used to shudder and blush, thinking myself utterly lost, when I got a one[1] in physics and did not get promoted; and how I thought myself utterly ruined after I had mismanaged that affair of my sister's that was entrusted to me. And yet, now that years have passed, I recall it and wonder that it could distress me so much. It will be the same thing, too, with this trouble. Time will go by and I shall not mind about this either."

But three months had passed and he had not stopped caring about it; and it was as painful for him to think of it as it had been those first days. He could not be at peace, because after dreaming so long of family life, and feeling himself so ripe for it, he was still not married, and was further than ever from marriage. He was painfully conscious himself, as were all about him, that at his age it is not good for a man to be alone. He remembered how before starting for Moscow he had once said to his cowman Nikolai, a simple-hearted peasant, whom he liked talking to: "Well, Nikolai! I intend getting married," and how Nikolai had promptly answered, as of a matter on which there could be no possible doubt: "And high time too, Konstantin Dmitrievich." But marriage had now become more remote than ever. The place was taken, and whenever he tried to imagine any of the girls he knew

---

[1] The lowest possible grade, i.e., A=5, B=4, C=3, D=2, E=1.

in that place, he felt that it was utterly impossible. Moreover, the recollection of the rejection and the part he had played in the affair tortured him with shame. However often he told himself that he was in no way to blame for it, that recollection, like other humiliating reminiscences of a similar kind, made him twinge and blush. There had been in his past, as in every man's, actions, recognized by him as bad, for which his conscience should have tormented him; but the memory of these evil actions was far from causing him so much suffering as those trivial but humiliating reminiscences. These wounds never healed. And with these memories was now ranged his rejection and the pitiful position in which he must have appeared to others that evening. But time and work did their part. Bitter memories were more and more covered up by the incidents—paltry in his eyes, but really important—of his country life. Every week he thought less often of Kitty. He was impatiently looking forward to the news that she was married, or just going to be married, hoping that such news would, like having a tooth out, completely cure him.

Meanwhile spring came on, beautiful and friendly, without the delays and treacheries of spring—one of those rare springs in which plants, beasts, and man rejoice alike. This lovely spring roused Levin still more, and strengthened him in his resolution of renouncing all his past and building up his lonely life firmly and independently. Though many of the plans with which he had returned to the country had not been carried out, still his most important resolution—that of chastity—had been kept by him. He was free from that shame, which had usually harassed him after a fall; and he could look everyone straight in the face. In February he had received a letter from Marya Nikolaevna telling him that his brother Nikolai's health was getting worse, but that he would not take advice, and in consequence of this letter Levin went to Moscow to his brother's, and succeeded in persuading him to see a doctor and to go to a spa abroad. He succeeded so well in persuading his brother, and in lending him money for the journey without irritating him, that he was satisfied with himself in that matter. In addition to his farming, which called for special attention in spring, in addition to reading, Levin had begun writing a book on agriculture that winter, the plan of which turned on taking into account the character of the laborer on the land as one of the unalterable data of the question, like the climate and the soil, and consequently deducing all the principles of scientific culture, not simply from the data of soil and climate, but from the data of soil, climate, and a certain unalterable character of the laborer. Thus, in spite of his solitude, or because of it, his life was exceedingly full. Only rarely he suffered from an unsatisfied desire to communicate his stray ideas to someone besides Agafya Mikhailovna. With her he not infrequently fell into discussions of physics, the theory of agriculture, and especially philosophy; philosophy was Agafya Mikhailovna's favorite subject.

Spring was slow in unfolding. For the last few weeks it had been steadily fine frosty weather. In the daytime it thawed in the sun, but at night there were even seven degrees of frost.[2] There was such a frozen surface on the snow that they drove the wagons without staying on the roads. Easter came in the snow. Then all of a sudden, on Easter Monday, a warm wind sprang up, storm clouds swooped down, and for three days and three nights the warm, driving rain fell in streams. On Thursday the wind dropped, and a thick gray fog brooded over the land as though hiding the mysteries of the transformations that were being wrought in nature. Behind the fog there was the flowing of water, the cracking and floating of ice, the swift rush of turbid, foaming torrents; and on the following Monday, in the evening, the fog parted, the storm clouds split up into little curling crests of cloud, the sky cleared, and the real spring had come. In the morning the sun rose brilliant and quickly wore away the thin layer of ice that covered the water, and all the warm air was quivering with the steam that rose up from the revivified earth. The old grass looked greener, and the young grass thrust up its tiny blades; the buds of the guelder rose and of the currant and the sticky birch buds were swollen with sap, and an exploring bee was humming about the golden blossoms that studded the willow. Larks trilled unseen above the velvety green fields and the ice-covered stubble; pewits wailed over the lowlands and marshes flooded by the pools; cranes and wild geese flew high across the sky uttering their spring calls. The cattle, bald in patches where the new hair had not grown yet, lowed in the

[2] I.e., sixteen degrees Fahrenheit.

pastures; the bowlegged lambs frisked around their bleating mothers. Nimble children ran about the drying paths, covered with the prints of bare feet. There was a merry chatter of peasant women over their linen at the pond, and the ring of axes in the yard, where the peasants were repairing plows and harrows. The real spring had come.

CHAPTER THIRTEEN

Levin put on his big boots and, for the first time, a cloth jacket instead of his fur cloak, and went out to look after his farm, stepping over streams of water that flashed in the sunshine and dazzled his eyes, and treading one minute on ice and the next into sticky mud.

Spring is the time of plans and projects. And, as he came out into the farmyard, Levin, like a tree in spring that knows not what form will be taken by the young shoots and twigs imprisoned in its swelling buds, hardly knew what undertakings he was going to begin upon now in the farm work that was so dear to him. But he felt he was full of the most splendid plans and projects. First of all he went to the cattle. The cows had been let out into their paddock, and their smooth sides were already shining with their new, sleek spring coats; they basked in the sunshine and lowed to go to the meadow. Levin gazed admiringly at the cows he knew so intimately to the minutest detail of their condition, and gave orders for them to be driven out into the meadow, and the calves to be let into the paddock. The herdsman ran gaily to get ready for the meadow. The cowherd girls, picking up their skirts, ran splashing through the mud with bare legs, still white, not yet brown from the sun, waving brushwood in their hands, chasing the calves that frolicked in the mirth of spring.

After admiring the young ones of that year, who were particularly fine—the early calves were the size of a peasant's cow, and Pava's daughter, at three months, was as big as a yearling—Levin gave orders for a trough to be brought out and for them to be fed in the paddock. But it appeared that as the paddock had not been used during the winter, the hurdles made in the autumn for it were broken. He sent for the carpenter, who, according to his orders, should have been at work on the threshing machine. But it appeared that the carpenter was repairing the harrows, which should have been repaired before Lent. This was very annoying to Levin. It was annoying to come upon that everlasting slovenliness in the farm work against which he had been striving with all his might for so many years. The hurdles, as he ascertained, not being wanted in winter, had been carried to the cart horses' stable, and there broken, as they were of light construction, meant only for folding calves. Moreover, it was apparent also that the harrows and all the agricultural implements, which he had directed to be looked over and repaired in the winter, for which very purpose he had hired three carpenters, had not been put into repair, and the harrows were being repaired when they should have been harrowing the field. Levin sent for his bailiff, but immediately went off himself to look for him. The bailiff, beaming all over, like everyone that day, in a sheepskin bordered with astrakhan, came out of the barn, twisting a bit of straw in his hands.

"Why isn't the carpenter working on the threshing machine?"

"Oh, I meant to tell you yesterday, the harrows need repairing. Here it's time they got to work in the fields."

"But what were they doing in the winter, then?"

"But what did you want the carpenter for?"

"Where are the hurdles for the calves' paddock?"

"I ordered them to be got ready. What would you have with those peasants!" said the bailiff, with a wave of his hand.

"It's not those peasants but this bailiff!" said Levin, getting angry. "Why, what do I keep you for?" he cried. But, thinking to himself that this would not help matters, he stopped short in the middle of a sentence, and merely sighed. "Well, what do you say? Can sowing begin?" he asked, after a pause.

"Behind Turkino tomorrow or next day they might begin."

"And the clover?"

"I've sent Vasily and Mishka; they're sowing. Only I don't know if they'll manage to get through; it's so slushy."

"How many acres?"

"About sixteen."

"Why not sow all?" cried Levin.

That they were sowing the clover only on sixteen acres instead of fifty was still more annoying to him. Clover, as he knew, both from books and from his own experience, never did well except when it was sown as early as possible, almost in the snow. And yet Levin could never get this done.

"There's no one to send. What can you do with such a set of peasants? Three haven't turned up. And there's Semyon—"

"Well, you should have taken some men from the thatching."

"And so I have, as it is."

"Where are the peasants, then?"

"Five are making compot" (he meant compost), "four are shifting the oats for fear of a touch of mildew, Konstantin Dmitrievich."

Levin knew very well that "a touch of mildew" meant that his English seed oats were already ruined. Again they had not done as he had ordered.

"Why, but I told you at Lent to put in ventilators," he cried.

"Don't worry; we'll get it all done in time."

Levin waved his hand angrily, went into the granary to glance at the oats, and then to the stable. The oats were not yet spoiled. But the peasants were carrying the oats in spades when they might simply let them slide down into the lower granary; and arranging for this to be done, and taking two workmen from there for sowing clover, Levin got over his vexation with the bailiff. Indeed, it was such a lovely day that one could not be angry.

"Ignat!" he called to the coachman, who, with his sleeves tucked up, was washing the carriage wheels, "saddle me—"

"Which, sir?"

"Well, let it be Kolpik."

"Yes, sir."

While they were saddling his horse, Levin again called the bailiff, who was hanging about in sight, to make it up with him, and began talking to him about the spring operations before them, and his plans for the farm.

The wagons were to begin carting manure earlier, so as to get everything done before the early mowing; and the plowing of the further land to go on without a break so as to let it ripen lying fallow; and the mowing to be done by hired labor, not on half-profits. The bailiff listened attentively, and obviously made an effort to approve of his employer's projects. But still he had that look Levin knew so well that always irritated him, a look of hopelessness and despondency. That look said: "That's all very well, but as God wills."

Nothing mortified Levin so much as that tone. But it was the tone common to all the bailiffs he had ever had. They had all taken up that attitude toward his plans, and so now he was not angered by it but mortified, and felt all the more roused to struggle against this, as it seemed, elemental force continually ranged against him, for which he could find no other expression than "as God wills."

"If we can manage it, Konstantin Dmitrievich," said the bailiff.

"Why shouldn't you manage it?"

"We positively must have another fifteen laborers. And they don't turn up. There were some here today asking seventy rubles for the summer."

Levin was silent. Again he was brought face to face with that opposing force. He knew that however they tried, they could not hire more than forty—thirty-seven, perhaps, or thirty-eight—laborers for a reasonable sum. About forty had been taken on, and there were no more. But still he could not help struggling against it.

"Send to Sury, to Chefirovka; if they don't come, we must look for them."

"Oh. I'll send, to be sure," said Vasily Fyodorovich despondently. "But there are the horses too, they're not good for much."

"We'll get some more. I know, of course," Levin added, laughing, "you always want to manage with as little and as poor quality as possible; but this year I'm not going to let you have things your own way. I'll see to everything myself."

"Why, I don't think you sleep too much as it is. It cheers us up to work under the master's eye . . ."

"So they're sowing clover behind Birch Dale? I'll go and have a look at them," he said, getting on to the little bay cob, Kolpik, who was led up by the coachman.

"You can't get across the streams, Konstantin Dmitrievich," the coachman shouted.

"All right, I'll go by the forest."

And Levin rode through the slush of the farmyard to the gate and out into the open country, his good little horse, after his long inactivity, stepping out gallantly, snorting over the pools, and asking, as it were, for guidance. If Levin had felt happy before in the cattle pens and farmyard, he felt happier yet in the open country. Swaying rhythmically with the ambling paces of his good little cob, drinking in the warm yet fresh scent of the snow and the air, as he rode through his forest over the crumbling, melting snow, still left in parts, and covered with dissolving tracks, he rejoiced over every tree, with the moss reviving on its bark and the buds swelling on its shoots. When he came out of the forest, in the immense plain before him, his grass fields stretched in an unbroken carpet of green, without one bare place or swamp, spotted only here and there in the hollows with patches of melting snow. He was not put out of temper even by the sight of the peasants' horses and colts trampling down his young grass (he told a peasant he met to drive them out), nor by the sarcastic and stupid reply of the peasant Ipat, whom he met on the way, and asked, "Well, Ipat, shall we soon be sowing?" "We must get the plowing done first, Konstantin Dmitrievich," answered Ipat. The further he rode, the happier he became, and plans for the land rose to his mind each better than the last; to plant all of his fields with hedges along the southern borders, so that the snow should not lie under them; to divide them up into six fields of arable and three of pasture and hay ; to build a cattle yard at the further end of the estate, and to dig a pond and to construct movable pens for the cattle as a means of manuring the land. And then eight hundred acres of wheat, three hundred of potatoes, and four hundred of clover, and not one acre exhausted.

Absorbed in such dreams, carefully keeping his horse by the hedges so as not to trample his young crops, he rode up to the laborers who had been sent to sow clover. A cart with the seed in it was standing, not at the edge, but in the middle of the crop, and the winter corn had been torn up by the wheels and trampled by the horse. Both the laborers were sitting in the hedge, probably smoking a pipe together. The earth in the cart, with which the seed was mixed, was not crushed to powder, but crusted together or adhering in clods. Seeing the master, the laborer, Vasily, went toward the cart, while Mishka set to work sowing. This was not as it should be, but with the laborers Levin seldom lost his temper. When Vasily came up, Levin told him to lead the horse to the hedge.

"It's all right, sir, it'll spring up again," responded Vasily.

"Please don't argue," said Levin, "but do as you're told."

"Yes, sir," answered Vasily, and he took the horse's head. "What a sowing, Konstantin Dmitrievich," he said, hesitating; "excellent. Only it's a job to move about! You drag a ton of earth on your shoes."

"Why is it you have earth that's not sifted?" said Levin.

"Well, we crumble it up," answered Vasily, taking up some seed and rolling the earth in his palms.

Vasily was not to blame for their having filled up his cart with unsifted earth, but still it was annoying.

Levin had more than once already tried a way he knew for stifling his anger and turning all that seemed dark right again, and he tried that way now. He watched how Mishka strode along, swinging the huge clods of earth that clung to each foot; and getting off his horse, he took the sieve from Vasily and started sowing himself.

"Where did you stop?"

Vasily pointed to the mark with his foot, and Levin went forward as best he could, scattering the seed on the land. Walking was as difficult as on a bog, and by the time Levin had ended the row he was in a great heat, and he stopped and gave the sieve to Vasily.

"Well, master, when summer's here, mind you don't scold me for that row," said Vasily.

"Eh?" said Levin cheerily, already feeling the effect of his method.

"Why, you'll see in the summertime. It'll look different. Look where I sowed last spring. How I did work at it! I do my best, Konstantin Dmitrievich, you see, as I would for my own father. I don't like bad work myself, nor would I let another man do it. What's good for the master's good for us too. To look out yonder now," said Vasily, pointing, "it does one's heart good."

"It's a lovely spring, Vasily."

"Why, it's a spring such as the old men don't remember the like of. I was up home; an old man up there has sown wheat too, about an acre of it. He was saying you wouldn't know it from rye."

"Have you been sowing wheat long?"

"Why, sir, it was you taught us the year before last. You gave me two measures. We sold about eight bushels and sowed a rood."

"Well, make certain you crumble up the clods," said Levin, going toward his horse, "and keep an eye on Mishka. And if there's a good crop you shall have half a ruble for every acre."

"Humbly thankful. We are very well content, sir, as it is."

Levin got on his horse and rode toward the field where last year's clover was, and the one that was plowed ready for the spring corn.

The crop of clover coming up in the stubble was magnificent. It had survived everything, and stood up vividly green through the broken stalks of last year's wheat. The horse sank in up to the pasterns, and he drew each hoof with a sucking sound out of the half-thawed ground. Over the plowland, riding was utterly impossible; the horse could keep a foothold only where there was ice, and in the thawing furrows he sank deep in at each step. The plowland was in splendid condition; in a couple of days it would be fit for harrowing and sowing. Everything was splendid, everything was encouraging. Levin rode back across the streams, hoping the water would have gone down. And he did in fact get across, and startled two ducks. "There must be snipe too," he thought, and just as he reached the turning homeward he met the forest keeper, who confirmed his theory about the snipe.

Levin went home at a trot, so as to have time to eat his dinner and get his gun ready for the evening.

CHAPTER FOURTEEN

As he rode up to the house in the happiest frame of mind, Levin heard the bell at the side of the main entrance of the house.

"Yes, that's someone from the railway station," he thought, "just the time to be here from the Moscow train . . . Who could it be? What if it's brother Nikolai? He did say: 'Maybe I'll go to the waters, or maybe I'll come down to you.' " He felt dismayed and vexed for the first minute that his brother Nikolai's presence should come to disturb his happy mood of spring. But he felt ashamed of the feeling, and at once he opened, as it were, the arms of his soul, and with a softened feeling of joy and expectation, now he hoped with all his heart that it was his brother. He pricked up his horse, and riding out from behind the acacias, he saw a hired three-horse sleigh from the railway station, and a gentleman in a fur coat. It was not his brother. "Oh, if only it were some nice person one could talk to a little!" he thought.

"Ah," cried Levin joyfully, flinging up both his hands. "Here's a delightful visitor! Ah, how glad I am to see you!" he shouted, recognizing Stepan Arkadyevich.

"I shall find out for certain whether she's married, or when she's going to be married," he thought. And on that delicious spring day he felt that the thought of her did not hurt him at all.

"Well, you didn't expect me, eh?" said Stepan Arkadyevich, getting out of the sleigh, splashed with mud on the bridge of his nose, on his cheek, and on his eyebrows, but radiant with health and good spirits. "I've come to see you, that's one thing," he said, embracing and kissing him, "to do some shooting, that's second, and to sell the forest at Yergushovo, that's third."

"Delightful! What a spring we're having! How did you manage in a sleigh?"

"In a cart it would have been worse still, Konstantin Dmitrievich," answered the driver, who knew him.

"Well, I'm very, very glad to see you," said Levin, with a genuine smile of childlike delight.

Levin led his friend to the room set apart for visitors, where Stepan Arkadyevich's things were carried also—a bag, a gun in a case, a pouch for cigars. Leaving him there to wash and change his clothes, Levin went off to the office to speak about the plowing and clover. Agafya Mikhailovna, always very anxious about the honor of the house, met him in the hall with inquiries about dinner.

"Do just as you like, only let it be as soon as possible," he said, and went to the bailiff.

When he came back, Stepan Arkadyevich, washed and combed, came out of his room with a beaming smile, and they went upstairs together.

"Well, I am glad I managed to get away to you! Now I shall understand what the mysterious business is that you are always absorbed in here. No, really, I envy you. What a house, how nice it all is! So bright, so cheerful!" said Stepan Arkadyevich, forgetting that it was not always spring and fine weather like that day. "And your old nurse is simply charming. A cute maid in a little apron might be even more desirable; but for your severe monastic style it does very well."

Stepan Arkadyevich told him many interesting pieces of news; especially interesting to Levin was the news that his brother, Sergey Ivanovich, was intending to pay him a visit in the summer.

Not one word did Stepan Arkadyevich say in reference to Kitty and the Shcherbatskys; he merely gave him greetings from his wife. Levin was grateful to him for his delicacy, and was very glad of his visitor. As always happened with him during his solitude, a mass of ideas and feelings had been accumulating within him, which he could not communicate to those about him. And now he poured out upon Stepan Arkadyevich his poetic joy in the spring, and his failures and plans for the land, and his thoughts and criticisms on the books he had been reading, and the idea of his own book, the basis of which really was, though he was unaware of it himself, a criticism of all the old books on agriculture. Stepan Arkadyevich, always charming, understanding everything at the slightest reference, was particularly charming on this visit, and Levin noticed in him a special tenderness, as it were, and a new tone of respect that flattered him.

The efforts of Agafya Mikhailovna and the chef, that the dinner should be particularly good, only ended in the two famished friends attacking the preliminary course, eating a great deal of bread and butter, smoked goose and salted mushrooms, and in Levin's finally ordering the soup to be served without the accompaniment of little pies, with which the chef had particularly meant to impress their visitor. But though Stepan Arkadyevich was accustomed to very different dinners, he thought everything excellent: the herb vodka, and the bread, and the butter, and above all the smoked goose and the mushrooms, and the nettle soup, and the chicken in white sauce, and the white Crimean wine—everything was superb and delicious.

"Splendid, splendid!" he said, lighting a fat cigar after the roast. "I feel as if, coming to you, I had landed on a peaceful shore after the noise and jolting of a steamer. And so you maintain that the laborer himself is an element to be studied and to regulate the choice of methods in agriculture. Of course, I'm an ignorant outsider; but I should imagine theory and its application will have its influence on the laborer too."

"Yes, but wait a moment. I'm not talking of political economy, I'm talking of the science of agriculture. It should be like the natural sciences, and to observe given phenomena and the laborer in his economic, ethnographical . . ."

At that instant Agafya Mikhailovna came in with jam.

"Oh, Agafya Mikhailovna," said Stepan Arkadyevich, kissing the tips of his plump fingers, "what smoked goose, what herb vodka! . . . What do you think, isn't it time to start, Kostya?" he added.

Levin looked out of the window at the sun sinking behind the bare trees of the forest.

"Yes, it's time," he said. "Kuzma, get the trap ready," [1] and he ran downstairs.

Stepan Arkadyevich, going down, carefully took the canvas cover off his varnished gun case with his own hands, and, opening it, began to get ready his expensive gun, which was one of the latest models. Kuzma, who already scented a big tip, never left Stepan Arkadyevich's side, and put on him both his stockings and boots, a task which Stepan Arkadyevich readily left him.

"Kostya, give orders that if the merchant Ryabinin comes—I told him to come today—he's to be brought in and to wait for me . . ."

"Why, do you mean to say you're selling the forest to Ryabinin?"

"Yes. Do you know him?"

"To be sure I do. I have had to do business with him, 'positively and conclusively.' "

Stepan Arkadyevich laughed. "Positively and conclusively" were the merchant's favorite words.

"Yes, it's wonderfully funny the way he talks. She knows where her master's going!" he added, patting Laska, who hung about Levin, whining and licking his hands, his boots, and his gun.

The trap was already at the steps when they went out.

"I told them to bring the trap around; or would you rather walk?"

"No, we'd better drive," said Stepan Arkadyevich, getting into the trap. He sat down, tucked the tigerskin rug around him, and lighted a cigar. "How is it you don't smoke? A cigar is a sort of thing, not

---

[1] *Lineika*, a long, flat, four-wheeled vehicle seating four or five back to back, facing its sides.

exactly a pleasure, but the crown and outward sign of pleasure. Come, this is life! How splendid it is! This is how I would like to live!"

"Why, who prevents you?" said Levin, smiling.

"No, you're a lucky man! You've got everything you like. You like horses—and you have them; dogs—you have them; shooting—you have it; farming—you have it."

"Perhaps because I rejoice in what I have, and don't bother about what I haven't," said Levin, thinking of Kitty.

Stepan Arkadyevich comprehended, looked at him, but said nothing.

Levin was grateful to Oblonsky for noticing, with his never failing tact, that he dreaded conversation about the Shcherbatskys, and so saying nothing about them. But now Levin was longing to find out what was tormenting him so, yet he had not the courage to begin.

"Come, tell me how things are going with you," said Levin, reminding himself that it was not nice of him to think only of himself.

Stepan Arkadyevich's eyes sparkled merrily.

"You don't agree, I know, that one can be fond of fresh rolls when one has had one's rations of bread—to your mind it's a crime; but I don't count life as life without love," he said, taking Levin's question in his own way. "What am I to do? I'm made that way. And really, one does so little harm to anyone, and gives oneself so much pleasure . . ."

"What! Is there something new, then?" queried Levin.

"Yes, my boy, there is! There, do you see, you know the Ossian type of woman[2] . . . Women such as one sees in dreams . . . Well, these women are sometimes to be met in reality . . . and these women are terrible. Woman, you know, is such a subject that however much you study it, it's always perfectly fresh."

"Well, then, it would be better not to study it."

"No. Some mathematician has said that enjoyment lies in the search for truth, not finding it."

Levin listened in silence, and in spite of all the efforts he made, he

[2] I.e., sensuous, romantic. Ossianic poems, purporting to be translations from a third-century Gaelic bard, Ossian, by James Macpherson (1736-96), were essentially the creation of Macpherson.

could not in the least sympathize with the feelings of his friend and understand his sentiments and the charm of studying such women.

CHAPTER FIFTEEN

The place fixed on for the shooting was not far above a stream in a little aspen copse. On reaching the copse, Levin got out of the trap and led Oblonsky to a corner of a mossy, swampy glade, already quite free from snow. He went back himself to a double birch tree on the other side, and leaning his gun on the fork of a dead lower branch, he took off his full overcoat, fastened his belt again, and worked his arms to see if they were free.

Gray old Laska, who had followed them, sat down warily opposite him and pricked up her ears. The sun was setting behind a thick forest, and in the glow of sunset the birch trees dotted about in the aspen copse stood out clearly with their hanging twigs, and their buds swollen almost to bursting.

From the thickest part of the copse, where the snow still remained, came the faint sound of narrow winding threads of water running away. Tiny birds twittered, and now and then fluttered from tree to tree.

In the pauses of complete stillness there came the rustle of last year's leaves, stirred by the thawing of the earth and the growth of the grass.

"Imagine! One can hear and see the grass growing!" Levin said to himself, noticing a wet, slate-colored aspen leaf moving beside a blade of young grass. He stood, listened, and sometimes gazed down at the wet mossy ground, sometimes at Laska listening all alert, sometimes at the sea of bare tree tops that stretched on the slope below him, sometimes at the darkening sky, covered with white streaks of cloud.

A hawk flew high over a forest far away with a slow sweep of its wings; another flew with exactly the same motion in the same direction and vanished. The birds twittered more and more loudly and busily in the thicket. An owl hooted not far off, and Laska, starting, stepped cautiously a few steps forward, and putting her head on one side, began to listen intently. Beyond the stream was heard the cuckoo. Twice she uttered her usual cuckoo call, and then gave a hoarse, hurried call and broke down.

"Imagine! The cuckoo already!" said Stepan Arkadyevich, coming out from behind a bush .

"Yes, I hear it," answered Levin, reluctantly breaking the stillness with his voice, which sounded harsh to him. "Now it's coming!"

Stepan Arkadyevich's figure again went behind the bush, and Levin saw nothing but the bright flash of a match, followed by the red glow and blue smoke of a cigarette.

"Click! click!" came the snapping sound as Stepan Arkadyevich cocked his gun.

"What's that cry?" asked Oblonsky, drawing Levin's attention to a prolonged cry, as though a colt were whinnying in a high voice, in play.

"Oh, don't you know it? That's the hare. But enough talking! Listen, it's flying!" Levin almost shrieked, cocking his gun.

They heard a shrill whistle in the distance, and in the exact time, so well known to the sportsman, two seconds later—another, a third, and after the third whistle the hoarse, guttural cry could be heard.

Levin looked about him to right and to left, and there, just facing him against the dusky blue sky above the confused mass of tender shoots of the aspens, he saw the flying bird. It was flying straight toward him; the guttural cry, like the sound made by tearing tightly stretched cloth, sounded close to his ear; the long beak and neck of the bird could be seen, and at the very instant when Levin was taking aim, behind the bush where Oblonsky stood, there was a flash of red lightning: the bird dropped like an arrow, and darted upward again. Again came the red flash and the sound of a blow, and fluttering its wings as though trying to keep up in the air, the bird halted, stopped still an instant, and fell with a heavy splash on the slushy ground.

"Can I have missed it?" shouted Stepan Arkadyevich, who could not see because of the smoke.

"Here it is!" said Levin, pointing to Laska, who, with one ear raised, wagged the end of her shaggy tail, came slowly back as though she would prolong the pleasure, and seeming almost to smile, brought the dead bird to her master. "Well, I'm glad you were successful," said Levin, who, at the same time felt envious because he had not succeeded in shooting the snipe.

"It was a bad shot from the right barrel," Stepan Arkadyevich responded, loading his gun. "Sh. . . it's flying!"

The shrill whistles rapidly following one another were heard again. Two snipe, playing and chasing one another, and only whistling, not crying, flew straight at the very heads of the sportsmen. There was the report of four shots, and, like swallows, the snipe turned swift somersaults in the air and vanished from sight.

⬥

The shooting was splendid. Stepan Arkadyevich shot two more birds and Levin two, one of which was not found. It began to get dark. Venus, bright and silvery, shone with her soft light low down in the west behind the birch trees, and high up in the east the red lights of Arcturus twinkled. Over his head Levin made out the stars of the Great Bear and lost them again. The snipe had ceased flying; but Levin resolved to stay a little longer, till Venus, which he saw below a branch of birch, should be above it, and the stars of the Great Bear should be perfectly plain. Venus had risen above the branch, and the chariot of the Great Bear with its shaft was now plainly visible against the dark blue sky, yet still he waited.

"Isn't it time to go home?" said Stepan Arkadyevich.

It was quite still now in the copse, and not a bird was stirring.

"Let's stay a little while," answered Levin.

"As you like."

They were standing now about fifteen paces from one another.

"Stiva!" said Levin unexpectedly: "how is it you don't tell me whether your sister-in-law's married yet, or when she's going to be?"

Levin felt so resolute and serene that he was convinced no answer could affect him. But he had never dreamed of what Stepan Arkadyevich replied.

"She's never thought of being married, and isn't thinking of it; but she's very ill, and the doctors have sent her abroad. They're afraid she may not live."

"What!" cried Levin. "Very ill? What is wrong with her? How has she . . . ?"

While they were saying this, Laska, with ears pricked up, was looking upward at the sky, and reproachfully at them.

"They have chosen a time to talk," she was thinking. "It's on the wing . . . Here it is, yes, it is. They'll miss it," thought Laska.

But at that very instant both suddenly heard a shrill whistle that seemed to hit them on their ears, and both suddenly seized their guns and two flashes gleamed, and two reports sounded at the very same instant. The snipe flying high above instantly folded its wings and fell into a thicket, bending down the delicate shoots.

"Splendid! Together!" cried Levin, and he ran with Laska into the thicket to look for the snipe.

"Oh, yes, what was it that was unpleasant?" he wondered. "Yes, Kitty's ill . . . Well, it can't be helped; I'm very sorry," he thought.

"She's found it! Isn't she a clever thing?" he said, taking the warm bird from Laska's mouth and packing it into the almost full game bag. "I've got it, Stiva!" he shouted.

CHAPTER SIXTEEN

On the way home, Levin asked all the details of Kitty's illness and the Shcherbatskys' plans, and though he would have been ashamed to admit it, he was pleased at what he heard. He was pleased that there was still hope, and still more pleased that she who had made him suffer so much was now suffering. But when Stepan Arkadyevich began to speak of the causes of Kitty's illness, and mentioned Vronsky's name, Levin cut him short.

"I have no right whatever to know family matters, and, to tell the truth, no interest in them either."

Stepan Arkadyevich smiled hardly perceptibly, catching the instantaneous change he knew so well in Levin's face, which had become as gloomy as it had been bright a minute before.

"Have you quite settled about the forest with Ryabinin?" asked Levin.

"Yes, it's settled. The price is excellent; thirty-eight thousand.

Eight at once, and the rest in six years. I've been bothering about it for a long time. No one would give more."

"Then you've as good as given away your forest for nothing," said Levin gloomily.

"How do you mean for nothing?" said Stepan Arkadyevich with a good-humored smile, knowing that nothing would be right in Levin's eyes now.

"Because the forest is worth at least a hundred and fifty rubles an acre," answered Levin.

"Oh, these farmers!" said Stepan Arkadyevich playfully.

"Your tone of contempt for us poor townsfolk! . . . But when it comes to business, we do it better than anyone. I assure you I have figured it all out," he said, "and the forest is bringing a very good price—so much so that I'm afraid of this fellow's changing his mind, in fact. You know, it's not 'timber,' " said Stepan Arkadyevich, hoping by this distinction to convince Levin completely of the unfairness of his doubts. "And it won't run to more than forty cubic yards of wood per acre, and he's paying me at the rate of seventy rubles an acre."

Levin smiled contemptuously. "I know," he thought, "that manner, not only in him, but in all city people, who, after being twice in ten years in the country, pick up two or three phrases and use them in season and out of season, firmly persuaded that they know all about it. 'Timber, run to, so many yards per acre.' He says those words without understanding them himself."

"I wouldn't attempt to teach you what you write about in your office," said he, "and if need arose, I should come to you to ask about it. But you're so positive you know all the lore of the forest. It's difficult. Have you counted the trees?"

"How count the trees?" said Stepan Arkadyevich, laughing, still trying to draw his friend out of his ill-temper. "Although a great mind could count the sands of the sea, the rays of the planets . . ." [1]

"Oh, well, the higher power of Ryabinin can. Not a single merchant ever buys a forest without counting the trees, unless they get it for nothing, as you're doing now. I know your forest. I go hunting there every year, and it's worth a hundred and fifty rubles an acre,

[1] By G. Derzhavin (1743-1816), from his ode "God."

cash, while he's giving you sixty by installments. So that in fact you're making him a present of thirty thousand."

"Come, don't let your imagination run away with you," said Stepan Arkadyevich piteously. "Why didn't anyone offer it, then?"

"Why, because he has an understanding with the merchants; he's bought them off. I've dealt with all of them; I know them. They're not merchants, you know: they're speculators. He wouldn't look at a bargain that gave him ten, fifteen per cent profit, but holds back to buy a ruble's worth for twenty kopeks."

"Well, enough of it! You're in a bad mood today."

"Not at all," said Levin gloomily, as they drove up to the house.

At the steps there stood a trap tightly covered with iron and leather, with a sleek horse tightly harnessed with broad collar straps. In the trap sat the chubby, tightly belted clerk who served Ryabinin as coachman. Ryabinin himself was already in the house, and met the friends in the hall. Ryabinin was a tall, thinnish, middle-aged man, with a mustache and a projecting clean-shaven chin, and prominent muddy-looking eyes. He was dressed in a long-skirted blue coat, with buttons below the waist at the back, and wore high boots wrinkled over the ankles and straight over the calf, with big galoshes drawn over them. He rubbed his face with his handkerchief, and wrapping around him his coat, which was extremely well positioned as it was, he greeted them with a smile, holding out his hand to Stepan Arkadyevich as though he wanted to catch something.

"So here you are," said Stepan Arkadyevich, giving him his hand. "That's marvelous."

"I did not venture to disregard Your Excellency's commands, though the road was extremely bad. I absolutely walked the whole way, but I am here on time. Konstantin Dmitrievich, my respects"; he turned to Levin, trying to seize his hand too. But Levin, scowling, pretended he did not notice his hand, and took out the snipe. "Your Honors have been diverting yourselves with the chase? What kind of bird may it be, pray?" added Ryabinin, looking contemptuously at the snipe: "a great delicacy, I suppose." And he shook his head disapprovingly, as though he had grave doubts whether this game was worth the candle.

"Would you like to go into my study?" Levin said in French to

Stepan Arkadyevich, scowling morosely. "Go into my study; you can talk there."

"As you wish," said Ryabinin with contemptuous dignity, as though wishing to make it felt that others might be in difficulties as to how to behave, but that he could never be in any difficulty about anything.

On entering the study, Ryabinin looked about, as his habit was, as though seeking the icon, but when he had found it, he did not cross himself. He scanned the bookcases and bookshelves, and with the same dubious air with which he had regarded the snipe, he smiled contemptuously and shook his head disapprovingly, as though by no means willing to admit that this game was worth the candle.

"Well, have you brought the money?" asked Oblonsky. "Sit down."

"Oh, don't worry about the money. I've come to see you to talk it over."

"What is there to talk over? But do sit down."

"I don't mind if I do," said Ryabinin, sitting down and leaning his elbows on the back of his chair in a position of the intensest discomfort to himself. "You must yield, Prince. It would be too bad. The money is ready to the last kopek. as for paying the money down, there'll be no hitch there."

Levin, who had meanwhile been putting his gun away in the cupboard, was just going out the door, but catching the merchant's words, he stopped.

"Why, you've got the forest for nothing as it is," he said. "He came to me too late, or I'd have fixed the price for him."

Ryabinin got up, and in silence, with a smile, he looked Levin up and down.

"Very tight about money is Konstantin Dmitrievich," he said with a smile, turning to Stepan Arkadyevich; "there's positively no dealing with him. I was bargaining for some wheat from him, and a pretty price I offered too."

"Why should I give you my goods for nothing? I didn't pick it up on the ground, or steal it either."

"Heaven help us! Nowadays there's no chance at all of stealing. With the public courts and everything done in style, nowadays there's no question of stealing. We are just talking things over like gentlemen. His Excellency's asking too much for the forest. I can't make any profit on it. I must ask for a little concession."

"But is the thing settled between you or not? If it's settled, it's useless haggling; but if it's not," said Levin, "I'll buy the forest."

The smile vanished at once from Ryabinin's face. A hawklike, greedy, cruel expression was left upon it. With rapid, bony fingers he unbuttoned his coat, revealing a shirt, bronze vest buttons, and a watch chain, and quickly pulled out a fat old wallet.

"Here you are, the forest is mine," he said, crossing himself quickly and holding out his hand. "Take the money; it's my forest. That's Ryabinin's way of doing business; he doesn't haggle over every kopek," he added, scowling and waving the wallet.

"I wouldn't be in a hurry if I were you," said Levin.

"Come, really," said Oblonsky in surprise, "I've given my word."

Levin went out of the room, slamming the door. Ryabinin looked toward the door and shook his head with a smile.

"It's all childishness—positively nothing but childishness. Why, I'm buying it, upon my honor, simply, believe me, for the glory of it so that Ryabinin, and no one else, will have bought Oblonsky's copse. And as to the profits, why, I must make what God gives. In God's name. If you would kindly sign the title . . ."

Within an hour the merchant, carefully patting his big overcoat into place, and hooking it up, with the agreement in his pocket, seated himself in his tightly covered trap and drove homeward.

"Ugh, these gentry!" he said to the clerk. "They—they're a nice bunch!"

"That's so," responded the clerk, handing him the reins and buttoning the leather apron. "But I can congratulate you on the purchase, Mikhail Ignatich?"

"Well, well . . ."

CHAPTER SEVENTEEN

Stepan Arkadyevich went upstairs with his pocket bulging with notes, which the merchant had paid him for three months in advance. The business of the forest was over, the money in his pocket; their shooting had been excellent, and Stepan Arkadyevich was in the happiest frame of mind, and so he felt especially anxious to dissipate the ill-humor that had come upon Levin. He wanted to finish the day at supper as pleasantly as it had been begun.

Levin certainly was out of humor, and in spite of his desire to be affectionate and cordial to his charming visitor, he could not control his mood. The intoxication of the news that Kitty was not married had gradually begun to work upon him.

Kitty was not married but ill, and ill from love for a man who had slighted her. This slight, it seems, fell upon him. Vronsky had slighted her, and she had slighted him, Levin. Consequently Vronsky had the right to despise Levin, and therefore he was his enemy. But all this Levin did not think out. He vaguely felt that there was something in it insulting to him, and he was not angry now at what had disturbed him but at everything that presented itself. The stupid sale of the forest, the fraud practiced upon Oblonsky and concluded in his house, exasperated him.

"Well, finished?" he said, meeting Stepan Arkadyevich upstairs. "Would you like supper?"

"Well, I wouldn't say no to it. What an appetite I get in the country! Wonderful! Why didn't you offer Ryabinin something?"

"Oh, damn him!"

"Still, how you treat him!" said Oblonsky. "You didn't even shake hands with him. Why not shake hands with him?"

"Because I don't shake hands with a footman, and a footman's a hundred times better than he is."

"What a reactionary you are, really! What about the amalgamation of classes?" said Oblonsky.

"Anyone who likes amalgamating is welcome to it, but it sickens me."

"You're a reactionary, I see."

"Really, I have never considered what I am. I am Konstantin Levin, and nothing else."

"And Konstantin Levin very much in a bad temper," said Stepan Arkadyevich, smiling.

"Yes, I am in a bad mood, and do you know why? Because—excuse me—of your stupid sale . . ."

Stepan Arkadyevich frowned good-naturedly, like one who feels himself upset and attacked for no fault of his own.

"Come, enough about it!" he said. "When did anybody ever sell anything without being told immediately after the sale, 'It was worth much more'? But when one wants to sell, no one will give anything . . . No, I see you've a grudge against that unlucky Ryabinin."

"Maybe I have. And do you know why? You'll say again that I'm a reactionary, or some other terrible word; but all the same it does annoy and anger me to see on all sides the impoverishing of the nobility to which I belong, and, in spite of the amalgamation of classes, I'm glad to belong. And their impoverishment is not due to extravagance—that would be nothing; living in good style—that's the proper thing for noblemen: it's only the nobles who know how to do it. Now the peasants about us buy land, and I don't mind that. The gentleman does nothing, while the peasant works and supplants the idle man. That's as it should be. And I'm very glad for the peasants. But I do mind seeing the process of impoverishment from a sort of—I don't know what to call it—innocence. Here a Polish speculator bought for half its value a magnificent estate from a young lady who lives in Nice. And there a merchant will get three acres of land worth ten rubles as security for the loan of one ruble. Here, for no reason, you've made that rascal a present of thirty thousand rubles."

"Well, what should I have done? Count every tree?"

"Of course, they must be counted. You didn't count them, but Ryabinin did. Ryabinin's children will have means of livelihood and education, while yours maybe will not!"

"Well, you must excuse me, but there's something despicable in this counting. We have our business and they have theirs, and they must make their profit. Anyway, the thing's done, and that's the end of it. And here come poached eggs, my favorite dish. And Agafya Mikhailovna will give us that marvelous herb vodka . . ."

Stepan Arkadyevich sat down at the table and began joking with Agafya Mikhailovna, assuring her that it was long since he had tasted such a dinner and such a supper.

"Well, you do praise it, anyway," said Agafya Mikhailovna, "but Konstantin Dmitrievich, give him what you will—a crust of bread—he'll eat it and walk away."

Though Levin tried to control himself, he was gloomy and silent. He wanted to put one question to Stepan Arkadyevich, but he could not bring himself to the point, and could not find the words or the moment in which to put it. Stepan Arkadyevich had gone down to his room, undressed, again washed, and attired in a goffered nightshirt, he had got into bed, but Levin still lingered in his room, talking of various trifling matters, and not daring to ask what he wanted to know.

"How wonderfully they make this soap," he said, gazing at a piece of soap he was handling, which Agafya Mikhailovna had made ready for the visitor but Oblonsky had not used. "Just look; why, it's a work of art."

"Yes, everything's brought to such a pitch of perfection nowadays," said Stepan Arkadyevich, with a moist and blissful yawn. "The theater, for instance, and the entertainments . . . a-a-a!" he yawned. "The electric light everywhere . . . a-a-a!"

"Yes, the electric light," said Levin. "Yes. Oh, and where's Vronsky now?" he asked suddenly, laying down the soap.

"Vronsky?" said Stepan Arkadyevich, checking his yawn; "he's in Petersburg. He left soon after you did, and he's not once been in Moscow since. And do you know, Kostya, I'll tell you the truth," he went on, leaning his elbow on the table and propping on his hand his handsome ruddy face, in which his moist, good-natured, sleepy eyes shone like stars. "It's your own fault. You took fright at the sight of your rival. But, as I told you at the time, I couldn't say which had the better chance. Why didn't you fight it out? I told you at the time that . . ." He yawned inwardly, without opening his mouth.

"Does he know, or doesn't he, that I did make a proposal?" Levin wondered, gazing at him. "Yes, there's something sly, diplomatic in his face," and feeling that he was blushing, he looked Stepan Arkadyevich straight in the face without speaking.

"If there was anything on her part at that time, it was nothing but a superficial attraction," pursued Oblonsky. "His being such a perfect aristocrat, you know, and his future position in society, had an influence not with her but with her mother."

Levin scowled. The humiliation of his rejection stung him to the heart, as though it was a fresh wound he had only just received. But he was at home, and the walls of home are a support.

"Wait, wait," he began, interrupting Oblonsky. "You talk of his being an aristocrat. But allow me to ask what it consists in, that aristocracy of Vronsky or of anybody else, beside which I can be looked down upon? You consider Vronsky an aristocrat, but I don't. A man whose father crawled up from nothing at all by intrigue, and whose mother—God knows whom she wasn't mixed up with . . . No, excuse me, but I consider myself aristocratic, and people like me, who can point back in the past to three or four honorable generations of their family, of the highest degree of breeding (talent and intellect, of course that's another matter), and have never curried favor with anyone, never depended on anyone for anything, like my father and my grandfather. And I know many such. You think it despicable of me to count the trees in my forest, while you make Ryabinin a present of thirty thousand; but you get rents from your lands and I don't know what, while I don't, and so I prize what's come to me from my ancestors or been won by hard work . . . We are aristocrats, and not those who can only exist by favor of the powerful of this world, and who can be bought for twenty kopeks."

"Well, but whom are you attacking? I agree with you," said Stepan Arkadyevich, sincerely and genially; though he was aware that in the class of those who could be bought for twenty kopeks Levin was counting him too. Levin's excitement gave him genuine pleasure. "Whom are you attacking? Though a good deal is not true that you say about Vronsky, but I won't talk about that. I tell you bluntly, if I were you, I would go back with me to Moscow, and—"

"No; I don't know whether you know it or not, but I don't care. And I tell you—I did propose and was rejected, and Katerina Alek-

sandrovna is nothing now to me but a painful and humiliating remi-
niscence."

"Why? What nonsense!"

"But we won't talk about it. Please forgive me if I've been nasty,"
said Levin. Now that he had opened his heart, he became as he had
been in the morning. "You're not angry with me, Stiva? Please don't
be angry," he said, and, smiling, he took his hand.

"Of course not; not a bit, and no reason to be. I'm glad we've spoken openly. And do you know, shooting in the early morning is usually good—why not go? I couldn't go to sleep after it, but I'll go
straight from there to the station."

"Excellent."

CHAPTER EIGHTEEN

Although Vronsky's whole inner life was absorbed in his passion, his
external life unalterably and inevitably followed along the old accustomed lines of his social and regimental ties and interests. The interests of his regiment took an important place in Vronsky's life, both
because he was fond of the regiment, and because the regiment was
fond of him. And they were not only fond of Vronsky, they respected
him too, and were proud of him; proud that this man, with his
immense wealth, his brilliant education and abilities, and the path
open before him to every kind of success, distinction, and ambition,
had disregarded all that, and of all the interests of life had the interests of his regiment and his comrades nearest to his heart. Vronsky
was aware of his comrades' opinion of him, and in addition to his liking for this life, he felt bound to keep up that reputation.

It need not be said that he did not speak of his love to any of his
comrades, nor did he betray his secret even in the wildest drinking
bouts (though indeed he was never so drunk as to lose all control of
himself). And he shut up any of his thoughtless comrades who
attempted to allude to his liaison. But in spite of that, his love was
known to the whole town; everyone guessed more or less correctly at
his relations with Madame Karenina. The majority of the younger
men envied him for just what was the most trying factor in his love—

the exalted position of Karenin, and the consequent publicity of their connection in society.

The greater number of the young women, who envied Anna and had long been weary of hearing her called *virtuous*, rejoiced at the fulfillment of their predictions, and were only waiting for a decisive turn in public opinion to fall upon her with the full weight of their scorn. They were already preparing the handfuls of mud they would fling at her when the right moment arrived. Most of the older people and those socially prominent were displeased at the prospect of the impending scandal in society.

Vronsky's mother, on hearing of his liaison, was at first pleased by it, because nothing to her mind gave such a finishing touch to a brilliant young man as an affair in the highest society; she was pleased, too, that Madame Karenina, who had so taken her fancy, and had talked so much of her son, was, after all, just like all other pretty and well-bred women—at least according to the Countess Vronskaya's ideas. But she had heard of late that her son had refused a position offered him of great importance to his career, simply in order to remain in the regiment, where he could constantly see Madame Karenina. She learned that important people were displeased with him because of this, and she changed her opinion. She was vexed, too, that from all she could learn of this liaison it was not that brilliant, graceful, worldly liaison which she would have welcomed, but a sort of Werther-like[1] desperate passion, so she was told, which might well lead him into something foolish. She had not seen him since his abrupt departure from Moscow, and she sent her elder son to bid him come to see her.

This elder son, too, was displeased with his younger brother. He did not distinguish what sort of love his might be, big or little, passionate or passionless, lasting or passing (he kept a ballet girl himself, though he was the father of a family, so he was lenient in this matter), but, knowing that this love affair displeased those whom it was necessary to please, he did not approve of his brother's conduct.

Besides the service and society, Vronsky had another great interest—horses; he was passionately fond of horses.

[1] The romantic hero of Goethe's *Werther*, who commits suicide.

That year races and a steeplechase had been arranged for the officers. Vronsky had put his name down, bought a thoroughbred English mare, and in spite of his love affair, he was looking forward to the races with intense, though reserved, excitement. . .

These two passions did not interfere with one another. On the contrary, he needed occupation and distraction quite apart from his love, so as to refresh and rest himself from the violent emotions that agitated him.

CHAPTER NINETEEN

On the day of the races at Krasnoe Selo, Vronsky had come earlier than usual to eat beefsteak in the officers' mess of the regiment. He had no need to be in strict training, as he had very quickly been brought down to the required weight of one hundred and sixty pounds, but still he had to avoid gaining weight, and he avoided starchy foods and desserts. He sat with his coat unbuttoned over a white vest, resting both elbows on the table, and while waiting for the steak he had ordered he looked at a French novel that lay open on his plate. He was looking at the book only to avoid conversation with the officers coming in and out; he was thinking.

He was thinking of Anna's promise to see him that day after the races. But he had not seen her for three days, and as her husband had just returned from abroad, he did not know whether she would be able to meet him today or not, and he did not know how to find out. He had last seen her at his cousin Betsy's summer villa. He visited the Karenins' summer villa as rarely as possible. Now he wanted to go there, and he pondered how to do it.

"Of course I can say Betsy has sent me to ask whether she's coming to the races. Of course, I'll go," he decided, lifting his head from the book. And as he vividly pictured the happiness of seeing her, his face lighted up.

"Send to my house, and tell them to prepare the troika as quickly as they can," he said to the servant, who handed him the steak on a hot silver dish, and moving the dish toward him, he began eating.

From the billiard room next door came the sound of balls knocking, of talk and laughter. Two officers appeared at the entrance door: one, a young fellow, with a feeble, delicate face, who had lately joined the regiment from the Corps of Pages; the other, a plump, elderly officer, with a bracelet on his wrist, and little eyes, lost in fat.

Vronsky glanced at them, frowned, and looking down at his book as though he had not noticed them, he proceeded to eat and read at the same time.

"What? Fortifying yourself for your work?" said the plump officer, sitting down beside him.

"As you see," responded Vronsky, knitting his brows, wiping his mouth, and not looking at the officer.

"So you're not afraid of getting fat?" said the latter, turning a chair around for the young officer.

"What?" said Vronsky angrily, making a wry face of disgust, and showing his even teeth.

"You're not afraid of getting fat?"

"Waiter, sherry!" said Vronsky without replying, and moving the book to the other side of him, he went on reading.

The plump officer took up the list of wines and turned to the young officer.

"You choose what we're to drink," he said, handing him the card and looking at him.

"Rhine wine, please," said the young officer, stealing a timid glance at Vronsky, and trying to pull his scarcely visible mustache. Seeing that Vronsky did not turn around, the young officer got up.

"Let's go into the billiard room," he said.

The plump officer rose submissively, and they moved toward the door.

At that moment there walked into the room the tall and well-built Captain Yashvin. Nodding with an air of lofty contempt to the two officers, he went up to Vronsky.

"Ah! Here he is!" he cried, bringing his big hand down heavily on his shoulder strap. Vronsky looked up angrily, but his face lighted up immediately with his characteristic expression of genial and firm friendliness.

"That's it, Aleksey," said the captain, in his loud baritone. "You must just eat a mouthful, now, and drink only one tiny glass."

"Oh, I'm not hungry."

"There go the inseparables," Yashvin said, glancing sarcastically at the two officers who were at that instant leaving the room. And he bent his long legs, encased in tight riding breeches, and sat down in the chair, which was too low for him, so that his knees were cramped up at a sharp angle.

"Why didn't you show up at the Krasnoe Selo Theater yesterday? Numerova wasn't at all bad. Where were you?"

"I stayed late at the Tverskoys'," said Vronsky.

"Ah!" Yashvin responded.

Yashvin, a gambler and a rake, a man not merely without moral principles, but of immoral principles—Yashvin was Vronsky's best friend in the regiment. Vronsky liked him both for his exceptional physical strength, which he showed for the most part by being able to drink like a fish, and do without sleep without being in the slightest degree affected by it; and for his great strength of character, which he showed in his relations with his comrades and superior officers, commanding both fear and respect, and also at cards, when he would play for tens of thousands and, regardless of how much he might have drunk, always with such skill and control that he was considered the best player at the English Club. Vronsky respected and liked Yashvin particularly because he felt that Yashvin liked him, not for his name and his money, but for himself. And of all men he was the only one to whom Vronsky would have liked to speak of his love. He felt that Yashvin, in spite of his apparent contempt for every sort of feeling, was the only man who could, so he thought, comprehend the intense passion which now filled his whole life. Moreover, he felt certain that Yashvin took no delight in gossip and scandal, and interpreted his feeling properly, that is to say, knew and believed that this passion was not a joke, not a pastime, but something more serious and important.

Vronsky had never spoken to him of his love, but he was aware that he knew all about it, and that he put the right interpretation on it, and he was glad to read this in his eyes.

"Ah, yes," he said, to the announcement that Vronsky had been at the Tverskoys'; and his black eyes shining, he plucked at his left mustache and began twisting it into his mouth, a bad habit he had.

"Well, and what did you do yesterday? Win anything?" asked Vronsky.

"Eight thousand. But three don't count; he won't pay up."

"Oh, then you can afford to lose on me," said Vronsky, laughing. (Yashvin had bet heavily on Vronsky's horse in the races.)

"No chance of my losing. Makhotin's the only one that's risky."

And the conversation passed to forecasts of the coming race, the only thing Vronsky could think of just now.

"Come along, I've finished," said Vronsky, and getting up, he went to the door. Yashvin got up too, stretching his long legs and his long back.

"It's too early for me to dine, but I must have a drink. I'll come along in a moment. Hey, wine!" he shouted in his rich voice, which always rang out so loudly at drill, and started the windows rattling now.

"No, I don't want any," he shouted again immediately after. "You're going home, so I'll go with you."

And he walked out with Vronsky.

CHAPTER TWENTY

Vronsky was staying in a roomy, clean Finnish hut, divided into two by a partition. Petritsky lived with him in camp too. Petritsky was asleep when Vronsky and Yashvin came into the hut.

"Get up, don't go on sleeping," said Yashvin, going behind the partition and giving Petritsky, who was lying with ruffled hair and with his nose in the pillow, a prod on the shoulder.

Petritsky jumped suddenly to his knees and looked around.

"Your brother's been here," he said to Vronsky. "He woke me up, damn him, and said he'd look in again." And pulling up the blanket, he flung himself back on the pillow. "Oh, do shut up, Yashvin!" he said, getting furious with Yashvin, who was pulling the blanket off him. "Shut up!" He turned over and opened his eyes. "You'd better tell me what to drink; such a foul taste in my mouth that—"

"Vodka's better than anything!" boomed Yashvin.

"Tereshchenko! Vodka for your master, and cucumbers," he shouted, obviously taking pleasure in the sound of his own voice.

"Vodka, do you think? Eh?" said Petritsky, blinking and rubbing his eyes. "And you'll drink something? All right, then, we'll have a drink together! Vronsky, have a drink?" said Petritsky, getting up and wrapping a tigerskin blanket around him. He went to the door of the partition wall, raised his hands, and sang in French, "There was a king in Th-u-le.' [1] Vronsky, will you have a drink?"

"Go to hell," said Vronsky, putting on the coat his valet handed him.

"Where are you off to?" asked Yashvin. "Oh, here is your troika," he added, seeing the carriage drive up.

"To the stables, and I've got to see Bryansky, too, about the horses," said Vronsky.

Vronsky had as a fact promised to call at Bryansky's, some seven miles from Peterhof, and to bring him some money for the horses; and he hoped to have time to do that too. But his comrades were at once aware that he was not only going there.

Petritsky, still humming, winked and made a pout with his lips, as though to say: "Oh, yes, we know your Bryansky."

"Careful you're not late!" was Yashvin's only comment; and to change the conversation: "How's my roan? Is he doing all right?" he inquired, looking out of the window at the middle horse, which he had sold to Vronsky.

"Wait!" cried Petritsky to Vronsky as he was just going out. "Your brother left a letter and a note for you. Wait a minute; where are they?"

Vronsky stopped.

"Well, where are they?"

"Where are they? That's exactly the question!" said Petritsky solemnly, moving his forefinger upward from his nose.

"Come, tell me; this is silly!" said Vronsky, smiling.

"I haven't lighted the fire. It's here somewhere."

"Come, enough fooling! Where is the letter!"

"No, I've forgotten. Or was it a dream? Wait a minute, wait a

---

[1] An aria from Gounod's opera *Faust*, which was based on Goethe's drama.

minute! But what's the use of getting in a rage. If you'd drunk four bottles yesterday as I did you'd forget where you were lying. Wait a minute, I'll remember!"

Petritsky went behind the partition and lay down on his bed.

"Wait a minute! This was how I was lying, and this was how he was standing. Yes—yes—yes . . . Here it is!" And Petritsky pulled a letter out from under the mattress, where he had hidden it.

Vronsky took the letter and his brother's note. It was the letter he was expecting—from his mother, reproaching him for not having been to see her—and the note was from his brother, saying that he must have a little talk with him. Vronsky knew that it was all about the same thing. "What business is it of theirs!" he thought, and crumpling up the letters, he thrust them between the buttons of his coat, intending to read them carefully on the road. On the porch of the hut he was met by two officers, one of his regiment and one of another.

Vronsky's quarters were always a meeting place for all the officers.

"Where are you off to?"

"I must go to Peterhof."

"Has the mare come from Tsarskoe?"

"Yes, but I've not seen her yet."

"They say Makhotin's Gladiator's lame."

"Nonsense! But how are you going to race in this mud?" said the other.

"Here are my saviors!" cried Petritsky, seeing them come in. Before him stood the orderly with a tray of vodka and pickled cucumbers. "Here's Yashvin ordering me to drink to freshen up."

"Well, you did give it to us yesterday," said one of those who had come in; "you didn't let us get a wink of sleep all night."

"Oh, didn't we make a pretty finish!" said Petritsky. "Volkov climbed out on the roof and began telling us how sad he was. I said: 'Let's have music, the funeral march!' He dropped asleep on the roof over the funeral march."

"Drink it up; you positively must drink the vodka, and then soda water and a lot of lemon," said Yashvin, standing over Petritsky like a mother making a child take medicine, "and then a little champagne—just a small bottle."

"Come, there's some sense in that. Wait a while, Vronsky. We'll all have a drink."

"No; good-by all of you. I'm not going to drink today."

"Why, are you gaining weight? All right, then, we must have it alone. Give us the club soda and lemon."

"Vronsky!" shouted someone when he was already outside.

"Well?"

"You'd better get your hair cut, it'll weigh you down, especially on the top."

Vronsky was in fact beginning, prematurely, to get a little bald. He laughed gaily, showing his even teeth, and pulling his cap over the bald patch, he went out and got into his carriage.

"To the stables!" he said, and was just pulling out the letters to read them through, when he thought better of it, and put off reading them so as not to distract his attention before looking at the mare. "Later! . . ."

CHAPTER TWENTY-ONE

The temporary stable, a wooden shed, had been put up close to the race track, and there his mare was to have been taken the previous day. He had not yet seen her there.

During the last few days he had not exercised her himself, but had put her in charge of the trainer, and so now he had no idea in what condition his mare had arrived yesterday and was today. He had scarcely got out of his carriage when his groom, the so-called stable boy, recognizing the carriage some way off, called the trainer. A lean Englishman, in high boots and a short jacket, clean shaven, except for a tuft below his chin, came to meet him, walking with the awkward gait of a jockey, his elbows sticking out and swaying from side to side.

"Well, how's Frou-Frou?" Vronsky asked in English.

"All right, sir," the Englishman's voice responded somewhere in the inside of his throat. "Better not go in," he added, touching his hat. "I've put a muzzle on her, and the mare's fidgety. Better not go in, it'll excite the mare."

"No, I'm going in. I want to look at her."

"Come along, then," said the Englishman, frowning, and speaking with his mouth shut, and, with swinging elbows, he went out in front with his loose gait.

They went into the little yard in front of the shed. A stable boy, spruce and smart in his holiday attire, met them with a broom in his hand, and followed them. In the shed there were five horses in their separate stalls, and Vronsky knew that his chief rival, Makhotin's Gladiator, a sixteen-hand chestnut horse, had been brought there, and must be standing among them. Even more than his mare, Vronsky longed to see Gladiator, whom he had never seen. But he knew that the etiquette of the race track dictated that it was not merely impossible for him to see the horse, but improper even to ask questions about him. Just as he was passing along the passage, the boy opened the door into the second horse box on the left, and Vronsky caught a glimpse of a big chestnut horse with white legs. He knew that this was Gladiator, but, with the feeling of a man turning away from the sight of another man's open letter, he turned around and went into Frou-Frou's stall.

"Here is the horse of Mak . . . Mak . . . I never can say the name," said the Englishman, over his shoulder, pointing his big finger and dirty nail toward Gladiator's stall.

"Makhotin? Yes, he's my most serious rival," said Vronsky.

"If you were riding him," said the Englishman, "I'd bet on you."

"Frou-Frou's more nervous; he's stronger," said Vronsky, smiling at the compliment to his riding.

"In a steeplechase it all depends on riding and on pluck," said the Englishman.

Of pluck—that is, energy and courage—Vronsky did not merely feel that he had enough; what was of far more importance, he was firmly convinced that no one in the world could have more of this "pluck" than he had.

"Don't you think more training was necessary?"

"Oh, no," answered the Englishman. "Please, don't speak loud. The mare's fidgety," he added, nodding toward the horse box, before which they were standing, and from which came the sound of restless stamping in the straw.

He opened the door, and Vronsky went into the horse box, dimly lighted by one little window. In the horse box stood a dark bay mare, with a muzzle on, picking at the fresh straw with her hoofs. Looking around him in the twilight of the horse box, Vronsky unconsciously took in once more in a comprehensive glance all the points of his favorite mare. Frou-Frou was a beast of medium size, not altogether free from blemish, from a breeder's point of view. She was small-boned all over; though her chest was extremely prominent in front, it was narrow. Her hindquarters were a little too tapered, and her legs, especially her hind legs, curved perceptibly inward. The muscles of both hind and fore legs were not very thick; but across her shoulders the mare was exceptionally broad, a peculiarity specially striking now that she was lean from training. The bones of her legs below the knees looked no thicker than a finger from in front, but were extraordinarily thick seen from the side. She looked, on the whole, except across the shoulders, squeezed in at the sides and drawn out in depth. But she had in the highest degree the quality that makes all defects forgotten: that quality was *blood*, the blood *that tells*, as the English expression has it. The muscles stood up sharply under the network of sinews, covered with the delicate, mobile skin, soft as satin, and they were hard as bone. Her lean head, with prominent, bright, spirited eyes, broadened out at the open nostrils, which showed the red blood in the cartilage within. Her whole figure, and especially her head, conveyed a certain expression of energy, and, at the same time, of softness. She was one of those creatures that seem mute only because the mechanism of their mouth does not allow them to speak.

To Vronsky, at any rate, it seemed that she understood all he felt at that moment, looking at her.

As soon as Vronsky went toward her, she drew in a deep breath, and, turning back her prominent eye till the white looked bloodshot, she started at the approaching figures from the opposite side, shaking her muzzle and shifting lightly from one leg to the other.

"There, you see how fidgety she is," said the Englishman.

"There, darling! There!" said Vronsky, going up to the mare and speaking soothingly to her.

But the nearer he came, the more excited she grew. Only when he stood by her head, she suddenly grew quieter, while the muscles quivered under her soft, delicate coat. Vronsky patted her strong neck, adjusted over her sharply defined withers a stray lock of her mane that had fallen on the wrong side, and moved his face near her dilated nostrils, as transparent as a bat's wing. She drew a loud breath and snorted out through her tense nostrils, started, pricked up her sharp ear, and put out her strong, black lip toward Vronsky, as though she would nip his sleeve. But remembering the muzzle, she shook it and again began restlessly stepping from one of her finely chiseled legs to the other.

"Quiet, darling, quiet!" he said, patting her again over her flank; and happy that his mare was in the best possible condition, he went out of the horse box.

The mare's excitement had infected Vronsky. He felt that his heart was throbbing, and that he, too, like the mare, longed to move, to bite; it was both dreadful and delicious.

"Well, I rely on you, then," he said to the Englishman; "half-past six on the track."

"All right," said the Englishman. "Oh, where are you going, my lord?" he asked suddenly, using the title "my lord," which he had scarcely ever used before.

Vronsky, in amazement, raised his head and stared, as he knew how to stare, not into the Englishman's eyes, but at his forehead, astounded at the impertinence of his question. But realizing that in asking this the Englishman had been looking at him not as an employer but as a jockey, he answered:

"I've got to go to Bryansky. I'll be home within an hour."

"How often I'm asked that question today!" he said to himself, and he blushed, a thing that rarely happened to him. The Englishman looked gravely at him; and as though he too knew where Vronsky was going, he added:

"The vital thing's to keep quiet before a race," said he; "don't get disturbed or upset about anything."

"All right," answered Vronsky, smiling; and jumping into his carriage, he told the man to drive to Peterhof.

Before he had driven many paces, the dark clouds that had been threatening rain all day broke, and there was a heavy downpour.

"What a pity!" thought Vronsky, putting up the roof of the carriage. "It was muddy before, now it will be an absolute swamp." As he sat in solitude in the closed carriage, he took out his mother's letter and his brother's note, and read them through.

Yes, it was the same thing over and over again. Everyone, his mother, his brother, everyone thought fit to interfere in the affairs of his heart. This interference aroused in him a feeling of angry hatred—a feeling he had rarely known before. "What business is it of theirs? Why does everybody feel called upon to concern himself about me? And why do they worry me so? Just because they see that this is something they can't understand. If it were a common, vulgar, worldly intrigue, they would have left me alone. They feel that this is something different, that this is not a mere pastime, that this woman is dearer to me than life. And this is incomprehensible, and that's why it annoys them. Whatever our destiny is or may be, we have made it ourselves, and we do not complain of it," he said, in the word "we" linking himself with Anna. "No, they must teach us how to live. They haven't an idea of what happiness is; they don't know that without our love, for us there is neither happiness nor unhappiness—no life at all," he thought.

He was angry with all of them for their interference just because he felt in his soul that they, all these people, were right. He felt that the love that bound him to Anna was not a momentary impulse, which would pass, as worldly intrigues do pass, leaving no other traces in the life of either but pleasant or unpleasant memories. He felt all the torture of his own and her position, all the difficulty there was for them, conspicuous as they were in the eyes of the whole world, in concealing their love, in lying, deceiving, feigning, and continually thinking of others, when the passion that united them was so intense that they were both oblivious of everything else but their love.

He vividly recalled all the constantly recurring instances of inevitable necessity for lying and deceit, which were so against his natural bent. He recalled particularly vividly the shame he had more than once detected in her at this necessity for lying and deceit. And he experienced the strange feeling that had sometimes come upon him since his secret love for Anna. This was a feeling of loathing for something—whether for Aleksey Aleksandrovich, or for himself, or for the whole world, he could not have said. But he always drove away this strange feeling. Now, too, he shook it off and continued the thread of his thoughts.

"Yes, she was unhappy before, but proud and at peace; and now she cannot be at peace and feel secure in her dignity, though she does not show it. Yes, we must put an end to it," he decided.

And for the first time the idea clearly presented itself that it was essential to put an end to this false position, the sooner the better. "Give up everything, she and I, and hide ourselves somewhere along with our love," he said to himself.

CHAPTER TWENTY-TWO

The rain did not last long, and by the time Vronsky arrived, his shaft horse trotting at full speed and dragging the trace horses galloping through the mud, with their reins hanging loose, the sun had peeped out again, the roofs of the summer villas and the old lime trees in the gardens on both sides of the principal streets sparkled with wet brilliance, and from the twigs came a pleasant drip and from the roofs rushing streams of water. He thought no more of the shower spoiling the race track, but was rejoicing now that—thanks to the rain—he would be sure to find her at home and alone, as he knew that Aleksey Aleksandrovich, who had lately returned from a foreign spa, had not moved from Petersburg.

Hoping to find her alone, Vronsky alighted, as he always did to avoid attracting attention, before crossing the bridge, and walked to the house. He did not use the steps to the front, but went through the yard.

"Has your master come?" he asked a gardener.

"No, sir. The mistress is at home. But will you please go to the front door; there are servants there," the gardener answered. "They'll open the door."

"No, I'll go in from the garden."

And feeling certain that she was alone, and wanting to take her by surprise, since he had not promised to be there today, and she would certainly not expect him to come before the races, he walked, holding his sword and stepping cautiously over the sandy path, bordered with flowers, to the terrace that looked out upon the garden. Vronsky forgot now all that he had thought of along the way, of the hardships and difficulties of their position. He thought of nothing but that he would see her very soon, not in imagination, but living, all of her, as she was in reality. He was just going in, stepping on his whole foot so as not to creak, up the worn steps of the terrace, when he suddenly remembered what he always forgot, and what caused the most torturing side of his relations with her: her son with his questioning—hostile, it seemed to him—eyes.

This boy was more often than anyone else a check upon their freedom. When he was present, both Vronsky and Anna did not merely avoid speaking of anything that they could not have repeated before everyone; they did not even allow themselves to refer by hints to anything the boy did not understand. They had made no agreement about this, it had determined itself. They would have felt it an insult to themselves to deceive the child. In his presence they talked like acquaintances. But in spite of this caution, Vronsky often saw the child's intent, bewildered glance fixed upon him, a strange shyness, uncertainty, at one time friendliness, at another, coldness and reserve, in the boy's manner to him; as though the child felt that between this man and his mother there existed some important bond, the significance of which he could not understand.

In fact, the boy did feel that he could not understand this relation, and he tried painfully, and was not able to make clear to himself what feeling he ought to have for this man. With a child's keen instinct for every manifestation of feeling, he saw distinctly that his father, his governess, his nurse—all did not merely dislike Vronsky, but looked on him with horror and aversion, though they never said anything about him, while his mother looked on him as her greatest friend.

"What does it mean? Who is he? How should I love him? If I don't know, it's my fault; either I'm stupid or a naughty boy," thought the child. And this was what caused his dubious, inquiring, sometimes hostile, expression, and the shyness and uncertainty which Vronsky found so irksome. This child's presence always and infallibly called up in Vronsky that strange feeling of inexplicable loathing which he had experienced of late. This child's presence called up both in Vronsky and in Anna a feeling akin to the feeling of a sailor who sees by the compass that the direction in which he is swiftly moving is far from the right one, but that to arrest his motion is not in his power, that every instant is carrying him further and further away, and that to admit to himself his deviation from the right direction is the same as admitting his certain ruin.

This child, with his innocent outlook upon life, was the compass that showed them the point to which they had departed from what they knew but did not want to know.

This time Seryozha was not at home, and she was completely alone. She was sitting on the terrace waiting for the return of her son, who had gone out for his walk and had been caught in the rain. She had sent a manservant and a maid out to look for him. Dressed in a white gown, deeply embroidered, she was sitting in a corner of the terrace behind some flowers, and did not hear him. Bending her curly black head, she pressed her forehead against a cool watering can that stood on the parapet, and both her lovely hands, with the rings he knew so well, clasped the pot. The beauty of her whole figure, her head, her neck, her hands, struck Vronsky every time as something new and unexpected. He stood still, gazing at her in ecstasy. But, as soon as he would have made a step to come nearer to her, she was aware of his presence, pushed away the watering can, and turned her flushed face toward him.

"What's the matter? You are ill?" he said to her, in French, going up to her. He would have run to her, but remembering that there might be spectators, he looked around toward the balcony door, and reddened a little, as he always reddened, feeling that he had to be afraid and on his guard.

"No, I'm well," she said, getting up and pressing his outstretched hand tightly. "I did not expect... you." [1]

"My God! What cold hands!" he said.

"You startled me," she said. "I'm alone, and expecting Seryozha; he's out for a walk; they'll come in from this side."

---

[1] She uses the informal *ty*. See note on page 64.

But in spite of her efforts to be calm, her lips were quivering.

"Forgive me for coming, but I couldn't pass the day without seeing you," he went on, speaking French, as he always did to avoid using "you," so impossibly cold in Russian, and the dangerously intimate singular.

"Forgive you? I'm so glad!"

"But you're ill or worried," he went on, not letting go her hands and bending over her. "What were you thinking of?"

"Always of the same thing," she said, with a smile.

She spoke the truth. If ever at any moment she had been asked what she was thinking of, she could have answered truly: of the same thing, of her happiness and her unhappiness. She was thinking, just when he came upon her, of this: why was it, she wondered, that for others, for Betsy (she knew of her secret liaison with Tushkevich), it was so easy, while for her it was such torture? Today her thought gained special poignancy from certain other considerations. She asked him about the races. He answered her questions, and, seeing that she was agitated, trying to calm her, he began telling her in the simplest tone the details of his preparations for the races.

"Tell him or not tell him?" she thought, looking into his quiet, affectionate eyes. "He is so happy, so absorbed in his races that he won't understand as he should, he won't understand the gravity of this fact to us."

"But you haven't told me what you were thinking of when I came in," he said, interrupting his narrative; "please tell me!"

She did not answer, and bending her head a little, she looked inquiringly at him from under her brows, her eyes shining under their long lashes. Her hand shook as it played with a leaf she had picked. He saw it, and his face expressed that utter subjection, that slavish devotion, which had done so much to win her.

"I can see something has happened. Do you suppose I can be at peace, knowing you have a trouble I am not sharing? Tell me, for God's sake," he repeated imploringly.

"Yes, I won't be able to forgive him if he does not realize the full gravity of it. Better not tell; why put him to the test?" she thought, still staring at him in the same way, and feeling that the hand that held the leaf was trembling more and more.

"For God's sake!" he repeated, taking her hand.

"Shall I tell you?"

"Yes, yes, yes . . ."

"I'm pregnant," she said, softly and deliberately. The leaf in her hand shook more violently, but she did not take her eyes off him, watching for his reaction. He turned white, would have said something, but stopped; he dropped her hand, and his head sank on his breast. "Yes, he realizes the full seriousness of it," she thought, and gratefully she pressed his hand.

But she was mistaken in thinking he realized the gravity of the fact as she, a woman realized it. On hearing it, he felt come upon him with tenfold intensity that strange feeling of loathing of someone. But at the same time, he felt that the turning point he had been longing for had come now; that it was impossible to go on concealing things from her husband, and it was inevitable in one way or another that they should soon put an end to their unnatural position. But, besides that, her emotion physically affected him in the same way. He looked at her with a look of submissive tenderness, kissed her hand, got up, and, in silence, paced up and down the terrace.

"Yes," he said, going up to her resolutely. "Neither you nor I have looked on our relations as a passing amusement, and now our fate is sealed. It is absolutely necessary to put an end"—he looked around as he spoke—"to the deception in which we are living."

"Put an end? How put an end, Aleksey?" she said softly.

She was calmer now, and her face lighted up with a tender smile.

"Leave your husband and make our life one."

"It is one as it is," she answered, scarcely audibly.

"Yes, but altogether; altogether."

"But how, Aleksey, tell me how?" she said in melancholy mockery at the hopelessness of her own position "Is there any way out of such a position? Am I not the wife of my husband?"

"There is a way out of every situation. We must make a decision," he said. "Anything's better than the situation in which you're living. Of course, I see how you torture yourself over everything—the world and your son and your husband."

"Oh, not over my husband," she said, with a quiet smile. "I don't know him, I don't think of him. He doesn't exist."

"You're not speaking sincerely. I know you. You worry about him too."

"Oh, he doesn't even know," she said, and suddenly a hot flush came over her face; her cheeks, her brow, her neck crimsoned, and tears of shame came into her eyes. "But we won't talk of him."

CHAPTER TWENTY-THREE

Vronsky had several times already, though not so resolutely as now, tried to get her to consider their situation, and every time he had been confronted by the same superficiality and triviality with which she met his appeal now. It was as though there were something in this which she could not or would not face, as though as soon as she began to speak of this, she, the real Anna, retreated somehow into herself, and another, strange and unaccountable woman came out, whom he did not love, and whom he feared, and who was in opposition to him. But today he was resolved to have it out.

"Whether he knows or not," said Vronsky, in his usual quiet and resolute tone, "that's nothing to do with us. We cannot . . . you cannot continue like this, especially now."

"What's to be done, according to you?" she asked with the same frivolous irony. She who had so feared he would take her condition too lightly was now vexed with him for deducing from it the necessity of taking some step.

"Tell him everything, and leave him."

"Very well, let us suppose I do that," she said. "Do you know what the result of that would be? I can tell you it all beforehand," and a wicked light gleamed in the eyes that had been so soft a minute before. " 'Eh, you love another man, and have entered into a criminal liaison with him?' " (Mimicking her husband, she threw an emphasis on the word "criminal," as Aleksey Aleksandrovich did.) " 'I warned you of the consequences from the religious, the civil, and the domestic points of view. You have not listened to me. Now I cannot let you disgrace my name—' " and my son, she had meant to say, but about her son she could not joke—" 'disgrace my name, and'— and more in the same style," she added. "In general terms, he'll say in his official manner, and with all distinctness and precision, that he cannot let me go, but will take all measures in his power to prevent scandal. And he will calmly and punctually act in accordance with his words. That's what will happen. He's not a man but a machine, and a spiteful machine when he's angry," she added, recalling Aleksey Aleksandrovich as she spoke, with all the peculiarities of his figure and manner of speaking, and setting against him every defect she could find in him, softening nothing for the great wrong she herself was doing him.

"But, Anna," said Vronsky, in a soft and persuasive voice, trying to soothe her, "we absolutely must, anyway, tell him, and then be guided by the line he takes."

"What, run away?"

"And why not run away? I don't see how we can keep on like this. And not for my sake—I see that you suffer."

"Yes, run away, and become your mistress," she said hastily.

"Anna," he said, with reproachful tenderness.

"Yes," she went on, "become your mistress, and complete the ruin of . . ."

Again she would have said "my son," but she could not utter that word.

Vronsky could not understand how she, with her strong and truthful nature, could endure this state of deceit, and not desire to get out of it. But he did not suspect that the chief cause of it was the word "son," which she could not bring herself to utter. When she thought of her son, and his future attitude toward his mother, who had abandoned his father, she felt such terror at what she had done that she could not face it; but, like a woman, could only try to comfort herself with lying assurances that everything would remain as it always had been, and that it was possible to forget the fearful question of what would be with her son.

"I beg you, I entreat you," she said suddenly, taking his hand, and speaking in quite a different tone, sincere and tender, "never speak to me of that!"

"But, Anna—"

"Never. Leave it to me. I know all the baseness, all the horror of my position; but it's not so easy to arrange as you think. And leave it to me, and do what I say. Never speak to me of it. Do you promise me? . . . No, no, promise! . . ."

"I promise everything, but I can't be at peace, especially after what you have told me. I can't be at peace when you can't be at peace . . ."

"I?" she repeated. "Yes, I am worried sometimes; but that will pass, if you will never talk about this. When you talk about it—it's only then it worries me."

"I don't understand," he said.

"I know," she interrupted him, "how hard it is for your truthful nature to lie, and I grieve for you. I often think that you have ruined your whole life for me."

"I was just thinking the very same thing," he said; "how could you sacrifice everything for my sake? I can't forgive myself that you're unhappy."

"I unhappy?" she said, coming closer to him, and looking at him with an ecstatic smile of love. "I am like a hungry man who has been given food. He may be cold, and dressed in rags, and ashamed, but he is not unhappy. I unhappy? No, this is my happiness . . ."

She could hear the sound of her son's voice coming toward them, and glancing swiftly around the terrace, she got up impulsively. Her eyes glowed with the fire he knew so well; with a rapid movement she raised her lovely hands, covered with rings, took his head, looked a long look into his face, and, putting her face to his, with smiling, parted lips, swiftly kissed his mouth and both eyes, and pushed him away. She would have gone, but he held her back.

"When?" he murmured in a whisper, gazing in ecstasy at her.

"Today, at one o'clock," she whispered, and, with a heavy sigh, she walked with her light, swift step to meet her son.

Seryozha had been caught by the rain in the big garden, and he and his nurse had taken shelter in an arbor.

"Well, good-by," she said to Vronsky. "I must soon be getting ready for the races. Betsy promised to fetch me."

Vronsky, looking at his watch, went away hurriedly.

CHAPTER TWENTY-FOUR

When Vronsky looked at his watch on the Karenins' balcony, he was so greatly agitated and lost in his thoughts that he saw the figures on the watch's face but could not realize what time it was. He came out onto the highroad and walked, picking his way carefully through the mud, to his carriage. He was so completely absorbed in his feeling for Anna that he did not even think what time it was, and whether he had time to go to Bryansky's. He had left him, as often happens, only the external faculty of memory which points out each step one has to take, one after the other. He went up to his coachman, who was dozing on the box in the shadow, already lengthening, of a thick lime tree; he admired the shifting clouds of midges circling over the sweating horses, and, waking the coachman, he jumped into the carriage and told him to drive to Bryansky's. It was only after driving nearly five miles that he had sufficiently recovered himself to look at his watch, and realize that it was half-past five, and he was late.

There were several races fixed for that day: the Life Guards' race, then the officers' mile-and-a-half race, then the three-mile race, and then the race for which he was entered. He could still be in time for his race, but if he went to Bryansky's he could just about be in time, and he would arrive when the whole of the court would be in their places. That would be a pity. But he had promised Bryansky to come, and so he decided to drive on, telling the coachman not to spare the horses.

He reached Bryansky's, spent five minutes there, and galloped back. This rapid drive calmed him. All that was painful in his relations with Anna, all the feeling of indefiniteness left by their conversation, had slipped out of his mind. He was thinking now with pleasure and excitement of the race, of his being, after all, on time, and now and then the thought of the blissful meeting awaiting him that night flashed across his imagination like a flaming light.

The excitement of the approaching race grew on him as he drove further and further into the atmosphere of the races, overtaking carriages driving up from the summer villas or out of Petersburg.

At his quarters no one was left at home; all were at the races, and his valet was waiting for him at the gate. While he was changing his clothes, his valet told him that the second race had begun already, that a lot of gentlemen had been to ask for him, and a boy had twice run up from the stables. Dressing without hurry (he never hurried himself, and never lost his self-possession), Vronsky drove to the sheds. From the sheds he could see a perfect sea of carriages, and people on foot, soldiers surrounding the track, and pavilions swarming with people. The second race was apparently going on, for just as he went into the sheds he heard a bell ringing. Going toward the stable, he met the white-legged chestnut, Makhotin's Gladiator, being led to the track in a blue-bordered orange covering, with what looked like huge ears edged with blue.

"Where's Cord?" he asked the stable boy.

"In the stable, putting on the saddle."

In the open horse box stood Frou-Frou saddled, ready. They were just going to lead her out.

"I'm not too late?"

"All right! All right!" said the Englishman; "don't upset yourself!"

Vronsky once more took in in one glance the exquisite lines of his favorite mare, who was quivering all over, and with an effort he tore himself from the sight of her, and went out of the stable. He went toward the pavilions at the best moment for escaping attention. The mile-and-a-half race was just finishing, and all eyes were fixed on the officer of the Horse Guards in front and the hussar behind, urging their horses on with a last effort close to the winning post. From the center and outside of the ring all were crowding to the winning post, and a group of soldiers and officers of the Horse Guards were shouting loudly their delight at the expected triumph of their officer and comrade. Vronsky moved into the middle of the crowd unnoticed, almost at the very moment when the bell rang at the finish of the race, and the tall, mud-spattered Horse Guards officer who came in first, bending over the saddle, let go the reins of his panting gray horse that looked dark with sweat.

The horse, stiffening out its legs, with an effort stopped its rapid course, and the officer of the Horse Guards looked about him like a man waking up from a heavy sleep, and just managed to smile. A crowd of friends and outsiders pressed around him.

Vronsky intentionally avoided that select crowd of the upper world, which was moving and talking freely but with discretion before the pavilions. He knew that Madame Karenina was there, and Betsy, and his brother's wife, and he purposely did not go near them for fear of something distracting his attention. But he was continually met and stopped by acquaintances, who told him about the previous races, and kept asking him why he was so late.

At the time when the racers had to go to the pavilion to receive the prizes, and all attention was directed to that point, Vronsky's elder brother, Aleksandr, a colonel with heavy fringed epaulets, came up to him. He was not tall, though as broadly built as Aleksey, and handsomer and ruddier than he; he had a red nose, and an open, drunken-looking face.

"Did you get my note?" he said. "One never can find you."

Aleksandr Vronsky, in spite of the dissolute life and, in particular, the drunken habits for which he was notorious, was quite a courtier.

Now, as he talked to his brother of a matter bound to be exceedingly disagreeable to him, knowing that the eyes of many people might be fixed upon him, he kept a smiling countenance, as though he was jesting with his brother about something of little importance.

"I got it, and I really can't make out what you are worrying yourself about," said Aleksey.

"I'm worrying myself because the remark has just been made to me that you weren't here, and that you were seen in Peterhof on Monday."

"There are matters that only concern those directly interested in them, and the matter you are so worried about is—"

"Yes, but if so, you may as well leave the service . . ."

"I beg you not to interfere, and that's all I have to say."

Aleksey Vronsky's frowning face turned white, and his prominent lower jaw quivered, which happened rarely with him. Being a man of very warm heart, he was seldom angry; but when he was angry, and when his chin quivered, then, as Aleksandr Vronsky knew, he was dangerous. Aleksandr Vronsky smiled gaily.

"I only wanted to give you Mother's letter. Answer it and don't worry about anything just before the race. *Bonne chance*," he added, smiling, and he moved away from him. But after him another friendly greeting brought Vronsky to a standstill.

"So you won't recognize your friends! How are you, *mon cher*?" said Stepan Arkadyevich, as conspicuously brilliant in the midst of all the Petersburg brilliance as he was in Moscow, his face rosy and his whiskers sleek and glossy. "I came up yesterday, and I'm delighted that I shall see your triumph. When shall we meet?"

"Come tomorrow to the mess," said Vronsky, and squeezing him by the sleeve of his coat, with apologies, he moved away to the center of the track, where the horses were being led for the great steeplechase.

The horses who had run in the last race were being led home, steaming and exhausted, by the stable boys, and one after another the fresh horses for the coming race made their appearance, for the most part English racers, wearing hoods, and looking with their girthed bellies like strange, huge birds. On the right, Frou-Frou was led in, lean and beautiful, lifting up her elastic, rather long pasterns, as though moved by springs. Not far from her they were taking the cloth off the lop-eared Gladiator. The strong, exquisite, perfectly correct lines of the stallion, with his superb hindquarters and excessively short pasterns almost over his hoofs attracted Vronsky's attention in spite of himself. He would have gone up to his mare, but he was again detained by an acquaintance.

"Oh, there's Karenin!" said the acquaintance with whom he was chatting. "He's looking for his wife, and she's in the middle of the pavilion. Didn't you see her?"

"No," answered Vronsky, and without even glancing around toward the pavilion where his friend was pointing out Madame Karenina, he went up to his mare.

Vronsky had not had time to look at the saddle, about which he had to give some direction, when the competitors were summoned to the pavilion to receive their numbers and places in the row at starting. Seventeen officers, looking serious and severe, many with pale faces, met together in the pavilion and drew the numbers. Vronsky drew the number seven. The cry was heard: "Mount!"

Feeling that with the other riding in the race, he was the center upon which all eyes were fastened, Vronsky walked up to his mare in that state of nervous tension in which he usually became deliberate and composed in his movements. Cord, in honor of the races, had put on his best clothes, a black coat buttoned up, a stiffly starched collar, which propped up his cheeks, a round black hat, and top boots. He was as calm and dignified as ever, and was with his own hands holding Frou-Frou by both reins, standing straight in front of her. Frou-Frou was still trembling as though in a fever. Her eye, full of fire, glanced sideways at Vronsky. Vronsky slipped his finger under the saddle girth. The mare glanced aslant at him, drew up her lip, and twitched her ear. The Englishman puckered up his lips, intending to indicate with a smile his amazement that anyone should have to verify his saddling.

"Get up; you won't feel so excited."

Vronsky looked around for the last time at his rivals. He knew that he would not see them during the race. Two were already riding forward to the point from which they were to start. Golitsyn, a friend of Vronsky's and one of his more formidable rivals, was moving around a bay horse that would not let him mount. A short hussar in tight riding breeches rode off at a gallop, crouched like a cat on the saddle, in imitation of English jockeys. Prince Kuzovlyov sat with a white face on his thoroughbred mare from the Grabovsky stud, while an English groom led her by the bridle. Vronsky and all his comrades knew Kuzovlyov and his peculiarity of "weak nerves" and terrible vanity. They knew that he was afraid of everything, afraid of riding a spirited horse. But now, just because it was terrifying, because people broke their necks, and there was a doctor standing at each obstacle, and an ambulance with a cross on it, and a nurse, he had made up his mind to take part in the race. Their eyes met, and Vronsky gave him a friendly and encouraging nod. Only one he did not see, his chief rival, Makhotin on Gladiator.

"Don't be in a hurry," said Cord to Vronsky, "and remember one thing: don't hold her in at the fences, and don't urge her on; let her go as she likes."

"All right, all right," said Vronsky, taking the reins.

"If you can, lead the race; but don't lose heart till the last minute, even if you're behind."

Before the mare had time to move, Vronsky stepped with an agile, vigorous movement into the steel-toothed stirrup, and lightly and firmly seated himself on the creaking leather of the saddle. Getting his right foot in the stirrup, he smoothed the double reins, as he always did, between his fingers, and Cord let go.

As though she did not know which foot to put first, Frou-Frou started, dragging at the reins with her long neck, and, as though she was on springs, shaking her rider from side to side. Cord quickened his step, following him. The excited mare, trying to shake off her rider first on one side and then on the other, pulled at the reins, and Vronsky tried in vain with voice and hand to soothe her.

They were just reaching the dammed-up stream on their way to the starting point. Several of the riders were in front and several behind, when suddenly Vronsky heard the sound of a horse galloping in the mud behind him, and he was overtaken by Makhotin on his white-legged, lop-eared Gladiator. Makhotin smiled, showing his long teeth, but Vronsky looked angrily at him. He did not like him, and regarded him now as his most formidable rival. He was angry with him for galloping past and exciting his mare. Frou-Frou started into a gallop, her left foot forward, made two bounds, and bothered by the tightened reins, passed into a jolting trot, bumping her rider up and down. Cord too scowled, and followed Vronsky almost at a trot.

CHAPTER TWENTY-FIVE

There were seventeen officers in all riding in this race. The track was a large three-mile elliptical ring in front of the pavilion. On this course nine obstacles had been arranged: the stream, a big and solid barrier five feet high, just before the pavilion, a dry ditch, a ditch full of water, a precipitous slope, an Irish barricade (one of the most difficult obstacles, consisting of a mound fenced with brushwood, beyond which was a ditch out of sight of the horses, so that the horse had to clear both obstacles or might be killed); then two more ditches filled with water, and one dry one; and the winning post faced the pavilion. But the race began not in the ring but two hundred yards away from it, and in that part of the course was the first obstacle, a dammed-up stream, seven feet in breadth, which the racers could leap or wade through as they preferred.

Three times they were lined up and ready to start, but each time some horse thrust itself out of line, and they had to begin again. The umpire who was starting them, Colonel Sestrin, was beginning to lose his temper, when at last for the fourth time he shouted "Away!" and the racers started.

Every eye, every field glass, was turned on the brightly colored group of riders at the moment they were in line to start.

"They're off! They're starting!" was heard on all sides after the hush of expectation.

And little groups and solitary figures among the public began running from place to place to get a better view. In the very first minute the close group of horsemen drew out, and it could be seen that they were approaching the stream in two's and three's and one behind another. To the spectators it seemed as though they had all started simultaneously, but to the racers there were seconds of difference that had great value to them.

Frou-Frou, excited and overnervous, lost in the first moment, and several horses had started before her, but before reaching the stream, Vronsky, who was holding in the mare with all his force as she tugged at the bridle, easily overtook three, and left in front of him were Makhotin's chestnut Gladiator, whose hindquarters were moving lightly and rhythmically up and down exactly in front of Vronsky, and in the lead the exquisite mare Diana bearing Kuzovlyov, more dead than alive.

For the first instant Vronsky was master of neither himself nor his mare. Up to the first obstacle, the stream, he could not guide the motions of his mare.

Gladiator and Diana came up to it together and almost at the same instant; simultaneously—up, up—they rose above the stream and flew across to the other side; Frou-Frou darted after them, as if flying; but at the very moment when Vronsky felt himself in the air, he suddenly saw almost under his mare's hoofs Kuzovlyov, who was floundering with Diana on the further side of the stream. (Kuzovlyov had let go the reins as he took the leap, and the mare had sent him flying over her head.) Those details Vronsky learned later; at the moment all he saw was that just under him, where Frou-Frou must alight, Diana's legs or head might be in the way. But Frou-Frou drew her legs up and back in the very act of leaping, like a falling cat, and clearing the other mare, alighted beyond her.

"Oh the darling!" thought Vronsky.

After crossing the stream, Vronsky had complete control of his mare, and began holding her in, intending to cross the great barrier behind Makhotin, and to try to overtake him in the clear ground of about five hundred yards that followed it.

The great barrier stood just in front of the imperial pavilion. The Tsar and the whole court and crowds of people were all gazing at them—at him, and at Makhotin a length ahead of him, as they drew near the "Devil," as the solid barrier was called. Vronsky was aware of those eyes fastened upon him from all sides, but he saw nothing except the ears and neck of his own mare, the ground racing to meet him, and the black and white legs of Gladiator beating time swiftly before him, and keeping always the same distance ahead. Gladiator rose, without touching anything. With a wave of his short tail he disappeared from Vronsky's sight.

"Bravo!" cried a voice.

At the same instant, under Vronsky's eyes, right before him flashed the palings of the barrier. Without the slightest change in her action his mare flew over it; the palings vanished, and he heard only a crash behind him. The mare, excited by Gladiator's keeping ahead, had risen too soon before the barrier, and grazed it with her hind hoofs. But her pace never changed, and Vronsky, feeling a spatter of mud in his face, realized that he was once more the same distance from Gladiator. Once more he perceived in front of him the same back and short tail, and again the same swiftly moving white legs that got no further away.

At the very moment Vronsky thought that now was the time to overtake Makhotin, Frou-Frou herself, understanding his thoughts without any urging on his part, gained considerable ground, and drew up alongside Makhotin on the best side, close to the inner rope. Makhotin would not let her pass that side. Vronsky had hardly formed the thought that he could perhaps pass on the outer side, when Frou-Frou shifted her pace and began overtaking him on the other side. Frou-Frou's shoulder, beginning by now to be dark with sweat, was even with Gladiator's back. For a few lengths they moved evenly. But before the obstacle they were approaching, Vronsky began working at the reins, anxious to avoid having to take the outer circle, and swiftly passed Makhotin just on the hillside. He caught a glimpse of his mud-spattered face as he flashed by. He even thought that he smiled. Vronsky passed Makhotin, but he was immediately aware of him close upon him, and he never ceased hearing the even gallop and the rapid and still quite fresh breathing of Gladiator.

The next two obstacles, the watercourse and the barrier, were easily crossed, but Vronsky began to hear the snorting and thud of Gladiator closer to him. He urged on his mare, and to his delight felt that she easily quickened her pace, and the thud of Gladiator's hoofs was again heard at the same distance away.

Vronsky was in the lead, just as he wanted to be and as Cord had advised, and now he felt sure of being the winner. His excitement, his delight, and his tenderness for Frou-Frou grew keener and keener. He longed to look around again, but he did not dare do this, and tried to be cool and not to urge on his mare, so to keep the same reserve of force in her as he felt that Gladiator still kept. There remained only one obstacle, the most difficult; if he could cross it ahead of the others, he would come in first. He was flying toward the Irish barricade, Frou-Frou and he both saw the barricade in the distance, and both the man and the mare had a moment's hesitation. He saw the uncertainty in the mare's ears and lifted the whip, but at the same time felt that his fears were groundless; the mare knew what was wanted. She quickened her pace and rose smoothly, just as he had thought she would, and as she left the ground she gave herself up to the force of her rush, which carried her far beyond the ditch; and with the same rhythm, without effort, with the same leg forward, Frou-Frou fell back into her pace again.

"Bravo, Vronsky!" He heard shouts from a knot of men—he knew they were his friends in the regiment—who were standing at the obstacle. He could not fail to recognize Yashvin's voice though he did not see him.

"Oh my sweet!" he said inwardly to Frou-Frou as he listened for what was happening behind. "He's cleared it!" he thought, catching the thud of Gladiator's hoofs behind him. There remained only the last ditch, filled with water and five feet wide. Vronsky did not even look at it, but anxious to win by a long way, first began working away at the reins, lifting the mare's head and letting it go in time with her paces. He felt that the mare was at her very last reserve of strength; not merely her neck and shoulders were wet, but the sweat was standing in drops on her mane, her head, her sharp ears; and her breath came in short, sharp gasps. But he knew that she had more than enough strength left for the remaining five hundred yards. It was only from feeling himself nearer the ground and from the peculiar smoothness of his motion that Vronsky knew how greatly the mare had quickened her pace. She flew over the ditch as though not noticing it. She flew over it like a bird; but at the same instant Vronsky, to his horror, felt that he had failed to keep up with the mare's pace, that he had, he did not know how, made a fearful, unpardonable mistake, in recovering his seat in the saddle. All at once his position had shifted and he knew something awful had happened. He could not yet make out what had happened, when the white legs of a chestnut horse flashed by close to him, and Makhotin passed at a swift gallop. Vronsky was touching the ground with one foot, and his mare was sinking on that foot. He just had time to free his leg when she fell on one side, gasping painfully, and making vain efforts to rise with her delicate, soaking neck, she fluttered on the ground at his feet like a shot bird. The clumsy movement made by Vronsky had broken her back. But that he found out only much later. At that moment he knew only that Makhotin had flown swiftly by, while he stood staggering alone on the muddy, motionless ground, and Frou-Frou lay gasping before him, bending her head back and gazing at him with her exquisite eyes. Still unable to realize what had happened, Vronsky tugged at his mare's reins. Again she struggled all over like a fish, and her shoulders setting the saddle heaving, she rose on her front legs, but unable to lift her back, she quivered all over and again fell on her side. With a face hideous with passion, his lower jaw trembling and his cheeks white, Vronsky kicked her with his heel in the stomach and again began tugging at the rein. She did not stir, but thrusting her nose into the ground, she simply gazed at her master with her speaking eyes.

"Ahhh!" groaned Vronsky, clutching at his head. "Ah, what have I done!" he cried. "The race lost! And my fault! shameful, unpardonable! And the poor darling, ruined mare! Ah, what have I done!"

A crowd of men, a doctor and his assistant, the officers of his regiment, ran up to him. To his misery, he felt that he was whole and unhurt. The mare had broken her back, and it was decided to shoot her. Vronsky could not answer questions, could not speak to anyone. He turned, and without picking up his cap, which had fallen off, he walked away from the track, not knowing where he was going. He felt utterly wretched. For the first time in his life he knew the bitterest sort of misfortune, misfortune beyond remedy, misfortune his own fault.

Yashvin overtook him with his cap, and led him home, and half an hour later Vronsky had regained his self-possession. But the memory of that race remained long in his heart, the cruelest and bitterest memory of his life.

CHAPTER TWENTY-SIX

Outwardly the relation of Aleksey Aleksandrovich and his wife had remained unchanged. The only difference lay in the fact that he was more busily occupied than ever. As in former years, at the beginning of the spring he had gone to a foreign spa for the sake of his health, weakened by the winter's work that every year grew heavier. And just as always, he returned in July and at once began to work as usual with increased energy. As usual, too, his wife had moved for the summer to a villa out of town, while he remained in Petersburg. From the date of their conversation after the party at Princess Tverskaya's he had never spoken again to Anna of his suspicions and his jealousies, and that habitual tone of his of bantering mimicry was the most convenient tone possible for his present attitude toward his wife. He was a little colder to her. He simply seemed to be slightly displeased with her for that first midnight conversation, which she had repelled. In his attitude toward her there was a shade of vexation, but nothing more. "You would not be frank with me," he seemed to say, mentally addressing her; "so much the worse for you. Now you may beg as you please, but I won't be frank with you. So much the worse for you!" he said mentally, like a man who, after vainly attempting to extinguish a fire, should fly into a rage with his vain efforts and say, "Oh, very well, then! You shall burn for this!" This man, so subtle and astute in official life, did not realize all the senselessness of such an attitude toward his wife. He did not realize it, because it was too terrible to him to realize his actual position, and he shut down and locked and sealed up in his heart that secret place where his feelings toward his family—that is, his wife and son—lay hidden. He who had been such a concerned father had from the end of that winter become peculiarly cold to his son, and adopted toward him just the same bantering tone he used with his wife. "Aha, young man!" was the greeting with which he met him.

Aleksey Aleksandrovich asserted and believed that he had never in any previous year had so much official business as that year. But he was not aware that he sought work for himself that year, that this was one of the means for keeping shut that secret place where his feelings toward his wife and son and his thoughts about them lay hidden, and which became more terrible the longer they lay there. If anyone had had the right to ask Aleksey Aleksandrovich what he thought of his wife's behavior, the mild and peaceable Aleksey Aleksandrovich would have made no answer, but he would have been greatly angered with any man who should question him on that subject. For this reason Aleksey Aleksandrovich's face took on a look of haughtiness and severity whenever anyone inquired after his wife's health. Aleksey Aleksandrovich did not want to think at all about his wife's behavior, and he actually succeeded in not thinking about it at all.

Karenin's permanent summer villa was in Peterhof, and the Countess Lydia Ivanovna used to, generally, spend the summer there, close to Anna, constantly seeing her. That year Countess Lydia Ivanovna declined to settle in Peterhof, was not once at Anna Arkadyevna's, and, in conversation with Aleksey Aleksandrovich, hinted at the unsuitability of Anna's intimacy with Betsy and Vronsky. Karenin sternly cut her short, roundly declaring his wife to be above suspicion, and from that time began to avoid the countess. He did not want to see, and did not see, that many people in society cast dubious glances on his wife; he did not want to understand, and did not understand, why his wife had so particularly insisted on staying at Tsarskoe, where Betsy was staying, not far from the camp of Vronsky's regiment. He did not allow himself to think about it, and he did not think about it; but, all the same, though he never admitted it to himself, and had no proof, not even suspicions, in the bottom of his heart he knew beyond all doubt that he was a deceived husband, and he was profoundly miserable about it.

How often during those eight years of happy life with his wife he had looked at other men's faithless wives and other deceived husbands and asked himself: "How can people descend to that? How is it they don't put an end to such a hideous situation?" But now, when the misfortune had come upon himself, he was so far from thinking of putting an end to the situation that he would not recognize it at all, would not recognize it just because it was too awful, too unnatural.

Since his return from abroad, Aleksey Aleksandrovich had been at their country villa twice. Once he dined there, the other time he spent the evening there with a party of friends, but neither time did he stay overnight, as it had been his habit to do in previous years.

The day of the races had been a very busy one for Aleksey Aleksandrovich; but when mentally sketching out the day in the morning, he made up his mind to go to their country house to see his wife immediately after dinner, and from there to the races, at which the whole Court would be, and at which he should be present. He was going to see his wife because he had determined to see her once a week to keep up appearances. And besides, on that day, as it was the fifteenth, he had to give his wife some money for her expenses, according to their usual arrangement.

With his habitual control over his thoughts, though he thought all this about his wife, he did not let his thoughts stray further in regard to her.

That morning was a very full one for Aleksey Aleksandrovich. The evening before, Countess Lydia Ivanovna had sent him a pamphlet by a celebrated traveler in China, who was staying in Petersburg and with it she enclosed a note begging him to see the traveler himself, as he was an extremely interesting person from various points of view, and likely to be interesting and useful to them. Karenin had not had time to read the pamphlet through in the evening, and finished it in the morning. Then people began arriving with petitions, and there came the reports, interviews, appointments, dismissals, apportionment of rewards, pensions, grants, notes, the workaday round, as he called it, that always took up so much time. Then there was private business of his own, a visit from the doctor and his manager. The manager did not take up much time. He simply gave Aleksey Aleksandrovich the money he needed with a brief statement of the condition of his affairs, which was not altogether satisfactory, as it had happened that during that year, owing to increased expenses, more had been paid out than usual and there was a deficit. But the doctor, a celebrated Petersburg doctor, who was an intimate acquaintance of Aleksey Aleksandrovich's, took up a great deal of time. Karenin had not expected him that day, and was surprised at his visit, still more so when the doctor questioned him very carefully about his health, listened to his breathing, and tapped at his liver. Karenin did not know that his friend Lydia Ivanovna, noticing that he was not as well as usual that year, had begged the doctor to go and examine him. "Do this for my sake," the countess had said to him.

"I will do it for the sake of Russia, Countess," replied the doctor.

"A priceless man!" said the countess.

The doctor was extremely dissatisfied with Aleksey Aleksandrovich. He found the liver considerably enlarged, and the digestive powers weakened, while the course of mineral waters had been quite without effect. He prescribed more physical exercise as far as possible, and as far as possible less mental strain, and above all no worry—in other words, just what was as much out of Aleksey Aleksandrovich's power as abstaining from breathing. Then he withdrew, leaving in Aleksey Aleksandrovich an unpleasant sense that something was wrong with him, and that there was no chance of curing it.

As he was coming away, the doctor chanced to meet on the staircase an acquaintance of his, Sliudin, who was Karenin's secretary. They had been comrades at the university, and though they rarely met, they thought highly of each other and were excellent friends, and so there was no one to whom the doctor would have given his opinion of a patient more freely.

"How glad I am you've been seeing him!" said Sliudin. "He's not well, and I think . . . Well, what do you think of him?"

"I'll tell you," said the doctor, beckoning over Sliudin's head to his coachman to bring the carriage round. "It's just this," said the doctor, taking a finger of his kid glove in his white hands and pulling it, "if you don't strain the strings, you'll find it difficult to break them, but strain a string to its very utmost, and the mere weight of one finger on the strained string will snap it. And with his close assiduity, his conscientious devotion to his work, he's strained to the utmost, and there's some outside burden weighing on him, and not a light one," concluded the doctor, raising his eyebrows significantly. "Will you be at the races?" he added, as he sank into his seat in the carriage.

"Yes, yes, to be sure; it does waste a lot of time," the doctor responded vaguely to some reply of Sliudin's he had not caught.

After the doctor, who had taken up so much time, came the celebrated traveler, and Aleksey Aleksandrovich, by means of the pamphlet he had just finished reading and his previous acquaintance with the subject, impressed the traveler by the depth of his knowledge of the subject and the breadth and enlightenment of his views.

At the same time as the traveler, there was announced a provincial marshal of nobility[1] on a visit to Petersburg, with whom Aleksey Aleksandrovich had to have some conversation. After his departure, he had to finish the daily routine of business with his secretary, and then he still had to drive round to call on a certain important person on a matter of grave and serious import. Aleksey Aleksandrovich just managed to be back by five o'clock, his dinner hour, and after dining with his secretary, he invited him to drive with him to his country villa and to the races.

Though he did not acknowledge it to himself, Karenin always tried nowadays to secure the presence of a third person in his interviews with his wife.

---

[1] Official elected by landlords of nobility. He had no real power, but would look into administrative matters, concern himself with philanthropic enterprises, etc.

CHAPTER TWENTY-SEVEN

Anna was upstairs standing in front of the mirror and, with Annushka's assistance, pinning the last ribbon on her gown when she heard carriage wheels crunching the gravel at the entrance.

"It's too early for Betsy," she thought, and glancing out of the window, she caught sight of the carriage and the black hat of Aleksey Aleksandrovich, and the ears she knew so well sticking up on each side of it. "How unfortunate! Can he be going to stay the night?" she wondered, and the thought of what might come of such a possibility struck her as so awful and terrible that, without dwelling on it for a moment, she went down to meet him with a bright and radiant face; and conscious of the presence of that spirit of falsehood and deceit in herself which she had come to know of late, she abandoned herself to that spirit and began talking, hardly knowing what she was saying.

"Ah, how nice of you!" she said, giving her husband her hand, and greeting Sliudin, who was like one of the family, with a smile. "You're staying for the night, I hope?" was the first word the spirit of falsehood prompted her to utter; "and now we'll go together. Only it's a pity I've promised Betsy. She's coming for me."

Aleksey Aleksandrovich knit his brows at Betsy's name.

"Oh, I'm not going to separate the inseparables," he said in his usual bantering tone. "I'm going with Mikhail Vasilievich. I'm ordered to exercise by the doctors too. I'll walk, and imagine myself at the spa again."

"There's no hurry," said Anna. "Would you like tea?"

She rang.

"Bring in tea, and tell Seryozha that Aleksey Aleksandrovich is here. Well, tell me, how have you been? Mikhail Vasilievich, you've not been to see me before. Look how lovely it is out on the terrace," she said, turning first to one and then to the other.

She spoke very simply and naturally, but too much and too fast. She was the more aware of this from noticing in the inquisitive look Mikhail Vasilievich turned on her that he was, as it were, keeping watch on her.

Mikhail Vasilievich promptly went out on the terrace.

She sat down beside her husband.

"You don't look well," she said.

"Yes," he said; "the doctor's been with me today and wasted an hour of my time. I feel that one of our friends must have sent him: my health's so precious, it seems."

"No; what did he say?"

She questioned him about his health and what he had been doing, and tried to persuade him to take a rest and come stay with her.

All this she said brightly, rapidly, and with a peculiar brilliance in her eyes. But Karenin did not now attach any special significance to this tone of hers. He heard only her words and gave them only the direct sense they bore. And he answered simply, though jestingly. There was nothing singular in this conversation, but Anna could never recall this brief scene without an agonizing pang of shame.

Seryozha came in preceded by his governess. If Aleksey Aleksandrovich had allowed himself to observe, he would have noticed the timid and bewildered eyes with which Seryozha glanced first at his father and then at his mother. But he would not see anything, and he did not see it.

"Ah, the young man! He's grown. Really, he's getting to be quite a man. How are you, young man?"

And he gave his hand to the scared child. Seryozha had been shy of his father before, and now, ever since Aleksey Aleksandrovich had begun calling him "young man," and since that insoluble question had occurred to him whether Vronsky was a friend or a foe, he avoided his father. He looked around toward his mother as though seeking shelter. It was only with his mother that he was at ease. Meanwhile, Aleksey Aleksandrovich was holding his son by the shoulder while he was speaking to the governess, and Seryozha was so miserably uncomfortable that Anna saw he was on the point of tears.

Anna, who had flushed a little the instant her son came in, noticing that Seryozha was uncomfortable, got up hurriedly, took Aleksey Aleksandrovich's hand from her son's shoulder, and, kissing the boy, led him out onto the terrace and quickly came back.

"It's time to start, though," said she, glancing at her watch. "How is it Betsy doesn't come? . . ."

"Yes," said Aleksey Aleksandrovich, and getting up, he folded his hands and cracked his knuckles. "I've come to bring you some money, too, for nightingales, we know, can't live on fairytales," he said. "You want it, I expect?"

"No, I don't . . . yes, I do," she said, not looking at him and crimsoning to the roots of her hair. "But you'll come back here after the races, I suppose?"

"Oh, yes!" answered Aleksey Aleksandrovich. "And here's the glory of Peterhof, Princess Tverskaya," he added, looking out of the window at the elegant English carriage with the tiny seats placed extremely high. "What elegance! Charming! Well, let us be starting too, then."

Princess Tverskaya did not get out of her carriage, but her groom, in high boots, a cape, and black hat, darted out at the entrance.

"I'm going; good-by!" said Anna, and kissing her son, she went up to Aleksey Aleksandrovich and held out her hand to him. "It was so nice of you to come."

Aleksey Aleksandrovich kissed her hand.

"Well, good-by, then! You'll come back for some tea; that's delightful!" she said, and went out, gay and radiant. But as soon as she no longer saw him, she was aware of the spot on her hand that his lips had touched, and she shuddered with repulsion.

CHAPTER TWENTY-EIGHT

When Aleksey Aleksandrovich reached the race track, Anna was already sitting in the pavilion beside Betsy, in that pavilion where all of the highest society had gathered. She caught sight of her husband in the distance. Two men, her husband and her lover, were the two centers of her existence, and unaided by her external senses, she was aware of their nearness. She was aware of her husband approaching a long way off, and she could not help following him in the surging crowd in the midst of which he was moving. She watched his progress toward the pavilion, saw him now responding condescendingly to an ingratiating bow, now exchanging friendly, nonchalant greetings with his equals, now assiduously trying to catch the eye of some great one of this world, and tipping his big round hat that squeezed the tip of his ears. All these ways of his she knew, and all were hateful to her. "Nothing but ambition, nothing but the desire to get ahead, that's all there is in his soul," she thought; "as for these lofty ideals, love of culture, religion, they are only so many tools for advancing."

From his glances toward the ladies' pavilion (he was staring straight at her, but did not distinguish his wife in the sea of muslin, ribbons, feathers, parasols and flowers), she saw that he was looking for her, but she purposely avoided noticing him.

"Aleksey Aleksandrovich!" Princess Betsy called to him; "I'm sure you don't see your wife: here she is."

He smiled his chilly smile.

"There's so much splendor here that one's eyes are dazzled," he said, and he went into the pavilion. He smiled to his wife as a man should smile on meeting his wife after only just parting from her, and greeted the princess and other acquaintances, giving to each what was due—that is to say, jesting with the ladies and dealing out friendly greetings among the men. Below, near the pavilion, was standing an adjutant general of whom Aleksey Aleksandrovich had a high opinion, noted for his intelligence and culture. Karenin entered into conversation with him.

There was an interval between the races, and so nothing hindered conversation. The adjutant general expressed his disapproval of races. Karenin replied defending them. Anna heard his high, measured tones, not losing one word, and every word struck her as false, and stabbed her ears with pain.

When the three-mile steeplechase was beginning, she bent forward and gazed with fixed eyes at Vronsky as he went up to his horse and mounted, and at the same time she heard that loathsome, never-ceasing voice of her husband. She was in an agony of terror for Vronsky, but a still greater agony was the never-ceasing, as it seemed to her, stream of her husband's shrill voice with its familiar intonations.

"I'm a wicked woman, a lost woman," she thought; "but I don't like lying, I can't endure falsehood, while as for *him*" (her husband) "it's the breath of his life—falsehood. He knows all about it, he sees it all; what does he care if he can talk so calmly? If he were to kill me, if he were to kill Vronsky, I might respect him. No, all he wants is falsehood and propriety," Anna said to herself, not considering exactly what it was she wanted of her husband, and how she would have liked to see him behave. She did not understand either that his peculiar loquacity that day, so exasperating to her, was merely the expression of his inward distress and uneasiness. As a child that has been hurt skips about, putting all his muscles into movement to drown the pain, in the same way Aleksey Aleksandrovich needed mental exercise to drown the thoughts of his wife which in her presence and in Vronsky's, and with the continual iteration of his name, would force themselves on his attention. And it was as natural for him to talk well and cleverly as it is natural for a child to skip about. He was saying:

"Danger in the races of officers, of cavalry men, is an essential element in the race. If England can point to the most brilliant feats of cavalry in military history, it is simply due to the fact that she has historically developed this force both in beasts and in men. Sport has, in my opinion, a great value, and as is always the case, we see nothing but what is most superficial."

"It's not superficial," said Princess Tverskaya. "One of the officers, they say, has broken two ribs."

Aleksey Aleksandrovich smiled his smile, which uncovered his teeth but revealed nothing more.

"We'll admit, Princess, that that's not superficial," he said, "but internal. But that's not the point," and he turned again to the general with whom he was talking seriously; "we mustn't forget that those who are taking part in the race are military men, who have chosen that career, and one must allow that every calling has its disagreeable side. It forms an integral part of the duties of an officer. Sports such as prize fighting or Spanish bullfights, disgraceful sports, are a sign of barbarity. But specialized trials of skill are a sign of progress."

"No, I shan't come another time; it's too exciting," said Princess Betsy. "Isn't it, Anna?"

"It is exciting, but one can't tear oneself away," said another lady. "If I'd been a Roman woman I would never have missed a single circus."

Anna said nothing, keeping her binoculars focused always on the same spot.

At that moment a tall general walked through the pavilion. Breaking off what he was saying, Aleksey Aleksandrovich got up hurriedly, though with dignity, and bowed low to the general.

"You're not racing?" the officer asked, chaffing him.

"My race is a harder one," Aleksey Aleksandrovich responded deferentially.

And though the answer meant nothing, the general looked as though he had heard a witty remark from a witty man, and fully relished *la pointe de la sauce*.[1]

"There are two aspects," Aleksey Aleksandrovich resumed: "those who take part and those who look on; and love for such spectacles is an unmistakable proof of a low degree of development in the spectator, I admit, but—"

"Princess, bets!" sounded Stepan Arkadyevich's voice from below, addressing Betsy. "Who's your favourite?"

"Anna and I are for Kuzovlyov," replied Betsy.

"I'm for Vronsky. A pair of gloves?"

"Done!"

"But it is a pretty sight, isn't it?"

Aleksey Aleksandrovich paused while there was talking about him, but he began again immediately.

"I admit that manly sports do not . . ." he was continuing.

But at that moment the racers started, and all conversation ceased. Aleksey Aleksandrovich too was silent, and everyone stood up and turned toward the stream. Aleksey Aleksandrovich took no interest in the race, and so he did not watch the racers but began listlessly scanning the spectators with his weary eyes. His eyes rested upon Anna.

Her face was white and set. She was obviously seeing nothing and no one but one man. Her hand had convulsively clutched her fan, and she held her breath. He looked at her and hastily turned away, scrutinizing other faces.

"But here's this lady too, and others very much moved as well; it's very natural," Aleksey Aleksandrovich told himself. He tried not to look at her, but unconsciously his eyes were drawn to her. He examined that face again, trying not to read what was so plainly written on

[1] "The flavor of the sauce."

it, and against his own will, with horror he read on it what he did not want to know.

The first fall—Kuzovlyov's, at the stream—agitated everyone, but Aleksey Aleksandrovich saw distinctly on Anna's pale, triumphant face that the man she was watching had not fallen. When, after Makhotin and Vronsky had cleared the worst barrier, the next officer had been thrown straight on his head at it and fatally injured, and a shudder of horror passed over the whole crowd, Aleksey Aleksandrovich saw that Anna did not even notice it, and had some difficulty in realizing what they were talking about all around her. But more and more often, and with greater persistence, he watcher her. Anna, wholly engrossed as she was with the race, became aware of her husband's cold eyes fixed upon her from one side.

She glanced around for an instant, looked inquiringly at him, and, with a slight frown, turned away again.

"Ah, I don't care!" she seemed to say to him, and she did not once glance at him again.

The race was an unlucky one, and of the seventeen officers who rode in it more than half were thrown and hurt. Toward the end of the race everyone was in a state of agitation, which was intensified by the fact the Tsar was displeased.

CHAPTER TWENTY-NINE

Everyone was loudly expressing disapprobation, everyone was repeating a phrase someone had uttered— "The lions and gladiators will be the next thing"—and everyone was feeling horrified; so that when Vronsky fell to the ground, and Anna moaned aloud, there was nothing very unusual about it. But afterwards a change came over Anna's face which really was beyond decorum. She utterly lost her head. She began fluttering like a caged bird, at one moment getting up as if to go, at the next turning to Betsy.

"Let us go, let us go!' she said.

But Betsy did not hear her. She was bending down, talking to a general who had come up to her.

Aleksey Aleksandrovich went up to Anna and courteously offered her his arm.

"Let us go, if you like," he said in French, but Anna was listening to the general and did not notice her husband.

"He's broken his leg too, so they say," the general was saying. "This is too much."

Without answering her husband, Anna lifted her binoculars and gazed toward the place where Vronsky had fallen; but it was so far off, and there was such a crowd of people around it, that she could make out nothing. She laid down the binoculars, about to move away, but at that moment an officer galloped up and made some announcement to the Tsar. Anna craned forward, listening.

"Stiva! Stiva!" she cried to her brother.

But her brother did not hear her. Again she started to leave.

"Once more I offer you my arm, if you wish to leave," said Aleksey Aleksandrovich, reaching toward her hand.

She drew back from him with aversion, and without looking in his face, she answered:

"No, no, let me be, I'll stay."

She saw now that from the place of Vronsky's accident an officer was running across the course toward the pavilion. Betsy waved her handkerchief to him. The officer brought the news that the rider was not killed, but the horse had broken its back.

On hearing this, Anna sat down hurriedly and hid her face in her fan. Aleksey Aleksandrovich saw that she was weeping, and could not control her tears, nor even the sobs that were shaking her bosom. Aleksey Aleksandrovich stood so as to screen her, giving her time to recover herself.

"For the third time I offer you my arm," he said to her after a little while, turning to her. Anna gazed at him and did not know what to say. Princess Betsy came to her rescue.

"No, Aleksey Aleksandrovich; I brought Anna and I promised to take her home," Betsy said

"Excuse me, Princess," he said, smiling courteously but looking her very firmly in the face, "but I see that Anna's not very well, and I wish her to come home with me."

Anna looked about her in a frightened way, got up submissively, and laid her hand on her husband's arm.

"I'll send to him and find out, and let you know," Betsy whispered to her.

As they left the pavilion, Aleksey Aleksandrovich, as always, talked to those he met, and Anna had, as always, to talk and answer; but she was utterly beside herself, and moved hanging on her husband's arm as though in a dream.

"Is he killed or not? Is it true? Will he come or not? Shall I see him today?" she was thinking.

She took her seat in her husband's carriage in silence, and in silence drove out of the crowd of carriages. In spite of all he had seen, Aleksey Aleksandrovich still did not allow himself to consider his wife's real condition. He merely saw the outward symptoms. He saw that she was behaving unbecomingly, and considered it his duty to tell her so. But it was very difficult for him not to say more, to tell her nothing but that. He opened his mouth to tell her she had behaved unbecomingly, but he could not help saying something utterly different.

"What an inclination we all have, though, for these cruel spectacles!" he said. "I observe—"

"What? I don't understand," said Anna contemptuously.

He was offended, and at once began to say what he had meant to say.

"I am obliged to tell you . . ." he began.

"So now we are to have it out," she thought, and she felt frightened.

"I am obliged to tell you that your behavior has been unbecoming today," he said to her in French.

"In what way has my behavior been unbecoming?" she said aloud, turning her head swiftly and looking him straight in the face, not with the bright expression that seemed masking something, but with a look of determination, under which she concealed with difficulty the dismay she was feeling.

"Careful," he said, pointing to the open window opposite the coachman.

He got up and pulled up the window.

"What did you consider unbecoming?" she repeated.

"The despair you were unable to conceal at the accident to one of the riders."

He waited for her to answer, but she was silent, looking straight before her.

"I have already begged you so to conduct yourself in society that even malicious tongues can find nothing to say against you. There was a time when I spoke of your inward attitude, but I am not speaking of that now. Now I speak only of your external attitude. You have behaved improperly, and I would wish it not to occur again."

She did not hear half of what he was saying; she felt panic-stricken before him, and was wondering whether it was true that Vronsky was not killed. Was it of him they were speaking when they said the rider was unhurt but the horse had broken its back? She merely smiled with a pretense of irony with he finished, and made no reply, because she had not heard what he said. Aleksey Aleksandrovich had begun to speak boldly, but as he realized plainly what he was speaking of, the dismay she was feeling infected him too. He saw the smile, and a strange misapprehension came over him.

"She is smiling at my suspicions. Yes, she will tell me now what she told me before; that there is no foundation for my suspicions, that it's absurd."

At that moment, when the revelation of everything was hanging over him, there was nothing he expected so much as that she would answer mockingly as before that his suspicions were absurd and utterly groundless. So terrible to him was that which he knew that now he was ready to believe anything. But the expression of her face, scared and gloomy, did not now promise even deception.

"Possibly I was mistaken," said he. "If so, I beg your pardon."

"No, you were not mistaken," she said deliberately, looking desperately into his cold face. "You were not mistaken. I was, and I could not help being in despair. I hear you, but I am thinking of him. I love him, I am his mistress; I can't bear you; I'm afraid of you, and I hate you . . . You can do what you like to me."

And dropping back into the corner of the carriage, she broke into

sobs, hiding her face in her hands. Aleksey Aleksandrovich did not
stir, and kept looking straight before him. But his whole face suddenly bore the solemn rigidity of the dead, and his expression did not
change during the whole time of the drive home. On reaching the
house, he turned his head to her, still with the same expression.

"Very well! But I expect a strict observance of the external forms
of propriety till such time"—his voice shook—"as I may take measures to protect my honor and communicate them to you."

He got out first and helped her to get out. Before the servants he
pressed her hand, took his seat in the carriage, and drove back to
Petersburg. Immediately afterwards a footman came from Princess
Betsy and brought Anna a note.

"I sent to Aleksey to find out how he is, and he writes me he is
quite well and unhurt, but in despair."

"So *he* will be here," she thought. "What a good thing I told him
everything!"

She glanced at her watch. She still had three hours to wait, and the
memories of their last meeting set her blood in flame.

"My God, how light it is! It's dreadful, but I love to see his face,
and I love this fantastic light . . . My husband! Oh, yes! . . . Well,
thank God everything's over with him!"

CHAPTER THIRTY

In the little German spa to which the Shcherbatskys had come, as in
all places where people are gathered together, the usual process, as
it were, of the crystallization of society went on, assigning to each
member of that society a definite and unalterable place. Just as the
particle of water in frost, definitely and unalterably, takes the special
form of the crystal of snow, so each new person who arrived at the
spa was at once placed in his special place.

Fürst Shcherbatsky, *sammt Gemahlin und Tochter*,[1] by the apartments
they took, and from their name and the friends they made, were
immediately crystallized into a definite place marked out for them.

---

[1] "Prince Shcherbatsky with his wife and daughter."

Visiting the spa that year was a real German *Fürstin*,[2] in consequence of which the crystallizing process went on more vigorously than ever. Princess Shcherbatsky wished, above all, to present her daughter to this German princess, and the day after their arrival she duly performed this rite. Kitty made a low and graceful curtsey in the *very simple*, that is to say, very elegant frock that had been ordered for her from Paris. The German princess said, "I hope the roses will soon come back to this pretty little face," and for the Shcherbatskys certain definite lines of existence were at once laid down from which there was no departing. The Shcherbatskys made the acquaintance too of the family of an English lady, of a German countess and her son, wounded in the last war,[3] of a learned Swede, and of Mr. Canut and his sister. But yet inevitably the Shcherbatskys were thrown most into the society of a Moscow lady, Marya Yevgenyevna Rtishcheva, and her daughter, whom Kitty disliked because she had fallen ill, like herself, over a love affair, and a Moscow colonel, whom Kitty had known from childhood and always seen in uniforms and epaulets, and who now, with his little eyes and his open neck and flowered cravat, was unusually ridiculous and tedious, because there was no getting rid of him. When all this was so firmly established, Kitty began to be very much bored, especially as the prince went away to Carlsbad and she was left alone with her mother. She took no interest in the people she knew, feeling that nothing fresh would come of them. Her chief interest in the spa consisted in watching and making theories about the people she did not know. It was characteristic of Kitty that she always saw people in the most favorable light possible, especially those she did not know. And now as she made surmises as to who people were, what their relations were to one another, and what they were like, Kitty endowed them with the most marvelous and noble characters, and found confirmation of her idea in her observations.

Of these people the one that attracted her most was a Russian girl who had come to the spa with an invalid Russian lady, Madame Stahl, as everyone called her. Madame Stahl belonged to the highest society, but she was so ill that she could not walk, and only on excep-

[2] "Princess."
[3] I.e., the Franco-Prussian War (1870-71).

tionally fine days she made her appearance at the spa in the wheel-chair. But it was not so much from ill health as from pride—so Princess Shcherbatsky interpreted it—that Madame Stahl had not made the acquaintance of anyone among the Russians there. The Russian girl looked after Madame Stahl, and besides that, she was, as Kitty observed, on friendly terms with all the invalids who were seriously ill, and there were many of them at the spa, and looked after them in the most natural way. The Russian girl was not, as Kitty gathered, related to Madame Stahl, nor was she a paid atten-dant. Madame Stahl called her "Varenka," and other people called her "Mademoiselle Varenka." Apart from the interest Kitty took in this girl's relations with Madame Stahl and with other unknown per-sons, as often happened, she felt an inexplicable attraction to Made-moiselle Varenka, and was aware when their eyes met that she too liked her.

Of Mademoiselle Varenka it could be said that she had passed her first youth, but that she seemed a creature without youth; she might have been taken for nineteen or for thirty. If her features were exam-ined separately, she was good-looking rather than plain, in spite of the sickly hue of her face. She would have had a good figure, too, if it had not been for her extreme thinness, and the size of her head, which was too large for her medium height. But she was not likely to be attractive to men. She was like a fine flower already past its bloom and without fragrance, though the petals were still unwith-ered. Moreover, she would have been unattractive to men also from the lack of just what Kitty had too much of—of the suppressed fire of vitality, and the consciousness of her own attractiveness.

She always seemed absorbed in work about which there could be no doubt, and so it seemed she could not take interest in anything outside it. It was just this contrast with her own position that was for Kitty the great attraction of Mademoiselle Varenka. Kitty felt that in her, in her manner of life, she would find an example of what she was now so painfully seeking: interest in life, a dignity in life—apart from the worldly relations of girls with men, which so revolted her, and appeared to her now as a shameful hawking about of goods in search of a purchaser. The more attentively Kitty watched her unknown friend, the more convinced she was that this girl was the perfect creature she imagined her to be, and the more eagerly she wished to make her acquaintance.

The two girls used to meet several times a day, and every time they met, Kitty's eyes said: "Who are you? What are you? Are you really the exquisite creature I imagine you to be? But for goodness' sake don't suppose," her eyes added, "that I would force my acquaintance on you, I simply admire you and like you." "I like you too, and you're very, very sweet. And I would like you better still, if I had time," answered the eyes of the unknown girl. Kitty saw indeed that she was always busy. Either she was taking the children of a Russian family home from the spa, or fetching a comforter for a sick lady and wrapping her up in it, or trying to interest an irritable invalid, or selecting and buying cakes for tea for someone.

Soon after the arrival of the Shcherbatskys there appeared in the morning crowd at the spa two persons who attracted universal and unfavorable attention. These were a tall man with a stooping figure, and huge hands, in an old coat too short for him, with black, simple, and yet terrible eyes, and a pockmarked, kind-looking woman, very badly and tastelessly dressed. Recognizing these persons as Russians, Kitty had already in her imagination begun constructing a delightful and touching romance about them. But the princess, having ascertained from the visitors' list that this was Nikolai Levin and Marya Nikolaevna, explained to Kitty what a bad man this Levin was, and all her dreams about these two people vanished. Not so much from what her mother told her, as from the fact that it was Konstantin's brother, this pair suddenly seemed to Kitty intensely unpleasant. This Levin, with his continual twitching of his head, aroused in her now an irrepressible feeling of disgust.

It seemed to her that his big, terrible eyes, which persistently pursued her, expressed a feeling of hatred and contempt, and she tried to avoid meeting him.

CHAPTER THIRTY-ONE

It was a wet day; it had been raining all morning, and the invalids, with their parasols, had flocked into the arcades.

Kitty was walking there with her mother and the Moscow colonel, smart and jaunty in his European coat, bought ready-made in Frankfort. They were walking on one side of the arcade, trying to avoid Levin, who was walking on the other side. Varenka, in her dark dress, in a black hat with a turn-down brim, was walking up and down the whole length of the arcade with a blind Frenchwoman, and, every time she met Kitty, they exchanged friendly glances.

"Mama, couldn't I speak to her?" said Kitty, watching her unknown friend, and noticing that she was going up to the spa, and that they might come there together.

"Oh, if you want to so much, I'll find out about her first and make her acquaintance myself," answered her mother. "What do you see in her that's so unusual? A companion, she must be. If you like, I'll make acquaintance with Madame Stahl; I used to know her *belle-soeur*," added the princess, lifting her head haughtily.

Kitty knew that the princess was offended that Madame Stahl had seemed to avoid making her acquaintance. Kitty did not insist.

"How wonderfully sweet she is!" she said, gazing at Varenka just as she handed a glass to the Frenchwoman. "Look how natural and sweet it all is."

"It's so funny to see your *engouements*,"[1] said the princess. "No, we'd better go back," she added, noticing Levin coming toward them with his companion and a German doctor, to whom he was talking very noisily and angrily.

They turned to go back, when suddenly they heard, not noisy talk, but shouting. Levin, stopping short, was shouting at the doctor, and the doctor, too, was excited. A crowd gathered around them. The princess and Kitty beat a hasty retreat, while the colonel joined the crowd to find out what was the matter.

A few minutes later the colonel overtook them.

"What was it?" inquired the princess.

"Scandalous and disgraceful!" answered the colonel. "The one thing to be dreaded is meeting Russians abroad. That tall gentleman was abusing the doctor, flinging all sorts of insults at him because he

[1] "Infatuations."

wasn't treating him quite as he liked, and he began waving his stick at him. It's simply a scandal!"

"Oh, how unpleasant!" said the princess. "Well, and how did it end?"

"Luckily at that point that—the one in the mushroom hat—intervened. A Russian lady, I think she is," said the colonel.

"Mademoiselle Varenka?" asked Kitty.

"Yes, yes. She came to the rescue before anyone; she took the man by the arm and led him away."

"There, Mama," said Kitty; "you wonder that I'm enthusiastic about her."

The next day, as she watched her unknown friend, Kitty noticed that Mademoiselle Varenka was already on the same terms with Levin and his companion as with her other protégés. She went up to them, entered into conversation with them, and served as interpreter for the woman, who could not speak any foreign language.

Kitty began to entreat her mother still more urgently to let her make friends with Varenka. And, disagreeable as it was to the princess to seem to take the first step in wishing to make the acquaintance of Madame Stahl, who thought fit to put on airs, she made inquiries about Varenka, and, having ascertained particulars about her tending to prove that there could be no harm though little good in the acquaintance, she herself approached Varenka and introduced herself.

Choosing a time when her daughter had gone to the spa, while Varenka had stopped outside the baker's, the princess went up to her.

"Allow me to make your acquaintance," she said, with her dignified smile. "My daughter has lost her heart to you," she said. "Possibly you do not know me. I am—"

"That feeling is more than reciprocal, Princess," Varenka answered hurriedly.

"What a good deed you did yesterday for our poor compatriot!" said the princess.

Varenka flushed a little. "I don't remember. I don't think I did anything," she said.

"Why, you saved that Levin from disagreeable consequences."

"Yes, *sa compagne*[2] called me, and I tried to pacify him; he's very ill, and was dissatisfied with the doctor. I'm used to looking after such invalids."

"Yes, I've heard you live at Mentone with your aunt—I think— Madame Stahl: I used to know her *belle-soeur*."

"No, she's not my aunt. I call her Mama, but I am not related to her; I was brought up by her," answered Varenka, flushing a little again.

This was so simply said, and so sweet was the truthful and candid expression of her face, that the princess saw why Kitty had taken such a liking to Varenka.

"Well, and what's this Levin going to do?" asked the princess.

"He's going away," answered Varenka.

At that instant Kitty came up from the spa beaming with delight that her mother had become acquainted with her unknown friend.

"Well, see, Kitty, your intense desire to make friends with Mademoiselle—"

"Varenka," Varenka offered, smiling, "That's what everyone calls me."

Kitty blushed with pleasure, and slowly, without speaking, pressed her new friend's hand, which did not respond to her pressure but lay motionless in her hand. The hand did not respond to her pressure, but Mademoiselle Varenka's face glowed with a soft, glad, though rather mournful smile that showed large but handsome teeth.

"I have long wished for this too," she said.

"But you are so busy."

"Oh, no, I'm not at all busy," answered Varenka, but at that moment she had to leave her new friends because two little Russian girls, children of an invalid, ran up to her.

"Varenka, Mama's calling!" they cried.

And Varenka went after them.

---

[2] "His companion."

CHAPTER THIRTY-TWO

The particulars which the princess had learned in regard to Varenka's past and her relations with Madame Stahl were as follows:

Madame Stahl, of whom some people said that she had worried her husband to death, while others said it was he who had made her wretched by his immoral behavior, had always been a woman of weak health and hysterical temperament. When, after her separation from her husband, she gave birth to her only child, the child had died almost immediately, and the family of Madame Stahl, knowing her sensibility, and fearing the news would kill her, had substituted another child, a baby born the same night and in the same house in Petersburg, the daughter of the chief cook of the palace. This was Varenka. Madame Stahl learned later on that Varenka was not her own child, but she continued bringing her up, especially because very soon afterwards Varenka had not a relation of her own living. Madame Stahl had now been living more than ten years continuously abroad, in the south, never leaving her couch. And some people said that she had made her social position as a philanthropic, highly religious woman; other people said she really was at heart the highly ethical being, living for nothing but the good of her fellow creatures, which she represented herself to be. No one knew what her faith was—Catholic, Protestant, or Greek Orthodox. But one fact was indubitable—she was in amicable relations with the highest dignitaries of all the churches and sects.

Varenka lived with her all the while abroad, and everyone who knew Madame Stahl knew and liked Mademoiselle Varenka, as everyone called her.

Having learned all these facts, the princess found nothing to object to in her daughter's intimacy with Varenka, especially since Varenka's breeding and education were of the best—she spoke French and English extremely well—and, what was of the most weight, brought a message from Madame Stahl expressing her regret that she was prevented by her ill health from making the acquaintance of the princess.

After getting to know Varenka, Kitty became more and more fascinated by her friend, and every day she discovered new virtues in her.

251

The princess, hearing that Varenka had a good voice, asked her to come and sing to them in the evening.

"Kitty plays, and we have a piano; not a good one, it's true, but you will give us so much pleasure," said the princess with her affected smile, which Kitty disliked particularly just then, because she noticed that Varenka had no inclination to sing. Varenka came, however, in the evening and brought a roll of music with her. The princess had invited Marya Yevgenyevna and her daughter and the colonel.

Varenka seemed quite unaffected by there being persons present she did not know, and she went right to the piano. She could not accompany herself, but she could read music very well. Kitty, who played well, accompanied her.

"You have an extraordinary talent," the princess said to her after Varenka had sung the first song extremely well.

Marya Yevgenyevna and her daughter expressed their thanks and admiration.

"Look," said the colonel, looking out of the window, "what an audience has collected to listen to you." There actually was quite a considerable crowd under the windows.

"I am very glad it gives you pleasure," Varenka answered simply.

Kitty looked with pride at her friend. She was enchanted by her talent, and her voice and her face, but most of all by her manner, by the way Varenka obviously thought nothing of her singing and was quite unmoved by their praises. She seemed only to be asking: "Am I to sing again, or is that enough?"

"If it had been me," thought Kitty, "how proud I would have been! How delighted I would have been to see that crowd under the windows! But she's utterly unmoved by it. Her only motive is to avoid refusing and to please Mama. What is there in her? What is it that gives her the power to disregard everything, to be calm independently of everything? How I should like to know it and to learn it from her!" thought Kitty, gazing into her serene face. The princess asked Varenka to sing again, and Varenka sang another song, also smoothly, distinctly, and well, standing erect at the piano and beating time on it with her thin, dark-skinned hand.

The next song in the book was an Italian one. Kitty played the opening bars, and looked round at Varenka.

"Let's skip that," said Varenka, flushing a little. Kitty let her eyes rest on Varenka's face with a look of dismay and inquiry.

"Very well, the next one," she said hurriedly, turning over the pages, and at once feeling that there was something connected with the song.

"No," answered Varenka with a smile, laying her hand on the music, "no, let's have that one." And she sang it just as quietly, as coolly, and as well as the others.

When she had finished, they all thanked her again, and went off to tea. Kitty and Varenka went out into the little garden that adjoined the house.

"Am I right, that you have some memories connected with that song?" said Kitty. "Don't tell me about it," she added hastily, "only say if I'm right."

"No, why not? I'll tell you," said Varenka simply, and without waiting for a reply, she went on: "Yes, it brings back memories, painful ones. I loved someone once, and I used to sing him that song."

Kitty, with big, wide-open eyes, gazed silently, sympathetically at Varenka.

"I loved him and he loved me; but his mother did not wish it, and he married another girl. He lives not far from us, and I see him sometimes. You didn't think I had a love affair too, did you?" she said, and there was a faint gleam in her beautiful face of that fire which Kitty felt must once have glowed all over her.

"I didn't think so? Why, if I were a man, I could never care for anyone else after knowing you. Only I can't understand how he could, to please his mother, forget you and make you unhappy; he had no heart."

"Oh, no, he's a very good man, and I'm not unhappy; quite the contrary, I'm very happy . . . Well, so we shan't be singing any more now," she added, turning toward the house.

"How good you are! How good you are!" cried Kitty, and stopping her, she kissed her. "If I could not be even a little like you!"

"Why should you be like anyone? You're nice as you are," said Varenka, smiling her gentle, weary smile.

"No, I'm not nice at all. Come, tell me . . . Stop a minute, let's sit down," said Kitty, making her sit down again beside her. "Tell me, isn't it humiliating to think that a man has disdained your love, that he hasn't cared for it?. . ."

"But he didn't disdain it; I believe he cared for me, but he was a dutiful son . . ."

"Yes, but if it hadn't been on account of his mother, if it had been his own doing? . . ." said Kitty, feeling she was giving away her secret, and that her face, burning with the flush of shame, had betrayed her already.

"In that case he would have done wrong, and I would not have regretted him," answered Varenka, evidently realizing that they were now talking not of her but of Kitty.

"But the humiliation," said Kitty, "the humiliation one can never forget, can never forget," she said, remembering her expression at the last ball during the pause in the music.

"Where is the humiliation? Why, you did nothing wrong?"

"Worse than wrong—shameful."

Varenka shook her head and laid her hand on Kitty's hand.

"Why, what is there shameful?" she said. "You didn't tell a man who didn't care for you that you loved him, did you?"

"Of course not; I never said a word, but he knew it. No, no, there are looks, there are ways; I can't forget it, if I live a hundred years."

"Why? I don't understand. The whole point is whether you love him now or not," said Varenka, who called everything by its name.

"I hate him; I can't forgive myself."

"Why, what for?"

"The shame, the humiliation!"

"Oh! If everyone were as sensitive as you are!" said Varenka. "There isn't a girl who hasn't been through the same. And it's all so unimportant."

"Why, what is important?" said Kitty, looking into her face with inquisitive wonder.

"Oh, there's so much that's important," said Varenka, smiling.

"Why, what?"

"Oh, so much that's more important," answered Varenka, not knowing what to say. But at that instant they heard the princess's voice from the window. "Kitty, it's cold! Either get a shawl, or come indoors."

"It really is time to go in!" said Varenka, getting up. "I have to go on to Madame Berthe's; she asked me to."

Kitty held her by the hand, and with passionate curiosity and entreaty her eyes asked her: "What is it, what is this of such importance that gives you such tranquillity? You know, tell me!" But Varenka did not even know what Kitty's eyes were asking her. She merely thought that she had to go to see Madame Berthe too that evening, and to hurry home in time for *maman's* tea at twelve o'clock. She went indoors, collected her music, and saying good-by to everyone, prepared to leave.

"Allow me to see you home," said the colonel.

"Yes, how can you go alone at night like this?" the princess chimed in. "Anyway, I'll send Parasha."

Kitty saw that Varenka could hardly restrain a smile at the idea that she needed an escort.

"No, I always go about alone and nothing ever happens to me," she said, taking her hat. And kissing Kitty once more, without saying what was important, she stepped out vigorously with the music under her arm and vanished into the twilight of the summer night, bearing away with her her secret of what was important and what gave her the calm and dignity so much to be envied.

CHAPTER THIRTY-THREE

Kitty made the acquaintance of Madame Stahl too, and this acquaintance, together with her friendship with Varenka, did not merely exercise a great influence on her, it also comforted her in her mental distress. She found this comfort through a completely new world being opened to her by means of this acquaintance, a world having nothing in common with her past, an exalted, noble world, from the height of which she could contemplate her past calmly. It was revealed to her that besides the instinctive life to which Kitty had given herself up till now there was a spiritual life. This life was disclosed in religion, but a religion having nothing in common with that one Kitty had known from childhood, and which found expression in masses and vespers at the Widow's Home, where one might meet one's friends, and in learning by heart Slavonic texts with the priest. This was a lofty, mysterious religion connected with a whole series of noble thoughts and feelings, which one could do more than believe merely because one was told to, which one could love.

Kitty found all this out not from words. Madame Stahl talked to Kitty as to a charming child that one looks on with pleasure as on the memory of one's youth, and only once she said in passing that in all human sorrows nothing gives comfort but love and faith, and that in the sight of Christ's compassion for us no sorrow is trifling—and immediately talked of other things. But in every gesture of Madame Stahl, in every word, in every heavenly—as Kitty called it—look, and above all in the whole story of her life, which she heard from Varenka, Kitty recognized that something "that was important," of which, till then, she had known nothing.

Yet, elevated as Madame Stahl's character was, touching as was her story, and exalted and moving as was her speech, Kitty could not help detecting in her some traits that perplexed her. She noticed that when questioning her about her family, Madame Stahl had smiled contemptuously, which was not in accord with Christian meekness. She noticed, too, that when she had found a Catholic priest with her, Madame Stahl had studiously kept her face in the shadow of the lamp shade and had smiled in a peculiar way. Trivial as these two observations were, they perplexed her, and she had her doubts about Madame Stahl. But on the other hand Varenka, alone in the world, without friends or relations, with a melancholy disappointment in the past, desiring nothing, regretting nothing, was just that perfection of which Kitty dared hardly dream. In Varenka she realized that one has but to forget oneself and love others, and one will be calm, happy, and noble. And that was what Kitty longed to be. Seeing now clearly what was the *most important*, Kitty was not satisfied with being enthusiastic over it; she at once surrendered her whole soul to the new life that was opening for her. From Varenka's accounts of the doings of Madame Stahl and other people whom she mentioned, Kitty had already constructed the plan of her own future life. She would, like Madame Stahl's niece, Aline, of whom Varenka had talked a great deal, seek out those who were in trouble, wherever she might be living, help them as far as she could, distribute Gospels, read the Gospel to the sick, the criminals, the dying. The idea of reading the Gospel to criminals, as Aline did, particularly fascinated Kitty. But all these were secret dreams, of which Kitty did not talk either to her mother or to Varenka.

While awaiting the time for carrying out her plans on a large scale, however, Kitty readily found a chance for practicing her new principles in imitation of Varenka at the spa, where there were so many people ill and unhappy.

At first the princess noticed nothing but that Kitty was much under the influence of her *engouement*, as she called it, for Madame Stahl, and still more for Varenka. She saw that Kitty did not merely imitate Varenka in her conduct, but unconsciously imitated her in her manner of walking, of talking, of blinking her eyes. But later on, the princess noticed that apart from this adoration, some kind of serious spiritual change was taking place in her daughter.

The princess saw that in the evening Kitty read the Gospels in French that Madame Stahl had given her—a thing she had never done before; that she avoided society acquaintances and associated with the sick people who were under Varenka's protection, and especially one poor family, that of a sick painter, Petrov. Kitty was unmistakably proud of playing the part of a sister of mercy in that family. All this was well enough, and the princess had nothing to say against it, especially as Petrov's wife was a perfectly nice sort of woman, and the German princess, noticing Kitty's devotion, praised her, calling her an angel of consolation. All this would have been very well if Kitty had not overdone it. But the princess saw that her daughter was rushing into extremes, and told her so.

"*Il ne faut jamais rien outrer,* "[1] she said to her.

Her daughter made no reply, but in her heart she thought that one could not talk about overdoing it where Christianity was concerned. How could one go too far in the practice of a doctrine wherein one was bidden to turn the other cheek when one was smitten, and give one's cloak if one's coat were taken? But the princess disliked this extreme behavior, and disliked even more the fact that she felt her daughter did not care to reveal her whole heart to her. Kitty did in

---

[1] "Never overdo anything."

fact conceal her new views and feelings from her mother. She concealed them not because she did not respect or did not love her mother, but simply because she was her mother. She would have revealed them to anyone sooner than to her mother.

"Why is it Anna Pavlovna's not been to see us for so long?" the princess said one day of Madame Petrova. "I've asked her, but she seems disturbed about something."

"No, I've not noticed it, *Maman*," said Kitty, flushing hotly.

"Is it long since you went to see them?"

"We intend to make an expedition to the mountain tomorrow," Kitty answered.

"Well, you can go," the princess said, gazing at her daughter's embarrassed face and trying to guess the cause of her embarrassment.

That day Varenka came to dinner and told them that Anna Pavlovna had changed her mind and given up the expedition for the morrow. And the princess noticed again that Kitty reddened.

"Kitty, haven't you had some misunderstanding with the Petrovs?" said the princess, when they were left alone. "Why has she given up sending the children and coming to see us?"

Kitty answered that nothing had happened between them, and that she could not tell why Anna Pavlovna seemed displeased with her. Kitty answered perfectly truly. She did not know the reason Anna Pavlovna had changed toward her, but she guessed it. She guessed at something which she could not tell her mother, which she did not put into words to herself. It was one of those things which one knows but which one can never speak of even to oneself, so terrible and shameful would it be mistaken.

Again and again she went over in her memory all her relations with the family. She remembered the simple delight expressed on the round, good-humored face of Anna Pavlovna at their meetings; she remembered their secret consultations about the invalid, their plots to draw him away from the work which was forbidden him and to get him out of doors; the devotion of the youngest boy, who used to call her "my Kitty," and would not go to bed without her. How nice it all was! Then she recalled the thin, terribly thin figure of Petrov, with his long neck, in his brown coat, his thin, curly hair, his questioning blue eyes that were so terrible to Kitty at first, and his painful attempts to seem hearty and lively in her presence. She recalled the efforts she had made at first to overcome the repugnance she felt for him, as for all consumptive people, and the pains it had cost her to think of things to say to him. She recalled the timid, softened look with which he gazed at her, and the strange feeling of compassion and awkwardness, and later of a sense of her own goodness, which she had felt at it. How nice it all was! But all that was at first. Now, a few days ago, everything was suddenly spoiled. Anna Pavlovna had met Kitty with effected cordiality, and had kept continual watch on her and on her husband.

Could that touching pleasure he showed when she came near be the cause of Anna Pavlovna's coolness?

"Yes," she mused, "there was something unnatural about Anna Pavlovna, and utterly unlike her good nature, when she said angrily the day before yesterday: 'There, he will keep waiting for you; he wouldn't drink his coffee without you, though he's grown so dreadfully weak.' "

"Yes, perhaps too she didn't like it when I gave him the comforter. It was all so simple, but he took it so awkwardly, and was so long thanking me, that I felt awkward too. And then that portrait of me he did so well. And most of all that look of confusion and tenderness! Yes, yes, that's it!" Kitty repeated to herself with horror. "No, it can't be, it shouldn't be! He's so much to be pitied!" she said to herself very soon after.

This doubt poisoned the charm of her new life.

CHAPTER THIRTY-FOUR

Before the end of the season at the spa, Prince Shcherbatsky, who had gone on from Carlsbad to Baden and Kissingen to Russian friends—to get a breath of Russian air, as he said—came back to his wife and daughter.

The views of the prince and of the princess on life abroad were completely opposed. The princess thought everything delightful, and in spite of her established position in Russian society, she tried abroad to be like a fashionable European lady, which she was not—for the simple reason that she was a typical Russian gentlewoman; and so she was affected, which did not altogether suit her. The prince, on the contrary, thought everything foreign detestable, got sick of European life, kept to his Russian habits, and purposely tried to appear less European than he was in reality.

The prince returned thinner, with the skin hanging in loose bags on his cheeks, but in the most cheerful frame of mind. His good humor was even greater when he saw Kitty completely recovered. The news of Kitty's friendship with Madame Stahl and Varenka, and the reports the princess gave him of some kind of change she had noticed in Kitty, troubled the prince and aroused his habitual feeling of jealousy of everything that drew his daughter away from him, and a dread that his daughter might have got out of the reach of his influence into regions inaccessible to him. But these unpleasant matters were all drowned in the sea of kindliness and good humor which was always within him, and more so than ever since the Carlsbad spa.

The day after his arrival the prince, in his long overcoat, with his Russian wrinkles and baggy cheeks propped up by a starched collar, went off with his daughter to the wells in the greatest good humor.

It was a lovely morning: the bright, cheerful houses with their little gardens, the sight of the red-faced, red-armed, beer-drinking German housemaids, working away merrily, did the heart good. But the nearer they got to the well, the oftener they met sick people; and their appearance seemed more pitiable than ever among the customary conditions of well-ordered German life. Kitty was no longer struck by this contrast. The bright sun, the brilliant green of the foliage, the strains of the music were for her the natural setting of all these familiar faces, with their changes for worse or for better, for which she watched. But to the prince the brightness and gaiety of the June morning, and the sound of the orchestra playing a gay waltz then in fashion, and above all, the appearance of the health attendants, seemed to be something inappropriate and monstrous, in conjunction with these slowly moving, dying figures gathered together from all parts of Europe. In spite of his feeling of pride and, as it were, of the return of youth, with his favorite daughter on his arm, he felt awkward, and almost ashamed of his vigorous step and his sturdy, stout limbs. He felt almost like a man naked in a crowd.

"Present me to your new friends," he said to his daughter, squeezing her hand with his elbow. "I like even your horrid Soden for making you so well again. Only it's sad, very sad here. Who's that?"

Kitty mentioned the names of all the people they met, some whom she was acquainted with and some not. At the entrance of the garden they met the blind lady, Madame Berthe, with her guide, and the prince was delighted to see the old Frenchwoman's face light up when she heard Kitty's voice. She at once began talking to him with exaggerated French politeness, applauding him for having such a delightful daughter, extolling Kitty to the skies before her face, and calling her a treasure, a pearl, and a consoling angel.

"Well, she's the second angel, then," said the prince, smiling. "She calls Mademoiselle Varenka angel number one."

"Oh! Mademoiselle Varenka, she's a real angel, *allez*," Madame Berthe assented.

In the arcade they met Varenka herself. She was walking rapidly toward them carrying an elegant red bag.

"Here is Papa," Kitty said to her, "he's just come."

Varenka made—simply and naturally, as she did everything—a movement between a bow and a curtsey, and immediately began talking to the prince without shyness, naturally, as she talked to everyone.

"Of course I know you; I know you very well," the prince said to her with a smile, in which Kitty detected with joy that her father liked her friend. "Where are you off to in such haste?"

"*Maman* is here," she said, turning to Kitty. "She has not slept all night, and the doctor advised her to go out. I'm taking her her work."

"So that's angel number one?" said the prince when Varenka had gone on.

Kitty saw that her father had meant to make fun of Varenka, but that he could not do it because he liked her.

"Come, so we shall see all your friends," he went on, "even Madame Stahl, if she sees fit to recognize me."

"Why, did you know her, Papa?" Kitty asked apprehensively, catching the gleam of irony that kindled in the prince's eyes at the mention of Madame Stahl.

"I used to know her husband, and her too a little before she'd joined the Pietists." [1]

"What is a Pietist, Papa?" asked Kitty, dismayed to find that what she prized so highly in Madame Stahl had a name.

"I don't quite know myself. I only know that she thanks God for everything, for every misfortune, and thanks God too that her husband died. And that's rather funny, because they didn't get along together.

"Who's that? What a piteous face!" he asked, noticing a sick man of medium height sitting on a bench, wearing a brown overcoat and white trousers that fell in strange folds about his long, fleshless legs. This man lifted his straw hat, showing his thin, curly hair and high forehead, painfully reddened by the pressure of the hat.

"That's Petrov, an artist," answered Kitty, blushing. "And that's his wife," she added, indicating Anna Pavlovna, who, as though on purpose, at the very instant they approached, walked away after a child who had run off along a path.

"Poor fellow! and what a nice face he has!" said the prince. "Why don't you go to him? He wanted to speak to you."

"Well, let us go, then," said Kitty, turning around resolutely. "How are you feeling today?" she asked Petrov.

Petrov got up, leaning on his stick, and looked shyly at the prince.

"This is my daughter," said the prince. "Let me introduce myself."

The painter bowed and smiled, showing his strangely dazzling white teeth.

"We expected you yesterday, Princess," he said to Kitty. He staggered as he said this, and then repeated the motion, trying to make it seem as if it had been intentional.

"I meant to come, but Varenka said that Anna Pavlovna sent word you were not going."

"Not going!" said Petrov, blushing and immediately beginning to cough, and his eyes sought his wife. "Aneta! Aneta!" he said loudly, and the swollen veins stood out like cords on his thin white neck.

Anna Pavlovna came up.

[1] A religious and philanthropic organization started by P. J. Spener (1635-1705), German Lutheran theologian, in 1675.

"So you sent word to the princess that we weren't going!" he whispered to her angrily, losing his voice.

"Good morning, Princess," said Anna Pavlovna, with an assumed smile utterly unlike her former manner. "Very glad to make your acquaintance," she said to the prince. "You've long been expected, Prince."

"Why did you send word to the princess that we weren't going?" the artist whispered hoarsely once more, still more angrily, obviously exasperated that his voice failed him, so that he could not give his words the expression he would have liked.

"Oh, goodness me, I thought we weren't going," his wife answered crossly.

"What, when . . ." He coughed and waved his hand. The prince took off his hat and moved away with his daughter.

"Ah! Ah!" he sighed deeply. "Oh, poor things!"

"Yes, Papa," answered Kitty. "And you must know they've three children, no servant and scarcely any means. He gets something from the Academy," she went on briskly, trying to drown the distress that the peculiar change in Anna Pavlovna's manner toward her had aroused in her.

"Oh, here's Madame Stahl," said Kitty, indicating a wheelchair, where, propped on pillows, something in gray and blue was lying under a sunshade. This was Madame Stahl. Behind her stood the gloomy, healthy-looking German workman who pushed the carriage. Close by was standing a flaxen-headed Swedish count, whom Kitty knew by name. Several invalids were lingering near the wheelchair, staring at the lady as though she was some curiosity.

The prince went up to her, and Kitty detected that disconcerting gleam of irony in his eyes. He addressed Madame Stahl with extreme courtesy and affability in that excellent French that so few speak nowadays.

"I don't know if you remember me, but I must recall myself to you to thank you for your kindness to my daughter," he said, taking off his hat and not putting it on again.

"Prince Aleksandr Shcherbatsky," said Madame Stahl, lifting upon him her heavenly eyes, in which Kitty discerned a look of annoyance. "Delighted! I have taken a great liking to your daughter."

"You are still in poor health?"

"Yes; I'm used to it," said Madame Stahl, and she introduced the prince to the Swedish count.

"You are scarcely changed at all," the prince said to her. "It's ten or eleven years since I had the honor of seeing you."

"Yes; God sends the cross and sends the strength to bear it. Often one wonders that the goal of this life is? . . . The other side!" she said angrily to Varenka, who had rearranged the comforter over her feet, not to her satisfaction.

"To do good, probably," said the prince with a twinkle in his eye.

"That is not for us to judge," said Madame Stahl, perceiving the shade of expression on the prince's face. "So you will send me that book, dear Count? I'm very grateful to you," she said to the young Swede.

"Ah!" cried the prince, catching sight of the Moscow colonel standing near, and with a bow to Madame Stahl, he walked away with his daughter and the Moscow colonel, who joined them.

"That's our aristocracy, Prince!" the Moscow colonel said with ironical intention. He cherished a grudge against Madame Stahl for not making his acquaintance.

"She's just the same," replied the prince.

"Did you know her before her illness, Prince—that is, before she took to her bed?"

"Yes. She took to her bed before my eyes," said the prince.

"They say it's ten years since she has stood on her feet."

"She doesn't stand up because her legs are too short. She had a very bad figure."

"Papa, it's not possible!" cried Kitty.

"That's what wicked tongues say, my darling. And your Varenka catches it too," he added. "Oh, these invalid ladies!"

"Oh, no, Papa!" Kitty objected warmly. "Varenka worships her. And then she does so much good! Ask anyone! Everyone knows her and Aline Stahl."

"Perhaps so," said the prince, pressing her hand with his elbow; "but it's better when one does good in such a manner that no one knows of it."

Kitty did not answer, not because she had nothing to say, but because she did not care to reveal her secret thoughts even to her father. But, strange to say, although she had made up her mind not to be influenced by her father's views, not to let him into her inmost sanctuary, she felt that the heavenly image of Madame Stahl, which she had carried for a whole month in her heart, had vanished, never to return, just as the fantastic figure made up of some clothes thrown down at random vanishes when one sees that it is only some garment lying there. All that was left was a woman with short legs, who lay down because she has a bad figure, and tormented patient Varenka for not arranging her comforter to her liking. And by no effort of the imagination could Kitty bring back the former Madame Stahl.

CHAPTER THIRTY-FIVE

The prince communicated his high spirits to his own family and his friends, and even to the German landlord in whose rooms the Shcherbatskys were staying.

On coming back with Kitty from the wells, the prince, who had asked the colonel and Marya Yevgenyevna and Varenka all to come and have coffee with them, gave orders for a table and chairs to be taken into the garden under the chestnut tree, and lunch to be laid there. The landlord and the servants, too, grew brisker under the influence of his high spirits. They knew his generous nature; and half an hour later the invalid doctor from Hamburg, who lived on the top floor, looked enviously out of the window at the merry party of healthy Russians assembled under the chestnut tree. In the trembling circles of shadow cast by the leaves, at a table covered with a white cloth and set with coffee pot, bread and butter, cheese, and cold game, sat the princess in a high cap with lilac ribbons, distributing cups of coffee and sandwiches. At the other end sat the prince, eating heartily, and talking loudly and merrily. The prince had spread out near him his purchases, carved boxes, knickknacks, paper knives of all sorts, of which he bought a heap at every spa, and bestowed them upon everyone, including Lieschen, the servant girl, and the landlord, with whom he jested in his comically bad German, assuring him that it was not the water that had cured Kitty but his splendid food, especially his prune soup. The princess laughed at her husband for his Russian ways, but she was more lively and good-humored than she had been all the while she had been at the spa. The colonel smiled, as he always did, at the prince's jokes, but as far as regards Europe, of which he believed himself to be making a careful study, he took the princess's side. The simple-hearted Marya Yevgenyevna simply roared with laughter at everything absurd the prince said, and his jokes made Varenka helpless with feeble but infectious laughter, which was something Kitty had never seen before.

Kitty was glad of all this, but she could not be light-hearted. She could not solve the problem her father had unconsciously created for her by his good-humored view of her friends, and of the life that had so attracted her. To this doubt there was joined the change in her relations with the Petrovs, which had been so conspicuously and unpleasantly marked that morning. Everyone was happy, but Kitty could not feel cheerful, and this increased her distress. She knew a feeling such as she had known in childhood when she had been locked in her room as a punishment, and had heard her sisters' merry laughter outside.

"Well, but what did you buy this mass of things for?" said the princess, smiling, and handing her husband a cup of coffee.

"One goes for a walk, one looks in a shop, and they ask you to buy. *Erlaucht, Excellenz, Durchlaucht.*[1] As soon as they get to '*Durchlaucht*' I can't hold out. I lose ten thalers."

"It's simply from boredom," said the princess.

"Of course it is. Such boredom, my dear, that one doesn't know what to do with oneself."

"How can you be bored, Prince? There's so much that's interesting now in Germany," said Marya Yevgenyevna.

"But I know everything that's interesting: the prune soup I know, and the pea sausages I know. I know everything."

"No, you may say what you like, Prince, their institutions are of interest," said the colonel.

"But what is there interesting about it? They're all as pleased as a shiny kopek. They've conquered everybody, and why am I to be

---

[1] "Eminence, Excellency, Serene Highness."

pleased at that? I haven't conquered anyone; and I'm obliged to take off my own boots, yes, and put them away too; in the morning, get up and dress at once, and go to the dining room to drink bad tea! How different it is at home! You get up in no haste, you get cross, grumble a little, and recover again. You've time to think things over. No need to hurry about anything."

"But time's money, you forget that," said the colonel.

"Time, indeed, that depends! Why, there's time one would give a month of for fifty kopeks, and time you wouldn't give half an hour of for any amount. Isn't that so, Katinka? What is it: why are you so depressed?"

"I'm not depressed."

"Where are you off to? Stay a little longer," he said to Varenka.

"I must be going home," said Varenka, getting up, and again she went off into a giggle. When she had recovered, she said good-by and went into the house to get her hat.

Kitty followed her. Even Varenka struck her as different. She was not worse, only different from what she had thought her before.

"Oh, dear! it's a long time since I've laughed so much!" said Varenka, gathering up her parasol and her bag. "How nice he is, your father!"

Kitty did not speak.

"When shall I see you again?" asked Varenka.

"Mama meant to go and see the Petrovs. Won't you be there?" said Kitty, testing Varenka.

"Yes," answered Varenka. "They're getting ready to go away, so I promised to help them pack."

"Well, I'll come too, then."

"No, why should you?"

"Why not? why not? why not?" said Kitty, opening her eyes wide, and clutching at Varenka's parasol so as not to let her go. "No, wait a minute; why not?"

"Oh, nothing; your father has come, and besides, they will feel awkward at your helping."

"No, tell me: why don't you want me to be at the Petrovs? You don't want me to—why not?"

"I didn't say that," said Varenka quietly.

"No, please tell me!"

"Tell you everything?" asked Varenka.

"Everything, everything!" Kitty assented.

"Well, there's really nothing of any consequence; only that Mikhail Alekseevich" (that was the artist's name) "had meant to leave earlier, and now he doesn't want to go away," said Varenka, smiling.

"Well, well?" Kitty urged impatiently, looking darkly at Varenka.

"Well, and for some reason Anna Pavlovna told him that he didn't want to because you are here. Of course, that was nonsense; but there was a dispute over it—over you. You know how irritable these sick people are."

Kitty, scowling more than ever, kept silent, and Varenka went on speaking alone, trying to soften or soothe her, and seeing a storm coming—she did not know whether of tears or of words.

"So you'd better not go . . . You understand; you won't be offended?"

"And it serves me right! And it serves me right!" Kitty cried quickly, snatching the parasol out of Varenka's hand and looking past her friend's face.

Varenka felt inclined to smile, looking at her childish fury, but she was afraid of hurting her.

"How does it serve you right? I don't understand," she said.

"It serves me right because it was all false; because it was all pretense, and not from the heart. What business had I to interfere with outsiders? And so it's happened that I'm the cause of a quarrel, and that I've done what nobody asked me to do. Because it was all a fake! A fake! A fake!"

"False! Why did you have to pretend?" said Varenka gently.

"Oh, it's idiotic, so hateful! There was no need whatever for me. . . Nothing but falseness!" she said, opening and shutting the parasol.

"But why?"

"To seem better to people, to myself, to God; to deceive everyone. No! Now I won't descend to that. I'll be bad; but anyway not a liar, a cheat."

"But who is a cheat?" said Varenka reproachfully. "You speak as if—"

But Kitty was in one of her gusts of fury, and she would not let her finish.

"I don't talk about you, not about you at all. You're perfection. Yes, yes, I know you're all perfection; but what am I to do if I'm bad? This would never have been if I weren't bad. So let me be what I am. I won't be a fake. What have I to do with Anna Pavlovna? Let them go their way, and me go mine. I can't be different . . . And yet it's not that, it's not that."

"What is not that?" asked Varenka in bewilderment.

"Everything. I can't act except from the heart, and you act from principle. I liked you because I liked you, but you probably only wanted to save me, to improve me."

"You are unfair," said Varenka.

"But I'm not speaking of other people, I'm speaking of myself."

"Kitty"—they heard her mother's voice—"Come here, show Papa your coral necklace."

Kitty, with a haughty air, without making peace with her friend, took the coral necklace from a little box on the table and went to her mother.

"What's the matter? Why are you so flushed?" her mother and father said to her with one voice.

"Nothing," she answered. "I'll be right back," and she ran back.

"She's still here," she thought. "What am I to say to her? Oh, dear! What have I done, what have I said? Why was I rude to her? What am I to do? What am I to say to her?" thought Kitty, and she stopped in the doorway.

Varenka, in her hat, and with the parasol in her hands, was sitting at the table examining the spring of her parasol which Kitty had broken. She lifted her head.

"Varenka, forgive me, do forgive me," whispered Kitty, going up to her. "I don't remember what I said. I—"

"I really didn't mean to hurt you," said Varenka, smiling.

Peace was made. But with her father's coming, the whole world in which she had been living was transformed for Kitty. She did not give up everything she had learned, but she became aware that she had deceived herself in supposing she could be what she wanted to be. Her eyes were, it seemed, opened; she felt all the difficulty of maintaining herself without hypocrisy and self-conceit on the pinnacle she had wished to mount. Moreover, she became aware of all the dreariness of the world of sorrow, of sick and dying people, in which she had been living. The efforts she had made to like it seemed to her intolerable,and she felt a longing to get back quickly into the fresh air, to Russia, to Yergushovo, where, as she knew from letters, her sister Dolly had already gone with her children.

But her affection for Varenka did not wane. As she said good-by Kitty begged her to come see them in Russia.

"I'll come when you get married," said Varenka.

"I shall never marry."

"Well, then, I shall never come."

"Well, then, I shall be married simply for that. Mind that you remember your promise," said Kitty.

The doctor's prediction was fulfilled. Kitty returned home to Russia cured. She was not as gay and thoughtless as before, but she was serene. Her Moscow troubles had become a memory.

PART THREE

CHAPTER ONE

Sergey Ivanovich Koznyshev wanted a rest from mental work, and instead of going abroad as he usually did, he went to stay in the country with his brother toward the end of May. In his judgment the best sort of life was a country life. He had come now to enjoy such a life at his brother's. Konstantin Levin was very glad to have him, especially as he did not expect his brother Nikolai that summer. But in spite of his affection and respect for Sergey Ivanovich, Konstantin Levin was uncomfortable with his brother in the country. It made him uncomfortable, and it positively annoyed him, to see his brother's attitude toward the country. To Konstantin Levin, the country was where one spent one's life, where there were pleasure, endeavors, labor. To Sergey Ivanovich, the country meant on one hand rest from work, on the other a valuable antidote to the corrupt influences of town, which he took with satisfaction and a sense of its utility. To Konstantin Levin, the country was especially good because it afforded an opportunity for labor, of the usefulness of which there could be no doubt. To Sergey Ivanovich, the country was particularly good because there it was possible and fitting to do nothing. Moreover, Sergey Ivanovich's attitude toward the peasants rather piqued Konstantin. Sergey Ivanovich used to say that he knew and liked the peasantry, and he often talked to the peasants, which he knew how to do without affectation or condescension, and from every such conversation he would deduce general conclusions in favor of the peasantry and in confirmation of his knowing them. Konstantin Levin did not like such an attitude toward the peasants. To Konstantin, the peasant was simply the chief partner in their common labor, and in spite of all the respect and the love, almost like that of kinship, he had for the peasant—imbibed probably, as he said himself, with the milk of his peasant nurse—still, as their partner, while sometimes enthu-

271

siastic over the vigor, gentleness, and justice of these men, he was very often, when their common labors called for other qualities, exasperated with the peasant for his carelessness, disorganization, drunkenness, and lying. If he had been asked whether he liked or didn't like the peasants, Konstantin Levin would have been absolutely at a loss as to what to reply. He liked and did not like the peasants, just as he liked and did not like men in general. Of course, being a good-hearted man, he liked men more than he disliked them, and so too with the peasants. But like or dislike the common people as something apart he could not, not only because he lived with them, and all his interests were bound up with theirs, but also because he regarded himself as a part of them, did not see any special qualities or failings distinguishing himself from the common people and could not contrast himself with them. Moreover, although he had lived so long in the closest relations with the peasants, as farmer and arbitrator, and what was more, as adviser (the peasants trusted him, and for thirty miles around they would come to ask his advice), he had no definite views of the peasantry, and would have been as much at a loss to answer the question whether he knew the common people as the question whether he liked them. For him to say he knew the peasantry would have been the same as to say he knew men. He was continually watching and getting to know people of all sorts, and among them peasants, whom he regarded as good and interesting people, and he was continually discovering new traits, altering his former views of them and forming new ones. With Sergey Ivanovich it was quite the contrary. Just as he liked and praised a country life in comparison with the life he did not like, so too he liked the peasantry in contradistinction to the class of men he did not like, and so too he knew the peasantry as something distinct from and opposed to men generally. In his methodical brain there were distinctly formulated certain aspects of peasant life, deduced partly from that life itself, but chiefly from contrast with other modes of life. He never changed his opinion of the peasantry and his sympathetic attitude toward them.

In the discussions that arose between the brothers on their views of the peasantry, Sergey Ivanovich always got the better of his brother, precisely because Sergey Ivanovich had definite ideas about the peasant—his character, his qualities, and his tastes. Konstantin Levin had no definite and unalterable idea on the subject, and so in their arguments Konstantin was readily convicted of contradicting himself.

In Sergey Ivanovich's eyes his younger brother was a splendid fellow, with his heart in the right place (as he expressed it in French), but with a mind which, thought fairly quick, was too much influenced by the impressions of the moment, and consequently filled with contradictions. With all the condescension of an elder brother he sometimes explained to him the true import of things, but he derived little satisfaction from arguing with him, because he got the better of him too easily.

Konstantin Levin regarded his brother as a man of immense intellect and culture, noble in the highest sense of the word, and possessed of a special faculty for working for the public good. But in the depths of his heart, the older he became, and the more intimately he knew his brother, the more and more frequently the thought struck him that this faculty of working for the public good, of which he felt himself utterly devoid, was possibly not so much a quality as a lack of something—not a lack of good, honest, noble desires and tastes, but a lack of vital force, of what is called heart, of that impulse which drives a man to choose one out of the innumerable paths of life and to care only for that one. The better he knew his brother, the more he noticed that Sergey Ivanovich, and many other people who worked for the public welfare, were not led by an impulse of the heart to care for the public good, but reasoned from intellectual considerations that it was a right thing to take interest in public affairs, and consequently took interest in them. Levin was confirmed in this generalization by observing that his brother did not take questions affecting the public welfare or the question of the immortality of the soul any more to heart than he did chess problems, or the ingenious construction of a new machine.

Besides this, Konstantin Levin was not at ease with his brother, because in summer in the country Levin was continually busy with work on the land, and the long summer day was not long enough for him to get through all he had to do, while Sergey Ivanovich was taking a holiday. But though he was taking a holiday now, that is to say, he was doing no writing, he was so used to intellectual activity that he liked to put into concise and eloquent shape the ideas that occurred to him, and liked to have someone listen to him. His most usual and natural listener was his brother. And so, in spite of the friendliness and directness of their relations, Konstantin felt an awkwardness in leaving him alone. Sergey Ivanovich liked to stretch himself on the grass in the sun, and to lie there, basking and chatting lazily.

"You wouldn't believe," he would say to his brother, "what a pleasure this rural laziness is to me. Not an idea in one's brain, as empty as a drum!"

But Konstantin Levin found it boring sitting and listening to him, especially when he knew that while he was away they would be carting manure to fields that were not plowed and ready for it, and heap it all up anyhow; and would not screw the shares in the plows, but would let them come off and then say that the new plows were a silly invention, and there was nothing like the old Andreevna plow,[1] and so on.

"Come, you've done enough trudging about in the heat," Sergey Ivanovich would say to him.

"No, I must just run to the office for a minute," Levin would answer, and he would run off to the fields.

CHAPTER TWO

Early in June it happened that Agafya Mikhailovna, the old nurse and housekeeper, in carrying to the cellar a jar of mushrooms she had just pickled, slipped, fell, and sprained her wrist. The district doctor, a talkative young medical student who had just finished his studies, came to see her. He examined the wrist, said it was not broken, was delighted at the chance of talking to the celebrated Sergey Ivanovich Koznyshev, and to show his advanced views of things, he told him all the gossip of the district, complaining of the poor state into which the district council had fallen. Sergey Ivanovich listened attentively, asked him questions, and, roused by a new listener, talked fluently,

[1] Comic name of primitive plow.

uttered a few keen and weighty observations, respectfully appreciated by the young doctor, and was soon in the eager frame of mind his brother knew so well, which inevitably followed a brilliant and eager conversation. After the departure of the doctor, he wanted to go with a fishing rod to the river. Sergey Ivanovich was fond of angling, and was, it seemed, proud of being fond of such a stupid occupation.

Konstantin Levin, whose presence was needed in the fields and the meadows, had come to take his brother in the trap.

It was that time of the year, the turning point of summer, when the crops of the present year are a certainty, when one begins to think of the sowing for next year, and the harvest is at hand; when the rye is formed, though its ears are still light, not yet full, and, gray-green, it waves in the wind; when the green oats, with tufts of yellow grass scattered here and there among it, droop irregularly over the late-sown fields; when the early buckwheat is already out and hiding the ground; when the fallow land, trodden hard as stone by the cattle, is half plowed over, with paths too hard to be touched by the plow; when, from the dry manure heaps carted onto the fields, there comes at sunset a smell of manure mingled with the honeyed odor of grasses, and on the low lands the riverside meadows are a thick sea of grass waiting for the mowing, with blackening heaps of sorrel stalks among it.

It was the time when there comes a brief pause in the toil of the fields before the beginning of the labors of harvest—every year recurring, every year straining every nerve of the peasants. The crop was a splendid one, and bright, hot summer days had set in with short, dewy nights.

The brothers had to drive through the woods to reach the meadows. Sergey Ivanovich was all the while admiring the beauty of the woods, which were a tangled mass of leaves, pointing out to his brother here an old lime tree on the point of flowering, dark on the shady side and brightly spotted with yellow stipules, there the young shoots of this year's saplings brilliant with emerald. Konstantin Levin did not like talking and hearing abut the beauty of nature. Words for him diminished the beauty of what he saw. He agreed to what his brother said, but he could not help beginning to think of other things. When they came out of the woods, his attention was completely engrossed by the view of the fallow land on the slope of a hill, in parts yellow with grass, in parts trampled and checkered with furrows, in parts dotted with ridges of manure, and in parts even plowed. A string of carts was moving across it. Levin counted the carts, and was pleased that all that were needed had been brought, and at the sight of the meadows his thoughts passed to the mowing. He always felt singularly excited at the haymaking. On reaching the meadow, Levin stopped the horse.

The morning dew was still lying on the thick undergrowth of the grass, and so that he might not get his feet wet, Sergey Ivanovich asked his brother to drive him in the trap up to the willow tree from which the carp was caught. Sorry as Konstantin Levin was to crush his grass, he drove him into the meadow. The high grass softly turned about the wheels and the horse's legs, leaving its seeds clinging to the wet axles and spokes of the wheels. His brother seated himself under a bush, arranging his tackle, while Levin led the horse away, tied him up, and walked into the vast gray-green sea of grass unmoved by the wind. The silky grass with its ripe seeds came almost to his waist in the dampest spots.

Crossing the meadow, Konstantin Levin came out onto the road, and met an old man with a swollen eye, carrying a beehive on his shoulder.

"What? Taken a stray swarm, Fomich?" he asked.

"No, indeed, Konstantin Mitrich![1] All we can do to keep our own! This is the second swarm that has flown away. . . . Luckily the boys caught them. They were plowing your field. They unyoked the horses and galloped after them."

"Well, what do you say, Fomich—start mowing or wait a while?"

"Eh, well. Our way's to wait till St. Peter's Day.[2] But you always mow sooner. Well, to be sure, please God, the hay's good. There'll be plenty for the beasts."

"What do you think about the weather?"

"That's in God's hands. Maybe it will be fine."

Levin went up to his brother.

[1] Peasant version of "Dmitrievich."
[2] Reckoning by Saints' days was common. The feast of both St. Peter and St. Paul fell on June 29 (O.S.).

Sergey Ivanovich had caught nothing, but he was not bored, and seemed in the most cheerful frame of mind. Levin saw that, stimulated by his conversation with the doctor, he wanted to talk. Levin, on the other hand, would have liked to get home as soon as possible to give orders about getting together the mowers for next day, and to set at rest his doubts about the mowing, which greatly absorbed him.

"Well, let's be going," he said.

"Why be in such a hurry? Let's stay a little. But how wet you are! Even though one catches nothing, it's nice. That's the best thing about every part of sport, that one has to do with nature. How exquisite this steely water is!" said Sergey Ivanovich. "These riverside banks always remind me of the riddle—do you know it? 'The grass says to the water: we sway and we sway.'"

"I don't know the riddle," answered Levin wearily.

CHAPTER THREE

"Do you know I've been thinking about you," said Sergey Ivanovich. "It's disgraceful what's being done in the district, according to what this doctor tells me. He's a very intelligent fellow. And as I've told you before, I tell you again: it's not right for you not to go to the meeting, and in general to keep out of the district business. If decent people won't go into it, of course it's bound to go all wrong. We pay the money, and it all goes in salaries, and there are no schools, or male nurses, or midwives, or pharmacies—nothing."

"Well, I did try, you know," Levin said slowly and unwillingly. "I can't! And so that's all there is to it."

"But why can't you? I must admit I can't understand. Indifference, incapacity—I won't admit; surely it's not simply laziness?"

"None of those things. I've tried, and I see I can do nothing," said Levin.

He had hardly grasped what his brother was saying. Looking toward the plowland across the river, he made out something black, but he could not distinguish whether it was only a horse or the bailiff on horseback.

"Why is it you can do nothing? You made an attempt and didn't succeed, so you think, and you give in. How can you have so little self-respect?"

"Self-respect!" said Levin, stung to the quick by his brother's words; "I don't understand. If they'd told me at college that other people understood the integral calculus and I didn't, then pride would have come in. But in this case one wants first to be convinced that one has certain qualifications for this sort of business, and especially that all this business is of great importance."

"What! Do you mean to say it's not of importance?" said Sergey Ivanovich, stung to the quick too at his brother's considering anything of no importance that interested him, and still more at his obviously paying little attention to what he was saying.

"I don't think it important; it does not excite me, I can't help it," answered Levin, making out that what he saw was the bailiff, and that the bailiff seemed to be taking the peasants off the plowing. They were turning the plow over. "Can they have finished plowing?" he wondered.

"Come, really," said the elder brother, with a frown on his handsome, intelligent face, "there's a limit to everything. It's all right to be eccentric, to be sincere, and to dislike hypocrisy—I know all about that; but really, what you're saying either has no meaning, or it has a very wrong meaning. How can you think it a matter of no importance whether the peasant, whom you love as you assert—"

"I never did assert it," thought Konstantin Levin.

"—dies without help? The ignorant midwives let the infants die, and the people stagnate in darkness, and are helpless in the hands of every village clerk, while you have at your disposal a means of helping them, and don't help them because to your mind it's of no importance."

And Sergey Ivanovich put before him the alternative: "Either you are so backward that you can't see all that you can do, or you won't sacrifice your comfort, your vanity, or whatever it is, to do it."

Konstantin Levin felt that there was no course open to him but to submit, or to confess to a lack of zeal for the public good. And this mortified him and hurt his feelings.

"It's both," he said resolutely. "I don't see that it was possible—"

"What! Was it impossible, if the money was put up, to provide medical aid?"

"Impossible, as it seems to me . . . For the three thousand square miles of our district, what with our thaws and the storms and the work in the fields, I don't see how it is possible to provide medical aid all over. And besides, I don't believe in medicine."

"Oh, well, that's unfair. . . . I can quote to you thousands of instances. . . . But the schools, anyway."

"Why have schools?"

"What do you mean? Can there be two opinions of the advantage of education? If it's a good thing for you, it's a good thing for everyone."

Konstantin Levin felt himself morally pinned against a wall, and so he got excited, and unconsciously blurted out the chief cause of his indifference to social issues.

"Perhaps it may all be very good; but why should I worry myself about establishing dispensaries which I shall never make use of, and schools to which I shall never send my children, to which even the peasants don't want to send their children, and to which I've no very firm faith that they ought to send them?" said he.

Sergey Ivanovich was for a minute surprised at this unexpected view of the subject; but he promptly made a new plan of attack. He was silent for a while, drew out a hook, threw it in again, and turned to his brother, smiling.

"Come, now . . . In the first place, the dispensary is needed. We ourselves sent for the district doctor for Agafya Mikhailovna."

"Oh, well, but I think her wrist will never be straight again anyway."

"That remains to be proved. . . . Next, the peasant who can read and write is as a workman of more use and value to you."

"No; you can ask anyone you like," Konstantin Levin answered with decision, "the man that can read and write is much inferior as a workman. And mending the roads is an impossibility; and as soon as they put up bridges they're stolen."

"Still, that's not the point," said Sergey Ivanovich, frowning. He disliked contradiction, and still more, arguments that were continually skipping from one thing to another, introducing new and disconnected points, so that there was no knowing to which to reply. "Do you admit that education is a benefit for the people?"

"Yes, I admit it," said Levin without thinking, and he was conscious immediately that he had said what he did not think. He felt that if he admitted that, it would be proved that he had been talking meaningless rubbish. How it would be proved he could not tell, but he knew that this would inevitably be logically proved to him, and he awaited that proof.

The argument turned out to be far simpler than he had expected.

"If you admit that it is a benefit," said Sergey Ivanovich, "then, as an honest man, you cannot help caring about it and sympathizing with the movement, and so wishing to work for it."

"But I still do not admit this movement to be just," said Konstantin Levin, reddening a little.

"What! But you said just now—"

"That's to say, I don't admit it's being either good or possible."

"That you can't tell without trying it."

"Well, supposing that's so," said Levin, though he did not suppose so at all, "supposing that is so, still I don't see, all the same, what I'm to worry myself about it for."

"How so?"

"No; since we are talking, explain it to me from the philosophical point of view," said Levin.

"I can't see where philosophy comes in," said Sergey Ivanovich, in a tone, Levin thought, as though he did not admit his brother's right to talk about philosophy. And that irritated Levin.

"I'll tell you, then," he said with excitement, "I imagine the mainspring of all our actions is, after all, self-interest. Now, in the local institutions I, as a nobleman, see nothing that could contribute to my prosperity, and the roads are not better and could not be better; my horses carry me well enough over bad ones. Doctors and dispensaries are no use to me. An arbitrator of disputes is no use to me. I never appeal to him, and never shall appeal to him. The schools are no good to me, but positively harmful, as I told you. For me the district councils simply mean I have to pay eighteen kopeks for every three acres, to drive into town, sleep with bugs, and listen to all sorts of idiocy and loathsomeness, and self-interest offers me no inducement."

"Excuse me," Sergey Ivanovich interposed with a smile, "self-interest did not induce us to work for the emancipation of the serfs, but we did work of it."

"No!" Konstantin Levin broke in, still more excitedly; "the emancipation of the serfs was a different matter. There self-interest did come in. One longed to throw off that yoke that crushed us, all decent people among us. But to be a town councilor and discuss how many outhouse men are needed, and how drains shall be constructed in a town in which I don't live—to serve on a jury and try a peasant who's stolen some ham, and listen for six hours at a stretch to all sorts of jabber from the counsel for the defense and the prosecution, and the president cross-examining my old half-witted Alyoshka, 'Do you admit, prisoner in the dock, the fact of the removal of the ham?' Eh?"

Konstantin Levin had warmed to his subject, and began mimicking the president and the half-witted Alyoshka: it seemed to him that it was all to the point.

But Sergey Ivanovich shrugged his shoulders.

"Well, what do you mean to say, then?"

"I simply mean to say that those rights that touch me . . . my interest, I shall always defend to the best of my ability; that when they made raids on us students, and the police read our letters, I was ready to defend those rights to the utmost, to defend my rights to education and freedom. I can understand compulsory military service, which affects my children, my brothers, and myself, I am ready to deliberate on what concerns me; but deliberating on how to spend forty thousand rubles of district council money, or judging the half-witted Alyoshka—I don't understand, and I can't do it."

Konstantin Levin spoke as though the floodgates of his speech had burst open. Sergey Ivanovich smiled.

"But tomorrow it'll be your turn to be tried; would it have suited your tastes better to be tried in the old criminal court?"

"I'm not going to be tried. I won't murder anybody, and I don't need anything like that. Well, I tell you what," he went on, again flying off to a subject quite beside the point, "our district self-government and all the rest of it—it's just like the birch branches we stick in the ground on Trinity Day, for instance, to look like the wood that has grown up by itself in Europe, and I can't gush over these birch branches and believe in them."

Sergey Ivanovich merely shrugged his shoulders, as though to express his amazement at how the birch branches had come into their argument at that point, though he did really understand at once what his brother meant.

"Excuse me, but you know one really can't argue in that way," he observed.

But Konstantin Levin wanted to justify himself for the failing, of which he was conscious, of lack of zeal for the public welfare, and he went on.

"I imagine," he said, "that no sort of activity is likely to be lasting if it is not founded on self-interest, that's a universal principle, a philosophical principle," he said, repeating the word "philosophical" with determination, as though wishing to show that he had as much right as anyone else to talk of philosophy.

Sergey Ivanovich smiled. "He too has a philosophy of his own at the service of his natural tendencies," he thought.

"Come, you'd better let philosophy alone," he said. "The chief problem of the philosophy of all ages consists just in finding the indispensable connection which exists between individual and social interests. But that's not to the point; what is to the point is a correction I must make in your comparison. The birches are not simply stuck in; some are sown and some are planted, and one must deal carefully with them. It's only those peoples that have an intuitive sense of what's of importance and significance in their institutions, and know how to value them, that have a future before them—it's only those people that one can truly call historical."

And Sergey Ivanovich carried the subject into the regions of philosophical history, where Konstantin Levin could not follow him, and showed him the incorrectness of his view.

"As for your dislike of it, excuse my saying so, that's simply our Russian laziness and haughty habits, and I'm convinced that in you it's a temporary error and will pass."

Konstantin was silent. He felt himself vanquished on all sides, but he felt at the same time that what he wanted to say was unintelligible to his brother. Only he could not make up his mind whether it was unintelligible because he was not capable of expressing his meaning clearly, or because his brother would not or could not understand him. But he did not pursue the speculation, and without replying, he began musing on a quite different and personal matter.

Sergey Ivanovich wound in the last line, untied the horse, and they drove off.

CHAPTER FOUR

The personal matter that absorbed Levin during his conversation with his brother was this: the previous year he had once gone to look at the mowing, and, being made very angry by the bailiff, he had recourse to his favorite means for regaining his temper—he took a scythe from a peasant and began mowing.

He liked the work so much that he had several times tried his hand at mowing since. He had cut all the meadow in front of his house, and this year, ever since the early spring, he had cherished a plan for mowing for whole days with the peasants. Ever since his brother's arrival, he had been in doubt whether to mow or not. He was loath to leave his brother alone all day long, and he was afraid his brother would laugh at him about it. But as he drove into the meadow, and recalled the sensations of mowing, he came near deciding that he would go mowing. After the irritating discussion with his brother, he pondered over this intention again.

"I must have physical exercise or my temper'll certainly be ruined," he thought, and he determined he would go mowing, however awkward he might feel about it with his brother or the peasants.

Toward evening Konstantin Levin went to his office, gave directions about the work to be done, and sent to the village to summon the mowers for the next day, to cut the hay in Kalinov meadow, the largest and best of his grasslands.

"And send my scythe, please, to Titus, for him to set it, and bring it around tomorrow. Perhaps I shall do some mowing myself too," he said, trying not to be embarrassed.

The bailiff smiled and said, "Yes, sir."

At tea the same evening Levin said to his brother:

"I think the fine weather will last. Tomorrow I shall start mowing."

"I like that form of field labor," said Sergey Ivanovich.

"I like it. I sometimes mow myself with the peasants, and tomorrow I want to try mowing the whole day."

Sergey Ivanovich lifted his head, and looked with interest at his brother.

"How do you mean? Just like one of the peasants, all day long?"

"Yes, it's very pleasant," said Levin.

"It's splendid as exercise, only you'll hardly be able to stand it," said Sergey Ivanovich, without a shade of irony.

"I've tried it. It's hard work at first, but you get used to it. I think I'll manage to keep up . . ."

"Really! What an idea! But tell me, how do the peasants look at it? I suppose they laugh in their sleeves at their master's being such a strange fish?"

"No, I don't think so; but it's so delightful, and at the same time such hard work, that one has no time to think about it."

"But what will you do about eating with them? To send you a bottle of Château Lafite and roast turkey out there would be a little awkward."

"No, I'll simply come home at the time of their noonday rest."

Next morning Konstantin Levin got up earlier than usual, but he was detained giving directions on the farm and when he reached the meadow the mowers were already at their second row.

From the uplands he could get a view of the shaded cut part of the meadow below, with its grayish ridges of cut grass, and the black heaps of coats, taken off by the mowers at the place from which they had started cutting.

Gradually, as he rode toward the meadow, the peasants came into sight, some in coats, some in their shirts, mowing, one behind another in a long string, swinging their scythes differently. He counted forty-two of them.

They were mowing slowly over the uneven bottom of the meadow, were there had been an old dam. Levin recognized some of his own men. Here was old Yermil in a very long white smock, bending forward to swing a scythe; there was a young fellow, Vaska, who had been a coachman of Levin's, taking every row with a wide sweep. Here, too, was Titus, Levin's teacher in the art of mowing, a thin little peasant. He was in front of everyone, and cut his wide row without bending, as though playing with the scythe.

Levin got off his mare and, fastening her by the roadside, went to meet Titus, who took a second scythe out of a bush and gave it to him.

"It's ready, sir, it's like a razor, cuts by itself," said Titus, taking off his cap with a smile and giving him the scythe.

Levin took the scythe, and began trying it. As they finished their rows, the mowers, sweating and cheerful, came out into the road one after another, and, laughing a little, greeted the master. They all stared at him, but no one made any remark till a tall old man, with a wrinkled, beardless face, wearing a short sheepskin jacket, came out into the road and accosted him.

"Look'ee now, master, once take hold of the rope there's no letting it go!" he said, and Levin heard smothered laughter among the mowers.

"I'll try not to let it go," he said, taking his stand behind Titus and waiting for the time to begin.

"Mind'ee," repeated the old man.

Titus made room, and Levin started behind him. The grass was short close to the road, and Levin, who had not done any mowing for a long while, and was disconcerted by the eyes fastened upon him, cut badly for the first moments, though he swung his scythe vigorously. Behind him he heard voices:

"It's not set right; handle's too high; see how he has to stoop to it," said one.

"Press more on the heel," said another.

"Never mind, he'll get on all right," the old man resumed.

"Look, he's made a start. . . . You swing it too wide, you'll tire yourself out. . . . The master, sure, does his best for himself! But see the grass missed! For such work us fellows would catch it!"

The grass became softer, and Levin, listening without answering, followed Titus, trying to do the best he could. They moved a hundred paces. Titus kept moving on, without stopping, not showing the slightest weariness, but Levin was already beginning to be afraid he would not be able to keep it up: he was so tired.

He felt as he swung his scythe that he was at the very end of his strength, and was making up his mind to ask Titus to stop. But at that very moment Titus stopped of his own accord, and, stooping down, picked up some grass, rubbed his scythe, and began whetting it. Levin straightened himself and, drawing a deep breath, looked around. Behind him came a peasant, and he too was evidently tired, for he stopped at once without waiting to mow up to Levin, and began whetting his scythe. Titus sharpened his scythe and Levin's and they went on. The next time it was just the same. Titus moved on with sweep after sweep of his scythe, not stopping or showing signs of weariness. Levin followed him trying not to get left behind, and he found it harder and harder: the moment came when he felt he had no strength left, but at that very moment Titus stopped again and whetted the scythes.

So they mowed the first row. And this long row seemed particularly hard work to Levin; but when the end was reached and Titus, shouldering his scythe, began with deliberate stride returning on the tracks left by his heels in the cut grass, and Levin walked back in the same way over the space he had cut, in spite of the sweat than ran in streams over his face and fell in drops down his nose, and drenched his back as though he had been soaked in water, he felt very happy. What delighted him particularly was that now he knew he would be able to hold out.

His pleasure was disturbed only by his row not being well cut. "I will swing less with my arm and more with my whole body," he thought, comparing Titus's row, which looked as if it had been cut with a line, with his own unevenly and irregularly scattered grass.

The first row, as Levin noticed, Titus had mowed specially quickly, probably wishing to put his master to the test, and the row happened to be a long one. The next rows were easier, but still Levin had to strain every nerve not to drop behind the peasants.

He thought of nothing, wished for nothing, but not to be left behind the peasants, and to do his work as well as possible. He heard nothing but the swish of scythes, and saw before him Titus's upright figure mowing away, the crescent-shaped curve of the cut grass, the grass and flower heads slowly and rhythmically falling before the blade of his scythe, and ahead of him the end of the row, where the rest would come.

Suddenly, in the midst of his toil, without understanding what it was or whence it came, he felt a pleasant sensation of chill on his hot, moist shoulders. He glanced at the sky during the interval for whetting the scythes. A heavy, lowering storm cloud had blown up, and big raindrops were falling. Some of the peasants went to their coats and put them on; others—like Levin—merely shrugged their shoulders, enjoying the pleasant coolness of it.

Another row, and yet another row, followed—long rows and short rows, with good grass and with poor grass. Levin lost all sense of time, and could not have told whether it was late or early now. A change began to come over his work, which gave him immense satisfaction. In the midst of his toil there were moments during which he forgot what he was doing, and it came easy to him, and at those same moments his row was almost as smooth and well cut as Titus's. But as soon as he recollected what he was doing, and began trying to do better, he was at once conscious of the difficulty of his task, and the row was badly mown.

On finishing yet another row, he would have gone back to the top of the meadow again to begin the next, but Titus stopped, and, going up to the old man, said something in a low voice to him. They both looked at the sun. "What are they talking about, and why doesn't he go back?" thought Levin, not guessing that the peasants had been mowing no less than four hours without stopping, and it was time for their lunch.

"Lunch, sir," said the old man.

"Is it really time? That's right; lunch, then."

Levin gave his scythe to Titus, and together with the peasants, who were crossing the long stretch of mown grass, slightly sprinkled with rain, to get their bread from the heap of coats, he went toward his horse. Only then did he suddenly awake to the fact that he had been wrong about the weather and the rain was drenching his hay.

"The hay will be spoiled," he said.

"No it won't be, sir. Mow in the rain, and you'll rake in fine weather!" said the old man.

Levin untied his horse and rode home to his coffee. Sergey Ivanovich was just getting up. When he had drunk his coffee, Levin rode back again to the mowing before Sergey Ivanovich had had time to dress and come down to the dining room.

CHAPTER FIVE

After lunch Levin was not in the same place in the string of mowers as before, but stood between the old man who had accosted him humorously, and now invited him to be his neighbor, and a young peasant, who had just been married in the autumn and who was mowing this summer for the first time.

The old man, holding himself erect, moved in front, with his feet turned out, taking long, regular strides, and with a precise and regular action which seemed to cost him no more effort than swinging one's arms in walking, as though it were in play, he laid the grass in the high, even rows. It was as though it was not he but the sharp scythe itself that was swishing through the juicy grass.

Behind Levin came the lad Mishka. His pleasant, boyish face, with a twist of fresh grass bound around his hair, was contorted with effort; but whenever anyone looked at him, he smiled. He would clearly have died sooner than admit it was hard work for him.

Levin kept between them. In the very heat of the day the mowing did not seem such hard work to him. The perspiration with which he was drenched cooled him, while the sun that burned his back, his head, and his arms, bare to the elbow, gave vigor and increased his perseverance to his labor; and more and more often now came those moments of unconsciousness, when it was possible not to think of what one was doing. The scythe cut by itself. These were happy moments. Still more delightful were the moments when they reached the stream where the rows ended, and the old man rubbed his scythe with the wet, thick grass, rinsed its blade in the fresh water of the stream, ladled out a little in a tin dipper, and offered Levin a drink.

"What do you say to kvas, eh? Good, eh?" said he, winking.

And truly Levin had never drunk anything so good as this warm water with bits of grass floating in it, and a taste of rust from the tin dipper. And immediately after this came the delicious, slow saunter, with his hand on the scythe, during which he could wipe away the streaming sweat, take deep breaths of air, and look about at the long string of mowers and at what was happening all around in the forest and the country.

The longer Levin mowed, the oftener he felt the moments of unconsciousness in which it seemed that the scythe was mowing by itself, a body full of life and consciousness of its own, and as though by magic, without thinking of it, the work turned out regular and precise by itself. These were the most blissful moments.

It was hard work only when he had to break off the motion, which had become unconscious, and think; when he had to mow around a mound or a tuft of sorrel. The old man did this easily. When a mound came, he changed his action, and at one time with the heel, at another with the tip of his scythe, he clipped the mound around both sides with short strokes. And while he did this he kept looking about and watching what came into his view: at one moment he picked a wild berry and ate it or offered it to Levin, then he flung away a twig with the blade of the scythe, then he looked at a quail's nest, from which the bird flew just under the scythe, or caught a snake that crossed his path and, lifting it on the scythe as though on a fork, showed it to Levin and threw it away.

For both Levin and the young peasant behind him, such changes of position were difficult. Both of them, repeating over and over again the same strained movement, were in a frenzy of toil, and were incapable of shifting their position and at the same time watching what was before them.

Levin did not notice how time was passing. If he had been asked how long he had been working, he would have said half an hour—and it was getting to be dinnertime. As they were walking back over the cut grass, the old man called Levin's attention to the little girls and boys who were coming from different directions, hardly visible through the long grass, and along the road toward the mowers, carrying sacks of bread, dragging their little hands down, and pitchers of kvas stoppered with rags.

"Look'ee, the little gnats crawling!" he said, pointing to them, and he shaded his eyes with his hand to look at the sun. They mowed two more rows; the old man stopped.

"Come, sir, dinnertime!" he said briskly. And, on reaching the stream, the mowers moved off across the lines of cut grass toward their pile of coats, where the children who had brought their dinners were sitting waiting for them. The peasants gathered into groups—those further away under a cart, those nearer under a willow bush.

Levin sat down by them; he felt he did not want to go away.

All constraint with the master had vanished long ago. The peasants got ready for dinner. Some washed, the young boys bathed in the stream, others made a place comfortable for a rest, untied their sacks of bread, and unstoppered the pitchers of kvas. The old man crumbled up some bread in a cup, stirred it with the handle of a spoon, poured water on it from the dipper, broke up some more bread, and, having seasoned it with salt, turned to the east to say his prayer.

"Come, master, taste my grub," said he, kneeling down before the cup.

The food was so good that Levin gave up the idea of going home. He dined with the old man, and talked to him about his family affairs, taking the keenest interest in them, and told him about his own affairs and all the circumstances that could be of interest to the old man. He felt much closer to him than to his brother, and could not help smiling at the affection he felt for this man. When the old man got up again, said his prayer, and lay down under a bush, putting some grass under his head for a pillow, Levin did the same, and in spite of the clinging flies that were so persistent in the sunshine, and the gnats that tickled his sweating face and body, he fell asleep at once and waked only when the sun had passed to the other side of the bush and reached him. The old man had been awake a long while, and was sitting up whetting the scythes of the younger boys.

Levin looked about him and hardly recognized the place, everything was so changed. The immense stretch of meadow had been mown and was sparkling with a peculiar fresh brilliance, with its lines of already sweet-smelling grass in the slanting rays of the evening sun. And the bushes about the river had been cut down, and the river itself, not visible before, now gleaming like steel in its bends, and the moving, ascending peasants, and the sharp wall of grass of the unmown part of the meadow, and the hawks hovering over the stripped meadow—all was perfectly new. Raising himself, Levin began considering how much had been cut and how much more could still be done that day.

The forty-two men had done a considerable amount. They had cut the whole of the big meadow, which had, in the years of serf labor, taken thirty scythes two days to mow. Only the corners remained to be done, where the rows were short. But Levin felt a longing to get as much mowing done that day as possible, and was vexed with the sun's sinking so quickly in the sky. He felt no weariness; all he wanted was to get his work done more and more quickly and as much done as possible.

"Could we cut Mashkin Upland too—what do you think?" he said to the old man.

"As God wills, the sun's not high. A little vodka for the boys?"

At the afternoon rest, when they were sitting down again, and those who smoked had lighted their pipes, the old man told the men: "Mashkin Upland's to be cut—there'll be some vodka."

"Why not cut it? Come on, Titus! We'll do it quickly! You can eat at night. Come on!" cried voices, and finishing their bread, the mowers went back to work.

"Come, boys, keep it up!" said Titus, and ran on ahead almost at a trot.

"Go on, go on!" said the old man, hurrying after him and easily overtaking him, "I'll mow you down, look out!"

And young and old mowed away, as though they were racing with one another. But however quickly they worked, they did not spoil the grass, and the rows were laid just as neatly and exactly. The little piece left uncut in the corner was mown in five minutes. The last of the mowers were just ending their rows, while the foremost snatched up their coats and slung them over their shoulders, and crossed the road toward Mashkin Upland.

The sun was already sinking into the trees when they went, with their tin boxes rattling,[1] into the wooden ravine of Mashkin Upland.

---

[1] I.e., the whetstone boxes.

The grass was up to their waists in the middle of the hollow, soft, tender, and broad-bladed, spotted here and there among the trees with wild pansies.

After a brief consultation—whether to take the rows lengthwise or diagonally—Prokor Yermilin, also a renowned mower, a huge, black-haired peasant, went on ahead. He went up to the top, turned back again, and started mowing, and they all proceeded to form in line behind him, going downhill through the hollow and uphill right up to the edge of the forest. The sun sank behind the forest. The dew was falling by now; the mowers were in the sun only on the hillside, but below, where a mist was rising, and on the opposite side, they mowed into the fresh, dewy shade. The work went rapidly. The grass cut with a juicy sound, and was at once laid in high, fragrant rows. The mowers from all sides, brought closer together in the short row, kept urging one another on to the sound of rattling tin boxes and clanging scythes, and the hiss of the whetstones sharpening them, and happy shouts.

Levin still kept between the young peasant and the old man. The old man, who had put on his short sheepskin jacket, was just as merry, jocose, and free in his movements. Among the trees, they were continually cutting with their scythes the birch mushrooms, swollen fat in the succulent grass. But the old man bent down every time he came across a mushroom, picked it up, and put it under his shirt. "Another present for my old woman," he said as he did so.

Easy as it was to mow the wet, soft grass, it was hard work going up and down the steep sides of the ravine. But this did not trouble the old man. Swinging his scythe just as usual, and moving his feet in their big bast shoes with firm little steps, he climbed slowly up the steep place, and though his breeches were hanging out below his smock, and his whole frame trembled with effort, he did not miss one blade of grass or one mushroom on his way, and kept making jokes with the peasants and Levin. Levin walked after him, thinking often that he would fall any minute, as he climbed with a scythe up a steep cliff where it would have been hard work to climb even without anything. But he climbed up and did what he had to do. He felt as though some external force was moving him.

CHAPTER SIX

Mashkin Upland was mown, the last row finished, and the peasants had put on their coats and were gaily trudging home. Levin got on his horse, and parting regretfully from the peasants, he rode homeward. On the hillside he looked back; he could not see them in the mist that had risen from the valley; he could only hear rough, merry voices, laughter, and the sound of clanking scythes.

Sergey Ivanovich had long ago finished dinner, and was drinking iced lemon and water in his own room, looking through the reviews and papers he had just received by mail, when Levin rushed into the room, talking merrily, with his wet and matted hair sticking to his forehead and his back and chest dark with sweat.

"We mowed the whole meadow! Oh, it is nice, delicious! And how have you been getting on?" said Levin, completely forgetting the disagreeable conversation of the previous day.

"Good heavens! What you look like!" said Sergey Ivanovich, for the first moment looking round with some dissatisfaction. "And the door, shut the door!" he cried. "You must have let in a dozen at least."

Sergey Ivanovich could not stand flies, and in his own room he never opened the window except at night, and carefully kept the door shut.

"Not one, on my honor. But if I have, I'll catch them. You wouldn't believe what a pleasure it is! How have you spent the day?"

"Very well. But have you really been mowing the whole day? You must be as hungry as a wolf. Kuzma has got everything ready for you."

"No, I don't even feel hungry. I had something to eat there. But I'll go and wash."

"Yes, go along, go along, and I'll come to you right away," said Sergey Ivanovich, shaking his head as he looked at his brother. "Go along, make haste," he added, smiling, and gathering up his books, he prepared to go too. Suddenly he felt happy too, and disinclined to leave his brother's side. "But what did you do while it was raining?"

"Rain? Why, there was scarcely a drop. I'll come soon. So you had a nice day too? That's fine." And Levin went off to change his clothes.

Five minutes later the brothers met in the dining room. Although it seemed to Levin that he was not hungry, and he sat down to dinner simply so as not to hurt Kuzma's feelings, when he began to eat, the dinner struck him as extraordinarily good. Sergey Ivanovich watched him with a smile.

"Oh, by the way, there's a letter for you," he said. "Kuzma, bring it, please. And be careful that you shut the doors."

The letter was from Oblonsky. Levin read it aloud. Oblonsky wrote to him from Petersburg:

I have had a letter from Dolly; she's at Yergushovo and everything seems to be going wrong there. Ride over and see her, please; help her with advice; you know all about it. She will be so glad to see you. She's quite alone, poor thing. My mother-in-law and all of them are still abroad.

"That's splendid! I will certainly ride over to her," said Levin. "Or we'll go together. She's such a splendid woman, isn't she?"

"They're not far from here, then?"

"Twenty-five miles. Or perhaps it is thirty. But a fine road. Splendid, we'll drive over."

"I shall be delighted," said Sergey Ivanovich, still smiling. The sight of his younger brother's appearance had immediately put him in a good humor.

"Well, you have an appetite!" he said, looking at his dark-red sunburned face and neck bent over the plate.

"Splendid! You can't imagine what an effectual remedy it is for every sort of foolishness. I want to enrich medicine with a new word: *Arbeitskur*."[1]

"Well, but you don't need it, I think."

"No, but for all sorts of nervous invalids."

"Yes, it ought to be tried. I had meant to come to the mowing to watch you, but it was so unbearably hot that I got no further than the forest. I sat there a little, and went on by the forest to the village, met your old nurse, and sounded her out as to the peasants' view of you. As far as I can make out, they don't approve of this. She said: 'It's not

[1] "Work cure."

a gentleman's work.' All in all, I think that in the people's ideas there are very clear and definite notions of certain, as they call it, 'gentlemanly' lines of action. And they don't sanction the gentry's moving outside bounds clearly laid down in their ideas."

"Perhaps; but anyway it's a pleasure such as I have never known in my life. And there's no harm in it, you know, is there?" Levin answered. "I can't help it if they don't like it. Besides, I think it's all right, eh?"

"On the whole," Sergey Ivanovich pursued, "you're satisfied with your day?"

"Quite satisfied. We cut the whole meadow. And such a splendid old man I made friends with there! You can't imagine how delightful he was!"

"Well, so you're content with your day. And so am I. First, I solved two chess problems, and one a real beauty—a pawn opening. I'll show it to you. And then—I thought over our conversation yesterday."

"Eh! Our conversation yesterday?" said Levin, blissfully dropping his eyelids and drawing deep breaths after finishing his dinner, and absolutely incapable of recalling what their conversation yesterday was about.

"I think you are partly right. Our difference of opinion amounts to this, that you make the mainspring self-interest, while I suppose that interest in the common good is bound to exist in every man of a certain degree of advancement. Possibly you are right, too, that action founded on material interest would be more desirable. You are altogether, as the French say, too *primesautière*[2] a nature; you must have intense, energetic action, or nothing."

Levin listened to his brother and did not understand a single word, and did not want to understand. He was only afraid his brother might ask him some question that would make it evident he had not heard.

"So that's what I think it is, my dear boy," said Sergey Ivanovich, touching him on the shoulder.

"Yes, of course. But, do you know? I won't stand up for my view," Levin answered, with a guilty, childlike smile. "What was it I was disputing about?" he wondered. "Of course, I'm right, and he's right,

[2] "Impulsive."

and it's all right. But I must get to the office and see to things." He got up, stretching and smiling. Sergey Ivanovich smiled too.

"If you want to go out, let's go together," he said, not wanting to be parted from his brother, who seemed to be positively exuding freshness and energy. "Come, we'll go to the office if you have to go there."

"Oh, heavens!" shouted Levin, so loudly that Sergey Ivanovich was quite frightened.

"What, what is the matter?"

"How's Agafya Mikhailovna's hand?" said Levin, slapping himself on the head. "I'd positively forgotten all about her."

"It's much better."

"Well, anyway, I'll run down to her. Before you've time to get your hat on, I'll be back."

And he ran downstairs, clattering his heels like a rattle.

CHAPTER SEVEN

Stepan Arkadyevich had gone to Petersburg to perform the most natural and essential official duty—so familiar to everyone in the government service, though incomprehensible to outsiders—that duty, but for which one could hardly be in government service, of reminding the ministry of his existence, and having, for the due performance of this rite, taken all the available cash from home, he was happily spending his days at the races and in the summer villas. Meanwhile, Dolly and the children had moved to the country to cut down expenses as much as possible. She had gone to Yergushovo, the estate that had been her dowry, and the one where in spring the forest had been sold. It was nearly forty miles from Levin's Pokrovskoe. The big old house at Yergushovo had been pulled down long ago, and the old prince had had the lodge done up and enlarged. Twenty years before, when Dolly was a child, the lodge had been roomy and comfortable, though, like all lodges, it stood sideways to the drive and faced the south. But by now this lodge was old and dilapidated. When Stepan Arkadyevich had gone down in the spring to sell the forest, Dolly had begged him to look over the house and order what repairs might be needed. Stepan Arkadyevich, like all unfaithful husbands, was very solicitous for his wife's comfort, and he himself had looked over the house and given instructions about everything that he considered necessary. What he considered necessary was to cover all the furniture with cretonne, to put up curtains, to weed the garden, to make a little bridge on the pond, and to plant flowers. But he forgot many other essential matters, the want of which greatly distressed Darya Aleksandrovna later on.

In spite of Stepan Arkadyevich's efforts to be an attentive father and husband, he never could keep in his mind that he had a wife and children. He had bachelor tastes, and it was in accordance with them that he shaped his life. On his return to Moscow, he informed his wife with pride that everything was ready, that the house would be a little paradise, and that he advised her most certainly to go. His wife's staying away in the country was very agreeable to Stepan Arkadyevich from every point of view: it did the children good, it decreased expenses, and it left him more at liberty. Darya Aleksandrovna regarded staying in the country for the summer as essential for the children, especially for the little girl, who had not succeeded in regaining her strength after the scarlet fever, and also as a means of escaping the petty humiliations, the small bills owing to the wood merchant, the fishmonger, the shoemaker, which made her miserable. Besides this, she was pleased to go away to the country because she was dreaming of getting her sister Kitty to stay with her there. Kitty was to be back from abroad in the middle of the summer, and bathing had been prescribed for her. Kitty wrote that no prospect was so alluring as to spend the summer with Dolly at Yergushovo, full of childhood memories for both of them.

The first days of her existence in the country were very hard for Dolly. She used to stay in the country as a child, and the impression she had retained of it was that the country was a refuge from all the unpleasantness of the town, that life there, though not luxurious— Dolly could easily make up her mind to that—was cheap and comfortable; that there was plenty of everything, everything was cheap, everything could be got, and children were happy. But now coming to the country as the head of a family, she perceived that it was all utterly unlike what she had expected.

The day after their arrival there was a heavy fall of rain and in the night the water came through in the hall and in the nursery, so that the beds had to be carried into the drawing room. There was no kitchenmaid to be found; of the nine cows, it appeared from the words of the dairymaids that some were about to calve, others had just calved, others were old, and others were hard-uddered; there was not butter or milk enough even for the children. There were no eggs. They could get no fowls; old, purplish, tough cocks were all they had for roasting and boiling. Impossible to get women to scrub the floors—all were potato-hoeing. Driving was out of the question, because one of the horses was restive, and bolted in the shafts. There was no place where they could bathe; the whole of the riverbank was trampled by the cattle and open to the road; even walks were impossible, for the cattle strayed into the garden through a gap in the hedge, and there was one terrible bull who bellowed and therefore might be expected to gore somebody. There were no proper cupboards for their clothes; what cupboards there were either would not close at all or burst open whenever anyone passed by them. There were no pots and pans; there was no copper in the wash house, nor even an ironing board in the maids' room.

Finding instead of peace and rest all these, from her point of view, fearful calamities, Darya Aleksandrovna was at first in despair. She exerted herself to the utmost, felt the hopelessness of the situation, and was every instant suppressing the tears that started into her eyes. The bailiff, a retired quartermaster, whom Stepan Arkadyevich had taken a fancy to and had appointed bailiff on account of his handsome and respectful appearance, showed no sympathy for Darya Aleksandrovna's woes. He said respectfully, "Nothing can be done, the peasants are such a wretched bunch," and did nothing to help her.

The situation seemed hopeless. But in the Oblonskys' household, as in all families indeed, there was one inconspicuous but most valuable and useful person, Matryona Filimonovna. She soothed her mistress, assured her that everything would work out (it was her expression, and Matvey had borrowed it from her), and without fuss or hurry proceeded to set to work herself. She had immediately made friends with the bailiff's wife, and on the very first day she drank tea with her and the bailiff under the acacias, and reviewed all the circumstances of the situation. Very soon Matryona Filimonovna had established her club, so to say, under the acacias, and there it was, in this club, consisting of the bailiff's wife, the village elder, and the office clerk, that the difficulties of existence were gradually smoothed away, and in a week's time everything actually had worked out. The roof was mended, a cook was found—a crony of the village elder's—hens were bought, the cows began giving milk, the garden hedge was stopped up with stakes, the carpenter made a mangle, hooks were put in the cupboards and they ceased to burst open spontaneously, and an ironing board covered with army cloth was placed across from the arm of a chair to the chest of drawers, and there was a smell of flatirons in the maid's room.

"Just see, now, and you were in despair," said Matryona Filimonovna, pointing to the ironing board. They even rigged up a bathing shed of straw hurdles. Lily began to bathe, and Darya Aleksandrovna began to realize, if only in part, her expectations, if not of a peaceful, at least of a comfortable, life in the country. Peaceful with six children Darya Aleksandrovna could not be. One would fall ill, another might easily become so, a third would be without something necessary, a fourth would show symptoms of a bad disposition, and so on. Rare indeed were the brief periods of peace. But these cares and anxieties were for Darya Aleksandrovna the sole happiness possible. Had it not been for them, she would have been left alone to brood over her husband who did not love her. And besides, hard though it was for the mother to bear the dread of illness, the illnesses themselves, and the grief of seeing signs of evil propensities in her children—the children themselves were even now repaying her in small joys for her sufferings. Those joys were so small that they passed unnoticed, like gold in sand, and at bad moments she could see nothing but the pain, nothing but sand; but there were good moments too when she saw nothing but the joy, nothing but gold.

Now in the solitude of the country, she began to be more and more frequently aware of those joys. Often, looking at them, she would make every possible effort to persuade herself that she was mistaken, that she as a mother was partial to her children. All the same, she could not help saying to herself that she had charming children, all six of them in different ways, but children such as are not often to be met, and she was happy in them, and proud of them.

CHAPTER EIGHT

Toward the end of May, when everything had been more or less satisfactorily arranged, she received her husband's answer to her complaints of the disorganized state of things in the country. He wrote begging her forgiveness for not having thought of everything before, and promised to come down at the first chance. This chance did not present itself, and till the beginning of June, Darya Aleksandrovna stayed alone in the country.

On Sunday, on St. Peter's Day, Darya Aleksandrovna drove to Mass with all her children to take Communion.[1] Darya Aleksandrovna, in her intimate, philosophical talks with her sister, her mother, and her friends, very often astonished them by the freedom of her views in regard to religion. She had a strange religion all her own, of transmigration of souls, in which she had firm faith, troubling herself little about the dogmas of the Church. But in her family she was strict in carrying out all that was required by the Church—and not merely in order to set an example, but with her whole heart in it. The fact that the children had not been to Communion for a year very much worried her, and with the full approval and sympathy of Matryona Filimonovna, she decided that this should take place now in the summer.

For several days before, Darya Aleksandrovna was busily deliberating on how to dress all the children. Frocks were made or altered and washed, seams and flounces were let out, buttons were sewn on, and ribbons got ready. One dress, Tanya's, which the English governess was altering, cost Darya Aleksandrovna much loss of temper. The English governess had made the seams in the wrong place, had taken up the sleeves too much, and altogether spoiled the dress. It was so narrow on Tanya's shoulders that it was quite painful to look

[1] In the Russian Orthodox Church, very young children receive Communion.

at her. But Matryona Filimonovna had the happy thought of putting in gussets, and adding a little shoulder cape. The dress was fixed, but there was nearly a quarrel with the English governess. Next morning, however, all was happily arranged, and toward ten o'clock—the time at which they had asked the priest to wait for them for the mass—the children in their new dresses, with beaming faces, stood on the step before the carriage waiting for their mother.

In the carriage, instead of the restive Raven, they had harnessed, thanks to the intercession of Matryona Filimonovna, the bailiff's horse, Brownie, and Darya Aleksandrovna, delayed by anxiety over her own attire, came out and got in, dressed in a white muslin gown.

Darya Aleksandrovna had done her hair, and dressed with care and excitement. In the old days she had dressed for her own sake to look pretty and be admired. Later on, as she got older, dressing up became more and more distasteful to her. She saw that she was losing her good looks. But now she began to feel pleasure and interest in dressing up again. Now she did not dress for her own sake, not for the sake of her own beauty, but simply so that as the mother of those exquisite creatures she might not spoil the general effect. And looking at herself for the last time in the mirror, she was satisfied with herself. She looked nice. Not nice as she would have wished to look nice in the old days at a ball, but nice for the object she now had in view.

In the church there was no one but the peasants, the servants, and their women. But Darya Aleksandrovna saw, or thought she saw, the sensation produced by her children and her. The children were not only beautiful to look at in their smart little dresses, but they were charming in the way they behaved. Alyosha, it is true, did not stand quite correctly; he kept turning around, trying to look at his little jacket from behind; but all the same he was wonderfully sweet. Tanya behaved like a grown-up person, and looked after the little ones. And the smallest, Lily, was bewitching in her naïve astonishment at everything, and it was difficult not to smile when, after taking the sacrament, she said in English, "Please, some more."

On the way home the children felt that something solemn had happened, and were very subdued.

Everything went happily at home too; but at lunch Grisha began whistling, and, what was worse, was disobedient to the English governess, and was forbidden to have any pie. Darya Aleksandrovna would not have let things go so far on such a day had she been present; but she had to support the English governess's authority, and she upheld her decision that Grisha should have no pie. This rather spoiled the general happiness. Grisha cried, declaring that Nikolinka had whistled too and he was not punished, and that he wasn't crying for the pie—he didn't care—but at being unjustly treated. This was really too tragic, and Darya Aleksandrovna made up her mind to persuade the English governess to forgive Grisha, and she went to speak to her. But on her way, as she passed the drawing room, she beheld a scene that filled her heart with such pleasure that the tears came into her eyes, and she forgave the delinquent herself.

The culprit was sitting at the window in the corner of the drawing room; beside him was standing Tanya with a plate. On the pretext of wanting to give some dinner to her dolls, she had asked the governess's permission to take her share of pie to the nursery, and had taken it instead to her brother. While still weeping over the injustice of his punishment, he was eating the pie, and kept saying through his sobs, "Eat yourself; let's eat it together . . . together."

Tanya had at first been under the influence of her pity for Grisha, then of a sense of her noble action, and tears were standing in her eyes too; but she did not refuse, and ate her share.

On catching sight of their mother, they were dismayed, but, looking into her face, they saw they were not doing wrong. They burst out laughing, and, with their mouths full of pie, they began wiping their smiling lips with their hands, and smearing their radiant faces all over with tears and jam.

"Heavens! Your new white frock; Tanya! Grisha!" said their mother, trying to save the frock, but with tears in her eyes, smiling a blissful, rapturous smile.

The new frocks were taken off, and orders were given for the little girls to have their blouses put on, and the boys their old jackets, and the trap to be harnessed with Brownie, to the bailiff's annoyance, again in the shafts; to drive out for mushroom picking and bathing. A roar of delighted shrieks arose in the nursery and never ceased till they had set off for the bathing place.

They gathered a whole basketful of mushrooms; even Lily found a birch mushroom. It had always happened before that Miss Hull found them and pointed them out to her; but this time she found a big one all by herself, and there was a general scream of delight: "Lily has found a mushroom!"

Then they reached the river, put the horses under the birch trees, and went to the bathing place. The coachman, Terenty, tied the horses, who kept whisking away the flies, to a tree, and treading down the grass, lay down in the shade of a birch and smoked his shag, while the never-ceasing shrieks of delight from the children floated across to him from the bathing place.

Though it was hard work to look after all the children and restrain their wild pranks, though it was difficult too to keep in one's head and not mix up all the stockings, little breeches, and shoes for the different legs, and to undo and to do up again all the tapes and buttons, Darya Aleksandrovna, who had always like bathing herself, and believed it to be very good for the children, enjoyed nothing so much as bathing with all the children. To go over all those fat little legs, pulling on their stockings, to take in her arms and dip those little naked bodies, and to hear their screams of delight and alarm, to see the breathless faces with wide-open, scared, and happy eyes of all her splashing cherubs was a great pleasure to her.

When half the children had been dressed, some peasant women in holiday dress, out picking herbs, came up to the bathing shed and stopped shyly. Matryona Filimonovna called one of them and handed her a sheet and a shirt that had dropped into the water for her to dry them, and Darya Aleksandrovna began to talk to the women. At first they laughed behind their hands and did not understand her questions, but soon they grew bolder and began to talk, winning Darya Aleksandrovna's heart at once by the genuine admiration of the children that they showed.

"My, what a beauty! As white as sugar," said one, admiring Tanichka and shaking her head; "but thin. . ."

"Yes, she has been ill."

"And so they've been bathing you too," said another to the baby.

"No; he's only three months old," answered Darya Aleksandrovna with pride.

"You don't say so!"

"And have you any children?"

"I've had four; I've two living—a boy and a girl. I weaned her before Lent."

"How old is she?"

"Why, two years old."

"Why did you nurse her so long?"

"It's our custom; for three fasts . . ."

And the conversation became most interesting to Darya Aleksandrovna. What sort of time did she have? What was the matter with the boy? Where was her husband? Did it often happen?

Darya Aleksandrovna felt disinclined to leave the peasant women, so interesting to her was their conversation, so completely identical were all their interests. What pleased her most of all was that she saw clearly what all the women admired more than anything was her having so many children, and such fine ones. The peasant women even made Darya Aleksandrovna laugh, and offended the English governess, because she was the cause of the laughter she did not understand. One of the younger women kept staring at the Englishwoman, who was dressing after all the rest, and when she put on her third petticoat she could not refrain from the remark, "My, she keeps putting on and putting on, and she'll never put enough on!" and they all went off into roars.

CHAPTER NINE

On the drive home, as Darya Aleksandrovna, with all her children around her, their heads still wet from their bath, and a kerchief tied over her own head, was getting near the house, the coachman said, "There's some gentleman coming: the master of Pokrovskoe, I do believe."

Darya Aleksandrovna peeped out in front, and was delighted when she recognized in the gray hat and gray coat the familiar figure of Levin walking to meet them. She was glad to see him at any time, but at this moment she was specially glad he should see her in all her glory. No one was better able to appreciate her grandeur than Levin.

Seeing her, he found himself face to face with one of the pictures of family life his imagination painted.

"You're like a hen with your chickens, Darya Aleksandrovna."

"Ah, how glad I am to see you!" she said, holding out her hand to him.

"Glad to see me, but you didn't let me know. My brother's staying with me. I got a note from Stiva that you were here."

"From Stiva?" Darya Aleksandrovna asked with surprise.

"Yes; he writes that you are here, and that he thinks you might allow me to be of use to you," said Levin, and as he said it he became suddenly embarrassed, and stopping abruptly, he walked on in silence by the trap, snapping off the buds of the lime trees and nibbling them. He was embarrassed through a sense that Darya Aleksandrovna would be annoyed by receiving from an outsider help that should by rights have come from her own husband. Darya Aleksandrovna certainly did not like this little way of Stepan Arkadyevich's of foisting his domestic duties on others. And she was at once aware that Levin was aware of this. It was just for the fineness of perception, for this delicacy, that Darya Aleksandrovna liked Levin.

"I know, of course," said Levin, "that that simply means that you would like to see me, and I'm exceedingly glad. Though I can imagine that, used to town housekeeping as you are, you must feel in the wilds here, and if there's anything needed, I'm altogether at your disposal."

"Oh, no!" said Dolly. "At first things were rather uncomfortable, but now we've settled everything wonderfully—thanks to my old nurse," she said, indicating Matryona Filimonovna, who, seeing that they were speaking of her, smiled brightly and cordially to Levin. She knew him, and knew that he would be a good match for the young lady, and was very keen to see the matter settled.

"Won't you get in, sir, we'll make room this side!" she said to him.

"No, I'll walk. Children, who'd like to race the horses with me?"

The children knew Levin very little, and could not remember when they had seen him, but they experienced none of that strange feeling of shyness and hostility toward him which children so often experience toward hypocritical, grown-up people, and for which they are so often and miserably punished. Hypocrisy in anything whatever may deceive the cleverest and most penetrating man, but the least wide-awake of children recognizes it, and is revolted by it, however ingeniously it may be disguised. Whatever fault Levin had, there was not a trace of hypocrisy in him, and so the children showed him the same friendliness that they saw in their mother's face. On his invitation, the two elder ones at once jumped out to him and ran with him as simply as they would have done with their nurse or Miss Hull or their mother. Lily, too, began begging to go to him, and her mother handed her to him; he sat her on his shoulder and ran along with her.

"Don't be afraid, don't be afraid, Darya Aleksandrovna!" he said, smiling brightly to the mother; "there's no chance of my hurting or dropping her."

And, looking at his strong, agile, very careful, and needlessly wary movements, the mother felt her mind at rest, and smiled gaily and approvingly as she watched him.

Here, in the country, with children, and with Darya Aleksandrovna, with whom he was in sympathy, Levin was in a mood not infrequent with him of childlike light-heartedness which she particularly liked in him. As he ran with the children, he taught them gymnastic feats, started Miss Hull laughing with his peculiar English accent, and talked to Darya Aleksandrovna of his pursuits in the country.

After dinner, Darya Aleksandrovna, sitting alone with him on the balcony, began to speak of Kitty.

"You know, Kitty's coming here, and is going to spend the summer with me."

"Really," he said, flushing, and at once, to change the conversation, he said: "Then shall I send you two cows? If you insist on a bill you shall pay me five rubles a month; but it's not nice of you."

"No, thank you. We can manage very well now."

"Oh, well, then, I'll have a look at your cows, and if you'll allow me, I'll give directions about their food. Everything depends on their food."

And Levin, to keep the conversation here, explained to Darya Aleksandrovna the theory of dairy farming, based on the principle that the cow is simply a machine for the transformation of food into milk, and so on.

He talked of this, and passionately longed to hear more of Kitty, and, at the same time, was afraid of hearing it. He dreaded the breaking up of the inward peace he had gained with such effort.

"Yes, but still all this has to be looked after, and who is there to look after it?" Darya Aleksandrovna responded, without interest.

She had by now got her household matters so satisfactorily arranged, thanks to Matryona Filimonovna, that she was disinclined to make any change in them; besides, she had no faith in Levin's knowledge of farming. General principles, as to the cow being a machine for the production of milk, she looked on with suspicion. It seemed to her that such principles could be only a hindrance in farm management. It all seemed to her a far simpler matter: all that was needed, as Matryona Filimonovna had explained, was to give Brindle and Whitebelly more food and drink, and not to let the cook carry all the kitchen slops to the laundress's cow. That was clear. But general propositions as to feeding on meal and on grass were doubtful and obscure. And, what was most important, she wanted to talk about Kitty.

CHAPTER TEN

"Kitty writes to me that there's nothing she longs for so much as peace and solitude," Dolly said after the silence that had followed.

"And how is she—better?" Levin asked in agitation.

"Thank God, she's quite well again. I never believed her lungs were affected."

"Oh, I'm very glad!" said Levin, and Dolly thought she saw something touching, helpless, in his face as he said this and looked silently into her face.

"Let me ask you, Konstantin Dmitrievich," said Darya Aleksandrovna, smiling her kindly and rather mocking smile, "Why is it you are angry with Kitty?"

"I? I'm not angry with her," said Levin.

"Yes, you are angry. Why was it you did not come to see us or them when you were in Moscow?"

"Darya Aleksandrovna," he said, blushing up to the roots of his hair, "I wonder really that with your kind heart you don't feel this. How is it you feel no pity for me, if nothing else, when you know—"

"What do I know?"

"You know I proposed and I was refused," said Levin, and all the tenderness he had been feeling for Kitty a minute before was replaced by a feeling of anger for the slight he had suffered.

"What makes you suppose I know?"

"Because everybody knows it . . ."

"That's just where you are mistaken; I did not know it, though I had guessed it was so."

"Well, now you know it."

"All I knew was that something had happened that made her dreadfully miserable, and that she begged me never to speak of it. And if she would not tell me, she would certainly not speak of it to anyone else. But what did pass between you? Tell me."

"I have told you."

"When was it?"

"When I was at their house the last time."

"Do you know," said Darya Aleksandrovna, "I am awfully, awfully sorry for her. You suffer only from pride . . ."

"Perhaps so," said Levin, "but—"

She interrupted him.

"But she, poor girl . . . I am awfully, awfully sorry for her. Now I see it all."

"Well, Darya Aleksandrovna, you must excuse me," he said, getting up. "Good-by, Darya Aleksandrovna, till we meet again."

"No, wait a minute," she said, clutching him by the sleeve. "Wait a minute, sit down."

"Please, please, don't let us talk of this," he said, sitting down, and at the same time feeling rise up and stir within his heart a hope he had believed to be buried.

"If I did not like you," she said, and tears came into her eyes; "if I did not know you, as I do know you . . ."

The feeling that had seemed dead revived more and more, rose up and took possession of Levin's heart.

"Yes, I understand it all now," said Darya Aleksandrovna. "You can't understand it; for you men, who are free and make your own choice, it's always clear whom you love. But a girl's in a position of suspense, with all a woman's or maiden's modesty, a girl who sees you men from afar, who takes everything on trust—a girl may have, and often has, such a feeling that she cannot tell what to say."

"Yes, if the heart does not speak—"

"No, the heart does speak; but just consider: you men have views about a girl, you come to the house, you make friends, you criticize, you wait to see if you have found what you love, and then, when you are sure you love her, you propose . . ."

"Well, that's not quite it."

"Anyway you propose, when your love is ripe or when the balance has completely turned between the two you are choosing from. But a girl is not asked. She is expected to make her choice, and yet she cannot choose, she can only answer 'yes' or 'no.' "

"Yes, to choose between me and Vronsky," thought Levin, and the dead thing that had come to life within him died again, and only weighed on his heart and set it aching.

"Darya Aleksandrovna," he said, "that's how one chooses a new dress, or some purchase or other, not love. The choice has been made, and so much the better . . . And there can be no repeating it."

"Ah, pride, pride!" said Darya Aleksandrovna, as though despising him for the baseness of this feeling in comparison with that other feeling which only women know. "At the time when you made Kitty an offer she was just in a position in which she could not answer. She was in doubt. Doubt between you and Vronsky. She was seeing him every day, and you she had not seen for a long while. Supposing she had been older . . . I, for instance, in her place could have felt no doubt. I always disliked him, and so it has turned out."

Levin recalled Kitty's answer. She had said: "*No, that cannot be. . .*"

"Darya Aleksandrovna," he said dryly, "I appreciate your confidence in me; I believe you are making a mistake. But whether I am right or wrong, the pride you so despise makes any thought of Katerina Aleksandrovna out of the question for me—you understand, utterly out of the question."

"I will only say one thing more: you know that I am speaking of my sister, whom I love as I love my own children. I don't say she cared for you, all I meant to say is that her refusal at that moment proves nothing."

"I don't know!" said Levin, jumping up. "If you only knew how you are hurting me. It's just as if a child of yours were dead, and they were to say to you: He would have been like this and like that, and he might have lived, and how happy you would have been in him. But he's dead, dead, dead! . . ."

"How absurd you are!" said Darya Aleksandrovna, looking with mournful tenderness at Levin's excitement. "Yes, I see it all more and more clearly," she went on musingly. "So you won't come to see us, then, when Kitty's here?"

"No, I will not come. Of course I won't avoid meeting Katerina Aleksandrovna, but as far as I can, I will try to save her the annoyance of my presence."

"You are very, very absurd," repeated Darya Aleksandrovna, looking with tenderness into his face. "Very well, then, let it be as though we had not spoken of this. What have you come for, Tanya?" she said in French to the little girl who had come in.

"Where's my spade, Mama?"

"I speak French, and you must too."

The little girl tried to say it in French, but could not remember the French for "spade"; the mother prompted her, and then told her in French where to look for the spade. And this made a disagreeable impression on Levin.

Everything in Darya Aleksandrovna's house and children struck him now as by no means so charming as a little while before. "And why does she talk French with the children?" he thought; "how unnatural and false it is! And the children feel it so: learning French and unlearning sincerity," he thought to himself, unaware that Darya Aleksandrovna had thought all that over twenty times already, and yet, even at the cost of some loss of sincerity, believed it necessary to teach her children French in that way.

"But why are you going? Do stay a little."

Levin stayed to tea; but his good humor had vanished, and he felt ill at ease.

After tea he went out into the hall to order his horses to be harnessed, and when he came back, he found Darya Aleksandrovna greatly disturbed, with a troubled face, and tears in her eyes. While Levin had been outside, an incident had occurred which had utterly shattered the happiness she had been feeling that day, and her pride in her children. Grisha and Tanya had been fighting over a ball. Darya Aleksandrovna, hearing a scream in the nursery, ran in and saw a terrible sight. Tanya was pulling Grisha's hair, while he, with a face hideous with rage, was beating her with his fists wherever he could get at her. Something snapped in Darya Aleksandrovna's heart when she saw this. It was as if darkness had swooped down upon her life; she felt that these children of hers, that she was so proud of, were not merely most ordinary, but positively bad, ill-bred children, with coarse, brutal propensities—wicked children.

She could not talk or think of anything else, and she could not speak to Levin of her misery.

Levin saw she was unhappy and tried to comfort her, saying that it showed nothing bad, that all children fight; but even as he said it, he was thinking in his heart: "No, I won't be artificial and talk French with my children; but my children won't be like that. All one has to do is not spoil children, not to distort their nature and they'll be delightful. No, my children won't be like that."

He said good-by and drove away, and she did not try to detain him.

CHAPTER ELEVEN

In the middle of July the elder of the village on Levin's sister's estate, about fifteen miles from Pokrovskoe, came to Levin to report on how things were going there and on the hay. The chief source of income on his sister's estate was from the riverside meadows. In former years the hay had been bought by the peasants for twenty rubles for every three acres. When Levin took over the management of the estate, he thought, on examining the grasslands, that they were worth more, and he fixed the price at twenty-five rubles for every three acres. The peasants would not give that price, and, as Levin suspected, discouraged other purchasers. Then Levin had driven over himself, and arranged to have the grass cut, partly by hired labor, partly at a payment of a certain proportion of the crop. His own peasants put every hindrance they could in the way of this new arrangement, but it was carried out, and the first year the meadows had yielded a profit almost double. The previous year—which was the third year—the peasants had maintained the same opposition to the arrangement, and the hay had been cut on the same system. This year the peasants were doing all the mowing for a third of the hay crop, and the village elder had come now to announce that that hay had been cut, and that, fearing rain, they had invited the estate clerk over, had divided the crop in his presence, and had raked together eleven stacks as the owner's share. From the vague answers to his question how much hay had been cut on the principal meadow, from the haste of the village elder to divide it without asking for permission, from the whole tone of the peasant, Levin perceived that there was something wrong in the division of the hay, and made up his mind to drive over himself to look into the matter.

Arriving for dinner at the village, and leaving his horse at the cottage of an old friend of his, the husband of his brother's wet nurse, Levin went to see the old man at his apiary, wanting to find out from him the truth about the hay. Parmenych, a talkative, stately old man, gave Levin a very warm welcome, showed him all he was doing, told him everything about his bees and the swarms of that year; but gave vague and unwilling answers to Levin's inquiries about the mowing. This confirmed Levin still more in his suspicions. He went to the hayfields and examined the stacks. The haystacks could not possibly contain fifty wagonloads each, and to convict the peasants, Levin ordered the wagons that had carried the hay to be brought at once, to lift one stack, and carry it into the barn. There turned out to be only thirty-two loads in the stack. In spite of the village elder's assertions about the compressibility of hay, and its having settled down in the stacks, and his swearing that everything had been done in the fear of God, Levin stuck to his point that the hay had been divided without his orders, and that therefore he would not accept that hay as fifty loads to a stack. After a prolonged dispute the matter was decided by the peasants taking these eleven stacks, counting them as fifty load each. The arguments and the division of the haycocks lasted the whole afternoon. When the last of the hay had been divided, Levin, entrusting the superintendence of the rest to the clerk, sat down on a haycock marked off by a stake of willow, and looked admiringly at the meadow swarming with peasants.

In front of him, in the bend of the river beyond the marsh, moved a bright-colored line of peasant women, and the scattered hay was being rapidly formed into gray winding rows over the pale green stubble. After the women came the men with pitchforks, and from the gray rows there were growing up broad, high, soft haycocks. To the left, carts were rumbling over the meadow that had already been cleared, and one after another the haycocks vanished, flung up in huge forkfuls, and in their place there were rising heavy cartloads of fragrant hay hanging over the horses' hindquarters.

"What weather for haying! What hay it'll be!" said an old man squatting down beside Levin. "It's tea, not hay! It's like scattering grain to the ducks, the way they pick it up!" he added, pointing to the growing haycocks. "Since dinnertime they've carried a good half of it."

"The last load, eh?" he shouted to a young peasant who drove by, standing in the front of an empty cart, shaking the cord reins.

"The last, Dad!" the lad shouted back, pulling in the horse, and, smiling, he looked around at a bright, rosy-cheeked peasant girl who sat in the cart smiling too, and drove on.

"Who's that? Your son?" asked Levin.

"My baby," said the old man with a tender smile.

"What a fine fellow!"

"The boy's all right."

"Married already?"

"Yes, it's two years last St. Filipp's Fast."[1]

"Any children?"

"Children indeed! Why, for over a year he was innocent as a babe himself, and bashful too," answered the old man. "Well, the hay! It's as fragrant as tea!" he repeated, wishing to change the subject.

Levin looked more attentively at Ivan Parmenov and his wife. They were loading a haycock onto the cart not far from him. Ivan Parmenov was standing on the cart, taking, laying in place, and

[1] I.e., November 14.

stamping down the huge bundles of hay, which his pretty young wife deftly handed up to him, at first in armfuls, and then on the pitchfork. The young wife worked easily, merrily, and dexterously. The close-packed hay did not once break away off her fork. First, she gathered it together, stuck the fork into it, then, with a rapid, supple movement, leaned the whole weight of her body on it, and at once with a bend of her back under the red belt she drew herself up, and arching her full bosom under the white smock, with a smart turn she swung the fork in her arms, and flung the bundle of hay high onto the cart. Ivan, obviously doing his best to save her every minute of unnecessary labor, made haste, opening wide his arms to clutch the bundle and lay it in the cart. As she raked together what was left of the hay, the young wife shook off the bits of hay that had fallen on her neck, and straightening the red kerchief that had dropped forward over her white brow, not browned like her face by the sun, she crept under the cart to tie up the load. Ivan directed her how to fasten the cord to the cross-piece, and at something she said he laughed aloud. In the expressions of both faces was to be seen vigorous, young, freshly awakened love.

CHAPTER TWELVE

The load was tied on. Ivan jumped down and took the quiet, sleek horse by the bridle. The young wife flung the rake up on the load, and with a bold step, swinging her arms, she went to join the women, who were forming a ring for the haymakers' dance. Ivan drove off to the road and fell into line with the other loaded carts. The peasant women, with their rakes on their shoulders, gay with bright flowers, and chattering with ringing, merry voices, walked behind the cart. One wild untrained female voice broke into a song, and sang it alone through a verse, and then the same verse was taken up and repeated by half a hundred strong, healthy voices of all sorts, coarse and fine, singing in unison.

The women, all singing, began to come close to Levin, and he felt as though a storm was swooping down upon him with a thunder of merriment. The storm swooped down, enveloped him and the haycock on which he was lying, and the other haycocks, and the carts, and the whole meadow and distant fields all seemed to be shaking and singing to the measures of this wild, merry song with its shouts and whistles and clapping. Levin felt envious of this health and mirthfulness; he longed to take part in the expression of this joy of life. But he could do nothing, and had to lie and look on and listen. When the peasants, with their singing, had vanished out of sight and hearing, a weary feeling of despondency at his own isolation, his physical inactivity, his alienation from this world, came over Levin.

Some of the very peasants who had been most active in wrangling with him over the hay, some whom he had treated with contempt, and who had tried to cheat him, those very peasants had greeted him cheerfully, and evidently had not, were incapable of having, any feeling of rancor against him, any regret, any recollection even of having tried to deceive him. All that was drowned in a sea of merry common labor. God gave the day, God gave the strength. And the day and the strength were consecrated to labor, and that labor was its own reward. For whom the labor? What would be its fruits? These were idle considerations—beside the point.

Often Levin had admired this life, often he had a sense of envy of the men who led this life; but today for the first time, especially under the influence of what he had seen in the attitude of Ivan Parmenov toward his young wife, the idea presented itself definitely to his mind that it was in his power to exchange the dreary, artificial, idle, and individualistic life he was leading for this laborious, pure, and delightful life.

The old man who had been sitting beside him had long ago gone home; the people had all separated. Those who lived near had gone home, while those who came from far were gathered into a group for supper, and to spend the night in the meadow. Levin, unobserved by the peasants, still lay on the haycock, and still looked on and listened and mused. The peasants who remained for the night in the meadow scarcely slept the whole short summer night. At first there was the sound of merry talk and laughter all together over the supper, then singing again and laughter.

The whole long day of toil had left no trace in them but lightness of heart. Before the early dawn all was hushed. Nothing was to be heard but the night sounds of the frogs that never ceased in the marsh, and the horses snorting in the mist that rose over the meadow before the morning. Rousing himself, Levin got up from the hay-cock, and looking at the stars, he saw that the night was over.

"Well, what am I going to do? How am I to do it?" he said to himself, trying to express to himself all the thoughts and feelings he had passed through in that brief night. All the thoughts and feel-ings he had passed through fell into three separate trains of thought. One was the renunciation of his old life, of his utterly useless edu-cation. This renunciation gave him satisfaction, and was easy and simple. Another series of thoughts and mental images related to the life he longed to live now. The simplicity, the purity, the sanity of this life he felt clearly and he was convinced he would find in it the content, the peace, and the dignity, of the lack of which he was so miserably conscious. But a third series of ideas turned upon the question of how to effect this transition from the old life to the new. And there nothing took clear shape for him. "Have a wife? Have work and the necessity of work? Leave Pokrovskoe? Buy land? Become a member of a peasant community? Marry a peasant girl? How am I to do it?" he asked himself again, and could not find an answer. "I haven't slept all night, though, and I can't think it out clearly," he said to himself. "I'll work it out later. One thing's cer-tain, this night has decided my fate. All my old dreams of married life were absurd, not the real thing," he told himself. "It's all really so much simpler and better. . ."

"How beautiful!" he thought, looking at the strange mother-of-pearl shell of white fleecy cloudlets resting right over his head in the middle of the sky. "How exquisite it all is in this exquisite night! And when was there time for that cloud shell to form? Just now I looked at the sky, and there was nothing in it—only two white streaks. Yes, and so imperceptibly too my views of life changed!"

He went out of the meadow and walked along the road toward the village. A slight wind arose, and the sky looked gray and sullen. The gloomy moment that usually precedes the dawn had come, the full triumph of light over darkness.

Shrinking from the cold, Levin walked rapidly, looking at the ground. "What's that? Something coming," he thought, catching the tinkle of bells and lifting his head. Forty paces from him a carriage with four horses harnessed abreast was driving toward him along the grassy road on which he was walking. The shaft horses were tilted against the shafts by the ruts, but the dexterous driver sitting on the box held the shaft over the ruts, so that the wheels ran on the smooth part of the road.

This was all Levin noticed, and without wondering who it could be, he gazed absently at the coach.

In the coach was an old lady dozing in one corner, and at the window, evidently only just awake, sat a young girl holding in both hands the ribbons of a white cap. With a face full of light and thought, full of a subtle, complex inner life that was remote from Levin, she was gazing beyond him at the glow of the sunrise.

At the very instant when this apparition was vanishing, the truthful eyes glanced at him. She recognized him, and her face lighted up with amazed delight.

He could not be mistaken. There were no other eyes like those in the world. There was only one creature in the world who could concentrate for him all the brightness and meaning of life. It was she. It was Kitty. He understood that she was driving to Yergushovo from the railway station. And everything that had been stirring Levin during that sleepless night, all the resolutions he had made, all vanished at once. He recalled with horror his dreams of marrying a peasant girl. Only there, in the carriage that had crossed over to the other side of the road and was rapidly disappearing, only there could he find the solution to the riddle of his life, which had weighed so agonizingly upon him of late.

She did not look out again. The sound of the carriage springs was no longer audible, the bells could scarcely be heard. The barking of dogs indicated that the carriage had reached the village, and all that was left were the empty fields all round, the village in front, and he himself isolated and apart from it all, wandering lonely the deserted road.

He glanced at the sky, expecting to find there the cloud shell he had been admiring and taking as the symbol of the ideas and feelings of that night. There was nothing in the sky in the least like a shell. There, in the remote heights above, a mysterious change had been accomplished. There was no trace of shell, and there was stretched over fully half the sky an even cover of tiny and ever tinier cloudlets. The sky had grown blue and bright; and with the same softness, but with the same remoteness, it met his questioning gaze.

"No," he said to himself, "however good that life of simplicity and toil may be, I cannot go back to it. I love *her*."

CHAPTER THIRTEEN

None but those who were most intimate with Aleksey Aleksandrovich Karenin knew that, while on the surface the coldest and most reasonable of men, he had one weakness quite opposed to the general trend of his character. Aleksey Aleksandrovich could not hear or see a child or woman crying without being moved. The sight of tears threw him into a state of nervous agitation, and he utterly lost all power of reflection. The chief secretary of his department and his private secretary were aware of this, and used to warn women who came with petitions on no account to give way to tears, if they did not want to ruin their chances. "He will get angry, and will not listen to you," they used to say. And as a fact, in such cases the emotional disturbance set up in Aleksey Aleksandrovich by the sight of tears found expression in hasty anger. "I can do nothing. Kindly leave the room!" he would commonly cry in such cases.

When returning from the races, Anna had informed him of her relations with Vronsky and immediately afterward had burst into tears, hiding her face in her hands, Aleksey Aleksandrovich, for all the fury aroused in him against her, was aware at the same time of a rush of that emotional disturbance always produced in him by tears. Conscious of it, and conscious that any expression of his feelings at that minute would be out of keeping with the situation, he tried to suppress every manifestation of life in himself, and so neither stirred nor looked at her. This was what had caused that strange expression of deathlike rigidity in his face which had so impressed Anna.

When they reached the house he helped her to get out of the carriage, and making an effort to master himself, he took leave of her with his usual urbanity, and uttered that phrase that bound him to nothing; he said that tomorrow he would let her know his decision.

His wife's words, confirming his worst suspicions, had sent a cruel pang to the heart of Aleksey Aleksandrovich. That pang was intensified by the strange feeling of physical pity for her set up by her tears. But when he was all alone in the carriage Aleksey Aleksandrovich, to his surprise and delight, felt complete relief both from this pity and from the doubts and agonies of jealousy.

He experienced the sensation of a man who has had a tooth out after suffering long from toothache. After a fearful agony and a sense of something huge, bigger than the head itself, being torn out of his jaw, the sufferer, hardly able to believe in his own good luck, feels all at once that what has so long poisoned his existence and enslaved his attention exists no longer, and that he can live and think again, and take interest in other things besides his tooth. This feeling Aleksey Aleksandrovich was experiencing. The agony had been strange and terrible, but now it was over; he felt that he could live again and think of something other than his wife.

"No honor, no heart, no religion; a corrupt woman. I always knew it and always saw it, though I tried to deceive myself to spare her," he said to himself. And it actually seemed to him that he always had seen it: he recalled incidents of their past life, in which he had never seen anything wrong before—now these incidents proved clearly that she had always been a corrupt woman. "I made a mistake in linking my life to hers; but there was nothing reprehensible in my mistake, and so I cannot be unhappy. It's not I that am to blame," he told himself, "but she. But I have nothing to do with her. She does not exist for me . . ."

Everything relating to her and her son, toward whom his sentiments were as much changed as toward her, ceased to interest him. The only thing that interested him now was the question of what way he could best, with most propriety and comfort for himself, and so with most justice, extricate himself from the mud with which she had spattered him in her fall, and then proceed along his path of active, honorable, and useful existence.

"I cannot be made unhappy by the fact that a contemptible woman has committed a crime. I have only to find the best way out of the difficult position in which she has placed me. And I shall find it," he said to himself, frowning more and more. "I'm not the first nor the last." And to say nothing of historical instances dating from the Menelaus and *La Belle Hélène*,[1] recently revived in the memory of all, a whole list of contemporary examples of husbands with unfaithful wives in the highest society rose before Aleksey Aleksandrovich's imagination. "Daryalov, Poltavsky, Prince Karibanov, Count Paskudin, Dram . . . Yes, even Dram, such an honest, capable fellow . . . Semyonov, Chagin, Sigonin," Aleksey Aleksandrovich remembered. "Admitting that a certain quite unreasonable *ridicule* falls to the lot of these men, yet I never saw anything but a misfortune in it, and always felt sympathy for it," he said to himself, though indeed this was not the fact, and he had never felt sympathy for misfortunes of that kind, but the more frequently he had heard of instances of unfaithful wives betraying their husbands, the more highly he had thought of himself. "It is a misfortune that may befall anyone. And this misfortune has befallen me. The only thing to be done is to make the best of the situation."

And he began mentally reviewing the course of action taken by men who had been in the same position that he was in.

"Daryalov fought a duel . . ."

The duel had particularly fascinated the thoughts of Aleksey Aleksandrovich in his youth, just because he was physically a coward and was himself well aware of the fact. Aleksey Aleksandrovich could not without horror contemplate the idea of a pistol aimed at himself, and never made use of any weapon in his life. This horror had in his youth started him pondering on dueling, and picturing himself in a position in which he would have to expose his life to danger. Having attained success and an established position in the world, he had long ago forgotten this feeling; but the old habit reasserted itself, and dread of his own cowardice proved even now so strong that Aleksey Aleksandrovich spent a long while thinking over the question of dueling in all its aspects, and playing with the idea of a duel, though he was fully aware beforehand that he would never under any circumstances fight one.

[1]Comic opera by Offenbach then very popular. Menelaus, in Greek mythology, was the husband of Helen of Troy. He lost her to Paris, Trojan prince.

"There's no doubt our society is still so barbarous (it's not the same in England) that very many"—and among these were those whose opinion Aleksey Aleksandrovich particularly valued—"look favorably on the duel; but what result is attained by it? Suppose I challenge him," Aleksey Aleksandrovich went on to himself, and vividly picturing the night he would spend after the challenge, and the pistol aimed at him, he shuddered, and knew that he never would do it. "Suppose I challenge him. Suppose I am taught," he went on musing, "to shoot. I press the trigger," he said to himself, closing his eyes, "and it turns out I have killed him," and he shook his head as though to dispel such silly ideas. "What sense is there in murdering a man in order to define one's relation to a guilty wife and son? I would still just as much have to decide what I ought to do with her. But what is more probable and what would doubtless occur—I would be killed or wounded. I, the innocent person, would be the victim— killed or wounded. It's even more senseless. But apart from that, a challenge to fight would be an act hardly honest on my side. Don't I know perfectly well that my friends would never allow me to fight a duel—would never allow the life of a statesman needed by Russia to be exposed to danger? Knowing perfectly well beforehand that the matter would never come to real danger, it would amount to my simply trying to gain a certain false glory by such a challenge. That would be dishonest, that would be false, that would be deceiving myself and others. A duel is quite unreasonable, and no one expects it of me. My aim is simply to safeguard my reputation, which is essential for the uninterrupted pursuit of my public duties." Official duties which had always been of great consequence in Aleksey Aleksandrovich's eyes, seemed of special importance to his mind at this moment. Considering and rejecting the duel, Aleksey Aleksandrovich turned to divorce—another solution selected by several of the husbands he remembered. Passing in mental review all the instances he knew of divorces (there were plenty of them in the very highest society with which he was very familiar), Aleksey Aleksandrovich could not find a single example in which the object of divorce was that which he had in view. In all these instances the husband had practically ceded or sold his unfaithful wife, and the very party which, being in fault, had not the right to contract a fresh marriage had formed counterfeit, pseudo-matrimonial ties with a self-styled husband. In his own case, Aleksey Aleksandrovich saw that a legal divorce, that is to say, one in which only the guilty wife would be repudiated, was impossible to get. He saw that the complex conditions of the life they led made the coarse proofs of his wife's guilt, required by the law, out of the question; he saw that a certain refinement in that life would not admit of such proofs being brought forward, even if he had them, and that to bring forward such proofs would damage him in the public estimation more than it would her.

An attempt at divorce could lead to nothing but a public scandal, which would be a perfect godsend to his enemies for calumny and attacks on his high position in society. His chief object, to define the position with the least amount of disturbance possible, would not be attained by divorce either. Moreover, in the event of divorce, or even of an attempt to obtain a divorce, it was obvious that the wife broke off all relations with the husband and threw in her lot with her lover. And in spite of the complete, as she supposed, contempt and indifference he now felt for his wife, at the bottom of his heart Aleksey Aleksandrovich still had one feeling left in regard to her— a disinclination to see her free to throw in her lot with Vronsky, so that her crime would be to her advantage. The mere notion of this so exasperated him that as soon as it occurred to him he groaned with inward agony, and got up and changed his place in the carriage, and for a long while after he sat with scowling brows, wrapping his numbed and bony legs in the fleecy blanket.

"Apart from formal divorce, one might still do like Karibanov, Paskudin, and that good fellow Dram—that is, separate from one's wife," he went on thinking, when he had regained his composure. But this step also presented the same drawback of public scandal as a divorce, and what was more, a separation, quite as much as a regular divorce, flung his wife into the arms of Vronsky. "No, it's out of the question, out of the question!" he said again, twisting his blanket tighter about him. "I cannot be unhappy, but neither she nor he ought to be happy."

The feeling of jealousy which had tortured him during the period of uncertainty had passed away at the instant when the tooth had been with agony extracted by his wife's words. But that feeling had been replaced by another, the desire, not merely that she should not be triumphant, but that she should get due retribution for her crime. He did not acknowledge this feeling, but deep in his heart he longed for her to suffer for having destroyed his peace of mind—his honor. And going over again the conditions inseparable from a duel, a divorce, a separation, and once again rejecting them, Aleksey Aleksandrovich felt convinced that there was only one solution—to keep her with him concealing what had happened from the world, and using every measure in his power to break off the intrigue, and still more—though this he did not admit to himself—to punish her. "I must inform her of my conclusion, that thinking over the terrible situation in which she has placed her family, all other solutions will be worse for both sides than an external *status quo*, and that such I agree to retain, on the strict condition of obedience on her part to my wishes, that is to say, cessation of all intercourse with her lover." When this decision had been finally adopted, another weighty consideration occurred to Aleksey Aleksandrovich in support of it. "By only such a course shall I be acting in accordance with the dictates of religion," he told himself. "In adopting this course, I am not casting off a guilty wife but giving her a chance of amendment; and, indeed, difficult as the task will be to me, I shall devote part of my energies to her reformation and salvation."

Though Aleksey Aleksandrovich was perfectly aware that he could not exert any moral influence over his wife, that such an attempt at reformation could lead to nothing but lies; though in passing through these difficult moments he had not once thought of seeking guidance in religion, yet now, when his conclusion corresponded, as it seemed to him, with the requirements of religion, this religious sanction to his decision gave him complete satisfaction, and to some extent restored his peace of mind. He was pleased to think that even in such an important crisis in life, no one would be able to say that he had not acted in accordance with the principles of that religion whose banner he had always held aloft amid the general apathy and indifference. As he pondered over subsequent developments, Aleksey Aleksandrovich did not see, indeed, why his relations with his wife should not remain practically the same as before. No doubt she could never regain his esteem, but there was not, and there could not be, any sort of reason that his existence should be troubled, and that he should suffer because she was a bad and faithless wife. "Yes, time will pass; time, which arranges all things, and the old relations will be restored," Aleksey Aleksandrovich told himself; "so far restored, that is, that I shall not be sensible of a break in the continuity of my life. She is bound to be unhappy, but I am not to blame, and so I cannot be unhappy."

CHAPTER FOURTEEN

As he neared Petersburg, Aleksey Aleksandrovich not only adhered entirely to his decision, he even composed in his head the letter he would write to his wife. Going into the porter's room, he glanced at the letters and papers brought from his office, and directed that they should be brought to him in his study.

"The horses can be unharnessed and I will see no one," he said, in answer to the porter, with a certain pleasure indicative of his agreeable frame of mind emphasizing the words "see no one."

In his study Aleksey Aleksandrovich walked up and down twice, and stopped at an immense writing table, on which six candles had already been lighted by the valet who had preceded him. He cracked his knuckles, and sat down, sorting out his writing materials. Putting his elbows on the table, he cocked his head to one side, thought a minute, and began to write without pausing for a second. He wrote without directly addressing her, and used French, making use of the plural "*vous*," which has not the same note of coldness as the corresponding Russian form:

> At our last conversation, I notified you of my intention to com-
> municate to you my decision in regard to the subject of that con-
> versation. Having carefully considered everything, I am writing
> now with the object of fulfilling that promise. My decision is as
> follows. Whatever your conduct may have been, I do not consider
> myself justified in breaking the ties in which we are bound by a
> Higher Power. The family cannot be broken up by a whim, a
> caprice, or even by the sin of one of the partners in the marriage,

and our life must go on as it has in the past. This is essential for me, for you, and for our son. I am fully convinced that you have repented and do repent of what has called forth the present let- ter, and that you will co-operate with me in eradicating the cause of our estrangement, and forgetting the past. In the contrary event, you can conjecture what awaits you and your son. All this I hope to discuss more in detail in a personal interview. As the sum- mer season is drawing to a close, I would beg you to return to Petersburg as quickly as possible, not later than Tuesday. All nec- essary preparations shall be made for your arrival here. I beg you to note that I attach particular significance to compliance with this request.

A. Karenin

P.S.—I enclose the money which may be needed for your expenses.

He read the letter through and felt pleased with it, and especially that he had remembered to enclose money: there was not a harsh word, not a reproach in it, nor was there undue indulgence. Most of all, it was a golden bridge for return. Folding the letter and smooth- ing it with a massive ivory knife, and putting it in an envelope with the money, he rang the bell with the gratification it always afforded him to use the well-arranged appointments of his writing table.

"Give this to the courier to be delivered to Anna Arkadyevna tomorrow at the summer villa," he said, getting up.

"Certainly, Your Excellency; tea to be served in the study?"

Aleksey Aleksandrovich ordered tea to be brought to the study, and playing with the massive paper knife, he moved to his armchair, near which there had been placed ready for him a lamp and the French work on the Eugubine Tables[1] that he had begun. Over the armchair there hung in a gold frame an oval portrait of Anna, a fine painting by a celebrated artist. Aleksey Aleksandrovich glanced at it. The unfathomable eyes gazed ironically and insolently at him. Insuf- ferably insolent and challenging was the effect, in Aleksey Aleksan- drovich's eyes, of the black lace about the head, admirably done by

[1] I.e., Tables discovered in Eugubium (now Gubbi, Italy) in 1444.

the painter, the black hair and handsome white hand with one finger lifted, covered with rings. After looking at the portrait for a minute, Aleksey Aleksandrovich shuddered, so that his lips quivered, and uttered the sound "brrr" and turned away. He made haste to sit down in his armchair, and opened the book. He tried to read, but he could not revive the very vivid interest he had felt before in Eugubine inscriptions. He looked at the book and thought of something else. He thought not of his wife but of a complication that had arisen in his official life, which at the time constituted the chief interest of it. He felt that he had penetrated more deeply than ever before into this intricate affair, and that he had originated a leading idea—he could say it without self-flattery—calculated to clear up the whole business, to strengthen him in his official career, to discomfort his enemies, and thereby to be of the greatest benefit to the government. As soon as the servant had set the tea and left the room, Aleksey Aleksandrovich got up and went to the writing table. Moving a portfolio of papers into the middle of the table, with a scarcely perceptible smile of self-satisfaction, he took a pencil from a rack and plunged into the perusal of a complex report relating to the present complication. The complication was of this nature: Aleksey Aleksandrovich's characteristic quality as a politician, that special individual qualification that every rising functionary possesses, the qualification that with his unflagging ambition, his reserve, his honesty, and his self-confidence had made his career, was his contempt for red tape, his cutting down of correspondence, his direct contact, wherever possible, with the living fact, and his economy. It happened that the famous Commission of the 2nd of June had set on foot an inquiry into the irrigation of lands in the Zaraisky province, which fell under Aleksey Aleksandrovich's department, and was a glaring example of fruitless expenditure and red tape. Aleksey Aleksandrovich was aware of the truth of this. The irrigation of these lands in the Zaraisky province had been initiated by the predecessor of Aleksey Aleksandrovich's predecessor. And vast sums of money had actually been spent and were still being spent on this business, and utterly unproductively, and the whole business could obviously lead to nothing whatever. Aleksey Aleksandrovich had perceived this at once on entering office, and would have liked to lay hands on the Board of Irrigation. But at first, when he did not yet feel secure in his position, he knew it would affect too many interests, and would be injudicious. Later on he had been engrossed in other questions, and had simply forgotten the Board of Irrigation. It went on by itself, like all such boards, by the mere force of inertia. (Many people gained their livelihood by the Board of Irrigation, especially one highly conscientious and musical family: all the daughters played stringed instruments, and Aleksey Aleksandrovich knew the family and had sponsored one of the elder daughters at her wedding.) The raising of this question by a hostile department was in Aleksey Aleksandrovich's opinion a dishonorable proceeding, seeing that in every department there were things similar and worse, which no one inquired into, for well-known reasons of official etiquette. However, now that the gauntlet had been thrown down, he had boldly picked it up and demanded the appointment of a special commission to investigate and verify the working of the Board of Irrigation of the lands in the Zaraisky province. But in compensation he gave no quarter to the enemy either. He demanded the appointment of another special commission to inquire into the question of regulating the affairs of the native population.[2] The question of regulating the affairs of the native population had been brought up incidentally in the Commission of the 2nd of June, and had been pressed forward actively by Aleksey Aleksandrovich as one admitting of no delay on account of the deplorable condition of the natives. In the commission this question had been a ground of contention between several departments. The department hostile to Aleksey Aleksandrovich proved that the condition of the natives was exceedingly flourishing, that the proposed reconstruction might be the ruin of their prosperity, and that if there was anything wrong, it arose mainly from the failure on the part of Aleksey Aleksandrovich's department to carry out the measures prescribed by law. Now Aleksey Aleksandrovich intended to demand: first, that a new commission should be formed which should be empowered to investigate the condition of the natives on the spot; second, if it should turn out that the condition of the natives actually was such as it appeared to be from the official documents in the hands of the committee, that another new scientific

[2]I.e., the alien, non-Russian minorities.

commission should be appointed to investigate the deplorable condition of the natives from the—(1) political, (2) administrative, (3) economic, (4) ethnographical, (5) material, and (6) religious points of
view; third, that evidence should be required from the rival department of the measures that had been taken during the last ten years
by that department for averting the disastrous conditions in which
the natives were now placed; and forth and finally, that that department be asked to explain why it had, as appeared from the evidence
before the committee, from No.17,015 and 18,308, from December
5, 1863, and June 7, 1864, acted in direct contravention of the intention of the law, volume . . . Act 18, and the footnote to Act 36. A flash
of eagerness suffused the face of Aleksey Aleksandrovich as he rapidly
wrote out a synopsis of these ideas for his own benefit. Having filled
a sheet of paper, he got up, rang, and sent a note to the chief secretary
of his department to look up certain necessary facts for him. Getting
up and walking about the room, he glanced again at the portrait,
frowned, and smiled contemptuously. After reading a little more of
the book on Eugubine inscriptions, and renewing his interest in it,
Aleksey Aleksandrovich went to bed at eleven o'clock, and recollecting as he lay in bed the incident with his wife, he no longer saw it in
such a gloomy light.

CHAPTER FIFTEEN

Though Anna had obstinately and with exasperation contradicted
Vronsky when he told her her position was impossible and tried to
convince her to tell everything to her husband, at the bottom of her
heart she regarded her own position as false and dishonorable, and
she longed with her whole soul to change it. On the way home from
the races she had told her husband the truth in a moment of excitement, and in spite of the agony she had suffered in doing so, she was
glad of it. After her husband had left her, she told herself that she was
glad, that now everything was out in the open, and at least there
would be no more lying and deception. It seemed to her beyond
doubt that her position was now made clear forever. It might be bad,
this new position, but it would be clear; there would be no indefi-

niteness or falsehood about it. The pain she had caused herself and her husband in uttering those words would be rewarded now by everything being made clear, she thought. That evening she saw Vronsky, but she did not tell him of what had passed between her and her husband, though, to make the position clear, it would be necessary to tell him.

When she awakened the next morning the first thing that came to her mind was what she had said to her husband, and this seemed to her so awful that she could not conceive now how she could have brought herself to utter those strange, coarse words, and could not imagine what would come of it. But the words were spoken, and Aleksey Aleksandrovich had gone away without saying anything. "I saw Vronsky and did not tell him. At the very instant he was going away I wanted to call him back and tell him, but I changed my mind, because it was strange that I had not told him the first minute. Why was it I wanted to tell him and did not tell him?" And in answer to this question a burning blush of shame spread over her face. She knew what had kept her from it, she knew that she had been ashamed. Her position, which had seemed to her clear the night before, suddenly struck her now as not only not simple but as absolutely hopeless. She felt terrified at the disgrace, of which she had not ever thought before. As soon as she thought of what her husband would do, the most terrible ideas came to her mind. She had a vision of being turned out of the house, of her shame being proclaimed to the whole world. She asked herself where she could go when she was turned out of the house, and she could not find an answer.

When she thought of Vronsky, it seemed to her that he did not love her, that he was already beginning to be tired of her, that she could not offer herself to him, and she felt bitter against him for it. It seemed to her that the words that she had spoken to her husband, and had continually repeated in her imagination, she had said to everyone, and everyone had heard them. She could not bring herself to look those of her own household in the face. She could not bring herself to call her maid, and still less go downstairs and see her son and his governess.

The maid, who had been listening at her door for a long while, came into her room of her own accord. Anna glanced inquiringly into her face, and blushed with fear. The maid begged her pardon for coming in, saying that she thought the bell rang. She brought her clothes and a note. The note was from Betsy. Betsy reminded her that Liza Merkalova and Baroness Stolz were coming to play croquet with her that morning with their admirers, Kaluzhsky and old Stremov. "Come, if only as a study in mores. I shall expect you," she finished.

Anna read the note and heaved a deep sigh.

"Nothing, I need nothing," she said to Annushka, who was rearranging the bottles and brushes on the dressing table. "You can go. I'll dress at once and come down. I need nothing."

Annushka went out, but Anna did not begin dressing, and sat in the same position, her head and hands hanging listlessly, and every now and then she shivered all over, seemed as though she would make some gesture, utter some word, and sank back into lifelessness again. She repeated continually, "My God! My God!" But neither "God" nor "my" had any meaning to her. The idea of seeking help in her difficulty in religion was as remote from her as seeking help from Aleksey Aleksandrovich himself, although she had never had doubts of the faith in which she had been brought up. She knew that the support of religion was possible only upon condition of renouncing what made up for her the whole meaning of life. She was not simply miserable, she began to feel alarm at the new emotional condition, never experienced before, in which she found herself. She felt as though everything was beginning to be doubled in her soul, just as objects sometimes appear doubled to overtired eyes. She hardly knew at times what it was she feared, and what she hoped for. Whether she feared or desired what had happened, or what was going to happen, and exactly what she longed for, she could not have said.

"Ah, what am I doing!" she said to herself, feeling a sudden thrill of pain in both sides of her head. When she came to herself, she saw that she was holding her hair in both hands, each side of her temples, and pulling it. She jumped up, and began walking about.

"The coffee is ready, and Mademoiselle and Seryozha are waiting," said Annushka, coming back again and finding Anna in the same position.

"Seryozha? What about Seryozha?" Anna asked, with sudden

eagerness, recollecting her son's existence for the first time that morning.

"He's been naughty, I think," answered Annushka with a smile.

"In what way?"

"Some peaches were lying on the table in the corner room. I think he slipped in and ate one of them on the sly."

The recollection of her son suddenly roused Anna from the helpless condition in which she found herself. She recalled the partly sincere, though greatly exaggerated, role of the mother living for her child, which she had taken up of late years, and she felt with joy that in the plight in which she found herself she had a support, quite apart from her relation to her husband or to Vronsky. This support was her son. In whatever position she might be placed, she could not lose her son. Her husband might put her to shame and turn her out, Vronsky might grow cold to her and go on living his own life apart (she thought of him again with bitterness and reproach); she could not leave her son. She had an aim in life. And she must act; act to secure this relation to her son, so that he might not be taken from her. Quickly indeed, as quickly as possible, she must take action before he was taken from her. She must take her son and go away. Here was the one thing she had to do now. She needed consolation. She must be calm, and get out of this insufferable position. The thought of immediate action binding her to her son, of going away somewhere with him, gave her this consolation.

She dressed quickly, went downstairs, and with resolute steps walked into the drawing room, where she found, as usual, waiting for her, the coffee, Seryozha, and his governess. Seryozha, all in white, with his back and head bent, was standing at a table under a mirror, and with an expression of intense concentration which she knew well, and in which he resembled his father, he was doing something to the flowers he carried.

The governess had a particularly severe expression. Seryozha screamed shrilly, as he often did, "Ah, Mama!" and stopped, hesitating whether to go to greet his mother and put down the flowers, or to finish making the wreath and go with the flowers.

The governess, after saying good morning, began a long and detailed account of Seryozha's naughtiness, but Anna did not hear her; she was considering whether she would take her with her or not. "No, I won't take her," she decided. "I'll go alone with my child."

"Yes, it's very wrong," said Anna, and taking her son by the shoulder, she looked at him, not severely, but with a timid glance that bewildered and delighted the boy, and she kissed him. "Leave him to me," she said to the astonished governess, and not letting go of her son, she sat down at the table, where coffee was set ready for her.

"Mama! I . . . I . . . didn't . . ." he said, trying to make out from her expression what was in store for him in regard to the peaches.

"Seryozha," she said, as soon as the governess had left the room, "that was wrong, but you'll never do it again, will you? . . . You love me?"

She felt that the tears were coming into her eyes. "Can I help loving him?" she said to herself, looking deeply into his scared and at the same time delighted eyes. "And can he ever join his father in punishing me? Is it possible he will not feel for me?" Tears were already flowing down her face, and to hide them she got up abruptly and almost ran out onto the terrace.

After the thundershowers of the last few days, cold, bright weather had set in. The air was cold in the bright sun that filtered through the freshly washed leaves.

She shivered, both from the cold and from the inward horror which had clutched her with fresh force in the open air.

"Run along, run along to Mariette," she said to Seryozha, who had followed her out, and she began walking up and down on the straw matting of the terrace. "Can it be that they won't forgive me, won't understand how it all couldn't be helped?" she said to herself.

Standing still, and looking at the tops of the aspen trees waving in the wind, with their freshly washed, brightly shining leaves in the cold sunshine, she knew that they would not forgive her, that everyone and everything would be merciless to her now as was that sky, that green. And again she felt that everything was split in two in her soul. "I mustn't, mustn't think," she said to herself. "I must get ready. To go where? When? Whom to take with me? Yes, to Moscow by the evening train. Annushka and Seryozha, and only the most necessary things. But first I must write to them both." She went quickly indoors into her boudoir, sat down at the table, and wrote to her husband:

After what has happened, I cannot remain any longer in your house. I am going away, and taking my son with me. I don't know the law, and so I don't know with which of the parents the son should remain; but I take him with me because I cannot live without him. Be generous, leave him to me.

Up to this point she wrote rapidly and naturally, but the appeal to his generosity, a quality she did not recognize in him, and the necessity of concluding the letter with something touching, made her stop. "Of my fault and my remorse I cannot speak, because . . ."

She stopped again, finding no connection in her ideas. "No," she said to herself, "this is unnecessary," and tearing up the letter, she wrote it again, leaving out the allusion to generosity, and sealed it.

Another letter had to be written, to Vronsky. "I have told my husband," she wrote, and she sat a long while unable to write more. It was so coarse, so unfeminine. "And what more am I to write him?" she said to herself. Again a flush of shame spread over her face; she recalled his composure, and a feeling of anger against him impelled her to tear the sheet with the phrase she had written into tiny bits. "No need to write anything," she said to herself, and closing her blotting pad, she went upstairs, told the governess and the servants that she was going that day to Moscow, and at once began to pack her things.

CHAPTER SIXTEEN

All the rooms of the summer villa were full of porters, gardeners, and footmen going to and fro carrying out things. Cupboards and chests were open; twice they had sent to the shop for cord; pieces of newspaper were tossing about on the floor. Two trunks, some bags, and strapped-up rugs had been carried down into the hall. The carriage and two hired cabs were waiting at the steps. Anna, forgetting her inward agitation in the work of packing, was standing at a table in her boudoir, packing her traveling bag, when Annushka called her attention to the rattle of a carriage driving up. Anna looked out of the window and saw Aleksey Aleksandrovich's courier on the steps, ringing at the front door bell.

"Run and find out what it is," she said, and with a calm sense of being prepared for anything, she sat down in an armchair, folding her hands on her knees. A footman brought in a thick envelope addressed in Aleksey Aleksandrovich's writing.

"The courier had orders to wait for an answer," he said.

"Very well," she said, and as soon as he had left the room, she tore open the letter with trembling fingers. A roll of unfolded notes done up in a wrapper fell out of it. She took out the letter and began reading it at the end. "Preparations shall be made for your arrival here . . . I attach particular significance to compliance . . ." she read. Then, going back, she read it all through, twice, from the beginning. When she had finished, she felt that she was cold all over, and that a fearful calamity such as she had not expected had burst upon her.

In the morning she had regretted that she had spoken to her husband, and wished for nothing so much as that those words could be unspoken. And here this letter regarded them as unspoken, and gave her what she had wanted. But now this letter seemed to her more terrible than anything she had been able to conceive.

"He's right!" she said; "of course, he's always right; he's a Christian, he's generous! Yes, vile, base creature! And no one understands it except me, and no one ever will; and I can't explain it. They say he's so religious, so high-principled, so upright, so clever; but they don't see what I've seen. They don't know how he had crushed my life for eight years, crushed everything that was living in me. He had not once given thought that I'm a live woman who must have love. They don't know how at every step he's humiliated me, and been just as pleased with himself. Haven't I tried, tried with all my strength, to find something to give meaning to my life? Haven't I struggled to love him, to love my son when I could not love my husband? But the time came when I knew that I couldn't cheat myself any longer, that I was alive, that I was not to blame, that God has made me so that I must love and live. And now what does he do? If he'd killed me, if he'd killed me I could have borne anything, I could have forgiven anything; but, no, he . . . How was it I didn't guess what he would do? He's doing just what's characteristic of his mean nature. He'll keep himself in the right, while me, in my ruin, he'll drive still lower to worse ruin yet . . ."

She recalled the words from the letter: "You can conjecture what awaits you and your son . . ." "That's a threat to take away my child, and most likely by their stupid law he can. But I know very well why he says it. He doesn't even believe in my love for my child, or he despises it (just as he always used to ridicule it). He despises that feeling in me, but he knows that I won't abandon my child, that I can't abandon my child, that there could be no life for me without my child, even with him whom I love; but that if I abandoned my child and ran away for him, I should be acting like the most infamous, basest of women. He knows that, and knows that I am incapable of doing that."

She recalled another sentence in the letter: "Our life must go on as it has done in the past . . ." "That life was miserable enough in the old days; it has been awful of late. What will it be now? And he knows all that; he knows that I can't repent that I breathe, that I love; he knows that it can lead to nothing but lying and deceit; but he wants to go on torturing me. I know him; I know that he's at home and happy in deceit, like a fish swimming in the water. No, I won't give him that happiness. I'll break through the spider web of lies in which he wants to catch me, come what may. Anything's better than lying and deceit.

"But how? My God! my God! Was ever a woman so miserable as I am? . . .

"No; I will break through it, I will break through it!" she cried, jumping up and keeping back her tears. And she went to the writing table to write him another letter. But at the bottom of her heart she felt that she was not strong enough to break through anything, that she was not strong enough to get out of her former position, however false and dishonorable it might be.

She sat down at the writing table, but instead of writing she clasped her hands on the table and, laying her head on them, burst into tears, with sobs and heaving breast like a child crying. She was weeping because her dream of her position being made clear and definite had been annihilated forever. She knew beforehand that everything would go on in the old way, and far worse, indeed, than in the old way. She felt that the position in the world that she enjoyed, and that had seemed to her of so little consequence in the morning, that this position was precious to her, that she would not have the strength to exchange it for the shameful position of a woman who has abandoned husband and child to join her lover; that however much she might struggle, she could not be stronger than herself. She would never know freedom in love, but would remain forever a guilty wife, with the menace of detection hanging over her at every instant; deceiving her husband for the sake of a shameful liaison with a man living apart and away from her, whose life she could never share. She knew that this was how it would be, and at the same time it was so awful that she could not even conceive what it would end in. And she cried without restraint, as children cry when they are punished.

The sound of the footman's steps forced her to rouse herself, and hiding her face from him, she pretended to be writing.

"The courier asks if there's an answer," the footman announced.

"An answer? Yes," said Anna. "Let him wait. I'll ring."

"What can I write?" she thought. "What can I decide upon alone? What do I know? What is there I care for?" Again she felt that her soul was beginning to be split in two. She was terrified again at this feeling, and clutched at the first pretext for doing something which might divert her thoughts from herself. "I ought to see Aleksey" (so she called Vronsky in her thoughts); "no one but he can tell me what I ought to do. I'll go to Betsy's, perhaps I shall see him there," she said to herself, completely forgetting that when she had told him the day before that she was not going to Princess Tverskaya's he had said that in that case he would not go either. She went up to the table, wrote to her husband, "I have received your letter.—A."; and, ringing the bell, gave it to the footman.

"We are not going," she said to Annushka as she came in.

"Not going at all?"

"No; don't unpack till tomorrow, and let the carriage wait. I'm going to the princess's."

"Which dress will you wear?"

CHAPTER SEVENTEEN

The croquet party to which the Princess Tverskaya had invited Anna was to consist of two ladies and their admirers. These two ladies were the chief representatives of a select new Petersburg circle, nicknamed, in imitation of some imitation, *les sept merveilles du monde*.[1] These ladies belonged to a circle which, though of the highest society, was utterly hostile to that in which Anna moved. Moreover, Stremov, one of the most influential people in Petersburg, and the elderly admirer of Liza Merkalova, was Aleksey Aleksandrovich's enemy in the political world. From all these considerations Anna had not meant to go, and the hints in Princess Tverskaya's note referred to her refusal. But now Anna was eager to go, in the hope of seeing Vronsky.

Anna arrived at Princess Tverskaya's earlier than the other guests.

At the same moment as she entered, Vronsky's footman, with side whiskers combed out like a chamberlain, went in too. He stopped at the door and, taking off his cap, let her pass. Anna recognized him, and only then recalled that Vronsky had told her the day before that he would not come. Most likely he was sending a note to say so.

As she took off her outer garment in the hall, she heard the footman, even pronouncing his *"r's"* like a chamberlain, say, "From the count for the princess," and deliver the note.

She longed to question him as to where his master was. She longed to turn back and send him a letter to come and see her, or to go see him herself. But neither the first nor the second nor the third course was possible. Already she heard bells ringing to announce her arrival ahead of her, and Princess Tverskaya's footman was standing at the open door waiting for her to go forward into the inner rooms.

"The princess is in the garden; they will inform her immediately. Would you be pleased to walk into the garden?" announced another footman in another room.

The position of uncertainty, of indecision, was still the same as at home—worse, in fact, since it was impossible to take any step, impossible to see Vronsky, and she had to remain here among out-

[1]"The seven wonders of the world."

siders, in company so uncongenial to her present mood. But she was wearing a dress that she knew suited her. She was not alone; all around was that luxurious setting of idleness that she was used to, and she felt less wretched than at home. She was not forced to think about what she was to do. Everything happened automatically. On meeting Betsy coming toward her in a white gown that struck her by its elegance, Anna smiled to her just as she always did. Princess Tverskaya was walking with Tushkevich and a young lady, a relation, who, to the great joy of her parents in the provinces, was spending the summer with the fashionable princess.

There was probably something unusual about Anna, for Betsy noticed it at once.

"I slept badly," answered Anna, looking intently at the footman who came to meet them, and, as she supposed, brought Vronsky's note.

"How glad I am you've come!" said Betsy. "I'm tired, and was just longing to have some tea before they come. You might go"—she turned to Tushkevich—"with Masha, and try the croquet lawn over there where they've been cutting it. We shall have time to talk a little over tea; we'll have a cozy chat, eh?" she said in English to Anna, with a smile, pressing the hand with which she held a parasol.

"Yes, especially as I can't stay very long with you. I'm forced to go on to old Madame Wrede. I've been promising to go for a century," said Anna, to whom lying, alien as it was to her nature, had become not merely simple and natural in society, but a positive source of satisfaction. Why she said this, which she had not thought of a second before, she could not have explained. She had said it simply from the reflection that as Vronsky would not be here, she had better secure her own freedom, and try to see him somehow. But why she had spoken of old Madame Wrede, whom she had to go and see, as she had to see many other people, she could not have explained; and yet, as it afterward turned out, had she contrived the most cunning devices to meet Vronsky, she could have thought of nothing better.

"No, I'm not going to let you go for anything," answered Betsy, looking intently into Anna's face. "Really, if I were not fond of you, I would feel offended. One would think you were afraid my society would compromise you. Tea in the small dining room, please," she said, half closing her eyes as she always did when addressing the footman.

Taking the note from him, she read it.

"Aleksey's playing us false," she said in French; "he writes that he can't come," she added in a tone as simple and natural as though it could never enter her head that Vronsky could mean anything more to Anna than a game of croquet. Anna knew that Betsy knew everything, but, hearing how she spoke of Vronsky before her, she almost felt persuaded for a minute that she knew nothing.

"Ah!" said Anna indifferently, as though not greatly interested in the matter, and she went on smiling. "How can you or your friends compromise anyone?"

This playing with words, this hiding of a secret, had a great fascination for Anna, as, indeed, it has for all women. And it was not the necessity of concealment, not the aim with which the concealment was contrived, but the process of concealment itself that attracted her.

"I can't be more Catholic than the Pope," she said. "Stremov and Liza Merkalova, why, they're the cream of the cream of society. Besides, they're received everywhere, and *I*"—she laid special stress on the "I"—"have never been strict and intolerant. It's simply that I haven't the time."

"No; you don't care, perhaps, to meet Stremov? Let him and Aleksey Aleksandrovich tilt at each other in the committee—that's no affair of ours. But in the world, he's the most amiable man I know, and a devoted croquet player. You will see. And in spite of his absurd position as Liza's lovesick swain at his age, you ought to see how he carries the absurd situation off. He's very nice. Sappho Stolz you don't know? Oh, that's a new kind, quite new."

Betsy said all this, and, at the same time, from her good-humored, shrewd glance, Anna felt that she partly guessed her plight, and was hatching something for her benefit. They were in the little study.

"I must write to Aleksey, though," and Betsy sat down at the table, scribbled a few lines, and put the note in an envelope.

"I'm writing him to come to dinner. I've one lady extra and no man to take her in. Look at what I've said, will that persuade him?

Excuse me, I must leave you for a minute. Would you seal it up, please, and send it off?" she said from the door: "I have to give some directions."

Without a moment's thought, Anna sat down at the table with Betsy's letter and, without reading it, wrote below: "It's essential for me to see you. Come to the Wrede garden. I shall be there at six o'clock." She sealed it up and, as Betsy was coming back, in her presence handed the note to be sent off.

At tea, which was brought them on a little tea table in the cool drawing room, the cozy chat promised by Princess Tverskaya before the arrival of her visitors really did come off between the two women. They criticized the people they were expecting, and the conversation fell upon Liza Merkalova.

"She's very sweet, and I always liked her," said Anna.

"You ought to like her. She raves about you. Yesterday she came up to me after the races and was in despair at not finding you. She says you're a real heroine out of a novel, and that if she were a man she would do all sorts of mad things for your sake. Stremov says she does that as it is."

"But do tell me, please, I never could make it out," said Anna, after being silent for some time, speaking in a tone that showed she was not asking an idle question, but what she was asking was of more importance to her than it should have been; "do tell me, please, what are her relations with Prince Kaluzhsky—Mishka, as he's called? I've met them so little. What are they?"

Betsy smiled with her eyes, and looked intently at Anna.

"It's a new fashion," she said. "They've all adopted it. They've flung their caps over the windmills.[2] But there are ways and ways of flinging them."

"Yes, but what are her relations precisely with Kaluzhsky?"

Betsy broke into unexpectedly mirthful and irrepressible laughter, a thing that rarely happened with her.

"You're encroaching on Princess Myahkaya's special domain now. That's the question of an *enfant terrible*," and Betsy obviously tried to

---

[2]From the French *jetter les bonnets pardessus les moulins*. Betsy often literally translates idiomatic French expressions into Russian. It means "to throw off all restraint."

restrain herself but could not, and went off into peals of that infectious laughter that people laugh who do not laugh often. "You'd better ask them," she said, between tears of laughter.

"No; you laugh," said Anna, laughing too in spite of herself, "but I never could understand it. I can't understand the husband's role in it."

"The husband? Liza Merkalova's husband carries her comforter, and is always ready to be of use. But anything more than that in reality, no one cares to inquire. You know, in decent society one doesn't talk or even think of certain details of dress. That's how it is with this."

"Will you be at Madame Rolandaki's fête?" asked Anna, to change the conversation.

"I don't think so," answered Betsy, and, without looking at her friend, she began filling the little transparent cups with fragrant tea. Putting a cup before Anna, she took out a cigarette, and, fitting it into a silver holder, she lighted it.

"It's like this, you see: I'm in a fortunate position," she began, quite serious now, as she took up her cup. "I understand you, and I understand Liza. Liza, now, is one of those naïve natures that, like children, don't know what's good and what's bad. Anyway, she didn't comprehend it when she was very young. And now she's aware that the lack of comprehension suits her. Now, perhaps, she doesn't know on purpose," said Betsy, with a subtle smile. "But, anyway, it suits her. The very same thing, don't you see, may be looked at tragically, and turned into a misery, or it may be looked at simply and even humorously. Possibly you are inclined to look at things too tragically."

"How I should like to know other people just as I know myself!" said Anna, seriously and dreamily. "Am I worse than other people, or better? I think I'm worse."

"*Enfant terrible, enfant terrible!*" Betsy repeated. "But here they are."

CHAPTER EIGHTEEN

They heard the sound of steps and a man's voice, then a woman's voice and laughter, and immediately thereafter there walked in the expected guests: Sappho Stolz, and a young man beaming with excess of health, known as Vaska. It was evident that ample supplies of beefsteak, truffles, and Burgundy never failed to reach him at the fitting hour. Vaska bowed to the two ladies and glanced at them, but only for one second. He walked after Sappho into the drawing room, and followed her about as though he were chained to her, keeping his sparkling eyes fixed on her as though he wanted to eat her. Sappho Stolz was a blond beauty with black eyes. She walked with brisk little steps in high-heeled shoes, and shook hands with the ladies vigorously like a man.

Anna had never met this new celebrity, and was struck by her beauty, the exaggerated extreme to which her dress was carried, and the boldness of her manners. On her head there was such a superstructure of soft golden hair—her own and artificial—that her head was equal in size to the elegantly rounded bust, of which so much was exposed in front. The impulsive abruptness of her movements was such that at every step the lines of her knees and the upper part of her legs were distinctly visible under her dress, and the question involuntarily arose as to where in the undulating, piled-up mountain of material at the back the real body of the woman, so small and slender, so naked in front, and so hidden behind and below, really came to an end.

Betsy made haste to introduce her to Anna.

"Just imagine, we all but ran over two soldiers," she began telling them at once, using her eyes, smiling and throwing back her train, which she had jerked too much to one side. "I drove here with Vaska . . . Ah, to be sure, you don't know each other." And mentioning his surname, she introduced the young man and, reddening a little, broke into a ringing laugh at her mistake—that is, at her having called him Vaska to a stranger. Vaska bowed once more to Anna, but he said nothing to her. He addressed Sappho: "You've lost your bet. We got here first. Pay up," said he, smiling. Sappho laughed still more festively.

"Not just now," said she.

"Oh, all right, I'll have it later."

"Very well, very well. Oh, yes." She turned suddenly to Princess Betsy: "How could I? . . . I positively forgot it . . . I've brought you a visitor. And here he comes." The unexpected young visitor, whom Sappho had invited and whom she had forgotten, was, however, a person of such importance that, in spite of his youth, both the ladies rose on his entrance.

He was a new admirer of Sappho's. He now dogged her footsteps, like Vaska.

Soon after, Prince Kaluzhsky arrived, and Liza Merkalova with Stremov. Liza Merkalova was a thin brunette, with an Oriental, languid type of face, and—as everyone used to say—exquisite enigmatic eyes. The tone of her dark dress (Anna immediately observed and appreciated the fact) was in perfect harmony with her style of beauty. Liza was as soft and relaxed as Sappho was smart and hard.

But to Anna's taste, Liza was far more attractive. Betsy had said to Anna that she had adopted the pose of an innocent child, but when Anna saw her, she felt that this was not the truth. She really was both innocent and corrupt, but a sweet and passive woman. It is true that her tone was the same as Sappho's; that, like Sappho, she had two men, one young and one old, tacked onto her, and devouring her with their eyes. But there was something in her that was superior to what surrounded her. There was in her the glow of the real diamond among imitations. This glow shone out in her exquisite, truly enigmatic eyes. The weary and at the same time passionate glance of those eyes, encircled by dark rings, impressed one by its perfect sincerity. Everyone looking into those eyes thought he knew her wholly, and knowing her, could not but love her. At the sight of Anna, her whole face lighted up at once with a smile of delight.

"Ah, how glad I am to see you!" she said, going up to her. "Yesterday at the races all I wanted was to get to you, but you'd gone away. I did so want to see you, yesterday especially. Wasn't it awful?" she said, looking at Anna with eyes that seemed to lay bare her soul.

"Yes; I had no idea it would be so thrilling," said Anna, blushing.

The company got up at this moment to go into the garden.

"I'm not going," said Liza, smiling and settling herself close to Anna. "You won't go either, will you? Who wants to play croquet?"

"Oh, I like it," said Anna.

"There, how do you manage never to be bored by things? It's delightful to look at you. You're alive, but I'm bored."

"How can you be bored? Why, you live in the liveliest set in Petersburg," said Anna.

"Possibly the people who are not of our set are even more bored; but we—I certainly—are not happy, but awfully, awfully bored."

Sappho, smoking a cigarette, went off into the garden with the two young men. Betsy and Stremov remained at the tea table.

"What, bored!" said Betsy. "Sappho says they did enjoy themselves tremendously at your house last night."

"Ah, how dreary it all was!" said Liza Merkalova. "We all drove back to my place after the races. And always the same people, always all the same. Always the same thing. We lounged about on sofas all evening. What is there to enjoy in that? No; do tell me how you manage never to be bored?" she said, addressing Anna again. "One has but to look at you and one sees, here's a woman who may be happy or unhappy, but she isn't bored. Tell me how you do it?"

"I do nothing," answered Anna, blushing at these searching questions.

"That's the best way," Stremov put in. Stremov was a man of fifty, partly gray, but still vigorous-looking, very ordinary, but with an intelligent face full of character. Liza Merkalova was his wife's niece, and he spent all his leisure hours with her. On meeting Anna Karenina, as he was Aleksey Aleksandrovich's enemy in the service, he tried, like a shrewd man and a man of the world, to be particularly cordial with her, the wife of his enemy.

"Nothing," he put in with a subtle smile, "that's the very best way. I told you long ago," he said, turning to Liza Merkalova, "that if you don't want to be bored, you mustn't think you're going to be bored. It's just as you mustn't be afraid of not being able to fall asleep, if you're afraid of sleeplessness. That's exactly what Anna Arkadyevna has just said."

"I would be very glad if I had said it, for it's not only clever but true," said Anna, smiling.

"No, do tell me why it is one can't go to sleep, and one can't help being bored?"

"To sleep well, one ought to work, and to enjoy oneself, one ought to work too."

"What am I to work for when my work is no use to anybody? And I can't and won't knowingly make a pretense about it."

"You're incorrigible," said Stremov, not looking at her, and he spoke again to Anna. Because he rarely met Anna, he could say nothing but commonplaces to her, but he said them, about when she was returning to Petersburg, and how fond Countess Lydia Ivanova was of her, with an expression which suggested that he longed with his whole soul to please her and show his regard for her and even more than that.

Tushkevich came in, announcing that everyone was awaiting the other players to begin croquet.

"No, don't go away, please don't," pleaded Liza Merkalova, hearing that Anna was going. Stremov joined in her entreaties.

"It's too violent a transition," he said, "to go from such company to old Madame Wrede. And besides, you will only give her a chance to talk scandal, while here you arouse very different feelings, of the most praiseworthy kind," he said to her.

Anna pondered for an instant in uncertainty. This shrewd man's flattering words, the naïve, childlike affection shown her by Liza Merkalova, and all the social atmosphere she was used to—it was all so easy, and what was in store for her was so difficult, that she was for a minute undecided whether to remain, to put off a little longer the painful moment of explanation. But remembering what was in store for her alone at home if she did not come to some decision, remembering that gesture—terrible even in memory—when she had clutched her hair in both hands, she said good-by and left.

CHAPTER NINETEEN

In spite of Vronsky's apparently frivolous life in society, he was a man who hated disorder. In his early youth in the Corps of Pages, he had experienced the humiliation of a refusal when he had tried, being in difficulties, to borrow money, and since then he had never once put himself in the same position again.

In order to keep his affairs straight, about five times a year (more or less frequently, according to circumstances) he would shut himself up alone and put all his affairs into shape. This he used to call his day of reckoning or *faire la lessive*.[1]

On waking up the day after the races, Vronsky put on a white linen tunic, and without shaving or taking his bath, he spread moneys, bills, and letters on the table and began to work. Petritsky, who knew he was ill-tempered on such occasions, on waking up and seeing his comrade at the writing table, quietly dressed and went out without getting in his way.

Every man who knows to the minutest details the complexity of the conditions surrounding him cannot help imagining that the complexity of these conditions, and the difficulty of making them clear, is something exceptional and personal, peculiar to himself, and never supposes that others are surrounded by just as complicated an array of personal affairs as he is. So indeed it seemed to Vronsky. And not without inward pride, and not without reason, he thought that any other man would long ago have been in difficulties, and would have been forced to some dishonorable course, if he had found himself in such a difficult position. But Vronsky felt that now especially it was essential for him to clear up and define his position if he were to avoid getting into difficulties.

What Vronsky attacked first as being the easiest was his money problems. Writing out on notepaper in his minute script all that he owed, he added up the amount and found that his debts amounted to 17,000 and some-odd hundreds, which he left out for the sake of simplicity. Reckoning up his money and his bankbook, he found that he had 1,800 rubles left, and nothing coming in before the new year. Going over again his list of debts, Vronsky copied it, dividing it into three categories. In the first he put the debts he would have to pay at once, or for which he must in any case have the money ready, so that on demand for payment there could not be a moment's delay in paying. Such debts amounted to about 4,000: 1,500 for a horse, and 2,500 as surety for a young comrade, Venevsky, who had lost that sum to a card shark in Vronsky's presence. Vronsky had wanted to pay the money at the time (he had that amount then), but Venevsky and

[1]"Doing the washing."

Yashvin had insisted that they would pay and not Vronsky, who had not played. That was very fine, but Vronsky knew that in this dirty business, though his only share in it was undertaking by word of mouth to be surety for Venevsky, it was absolutely necessary for him to have the 2,500 rubles so as to be able to fling it at the swindler and have no more words with him. And so for this first and most important category he had to have 4,000 rubles. The second category— 8,000 rubles—consisted of less important debts. These were principally accounts incurred in connection with his race horses, to the purveyor of oats and hay, the English trainer, and so on. He would have to pay some 2,000 rubles on these debts too, in order to be quite free from anxiety. The last category of debts—to shops, to hotels, to his tailor—were such as need not be considered. So that he needed at least 6,000 rubles for current expenses, and he had only 1,800. For a man with 100,000 rubles of revenue, which was what everyone fixed as Vronsky's income, such debts, one would suppose, could hardly be embarrassing; but the fact was that he was far from having 100,000. His father's immense property, which alone yielded a yearly income of 200,000, was left undivided between the brothers. At the time when the elder brother, with a mass of debts, married Princess Varya Chirkova, the daughter of a Decembrist[2] without any fortune whatever, Aleksey had given up to his elder brother almost the whole income from his father's estate, reserving for himself only 25,000 a year from it. Aleksey had said at the time to his brother that that sum would be sufficient for him until he married, which he probably would never do. And his brother, who was in command of one of the most expensive regiments, and was only just married, could not decline the gift. His mother, who had her own separate property, had allowed Aleksey 20,000 every year in addition to the 25,000 he had reserved, and Aleksey had spent it all. Of late his mother, incensed with him on account of his love affair and his leaving Moscow, had given up sending him the money. And in consequence of this, Vronsky, who had been in the habit of living on the scale of 45,000 a year, having received only 25,000 that year, now found himself in difficul-

[2] I.e., a member of a revolutionary movement of liberal noblemen who, in December of 1825, upon the death of Aleksandr I, led an uprising against the future Tsar, Nicholas I.

ties. To get out of these difficulties, he could not apply to his mother for money. Her last letter, which he had received the day before, had particularly exasperated him by the hints in it that she was quite ready to help him to succeed in the world and in the army, but not to lead a life that was a scandal to all good society. His mother's attempt to buy him stung him to the quick and made him feel colder than ever toward her. But he could not renege on the generous word when once it was uttered, even though he felt now, vaguely foreseeing certain eventualities in his intrigue with Madame Karenina, that this generous word had been spoken thoughtlessly, and that even though he was not married, he might need all 100,000 of his income. But it was impossible to renege. He had only to recall his brother's wife, to remember how that sweet, delightful Varya sought, at every convenient opportunity, to remind him that she remembered his generosity and appreciated it, to grasp the impossibility of taking back his gift. It was as impossible as beating a woman, stealing, or lying. Only one thing could and should be done, and Vronsky determined upon it without an instant's hesitation: to borrow money from a moneylender, 10,000 rubles, a proceeding that presented no difficulty, to cut down his expenses generally, and to sell his race horses. Resolving on this, he promptly wrote a note to Rolandaki, who had more than once offered to buy horses from him. Then he sent for the Englishman and the moneylender, and divided what money he had according to the accounts he intended to pay. Having finished this business, he wrote a cold and cutting answer to his mother. Then he took out of his notebook three notes of Anna's, read them again, burned them, and remembering their conversation of the previous day, he sank into meditation.

CHAPTER TWENTY

Vronsky's life was particularly happy in that he had a code of principles, which defined with unfailing certitude what he should and what he should not do. This code of principles covered only a very small circle of contingencies, but then the principles were never doubtful, and Vronsky, because he never went outside that circle, had never had a moment's hesitation about doing what he ought to do. These principles laid down as invariable rules: that one must pay a card shark, but need not pay a tailor; that one must never tell a lie to a man, but one may to a woman; that one must never cheat anyone, but one may cheat a husband; that one must never pardon an insult, but one may give one, and so on. These principles were possibly not reasonable and not good, but they were of unfailing certainty, and as long as he adhered to them, Vronsky felt that his heart was at peace and he could hold his head up. Only quite lately, in regard to his relations with Anna, Vronsky had begun to feel that his code of principles did not fully cover all possible contingencies, and to foresee in the future, difficulties and perplexities for which he could find no guiding clue.

His present relation to Anna and to her husband was to his mind clear and simple. It was clearly and precisely defined in the code of principles by which he was guided.

She was an honorable woman who had bestowed her love upon him, and he loved her, and therefore she was in his eyes a woman who had a right to the same, or even more, respect than a lawful wife. He would have had his hand chopped off before he would have allowed himself by a word, by a hint, to humiliate her, or even to fall short of the fullest respect a woman could look for.

His attitude toward society, too, was clear. Everybody might know, might suspect it, but no one would dare speak of it. If anyone did so, he was ready to force him to be silent and to respect the nonexistent honor of the woman he loved.

His attitude toward the husband was the clearest of all. From the moment that Anna loved Vronsky, he had regarded his own right over her as the one thing unassailable. Her husband was simply a superfluous and tiresome person. No doubt he was in a pitiable position, but how could that be helped? The one thing the husband had a right to was to demand satisfaction with a weapon in his hand, and Vronsky was prepared for this at any minute.

But of late, new inner relations had arisen between him and her which frightened Vronsky by their vagueness. Only the day before she had told him that she was pregnant. And he felt that this fact and what she expected of him called for something not fully defined in that code of principles by which he had hitherto steered his course in life. And he had been indeed caught unawares, and at the first moment when she spoke to him of her situation, his heart had prompted him to beg her to leave her husband. He had said that, but now, thinking things over, he saw clearly that it would be better to manage to avoid that; and at the same time, while he told himself so, he was afraid whether it was not wrong.

"If I told her to leave her husband, that must mean uniting her life with mine; am I prepared for that? How can I take her away now, when I have no money? Supposing I could arrange . . . But how can I take her away while I'm in the service? If I say that, I should be prepared to do it, that is, I should have the money and retire from the army."

And he grew thoughtful. The question of whether to retire from the service or not brought him to the other and perhaps the chief though hidden interest of his life, of which none know but he.

Ambition was the old dream of his youth and childhood, a dream which he did not confess even to himself, though it was so strong that now this passion was even doing battle with his love. His first steps in the world and in the service had been successful, but two years before he had made a great mistake. Anxious to show his independence and to advance, he had refused a post that had been offered him, hoping that this refusal would heighten his value; but it turned out that he had been too bold, and he was passed over. And having, whether he liked or not, taken the position of an independent man, he carried it off with great tact and good sense, behaving as though he bore no grudge against anyone, did not regard himself as injured in any way, and cared for nothing but to be left alone, since he was enjoying himself. In reality he had ceased to enjoy himself as long ago as the year before, when he went away to Moscow. He felt that this independent attitude of a man who might have done anything but cared to do nothing was already beginning to pall, that many people were beginning to think that he was not really capable of anything but being a straightforward, good-natured fellow. His affair with Madame Karenina, by creating so much sensation and attracting general attention, had given him a fresh distinction which soothed his gnawing worm of ambition for a while, but a week before that worm had been roused up again with fresh force. The friend of his childhood, a man of the same set, of the same coterie, his comrade in the Corps of Pages, Serpukhovskoy, who had left school with him and had been his rival in class, in gymnastics, in their scrapes and their dreams of glory, had come back a few days before from Central Asia, where he had gained two steps up in rank, and an order rarely bestowed upon generals so young.

As soon as he arrived in Petersburg, people began to talk about him as a newly risen star of the first magnitude. A classmate of Vronsky's and of the same age, he was a general and was expecting a command which might have influence on the course of political events; while Vronsky, independent and brilliant and beloved by a charming woman though he was, was simply a cavalry captain who was readily allowed to be as independent as he liked. "Of course I don't envy Serpukhovskoy and never could envy him; but his advancement shows me that one has but to watch one's opportunity, and the career of a man like me may be very rapidly made. Three years ago he was in just the same position as I am in now. If I retire, I burn my ships. If I remain in the army, I lose nothing. She said herself she did not wish to change her position. And with her love I cannot feel envious of Serpukhovskoy." And slowly twirling his mustaches, he got up from the table and walked about the room. His eyes shone particularly brightly, and he enjoyed that confident, calm, and happy frame of mind which always came after he had thoroughly faced his situation. Everything was straight and clear, just as after former days of stocktaking. He shaved, took a cold bath, dressed, and went out.

CHAPTER TWENTY-ONE

"I've come to fetch you. Your washing lasted a good time today," said Petritsky. "Well, is it over?"

"It is over," answered Vronsky, smiling with his eyes only, and twirling the tips of his mustaches as circumspectly as though, after the perfect order into which his affairs had been brought, any overbold or rapid movement might disturb it.

"You're always just as if you'd come out of a bath after it," said

Petritsky. "I've come from Gritsko's" (that was what they called the colonel); "they're expecting you."

Vronsky, without answering, looked at his comrade, thinking of something else.

"Yes, is that music from his place?" he said, listening to the familiar sounds of polkas and waltzes floating across to him. "What's the occasion?"

"Serpukhovskoy's come."

"Aha!" said Vronsky. "Why, I didn't know."

The smile in his eyes gleamed more brightly than ever.

Having once made up his mind that he was happy in his love, that he sacrificed his ambition to it—having anyway taken up this position, Vronsky was incapable of feeling either envious of Serpukhovskoy or vexed with him for not coming first to him when he came to the regiment. Serpukhovskoy was a good friend, and he was delighted he had come.

"Ah, I'm very glad!"

The colonel, Dyomin, had taken a large country house. The whole party were in the wide lower balcony. In the courtyard the first objects that met Vronsky's eyes were a band of singers in while linen tunics, standing near a barrel of vodka, and the robust figure of the colonel surrounded by officers. He had gone out as far as the first step of the balcony and was loudly shouting over the band, which was playing an Offenbach quadrille, waving his arms and giving some orders to a few soldiers standing on one side. A group of soldiers, a sergeant, and several other non-commissioned officers came up to the balcony with Vronsky. The colonel returned to the table, went out again onto the steps with a tumbler in his hand, and proposed the toast: "To the health of our former comrade, the gallant general, Prince Serpukhovskoy. Hurrah!"

The colonel was followed by Serpukhovskoy, who came out onto the steps smiling, with a glass in his hand.

"You always get younger, Bondarenko," he said to the ruddy-cheeked, smart-looking sergeant standing just before him still youngish-looking though doing his second term of service.

It was three years since Vronsky had seen Serpukhovskoy. He looked more robust, had let his whiskers grow, but was still the same graceful creature, striking, not because of his good looks, but because of the delicacy and nobility of his face and figure. The only change Vronsky detected in him was that subdued, continual radiance of beaming content which settles on the faces of men who are successful and are sure of the recognition of their success by everyone. Vronsky knew that radiant air, and immediately observed it in Serpukhovskoy.

As Serpukhovskoy came down the steps he saw Vronsky. A smile of pleasure lighted up his face. He tossed his head upward and waved the glass in his hand, greeting Vronsky, and showing him by the gesture that he could not come to him before he went to the sergeant, who stood puckering up his lips ready to be kissed.

"Here he is!" shouted the colonel. "Yashvin told me you were in one of your gloomy moods."

Serpukhovskoy kissed the moist, fresh lips of the gallant-looking sergeant, and wiping his mouth with his handkerchief, he went up to Vronsky.

"How glad I am!" he said, squeezing his hand and drawing him to one side.

"You look after him," the colonel shouted to Yashvin, pointing to Vronsky; and he went down below to the soldiers.

"Why, weren't you at the races yesterday? I expected to see you there," said Vronsky, scrutinizing Serpukhovskoy.

"I did go, but late. Pardon me," he added, and he turned to his adjutant: "Please have this equally distributed among the men." And he hurriedly took three 100-ruble notes from his wallet, blushing a little.

"Vronsky! Have anything to eat or drink?" asked Yashvin. "Hey, something for the count to eat! Ah, here it is: have a glass!"

The party at the colonel's lasted a long while. There was a great deal of drinking. They tossed Serpukhovskoy in the air and caught him again several times. Then they did the same to the colonel. Then, to the accompaniment of the band, the colonel himself danced with Petritsky. Then the colonel, who began to show signs of shakiness, sat down on a bench in the courtyard and began demonstrating to Yashvin the superiority of Russia over Prussia, especially in cavalry attack, and there was a lull in the revelry for a moment. Serpukhovskoy went into the house to the washroom to wash his hands and found Vronsky there: Vronsky was drenching his head with water. He had taken off his coat and put his sunburned, hairy neck under the tap, and was rubbing it and his head with his hands. When he had finished, Vronsky sat down next to Serpukhovskoy. They both sat down in the washroom on a lounge, and a conversation began which was very interesting to both of them.

"I've always been hearing about you through my wife," said Serpukhovskoy. "I am glad you've been seeing her pretty often."

"She's friendly with Varya, and they're the only women in Petersburg I care about seeing," answered Vronsky, smiling. He smiled because he foresaw the turn the conversation would take and he was glad of it.

"The only ones?" Serpukhovskoy queried, smiling.

"Yes; and I heard news of you, but not only through your wife," said Vronsky, checking his hint by a stern expression. "I was greatly delighted to hear of your success, but not a bit surprised. I expected even more."

Serpukhovskoy smiled. Such an opinion of him was obviously agreeable to him, and he did not think it necessary to conceal it.

"Well, I on the contrary expected less—I'll admit frankly. But I'm glad, very glad. I'm ambitious; that's my weakness, and I confess to it."

"Perhaps you wouldn't confess to it if you hadn't been successful," said Vronsky.

"I don't suppose so," said Serpukhovskoy, smiling again. "I won't say life wouldn't be worth living without it, but it would be dull. Of course I may be mistaken, but I think I have a certain capacity for the line I've chosen, and that power of any sort in my hands, if it is to be, will be better than in the hands of a good many people I know," said Serpukhovskoy, with beaming consciousness of success; "and the nearer I get to it, the better pleased I am."

"Perhaps that is true for you, but not for everyone. I used to think so too, but here I live and think life worth living not only for that."

"There it's out! Here it comes!" said Serpukhovskoy, laughing. "Ever since I heard about you, about your refusal, I began . . . Of course, I approved of what you did. But there are ways of doing everything. And I think your action was good in itself, but you didn't do it quite in the way you should have done it."

"What's done can't be undone, and you know I never go back on what I've done. And besides, I'm all right."

"All right—for the time. But you're not satisfied with that. I wouldn't say this to your brother. He's a nice child, like our host here. There he goes!" he added, listening to the roar of "hurrah!"—"and he's happy, but that does not satisfy you."

"I didn't say it did satisfy me."

"Yes, but that's not the only thing. Such men as you are wanted."

"By whom?"

"By whom? By society, by Russia. Russia needs men; she needs a political party, or else everything goes and will go to the dogs."

"How do you mean? Bertenev's party against the Russian communists?"

"No," said Serpukhovskoy, frowning with vexation at being suspected of such an absurdity. "*Tout ça est une blague.*[1] That's always been and always will be. There are no communists. But intriguing people have to invent a noxious, dangerous party. It's an old trick. No, what's wanted is a powerful party of independent men like you and me."

"But why so?" Vronsky mentioned a few men who were in power. "Why aren't they independent men?"

"Simply because they have not, or have not had from birth, an independent fortune; they've not had a name, they've not been born as close to the sun as we were. They can be bought either by money or by favor. And they have to find a support for themselves in inventing a policy. And they bring forward some notion, some policy that they don't believe in, that does harm; and the whole policy is really only a means to a government house and so much income. *Cela n'est pas plus fin que ça,*[2] when you get a peep at their cards. I may be inferior to them, stupider perhaps, though I don't see why I should be inferior to them. But you and I have one important advantage over

[1] "All that is a joke."
[2] "That's all it is."

them for certain, in being more difficult to buy. And such men are more needed than ever."

Vronsky listened attentively, but he was not so much interested in the meaning of the words as by the attitude of Serpukhovskoy, who was already contemplating a struggle with the existing powers, and already had his likes and dislikes in that higher world, while his own interest in the governing world did not go beyond the interests of his regiment. Vronsky felt, too, how powerful Serpukhovskoy might become through his obvious faculty for thinking things out and for taking things in, through his intelligence and gift of words, so rarely met with in the world in which he moved. And, ashamed as he was of the feeling, he felt envious.

"Still, I haven't the one thing of most importance for that," he answered; "I haven't the desire for power. I had it once, but it's gone."

"Excuse me, that's not true," said Serpukhovskoy, smiling.

"Yes, it is true, it is true . . . now!" Vronsky added, to be truthful.

"Yes, it's true *now*, that's another thing; but that *now* won't last for-ever."

"Perhaps," answered Vronsky.

"You say 'perhaps,' " Serpukhovskoy went on, as though guessing his thoughts, "but I say for *certain*. And that's why I wanted to see you. Your action was just what it should have been. I see that, but you ought not to *persevere* in it. I only ask you to give me *carte blanche*. I'm not going to offer you my protection. . . though, indeed, why shouldn't I protect you?—you've protected me often enough! I should hope our friendship rises above all that sort of thing. Yes," he said, smiling to him as tenderly as a woman, "give me *carte blanche*, retire from the regiment, and I'll draw you up imperceptibly."

"But you must understand that I want nothing," said Vronsky, "except that all should be as it is."

Serpukhovskoy got up and stood facing him.

"You say that all should be as it is. I understand what that means. But listen: we're the same age, you've known a greater number of women perhaps than I have." Serpukhovskoy's smile and gestures told Vronsky that he mustn't be afraid, that he would be tender and careful in touching the sore spot. "But I'm married, and believe me, in getting to know thoroughly one's wife, if one loves her, as someone has said, one gets to know all women better than if one knew thousands of them."

"We're coming right away!" Vronsky shouted to an officer who looked into the room and called them to the colonel.

Vronsky was longing now to hear to the end and know what Serpukhovskoy would say to him.

"And here's my opinion for you. Women are the chief stumbling block in a man's career. It's hard to love a woman and do anything. There's only one way of having love conveniently without its being a hindrance—that's marriage. How, how am I to tell you what I mean?" said Serpukhovskoy, who liked similes. "Wait a minute, wait a minute! Yes, just as you can only carry a *fardeau*[3] and do something with your hands when the *fardeau* is tied on your back, and that's marriage. And that's what I felt when I was married. My hands were suddenly set free. But to drag that *fardeau* about with you without marriage, your hands will always be so full that you can do nothing. Look at Mazankov, at Krupov. They've ruined their careers for the sake of women."

"What women!" said Vronsky, recalling the Frenchwoman and the actress with whom the two men he had mentioned were associated.

"The firmer the woman's footing in society, the worse it is. That's much the same as not merely carrying the *fardeau* in your arms, but tearing it away from someone else."

"You have never loved," Vronsky said softly, looking straight before him and thinking of Anna.

"Perhaps. But you remember what I've said to you. And another thing, women are all more materialistic than men. We make something immense out of love, but they are always *terre-à-terre*."[4]

"Coming, coming!" he cried to a footman who came in. But the footman had not come to call them again, as he supposed. The footman brought Vronsky a note.

"A man brought it from Princess Tverskaya."

Vronsky opened the letter, and flushed crimson.

[3]"Load."
[4]"Matter-of-fact."

"My head's begun to ache; I'm going home," he said to Serpukhovskoy.

"Well, good-by, then. Do you give me *carte blanche*?"

"We'll talk about it later on; I'll look you up in Petersburg."

CHAPTER TWENTY-TWO

It was past five already, and so, in order to be there quickly, and at the same time not to drive with his own horses, known to everyone, Vronsky got into Yashvin's hired carriage and told the driver to drive as quickly as possible. It was a roomy, old-fashioned carriage, with seats for four. He sat in one corner, stretched his legs out on the front seat, and sank into meditation.

A vague sense of the order into which his affairs had been brought, a vague recollection of the friendliness and flattery of Serpukhovskoy, who had considered him a man that was needed, and most of all, the anticipation of the interview before him—all blended into a general, joyous sense of life. This feeling was so strong that he could not help smiling. He dropped his legs, crossed one leg over the other knee, and, taking it in his hand, felt the springy muscle of the calf, where it had been grazed the day before by his fall, and leaning back, he drew several deep breaths.

"I'm happy, very happy!" he said to himself. He had often before had this sense of physical joy in his own body, but he had never felt so fond of himself, of his own body, as at that moment. He enjoyed the slight ache in his strong leg, he enjoyed the muscular sensation of movement in his chest as he breathed. The bright, cold August day, which had made Anna feel so hopeless, seemed to him keenly stimulating, and refreshed his face and neck, which still tingled from the cold water. The scent of brilliantine on his whiskers struck him as particularly pleasant in the fresh air. Everything he saw from the carriage window, everything in that cold pure air, in the pale light of the sunset, was as fresh, and gay, and strong as he was himself: the roofs of the houses shining in the rays of the setting sun, the sharp outlines of fences and angles of buildings, the figures of passers-by, the carriages that met him now and then, the motionless green of the trees and grass, the fields with evenly drawn furrows of potatoes, and the slanting shadows that fell from the houses, and trees, and bushes, and even from the rows of potatoes—everything was bright like a pretty landscape just finished and freshly varnished.

"Faster, faster!" he said to the driver, putting his head out of the window, and pulling a three-ruble note out of his pocket, he handed it to the man as he looked around. The driver's hand fumbled with something at the lamp, the whip cracked, and the carriage rolled rapidly along the smooth highroad.

"I want nothing, nothing but this happiness," he thought, staring at the ivory button of the bell in the space between the windows, and picturing to himself Anna just as he had seen her last time. "And as I go on, I love her more and more. Here's the garden of the Wrede country house. Where will she be? Where? How? Why did she decide on this place to meet me, and why does she write in Betsy's letter?" he thought, wondering now for the first time about it. But there was no time now for wonder. He called to the driver to stop before reaching the avenue, and opening the door, he jumped out while the carriage was moving, and went into the avenue that led up to the house. There was no one in the avenue; but looking around to the right, he caught sight of her. Her face was hidden by a veil, but he drank in with joyous eyes the special movement in walking, peculiar to her alone, the slope of the shoulders, and the set of the head, and at once a sort of electric shock ran through him. With fresh force, he felt conscious of himself from the springy motions of his legs to the movements of his lungs as he breathed, and something set his lips twitching.

Joining him, she pressed his hand tightly.

"You're not angry that I sent for you? I absolutely had to see you," she said; and the serious and set line of her lips which he saw under the veil, transformed his mood at once.

"I angry? But how have you come, where from?"

"Never mind," she said, laying her hand on his, "come along, I must talk to you."

He saw that something had happened, and that the meeting would not be a joyous one. In her presence he had no will of his own: without knowing the grounds of her distress, he already felt the same distress unconsciously passing over him.

"What is it? What?" he asked her, pressing her arm with his elbow, and trying to read her thoughts in her face.

She walked on a few steps in silence, gathering up her courage; then suddenly she stopped.

"I did not tell you yesterday," she began, breathing quickly and painfully, "that coming home with Aleksey Aleksandrovich I told him everything . . . told him I could not be his wife, that . . . and told him everything."

He heard her, unconsciously bending his whole figure down to her as though hoping in this way to soften the seriousness of her position for her. But as soon as she had said this, he suddenly drew himself up, and a proud and stern expression came over his face.

"Yes, yes, that's better, a thousand times better! I know how painful it was," he said. But she was not listening to his words, she was reading his thoughts from the expression of his face. She could not guess that that expression arose from the first idea that presented itself to Vronsky—that a duel was now inevitable. The idea of a duel had never crossed her mind, and so she put a different interpretation on this stern expression.

When she got her husband's letter, she knew then at the bottom of her heart that everything would go on in the old way, that she would not have the strength of will to forego her position, to abandon her son, and to join her lover. The morning spent at Princess Tverskaya's had confirmed her still more in this. But this interview was still of the utmost gravity for her. She hoped that this interview would transform her position, and save her. If on hearing this news he were to say to her resolutely, passionately, without an instant's wavering: "Give up everything and come with me!" she would give up her son and go away with him. But this news had not produced what she had expected in him; he simply seemed as though he was offended by something.

"It was not in the least painful for me. It happened by itself," she said irritably, "and see . . ." She pulled her husband's letter out of her glove.

"I understand, I understand," he interrupted her, taking the letter but not reading it, and trying to soothe her. "The one thing I longed for, the one thing I prayed for, was to cut short this position so as to devote my life to your happiness."

"Why do you tell me that?" she said. "Do you suppose I can doubt it? If I doubted—"

"Who's that coming?" said Vronsky suddenly, pointing to two ladies walking toward them. "Perhaps they know us!" and he hurriedly drew her after him into a side path.

"Oh, I don't care!" she said. Her lips were quivering. And he thought that her eyes looked at him from under the veil with strange anger. "I tell you that's not the point—I can't doubt that; but see what he writes to me. Read it." She stood still again.

Again, just as at the first moment of hearing of her break with her husband, Vronsky, on reading the letter, was unconsciously carried away by the natural feeling aroused in him by his own relation to the betrayed husband. Now while he held his letter in his hands, he could not help picturing the challenge, which he would most likely find at home today or tomorrow, and the duel itself, in which, with the same cold and haughty expression that his face was assuming at this moment he would await the injured husband's shot, after having himself fired into the air. And at that instant there flashed across his mind the thought of what Serpukhovskoy had just said to him, and what he had himself been thinking in the morning—that it was better not to bind himself—and he knew that this thought he could not tell her.

Having read the letter, he raised his eyes to her, and there was no determination in them. She saw at once that he had been thinking about it before by himself. She knew that whatever he might say to her, he would not say all he thought. And she knew that her last hope had failed her. This was not what she had been expecting.

"You see the sort of man he is," she said, with a shaking voice; "he. . ."

"Forgive me, but I rejoice at it," Vronsky interrupted. "For God's sake, let me finish!" he added, his eyes imploring her to give him time to explain his words. "I rejoice, because things cannot, cannot possibly remain as he supposes."

"Why can't they?" Anna said, restraining her tears, and obviously attaching no sort of importance to what he said. She felt that her fate was sealed.

Vronsky meant that after the duel—inevitable, he thought—things could not go on as before, but he said something different.

"It can't go on. I hope that now you will leave him. I hope"—he was confused, and reddened—"that you will let me arrange and plan our life. Tomorrow . . ." he was beginning.

She did not let him go on.

"But my child!" she shrieked. "You see what he writes! I would have to leave him, and I can't and won't do that."

"But, for God's sake, which is better?—leave your child, or keep up this degrading position?"

"To whom is it degrading?"

"To all, and most of all to you."

"You say 'degrading'. . . Don't say that. Those words have no meaning for me," she said in a shaking voice. She did not want him now to say what was untrue. She had nothing left her but his love, and she wanted to love him. "Don't you understand that from the day I loved you everything has changed for me? For me there is one thing, and one thing only—your love. If that's mine, I feel so exalted, so strong, that nothing can be humiliating to me. I am proud of my position, because . . . proud of being . . . proud . . ." She could not say what she was proud of. Tears of shame and despair choked her utterance. She stood still and sobbed.

He felt, too, something swelling in his throat and twitching in his nose, and for the first time in his life he felt on the point of weeping. He could not have said exactly what it was that touched him so. He felt sorry for her, and he felt he could not help her, and with that he knew that he was to blame for her wretchedness, and that he had done something wrong.

"Isn't a divorce possible?" he said feebly. She shook her head, not answering. "Couldn't you take your son and still leave him?"

"Yes; but it all depends on him. Now I must go to him," she said shortly. Her presentiment that all would again go on in the old way had not deceived her.

"On Tuesday I shall be in Petersburg, and everything can be settled."

"Yes," she said. "But don't let us talk any more of it."

Anna's carriage, which she had sent away and ordered to come back to the little gate of the Wrede garden, drove up. Anna said good-by to Vronsky, and drove home.

CHAPTER TWENTY-THREE

On Monday there was the usual sitting of the Commission of the 2nd of June. Aleksey Aleksandrovich walked into the hall where the sitting was held, greeting the members and the president, as usual, and sat down in his place, putting his hand on the papers laid ready before him. Among these papers lay the necessary evidence and a rough outline of the speech he intended to make. But he did not really need these documents. He remembered every point, and did not think it necessary to go over in his memory what he would say. He knew that when the time came, and when he saw his enemy facing him and studiously endeavoring to assume an expression of indifference, his speech would flow by itself better than he could prepare it now. He felt that the import of his speech was of such magnitude that every word of it would have weight. Meantime, as he listened to the usual report, he had the most innocent and inoffensive air. No one looking at his white hands, with their swollen veins and long fingers, so softly stroking the edges of the white paper that lay before him, and at the air of weariness with which his head drooped on one side, would have suspected that in a few minutes a torrent of words would flow from his lips that would arouse a fearful storm, set the members shouting and attacking one another, and force the president to call for order. When the report was over, Aleksey Aleksandrovich announced in his subdued, delicate voice that he had several points to bring before the meeting regarding the settlement of the native population. All attention was turned upon him. Aleksey Aleksandrovich cleared his throat, and not looking at his opponent, but selecting, as he always did while he was delivering his speeches, the first person sitting opposite him, an inoffensive little old man who never had an opinion of any sort in the commission, he began to expound his views. When he reached the point about the fundamental and radical law, his opponent jumped up and began to protest. Stremov, who was also a member of the commission, and also stung to the quick, began defending himself, and altogether a stormy sitting followed; but Aleksey Aleksandrovich triumphed, and his motion was carried, three new commissions were appointed, and the next day in a certain Petersburg circle nothing else was talked of but this meeting. Aleksey Aleksandrovich's success had been even greater than he had anticipated.

The next morning, Tuesday, Aleksey Aleksandrovich on waking up, recollected with pleasure his triumph of the previous day, and he could not help smiling, though he tried to appear indifferent when the chief secretary of his department, anxious to flatter him, informed him of the rumors that had reached him concerning what had happened in the commission.

Absorbed in business with the chief secretary, Aleksey Aleksandrovich had completely forgotten that it was Tuesday, the day fixed by him for the return of Anna Arkadyevna, and he was surprised and received a shock of annoyance when a servant came in to inform him of her arrival.

Anna had arrived in Petersburg early in the morning; the carriage had been sent to meet her in accordance with her telegram, and Aleksey Aleksandrovich should have known of her arrival. But when she arrived, he did not meet her. She was told that he had not yet gone out, but was busy with his secretary. She sent word to her husband that she had come, went to her own room, and occupied herself in sorting out her things, expecting that he would come to her. But an hour passed; he did not come. She went into the dining room on the pretext of giving some orders, and spoke loudly on purpose, expecting him to come out; but he did not come, though she heard him go to the door of his study as he parted from the chief secretary. She knew that he usually went out quickly to his office, and she wanted to see him before that, so that their attitude to one another might be defined.

She walked across the drawing room and went resolutely to him. When she went into his study, he was in official uniform, obviously ready to go out, sitting at a little table on which he rested his elbows, looking dejectedly before him. She saw him before he saw her, and she saw that he was thinking of her.

On seeing her, he began to rise, but changed his mind; then his face flushed hotly—a thing Anna had never seen before, and he got up quickly and went to meet her, looking not at her eyes but above them at her forehead and hair. He went up to her, took her by the hand, and asked her to sit down.

"I am very glad you have come," he said, sitting down beside her, and obviously wishing to say something, he stuttered. Several times he tried to begin to speak, but stopped. In spite of the fact that, preparing herself for meeting him, she had schooled herself to despise and reproach him, she did not know what to say to him and she felt sorry for him. And so the silence lasted for some time. "Is Seryozha well?" he said, and not waiting for an answer, he added: "I will not be dining at home today, and I have got to go out at once."

"I had thought of going to Moscow," she said.

"No, you did quite, quite right to come," he said, and was silent again.

Seeing that he was powerless to begin the conversation, she began herself.

"Aleksey Aleksandrovich," she said, looking at him and not lowering her eyes under his persistent gaze at her hair, "I'm a guilty woman, I'm a bad woman, but I am the same as I was, as I told you then, and I have come to tell you that I can change nothing."

"I have asked you nothing about that," he said, all at once, resolutely, and with hatred looking her straight in the face; "that was as I had supposed." Under the influence of anger he apparently regained complete possession of all his faculties. "But as I told you then, and have written to you," he said in a thin, shrill voice, "I repeat now, that I am not bound to know this. I ignore it. Not all wives are as kind as you, to be in such a hurry to communicate such pleasant news to their husbands." He laid special emphasis on the word "pleasant." "I shall ignore it as long as the world knows nothing of it, as long as my name is not disgraced. And so I simply inform you that our relations must be just as they have always been, and that only in the event of your letting yourself be compromised shall I be obliged to take steps to secure my honor."

"But our relations cannot be the same as before," Anna began in a timid voice, looking at him with dismay.

When she saw once more those composed gestures, heard that shrill, childish, and sarcastic voice, her aversion for him extinguished her pity for him and she felt only afraid, but at all costs she wanted to make clear her position.

"I cannot be your wife while I—" she began.

He laughed a cold and venomous laugh.

"The manner of life you have chosen is reflected, I suppose, in your ideas. I have too much respect or contempt, or both . . . I respect your past and despise your present . . . that I was far from the interpretation you put on my words."

Anna sighed and bowed her head.

"Though indeed I fail to comprehend how, with the independence you show," he went on, getting heated, "telling your husband of your infidelity and apparently seeing nothing reprehensible in it, you should consider it reprehensible to perform a wife's duties to her husband."

"Aleksey Aleksandrovich! What is it you want of me?"

"I want you not to meet that man here, and to conduct yourself so that neither the *world* nor the *servants* can reproach you. . . not to see him. That's not much, I think. And in return you will enjoy all the privileges of a faithful wife without fulfilling her duties. That's all I have to say to you. Now it's time for me to go. I'm not dining at home." He got up and moved toward the door.

Anna got up too. Bowing in silence, he let her pass before him.

CHAPTER TWENTY-FOUR

The night spent by Levin on the haycock did not pass without leaving its mark. The way in which he had been managing his land revolted him and had lost all attraction for him. In spite of the magnificent harvest, never had there been, or, at least, never it seemed to him had there been so many hindrances and so many quarrels between him and the peasants as that year, and the origin of these failures and this hostility was now perfectly comprehensible to him. The delight he had experienced in the work itself, and the consequent greater intimacy with the peasants, the envy he felt of them, of their life, the desire to adopt that life, which had been to him that night not a dream but an intention, the execution of which he had thought out in detail—all this had so transformed his view of the farming of the land as he had managed it, that he could not take his former interest in it, and could not help seeing that unpleasant relation between him and the work people which was the foundation of it all. The herd of improved cows such as Pava, the whole land plowed over and manured, the nine level fields surrounded with willows, the two hundred and forty acres heavily manured, the seed drills, and all the rest of it—it was all splendid if only the work had been done for themselves, or for themselves and comrades—people in sympathy with them. But he saw clearly now (his work on a book of agriculture, in which the chief element in husbandry was to have been the laborer, greatly assisted him in this) that the sort of farming he was carrying on was nothing but a cruel and stubborn struggle between him and the laborers, in which there was on one side—his side—a continual intense effort to change everything to a pattern he considered better; on the other side, the natural order of things. And in this struggle he saw that with immense expenditure of force on his side, and with no effort or even intention on the other side, all that resulted was that the work did not go to the liking of either side, and that splendid tools, splendid cattle, and land were spoiled with no good to anyone. Worst of all, the energy expended on this work was not simply wasted. He could not help feeling now, since the meaning of this system had become clear to him, that the aim of his energy was a most unworthy one. In reality, what was the struggle about? He was struggling for every kopek of his share (and he could not help it, for he had only to relax his efforts, and he would not have had the money to pay his laborers' wages) while they were struggling only to be able to do their work easily and agreeably, that is to say, as they were used to doing it. It was for his interests that every laborer should work as hard as possible, and that while doing so he should keep his wits about him, so as to try not to break the winnowing machines, the horse rakes, the threshing machines, that he should attend to what he was doing. What the laborer wanted was to work as pleasantly as possible, with rests, and above all, carelessly and heedlessly, without thinking. That summer Levin saw this at every step. He sent the men to mow some clover for hay, picking out the worst patches where the clover was overgrown with grass and wormwood and of no use for seed; again and again they mowed the best acres of clover, justifying themselves by the pretense that the bailiff had told them to, and trying to pacify him with the assurance that it would be splendid hay; but he knew that it was because those acres were so much easier to mow. He sent out a hay machine for pitching the hay—it was broken at the first row because it was boring work for a peasant to sit on the seat in front with the great wings waving above him. And he was told, "Don't trouble, sir, sure, the women will pitch it quick enough." The plows were practically useless, because it never occurred to the laborer to raise the share when he turned the plow, and forcing it around, he strained the horses and tore up the ground, and Levin was begged not to worry. The horses were allowed to stray into the wheat, because not a single laborer would consent to be night watchman, and in spite of orders to the contrary, the laborers insisted on taking turns for night duty, and Ivan, after working all day long, fell asleep, and was very penitent for his fault, saying "Do what you will to me, Your Honor."

They let three of the best calves die by letting them into the clover without any water to drink, and nothing would make the men believe that they had been swelled up by the clover, but they told him by way of consolation that one of his neighbors had lost a hundred and twelve head of cattle in three days. All this happened, not because anyone felt ill-will toward Levin or his farm; on the contrary, he knew that they liked him, thought him a simple gentleman (their highest praise); but it happened simply because all they wanted was to work merrily and carelessly, and his interests were not only remote and incomprehensible to them, but fatally opposed to their most just claims. Long before, Levin had felt dissatisfaction with his own position in regard to the land. He saw where his boat leaked, but he did not look for the leak, perhaps purposely deceiving himself. But now he could deceive himself no longer. The farming of the land, as he was managing it, had become not merely unattractive but revolting to him and he could take no further interest in it.

To this now was joined the presence, only twenty-five miles off, of Kitty Shcherbatskaya, whom he longed to see and could not see. Darya Aleksandrovna Oblonskaya had invited him, when he was over there, to come; to come with the object of renewing his proposal to her sister, who would, so she made him understand, accept him now. Levin himself had felt, on seeing Kitty Shcherbatskaya, that he had never ceased to love her, but he could not go over to the Oblonskys' knowing she was there. The fact that he had proposed and that she had refused him had placed an insuperable barrier between her and him. "I can't ask her to be my wife merely because she can't be the wife of the man she wanted to marry," he said to himself. The thought of this made him cold and hostile toward her. "I will not be able to speak to her without a feeling of reproach; I could not look at her without anger; and she will only hate me all the more, as it's right she should. And besides, how can I now, after what Darya Aleksandrovna told me, go see them? Can I help showing that I know what she told me? And to go magnanimously to forgive her, and have pity on her! Me go through a performance before her of forgiving, and designing to bestow my love on her! . . . What induced Darya Aleksandrovna to tell me that? By chance I might have seen her, then everything would have happened naturally, but, as it is, it's out of the question, out of the question!"

Darya Aleksandrovna sent him a letter, asking him for a sidesaddle for Kitty's use. "I'm told you have a sidesaddle," she wrote to him; "I hope you will bring it over yourself."

This was more than he could stand. How could a woman of any intelligence, of any delicacy, put her sister in such a humiliating position! He wrote ten notes, and tore them all up, and sent the saddle without any reply. To write that he would go was impossible, because he could not go; to write that he could not come because something prevented him, or that he would be away, that was still worse. He sent the saddle without an answer, and with a sense of having done something shameful; he handed over all the now revolting business of the estate to his bailiff, and set off the next day to a remote district to see his friend Sviazhsky, who had splendid marshes for snipe in his neighborhood, and had lately written to ask him to keep a long-standing promise to stay with him. The snipe marsh, in the Surovsky district, had long tempted Levin, but he had continually put off this visit because of his work on the estate. Now he was glad to get away from the neighborhood of the Shcherbatskys, and most of all from his farm work, especially on a shooting expedition, which always served as the best consolation in all his troubles.

CHAPTER TWENTY-FIVE

In the Surovsky district there was no railway or service of post horses, and Levin drove there with his own horses in his big old-fashioned carriage.

He stopped halfway at a well-to-do peasant's to feed his horses. A bald, well-preserved man with a broad, red beard, gray on his cheeks, opened the gate, squeezing against the gate post to let the three horses pass. Directing the coachman to a place under the shed in the big, clean, tidy yard, with charred, old-fashioned plows in it, the old man asked Levin to come into the parlor. A cleanly dressed young woman, with galoshes on her bare feet, was scrubbing the floor in the new outer room. She was frightened of the dog, which ran in after Levin, and uttered a shriek, but began laughing at her own fright at once when she was told the dog would not hurt her. Pointing Levin to the door into the parlor with her bare arm, she bent down again, hiding her handsome face, and went on scrubbing.

"Would you like the samovar?" she asked.

"Yes, please."

The parlor was a big room, with a Dutch stove, and a partition dividing it into two. Under the icons stood a table painted in patterns, a bench, and two chairs. Near the entrance was a dresser full of crockery. The shutters were closed, there were few flies, and it was so clean that Levin was anxious that Laska, who had been running along the road and bathing in puddles, should not muddy the floor, and ordered her to a place in the corner by the door. After looking around the parlor, Levin went out in the back yard. The good-looking young woman in galoshes, swinging the empty pails on the yoke, ran on before him to the well for water.

"Look alive, my girl!" the old man shouted after her merrily, and he went up to Levin. "Well, sir, are you going to Nikolai Ivanovich Sviazhsky? His Honor comes to us too," he began chatting, leaning his elbows on the railing of the steps. In the middle of the old man's account of his acquaintance with Sviazhsky, the gates creaked again, and laborers came into the yard from the fields, with wooden plows and harrows. The horses harnessed to the plows and harrows were sleek and well fed. The laborers were obviously of the household: two were young men in cotton shirts and caps, the two others were hired laborers in homespun shirts, one an old man, the other a young fellow. Moving off from the steps, the old man went up to the horses and began unharnessing them.

"What have they been plowing?" asked Levin.

"Plowing up the potatoes. We rent a bit of land too. Fedot, don't let out the gelding, but take it to the trough, and we'll put the other in harness."

"Oh, Father, has he brought the plowshares I ordered?" asked the big, healthy-looking fellow, obviously the old man's son.

"There . . . in the outer room," answered the old man, bundling together the harness he had taken off and flinging it on the ground. "You can put them on while they have dinner."

The good-looking young woman came into the outer room with the full pails dragging at her shoulders. More women came on the scene from somewhere, young and handsome, middle-aged, old and ugly, with children and without children.

The samovar was beginning to sing; the laborers and the family, having disposed of the horses, came in to dinner. Levin, getting his provisions out of his carriage, invited the old man to have tea with him.

"Well, I have had some today already," said the old man, obviously accepting the invitation with pleasure. "But just a glass for company."

Over their tea Levin heard all about the old man's farming. Ten years before, the old man had rented three hundred acres from the lady who owned them, and a year ago he had bought them and rented another three hundred from a neighboring landowner. A small part of the land—the worst part—he rented out, while a hundred and twenty acres of arable land he cultivated himself with his family and two hired laborers. The old man complained that things were going badly. But Levin saw that he simply did so from a feeling of propriety, and that his farm was in a flourishing condition. If it had been successful he would not have bought land at thirty-five rubles an acre, he would not have married off his three sons and a nephew, he would not have rebuilt twice after fires, and each time on a larger scale. In spite of the old man's complaints, it was evident that he was proud, and justly proud, of his prosperity, proud of his sons, his nephew, his sons' wives, his horses and his cows, and especially of the fact that he was keeping all this farming going. From his conversation with the old man, Levin thought he was not averse to new methods, either. He had planted a great many potatoes, and his potatoes, as Levin had seen driving past, were already past flowering and beginning to form fruit, while Levin's were only just coming into flower. He earthed up his potatoes with a modern plow borrowed from a neighboring landowner. He sowed wheat. The trifling fact that, thinning out his rye, the old man used the rye he thinned out for his horses specially struck Levin. How many times had Levin seen this splendid fodder wasted, and tried to get it saved; but always it had turned out to be impossible. The peasant got this done, and he could not say enough in praise of it as food for the beasts.

"What have the wenches to do? They carry it out in bundles to the roadside, and the cart brings it away."

"Well, we landowners can't manage well with our laborers," said Levin, handing him a glass of tea.

"Thank you," said the old man, and he took the glass, but refused sugar, pointing to a lump he had left. "They're ruination," said he. "Look at Sviazhsky's, for instance. We know what the land's like—excellent, yet there's not much of a crop to boast of. It's not looked after enough—that's all it is!"

"But you work your land with hired laborers?"

"We're all peasants together. We supervise everything ourselves. If a man's no good, he can go, and we can manage by ourselves."

"Father, Finogen needs some tar," said the young woman in the galoshes, coming in.

"Yes, yes, that's how it is, sir!" said the old man, and getting up, he crossed himself deliberately, thanked Levin, and went out.

When Levin went into the kitchen to call his coachman he saw the whole family at dinner. The women were standing up serving. The young, sturdy-looking son was telling something funny with his mouth full of *kasha*, and they were all laughing, the woman in the galoshes, who was pouring cabbage soup into a bowl, laughing most merrily of all.

Very probably the good-looking face of the young woman in the galoshes had a good deal to do with the impression of well-being this peasant household made upon Levin, but the impression was so strong that Levin could never get rid of it. And all the way from the old peasant's to Sviazhsky's he kept recalling this peasant farm as though there were something in this impression that demanded his special attention.

CHAPTER TWENTY-SIX

Sviazhsky was the marshal of nobility of his district. He was five years older than Levin, and had long been married. His sister-in-law, a young girl Levin liked very much, lived in his house; and Levin knew that Sviazhsky and his wife would have greatly liked to marry the girl to him. He knew this with certainty, as so-called eligible young men always know it, though he could never have brought himself to speak of it to anyone; and he knew too that, although he wanted to get married, and although by every token this very attractive girl would make an excellent wife, he could no more have married her, even if he had not been in love with Kitty Shcherbatskaya, than he could have flown up to the sky. And this knowledge poisoned the pleasure he had hoped to find in the visit to Sviazhsky.

On getting Sviazhsky's letter with the invitation for shooting, Levin had immediately thought of this; but in spite of it he had made up his mind that this idea of Sviazhsky's intentions was based on his own groundless supposition, and so he would go all the same. Besides, at the bottom of his heart he had a desire to test himself in regard to this girl. The Sviazhskys' home life was exceedingly pleasant, and Sviazhsky himself, the best type of man taking part in local affairs that Levin knew, was very interesting to him.

Sviazhsky was one of those people, always a source of wonder to Levin, whose convictions, very logical though never original, go one way by themselves, while their life, exceedingly definite and firm in its

directions, goes its way quite apart and almost always in direct contradiction to their convictions. Sviazhsky was an extremely liberal
man. He despised the nobility, and believed the mass of nobility to
be secretly in favor of serfdom, concealing their views only because of
cowardice. He regarded Russia as a doomed country, like Turkey, and
the government of Russia as so bad that he never permitted himself to
criticize its doings seriously, and yet he was a functionary of that government and a model marshal of nobility, and when he drove about he
always wore the cockade of office and the cap with the red band. He
considered human life tolerable only abroad, and went abroad to stay
at every opportunity, and at the same time he carried on a complex
and improved system of agriculture in Russia, and with extreme interest followed everything and knew everything that was being done in
Russia. He considered the Russian peasant as occupying a stage of
development intermediate between the ape and man, and at the same
time in the local assemblies no one was readier to shake hands with
the peasants and listen to their opinion. He believed in neither God
nor the devil, but was much concerned about the question of
improvement of the clergy and the maintenance of their revenues,
and took special trouble to keep up the church in his village.

On the woman question he was on the side of the extreme advocates of complete liberty for women, and especially their right to
labor. But he lived with his wife on such terms that their affectionate childless home life was the admiration of everyone, and he
arranged his wife's life so that she did nothing and could do nothing
but share her husband's efforts to make her time pass as happily and
as agreeably as possible.

If it had not been a characteristic of Levin's to put the most favorable interpretation on people, Sviazhsky's character would have presented no doubt or difficulty to him: he would have said to himself,
"a fool or a scoundrel," and everything would have seemed clear. But
he could not say "a fool," because Sviazhsky was unmistakably intelligent and, moreover, a highly cultivated man, who was exceptionally
modest concerning his culture. There was not a subject he did not
know something about. But he did not display his knowledge except
when he was compelled to do so. Still less could Levin say that he was
a scoundrel, as Sviazhsky was unmistakably an honest, good-hearted,

sensible man, who worked cheerfully, keenly, and perseveringly at his work; he was held in high honor by everyone about him, and certainly had never consciously done, and was indeed incapable of doing anything base.

Levin tried to understand him, and could not understand him, and looked at him and his life as at a living enigma.

Levin and he were very friendly, and so Levin used to venture to sound out Sviazhsky, to try to get at the very foundation of his view of life; but it was always in vain. Every time Levin tried to penetrate beyond the outer chambers of Sviazhsky's mind, which were hospitably open to all, he noticed that Sviazhsky was slightly disconcerted; faint signs of alarm were visible in his eyes, as though he was afraid Levin would understand him, and he would give him a kindly, good-humored rebuff.

Just now, since his disenchantment with farming, Levin was particularly glad to stay with Sviazhsky. Apart from the fact that the sight of this happy and affectionate couple, so pleased with themselves and everyone else, and their comfortable home always had a cheering effect on Levin, he felt a longing, now that he was so dissatisfied with his own life, to get at that secret in Sviazhsky that gave him such clearness, definiteness, and courage. Moreover, Levin knew that at Sviazhsky's he would meet the landowners of the neighborhood, and it was particularly interesting for him just now to hear and take part in those rural conversations concerning crops, laborers' wages, and so on, which, he was aware, are conventionally regarded as something beneath dignity, but which seemed to him just now to constitute the one subject of importance. "It was not, perhaps, of importance in the days of serfdom, and it may not be of importance in England. In both cases the conditions of agriculture are firmly established; but among us now, when everything has been turned upside down and is only just taking shape, the question of what form these conditions will take is the one question of importance in Russia," thought Levin.

The shooting turned out to be worse than Levin had expected. The marsh was dry and there were no snipe at all. He walked about the whole day and brought back only three birds, but to make up for that, he brought back, as he always did from shooting, an excellent appetite, excellent spirits, and that keen intellectual mood which with him always accompanied violent physical exertion. And while out shooting, when he seemed to be thinking of nothing at all, suddenly the old man and his family kept coming back to his mind, and the impression of them seemed to claim not merely his attention but also the solution of some question connected with them.

In the evening at tea, two landowners who had come about some business connected with a wardship were present, and the interesting conversation Levin had been looking forward to sprang up.

Levin was sitting beside his hostess at the tea table, and was obliged to keep up a conversation with her and her sister, who was sitting opposite him. Madame Sviazhskaya was a round-faced, fair-haired, rather short woman, all smiles and dimples. Levin tried through her to get at a solution of the weighty enigma her husband presented to his mind; but he had not complete freedom of ideas, because he was in an agony of embarrassment. This agony of embarrassment was due to the fact that the sister-in-law was wearing a dress specially put on, he thought, for his benefit, cut particularly low, in the shape of a trapeze, on her white bosom. This square opening, in spite of the bosom's being very white, or just because it was very white, deprived Levin of the full use of his faculties. He imagined, probably mistakenly, that this low-necked bodice had been made on his account, and felt that he had no right to look at it, and tried not to look at it; but he felt that he was to blame for the very fact of the low-necked bodice having been made. It seemed to Levin that he had deceived someone, that he ought to explain something, but that to explain it was impossible, and for that reason he was continually blushing, was ill at ease and awkward. His awkwardness infected the pretty sister-in-law too. But their hostess appeared not to observe this, and kept purposely drawing her into the conversation.

"You say," she said, pursuing the subject that had been started, "that my husband cannot be interested in what's Russian. It's quite the contrary; he is always in cheerful spirits abroad, but not as he is here. Here, he feels in his proper place. He has so much to do, and he has the faculty of interesting himself in everything. Oh, you've not been to see our school, have you?"

"I've seen it . . . The little house covered with ivy, isn't it?"

"Yes; that's Nastya's work," she said, indicating her sister.

"You teach in it yourself?" asked Levin, trying to look above the open neck, but feeling that wherever he looked in that direction he would see it.

"Yes; I used to teach in it myself, and do teach still, but we have a first-rate schoolmistress now. And we've started gymnastic exercises."

"No, thank you, I won't have any more tea," said Levin, and conscious of doing a rude thing, but incapable of continuing the conversation, he got up, blushing. "I hear a very interesting conversation," he added, and walked to the other end of the table, where Sviazhsky was sitting with the two gentlemen of the neighborhood. Sviazhsky was sitting sideways, with one elbow on the table, and a cup in one hand, while with the other hand he gathered up his beard, held it to his nose and let it drop again, as though he were smelling it. His brilliant black eyes were looking straight at the excited country gentleman with gray whiskers, and apparently he derived amusement from his remarks. The gentleman was complaining of the peasants. It was evident to Levin that Sviazhsky knew an answer to this gentleman's complaints, which would at once demolish his whole contention, but that in his position he could not give utterance to this answer, and listened, not without pleasure, to the landowner's comic speeches.

The gentleman with the gray mustache was obviously an inveterate adherent of serfdom and a devoted agriculturist, who had lived all his life in the country. Levin saw proofs of this in his dress, in the old-fashioned threadbare coat, obviously not his everyday attire, in his shrewd, deep-set eyes, in his idiomatic, fluent Russian, in the imperious tone that had become habitual from long use, and in the resolute gestures of his large, red, sunburned hands, with an old engagement ring on the little finger.

CHAPTER TWENTY-SEVEN

"If I'd only the heart to give up what's been set going . . . such a lot of trouble wasted . . . I'd turn my back on the whole business, sell it all, go off like Nikolai Ivanovich . . . to her *La Belle Hélène*," said the landowner, a pleasant smile lighting up his shrewd old face.

"But you see you don't give it up," said Nikolai Ivanovich Sviazhsky; "so there must be some advantages."

"The only advantage is that I live in my own house, neither bought nor rented. Besides, one keeps hoping the people will learn sense. Though, instead of that, you'd never believe it—the drunkenness, the debauchery! They keep chopping and changing their bits of land. Not a sight of a horse or a cow. The peasant's dying of hunger, but just go and take him on as a laborer, he'll do his best to do mischief, and then bring you up before the justice of the peace."

"But then you make complaints to the justice, too," said Sviazhsky.

"I lodge complaints? Not for anything in the world! Such gossip that one would have cause to regret it. At the mill, for instance, they pocketed the advance money and made off. What did the justice do? Why, acquitted them. Nothing keeps them in line but their own communal court and their village elder. He'll flog them in the good old style! But for that there'd be no choice but to give it all up and run away."

Obviously the landowner was teasing Sviazhsky, who, far from resenting it, was apparently amused by it.

"But you see we manage our land without such extreme measures," said he, smiling: "Levin and I and this gentleman."

He indicated the other landowner.

"Yes, the thing's done at Mikhail Petrovich's, but ask him how it's done. Do you call that a rational system?" said the landowner, obviously rather proud of the word "rational."

"My system's very simple," said Mikhail Petrovich, "thank God. All my management rests on getting the money ready for the autumn taxes, and the peasants come to me, 'Father, master, help us!' Well, the peasants are all one's neighbors; one feels for them. So one advances them a third, but one says: 'Remember, boys, I have helped you, and you must help me when I need it—whether it's the sowing of the oats, or the hay cutting, or the harvest'; and well, one agrees, so much for each taxpayer—though there are dishonest ones among them too, it's true."

Levin, who had long been familiar with these patriarchal methods, exchanged glances with Sviazhsky and interrupted Mikhail Petrovich, turning again to the gentleman with the gray mustache.

"Then what do you think?" he asked; "what system is one to adopt nowadays?"

"Why, manage like Mikhail Petrovich, or let the land for half the crop or for rent to the peasants; that one can do—only that's just how the general prosperity of the country is being ruined. Where the land with serf labor and good management gave a yield of nine to one, on the half-crop system it yields three to one. Russia has been ruined by the emancipation!"

Sviazhsky looked with smiling eyes at Levin, and even made a faint gesture of irony to him; but Levin did not think the landowner's words absurd, he understood them better than he did Sviazhsky. A great deal more of what the gentleman with the gray mustache said to show in what way Russia was ruined by the emancipation struck him indeed as very true, new to him, and quite incontestable. The landowner unmistakably spoke his own individual thought—a thing that rarely happens—and a thought to which he had been brought not by a desire of finding some exercise for an idle brain, but a thought which had grown up out of the conditions of his life, which he had brooded over in the solitude of his village, and had considered in every aspect.

"The point is, don't you see, that progress of every sort is made only by the use of authority," he said, evidently wishing to show he was not without culture. "Take the reforms of Peter, of Catherine, of Aleksandr. Take European history. And progress in agriculture more than anything else—the potato, for instance, that was introduced among us by force. The wooden plow too wasn't always used. It was introduced maybe in the days of medieval Russia, but it was probably brought in by force. Now, in our own day, we landowners in the serf times used various improvements in our husbandry: drying machines and threshing machines, and carting manure and all the modern implements—all that we brought into use by our authority, and the peasants opposed it at first, and ended by imitating us. Now by the abolition of serfdom we have been deprived of our authority; and so our husbandry, where it had been raised to a high level, is bound to sink to the most savage primitive condition. That's how I see it."

"But why so? If it's rational, you'll be able to keep up the same system with hired labor," said Sviazhsky.

"We've no power over them. With whom am I going to work the system, allow me to ask?"

"There it is—the labor force—the chief element in agriculture," thought Levin.

"With laborers."

"The laborers won't work well, and won't work with good implements. Our laborers can do nothing but get drunk like a pig, and when he's drunk he ruins everything you give him. He makes the horses ill with too much water, cuts good harness, barters the tires off the wheels for drink, drops a bolt into the threshing machine, so as to break it. He loathes the sight of anything that's not after his fashion. And that's how it is that the whole level of husbandry has fallen. Lands gone out of cultivation, overgrown with weeds, or divided among the peasants, and where millions of bushels were raised you get a hundred thousand; the wealth of the country has decreased. If the same thing had been done, but with care that . . ."

And he proceeded to unfold his own scheme of emancipation by means of which these drawbacks might have been avoided.

This did not interest Levin, but when he had finished, Levin went back to his first proposition, and addressing Sviazhsky, he tried to draw him into expressing his serious opinion:

"That the standard of culture is falling, and that with our present relations to the peasants there is no possibility of farming on a rational system to yield a profit—that's perfectly true," said he.

"I don't believe it," Sviazhsky replied quite seriously; "all I see is that we don't know how to cultivate the land, and that our system of agriculture in the serf days was by no means too high, but too low. We have no machines, no good stock, no efficient supervision; we don't even know how to keep accounts. Ask any landowner; he won't be able to tell you what crop's profitable and what's not."

"Italian bookkeeping," said the gentleman of the gray mustache ironically. "You may keep your books as you like, but if the peasants spoil everything for you, there won't be any profit."

"Why do they spoil things? An inferior threshing machine of Russian quality they will break, but my steam threshing machine they don't break. A wretched Russian nag they'll ruin, but keep good dray horses or cart horses—they won't ruin them. And so it is all around. We must raise our farming to a higher level."

"Oh, if one only had the means to do it, Nikolai Ivanovich! It's all very well for you; but for me, with a son to keep at the university, boys to be educated at the high school—how am I going to buy these dray horses?"

"Well, that's what the banks are for."

"To get what's left me sold by auction? No, thank you."

"I don't agree that it's necessary or possible to raise the level of agriculture still higher," said Levin. "I devote myself to it, and I have means, but I can do nothing. As to the banks, I don't know to whom they're any good. For my part, anyway, whatever I've spent money on in the way of husbandry, it has been a loss: stock—a loss, machinery—a loss."

"That's true enough," the gentleman with the gray mustache chimed in, actually laughing with satisfaction.

"And I'm not the only one," pursued Levin. "I mix with all the neighboring landowners, who are cultivating their land on a rational system; they all, with rare exceptions, are doing so at a loss. Come, tell us, how does your land do—does it pay?" said Levin, and at once in Sviazhsky's eyes he detected that fleeting expression of alarm which he had noticed whenever he had tried to penetrate beyond the outer chambers of Sviazhsky's mind.

Moreover, this question on Levin's part was not quite in good faith. Madame Sviazhskaya had just told him at tea that they had that summer invited a German expert in bookkeeping from Moscow, who for a consideration of five hundred rubles had investigated the management of their property, and found that it was costing them a loss of three thousand-odd rubles. She did not remember the precise sum, but it appeared that the German had worked it out to the fraction of a kopek.

The gray-mustached landowner smiled at the mention of the profits of Sviazhsky's farming, obviously aware how much gain his neighbor and marshal was likely to be making.

"Possibly it does not pay," answered Sviazhsky. "That merely proves either that I'm a bad manager or that I've sunk my capital to increase my rents."

"Oh, rent!" Levin cried with horror. "Rent there may be in Europe, where land has been improved by the labor put into it; but with us all the land is deteriorating from the labor put into it—in other words, they're working it out; so there's no question of rent."

"How no rent? It's a natural law."

"Then we're outside the law; rent explains nothing for us, but simply confuses us. No, tell me how there can be a theory of rent? . . ."

"Will you have some sour milk? Masha, pass us some sour milk or raspberries." He turned to his wife. "The raspberries are lasting extraordinarily late this year."

And in the happiest frame of mind Sviazhsky got up and walked off, apparently supposing the conversation to have ended at the very point when to Levin it seemed that it was only just beginning.

Having lost his antagonist, Levin continued the conversation with the gray-mustached landowner, trying to prove to him that all the difficulty arises from the fact that we don't find out the peculiarities and habits of our laborer; but the landowner, like all men who think independently and in isolation, was slow in absorbing any person's ideas and remained particularly partial to his own. He insisted that the Russian peasant is a pig and likes piggishness, and that to get him out of his piggishness one must have authority, and there is none; one must have the stick, and we have become so liberal that we have all of a sudden replaced the stick that served us for a thousand years with lawyers and model prisons, where the worthless, stinking peasant is fed on good soup and has a fixed allowance of cubic feet of air.

"What makes you think," said Levin, trying to get back to the question, "that it's impossible to find some relationship with the laborer in which the labor would become productive?"

"That never could be so with the Russian peasantry; we've no power over them," answered the landowner.

"How can new conditions be found?" asked Sviazhsky. Having eaten some sour milk and lit a cigarette, he came back to the discussion. "All possible relations to the labor force have been defined and studied," he said. "The relic of barbarism, the primitive commune with mutual guarantee, will disappear by itself; serfdom has been abolished—there remains nothing but free labor, and its forms are fixed and ready made, and must be adopted. Permanent hands, day laborers, farmers—you can't get out of those forms."

"But Europe is dissatisfied with these forms."

"Dissatisfied, and seeking new ones. And will find them, in all probability."

"That's just what I mean," answered Levin. "Why shouldn't we seek them for ourselves?"

"Because it would be just like inventing afresh the means for constructing railways. They are ready, invented."

"But if they don't do for us, if they're stupid?" said Levin.

And again he detected the expression of alarm in the eyes of Sviazhsky.

"Oh, yes; we'll bury the world under our caps! We've found the secret Europe was seeking! I've heard all that; but, forgive me, do you know all that's been done in Europe on the question of the organization of labor?"

"No, very little."

"That question is now absorbing the best minds in Europe. The Schulze-Delitzsch[1] movement. . . . And then all this enormous amount of literature on the labor question of the most liberal Lassalle[2] trend . . . the Mulhausen[3] system? That's a fact by now, as you're probably aware."

"I have some idea of it, but very vague."

"No, you only say that; no doubt you know all about it as well as I do. I'm not a professor of sociology, of course, but it interested me, and really, if it interests you, you ought to study it."

"But what conclusion have they come to?"

"Excuse me. . ."

---

[1]Franz Hermann Schulze-Delitzsch (1808-83), a German economist, withdrew from public appointments in 1851 and devoted himself to the organization of co-operative societies and people's banks.

[2]Ferdinand Lassalle (1825-64), German socialist who, in contrast to Marx, emphasized the role of the state, favored a system of workers' co-operative.

[3]French town where, in 1853, an interesting attempt at industrial town planning was made.

The two neighbors had risen, and Sviazhsky, once more checking Levin in his inconvenient habit of peeping into what was beyond the outer chambers of his mind, went to see his guests out.

CHAPTER TWENTY-EIGHT

Levin was insufferably bored that evening with the ladies; he was stirred as he had never been before by the idea that the dissatisfaction he was feeling with his system of managing his land was not an exceptional case, but the general condition of things in Russia; that the organization of some relation of the laborers to the soil in which they would work, as with the peasant he had met on the way to the Sviazhskys', was not a dream, but a problem which must be solved. And it seemed to him that the problem could be solved, and that he ought to try and solve it.

After saying good night to the ladies, and promising to stay the whole of the next day, so as to make an expedition on horseback with them to see an interesting ruin in the crown forest, Levin went, before going to bed, into his host's study to get the books on the labor question that Sviazhsky had offered him. Sviazhsky's study was a huge room, surrounded by bookcases and with two tables in it— one a massive writing table, standing in the middle of the room, and the other a round table, covered with recent issues of reviews and journals in different languages, ranged like the rays of a star round the lamp. On the writing table was a stand of drawers marked with gold lettering, and full of papers of various sorts.

Sviazhsky took out the books, and sat down in a rocking chair.

"What are you looking at there?" he said to Levin, who was standing at the round table looking through the reviews.

"Oh, yes, there's a very interesting article here," said Sviazhsky of the review Levin was holding in his hand. "It appears," he went on, with eager interest, "that Frederick[1] was not, after all, the person chiefly responsible for the partition of Poland. It is proved . . ."

And, with his characteristic clearness, he summed up those new,

[1] Frederick the Great (1712-86), who became king of Prussia in 1740.

very important, and interesting revelations. Although Levin was engrossed at the moment by his ideas about the problem of the land, he wondered, as he heard Sviazhsky: "What is there inside of him? And why, why is he interested in the partition of Poland?" When Sviazhsky had finished, Levin could not help asking: "Well, and what then?" But there was nothing to follow. It was simply interesting that it had been proved to be so and so. But Sviazhsky did not explain, and saw no need to explain why it was interesting to him.

"Yes, but I was very much interested by your irritable neighbor," said Levin, sighing. "He's a clever fellow, and said a lot that was true."

"Oh, get along with you! An inveterate supporter of serfdom at heart, like all of them!" said Sviazhsky.

"Whose marshal you are."

"Yes, only I marshal them in the other direction," said Sviazhsky, laughing.

"I'll tell you what interests me very much," said Levin. "He's right that our system, that is to say, of rational farming, has failed, that the only thing that succeeds is the moneylender system, like that meek-looking gentleman's, or else the very simplest. . . Whose fault is it?"

"Our own, of course. Besides, it's not true that it doesn't succeed. It does with Vasilchikov."

"A factory . . ."

"But I really don't know what it is you are surprised at. The people are at such a low stage of rational and moral development that it's obvious they're bound to oppose everything that's strange to them. In Europe, a rational system succeeds because the people are educated; it follows that we must educate the people—that's all."

"But how are we to educate the people?"

"To educate the people three things are needed: schools, and schools, and schools."

"But you said yourself the people are at such a low stage of material development: what help are schools for that?"

"Do you know, you remind me of the story of the advice given to the sick man— You should try a laxative. Taken: worse. Try leeches. Tried them: worse. Well, then, there's nothing left but to pray to God. Tried it: worse. That's just how it is with us. I say political economy; you say—worse. I say socialism: worse. Education: worse."

"But how do schools help matters?"

"They give the peasant fresh needs."

"Well, that's a thing I've never understood," Levin replied with heat. "In what way are schools going to help the people to improve their material position? You say schools, education, will give them fresh needs. So much the worse, since they won't be capable of satisfying them. And in what way a knowledge of addition and subtraction and the catechism is going to improve their material condition, I never could make out. The day before yesterday, I met a peasant woman in the evening with a little baby, and asked her where she was going. She said she was going to the village sorceress; her boy had screaming fits, so she was taking him to be doctored. I asked, 'Why, how does the wise woman cure screaming fits?' 'She puts the child on the hen roost and repeats some charm . . .' "

"Well, you're saying it yourself! What's needed to prevent her taking her child to the hen roost to cure it of screaming fits is just . . ." Sviazhsky said, smiling good-humoredly.

"Oh, no!" said Levin with annoyance; "that method of doctoring I merely meant as a simile for doctoring the people with schools. The people are poor and ignorant—that we see as surely as the peasant woman sees the baby is ill because it screams. But in what way this trouble of poverty and ignorance is to be cured by schools is as incomprehensible as how the hen roost affects the screaming. What has to be cured is what makes him poor."

"Well, in that, at least, you're in agreement with Spencer,[1] whom you dislike so much. He says, too, that education may be the consequence of greater prosperity and comfort, of more frequent washing, as he says, but not of being able to read and write . . ."

"Well, then, I'm very glad—or the contrary, very sorry, that I'm in agreement with Spencer; only I've known it a long while. Schools can do no good; what will do good is an economic organization in which the people will become richer, will have more leisure—and then there will be schools."

"Still, all over Europe now schools are obligatory."

[1]Herbert Spencer (1820-1903), English philosopher.

"And how far do you agree with Spencer yourself about it?" asked Levin.

But there was a gleam of alarm in Sviazhsky's eyes, and he said, smiling:

"No; that screaming-fit story is positively marvelous! Did you really hear it yourself?"

Levin saw that he was not to discover the connection between this man's life and his thoughts. Obviously he did not care in the least what his reasoning led him to; all he wanted was the process of reasoning. And he did not like it when the process of reasoning brought him into a blind alley. That was the only thing he disliked, and avoided by changing the conversation to something agreeable and amusing.

All the impressions of the day, beginning with the impression made by the old peasant, which served, as it were, as the fundamental basis of all the conceptions and ideas of the day, threw Levin into violent excitement. This dear good Sviazhsky, keeping a stock of ideas simply for social purposes, obviously having some other principles hidden from Levin, while with the crowd, whose name is legion, he guided public opinion by ideas he did not share; that irascible country gentleman, perfectly correct in his conclusions that he had been worried into by life, but wrong in the exasperations against a whole class, and that the best class in Russia; his own dissatisfaction with the work he had been doing, and the vague hope of finding a remedy for all this—all was blended in a sense of inner turmoil, and anticipation of some solution near at hand.

Left alone in the room assigned him, lying on a spring mattress that yielded unexpectedly at every movement of his arm or his leg, Levin did not fall asleep for a long while. Not one conversation with Sviazhsky, though he had said a great deal that was clever, had interested Levin; but the conclusions of the irascible landowner required consideration. Levin could not help recalling every word he had said, and in imagination amending his own replies.

"Yes, I should have said to him: 'You say that our husbandry does not succeed because the peasant hates improvements, and that they must be forced on him by authority. If no system of husbandry succeeded at all without these improvements, you would be quite right. But the only system that does succeed is when the laborer is working in accordance with his habits, just as on the old peasant's land halfway here. Your and our general dissatisfaction with the system shows that either we or the laborers are to blame. We have gone our way—the European way—a long while, without asking ourselves about the qualities of our labor force. Let us try to look upon the labor force not as the ideal labor *force*, but as the *Russian peasant* with his instincts, and we shall arrange our system of culture in accordance with that. Imagine,' I should have said to him, 'that you have the same system as the old peasant has, that you have found means of making your laborers take an interest in the success of the work, and have found the happy mean in the way of improvements which they will admit—and you will, without exhausting the soil, get twice or three times the yield you got before. Divide it in halves, give half as the share of labor, the surplus left you will be greater, and the share of labor will be greater too. And to do this one must lower the standard of husbandry and interest the laborers in its success. How to do this?—that's a matter of detail; but undoubtedly it can be done.' "

This idea threw Levin into a great excitement. He did not sleep half the night, thinking over in detail the putting of his idea into practice. He had not intended to leave the next day, but he now determined to go home early in the morning. Besides, the sister-in-law with her low-necked bodice aroused in him a feeling akin to shame and remorse for some utterly base action. Most important of all—he must get back without delay: he would have to make haste to put his new project to the peasants before the sowing of the winter wheat, so that the sowing might be undertaken on a new basis. He had made up his mind to revolutionize his whole system.

CHAPTER TWENTY-NINE

The carrying out of Levin's plan presented many difficulties; but he struggled on, doing his utmost, and attained a result which, though not what he desired, was enough to enable him, without self-deception, to believe that the attempt was worth the trouble. One of the chief difficulties was that the process of cultivating the land was in full swing, that it was impossible to stop everything and begin it all again from the beginning, and the machine had to be overhauled while in motion.

When on the evening that he arrived home he informed the bailiff of his plans, the latter with visible pleasure agreed with what he said so long as he was pointing out that all that had been done up to that time was stupid and useless. The bailiff said that he had said so a long while ago, but no heed had been paid him. But as for the proposal made by Levin—to take a part as shareholder with his laborers in each agricultural undertaking—at this the bailiff simply expressed a profound despondency, and offered no definite opinion, but began immediately talking of the urgent necessity of carrying the remaining sheaves of rye the next day, and of sending the men out for the second plowing, so that Levin felt that this was not the time for discussing it.

On beginning to talk to the peasants about it, and making a proposition to cede them the land on new terms, he came into collision with the same great difficulty: they were so much absorbed by the current work of the day that they did not have time to consider the advantages and disadvantages of the proposed scheme.

The naïve Ivan, the cowherd, seemed completely to grasp Levin's proposal—that he and his family should take a share of the profits of the dairy farm—and he was in complete sympathy with the plan. But when Levin hinted at the future advantages, Ivan's face expressed alarm and regret that he could not hear all he had to say, and he made haste to find himself some task that could not be delayed: he either snatched up the fork to pitch the hay out of the pens, or ran to get water, or cleaned out the manure.

Another difficulty lay in the invincible disbelief of the peasant that a landowner's object could be anything else than a desire to squeeze all he could out of them. They were firmly convinced that his real aim (whatever he might say to them) would always be in what he did not say to them. And they themselves, in giving their opinion, said a great deal but never said what was their real object. Moreover (Levin felt that the irascible landowner had been right), the peasants made as the first and unalterable condition of any agreement whatever that they should not be forced to any new methods of tillage of any kind, or to use new implements. They agreed that the modern plow plowed better, that the scarifier did the work more quickly, but they found thousands of reasons that made it out of the question for them to use either of them; and though he had accepted the conviction that he would have to lower the standard of cultivation, he felt sorry to give up improved methods, the advantages of which were so obvious. But in spite of all these difficulties he got his way, and by autumn the system was working, or so at least it seemed to him.

At first Levin had thought of giving up the whole farming of the land just as it was to the peasants, the laborers, and the bailiff on new conditions of partnership; but he was very soon convinced that this was impossible, and determined to divide it up. The cattle yard, the garden, hayfields, and arable land, divided into several parts, had to be made into separate lots. The naïve cowherd, Ivan, who, Levin thought, understood the matter better than any of them, collecting together a gang of workers, principally of his own family, became a partner in the dairy farm. A distant part of the estate, a tract of waste land that had lain fallow for eight years, was, with the help of the clever carpenter, Fyodor Rezunov, taken by six families of peasants on new conditions of partnership, and the peasant Shurayev took the management of all the vegetable gardens on the same terms. The remainder of the land was still worked on the old system, but these three associated partnerships were the first step to a new organization of the whole, and they completely took up Levin's time.

It is true that in the dairy farm things went no better than before, and Ivan strenuously opposed warm housing for the cows and butter made of fresh cream, affirming that cows require less food if kept cold, and that butter is more profitable made from sour cream, and he asked for wages just as under the old system, and took not the slightest interest in the fact that the money he received was not wages but an advance out of his future share in the profits.

It is true that Fyodor Rezunov's group did not plow the ground twice before sowing, as had been agreed, justifying themselves on the plea that the time was too short. It is true that the peasants of the same group, though they had agreed to work the land on the new conditions, always spoke of the land, not as held in partnership, but as rented for half the crop, and more than once the peasants and Rezunov himself said to Levin, "If you would take rent for the land, it would save you trouble, and we would be more free." Moreover, the same peasants kept putting off, on various excuses, the building of a cattle yard and barn on the land as agreed upon, and delayed doing it till winter.

It is true that Shurayev would have liked to sublease the vegetable gardens in small lots to the peasants. He evidently quite misunderstood, and apparently intentionally misunderstood, the conditions upon which the land had been given to him.

Often, too, talking to the peasants and explaining to them all the advantages of the plan, Levin felt that they heard nothing but the sound of his voice, and were firmly resolved, whatever he might say, not to let themselves be taken in. He felt this especially when he talked to the cleverest of the peasants, Rezunov, and detected the gleam in his eyes which showed so plainly both ironical amusement at Levin, and the firm conviction that, if anyone were to be taken in, it would not be he, Rezunov. But in spite of all this Levin thought the system worked, and that by keeping accounts strictly and insisting on his own way, he would prove to them in the future the advantages of the arrangement, and then the system would work automatically.

These matters, together with the management of the land still left on his hands, and the indoor work over his book, so engrossed Levin the whole summer that he scarcely ever went out shooting. At the end of August he heard, from their servant who brought back the saddle, that the Oblonskys had gone away to Moscow. He felt that in not answering Darya Aleksandrovna's letter he had, by his rudeness, of which he could not think without a flush of shame, burned his ships, and that he would never go and see them again. He had been just as rude with the Sviazhskys, leaving them without saying good-by. But he would never go to see them again either. He did not care about that now. The business of reorganizing the farming of his land absorbed him as completely as though there would never be anything else in his life. He read the books lent him by Sviazhsky, and copying out what he did not have, he read books on both the economic and the socialistic aspects of the subject, but, as he had anticipated, found nothing bearing on the scheme he had undertaken. In the books on political economy—in Mill, for instance—whom he studied first with great ardor, hoping every minute to find an answer to the questions

that were engrossing him, he found laws deduced from the condition
of land culture in Europe; but he did not see why these laws, which
did not apply in Russia, must be general. He saw just the same thing
in the books on socialism: either they were the beautiful but imprac-
ticable fantasies which had fascinated him when he was a student, or
they were attempts at improving, rectifying the economic position in
which Europe was placed, with which the system of land tenure in
Russia had nothing in common. Political economy told him that the
laws by which the wealth of Europe had been developed, and was
developing, were universal and unvarying. Socialism told him that
development along these lines leads to ruin. And neither of them gave
an answer, or even a hint, in reply to the question of what he, Levin,
and all the Russian peasants and landowners, were to do with their
millions of hands and millions of acres, to make them as productive as
possible for the common good.

Having once taken up the subject, he read conscientiously everything bearing on it, and intended in the autumn to go abroad to
study land systems on the spot, in order that he might not on this
question be confronted with what so often met him on various subjects. Often, just as he was beginning to understand the idea in the
mind of anyone he was talking to, and was beginning to explain his
own, he would suddenly be told: "But Kaufmann, but Jones, but
Dubois, but Micelli?[1] You haven't read them; they've thrashed that
question out thoroughly."

He saw now distinctly that Kaufmann and Micelli had nothing
to tell him. He knew what he wanted. He saw that Russia has splendid land, splendid laborers, and that in certain cases, as at the peasant's on the way to Sviazhsky's, the produce raised by the laborers
and the land is great—in the majority of cases when capital is
applied in the European way the produce is small, and that this simply arises from the fact that the laborers want to work and work well
only in their own peculiar way, and that this antagonism is not incidental but invariable, and has its roots in the national spirit. He
thought that the Russian people whose task it was to colonize and

---

[1]These four are invented by Tolstoy. He creates a German, an Englishman, a
Frenchman, and an Italian to ridicule European science.

cultivate vast tracts of unoccupied land, consciously adhered, till all their land was occupied, to the methods suitable to their purpose, and that their methods were by no means so bad as was generally supposed. And he wanted to prove this theoretically in his book and practically on his land.

CHAPTER THIRTY

At the end of September the timber had been carted for building the cattle yard on the land that had been rented to the association of peasants, and the butter from the cows was sold and the profits divided. In practice the system worked wonderfully, or, at least, so it seemed to Levin. In order to work out the whole subject theoretically and to complete his book—which, in Levin's daydreams, was not merely to effect a revolution in political economy, but to annihilate that science entirely and to lay the foundation of a new science of the relation of the people to the soil—all that was left to do was to make a tour abroad, and to study on the spot all that had been done in the same direction, and to collect conclusive evidence that all that had been done there was not what was wanted. Levin was only waiting for the delivery of his wheat to receive the money for it and go abroad. But the rains began, preventing the harvesting of the corn and potatoes left in the fields, and putting a stop to all work, even to the delivery of the wheat.

The mud was impassable along the roads; two mills were carried away, and the weather got worse and worse.

On September 30 the sun came out in the morning, and hoping for fine weather, Levin began making final preparations for his journey. He gave orders for the wheat to be delivered, sent the bailiff to the merchant to get the money owed him, and went out himself to give some final instructions on the estate before setting off.

Having finished all his business, soaked through with the streams of water which kept running down the leather behind his neck and his high boots, but in the keenest and most confident temper, Levin returned homeward in the evening. The weather had become worse than ever toward evening; the hail lashed the drenched mare so cruelly that she went along sideways, shaking her head and ears; but Levin was all right under his hood, and he looked cheerfully about him at the muddy streams running under the wheels, at the drops hanging on every bare twig, at the whiteness of the patch of unmelted hailstones on the planks of the bridge, at the thick layer of still juicy, fleshy leaves that lay heaped up about the naked elm tree. In spite of the gloominess of nature around him, he felt peculiarly elated. The talks he had been having with the peasants in the further village had shown that they were beginning to get used to their new position. The old servant to whose hut he had gone to get dry evidently approved of Levin's plan, and of his own accord proposed to enter the partnership by the purchase of cattle.

"I need only continue stubbornly on toward my aim, and I will attain my end," thought Levin; "and it's something to work and take trouble for. This is not a matter of myself individually, the question of the public welfare enters into it. The whole system of culture, the chief element in the condition of the people, must be completely transformed. Instead of poverty, general prosperity and content; instead of hostility, harmony and unity of interests. In short, a bloodless revolution, but a revolution of the greatest magnitude, beginning in the little circle of our district, then the province, then Russia, then the whole world. Because a just idea cannot but be fruitful. Yes, it's an aim worth working for. And it's being me, Kostya Levin, who went to a ball in a black tie, and was refused by the Shcherbatskaya girl, and who was intrinsically such a pitiful, worthless creature—that proves nothing; I feel sure Franklin felt just as worthless, and he too had no faith in himself when summing himself up. That means nothing. And he too, most likely, had an Agafya Mikhailovna to whom he confided his secrets."

Musing on such thoughts, Levin reached home in the darkness.

The bailiff, who had been to the merchant, had come back and brought part of the money for the wheat. An agreement had been made with the old servant, and on the road the bailiff had learned that everywhere the corn was still standing in the fields, so that his one hundred and sixty shocks still in the fields were nothing in comparison with the losses of others.

After dinner Levin was sitting, as he usually did, in an armchair with a book, and as he read he went on thinking of the journey before him in connection with his book. Today all the significance of his book rose before him with special distinctness, and whole periods ranged themselves in his mind in illustration of his theories. "I must write that down," he thought. "That should make a brief introduction, which I thought unnecessary before." He got up to go to his writing table, and Laska, lying at his feet, got up too, stretching and looking at him as though to inquire where to go. But he had no time to write it down, for the head peasants had come to see him, and Levin went out into hall to receive them.

After giving directions about the labors of the next day, and seeing all the peasants who had business with him, Levin went back to his study and sat down to work.

Laska lay under the table; Agafya Mikhailovna settled herself in her place with her knitting.

After writing for a little while, Levin suddenly thought with exceptional vividness of Kitty, her refusal, and their last meeting. He got up and began walking about the room.

"What's the use of being dreary?" said Agafya Mikhailovna. "Come, why do you stay at home? You ought to go to some spa, especially now that you're ready for the journey."

"Well, I am going away the day after tomorrow, Agafya Mikhailovna; I must finish my work."

"There, there, your work, you say! As if you hadn't done enough for the peasants! Why, as it is, they're saying, 'Your master will be getting some honor from the Tsar for it.' Indeed, and it is a strange thing; why need you worry about the peasants?"

"I'm not worrying about them; I'm doing it for my own good."

Agafya Mikhailovna knew every detail of Levin's plans for his land. Levin often put his views before her in all their complexity, and not uncommonly he argued with her and did not agree with her comments. But on this occasion she entirely misinterpreted what he had said.

"Of one's soul's salvation we all know and must think before all else," she said with a sigh. "Parfyon Denisych, now, though he was no scholar, died a death that God grant every one of us," she said, referring to a servant who had died recently. "Took the sacrament and all."

"That's not what I mean," said he. "I mean that I'm acting for my own advantage. It's to my advantage if the peasants do their work better."

"Well, whatever you do, if he's a lazy good-for-nothing, everything'll be messed up. If he has a conscience, he'll work, and if not, there's no doing anything."

"Oh, come, you say yourself Ivan has begun looking after the cattle better."

"All I say is," answered Agafya Mikhailovna, evidently not speaking at random, but in strict sequence of ideas, "that you should get married, that's what I say."

Agafya Mikhailovna's allusion to the very subject he had just been thinking about hurt and stung him. Levin scowled, and without answering her, he sat down again to his work, repeating to himself all that he had been thinking about the real significance of that work. Only at intervals he listened in the stillness to the click of Agafya Mikhailovna's needles, and recollecting what he did not want to remember, he frowned again.

At nine o'clock they heard the bell and the faint vibration of a carriage through the mud.

"Well, here's visitors come to us, and you won't be bored," said Agafya Mikhailovna, getting up and going to the door. But Levin overtook her. His work was not going well now, and he was glad of a visitor, whoever it might be.

CHAPTER THIRTY-ONE

Running halfway down the staircase, Levin caught a sound he knew, a familiar cough in the hall. But he heard it indistinctly through the sound of his own footsteps, and hoped he was mistaken. Then he caught sight of a long, bony, familiar figure, and now it seemed there was no possibility of mistake; and yet he still went on hoping that this tall man taking off his fur cloak and coughing was not his brother Nikolai.

Levin loved his brother, but being with him was always a torture. Just now, when Levin, under the influence of the thoughts that had come to him, and Agafya Mikhailovna's hint, was in a troubled and uncertain mood, the meeting he had to face with his brother seemed particularly difficult. Instead of a lively, healthy visitor, some outsider who would cheer him up in his uncertain humor, he had to see his brother, who knew him through and through, who would call forth all the thoughts nearest his heart, would force him to show himself fully. And that he was not disposed to do.

Angry with himself for so base a feeling, Levin ran into the hall; as soon as he had seen his brother close, this feeling of selfish disappointment vanished instantly and was replaced by pity. Terrible as his brother Nikolai had been before in his emaciation and sickliness, he now looked still more emaciated, still more wasted. He was a skeleton covered by skin.

He stood in the hall, jerking his long, thin neck and pulling the scarf off it, and smiled a strange and pitiful smile. When he saw that smile, submissive and humble, Levin felt something clutching at his throat.

"You see, I've come to you," said Nikolai in a thick voice, never for one second taking his eyes off his brother's face. "I've been meaning to for a long while, but I've been sick all the time. Now I'm so much better," he said, rubbing his beard with his big, thin hands.

"Yes, yes!" answered Levin. And he felt still more frightened when, kissing him, he felt with his lips the dryness of his brother's skin and saw close to him his big eyes, full of a strange light.

A few weeks before, Konstantin Levin had written to his brother that through the sale of the small part of the property that had remained undivided, there was a sum of about two thousand rubles due him as his share.

Nikolai said that he had come now to take this money and, what was more important, to stay a while in the old nest, to get in touch with the earth so as to renew his strength like the heroes of old for the work that lay before him. In spite of his exaggerated stoop, and the emaciation that was so striking from his height, his movements were as rapid and abrupt as ever. Levin led him into his study.

His brother, dressed with particular care—a thing he never used to do—combed his thin, lank hair, and, smiling, went upstairs.

He was in the most affectionate and good-humored mood, just as Levin often remembered him in childhood. He even referred to Sergey Ivanovich without rancor. When he saw Agafya Mikhailovna he made jokes with her and asked about the old servants. The news of the death of Parfyon Denisych made a painful impression on him. A look of fear crossed his face, but he regained his serenity immediately.

"Of course he was quite old," he said, and changed the subject. "Well, I'll spend a month or two with you, and then I'm off to Moscow. Do you know, Myahkov has promised me a place there, and I'm going into the civil service. Now I'm going to arrange my life quite differently," he went on. "You know I got rid of that woman."

"Marya Nikolaevna? Why, what for?"

"Oh, she was a horrible woman! She caused me all sorts of trouble." But he did not say what the trouble was. He could not say that he had cast off Marya Nikolaevna because the tea was weak, and, above all, because she would look after him as though he were an invalid.

"Besides, I want to turn over a new leaf completely now. I've done silly things, of course, like everyone else, but money's the last consideration; I don't regret it. So long as there's health, and my health, thank God, is quite restored."

Levin listened and racked his brains, but could think of nothing to say. Nikolai probably felt the same; he began questioning his brother about his affairs; and Levin was glad to talk about himself, because then he could speak without hypocrisy. He told his brother of his plans and his doings.

His brother listened, but evidently he was not interested by it.

These two men were so akin, so near each other, that the slightest gesture, the tone of voice, told both more than could be said in words.

Both of them now had only one thought—the illness of Nikolai and the nearness of his death—which stifled all else. But neither of them dared to speak of it, and so whatever they said—not uttering the one thought that filled their minds—was all falsehood. Never had Levin been so glad when an evening was over and it was time to go to bed. Never with any outside person, never on any official visit had he been so unnatural and false as he was that evening. And the consciousness of this unnaturalness, and the remorse he felt at it, made him even more unnatural. He wanted to weep over his dying, dearly beloved brother, and he had to listen and keep on talking of how he meant to live.

As the house was damp, and only one bedroom had been kept heated, Levin put his brother to sleep in his own bedroom behind a partition.

His brother got into bed, and whether he slept or did not sleep, he tossed about like a sick man, coughed, and, when he could not get his throat clear, mumbled something. Sometimes when his breathing was painful he said, "Oh, my God!" Sometimes when he was choking he muttered angrily, "Ah hell!" Levin could not sleep for a long while, hearing him. His thoughts were of all sorts of things, but the end of all his thoughts was the same—death. Death, the inevitable end of all, for the first time presented itself to him with irresistible force. And death, which was here in this beloved brother, groaning, half asleep and from habit calling without distinction on God and the devil, was not so remote as it had hitherto seemed to him. It was in himself too; he felt that. If not today, tomorrow, if not tomorrow, in thirty years, wasn't it all the same! And what was this inevitable death—he did not know, had never thought about it, and, what was more, had not the power, had not the courage to think about it.

"I work, I want to do something, but I had forgotten it must all end; I had forgotten—death."

He sat on his bed in the darkness, crouched up, hugging his knees, and holding his breath from the strain of thought, he pondered. But the more intensely he thought, the clearer it became to him that it was indubitably so, that in reality, looking upon life, he had forgotten one little facet—that death will come, and all ends; that nothing was even worth beginning, and that there was nothing that could be done about it anyway. Yes, it was awful, but it was so.

"But I am alive still. Now what's to be done? What's to be done?"

he said in despair. He lit a candle, got up cautiously, and went to the mirror and began looking at his face and hair. Yes, there were gray hairs about his temples. He opened his mouth. His back teeth were beginning to decay. He bared his muscular arms. Yes, there was strength in them. But Nikolai, who lay there breathing with what was left of lungs, had had a strong, healthy body too. And suddenly he recalled how they used to go to bed together as children, and how they waited only till Fyodor Bogdanych was out of the room to fling pillows at each other and laugh, laugh irrepressibly, so that even their awe of Fyodor Bogdanych could not check the effervescing, overbrimming sense of life and happiness. "And now that bent, hollow chest . . . and I, not knowing what will become of me, or wherefore . . ."

"K . . . ha! K . . . ha! Hell! Why do you keep fidgeting, why don't you go to sleep?" his brother's voice called to him.

"Oh, I don't know; I'm not sleepy."

"I have had a good sleep, I'm not in a sweat now. Just see, feel my shirt; it's not wet, is it?"

Levin felt, withdrew behind the screen, and put out the candle, but for a long while he could not sleep. The question of how to live had hardly begun to grow a little clearer to him when a new, insoluble question presented itself—death.

"Why, he's dying—yes, he'll die in the spring, and how can I help him? What can I say to him? What do I know about it? I'd even forgotten that it existed at all."

CHAPTER THIRTY-TWO

Levin had long before made the observation that when one is uncomfortable with people from their being excessively amenable and meek, one is apt very soon after to find things intolerable because of their touchiness and irritability. He felt that this was how it would be with his brother. And his brother Nikolai's gentleness did in fact not last for long. The very next morning he began to be irritable, and seemed to be doing his best to find fault with his brother, attacking him on his tenderest points.

Levin felt himself to blame, and could not set things right. He felt that if they had both not kept up appearances but had spoken from the heart—that is to say, had said just what they were thinking and feeling—they would simply have looked into each other's faces, and Konstantin could only have said, "You're dying, you're dying," and Nikolai could only have answered, "I know I'm dying, but I'm afraid, I'm afraid!" And they could have said nothing more if they had said only what was in their hearts. But life like that was impossible, and so Konstantin tried to do what he had been trying to do all his life and never could learn to do, though, as far as he could observe, many people knew so well how to do it, and without it there was no living at all. He tried to say what he was not thinking, but he felt continually that it had a ring of falsehood, that his brother detected him in it, and was exasperated at it.

The third day Nikolai induced his brother to explain his plan to him again, and began not merely attacking it, but intentionally confusing it with communism.

"You've simply borrowed an idea that's not your own, but you've distorted it, and are trying to apply it where it's not applicable."

"But I tell you it has nothing to do with it. They deny the justice of property, of capital, of inheritance, while I do not deny this chief stimulus." (Levin felt disgusted at himself for using such words, but ever since he had been engrossed by his work, he had unconsciously come more and more frequently to use words not Russian.) "All I want is to regulate labor."

"Which means, you've borrowed an idea, stripped it of all that gave it its force, and want to make believe that it's something new," said Nikolai, angrily tugging at his necktie.

"But my idea has nothing in common . . ."

"That, anyway," said Nikolai Levin, with an ironical smile, his eyes flashing malignantly, "has the charm of—what's one to call it?—geometrical symmetry, of clearness, of definiteness. It may be a Utopia. But if once one allows the possibility of making of all the past a *tabula rasa*[1]—no property, no family—then labor would organize itself. But you gain nothing . . ."

---

[1]"Clean slate."

"Why do you mix things up? I've never been a communist."

"But I have, and I consider it premature but rational, and it has a future, just like Christianity in its first centuries."

"All that I maintain is that the labor force ought to be investigated from the point of view of natural science; that is to say, it ought to be studied, its qualities ascertained . . ."

"But that's an utter waste of time. That force finds a certain form of activity itself, according to the stage of its development. There have been slaves first everywhere, then tenants; and we have the share-crop system, rent, and day laborers. What are you trying to find?"

Levin suddenly lost his temper at these words, because at the bottom of his heart he was afraid that it was true—true that he was trying to hold the balance even between communism and the existing forms, and that this was hardly possible.

"I am trying to find means of working productively for myself and for the laborers. I want to organize—" he answered hotly.

"You don't want to organize anything; it's simply just as you've been all your life, that you want to be original, to show that you are not simply exploiting the peasants but have some idea in view."

"Oh, all right, that's what you think—and let me alone!" answered Levin, feeling the muscles of his left cheek twitching uncontrollably.

"You've never had, and never have, convictions; all you want is to please your vanity."

"Oh, very well; then let me alone!"

"And I will let you alone! And it's high time I did, and go to hell! and I'm very sorry I ever came!"

In spite of all Levin's efforts to soothe his brother afterward, Nikolai would listen to nothing he said, declaring that it was better to part, and Konstantin saw that it was simply that life was unbearable to him.

Nikolai was just getting ready to go when Konstantin went in to him again and begged him, rather unnaturally, to forgive him if he had hurt his feelings in any way.

"Ah, generosity!" said Nikolai, and he smiled. "If you want to be right, I can give you that satisfaction. You're right; but I'm going all the same."

It was only at parting that Nikolai kissed him and said, looking with sudden strangeness and seriousness at his brother:

"Anyway, don't remember evil against me, Kostya!" and his voice quivered. These were the only words that had been spoken sincerely between them. Levin knew that those words meant, "You see and you know that I'm in a bad way, and maybe we shall not see each other again." Levin knew this, and the tears gushed from his eyes. He kissed his brother once more, but he could not speak, and knew not what to say.

Three days after his brother's departure, Levin too set off for his foreign tour. Happening to meet Shcherbatsky, Kitty's cousin, in the railway train, Levin greatly astonished him by his depression.

"What's the matter with you?" Shcherbatsky asked him.

"Oh, nothing; there's not much happiness in life."

"Not much? You come with me to Paris instead of to Mulhausen. You shall see how to be happy."

"No, I'm finished with it all. It's time I was dead."

"Well, that's a good one!" said Shcherbatsky, laughing, "why, I'm only just getting ready to begin."

"Yes, I thought the same not long ago, but now I know I shall soon be dead."

Levin said what he had genuinely been thinking of late. He saw nothing but death or the advance toward death in everything. But his cherished scheme only engrossed him all the more. Life had to be got through somehow till death did come. Darkness had fallen upon everything for him; but just because of this darkness he felt that the one guiding clue in the darkness was his work, and he clutched it and clung to it with all his strength.

PART FOUR

CHAPTER ONE

The Karenins, husband and wife, continued living in the same house, met every day, but were complete strangers to one another. Aleksey Aleksandrovich made it a rule to see his wife every day, so that the servants might have no grounds for suppositions, but avoided dining at home. Vronsky was never at Aleksey Aleksandrovich's house, but Anna saw him away from home, and her husband was aware of it.

The position was one of misery for all three; and not one of them would have been equal to enduring this position for a single day if it had not been for the expectation that it would change, that it was merely a temporary painful ordeal which would pass over. Aleksey Aleksandrovich hoped that this passion would pass, as everything does pass, that everyone would forget about it, and his name would remain unsullied. Anna, who was responsible for the situation, and for whom it was more miserable than for anyone, endured it because she not merely hoped, but firmly believed, that it would all very soon be settled and alleviated. She had not the least idea what would settle the situation, but she firmly believed that something would turn up very soon. Vronsky, against his own will or wishes, followed her lead, hoped too that something, apart from his own action, would be sure to solve all difficulties.

In the middle of the winter Vronsky spent a very tiresome week. A foreign prince, who had come on a visit to Petersburg, was put under his charge, and he had to show him the sights worth seeing. Vronsky was of distinguished appearance; he possessed, moreover, the art of behaving with respectful dignity, and was used to dealing with such important dignitaries—that was why he came to be put in charge of the prince. But he felt his duties very irksome. The prince was anxious to miss nothing of which he would be asked at home, had he seen that in Russia? And on his own account he was anxious to enjoy to the utmost all Russian forms of amusement. Vronsky was obliged to be his guide in satisfying both these inclinations. The mornings they spent driving to look at places of interest; the evenings they passed enjoying the national entertainments. The prince rejoiced in health exceptional even among princes. By gymnastics and careful attention to his health he had brought himself to such a point that in spite of his excesses in pleasure he looked as fresh as a big glossy green Dutch cucumber. The prince had traveled a great deal, and considered that one of the chief advantages of modern facilities of communication was the accessibility of the pleasures of all nations.

He had been in Spain, and there had indulged in serenades and had made friends with a Spanish girl who played the mandolin. In Switzerland he had killed a chamois. In England he had galloped in a red coat over hedges and killed two hundred pheasants for a bet. In Turkey he had got into a harem; in India he had hunted on an elephant, and now in Russia he wished to taste all the typically Russian forms of pleasure.

Vronsky, who was, as it were, chief master of ceremonies, was at great pains to arrange all the Russian amusements suggested by various persons to the prince: races, and Russian pancakes, and bear hunts, and troikas, and gypsies, and drinking feasts with the Russian accompaniment of broken crockery. And the prince, with surprising ease, fell in with the Russian spirit, smashed trays full of crockery, sat with a gypsy girl on his knee, and seemed to be asking—what more, and does the whole Russian spirit consist in just this?

In reality, of all the Russian entertainments, the prince liked best French actresses and ballet dancers and white-seal champagne. Vronsky was used to princes, but, either because he had himself changed of late, or because he was in too close proximity to the prince, that week seemed fearfully wearisome to him. The whole of that week he experienced a sensation such as a man might have who had been placed in charge of a dangerous madman, afraid of the madman, and at the same time, from being with him, afraid for his own reason. Vronsky was continually conscious of the necessity of never for a second relaxing the tone of stern official respectfulness, so that he might not himself be insulted. The prince's manner of treating the very people who, to Vronsky's surprise, were ready to descend to any depths to provide him with Russian amusements, was contemptuous. His criticism of Russian women, whom he wished to study, more than once made Vronsky crimson with indignation. The chief reason why the prince was so particularly disagreeable to Vronsky was that he could not help seeing himself in him. And what he saw in this mirror did not gratify his self-esteem. He was a very stupid and very self-satisfied and very healthy and very immaculate man, and nothing else. He was a gentleman—that was true, and Vronsky could not deny it. He was equable and did not cringe before his superiors, was free and ingratiating in his behavior with his equals, and was contemptuously indulgent with his inferiors. Vronsky was himself the same, and regarded it as a great merit to be so. But for this prince he was an inferior, and his contemptuous and indulgent attitude toward himself revolted Vronsky.

"Brainless beef! Can I be like that?" he thought.

Be that as it might, when, on the seventh day, he parted from the prince, who was starting for Moscow, and received his thanks, he was happy to be rid of his uncomfortable situation and the unpleasant reflection of himself. He said good-by to him at the station on their return from a bear hunt, at which they had had a display of Russian prowess kept up all night.

CHAPTER TWO

When he got home, Vronsky found a note from Anna. She wrote:

> I am ill and unhappy. I cannot come out, but cannot go on longer without seeing you. Come this evening. Aleksey Aleksandrovich goes to the council at seven and will be there till ten.

Thinking for an instant of the strangeness of her bidding him to come straight to her, in spite of her husband's insisting on her not receiving him, he decided to go.

Vronsky had that winter got his promotion, was now a colonel, had left the regimental quarters, and was living alone. After having some lunch, he lay down on the sofa immediately, and in five minutes memories of the hideous scenes he had witnessed during the last few days were mixed together and joined to a mental image of Anna and of the peasant who had played an important part in the bear hunt, and Vronsky fell asleep. He awoke in the dark, trembling with horror, and made haste to light a candle. "What was it? What? What was the dreadful thing I dreamed? Yes, yes; I think a short, filthy man with a disheveled beard was stooping down doing something, and all of a sudden he began saying some strange words in French. Yes, there was nothing else in the dream," he said to himself. "But why was it so awful?" He vividly recalled the peasant again and those incomprehensible French words the peasant had uttered, and a chill of horror ran down his spine.

"What nonsense!" thought Vronsky, and glanced at his watch.

It was half-past eight already. He rang for his servant, dressed in haste, and went out onto the steps, completely forgetting the dream, and only worried about being late. As he drove up to the Karenins' entrance he looked at his watch and saw that it was ten minutes to nine. A high, narrow carriage with a pair of grays was standing at the entrance. He recognized Anna's carriage. "She is coming to me," thought Vronsky, "and it's better. I don't like going into that house. But no matter; I can't hide myself," he thought, and with that manner peculiar to him from childhood, as of a man who has nothing to be ashamed of, Vronsky got out of his sleigh and went to the door. The door opened, and the hall porter, with a comforter on his arm, called the carriage. Vronsky, though he did not usually notice details, noticed at this moment the amazed expression with which the porter glanced at him. In the doorway Vronsky almost ran up against Aleksey Aleksandrovich. The gas jet threw its full light on the bloodless, sunken face under the black hat and on the white cravat, brilliant against the beaver of the coat. Karenin's fixed, dull eyes were fastened upon Vronsky's face. Vronsky bowed, and Aleksey Aleksandrovich, compressing his lips as if chewing, lifted his hand to his hat and went out. Vronsky saw him get into the carriage without looking around, pick up the comforter and the opera glasses, and disappear. Vronsky went into the hall. His brows were scowling, and his eyes gleamed with a proud and angry light in them.

"What a situation!" he thought. "If he would fight, would stand up for his honor, I could act, could express my feelings; but this weakness or baseness . . . He puts me in the position of a deceiver, which I never was and never meant to be."

Vronsky's ideas had changed since the day of his conversation with Anna in the Wrede garden. Unconsciously yielding to the weakness of Anna—who had surrendered herself up to him, utterly, and simply looked to him to decide her fate, ready to submit to anything—he had long ceased to think that their union might end as he had thought then. His ambitious plans had retreated into the background again, and feeling that he had got out of that circle of activity in which everything was definite, he had given himself entirely to his passion, and that passion was binding him more and more closely to her.

He was still in the hall when he caught the sound of her retreating footsteps. He knew she had been expecting him, had listened for him, and was now going back to the drawing room.

"No," she cried, on seeing him, and at the first sound of her voice the tears came into her eyes. "No; if things are to go on like this, the end will come much, much too soon."

"What is it, dear one?"

"What? I've been waiting in agony for an hour, two hours. . . No, I won't . . . I can't quarrel with you. Of course you couldn't come. No, I won't." She laid her hands on his shoulders, and looked a long while at him with a profound, passionate, and at the same time searching look. She was studying his face to make up for the time she had not seen him. She was, every time she saw him, comparing the picture she painted of him in her imagination (incomparably superior, impossible in reality) with him as he really was.

CHAPTER THREE

"You met him?" she asked, when they had sat down at the table in the lamplight. "You're punished, you see, for being late."

"Yes; but how did it happen? Wasn't he to be at the council?"

"He had been and came back, and was going out somewhere again. But that's no matter. Don't talk about it. Where have you been? With the prince still?"

She knew every detail of his existence. He was going to say that he had been up all night and had dropped asleep, but looking at her thrilled and rapturous face, he was ashamed. And he said he had had to go to report on the prince's departure.

"But it's over now? He is gone!"

"Thank God it's over! You wouldn't believe how insufferable it's been for me."

"Why so? Isn't it the life all of you, all young men, always lead?" she said, knitting her brows; and taking up the crocheting that was lying on the table, she began drawing the hook out of it, without looking at Vronsky.

"I gave that life up long ago," said he, wondering at the change in her face, and trying to divine its meaning. "And I confess," he said, with a smile, showing his tightly packed white teeth, "watching that life, I didn't like it."

She held the work in her hands, but did not crochet, and looked at him with strange, shining, and hostile eyes.

"This morning Liza came to see me—they're not afraid to call on me in spite of Countess Lydia Ivanovna," she put in—"and she told me about your orgy. How loathsome!"

"I was just going to say—"

She interrupted him.

"Was it that Thérèse you used to know?"

"I was just saying—"

"How disgusting you are, you men! How is it you can't understand that a woman can never forget that," she said, getting more and more angry, and so letting him see the cause of her irritation, "especially a woman who cannot know your life? What do I know? What have I ever known?" she said, "what you tell me. And how do I know whether you tell me the truth? . . ."

"Anna, you hurt me. Don't you trust me? Haven't I told you that I haven't a thought I wouldn't lay bare to you?"

"Yes, yes," she said, evidently trying to suppress her jealous thoughts. "But if only you know how wretched I am! I believe you, I believe you . . . What were you saying?"

But he could not at once recall what he had been going to say. These fits of jealousy, which of late had been more and more frequent with her, horrified him, and however much he tried to disguise the fact, made him feel cold to her, although he knew the cause of her jealousy was her love for him. How often he had told himself that her love was happiness; and now she loved him as a woman can love when love has outweighed for her all the good things of life—and he was much further from happiness than when he had followed her from Moscow. Then he had thought himself unhappy, but happiness was before him; now he felt that the best happiness was already left behind. She was utterly unlike what she had been when he first saw her. Both morally and physically she had changed for the worse. She had broadened out all over, and in her face at the time when she was speaking of the actress there was a malevolent expression of hatred that distorted it. He looked at her as a man looks at a faded flower he has gathered, with difficulty recognizing in it the beauty for which he picked and ruined it. And in spite of this he felt that then, when his love was stronger, he could, if he had greatly wished it, have torn that love out of his heart: but now, when as at that moment it seemed to him he felt no love for her, he knew that what bound him to her could not be broken.

"Well, well, what was it you were going to say about the prince? I have driven away the fiend," she added. The fiend was the name they had given her jealousy. "What did you begin to tell me about the prince? Why did you find it so tiresome?"

"Oh, it was intolerable!" he said, trying to pick up the thread of his interrupted thought. "He does not improve on closer acquaintance. If you want him defined, here he is: a prime, well-fed beast, the kind that wins medals at the cattle shows, and nothing more," he said, with a tone of vexation that interested her.

"No; how so?" she replied. "He's seen a great deal, anyway; he's cultured?"

"It's an utterly different culture—their culture. He's cultivated, one sees, simply to be able to despise culture, as they despise everything but animal pleasures."

"But don't you all care for these animal pleasures?" she said, and again he noticed a dark look in her eyes that avoided him.

"How is it you're defending him?" he said, smiling.

"I'm not defending him, it's nothing to me; but I imagine if you had not cared for those pleasures yourself, you might have got out of them. But if it affords you satisfaction to gaze at Thérèse in the costume of Eve . . ."

"Again, the devil again!" Vronsky said, taking the hand she laid on the table and kissing it.

"Yes; but I can't help it! You don't know what I have suffered waiting for you. I believe I'm not jealous. I'm not jealous: I believe you when you're here; but when you're away somewhere leading your life, so incomprehensible to me . . ."

She turned away from him, pulled the hook at last out of the crochet work, and rapidly, with the help of her forefinger, began working loop after loop of the wool that was dazzling white in the lamplight, while the slender wrist moved swiftly, nervously in the embroidered cuff.

"How was it, then? Where did you meet Aleksey Aleksandrovich?" The tone of her voice was unnatural and jarring.

"We ran up against each other in the doorway."

"And he bowed to you like this?"

She drew a long face and, half-closing her eyes, quickly transformed her expression, folded her hands, and Vronsky suddenly saw in her beautiful face the very expression with which Aleksey Aleksandrovich had bowed to him. He smiled, while she laughed gaily, with that sweet, deep laugh which was one of her greatest charms.

"I don't understand him in the least," said Vronsky. "If after your talk to him at your country house he had broken with you, if he had challenged me—but this I can't understand. How can he put up with such a situation? He feels it, that's evident."

"He?" she said sneeringly. "He's perfectly satisfied."

"Why are we all miserable, when everything might be so happy?"

"Not him. Don't I know him, the falsity in which he's utterly steeped? . . . Could one, with any feeling, live as he is living with me? He understands nothing, and feels nothing. Could a man of any feeling live in the same house with his unfaithful wife? Could he talk to her, call her 'my dear'?"

And again she could not help mimicking him: " 'Anna, *ma chère*; Anna, dear!'

"He's not a man, not a human being—he's a puppet! No one

knows him; but I know him. Oh, if I'd been in his place, I'd long ago have killed, have torn to pieces a wife like me. I wouldn't have said, 'Anna, *ma chère*'! He's not a man, he's an official machine. He doesn't understand that I'm your wife, that he's outside, that he's superfluous . . . Don't let's talk of him! . . ."

"You're unfair, very unfair, dearest," said Vronsky, trying to soothe her. "But never mind, don't let's talk of him. Tell me what you've been doing? What is the matter? What has been wrong with you, and what did the doctor say?"

She looked at him with mocking amusement. Evidently she had hit on other absurd and grotesque aspects in her husband and was awaiting the moment to give expression to them.

But he went on:

"I imagine that it's not illness, but your condition. When will it be?"

The ironical light died away in her eyes, but a different smile, a consciousness of something, he did not know what, and of quiet melancholy, came over her face.

"Soon, soon. You say that our situation is miserable, that we must put an end to it. If you knew how terrible it is to me, what I would give to be able to love you freely and boldly! I should not torture myself and torture you with my jealousy . . . And it will come soon but not as we expect."

And at the thought of how it would come, she was so sorry for herself that tears came into her eyes, and she could not go on. She laid her hand on his sleeve, dazzling and white with its rings in the lamplight.

"It won't come as we suppose. I didn't mean to say this to you, but you've made me. Soon, soon, all will be over, and we shall all, all be at peace, and suffer no more."

"I don't understand," he said, understanding her.

"You asked when? Soon. And I will not live through it. Don't interrupt me!" and she made haste to speak. "I know it; I know for certain. I shall die; and I'm very glad I shall die, and release myself and you."

Tears dropped from her eyes; he bent down over her hand and began kissing it, trying to hide his emotion, which, he knew, had no foundation, though he could not control it.

"Yes, it's better so," she said, tightly gripping his hand. "That's the only way, the only way left us."

He had recovered himself, and lifted his head.

"How absurd! What absurd nonsense you are talking!"

"No, it's the truth."

"What, what's the truth?"

"That I shall die. I have had a dream."

"A dream?" repeated Vronsky, and instantly he recalled the peasant of his dream.

"Yes, a dream," she said. "It's a long while since I dreamed it. I dreamed that I ran into my bedroom, that I had to get something there, to find out something; you know how it is in dreams," she said, her eyes wide with horror; "and in the bedroom, in the corner, stood something."

"Oh, what nonsense! How can you believe . . ."

But she would not let him interrupt her. What she was saying was too important to her.

"And the something turned round, and I saw it was a peasant with a disheveled beard, small, and dreadful-looking. I wanted to run away, but he bent down over a sack, and was fumbling there with his hands . . ."

She showed how he had moved his hands. There was terror in her face. And Vronsky, remembering his dream, felt the same terror filling his soul.

"He was fumbling and kept talking quickly in French, you know: *Il faut le battre, le fer, le broyer, le petrir*[1] . . . And in my horror I tried to wake up, and woke up . . . but woke up in another dream. And I began asking myself what it meant. And Korney said to me: 'In childbirth you'll die, ma'am, you'll die . . .' And I woke up."

"What nonsense, what nonsense!" said Vronsky; but he felt himself that there was no conviction in his voice.

"But let's not talk about it. Ring the bell, I'll have tea. And stay a little, now; it will not be long I shall . . ."

But all at once she stopped. The expression of her face instantaneously changed. Horror and agitation were suddenly replaced by a

---

[1]"The iron must be beaten, pound it, mold it."

look of soft, solemn, blissful attention. He could not comprehend the meaning of the change. She was listening to the stirring of a new life within her.

CHAPTER FOUR

Aleksey Aleksandrovich, after meeting Vronsky on his own steps, drove, as he had intended, to the Italian opera. He sat through two acts there, and saw everyone he had wanted to see. On returning home, he carefully scrutinized the coat stand, and noticing that there was not a military overcoat there, he went as usual to his own room. But, contrary to his usual habit, he did not go to bed; he walked up and down his study till three o'clock in the morning. The feeling of furious anger with his wife, who would not observe the proprieties and keep to the one stipulation he had laid on her, not to receive her lover in her own house, gave him no peace. She had not complied with his request, and he was bound to punish her and carry out his threat—obtain a divorce and take away his son. He knew all the difficulties connected with this course, but he had said he would do it, and now he must carry out his threat. Countess Lydia Ivanovna had hinted that this was the best way out of his situation, and of late the obtaining of divorces had been brought to such perfection that Aleksey Aleksandrovich saw a possibility of overcoming the formal difficulties. Misfortunes never come singly, and the affairs of the reorganization of the native population, and of the irrigation of the lands of the Zaraisky province, had brought such official worries upon Aleksey Aleksandrovich that he had been of late in a continual condition of extreme irritability.

He did not sleep the whole night, and his fury growing in a sort of giant progression, reached its highest limits in the morning. He dressed in haste, and as though carrying his cup full of wrath, and fearing to spill any over, fearing to lose with his wrath the energy necessary for the interview with his wife, he went into her room as soon as he heard she was up.

Anna, who had thought she knew her husband so well, was

amazed at his appearance when he went in to her. His brow was furrowed, and his eyes stared darkly before him, avoiding her eyes; his mouth was tightly and contemptuously shut. In his walk, in his gestures, in the sound of his voice there was a determination and firmness such as his wife had never seen in him. He went into her room, and without greeting her, walked straight up to her writing table and, taking her keys, opened a drawer.

"What do you want?" she cried.

"Your lover's letters," he said.

"They're not here," she said, shutting the drawer; but from that action he saw he had guessed correctly, and roughly pushing away her hand, he quickly snatched a portfolio in which he knew she used to put her most important papers. She tried to pull the portfolio away, but he pushed her back.

"Sit down! I have to speak to you," he said, putting the portfolio under his arm, and squeezing it so tightly with his elbow that his shoulder lifted up. Amazed and intimidated, she gazed at him in silence.

"I told you that I would not allow you to receive your lover in this house."

"I had to see him to . . ."

She stopped, not finding a reason.

"I do not enter into the details of why a woman wants to see her lover."

"I meant, I only . . ." she said, flushing hotly. This coarseness of his angered her, and gave her courage. "Surely you must feel how easy it is for you to insult me?" she said.

"An honest man and an honest woman may be insulted, but to tell a thief he's a thief is simply *la constatation d'un fait*."[1]

"This cruelty is something I did not know in you before."

"You call it cruelty for a husband to give his wife freedom, giving her the honorable protection of his name, simply on the condition of observing the proprieties: is that cruelty?"

---

[1] "The statement of a fact."

"It's worse than cruel—it's base, if you want to know!" Anna cried, in a rush of hatred, and getting up, she began to leave.

"No!" he shrieked in his shrill voice, which rose a note higher than usual, and his big hands clutching her by the arm so violently that red marks were left from the bracelet he was squeezing, he forcibly sat her down in her place.

"Base! If you care to use that word, what is base is to forsake husband and child for a lover, while you eat your husband's bread!"

She bowed her head. She did not say what she had said the evening before to her lover, that *he* was her husband, and her husband was superfluous; she did not even think that. She felt the full justice of his words, and only said softly:

"You cannot describe my position as worse than I feel it to be myself; but what are you saying all this for?"

"What am I saying it for? What for?" he went on, as angrily. "That you may know that since you have not carried out my wishes in regard to observing outward decorum, I will take measures to put an end to this state of affairs."

"Soon, very soon, it will end, anyway," she said; and again, at the thought of death near at hand and now desired, tears came into her eyes.

"It will end sooner than you and your lover have planned! If you must have the satisfaction of animal passion . . ."

"Aleksey Aleksandrovich! I won't say it's not generous, but it's not like a gentleman to strike one who's down."

"Yes, you only think of yourself! But the sufferings of a man who was your husband have no interest for you. You don't care that his whole life is ruined, that he is thuff . . . thuff . . ."

Aleksey Aleksandrovich was speaking so quickly that he stammered, and was utterly unable to articulate the word "suffering." In the end he pronounced it "thuffering." She wanted to laugh, and was immediately ashamed that anything could amuse her at such a moment. And for the first time, for an instant, she felt for him, put herself in his place, and was sorry for him. But what could she say or do? Her head sank, and she sat silent. He too was silent for some time, and then began speaking in a frigid, less shrill voice, emphasizing random words that had no special significance.

"I came to tell you . . ." he said.

She glanced at him. "No, it was my imagination," she thought, recalling the expression of his face when he stumbled over the word "suffering." "No; can a man with those dull eyes, with that self-satisfied complacency, feel anything?"

"I cannot change anything," she whispered.

"I have come to tell you that I am going to Moscow tomorrow, and shall not return again to this house, and you will receive notice of what I decide through the lawyer into whose hands I shall entrust the task of getting a divorce. My son is going to my sister's," said Aleksey Aleksandrovich, with an effort recalling what he had meant to say about his son.

"You take Seryozha to hurt me," she said, looking at him from under brows. "You do not love him . . . Leave me Seryozha!"

"Yes, I have lost even my affection for my son, because he is associated with the revulsion I feel for you. But still I shall take him. Good-by!"

And he was going away, but now she detained him.

"Aleksey Aleksandrovich, leave me Seryozha!" she whispered once more. "I have nothing else to say. Leave Seryozha till my—I shall soon be confined; leave him!"

Aleksey Aleksandrovich flew into a rage, and, snatching his hand from her, he went out of the room without a word.

CHAPTER FIVE

The waiting room of the celebrated Petersburg lawyer was full when Aleksey Aleksandrovich entered it. Three ladies—an old lady, a young lady, and a merchant's wife—and three gentlemen—one a German banker with a ring on his finger, the second a merchant with a beard, and the third a wrathful-looking government clerk in official uniform, with an order[1] on his neck—had obviously been waiting a long while already. Two clerks were writing at tables with scratching pens. The materials of the writing tables, about which

[1]Decoration for service to the State.

Aleksey Aleksandrovich was himself very fastidious, were exceptionally good. He could not help observing this. One of the clerks, without getting up, turned wrathfully to Aleksey Aleksandrovich, half-closing his eyes.

"What do you want?"

He replied that he had to see the lawyer on some business.

"He is engaged," the clerk responded severely, and he pointed with his pen at the persons waiting, and went on writing.

"Can't he spare time to see me?" said Aleksey Aleksandrovich.

"He has no time free; he is always busy. Kindly wait your turn."

"Then I must trouble you to give him my card," Aleksey Aleksandrovich said with dignity, seeing the impossibility of preserving his incognito.

The clerk took the card and, obviously not approving of what he read on it, went to the door.

Aleksey Aleksandrovich was, on principle, in favor of public trials, though for some higher official considerations he disliked the application of the principle in Russia, and disapproved of it, as far as he could disapprove of anything instituted by authority of the Emperor. His whole life had been spent in administrative work, and consequently, when he did not approve of anything, his disapproval was softened by the recognition of the inevitability of mistakes and the possibility of reform in every department. In the new public law courts he disliked the restriction laid on the lawyers conducting cases. But till then he had nothing to do with the courts, and so had disapproved of them simply in theory; now his disapprobation was strengthened by the unpleasant impression made on him in the lawyer's waiting room.

"Coming immediately," said the clerk; and two minutes later there did actually appear in the doorway the large figure of an old solicitor who had been consulting with the lawyer himself.

The lawyer was a little, squat, bald man, with a dark, reddish beard, light-colored long eyebrows, and an overhanging brow. He was attired as though for a wedding, from his cravat to his double watch-chain and patent leather shoes. His face was intelligent and peasant-like, but his clothes were dandified and in bad taste.

"Pray walk in," said the lawyer, addressing Aleksey Aleksandrovich; and, gloomily ushering Karenin in before him, he closed the door.

"Won't you sit down?" He indicated an armchair at a writing table covered with papers. He sat down himself, and, rubbing his little hands with short fingers covered with white hairs, he bent his head to one side. But as soon as he was settled in this position a moth flew over the table. The lawyer, with a swiftness that could never have been expected of him, opened his hands, caught the moth, and resumed his former attitude.

"Before beginning to speak of my business," said Aleksey Aleksandrovich, following the lawyer's movements with astonishment, "I ought to observe that the business about which I have to speak to you is to be strictly private."

The lawyer's drooping reddish mustaches were parted in a scarcely perceptible smile.

"I should not be a lawyer if I could not keep the secrets confided to me. But if you would like proof . . ."

Aleksey Aleksandrovich glanced at his face, and saw that the shrewd, gray eyes were laughing, and seemed to know all about it already.

"You know my name?" Aleksey Aleksandrovich resumed.

"I know you and the good"—again he caught a moth—"work you are doing, like every Russian," said the lawyer, bowing.

Aleksey Aleksandrovich sighed, plucking up his courage. But having once made up his mind he went on in his shrill voice, without timidity or hesitation, accentuating here and there a word.

"I have the misfortune," Aleksey Aleksandrovich began, "to have been deceived in my married life, and I desire to break off all relations with my wife by legal means—that is, to be divorced, but to do this so that my son may not remain with his mother."

The lawyer's gray eyes tried not to laugh, but they were dancing with irrepressible glee, and Aleksey Aleksandrovich saw that it was not simply the delight of a man who has just got a profitable job: there was triumph and joy, there was a gleam like the malignant gleam he saw in his wife's eyes.

"You desire my assistance in securing a divorce?"

"Yes, precisely so; but I ought to warn you that I may be wasting your time and attention. I have come simply to consult you as a preliminary step. I want a divorce, but the form in which it is possible is of great consequence to me. It is very possible that if that form does not correspond with my requirements, I may give up a legal divorce."

"Oh, that's always the case," said the lawyer, "and that's always for you to decide."

He let his eyes rest on Aleksey Aleksandrovich's feet, feeling that he might offend his client by the sight of his irrepressible amusement. He looked at a moth that flew before his nose, and moved his hand, but did not catch it out of regard for Aleksey Aleksandrovich's position.

"Though in their general features our laws on this subject are known to me," pursued Aleksey Aleksandrovich, "I should like to have an idea of the forms in which such things are done in practice."

"You would like," the lawyer, without lifting his eyes, responded, adopting, with a certain satisfaction, the tone of his client's remarks, "for me to lay before you all the methods by which you could secure what you desire?"

And on receiving an assenting nod from Aleksey Aleksandrovich, he went on, stealing a glance now and then at Aleksey Aleksandrovich's face, which was growing red in patches.

"Divorce by our laws," he said, with a slight shade of disapprobation of the laws, "is possible, as you are aware, in the following cases . . . Wait a minute!" he called to a clerk who put his head in at the door, but he got up all the same, said a few words to him, and sat down again. ". . .In the following cases: physical defect in the married parties, desertion without communication for five years," he said, crooking a short finger covered with hair, "adultery" (this word he pronounced with obvious satisfaction), "subdivided as follows" (he continued to crook his fat fingers, though the three cases and their subdivisions could obviously not be classified together): "physical defect of the husband or of the wife, adultery of the husband or of the wife." Since by now all his fingers were used up, he uncrooked all of them and went on: "This is the theoretical view; but I imagine you have done me the honor to apply to me in order to learn its application in practice. And therefore, guided by precedents, I must inform you that in practice cases of divorce may all be reduced to the following—there's no physical defect, I may assume, nor desertion? . . ."

Aleksey Aleksandrovich bowed his head in assent.

". . . May be reduced to the following: adultery of one of the married parties, and the detection in the fact of the guilty party by mutual agreement, and failing such agreement, accidental detection. It must be admitted that the latter case is rarely met with in practice," said the lawyer, and stealing a glance at Aleksey Aleksandrovich he paused, as a man selling pistols, after enlarging on the advantages of each weapon, might await his customer's choice. But Aleksey Aleksandrovich said nothing, and therefore the lawyer went on: "The most usual and simple, the sensible course, I consider, is adultery by mutual consent. I should not permit myself to express it so, speaking with a man of no education," he said, "but I imagine that to you this is comprehensible."

Aleksey Aleksandrovich was, however, so perturbed that he did not immediately comprehend the reasonableness of adultery by mutual consent, and his eyes expressed this uncertainty; but the lawyer promptly came to his assistance.

"People cannot go on living together—here you have a fact. And if both are agreed about it, the details and formalities become a matter of no importance. And at the same time this is the simplest and most certain method."

Aleksey Aleksandrovich fully understood now. But he had religious scruples, which hindered the execution of such a plan.

"That is out of the question in the present case," he said. "Only one alternative is possible: undesigned detection, supported by letters which I have."

At the mention of letters the lawyer pursed his lips, and gave utterance to a thin little compassionate and contemptuous sound.

"Kindly consider," he began, "cases of that kind are, as you are aware, under ecclesiastical jurisdiction; the reverend fathers are fond of going into the minutest details in cases of that kind," he said with a smile, which betrayed his sympathy with the reverend fathers' taste. "Letters may, of course, be a partial confirmation; but detection in the fact, there must be of the most direct kind, that is, by eyewitness.

In fact, if you do me the honor to entrust your confidence to me, you will do well to leave me the choice of the measures to be employed. If one wants the result, one must accept the means."

"If it is so . . ." Aleksey Aleksandrovich began, suddenly turning white; but at that moment the lawyer rose and again went to the door to speak to the intruding clerk.

"Tell her we don't haggle over fees!" he said, and returned to Aleksey Aleksandrovich.

On his way back he caught unobserved another moth. "Nice state my rep curtains will be in by the summer!" he thought, frowning.

"And so you were saying? . . ." he said.

"I will communicate my decision to you by letter," said Aleksey Alexandrovich, getting up, and he clutched at the table. After standing a moment in silence, he said: "From your words I may consequently conclude that a divorce may be obtained? I would ask you to let me know what are your terms."

"It may be obtained if you give me complete liberty of action," said the lawyer, not answering his question. "When can I count on receiving information from you?" he asked, moving toward the door, his eyes and his patent leather shoes shining.

"In a week's time. Your answer as to whether you will undertake to conduct the case, and on what terms, you will be so good as to communicate to me."

"Very good."

The lawyer bowed respectfully, let his client out of the door, and, left alone, gave himself up to his sense of amusement. He felt so mirthful that, contrary to his rules, he made a reduction in his terms to the haggling lady, and gave up catching moths, finally deciding that next winter he must have the furniture covered with velvet, like Sigonin's.

CHAPTER SIX

Aleksey Aleksandrovich had gained a brilliant victory at the meeting of the Commission of the 17th of August, but the consequence of this victory cut the ground from under his feet. The new commission for the inquiry into the condition of the native population in all its branches had been formed and despatched to its destination with an unusual speed and energy inspired by Aleksey Aleksandrovich. Within three months a report was presented. The condition of the natives was investigated in its political, administrative, economic, ethnographic, material, and religious aspects. To all these questions there were answers admirably stated, and answers admitting no shade of doubt, since they were not a product of human thought, always liable to error, but were all the product of official activity. The answers were all based on official data furnished by governors and heads of churches, and founded on the reports of district magistrates and ecclesiastical superintendents, founded in their turn on the reports of parochial overseers and parish priests; and so all of these answers were unhesitating and certain. All such questions as, for instance, of the cause of failure of crops, of the adherence of certain natives to their ancient beliefs, etc.—questions which, but for the convenient intervention of the official machine, are not, and cannot be solved for ages—received full, unhesitating solution. And this solution was in favor of Aleksey Aleksandrovich's contention. But Stremov, who had felt stung to the quick at the last meeting, had, on the reception of the commission's report, resorted to tactics which Aleksey Aleksandrovich had not anticipated. Stremov, bringing with him several other members, went over to Aleksey Aleksandrovich's side, and not contenting himself with warmly defending the measure proposed by Karenin, proposed other more extreme measures in the same direction. These measures, very much exaggerating Aleksey Aleksandrovich's fundamental idea, were passed by the commission, and then the aim of Stremov's tactics became apparent. Carried to an extreme, the measures seemed at once to be so absurd that the highest authorities, and public opinion, and intellectual ladies, and the newspapers, all at the same time attacked them, expressing their indignation both with the measures and their nominal father, Aleksey Aleksandrovich. Stremov drew back, affecting to have blindly followed Karenin, and to be astounded and distressed at what had been done. This meant the defeat of Aleksey Aleksandrovich. But in spite of failing health, in spite of his domestic griefs, he did not give in. There was a split in

the commission. Some members, with Stremov at their head, justified their mistake on the ground that they had put faith in the commission of revision, instituted by Aleksey Aleksandrovich, and
maintained that the report of the commission was rubbish, and simply so much waste paper. Aleksey Aleksandrovich, with a following
of those who saw the danger of so revolutionary an attitude to official documents, persisted in upholding the statements obtained by
the revising commission. In consequence of this, in the higher
spheres, and even in society, all was chaos, and although everyone
was interested, no one could tell whether the natives really were
becoming impoverished and ruined, or whether they were in a
flourishing condition. The position of Aleksey Aleksandrovich due
to this, and partly due to the contempt lavished on him for his wife's
infidelity, became very precarious. And in this position he took an
important resolution. To the astonishment of the commission, he
announced that he would ask permission to go himself to investigate
the question on the spot. And having obtained permission, Aleksey
Aleksandrovich prepared to set off to these remote provinces.

His departure created a great sensation, the more so because just
before he started he officially returned the traveling expense money
allowed him for twelve horses, with which to drive to his destination.

"I think it very noble," Betsy said to the Princess Myahkaya.
"Why take money for post horses when everyone knows that there
are railways everywhere now?"

But Princess Myahkaya did not agree, and the Princess Tverskaya's opinion annoyed her.

"It's all very well for you to talk," said she, "when you have I don't
know how many millions; but I am very glad when my husband goes
on an inspection tour in the summer. It's very good for him and he
enjoys traveling about, and we have an understanding by which I
keep a carriage and coachman on that money."

On his way to the remote provinces Aleksey Aleksandrovich
stopped for three days in Moscow.

The day after his arrival he was driving back from calling on the
governor-general. At the crossing by Gazetny Lane, where there are
always crowds of carriages and sleighs, Aleksey Aleksandrovich suddenly heard his name called out in such a loud and cheerful voice that

he could not help looking around. At the corner of the sidewalk, in a short, stylish overcoat and a low-crowned fashionable hat, jauntily askew, with a smile that showed a gleam of white teeth and red lips, stood Stepan Arkadyevich, radiant, young, and beaming. He called him vigorously and urgently, and insisted on his stopping. He had one arm on the window of a carriage that was stopping at the corner, and out of the window were thrust the heads of a lady in a velvet hat, and two children. Stepan Arkadyevich was smiling and beckoning to his brother-in-law. The lady smiled a kindly smile too, and waved her hand to Aleksey Aleksandrovich. It was Dolly with her children.

Aleksey Aleksandrovich did not want to see anyone in Moscow, and least of all his wife's brother. He raised his hat and would have driven on, but Stepan Arkadyevich told his coachman to stop, and ran across the snow to him.

"Well, what a shame not to have let us know! Been here long? I was at Dussot's yesterday and saw 'Karenin' on the visitor's list, but it never entered my head that it was you," said Stepan Arkadyevich, sticking his head in at the window of the carriage, "or I would have looked you up. I am glad to see you!" he said, knocking one foot against the other to shake off the snow. "What a shame not to let us know!" he repeated.

"I had no time; I am very busy," Aleksey Aleksandrovich responded dryly.

"Come say hello to my wife, she does so want to see you."

Aleksey Aleksandrovich unfolded the comforter in which his frozen feet were wrapped, and getting out of his carriage, he made his way over the snow to Darya Aleksandrovna.

"Why, Aleksey Aleksandrovich, why are you avoiding us like this?" said Dolly, smiling.

"I was very busy. Delighted to see you!" he said in a tone clearly indicating that he was annoyed by it. "How are you?"

"Tell me, how is my darling Anna?"

Aleksey Aleksandrovich mumbled something and was about to leave, but Stepan Arkadyevich stopped him.

"I tell you what we'll do tomorrow. Dolly, ask him to dinner. We'll ask Koznyshev and Pestsov, so as to treat him to our Moscow intelligentsia."

"Yes, please, do come," said Dolly; "we will expect you at five or six o'clock, if you like. How is my darling Anna? How long . . ."

"She is quite well," Aleksey Aleksandrovich mumbled, frowning. "Delighted!" and he moved away toward his carriage.

"You will come?" Dolly called after him.

Aleksey Aleksandrovich said something that Dolly could not catch in the noise of the moving carriages.

"I shall come over tomorrow!" Stepan Arkadyevich shouted to him.

Aleksey Aleksandrovich got into his carriage and buried himself in it so as neither to see nor to be seen.

"Strange fish!" said Stepan Arkadyevich to his wife, and glancing at his watch, he made a motion of his hand before his face, indicating a caress to his wife and children, and walked jauntily along the pavement.

"Stiva! Stiva!" Dolly called, reddening.

He turned around.

"I must get coats, you know, for Grisha and Tanya. Give me the money."

"Never mind; you tell them I'll pay the bill!" and he vanished, nodding genially to an acquaintance who drove by.

CHAPTER SEVEN

The next day was Sunday. Stepan Arkadyevich went to the Bolshoi Theater to a rehearsal of the ballet, and gave Masha Chibisova, a pretty dancer whom he had just taken under his patronage, the coral necklace he had promised her the evening before, and behind the scenery in the dim daylight of the theater, he managed to kiss her pretty little face, radiant over her present. Besides the gift of the necklace, he wanted to arrange their meeting after the ballet. After explaining that he could not come at the beginning of the ballet, he promised he would come for the last act and take her to supper. From the theater Stepan Arkadyevich drove to Okhotny Row, the market, selected himself the fish and asparagus for dinner, and by twelve o'clock was at Dussot's, where he had to see three people, luckily all staying at the same hotel: Levin, who had recently come back from abroad and was staying there; the new head of his department, who had just been promoted to that position and had come on an inspection tour to Moscow; and his brother-in-law, Karenin, whom he must see, so as to be sure of bringing him to dinner.

Stepan Arkadyevich liked dining, but still better he liked to give a dinner, small but very choice, both as regards the food and drink and as regards the selection of guests. He particularly liked the menu of that day's dinner. There would be fresh perch, asparagus, and *la pièce de résistance*—first-rate, but quite plain, roast beef, and the appropriate wines; so much for the eating and drinking. Kitty and Levin would be guests, and so that this might not be too obvious, there would be a girl cousin too, and young Shcherbatsky, and *la pièce de résistance* among the guests—Sergey Koznyshev and Aleksey Aleksandrovich Karenin. Sergey Ivanovich was a Moscow man, and a philosopher; Aleksey Aleksandrovich a Petersburger, and a practical politician. He was asking, too, the well-known eccentric enthusiast Pestsov, a liberal, a great talker, a musician, a historian, and the most delightfully youthful person of fifty, who would be sauce and garnish for Koznyshev and Karenin. He would provoke them and set them off.

The second installment of the forest money had been received from the merchant and was not yet exhausted; Dolly had been very amiable and good-humored of late, and the idea of the dinner pleased Stepan Arkadyevich from every point of view. He was in the most light-hearted mood. There were two circumstances a little unpleasant, but these two circumstances were drowned in the sea of good-humored gaiety which flooded the soul of Stepan Arkadyevich. These two circumstances were: first, that on meeting Aleksey Aleksandrovich the day before in the street, he had noticed that he was cold and reserved with him, and putting together the expression of Aleksey Aleksandrovich's face and the fact that he had not come to see them or let them know of his arrival with the rumors he had heard about Anna and Vronsky, Stepan Arkadyevich guessed that something was wrong between husband and wife.

That was one disagreeable thing. The other slightly disagreeable fact was that the new head of his department, like all new heads, had the reputation already of a terrible person, who got up at six o'clock in the morning, worked like a horse, and insisted on his subordinates working in the same way. Moreover, this new head had the further reputation of being a bear in his manners, and was, according to all rumors, a man of a class in all respects the opposite of that to which his predecessor had belonged, and to which Stepan Arkadyevich had hitherto belonged himself. On the previous day Stepan Arkadyevich had appeared at the office in uniform, and the new chief had been very affable and had talked to him as to an acquaintance. Consequently Stepan Arkadyevich deemed it his duty to call upon him in his frock coat. The thought that the new chief might not give him a warm reception was the other unpleasant thing. But Stepan Arkadyevich instinctively felt that everything would "work out" all right. "They're all people, all men, like us poor sinners; why be nasty and quarrelsome?" he thought as he went into the hotel.

"Good day, Vasily," he said, walking into the corridor with his hat cocked to one side, and addressing a footman he knew; "why, you've let your whiskers grow! Levin, number seven, eh? Take me up, please. And find out whether Count Anichkin" (this was the new head) "is receiving."

"Yes, sir," Vasily responded smiling. "You've not been to see us for a long while."

"I was here yesterday, but at the other entrance. Is this number seven?"

Levin was standing with a peasant from Tver in the middle of the room, measuring a fresh bearskin, when Stepan Arkadyevich went in.

"What! You killed him?" cried Stepan Arkadyevich. "Well done! A she-bear? How are you, Arkhip!"

He shook hands with the peasant and sat down on the edge of a chair without taking off his coat and hat.

"Come, take off your coat and stay a little," said Levin, taking his hat.

"No, I haven't time; I've only looked in for a second," answered Stepan Arkadyevich. He threw open his coat, but afterwards did take it off, and stayed for a whole hour, talking to Levin about hunting and the most intimate subjects.

"Come, tell me, please, what you did abroad? Where have you been?" said Stepan Arkadyevich, when the peasant had gone.

"Oh, I stayed in Germany, in Prussia, in France, and in England—not in the capitals, but in the manufacturing towns, and saw a great deal that was new to me. And I'm glad I went."

"Yes, I knew your idea of the solution of the labor question."

"Not at all: in Russia there can be no labor question. In Russia the question is that of the relation of the working people to the land; though the question exists there too—but there it's a matter of repairing what's been ruined, while with us . . ."

Stepan Arkadyevich listened attentively to Levin.

"Yes, yes!" he said. "It's very possible you're right. But I'm glad you're in good spirits, and are hunting bears, and working, and interested. Shcherbatsky told me another story—he met you—that you were in such a depressed state, talking of nothing but death . . ."

"Well, what of it? I've not given up thinking of death," said Levin. "It's true that it's high time I was dead; and that all this is nonsense. It's the truth I'm telling you. I do value my idea and my work very highly; but in reality only consider this: all this world of ours is nothing but a speck of mildew, which has grown up on a tiny planet. And for us to suppose we can have something great—ideas, work—it's all grains of sand."

"But all that's as old as the hills, my boy!"

"It is old; but do you know, when you grasp this fully, then somehow everything becomes of no consequence. When you understand that you will die tomorrow, if not today, and nothing will be left, then everything is so unimportant! And I consider my ideas very important, but they turn out to be as unimportant, even if they were carried out, as walking around this bearskin. So one goes on living, amusing oneself with hunting, with work—anything so as not to think of death!"

Stepan Arkadyevich smiled a subtle and affectionate smile as he listened to Levin.

"Well, of course! Here you've come round to my point. Do you remember you attacked me for seeking enjoyment in life? Don't be so severe, O moralist!"

"No; all the same, what's fine in life is . . ." Levin hesitated—"Oh, I don't know. All I know is that we shall soon be dead."

"Why so soon?"

"And do you know, there's less charm in life when one thinks of death, but there's more peace."

"On the contrary, the finish is always the best. But I must be going," said Stepan Arkadyevich, getting up for the tenth time.

"Oh, no, stay a while!" said Levin, detaining him. "Now, when shall we see each other again? I'm going tomorrow."

"I'm a prize package! Why, that's just what I came for! You simply must come to dinner with us today. Your brother's coming, and Karenin, my brother-in-law."

"You don't mean to say he's here?" said Levin, and he wanted to inquire about Kitty. He had heard at the beginning of the winter that she was in Petersburg with her sister, the wife of the diplomat, and he did not know whether she had come back or not; but he changed his mind and did not ask. "Whether she's coming or not, I don't care," he said to himself.

"So you'll come?"

"Of course."

"At five o'clock, then, and not in evening dress."

And Stepan Arkadyevich got up and went down below to the new head of his department. Instinct had not misled Stepan Arkadyevich. The terrible new head turned out to be an extremely amiable person, and Stepan Arkadyevich lunched with him and stayed on, so that it was four o'clock before he got to Aleksey Aleksandrovich.

CHAPTER EIGHT

Aleksey Aleksandrovich, on coming back from church service, had spent the whole morning indoors. He had two pieces of business before him that morning: first, to receive and send on a deputation from the native population which was on its way to Petersburg, and now at Moscow; second, to write the promised letter to the lawyer. The deputation, though it had been summoned at Aleksey Aleksandrovich's instigation, was not without its discomforting and even dangerous aspect, and he was glad he had found it in Moscow. The members of this deputation had not the slightest conception of their duty and the part they were to play. They naïvely believed that it was their business to lay before the commission their needs and the actual condition of things, and to ask assistance of the government, and utterly failed to grasp that some of their statements and requests supported the contention of the enemy's side, and so spoiled the whole business. Aleksey Aleksandrovich was busily engaged with them for a long while, drew up a program for them, from which they were not to deviate, and, on dismissing them, wrote a letter to Petersburg for the guidance of the deputation. He had his chief support in this affair in the Countess Lydia Ivanovna. She was a specialist in the matter of deputations, and no one knew better than she how to manage them, and guide them in the proper direction. Having completed this task, Aleksey Aleksandrovich wrote the letter to the lawyer. Without the slightest hesitation he gave him permission to act as he thought best. In the letter he enclosed three of Vronsky's notes to Anna, which were in the portfolio he had taken away.

Since Aleksey Aleksandrovich had left home with the intention of not returning to his family again, and since he had been at the lawyer's and had spoken, though only to one man, of his intention, and especially since he had translated the matter from the world of real life to the world of ink and paper, he had grown more and more used to his own intention, and by now distinctly perceived the feasibility of its execution.

He was sealing the envelope to the lawyer when he heard the loud tones of Stepan Arkadyevich's voice. Stepan Arkadyevich was arguing with Aleksey Aleksandrovich's servant, and insisting on being announced.

"No matter," thought Aleksey Aleksandrovich, "so much the better. I will inform him at once of my position in regard to his sister, and explain why it is that I can't dine with him."

"Come in!" he said loudly, collecting his papers and putting them in the folder.

"There, you see, you're talking nonsense, and he's at home!" responded Stepan Arkadyevich's voice, addressing the servant, who had refused to let him in, and taking off his coat as he went, Oblonsky walked into the room. "Well, I'm awfully glad I've found you! So I hope . . ." Stepan Arkadyevich began cheerfully.

"I cannot come," Aleksey Aleksandrovich said coldly, standing and not asking his visitor to sit down.

Aleksey Aleksandrovich had expected to enter at once into those cold relations in which he ought to be with the brother of a wife against whom he was beginning a suit for divorce. But he had not taken into account the ocean of kindliness brimming over in the heart of Stepan Arkadyevich.

Stepan Arkadyevich opened wide his clear, shining eyes.

"Why can't you? What do you mean?" he asked in perplexity, speaking in French, "Oh, but it's a promise. And we're all counting on you."

"I want to tell you that I can't dine at your house because the family relationship which has existed between us must cease."

"How? How do you mean? What for?" said Stepan Arkadyevich with a smile.

"Because I am beginning an action for divorce against your sister, my wife. I ought to have—"

But before Aleksey Aleksandrovich had time to finish his sentence, Stepan Arkadyevich behaved not at all as he had expected. He groaned and sank into an armchair.

"No, Aleksey Aleksandrovich! What are you saying?" cried Oblonsky, and his suffering was apparent in his face.

"It is so."

"Excuse me, I can't, I can't believe it!"

Aleksey Aleksandrovich sat down, feeling that his words had not had the effect he anticipated, and that it would be unavoidable for him to explain his position, and that, whatever explanations he might make, his relations with his brother-in-law would remain unchanged.

"Yes, I am brought to the painful necessity of seeking a divorce," he said.

"I will say one thing, Aleksey Aleksandrovich. I know you for an excellent, upright man; I know Anna—excuse me, I can't change my opinion of her—for a good, an excellent woman; and so excuse me, I cannot believe it. There is some misunderstanding," said he.

"Oh, if it were merely a misunderstanding!"

"Wait, I understand," interposed Stepan Arkadyevich. "But of course . . . One thing: you must not act in haste. You must not, you must not act in haste!"

"I am not acting in haste," Aleksey Aleksandrovich said coldly, "but one cannot ask advice of anyone in such a matter. I have made up my mind."

"This is awful!" said Stepan Arkadyevich. "I would do one thing, Aleksey Aleksandrovich. I beseech you, do it!" he said. "No action has yet been taken, if I understand rightly. Before you take advice, see my wife, talk to her. She loves Anna like a sister, she loves you, and she's a wonderful woman. For God's sake, talk to her! Do me that favor, I beseech you!"

Aleksey Aleksandrovich pondered, and Stepan Arkadyevich looked at him sympathetically, without interrupting his silence.

"You will go to see her?"

"I don't know. That was just why I have not been to see you. I imagine our relations must change."

"Why so? I don't see that. Allow me to believe that apart from our family connection you have for me, at least in part, the same friendly feeling I have always had for you . . . and sincere esteem," said Stepan Arkadyevich, pressing his hand. "Even if your worst suppositions were correct, I don't—and never would—take on myself to judge either side, and I see no reason why our relations should be affected. But now, do this, come and see my wife."

"Well, we look at the matter differently," said Aleksey Aleksandrovich coldly. "However, we won't discuss it."

"No; why shouldn't you come today to dine, anyway? My wife's expecting you. Please, do come. And, above all, talk it over with her. She's a wonderful woman. For God's sake, on my knees, I implore you!"

"If you so much wish it, I will come," said Aleksey Aleksandrovich, sighing.

And, anxious to change the conversation, he inquired about what interested them both—the new head of Stepan Arkadyevich's department, a man not yet old, who had suddenly been promoted to so high a position.

Aleksey Aleksandrovich had previously felt no liking for Count Anichkin, and had always differed from him in his opinions. But now, from a feeling readily comprehensible to officials—that hatred felt by one who has suffered a defeat in the service for one who has received a promotion, he could not endure him.

"Well, have you seen him?" said Aleksey Aleksandrovich with a malignant smile.

"Of course; he was at our meeting yesterday. He seems to know his work perfectly, and to be very energetic."

"Yes, but what is his energy directed to?" said Aleksey Aleksandrovich. "Is he aiming at doing anything, or simply undoing what's been done? It's the great misfortune of our government—this redtape administration, of which he's a worthy representative."

"Really, I don't know what fault one could find with him. His policy I don't know, but one thing—he's a very nice fellow," answered Stepan Arkadyevich. "I've just been seeing him, and he's really a nice fellow. We lunched together, and I taught him how to make, you know, that drink, wine and oranges. It's so cooling. And it's a wonder he didn't know it. He liked it very much. No, really he's a nice fellow."

Stepan Arkadyevich glanced at his watch.

"Why, good heavens, it's after four already, and I've still got to go to Dolgovushin's! So please come to dinner. You can't imagine how you will grieve my wife and me if you don't."

The way in which Aleksey Aleksandrovich saw his brother-in-law out was very different from the manner in which he had met him.

"I've promised, and I'll come," he answered wearily.

"Believe me, I appreciate it, and I hope you won't regret it," answered Stepan Arkadyevich, smiling.

And, putting on his coat as he went, he patted the footman on the head, chuckled, and went out.

"At five o'clock, and not in evening dress, please," he shouted once more, turning at the door.

CHAPTER NINE

It was past five, and several guests had already arrived, before the host himself got home. He went in together with Sergey Ivanovich

Koznyshev and Pestsov, who had reached the street door at the same moment. These were the two leading representatives of the Moscow intelligentsia, as Oblonsky had called them. Both were men respected for their character and their intelligence. They respected each other, but were in complete and hopeless disagreement upon almost every subject, not because they belonged to opposite parties, but precisely because they were of the same party (their enemies refused to see any distinction between their views); but, in that party, each had his own special shade of opinion. And since no difference is less easily overcome than the difference of opinion about semiabstract questions, they never agreed in any opinion, and had long, indeed, been accustomed to jeer without anger, each at the other's incorrigible aberrations.

They were just going in at the door, talking of the weather, when Stepan Arkadyevich overtook them. Prince Aleksandr Dmitrievich Shcherbatsky, Oblonsky's father-in-law, young Shcherbatsky, Turovtsyn, Kitty, and Karenin were already in the drawing room.

Stepan Arkadyevich saw immediately that things were not going well in the drawing room without him. Darya Aleksandrovna, in her best gray silk gown, obviously worried about the children, who were to have their dinner by themselves in the nursery, and by her husband's absence, was not equal to the task of making the party mix without him. All were sitting like so many priests' daughters on a visit (so the old prince expressed it), obviously wondering why they were there, and pumping up remarks simply to avoid being silent. Turovtsyn—good, simple man—felt unmistakably like a fish out of water, and the smile with which his thick lips greeted Stepan Arkadyevich said as plainly as words: "Well, dear fellow, you have popped me down in a bunch of brains! A drinking party, now, or the Château des Fleurs would be more in my line!" The old prince sat in silence, his bright little eyes watching Karenin from one side, and Stepan Arkadyevich saw that he had already formed a phrase to sum up that politician of whom guests were invited to partake as though he were a sturgeon. Kitty was looking at the door, calling up all her energies to keep from blushing at the entrance of Konstantin Levin. Young Shcherbatsky, who had not been introduced to Karenin, was trying to look as though he were not in the least conscious of it.

Karenin himself had followed the Petersburg fashion for a dinner with ladies and was wearing evening dress and a white tie. Stepan Arkadyevich saw by his face that he had come simply to keep his promise, and was performing a disagreeable duty in being present at this gathering. He was indeed the person chiefly responsible for the chill benumbing all the guests before Stepan Arkadyevich came in.

On entering the drawing room, Stepan Arkadyevich apologized, explaining that he had been detained by that prince who was always the scapegoat for all his absences and latenesses, and in one moment he had made all the guests acquainted with each other, and bringing together Aleksey Aleksandrovich and Sergey Koznyshev, he started them on a discussion of the Russification of Poland, into which they immediately plunged with Pestsov. Slapping Turovtsyn on the shoulder, he whispered something comic in his ear, and set him down by his wife and the old prince. Then he told Kitty she was looking very pretty that evening, and presented Shcherbatsky to Karenin. In a moment he had so kneaded together the social dough that the drawing room became very lively, and there was a merry buzz of voices. Konstantin Levin was the only person who had not arrived. But this was so much the better, as going into the dining room, Stepan Arkadyevich found to his horror that the port and sherry had been procured from Depré, and not from Levé, and directing that the coachman should be sent off as speedily as possible to Levé's, he started back to the drawing room.

In the dining room he was met by Konstantin Levin.

"I'm not late?"

"You can never help being late!" said Stepan Arkadyevich, taking his arm.

"Have you a lot of people? Who's here?" asked Levin, unable to help blushing, as he knocked the snow off his cap with his glove.

"All our own people. Kitty's here. Come along, I'll introduce you to Karenin."

Stepan Arkadyevich, for all his liberal views, was well aware that to meet Karenin was sure to be felt a flattering distinction, and so treated his best friend to this honor. But at that instant Konstantin Levin was not in condition to feel all the gratification of making such an acquaintance. He had not seen Kitty since that memorable evening when he met Vronsky, not counting, that is, the moment when he had had a glimpse of her on the highroad. He had known at the bottom of his heart that he would see her here today. But to keep his thoughts free, he had tried to persuade himself that he did not know it. Now when he heard that she was here, he was suddenly conscious of such delight, and at the same time of such dread, that his breath failed him and he could not utter what he wanted to say.

"What is she like, what is she like? Like what she used to be, or like what she was in the carriage? What if Darya Aleksandrovna told the truth? Why shouldn't it be the truth?" he thought.

"Oh, please, introduce me to Karenin," he said with an effort, and with a desperately determined step he walked into the drawing room and beheld her.

She was not the same as she used to be, nor was she as she had been in the carriage; she was quite different.

She was frightened, shy, shame-faced, and still more charming because of it. She saw him the very instant he walked into the room. She had been expecting him. She was delighted, and so confused at her own delight that there was a moment, the moment when he went up to her sister and glanced again at her, when she, and he, and Dolly, who saw it all, thought she would break down and would begin to cry. She crimsoned, turned white, crimsoned again, and grew faint, waiting with quivering lips for him to come to her. He went up to her, bowed, and held out his hand without speaking. Except for the slight quiver of her lips and the moisture in her eyes that made them brighter, her smile was almost calm as she said:

"How long it is since we've seen each other!" and with desperate determination she pressed his hand with her cold hand.

"You've not seen me, but I've seen you," said Levin, with a radiant smile of happiness. "I saw you when you were driving from the railway station to Yergushovo."

"When?" she asked, wondering.

"You were driving to Yergushovo," said Levin, feeling as if he would sob with the rapture that was flooding his heart. "How dared I associate anything not innocent with this touching creature? And, yes, I do believe it's true what Darya Aleksandrovna told me," he thought.

Stepan Arkadyevich took him by the arm and led him away to Karenin.

"Let me introduce you." He mentioned their names.

"Very glad to meet you again," said Aleksey Aleksandrovich coldly, shaking hands with Levin.

"You are acquainted?" Stepan Arkadyevich asked in surprise.

"We spent three hours together in the train," said Levin, smiling, "but got out, just as in a masquerade, quite mystified—at least I was."

"Nonsense! Come along, please," said Stepan Arkadyevich, pointing in the direction of the dining room.

The men went into the dinning room and went up to a table laid with six kinds of vodka and as many kinds of cheese, some with little silver spades and some without, caviars, herrings, preserves of various kinds, and plates with slices of French bread.

The men stood around the fragrant vodkas and appetizers, and the discussion of the Russification of Poland between Koznyshev, Karenin, and Pestsov died down in anticipation of dinner.

Sergey Ivanovich was unequaled in his skill in winding up the most heated and serious argument by some unexpected pinch of Attic salt[1] that changed the disposition of his opponent. He did this now.

Aleksey Aleksandrovich had been maintaining that the Russification of Poland could be accomplished only as a result of highest principles, which ought to be introduced by the Russian government.

Pestsov insisted that one country can assimilate only when it is more densely populated.

Koznyshev admitted both points, but with limitations. As they were going out of the drawing room to conclude the argument, Koznyshev said, smiling:

"So, then, for the Russification of our foreign populations that is but one method—to bring up as many children as one can. My brother and I are terribly at fault, I see. You married men, especially you, Stepan Arkadyevich, are the real patriots: How many have you?" he said, smiling genially at their host and holding out a tiny vodka glass to him.

[1] I.e., dry, graceful wit.

Everyone laughed, and Stepan Arkadyevich with particular good-humor.

"Oh, yes, that's the best method!" he said, munching cheese and filling the glass before him with a special sort of vodka. The conversation dropped at the jest.

"This cheese is not bad. Shall I give you some?" said the host. "Why, have you been going in for gymnastics again?" he asked Levin, pinching his muscle with his left hand. Levin smiled, bent his arm, and under Stepan Arkadyevich's fingers the muscles bulged like a Dutch cheese, hard as steel, through the fine cloth of the coat.

"What biceps! A real Samson!"

"I imagine great strength is needed for hunting bears," observed Aleksey Aleksandrovich, who had only the mistiest notions about hunting. He cut off and spread with cheese a thin slice of bread fine as a cobweb.

Levin smiled.

"Not at all. Quite the contrary; a child can kill a bear," he said, with a slight bow moving aside for the ladies, who were approaching the table.

"You have killed a bear, I've been told!" said Kitty, vainly trying to catch with her fork a perverse mushroom that would slip away, and setting the lace quivering over her white arm. "Are there bears on your place?" she added, turning her lovely little head to him and smiling.

There was apparently nothing extraordinary in what she said, but what unutterable meaning there was for him in every sound, in every turn of her lips, her eyes, her hand as she said it! There was entreaty for forgiveness, and trust in him and tenderness—soft, timid tenderness—and promise and hope and love for him, which he could not but believe in and which choked him with happiness.

"No, we've been hunting in the Tverskoy province. It was coming back from there that I met your *beau-frère*[2] in the train, or your *beau-frère*'s brother-in-law," he said with a smile. "It was an amusing meeting."

---

[2] "Brother-in-law."

And he began telling with droll good-humor how, after not sleeping all night, he had, wearing an old sheep-lined coat, got into Aleksey Aleksandrovich's compartment.

"The conductor, regardless of the proverb,[3] would have chucked me out on account of my attire; but thereupon I began expressing my feelings in fancy language, and . . . you too," he said, addressing Karenin and forgetting his name, "at first would have ejected me because of the old coat, but afterwards you took my part, for which I am extremely grateful."

"The rights of passengers, generally, to choose their seats are too ill-defined," said Aleksey Aleksandrovich, rubbing the tips of his fingers on his handkerchief.

"I saw you were uncertain about me," said Levin, smiling good-naturedly, "but I made haste to plunge into intellectual conversation to smooth over the defects of my attire."

Sergey Ivanovich, while keeping up a conversation with their hostess, had one ear cocked for his brother, and he glanced askance at him. "What is the matter with him today? Why such a conquering hero?" he thought. He did not know that Levin was feeling as though he had grown wings. Levin knew *she* was listening to his words and that she was glad to listen to him. And this was the only thing that interested him. Not in that room only, but in the whole world, there existed for him only himself, with enormously increased importance and dignity in his own eyes, and here. He felt himself on a pinnacle that made him giddy, and far away down below were all those nice excellent Karenins, Oblonskys, and all the world.

Quite without attracting notice, without glancing at them, as though there were no other places left, Stepan Arkadyevich seated Levin and Kitty side by side.

"Oh, you may as well sit here," he said to Levin.

The dinner was as choice as the china, of which Stepan Arkadyevich was a connoisseur. The *potage Marie-Louise* was a splendid success; the tiny pies eaten with it melted in the mouth and were irreproachable. The two footmen and Matvey, in white cravats, did

[3] I.e.,"Upon meeting, you're judged by your clothes, upon parting, you're judged by your wits."

their duty with the dishes and wines unobtrusively, quietly, and swiftly. On the material side the dinner was a success; it was no less so on the non-material. The conversation, at times general and at times between individuals, never ceased, and toward the end the company was so lively that the men rose from the table still talking, and even Aleksey Aleksandrovich thawed.

CHAPTER TEN

Pestsov liked thrashing an argument out to a conclusion, and was not satisfied with Sergey Ivanovich's words, especially as he felt the injustice of his view.

"I did not mean," he said over the soup, addressing Aleksey Aleksandrovich, "mere density of population alone, but in conjunction with fundamental ideas, and not by means of principles."

"It seems to me," Aleksey Aleksandrovich said languidly, and with no haste, "that's the same thing. In my opinion, influence over another people is possible only to the people which has the higher development, which—"

"But that's just the question," Pestov broke in in his bass.

He was always in a hurry to speak, and seemed always to put his whole soul into what he was saying: "Of what are we to make higher development consist? The English, the French, the Germans—which is at the highest state of development? Which of them will nationalize the other? We see the Rhine provinces have been turned French, but the Germans are not at a lower stage!" he shouted. "There is another law at work there."

"I imagine that the greater influence is always on the side of true civilization," said Aleksey Aleksandrovich, slightly lifting his eyebrows.

"But what are we to lay down as the outward signs of true civilization?" said Pestsov.

"I imagine such signs are generally very well known," said Aleksey Aleksandrovich.

"But are they fully known?" Sergey Ivanovich put in with a subtle smile. "It is the accepted view now that real culture must be purely classical; but we see most intense disputes on each side of the question, and there is no denying that the opposite camp has strong points in its favor."

"You are a classicist, Sergey Ivanovich. Will you have red wine?" said Stepan Arkadyevich.

"I am not expressing my own opinion of either form of culture," Sergey Ivanovich said, holding out his glass with a smile of condescension, as to a child. "I say only that both sides have strong arguments to support them," he went on, addressing Aleksey Aleksandrovich. "My sympathies are classical from education, but in this discussion I am personally unable to arrive at a conclusion. I see no distinct grounds for classical studies being given a pre-eminence over scientific studies."

"The natural sciences have just as great an educational value," put in Pestsov. "Take astronomy, take botany, or zoölogy with its system of general laws."

"I cannot quite agree with that," responded Aleksey Aleksandrovich. "It seems to me that one must admit that the very process of studying the forms of language has a peculiarly favorable influence on intellectual development. Moreover, it cannot be denied that the influence of the classical authors is in the highest degree moral, while, unfortunately, with the study of the natural sciences are associated the false and noxious doctrines which are the curse of our day."

Sergey Ivanovich would have said something, but Pestsov interrupted him in his rich bass. He began warmly contesting the justice of this view. Sergey Ivanovich waited serenely to speak, obviously with a convincing reply ready.

"But," said Sergey Ivanovich, smiling subtly, and addressing Karenin, "one must admit that to weigh all the advantages and disadvantages of classical and scientific education is a difficult task, and the question of which form of education is preferable would not have been so quickly and conclusively decided if there had not been in favor of classical education, as you expressed it just now, its moral—*disons le mot*[1]—antinihilist influence."

"Undoubtedly."

[1]"Let's say the word."

"If it had not been for the distinctive property of antinihilistic influence on the side of classical studies, we should have considered the subject more, have weighed the arguments on both sides," said Sergey Ivanovich with a subtle smile, "we should have given elbow room to both tendencies. But now we know that these little pills of classical learning possess the medicinal property of antinihilism, and we boldly prescribe them to our patients . . . But what if they had no such medicinal property?" he wound up, sprinkling his Attic salt.

At Sergey Ivanovich's little pills, everyone laughed; Turovtsyn especially roared loudly and jovially, glad at last to have found something to laugh at (all he ever looked for in listening to conversation).

Stepan Arkadyevich had not made a mistake in inviting Pestsov. With Pestsov intellectual conversation never flagged for an instant. As soon as Sergey Ivanovich had concluded the conversation with his jest, Pestsov promptly started a new one.

"I can't agree even," said he, "that the government had that aim. The government obviously is guided by abstract considerations, and remains indifferent to the influence its measures may exercise. The education of women, for instance, would naturally be regarded as likely to be harmful, but the government opens schools and universities for women."

And the conversation at once passed to the new subject of the education of women.

Aleksey Aleksandrovich expressed the idea that the education of women is apt to be confused with the emancipation of women, and that it is only so that it can be considered dangerous.

"I consider, on the contrary, that the two questions are inseparably connected together," said Pestsov; "it is a vicious circle. Woman is deprived of rights from lack of education, and the lack of education results from the absence of rights. We must not forget that the subjection of women is so complete, and dates from such ages back, that we are often unwilling to recognize the gulf that separates them from us," said he.

"You said rights," said Sergey Ivanovich, waiting till Pestsov had finished, "meaning the right of sitting on juries, of voting, of presiding at official meetings, the right of entering the civil service, of sitting in parliament . . ."

"Undoubtedly."

"But if women, as a rare exception, can occupy such positions, it seems to me you are wrong in using the expression 'rights.' It would be more correct to say 'duties.' Every man will agree that in performing the functions of a juryman, a town councilor, a telegraph clerk, we feel we are performing duties. And therefore it would be correct to say that women are seeking duties, and quite legitimately. And one can sympathize with this desire to assist in the general labor of man."

"Quite so," Aleksey Aleksandrovich assented. "The question, I imagine, is simply whether they are fitted for such duties."

"They will most likely be perfectly fitted," said Stepan Arkadyevich, "when education has become general among them. We see this—"

"How about the proverb?" said the prince, who had a long while been intent on the conversation, his little comical eyes twinkling. "I can say it before my daughters: her hair is long, because her wit is—"[2]

"Just what they thought of the Negroes before their emancipation!" said Pestsov angrily.

"What seems strange to me is that women should seek fresh duties," said Sergey Ivanovich, "while we see, unhappily, that men usually try to avoid them."

"Duties are bound up with rights—power, money, honor; those are what women are seeking," said Pestov.

"Just as though I should seek the right to be a wet nurse and feel injured because women are paid for the work, while no one will take me," said the old prince.

Turovtsyn exploded in a loud roar of laughter and Sergey Ivanovich regretted that he had not made this comparison. Even Aleksey Aleksandrovich smiled.

"Yes, but a man can't nurse a baby," said Pestsov, "while a woman—"

"No, there was an Englishman who did suckle his baby on board ship," said the old prince, feeling this freedom in conversation permissible before his own daughters.

[2]The full proverb: "Where the hair is long, the wit is short."

"There are many such Englishmen as there would be women officials," said Sergey Ivanovich.

"Yes, but what is a girl to do who has no family?" put in Stepan Arkadyevich, thinking of Masha Chibisova, whom he had had in mind all along in sympathizing with Pestsov and supporting him.

"If the story of such a girl were thoroughly sifted, you would find she had abandoned a family—her own or a sister's, where she might have found a woman's duties," Darya Aleksandrovna broke in unexpectedly in a tone of exasperation, probably suspecting what sort of girl Stepan Arkadyevich was thinking of.

"But we take our stand on principle as the ideal," replied Pestsov in his mellow bass. "Woman desires to have rights, to be independent, educated. She is oppressed, humiliated by the consciousness that this is impossible for her."

"And I'm opposed and humiliated that they won't engage me at the Foundling,"[3] the old prince said again, to the huge delight of Turovtsyn, who in his mirth dropped his asparagus with the thick end in the sauce.

CHAPTER ELEVEN

Everyone took part in the conversation except Kitty and Levin. At first, when they were talking of the influence that one people has on another, there rose to Levin's mind what he had to say on the subject. But these ideas, once of such importance in his eyes, seemed to come into his brain as in a dream, and had now not the slightest interest for him. It even struck him as strange that they should be so eager to talk of what was of no use to anyone. One would have supposed that Kitty, too, would have been interested in what they were saying of the rights and education of women. How often she had mused on the subject, thinking of her friend abroad, Varenka, of her painful state of dependence, how often she had wondered about herself and what would become of her if she did not marry, and how often she had argued with her sister about it! But it did not interest her at all. She

---

[3]I.e., foundling hospital, as a wet nurse.

and Levin had a conversation of their own, yet not a conversation, but a sort of mysterious communication, which brought them every moment nearer, and stirred in both a sense of joyful terror before the unknown into which they were entering.

At first Levin, in answer to Kitty's question how he could have seen her last year in the carriage, told her how he had been coming home from the mowing along the highroad and had met her.

"It was very, very early in the morning. You were probably only just awake. Your mother was asleep in the corner. It was an exquisite morning. I was walking along wondering who it could be in a four-in-hand. It was a splendid team of horses with bells, and in a second you flashed by, and I saw you at the window—you were sitting like this, holding the strings of your cap in both hands, and thinking very deeply about something," he said, smiling. "How I should like to know what you were thinking about then! Something important?"

"Wasn't I dreadfully untidy?" she wondered, but seeing the smile of ecstasy these reminiscences called up, she felt that the impression she had made had been very good. She blushed and laughed with delight: "Really I don't remember."

"How nicely Turovtsyn laughs!" said Levin, admiring his moist eyes and shaking chest.

"Have you known him long?" asked Kitty.

"Oh, everyone knows him!"

"And I see you think he's a horrid man?"

"Not horrid, but worthless."

"Oh, you're wrong! And you must stop thinking so at once!" said Kitty. "I used to have a very poor opinion of him too, but he, he's an awfully nice and wonderfully goodhearted man. He has a heart of gold."

"How could you find out what sort of heart he has?"

"We are great friends. I know him very well. Last winter soon after . . . you came to see us," she said, with a guilty and at the same time confiding smile, "all Dolly's children had scarlet fever, and he happened to come and see her. And just imagine," she said in a whisper, "he felt so sorry for her that he stayed and began to help her look after the children. Yes, and for three weeks he was with them, and looked after the children like a nurse."

"I am telling Konstantin Dmitrievich about Turovtsyn in the scarlet fever," she said, bending over to her sister.

"Yes, it was wonderful, noble!" said Dolly, glancing toward Turovtsyn, who had become aware they were talking of him and smiling gently to him. Levin glanced once more at Turovtsyn, and wondered how it was he had not realized all this man's goodness before.

"I'm sorry, I'm sorry, and I'll never think ill of people again!" he said gaily, genuinely expressing what he felt at the moment.

CHAPTER TWELVE

Connected with the conversation that had sprung up on the rights of women there were certain questions as to the inequality of rights in marriages improper to discuss before the ladies. Pestsov had several times during dinner touched upon these questions, but Sergey Ivanovich and Stepan Arkadyevich carefully drew him off them.

When they rose from the table and the ladies had gone out, Pestsov did not follow them, but addressing Aleksey Aleksandrovich, began to expound the chief ground of inequality. The inequality in marriage, in his opinion, lay in the fact that the infidelity of the wife and the infidelity of the husband are punished unequally, both by the law and by public opinion. Stepan Arkadyevich went hurriedly up to Aleksey Aleksandrovich and offered him a cigar.

"No, I don't smoke," Aleksey Aleksandrovich answered calmly, and as though purposely wishing to show that he was not afraid of the subject, he turned to Pestsov with a chilly smile.

"I imagine that such a view has a foundation in the very nature of things," he said, about to go into the drawing room. But at this point Turovtsyn suddenly and unexpectedly broke into the conversation, addressing Aleksey Aleksandrovich.

"You heard, perhaps, about Pryachnikov?" said Turovtsyn, warmed up by the champagne he had drunk, and long waiting for an opportunity to break the silence that had weighed on him. "Vasya Pryachnikov," he said, with a good-natured smile on his damp, red lips, addressing himself principally to the most important guest,

Aleksey Aleksandrovich. "They told me today he fought a duel with Kvytsky at Tver, and killed him."

Just as it always seems that one bruises oneself on a sore place, so Stepan Arkadyevich felt now that the conversation would by ill luck fall every moment on Aleksey Aleksandrovich's sore spot. He would again have got his brother-in-law away, but Aleksey Aleksandrovich himself inquired, with curiosity:

"What did Pryachnikov fight about?"

"His wife. Acted like a man, he did! Challenged and shot him!"

"Ah!" said Aleksey Aleksandrovich indifferently, and lifting his eyebrows, he went into the drawing room.

"How glad I am you have come," Dolly said with a frightened smile, meeting him in the outer drawing room. "I must talk to you. Let's sit here."

Aleksey Aleksandrovich, with the same expression of indifference given him by his lifted eyebrows, sat down beside Darya Aleksandrovna, and smiled affectedly.

"It's fortunate," said he, "especially as I was meaning to ask you to excuse me, and to be leaving. I have to start tomorrow."

Darya Aleksandrovna was firmly convinced of Anna's innocence, and she felt herself growing pale and her lips quivering with anger at this cold, unfeeling man who was so calmly intending to ruin her innocent friend.

"Aleksey Aleksandrovich," she said, with desperate resolution, looking him in the face, "I asked you about Anna; you made me no answer. How is she?"

"She is, I believe, quite well, Darya Aleksandrovna," replied Aleksey Aleksandrovich, not looking at her.

"Aleksey Aleksandrovich, forgive me, I have no right . . . but I love Anna as a sister, and esteem her; I beg, I beseech you to tell me what is wrong between you? What fault do you find with her?"

Aleksey Aleksandrovich frowned, and almost closing his eyes, he lowered his head.

"I presume that your husband has told you the grounds on which I consider it necessary to change my relations with Anna Arkadyevna?" he said, not looking her in the face, but eyeing with displeasure Shcherbatsky, who was walking across the drawing room.

"I don't believe it, I don't believe it, I can't believe it!" Dolly said, clasping her bony hands before her with a vigorous gesture. She rose quickly, and laid her hand on Aleksey Aleksandrovich's sleeve. "We shall be disturbed here. Come this way, please."

Dolly's agitation had an effect on Aleksey Aleksandrovich. He got up and submissively followed her to the classroom. They sat down at a table covered with an oilcloth cut in slits by penknives.

"I don't, I don't believe it!" Dolly said, trying to catch his glance that avoided her.

"One cannot disbelieve facts, Darya Alexandrovna," said he, with an emphasis on the word "facts."

"But what has she done?" said Darya Aleksandrovna. "What precisely has she done?"

"She has forsaken her duty, and deceived her husband. That's what she has done," said he.

"No, no, it can't be! No, for God's sake, you are mistaken," said Dolly, putting her hands to her temples and closing her eyes.

Aleksey Aleksandrovich smiled coldly, with his lips alone, meaning to signify to her and himself the firmness of his conviction; but this warm defense, though it could not shake him, reopened his wound. He began to speak with greater heat.

"It is extremely difficult to be mistaken when a wife herself informs her husband of the fact—informs him that eight years of her life, and a son, all that's a mistake, and that she wants to begin life again," he said angrily, with a snort.

"Anna and sin—I cannot connect them, I cannot believe it!"

"Darya Aleksandrovna," he said, now looking straight into Dolly's kindly, troubled face, and feeling that his tongue was being loosened in spite of himself, "I would give a great deal for doubt to be still possible. When I doubted, I was miserable, but it was better than now. When I doubted, I had hope; but now there is no hope, and still I doubt everything. I am in such doubt of everything that I even hate my son, and sometimes do not believe he is my son. I am very unhappy."

He had no need to say that. Darya Aleksandrovna had seen that as soon as he glanced into her face; and she felt sorry for him, and her faith in the innocence of her friend began to totter.

"Oh, this is awful, awful! But can it be true that you are resolved on a divorce?"

"I am resolved on extreme measures. There is nothing else for me to do."

"Nothing else to do, nothing else to do . . ." she replied, with tears in her eyes. "Oh no, don't say nothing else to do!" she said.

"What is horrible in a trouble of this kind is that one cannot, as in any other—in loss, in death—bear one's trouble in peace, but that one must act," said he, as though guessing her thought. "One must get out of the humiliating position in which one is placed; one can't live *à trois*."[1]

"I understand, I quite understand that," said Dolly, and her head sank. She was silent for a little, thinking of herself, of her own grief in her family, and all at once, with an impulsive movement, she raised her head and clasped her hands with an imploring gesture. "But wait! You are a Christian. Think of her! What will become of her if you cast her off?"

"I have thought, Darya Aleksandrovna, I have thought a great deal," said Aleksey Aleksandrovich. His face turned red in patches, and his dim eyes looked straight before him. Darya Aleksandrovna at that moment pitied him with all her heart. "That was what I did when she herself made known to me my humiliation; I left everything as before. I gave her a chance to reform, I tried to save her. And with what result? She would not regard the slightest request—that she should observe decorum," he said, getting heated. "One may save anyone who does not want to be ruined; but if the whole nature is so corrupt, so depraved, that ruin itself seems to her salvation, what's to be done?"

"Anything, only not divorce!" answered Darya Aleksandrovna.

"But what is anything?"

"No, it is awful! She will be no one's wife; she will be lost!"

"What can I do?" said Aleksey Aleksandrovich, raising his shoulders and his eyebrows. The recollection of his wife's last act had so incensed him that he had become cold, as at the beginning of the

---

[1] "Three together."

conversation. "I am very grateful for your sympathy, but I must be going," he said, getting up.

"No, wait a minute. You must not ruin her. Wait! I will tell you about myself. I was married, and my husband deceived me; in anger and jealousy, I would have given up everything, I would myself . . . But I came to myself again; and who did it? Anna saved me. And here I am living on. The children are growing up, my husband has come back to his family, and feels his fault, is growing purer, better, and I live on . . . I have forgiven it, and you ought to forgive!"

Aleksey Aleksandrovich heard her, but her words had no effect on him now. All the hatred of that day when he had resolved on a divorce had sprung up again in his soul. He shook himself, and said in a shrill, loud voice:

"Forgive I cannot, and do not wish to, and I regard it as wrong. I have done everything for this woman, and she trampled it all in the mud to which she is akin. I am not a spiteful man, I have never hated anyone, but I hate her with my whole soul, and I cannot even forgive her, because I hate her too much for all the wrong she has done me!" he said, with tones of hatred in his voice.

"Love them that hate you . . ." Darya Aleksandrovna whispered timorously.

Aleksey Aleksandrovich smiled contemptuously. That he knew long ago, but it could not be applied to his case.

"Love them that hate you, but to love those one hates is impossible. Forgive me for having troubled you. Everyone has enough to bear in his own grief!" And regaining his self-possession, Aleksey Aleksandrovich quietly look leave and went away.

CHAPTER THIRTEEN

When they rose from the table, Levin would have liked to follow Kitty into the drawing room; but he was afraid she might dislike this, because he would be too obviously paying her attention. He remained in the little ring of men, taking part in the general conversation and, without looking at Kitty, was aware of her movements, her looks, and the place where she was in the drawing room.

He did at once, and without the smallest effort, keep the promise he had made her—always to think well of all men, and to like everyone always. The conversation fell on the village commune, in which Pestsov saw a sort of special principle, called by him "the choral principle." Levin did not agree with Pestsov, nor with his brother, who had a special attitude of his own, both admitting and not admitting the significance of the Russian commune. But he talked to them, simply trying to reconcile and soften their differences. He was not in the least interested in what he said himself, and even less so in what they said; all he wanted was that they and everyone should be happy and contented. He knew now the one thing of importance; and that one thing was at first there, in the drawing room, and then began moving across and came to a stop at the door. Without turning around he felt the eyes fixed on him, and the smile, and he could not help turning around. She was standing in the doorway with Shcherbatsky, looking at him.

"I thought you were going toward the piano," said he, going up to her. "That's something I miss in the country—music."

"No; we only came to fetch you and thank you," she said, rewarding him with a smile that was like a gift, "for coming. Why do they want to argue? No one ever convinces anyone, you know."

"Yes; that's true," said Levin; "it generally happens that one argues warmly simply because one can't make out what one's opponent wants to prove."

Levin had often noticed in discussions between the most intelligent people that after enormous efforts, and an enormous expenditure of logical subtleties and words, the disputants finally came to be aware that what they had so long been struggling to prove to one another had long ago, from the beginning of the argument, been known to both, but that they liked different things, and would not define what they liked for fear of its being attacked. He had often had the experience of suddenly in a discussion grasping what it was his opponent liked and at once liking it too, and immediately he found himself agreeing, and then all arguments fell away as useless. Sometimes, too, he had experienced the opposite, expressing at last what he liked himself, which he was devising arguments to defend, and, chancing to express it well and genuinely, he had found his opponent at once agreeing and ceasing to dispute his position. He tried to say this.

She knitted her brow, trying to understand. But as soon as he began to illustrate his meaning, she understood at once.

"I know: one must find out what he is arguing for, what is precious to him, then one can . . ."

She had completely guessed and expressed his badly expressed idea. Levin smiled joyfully; he was struck by this transition from the confused, verbose discussion with Pestsov and his brother to this laconic, clear, almost wordless communication of the most complex ideas.

Shcherbatsky moved away from them, and Kitty, going up to a card table, sat down and, picking up the chalk, began drawing spirals over the new green cloth.

They began again on the subject that had been started at dinner—the liberty and occupations of women. Levin was of the opinion of Darya Aleksandrovna, that a girl who did not marry should find a woman's duties in a family. He supported this view by the fact that no family can get on without women to help; that in every family, poor or rich, there are and must be nurses, either relations or hired.

"No," said Kitty, blushing, but looking at him all the more boldly with her truthful eyes; "a girl may be in such a situation that she cannot live in the family without humiliation, while she herself . . ."

At the hint he understood her.

"Oh, yes," he said. "Yes, yes, yes—you're right; you're right!"

And he saw all that Pestsov had been maintaining at dinner about the freedom of woman, simply from getting a glimpse of the terror of an old maid's existence and its humiliation in Kitty's heart; and loving her, he felt that terror and humiliation, and at once gave up his arguments.

A silence followed. She was still drawing with the chalk on the table. Her eyes were shining with a soft light. Under the influence of her mood he felt in all his being a continually growing tension of happiness.

"Ah! I've scribbled all over the table!" she said, and laying down the chalk, she made a movement as though to get up.

"What! Shall I be left alone—without her?" he thought with horror, and he took the chalk. "Wait a minute," he said, sitting down to the table. "I've long wanted to ask you one thing."

He looked straight into her caressing, though frightened eyes.

"Please, ask it."

"Here," he said; and he wrote the initial letters *w, y, t, m, i, c, n, b, d, t, m, n, o, t.* These letters meant, "When you told me it could never be, did that mean never, or then?" There seemed no likelihood that she could make out this complicated sentence; but he looked at her as though his life depended on her understanding the words. She glanced at him seriously, then leaned her puckered brow on her hands and began to read. Once or twice she stole a look at him, as though asking him, "Is it what I think?"

"I understand," she said, flushing a little.

"What is this word?" he said, pointing to the *n* that stood for *never*.

"It means *never*," she said; "but that's not true!"

He quickly rubbed out what he had written, gave her the chalk, and stood up. She wrote *t, i, c, n, a, d.*

Dolly was completely comforted in the depression caused by her conversation with Aleksey Aleksandrovich when she caught sight of the two figures: Kitty with the chalk in her hand, with a shy and happy smile looking up at Levin, and his handsome figure bending over the table with glowing eyes fastened one minute on the table and the next on her. He was suddenly radiant: he had understood. It meant, "Then I could not answer differently."

He glanced at her questioningly, timidly.

"Only then?"

"Yes," her smile answered.

"And n . . . and now?" he asked.

"Well, read this. I'll tell you what I would like—would like so much!" She wrote the initial letters *i, y, c, f, a, f, w, h.* This meant, "If you could forget and forgive what happened."

He snatched the chalk with nervous, trembling fingers, and, breaking it, wrote the initial letters of the following phrase, "I have nothing to forget and to forgive; I have never ceased to love you."

She glanced at him with a smile that did not waver.

"I understand," she said in a whisper.

He sat down and wrote a long phrase. She understood it all, and without asking him "Is it this?" took the chalk and at once answered.

For a long while he could not understand what she had written, and often looked into her eyes. He was stupefied with happiness. He could not supply the words she had meant; but in her charming eyes, beaming with happiness, he saw all he needed to know. And he wrote three letters. But he had hardly finished writing when she read them over her arm, and herself finished and wrote the answer, "Yes."

"You're playing *secrétaire*?" said the old prince. "But we must really be getting along if you want to be in time at the theater."

Levin got up and escorted Kitty to the door.

In their conversation everything had been said; it had been said that she loved him, and that she would tell her father and mother that he would come tomorrow morning.

CHAPTER FOURTEEN

When Kitty had gone and Levin was left alone, he felt such uneasiness without her and such an impatient longing to get as quickly, as quickly as possible, to tomorrow morning, when he would see her again and be plighted to her forever, that he felt afraid, as though of death, of those fourteen hours that he had to get through without her. It was essential for him to be with someone to talk to, so as not to be left alone, to kill time. Stepan Arkadyevich would have been the companion most congenial to him but he was going out, he said, to a soirée, in reality to the ballet. Levin had time only to tell him he was happy, and that he loved him, and would never, never forget what he had done for him. The eyes and the smile of Stepan Arkadyevich showed Levin that he comprehended that feeling correctly.

"Oh, so it's not time to die yet?" said Stepan Arkadyevich, pressing Levin's hand with emotion.

"N-n-no!" said Levin.

Darya Aleksandrovna too, as she said good-by to him, seemed to congratulate him, saying, "How glad I am you have met Kitty again! One must value old friends." Levin did not like these words of Darya

Aleksandrovna's. She could not understand how lofty and beyond her it all was, and she ought not to have dared to allude to it. Levin said good-by to them, but, not to be left alone, he attached himself to his brother.

"Where are you going?"

"I'm going to a meeting."

"Well, I'll come with you. Can I?"

"What for? Yes, come along," said Sergey Ivanovich, smiling, "What is the matter with you today?"

"With me? Happiness is the matter with me!" said Levin, letting down the window of the carriage they were driving in. "You don't mind?—it's so stifling. It's happiness is the matter with me! Why is it you have never married?"

Sergey Ivanovich smiled.

"I am very glad, she seems a nice gi—" Sergey Ivanovich was beginning.

"Don't say it! Don't say it!" shouted Levin, clutching at the collar of his fur coat with both hands, and muffling him up in it. "She's a nice girl" were such simple, humble words, so out of harmony with his feeling.

Sergey Ivanovich laughed outright a merry laugh, which was rare with him.

"Well, anyway, I may say that I'm very glad of it."

"That you may do tomorrow, tomorrow, and nothing more! 'Nothing, nothing, silence,' "[1] said Levin, and muffling him once more in his fur coat, he added: "I like you so much! Well, is it possible for me to be present at the meeting?"

"Of course it is."

"What is your discussion about today?" asked Levin, never ceasing smiling.

They arrived at the meeting. Levin heard the secretary hesitatingly read the minutes which he obviously did not himself understand; but Levin saw from this secretary's face what a good, nice, kind-hearted person he was. This was evident from his confusion and embarrassment in reading the minutes. Then the discussion began.

[1] From Gogol's *Diary of a Madman.*

They were disputing about the misappropriation of certain sums and the laying of certain pipes, and Sergey Ivanovich was very cutting to two members, and said something at great length with an air of triumph; and another member, scribbling something on a bit of paper, began timidly at first, but afterwards answered him very venomously and charmingly. And then Sviazhsky (he was there too) said something, very handsomely and nobly. Levin listened to them, and saw clearly that these missing sums and these pipes were not anything real, and that these people were not at all angry but were all the nicest, kindest people, and everything was as happy and charming as possible between them. They did no harm to anyone, and were all enjoying it. What struck Levin was that he could see through them all today, and from little, almost imperceptible signs he knew the soul of each, and saw distinctly that they were all good at heart. And they were all extremely fond of Levin, in particular, that day. That was evident from the way they spoke to him, from the friendly, affectionate way even those he did not know looked at him.

"Well, did you like it?" Sergey Ivanovich asked him.

"Very much. I never supposed it was so interesting! Marvelous! Splendid!"

Sviazhsky went up to Levin and invited him to have tea with him. Levin was utterly at a loss to comprehend or recall what it was he had disliked in Sviazhsky, what he had failed to find in him. He was an intelligent and wonderfully good-hearted man.

"Most delighted," he said, and asked after his wife and sister-in-law. And from a strange association of ideas, because in his imagination the idea of Sviazhsky's sister-in-law was connected with marriage, it occurred to him that there was no one to whom he could more suitably speak of his happiness, and he was very glad to go and see them.

Sviazhsky questioned him about his improvements on his estate, presupposing, as he always did, that there was no possibility of doing anything not done already in Europe, and now this did not in the least annoy Levin. On the contrary, he felt that Sviazhsky was right, that the whole business was of little value, and he saw the wonderful softness and consideration with which Sviazhsky avoided fully expressing his correct view. The ladies of the Sviazhsky household were particularly delightful. It seemed to Levin that they knew all about it already and sympathized with him, saying nothing merely from delicacy. He stayed with them one hour, two, three, talking of all sorts of subjects but the one thing that filled his heart, and did not observe that he was boring them dreadfully, and that it was long past their bedtime.

Sviazhsky went with him into the hall, yawning and wondering at the strange mood his friend was in. It was past one o'clock. Levin went back to his hotel, and was dismayed at the thought that, all alone now with his impatience, he had ten hours still left to get through. The servant, whose turn it was to be up all night, lighted his candles, and would have gone away, but Levin stopped him. This servant, Yegor, whom Levin had noticed before, struck him as a very intelligent, excellent, and, above all, good-hearted man.

"Well, Yegor, it's hard work not sleeping, isn't it?"

"One's got to put up with it! It's part of our work, you see. In a gentleman's house it's easier; but then here one makes more."

It appeared that Yegor had a family, three boys and a daughter, a seamstress, whom he wanted to marry to a salesman in a saddler's shop.

Levin, on hearing this, informed Yegor that, in his opinion, in marriage the main thing was love, and that with love one would always be happy, for happiness lies only within oneself.

Yegor listened attentively, and obviously quite took in Levin's idea, but by way of assent to it he enunciated, greatly to Levin's surprise, the observation that when he had lived with good masters he had always been satisfied with his masters, and now was perfectly satisfied with his employer, though he was a Frenchman.

"Wonderfully good-hearted fellow!" thought Levin.

"Well, but you yourself, Yegor, when you got married, did you love your wife?"

"Ay! And why not?" responded Yegor.

And Levin saw that Yegor too was in an excited state and intended to express all his most heartfelt emotions.

"My life, too, has been a wonderful one. From a child up. . ." he was beginning with flashing eyes, apparently catching Levin's enthusiasm, just as people catch yawning.

But at that moment a ring was heard. Yegor departed, and Levin was left alone. He had eaten scarcely anything at dinner, had refused tea and supper at Sviazhsky's, but he was incapable of thinking of supper. He had not slept the previous night, but was incapable of thinking of sleep either. His room was cold, but he was oppressed by heat. He opened both the movable panes in his window and sat down to the table opposite the open panes. Over the snow-covered roofs could be seen a gilt fretwork cross decorated with chains, and above it the rising triangle of the Charioteer with the yellowish light of Capella. He gazed at the cross, then at the stars, drank in the fresh freezing air that flowed evenly into the room, and followed as through in a dream the images and memories that rose in his imagination. At four o'clock he heard steps in the passage and peeped out at the door. It was the gambler Myaskin, whom he knew, coming from the club. He walked gloomily, frowning and coughing. "Poor, unlucky fellow!" thought Levin, and tears came into his eyes from love and pity for this man. He would have talked with him, comforted him, but remembering that he had nothing but his shirt on, he changed his mind and sat down again at the open pane to bathe in the cold air and gaze at the exquisite lines of the cross, silent, but full of meaning for him, and the rising bright yellow star. At seven o'clock there was a noise of people polishing the floors, and bells ringing for service, and Levin felt that he was beginning to get frozen. He closed the pane, washed, dressed, and went out into the street.

CHAPTER FIFTEEN

The streets were still empty. Levin went to the Shcherbatskys'. The visitors' doors were closed and everyone was asleep. He walked back, went into his room again, and asked for coffee. The day servant, not Yegor this time, brought it to him. Levin would have entered into conversation with him, but a bell rang for the servant, and he went out. Levin tried to drink coffee and put a piece of roll in his mouth, but his mouth was quite at a loss as to what to do with it. Levin, spitting out the roll, put on his coat and went out again for a walk. It was nine o'clock when he reached the Shcherbatskys' steps the second time. In the house they were just up, and the cook came out to go marketing. He had to get through at least two hours more.

All that night and morning Levin lived perfectly unconsciously, and felt perfectly lifted out of the conditions of material life. He had eaten nothing for a whole day, he had not slept for two nights, had spent several hours undressed in the frozen air, and felt not simply fresher and stronger than ever, but utterly independent of his body; he moved without effort of his muscles, and felt as if he could do anything. He was convinced he could fly upward or lift the corner of the house, if need be. He spent the remainder of the time in the street, incessantly looking at his watch and gazing about him.

And what he saw then, he never saw again. Especially the children going to school, the bluish pigeons flying down from the roof to the sidewalk, and the little loaves covered with flour, thrust out by an unseen hand—all touched him. Those loaves, those pigeons, and those two boys were not earthly creatures. It all happened at the same time: a boy ran toward a dove and glanced smiling at Levin; the dove with a whir of her wings, darted away, flashing in the sun amid grains of snow that quivered in the air, while from a little window there came a smell of fresh-baked bread, and the loaves were put out. All of this together was so extraordinarily nice that Levin laughed and cried with delight. Going a long way round by Gazetny Lane and Kislovka, he went back again to the hotel, and putting his watch before him, he sat down to wait for twelve o'clock. In the next room they were talking about some sort of machines, and swindling, and coughing their morning coughs. They did not realize that the hand was near twelve. The hand reached it. Levin went out onto the steps. The sleigh drivers obviously knew all about it. They crowded around Levin with happy faces, quarreling among themselves, and offering their services. Trying not to offend the other sleigh drivers, and promising to drive with them too, Levin took one and told him to drive to the Shcherbatskys'. The sleigh driver was splendid in a white shirt collar sticking out over his overcoat and fitting tightly around his strong, thick, red neck. The sleigh was high and comfortable, altogether one the likes of which Levin never drove in after, and the horse was a good one, and tried to gallop but didn't seem to move.

The driver knew the Shcherbatskys' house, and drew up at the entrance with a curve of his arm and a "Wo!" especially indicative of respect for his fare. The Shcherbatskys' hall porter certainly knew all about it. This was evident from the smile in his eyes and the way he said:

"Well, it's a long while since you've been to see us, Konstantin Dmitrievich!"

Not only did he know all about it, but he was unmistakably delighted and making efforts to conceal his joy. Looking into his kindly old eyes, Levin realized something new even in his happiness.

"Are they up?"

"Please walk in! Leave it here," said he, smiling, as Levin would have come back to take his hat. That meant something.

"To whom shall I announce your honor?" asked the footman.

The footman, though a young man, and one of the new school of footmen, a dandy, was a very kind-hearted, good fellow, and he too knew all about it.

"The princess . . . the prince . . . the young princess . . ." said Levin.

The first person he saw was Mademoiselle Linon. She walked across the room, and her ringlets and her face were beaming. He had only just spoken to her, when suddenly he heard the rustle of a skirt at the door, and Mademoiselle Linon vanished from Levin's eyes, and a joyful terror came over him at the nearness of his happiness. Mademoiselle Linon was in great haste, and leaving him, went out at the other door. As soon as she had gone out, swift, swift light steps sounded on the parquet, and his bliss, his life, himself—what was best in himself, what he had so long sought and longed for—was quickly, so quickly approaching him. She did not walk but seemed, by some unseen force, to float to him. He saw nothing but her clear, truthful eyes, frightened by the same bliss of love that flooded his heart. Those eyes were shining nearer and nearer, blinding him with their light of love. She stopped close to him, touching him. Her hands rose and dropped on his shoulders.

She had done all she could—she had run up to him and given herself up entirely, shyly, blissfully. He put his arms around her and pressed his lips to her mouth that sought his kiss.

She too had not slept all night, and had been expecting him all morning. Her mother and father had consented without qualification, and were happy in her happiness. She had been waiting for him. She wanted to be the first to tell him of her happiness and his. She had got ready to see him alone, and had been delighted at the idea, and had been shy and ashamed, and did not know herself what she was doing. She had heard his steps and voice and had waited at the door for Mademoiselle Linon to go. Mademoiselle Linon had gone away. Without thinking, without asking herself how and what, she had gone up to him, and did as she was doing.

"Let us go to Mama!" she said, taking him by the hand. For a long while he could say nothing, not so much because he was afraid of desecrating the loftiness of his emotion by a word, as that every time he tried to say something, instead of words he felt that tears of happiness were welling up. He took her hand and kissed it.

"Can it be true?" he said at last in a choked voice. "I can't believe you love me, dear!"

She smiled at that "dear," and at the timidity with which he glanced at her.

"Yes!" she said significantly, deliberately. "I am so happy!"

Not letting go his hands, she went into the drawing room. The princess, seeing them, breathed quickly, and immediately began to cry and then immediately began to laugh and with a vigorous step Levin had not expected, ran up to him, and hugging his head, kissed him, wetting his cheeks with her tears.

"So it is all settled! I am glad. Love her. I am glad . . . Kitty!"

"You've not been long settling things," said the old prince, trying to seem unmoved; but Levin noticed that his eyes were wet when he turned to him.

"I've long, always wished for this!" said the prince, taking Levin by the arm and drawing him toward himself. "Even when this little scatterbrain thought—"

"Papa!" shrieked Kitty, and shut his mouth with her hands.

"Well, I won't!" he said. "I'm very, very . . . plea . . . Oh, what a fool I am . . ."

He embraced Kitty, kissed her face, her hand, her face again, and made the sign of the cross over her.

And there came over Levin a new feeling of love for this man, till then so little known to him, when he saw how slowly and tenderly Kitty kissed his fleshy hand.

CHAPTER SIXTEEN

The princess sat in her armchair, silent and smiling; the prince sat down beside her. Kitty stood by her father's chair, still holding his hand. All were silent.

The princess was the first to put everything into words, and to translate all thoughts and feelings into practical questions. And all equally felt this strange and painful for the first minute.

"When is it to be? We must have the benediction and announcement. And when's the wedding to be? What do you think, Aleksandr?"

"Here he is," said the old prince, pointing to Levin—"he's the principal person in the matter."

"When?" said Levin, blushing. "Tomorrow. If you ask me, I should say the benediction today and the wedding tomorrow."

"Come, *mon cher*, that's nonsense!"

"Well, in a week."

"He's quite mad."

"No, why so?"

"Well, upon my word!" said the mother, smiling, delighted at his haste. "How about the trousseau?"

"Will there really be a trousseau and all that?" Levin thought with horror. "But can the trousseau and the benediction and all that—can it spoil my happiness? Nothing can spoil it!" He glanced at Kitty, and noticed that she was not in the least, not in the very least, disturbed by the idea of the trousseau. "Then it must be all right," he thought.

"Oh, I know nothing about it; I only said what I would like," he said apologetically.

"We'll talk it over, then. The benediction and announcement can take place now. That's very well."

The princess went up to her husband, kissed him, and was about to leave, but he held on to her, embraced her, and, tenderly as a young lover, kissed her several times, smiling. The old people were obviously muddled for a moment, and did not quite know whether it was they who were in love again or their daughter. When the prince and the princess had gone, Levin went up to his betrothed and took her hand. He was self-possessed now and could speak, and he had a great deal he wanted to tell her. But he said not at all what he had to say.

"I knew it would be so! I never hoped for it; and yet in my heart I was always sure," he said. "I believe that it was ordained."

"And I!" she said. "Even when . . ." She stopped and went on again, looking at him resolutely with her truthful eyes: "Even when I thrust from me my happiness. I always loved you alone, but I was carried away. I ought to tell you . . . Can you forgive it?"

"Perhaps it was for the best. You will have to forgive me so much. I ought to tell you . . ."

This was one of the things he had meant to speak about. He had resolved from the first to tell her two things—that he was not chaste as she was, and that he was not a believer. It was agonizing, but he considered he ought to tell her both these facts.

"No, not now, later!" he said.

"Very well, later, but you must certainly tell me. I'm not afraid of anything. I want to know everything. Now it is settled."

He added: "Settled that you'll take me whatever I may be—you won't give me up? Yes?"

"Yes, yes."

Their conversation was interrupted by Mademoiselle Linon, who with an affected but tender smile came to congratulate her favorite pupil. Before she had gone, the servants came in with their congratulations. Then relations arrived, and there began that state of blissful absurdity from which Levin did not emerge till the day after his wedding. Levin was in a continual state of awkwardness and discomfort, but the intensity of his happiness kept on increasing. He felt continually that a great deal was being expected of him—what, he did not know; and he did everything he was told, and it all gave him happiness. He had thought his engagement would have nothing about it like others, that the ordinary conditions of engaged couples would spoil his special happiness; but it ended in his doing exactly as other people did, and his happiness being only increased thereby and becoming more and more special, more and more unlike anything that had ever happened.

"Now we shall have sweets to eat," said Mademoiselle Linon—and Levin drove off to buy sweets.

"Well, I'm very glad," said Sviazhsky. "I advise you to get the bouquets from Fomin's."

"Oh, are they needed?" And he drove to Fomin's.

His brother offered to lend him money, as he would have so many expenses, presents to give . . .

"Oh, are presents needed?" And he galloped to Fulde's.

And at the confectioner's, and at Fomin's, and at Fulde's he saw that he was expected; that they were pleased to see him, and prided themselves on his happiness, just as everyone whom he had to deal with during those days. What was extraordinary was not only that everyone liked him, but that even people previously unsympathetic, cold, and callous were enthusiastic over him, gave way to him in everything, treated his feeling with tenderness and delicacy, and shared his conviction that he was the happiest man in the world because his betrothed was beyond perfection. Kitty too felt the same thing. When Countess Nordston ventured to hint that she had hoped for something better, Kitty was so angry and proved so conclusively that nothing in the world could be better than Levin, that Countess Nordston had to admit it, and in Kitty's presence she never met Levin without a smile of ecstatic admiration.

The confession he had promised was the one painful incident of this time. He consulted the old prince, and, with his sanction gave Kitty his diary, in which there was written the confession that tortured him. He had written this diary at the time with a view to his future wife. Two things caused him anguish: his lack of purity and his lack of faith. His confession of unbelief passed unnoticed. She was religious, had never doubted the truths of religion, but his external unbelief did not affect her in the least. Through love she knew all his soul, and in his soul she saw what she wanted, and that such a state of soul should be called unbelieving was to her a matter of no account. The other confession set her weeping bitterly.

Levin, not without an inner struggle, handed her his diary. He knew that between him and her there could not be, and should not be, secrets, and so he had decided that so it must be. But he had not realized what an effect it would have on her, he had not put himself in her place. It was only when the same evening he came to their house before the theater, went into her room and saw her tear-stained, pitiful, sweet face, miserable with suffering he had caused and nothing could undo, he felt the abyss that separated his shameful past from her dovelike purity, and was appalled at what he had done.

"Take them, take these dreadful books!" she said, pushing away the notebooks lying before her on the table. "Why did you give them to me? No, it was better anyway," she added, touched by his despairing face. "But it's awful, awful!"

His head sank, and he was silent. He could say nothing.

"You can't forgive me," he whispered.

"Yes, I forgive you; but it's terrible!"

But his happiness was so immense that this confession did not shatter it, it only added another shade to it. She forgave him; but from that time more than ever he considered himself unworthy of her, morally bowed down lower than ever before her, and prized more highly than ever his undeserved happiness.

CHAPTER SEVENTEEN

Unconsciously going over in his memory the conversations that had taken place during and after dinner, Aleksey Aleksandrovich returned to his solitary room. Darya Aleksandrovna's words about forgiveness had aroused in him nothing but annoyance. The applicability or nonapplicability of the Christian precept to his own case was too difficult a question to be discussed lightly, and this question had long ago been answered by Aleksey Aleksandrovich in the negative. Of all that had been said, what stuck most in his memory was the phrase of silly, good-natured Turovtsyn—"*Acted like a man, he did! Challenged him and shot him!*" Everyone had apparently shared this feeling, though from politeness they had not expressed it.

"But the matter is settled, it's useless thinking about it," Aleksey Aleksandrovich told himself. And thinking of nothing but the journey before him, and the inspection work he had to do, he went into his room and asked the porter who escorted him where his valet was. The porter said that the valet had just gone out. Aleksey Aleksandrovich ordered tea to be sent him, sat down at the table, and, taking the railway timetable, began considering the route of his journey.

"Two telegrams," said his valet, coming into the room. "I beg your pardon, Your Excellency; I'd only just that minute gone out."

Aleksey Aleksandrovich took the telegrams and opened them. The first telegram was the announcement of Stremov's appointment to the very post Karenin had coveted. Aleksey Aleksandrovich flung the telegram down, and, flushing a little, got up and began to pace up and down the room. "*Quos vult perdere dementat,*"[1] he said, meaning by "*quos*" the persons responsible for this appointment. He was not so much annoyed that he had not received the post, that he had been conspicuously passed over; but it was incomprehensible, amazing to him that they did not see that the wordy phrase-monger Stremov was the last man fit for it. How could they fail to see how they were ruining themselves, lowering their *prestige* by this appointment?

"Something else in the same line" he said to himself bitterly, opening the second telegram. The telegram was from his wife. Her name, written in blue pencil, "Anna," was the first thing that caught his eye. "I am dying; I beg, I implore you to come. I shall die easier with your forgiveness," he read. He smiled contemptuously, and flung down the telegram. This was a trick and a fraud—of that, he thought for the first minute, there could be no doubt.

"There is no deceit she would not try. She is near her confinement. Perhaps it is the confinement. But what can be their aim? To legitimize the child, to compromise me, and prevent a divorce," he thought. "But something was said in it: 'I am dying . . .'" He read the telegram again, and suddenly the plain meaning of what was said in it struck him.

"And if it is true?" he said to himself. "If it is true that in the moment of agony and nearness to death she is genuinely penitent, and I, taking it for a trick, refuse to go? That would not only be

---

[1]For some reason, *Deus* (God), which should be the second word of this famous Latin expression, was left out by Tolstoy (or deleted by the censor). The line should read: "Whom God wants to destroy He deprives of his reason."

cruel, and everyone would blame me, but it would be stupid on my part."

"Piotr, call a coach; I am going to Petersburg," he said to his servant.

Aleksey Aleksandrovich decided that he would go to Petersburg and see his wife. If her illness was a trick, he would say nothing and go away again. If she was really in danger, and wished to see him before her death, he would forgive her if he found her alive, and pay her the last duties if he came too late.

All the way he thought no more of what he ought to do.

With the sense of weariness and feeling dirty from the night spent in the train, in the early fog of Petersburg, Aleksey Aleksandrovich drove through the deserted Nevsky Prospekt and stared straight before him, not thinking of what was awaiting him. He could not think about it, because in picturing what would happen, he could not drive away the reflection that her death would at once remove all the difficulty of his position. Bakers, closed shops, night cabmen, porters sweeping the pavements flashed past his eyes, and he watched it all, trying to smother the thought of what was awaiting him, and what he dared not hope for and yet was hoping for. He drove up to the steps. A sleigh and a carriage with the coachman asleep stood at the entrance. As he went into the entry, Aleksey Aleksandrovich seemed to draw his resolution from the remotest corner of his brain, and mastered it thoroughly. Its meaning ran: "If truth, do what is proper."

The porter opened the door before Aleksey Aleksandrovich rang. Petrov, otherwise known as Kapitonich, looked strange in an old coat, without a tie, and in slippers.

"How is your mistress?"

"A successful delivery yesterday."

Aleksey Aleksandrovich stopped short and turned white. He felt distinctly now how intensely he had longed for her death.

"And how is she?"

Korney, in his morning apron, ran downstairs.

"Very ill," he answered. "There was a consultation yesterday, and the doctor's here now."

"Take my things," said Aleksey Aleksandrovich, and feeling some relief at the news that there was still hope of her death, he went into the hall.

On the hat stand there was a military overcoat. Aleksey Aleksandrovich noticed it and asked:

"Who is here?"

"The doctor, the midwife, and Count Vronsky."

Aleksey Aleksandrovich went into the inner rooms.

In the drawing room there was no one; at the sound of his steps the midwife, in a cap with lilac ribbons, came out of the boudoir.

She went up to Aleksey Aleksandrovich, and with the familiarity given by the approach of death, she took him by the arm and drew him toward the bedroom.

"Thank God you've come! She keeps talking about you and nothing but you," she said.

"Make haste with the ice!" the doctor's peremptory voice said from the bedroom.

Aleksey Aleksandrovich went into her boudoir.

At the table, sitting sideways in a low chair, was Vronsky, his face hidden in his hands, weeping. He jumped up at the doctor's voice, took his hands from his face, and saw Aleksey Aleksandrovich. Seeing the husband, he was so overwhelmed that he sat down again, drawing his head down between his shoulders, as if he wanted to disappear; but he made an effort over himself, got up, and said:

"She is dying. The doctors say there is no hope. I am entirely in your power, only let me be here . . . though I am at your disposal. I . . ."

Aleksey Aleksandrovich, seeing Vronsky's tears, felt a rush of that nervous emotion always produced in him by the sight of other people's sufferings, and turning away his face, he moved hurriedly to the door, without hearing the rest of his words. From the bedroom came the sound of Anna's voice saying something. Her voice was lively, eager, with exceedingly distinct intonations. Aleksey Aleksandrovich went into the bedroom, and went up to the bed. She was lying turned with her face toward him. Her cheeks were flushed crimson, her eyes glittered, her little white hands thrust out from the sleeves of her dressing gown were playing with the quilt, twisting it about. It seemed as though she was not only well and blooming, but in the happiest frame of mind. She was talking rapidly, musically, and with exceptionally correct articulation and expressive intonation.

"For Aleksey—I am speaking of Aleksey Aleksandrovich (what a strange and awful thing that both are Aleksey, isn't it?)—Aleksey would not refuse me. I would forget, he would forgive . . . But why doesn't he come? He's so good, he doesn't know himself how good he is. Ah, my God, what agony! Give me some water, quick! Oh, that will be bad for her, my little girl! Oh, very well then, give her to a nurse. Yes, I agree, it's better in fact. He'll be coming; it will hurt him to see her. Give her to the nurse."

"Anna Arkadyevna, he has come. Here he is!" said the midwife, trying to attract her attention to Aleksey Aleksandrovich.

"Oh, what nonsense!" Anna went on, not seeing her husband. "No, give her to me; give me my little one! He has not come yet. You say he won't forgive me because you don't know him. No one knows him. I'm the only one, and it was hard even for me. His eyes I ought to know—Seryozha has just the same eyes—and I can't bear to see them because of it. Has Seryozha had his dinner? I know everyone will forget him. He would not forget. Seryozha must be moved into the corner room, and Mariette must be asked to sleep with him."

All of a sudden she shrank back, was silent; and in terror, as though expecting a blow, as though to defend herself, she raised her hands to her face. She had seen her husband.

"No, no!" she began. "I am not afraid of him; I am afraid of death. Aleksey, come here. I am in a hurry because I've no time; I've not long left to live; the fever will begin soon and I shall understand nothing more. Now I understand, I understand it all, I see it all!"

Aleksey Aleksandrovich's wrinkled face wore an expression of agony; he took her by the hand and tried to say something, but he could not utter it; his lower lip quivered, but he still went on struggling with his emotion, and only now and then glanced at her. And each time he glanced at her, he saw her eyes gazing at him with such passionate and triumphant tenderness as he had never seen in them.

"Wait a minute, you don't know . . . stay a minute, stay! . . ." She stopped, as though collecting her ideas. "Yes," she began; "yes, yes, yes. This is what I wanted to say. Don't be surprised at me. I'm still the same . . . But there is another woman in me, I'm afraid of her: she loved that man, and I tried to hate you, and could not forget about her that used to be. I'm not that woman. Now I'm my real self, all myself. I'm dying now, I know I shall die, ask him. Even now I feel— see here, the weights on my feet, on my hands, on my fingers. My fingers—see how huge they are! But this will soon all be over. . . Only one thing I want: forgive me, forgive me completely. I'm terrible, but my nurse used to tell me; the holy martyr—what was her name? She was worse. And I'll go to Rome; there's a wilderness, and there I shall be no trouble to anyone, only I'll take Seryozha and the little one . . . No, you can't forgive me! I know, it can't be forgiven! No, no, go away, you're too good!" She held his hand in one burning hand, while she pushed him away with the other.

The nervous agitation of Aleksey Aleksandrovich kept increasing, and had by now reached such a point that he ceased to struggle with it. He suddenly felt that what he had regarded as nervous agitation was on the contrary a blissful spiritual condition that gave him all at once a new happiness he had never known. He did not think that the Christian law that he had been all his life trying to follow enjoined him to forgive and love his enemies; but a happy feeling of love and forgiveness for his enemies filled his heart. He knelt down, and laying his head in the curve of her arm, which burned him as with fire through the sleeve, he sobbed like a little child. She put her arm around his head, moved toward him, and, with defiant pride, raised her eyes.

"That is he. I knew him! Now, forgive me, everyone, forgive me! . . . They've come again; why don't they go away? . . . Oh, take these cloaks off me!"

The doctor unloosed her hands, carefully laying her on the pillow, and covered her up to the shoulders. She lay back submissively, and looked before her with beaming eyes.

"Remember one thing, that I needed nothing but forgiveness, and I want nothing more . . . Why doesn't *he* come?" she said, turning to the door toward Vronsky. "Do come, do come! Give him your hand."

Vronsky came to the side of the bed, and seeing Anna, he again hid his face in his hands.

"Uncover your face—look at him! He's a saint," she said. "Oh!

Uncover your face, do uncover it!" she said angrily. "Aleksey Aleksandrovich, do uncover his face! I want to see him."

Aleksey Aleksandrovich took Vronsky's hands and drew them away from his face, which was awful with the expression of agony and shame upon it.

"Give him your hand. Forgive him."

Aleksey Aleksandrovich gave him his hand, not attempting to restrain the tears that streamed from his eyes.

"Thank God, thank God!" she said. "Now everything is ready. Only to stretch my legs a little. There, that's wonderful. How badly these flowers are done—not a bit like a violet," she said, pointing to the wallpaper. "My God, my God! When will it end? Give me some morphine. Doctor, give me some morphine! Oh, my God, my God!"

And she tossed about on the bed.

The doctors said that it was puerperal fever, and that it was ninety-nine chances in a hundred that it would end in death. The whole day long there was fever, delirium, and unconsciousness. At midnight the patient lay without consciousness, and almost without pulse.

The end was expected every minute.

Vronsky had gone home, but in the morning he came to inquire, and Aleksey Aleksandrovich meeting him in the hall, said: "Better stay, she might ask for you," and himself led him to his wife's boudoir. Toward morning there was a return again of excitement, rapid thought and talk, and again it ended in unconsciousness. On the third day it was the same thing, and the doctors said there was hope. That day Aleksey Aleksandrovich went into the boudoir where Vronsky was sitting, and, closing the door, sat down opposite him.

"Aleksey Aleksandrovich," said Vronsky, feeling that an explanation was coming, "I can't speak, I can't understand. Spare me! However hard it is for you, believe me, it is more terrible for me."

He would have risen, but Aleksey Aleksandrovich took him by the hand and said:

"I beg you to hear me out; it is necessary. I must explain my feelings, the feelings that have guided me and will guide me, so that you may not be in error regarding me. You know I had resolved on a divorce, and had even begun to take proceedings. I won't conceal from you that in beginning this I was in uncertainty, I was in misery; I will confess that I was pursued by a desire to revenge myself on you and on her. When I got the telegram, I came here with the same feelings; I will say more, I longed for her death. But . . ." He paused, pondering whether to disclose or not to disclose his feeling to him. "But I saw her and forgave her. And the happiness of forgiveness has revealed to me my duty. I forgive completely. I would offer the other cheek, I would give my cloak if my coat be taken. I pray to God only not to take from me the bliss of forgiveness!"

Tears stood in his eyes, and the luminous, serene look in them impressed Vronsky.

"This is my position: you can trample me in the mud, make me the laughingstock of the world, I will not abandon her, and I will never utter a word of reproach to you, " Aleksey Aleksandrovich went on. "My duty is clearly marked for me; I should be with her, and I will be. If she wishes to see you, I will let you know, but now I suppose it would be better for you to go away."

He got up, and sobs cut short his words. Vronsky too was getting up, and in a stooping, not yet erect posture, he looked up at him from under his brows. He did not understand Aleksey Aleksandrovich's feeling, but he felt that it was something beyond him, even unattainable for him with his outlook on life.

CHAPTER EIGHTEEN

After the conversation with Aleksey Aleksandrovich, Vronsky went out onto the steps of the Karenin house and stood still, with difficulty remembering where he was and where he should walk or drive. He felt disgraced, humiliated, guilty, and deprived of all possibility of washing away his humiliation. He felt thrust out of the beaten track along which he had so proudly and lightly walked till then. All the habits and rules of his life that had seemed so firm had turned out suddenly false and inapplicable. The betrayed husband, who had figured till that time as a pitiful creature, an incidental and somewhat ludicrous obstacle to his happiness, had suddenly been summoned by her herself, elevated to an awe-inspiring pinnacle, and on the pinnacle that husband had shown himself not malignant, not false or ludicrous, but kind and straightforward and dignified. Vronsky could not but feel this, and the parts were suddenly reversed. Vronsky felt Karenin's elevation and his own abasement, Karenin's rightness, his own wrongdoing. He felt that the husband was magnanimous even in his sorrow, while he had been base and petty in his deceit. But this sense of his own humiliation before the man he had unjustly despised made up only a small part of his misery. He felt unutterably wretched now, for his passion for Anna, which had seemed to him of late to be growing cooler, now that he knew he had lost her forever, was stronger than it had ever been. He had learned to know her completely in her illness, had come to know her very soul, and it seemed to him that he had never loved her till then. And now, when he had learned to know her, to love her as she should be loved, he had been humiliated before her, and had lost her forever, leaving with her nothing of himself but a shameful memory. Most terrible of all had been his ludicrous, shameful position when Aleksey Aleksandrovich had pulled his hands away from his humiliated face. He stood on the steps of the Karenin house like one distraught, and did not know what to do.

"A sleigh, sir?" asked the porter.

"Yes, a sleigh."

On getting home, after three sleepless nights, Vronsky, without undressing, lay down flat on the sofa, clasping his hands and laying his head on them. His head was heavy. Images, memories, and ideas of the strangest description followed one another with extraordinary rapidity and vividness. First it was the medicine he had poured out for the patient and spilled over the spoon, then the midwife's white hands, then the strange position of Aleksey Aleksandrovich on the floor beside the bed.

"To sleep! To forget!" he said to himself with the serene confidence of a healthy man who, if he is tired and sleepy, will go to sleep at once. And the same instant his head did begin to feel drowsy and he began to drop off into forgetfulness. The waves of the sea of unconsciousness had begun to close over his head, when all at once—it was as though a violent shock of electricity had passed over him, he started so that he leaped up on the springs of the sofa, and, leaning on his arms, got to his knees in panic. His eyes were wide open as though he had not been asleep. The heaviness in his head and the weariness in his limbs that he had felt a minute before had suddenly gone.

"You may trample me in the mud"—he heard Aleksey Aleksandrovich's words and saw him standing before him, and saw Anna's face with its burning cheeks and glittering eyes, gazing with love and tenderness not at him but at Aleksey Aleksandrovich; he saw his own, as he imagined, foolish and ludicrous figure when Aleksey Aleksandrovich took his hands away from his face. He stretched out his legs again and flung himself on the sofa in the same position and shut his eyes.

"To sleep! To sleep!" he repeated to himself. But with his eyes shut he saw more distinctly than ever Anna's face as it had been on the memorable evening before the races.

"That is not and will not be, and she wants to wipe it out of her memory. But I cannot live without it. How can we be reconciled? How can we be reconciled?" he said aloud, and unconsciously began to repeat these words. This repetition prevented fresh images and memories, which he felt were thronging in his brain. But repeating words did not check his imagination for long. Again, in extraordinarily rapid succession, his happiest moments rose before his mind, and then his recent humiliation. "Take away his hands," Anna's voice says. He takes away his hands and feels the shame-struck and idiotic expression on his face.

He still lay down, trying to sleep, though he felt there was not the smallest hope of it, and kept repeating stray words from some chain of thought, trying by this to check the rising flood of fresh images. He listened, and heard in a strange, mad whisper words repeated: *"I did not appreciate it, did not make enough of it. I did not appreciate it, did not make enough of it."*

"What's this? Am I going out of my mind?" he said to himself. "Perhaps. What makes men go out of their minds; what makes men shoot themselves?" he answered himself, and opening his eyes, he saw with wonder an embroidered cushion beside him, done by Varya, his brother's wife. He touched the tassel of the cushion, and tried to think of Varya, of when he had seen her last. But to think of anything extraneous was an agonizing effort. "No, I must sleep!" He moved the cushion up and pressed his head into it, but he had to make an effort to keep his eyes shut. He jumped up and sat down. "That's all over for me," he said to himself. "I must think of what to do. What is left?" His mind rapidly ran through his life apart from his love of Anna.

"Ambition? Serpukhovskoy? Society? Court?" He could not come to a pause anywhere. All of it had had meaning before, but now there was no reality in it. He got up from the sofa, took off his coat, undid his belt, and, uncovering his hairy chest to breathe more freely, walked up and down the room. "This is how people go mad," he repeated, "and how they shoot themselves . . . to escape humiliation," he added slowly.

He went to the door and closed it; then, with staring eyes and clenched teeth, he went to the table, took a revolver, looked around him, turned it to a loaded chamber, and sank into thought. For two minutes, his head bent forward, an expression of intense concentration on his face, he stood with the revolver in his hand, motionless, thinking.

"Of course," he said to himself, as though a logical, continuous, and clear chain of reasoning had brought him to an indubitable conclusion. In reality this "of course" that seemed convincing to him was simply the result of exactly the same circle of memories and images through which he had passed ten times already during the last hour—memories of happiness lost forever. There was the same conception of the senselessness of everything to come in life, the same consciousness of humiliation. Even the sequence of these images and emotions was the same.

"Of course," he repeated, when for the third time his thought passed again around the same spellbound circle of memories and images, and pulling the revolver to the left side of his chest, clutching it vigorously with his whole hand, as though clenching his fist, he pulled the trigger. He did not hear the sound of the shot, but a violent blow on his chest sent him reeling. He tried to clutch at the edge of the table, dropped the revolver, staggered, and sat down on the floor, looking about him in astonishment. He did not recognize his room as he looked up from the floor at the curved legs of the table, at the waste-paper basket, and the tigerskin rug. The hurried, creaking steps of his servant coming through the drawing room brought him to his senses. He made an effort at thought, and was aware that he was on the floor; and seeing blood on the tigerskin rug and on his arm, he knew he had shot himself.

"Idiotic! Missed!" he said, fumbling for the revolver. The revolver was close to him—he searched further away. Still feeling for it, he stretched out to the other side, and not being strong enough to keep his balance, he fell over, streaming with blood.

The elegant, whiskered servant, who used to continually complain to his acquaintances of the delicacy of his nerves, was so panic-stricken on seeing his master lying on the floor that he left him to bleed to death while he ran for assistance. An hour later Varya, his brother's wife, had arrived, and with the assistance of three doctors, whom she had sent for in all directions, and who all appeared at the same moment, she got the wounded man to bed, and remained to nurse him.

CHAPTER NINETEEN

The mistake made by Aleksey Aleksandrovich—that when preparing to see his wife he had overlooked the possibility that her repentance might be sincere, that he might forgive her, that she might not die—this mistake was brought home to him in all its significance two months after his return from Moscow. But the mistake made by him had arisen not simply from his having overlooked that contingency, but also from the fact that until the day he looked at his dying wife, he had not known his own heart. At his sick wife's bedside he had for the first time in his life given way to that feeling of warm compassion always roused in him by the suffering of others, and hitherto looked on by him with shame as a harmful weakness. And pity for her, and remorse for having desired her death, and, most of all the joy of forgiveness made him at once conscious, not merely of the relief of his own sufferings, but also of a spiritual peace he had never experienced before. He suddenly felt that the very thing that was the source of his sufferings had become the source of his spiritual joy; that what had seemed insoluble while he was judging, blaming, and hating had become clear and simple when he forgave and loved.

He forgave his wife and pitied her for her sufferings and her remorse. He forgave Vronsky and pitied him, especially after reports reached him of his desperate action. He felt more for his son than before. And he blamed himself now for having taken too little interest in him. But for the newborn little girl he felt a special sentiment, not of pity only, but of tenderness. At first, from a feeling of compassion alone, he had been interested in the delicate little creature who was not his child, and who was cast to one side during her mother's illness, and would certainly have died if he had not troubled about her, and he did not himself observe how fond he became of her. He would go into the nursery several times a day and sit there for a long while, so that the nurses, who were at first afraid of him, got quite used to his presence. Sometimes for half an hour at a stretch he would sit silently gazing at the saffron-red, downy, wrinkled face of the sleeping baby, watching the movements of the frowning brows, and the fat little hands, with clenched fingers, that rubbed the little eyes and nose. At such moments particularly, Aleksey Aleksandrovich had a sense of perfect peace and inner harmony, and saw nothing extraordinary in his position, nothing that ought to be changed.

But as time went on, he saw more and more distinctly that however natural the position now seemed to him, he would not long be allowed to remain in it. He felt that besides the blessed spiritual force controlling his soul, there was another, a brutal force, as powerful, or more powerful, which controlled his life, and that this force would not allow him that humble peace he longed for. He felt that everyone was looking at him with questioning amazement, that he was not understood, and that something was expected of him. Above all, he felt the instability and unnaturalness of his relations with his wife.

When the softening effect of the near approach of death had passed away, Aleksey Aleksandrovich began to notice that Anna was afraid of him, ill at ease with him, and could not look him straight in the face. She seemed to be wanting, and not daring, to tell him something; and as though foreseeing that their present relations could not continue, she seemed to be expecting something from him.

Toward the end of February it happened that Anna's baby daughter, who had been named Anna too, fell ill. Aleksey Aleksandrovich was in the nursery in the morning, and leaving orders for the doctor to be sent for, he went to his office. On finishing his work, he returned home at four. Going into the hall he saw a handsome footman in a braided livery and bearskin cape, holding a white fur cloak.

"Who is here?" asked Aleksey Aleksandrovich.

"Princess Elizaveta Fyodorovna Tverskaya," the groom answered, and it seemed to Aleksey Aleksandrovich that he grinned.

During all this difficult time Aleksey Aleksandrovich had noticed that his worldly acquaintances, especially women, took a peculiar interest in him and his wife. All these acquaintances, he observed, had difficulty concealing a kind of mirth—the same mirth that he had perceived in the lawyer's eyes, and just now in the eyes of this groom. Everyone seemed, somehow, enormously delighted, as though they had just been to a wedding. When they met him, they inquired about his wife's health with hardly disguised glee. The presence of Princess Tverskaya was unpleasant to Aleksey Aleksandrovich because of the memories associated with her, and also because he disliked her, and he went straight to the nursery. In the front nursery Seryozha, lying on the table with his legs on a chair, was drawing and chatting away merrily. The English governess, who had during Anna's illness replaced the French one, was sitting near the boy crocheting. She hurriedly got up, curtsied, and nudged Seryozha.

Aleksey Aleksandrovich stroked his son's hair, answered the governess's inquiries about his wife, and asked what the doctor had said of the baby.

"The doctor said it was nothing serious, and he ordered baths, sir."

"But she is still in pain," said Aleksey Aleksandrovich, listening to the baby's screaming in the next room.

"I think it's because of the wet nurse, sir," the Englishwoman said firmly.

"What makes you think so?" he asked, stopping short.

"It's just as it was at Countess Pohl's, sir. They gave the baby medicine, and it turned out that the baby was simply hungry; the nurse
had no milk, sir."

Aleksey Aleksandrovich pondered, and after standing still a few
seconds he went in the other door. The baby was lying with her head
thrown back, stiffening herself in the nurse's arms, and would not
take the plump breast offered her; and she never ceased screaming
in spite of the hushing of the wet nurse and the other nurse, who
was bending over her.

"Still no better?" said Aleksey Aleksandrovich.

"She's very restless," answered the nurse in a whisper.

"Miss Edward says that perhaps the wet nurse has no milk," he
said.

"I think so too, Aleksey Aleksandrovich."

"Then why didn't you say so?"

"Who's one to say it to? Anna Arkadyevna still ill . . ." said the
nurse resentfully.

The nurse was an old servant of the family. And in her simple
words there seemed to Aleksey Aleksandrovich an allusion to his
position.

The baby screamed louder than ever, struggling and sobbing. The
nurse, with a gesture of despair, went to her, took her from the wet
nurse's arms, and began walking up and down, rocking her.

"You must ask the doctor to examine the wet nurse," said Aleksey
Aleksandrovich. The smartly dressed and healthy-looking nurse,
frightened at the idea of losing her job, muttered something to herself, and, covering her bosom, smiled contemptuously at the idea of
doubts being cast on her abundance of milk. In that smile, too, Aleksey Aleksandrovich saw a sneer at his position.

"Luckless child!" said the nurse, hushing the baby, and still walking up and down with her.

Aleksey Aleksandrovich sat down, and, with the despondent and
suffering face, watched the nurse walking to and fro.

When the child at last was still, and had been put in a cot, and the
nurse, after smoothing the little pillow, had left her, Aleksey Aleksandrovich got up and, walking awkwardly on tiptoe, approached the

baby. For a minute he was still, and gazed at the baby with the same despondent face; but all at once a smile, which wrinkled the skin on his forehead and made his hair move, came out on his face, and he went softly out of the room.

In the dining room he rang the bell and told the servant who came in to send again for the doctor. He felt annoyed with his wife for not being anxious about this delightful baby, and in this mood he had no wish to go to her; he had no wish, either, to see Princess Betsy. But his wife might wonder why he did not go to her as usual; and so, overcoming his disinclination, he went toward the bedroom. As he walked over the soft rug toward the door, he could not help overhearing a conversation he did not want to hear.

"If he hadn't been going away, I could have understood your answer and his too. But your husband ought to be above that," Betsy was saying.

"It's not for my husband but for myself that I don't wish it. Don't say that!" answered Anna's excited voice.

"Yes, but you must certainly say good-by to a man who has tried to shoot himself on your account. "

"That's just why I don't want to."

With a frightened and guilty expression, Aleksey Aleksandrovich stopped, and considered going back unobserved. But reflecting that this would be undignified, he turned back again, and clearing his throat, he went to the bedroom. The voices fell silent, and he went in.

Anna, in a gray dressing gown, with her black hair cut short but growing in like a thick brush over her round head, was sitting on a settee. The animation left her face, as it always did, at the sight of her husband; she lowered her head and looked around uneasily at Betsy. Betsy, dressed in the height of the latest fashion, in a hat that soared somewhere over her head like a shade on a lamp, in a dove-colored gown with very pronounced diagonal stripes going one way on the bodice and the other way on the skirt, was sitting beside Anna, her tall, flat figure held erect. Bowing her head, she greeted Aleksey Aleksandrovich with an ironical smile.

"Ah!" she said, as though surprised. "I'm very glad you're home. You never put in an appearance anywhere, and I haven't seen you ever since Anna has been ill. I have heard all about it—your troubles. Yes, you're a wonderful husband!" she said, with a significant and affable air, as though she were bestowing an order of magnanimity on him for his conduct to his wife.

Aleksey Aleksandrovich bowed coldly, and, kissing his wife's hand, asked how she was.

"Better, I think," she said, avoiding his eyes.

"But you look feverish," he said, laying stress on the word "feverish."

"We've been talking too much," said Betsy. "I feel it's selfishness on my part, and I'm going."

She got up, but Anna, suddenly flushing, quickly seized her hand.

"No, wait a minute, please. I must tell you . . . no, you." She turned to Aleksey Aleksandrovich, and her neck and brow were suffused with crimson. "I won't and can't keep anything secret from you," she said.

Aleksey Aleksandrovich cracked his knuckles and bowed his head.

"Betsy's been telling me that Count Vronsky wants to come here to say good-by before his departure for Tashkent." She did not look at her husband, and was evidently in haste to have everything out, however hard it might be for her. "I told her I could not receive him."

"You said, my dear, that it would depend on Aleksey Aleksandrovich," Betsy corrected her.

"Oh, no, I can't receive him and it wouldn't do any—" She stopped suddenly, and glanced inquiringly at her husband (he did not look at her). "In short, I don't wish it. . . ."

Aleksey Aleksandrovich advanced and reached out his hand.

Her first impulse was to jerk back her hand from the damp hand with big swollen veins that sought hers, but with an obvious effort to control herself she pressed his hand.

"I am very grateful to you for your confidence, but . . ." he said, feeling with confusion and annoyance that what he could decide easily and clearly by himself, he could not discuss before Princess Tverskaya, who to him represented the incarnation of that brute force which would inevitably control him in the life he led in the eyes of the world and hinder him from giving way to his feeling of love and forgiveness. He stopped short, looking at Princess Tverskaya.

"Well, good-by, my darling," said Betsy, getting up. She kissed Anna and went out. Aleksey Aleksandrovich escorted her out.

"Aleksey Aleksandrovich! I know you are a truly magnanimous man," said Betsy, stopping in the little drawing room and with special warmth shaking hands with him once more. "I am an outsider, but I so love her and respect you that I venture to advise. Receive him. Aleksey Vronsky is the soul of honor, and he is going away to Tashkent."

"Thank you, Princess, for your sympathy and advice. But the question of whether my wife can or cannot see anyone she must decide herself."

He said this from habit, lifting his brows with dignity, and reflected immediately that whatever his words might be, there could be no dignity in his position. And he saw this by the suppressed, malicious, and ironical smile with which Betsy glanced at him after this phrase.

CHAPTER TWENTY

Aleksey Aleksandrovich took leave of Betsy in the drawing room, and went to his wife. She was lying down, but hearing his steps, she sat up hastily in her former place and looked at him apprehensively. He saw that she had been crying.

"I am very grateful for your confidence in me." He repeated gently in Russian the phrase he had said in Betsy's presence in French, and sat down beside her. When he spoke to her in Russian, using "thou," it was insufferably irritating to Anna. "And I am very grateful for your decision. I, too, imagine that since he is going away, there is no need whatever for Count Vronsky to come here. However, if—"

"But I've said so already, so why repeat it?" Anna suddenly interrupted him with an irritation she could not succeed in repressing. "No need whatever," she thought, "for a man to come and say good-by to the woman he loves, for whom he was ready to kill himself, for whom he has ruined himself, and who cannot live without him. No need whatever!" She compressed her lips, and turned her glittering eyes to his hands, with their swollen veins. They were rubbing each other.

"Let us never speak of it," she added more calmly.

"I have left this question for you to decide, and I am very glad to see—" Aleksey Aleksandrovich was beginning.

"That my wish coincides with your own," she finished quickly, exasperated at his talking so slowly when she knew beforehand all he would say.

"Yes," he assented; "and Princess Tverskaya's interference in the most difficult private affairs is utterly uncalled for. She especially—"

"I don't believe a word of what's said about her," said Anna quickly. "I know she really cares for me."

Aleksey Aleksandrovich sighed and said nothing. She played nervously with the tassel of her dressing gown, glancing at him with that torturing sensation of physical loathing for which she blamed herself, though she could not control it. Her only desire now was to be rid of his oppressive presence.

"I have just sent for the doctor," said Aleksey Aleksandrovich.

"I am very well; what do I want the doctor for?"

"No, the little one cries, and they say the nurse hasn't enough milk."

"Why didn't you let me nurse her when I begged to? Anyway" (Aleksey Aleksandrovich knew what was meant by that "anyway"), "she's a baby, and they're killing her." She rang the bell and ordered the baby to be brought her. "I begged to nurse her, I wasn't allowed to, and now I'm blamed for it."

"I don't blame—"

"Yes, you do blame me! My God! Why didn't I die!" And she broke into sobs. "Forgive me, I'm upset, I'm unfair," she said, controlling herself, "but go . . ."

"No, it can't go on like this," Aleksey Aleksandrovich said to himself firmly as he left his wife's room.

Never had the impossibility of his situation in the world's eyes, and his wife's hatred of him, and altogether the power of that mysterious brutal force that guided his life contrary to his inner mood, and exacted conformity with its decrees and change in his attitude toward his wife, been presented to him with such distinctness as that day. He saw clearly that the world as a whole, and his wife, demanded—but what exactly, he could not make out. He felt that this was rousing in his soul a feeling of anger destructive of his peace of mind and achievement of any value. He believed that for Anna herself it would be better to break off all relations with Vronsky; but if they all thought this out of the question, he was even ready to allow these relations to be renewed, so long as the children were not disgraced and he was not deprived of them or forced to change his position. Bad as this might be, it was better than a complete break, which would put her in a hopeless and shameful position and deprive him of everything he cared for. But he felt helpless; he knew beforehand that everyone was against him, and that he would not be allowed to do what seemed to him now so natural and good, but would be forced to do what was wrong, though it seemed the proper thing to them.

CHAPTER TWENTY-ONE

Before Betsy had time to walk out of the drawing room, she was met in the doorway by Stepan Arkadyevich, who had just come from Yeliseyev's, where a consignment of fresh oysters had been received.

"Ah! Princess! What a delightful meeting!" he began. "I've been to see you."

"We meet but for a moment, for I'm going," said Betsy, smiling and putting on her glove.

"Don't put on your glove yet, Princess; let me kiss your hand. There's nothing I'm so thankful for as the revival of the old custom of hand-kissing." He kissed Betsy's hand. "When shall we see each other?"

"You don't deserve it," answered Betsy, smiling.

"Oh, yes, I deserve a great deal, for I've become a most serious person. I don't only manage my own affairs but other people's too," he said with a significant glance.

"Oh, I'm so glad!" answered Betsy, at once understanding that he was speaking of Anna. And going back into the drawing room, they stood in a corner. "He'll kill her," said Betsy in a whisper full of meaning. "It's impossible, impossible . . ."

"I'm so glad you think so," said Stepan Arkadyevich, shaking his head with a serious expression of commiseration. "That's what I've come to Petersburg for."

"The whole town's talking about it," she said. "It's an impossible situation. She pines, pines away. He doesn't understand that she's one of those women who can't trifle with their feelings. One of two things: either let him take her away, act with energy, or give her a divorce. This is stifling her."

"Yes, yes . . . just so . . ." Oblonsky said, sighing. "That's what I've come for. Well, not solely for that . . . I've been made a chamberlain; of course, one has to say thank you. But the chief thing was having to settle this."

"Well, God help you!" said Betsy.

After accompanying Betsy to the outside hall, once more kissing her hand above the glove at the point where the pulse beats, and murmuring to her such indecent nonsense that she did not know whether to laugh or be angry, Stepan Arkadyevich went to his sister. He found her in tears.

Although he happened to be bubbling over with good spirits, Stepan Arkadyevich immediately and quite naturally fell into the sympathetic, poetically emotional tone which harmonized with her mood. He asked her how she was, and how she had spent the morning.

"Very, very miserably. Today and this morning and all past days and days to come," she said.

"I think you're giving way to melancholy. You must rouse yourself; you must look life in the face. I know it's hard, but—"

"I have heard it said that women love men even for their vices," Anna began suddenly, "but I hate him for his virtues. I can't live with him. Do you understand? The sight of him has a physical effect on me, it enrages me. I can't, I can't live with him. What am I to do? I was unhappy, and used to think one couldn't be more unhappy, but the terrible state of things I am going through now I could never have conceived. Would you believe it, that knowing he's a good man, a splendid man, that I'm not worth his little finger, still I hate him. I hate him for his generosity. And there's nothing left for me but—"

She would have said "death," but Stepan Arkadyevich would not let her finish.

"You are ill and overwrought," he said; "believe me, you're greatly exaggerating. There's nothing so terrible about it."

And Stepan Arkadyevich smiled. No one else in Stepan Arkadyevich's place, dealing with such despair, would have ventured to smile (the smile would have seemed brutal); but in his smile there was so much sweetness and almost feminine tenderness that his smile did not hurt but comforted and soothed. His gentle, soothing words and smiles were as soothing and comforting as almond oil, and Anna soon felt this.

"No, Stiva," she said, "I'm lost, lost! Worse than lost! I can't say yet that all is over; on the contrary, I feel that it's not over. I'm an overstrained string that must snap. But it's not ended yet . . . and it will have a fearful end."

"No matter, we must let the string be loosened, little by little. There's no situation from which there is no way of escape."

"I have thought and thought. Only one . . ."

Again he knew from her terrified eyes that this one way of escape in her thoughts was death, and he would not let her say it.

"Not at all," he said. "Listen to me. You can't see your own situation as I can. Let me candidly tell you my opinion." Again he smiled, his discreetly almond-oil smile. "I'll begin from the beginning. You married a man twenty years older than yourself. You married him without love and not knowing what love was. It was a mistake, let's say."

"A fearful mistake!" said Anna.

"But I repeat, it's an accomplished fact. Then you had, let us say, the misfortune to love a man not your husband. That was a misfortune; but that, too, is an accomplished fact. And your husband knew it and forgave it." He stopped at each sentence, waiting for her to object, but she made no answer. "That's so. Now the question is: can you go on living with your husband? Do you wish it? Does he wish it?"

"I don't know, I don't know."

"But you said yourself that you can't stand him."

"No, I didn't say so. I deny it. I can't tell, I don't know anything."

"Yes, but let—"

"You can't understand. I feel I'm flying head first over a precipice, but must not even try to save myself. And I can't—"

"Never mind, we'll spread something out to catch you. I understand you; I understand that you can't take it on yourself to express your wishes, your feelings."

"There's nothing, nothing I wish . . . except for it to be all over."

"But he sees this and knows it. And do you suppose it weighs on him any less than on you? You're wretched, he's wretched, and what good can come of it? While divorce would solve the whole difficulty." With some effort Stepan Arkadyevich brought out his central idea, and looked at her significantly.

She said nothing, and shook her cropped head is dissent. But from the look on her face, which suddenly brightened into its old beauty, he saw that if she did not desire this, it was simply because it seemed to her unattainable happiness.

"I'm terribly sorry for you! And how happy I would be if I could arrange things!" said Stepan Arkadyevich, smiling more boldly. "Don't speak, don't say a word! God grant only that I may speak as I feel. I'm going to him."

Anna looked at him with dreamy, shining eyes, and said nothing.

CHAPTER TWENTY-TWO

Stepan Arkadyevich, with the same somewhat solemn expression with which he used to take his chair at council meetings, walked into Aleksey Aleksandrovich's room. Aleksey Aleksandrovich was walking about his room with his hands behind his back, thinking of just what Stepan Arkadyevich had been discussing with his wife.

"I'm not disturbing you?" said Stepan Arkadyevich, at the sight of his brother-in-law becoming suddenly aware of a sense of embarrassment unusual in him. To conceal this embarrassment, he took a cigarette case he had just bought that opened in a new way and, sniffing the leather, took a cigarette out of it.

"No. Do you want anything?" Aleksey Aleksandrovich asked without eagerness.

"Yes, I wished . . . I wanted . . . yes, I wanted to talk to you," said Stepan Arkadyevich, with surprise aware of an unaccustomed timidity.

This feeling was so unexpected and so strange that he did not believe it was the voice of conscience telling him that what he was about to do was wrong.

Stepan Arkadyevich made an effort and struggled with the timidity that had come over him.

"I hope you believe in my love for my sister and my sincere affection and respect for you," he said, reddening.

Aleksey Aleksandrovich stood still and said nothing, but his face struck Stepan Arkadyevich by its expression of submissive self-sacrifice.

"I intended . . . I wanted to have a little talk with you about my sister and your mutual position," he said, still struggling with an unaccustomed timidity.

Aleksey Aleksandrovich smiled mournfully, looked at his brother-in-law, and, without answering, went up to the table, took from it an unfinished letter, and handed it to him.

"I think unceasingly of the same thing. And here is what I had begun writing, thinking I could say it better by letter, and that my presence irritates her," he said, as he gave him the letter.

Stepan Arkadyevich took the letter, looked with incredulous surprise at the lusterless eyes fixed so immovably on him, and began to read:

I see that my presence is irksome to you. Painful as it is for me to believe it, I see that it is so, and cannot be otherwise. I don't blame you, and God is my witness that on seeing you at the time of your illness I resolved with my whole heart to forget all that had passed between us and to begin a new life. I do not regret, and shall never regret, what I have done: but I have desired one thing—your good, the good of your soul—and now I see I have not attained that. Tell me yourself what will give you true happiness and peace of mind. I put myself entirely in your hands and trust to your feeling of justice.

Stepan Arkadyevich handed back the letter, and, with the same surprise, continued looking at his brother-in-law, not knowing what to say. This silence was so awkward for both of them that Stepan Arkadyevich's lips began twitching nervously, while he still gazed without speaking at Karenin's face.

"That's what I wanted to say to her," said Aleksey Aleksandrovich, turning away.

"Yes, yes . . ." said Stepan Arkadyevich, not able to answer because of the tears that were choking him.

"Yes, yes, I understand you," he brought out at last.

"I want to know what she wants," said Aleksey Aleksandrovich.

"I am afraid she does not understand her own situation. She is not a judge of it," said Stepan Arkadyevich, taking hold of himself. "She is crushed, simply crushed by your generosity. If she were to read this letter she would be incapable of saying anything, she would only hang her head lower than ever."

"Yes, but what's to be done in that case? How explain . . . how find out her wishes?"

"If you will allow me to give my opinion, I think it is for you to point out clearly the steps you consider necessary to end the situation."

"So you think it must be ended?" Aleksey Aleksandrovich interrupted him. "But how?" he added, passing his hands across his eyes, a gesture unusual with him. "I see no possible way out of it."

"There is some way of getting out of every situation," said Stepan Arkadyevich, standing up and becoming more animated. "There was a time when you thought of breaking off . . . If you are convinced now that you cannot make each other happy . . ."

"Happiness may be variously understood. But suppose that I agree to everything, that I want nothing: what way is there of getting out of our situation?"

"If you care to know my opinion," said Stepan Arkadyevich with the same smile of soothing, almond-oil tenderness with which he had been talking to Anna. His kindly smile was so convincing that Aleksey Aleksandrovich, feeling his own weakness and unconsciously swayed by it, was ready to believe what Stepan Arkadyevich was saying.

"She will never speak out about it. But one thing is possible, one thing she might desire," he went on. "That is the cessation of your relations and all memories associated with them. To my thinking, in your case what's essential is the classification of your new relationship to one another. And this new relationship depends on both sides being free."

"Divorce," Aleksey Aleksandrovich interrupted, with disgust.

"Yes, I think divorce—yes, divorce," Stepan Arkadyevich repeated, reddening. "That is from every point of view the most rational course for married people who find themselves in the position you are in. What can be done if married people find that life is impossible for them together? That can always happen."

Aleksey Aleksandrovich sighed heavily and closed his eyes.

"There's only one point to be considered: is either of the parties desirous of remarrying? If not, it is very simple," said Stepan Arkadyevich, more and more overcoming his embarrassment.

Aleksey Aleksandrovich, his face drawn with distress, muttered something to himself, and made no answer. All that seemed so simple to Stepan Arkadyevich, Aleksey Aleksandrovich had thought over thousands of times. And, far from being simple, it all seemed to him utterly impossible. Divorce, the details of which he knew by this time, seemed to him now out of the question, because the sense of his own dignity and respect for religion forbade his pleading guilty to a fictitious charge of adultery, and still more allowing his wife, pardoned and beloved by him, to be exposed and put to public shame. Divorce appeared to him impossible for still more important reasons.

What would become of his son in case of divorce? To leave him with his mother was out of the question. The divorced mother would have her own illegitimate family, in which his position as a stepson and his education would not be good. Keep him with him? He knew that would be an act of vengeance on his part, and that he did not want. But apart from this, what more than anything made divorce seem impossible to Aleksey Aleksandrovich was that by consenting to a divorce he would be completely ruining Anna. The words of Darya Aleksandrovna at Moscow, that in deciding on a divorce he was thinking of himself and not considering that by this he would be ruining her irrevocably, had sunk into his heart. And connecting this with his forgiveness of her, with his devotion to the children, he understood it now in his own way. To consent to a divorce, to give her her freedom, meant in his thoughts to take from himself the last tie that bound him to life—the children whom he loved; and to take from her the last prop that supported her on the path of virtue and cast her down to her ruin. If she were divorced, he knew she would join her life to Vronsky's, and their tie would be an illegitimate and criminal one, since a wife, by the interpretation of the ecclesiastical law, could not marry while her husband was living. "She will join him, and in a year or two he will abandon her, or she will have a new liaison," thought Aleksey Aleksandrovich. "And I, by agreeing to an unlawful divorce, shall be to blame for her ruin." He had thought it all over hundreds of times, and was convinced that a divorce was not at all simple, as Stepan Arkadyevich had said, but was utterly impossible. He did not believe a single word Stepan Arkadyevich said to him; to every word he had a thousand objections to make, but he listened, feeling that his words were the expression of that powerful brutal force which controlled his life and to which he would have to submit.

"The only question is on what terms you agree to give her a divorce. She does not want anything, does not dare ask you for anything, she leaves it all to your generosity."

"My God, my God! What for?" thought Aleksey Aleksandrovich, remembering the details of divorce proceedings in which the husband took the blame on himself, and with the same gesture with which Vronsky had covered his face, he hid his face in shame in his hands.

"You are distressed, I understand that. But if you think it over . . ."

"Whosoever shall smite thee on thy right cheek, turn to him the other also; and if any man take away thy coat, let him have thy cloak also," thought Aleksey Aleksandrovich.

"Yes, yes!" he cried in a shrill voice. "I will take the disgrace on myself, I will give up even my son, but . . . but wouldn't it be better to leave it alone? However, you may do as you like . . ."

And turning away so that his brother-in-law could not see him, he sat down on a chair by the window. There was bitterness, there was shame in his heart, but with bitterness and shame he felt joy and emotion at the greatness of his own humility.

Stepan Arkadyevich was touched. He was silent for a while.

"Aleksey Aleksandrovich, believe me, she appreciates your generosity," he said. "But it seems it was the will of God," he added, and as he said it he felt how stupid a remark it was, and with difficulty repressed a smile at his own stupidity.

Aleksey Aleksandrovich would have made some reply, but tears stopped him.

"This calamity is fatal, and one must accept it as such. I accept the calamity as an accomplished fact, and am doing my best to help both her and you," said Stepan Arkadyevich.

When he went out of his brother-in-law's room he was touched, but that did not prevent him from being glad he had successfully brought the matter to a conclusion, for he felt certain Aleksey Aleksandrovich would not go back on his words.

To this satisfaction was added the fact that a thought had just struck him for a riddle turning on his successful achievement, that when the affair was over he would ask his wife and most intimate friends: "What is the difference between me and the Tsar? The Tsar divorces himself from his subjects and no one is happier, I arrange a divorce and three people are happier . . . Or, what similarity is there . . . But I'll work it out better than that," he said to himself with a smile.

CHAPTER TWENTY-THREE

Vronsky's wound had been a dangerous one, thought it did not touch the heart, and for several days he had lain between life and death. The first time he was able to speak, Varya, his brother's wife, was alone with him in the room.

"Varya," he said, looking sternly at her, "I shot myself by accident. And please never speak of it, and tell everyone that. Otherwise it's too ridiculous."

Without answering his words, Varya bent over him, and with a delighted smile gazed into his face. His eyes were clear, not feverish; but their expression was stern.

"Thank God!" she said. "You're not in pain?"

"A little here." He pointed to his breast.

"Then let me change your bandages."

In silence, setting his broad jaws, he looked at her while she bandaged him up. When she had finished he said:

"I'm not delirious. Please manage it so that there will be no talk of my having shot myself on purpose."

"No one says so. But I hope you won't shoot yourself by accident any more," she said, with a questioning smile.

"Of course I won't, but it would have been better . . ."

And he smiled gloomily.

In spite of these words and this smile, which so frightened Varya, when the inflammation was over and he began to recover, he felt that he was completely free from one part of his misery. By his action he had, as it were, washed away the shame and humiliation he had felt before. He could now think calmly of Aleksey Aleksandrovich. He recognized all his magnanimity, but he did not now feel himself humiliated by it. Besides, he had got back into his old rut again. He saw the possibility of looking men in the face again without shame, and he could live in accordance with his own habits. One thing he could not tear out of his heart, though he never ceased struggling with it, was the regret, amounting to despair, that he had lost her forever. Having expiated his sin against the husband, he was bound to renounce her and never in the future to stand between her, with her repentance, and her husband—that he had firmly decided in his heart; but he could not tear out of his heart his regret at the loss of her love, he could not erase from his memory those moments of happiness that he had so little prized at the time, and that haunted him in all their charm.

Serpukhovskoy had planned his appointment at Tashkent, and Vronsky agreed to the proposition without the slightest hesitation. But the nearer the time of departure came, the bitterer was the sacrifice he was making to what he thought his duty.

His wound was healed, and he was driving about making preparations for his departure for Tashkent.

"To see her once and then to bury myself to die," he thought, and as he was paying farewell visits, he uttered this thought to Betsy.

Charged with this commission, Betsy had gone to Anna, and brought back a negative reply.

"So much the better," thought Vronsky when he received the news. "It was a weakness that would have shattered what strength I have left."

Next day Betsy herself came to him in the morning, and announced that she had heard through Oblonsky as a positive fact that Aleksey Aleksandrovich had agreed to a divorce, and that therefore Vronsky could see Anna.

Without even troubling himself to see Betsy out of his apartment, forgetting all his resolutions, and without asking when he could see her or where her husband was, Vronsky drove straight to the Karenins'. He ran up the stairs seeing no one and nothing, and with a rapid step, almost breaking into a run, he went into her room. And without considering, without noticing whether there was anyone in the room or not, he flung his arms around her and began to cover her face, her hands, her neck with kisses.

Anna had been preparing herself for this meeting, had thought what she would say to him, but she did not succeed in saying any of it; his passion overwhelmed her. She tried to calm him, to calm herself, but it was too late. His feeling infected her. Her lips trembled, so that for a long while she could say nothing.

"Yes, you have conquered me, and I am yours," she said at last, pressing his hands to her bosom.

"So it had to be," he said. "So long as we live, it must be so. I know it now."

"That's true," she said, getting whiter and whiter, and putting her arms around his head. "Still there is something terrible in it after all that has happened."

"It will all pass, it will all pass; we shall be so happy. Our love, if it *could* be stronger, will be strengthened because there is something terrible in it," he said, lifting his head and parting his strong teeth in a smile.

And she could not but respond with a smile—not to his words, but to the love in his eyes. She took his hand and stroked her cold cheeks and cropped hair with it.

"I hardly know you with this short hair. You've grown so lovely. Like a little boy. But how pale you are!"

"Yes, I'm very weak," she said, smiling. And her lips began trembling again.

"We'll go to Italy; you will grow strong," he said.

"Can it be possible we could be like husband and wife, alone, our own family?" she said, looking close into his eyes.

"It only seems strange to me that it could ever have been otherwise."

"Stiva says that *he* has agreed to everything, but I can't accept *his* generosity," she said, looking dreamily past Vronsky's face. "I don't want a divorce; it's all the same to me now. Only I don't know what he will decide about Seryozha."

He could not conceive how at this moment of their meeting she could remember and think of her son, of divorce. What did it all matter?

"Don't speak of that, don't think of it," he said, turning her hand in his, and trying to draw her attention to him; but still she did not look at him.

"Oh, why didn't I die? It would have been better!" she said, and tears flowed silently down both her cheeks; but she tried to smile so as not to hurt him.

To decline the flattering and dangerous mission to Tashkent would have been, Vronsky had till then considered, disgraceful and impossible. But now, without an instant's consideration, he declined it, and noticing the dissatisfaction of his superiors, he immediately retired from the army.

A month later Aleksey Aleksandrovich was left alone with his son in his house at Petersburg, while Anna and Vronsky had gone abroad, not having obtained a divorce, but having absolutely refused one.

PART FIVE

CHAPTER ONE

Princess Shcherbatskaya considered that it was out of the question for the wedding to take place before Lent, just five weeks off, since not half the trousseau could possibly be ready by that time. But she could not but agree with Levin that to fix it for after Lent would be putting it off too late, as an old aunt of Prince Shcherbatsky's was seriously ill and might die, and then the mourning would delay the wedding still longer. And therefore, deciding to divide the trousseau into two parts—a larger and smaller trousseau—the princess consented to have the wedding before Lent. She determined that she would get the smaller part of the trousseau all ready now, and the larger part should be made later, and she was very angry with Levin because he was incapable of giving her a serious answer to the question whether he agreed to this arrangement or not. The arrangement was the more convenient because, immediately after the wedding the young people were to go to the country, where the more important part of the trousseau would not be needed.

Levin still continued in the same delirious condition in which it seemed to him that he and his happiness constituted the chief and sole aim of all existence, and that he need not now think or care about anything, that everything was being done and would be done for him by others. He had not even plans and aims for the future; he left its arrangement to others, knowing that everything would be delightful. His brother Sergey Ivanovich, Stepan Arkadyevich, and the princess directed him in doing what he had to do. All he did was to agree entirely with everything suggested to him. His brother raised money for him,[1] the princess advised him to leave Moscow

[1] Levin's lack of cash was in no sense unusual. Capital was almost always completely tied up in the land, and it was only during harvest time that cash would normally be available.

after the wedding, Stepan Arkadyevich advised him to go abroad. He agreed to everything. "Do what you like, if it amuses you. I'm happy, and my happiness can be no greater and no less because of anything you do," he thought. When he told Kitty of Stepan Arkadyevich's suggestion that they go abroad, he was much surprised that she did not agree to this, and had some definite proposals of her own regarding their future. She knew Levin had work he loved in the country. She did not, as he saw it, understand this work, she did not even care to understand it. But that did not prevent her from regarding it as a matter of great importance. And besides, she knew their home would be in the country, and she wanted to go, not abroad where she was not going to live, but to the place where their home would be. This strongly expressed intention astonished Levin. But since he did not care either way, he immediately asked Stepan Arkadyevich, as though it was his duty, to go down to the country and to arrange everything there according to his own good taste, of which he had so much.

"But look," Stepan Arkadyevich said to him one day after he had come back from the country, where he had got everything ready for the young people's arrival, "have you a certificate showing you have received Communion?"

"No. But what of it?"

You can't be married without it."

"*Aie, aie, aie!*" cried Levin, "Why, I think it's nine years since I've been to Communion! I never thought of it."

"You're a prize package!" said Stepan Arkadyevich, laughing, "and you call *me* a nihilist! But this won't do, you know. You must confess and take the sacrament."

"When? There are only four days left now."

Stepan Arkadyevich arranged this also, and Levin had to prepare himself for confession. To Levin, as to any unbeliever who respects the beliefs of others, it was exceedingly disagreeable to be present at and take part in church ceremonies. At this moment, in his present softened state of feeling, sensitive to everything, this inevitable act of hypocrisy was not merely painful to Levin, it seemed to him utterly impossible. Now, in the heyday of his glory, his fullest flowering, he would have to be a liar or a blasphemer. He felt incapable of being either. But though he repeatedly plied Stepan Arkadyevich with questions as to the possibility of obtaining a certificate without going to Communion, Stepan Arkadyevich maintained that it was out of the question.

"Besides, what is it to you—two days? And the priest is a very nice and sensible old man. He'll pull the tooth out for you so gently, you won't notice it."

Standing at the first mass, Levin attempted to revive in himself his youthful recollections of the intense religious emotion he had passed through between the ages of sixteen and seventeen.

But he was at once convinced that it was utterly impossible for him. He attempted to look at it all as an empty custom, having no sort of meaning, like the custom of paying calls. But he felt that he could not do that either. Levin found himself, like the majority of his contemporaries, in the vaguest position in regard to religion. Believe he could not, and at the same time he had no firm conviction that it was all wrong. And consequently, not being able to believe in the significance of what he was doing or to regard it with indifference as an empty formality, during the whole period of preparing for the sacrament he was conscious of a feeling of discomfort and shame at doing what he did not himself understand, and what, as an inner voice told him, was therefore false and wrong.

During the service he would first listen to the prayers, trying to attach some meaning to them not in conflict with his own views; then, feeling that he could not understand and must condemn them, he tried not to listen to them, but to attend to the thoughts, observations, and memories which floated through his brain with extreme vividness during the time he was standing idly in church.

He stood through the mass, vespers, and evensong, and the next day he got up earlier than usual and, without having tea, went to the church at eight o'clock in the morning for the morning service and the confession.

There was no one in the church but a beggar soldier, two old women, and the church officials. A young deacon, whose long back showed in two distinct halves through his thin undercassock, met him, and at once, going to a small table by the wall, read the prayers. During the reading, especially at the frequent and rapid repetition of the same words, "Lord, have mercy on us!" which sounded like

"Lorhavmercypons,"[2] Levin felt that his mind was shut and sealed up, and that it must not be touched or stirred now or confusion would be the result; and so, standing behind the deacon, he went on thinking of his own affairs, neither listening nor examining what was said. "It's wonderful what expression there is in her hand," he thought, remembering how they had been sitting the day before at a corner table. They had nothing to talk about, as was almost always the case at this time, and laying her hand on the table, she kept opening and shutting it, and laughed herself as she watched her action. He remembered how he had kissed it and then had examined the lines on the pink palm. "Again 'Lorhavmercypons,' " thought Levin, crossing himself, bowing, and looking at the supple movements of the deacon's back bowing before him. "She took my hand then and examined the lines. 'You've got a splendid hand,' she said." And he looked at his own and at the stumpy hand of the deacon. "Yes, now it will soon be over," he thought. "No, it seems to be beginning again," he thought, listening to the prayers. "No, it's just ending: here he is bowing down to the ground. That's always at the end."

The deacon's hand in a velvet cuff stealthily accepted a three-ruble note, and he said he would put down Levin's name; his new boots clattered over the flagstones of the empty church as he went jauntily to the chancel. A moment later he peeped out and beckoned to Levin. Thought, till then locked up, began to stir in Levin's head, but he made haste to drive it away. "It will come right somehow," he thought, and went toward the ambo. He went up the steps, and, turning to the right, saw the priest. The priest, a little old man with a scant, grizzled beard and weary, good-natured eyes, was standing near the lectern, turning over the pages of a missal. With a slight bow to Levin, he began immediately reading prayers in the stereotyped voice. When he had finished them he bowed down to the ground and turned, facing Levin.

"Christ is present here unseen, receiving your confession," he said, pointing to the crucifix. "Do you believe in all the doctrines of the Holy Apostolic Church?" the priest went on, turning his eyes away from Levin's face and folding his hands under his stole.

---

[2] I.e., *Gospodi pomiluv* sounded like *pomilos, pomilos.*

"I have doubted and I still doubt everything," said Levin in a voice unpleasant to him, and he ceased speaking.

The priest waited a few seconds to see if he would add anything more, and closing his eyes he said quickly, with a broad Vladimir accent,[3] emphasizing the *o's*:

"Doubt is natural to the weakness of mankind, but we must pray that God in His mercy will strengthen us. What are your particular sins?" he added, without the slightest pause, as though anxious not to waste time.

"My chief sin is doubt. I have doubts about everything, and am most of the time in doubt."

"Doubt is natural to the weakness of mankind," the priest repeated the same words. "What do you doubt particularly?"

"I doubt everything. I sometimes even have doubts of the existence of God," Levin could not help saying, and he was horrified at the impropriety of what he was saying. But Levin's words did not, it seemed, make much impression on the priest.

"What sort of doubt can there be of the existence of God?" he said hurriedly, with a barely perceptible smile.

Levin did not speak.

"What doubt can you have of the Creator when you behold His creation?" the priest went on in the rapid customary jargon. "Who has decked the heavenly firmament with its stars? Who has clothed the earth in its beauty? How could it be without the Creator?" he said, looking inquiringly at Levin.

Levin felt that it would be improper to enter upon a metaphysical discussion with the priest, and so he said in reply merely what was a direct answer to the question.

"I don't know," he said.

"You don't know! Then how can you doubt that God created all?" the priest said, with good-humored perplexity.

"I don't understand it all," said Levin, blushing, feeling that his words were stupid, and that they could not be anything but stupid in such a situation.

"Pray to God and beseech Him. Even the holy fathers had doubts,

[3] I.e., a strong provincial accent.

and prayed to God to strengthen their faith. The devil has great power, and we must resist him. Pray to God, beseech Him. Pray to God," he repeated hurriedly.

The priest paused for some time, as though meditating.

"You're about, I hear, to marry the daughter of my parishioner and spiritual son, Prince Shcherbatsky?" he resumed, with a smile. "An excellent young lady."

"Yes," answered Levin, blushing for the priest. "Why does he want to ask me about this at confession?" he thought.

And, as though answering his thought, the priest said to him:

"You are about to enter into holy matrimony, and God may bless you with offspring. Well, what sort of education can you give your babes if you do not overcome the temptation of the devil, enticing you to infidelity?" he said, with gentle reproachfulness. "If you love your child as a good father, you will desire not only wealth, luxury, honor for your infant; you will be anxious for his salvation, his spiritual enlightenment with the light of truth. Eh? What answer will you make him when the innocent babe asks you: 'Papa! Who made all that enchants me in this world—the earth, the waters, the sun, the flowers, the grass?' Can you say to him: 'I don't know'? You cannot but know, since the Lord God in His infinite mercy has revealed it to us. Or your child will ask you: 'What awaits me in the life beyond the tomb?' What will you say to him when you know nothing? How will you answer him? Will you leave him to the temptations of the world and the devil? That's not right," he said, and he stopped, putting his head on one side and looking at Levin with his kindly, gentle eyes.

Levin made no answer this time, not because he did not want to enter upon a discussion with the priest, but because, so far, no one had ever asked him such questions, and when his babes did ask him those questions, it would be time enough to think about answering them.

"You are entering upon a time of life," pursued the priest, "when you must choose your path and keep to it. Pray to God that He may in His mercy aid you and have mercy on you!" he concluded. "May our Lord Jesus Christ, in the abundance and riches of His loving-kindness, forgive this His child . . ." and, finishing the prayer of absolution, the priest blessed him and let him go.

On getting home that day, Levin had a delightful sense of relief at the awkward position being over and having been through it without his having to tell a lie. Apart from this, there remained a vague memory that what the kind, nice old fellow had said had not been at all so stupid as he had thought at first, and that there was something in it that must be cleared up.

"Of course, not now," thought Levin, "but someday later on." Levin felt more than ever now that there was something not clear and not clean in his soul, and that, in regard to religion, he was in the same position he perceived so clearly and disliked in others, and for which he blamed his friend Sviazhsky.

Levin spent that evening with his betrothed at Dolly's, and was in very high spirits. To explain to Stepan Arkadyevich the state of excitement in which he found himself, he said that he was as happy as a dog being trained to jump through a hoop, who, having at last caught the idea and done what was required of it, whines and wags its tail, and jumps for joy on the table and the window sills.

CHAPTER TWO

On the day of the wedding, according to the Russian custom (the princess and Darya Aleksandrovna insisted on strictly keeping all the customs), Levin did not see his bride, and dined at his hotel with three bachelor friends, casually brought together in his rooms. These were Sergey Ivanovich, Katavasov, a university friend, now professor of natural science, whom Levin had met in the street and insisted on taking home with him, and Chirikov, his best man, a Moscow magistrate, Levin's companion in his bear hunts. The dinner was a very merry one: Sergey Ivanovich was in his happiest mood, and was much amused by Katavasov's originality. Katavasov, feeling that his originality was appreciated and understood, made the most of it. Chirikov always gave lively and good-humored support to conversation of any sort.

"See, now," said Katavasov with a drawl, a habit acquired in the lecture room, "what a capable fellow our friend Konstantin Dmitrievich was. I'm not speaking of present company, for he's not with us any longer. At the time he left the university he was fond of science, took an interest in humanity; now one half of his abilities is devoted to deceiving himself, and the other to justifying the deceit."

"A more determined enemy of matrimony than you I never saw," said Sergey Ivanovich.

"Oh, no, I'm not an enemy of matrimony. I'm in favor of division of labor. People who can do nothing else ought to propagate while the rest work for their happiness and enlightenment. That's how I look at it. To muddle up two trades is the error of the amateur; I'm not one of them."

"How happy I shall be when I hear that you're in love!" said Levin. "Please invite me to the wedding."

"I'm in love already."

"Yes, with a cuttlefish! You know"—Levin turned to his brother—"Mikhail Semyonovich is writing a work on the digestive organs of the—"

"Now, make a mess of it! It doesn't matter what about. And the fact is, I certainly do love cuttlefish."

"But that's no hindrance to your loving your wife."

"The cuttlefish is no hindrance. The wife is the hindrance."

"Why so?"

"Oh, you'll see! You care about farming, hunting,—well, you'll find out!"

"Arkhip was here today; he said there were a lot of elks in Prudnoe, and two bears," said Chirikov.

"Well, you must go and get them without me."

"Ah, that's the truth," said Sergey Ivanovich. "And you may say good-by to bear hunting for the future—your wife won't allow it!"

Levin smiled. The picture of his wife not letting him go was so pleasant that he was ready to renounce the delights of seeing bears forever.

"Still, it's a pity they should get those two bears without you. Do you remember last time at Khapilovo? That was a delightful hunt!" said Chirikov.

Levin had not the heart to disillusion him of the notion that there could be something delightful apart from her, and so said nothing.

"There's some sense in this custom of saying good-by to bachelor life," said Sergey Ivanovich. "However happy you may be, you must regret your freedom."

"And confess you feel that you want to jump out of the window, like Gogol's bridegroom?"[1]

"Of course he does, but he won't admit it," said Katavasov, and he broke into loud laughter.

"Oh, well, the window's open. Let's start this instant to Tver! There's a big she-bear; one can go right up to the lair. Seriously, let's go by the five o'clock. And let them do what they like here," said Chirikov, smiling.

"Well, now, on my honor," said Levin, smiling, "I can't find in my heart that feeling of regret for my freedom."

"Yes, there's such chaos in your heart just now that you can't find anything there," said Katavasov. "Wait a while, when you've settled down, you'll find it!"

"No; if so, I should have felt a little, apart from my feeling" (he did not want to say "love" before them) "and happiness, a certain regret at losing my freedom . . . "

"Awful! It's a hopeless case!" said Katavasov. "Well, let's drink to his recovery, or wish that a hundredth part of his dreams may be realized—and that would be happiness such as never has been seen on earth!"

Soon after dinner the guests went away to be in time to get dressed for the wedding.

When he was left alone, and recalled the conversation of these bachelor friends, Levin asked himself: had he in his heart that regret for his freedom of which they had spoken? He smiled at the question. "Freedom! What is freedom for? Happiness is only in loving and wishing her wishes, thinking her thoughts, that is to say, not freedom at all—that's happiness!"

"But do I know her ideas, her wishes, her feelings?" some voice suddenly whispered to him. The smile died on his face and he grew thoughtful. And suddenly a strange feeling came upon him. There came over him a dread and doubt—doubt of everything.

"What if she does not love me? What if she's marrying me sim-

[1]The marriage-shy Podkoliosin in Gogol's play *Marriage*.

ply to be married? What if she doesn't know herself what she's doing?" he asked himself. "She may come to her senses, and only when she is being married realize that she does not and cannot love me." And strange, most evil thoughts of her began to come to him. He was jealous of Vronsky, as he had been a year ago, as though the evening he had seen her with Vronsky had been yesterday. He suspected she had not told him everything.

He jumped up quickly. "No, this can't go on!" he said to himself in despair. "I'll go to her; I'll ask her; I'll say for the last time: we are free, and hadn't we better remain so? Anything's better than endless misery, disgrace, infidelity!" With despair in his heart and bitter anger against all men, against himself, against her, he went out of the hotel and drove to her house.

He found her in one of the back rooms. She was sitting on a trunk and making some arrangements with her maid, sorting out piles of dresses of different colors, spread on the backs of chairs and on the floor.

"Ah!" she cried, seeing him, and beaming with delight. "Is it thou? Is it you?" (To this very day she sometimes said "thou," sometimes "you.")[2] "I didn't expect you! I'm going through my wardrobe to see what's for whom . . . "

"Oh! That's very nice!" he said gloomily, looking at the maid.

"You can go, Dunyasha, I'll call you presently," said Kitty. "Kostya, what's the matter?" she asked, definitely adopting the familiar name as soon as the maid had gone out. She noticed his strange face, agitated and gloomy, and panic came over her.

"Kitty! I'm tortured, I can't suffer alone," he said with despair in his voice, standing before her and looking imploringly into her eyes. He saw already from her loving, truthful face that nothing could come of what he had meant to say, but yet he wanted her to reassure him herself. "I've come to say that there's still time. This can be stopped and put right."

"What? I don't understand. What is the matter?"

"What I have said a thousand times over, and can't help thinking . . . that I'm not worthy of you. You couldn't consent to marry me. Think a little. You've made a mistake. Think it over thoroughly. You can't love me. . . . If . . . better say so," he said, not looking at her. "I shall be wretched. Let people say what they like; anything's better than misery . . . Far better now while there's still time . . . "

"I don't understand," she answered, panic-stricken; "you mean you want to give it up . . . don't want it?"

"Yes, if you don't love me."

"You're mad!" she cried, turning crimson with vexation. But his face was so piteous that she restrained her vexation, and flinging some clothes off an armchair, she sat down beside him. "What are you thinking? Tell me all."

"I am thinking you can't love me. What can you love me for?"

"My God! What can I do? . . . " she said, and burst into tears.

"Oh! What have I done?" he cried, and kneeling before her, he started kissing her hands.

When the princess came into the room five minutes later, she found them completely reconciled. Kitty had not simply assured him that she loved him, but had gone so far—in answer to his question, what she loved him for—as to explain why. She told him that she loved him because she understood him completely, because she knew what he would like, and because everything he liked was good. And this seemed to him perfectly clear. When the princess came to them, they were sitting side by side on the trunk, sorting the dresses and disputing over Kitty's wanting to give Dunyasha the brown dress she had been wearing when Levin proposed to her, while he insisted that that dress must never be given away, but Dunyasha must have the blue one.

"How is it you don't see? She's a brunette, and it won't suit her . . . I've worked it all out."

Hearing why he had come, the princess was half humorously, half seriously angry with him, and sent him home to dress and not to hinder Kitty, whose hair was to be done, as Charles the hairdresser was expected at once.

"As it is, she's been eating nothing lately and is losing her looks, and then you come and upset her with your nonsense," she said to him. "Get along with you, my dear fellow!"

Levin, guilty and shame-faced, but pacified, went back to his hotel. His brother, Darya Aleksandrovna, and Stepan Arkadyevich, all in full dress, were waiting for him to bless him with the icon. There was no time to lose. Darya Aleksandrovna had to drive home again to fetch her curled and pomaded son, who was to drive in the bride's carriage with the icon. Then a carriage had to be sent for the best man, and another that would take Sergey Ivanovich away would have to be sent back . . . Altogether there were a great many most complicated matters to be considered and arranged. One thing was certain: there must be no delay, as it was already half-past six.

The ceremony of benediction was anything but solemn. Stepan Arkadyevich stood in a comically solemn pose beside his wife, took the icon, and telling Levin to bow down to the ground, he blessed him with his kindly, ironical smile, and kissed him three times; Darya Aleksandrovna did the same, and immediately was in a hurry to get off, and again plunged into intricate questions of the destinations of the various carriages.

"Come, I'll tell you how we'll manage; you drive in our carriage to fetch him, and Sergey Ivanovich, if he'll be so good, will drive there and then send his carriage."

"Of course; I shall be delighted."

"We'll come immediately with him. Are your things sent off?" said Stepan Arkadyevich.

"Yes," answered Levin, and he told Kuzma to lay out his clothes.

CHAPTER THREE

A crowd of people, principally women, was thronging around the church, lighted up for the wedding. Those who had not succeeded in getting into the main entrance were crowding about the windows, pushing, wrangling, and peeping through the gratings.

More than twenty carriages had already been drawn up in ranks along the street by the police. A police officer, ignoring the frost, stood at the entrance, resplendent in his uniform. More carriages were continually driving up, and ladies were wearing flowers in their hair and carrying their trains, and men were taking off their military caps or black hats as they entered the church. Inside the church both chandeliers and all the candles before the icons were lighted. The golden glitter of the crimson background of the iconostasis, the gilt chasing of the icons, the silver of the chandeliers and candlesticks, the flagstone of the floor, the mats, the banners above the choir, the steps of the ambo, the books blackened with age, the cassocks and surplices—all were flooded with light. On the right side of the warm church, in the crowd of frock coats and white ties, uniforms and broadcloth, velvet, satin, hair and flowers, bare shoulders and arms and long gloves, there was discreet but lively conversation that echoed strangely in the high cupola. Every time the creak of the opened door was heard the conversation in the crowd died away, and everybody looked around expecting to see the bride and bridegroom come in. But the door had opened more than ten times, and each time it was either a belated guest or guests, who joined the circle of the invited on the right, or a spectator who had eluded or softened the police officer, and went to join the crowd of outsiders on the left. Both the guests and the outside public had by now passed through all the phases of anticipation.

At first they imagined that the bride and bridegroom would arrive immediately, and attached no importance at all to their being late. Then they began to look more and more often toward the door, and to talk of whether anything could have happened. Then the long delay began to be positively discomforting, and relations and guests tried to look as if they were not thinking of the bridegroom but were engrossed in conversation.

The archdeacon, as though to remind them of the value of his time, coughed impatiently, making the windowpanes quiver in their frames. In the choir the bored choristers could be heard trying their voices and blowing their noses. The priest was continually sending first the beadle and then the deacon to find out whether the bridegroom had come; more and more often he went himself, in a lilac vestment and an embroidered sash, to the side door, expecting to see the bridegroom. At last one of the ladies, glancing at her watch, said, "It really is strange, though!" and all the guests became uneasy and began loudly expressing their wonder and dissatisfaction. One of the bridegroom's best men went to find out what had happened. Kitty meanwhile had long since been ready, and in her white dress and long veil and wreath of orange blossoms she was standing in the drawing room of the Shcherbatskys' house with her sister, Madame Lvova, who was her nuptial godmother. She was looking out of the window, and for over half an hour had been anxiously expecting to hear from the best man that her bridegroom was at the church.

Levin, meanwhile, in his trousers but without his coat and vest, was walking to and fro in his room at the hotel, continually putting his head out of the door and looking up and down the corridor. But in the corridor there was no sign of the person he was looking for and he came back in despair, and frantically waving his hands, he addressed Stepan Arkadyevich, who was smoking serenely.

"Was ever a man in such an absolutely idiotic situation?" he said.

"Yes, it is stupid," Stepan Arkadyevich assented, smiling soothingly. "But don't worry, it'll be brought in a minute."

"No, what is to be done!" said Levin, with smothered fury. "And these idiotic open vests! Out of the question!" he said, looking at the crumpled front of his shirt. "And what if the things have been taken to the railway station!" he roared in desperation.

"Then you must put on mine."

"I should have done so long ago."

"It's not nice to look ridiculous . . . Wait! It will *work out*."

What happened was that when Levin asked for his evening suit, Kuzma, his old servant, had brought him the coat, vest, and everything that was needed.

"But the shirt!" cried Levin.

"You've got a shirt on," Kuzma answered, with a placid smile.

Kuzma had not thought of leaving out a clean shirt, and on receiving instructions to pack up everything and send it round to the Shcherbatskys' house, from which the young people were to set out the same evening, he had done so, packing everything but the dress suit. The shirt, worn since the morning, was crumpled and out of the question with the fashionable open vest. It was a long way to send to the Shcherbatskys'. They sent out to buy a shirt. The servant came back; everything was locked up—it was Sunday. They sent to Stepan Arkadyevich's and brought a shirt—it was impossibly wide and short. They sent finally to the Shcherbatskys' to unpack the things. The bridegroom was expected at the church while he was pacing up and down his room like a wild beast in a cage, peeping out into the corridor, and with horror and despair recalling what absurd things he had said to Kitty and what she might be thinking now.

At last the guilty Kuzma flew panting into the room with the shirt. "Just in time. They were just lifting it into the van," said Kuzma.

Three minutes later Levin ran full speed into the corridor, not looking at his watch for fear of aggravating his sufferings.

"You won't help matters like this," said Stepan Arkadyevich with a smile, following without haste. "It will *work out*, it will *work out*, I tell you."

CHAPTER FOUR

"They've come!" "Here he is!" "Which one?" "The younger one, eh?" "Why, poor dear, she looks more dead than alive!" were the comments in the crowd when Levin, meeting his bride in the entrance, walked with her into the church.

Stepan Arkadyevich told his wife the cause of the delay, and the guests were whispering it with smiles to one another. Levin saw nothing and no one; he did not take his eyes off his bride.

Everyone said she had lost her looks the last few days and was not nearly so pretty in her wedding dress as usual; but Levin did not think so. He looked at her hair done up high, with the long white veil and white flowers and the high, stand-up scalloped collar that in such a maidenly fashion hid her long neck at the sides and only showed it in front, at her strikingly slender figure, and it seemed to him that she looked better than ever—not because these flowers, this veil, this gown from Paris added anything to her beauty; but because, in spite of the elaborate sumptuousness of her attire, the expression of her sweet face, of her eyes, of her lips was still her own characteristic expression of guileless truthfulness.

"I was beginning to think you meant to run away," she said, and smiled to him.

"It's so stupid, what happened to me, I'm ashamed to speak of it!" he said, reddening, and he was obliged to turn to Sergey Ivanovich, who came up to him.

"Lovely story of yours about the shirt!" said Sergey Ivanovich, shaking his head and smiling.

"Yes, yes!" answered Levin, without any idea of what they were talking about.

"Now, Kostya, you have to decide," said Stepan Arkadyevich with an air of mock dismay, "a weighty question. You are at this moment just in the mood to appreciate all its gravity. They ask me, are they to light the candles that have been lighted before or candles that have never been lighted? It's a matter of ten rubles," he added, relaxing his lips into a smile. "I have decided, but I was afraid you might not agree."

Levin saw that it was a joke, but he could not smile.

"Well, how's it to be, then?—unlighted or lighted candles? That is the question."

"Yes, yes, unlighted."

"Oh, I'm very glad. The question's decided!" said Stepan Arkadyevich, smiling. "How stupid men are, though, in this situation," he said to Chirikov, when Levin, after looking absently at him, had moved back to his bride.

"Kitty, careful you're the first to step on the carpet," said Countess Nordston, coming up. "You're something!" she said to Levin.

"Aren't you frightened, eh?" said Marya Dmitrievna, an old aunt.

"Are you cold? You're pale. Stop a minute, stoop down," said Kitty's sister, Madame Lvova, and with her plump, beautiful arms she smilingly arranged the flowers on her head.

Dolly came up, tried to say something, but could not speak, cried, and then laughed unnaturally.

Kitty looked at all of them with the same faraway eyes as Levin. Her only response to everything said to her was a smile of happiness, which came naturally to her now.

Meanwhile, the officiating clergy had got into their vestments, and the priest and deacon came out to the lectern, which stood in the forepart of the church. The priest turned to Levin saying something. Levin did not hear what the priest said.

"Take the bride's hand and lead her," the best man said to Levin.

It was a long while before Levin could make out what was

expected of him. For a long time they tried to put him right and made him begin again—because he kept taking Kitty by the wrong arm or with the wrong arm—till he understood at last that what he had to do was, without changing his position, take her right hand in his right hand. When at last he had taken the bride's hand in the correct way, the priest walked a few paces in front of them and stopped at the lectern. The crowd of friends and relations moving after them, with a buzz of talk and a rustle of skirts. Someone stooped down and pulled out the bride's train. The church became so still that the drops of wax could be heard falling from the candles.

The little old priest in his ecclesiastical cap, with his locks of gray hair glistening like silver, combed back behind his ears, was fumbling with something at the lectern, freeing his little old hands from under the heavy silver vestment with the gold cross on the back of it.

Stepan Arkadyevich approached him cautiously, whispered something, and, making a sign to Levin, walked back again.

The priest lighted two candles wreathed with flowers, and holding them sideways so that the wax dropped slowly from them, he turned, facing the bridal pair. The priest was the same old man who had confessed Levin. He looked with weary and melancholy eyes at the bride and bridegroom, sighed, and, putting his right hand out from his vestment, blessed the bridegroom with it, and also, with a shade of solicitous tenderness laid the crossed fingers on the bowed head of Kitty. Then he gave them the candles, and taking the censer, he moved slowly away from them.

"Can it be true?" thought Levin, and he looked around at his bride. Looking down at her, he saw her face in profile, and from the scarcely perceptible quiver of her lips and eyelashes he knew she was aware of his eyes upon her. She did not look around, but the high scalloped collar, which reached her little pink ear, trembled faintly. He saw that a sigh was held back in her throat, and the little hand in the long glove shook as it held the candle.

All the fuss of the shirt, of being late, all the talk of friends and relations, their annoyance, his ludicrous situation—all suddenly passed away and he was filled with joy and dread.

The handsome, stately senior deacon, wearing a silver robe and his curled locks parted in the middle, stepped smartly forward, and lifting his stole with the practiced movement of two fingers, he stood opposite the priest.

"Blessed be the name of the Lord," the solemn syllables rang out slowly one after another, setting the air quivering with waves of sound.

"Blessed be the name of our God, now and hereafter," the little old priest answered in a submissive, piping voice, still fingering something at the lectern. And the full chorus of the unseen choir rose up, filling the whole church from the windows to the vaulted roof with broad waves of melody. It grew stronger, rested for an instant, and slowly died away.

They prayed, as they always do, for peace from on high and for salvation, for the Holy Synod, and for the Tsar; they prayed, too, for the servants of God, Konstantin and Yekaterina, now plighting their troth.

"Vouchsafe to them love made perfect, peace and help, O Lord, we beseech Thee," the whole church seemed to breathe with the voice of the senior deacon.

Levin heard the words, and they impressed him. "How did they guess that it is help, just help that one needs?" he thought, recalling all his fears and doubts of late. "What do I know? What can I do in this fearful business," he thought, "without help? Yes, it is help I need now."

When the deacon had finished the liturgical prayer, the priest turned to the bridal pair with a book: "Eternal God, that joinest together in love them that were separate," he read in a gentle, piping voice: "who hath ordained the union of holy wedlock that cannot be set asunder, Thou who didst bless Isaac and Rebecca and their descendants, according to Thy Holy Covenant; bless Thy servants, Konstantin and Yekaterina, leading them in the path of all good works. For gracious and merciful art Thou, our Lord, and glory be to Thee, the Father, the Son, and the Holy Ghost, now and forever and ever."

"Amen!" the unseen choir sent floating again through the air.

" 'Joinest together in love them that were separate.' What deep meaning in those words, and how they correspond with what one feels at this moment," thought Levin. "Is she feeling the same as I?"

And looking around, he met her eyes, and from their expression he concluded that she was understanding it just as he was. But this was a mistake; she almost completely missed the meaning of the words of the service; she had not heard them, in fact. She could not listen to them and take them in, so strong was the one feeling that filled her breast and grew stronger and stronger. That feeling was joy at the completion of the process that for the last month and a half had been going on in her soul, and had during those six weeks been a joy and a torture to her. On the day when in the drawing room of the house on Arbat she had gone up to him in her brown dress, and accepted him without a word—on that day, at that hour, there took place in her heart a complete severance from her old life, and a quite different, new, utterly strange life had begun for her, while the old life was actually going on as before. Those six weeks had for her been a time of the utmost bliss and the utmost misery. All her life, all her desires and hopes were concentrated on this one man, still not understood by her, to whom she was bound by a feeling of alternate attraction and repulsion, even less comprehended than the man himself, and all the while she was going on living in the outward conditions of her old life. Living the old life, she was horrified at herself, at her utter insurmountable callousness to her own past, to things, to habits, to the people she had loved, who loved her—to her mother, who was wounded by her indifference, to her kind, tender father, till then dearer than all the world. At one moment she was horrified at this indifference, at another she rejoiced at what had brought her to this indifference. She could not frame a thought, not a wish apart from life with this man; but this new life was not yet, and she could not even picture it clearly to herself. There was only anticipation, the dread and joy of the new and the unknown. And now behold—anticipation and uncertainty and remorse at the abandonment of the old life—all was ending, and the new was beginning. This new life could not but have terrors for her inexperience; but, terrible or not, the change had been wrought six weeks before in her soul, and this was merely the final sanction of what had long been completed in her heart.

Turning again to the lectern, the priest with some difficulty picked up Kitty's little ring, and asking Levin for his hand, he put it on the tip of his finger. "The servant of God, Konstantin, plights his troth to the servant of God, Yekaterina." And putting the big ring on Kitty's touchingly weak, rosy little finger, the priest said the same thing.

And the bridal pair tried several times to understand what they had to do, and each time made some mistake and were corrected by the priest in a whisper. At last, having duly done what was necessary, having made the sign of the cross over them with the rings, the priest handed Kitty the big ring, and Levin the little one. Again they were puzzled, and passed the rings from hand to hand, still without doing what was expected.

Dolly, Chirikov, and Stepan Arkadyevich stepped forward to help them. There was an interval of hesitation, whispering, and smiles; but the expression of solemn emotion on the faces of the betrothed pair did not change; on the contrary, in their perplexity over their hands they looked more grave and deeply moved than before, and the smile with which Stepan Arkadyevich whispered to them that now they would each put on their own ring died away on his lips. He had a feeling that any smile would pain them.

"Thou who didst from the beginning create male and female," the priest read after the exchange of rings, "from Thee woman was given to man to be a helpmeet to him, and for the procreation of children. O Lord, our God, who hast poured down the blessings of Thy Truth according to Thy Holy Covenant upon Thy chosen servants, our fathers, from generation to generation, bless Thy servants Konstantin and Yekaterina and make their troth fast in faith, and union of hearts, and truth, and love . . ."

Levin felt more and more that all his ideas of marriage, all his dreams of how he would arrange his life, were mere childishness, and that it was something he had never understood, and now understood less than ever, though it was happening to him. In his breast a tremor rose higher and higher, and tears that would not be checked came into his eyes.

CHAPTER FIVE

In the church there was all Moscow, all the friends and relations; and during the ceremony of plighting troth, in the brilliantly lighted church, there was an incessant flow of discreetly subdued talk in the circle of gaily dressed women and girls, and men in white ties, frock coats, and uniforms. The talk was principally kept up by the men, while the women were absorbed in watching every detail of the ceremony, which always means so much to them.

In the little group nearest to the bride were her two sisters: Dolly, and the elder one, the calm beauty, Madame Lvova, who had just arrived from abroad.

"Why is it Marie's in lilac, as bad as black, at a wedding?" said Madame Korsunskaya.

"With her complexion, it's the one salvation," Princess Drubetskaya responded. "I wonder why they had the wedding in the evening. It's like what tradespeople do . . ."

"So much prettier. I was married in the evening too . . . " answered Madame Korsunskaya, and she sighed, remembering how charming she had been that day, and how absurdly in love her husband was, and how different it all was now.

"They say if anyone's best man more than ten times, he'll never be married. I wanted to be for the tenth time, but the post was taken," said Count Sinyavin to the pretty Princess Charskaya, who had designs on him.

Princess Charskaya only answered with a smile. She looked at Kitty, thinking how and when she would stand with Count Sinyavin in Kitty's place, and how she would remind him then of his joke today.

Young Shcherbatsky told the old lady in waiting, Madame Nikolaeva, that he meant to put the crown on Kitty's chignon for luck.[1]

"She should not have worn a chignon," answered Madame Nikolaeva, who had long ago made up her mind that if the elderly widower she was angling for married her, the wedding should be of the simplest. "I don't like such grandeur."

[1] During specific parts of the marriage ceremony, heavy metal crowns are held above the heads of the bride and bridegroom. It is felt that if the crowns are actually put on, singular luck will follow.

Sergey Ivanovich was talking to Darya Dmitrievna, jestingly assuring her that the custom of going away after the wedding was becoming common because newly married people always felt a little ashamed of themselves.

"Your brother may feel proud of himself. She's a marvel of sweetness. I believe you're envious."

"Oh, I've got over that, Darya Dmitrievna," he answered, and a melancholy and serious expression suddenly came over his face.

Stepan Arkadyevich was telling his sister-in-law his joke about divorce.

"The wreath needs to be put straight," she answered, not listening to him.

"What a pity she's lost her looks so," Countess Nordston said to Madame Lvova. "Still he's not worth her little finger, is he?"

"Oh, I like him so . . . not because he's my future *beau-frère*," answered Madame Lvova. "And how well he's behaving! It's so difficult, too, to behave well in such a situation, not to look ridiculous. And he's not ridiculous, and not affected; one can see he's moved."

"You expected it, I suppose?"

"Almost. She always cared for him."

"Well, we shall see which of them will step on the mat first.[2] I warned Kitty."

"It will make no difference," said Madame Lvova; "we're all obedient wives; it's in our family."

"Oh, I stepped on the mat before Vasily on purpose. And you, Dolly?"

Dolly stood beside them, she heard them, but she did not answer. She was deeply moved. The tears stood in her eyes, and she could not have spoken without crying. She was rejoicing over Kitty and Levin; going back in thought to her own wedding, she glanced at the radiant figure of Stepan Arkadyevich, forgot the present, and remembered only her own innocent love. She recalled not only herself, but all the women she was intimate with or with whom she was acquainted. She thought of them on the one day of their triumph,

---

[2]Those getting married stand on a small silk mat during part of the ceremony, and it is said that the one who steps on it first will become head of the house.

when they had stood like Kitty under the wedding crown, with love and hope and dread in their hearts, renouncing the past and stepping forward into the mysterious future. Among the brides that came back to her memory, she thought too of her darling Anna, of whose proposed divorce she had just been hearing. And she had stood just as innocent in orange flowers and bridal veil. And now? "It's terribly strange," she said to herself.

It was not merely the sisters, the friends and relations of the bride who were following every detail of the ceremony. Women who were complete strangers, mere spectators, were watching it excitedly, holding their breath, in fear of losing a single movement or expression of the bride and bridegroom, and angrily not answering, often not hearing, the remarks of the callous men, who kept making jocular or irrelevant observations.

"Why has she been crying? Is she being married against her will?"

"Against her will to a fine fellow like that? A prince, isn't he?"

"Is that her sister in the white satin? Just listen how the deacon booms out, 'and obey thy husband.' "

"Are the choristers from Chudovo?"[3]

"No, from the Synod."

"I asked the footman. He says he's going to take her home to his country place at once. Terribly rich, they say. That's why she's being married to him."

"No, they're a very nice couple."

"Marya Vasilievna, you were saying that crinolines were not being worn fuller at the sides. Just look at her in the puce dress . . . an ambassador's wife, they say she is—how her skirt bounces out from side to side!"

"What a pretty dear the bride is—like a lamb decked with flowers! Well, say what you will, we women feel for our sister."

Such were the comments in the crowd of women spectators who had succeeded in slipping in at the church doors.

---

[3]Monastery famous for its choirs.

CHAPTER SIX

When the ceremony of plighting troth was over, the verger spread before the lectern in the middle of the church a piece of pink silk cloth, the choir sang a complicated and elaborate psalm, in which the bass and tenor sang responses to one another, and the priest, turning around, pointed the bridal pair to the pink silk mat. Though both had often heard a great deal about the saying that the one who steps first on the mat will be the head of the house, neither Levin nor Kitty were capable of thinking of it as they took the few steps toward it. They did not hear the loud remarks and disputes that followed, some maintaining he had stepped on first, and others that both had stepped on together.

After the customary questions, whether they desired to enter upon matrimony, and whether they were pledged to anyone else, and their answers, which sounded strange to themselves, the second part of the ceremony began. Kitty listened to the words of the prayer, trying to make out their meaning, but she could not. The feeling of triumph and radiant happiness flooded her soul more and more as the ceremony went on, and deprived her of all power of attention.

They prayed:

"Endow them with continence and fruitfulness, and vouchsafe that their hearts may rejoice looking upon their sons and daughters." They alluded to God's creation of a wife from Adam's rib, "and for this cause a man shall leave father and mother, and cleave unto his wife, and they two shall be one flesh," and that "this is a great mystery"; they prayed that God would make them fruitful and bless them, like Isaac and Rebecca, Joseph, Moses and Zipporah, and that they might look upon their children's children. "It's all beautiful," thought Kitty, catching the words, "just as it should be," and a smile of happiness, unconsciously reflected in everyone who looked at her, beamed on her radiant face.

"Put it entirely on," voices were heard urging when the priest had put on the wedding crowns, and Shcherbatsky, his hand shaking in its three-button glove, held the crown high above her head.

"Put it on!" she whispered, smiling.

Levin looked around at her, and was struck by the joyful radiance on her face, and unconsciously her feeling infected him. He too, like her, felt glad and happy.

They enjoyed hearing the epistle read, and the roll of the senior deacon's voice at the last verse, awaited with such impatience by the outsiders. They enjoyed drinking out of the shallow cup of warm red wine and water, and they were still more pleased when the priest, flinging back his stole and taking both their hands in his, led them round the lectern to the accompaniment of bass voices chanting "Rejoice, O Isaiah!"

Shcherbatsky and Chirikov, supporting the crowns and entangled in the bride's train, smiling too and happy without knowing why, were at one moment lagging behind, at the next stumbling over the bridal pair as the priest came to a halt. The spark of joy kindled in Kitty seemed to have infected everyone in the church. It seemed to Levin that the priest and the deacon too wanted to smile just as he did.

Taking the crowns off their heads, the priest read the last prayer and congratulated the young people. Levin looked at Kitty, and he had never before seen her look as she did. She was charming with the new radiance of happiness in her face. Levin longed to say something to her, but he did not know whether it was all over. The priest got him out of his difficulty. He smiled his kindly smile and said gently, "Kiss your wife, and you kiss your husband," and took the candles out of their hands.

Levin kissed her smiling lips with timid care, gave her his arm, and, with a new strange sense of closeness, walked out of the church. He did not believe, he could not believe, that it was true. It was only when their surprised and timid eyes met that he believed in it, because he felt that they were one.

After supper, the same night, the young couple left for the country.

CHAPTER SEVEN

Vronsky and Anna had been traveling for three months together in Europe. They had visited Venice, Rome, and Naples, and had just arrived at a small Italian town where they meant to stay some time.

A handsome head waiter, with thick pomaded hair parted from the neck upward, an evening coat, a broad white cambric shirt front, and a bunch of charms dangling on his round stomach, stood with his hands in the full curve of his pockets, looking contemptuously from under his eyelids while he gave some reply in a severe tone to a gentleman who had stopped him. Catching the sound of footsteps coming from the other side of the entry toward the staircase, the head waiter turned around, and seeing the Russian count, who had taken their best rooms, he took his hands out of his pockets deferentially, and with a bow informed him that a courier had been, and that the business about the palazzo had been arranged. The steward was prepared to sign the agreement.

"Ah! I'm glad to hear it," said Vronsky. "Is madame at home or not?"

"Madame has been out for a walk but has returned now," answered the waiter.

Vronsky took off his soft, wide-brimmed hat and passed his handkerchief over his perspiring brow and hair, which had grown well over his ears, and was brushed back covering the bald patch on his head. And glancing casually at the gentleman, who still stood there gazing intently at him, he would have gone in.

"This gentleman is a Russian, and was inquiring after you," said the head waiter.

With mingled feelings of annoyance at never being able to get away from acquaintances anywhere, and longing to find some sort of diversion from the monotony of his life, Vronsky looked once more at the gentleman, who had retreated and stood still again, and at the same moment a light came into the eyes of both.

"Golenishchev!"

"Vronsky!"

It really was Golenishchev, a comrade of Vronsky's in the Corps of Pages. In the corps, Golenishchev had belonged to the liberal party; he left the corps without entering the army, and had never taken office under the government. Vronsky and he had gone completely different ways on leaving the corps, and had met only once since.

At that meeting Vronsky perceived that Golenishchev had taken up a sort of lofty intellectually liberal line, and was consequently disposed to look down upon Vronsky's interests and calling in life. Hence Vronsky had met him with the chilling and haughty manner he so well knew how to assume, the meaning of which was: "You may like or dislike my way of life, that's a matter of the most perfect indifference to me; you will have to treat me with respect if you want to know me." Golenishchev had been contemptuously indifferent to the tone taken by Vronsky. This second meeting might have been expected, one would have supposed, to estrange them still more. But now they beamed and exclaimed with delight on recognizing one another. Vronsky would never have expected to be so pleased to see Golenishchev, but probably he was not himself aware how bored he was. He forgot the disagreeable impression of their last meeting, and, with a face of frank delight, held out his hand to his old comrade. The same expression of delight replaced the look of uneasiness on Golenishchev's face.

"How glad I am to meet you!" said Vronsky, showing his strong white teeth in a friendly smile.

"I heard the name Vronsky, but I didn't know which one. I'm very, very glad!"

"Let's go in. Come, tell me what you're doing."

"I've been living here for two years. I'm working."

"Ah!" said Vronsky, with interest, "let's go in." And with the habit common with Russians, instead of saying in Russian what he wanted to keep from the servants, he began to speak in French.

"Do you know Madame Karenina? We are traveling together. I am going to see her now," he said in French, carefully scrutinizing Golenishchev's face.

"Ah! I did not know" (though he did know), Golenishchev answered indifferently. "Have you been here long?" he added.

"Four days," Vronsky answered, once more scrutinizing his friend's face intently.

"Yes, he's a decent fellow, and will look at the thing properly," Vronsky said to himself, catching the significance of Golenishchev's face and the change of subject. "I can introduce him to Anna."

During those three months that Vronsky had spent abroad with Anna, he had always on meeting new people asked himself how the new person would look at his relations with Anna, and for the most part, in men, he had met with the "proper" way of looking at it. But if he had been asked, and those who looked at it "properly" had been asked, exactly how they did look at it, both he and they would have been greatly puzzled as to how to answer.

In reality, those who in Vronsky's opinion had the "proper" view had no sort of view at all, but behaved in general as well-bred persons behave in regard to all the complex and insoluble problems with which life is encompassed on all sides; they behaved with propriety, avoiding allusions and unpleasant questions. They assumed an air of fully comprehending the import and force of the situation, of accepting and even approving of it, but of considering it superfluous and uncalled for to put all this into words.

Vronsky at once divined that Golenishchev was of this kind, and therefore was doubly pleased to see him. And in fact, Golenishchev's manner toward Madame Karenina, when he was taken to call on her, was all that Vronsky could have desired. Evidently without the slightest effort he steered clear of all subjects that might lead to embarrassment.

He had never met Anna before, and was struck by her beauty, and still more by the frankness with which she accepted her position. She blushed when Vronsky brought in Golenishchev, and he was extremely charmed by this childish blush overspreading her candid and beautiful face. But what he liked particularly was the way in which at once, as though on purpose so that there might be no misunderstanding with an outsider, she called Vronsky simply Aleksey, and said they were moving into a house they had just taken, what was locally called a palazzo. Golenishchev liked this direct and simple attitude toward her own position. Looking at Anna's manner of simple-hearted, spirited gaiety, and knowing Aleksey Aleksandrovich and Vronsky, Golenishchev thought that he understood her perfectly. He thought that he understood what she was utterly unable to understand: how it was that having made her husband wretched, having abandoned him and her son and lost her good name, she yet felt full of energy, gaiety, and happiness.

"It's in the guidebook," said Golenishchev, referring to the palazzo

Vronsky had taken. "There's a first-rate Tintoretto[1] there. One of his last period."

"I tell you what: it's a lovely day, let's go and have another look at it," said Vronsky, addressing Anna.

"I shall be very glad to; I'll go and put on my hat. You say it's hot?" she said, stopping at the door and looking inquiringly at Vronsky. And again a vivid flush overspread her face.

Vronsky saw from her eyes that she did not know on what terms he cared to be with Golenishchev, and so was afraid of not behaving as he would wish.

He looked at her with a long, tender look.

"No, not very," he said.

And it seemed to her that she understood everything, most of all that he was pleased with her; and smiling to him, she walked out with her rapid step.

The friends glanced at one another, and a look of hesitation came into both faces, as though Golenishchev, unmistakably admiring her, would have liked to say something about her, and could not find the right thing to say, while Vronsky desired and dreaded his doing so.

"Well, then . . . " Vronsky began to start a conversation of some sort. "So you're settled here? You're still at the same work, then?" he went on, recalling that he had been told Golenishchev was writing something.

"Yes, I'm writing the second part of the *Two Principles*," said Golenishchev, coloring with pleasure at the question—"that is, to be exact, I am not writing it yet; I am preparing, collecting materials. It will be of far wider scope, and will touch on almost all questions. We in Russia refuse to see that we are the heirs of Byzantium," and he launched into a long and heated explanation of his views.

Vronsky at the first moment felt embarrassed at not even knowing of the first part of the *Two Principles*, of which the author spoke as something well known. But as Golenishchev began to lay down his opinions and Vronsky was able to follow them even without knowing

---

[1](1518-94), Venetian painter, one of the great masters of the Renaissance. The works of his last period are especially marked by dramatic lighting and broad impressionistic brush-work.

the *Two Principles*, he listened to him with some interest, for Golen-ishchev spoke well. But Vronsky was startled and annoyed by the irri-table excitement with which Golenishchev talked of the subject that engrossed him. As he went on talking, his eyes glittered more and more angrily; he was more and more hurried in his replies to imagi-nary opponents, and his face grew more and more excited and wor-ried. Remembering Golenishchev, a thin, lively, good-natured, and well-bred boy, always at the head of the class, Vronsky could not make out the reason for his irritability, and he did not like it. What he particularly disliked was that Golenishchev, a man belonging to good society, should put himself on a level with some scribblers, with whom he was irritated and angry. Was it worth it? Vronsky disliked it, yet he felt that Golenishchev was unhappy, and was sorry for him. Unhappiness, almost insanity, was visible on his mobile, rather hand-some face, while without even noticing Anna's coming in, he went on hurriedly and hotly expressing his views.

When Anna came back in her hat and cape, her lovely hand rapidly swinging her parasol, and stood beside him, it was with a feeling of relief that Vronsky broke away from the plaintive eyes of Golenishchev which fastened persistently upon him, and with a fresh rush of love looked at his charming companion, full of life and happiness. Golen-ishchev recovered himself with an effort, and at first was dejected and gloomy, but Anna, disposed to feel friendly with everyone as she was at that time, soon revived his spirits by her direct and lively manner. After trying various subjects of conversation, she got him on to painting, of which he talked very well, and she listened to him attentively. They walked to the house they had taken, and went over it.

"I am very glad of one thing," said Anna to Golenishchev when they were on their way back, "Aleksey will have a wonderful *atelier*.[2] You must certainly take that room," she said to Vronsky in Russian, using the familiarity as though she saw that Golenishchev would become intimate with them in their isolation, and that there was no need for reserve before him.

"Do you paint?" said Golenishchev, turning around quickly to Vronsky.

[2]"Studio."

"Yes, I used to study long ago, and now I have begun to do a little," said Vronsky, reddening.

"He has great talent," said Anna with a delighted smile. "I'm no judge, of course. But good judges have said the same."

CHAPTER EIGHT

Anna, in that first period of her emancipation and rapid return to health, felt herself unpardonably happy and full of the joy of life. The thought of her husband's unhappiness did not poison her happiness. On one side that memory was too awful to be thought of. On the other side her husband's unhappiness had given her too much happiness to be regretted. The memory of all that had happened after her illness: her reconciliation with her husband, its breakdown, the news of Vronsky's wound, his visit, the preparations for divorce, the departure from her husband's house, the parting from her son—all that seemed to her like a delirious dream, from which she had awakened abroad and alone with Vronsky. The thought of the harm caused to her husband aroused in her a feeling like repulsion, like what a drowning man might feel who has shaken off another man clinging to him. That man did drown. It was wrong, of course, but it was the sole means of escape, and better not to brood over such horrible details.

One consolatory reflection upon her conduct had occurred to her at the first moment of the final break, and when now she recalled all the past, she remembered that one reflection, "I have inevitably made that man wretched," she thought; "but I don't want to profit by his misery. I too am suffering, and shall suffer; I don't want a divorce, and shall suffer from my shame and separation from my child." But, however sincerely Anna had meant to suffer, she was not suffering. Shame there was not. With the tact of which both had such a large share, they had succeeded in avoiding Russian ladies abroad, and so had never placed themselves in a false position, and everywhere they had met people who pretended that they perfectly understood their position, far better indeed than they did themselves. Separation from the son she loved—even that did not cause her anguish in these early days. The baby girl—*his* child—was so sweet, and had so won Anna's heart, since she was all that was left her, that Anna rarely thought of her son.

The desire for life, waxing stronger with recovered health, was so intense, and the conditions of life were so new and pleasant, that Anna felt unpardonably happy. The more she got to know Vronsky, the more she loved him. She loved him for himself, and for his love for her. Her complete ownership of him was a continual joy to her. His presence was always sweet to her. All the traits of his character, which she learned to know better and better, were unutterably precious to her. His appearance, changed by his civilian dress, was as fascinating to her as though she were some young girl in love. In everything he said, thought, did, she saw something particularly noble and elevated. Her adoration of him alarmed her; she sought and could not find in him anything not beautiful. She dared not show him her feeling of her own inferiority beside him. It seemed to her that, knowing this, he might sooner cease to love her; and she dreaded nothing now so much as losing his love, though she had no grounds for fearing it. But she could not help being grateful to him for his attitude toward her, and showing that she appreciated it. He, who had in her opinion such a marked aptitude for a political career, in which he would have been certain to play a leading part—he had sacrificed his ambition for her sake, and never betrayed the slightest regret. He was more lovingly respectful to her than ever, and the constant care that she should not feel the awkwardness of her position never deserted him for a single instant. He, so manly a man, never opposed her, had indeed, with her, no will of his own, and was anxious, it seemed, for nothing but to anticipate her wishes. And she could not but appreciate this, even though the very intensity of his solicitude for her, the atmosphere of care with which he surrounded her, sometimes weighted upon her.

Vronsky, meanwhile, in spite of the complete realization of what he had so long desired, was not perfectly happy. He soon felt that the realization of his desires gave him no more than a grain of sand of the mountain of happiness he had expected. It showed him the mistake men make in picturing to themselves happiness as the realization of their desires. For a time after joining his life to hers, and putting on civilian dress, he had felt all the delight of freedom in general, of which he had known nothing before, and of freedom in his love—and he was content, but not for long. He was soon aware that there was springing up in his heart a desire for desires—*ennui*. Without conscious intention he began to clutch at every passing caprice, taking it for a desire and an object. Sixteen hours of the day must be occupied in some way, since they were living abroad in complete freedom, outside the conditions of social life which filled up time in Petersburg. As for the amusements of bachelor existence, which had provided Vronsky with entertainment on previous tours abroad, they could not be thought of, since the sole attempt of the sort had led to a sudden attack of depression in Anna, quite out of proportion with the cause—a late supper with bachelor friends. Relations with the society of the place—foreign and Russian—were equally out of the question owing to the irregularity of their position. The inspection of objects of interest, apart from the fact that everything had been seen already, had not for Vronsky, a Russian and a sensible man, the immense significance Englishmen are able to attach to that pursuit.

And just as the hungry stomach eagerly accepts every object it can get, hoping to find nourishment in it, Vronsky quite unconsciously clutched first at politics, then at new books, and then at pictures.

As he had from childhood a taste for painting, and as, not knowing what to spend his money on, he had begun collecting engravings, he came to a stop at painting, began to take interest in it, and concentrated upon it the unoccupied mass of desires which demanded satisfaction.

He had a ready appreciation of art, and for accurately and tastefully imitating it, and he supposed himself to have the real qualities essential for an artist, and after hesitating for some time about which style of painting to select—religious, historical, realistic, or genre painting—he began painting. He appreciated all kinds, and could have felt inspired by any of them; but he had no conception of the possibility of knowing nothing at all of any school of painting, and of being inspired directly by what is within the soul, without caring whether what is painted will belong to any recognized school. Since he knew nothing of this, and drew his inspiration, not directly from life, but indirectly from life embodied in art, his inspiration came very quickly and easily, and as quickly and easily came his success in painting something very similar to the sort of painting he was trying to imitate.

More than any other style he liked the French—graceful and effective—and in that style he began to paint Anna's portrait in Italian costume, and the portrait seemed to him, and to everyone who saw it, extremely successful.

CHAPTER NINE

The old neglected palazzo, with its lofty stucco ceilings and frescoes on the walls, with its floors of mosaic, with its heavy yellow damask curtains on the windows, with its vases on pedestals, and its open fireplaces, its carved doors and gloomy rooms, hung with pictures—this palazzo did much, by its very appearance after they had moved into it, to confirm in Vronsky the agreeable illusion that he was not so much a Russian country gentleman, an equerry without a post, as an enlightened amateur and patron of the arts, himself a modest artist who had renounced the world, his connections, and his ambition for the sake of the woman he loved.

The role chosen by Vronsky with their removal into the palazzo was completely successful, and having, through Golenishchev, made acquaintance with a few interesting people, for a time he was satisfied. He painted studies from nature under the guidance of an Italian professor of painting, and studied medieval Italian life. Medieval Italian life so fascinated Vronsky that he even wore a hat and flung a cloak over his shoulder in the medieval style, which, indeed, was extremely becoming to him.

"Here we live and know nothing of what's going on," Vronsky said to Golenishchev as he came to see him one morning. "Have you seen Mikhailov's picture?" he said, handing him a Russian paper he had received that morning, and pointing to an article on a Russian artist, living in the very same town, who was just finishing a picture that had long been talked about, and had been bought before it had been finished. The article criticized the government and the Academy for letting so remarkable an artist be left without encouragement and support.

"I've seen it," answered Golenishchev. "Of course, he's not without talent, but it's all in a wrong direction. It's all the Ivanov-Strauss-Renan[1] attitude of Christ and to religious painting."

"What is the subject of the picture?" asked Anna.

"Christ before Pilate. Christ is represented as a Jew with all the realism of the new school."

And the question of the subject of the picture having brought him to one of his favorite theories, Golenishchev launched forth into a disquisition on it.

"I can't understand how they can fall into such a gross mistake. Christ always has his definite embodiment in the art of the great masters. And therefore, if they want to depict not God but a revolutionist or a sage, let them take from history a Socrates, a Franklin, a Charlotte Corday,[2] but not Christ. They take the very figure which cannot be taken for their art, and then—"

"And is it true that this Mikhailov is in such poverty?" asked Vronsky, thinking that, as a Russian Maecenas,[3] it was his duty to assist the artist regardless of whether the picture was good or bad.

"I should say not. He's a remarkable portrait painter. Have you ever seen his portrait of Madame Vasilchikova? But I believe he doesn't care about painting any more portraits, and so very likely he is in want. I maintain that—"

"Couldn't we ask him to paint a portrait of Anna Arkadyevna?" said Vronsky.

"Why mine?" said Anna. "After yours I don't want another portrait. Better have one of Annie" (as she called her little girl). "Here she is," she added, looking out of the window at the handsome Italian nurse who was carrying the child into the garden, and immedi-

[1]Aleksandr Andreevich Ivanov (1806-58), whose paintings of Christ were realistic; David Friedrich Strauss (1808-74), German theologian and philosopher whose *Das Leben Jesu* (*The Life of Jesus*) treated the Gospel story as myth; Ernest Renan (1823-92), French historian and critic, apostle of the scientific approach to religion, author of *Vie de Jesus* (*Life of Jesus*).

[2](1768-93), Girondist (moderate republican) sympathizer, who stabbed Marat (French revolutionist) to death and was guillotined.

[3]I,e., patron of the arts.

ately glancing unnoticed at Vronsky. The handsome nurse, whose head Vronsky was painting for his picture, was the one hidden grief in Anna's life. He painted with her as his model, admired her beauty and "medievalness," and Anna dared not confess to herself that she was afraid of becoming jealous of this nurse, and was for that reason particularly gracious and condescending both to her and her little son. Vronsky, too, glanced out of the window and into Anna's eyes, and, turning at once to Golenishchev, he said:

"Do you know this Mikhailov?"

"I have met him. But he's a strange fish, and quite without breeding. You know, one of those uncouth new people one's so often coming across nowadays, one of those freethinkers, you know, who are reared *d'emblée*[4] in theories of atheism, skepticism, and materialism. In former days," said Golenishchev, not observing, or not willing to observe, that both Anna and Vronsky wanted to speak, "in former days the freethinker was a man who had been brought up in ideas of religion, law, and morality, and only through conflict and struggle became a freethinker; but now there has sprung up a new type of born freethinker who grows up without even having heard of principles of morality or of religion, of the existence of authorities, who grows up in ideas of negation in everything, that is to say, a savage. Well, he's of that class. He's the son, it appears, of some Moscow butler, and has never had any sort of education. When he got into the Academy and made his reputation he tried, as he's no fool, to educate himself. And he turned to what seemed to him the very source of culture—the magazines. In old times, you see, a man who wanted to educate himself—a Frenchman, for instance—would have begun to study all the classics and theologians and tragedians and historians and philosophers, and what mental work came his way. But in our day he goes straight for the literature of negation, very quickly assimilates all the extracts of the science of negation, and he's ready. And that's not all—twenty years ago he would have found in that literature traces of conflict with authorities, with the creeds of the ages; he would have perceived from this conflict that something else existed; but now he comes at once upon a literature in

4"From the first."

which the old creeds do not even furnish matter for discussion, but it is stated baldly that there is nothing else—evolution, natural selection, struggle for existence—and that's all. In my article I've—"

"I tell you what," said Anna, who had for a long while been exchanging wary glances with Vronsky, and knew that he was not in the least interested in the education of this artist, but was simply absorbed by the idea of assisting him, and commissioning him to do a portrait. "I tell you what," she said, resolutely interrupting Golenishchev, who was still talking away. "Let's go and see him!"

Golenishchev recovered his poise and readily agreed. But since the artist lived in a remote suburb, it was decided to take the carriage.

An hour later Anna, with Golenishchev by her side and Vronsky on the front seat of the carriage, facing them, drove up to an ugly new house in the remote suburb. On learning from the porter's wife, who came out to meet them, that Mikhailov saw visitors at his studio, but that at that moment he was in his lodging only a couple of steps away, they sent her to him with their cards, asking permission to see his pictures.

CHAPTER TEN

The artist Mikhailov was, as always, at work when the cards of Count Vronsky and Golenishchev were brought to him. In the morning he had been working in his studio at his big picture. On getting home, he flew into a rage with his wife for not having managed to put off the landlady, who had been asking for money.

"I've told you twenty times not to start an argument. You're fool enough at all times, and when you start explaining things in Italian you're a fool three times as foolish," he said after a long dispute.

"Then don't get so behind; it's not my fault. If I had the money—"

"Leave me in peace, for God's sake!" Mikhailov shrieked, with tears in his voice, and stopping his ears, he went off into his workroom, the other side of a partition wall, and closed the door after him. "Idiotic woman!" he said to himself, and, sitting down at the table, he opened a portfolio and set to work at once with peculiar fervor on a sketch he had begun.

Never did he work with such fervor and success as when things went badly with him, and especially when he quarreled with his wife. "Oh, damn them all!" he thought as he went on working. He was making a sketch for the figure of a man in a violent rage. A sketch had been made before, but he was dissatisfied with it. "No, that one was better . . . where is it?" He went back to his wife, and, scowling and not looking at her, asked his eldest little girl where was that piece of paper he had given them. The paper with the discarded sketch on it was found, but it was dirty and spotted with candle grease. Still, he took the sketch, laid it on his table, and, moving a little away, screwing up his eyes, began examining it. All at once he smiled and gesticulated gleefully.

"That's it!" he said, and, at once picking up the pencil, he began rapidly drawing. The spot of tallow had given the figure a new pose.

He had sketched this new pose when all at once he recalled the face of a shopkeeper from whom he had bought cigars, a vigorous face with a prominent chin, and he sketched this very face, this chin, on to the figure of the man. He laughed aloud with delight. The figure, from a lifeless imagined thing, had become alive and could not be changed. The figure lived, and was clearly and unmistakably defined. The sketch might be corrected in accordance with the requirements of the figure, the legs, indeed, could and must be put differently, and the position of the left arm must be considerably altered; the hair too might be thrown back. But in making these corrections, he was not altering the figure; he was simply getting rid of what concealed the figure. He was, as it were, stripping off the coverings which hindered it from being distinctly seen. Each new feature only brought out the whole figure in all its force and vigor, as it had suddenly come to him from the spot of tallow. He was carefully finishing the figure when the cards were brought to him.

"Coming, coming!"

He went to his wife.

"Come, Sasha, don't be angry!" he said, smiling timidly and affectionately at her. "You were to blame. I was to blame. I'll make it all right." And having made peace with his wife, he put on an olive-green overcoat with a velvet collar, and a hat, and went toward his studio. The successful figure he had already forgotten. Now he was delighted and excited at the visit of these people of consequence, Russians, who had come in their carriage.

Of his picture, the one that now stood on his easel, he had at the bottom of his heart one conviction—that no one had ever painted a picture like it. He did not believe that his picture was better than all the pictures of Raphael, but he knew that what he tried to convey in that picture no one had ever conveyed. This he knew positively, and had known a long while, ever since he had begun to paint it. But, nevertheless, other people's criticisms, whatever they might be, had immense consequence in his eyes, and they agitated him to the depths of his soul. Any remark, the most insignificant, that showed that the critic saw even the tiniest part of what he saw in the picture agitated him to the depths of his soul. He always attributed to his critics a more profound comprehension than he had himself, and always expected from them something he did not himself see in the picture. And often in their criticisms he imagined that he had found this.

He walked rapidly to the door of his studio, and in spite of his excitement he was struck by the soft light on Anna's figure as she stood in the shade of the entrance listening to Golenishchev, who was eagerly telling her something, while she evidently wanted to look round at the artist. He did not himself notice how, as he approached them, he seized on this impression and absorbed it, as he had the chin of the shopkeeper who had sold him the cigars, and put it away somewhere to be brought out when he wanted it. The visitors, not agreeably impressed beforehand by Golenishchev's account of the artist, were still less so by his personal appearance. Thickset and of medium height, with his nervous gait, with his brown hat, olive-green coat, and narrow trousers—though wide trousers had been the fashion for a long time—most of all, with the ordinariness of his broad face, and the combined expression of timidity and anxiety to keep up his dignity, Mikhailov made an unpleasant impression. ·

"Please step in," he said, trying to look indifferent, and going into the passage, he took a key out of his pocket and opened the door.

CHAPTER ELEVEN

On entering the studio, Mikhailov once more scanned his visitors and made a mental note of Vronsky's face, especially his cheekbones. Although his artistic sense was unceasingly at work collecting materials, although he felt a continually increasing excitement as the moment of criticizing his work drew nearer, he rapidly and subtly formed, from imperceptible signs, a mental image of these three persons.

That fellow (Golenishchev) was a Russian living here. Mikhailov did not remember his surname, or where he had met him, or what he had said to him. He remembered only his face, as he remembered all the faces he had ever seen; but he remembered, too, that it was one of the faces laid by in his memory in the immense class of the falsely consequential and lacking in expression. The abundant hair and very open forehead gave an appearance of consequence to the face, which had only one expression—a petty, childish, peevish expression, concentrated just above the bridge of the narrow nose. Vronsky and Madame Karenina must be, Mikhailov supposed, distinguished and wealthy Russians, knowing nothing about art, like all those wealthy Russians, but posing as amateurs and connoisseurs. "Most likely they've already looked at all the antiques, and now they're making the round of the studios of the new people, the German humbug and the cracked Pre-Raphaelite English fellow, and have only come to me to make the point of view complete," he thought. He was well acquainted with the way dilettanti have (the cleverer they were, the worse he found them) of looking at the works of contemporary artists with the sole object of being in a position to say that art is a thing of the past, and that the more one sees of the new men, the more one sees how inimitable the works of the great old masters have remained. He expected all this; he saw it all in their faces, he saw it in the careless indifference with which they talked among themselves, stared at the lay figures and busts, and walked about in leisurely fashion, waiting for him to uncover his picture. But in spite of this, while he was turning over his studies, pulling up the blinds and taking off the sheet, he was in intense excitement, especially as, in spite of his conviction that all distinguished and wealthy

Russians were certain to be beasts and fools, he liked Vronsky, and still more Anna.

"Here, if you please," he said, moving on one side with his nimble gait and pointing to his picture, "it's 'Pilate's Admonition'—Matthew, chapter twenty-seven," he said, feeling his lips beginning to tremble with emotion. He moved away and stood behind them.

For the few seconds during which the visitors were gazing at the picture in silence, Mikhailov too gazed at it with the indifferent eye of an outsider. For those few seconds he was sure in anticipation that a higher, juster criticism would be uttered by them, by those very visitors whom he had so despised a moment before. He forgot all he had thought about his picture during the three years he had been painting it; he forgot all the qualities that had been absolutely certain to him; he saw the picture with their indifferent, new, outside eyes, and saw nothing good in it. He saw in the foreground Pilate's irritated face and the serene face of Christ, and in the background the figures of Pilate's servants and the face of John watching what was happening. Every face that with such agony, such blunders and corrections, had grown up within him with its special character, every face that had given him such torments and such raptures, and all these faces so many times transposed for the sake of the harmony of the whole, all the shades of color and tones that he had attained with such labor—all of this together seemed to him now, looking at it with their eyes, the merest vulgarity, something that had been done a thousand times over. The face dearest to him, the face of Christ, the center of the picture, which had given him such ecstasy as it unfolded itself to him, was utterly lost to him when he looked at the picture with their eyes. He saw a well-painted (no, not even that—now he distinctly saw a mass of defects) repetition of those endless Christs of Titian, Raphael, Rubens, the same soldiers, the same Pilates. It was all common, poor and stale, and positively badly painted—weak and unharmonious. They would be justified in repeating hypocritically civil speeches in the presence of the painter, and pitying him and laughing at him when they were alone again.

The silence (though it lasted no more than a minute) became too intolerable for him. To break it, and to show that he was not agitated, he made an effort and addressed Golenishchev.

"I think I've had the pleasure of meeting you," he said, looking uneasily first at Anna, then at Vronsky, for fear of losing any shade of their expression.

"To be sure! We met at Rossi's, do you remember, at that soirée when that Italian lady—the new Rachel[1]—recited?" Golenishchev answered easily, looking away without the slightest regret from the picture and turning to the artist.

Noticing, however, that Mikhailov was expecting criticism of the picture, he said:

"Your picture has progressed a great deal since I saw it last time; and what strikes me particularly now, as it did then, is the figure of Pilate. One so knows the man: a good-natured, kind fellow, but an official through and through, who does not know what it is he's doing. But I think . . ."

All of Mikhailov's mobile face beamed at once; his eyes sparkled. He tried to say something, but he could not speak for excitement, and pretended to be coughing. Low as was his opinion of Golenishchev's capacity for understanding art, trifling as was the true remark upon the fidelity of the expression of Pilate as an official, and offensive as might have seemed the utterance of so unimportant an observation while nothing was said of more serious points, Mikhailov was in an ecstasy of delight at this observation. He had himself thought about Pilate's figure just what Golenishchev said. The fact that this reflection was but one of millions of reflections, which as Mikhailov knew for certain would be true, did not diminish for him the significance of Golenishchev's remark. His heart warmed to Golenishchev for this remark, and from a state of depression he suddenly passed to ecstasy. At once the whole of his picture lived before him in all the indescribable complexity of everything living. Mikhailov again tried to say that that was how he understood Pilate, but his lips quivered intractably, and he could not pronounce the words. Vronsky and Anna too said something in that subdued voice in which, partly to avoid hurting the artist's feelings and partly to avoid saying out loud something silly—so easily said when talking of art—people usually speak at exhibitions of pictures. Mikhailov

[1]Famous French actress (1820-58).

thought that the picture had made an impression on them too. He went up to them.

"How marvelous Christ's expression is!" said Anna. Of all she saw she liked that expression most of all, and felt that it was the center of the picture, and so praise of it would be pleasant to the artist. "One can see that He is pitying Pilate."

This again was one of the million true reflections that could be found in his picture and in the figure of Christ. She said that He was pitying Pilate. In Christ's expression there ought to be indeed an expression of pity, since there is an expression of love, of heavenly peace, of readiness for death, and a sense of the vanity of words. Of course there is the expression of an official in Pilate and of pity in Christ, seeing that one is the incarnation of the fleshly and the other of the spiritual life. All this and much more flashed into Mikhailov's thoughts.

"Yes, and how that figure is done—how airy! One can walk around it," said Golenishchev, unmistakably betraying by this remark that he did not approve of the meaning and idea of the figure.

"Yes, wonderful craftsmanship!" said Vronsky. "How those figures in the background stand out! There you have technique," he said, addressing Golenishchev, alluding to a conversation between them about Vronsky's despair of attaining this technique.

"Yes, yes, marvelous!" Golenishchev and Anna assented. In spite of the excited condition in which he was, the sentence about technique had sent a pang to Mikhailov's heart, and looking angrily at Vronsky, he suddenly scowled. He had often heard this word "technique," and was utterly unable to understand what was meant by it. He knew that by this term was meant a mechanical facility for painting or drawing, entirely apart from its subject. He had noticed often that even in actual praise technique was opposed to essential quality, as though one could paint well something that was bad. He knew that a great deal of attention and care was necessary in taking off the coverings, to avoid injuring the creation itself, and to take off the coverings; but there was no art of painting—no technique of any sort—about it. If to a little child or to his cook were revealed what we saw, it or she would have been able to peel the wrappings off what was seen. And the most experienced and adroit painter could not by mere mechanical facility paint anything if the lines of the subject were not revealed to him first. Besides, he saw that if it came to talking about technique, it was impossible to praise him for it. In all he had painted and repainted he saw faults that hurt his eyes, coming from want of care in taking off the coverings—faults he could not correct now without spoiling the whole. And in almost all the figures and faces he saw, too, remnants of the coverings not perfectly removed that spoiled the picture.

"One thing might be said, if you will allow me to make the remark . . ." observed Golenishchev.

"Oh, I shall be delighted, I beg you," said Mikhailov with a forced smile.

"That is, that you make Him the man-god, and not a God-man. But I know that was what you meant to do."

"I cannot paint a Christ that is not in my heart," said Mikhailov gloomily.

"Yes; but in that case, if you will allow me to say what I think . . . Your picture is so fine that my observation cannot detract from it, and, besides, it is only my personal opinion. With you it is different. Your very motive is different. But let us take Ivanov. I imagine that if Christ is brought down to the level of a historical character, it would have been better for Ivanov to select some other historical subject, fresh, untouched."

"But if this is the greatest subject presented to art?"

"If one looked one would find others. But the point is that art cannot suffer doubt and discussion. And before the picture of Ivanov the question arises for the believer and the unbeliever alike, 'Is it God, or is it not God?' and the unity of the impression is destroyed."

"Why so? I think that for educated people," said Mikhailov, "the question cannot exist."

Golenishchev did not agree with this, and confounded Mikhailov by his support of this first idea of the unity of the impression being essential to art.

Mikhailov was greatly perturbed, but he could say nothing in defense of his own idea.

CHAPTER TWELVE

Anna and Vronsky had long been exchanging glances, regretting their friend's flow of cleverness. At last Vronsky, without waiting for the artist, walked away to another small picture.

"Oh, how exquisite! What a lovely thing! A gem! How exquisite!" they cried with one voice.

"What is it they're so pleased with?" thought Mikhailov. He had positively forgotten that picture he had painted three years ago. He had forgotten all the agonies and the ecstasies he had lived through with that picture when for several months it had been the one thought haunting him day and night. He had forgotten, as he always forgot, the pictures he had finished. He did not even like to look at it, and had brought it out only because he was expecting an Englishman who wanted to buy it.

"Oh, that's only an old study," he said.

"How fine!" said Golenishchev, he too, with unmistakable sincerity, falling under the spell of the picture.

Two boys were angling in the shade of a willow tree. The elder had just dropped in the hook, and was carefully pulling the float from behind a bush, entirely absorbed in what he was doing. The other, a little younger, was lying in the grass leaning on his elbows, with his tangled, flaxen head in his hands, staring at the water with his dreamy blue eyes. What was he thinking of?

The enthusiasm over this picture stirred some of the old feeling for it in Mikhailov, but he feared and disliked this waste of feeling for things past, and so, even though this praise was pleasurable to him, he tried to draw his visitors away to a third picture.

But Vronsky asked whether the picture was for sale. To Mikhailov at that moment, excited by visitors, it was extremely distasteful to speak of money matters.

"It is put up there to be sold," he answered, scowling gloomily.

When the visitors had gone, Mikhailov sat down opposite the picture of Pilate and Christ, and in his mind went over what had been said, and what, though not said, had been implied by those visitors. And, strange to say, what had had such weight with him while they were there and while he mentally put himself in their point of view, suddenly lost all importance for him. He began to look at his picture with his own full artist vision, and was soon in that mood of conviction of the perfectibility, and so of the significance, of his picture—a conviction essential to the intensest fervor, excluding all other interests—in which alone he could work.

Christ's foreshortened foot was not right, though. He took his palette and began to work. As he corrected the foot he looked continually at the figure of John in the background, which his visitors had not even noticed, but which he knew was beyond perfection. When he had finished the foot he wanted to touch up that figure, but he felt too excited for it. He was equally unable to work when he was indifferent and when he was too overwrought and saw everything too clearly. There was only one stage in the transition from indifference to inspiration at which work was possible. Today he was too much agitated. He would have covered the picture, but he stopped, holding the cloth in his hand, and, smiling blissfully, looked for a long while at the figure of John. At last, regretfully tearing himself away, he dropped the cloth and, exhausted but happy, went home.

Vronsky, Anna, and Golenishchev were particularly lively and cheerful on their way home. They talked of Mikhailov and his pictures. The word "*talent*," by which they meant an inborn and almost physical aptitude apart from brain and heart, and in which they tried to find an expression for all the artist had gained from life, recurred particularly often in their talk, as though it were necessary for them to sum up what they had no conception of, though they wanted to talk of it. They said that there was no denying his talent, but that his talent could not develop for want of education—the common defect of our Russian artists. But the picture of the boys had imprinted itself on their memories, and they were continually coming back to it. "What an exquisite thing! How he has succeeded in it, and how simply! He doesn't even comprehend how good it is. Yes, I mustn't let it slip by; I must buy it," said Vronsky.

CHAPTER THIRTEEN

Mikhailov sold Vronsky his picture, and agreed to paint a portrait of Anna. On the day fixed he came and began the work.

From the fifth sitting the portrait impressed everyone, especially Vronsky, not only by its likeness, but by its characteristic beauty. It was strange how Mikhailov could have discovered her special beauty. "One needs to know and love her as I have loved her to discover the very sweetest expression of her soul," Vronsky thought, though it was only from this portrait that he had himself learned this sweetest expression of her soul. But the expression was so true that he, and others too, thought they had long known it.

"I have been struggling on forever without doing anything," he said of his own portrait of her, "and he just looked and painted it. That's where technique comes in."

"That will come," was the consoling reassurance given him by Golenishchev, in whose view Vronsky had both talent and, what was most important, culture, giving him a wider outlook on art. Golenishchev's faith in Vronsky's talent was propped up by his own need of Vronsky's sympathy and approval for his own articles and ideas, and he felt that the praise and support must be mutual.

In another man's house, and especially in Vronsky's palazzo, Mikhailov was quite a different man from what he was in his studio. He behaved with hostile politeness, as though he were afraid of coming closer to people he did not respect. He called Vronsky "Your Excellency," and notwithstanding Anna's and Vronsky's invitations, he would never stay to dinner, or come except for the sittings. Anna was even more friendly to him than to other people and was very grateful for her portrait. Vronsky was more than cordial with him, and was obviously interested to know the artist's opinion of his picture. Golenishchev never let slip an opportunity of instilling sound ideas about art into Mikhailov. But Mikhailov remained equally chilly to all of them. Anna was aware from his eyes that he liked looking at her, but he avoided conversation with her. Vronsky's talk about his painting he met with stubborn silence, and he was as stubbornly silent when he was shown Vronsky's picture. He was unmistakably bored by Golenishchev's conversation, and he did not attempt to oppose him.

Altogether Mikhailov, with his reserved and disagreeable, as it were, hostile attitude, made them dislike him as they got to know him better; and they were glad when the sittings were over, and they were left with a magnificent portrait in their possession, and he gave up coming. Golenishchev was the first to give expression to an idea that had occurred to all of them, which was that Mikhailov was simply jealous of Vronsky.

"Not jealous, let us say, since he has *talent*; but it annoys him that a wealthy man of the highest society, and a count, too (you know they all detest a title), can, without any particular trouble, do as well, if not better, than he who has devoted all his life to it. And more than anything, it's a question of culture, which he is without."

Vronsky defended Mikhailov, but at the bottom of his heart he believed it, because in his view a man of a different, lower world would be sure to be envious.

Anna's portrait—the same subject painted from nature both by him and by Mikhailov—should have shown Vronsky the difference between him and Mikhailov; but he did not see it. But after Mikhailov's portrait was painted he stopped painting his portrait of Anna, deciding that is was now not needed. His picture of medieval life he went on with. And he himself, and Golenishchev, and still more Anna, thought it very good, because it was far more like the celebrated pictures they knew than Mikhailov's picture.

Mikhailov meanwhile, although Anna's portrait greatly fascinated him, was even more glad than they were when the sittings were over, and he had no longer to listen to Golenishchev's disquisitions upon art, and could forget about Vronsky's painting. He knew that Vronsky could not be prevented from amusing himself with painting; he knew that he and all dilettanti had a perfect right to paint what they liked, but it was distasteful to him. A man could not be prevented from making himself a big wax doll and kissing it. But if the man were to come with the doll as the lover before a man in love, and begin caressing his doll as the lover caressed the woman he loved, it would be distasteful to the lover. Just such a distasteful sensation was what Mikhailov felt at the sight of Vronsky's painting: he felt it both ludicrous and irritating, both pitiable and offensive.

Vronsky's interest in painting and the Middle Ages did not last long. He had enough taste for painting to be unable to finish his picture. The picture came to a standstill. He was vaguely aware that its defects, inconspicuous at first, would be glaring if he were to go on with it. The same experience befell him as Golenishchev, who felt that he had nothing to say, and continually deceived himself with the theory that his idea was not yet mature, that he was working it out and collecting materials. This exasperated and tortured Golenishchev, but Vronsky was incapable of deceiving and torturing himself, and even more incapable of exasperation. With his characteristic decision, without explanation or apology, he simply ceased working at painting.

But without this occupation, the life of Vronsky and of Anna, who wondered at his loss of interest in it, struck them as intolerably tedious in an Italian town. The palazzo suddenly seemed so obtrusively old and dirty, the spots on the curtains, the cracks in the floors, the broken plaster on the cornices became so disagreeably obvious, and the everlasting sameness of Golenishchev and the Italian professor and the German traveler became so wearisome that they had to make some change. They resolved to go to Russia, to the country. In Petersburg, Vronsky intended to arrange a division of the land with his brother, while Anna meant to see her son. The summer they intended to spend on Vronsky's large family estate.

CHAPTER FOURTEEN

Levin had been married three months. He was happy, but not at all in the way he had expected to be. At every step he found his former dreams disappointed, and new, unexpected surprises of happiness. He was happy; but on entering upon family life, he saw at every step that it was utterly different from what he had imagined. At every step he experienced what a man would experience who, after admiring the smooth, happy course of the little boat on a lake, should get himself into that little boat. He saw that it was not all sitting still, floating smoothly; that one had think too, not for an instant to forget where one was floating; and that there was water under one, and that one must row; and that his unaccustomed hands would be sore; and that it was only to look at it that was easy; but that doing it, though very delightful, was very difficult.

As a bachelor, when he had watched other people's married life, seen the petty cares, the squabbles, the jealousy, he had only smiled contemptuously in his heart. In his future married life there could be, he was convinced, nothing of that sort; even the external forms, he thought, must be utterly unlike the life of others in everything. And all of a sudden, instead of his life with his wife being made on an individual pattern, it was on the contrary entirely made up of the pettiest details, which he had so despised before, but which now, by no will of his own, had gained an extraordinary importance that it was useless to contend against. And Levin saw that the organization of all these details was by no means as easy as he had imagined. Although Levin thought he had the most exact ideas about domestic life, like all men, he had imagined married life to consist merely of the enjoyment of love, which nothing must hinder and from which no petty cares must distract. He should, as he conceived the position, do his work, and find repose from it in the happiness of love. She be loved, nothing more. But, like all men, he forgot that she, his poetic, exquisite Kitty, could not merely in the first weeks, but even in the first days of their married life, think, remember, and busy herself about tablecloths and furniture, about mattresses for visitors, about a tray, about the cook and the dinner, and so on. While they were still engaged, he had been struck by the definiteness with which she had declined the tour abroad and decided to go into the country, as though she knew of something she wanted, and could still think of something outside her love. This had hurt him then, and now her trivial cares and anxieties hurt him several times. But he saw that this was essential for her. And, loving her as he did, though he did not understand the reason behind them, and laughed at these domestic pursuits, he could not help admiring them. He laughed at the way in which she arranged the furniture they brought from Moscow; rearranged their room; hung up curtains; prepared rooms for visitors; a room for Dolly; saw after a room for her new maid; ordered dinner from the old cook; had words with Agafya Mikailovna, taking from her charge of the supplies. He saw how the old cook smiled, admiring her, and listening to her inexperienced, impossible orders, how mournfully and tenderly Agafya Mikhailovna shook her head over the young mistress's new arrangements. He saw that Kitty was extraordinarily sweet when, laughing and crying, she came to tell him that her maid, Masha, was used to looking upon her as her young girl, and so no one obeyed her. It seemed to him sweet but strange, and he thought it would have been better without this.

He did not know how great a sense of change she was experiencing; she, who at home had sometimes wanted some cabbage and kvas, or sweets, without the possibility of getting either, now could order what she liked, buy pounds of sweets, spend as much money as she liked, and order any desserts she pleased.

She was dreaming with delight now of Dolly's coming to them with her children, especially because she would order for the children their favorite puddings and Dolly would appreciate her new arrangements. She herself did not know why, but the arranging of her house had an irresistible attraction for her. Instinctively feeling the approach of spring, and knowing that there would be days of rough weather too, she built her nest as best she could, and was in haste at the same time to build it while still learning how to do it.

This care for domestic details in Kitty, so opposed to Levin's ideal of exalted happiness, was at first one of his disappointments; and this sweet care of her household, the aim of which he did not understand but could not help loving, was one of the new happy surprises.

Another disappointment and happy surprise came in their quarrels. Levin could never have conceived that between him and his wife any relations could arise other than tender, respectful, and loving, and all at once in the very early days they quarreled, so that she said he did not care for her, that he cared for no one but himself, burst into tears, and wrung her hands.

This first quarrel arose from Levin's having gone out to a new farmhouse and having been away half an hour too long, because he had tried to get home by a short cut and had lost his way. He drove home thinking of nothing but her, of her love, of his own happiness, and the nearer he drew to home, the warmer was his tenderness for her. He ran into the room with the same feeling, with an even stronger feeling than he had had when he reached the Shcherbatskys' house to propose. And suddenly he was met by a grim expression he had never seen on her face. He tried to kiss her, but she pushed him away.

"What is it?"

"You've been enjoying yourself," she began, trying to appear calm and spiteful. But as soon as she opened her mouth, a stream of reproach, of senseless jealousy, of all that had been torturing her during that half-hour which she had spent sitting motionless at the window, burst from her. It was only then, for the first time, that he clearly understood what he had not understood when he led her out of the church after the wedding. He felt now that he was not simply close to her, but that he did not know where he ended and she began. He felt this from the agonizing sensation of division that he experienced at that instant. He was offended for the first instant, but the very same second he felt that he could not be offended by her, that she was himself. He felt for the first moment as a man feels when, having suddenly received a violent blow from behind, turns around, angry and eager to avenge himself, to look for his antagonist, and finds that it is he himself who has accidentally struck himself, that there is no one to be angry with, and that he must put up with and try to soothe the pain.

Never afterward did he feel it with such intensity, but this first time he could not for a long while get over it. His natural feeling urged him to defend himself, to prove to her she was wrong; but to prove her wrong would mean irritating her still more and widening the breach that was the cause of all his suffering. One habitual impulse impelled him to get rid of the blame and to lay it on her. Another feeling, even stronger, impelled him as quickly as possible to smooth over the breach without letting it grow wider. To remain under such undeserved reproach was wretched, but to make her suffer by justifying himself was wrong still. Like a man half-awake in an agony of pain, he wanted to tear out, to fling away the aching part and, coming to his senses, he felt that the aching part was himself. He could do nothing but try to help the aching part to bear it, and this he tried to do.

They made peace. She, recognizing that she was wrong, though she did not say so, became tenderer to him, and they experienced new, redoubled happiness in their love. But that did not prevent such quarrels from happening again, and exceedingly often too, on the most unexpected and trivial grounds. These quarrels frequently arose from the fact that they did not yet know what was of importance to each other, and that during this early period they were both often in a bad mood. When one was in a good mood, and the other in a bad mood, the peace was not broken; but when both happened to be in ill-humor, quarrels sprang up from such incomprehensibly trifling causes that they could never remember afterward what they had quarreled about. It is true that when they were both in a good mood their enjoyment of life was redoubled. But still this first period of their married life was a difficult time for them.

During all this early time they had a peculiarly vivid sense of tension, as it were, a tugging in opposite directions of the chain by which they were bound. Altogether their honeymoon—that is to say, the month after their wedding—from which by tradition Levin expected so much, was not merely not a time of sweetness, but remained in the memories of both as the bitterest and most humiliating period in their lives. They both tried in later life to blot out from their memories all the monstrous, shameful incidents of that morbid period, when both were rarely in a normal frame of mind, both were rarely quite themselves.

It was only in the third month of their married life, after their return from Moscow, where they had been staying for a month, that their life began to flow more smoothly.

CHAPTER FIFTEEN

They had just come from Moscow, and were glad to be alone. He was sitting in his study, writing. She, wearing the dark lilac dress she had worn during the first days of their married life, and put on again today, a dress particularly remembered and loved by him, was sitting on the sofa, the same old-fashioned leather sofa which had always stood in the study in Levin's father's and grandfather's day. She was embroidering *broderie anglaise*. He thought and wrote, never losing the happy consciousness of her presence. His work, both on the land and on the book, in which the principles of the new land system were to be laid down, had not been abandoned; but just as formerly these pursuits and ideas had seemed to him petty and trivial in comparison with the darkness that overspread his whole life, now they seemed as unimportant and petty in comparison with life that lay before him suffused with the brilliant light of happiness. He went on with his work, but he felt now that the center of gravity of his attention had passed to something else, and that consequently he looked at his work quite differently and more clearly. Formerly this work had been for him an escape from life. Formerly he had felt that without this work his life would be too gloomy. Now these pursuits were necessary for him so that life might not be too uniformly bright. Taking up his manuscript, reading through what he had written, he found with pleasure that the work was worth his working at. Many of his old ideas seemed to him superfluous and extreme, but many blanks became distinct to him when he reviewed the whole thing in his memory. He was now writing a new chapter on the causes of the present disastrous condition of agriculture in Russia. He maintained that the poverty of Russia arose, not merely from the anomalous distribution of landed property and misdirected reforms, but that what had contributed of late years to this result was the civilization from without artificially grafted upon Russia, especially means of communication, that is, railways, leading to centralization in towns, increased leisure, and the consequent development of industries, credit, and its concomitant, speculation—all to the detriment of agriculture. It seemed to him that in a normal development of wealth in a state all these phenomena would arise only when it had come under regular, or at least definite, conditions; that the wealth of a country ought to increase proportionally, and especially in such a way that other sources of wealth should not outstrip agriculture; that in harmony with a certain stage of agriculture there should be means of communication corresponding to it, and that in our unsettled condition of the land, railways, called into being by political and not by economic needs, were premature, and instead of promoting agriculture, as was expected of them, they were competing with agriculture and promoting the development of industry and credit, and so arresting its progress; and that just as the one-sided and premature development of one organ in an animal would hinder its general development, so in the general development of wealth in Russia, credit, facilities of communication, manufacturing activity, indubitably necessary in Europe,[1] where they had arisen in their proper time, had with us only done harm, by throwing into the background the chief question calling for solution—the question of the organisation of agriculture.

While he was writing his ideas she was thinking how unnaturally polite her husband had been to young Prince Charsky, who had, with great want of tact, flirted with her the day before they left Moscow. "He's jealous," she thought. "Goodness! How sweet and stupid he is! He's jealous of me! If he knew that I think no more of them than of Piotr the cook," she thought, looking at the nape of his red neck with a feeling of possession strange to her. "Though it's a pity to take him from his work (but he had plenty of time!), I must look at his face; will he feel I'm looking at him? I wish he'd turn around . . . I'll *will* him to!" and she opened her eyes wide, as though to intensify the influence of her look.

"Yes, they draw away all the sap and give a false appearance of prosperity," he muttered, stopping to write, and, feeling that she was looking at him and smiling, he looked around.

"Well?" he queried, smiling and getting up.

"He looked around," she thought.

"It's nothing; I wanted you to look around," she said, watching him and trying to guess whether or not he was vexed at being interrupted.

"How happy we are alone together!—I am, that is," he said, going up to her with a radiant smile of happiness.

"I'm just as happy. I'll never go anywhere, especially not to Moscow."

"And what were you thinking about?"

"I? I was thinking . . . No, no, go along, go on writing; don't break off," she said, pursing up her lips, "and I must cut out these little holes now, do you see?"

She took up her scissors and began cutting them out.

"No; tell me, what was it?" he said, sitting down beside her and watching the circular motion of the tiny scissors.

"Oh! What was I thinking about? I was thinking about Moscow, about the back of your neck."

[1]Russians often view themselves as separate from the rest of Europe.

"Why should I, of all people, have such happiness! It's unnatural, too good," he said, kissing her hand.

"I feel quite the opposite; the better things are, the more natural it seems to me."

"And you've got a little curl loose," he said, carefully turning her head around.

"A little curl, oh yes. No, no, we are busy at our work!"

Work did not progress further, and they darted apart from one another like culprits when Kuzma came in to announce that tea was ready.

"Have they come from the town?" Levin asked Kuzma.

"They've just come; they're unpacking the things."

"Come quickly," she said to him as she went out of the study, "or else I shall read your letters without you."

Left alone, after putting his manuscripts away in the new portfolio bought by her, he washed his hands at the new washstand with the elegant fixtures, which had all made their appearance with her. Levin smiled at his own thoughts, and shook his head disapprovingly at those thoughts; a feeling like remorse bothered him. There was something shameful, effeminate, Capuan[2], as he called it, in his present mode of life. "It's not right to go on like this," he thought. "It'll soon be three months, and I'm doing next to nothing. Today, almost for the first time, I set to work seriously, and what happened? I did nothing but begin and throw it aside. Even my ordinary pursuits I have almost given up. I scarcely walk or drive about at all to look after the farm work. Either I am loath to leave her, or I see she's bored alone. And I used to think that before marriage life was nothing much, somehow didn't count, but that after marriage life began in earnest. And here almost three months have passed, and I have spent my time so idly and unprofitably. No, this won't do; I must begin. Of course, it's not her fault. She's not to blame in any way. I ought myself to be firmer, to maintain my masculine independence; this way I'll get into bad habits, and encourage her too . . . Of course she's not to blame," he told himself.

[2]From Joseph Capoul, French actor and dandy, who was a "lawmaker" of masculine fashion. A hairdo *à la Capoul* was a special way of cutting a man's hair.

But it is hard for anyone who is dissatisfied not to blame someone else, and especially the person nearest of all to him, for the ground of his dissatisfaction. And it vaguely entered Levin's mind that it was not she herself that was to blame (she could not be to blame for anything) but her education, which had been too superficial and frivolous. ("That fool Charsky: she wanted to stop him, I know, but didn't know how to.") "Yes, apart from her interest in the house (she has that), apart from clothes and *broderie anglaise*, she had no serious interests. No interest in her work, in the estate, in the peasants, not in music, though she's rather good at it, nor in reading. She does nothing, and is perfectly satisfied." Levin, in his heart, condemned this, and did not as yet understand that she was preparing for that period of activity which was to come for her when she would at once be the wife of her husband and mistress of the house, and would bear, and nurse, and bring up children. He knew not that she was instinctively aware of this, and preparing herself for this time of terrible toil, did not reproach herself for the carefree moments of happiness in her love that she enjoyed now while gaily building her nest for the future.

CHAPTER SIXTEEN

When Levin went upstairs, his wife was sitting near the new silver samovar behind the new tea service, and, having made Agafya Mikhailovna sit down at a little table with a full cup of tea, was reading a letter from Dolly, with whom they were in continual and frequent correspondence.

"You see, your lady's made me sit with her," said Agafya Mikhailovna, smiling affectionately at Kitty.

In these words of Agafya Milkailovna, Levin read the final act of the drama that had been enacted of late between her and Kitty. He saw that in spite of Agafya Mikhailovna's feelings being hurt by a new mistress taking the reins of government out of her hands, Kitty had yet conquered her and made her love her.

"Here, I opened your letter too," said Kitty, handing him a badly written letter. "It's from that woman, I think, your brother's . . ." she said. "I did not read it through. This is from my people and from

Dolly. Imagine! Dolly took Tanya and Grisha to a children's ball at the Sarmatskys': Tanya went as a French marquise."

But Levin did not hear her. Flushing, he took the letter from Marya Nikolaevna, his brother's former mistress, and began to read it. This was the second letter he had received from Marya Nikolaevna. In the first letter Marya Nikolaevna wrote that his brother had sent her away for no fault of hers, and, with touching simplicity, added that though she was in want again, she asked for nothing and wished for nothing, but was only tormented by the thought that Nikolai Dmitrievich would come to grief without her, owing to the weak state of his health, and begged his brother to look after him. Now she wrote quiet differently. She had found Nikolai Dmitrievich, had again made up with him in Moscow, and had moved with him to a provincial town, where he had received a post in the government service. But that he had quarreled with the head official, and was on his way back to Moscow, only he had been taken so ill on the road that it was doubtful if he would ever leave his bed again, she wrote. "It's always of you he has talked, and, besides, he had no more money left."

"Read this; Dolly writes about you," Kitty was beginning, with a smile; but she stopped suddenly, noticing the changed expression of her husband's face.

"What is it? What's the matter?"

"She writes to me that Nikolai, my brother, is at death's door. I shall go to him."

Kitty's face changed at once. Thoughts of Tanya as a marquise, of Dolly, all had vanished.

"When are you going?" she said.

"Tomorrow."

"And I will go with you, can I?" she said.

"Kitty! What are you thinking of?" he said reproachfully.

"How do you mean?" she said, offended that he should seem to take her suggestion unwillingly and with vexation. "Why shouldn't I go? I won't be in your way. I—"

"I'm going because my brother is dying," said Levin. "Why should you—"

"Why? For the same reason as you."

"At a moment of such gravity for me, she only thinks of her being bored by herself," thought Levin. And her answer in a matter of such gravity infuriated him.

"It's out of the question," he said sternly.

Agafya Mikhailovna, seeing that it was coming to a quarrel, gently put down her cup and withdrew. Kitty did not even notice her. The tone in which her husband had said the last words wounded her, especially because he evidently did not believe what she had said.

"I tell you that if you go, I shall come with you; I shall certainly come," she said hastily and wrathfully. "Why out of the question? Why do you say it's out of the question?"

"Because it'll be going God knows where, by all sorts of roads and to all sorts of hotels. You would be a hindrance to me," said Levin, trying to keep cool.

"Not at all. I don't want anything. Where you can go, I can—"

"Well, for one thing, then, because this woman's there whom you can't associate with."

"I don't know and don't care to know who's there and what. I know that my husband's brother is dying and my husband is going to him, and I go with my husband too . . ."

"Kitty! Don't get angry. But just think a little: this is a matter of such importance that I can't bear to think that you're mixing it up with a feeling of weakness, dislike of being left alone. If you'll be bored alone, go to Moscow."

"There, you always ascribe base, vile motives to me," she said with tears of wounded pride and fury. "I didn't mean, it wasn't weakness, it wasn't . . . I feel that it's my duty to be with my husband when he's in trouble, but you try on purpose to hurt me, you try on purpose not to understand . . ."

"No, this is awful! To be such a slave!" cried Levin, getting up, unable to restrain his anger any longer. But at the same second he felt that he was beating himself.

"Then why did you marry? You could have been free. Why did you, if you regret it?" she said, getting up and running away into the drawing room.

When he went to her, she was sobbing.

He began to speak, trying to find words not to dissuade but simply to soothe her. But she did not heed him, and would not agree to anything. He bent down to her and took her hand, which resisted him. He kissed her hand, kissed her hair, kissed her hand again—still she was silent. But when he took her face in both hands and said "Kitty!" she suddenly recovered herself, cried a little, and they were reconciled.

It was decided that they should go together the next day. Levin told his wife that he believed she wanted to go simply in order to be of use, agreed that Marya Nikolaevna's being with his brother did not make her going improper, but at the bottom of his heart he was dissatisfied both with her and with himself. He was dissatisfied with her for being unable to make up her mind to let him go when it was necessary (and how strange it was for him to think that he, so lately hardly daring to believe in such happiness as that she could love him, now was unhappy because she loved him too much!), and he was dissatisfied with himself for not showing more strength of will. Still less could he agree with any conviction that it did not matter if she did not have anything to do with the woman who was with his brother, and he thought with horror of all the contingencies they might meet with. The mere idea of his wife, his Kitty, being in the same room with a prostitute set him shuddering with horror and loathing.

CHAPTER SEVENTEEN

The hotel in the provincial town where Nikolai Levin was lying ill was one of those provincial hotels which are constructed with the most modern improvements, with the best intentions of cleanliness, comfort, and even elegance, but, owing to the public that patronizes them, are, with astounding rapidity, transformed into filthy taverns with pretensions to modern improvements, these pretensions only making them worse than the old-fashioned hotels, which were simply filthy. This hotel had already reached that stage, and the soldier in a filthy uniform smoking in the entry supposed to be a hall porter, and the cast-iron, slippery, dark, and unpleasant staircase, and the impertinent waiter in a filthy frock coat, and the common dining room with a dusty bouquet of wax flowers adorning the table, and filth, dust, and disorder everywhere, and at the same time the sort of modern up-to-date self-complacent railway-induced bustle—everything aroused a most painful feeling in Levin after their fresh home life, especially because the impression of artificiality made by the hotel was so out of keeping with what awaited them.

As is invariably the case, after they had been asked at what price they wanted rooms, it appeared that there was not one decent room for them; one decent room had been taken by the inspector of railroads, another by a lawyer from Moscow, a third by Princess Astaflieva from the country. There remained only one filthy room, next to which they promised that another would be empty by the evening. Feeling angry with his wife because what he had expected had come to pass, which was that at the moment of arrival, when his heart throbbed with emotion and anxiety to know how his brother was getting on, he should have to be looking after her instead of rushing straight to his brother, Levin conducted her to the room assigned them.

"Go, go!" she said, looking at him with timid and guilty eyes.

He went out of the room without a word, and at once stumbled over Marya Nikolaevna, who had heard of his arrival and had not dared to go in to see him. She was just the same as when he had seen her in Moscow: the same woolen dress and bare arms and neck, and the same good-natured, dull, pockmarked face, only a little plumper.

"Well, how is he? How is he?"

"Very bad. He can't get up. He has constantly been expecting you. He . . . Are you . . . with your wife?"

Levin did not at first understand what it was that embarrassed her, but she immediately enlightened him.

"I'll go away. I'll go down to the kitchen," she said. "Nikolai Dmitrievich will be delighted. He heard about it, and knows your lady, and remembers her abroad."

Levin realized that she meant his wife, and did not know what answer to make.

"Come along, come along to him!" he said.

But as soon as he moved, the door of his room opened and Kitty peeped out. Levin crimsoned both from shame and from anger with his wife, who had put herself and him in such a difficult position; but Marya Nikolaevna crimsoned still more. She positively shrank and flushed to the point of tears, and clutching the ends of her apron in both hands, she twisted them in red fingers without knowing what to say or do.

For the first instant Levin saw an expression of eager curiosity in the eyes with which Kitty looked at this awful woman, so incomprehensible to her; but it lasted only a single instant.

"Well! How is he?" She turned to her husband and then to her.

"But one can't go on talking in the passage like this!" Levin said, looking angrily at a gentleman who walked jauntily across the corridor at that moment, going about his own business.

"Well, then, come in," said Kitty, turning to Marya Nikolaevna, who had recovered herself, but noticing her husband's frightened face: "or go on; go, and then come for me," she said, and went back into the room. Levin went to his brother's room.

He had not in the least expected what he saw and felt in his brother's room. He had expected to find him in the same state of self-deception which he had heard was so frequent with the consumptive, and which had struck him so much during his brother's visit in the autumn. He had expected to find the physical signs of the approach of death more marked—greater weakness, greater emaciation—but still almost the same condition of things. He had expected himself to feel the same distress at the loss of the brother he loved and the same horror in the face of death he had felt then, only in a greater degree. And he had prepared himself for this; but he found something utterly different.

In a little dirty room with the painted panels of its walls filthy with spittle, and conversation audible through the thin partition from the next room, in a stifling atmosphere saturated with excrement, on a bed moved away from the wall, there lay covered with a blanket a body. One arm of this body was above the blanket, and the wrist, as huge as a rakehandle, was attached, inconceivable as it seemed, to a thin, long spindle that was straight from the end to the middle. The head lay sideways on the pillow. Levin could see the thin hair wet with sweat on the temples and the drawn, transparent-looking forehead.

"It cannot be that that terrible body is my brother Nikolai?" thought Levin. But he went closer, saw the face, and doubt became impossible. In spite of the terrible change in the face, Levin had only to glance at those eager eyes raised at his approach, only at catch the faint movement of the mouth under the sticky mustache, to realize the terrible truth that this dead body was his living brother.

The glittering eyes looked sternly and reproachfully at his brother as he drew near. And immediately this glance established a living relationship between living men. Levin immediately felt the reproach in the eyes fixed on him, and felt remorse at his own happiness.

When Konstantin took him by the hand, Nikolai smiled. The smile was faint, scarcely perceptible, and in spite of the smile the stern expression of the eyes was unchanged.

"You did not expect to find me like this," he articulated with effort.

"Yes . . . no," said Levin, hesitating over his words. "How was it you didn't let me know before, that is, at the time of my wedding? I made inquiries in all directions."

He had to talk so as not to be silent, and he did not know what to say, especially as his brother made no reply, and simply stared without lowering his eyes, and evidently penetrated to the inner meaning of each word. Levin told his brother that his wife had come with him. Nikolai expressed pleasure, but said he was afraid of frightening her by his condition. A silence followed. Suddenly Nikolai stirred, and began to say something. From the look on his face, Levin expected something of peculiar gravity and importance, but Nikolai began speaking of his health. He found fault with the doctor, regretting that he had not a celebrated Moscow doctor. Levin saw that he still hoped.

Seizing the first moment of silence, Levin got up, anxious to escape, if only for an instant, from his agonizing emotion, and said that he would go and fetch his wife.

"Very well, and I'll tell her to clean up here. It's dirty and stinking here, I expect. Marya! Clean up the room," the sick man said with effort. "Oh, and when you've cleaned up, go away yourself," he added, looking inquiringly at his brother.

Levin made no answer. Going out into the corridor, he stopped short. He had said he would fetch his wife, but now, taking stock of the emotion he was feeling, he decided that he would try on the contrary to persuade her not to go in to the sick man. "Why should she suffer as I am suffering?" he thought.

"Well, how is he?" Kitty asked with a frightened face.

"Oh, it's awful, it's awful! What did you come for?" said Levin.

Kitty was silent for a few seconds, looking timidly and ruefully at her husband; then she went up and took him by the elbow with both hands.

"Kostya! take me to him; it will be easier for us to bear it together. You only take me, take me to him, please, and go away," she said. "You must understand that for me to see you, and not to see him, is far more painful. There I might be a help to you and to him. Please, let me!" she besought her husband, as though the happiness of her life depended on it.

Levin was obliged to agree, and regaining his composure, and completely forgetting about Marya Nikolaevna by now, he went in again to his brother with Kitty.

Stepping lightly, and continually glancing at her husband, showing him a valorous and sympathetic face, Kitty went into the sick man's room and, turning without haste, noiselessly closed the door. With inaudible steps she went quickly to the sick man's bedside, and going up so that he didn't have to turn his head, she immediately clasped in her fresh young hand the skeleton of his huge hand, pressed it, and began speaking with that soft eagerness, sympathetic and not offensive, which is peculiar to women.

"We have met, though we were not acquainted, at Soden," she said. "You never thought I was to be your sister?"

"You would not have recognized me?" he said, with a radiant smile at her entrance.

"Yes, I would. What a good thing you let us know! Not a day has passed that Kostya has not mentioned you, and been anxious."

But the sick man's animation did not last long.

Before she had finished speaking, there had come back into his face the stern, reproachful expression of the dying man's envy of the living.

"I am afraid you are not quite comfortable here," she said, turning away from his fixed stare and looking about the room. "We must ask about another room," she said to her husband, "so that we might be nearer."

CHAPTER EIGHTEEN

Levin could not look calmly at his brother; he could not himself be natural and calm in his presence. When he went in to the sick man, his eyes and his attention were unconsciously dimmed, and he did not see and did not distinguish the details of his brother's condition. He smelled the awful odor, saw the dirt, disorder, and miserable condition, and heard the groans, and felt that nothing could be done to help. It never entered his head to analyze the details of the sick man's situation, to consider how that body was lying under the blanket, how those emaciated legs and thighs and spine were lying huddled up, and whether they could not be made more comfortable, whether anything could not be done to make things, if not better, at least less bad. It made his blood run cold when he began to think of all these details. He was absolutely convinced that nothing could be done to prolong his brother's life or to relieve his suffering. But a sense of his regarding all aid as out of the question was felt by the sick man, and exasperated him. And this made it still more painful to Levin. To be in the sickroom was agony to him, not to be there still worse. And he was continually, on various pretexts, going out of the room and coming in again, because he was unable to remain alone.

But Kitty thought, and felt, and acted quite differently. On seeing the sick man, she pitied him. And pity in her womanly heart did not arouse at all the feeling of horror and loathing that it aroused in her husband, but a desire to act, to find out the details of his condition, and to remedy them. And since she had not the slightest doubt that it was her duty to help him, she had no doubt either that it was possible, and immediately set to work. The very details, the mere thought of which reduced her husband to terror, immediately engaged her attention. She sent for the doctor, sent to the chemist's, sent the maid who had come with her and Marya Nikolaevna to sweep and dust and scrub; she herself washed up something, washed out something else, laid something under the blanket. Something was by her directions brought into the sickroom, something else was carried out. She herself went several times to her room, regardless of the people she met in the corridor, got out and brought in sheets, pillow-cases, towels, and shirts.

561

The waiter, who was busy serving a meal to a party of engineers in the dining room, came several times with an irate countenance in answer to her summons, and could not avoid carrying out her orders, as she gave them with such gracious insistence that there was no evading her. Levin did not approve of all this; he did not believe it would be any good to the patient. Above all, he was afraid the patient would be angry at it. But the sick man, though he seemed and was indifferent about it, was not angry, but only ashamed, and on the whole seemed interested in what she was doing for him. Coming back from the doctor to whom Kitty had sent him, Levin, on opening the door, came upon the sick man at the instant when, by Kitty's directions, they were changing his shirt. The long white skeletal back, with the huge, prominent shoulder blades and protruding ribs and vertebrae, was bare, and Marya Nikolaevna and the waiter were struggling with the sleeve of the shirt, and could not get the long, limp arm into it. Kitty, hurriedly closing the door after Levin, was not looking that way; but the sick man groaned, and she moved rapidly toward him.

"Hurry up," she said.

"Oh, don't you come," said the sick man angrily. "I'll do it myself . . . "

"What say?" queried Marya Nikolaevna. But Kitty heard and saw that he was ashamed and uncomfortable at being naked before her.

"I'm not looking. I'm not looking!" she said, putting the arm in. "Marya Nikolaevna, you come to this side, you do it," she added.

"Please go for me, there's a little bottle in my handbag," she said, turning to her husband, "you know, in the side pocket; bring it, please, and meanwhile they'll finish up here."

Returning with the bottle, Levin found the sick man settled comfortably and everything about him completely changed. The foul smell was replaced by the smell of aromatic vinegar, which Kitty, with pouting lips and puffed-out, rosy cheeks, was blowing through a little tube. There was no dust visible anywhere, a mat was laid by the bedside. On the table stood medicine bottles and decanters tidily arranged, and the linen needed was folded up there, and Kitty's *broderie anglaise*. On the other table by the patient's bed there was a candle and drink and powders. The sick man himself, washed and combed, lay in clean sheets on high pillows, in a clean shirt with a white collar about his astoundingly thin neck, and with a new expression of hope, he looked fixedly at Kitty.

The doctor brought by Levin, and found by him at the club, was not the one who had been attending Nikolai Levin, with whom the patient was dissatisfied. The new doctor took up a stethoscope and sounded the patient, shook his head, prescribed medicine and then what diet was to be kept to. He advised eggs, raw or lightly boiled, and seltzer water, with fresh milk at a certain temperature. When the doctor had gone away, the sick man said something to his brother, of which Levin could distinguish only the last words—"your Katya." By the expression with which he gazed at her, Levin saw that he was praising her. He asked Katya, as he called her, to come closer.

"I'm much better already," he said. "Why, with you I should have got well long ago. How nice it feels!" He took her hand and drew it toward his lips, but as though afraid she would dislike it, he changed his mind, let it go, and only stroked it. Kitty took his hand in both hers and pressed it.

"Now turn me over on the left side and go to bed," he said.

No one could make out what he said but Kitty; she alone understood. She understood because she was all the while mentally keeping watch on what he needed.

"On the other side," she said to her husband, "he always sleeps on that side. Turn him over, it's so disagreeable calling the servants. I'm not strong enough. Can you?" she said to Marya Nikolaevna.

"I'm afraid not," answered Marya Nikolaevna.

Terrible as it was to Levin to put his arms around that terrible body, to take hold of that under the blanket of which he preferred to know nothing, under his wife's influence he made his resolute face that she knew so well, and putting his arms into the bed, he took hold of the body, but in spite of his own strength he was struck by the strange heaviness of those powerless limbs. While he was turning him over, conscious of the huge emaciated arm about his neck, Kitty swiftly and noiselessly turned the pillow, fluffed it up, and settled in it the sick man's head, smoothing back his hair, which was sticking again to his moist brow.

The sick man kept his brother's hand in his own. Levin felt that he meant to do something with his hand and was pulling it somewhere.

Levin yielded with a sinking heart: yes, he drew it to his mouth and kissed it. Levin, shaking with sobs and unable to articulate a word, went out of the room.

CHAPTER NINETEEN

"Thou hast hid these things from the wise and prudent, and hast revealed them unto babes." So Levin thought about his wife as he talked to her that night.

Levin thought of the text, not because he considered himself "wise and prudent." He did not so consider himself, but he could not help knowing that he was more intelligent than his wife and Agafya Mikhailovna, and he could not help knowing that when he thought of death, he thought with his whole heart and soul. He knew too that the brains of many great men, whose thoughts he had read, had brooded over death, and yet knew not a hundredth part of what his wife and Agafya Milkailovna knew about it. Different as those two women were, Agafya Mikhailovna and Katya, as his brother Nikolai had called her, and as Levin particularly liked to call her now, they were quite alike in this. Both knew, without a shade of doubt, what sort of thing life was and what death was, and though neither of them could have answered, even have understood the questions that presented themselves to Levin, both had no doubt of the significance of this event, and were precisely alike in their way of looking at it, which they shared with millions of people. The proof that they knew for a certainty the nature of death lay in the fact that they knew without a second of hesitation how to deal with the dying, and were not frightened of them. Levin and other men like him, though they could have said a great deal about death, obviously did not know this, since they were afraid of death, and were absolutely at a loss about what to do when people were dying. If Levin had been alone now with his brother Nikolai, he would have looked at him with terror, and with still greater terror waited, and would not have known what else to do.

More than that, he did not know what to say, how to look, how to move. To talk of outside things seemed to him shocking, impossible, to talk of death and depressing subjects—also impossible. To be silent, also impossible. "If I look at him he will think I am studying him, I am afraid; if I don't look at him, he'll think I'm thinking of other things. If I walk on tiptoe, he will be vexed; to tread firmly, I'm ashamed." Kitty evidently did not think of herself, and had no time to think about herself: she was thinking about him because she knew something, and all went well. She told him about herself and about her wedding, and smiled and sympathized with him and petted him, and talked of cases of recovery and all went well; so then she must know. The proof that her behavior and Agafya Mikailovna's was not instinctive, animal, irrational, was that apart from the physical treatment, the relief of suffering, both Agafya Mikhailovna, speaking of the old man who had just died, had said: "Well, thank God, he took the sacrament and received extreme unction; God grant each one of us such a death." Katya in just the same way, besides all her care about linen, bedsores, drink, found time the very first day to persuade the sick man of the necessity of taking the sacrament and receiving extreme unction.

On getting back from the sickroom to their own two rooms for the night, Levin sat with hanging head not knowing what to do. Not to speak of supper, of preparing for bed, of considering what they were going to do, he could not even talk to his wife; he was ashamed to. Kitty, on the contrary, was more active than usual. She was even livelier than usual. She ordered supper to be brought, herself unpacked their things, and herself helped to make the beds and did not even forget to sprinkle them with insect powder. She showed the alertness, that swiftness of reflection which comes out in a man before a battle, in conflict, in the dangerous and decisive moments of life—those moments when a man shows once and for all his mettle, and that all his past has not been wasted but has been a preparation for these moments.

Everything went rapidly in her hands, and before it was twelve o'clock all their things were arranged cleanly and tidily in her rooms, in such a way that the hotel rooms seemed like home; the beds were made, brushes, combs, mirrors laid out, table napkins were spread.

Levin felt that it was unpardonable to eat, to sleep, to talk even now, and it seemed to him that every movement he made was improper. She arranged the brushes, but she did it all so that there was nothing offensive about it.

They could neither of them eat, however, and for a long while they could not sleep, and did not even go to bed.

"I am very glad I persuaded him to receive extreme unction tomorrow," she said, sitting in her bed jacket before her folding mirror, combing her soft, fragrant hair with a fine comb. "I have never seen it, but I know, Mama has told me, there are prayers said for recovery."

"Do you suppose he can possibly recover?" said Levin, looking at the back of her round little head, at the narrow part which closed every time she drew the comb forward.

"I asked the doctor; he said he couldn't live more than three days. But can they be sure? I'm very glad, anyway, that I persuaded him," she said, peering at her husband through her hair. "Anything is possible," she added with that peculiar, rather sly expression that was always in her face when she spoke of religion.

Since their conversation about religion when they were engaged, neither of them had even started a discussion of the subject, but she performed all the ceremonies of going to church, saying her prayers, and so on, always with the unvarying conviction that this ought to be so. In spite of his assertion to the contrary, she was firmly persuaded that he was as much a Christian as she, and indeed a far better one; and all that he said about it was simply one of his amusing masculine whims, like what he would say about her *broderie anglaise:* that good people darn holes but that she cut them on purpose, and so on.

"Yes, you see, this woman, Marya Nikolaevna, did not know how to manage all this," said Levin. "And . . . I must admit I'm very, very glad you came. You are such purity that . . . " He took her hand and did not kiss it (to kiss her hand in such closeness to death seemed to him improper); he merely squeezed it with a penitent air, looking at her brightening eyes.

"It would have been miserable for you to be alone," she said, and lifting her hands, which hid her cheeks flushing with pleasure, she twisted a coil of hair on the nape of her neck and pinned it there. "No," she went on, "she did not know how . . . Luckily, I learned a lot at Soden."

"Surely there are not people there so ill?"

"Worse."

"What's so awful to me is that I can't help seeing him as he was when he was young. You would not believe how charming he was as a youth, but I did not understand him then."

"I can very much believe it. Now I feel that we *might* have been friends!" she said; and, distressed at what she had said, she looked around at her husband, and tears came into her eyes.

"Yes, *might have been*," he said mournfully. "He's just one of those people of whom they say they're not for this world."

"But we have many hard days before us; we must go to bed," said Kitty, glancing at her tiny watch.

CHAPTER TWENTY

DEATH

The next day the sick man received communion and extreme unction. During the ceremony Nikolai Levin prayed fervently. His large eyes, fastened on the icon that was set out on a card table covered with a colored napkin, expressed such passionate prayer and hope that it was terrible for Levin to see it. Levin knew that this passionate prayer and hope would only make him feel more bitter at having to part from the life he so loved. Levin knew his brother and the workings of his mind: he knew that his skepticism came, not from life being easier for him without faith, but arose because step by step the contemporary scientific interpretation of natural phenomena crushed the possibility of faith; and so he knew that his present return to faith was not a legitimate one, brought about by way of the same working of his mind, but simply a temporary, selfish return to faith in desperate hope of recovery. Levin knew too that Kitty had strengthened his hope by accounts of the marvelous recoveries she had heard of. Levin knew all this; and it was agonizingly painful to him to behold the supplicating hopeful eyes and the emaciated wrist, lifted with difficulty, making the sign of the cross on the drawn brow, and the prominent shoulders and hollow, rattling chest, which one could not feel consistent with the life the sick man was praying for.

During the sacrament Levin also prayed, did what he, an unbeliever, had done a thousand times. He said, addressing God, "If Thou dost exist, make this man to recover" (of course this same thing had happened many times), "and Thou wilt save him and me."

After extreme unction the sick man became suddenly much better. He did not cough once in the course of an hour, smiled, kissed Kitty's hand, thanking her with tears, and said he was comfortable, free from pain, and that he felt strong and had an appetite. He even raised himself when his soup was brought and asked for a cutlet as well. Hopelessly ill as he was, obvious as it was at the first glance that he could not recover, Levin and Kitty were for that hour both in the same state of excitement, happy, though fearful of being mistaken.

"Is he better?"

"Yes, much."

"It's wonderful."

"There's nothing wonderful in it."

"Anyway, he's better," they said in a whisper, smiling to one another.

This illusion was not of long duration. The sick man fell into a peaceful sleep, but he was awakened half an hour later by his cough. And all at once every hope vanished in those about him and in himself. The reality of his suffering crushed all hopes in Levin and Kitty and in the sick man himself, leaving no doubt, no memory even of past hopes.

Without referring to what he had believed in half an hour before, as though ashamed even to recall it, he asked for iodine to inhale in a bottle covered with perforated paper. Levin gave him the bottle, and the same look of passionate hope with which he had taken the sacrament was now fastened on his brother, demanding from him the confirmation of the doctor's words that inhaling iodine worked wonders.

"Is Katya not here?" he gasped, looking around while Levin reluctantly confirmed the doctor's words. "No; so I can say it . . . it was for her sake I went through that farce. She's so sweet; but you and I can't deceive ourselves. This is what I believe in," he said, and, squeezing the bottle in his bony hand, he began inhaling from it.

At eight o'clock in the evening Levin and his wife were drinking tea in their room, when Marya Nikolaevna ran in to them breathlessly. She was pale, and her lips were quivering. "He is dying!" she whispered. "I'm afraid he will die immediately."

Both of them ran to him. He was sitting raised up with one elbow on the bed, his long back bent, and his head hanging low.

"How do you feel?" Levin asked in a whisper, after a silence.

"I feel I'm going," Nikolai said with difficulty but with extreme distinctness, slowly squeezing the words out of himself. He did not raise his head, but simply turned his eyes upward, without their reaching his brother's face. "Katya, go away!" he added.

Levin jumped up and, with a peremptory whisper, made her go out.

"I'm going," he said again.

"Why do you think so?" said Levin so as to say something.

"Because I'm going," he repeated, as though he had a liking for the phrase. "It's the end."

Marya Nikolaevna went up to him.

"You had better lie down; you'd feel better," she said.

"I'll lie down soon enough," he pronounced slowly, "when I'm dead," he said sarcastically, wrathfully. "Well, you can lay me down if you like."

Levin laid his brother on his back, sat down beside him, and gazed at his face, holding his breath. The dying man lay with closed eyes, but the muscles twitched from time to time on his forehead, as if he were thinking deeply and intensely. Levin involuntarily thought with him of what it was that was happening to him now, but in spite of all his mental efforts to go along with him, he saw by the expression of that calm, stern face that for the dying man all was growing clearer and clearer that was still as dark as ever for Levin.

"Yes, yes, that's so," the dying man articulated slowly at intervals. "Wait a while." He was silent. "That's so!" he pronounced suddenly, as though all were solved for him. "Oh Lord!" he murmured, and sighed deeply.

Marya Nikolaevna felt his feet. "They're getting cold," she whispered.

For a long while, a very long while, it seemed to Levin, the sick man lay motionless. But he was still alive, and from time to time he sighed. Levin by now was exhausted from mental strain. He felt that despite his mental efforts he could not understand what was so. He could not even think of the problem of death itself, but with no will of his own, thoughts kept coming to him of what he had to do next: closing the dead man's eyes, dressing him, ordering the coffin. And, strange to say, he felt utterly indifferent, and was not conscious of sorrow or of loss; less still of pity for his brother. If he had any feeling for his brother at that moment it was envy for the knowledge the dying man had now that he could not have.

A long time more he sat over him like that, continually expecting the end. But the end did not come. The door opened and Kitty appeared. Levin got up to stop her. But at the moment he was getting up, he caught the sound of the dying man stirring.

"Don't go away," said Nikolai, and held out his hand. Levin gave him his, and angrily waved to his wife to go away.

With the dying man's hand in his hand, he sat for half an hour, an hour, another hour. He did not think of death at all now. He wondered what Kitty was doing; who lived in the next room; whether the doctor lived in a house of his own. He longed for food and for sleep. He cautiously drew away his hand and felt the feet. The feet were cold, but the sick man was still breathing. Levin tried again to move away on tiptoe, but the sick man stirred again and said: "Don't go."

The dawn came; the sick man's condition was unchanged. Levin stealthily withdrew his hand, and, without looking at the dying man, went off to his own room and went to sleep. When he woke up, instead of news of his brother's death which he expected, he learned that the sick man had returned to his earlier condition. He had begun sitting up again, coughing, had begun eating again, talking again, and again had ceased to talk of death, again had begun to express hope of his recovery, and had become more irritable and gloomier than ever. No one, neither his brother nor Kitty, could soothe him. He was angry with everyone, and said nasty things to everyone, reproached everyone for his sufferings, and insisted that they should get him a celebrated doctor from Moscow. To all inquiries about how he felt, he made the same answer with an expression of vindictive reproachfulness: "I'm suffering horribly, intolerably!"

The sick man was suffering more and more, especially from bed-sores, which it was impossible now to remedy, and grew more and more angry with everyone about him, blaming them for everything, and especially for not having brought him a doctor from Moscow. Kitty tried in every possible way to relieve him, to soothe him; but it was all in vain, and Levin saw that she herself was exhausted both physically and mentally, though she would not admit it. The aura of death, which had been evoked in all by his taking leave of life on the night when he had sent for his brother, was destroyed. Everyone knew that he must inevitably die soon, that he was half dead already. Every-one wished for nothing but that he should die as soon as possible, and everyone, concealing this, gave him medicines, tried to find remedies and doctors, and deceived him and themselves and each other. All this was falsehood, disgusting, irreverent deceit. And owing to the bent of his character, and because he loved the dying man more than any-one else did, Levin was most painfully conscious of this deceit.

Levin, who had long been possessed by the idea of reconciling his brothers, at least in the face of death, had written to his brother Sergey Ivanovich, and having received an answer from him, he read this letter to the sick man. Sergey Ivanovich wrote that he could not come himself, and in touching terms he begged his brother's for-giveness.

The sick man said nothing.

"What am I to write to him?" said Levin. "I hope you are not angry with him?"

"No, not the least!" Nikolai answered, vexed at the question. "Tell him to send me a doctor."

Three more days of agony followed; the sick man was still in the same condition. The sense of longing for his death was felt by every-one now at the mere sight of him, by the waiters and the proprietor and all the people staying in the hotel, and the doctor and Marya Nikolaevna and Levin and Kitty. The sick man alone did not express this desire, but, on the contrary, was furious at their not getting him doctors, and went on taking medicine and talking of life. Only at rare moments, when the opium gave him an instant's relief from the never-ceasing pain, he would sometimes, half asleep, utter what was felt more intensely in his heart than any of the others: "Oh, if it were only the end!" or: "When will it be over?"

His sufferings, steadily growing more intense, did their work and prepared him for death. There was no position in which he was not in pain, there was not a minute in which he was unconscious of it, not a limb, not a part of his body that did not ache and cause him agony. Even the memories, the impressions, the thoughts of this body awakened in him now the same aversion as the body itself. The sight of other people, their remarks, his own reminiscences, everything was for him a source of agony. Those about him felt this, and instinctively did not allow themselves to move freely, to talk, to express their wishes before him. All his life was merged in the one feeling of suffering and desire to be rid of it.

There was evidently coming over him that revulsion that would make him look upon death as the goal of his desires, as happiness. Hitherto each individual desire, aroused by suffering or privation, such as hunger, fatigue, thirst, had been satisfied by some bodily function giving pleasure. But now no physical craving or suffering received relief, and the effort to relieve them only caused fresh suffering. And so all desires were merged in one—the desire to be rid of all his sufferings and their source, the body. But he had no words to express this desire of deliverance, and so he did not speak of it, and from habit asked for the satisfaction of desires which could not now be satisfied. "Turn me over on the other side," he would say, and immediately after he would ask to turn back again as before. "Give me some broth. Take away the broth. Talk of something: why are you silent?" And as soon as they began to talk he would close his eyes, and would show weariness, indifference, and loathing.

On the tenth day after their arrival in town, Kitty fell ill. She suffered from headache and vomiting, and she could not get up all morning.

The doctor explained that the indisposition arose from fatigue and excitement, and prescribed rest.

After dinner, however, Kitty got up and went as usual with her embroidery to the sick man. He looked at her sternly when she came in, and smiled contemptuously when she said she had been sick. That day he was continually blowing his nose, and groaning piteously.

"How do you feel?" she asked him.

"Worse," he articulated with difficulty. "In pain!"

"In pain, where?"

"Everywhere."

"It will be over today, you will see," said Marya Nikolaevna. Though it was said in a whisper, the sick man, whose hearing Levin had noticed was very keen, must have heard. Levin said hush to her, and looked around at the sick man. Nikolai had heard; but these words produced no effect on him. His eyes had still the same intense reproachful look.

"Why do you think so?" Levin asked her, when she had followed him into the corridor.

"He has begun picking at himself," said Marya Nikolaevna.

"How do you mean?"

"Like this," she said, tugging at the folds of her wool dress. Levin noticed, indeed, that all that day the patient pulled at himself as if trying to snatch something away.

Marya Nikolaevna's prediction came true. Toward night the sick man was not able to life his hands, and could only gaze before him with the same intensely concentrated expression in his eyes. Even when his brother or Kitty bent over him, so that he could see them, he looked just the same. Kitty sent for the priest to read the prayer for the dying.

While the priest was reading it, the dying man did not show any sign off life; his eyes were closed. Levin, Kitty, and Marya Nikolaevna stood at the bedside. The priest had not quite finished reading the prayer when the dying man stretched, sighed, and opened his eyes. The priest, on finishing the prayers, put the cross to the cold forehead, then slowly returned it to the stand, and after standing for two minutes more in silence, he touched the huge, bloodless hand that was turning cold.

"He is gone," said the priest, and was about to move away when suddenly there was a faint stir in the clammy mustache of the dead man and quite distinctly through the stillness they heard from the depth of his chest the sharply distinct sounds:

"Not yet . . . soon."

And a minute later the face brightened, a smile came out under the mustache, and the women who had gathered around began carefully laying out the body.

The sight of his brother and the nearness of death revived in Levin that sense of horror in the face of the insoluble enigma, together with the nearness and inevitability of death, that had come upon him that autumn evening when his brother had come to him. This feeling was now even stronger than before; even less than before did he feel capable of apprehending the meaning of death, and its inevitability rose up before him more terrible than ever. But now, thanks to his wife's presence, that feeling did not reduce him to despair. In spite of death, he felt the need for life and love. He felt that love saved him from despair, and that this love, under the threat of despair, had become still stronger and purer. The one mystery of death, still unsolved, had scarcely passed before his eyes, when another mystery had arisen, as insoluble, calling to love and to life.

The doctor confirmed his suspicion about Kitty. Her indisposition was pregnancy.

CHAPTER TWENTY-ONE

From the moment when Aleksey Aleksandrovich Karenin understood from his interviews with Betsy and with Stepan Arkadyevich that all that was expected of him was to leave his wife in peace, without burdening her with his presence, and that his wife herself desired this, he felt so distraught that he could come to no decision by himself; he did not know what he wanted now, and putting himself in the hands of those who were so pleased to interest themselves in his affairs, he met everything with unqualified assent. It was only when Anna had left his house, and the English governess sent to ask him whether she should dine with him or separately, that for the first time he clearly comprehended his position, and was appalled by it. Most difficult of all in this position was the fact that he could not in any way connect and reconcile his past with what was now. It was not the past when he had lived happily with his wife that troubled him.

The transition from that past to a knowledge of his wife's infidelity he had lived through miserably already; that state was painful, but he could understand it. If his wife had then, on declaring to him her infidelity, left him, he would have been hurt, unhappy, but he would not have been in the hopeless position—incomprehensible to him— in which he felt himself now. He could not now reconcile his immediate past, his tenderness, his love for his sick wife and for the other man's child with what was now the case, that is with the fact that, as if in return for all this, he now found himself alone, put to shame, ridiculed, needed by no one, and despised by everyone.

For the first two days after his wife's departure Aleksey Aleksandrovich received petitioners and his private secretary, drove to the committee, and went to dinner in the dining room as usual. Without giving himself a reason for what he was doing, he strained every nerve of his being for those two days, simply to preserve an appearance of composure, and even of indifference. Answering inquiries about the disposition of Anna Arkadyevna's rooms and belongings, he had exercised immense self-control to appear like a man in whose eyes what had occurred was not unforeseen or out of the ordinary course of events, and he attained his aim: no one could have detected in him signs of despair. But on the second day after her departure, when Korney gave him a bill from a fashionable milliner's which Anna had forgotten to pay, and announced that the manager of the shop had personally come, Aleksey Aleksandrovich told him to show him up.

"Excuse me, Your Excellency, for venturing to trouble you. But if you direct us to apply to Her Excellency, would you graciously oblige us with her address?"

Aleksey Aleksandrovich pondered, it seemed to the manager, and all at once, turning around, he sat down at the table. Letting his head sink into his hands, he sat for a long while in that position, several times attempted to speak, and stopped short. Korney, perceiving his master's emotion, asked the manager to call another time. Left alone, Aleksey Aleksandrovich recognized that he had not the strength to keep up the line of firmness and composure any longer. He gave orders for the carriage that was awaiting him to be taken back, and for no one to be admitted, and he did not go down to dinner.

He felt that he could not endure the weight of universal contempt and exasperation which he had distinctly seen in the face of the clerk and of Korney and of everyone, without exception, whom he had met during those two days. He felt that he could not turn aside the hatred of men, because that hatred did not come from his being bad (in that case he could have tried to be better), but from his being shamefully and repulsively unhappy. He knew that for this, for the very fact that his heart was torn with grief, they would be merciless to him. He felt that men would crush him as dogs rip the throat of a crippled dog yelping with pain. He knew that his sole means of security against people was to hide his wounds from them, and instinctively he tried to do this for two days, but now he felt incapable of keeping up the unequal struggle.

His despair was even intensified by the consciousness that he was utterly alone in his sorrow. In all Petersburg there was not a human being to whom he could express what he was feeling, who would feel for him, not as a high official, not as a member of society, but simply as a suffering man; indeed, he had not such a friend in the whole world.

Aleksey Aleksandrovich grew up an orphan. There were two brothers. They did not remember their father, and their mother died when Aleksey Aleksandrovich was ten years old. The property was a small one. Their uncle Karenin, a government official of high standing, at one time a favorite of the late emperor, had brought them up.

On completing his high school and university courses with honors, Aleksey Aleksandrovich had, with his uncle's aid, immediately started in a prominent position in the service, and from that time forward he had devoted himself exclusively to political ambition. In high school and in the university, and afterward in the service, Aleksey Aleksandrovich had never formed a close friendship with anyone. His brother had been the person nearest to his heart, but he had a post in the Ministry of Foreign Affairs, and was always abroad, where he had died shortly after Aleksey Aleksandrovich's marriage.

While he was governor of a province, Anna's aunt, a wealthy provincial lady, had brought him together—middle-aged as he was, though young for a governor—with her niece, and had succeeded in putting him in such a position that he had either to propose or to leave town. Aleksey Aleksandrovich hesitated for a long time. There were at the time as many reasons for the step as against it, and there was no decisive consideration to outweigh his invariable rule of refraining when in doubt. But Anna's aunt had, through a mutual acquaintance, insinuated that he had already compromised the girl, and that he was in honor bound to propose. He proposed, and concentrated on his betrothed and his wife all the feeling of which he was capable.

The attachment he felt to Anna precluded every need of intimate relations with others. And now among all his acquaintances he had not one friend. He had plenty of so-called connections, but no friendships. Aleksey Aleksandrovich had plenty of people whom he could invite to dinner, to whose sympathy he could appeal in any public affair he was concerned about, whose interest he could count upon for anyone he wished to help, with whom he could candidly discuss other people's business and affairs of state. But his relations with these people were confined to one clearly defined channel, and had a certain routine from which it was impossible to depart. There was one man, a comrade of his at the university, with whom he had made friends later, and with whom he could have spoken of personal sorrow; but this friend had a post in the Department of Education in a remote part of Russia. Of the people in Petersburg with whom he was most intimate and in whom he could confide, there were his chief secretary and his doctor.

Mikhail Vasilievich, the chief secretary, was a straightforward, intelligent, good-hearted, and conscientious man, and Aleksey Aleksandrovich was aware of his personal good will. But their five years of official work together seemed to have put a barrier between them that prevented more intimate confidences.

After signing the papers brought him, Aleksey Aleksandrovich had sat for a long while in silence, glancing at Mikhail Vasilievich, and several times he attempted to speak, but could not. He had already prepared the phrase: "You have heard of my trouble?" But he ended by saying, as usual: "So you'll get this ready for me?" and with that dismissed him.

The other person was the doctor, who had also a kindly feeling for him; but there had long existed a tacit understanding between them that both were weighed down by work, and always in a hurry.

Of his women friends, foremost among them Countess Lydia

Ivanovna, Aleksey Aleksandrovich never thought. All women, simply as women, were dreadful and repulsive.

CHAPTER TWENTY-TWO

Aleksey Aleksandrovich had forgotten the Countess Lydia Ivanovna, but she had not forgotten him. At the bitterest moment of his lonely despair she came to him, and, without waiting to be announced, walked straight into his study. She found him as he had been sitting, with his head in both hands.

"*J'ai forcé la consigne,*"[1] she said, walking in rapidly and breathing hard from excitement and exercise. "I have heard all! Aleksey Aleksandrovich! Dear friend!" she went on, warmly squeezing his hand in both of hers and gazing with her beautiful, dreamy eyes into his.

Aleksey Aleksandrovich, frowning, got up and, disengaging his hand, moved a chair toward her.

"Won't you sit down, Countess? I'm seeing no one because I'm not well, Countess," he said, and his lips twitched.

"Dear friend!" repeated Countess Lydia Ivanovna, never taking her eyes off his, and suddenly her eyebrows rose at the inner corners, forming a triangle on her forehead; her plain yellow face became still plainer, but Aleksey Aleksandrovich felt that she was sorry for him and was preparing to cry. And he too was moved; he snatched her plump hand and proceeded to kiss it.

"Dear friend!" she said in a voice breaking with emotion. "You must not give way to grief. Your sorrow is great, but you must find consolation."

"I am crushed, I am annihilated, I am no longer a man!" said Aleksey Aleksandrovich, releasing her hand but still gazing into her brimming eyes. "My position is so awful because I can nowhere find support, not even in myself."

"You will find support; seek it—not in me, though I beseech you to believe in my friendship," she said, with a sigh. "Our support is love, that love that He has vouchsafed us. His burden is light," she

---

[1] "I've forced my way in."

said, with the look of ecstasy Aleksey Aleksandrovich knew so well. "He will be your support and your succor."

Though it seemed evident that she was moved by her own lofty sentiments, and by that new mystical fervor which had lately gained ground in Petersburg, and which seemed to Aleksey Aleksandrovich excessive, still it was gratifying to hear this now.

"I am weak. I am crushed. I foresaw nothing, and now I understand nothing."

"Dear friend," repeated Lydia Ivanovna.

"It's not the loss of what no longer is, it's not that," pursued Aleksey Aleksandrovich. "I do not grieve for that. But I cannot help feeling humiliated before other people for the position I am placed in. It is wrong, but I can't help it, I can't help it."

"Not you it was performed that noble act of forgiveness, at which I and everyone was moved to rapture, but He, working within your heart," said Countess Lydia Ivanovna, raising her eyes ecstatically, "and so you cannot be ashamed of your act."

Aleksey Aleksandrovich knitted his brows and, crooking his hands, he cracked the joints of his fingers.

"One must know all the facts," he said in his thin voice. "A man's strength has its limits, Countess, and I have reached my limits. The whole day I have had to be making arrangements, arrangements about household matters arising" (he emphasized the word "arising") "from my new, solitary position. The servants, the governess, the accounts . . . These petty flames have seared me, and I have not the strength to bear it. At dinner . . . yesterday, I almost left the table. I could not bear the way my son looked at me. He did not ask me the meaning of it all, but he wanted to ask, and I could not bear the look in his eyes. He was afraid to look at me, but that is not all . . ." Aleksey Aleksandrovich would have referred to the bill that had been brought to him, but his voice shook, and he stopped. That bill on blue paper, for a hat and ribbons, he could not recall without a rush of self-pity.

"I understand, dear friend," said Lydia Ivanovna. "I understand it all. Succor and comfort you will find not in me, though I have come only to aid you if I can. If I could lift from your shoulders all these petty, humiliating cares . . . I understand that a woman's word, a woman's direction is needed. You will entrust it to me?"

Silently and gratefully Aleksey Aleksandrovich pressed her hand.

"Together we will take care of Seryozha. Practical affairs are not my strong point. But I will do it. I will be your housekeeper. Don't thank me. I do it not from myself . . . "

"I cannot help thanking you."

"But, dear friend, do not give way to the feeling of which you spoke—being ashamed of what is the Christian's highest glory: 'he that humbleth himself shall be exalted.' And you cannot thank me. You must thank Him, and pray to Him for succor. In Him alone we find peace, consolation, salvation, and love," she said, and turning her eyes heavenward, she began praying, as Aleksey Aleksandrovich gathered from her silence.

Aleksey Aleksandrovich listened to her now, and those expressions which had seemed to him, if not distasteful, at least exaggerated, now seemed to him natural and consolatory. Aleksey Aleksandrovich had disliked this new ecstatic fervor. He was a believer who was interested in religion primarily in its political aspect, and the new doctrine which ventured upon several new interpretations, just because it paved the way to discussion and analysis, was in principle disagreeable to him. He had hitherto taken up a cold and even antagonistic attitude toward this new doctrine, and with Countess Lydia Ivanovna, who had been carried away by it, he had never argued, but by silence had assiduously parried her attempts to provoke him into argument. Now for the first time he heard her words with pleasure, and did not inwardly oppose them.

"I am very, very grateful to you, both for your deeds and for your words," he said, when she had finished praying.

Countess Lydia Ivanovna once more pressed both her friend's hands.

"Now I will enter upon my duties," she said with a smile after a pause, as she wiped away the traces of tears. "I am going to Seryozha. Only as the last resort shall I apply to you." And she got up and went out.

Countess Lydia Ivanovna went into Seryozha's part of the house, and dropping tears on the scared child's cheeks, she told him that his father was a saint and his mother was dead.

Countess Lydia Ivanovna kept her promise. She did actually take

upon herself the care of the organization and management of Aleksey Aleksandrovich's household. But she had not overstated the case
when saying that practical affairs were not her strong point. All her
arrangements had to be modified because they could not be carried
out, and they were modified by Korney, Aleksey Aleksandrovich's
valet, who, though no one was aware of the fact, now managed
Karenin's household, and quietly and discreetly reported to his master, while helping him dress, all it was necessary for him to know. But
Lydia Ivanovna's help was nonetheless real; she gave Aleksey Aleksandrovich moral support in the consciousness of her love and
respect for him, and still more, as it was soothing for her to believe,
in that she almost turned him to Christianity—that is, from an indifferent and apathetic believer she turned him into an ardent and
steadfast adherent of the new interpretation of Christian doctrine,
which had been gaining ground of late in Petersburg. It was easy for
Aleksey Aleksandrovich to believe in this teaching. Aleksey Aleksandrovich, like Lydia Ivanovna, and others who shared their views, was
completely devoid of that depth of imaginative faculty, that spiritual
faculty in virtue of which the conceptions evoked by the imagination become so vivid that they demand being brought into harmony
with other conceptions, and with actual fact. He saw nothing impossible and inconceivable in the idea that death, though existing for
unbelievers, did not exist for him, and that, as he was possessed of the
most perfect faith, of the measure of which he was himself the judge,
therefore there was no sin in his soul, and he was experiencing complete salvation here on earth.

It is true that the erroneousness and shallowness of the conception
of his faith was dimly perceptible to Aleksey Aleksandrovich, and he
knew that when, without the slightest idea that his forgiveness was
the action of a higher power, he had surrendered directly to the feeling of forgiveness, he had felt more happiness than now when he was
thinking every instant that Christ was in his heart, and that in signing official papers he was doing His will. But for Aleksey Aleksandrovich it was a necessity to think that way; it was such a necessity for
him in his humiliation to have at least some elevation, however imaginary, from which, looked down upon by all, he could look down on
others, that he clung to his mock salvation as if it were genuine.

CHAPTER TWENTY-THREE

The Countess Lydia Ivanovna had, as a very young and rhapsodical girl, been married to a wealthy man of high rank, a very good-natured, jovial, and extremely dissipated rake. Two months after marriage her husband abandoned her, and her impassioned protestations of affection he met with a sarcasm and even hostility that people knowing the count's good heart, and seeing no defects in the ecstatic Lydia, were at a loss to explain. Though they were not divorced, they lived apart, and whenever the husband met the wife, he invariably behaved to her with the same venomous irony, the cause of which was incomprehensible.

Countess Lydia Ivanovna had long ceased being in love with her husband, but from that time she had never ceased being in love with someone. She was in love with several people at once, both men and women; she had been in love with almost everyone who had been particularly distinguished in any way. She was in love with all the new princes and princesses who married into the Imperial family; she had been in love with a metropolitan, a vicar, and a priest; she had been in love with a journalist, three Slavs, with Komisarov, a minister, a doctor, an English missionary, and Karenin. All these passions, constantly waning or growing more ardent; did not prevent her from keeping up the most extended and complicated relations with the court high society. But from the time after Karenin's trouble she took him under her special protection, from the time she set to work in Karenin's household looking after his welfare, she felt that all her other attachments were not the real thing, and that she was now genuinely in love, and with no one but Karenin. The feeling she now experienced for him seemed to her stronger than any of her former feelings. Analyzing her feeling, and comparing it with former passions, she distinctly perceived that she would not have been in love with Komisarov if he had not saved the life of the Tsar,[1] that she would not have been in love with Ristich-Kudzhitsky if there had been no Slav question,[2] but that she loved Karenin for himself, for

---

[1]Komisarov saved Aleksandr II from being shot by knocking the pistol from the hand of a would-be assassin.
[2]In 1875 there was an uprising of Bosnia and Herzegovina against the Turks, and the

his lofty, misunderstood soul, for the—to her—high-pitched sound of his voice, for his drawling inflections which she thought charming, his weary eyes, his character, and his soft white hands with their swollen veins. She was not simply overjoyed at meeting him, but she sought in his face signs of the impression she was making on him. She tried to please him, not only by her words, but also in her whole person. For his sake it was that she now lavished more care on her dress than before. She caught herself in reveries on what might have been if she had not been married and he had been free. She blushed with excitement when he came into the room; she could repress a smile of rapture when he said anything friendly to her.

For several days, now, Countess Lydia Ivanovna had been in a state of intense excitement. She had learned that Anna and Vronsky were in Petersburg. Aleksey Aleksandrovich must be saved from seeing her, he must be saved even from the torturing knowledge that that awful woman was in the same town as he, and that he might meet her any minute.

Lydia Ivanovna made inquiries through her friends as to what *those disgusting people*, as she called Anna and Vronsky, intended doing, and she endeavored so to guide every movement of her friend during those days that he could not come across them. The young adjutant, an acquaintance of Vronsky's, through whom she obtained her information, and who hoped through Countess Lydia Ivanovna to obtain a concession, told her that they had finished their business and were going away the next day. Lydia Ivanovna had already begun to calm down, when the next morning a note was brought to her, the handwriting of which she recognized with horror. It was the handwriting of Anna Karenina. The envelope was of paper as thick as parchment; on the oblong yellow paper there was a huge monogram, and the letter smelled of delicious perfume.

"Who brought it?"

"A commissionaire from the hotel."

---

same year there occurred the "Bulgarian atrocities" (i.e., the murder of thousands by the Turks). In 1876, joining Serbia and Montenegro, Russia (which had been sending volunteers to aid the insurgents) went to war with Turkey, for the "defense of Slavic brethren." Jovan Ristich-Kudzhitsky, prominent Serbian statesman, was Minister of Foreign Affairs during the war.

It was some time before Countess Lydia Ivanovna could sit down to read the letter. Her excitement brought on an attack of asthma, to which she was subject. When she had recovered her composure, she read the following letter, written in French:

Madame La Comtesse—The Christian feelings with which your heart is filled give me the, I feel, unpardonable boldness to write to you. I am miserable at being separated from my son. I entreat permission to see him once before my departure. Forgive me for recalling myself to your memory. I apply to you and not to Aleksey Aleksandrovich simply because I do not wish to cause that generous man to suffer in remembering me. Knowing your friendship for him, I know you will understand me. Could you send Seryozha to me, or should I come to the house at some fixed hour, or will you let me know when and where I could see him away from home? I do not anticipate a refusal, knowing the magnanimity of him with whom it rests. You cannot conceive the craving I have to see my son, and so cannot conceive the gratitude your help will arouse in me.

Anna

Everything in this letter exasperated Countess Lydia Ivanovna; its contents and the allusion to magnanimity, and especially what seemed to her its free and easy tone.

"Say that there is no answer," said Countess Lydia Ivanovna, and immediately opening her blotting pad, she wrote to Aleksey Aleksandrovich that she hoped to see him at one o'clock at the reception.

"I must talk with you of a grave and painful subject. There we will arrange where to meet. Best of all at my house, where I will have your tea ready. Urgent. He sends a cross, but He sends the strength to bear it," she added, so as to prepare him somewhat. Countess Lydia Ivanovna usually wrote some two or three letters a day to Aleksey Aleksandrovich. She enjoyed that form of communication, which gave opportunity for elegance and an air of mystery not afforded by their personal relationship.

CHAPTER TWENTY-FOUR

The reception was drawing to a close. People met as they were going away, and gossiped of the latest news, of the newly bestowed honors, and the changes in the positions of the highest officials.

"If only Countess Marya Borisovna were Minister of War, and Princess Vatkovskaya were Commander-in-chief," said a gray-headed little old man in a gold-embroidered uniform, addressing a tall, beautiful Lady in Waiting, who had questioned him about the new appointments.

"And me the aide-de-camp," said the Lady in Waiting, smiling.

"You have an appointment already. You're over in the ecclesiastical department. And your assistant's Karenin."

"He and Putyatov had received the Aleksandr Nevsky." [1]

"I thought he had it already."

"No. Just look at him," said the little old man, pointing with his embroidered hat to Karenin in a court uniform with the new red sash across his shoulders, standing in the doorway of the hall with an influential member of the State Council. "Pleased and happy as a brass kopek," he added, stopping to shake hands with a handsome, athletic chamberlain.

"No; he's looking older," said the gentleman of the bedchamber.

"From overwork. He's always drawing up projects nowadays. He won't let a poor devil go nowadays till he's explained it all to him point by point."

"Looking older, did you say? *Il fait des passions.*[2] I believe Countess Lydia Ivanovna's jealous now of his wife."

"Oh, come now, please don't say anything bad about Countess Lydia Ivanovna."

"Why, is there any harm in her being in love with Karenin?"

"But is it true Madame Karenina's here?"

"Well, not here in the palace, but in Petersburg. I met her yesterday with Aleksey Vronsky, *bras dessus, bras dessous,*[3] in the Morskaya."

[1] One of the highest orders in Tsarist Russia.
[2] "He arouses passions."
[3] "Arm in arm."

"*C'est un homme qui n'a pas*[4] . . ." the chamberlain was beginning, but he stopped to make room, bowing for a member of the Imperial family to pass.

Thus people talked incessantly of Aleksey Aleksandrovich, finding fault with him and laughing at him, while he, blocking the way of the member of the State Council he had captured, was explaining to him point by point his new financial project, never interrupting his discourse for an instant for fear he might escape.

Almost at the same time that his wife left Aleksey Aleksandrovich, there had come to him that bitterest moment in the life of an official—the moment when his upward career comes to a full stop. This full stop had arrived and everyone perceived it, but Aleksey Aleksandrovich himself was not yet aware that his career was over. Whether it was due to his feud with Stremov, or his misfortune with his wife, or simply that he had reached his destined limits, it had become evident to everyone in the course of that year that his career was at an end. He still filled a position of consequence, he sat on many commissions and committees, but he was a man whose day was over, and from whom nothing was expected. Whatever he said, whatever he proposed, was heard as though it was something long familiar, and the very thing that was not needed. But Aleksey Aleksandrovich was not aware of this, and, on the contrary, being cut off from direct participation in governmental activity, he saw more clearly than ever the errors and defects in the action of others, and thought it his duty to point out means of their correction. Shortly after his separation from his wife, he began writing his first note on the new judicial procedure, the first of the endless series of notes he was destined to write in the future.

Aleksey Aleksandrovich did not merely fail to observe his hopeless position in the official world, he was not merely free from anxiety, he was positively more satisfied than ever with his own activity.

"He that is unmarried careth for the things that belong to the Lord, how he may please the Lord: but he that is married careth for the things of the world, how he may please his wife," says the Apostle Paul, and Aleksey Aleksandrovich, who was now guided in every

---

[4] "That's a man who has no . . . "

action by Scripture, often recalled this text. It seemed to him that ever since he had been left without a wife he had in these very projects of reform been serving the Lord more zealously than before.

The unmistakable impatience of the member of the State Council trying to get away from him did not trouble Aleksey Aleksandrovich; he gave up his exposition only when the member of the Council, seizing his chance when one of the royal family was passing, slipped away from him.

Left alone, Aleksey Aleksandrovich looked down, collecting his thoughts, then looked casually about him and walked toward the door, where he hoped to meet Countess Lydia Ivanovna.

"And how strong they all are, how sound physically," thought Aleksey Aleksandrovich, looking at the powerfully built chamberlain with his well-brushed, perfumed whiskers, and at the red neck of the prince, pinched by his tight uniform. He had to pass them on his way. "Truly is it said that all the world is evil," he thought, with another sidelong glance at the calves of the chamberlain.

Moving forward deliberately, Aleksey Aleksandrovich bowed with his customary air of weariness and dignity to the gentlemen who had been talking about him, and looking toward the door, his eyes sought Countess Lydia Ivanovna.

"Ah! Aleksey Aleksandrovich!" said the little old man with a malicious light in his eyes at the moment when Karenin passed him, nodding with a cold gesture. "I haven't congratulated you yet," said the old man, pointing to his newly received order.

"Thank you," answered Aleksey Aleksandrovich. "What an *exquisite* day today," he added, laying emphasis in his peculiar way on the word "exquisite."

That they laughed at him he was well aware, but he did not expect anything but hostility from them; he was used to that by now.

Catching sight of the yellow shoulders of Lydia Ivanovna jutting out above her bodice, and her beautiful, dreamy eyes bidding him to her, Aleksey Aleksandrovich smiled, revealing untarnished white teeth, and went toward her.

Lydia Ivanovna's dress had cost her great pains, as indeed all her dresses had done of late. Her aim in dress was now quite the reverse of that she had pursued thirty years ago. Then her desire had been to adorn herself for something, and the more adorned the better. Now, on the contrary, she was perforce decked out in a way so inconsistent with her age and her figure that her one anxiety was to contrive that the contrast between these adornments and her own exterior should not be too appalling. And as far as Aleksey Aleksandrovich was concerned, she succeeded, and was in his eyes attractive. For him she was the one island, not only of good will, but also of love in the midst of the sea of hostility and sneers that surrounded him.

Running the gauntlet of those mocking eyes, he was drawn as naturally to her loving glance as a plant to the sun.

"I congratulate you," she said to him, her eyes on his ribbon.

Suppressing a smile of pleasure, he shrugged his shoulders, closing his eyes, as though to say that that could not be a source of joy to him. Countess Lydia Ivanovna was very well aware that it was one of his chief sources of satisfaction, though he never admitted it.

"How is our angel?" asked Countess Lydia Ivanovna, meaning Seryozha.

"I can't say I am wholly pleased with him," said Aleksey Aleksandrovich, raising his eyebrows and opening his eyes. "And Sitnikov is not satisfied with him." (Sitnikov was the tutor to whom Seryozha's secular education had been entrusted.) "As I have mentioned to you, there's a sort of coldness in him toward the most important questions which ought to touch the heart of every man and child . . ." Aleksey Aleksandrovich began expounding his views on the sole question that interested him besides the service—the education of his son.

When Aleksey Aleksandrovich, with Lydia Ivanovna's help, had been brought back anew to life and activity, he felt it his duty to undertake the education to the son left on his hands. Having never before taken any interest in educational questions, Aleksey Aleksandrovich devoted some time to the theoretical study of the subject. After reading several books on anthropology, pedagogics, and didactics, Aleksey Aleksandrovich drew up a plan of education, and engaging the best tutor in Petersburg to supervise it, he set to work, and the subject continually absorbed him.

"Yes, but the heart. I see in him his father's heart, and with such a heart a child cannot go far wrong," said Lydia Ivanovna with enthusiasm.

"Yes, perhaps . . . As for me, I do my duty. It's all I can do."

"You must come and see me," said Countess Lydia Ivanovna, after a pause; "we have to speak of a subject painful to you. I would give anything to have spared you certain memories, but others are not of the same mind. I have received a letter from *her. She* is here in Petersburg."

Aleksey Aleksandrovich shuddered at the allusion to his wife, but immediately his face assumed the deathlike rigidity which expressed utter helplessness in the matter.

"I was expecting it," he said.

Countess Lydia Ivanovna looked at him ecstatically, and tears of rapture at the grandeur of his soul came into her eyes.

CHAPTER TWENTY-FIVE

When Aleksey Aleksandrovich came into the Countess Lydia Ivanovna's snug little boudoir, decorated with old china and hung with portraits, the lady herself had not yet made her appearance.

She was changing her dress.

A cloth was laid on a round table, and on it stood a china tea service and a silver spirit lamp and teakettle. Aleksey Aleksandrovich looked idly about at the countless familiar portraits which adorned the room, and sitting down at the table, he opened a New Testament lying upon it. The rustle of the countess's silk dress drew his attention away.

"Well now, we can sit quietly," said Countess Lydia Ivanovna, slipping hurriedly with an agitated smile between the table and the sofa, "and talk over our tea."

After some words of preparation, Countess Lydia Ivanovna, breathing hard and flushing crimson, put into Aleksey Aleksandrovich's hands the letter she had received.

After reading the letter, he sat a long while in silence.

"I don't think I have the right to refuse her," he said, timidly raising his eyes.

"Dear friend, you never see evil in anyone!"

"On the contrary, I see that all is evil. But whether it is fair—"

His face showed irresolution, was seeking counsel, support, and guidance in a matter he did not understand.

"No," Countess Lydia Ivanovna interrupted him, "there are limits to everything. I can understand immorality," she said, not quite truthfully, since she never could understand that which leads women to immorality, "but I can't understand cruelty, and to whom? To you! How can she stay in the town where you are? No, the longer one lives, the more one learns. And I'm learning to understand your loftiness and her baseness."

"Who is to throw a stone?" said Aleksey Aleksandrovich, unmistakably pleased with the part he had to play. "I have forgiven all, and so I cannot deprive her of what is exacted by love in her—by her love for her son . . ."

"But is that love, my friend? Is it sincere? Admitting that you have forgiven—that you forgive—have we the right to work on the feelings of that angel? He looks on her as dead. He prays for her, and beseeches God to have mercy on her sins. And it is better so. But now what will he think?"

"I had not thought of that," said Aleksey Aleksandrovich, evidently agreeing.

Countess Lydia Ivanovna hid her face in her hands and was silent. She was praying.

"If you ask my advice," she said, having finished her prayer and uncovered her face, "I do not advise you to do this. Do you suppose I don't see how you are suffering, how this has torn open your wounds? But supposing that, as always, you don't think of yourself, what can it lead to?—to fresh suffering for you, to torture for the child. If there were a trace of humanity left in her she ought not to wish for it herself. No, I have no hesitation in saying I advise not, and if you will entrust it to me, I will write to her."

And Aleksey Aleksandrovich consented, and Countess Lydia Ivanovna sent the following letter in French:

Dear Madame—To be reminded of you might lead your son to asking questions which could not be answered without implanting in the child's soul a spirit of censure toward what should be for him sacred, and therefore I beg you to interpret your husband's refusal in the spirit of Christian love. I pray to Almighty God to have mercy on you.

Countess Lydia

This letter accomplished the secret purpose which Countess Lydia Ivanovna had concealed even from herself. It wounded Anna to the quick.

For his part, Aleksey Aleksandrovich, on returning home from Lydia Ivanovna's, could not all that day concentrate on his usual pursuits, and find that spiritual peace of a believer who has found salvation which he had felt of late.

The thought of his wife, who had so greatly sinned against him, and toward whom he had been so saintly, as Countess Lydia Ivanovna had so justly told him, should not have troubled him, but he was not at ease; he could not understand the book he was reading; he could not drive away harassing recollections of his relations with her, of the mistake which, it now seemed, he had made in regard to her. The memory of how he had received her confession of infidelity on their way home from the races (especially that he had insisted only on the observance of external decorum, and had not sent a challenge) tortured him like remorse. He was tortured, too, by the thought of the letter he had written her; and most of all by his forgiveness, which nobody wanted, and his care of the other man's child made his heart burn with shame and remorse.

And exactly the same feeling of shame and regret he felt now, as he reviewed his past with her, recalling the awkward words in which, after long hesitating, he had proposed.

"But have I been to blame?" he said to himself. And this question always excited another question in him—whether they felt differently, did their loving and marrying differently, these Vronskys and Oblonskys . . . these fat-calved chamberlains. And there passed before his mind a whole series of those juicy, vigorous, self-confident men, who always and everywhere drew his inquisitive attention in spite of himself. He tried to dispel these thoughts, he tried to persuade himself that he was not living for this transient life but for the life of eternity, and that there was peace and love in his heart.

But the fact that he had in this transient, trivial life made, as it seemed to him, a few trivial mistakes tortured him as though the eternal salvation in which he believed had no existence. But this temptation did not last long, and soon there was re-established once more in Aleksey Aleksandrovich's soul the peace and the loftiness by virtue of which he could forget what he did not wish to remember.

CHAPTER TWENTY-SIX

"Well, Kapitonich?" said Seryozha, coming back rosy and cheerful from his walk the day before his birthday, and giving his overcoat to the tall old hall porter, who smiled down at the little fellow from the height of his long figure. "Well, has the muffled-up man been here today? Did Papa see him?"

"He saw him. The minute the secretary came out, I announced him," said the hall porter with a good-humored wink. "Here, I'll take it off."

"Seryozha!" said the tutor, stopping in the doorway leading to the inner rooms. "Take it off yourself." But Seryozha, though he heard his tutor's feeble voice, did not pay attention to it. He stood, keeping hold of the hall porter's shoulder strap and gazing into his face.

"Well, and did Papa do what he wanted?"

The hall porter nodded his head affirmatively. The muffled-up man, who had already been seven times to ask some favor of Aleksey Aleksandrovich, interested both Seryozha and the hall porter. Seryozha had come upon him in the hall, and had heard him plaintively beg the hall porter to announce him, saying that he and his children had death staring them in the face.

Since then Seryozha, having met him a second time in the hall, took great interest in him.

"Well, was he very glad? he asked.

"Glad? I should think so! Almost dancing as he walked away."

"And has anything come?" asked Seryozha, after a pause.

"Come, sir," said the hall porter; then, with a shake of his head, he whispered, "Something from the countess."

Seryozha understood at once that what the hall porter was speaking of was a present from Countess Lydia Ivanovna for his birthday.

"You don't say? Where?"

"Korney took it to your papa. A fine thing it must be too!"

"How big? Like this?"

"Not quite, but a fine thing."

"A book."

"No, a thing. Run along, run along. Vasily Lukich is calling you," said the porter, hearing the tutor's steps approaching, and carefully taking away from his shoulder strap the little hand in the glove half pulled off, he motioned with his head toward the tutor.

"Vasily Lukich, in a tiny minute!" answered Seryozha with that gay and loving smile which always won over the conscientious Vasily Lukich.

Seryozha was too happy, everything was too delightful, for him to be able to help sharing with his friend, the porter, the family good fortune of which he had heard during his walk in the public gardens from Lydia Ivanovna's niece. This piece of good news seemed to him particularly important because it came at the same time with the happiness of the muffled-up official and his own happiness at a present having come for him. It seemed to Seryozha that this was a day on which everyone ought to be glad and happy.

"You know Papa's received the Aleksandr Nevsky today?"

"To be sure I do! People have been to congratulate him already."

"And is he glad?"

"Glad at the Tsar's gracious favor! I should think so! It's proof he's deserved it," said the porter sternly and seriously.

Seryozha became thoughtful, gazing up at the face of the porter, which he had thoroughly studied in every detail, especially the chin that hung down between the gray whiskers, never seen by anyone but Seryozha, who saw him only from below.

"Well, and has your daughter been to see you lately?"

The porter's daughter was a ballet dancer.

"When is she to come, on week days? They've their lessons to learn, too. And you've your lesson, sir; run along."

On coming into the room, Seryozha, instead of sitting down to his lessons, told his tutor of his guess that what had been brought him must be a machine. "What do you think?" he inquired.

But Vasily Lukich was thinking of nothing but the necessity of learning the grammar lesson for the teacher, who was coming at two.

"No, do just tell me, Vasily Lukich," he asked suddenly, when he was seated at the desk with the book in his hands, "what is greater than the Aleksandr Nevsky? You know Papa's received the Aleksandr Nevsky?"

Vasily Lukich replied that the Vladimir was greater than the Aleksandr Nevsky.

"And higher still?"

"Well, highest of all is the Andrey Pervozvanny."

"And higher than the Andrey?"

"I don't know."

"What, you don't know?" said Seryozha, leaning on his elbows; and he sank into deep meditation.

His reflections were of the most complex and diverse character. He imagined his father's having suddenly been presented with both the Vladimir and the Andrey today, and in consequence being much kinder at his lesson, and dreamed how, when he was grown up, he would himself receive all the orders, and what they might invent higher than the Andrey. As soon as any higher order was invented, he would win it. They would make a higher one still, and he would immediately win that, too.

The time passed in such reflections, and when the teacher came, the lesson about the adverbs of place and time and manner of action was not ready, and the teacher was not only displeased but hurt. This touched Seryozha. He felt he was not to blame for not having learned the lesson; however much he tried, he was utterly unable to do it. As long as the teacher was explaining to him, he believed him and seemed to comprehend, but as soon as he was left alone, he was positively unable to recollect and to understand that the short and familiar word "suddenly" is *an adverb of manner of action*. Still, he was sorry that he had disappointed the teacher.

He chose a moment when the teacher was looking in silence at the book.

"Mikhail Ivanovich, when is your birthday?" he asked suddenly.

"You'd much better be thinking about your work. Birthdays are of no importance to a rational being. It's a day like any other on which one has to do one's work."

Seryozha looked intently at the teacher, at his scanty beard, at his spectacles, which had slipped down below the ridge on his nose, and fell into so deep a reverie that he heard nothing of what the teacher was explaining to him. He knew that the teacher did not believe what he said; he felt it from the tone in which it was said. "But why have they all agreed to speak just in the same manner about the dreariest and most useless stuff? Why does he repulse me? Why doesn't he love me?" he asked himself mournfully, and could not think of an answer.

CHAPTER TWENTY-SEVEN

After the lesson with the grammar teacher came his father's lesson. While waiting for his father, Seryozha sat at the table playing with a penknife, and started thinking. Among Seryozha's favorite occupations was searching for his mother during his walks. He did not believe in death generally, and in her death in particular, in spite of what Lydia Ivanovna had told him and his father had confirmed, and it was just because of that, after he had been told she was dead, that he had begun looking for her when out for a walk. Every woman of full, graceful figure with dark hair was his mother. At the sight of such a woman, such a feeling of tenderness was stirred within him that his breath failed him, and tears came into his eyes. And he expected that she would come up to him, would lift her veil. Her face would be visible, she would smile, she would hug him, he would smell her fragrance, feel the softness of her arms, and cry with happiness, just as one evening he had lain on her lap while she tickled him, and he laughed and bit her white, ring-covered fingers. Later, when he accidentally learned from his old nurse that his mother was not dead, and his father and Lydia Ivanovna had explained that she was dead to him because she was wicked (which he could not possibly believe, because he loved her), he went on seeking her and expecting her in the same way. That day in the Summer Garden there had been a lady in a lilac veil whom he had watched with a throbbing heart, believing it to be her as she came toward them along the path. The lady had not come up to them, but had disappeared somewhere. That day, more intensely than ever, Seryozha felt a rush of love for her, and now, waiting for his father, he forgot everything, and notched the whole edge of the table with his penknife, staring straight before him with sparkling eyes and dreaming of her.

"Here is your papa!" said Vasily Lukich, rousing him.

Seryozha jumped up and went up to his father, and kissing his hand, he looked at him intently, trying to discover signs of his joy at receiving the Aleksandr Nevsky.

"Did you have a nice walk?" said Aleksey Aleksandrovich, sitting down in his easy chair, pulling the volume of the Old Testament to him and opening it. Although Aleksey Aleksandrovich had more than once told Seryozha that every Christian ought to know Scripture history thoroughly, he often referred to the Bible himself during the lessons, and Seryozha observed this.

"Yes, it was very nice, Papa," said Seryozha, sitting sideways on his chair and rocking it, which was forbidden. "I saw Nadenka" (Nadenka was a niece of Lydia Ivanovna's who was being brought up in her house). "She told me you'd been given a new star. Are you glad, Papa?"

"First of all, don't rock your chair, please," said Aleksey Aleksandrovich. "And secondly, it's not the reward that's precious, but the work itself. And I wish you'd understand that. Now if you are going to work, to study in order to win a reward, then the work will seem hard to you; but when you work" (Aleksey Aleksandrovich, as he spoke, thought of how he had been sustained by a sense of duty through the wearisome labor of the morning, consisting of signing one hundred and eighteen papers), "loving your work, you will find your reward in it."

Seryozha's eyes, which had been shining with gaiety and tenderness, grew dull and drooped before his father's gaze. This was the same long-familiar tone his father always took with him, and Seryozha had learned by now to fall in with it. His father always talked to him—so Seryozha felt—as though he were addressing some boy of his own imagination, one of those boys who existed in books, utterly unlike himself. And Seryozha always tried, with his father, to act like the storybook boy.

"You understand that, I hope?" said his father.

"Yes, Papa," answered Seryozha, acting the part of the imaginary boy.

The lesson consisted of learning by heart several verses of the Gospel, and the repetition of the beginning of the Old Testament. The verses from the Gospel Seryozha knew fairly well, but at the moment when he was saying them he became so absorbed in watching a bone in his father's forehead that he lost thread, and he transposed the end of one verse and the beginning of the other. So it was evident to Aleksey Aleksandrovich that Seryozha did not understand what he was saying, and that irritated him.

He frowned, and began explaining what Seryozha had heard many times before and never could remember, because he understood it too well, just as he understood that "suddenly" is *an adverb of manner of action.* Seryozha looked with frightened eyes at his father, and could think of nothing but whether his father would make him repeat what he had said, as he sometimes did. And this thought so alarmed Seryozha that he now understood nothing. But his father did not make him repeat it, and passed on to the lesson out of the Old Testament. Seryozha recounted the events themselves well enough, but when he had to answer questions as to what certain events prefigured, he knew nothing, though he had already been punished over this lesson. The passage at which he was utterly unable to say anything, and began fidgeting and cutting the table and swinging his chair, was the one about the partriachs before the Flood. He did not know one of them except Enoch, who had been taken up alive to heaven. Last time he had remembered their names, but now he had forgotten them utterly, chiefly because Enoch was the character he liked best in the whole of the Old Testament, and Enoch's being taken to heaven was connected in his mind with the whole long train of thought, in which he became absorbed now while he gazed with fascinated eyes at his father's watch chain and a half-unbuttoned button on his vest.

In death, of which they talked to him so often, Seryozha disbelieved entirely. He did not believe that those he loved could die—

above all, that he himself would die. That was to him something utterly inconceivable and impossible. But he had been told that all men die; he had asked people, those whom he trusted, and they too had confirmed it; his old nurse, too, said the same, though reluctantly. But Enoch had not died, and so it followed that not everyone did die. "And why cannot anyone else so serve God and be taken alive to heaven?" thought Seryozha. Bad people, that is, those Seryozha did not like, they might die, but the good might all be like Enoch.

"Well, what are the names of the patriarchs?"

"Enoch, Enos . . ."

"But you have said that already. This is bad, Seryozha, very bad. If you don't try to learn what is more necessary than anything for a Christian," said his father, getting up, "whatever can interest you? I am displeased with you, and Piotr Ignatich" (the most important of his teachers) "is displeased with you. I shall have to punish you."

His father and his teacher were both displeased with Seryozha, and he certainly did learn his lessons very badly. But still it could not be said that he was stupid boy. On the contrary, he was far more clever than the boys his teacher held up as examples to him. In his father's opinion, he did not want to learn what he was taught. In reality he could not learn that. He could not because the claims of his own soul were more binding on him than those claims his father and his teacher made upon him. Those claims were in opposition, and he was in direct conflict with his education. He was nine years old; he was a child, but he knew his own soul. His teachers complained that he would not learn, while his soul was brimming over with thirst for knowledge. And he learned from Kapitonich, from his nurse, from Nadenka, from Vasily Lukich, but not from his teachers. The water his father and his teachers counted upon to turn their mill wheels had long since leaked out and did its work in another channel.

His father punished Seryozha by not letting him go to see Nadenka, Lydia Ivanovna's niece; but this punishment turned out happily for Seryozha. Vasily Lukich was in good humor, and showed him how to make windmills. The whole evening passed in this work and in dreaming of how to make a windmill on which he could turn himself—clutching at the sails or tying himself on and whirling around. Seryozha did not think of his mother the whole evening, but when he had gone to bed, he suddenly remembered her, and prayed in his own words that she would stop hiding herself and come to him tomorrow for his birthday.

"Vasily Lukich, do you know what I prayed for extra?"

"That you might learn your lessons better?"

"No."

"Toys?"

"No. You'll never guess. A splendid thing; but it's a secret! When it comes to pass, I'll tell you. Can't you guess?"

"No, I can't guess. You tell me," said Vasily Lukich with a smile, which was rare for him. "Come, lie down, I'm putting out the candle.

"Without the candle I can see better what I prayed for. There! I was almost telling the secret!" said Seryozha, laughing gaily.

When the candle was taken away, Seryozha heard and felt his mother. She stood over him and with loving eyes caressed him. But then came windmills, a knife, everything began to get mixed up, and he fell asleep.

CHAPTER TWENTY-EIGHT

On arriving in Petersburg, Vronsky and Anna stayed at one of the best hotels, Vronsky alone on the lower floor, Anna above, with her child, her nurse, and her maid, in a large suite of four rooms.

On the day of his arrival Vronsky went to his brother's. There he found his mother, who had come from Moscow on business. His mother and sister-in-law greeted him as usual: they asked him about his stay abroad, and talked of their common acquaintances, but did not let drop a single word about his liaison with Anna. His brother came the next morning to see him, and of his own accord asked him about her, and Vronsky told him frankly that he looked upon his union with Madame Karenina as marriage; that he hoped to arrange a divorce and then to marry her, and until then he considered her as much a wife as any other wife, and he begged him to tell their mother and his wife so.

"If the world disapproves, I don't care," said Vronsky; "but if my relatives want to be treated as such, they will have to act like relatives toward my wife."

The elder brother, who had always had a respect for his younger brother's judgment, could not quite tell whether he was right or not till the world had decided the question; for his part he had nothing against it, and with Aleksey he went up to see Anna.

Before his brother, as before everyone, Vronsky addressed Anna with a certain formality, treating her as he might a good friend, but it was understood that his brother knew their real relations, and they talked about Anna's going to Vronsky's estate.

In spite of all his social experience, Vronsky was, in consequence of the new position in which he was placed, laboring under a strange delusion. One would have thought he must have understood that society was closed to him and Anna; but now some vague ideas had sprung up in his brain that this was only the case in old-fashioned days, and that now with the rapidity of modern progress (he had unconsciously become by now a partisan of every sort of progress) the views of society had changed, and that the question of whether they would be received in society was not a foregone conclusion. "Of course," he thought, "she would not be received at court, but intimate friends can and must look at it in the proper light." One may sit for several hours at a stretch with one's legs crossed in the same position if one knows that there's nothing to prevent one's changing one's position; but if a man knows that he must remain sitting so with crossed legs, then cramps come on, the legs begin to draw them. This was what Vronsky was experiencing in regard to the world. Though at the bottom of his heart he knew that the world was shut to them, he put it to the test whether the world had not changed by now and would not receive them. But he very quickly perceived that though the world was open for him personally, it was closed for Anna. Just as in the game of cat and mouse, the hands raised for him and were dropped to bar the way for Anna.

One of the first ladies of Petersburg society whom Vronsky saw was his cousin Betsy.

"At last!" she greeted him joyfully. "And Anna? How glad I am! Where are you stopping? I can imagine that after your delightful travel you must find our poor Petersburg horrid. I can imagine your honeymoon in Rome. How about the divorce? Is that all over?"

Vronsky noticed that Betsy's enthusiasm waned when she learned that no divorce had as yet taken place.

"People will throw stones at me, I know," she said, "but I shall come and see Anna; yes, I shall certainly come. You won't be here long, I suppose?"

And she certainly did come to see Anna the same day, but her tone was not at all the same as in former days. It was clear that she prided herself on her courage, and wished Anna to appreciate that fidelity of her friendship. She stayed only ten minutes, talking of society gossip, and on leaving, she said:

"You've never told me when the divorce is to be! I've flung convention to the wind, but others, strait-laced people, will give you the cold shoulder until you're married. And that's so simple nowadays. *Ça se fait.*[1] So you're going on Friday? Sorry we shan't see each other again."

From Betsy's tone, Vronsky might have grasped what he had to expect from the world; but he made another effort in his own family. His mother he did not count upon. He knew that his mother, who had been so enthusiastic over Anna at their first acquaintance, would have no mercy on her now for having ruined her son's career. But he had more hope of Varya, his brother's wife. He thought she would not cast stones, and would go simply and directly to see Anna, and would receive her in her own house.

The day after his arrival, Vronsky went to her, and finding her alone, he expressed his wishes frankly.

"You know, Aleksey," she said after hearing him, "how fond I am of you, and how ready I am to do anything for you; but I have not spoken because I knew I could be of no use to you and to Anna Arkadyevna," she said, articulating the name "Anna Arkadyevna" with particular care. "Don't suppose, please, that I judge her. Never; perhaps in her place I would have done the same. I don't and can't enter into that," she said, glancing timidly at his gloomy face. "But one must call things by their names. You want me to go and see her,

---

[1] "It's done."

to ask her here, and to rehabilitate her in society; but do understand that I cannot do so. I *cannot* do so. I have daughters growing up, and I must mix in society for my husband's sake. Well, I'm ready to come and see Anna Arkadyevna: she will understand that I can't ask her here, or I would have to do so in such a way that she would not meet people who look at things differently; that would offend her. I can't raise her—"

"Oh, I don't regard her as more fallen than hundreds of women you do receive!" Vronsky interrupted her still more gloomily, and he got up in silence, understanding that his sister-in-law's decision was not to be shaken.

"Aleksey! Don't be angry with me. Please understand that I'm not to blame," Varya began, looking at him with a timid smile.

I'm not angry with you," he said just as gloomily; "but I'm sorry in two ways. I'm sorry, too, that this means breaking up our friendship—if not breaking up, at least weakening it. You will understand that for me, too, it cannot be otherwise."

And with that he left her.

Vronsky knew that further efforts were useless, and that he had to spend these few days in Petersburg as though in a strange town, avoiding every sort of relation with his own old circle in order not to be exposed to the annoyance and humiliations which were so intolerable to him. One of the most unpleasant features of his position in Petersburg was that Aleksey Aleksandrovich and his name seemed to meet him everywhere. He could not begin to talk of anything without the conversation turning to Aleksey Aleksandrovich, he could not go anywhere without risk of meeting him. So at least it seemed to Vronsky, just as it seems to a man with a sore finger that he is continually, as though on purpose, knocking his sore finger on everything.

Their stay in Petersburg was the more painful to Vronsky because he perceived all the time a sort of new mood that he could not understand in Anna. At one time she would seem in love with him, and then she would become cold, irritable, and impenetrable. She was worrying about something, and keeping something back from him, and did not seem to notice the humiliations which poisoned his existence and for her, with her acute perception, must have been still more unbearable.

CHAPTER TWENTY-NINE

One of Anna's reasons for coming back to Russia had been to see her son. From the day she left Italy the thought of it had never ceased to agitate her. And as she got nearer to Petersburg, the delight and importance of this meeting grew ever greater in her imagination. She did not even put to herself the question of how to arrange it. It seemed to her natural and simple to see her son when she should be in the same town as he. But on her arrival in Petersburg, she was suddenly made distinctly aware of her present position in society, and she grasped the fact that to arrange this meeting was no easy matter.

She had now been in Petersburg two days. The thought of her son never left her for a single instant, but she had not yet seen him. To go straight to the house, where she might meet Aleksey Aleksandrovich, she felt she had no right to do. She might be refused admittance and insulted. To write and so enter into relations with her husband—that made her miserable to think of doing; she could be at peace only when she did not think of her husband. To get a glimpse of her son out walking, finding out where and when he went out, was not enough for her; she had so looked forward to this meeting, she had so much to say to him, she so longed to embrace him, to kiss him. Seryozha's old nurse might be a help to her and show her what to do. But the nurse was no longer living in Aleksey Aleksandrovich's house. In this uncertainty, and in efforts to find the nurse, two days had slipped by.

Hearing of the intimate friendship between Aleksey Aleksandrovich and Countess Lydia Ivanovna, Anna decided on the third day to write her a letter, which cost her great pains, and in which she intentionally said that permission to see her son must depend on her husband's generosity. She knew that if the letter was shown to her husband he would keep up his character of magnanimity and would not refuse her request.

The commissionaire who took the letter had brought her back the most cruel and unexpected answer—that there was no answer. She had never felt so humiliated as at the moment when, sending for the commissionaire, she heard from him the exact account of how he had waited, and how afterward he had been told there was no answer.

Anna felt humiliated, insulted, but she saw that from her point of view Countess Lydia Ivanovna was right. Her suffering was the more poignant because she had to bear it in solitude. She could not and would not share it with Vronsky. She knew that to him, although he was the primary cause of her distress, the question of her seeing her son would seem a matter of very little consequence. She knew that he would never be capable of understanding the depth of her suffering, that for his cold tone at any allusion to it she would begin to hate him. And she dreaded that more than anything in the world, and so she hid from him everything that related to her son. Spending the whole day at home, she considered ways of seeing her son, and had reached a decision to write to her husband. She was just composing this letter when she was handed the letter from Lydia Ivanovna. The countess's silence had subdued and depressed her, but the letters, all that she read between the lines in it, so exasperated her, this malice was so revolting beside her passionate, legitimate tenderness for her son, that she turned against other people and stopped blaming herself.

"This coldness—this pretense of feeling!" she said to herself. "They only want to insult me and torture the child, and I am to submit to it! Not on any consideration! She is worse than I am. I don't lie, anyway." And she decided on the spot that next day, Seryozha's birthday, she would go straight to her husband's house, bribe or deceive the servants, but at any cost see her son and overturn the hideous deception with which they were surrounding the unfortunate child.

She went to a toy shop, bought toys, and thought over a plan of action. She would go early in the morning, at eight o'clock, when Aleksey Aleksandrovich would be certain not to be up. She would have money in her hand to give the hall porter and the footman, so that they should let her in, and raising her veil, she would say that she had come from Seryozha's godfather to congratulate him, and that she had been charged to leave the toys at his bedside. She had prepared everything but the words she would say to her son. Much as she thought of it, she could not prepare what to say.

The next day, at eight o'clock in the morning, Anna got out of a hired sleigh and rang at the front entrance of her former home.

"Run and see what's wanted. Some lady," said Kapitonich, who, not yet dressed, in his overcoat and galoshes, had peeped out of the window and seen a lady in a veil standing close to the door. His assistant, a lad Anna did not know, had no sooner opened the door than she came in and, pulling a three-ruble note out of her muff, put it hurriedly into his hand.

"Seryozha—Sergey Alekseyich," she said, and walked in. Scrutinizing the note, the porter's assistant stopped her at the second glass door.

"Whom do you want?" he asked.

She did not hear his words and made no answer.

Noticing the embarrassment of the unknown lady, Kapitonich went to her, opened the second door for her, and asked her what she wanted.

"From Prince Skorodumov for Sergey Alekseyich," she said.

"He is not up yet," said the porter, looking at her attentively.

Anna had not anticipated that the absolutely unchanged hall of the house where she had lived for nine years would so greatly affect her. Memories sweet and painful rose one after another in her heart, and for a moment she forgot what she was there for.

"Would you kindly wait?" said Kapitonich, taking off her fur cloak.

As he took off the cloak, Kapitonich glanced at her face, recognized her, and made her a low bow in silence.

"Please walk in, Your Excellency," he said to her.

She tried to say something, but her voice refused to utter any sound; with a guilty and imploring glance at the old man, she went with light, swift steps up the stairs. Bent double, and his galoshes catching in the steps, Kapitonich ran after her, trying to overtake her.

"The tutor's there; maybe he's not dressed. I'll let him know."

Anna still mounted the familiar staircase, not understanding what the old man was saying.

"This way, to the left, if you please. Excuse its not being tidy. His honor's in the old parlor now," the hall porter said, panting. "Excuse me, wait a minute, Your Excellency; I'll just see," he said, and overtaking her, he opened the high door and disappeared behind it. Anna stood still, waiting. "He's only just awake," said the hall porter, coming out. And at the very instant the porter said this, Anna caught the sound of a childish yawn. From the sound of this yawn alone she knew her son and seemed to see him living before her eyes.

"Let me in; go away!" she said, and went in through the high doorway. On the right of the door stood a bed, and sitting up in the bed was the boy. His little body bent forward with his night shirt unbuttoned, he was stretching and still yawning. The instant his lips came together they curved into a blissfully sleepy smile, and with that smile he slowly and deliciously rolled back again.

"Seryozha!" she whispered, going noiselessly up to him.

During the time they had been separated and more recently when she had been feeling a fresh rush of love for him, she had pictured him as he was at four, when she had loved him most of all. Now he was not even the same as when she had left him; he was still further from the four-year-old baby, taller and thinner. How thin his face was, how short his hair was! What long hands! How he had changed since she left him! But it was he, the shape of his head, his lips, his soft neck, and broad little shoulders.

"Seryozha!" she repeated almost in the child's ear.

He raised himself again on his elbow, turned his tousled head from side to side as though looking for something, and opened his eyes. Slowly and inquiringly he looked for several seconds at his mother standing motionless before him; then all at once he smiled a blissful smile and, shutting his eyes, rolled not backward but toward her into her arms.

"Seryozha! My darling boy!" she said, breathing hard and putting her arms around his plump little body. "Mama!" he said, wriggling about in her arms so as to touch her arms with different parts of his body.

Smiling sleepily, still with closed eyes, he flung his fat little arms around her shoulders, rolled toward her with the delicious sleepy warmth and fragrance that is found only in children, and began rubbing his face against her neck and shoulders.

"I knew," he said, opening his eyes, "it's my birthday today. I knew you'd come. I'll get up now . . ."

And saying that, he dropped back to sleep.

Anna looked at him hungrily; she saw how he had grown and changed in her absence. She knew, and did not know, the bare legs, so long now, that were thrust out below the blanket, and his cheeks, now thinner, those short curls on his neck where she had so often kissed him. She touched all this and could not say anything; tears choked her.

"What are you crying for, Mama?" he said, waking up completely. "Mama, what are you crying for?" he cried in a tearful voice.

"I won't cry . . . I'm crying for joy. It's so long since I've seen you. I won't, I won't," she said, gulping down her tears and turning away. "Come, it's time for you to dress now," she added after a pause, and, never letting go of his hands, she sat down by his bedside on the chair, where his clothes were laid out for him.

"How do you dress without me? How . . ." She tried to begin talking simply and cheerfully, but she could not, and again she turned away.

"I don't have a cold bath. Papa says I shouldn't. And you've not seen Vasily Lukich? He'll come in soon. Why, you're sitting on my clothes!"

And Seryozha went off into a peal of laughter. She looked at him and smiled.

"Mama! Darling Mama!" he shouted, flinging himself on her again and hugging her. It was as though only now, on seeing her smile, he fully grasped what had happened.

"You don't want that," he said, taking off her hat. And, as though seeing her afresh, he began kissing her again.

"But what did you think about me? You didn't think I was dead?"

"I never believed it."

"You didn't believe it, my sweet?"

"I knew, I knew!" he repeated his favorite phrase, and snatching the hand that was stroking his hair, he pressed the open palm to his mouth and kissed it.

CHAPTER THIRTY

Meanwhile Vasily Lukich had not at first understood who this lady was, but had learned from their conversation that it was no other person than the mother who had left her husband and whom he had not seen, since he had entered the house after her departure. He was in doubt whether to go in or out, or whether to communicate with Aleksey Aleksandrovich. Reflecting finally that his duty was to get Seryozha up at the hour fixed, and that it was therefore not his business to consider who was there, the mother or anyone else, but simply to do his duty, he finished dressing, went to the door, and opened it.

But the embraces of the mother and child, the sound of their voices, and what they were saying, made him change his mind.

He shook his head, and with a sigh, he closed the door. "I'll wait another ten minutes," he said to himself, clearing his throat and wiping away tears.

Among the servants of the household there was intense excitement all this time. All had heard that their mistress had come, and that Kapitonich had let her in, and that she was even now in the nursery, and that their master always went in person to the nursery after eight, and everyone fully comprehended that it was impossible for the husband and wife to meet, and that they must prevent it. Korney, the valet, going down to the hall porter's room, asked who had let her in, and how it was he had done so, and learning that Kapitonich had admitted her and shown her up, he reprimanded the old man. The hall porter was doggedly silent, but when Korney told him she ought to be sent away, Kapitonich darted up to him, and waving his hands in Korney's face, he said:

"Oh yes, to be sure, you'd not have let her in! After ten years' service, and never a word but of kindness, and there you'd go up and say, 'Get out of here!' Oh yes, you're a shrewd one you are! You don't need to be taught how to swindle the master, and to filch fur coats!"

"Boor!"[1] said Korney contemptuously, and he turned to the nurse, who was coming in. "Here, what do you think, Marya Efimovna: he let her in without a word to anyone," Korney said, addressing her. "Aleksey Aleksandrovich will be down immediately—and go into the nursery!"

"A pretty business, a pretty business!" said the nurse. "You, Kor-

---

[1]Literally "soldier," but, as such, its strongly deprecatory connotative value in Russian cannot be conveyed.

ney Vasilievich, you'd best keep him some way or other, the master, while I run and get her away somehow. A pretty business!"

When the nurse went into the nursery, Seryozha was telling his mother how he and Nadenka had had a fall while sledding downhill, and had turned over three times. She was listening to the sound of his voice, watching his face and the play of expression on it, touching his hand, but she did not follow what he was saying. She must go, she must leave him—this was the only thing she was thinking and feeling. She heard the steps of Vasily Lukich coming up to the door, and coughing; she heard, too, the steps of the nurse as she came near; but she sat like one turned to stone, incapable of speaking or getting up.

"Madam, dear madam!" the nurse began, going up to Anna and kissing her hands and shoulders. "God has brought joy indeed to our boy on his birthday. You aren't changed one bit."

"Oh, nurse, dear, I didn't know you were in the house," said Anna, rousing herself for a moment.

"I'm not living here, I'm living with my daughter. I came for the birthday, Anna Arkadyevna, my dear!"

The nurse suddenly burst into tears, and began kissing her hand again.

Seryozha, with radiant eyes and smiles, holding his mother by one hand and his nurse by the other, jumped on the rug with his little bare feet. The tenderness shown by his beloved nurse to his mother threw him into ecstasy.

"Mama! She often comes to see me, and when she comes . . ." he was beginning, but he stopped, noticing that the nurse was saying something in a whisper to his mother, and that in his mother's face there was a look of dread and something like shame, which was so strangely unbecoming to her.

She went up to him.

"My sweet!" she said.

She could not say "*good-by*," but the expression on her face said it, and he understood. "Darling, darling Kutik!"—she used the name she had called him when he was a baby—"you won't forget me? You . . ." But she could not say more.

How often, afterward, she thought of words she might have said.

But now she did not know how to say it, and could say nothing. But Seryozha knew all she wanted to say to him. He understood that she was unhappy and loved him. He understood even what the nurse had whispered. He had caught the words "always after eight," and he knew that this was said of his father, and that his father and mother could not meet. That he understood, but one thing he could not understand—why there should be a look of dread and shame in her face. She was not at fault, but she was afraid of him and ashamed of something. He would have liked to put a question that would have set at rest this doubt, but he did not dare; he saw she was miserable, and he felt for her. Silently he pressed close to her and whispered, "Don't go yet. He won't come just yet."

The mother held him away from her to see what he was thinking, what to say to him, and in his frightened face she read, not only that he was speaking of his father, but, as it were, asking her what he ought to think about his father.

"Seryozha, my darling," she said, "love him; he's better and kinder than I am and I have done him wrong. When you grow up you will judge."

"There's no one better than you!" he cried in despair through his tears, and clutching her by the shoulders, he began squeezing her with all his might to him, his arms trembling with the strain.

"My sweet, my little one!" said Anna, and she cried as weakly and childishly as he.

At that moment the door opened. Vasily Lukich came in.

At the other door there was the sound of steps, and the nurse in a scared whisper said, "He's coming," and gave Anna her hat.

Seryozha sank onto the bed and sobbed, hiding his face in his hands. Anna removed his hands, once more kissed his face, and with rapid steps went to the door. Aleksey Aleksandrovich walked in, meeting her. Seeing her, he stopped short and bowed his head.

Although she had just said he was better and kinder than she, in the rapid glance she flung at him, taking in his whole figure in all its details, feelings of revulsion and hatred for him and jealousy over her son took possession of her. With a swift gesture she put down her veil, and quickening her pace, almost ran out of the room.

She had not time to unwrap them, and so carried back with her the parcel of toys she had chosen the day before in a toy shop with such love and sorrow.

CHAPTER THIRTY-ONE

Intensely as Anna had longed to see her son, and much as she had been thinking of it and preparing herself for it, she had not in the least expected that seeing him would affect her so deeply. On getting back to her lonely rooms in the hotel, she could not for a long while understand why she was there. "Yes, it's all over, and I am again alone," she said to herself, and without taking off her hat, she sat down in a low chair by the hearth. Fixing her eyes on a bronze clock standing on a table between the windows, she tried to think.

The French maid brought from abroad came in to suggest she should dress. She gazed at her wonderingly and said, "Presently." A footman offered her coffee. "Later," she said.

The Italian nurse, having dressed the baby, brought her to Anna. The plump, well-fed little baby, on seeing her mother, held out her fat little hands as she always did—so fat that they looked as if thread had been tightly tied around the wrists—and, with a smile on her toothless little mouth, began, like a fish waving its fins, beating the air, making the starched folds of her embroidered skirt rustle. It was impossible not to smile, not to kiss the baby; impossible not to hold out a finger for her to clutch, crowing with joy, and wriggling all over; impossible not to offer her a lip which she sucked into her little mouth by way of a kiss. And all this Anna did, and took her in her arms and made her dance, and kissed her fresh little cheek and bare little elbows; but at the sight of this child it was plainer than ever to her that the feeling she had for her could not be called love in comparison with what she felt for Seryozha. Everything about this baby was charming, but for some reason all this did not penetrate deep to her heart. On her first child, though the child of an unloved father, had been concentrated all the love that had never found satisfaction. Her baby girl had been born in the most painful circumstances and had not had a hundredth part of the care and thought which had been concentrated on her first child. Besides, for the little girl, every-thing was still in the future, while Seryozha was by now almost a per-sonality, and a personality dearly loved. In him there was a conflict of thought and feeling; he understood her, he loved her, he judged her, she thought, recalling his words and his eyes. And she was forever—not only physically but also spiritually—divided from him, and it was impossible to set this right.

She gave the baby back to the nurse, let her go, and opened the locket in which there was Seryozha's portrait when he was almost the same age as the girl. She got up, and, taking off her hat, took up from a little table an album in which there were photographs of her son at different ages. She wanted to compare them, and began taking them out of the album. She took them all out except one, the latest and best photograph. In it he was in a white smock, sitting astride a chair, with frowning eyes and smiling lips. It was his best, most char-acteristic expression. With her deft little hands, her white, delicate fingers that moved with a peculiar intensity today, she pulled at a cor-ner of the photograph, but the photograph had caught somewhere, and she could not get it out. There was no paper knife on the table, and so, pulling out the photograph that was next to her son's (it was a photograph of Vronsky taken at Rome in a round hat and with long hair), she used it to push out her son's photograph. "Oh, here he is!" she said, glancing at the portrait of Vronsky, and she suddenly recalled that he was the cause of her present misery. She had not once thought of him all morning. But now, coming all at once upon that manly, noble face, so familiar and so dear to her, she felt a sud-den rush of love for him.

"But where is he? How is it he leaves me alone in my misery?" she thought all at once with a feeling of reproach, forgetting she had herself kept from him everything concerning her son. She sent to ask him to come to her immediately; with a throbbing heart she awaited him, rehearsing to herself the words in which she would tell him all, and the expressions of love with which he would console her. The messenger returned with the answer that he had a visitor with him, but that he would come immediately, and that he asked whether she would let him bring with him Prince Yashvin, who had just arrived in Petersburg. "He's not coming alone, and since dinner yesterday he has not seen me," she thought; "he's not coming so that I could tell him everything, but coming with Yashvin." And all at once a strange idea came to her: what if he had ceased to love her?

And going over the events of the last few days, it seemed to her that she saw in everything a confirmation of this terrible idea. The fact that he had not dined at home yesterday, and the fact that he had insisted on their taking separate sets of rooms at Petersburg, and that even now he was not coming to her alone, as though he were trying to avoid meeting her face to face.

"But he ought to tell me. I must know that it is so. If I know it, then I'll know what I should do," she said to herself, utterly unable to picture to herself the position she would be in if she were convinced of his not caring for her. She thought he had ceased to love her, she felt close to despair, and consequently she felt exceptionally excited. She rang for her maid and went to her dressing room. As she dressed, she took more care over her appearance than she had done all those days, as though he might, if he had grown cold to her, fall in love with her again because she had dressed and arranged her hair in the way most becoming to her.

She heard the bell ring before she was ready.

When she went into the drawing room it was not he but Yashvin who met her eyes. Vronsky was looking through the photographs of her son which she had forgotten on the table, and he made no haste to look around at her.

"We have met already," she said, putting her little hand into the huge hand of Yashvin (whose bashfulness was so strangely out of keeping with his powerful frame and coarse face). "We met last year at the races. Give them to me," she said, with a rapid movement snatching from Vronsky the photographs of her son, and glancing significantly at him with flashing eyes. "Were the races good this year? Instead of them I saw the races on the Corso in Rome. But you don't care for life abroad," she said with a cordial smile. "I know you and all your tastes, though I have seen so little of you."

"I'm awfully sorry about that, for my tastes are mostly bad," said Yashvin, gnawing at his left mustache.

Having talked a little while, and noticing that Vronsky glanced at the clock, Yashvin asked her whether she would be staying much longer in Petersburg, and unbending his huge figure, he reached for his hat.

"Not long, I think," she said hesitatingly, glancing at Vronsky.

"So, then, we shall not meet again?"

"Come and dine with me," said Anna resolutely, angry with herself for her embarrassment, but flushing as she always did when she defined her position before another person. "The dinner here is not good, but at least you will see each other. There is not one of his old friends in the regiment Aleksey cares for as he does for you."

"Delighted," said Yashvin with a smile, from which Vronsky could see that he liked Anna very much.

Yashvin said good-by and went away; Vronsky stayed behind.

"Are you going too?" she said to him.

"I'm late already," he answered. "Run along! I'll catch up with you in a moment," he called to Yashvin.

She took him by the hand, and without taking her eyes off him, gazed at him while she ransacked her mind for the words that would keep him.

"Wait a minute, there's something I want to say to you," she said, and taking his broad hand, she pressed it on her neck. "Oh, was it right my asking him to dinner?"

"You did quite right," he said with a serene smile that showed his even teeth, and he kissed her hand.

"Aleksey, you have not changed toward me?" she said, pressing his hand in both of hers. "Aleksey, I am miserable here. When are we going away?"

"Soon, soon. You wouldn't believe how disagreeable our way of living here is to me too," he said, and he drew away his hand.

"Well, go, go!" she said in a hurt tone, and she walked quickly away from him.

CHAPTER THIRTY-TWO

When Vronsky returned home, Anna was not yet home. Soon after he had left, some lady, so they told him, had come to see her, and she had gone out with her. That she had gone out without leaving word where she was going, that she had not yet come back and that all morning she had been going about somewhere without a word to him—all this, together with the strange look of excitement in her face in the morning, and the recollection of the hostile tone with which she had almost snatched her son's photographs out of his hands in front of Yashvin, started him thinking. He decided he absolutely must speak frankly with her. And he waited for her in her drawing room. But Anna did not return alone; she brought with her her old unmarried aunt, Princess Oblonskaya. This was the lady who had come in the morning, and with whom Anna had gone out shopping. Anna appeared not to notice Vronsky's worried and inquiring expression, and began a lively account of her morning's shopping. He saw that there was something going on within her; in her flashing eyes, when they rested for a moment on him, there was an intense concentration, and in her words and movements there was that nervous rapidity and grace which, during the early days of their intimacy, had so fascinated him, but which now disturbed and alarmed him.

The dinner was laid for four. All were gathered together and about to go into the little dining room, when Tushkevich made his appearance with a message from Princess Betsy. Princess Betsy begged her to excuse her not having come to say good-by; she had been indisposed, but begged Anna to come to her between half-past six and nine o'clock. Vronsky glanced at Anna because of the specific limit of time, which indicated that steps had been taken so that she should meet no one; but Anna appeared not to notice it.

"Very sorry that I can't come just between half-past six and nine," she said with a faint smile.

"The princess will be very sorry."

"And so am I."

"You're going, no doubt, to hear Patti?[1] said Tushkevich.

"Patti? You suggest the idea to me. I would go if it were possible to get a box."

"I can get one," Tushkevich offered.

"I would be very, very grateful to you," said Anna. "But won't you dine with us?"

[1]Famous Italian soprano.

Vronsky gave a hardly perceptible shrug. He was at a complete loss to understand what Anna was doing. Why had she brought the old Princess Oblonskaya home, why had she made Tushkevich stay to dinner, and, most amazing of all, why was she sending him for a box? Could she possibly, in her position, think of going to Patti's benefit, where the entire circle of her acquaintances would be? He looked at her with searching eyes, but she responded with that defiant, half-mirthful, half-desperate look, the meaning of which he could not comprehend. At dinner Anna was in aggressively high spirits—she almost flirted both with Tushkevich and with Yashvin. When they got up from dinner and Tushkevich had gone to get a box at the opera, Yashvin went to smoke, and Vronsky went down with him to his own rooms. After sitting there for some time, he ran upstairs. Anna was already dressed in a low-necked gown of light silk and velvet that she had had made in Paris, with costly white lace on her head that framed her face and was particularly becoming, setting off her dazzling beauty.

"Are you really going to the theater?" he said, trying not to look at her.

"Why do you ask with such alarm?" she said, wounded again at his not looking at her. "Why shouldn't I go?"

She appeared not to understand the motive of his words.

"Oh, of course there's no reason whatever," he said, frowning.

"That's just what I say," she said, willfully refusing to see the irony of his tone, and quietly pulling up her long, perfumed glove.

"Anna, for God's sake! What is the matter with you?" he said, appealing to her exactly as once her husband had done.

"I don't understand what you mean."

"You know that it's out of the question to go."

"Why not? I'm not going alone. Princess Varvara has gone to dress; she is going with me."

He shrugged his shoulders with an air of perplexity and despair.

"But do you mean to say you don't know? . . ." he began.

"But I don't care to know!" she shrieked. "I don't care to. Do I regret what I have done? No, no, no! If it were all to do again from the beginning, it would be the same. For us, for you and for me, there is only one thing that matters, whether we love each other.

Other people we need not consider. Why are we living here apart and not seeing each other? Why can't I go? I love you, and nothing else matters," she said in Russian, glancing at him with a peculiar gleam in her eyes that he could not understand, "if you have not changed toward me. Why don't you look at me?"

He looked at her. He saw all the beauty of her face and full evening dress, always so becoming to her. But now her beauty and elegance were just what irritated him.

"My feeling cannot change, you know, but I beg you, I entreat you," he said again in French, with a note of tender supplication in his voice, but with coldness in his eyes.

She did not hear his words, but she saw the coldness of his eyes, and answered with irritation:

"And I beg you to explain why I should not go."

"Because it might cause you . . ." He hesitated.

"I don't understand. Yashvin *n'est pas compromettant*,[2] and Princess Varvara is no worse than others. Oh, here she is!"

CHAPTER THIRTY-THREE

Vronsky for the first time experienced a feeling of anger against Anna, almost hate, for her willfully refusing to understand her own position. This feeling was aggravated by his being unable to tell her plainly the cause of his anger. If he had told her frankly what he was thinking, he would have said:

"In that dress, with a princess only too well known to everyone, to show yourself at the theater is equivalent not merely to acknowledging your position as a fallen woman, but is flinging down the gauntlet to society, that is to say, cutting yourself off from it forever."

He could not say that to her. "But how can she fail to see it, and what is going on in her mind?" he said to himself. He felt at the same time that his respect for her was diminished while his sense of her beauty was intensified.

[2]"Yashvin's company is not compromising."

He went back scowling to his rooms, and sitting down beside Yashvin, who, with his long legs stretched out on a chair, was drinking brandy and club soda, he ordered a glass of the same for himself.

"You were talking of Lankovsky's Powerful. That's a fine horse, and I would advise you to buy him," said Yashvin, glancing at his comrade's gloomy face. "His hindquarters aren't quite first rate, but the legs and head—one couldn't wish for anything better."

"I think I will take him," answered Vronsky.

Their conversation about horses interested him, but he did not for an instant forget Anna, and could not help listening to the sound of steps in the corridor and looking at the clock on the mantelpiece.

"Anna Arkadyevna gave orders to announce that she has gone to the theater."

Yashvin, tipping another glass of brandy into the soda water, drank it and got up, buttoning his coat.

"Well, let's go," he said, faintly smiling under his mustache, and showing by this smile that he knew the cause of Vronsky's gloominess, and did not attach any significance to it.

"I'm not going," Vronsky answered gloomily.

"Well, I must, I promised to. Good-by, then. If you do, come to the stalls; you can take Krasinsky's stall," he added as he went out.

"No, I'm busy."

"A wife is a worry, but it's worse when she's not a wife," thought Yashvin, as he walked out of the hotel.

Vronsky, left alone, got up from his chair and began pacing up and down the room.

"And what's today? The fourth subscription night . . . Yegor and his wife are there, and my mother, most likely. Of course all Petersburg's there. Now she's gone in, taken off her cloak, and come into the light. Tushkevich, Yashvin, Princess Varvara . . ." He pictured them to himself . . . "What about me? Either that I'm frightened or have given up to Tushkevich the right to protect her? From every point of view—stupid, stupid! . . . And why is she putting me in such a position?" he said with a gesture of despair.

With that gesture he knocked against the table on which the soda water and the decanter of brandy were standing, and almost upset it.

He tried to catch it, let it slip, and angrily kicked the table over and rang.

"If you care to be in my service," he said to the valet who came in, "you had better remember your duties. This shouldn't be here. You ought to have cleared it away."

The valet, conscious of his own innocence, would have defended himself, but glancing at his master he saw from his face that the only thing to do was to be silent, and hurriedly threading his way in and out, he dropped down on the carpet and began gathering up the whole and broken glasses and bottles.

"That's not your duty; send the waiter to clear it away, and get my dress suit out."

Vronsky went into the theater at half-past eight. The performance was in full swing. The little old box keeper, recognizing Vronsky as he helped him off with his fur coat, called him "Your Excellency," and suggested he should not take a number but should simply call "Fyodor" when he wanted his coat. In the brightly lighted corridor there was no one but the box attendant and two footmen with fur cloaks on their arms listening at the doors. Through the closed doors came the sounds of the discreet staccato accompaniment of the orchestra, and a single female voice rendering distinctly a musical phrase. The door opened to let an attendant slip through, and the phrase drawing to a close reached Vronsky's hearing clearly. But the doors were closed again at once, and Vronsky did not hear the end of the phrase and the cadenza after it, though he knew from the thunder of applause that it was over. When he entered the theater, brilliantly lighted with chandeliers and bronze gas-brackets, the noise was still going on. On the stage the prima donna, bowing and smiling, with bare shoulders flashing with diamonds, was, with the help of the tenor who had given her his arm, gathering up the bouquets that were flying awkwardly over the footlights. Then she went up to a gentleman with glossy pomaded hair parted down the center, who was stretching across the footlights holding out something to her, and all the public in the stalls as well as in the boxes was in excitement, craning forward, shouting and clapping. The conductor, from his raised chair, assisted in passing the offering, and straightened his white tie. Vronsky walked into the middle of the stalls and, standing still, began looking about him. That day less than ever was his attention turned upon the familiar, habitual surroundings: the stage, the noise, all the familiar, uninteresting, multicolored herd of spectators in the packed theater.

There were, as always, the same ladies of some sort with officers of some sort in the back of the boxes; the same gaily dressed women—God knows who—and uniforms and black coats; the same dirty crowd in the upper gallery, and among the crowd, in the boxes and in the front rows, were some forty of the *real* people. And to these oases Vronsky at once directed his attention, and exchanged greetings with them.

The act was over when he went in, and so he did not go straight to his brother's box but, going up to the first row of stalls, stopped beside Serpukhovskoy, who, standing at the footlights, with one knee raised tapping the wall of the orchestra with his heel, caught sight of him in the distance and beckoned to him, smiling.

Vronsky had not yet seen Anna. He purposely avoided looking in her direction. But he knew by the direction of people's eyes where she was. He looked around discreetly, but he was not seeking her; expecting the worst, his eyes sought Aleksey Aleksandrovich Karenin. To his relief, Aleksey Aleksandrovich was not in the theater that evening.

"How little of the military man there is left in you!" Serpukhovskoy was saying to him. "A diplomat, an artist, something of that sort, one would say."

"Yes, as soon as I got home I put on a black coat," answered Vronsky, smiling and slowly taking out his opera glasses.

"Well, I'll confess I envy you there. When I come back from abroad and put on this"—he touched his epaulets—"I regret my lost freedom."

Serpukhovskoy had long given up all hope of Vronsky's career, but he liked him as before, and was now particularly cordial to him.

"What a pity you were not in time for the first act!"

Vronsky, listening with one ear, moved his opera glasses from the stalls and scanned the boxes. Near a lady in a turban and a bald old man, who seemed to blink angrily in the moving opera glasses, Vronsky suddenly caught sight of Anna's head, proud, strikingly beautiful, and smiling in the frame of lace. She was in the fifth box, twenty paces from him. She was sitting in front, and slightly turning, was saying something to Yashvin. The setting of her head on her beautiful, broad shoulders, and the restrained excitement and brilliance of her eyes and her whole face reminded him of her just as he had seen her at the ball in Moscow. But he felt utterly different toward her beauty now. In his feeling for her now there was no element of mystery, and so her beauty, though it attracted him even more intensely than before, now offended him too. She was not looking in his direction, but Vronsky felt that she had seen him already.

When Vronsky turned the opera glasses again in that direction, he noticed that Princess Varvara was particularly red in the face, and kept laughing unnaturally and looking round at the next box. Anna, folding her fan and tapping it on the red plush of the next box, was looking away and did not see, and obviously did not wish to see, what was taking place in the next box. Yashvin's face wore the expression that was common when he was losing at cards. Scowling, he sucked the left end of his mustache further and further into his mouth, and cast sidelong glances at the next box.

In that box, on the left, were the Kartasovs. Vronsky knew them, and knew that Anna was acquainted with them. Madame Kartasova, a thin little woman, was standing up in her box, and, her back turned to Anna, was putting on a mantle that her husband was holding for her. Her face was pale and angry, and she was talking excitedly. Kartasov, a fat, bald man, was continually looking round at Anna, while attempting to soothe his wife. When the wife had gone out, the husband lingered a long while, and tried to catch Anna's eye, obviously anxious to bow to her. But Anna, with unmistakable intention, avoided noticing him, and talked to Yashvin, whose cropped head was bent down to her. Kartasov went out without making his salutation, and the box was left empty.

Vronsky could not understand exactly what had passed between the Kartasovs and Anna, but he was certain that something humiliating for Anna had happened. He knew this both from what he had seen and, most of all, from the face of Anna, who, he could see, was taxing every nerve to carry through the role she had undertaken. And, in maintaining this attitude of external composure, she was completely successful. Anyone who did not know her and her circle, who had not heard all the utterances of the women expressive of commiseration, indignation, and amazement that she should show herself in society, and show herself so conspicuously with her lace and her beauty, would have admired the serenity and loveliness of this woman without a suspicion that she was undergoing the sensations of someone in the stocks.

Knowing that something had happened, but not knowing precisely what, Vronsky felt a thrill of painful agitation, and hoping to find out something, he went toward his brother's box. Purposely choosing the way round furthest from Anna's box, he ran into the colonel of his old regiment talking to two acquaintances. Vronsky heard the name of Madame Karenina, and noticed how the colonel hastened to address Vronsky loudly by name, with a meaningful glance at his companions.

"Ah, Vronsky! When are you coming to the regiment? We can't let you off without a supper. You're one of the old set," said the colonel of his regiment.

"I can't stop, very sorry, another time," said Vronsky, and he ran upstairs toward his brother's box. Varya, with the young Princess Sorokina, met him in the corridor.

Leaving the Princess Sorokina with her mother, Varya held out her hand to her brother-in-law, and began immediately to speak of what interested him. She was more excited than he had ever seen her.

"I think it's mean and hateful, and Madame Kartasova had no right to do it. Madame Karenina . . . " she began.

"But what is it? I don't know."

"What? You've not heard?"

"You know I would be the last person to hear of it."

"There isn't a more spiteful creature than that Madame Kartasova!"

"But what did she do?"

"My husband told me . . . She has insulted Madame Karenina. Her husband began talking to her across the box, and Madame Kartasova made a scene. She said something aloud, he says, something insulting, and went away."

"Count, your *maman* is asking for you," said the young Princess Sorokina, peeping out of the door of the box.

"I've been expecting you all the while," said his mother, smiling sarcastically. "You were nowhere to be seen."

Her son saw that she could not suppress a smile of delight.

"Good evening, *Maman*. I was coming to you," he said coldly.

"Why aren't you going to *faire la cour à*[1] *Madame Karenina*?" she went on, when Princess Sorokina had moved away. "*Elle fait sensation. On oublie la Patti pour elle.*"[2]

"*Maman*, I have asked you not to say anything to me of that," he answered, scowling.

"I'm only saying what everyone's saying."

Vronsky made no reply, and saying a few words to Princess Sorokina, he left. At the door he met his brother.

"Ah, Aleksey!" said his brother. "How disgusting! Idiot of a woman, nothing else . . . I wanted to go straight to her. Let's go together."

Vronsky did not hear him. With rapid steps he went downstairs; he felt that he must do something, but he did not know what. Anger with her for having put herself and him in such a false position, together with pity for her suffering, filled his heart. He went down, and made straight for Anna's box. At her box stood Stremov, talking to her.

"There are no more tenors. *Le moule en est brise!*"[3]

Vronsky bowed to her and stopped to greet Stremov.

"You came in late, I think, and have missed the best aria," Anna said to Vronsky, glancing ironically, he thought, at him.

"I am a poor judge of music," he said, looking sternly at her.

"Like Prince Yashvin," she said, smiling, "who maintains that Patti sings too loud. Thank you," she said, her little hand in its long glove taking the playbill Vronsky picked up, and suddenly at that instant her lovely face quivered. She got up and went into the interior of the box.

[1] "Pay court to . . . "
[2] "She is creating a sensation. They ignore Patti because of her."
[3] "The mold for them is shattered."

Noticing in the next act that her box was empty, Vronsky, rousing murmurs of "hush" from the audience, which had grown quiet as a *cavatina* began, left the orchestra and drove home.

Anna was already at home. When Vronsky went up to her, she was in the same dress she had worn at the theater. She was sitting in the first armchair against the wall, looking straight before her. She looked at him, and at once resumed her former position.

"Anna," he said.

"You, you are to blame for everything!" she cried, with tears of despair and anger in her voice, getting up.

"I begged, I implored you not to go; I knew it would be unpleasant . . ."

"Unpleasant!" she cried. "Hideous! As long as I live I shall never forget it. She said it was a disgrace to sit beside me."

"A silly woman's chatter," he said. "But why risk it, why provoke—"

"I hate your calm. You shouldn't have brought me to this. If you had loved me . . ."

"Anna! How does the question of my love come in?"

"Oh, if you loved me as I love, if you were tortured as I am!" she said, looking at him with an expression of terror.

He was sorry for her, and angry all the same. He assured her of his love because he saw that this was the only means of soothing her, and he did not reproach her in words, but in his heart he reproached her.

And the assurances of his love, which seemed to him so vulgar that he was ashamed to utter them, she drank in eagerly, and gradually became calmer. The next day, completely reconciled, they left for the country.

PART SIX

CHAPTER ONE

Darya Aleksandrovna spent the summer with her children at Pokrovskoe, at her sister Kitty Levin's. The house on her own estate was quite in ruins, and Levin and his wife had persuaded her to spend the summer with them. Stepan Arkadyevich greatly approved of the arrangement. He said he was very sorry his official duties prevented him from spending the summer in the country with his family, which would have been the greatest happiness for him; and remaining in Moscow, he came down to the country from time to time for a day or two. Besides the Oblonskys, with all their children and their governess, the old princess too came to stay that summer with the Levins, as she considered it her duty to watch over her inexperienced daughter in her *interesting condition*. Moreover, Varenka, Kitty's friend abroad, kept her promise to come to Kitty when she was married, and stayed with her friend. All of these were friends or relations of Levin's wife. And though he liked them all, he rather regretted his own Levin world and ways, which was smothered by this influx of the "Shcherbatsky element," as he called it. Of his own relations, only Sergey Ivanovich stayed with him, but he too was a man of the Koznyshev and not the Levin stamp, so that the Levin spirit was utterly obliterated.

In the Levins' house, so long deserted, there were now so many people that almost all the rooms were occupied, and almost every day it happened that the old princess, sitting down at the table, counted them all over, and put the thirteenth grandson or grand-daughter at a separate table.[1] And Kitty, with her careful housekeeping, had no little trouble to get all the chickens, turkeys, and geese, of which so

---

[1]Because superstition holds that if there are thirteen seated at a table, one will die during the year that follows.

many were needed to satisfy the summer appetites of the visitors and children.

The whole family were sitting at dinner. Dolly's children, with their governess and Varenka, were making plans for going to look for mushrooms. Sergey Ivanovich, who was looked up to by all the party for his intellect and learning, and commanded a respect that almost amounted to awe, surprised everyone by joining in the conversation about mushrooms.

"Take me with you. I am very fond of picking mushrooms," he said, looking at Varenka; "I think it's a very nice occupation."

"Oh, we shall be delighted," answered Varenka, coloring a little. Kitty exchanged meaningful glances with Dolly. The proposal of the learned and intellectual Sergey Ivanovich to go looking for mushrooms with Varenka confirmed certain theories of Kitty's with which her mind had been very busy of late. She made haste to address some remark to her mother, so that her look should not be noticed. After dinner Sergey Ivanovich sat with his cup of coffee at the drawing room window, and while he took part in a conversation he had begun with his brother, he watched the door through which the children would start on the mushroom-picking expedition. Levin was sitting on the window sill near his brother.

Kitty stood beside her husband, evidently awaiting the end of a conversation that had no interest for her, in order to tell him something.

"You have changed in many respects since your marriage, and for the better," said Sergey Ivanovich, smiling to Kitty, and obviously little interested in the conversation, "but you have remained true to your passion for defending the most paradoxical theories."

"Katya, it's not good for you to stand," her husband said to her, moving a chair toward her and looking significantly at her.

"Oh, there's no time now," added Sergey Ivanovich, seeing the children running out.

At the head of them all Tanya galloped sideways, in her tightly drawn stockings, and waving a basket and Sergey Ivanovich's hat, she ran straight up to him.

Boldly running up to Sergey Ivanovich with shining eyes, so like her father's fine eyes, she handed him his hat and made as though she would put it on for him, softening her daring by a shy and friendly smile.

"Varenka's waiting," she said, carefully putting his hat on, seeing from Sergey Ivanovich's smile that she might do so.

Varenka was standing at the door, dressed in a yellow print dress, with a white kerchief on her head.

"I'm coming, I'm coming, Varvara Andreevna," said Sergey Ivanovich, finishing his cup of coffee, and putting into their separate pockets his handkerchief and cigar case.

"And how sweet my Varenka is, eh?" said Kitty to her husband, as soon as Sergey Ivanovich rose. She spoke so that Sergey Ivanovich could hear, and it was clear that she meant him to do so. "And how pretty she is—such a refined beauty! Varenka!" Kitty shouted. "Will you be in the mill copse? We'll come out to you."

"You certainly forget your condition, Kitty," said the old princess, hurriedly coming out at the door. "You mustn't shout like that."

Varenka, hearing Kitty's voice and her mother's reprimand, went with light, rapid steps up to Kitty. The rapidity of her movement, her flushed and eager face, everything betrayed that something out of the ordinary was going on in her. Kitty knew what this was, and had been watching her intently. She called Varenka at that moment merely in order mentally to give her a blessing for the important event which, as Kitty imagined, was bound to come to pass that day after dinner in the woods.

"Varenka, I would be very happy if a certain something were to happen," she whispered as she kissed her.

"And are you coming with us?" Varenka said to Levin in confusion, pretending not to have heard what had been said.

"I am coming, but only as far as the threshing floor, and there I shall stop."

"Why, what do you want there?" said Kitty.

"I must go have a look at the new wagons, and check their capacity," said Levin. "And where will you be?"

"On the terrace."

CHAPTER TWO

On the terrace were assembled all the ladies of the party. They always liked sitting there after dinner, and that day they had work to do there, too. Besides the sewing of baby clothes and knitting of swaddling bands, with which all of them were now busy, jam was being made on the terrace by a method new to Agafya Mikhailovna, without the addition of water. Kitty had introduced this new method, which had been in use in her home. Agafya Mikhailovna, to whom the task of jam-making had always been entrusted, considering that what had been done in the Levin household could not be amiss, had nevertheless put water with the strawberries, maintaining that the jam could not be made without it. She had been caught in the act, and was now making jam before everyone, and it was to be proved to her conclusively that jam could be very well made without water.

Agafya Mikhailovna, her face flushed and angry, her hair untidy, and her thin arms bare to the elbows, was moving the preserving pan over the brazier with a circular motion, looking darkly at the raspberries and devoutly hoping they would stick and not cook properly. The princess, conscious that Agafya Mikhailovna's wrath must be chiefly directed against her, as the person responsible for the raspberry jam–making, tried to appear to be absorbed in other things and not interested in the jam, talked of other matters, but cast stealthy glances in the direction of the stove.

"I always buy my maids' dresses myself, of some cheap material," the princess said, continuing the previous conversation. "Isn't it time to skim it, my dear?" she added, addressing Agafya Mikhailovna. "There's not the slightest need for you to do it, and it's hot for you," she said, stopping Kitty.

"I'll do it," said Dolly, and getting up, she carefully passed the spoon over the frothing sugar, and from time to time shook the clinging jam from the spoon by knocking it on a plate that was covered with yellow scum and blood syrup. "How they'll enjoy this at teatime!" she thought of her children, remembering how she herself, as a child, had wondered how it was the grownups did not eat what was best of all—the scum of the jam.

"Stiva says it's much better to give money." Dolly meanwhile took up the weighty subject under discussion, what presents should be made to servants. "But—"

"Money's out of the question!" the princess and Kitty exclaimed with one voice. "They appreciate a present."

"Well, last year, for instance, I bought our Matryona Semyonovna, not a poplin, but something of that sort," said the princess.

"I remember she was wearing it on your nameday."[1]

"A charming pattern—so simple and refined—I would have liked it myself, if she hadn't had it. Something like Varenka's. So pretty and inexpensive."

"Well, now I think it's done," said Dolly, dropping the syrup from the spoon.

"When it begins to set, it's ready. Cook it a little longer, Agafya Mikhailovna."

"The flies!" said Agafya Mikhailovna angrily. "It'll be just the same," she added.

"Ah! How sweet it is! Don't frighten it!" Kitty said suddenly, looking at a sparrow that had settled on the balustrade and was pecking at the center of a raspberry.

"Yes, but you keep a little further from the stove," said her mother.

"*A propos de Varenka*,"[2] said Kitty, speaking in French, as they had been doing all the while, so that Agafya Mikhailovna would not understand them, "you know, Mama, I somehow expect things to be settled today. You know what I mean. How splendid it would be!"

"But what a famous matchmaker she is!" said Dolly. "How carefully and cleverly she throws them together!"

"No; tell me, Mama, what do you think?"

"Why, what is one to think? He" (Sergey Ivanovich) "could have been a match for anyone in Russia; now, of course, he's not quite a young man, still I know ever so many girls who would be glad to marry him even now. She's a very nice girl, but he might—"

"Oh, no, Mama, do understand why, for him and for her, too, nothing better could be imagined. In the first place, she's charming!" said Kitty, crooking one of her fingers.

[1]An Orthodox Russian celebrates the feast day of his patron saint, after whom he was christened, as his birthday.
[2]"As to Varenka."

"He thinks her very attractive that's certain," Dolly assented.

"Then he occupies such a position in society that he has no need to look for either fortune or position in his wife. All he needs is a good, sweet wife—a quiet one."

"Well, with her he would certainly have it quiet enough," Dolly said.

"Thirdly, that she should love him. And so it is . . . that is, it would be, so splendid! . . . I look forward to seeing them coming out of the woods—and everything settled. I shall see at once by their eyes. I would be so delighted! What do you think, Dolly?"

"But don't excite yourself. It's not at all the thing for you to be excited," said her mother.

"Oh, I'm not excited, Mama. I think he will propose today."

"Ah, that's so strange, how and when a man proposes! There is a sort of barrier, and all at once it's broken down," said Dolly, smiling pensively and recalling her past with Stepan Arkadyevich.

"Mama, how did Papa propose?" Kitty asked suddenly.

"There was nothing unusual, it was very simple," answered the princess, but her face beamed all over at the recollection.

"Oh, but how was it? You loved him, anyway, before you were allowed to speak?"

Kitty felt a peculiar pleasure in being able now to talk to her mother on equal terms about those questions of such paramount interest in a woman's life.

"Of course I did; he had come to stay with us in the country. You imagine, I suppose, that you invented something new? It's always just the same: it was settled by the eyes, by smiles . . ."

"How nicely you said that, Mama! It's just by the eyes, by smiles that it's done," Dolly assented.

"But what words did he say?"

"What did Kostya say to you?"

"He wrote it in chalk. It was wonderful . . . How long ago it seems!" she said.

And the three women all thought about the same thing. Kitty was the first to break the silence. She remembered all of that last winter before her marriage, and her passion for Vronsky.

"There's one thing . . . that old love affair of Varenka's," she said, a natural chain of ideas bringing her to this point. "I would have liked to say something to Sergey Ivanovich, to prepare him. They're all—all men, I mean," she added—"awfully jealous over our past."

"Not all," said Dolly. "You judge by your own husband. It makes him miserable even now to remember Vronsky. Eh? That's true, isn't it?"

"Yes," Kitty answered, a pensive smile in her eyes.

"But I really don't know," the mother put in, in defense of her motherly care of her daughter, "what there was in your past that could worry him. That Vronsky paid you attentions—that happens to every girl."

"Oh, yes, but we didn't mean that," Kitty said, flushing a little.

"No, let me speak," her mother went on. "Why, you yourself would not let me have a talk with Vronsky. Don't you remember?"

"Oh, Mama!" said Kitty, with an expression of suffering.

"There's no keeping you young people in check nowadays . . . Your friendship could not have gone beyond what was suitable. I should myself have called upon him to explain himself. But, my darling, it's not right for you to be excited. Please remember that and calm yourself."

"I'm perfectly calm, *Maman*."

"How fortunate it was for Kitty that Anna came then," said Dolly, "and how unfortunate for her. It turned out quite the opposite," she said, struck by her own ideas. "Then Anna was so happy, and Kitty thought herself unhappy. Now it is just the opposite. I often think of her."

"A nice person to think about! Horrid, repulsive woman—no heart," said her mother, who could not forget that Kitty had married not Vronsky but Levin.

"What do you want to talk of it for?" Kitty said with annoyance. "I never think about it, and I don't want to think of it . . . No, I don't want to think of it," she said, catching the sound of her husband's familiar step on the terrace.

"What's that you don't want to think about?" inquired Levin, coming onto the terrace.

But no one answered him, and he did not repeat the question.

"I'm sorry I've broken in on your feminine parliament," he said, looking round at everyone discontentedly, perceiving that they had been talking of something they would not talk about before him.

For a second he felt that he was sharing the feeling of Agafya Mikhailovna, vexation at their making jam without water, and altogether at the alien Shcherbatsky element. He smiled, however, and went up to Kitty.

"Well, how are you?" he asked her, looking at her with the expression with which everyone looked at her now.

"Oh, very well," said Kitty, smiling, "and how have things gone with you?"

"The wagons hold three times as much as the old carts did. Well, are we going for the children? I've ordered the horses to be put in."

"What! You want to take Kitty in the trap?" her mother said reproachfully.

"Yes, at a walking pace, Princess."

Levin never called the princess "*Maman*," as men often do call their mothers-in-law, and the princess disliked his not doing so. But though he liked and respected the princess, Levin could not call her so without a sense of profaning his feeling for his dead mother.

"Come with us, *Maman*," said Kitty.

"I don't like to see such imprudence."

"Well, I'll walk, then; it's good for me." Kitty got up and went to her husband and took his hand.

"It may be good for you, but everything in moderation," said the princess.

"Well, Agafya Mikhailovna, is the jam done?" said Levin, smiling to Agafya Mikhailovna, and trying to cheer her up. "Is it all right in the new way?"

"I suppose it's all right. To our way of thinking, it's boiled too long."

"It'll be all the better, Agafya Mikhailovna, it won't mildew, even though our ice has begun to thaw already, so that we've no cool cellar to store it," said Kitty, at once divining her husband's motive, and addressing the old housekeeper with the same feeling; "but your pickle's so good—Mama says she never tasted any like it," she added, smiling, and putting her kerchief straight.

Agafya Mikhailovna looked angrily at Kitty.

"You needn't try to console me, mistress. I need only to look at you with him and I feel happy," she said, and something in the rough familiarity of that "him" touched Kitty.

"Come along with us to look for mushrooms, you will show us the best places." Agafya Mikhailovna smiled and shook her head as though to say: "I would like to be angry with you too, but I can't."

"Please follow my advice," said the princess; "put some paper over the jam and moisten it with a little rum, and even without ice it will never go mildewy."

CHAPTER THREE

Kitty was particularly glad of a chance of being alone with her husband, for she had noticed the shade of mortification that had passed over his face—always so quick to reflect every feeling—at the moment when he had come onto the terrace and asked what they were talking of, and had got no answer.

When they had set off on foot ahead of the others, and had come out of sight of the house onto the hard, dusty road, strewn with rye ears and grain, she leaned more heavily on his arm and pressed it closer to her. He had quite forgotten the momentary unpleasant impression, and alone with her he felt, now that the thought of her approaching motherhood was never for a moment absent from his mind, a new and delicious bliss, quite pure from sensuality, in being near the woman he loved. There was no need for speech, yet he longed to hear the sound of her voice, which, like her eyes, had changed since she had been with child. In her voice, as in her eyes, there was that softness and gravity which is found in people continually concentrated on some cherished pursuit.

"So you're not tired? Lean more on me," said he.

"No, I'm so glad of a chance of being alone with you, and I must confess, though I'm happy with them, I do miss our winter evenings alone."

"That was good, but this is even better. Both are better," he said, squeezing her hand.

"Do you know what we were talking about when you came in?"

"About jam?"

"Oh, yes, about jam too; but afterward—about how men propose."

"Ah!" said Levin, listening more to the sound of her voice than to the words she was saying, and all the while paying attention to the road, which passed now through the woods, and avoiding places where she might make a false step.

"And about Sergey Ivanovich and Varenka. You've noticed? . . . I'm very eager for it," she went on. "What do you think about it?" And she peered into his face.

"I don't know what to think," Levin answered, smiling. "Sergey seems very strange to me in that way. I told you, you know . . ."

"Yes, that he was in love with that girl who died . . ."

"That was when I was a child; I know about it from hearsay and tradition. I remember him then. He was wonderfully sweet. But I've watched him since with women; he is friendly, some of them he likes, but one feels that to him they're simply people, not women."

"Yes, but now with Varenka . . . I think there's something . . ."

"Perhaps there is . . . but one has to know him. He's a peculiar, wonderful person. He lives a spiritual life only. He's too pure, too exalted a nature."

"Why? Would this lower him, then?"

"No, but he's so used to a spiritual life that he can't reconcile himself with actual fact, and Varenka is, after all, fact."

Levin had grown used by now to uttering his thoughts boldly, without taking the trouble to dress them in precise language. He knew that his wife, in such moments of loving tenderness as now, would understand what he meant to say from a hint, and she did understand him.

"Yes, but there's not so much of that actual fact about her as about me. I can see that he would never have cared for me. She is altogether spiritual."

"Oh, no, he is so fond of you, and I am always so glad when my people like you . . ."

"Yes, he's very nice to me; but . . ."

"It's not as it was with poor Nikolai . . . you really cared for each other," Levin finished. "Why not speak of him?" he added. "I sometimes blame myself for not; it ends in one's forgetting. Ah, how terrible and charming he was! . . . Yes, what were we talking about?" Levin said, after a pause.

"You think he can't fall in love," said Kitty, translating into her own language.

"It's not so much that he can't fall in love," Levin said, smiling, "but he has not the weakness necessary . . . I've always envied him, and even now, when I'm so happy, I still envy him."

"You envy him for not being able to fall in love?"

"I envy him for being better than me," said Levin. "He does not live for himself. His whole life is subordinated to his duty. And that's why he can be calm and contented."

"And you?" Kitty asked, with an ironical and loving smile.

She could never have explained the chain of thought that made her smile; but the last link in it was that her husband, in exalting his brother and abasing himself, was not quite sincere. Kitty knew that this insincerity came from his love for his brother, from his sense of shame at being too happy, and above all from his unflagging craving to be better—she loved it in him, and so she smiled.

"And you? What are you dissatisfied with?" she asked, with the same smile.

Her disbelief in his self-dissatisfaction delighted him, and unconsciously he tried to draw her into giving utterance to the grounds of her disbelief.

"I am happy, but dissatisfied with myself," he said.

"Why, how can you be dissatisfied with yourself if you are happy?"

"Well, how shall I say? . . . In my heart I really care for nothing whatever but that you should not stumble—see? Oh, but really you mustn't skip about like that!" he cried, breaking off to scold her for too agile a movement in stepping over a branch that lay in the path. "But when I think about myself, and compare myself with others, especially with my brother, I feel I'm a poor creature."

"But in what way?" Kitty pursued with the same smile. "Don't you too work for others? What about your co-operative settlement, and your work on the estate, and your book?"

"Oh, but I feel, and particularly just now—it's your fault," he said, pressing her hand—"that all that doesn't count. I do it half-heartedly.

If I could care for all that as I care for you! . . . Instead of that, I do it these days like a task that is set me."

"Well, what would you say about Papa?" asked Kitty. "Is he a poor creature, then, as he does nothing for the public good?"

"He? No! But then one must have the simplicity, the straightforwardness, the goodness, of your father: and I haven't got that. I do nothing, and I fret about it. It's all your doing. Before there was you—and *this* too," he added with a glance toward her belly which she understood—"I put all my energies into work; now I can't, and I'm ashamed; I do it just as though it were a task set me, I'm pretending . . ."

"Well, but would you like to change this minute with Sergey Ivanovich?" said Kitty. "Would you like to do this work for the general good, and to love the task set you, as he does, and nothing else?"

"Of course not," said Levin. "But I'm so happy that I don't understand anything. So you think he'll propose today?" he added after a brief silence.

"I think so, and I don't think so. But I'm so eager for it. Here, wait a minute." She stooped down and picked a wild camomile at the edge of the path. "Come, count: he will propose, he won't . . ." she said, giving him the flower.

"He will, he won't," said Levin, tearing off the narrow white petals.

"No, no!" Kitty, snatching at his hand, stopped him. She had been watching his fingers with interest. "You picked off two."

"Then we won't count this little one," said Levin, tearing off a little half-grown petal. "Here's the trap overtaking us."

"Aren't you tired, Kitty?" called the princess.

"Not in the least."

"If you are you can get in, if the horses are quiet and go at a walking pace."

But it was not worthwhile to get in, they were quite near the place, and all walked on together.

CHAPTER FOUR

Varenka, with her white kerchief over her black hair, surrounded by the children, gaily and good-humoredly looking after them and at the same time visibly excited at the possibility of receiving a proposal from the man she cared for, looked very attractive. Sergey Ivanovich walked beside her, and never stopped admiring her. Looking at her, he recalled all the delightful things he had heard from her lips, all the good he knew about her, and became more and more conscious that the feeling he had for her was something special that he had felt long, long ago, and only once, in his early youth. The feeling of happiness in being near her continually grew, and at last reached such a point that, as he put a huge birch mushroom with a slender stalk and an up-curling rim in her basket, he looked straight into her face, and noticing the flush of joyful and alarmed excitement that overspread her face, he was confused himself, and smiled to her in silence a smile that said too much.

"If so," he said to himself, "I ought to think it over and make up my mind, and not give way like a boy to the impulse of a moment."

"I'm going by myself to pick apart from all the rest, or else my efforts will not be noticed," he said, and he left the edge of the wood, where they were walking on low silky grass between old birch trees standing far apart, and went more into the heart of the wood, where between the white birch trunks there were gray trunks of aspen and dark bushes of hazel. Walking some forty paces away, Sergey Ivanovich, knowing he was out of sight, stood still behind a bushy spindle tree in full flower with its pinkish-red catkins. It was perfectly still all round him. Only overhead in the birches under which he stood, the flies, like a swarm of bees, buzzed unceasingly, and from time to time the children's voices floated across to him. All at once he heard, not far from the edge of the wood, the sound of Varenka's contralto voice calling Grisha, and a smile of delight passed over Sergey Ivanovich's face. Conscious of this smile, he shook his head disapprovingly at his own condition, and taking out a cigar, he began lighting it. For a long while he could not strike a match against the trunk of a birch. The soft scales of the white bark rubbed off the phosphorus, and the light went out. At last one of the matches burned, and the fragrant cigar smoke, hovering uncertainly like a broad sheet, stretched forward and upward over a bush under the drooping branches of the birch. Watching the streak of smoke, Sergey Ivanovich walked slowly on, deliberating on his position.

"Why not?" he thought. "If it were only a passing fancy or a passion, if it were only this attraction—this mutual attraction (I can call it a *mutual* attraction), but I felt that it was in contradiction with the whole bent of my life—if I felt that in giving way to this attraction I should be false to my vocation and my duty . . . but it's not so. The only thing I can say against it is that, when I lost Marie, I said to myself that I would remain faithful to her memory. That's the only thing I can say against my feeling . . . That's important," Sergey Ivanovich said to himself, feeling at the same time that this consideration had not the slightest importance for him personally, but would only perhaps detract from his romantic role in the eyes of others. "But apart from that, however much I searched, I would never find anything to say against my feeling. If I were choosing by considerations of suitability alone, I could not have found anything better."

However many women and girls he thought of whom he knew, he could not think of a girl who united to such a degree all, positively all, the qualities he would wish to see in his wife. She had all the charm and freshness of youth, but she was not a child; and if she loved him, she loved him consciously as a woman ought to love; that was one thing. Another point: she was not only far from being worldly, but had an unmistakable distaste for worldly society, and at the same time she knew the world, and had all the ways of a woman of the best society, which were absolutely essential to Sergey Ivanovich's conception of the woman who was to share his life. Third: she was religious, and not like a child, unconsciously religious and good, as Kitty, for example, was, but her life was founded on religious principles. Even in trifling matters, Sergey Ivanovich found in her all that he wanted in his wife: she was poor and alone in the world, so she would not bring with her a mass of relations and their influence into her husband's house, as he saw now in Kitty's case. She would owe everything to her husband, which was what he had always desired too for his future family life. And this girl, who united all these qualities, loved him. He was a modest man, but he could not help seeing it. And he loved her. There was one consideration against it—his age. But he was of a long-lived family, he had not a single gray hair, no one would have taken him for forty, and he remembered Varenka's saying that it was only in Russia that men of fifty thought themselves old, and that in France a man of fifty considers himself *dans la force de l'age*,[1] while a man of forty is *un jeune homme*.[2] But what did the mere reckoning of years matter when he felt as young in heart as he had been twenty years ago? Was it not youth to feel as he felt now, when coming from the other side to the edge of the wood he saw in the glowing light of the slanting sunbeams the graceful figure of Varenka in her yellow dress with her basket, walking lightly by the trunk of an old birch tree, and when this impression of the sight of Varenka blended so harmoniously with the beauty of the view, of the yellow oatfield lying bathed in the slanting sunshine, and beyond it the distant ancient forest flecked with yellow and melting into the blue of the distance? His heart throbbed joyously. A tender feeling came over him. He felt that he had made up his mind. Varenka, who had just crouched down to pick a mushroom, rose with a supple movement and looked around. Flinging away the cigar, Sergey Ivanovich advanced with resolute steps toward her.

CHAPTER FIVE

"Varvara Andreevna, when I was very young, I set before myself the ideal of the woman I loved and would be happy to call my wife. I have lived through a long life, and now for the first time I have met what I sought—in you. I love you, and offer you my hand."

Sergey Ivanovich was saying this to himself while he was ten paces from Varenka. Kneeling down, with her hands over the mushrooms to guard them from Grisha, she was calling little Masha.

"Come here, little ones! There are so many!" she was saying in her sweet, deep voice.

[1]"In the prime of life."
[2]"A young man."

Seeing Sergey Ivanovich approaching, she did not get up and did not change her position, but everything told him that she felt his presence and was glad of it.

"Well, did you find some?" she asked from under the white kerchief, turning her beautiful, gently smiling face to him.

"Not one," said Sergey Ivanovich. "Did you?"

She did not answer, busy with the children who thronged about her.

"That one too, near the twig." She pointed out to little Masha a mushroom, split in half across its rosy cap by the dry grass from under which it thrust itself. Varenka got up while Masha picked the mushroom, breaking it into two white halves. "This brings back my childhood," she added, moving apart from the children by Sergey Ivanovich.

They walked on for some steps in silence. Varenka saw that he wanted to speak; she guessed of what, and felt faint with joy and panic. They had walked so far away that no one could hear them now, but still he did not begin to speak. It would have been better for Varenka to be silent. After a silence it would have been easier for them to say what they wanted to say than after talking about mushrooms. But against her own will, as it were accidentally, Varenka said:

"So you found nothing? In the middle of the wood there are always fewer, though." Sergey Ivanovich sighed and made no answer. He was annoyed that she had spoken about the mushrooms. He wanted to bring her back to the first words she had uttered about her childhood; but after a pause of some length, as though against his own will, he made an observation in response to her last words.

"I have heard that the white edible mushrooms are found principally at the edge of the wood, though I can't tell them apart."

Some minutes more passed, they moved still further away from the children, and were quite alone. Varenka's heart throbbed so that she heard it beating, and felt that she was turning red and pale and red again.

To be the wife of a man like Koznyshev, after her position with Madame Stahl, was to her imagination the height of happiness. Besides, she was almost certain that she was in love with him. And this moment it would have to be decided. She felt frightened. She dreaded both his speaking and his not speaking.

Now or never it must be said—that Sergey Ivanovich felt too. Everything in the expression, the flushed cheeks and the downcast eyes of Varenka betrayed a painful suspense. Sergey Ivanovich saw it and felt sorry for her. He felt even that to say nothing now would be a slight to her. Rapidly in his own mind he ran over all the arguments in support of his decision. He even said over to himself the words in which he meant to propose, but instead of those words, some utterly unexpected reflection that occurred to him made him ask:

"What is the difference between the birch mushroom and the white mushroom?"

Varenka's lips quivered with emotion as she answered:

"In the top part there is scarcely any difference, it's in the stalk."

And as soon as these words were uttered, both he and she felt that it was over, that what was to have been said would not be said; and their emotion, which had up to then been continually growing more intense, began to subside.

"The birch mushroom's stalk suggests a dark man's chin after two days without shaving," said Sergey Ivanovich, speaking quite calmly now.

"Yes, that's true," answered Varenka, smiling, and unconsciously the direction of their walk changed. They began to turn toward the children. Varenka felt both hurt and ashamed; at the same time she had a sense of relief.

When he had got home again and went over the whole subject, Sergey Ivanovich thought his previous decision had been a mistaken one. He could not be false to the memory of Marie.

"Gently, children, gently!" Levin shouted quite angrily to the children, standing before his wife to protect her when the crowd of children flew with shrieks of delight to meet them.

Behind the children Sergey Ivanovich and Varenka walked out of the wood. Kitty had no need to ask Varenka; she saw from the calm and somewhat crestfallen faces of both that her plans had not come off.

"Well?" her husband questioned her as they were going home again.

"It didn't bite," said Kitty, her smile and manner of speaking recalling her father, a likeness Levin often noticed with pleasure.

"How didn't bite?"

"I'll show you," she said, taking her husband's hand, lifting it to her mouth, and just faintly brushing it with closed lips. "Like a kiss on a bishop's hand."

"Which didn't bite?" he said, laughing.

"Both. But it should have been like this . . ."

"There are some peasants coming . . ."

"Oh, they didn't see."

CHAPTER SIX

During the time of the children's tea the grownups sat in the balcony and talked as though nothing had happened though they all, especially Sergey Ivanovich and Varenka, were very well aware that there had happened an event which, though negative, was of very great importance. They both had the same feeling, rather like that of a schoolboy after an examination which has left him in the same class or shut him out of the school forever. Everyone present, feeling too that something had happened, talked eagerly about extraneous subjects. Levin and Kitty were particularly happy and conscious of their love that evening. And their happiness in their love seemed to imply a disagreeable slur on those who would have liked to feel the same and could not— and they felt a prick of conscience.

"Mark my words, Aleksandr will not come," said the old princess.

That evening they were expecting Stepan Arkadyevich Oblonsky to come down by train, and the old prince had written that possibly he might come too.

"And I know why," the princess went on; "he says that young people ought to be left alone for a while at first."

"But Papa has left us alone. We've never seen him," said Kitty.

"Besides, we're not young people!— we're old married people by now."

"Only if he doesn't come, I shall say good-by to you children," said the princess, sighing mournfully.

"What nonsense, Mama!" both the daughters said, falling upon her at once.

"How do you suppose he is feeling? Why, now . . . "

And suddenly there was an unexpected quiver in the princess's voice. Her daughters were silent, and looked at one another. "*Maman* always finds something to be miserable about," they said in that glance. They did not know that, happy as the princess was in her daughter's house, and useful as she felt herself to be there, she had been extremely miserable, both on her own account and her husband's, ever since they had married their last and favorite daughter, and the old home had been left empty.

"What is it, Agafya Mikhailovna?" Kitty asked suddenly of Agafya Mikhailovna, who was standing with a mysterious air, and a face full of meaning.

"About supper."

"Well, that's right," said Dolly; "you go and arrange it, and I'll go and hear Grisha repeat his lesson, or else he will have done nothing all day."

"That's my lesson! No, Dolly, I'm going," said Levin, jumping up.

Grisha, who was by now in high school, had to go over the lessons of the term in the summer holidays. Darya Aleksandrovna, who had been studying Latin with her son in Moscow before, had made it a rule on coming to the Levins' to go over with him, at least once a day, the most difficult lessons of Latin and arithmetic. Levin had offered to take her place, but the mother, having once overheard Levin's lesson, and noticing that it was not given exactly as the teacher in Moscow had given it, said resolutely, though with much embarrassment and anxiety not to mortify Levin, that they must keep strictly to the book as the teacher had done, and that she had better undertake it again herself. Levin was amazed both at Stepan Arkadyevich, who, by neglecting his duty, threw upon the mother the supervision of studies of which she had no comprehension, and at the teachers for teaching the children so badly. But he promised his sister-in-law to give the lessons exactly as she wished. And he went on teaching Grisha, not in his own way, but by the book, and so took little interest in it, and often forgot the hour of the lesson. So it had been today.

"No, I'm going, Dolly, you sit still," he said. "We'll do it all properly, like the book. Only when Stiva comes, and we go out shooting, then we shall have to miss it."

And Levin sent to Grisha.

Varenka was saying the same thing to Kitty. Even in the happy, well-ordered household of the Levins, Varenka had succeeded in making herself useful.

"I'll see the supper, you sit still," she said, and got up to go to Agafya Mikhailovna.

"Yes, yes, most likely they've not been able to get chickens. If so, ours—"

"Agafya Mikhailovna and I will see about it," and Varenka vanished with her.

"What a nice girl!" said the princess.

"Not nice, *Maman*; she's an exquisite girl; there's no one else like her."

"So you are expecting Stepan Arkadyevich today?" said Sergey Ivanovich, evidently not disposed to pursue the conversation about Varenka. "It would be difficult to find two brothers-in-law more unlike than yours," he said with a subtle smile. "One always on the move, living only in society, like a fish in water; the other our Kostya, lively, alert, quick in everything, but as soon as he is in society, he either sinks into apathy or struggles helplessly like a fish on land."

"Yes, he's very thoughtless," said the princess, addressing Sergey Ivanovich. "I've been meaning, indeed, to ask you to tell him that it's out of the question for her" (she indicated Kitty) "to stay here; that she positively must come to Moscow. He talks of getting a doctor down . . . "

"*Maman*, he'll do everything; he has agreed to everything," Kitty said, angry with her mother for appealing to Sergey Ivanovich to judge in such a matter.

In the middle of their conversation they heard the snorting of horses and the sound of wheels on gravel. Dolly had not time to get up to go and meet her husband, when from the window of the room below, where Grisha was having his lesson, Levin leaped out and helped Grisha out after him.

"It's Stiva!" Levin shouted from under the balcony. "We've finished, Dolly, don't be afraid!" he added, and started running like a boy to meet the carriage.

"*Is, ea, id, ejus, ejus, ejus!*[1] shouted Grisha, skipping along the avenue.

"And someone else too! Papa, of course!" cried Levin, stopping at the entrance of the avenue. "Kitty, don't come down the steep staircase, go around."

But Levin had been mistaken in taking the person sitting in the carriage for the old prince. As he got nearer to the carriage he saw beside Stepan Arkadyevich not the prince but a handsome, stout young man in a Scotch cap, with long ribbons behind. This was Vasenka Veslovsky, a distant cousin of the Shcherbatskys, a brilliant young gentleman in Petersburg and Moscow society. "A wonderful fellow, and a keen sportsman," as Stepan Arkadyevich said, introducing him.

Not a whit abashed by the disappointment caused by his having come in place of the old prince, Veslovsky greeted Levin gaily, claiming acquaintance with him in the past, and snatching up Grisha into the carriage, he lifted him over the pointer that Stepan Arkadyevich had brought with him.

Levin did not get into the carriage but walked behind. He was rather vexed at the non-arrival of the old prince, whom he liked more and more the more he saw of him, and also at the arrival of this Vasenka Veslovsky, a quite uncongenial and superfluous person. He seemed to him still more uncongenial and superfluous when, on approaching the steps where the whole party, children and grownups, were gathered together in much excitement, Levin saw Vasenka Veslovsky, with a particularly warm and gallant air, kissing Kitty's hand.

"Your wife and I are cousins and very old friends," said Vasenka Veslovsky, once more shaking Levin's hand with great warmth.

"Well, are there plenty of birds?" Stepan Arkadyevich asked Levin, hardly leaving time for everyone to utter their greetings. "We've come with the most savage intentions. Why, *Maman*, they've not been in Moscow since! Look, Tanya, here's something for you!

[1]Declension of the Latin personal pronoun: "He, she, it, his, hers, its."

Get it, please, it's in the carriage, behind!" he said, talking in all directions. "How pretty you've grown, Dolly," he said to his wife, once more kissing her hand, holding it in one of his and patting it with other.

Levin, who a minute before had been in the happiest frame of mind, now looked darkly at everyone, and everything displeased him.

"Who was it he kissed yesterday with those lips?" he thought, looking at Stepan Arkadyevich's tender demonstrations to his wife. He looked at Dolly, and he did not like her either.

"She doesn't believe in his love. So what is she so pleased about? Revolting!" thought Levin.

He looked at the princess, who had been so dear to him a minute before, and he did not like the manner in which she welcomed this Vasenka, with his ribbons, just as though she were in her own house.

Even Sergey Ivanovich, who had also come out onto the steps, seemed to him unpleasant with the show of cordiality with which he met Stepan Arkadyevich, though Levin knew that his brother neither liked nor respected Oblonsky.

And Varenka, even she seemed hateful, with her *sainte nitouche*[2] air, making the acquaintance of this gentleman, yet all the while she was thinking of nothing but getting married.

And more hateful than anyone was Kitty for falling in with the tone of gaiety with which this gentleman regarded his visit in the country, as though it was a holiday for himself and everyone else. And unpleasant above all was that particular smile with which she responded to his smile.

Talking noisily, they all went into the house; but as soon as they were all seated, Levin turned and went out.

Kitty saw that something was bothering her husband. She tried to seize a moment to speak to him alone, but he made haste to get away from her, saying he was needed at the office. It was long since that his own work on the estate had seemed to him so important as at that moment. "It's all holiday for them," he thought; "but these are no holiday matters, they won't wait, and there's no living without them."

[2]"Holy unapproachable."

Levin came back to the house only when they sent to summon him to supper. Kitty and Agafya Mikhailovna were standing on the stairs, consulting about wines for supper.

"But why are you making all this fuss? Have what we usually do."

"No, Stiva doesn't drink . . . Kostya, stop, what's the matter?" Kitty began, hurrying after him, but he strode ruthlessly away to the dining room without waiting for her, and at once joined in the lively general conversation which was being maintained there by Vasenka Veslovsky and Stepan Arkadyevich.

"Well, what do you say, are we going shooting tomorrow?" said Stepan Arkadyevich.

"Please, let's go," said Veslovsky, moving to another chair, where he sat down sideways, with one fat leg tucked under him.

"I shall be delighted, we will go. And have you had any shooting yet this year?" said Levin to Veslovsky, looking intently at his leg, but speaking with that forced amiability that Kitty knew so well in him, and that was so out of keeping with him. "I can't answer for our finding grouse, but there are plenty of snipe. Only we ought to start early. You're not tired? Are you tired, Stiva?"

"Me tired? I've never been tired. Suppose we stay up all night. Let's go for a walk!"

"Yes, really, let's not go to bed at all! Excellent!" Veslovksy chimed in.

"Oh, we all know you can do without sleep, and keep other people up too," Dolly said to her husband, with that faint note of irony in her voice which she almost always had now with him. "But to my thinking, it's time for bed now. . . . I'm going, I don't want supper."

"No, do stay a while, Dolly, dear," said Stepan Arkadyevich, going round to her side behind the table where they were having supper. "I've so much still to tell you."

"Nothing much, I suppose."

"Do you know Veslovsky has been at Anna's, and he's going to them again? You know they're hardly fifty miles from us, and I too must certainly go over there. Veslovsky, come here!"

Vasenka crossed over to the ladies, and sat down beside Kitty.

"Ah, do tell me, please; you have stayed with her? How was she?" Darya Aleksandrovna appealed to him.

Levin was left at the other end of the table, and though he never paused in his conversation with the princess and Varenka, he saw that there was an eager and mysterious conversation going on between Stepan Arkadyevich, Dolly, Kitty, and Veslovsky. And that was not all. He saw on his wife's face an expression of deep feeling as she gazed with fixed eyes on the handsome face of Vasenka, who was telling them something with great animation.

"It's exceedingly nice at their place," Veslovsky was telling them about Vronsky and Anna. "I can't, of course, take it upon myself to judge, but in their house you feel the real feeling of home."

"What do they intend doing?"

"I believe they think of going to Moscow."

"How jolly it would be for us all to go over to them together! When are you going there?" Stepan Arkadyevich asked Vasenka.

"I'm spending July there."

"Will you go?" Stepan Arkadyevich asked his wife.

"I've been wanting to a long while; I shall certainly go," said Dolly. "I am sorry for her, and I know her. She's a splendid woman. I will go alone, when you go back, and then I shall be in no one's way. And it will be better without you."

"To be sure," said Stepan Arkadyevich. "And you, Kitty?"

"I? Why should I go?" Kitty said, flushing all over, and she glanced around at her husband.

"Do you know Anna Arkadyevna, then?" Veslovsky asked her. "She's a very fascinating woman."

"Yes," she answered Veslovsky, crimsoning still more. She got up and walked across to her husband.

"Are you going shooting, then, tomorrow?" she asked.

His jealousy had in these few moments, especially at the flush that had overspread her cheeks while she was talking to Veslovsky, gone far indeed. Now as he heard her words, he construed them in his own fashion. Strange as it was to him afterward to recall it, it seemed to him at the moment clear that in asking whether he was going shooting, all she cared to know was whether he would give that pleasure to Vasenka Veslovsky, with whom, he imagined, she was in love.

"Yes, I'm going," he answered her in an unnatural voice, disagreeable to himself.

"No, better spend the day here tomorrow, or Dolly won't see anything of her husband, and set off the day after," said Kitty.

The motive of Kitty's words was interpreted by Levin thus: "Don't separate me from *him*. I don't care about your going, but do let me enjoy the company of this delightful young man."

"Oh, if you wish, we'll stay here tomorrow," Levin answered, with peculiar amiability.

Vasenka meanwhile, utterly unsuspecting the misery his presence had occasioned, got up from the table after Kitty, and watching her with smiling and admiring eyes, he followed her.

Levin saw that look. He turned white, and for a minute he could hardly breathe. "How dare he look at my wife like that!" was the feeling that boiled within him.

"Tomorrow, then? Do, please, let us go," said Vasenka, sitting down on a chair, and again tucking his leg under him, as was his habit.

Levin's jealousy went further still. Already he saw himself a deceived husband, looked upon by his wife and her lover as simply necessary to provide them with the conveniences and pleasures of life . . . But in spite of that he made polite and hospitable inquiries of Vasenka about his shooting, his gun, and his boots, and agreed to go shooting the next day.

Happily for Levin, the old princess cut short his agonies by getting up herself and advising Kitty to go to bed. But even at this point Levin could not escape another agony. As Vasenka said good night to his hostess, he leaned down to kiss her hand again, but Kitty, reddening, drew back her hand and said with a native bluntness, for which the old princess scolded her afterward:

"That's not customary in our house."

In Levin's eyes she was to blame for having allowed such relations to arise, and still more to blame for showing so awkwardly that she did not like them.

"Why, how can one want to go to bed!" said Stepan Arkadyevich, who, after drinking several glasses of wine at supper, was now in his most charming and poetical mood. "Look, Kitty," he said, pointing to the moon, which had just risen behind the lime trees—"how exquisite! Veslovsky, this is the time for a serenade. You know, he has a splendid voice; we practiced songs together along the road. He has brought some lovely songs with him, two new ones. Varvara Andreevna and he must sing some duets."

When the party had broken up, Stepan Arkadyevich walked a long while about the avenue with Veslovsky; their voices could be heard singing one of the new songs.

Levin, hearing these voices, sat scowling in an armchair in his wife's bedroom, and maintained an obstinate silence when she asked him what was wrong. But when at last, with a timid glance, she hazarded the question: "Was there perhaps something you disliked about Veslovsky?" it burst out, and he told her all. He was humiliated himself at what he was saying, and that exasperated him all the more.

He stood facing her with his eyes glittering menacingly under his scowling brows, and he pressed his strong arms across his chest, as though he were straining every nerve to hold himself in. The expression on his face would have been grim, and even cruel, if it had not at the same time had a look of suffering which touched her. His jaws were twitching, and his voice kept breaking.

"You must understand that I'm not jealous, that's a nasty word. I can't be jealous, and believe that . . . I can't say what I feel, but this is awful . . . I'm not jealous, but I'm offended, humiliated that anybody dare think, that anybody dare look at you with eyes like that."

"Eyes like what?" said Kitty, trying as conscientiously as possible to recall every word and gesture of that evening and every shade implied in them.

In the very depths of her heart she did think there had been something precisely at the moment when Vasenka had followed her to the other end of the table; but she dared not admit it even to herself, and would have been even more unable to bring herself to say to him, and so increase his suffering.

"And what can there possibly be attractive about me as I am now? . . . "

"Ah!" he cried, clutching at his head, "you shouldn't say that! . . . If you had been attractive then . . . "

"Oh, no, Kostya, oh, wait a minute, oh, do listen!" she said, looking at him with an expression of compassionate pain. "Why, what can you be thinking about! When for me there's no one in the world, no one, no one! . . . Would you like me never to see anyone?"

For the first minute she had been offended at his jealousy; she was angry that the slightest amusement, even the most innocent, should be forbidden her; but now she would readily have sacrificed, not merely such trifles, but everything for his peace of mind, to save him from the agony he was suffering.

"You must understand the horror and absurdity of my position," he went on in a desperate whisper; "that he's in my house, that he's done nothing improper, after all, except his free and easy manner and the way he sits on his legs. He thinks it's the best possible form, and so I'm obliged to be civil to him."

"But, Kostya, you're exaggerating," said Kitty, at the bottom of her heart rejoicing at the depth of his love for her, shown now in his jealousy.

"The most awful part of it all is that you're just as you always are, and especially now when to me you're something sacred, and we're so happy, so particularly happy—and all of a sudden this trash . . . He's not trash; why should I abuse him? I have nothing to do with him. But why should my, and your, happiness . . . "

"Do you know, I understand now what it's all come from," Kitty was beginning.

"Well, what? What?"

"I saw how you looked while we were talking at supper."

"Well, well!" Levin said in dismay.

She told him what they had been talking about. And as she told him, she was breathless with emotion. Levin was silent for a time, then he scanned her pale and distressed face, and suddenly he clutched at his head.

"Katya, I've been worrying you! Darling, forgive me! It's madness! Katya, I'm a criminal. And how could you be so distressed at such idiocy?"

"Oh, I was sorry for you."

"For me? For me? How mad I am! . . . But why make you miserable? It's awful to think that any outsider can shatter our happiness."

"It's humiliating too, of course."

"Oh, then I'll keep him here all summer, and will overwhelm him with civility," said Levin, kissing her hands. "You shall see. Tomorrow . . . Oh, yes, we are going shooting tomorrow."

CHAPTER EIGHT

The next day, before the ladies were up, a shooting brake and a cart were at the door waiting for them, and Laska, aware since early morning that they were going shooting, after much whining and darting to and fro, had sat herself down in the cart beside the coachman, and, disapproving of the delay, was excitedly watching the door from which the sportsmen still did not come out. The first to come out was Vasenka Veslovsky, in new high boots that reached halfway up his thick thighs, in a green shirt, with a new leather cartridge belt, and in his Scotch cap with streamers, with a brand-new English hammerless gun without a sling. Laska flew up to welcome him and, jumping up, asked him in her own way whether the others were coming soon, but getting no answer, she returned to her observation post and sank into repose again, her head on one side and one ear pricked up to listen. At last the door opened with a creak, and Stepan Arkadyevich's spotted tan pointer, Krak, flew out, running round and round and turning over in the air. Stepan Arkadyevich himself followed, with a gun in his hand and a cigar in his mouth.

"Good dog, good dog, Krak!" he cried encouragingly to the dog, who put his paws up on his chest, catching at his game bag. Stepan Arkadyevich was dressed in rough leggings and linen bands wrapped around his feet, torn trousers, and a short coat. On his head there was a wreck of a hat of indefinite form, but his gun of a new patent was a perfect gem, and his game bag and cartridge belt, though worn, were of the very best quality.

Vasenka Veslovsky had no notion before that it was truly *chic* to be in tatters, but to have a shooting outfit of the best quality. He saw it now as he looked at Stepan Arkadyevich, radiant in his rags, graceful, well fed, and joyous, a typical gentleman. And he made up his mind that next time he went shooting he would certainly adopt the same get-up.

"Well, and what about our host?" he asked.

"A young wife," said Stepan Arkadyevich, smiling.

"Yes, and such a charming one!"

"He came down dressed. No doubt he's run up to her again."

Stepan Arkadyevich guessed right. Levin had run up again to his wife to ask her once more if she forgave him for his idiocy yesterday, and, moreover, to beg her for heaven's sake to be more careful. The important thing was for her to keep away from the children—they might any minute push against her. Then he had once more to hear her declare that she was not angry with him for going away for two days, and to beg her to be sure to send him a note the next morning by a servant on horseback, to write him, if only two words, to let him know that all was well with her.

Kitty was distressed, as she always was, at parting for a couple of days from her husband, but when she saw his animated figure, looking big and strong in his shooting boots and his white shirt and his radiant excitement, incomprehensible to her, she forgot her own chagrin for the sake of his pleasure, and said good-by to him cheerfully.

"Sorry, gentlemen!" he said, running out onto the steps. "Have you put the lunch in? Why is the chestnut on the right? Well, it doesn't matter. Laska, down; go and lie down!"

"Put it with the heifers," he said to the herdsman, who was waiting for him at the steps with some question. "Excuse me, here comes another villain."

Levin jumped out of the shooting brake, in which he had already taken his seat, to meet the carpenter, who came toward the steps with a ruler in his hand.

"You didn't come to the office yesterday, and now you're detaining me. Well, what is it?"

"Would your honor let me make another turning? It's only three steps to add. And we make it just fit at the same time. It would be much more convenient."

"You should have listened to me," Levin answered with annoyance. "I said fix the stringboards first and then fit the treads. Now there's no way of changing it . Do as I tell you, and make a new staircase."

The point was that in the lodge that was being built the carpenter had spoiled the staircase, fitting it together without calculating the elevation, so that the steps all sloped when put into place. Now the carpenter wanted to keep the same staircase, to add three steps.

"It will be much better."

"But where's your staircase going to reach with its three steps?"

"Why, my heavens, sir," the carpenter said with a contemptuous smile, "it comes out right at the very spot. It starts from the bottom," he said, with a persuasive gesture; "it will go up and up till it gets there."

"But three steps will add to the length, too . . . where is it to come out?"

"Why, to be sure, it'll start from the bottom and it's certain to get there," the carpenter said obstinately and convincingly.

"It'll reach the ceiling and go up the wall."

"Heavens, no, sir! Why, it'll go up till it gets there."

Levin took out a ramrod and began sketching the plan of the staircase in the dust.

"There, do you see?"

"As your honor likes," said the carpenter, with a sudden gleam in his eyes, obviously understanding the thing at last. "It seems it'll be best to make a new one."

"Well, then, do it as you're told," Levin shouted, seating himself in the shooting brake. "We're off! Hold the dogs, Filipp!"

Levin felt now, on leaving behind his family and all the household cares, such an eager sense of joy in life and expectation that he was not disposed to talk. Besides that, he had that feeling of concentrated excitement that every sportsman experiences as he approaches the scene of action. If he had anything on his mind at that moment, it was only the doubt of whether they would find anything in the Kolpensky marsh, whether Laska would show to advantage in comparison with Krak, and whether he would shoot well that day himself. Not to disgrace himself before a new spectator—not to be outdone by Oblonsky—that too was a thought that crossed his mind.

Oblonsky was feeling the same, and he too was not talkative.

Vasenka Veslovsky alone kept up a ceaseless flow of cheerful chatter. As he listened to him now, Levin felt ashamed to think how unfair he had been to him the day before. Vasenka was really a nice fellow, simple, good-hearted, and very good-humored. If Levin had met him before he was married, he would have made friends with him. Levin rather disliked his way of treating life as a never-ending holiday, and the sort of free and easy air of elegance about him. It was as though he assumed a high degree of importance in himself that could not be disputed, because he had long nails and a Scotch cap, and everything else to correspond; but this could be forgiven for the sake of his good nature and good breeding. Levin liked him for his good education, for speaking excellent French and English, and for being a man of the world.

Vasenka was extremely delighted with the left horse, a horse of the Don steppes. He kept praising him enthusiastically. "How fine it must be galloping over the steppes on a Cossack horse! Eh? Isn't it?" he said. He had imagined riding on a Cossack horse as something wild and romantic, and it turned out to be nothing of the sort. But his simplicity, particularly in conjunction with his good looks, his amiable smile, and the grace of his movements, was very attractive. Either because his nature was sympathetic to Levin, or because Levin was trying to atone for his sins of the previous evening by seeing nothing but what was good in him, Levin liked his company.

After they had driven about two miles from home, Veslovsky missed his cigars and wallet, and did not know whether he had lost them or left them on the table. In the pocketbook there were three hundred and seventy rubles, and so the matter could not be left in uncertainty.

"Do you know what, Levin, I'll gallop home on that left trace horse. That will be splendid, eh?" he said, preparing to get out.

"No, why should you?" answered Levin, calculating that Vasenka could hardly weigh less than two hundred and forty pounds. "I'll send the coachman."

The coachman rode back on the trace horse, and Levin himself drove the remaining pair.

CHAPTER NINE

"Well, now, what's our schedule? Tell us all about it," said Stepan Arkadyevich.

"Our plan is this. Now we're driving to Gvozdevo. In Gvozdevo there's a grouse marsh on this side, and beyond Gvozdevo come some magnificent snipe marshes where there are grouse too. It's hot now, and we'll get there—it's fifteen miles or so—toward evening and have some evening shooting; we'll spend the night there and go on tomorrow to the bigger marshes."

"And is there nothing on the way?"

"Yes; but we'll reserve ourselves; besides, it's hot. There are two nice little places, but I doubt there being anything to shoot."

Levin would himself have liked to go into these little places, but they were near home; he could shoot there any time, and they were only little places—there would hardly be room for three to shoot. And so, with some insincerity, he said that he doubted there being anything to shoot. When they reached a little marsh, Levin would have driven by, but Stepan Arkadyevich, with the experienced eye of a sportsman, at once detected reeds visible from the road.

"Shall we try that?" he said, pointing to the little marsh.

"Levin, do, please! How delightful!" Vasenka Veslovsky began begging, and Levin had to consent.

Before they had time to stop, the dogs had flown one before the other into the marsh.

"Krak! Laska! . . . "

The dogs came back.

"There won't be room for three. I'll stay here," said Levin, hoping they would find nothing but peesweeps, which had been flushed by the dogs and, turning over in their flight, were plaintively wailing above the marsh.

"No! Come along, Levin, let's go together!" Veslovsky called.

"Really, there's not room. Laska, back, Laska! You won't need another dog, will you?"

Levin remained with the brake, and looked enviously at the sportsmen. They walked right across the marsh. Except for a moorhen and peesweeps, one of which Vasenka killed, there was nothing in the marsh.

"Come, you see now that it was not that I grudged the marsh," said Levin, "only it's wasting time."

"Oh, no, it was fun all the same. Did you see us?" asked Vasenka Veslovsky, clambering awkwardly into the brake with his gun and his peesweep in his hands. "How splendidly I shot this bird! Didn't I? Well, shall we soon be getting to the real place?"

The horses started off suddenly, Levin knocked his head against the barrel of someone's gun, and there was the report of a shot. The gun did actually go off first, but that was not how it seemed to Levin. What happened was that Vasenka Veslovsky, while uncocking one trigger, had pulled the other. The charge flew into the ground without doing harm to anyone. Stepan Arkadyevich shook his head and laughed reprovingly at Veslovsky. But Levin had not the heart to reprove him. In the first place, any reproach would have seemed to be called forth by the danger he had incurred and the bump that had come up on Levin's forehead. And besides, Veslovsky was at first so naïvely distressed, and then laughed so good-humoredly and infectiously at their general dismay, that one could not but laugh with him.

When they reached the second marsh, which was fairly large and would inevitably take some time to go over, Levin tried to persuade them to pass it by. But Veslovsky again persuaded him. Again, as the marsh was narrow, Levin, like a good host, remained with the brake.

Krak made straight for some clumps of sedge. Vasenka Veslovsky was the first to run after the dog. Before Stepan Arkadyevich had time to come up, a grouse flew out. Veslovsky missed it and it flew into an unknown meadow. This grouse was left for Veslovsky to follow up. Krak found it again and pointed, and Veslovsky shot it and went back to the carriages. "Now you go and I'll stay with the horses," he said.

Levin had begun to feel the pangs of a sportsman's envy. He handed the reins to Veslovsky and walked into the marsh.

Laska, who had been plaintively whining and fretting against the injustice of her treatment, flew straight ahead to a promising place that Levin knew well, and that Krak had not yet come upon.

"Why don't you stop her?" shouted Stepan Arkadyevich.

"She won't scare them," answered Levin, sympathizing with his bitch's pleasure and hurrying after her.

As she came nearer and nearer to the familiar breeding places, there was more and more earnestness in Laska's exploration. A little marsh bird did not divert her attention for more than an instant. She circled once in front of the hummocks, was beginning again, and suddenly quivered with excitement and became motionless.

"Come, come, Stiva!" shouted Levin, feeling his heart beginning to beat more violently; and all of a sudden, as though some sort of shutter had been drawn back from his straining ears, all sounds, confused but loud, began to beat on his hearing, losing all sense of distance. He heard the steps of Stepan Arkadyevich, mistaking them for the tramp of the horses in the distance, he herd the brittle sound of the edge of a hummock on which he had trodden, taking this sound for the flying of a grouse. He heard too, not far behind him, a splashing in the water, which he could not explain to himself.

Picking his way, he moved up to the dog.

"Fetch it!"

Not a grouse but a snipe flew up from beside the dog. Levin had lifted his gun, but at the very instant when he was taking aim, the sound of splashing grew louder, came closer, and was joined with the sound of Veslovsky's voice, shouting something behind the snipe, but still he fired.

When he had made sure he had missed, Levin looked around and saw the horses and the brake not on the road but in the marsh.

Veslovsky, eager to see the shooting, had driven into the marsh, and got the horses stuck in the mud.

"Damn the fellow!" Levin said to himself as he went back to the carriage that had sunk in the mire. "What did you drive in for?" he said to him dryly, and calling the coachman, he began pulling the horses out.

Levin was vexed both at being hindered from shooting and at his horses getting stuck in the mud, and still more at the fact that neither Stepan Arkadyevich nor Veslovsky helped him and the coachman unharness the horses and get them out, since neither of them had the slightest notion of harnessing. Without uttering a syllable in reply to Vasenka's protestations that it had been quite dry there, Levin worked in silence with the coachman at extricating the horses. But then, as he got warm at the work and saw how assiduously Veslovsky was tugging at the brake by one of the mudguards, so that he finally broke it, Levin blamed himself for having under the influence of yesterday's feelings been too cold to Veslovsky, and tried to be particularly genial so as to smooth over his chilliness. When everything had been put right, and the carriage had been brought back to the road, Levin had the lunch served.

"*Bon appétit—bonne conscience! Ce poulet va tomber jusqu'au fond de mes bottes.*"[1] Vasenka, who had recovered his spirits, quoted the French saying as he finished his second chicken. "Well, now our troubles are over, now everything's going to go well. Only, to atone for my sins, I'm bound to sit on the box. That's so, eh? No, no! I'll be your Automedon.[2] You wait and see how I'll get you along," he answered, not letting go the rein, when Levin begged him to let the coachman drive. "No, I must atone for my sins, and I'm very comfortable on the box." And he drove.

Levin was a little afraid he would exhaust the horses, especially the chestnut, whom he did not know to hold in; but unconsciously he fell under the influence of his gaiety and listened to the songs he sang all the way on the box, or the stories he told, and his imitation of driving in the English fashion, four-in-hand; and it was in the very best of spirits that after lunch they drove to the Gvozdevo marsh.

CHAPTER TEN

Vasenka drove the horses so fast that they reached the marsh too early, while it was still hot.

As they drew near this real marsh, the chief aim of their expedition, Levin could not help considering how he could get rid of Vasenka and be free in his movements. Stepan Arkadyevich evidently

[1]"Good appetite—good conscience! This chicken will go down to the bottom of my boots."
[2]Charioteer of Achilles in Homer's *Iliad*.

had the same desire, and Levin saw on his face the look of anxiety always present in a true sportsman when beginning a shoot, together with a certain good-humored slyness characteristic of him.

"How shall we go? It's a splendid marsh, I see, and there are hawks," said Stepan Arkadyevich, pointing to two great birds hovering over the reeds. "Where there are hawks, there is sure to be game."

"Now, gentlemen," said Levin, pulling up his boots and examining the caps of his gun with rather a gloomy expression, "do you see those reeds?" He pointed to an oasis of blackish green in the huge half-mown wet meadow that stretched along the right bank of the river. "The marsh begins here, straight in front of us, do you see—where it is the greener? From here it runs to the right where the horses are: there are breeding places there, and grouse, and all around those reeds as far as that alder, and right up to the mill. Over there, do you see where the pools are? That's the best place. There I once shot seventeen snipe. We'll separate with the dogs and go in different directions, and then meet over there at the mill."

"Well, who shall go to the left and who to the right?" asked Stepan Arkadyevich. "It's wider to the right: you two go that way and I'll take the left," he said with apparent indifference.

"Fine! We'll make the bigger bag! Yes, come along, come along!" Vasenka exclaimed.

Levin could do nothing but agree, and they separated.

As soon as they entered the marsh, the two dogs began hunting about together and made toward the green, slime-covered pool. Levin knew Laska's method, wary and indefinite: he knew the place, too, and expected a whole covey of snipe.

"Veslovsky! Beside me, walk beside me!" he said in a faint voice to his companion splashing in the water behind him. Levin could not help feeling an interest in the direction his gun was pointed, after that casual shot near the Kolpensky marsh.

"Oh, I won't get in your way, don't trouble about me."

But Levin could not keep troubling, and recalling Kitty's words at parting: "Mind you don't shoot one another." The dogs came nearer and nearer, passed each other, each pursuing its own scent. The expectation of snipe was so intense that to Levin the squishing sound of his own heel as he drew it up out of the mire seemed to be the call of a snipe, and he clutched and pressed the butt of his gun.

"Bang! Bang!" sounded almost in his ear. Vasenka had fired at a flock of ducks which was hovering over the marsh and flying at that moment toward the sportsmen, far out of range. Before Levin had time to look around, there was the whir of one snipe, another, a third, and some eight more rose one after another.

Stepan Arkadyevich hit one at the very moment when it was beginning its zigzag movements, and the snipe fell in a heap into the mud. Oblonsky aimed deliberately at another, still flying low in the reeds, and together with the report of the shot, that snipe too fell, and it could be seen fluttering out where the sedge had been cut, its unhurt wing showing white beneath.

Levin was not so lucky: he aimed at his first bird too low, and missed; he aimed at it again, just as it was rising, but at that instant another snipe flew up at his very feet, distracting him so that he missed again.

While they were loading their guns, another snipe rose, and Veslovsky, who had time to load again, sent two charges of small shot into the water. Stepan Arkadyevich picked up his snipe, and with sparkling eyes looked at Levin.

"Well, now let us separate," said Stepan Arkadyevich, and limping on his left foot, holding his gun in readiness and whistling to his dog, he walked off in one direction. Levin and Veslovsky walked in the other.

It always happened with Levin that when his first shots were a failure he got excited and out of temper, and shot badly the whole day. So it was that day. The snipe showed themselves in numbers. They kept flying up from just under the dogs, from under the sportsmen's legs, and Levin might have retrieved his ill-luck. But the more he shot, the more he felt disgraced in the eyes of Veslovsky, who kept popping away merrily and indiscriminately, killing nothing, and not in the slightest abashed by it. Levin, in feverish haste, could not restrain himself, got more and more out of temper, and ended by shooting almost without a hope of hitting. Laska, indeed, seemed to understand this. She began looking more languidly, and gazed back at the sportsmen, as it were, with perplexity or reproach in her eyes. Shots followed shots in rapid succession. The smoke of the powder hung about the sportsmen, while in the great roomy net of the game bag there were only three light little snipe. And of these one had been killed by Veslovsky alone, and one by both of them together. Meanwhile from the other side of the marsh came the sound of Stepan Arkadyevich's shots, not frequent, but, as Levin imagined, well directed, for almost after each they heard "Krak, Krak, fetch!"

This excited Levin still more. The snipe were floating continually in the air over the reeds. Their whirring wings close to the earth, and their harsh cries high in the air, could be heard on all sides; the snipe that had risen first and flown up into the air settled again before the sportsmen. Instead of two hawks there were now dozens of them hovering with shrill cries over the marsh.

After walking through the larger half of the marsh, Levin and Veslovsky reached the place where the peasants' meadowland was divided into long strips reaching to the reeds, marked off in one place by the trampled grass, in another by a path mown through it. Half of these strips had already been mown.

Though there was not so much hope of finding birds in the uncut part as the cut part, Levin had promised Stepan Arkadyevich to meet him, and so he walked on with his companion through the cut and uncut patches.

"Hey, sportsmen!" shouted one of a group of peasants, sitting on an unharnessed cart; "come have some lunch with us! Have a drop!"

Levin looked around.

"Come along, it's all right!" shouted a merry-looking bearded peasant with a red face, showing his white teeth in a grin, and holding up a greenish bottle that flashed in the sunlight.

"*Qu'est-ce qu'ils disent?*"[1] asked Veslovsky.

"They invite you to have some vodka. Most likely they've been dividing the meadow into lots. I would have some," said Levin, not without some guile, hoping Veslovsky would be tempted by the vodka and go away to them.

"Why do they offer it?"

_____
[1]"What are they saying?"

"Oh, they're merry-making. Really, you should join them. You would be interested."

"*Allons, c'est curieux.*"[2]

"You go, you go, you'll find the way to the mill!" cried Levin, and looking around, he perceived with satisfaction that Veslovsky, bent and stumbling with weariness, holding his gun out at arm's length, was making his way out of the marsh toward the peasants.

"You come too!" the peasant shouted to Levin. "Never fear! Taste our pie!"

Levin felt a strong inclination to drink a little vodka and eat some bread. He was exhausted, and felt it a great effort to drag his staggering legs out of the mire, and for a minute he hesitated. But Laska was pointing. And immediately all his weariness vanished, and he walked lightly through the swamp toward the dog. A snipe flew up at his feet; he fired and killed it. Laska still pointed. "Fetch it!" Another bird flew up close to the dog. Levin fired. But it was an unlucky day for him; he missed it, and when he went to look for the one he had shot, he could not find that either. He wandered all about the reeds, but Laska did not believe he had shot it, and when he sent her to find it, she pretended to hunt for it, but did not really. And in the absence of Vasenka, on whom Levin threw the blame for his failure, things went no better. There were plenty of snipe still, but Levin made one miss after another.

The slanting rays of the sun were still hot; his clothes, soaked through with perspiration, stuck to his body; his left boot, full of water, weighed heavily on his leg and squeaked at every step; the sweat ran in drops down his nose of the smell of powder and stagnant water; his ears were ringing with the incessant whir of the snipe; he could not touch the barrels of his gun, they were so hot; his heart beat with short, rapid throbs; his hands shook with excitement; and his weary legs stumbled and staggered over the hillocks and in the swamp—but still he walked on and still he shot. At last, after a disgraceful miss, he flung his gun and hat on the ground.

"No, I must control myself," he said to himself. Picking up his gun and hat, he called Laska, and went out of the swamp. When he got to

[2]"Come, it's interesting."

dry ground he sat down, pulled off his boot and emptied it, then walked to the marsh, drank some stagnant-tasting water, moistened the heated barrels, and washed his face and hands. Feeling refreshed, he went back to the spot where a snipe had settled, firmly resolved to keep cool.

He tried to be calm, but it was the same again. His finger pulled the trigger before he had taken good aim at the bird. It got worse and worse.

He had only five birds in his game bag when he walked out of the marsh toward the alders where he was to rejoin Stepan Arkadyevich.

Before he caught sight of Stepan Arkadyevich he saw his dog. Krak darted out from behind the twisted root of an alder, black all over with the stinking mire of the marsh, and with the air of a conqueror sniffed at Laska. Behind Krak there came into view, in the shade of the alder tree, the stately figure of Stepan Arkadyevich. He came to meet him, red and perspiring, with unbuttoned collar, still limping in the same way.

"Well? You have been popping away!" he said, smiling good-humoredly.

"How have you got on?" queried Levin. But there was no need to ask, for he had already seen the full game bag.

"Oh, pretty fair."

He had fourteen birds.

"A splendid marsh! I've no doubt Veslovsky got in your way. It's awkward too, shooting with one dog," said Stepan Arkadyevich, to soften his triumph.

CHAPTER ELEVEN

When Levin and Stepan Arkadyevich reached the peasant's hut where Levin always used to stay, Veslovsky was already there. He was sitting in the middle of the hut, clinging with both hands to the bench from which he was being pulled by a soldier, the brother of the peasant's wife, who was helping him off with his slimy boots. Veslovsky was laughing his infectious, good-humored laugh.

"I've only just come. *Ils ont été charmants.*[1] Just imagine, they gave me drink, fed me! Such bread, it was exquisite! *Délicieux!* And the vodka, I never tasted any better. And they would not take a kopek for anything. And they kept saying: 'Excuse our homely ways.' "

"What should they take anything for? They were entertaining you, to be sure. Do you suppose they keep vodka for sale?" said the soldier, succeeding at last in pulling the soaked boot off the blackened stocking.

In spite of the dirtiness of the hut, which was all muddied by their boots and the filthy dogs licking themselves clean, and the smell of marsh mud and powder that filled the room, and the absence of knives and forks, the party drank their tea and ate their supper with a relish known only to sportsmen. Washed and clean, they went into a hay barn swept ready for them, where the coachman had been making up beds for the gentlemen.

Though it was dusk, not one of them wanted to go to sleep.

After exchanging reminiscences and anecdotes of guns, of dogs, and of former shooting parties, the conversation focused on a topic that interested all of them. After Vasenka had several times over expressed his appreciation of this delightful sleeping place among the fragrant hay, this delightful broken cart (he supposed it to be broken because the shafts had been taken out), of the good nature of the peasants who had treated him to vodka, of the dogs who lay at the feet of their respective masters, Oblonsky began telling them of a delightful shooting party at Malthus's, where he had stayed the previous summer.

Malthus was a well-known railway magnate. Stepan Arkadyevich described what grouse moors this Malthus had bought in Tverskoy province, and how they were preserved, and of the carriages and dogcarts in which the shooting party had been driven, and the luncheon pavilion that had been rigged up at the marsh.

"I don't understand you," said Levin, sitting up in the hay: "how is it such people don't disgust you? I can understand a lunch with Château Lafite is all very pleasant, but don't you dislike just that very sumptuousness? All these people, just like our liquor monopo-

[1] "They were charming."

lists in old days, get their money in a way that gains them the contempt of everyone. They don't care about this contempt, and then they use their dishonest gains to buy off the contempt they have deserved."

"Perfectly true!" chimed in Vasenka Veslovsky. "Perfectly! Oblonsky, of course, goes out of *bonhomie*,[2] but other people say: 'Well, Oblonsky stays with them . . .'"

"Not at all." Levin could hear that Oblonsky was smiling as he spoke. "I simply don't consider him more dishonest than any other wealthy merchant or nobleman. They've all made their money alike—by their work and their intelligence."

"Oh, by what work? Do you call it work to get hold of a concession and speculate with it?"

"Of course it's work. Work in the sense that if it were not for him and others like him there would have been no railways."

"But that's not work, like the work of a peasant or a scholar."

"Granted, but it's work in the sense that his activity produces a result—the railways. But of course you think the railways useless."

"No, that's another question; I am prepared to admit that they're useful. But all profit that is out of proportion to the labor expended is dishonest."

"But who is to define what is proportionate?"

"Making profit by dishonest means, by trickery," said Levin, conscious that he could not draw a distinct line between honesty and dishonesty. "Such as banking, for instance," he went on. "It's an evil—the amassing of huge fortunes without labor, just the same thing as with the liquor monopolies, it's only the form that's changed. *Le roi est mort, vive le roi!*[3] No sooner were the liquor monopolies abolished than the railways came up, and banking companies; that, too, is profit without work."

"Yes, that may all be very true and clever . . . Lie down, Krak!" Stepan Arkadyevich called to his dog, who was scratching and turning over the hay. He was obviously convinced of the correctness of

[2] "Good nature."
[3] "The king is dead, long live the king!"

his position, and so talked serenely and without haste. "But you have not drawn the line between honest and dishonest work. That I receive a bigger salary than my chief clerk, though he knows more about the work than I do—that's dishonest, I suppose?"

"I can't say."

"Well, but I can tell you: your receiving some five thousand, let's say, for your work on the land, while our host, the peasant here, however hard he works, can never get more than fifty rubles, is just as dishonest as my earning more than my chief clerk, and Malthus getting more than a railway mechanic. No, quite the contrary; I see that society takes up a sort of antagonistic attitude to these people, which is utterly baseless, and I hold there's envy at the bottom of it . . ."

"No, that's unfair," said Veslovsky; "how could envy come in? There is something ugly about that sort of business."

"You say," Levin went on, "that it's unjust for me to receive five thousand, while the peasant has fifty; that's true. It is unfair, and I feel it, but—"

"It really is. Why is it we spend our time riding, drinking, shooting, doing nothing, while they are forever at work?" said Vasenka Veslovsky, obviously for the first time in his life reflecting on the question, and consequently considering it with perfect sincerity.

"Yes, you feel it, but you don't give him your property," said Stepan Arkadyevich, intentionally, as it seemed, provoking Levin.

There had arisen of late something like a covert antagonism between the two brothers-in-law; as though, since they had married sisters, a kind of rivalry had sprung up between them as to which was ordering his life best, and now this hostility showed itself in the conversation, as it began to take a personal note.

"I don't give it away because no one demands that from me, and if I wanted to, I could not give it away," answered Levin, "and I have no one to give it to."

"Give it to this peasant; he would not refuse it."

"Yes, but how am I to give it up? Am I to go to him and make a deed of conveyance?"

"I don't know; but if you are convinced that you have no right . . ."

"I'm not at all convinced. On the contrary, I feel I have no right to give it up, that I have duties both to the land and to my family."

"No, excuse me, but if you consider this inequality unjust, why is it you don't act accordingly?"

"Well, I do act negatively on that idea, so far as not trying to increase the difference of position existing between him and me."

"No, excuse me, that's a paradox."

"Yes, there's something of a sophistry about that," Veslovsky agreed. "Ah! Our host; so you're not asleep yet?" he said to the peasant who came into the barn, opening the creaking door. "How is it you're not asleep?"

"No, how's one to sleep! I thought our gentlemen would be asleep, but I heard them chattering. I want to get a hook from here. She won't bite?" he added, stepping cautiously around Krak with his bare feet.

"And where are you going to sleep?"

"We are going to take the horses to graze tonight."

"Ah, what a night!" said Veslovsky, looking out through the huge frame of the open barn doors at a corner of the hut and the unharnessed brake that could be seen in the faint light of the evening glow. "But listen, there are women's voices singing, and not badly, either. Who's that singing, my friend?"

"The maidservants close by."

"Let's go, let's have a walk! We shan't go to sleep, you know. Oblonsky, come along!"

"If one could only do both, lie here and go," answered Oblonsky, stretching. "It's marvelous lying here."

"Well, I shall go by myself," said Veslovsky, getting up eagerly and putting on his shoes and stockings. "Good-by, gentlemen. If it's fun, I'll fetch you. You've treated me to some good sport, and I won't forget you."

"He really is a splendid fellow, isn't he?" said Stepan Arkadyevich, when Veslovsky had gone out and the peasant had closed the door after him.

"Yes, splendid," answered Levin, still thinking of the subject of their conversation just before. It seemed to him that he had clearly expressed his thoughts and feelings to the best of his capacity, and yet both his brother and Veslovsky, straightforward men and not fools, had said with one voice that he was comforting himself with sophistries. This disconcerted him.

"It's just this, my dear boy. One must do one of two things: either admit that the existing order of society is just, and then stick up for one's rights in it; or acknowledge that you are enjoying unjust privileges, as I do, and then enjoy them and all the pleasure you can out of them."

"No, if it were unjust, you could not enjoy these advantages and be satisfied—at least I could not. The important thing for me is to feel that I'm not guilty."

"What do you say, why not go after all?" said Stepan Arkadyevich, evidently weary of the strain of thought. "We won't go to sleep, you know. Come, let's go!"

Levin did not answer. What they had said in the conversation about his having acted justly only in a negative sense absorbed his thoughts. "Can it be that it's possible to be just only negatively?" he was asking himself.

"How strong the smell of the fresh hay is, though," said Stepan Arkadyevich, getting up. "There's not a chance of sleeping. Vasenka is up to something there. Do you hear the laughing and his voice?" Hadn't we better go? Come along!"

"No, I'm not coming," answered Levin.

"Surely that's not a matter of principle, too," said Stepan Arkadyevich, smiling, as he felt about in the dark for his cap.

"It's not a matter of principle, but why should I go?"

"But do you know, you are preparing trouble for yourself," said Stepan Arkadyevich, finding his cap and getting up.

"How so?"

"Do you suppose I don't see the line you've taken up with your wife? I heard how it's a question of the greatest consequence whether or not you're to be away for a couple of days' shooting. That's all very well as an idyllic episode, but for your whole life that won't do. A man must be independent; he has his masculine interests. A man has to be manly," said Oblonsky, opening the door.

"In what way? To go running after servant girls?" said Levin.

"Why not, if it amuses you? *Ça ne tire pas à conséquence.*[4] It won't do my wife any harm, and it'll amuse me. The great thing is to respect the sanctity of the home. There should be no disturbance in the home. But don't tie your own hands."

"Perhaps so," said Levin dryly, and he turned on his side. "Tomorrow, early, I want to go shooting, and I won't wake anyone, I'll set off at daybreak."

"*Messieurs, venez vite!*"[5] they heard the voice of Veslovsky coming back. "*Charmante!* I've made such a discovery. *Charmante!* A perfect Gretchen, and I've already made friends with her. Really, exceedingly pretty," he declared in a tone of approval, as though she had been made pretty entirely on his account, and he was expressing his satisfaction with the maker.

Levin pretended to be asleep, while Oblonsky, putting on his slippers and lighting a cigar, walked out of the barn, and soon their voices were lost.

For a long while Levin could not get to sleep. He heard the horses munching hay, then he heard the peasant and his elder boy getting ready for the night, and going off for the night watch with the beasts, then he heard the soldier arranging his bed on the other side of the barn, with his nephew, the younger son of their peasant host. He heard the boy in his shrill little voice telling his uncle what he thought about the dogs, who seemed to him huge and terrible creatures, and asking what the dogs were going to hunt next day, and the soldier, in a husky, sleepy voice, telling him the sportsmen were going in the morning to the marsh, and would shoot with their guns; and then, to check the boy's questions, he said, "Go to sleep, Vaska; or you'll catch it," and soon he began snoring himself, and everything was still. He could hear only the snort of the horses and the guttural cry of a snipe.

"Is it really only negative?" he repeated to himself. "Well, what of it? It's not my fault." And he began thinking about the next day.

"Tomorrow I'll go out early, and I'll make a point of keeping cool.

---

[4] "It's of no consequence."
[5] "Gentlemen, come quickly!"

There are lots of snipe; and there are grouse too. When I come back there'll be the note from Kitty. Yes, Stiva may be right, I'm not manly with her, I'm tied to her apron strings . . . Well, it can't be helped! Negative again . . ."

Half asleep, he heard the laughter and mirthful talk of Veslovsky and Stepan Arkadyevich. For an instant he opened his eyes: the moon was up, and in the open doorway, brightly lighted up by the moonlight, they were standing talking. Stepan Arkadyevich was saying something of the freshness of one girl, comparing her to a freshly shelled nut, and Veslovsky with his infectious laugh was repeating some words, probably said to him by a peasant: "Ah, you better get your own girl!" Levin, half asleep, said:

"Gentlemen, tomorrow before daylight!" and fell asleep.

CHAPTER TWELVE

Waking up at daybreak, Levin tried to wake his companions. Vasenka, lying on his stomach, with one leg in a stocking thrust out, was sleeping so soundly that he could elicit no response. Oblonsky, half asleep, declined to get up so early. Even Laska, who was asleep, curled up in the hay, got up unwillingly, and lazily stretched out and straightened her hind legs one after the other. Getting on his boots and stockings, taking his gun, and carefully opening the creaking door of the barn, Levin went out into the road. The coachmen were sleeping in their carriages, the horses were dozing. One was lazily eating oats, dipping its nose into the manger. It was still gray out of doors.

"Why are you up so early, my dear?" the old woman, their hostess, said, coming out of the hut and addressing him affectionately as an old friend.

"Going shooting, Granny. Do I go this way to the marsh?"

"Straight out at the back; by our threshing floor, my dear, and across hemp patches; there's a little footpath." Stepping carefully with her sunburned bare feet, the old woman conducted Levin, and moved back the fence for him by the threshing floor.

"Straight on and you'll come to the marsh. Our lads drove the cattle there yesterday evening."

Laska ran forward eagerly along the little path. Levin followed her with a light, rapid step, continually looking at the sky. He hoped the sun would not be up before he reached the marsh. But the sun did not delay. The moon, which had been bright when he went out, by now shone only like a crescent of quicksilver. The morning star, which one could not help seeing before, now had to be sought to be discerned at all. What were before undefined, vague blurs in the distant countryside, could now be distinctly seen. They were sheaves of rye. The dew, not visible till the sun was up, wet Levin's legs and his shirt above his belt in the high-growing, fragrant hemp patch, from which the pollen had already fallen out. In the transparent stillness of morning the smallest sounds were audible. A bee flew by Levin's ear with the whizzing sound of a bullet. He looked carefully, and saw a second and a third. They were all flying from the beehives behind the hedge, and they disappeared over the hemp patch in the direction of the marsh. The path led straight to the marsh. The marsh could be recognized by the mist which rose from it, thicker in one place and thinner in another, so that the reeds and willow bushes swayed like islands in this mist. At the edge of the marsh and the road, peasant boys and men, who had been herding for the night, were lying, and in the dawn all were asleep under their coats. Not far from them were three hobbled horses. One of them clanked a chain. Laska walked beside her master, pressing a little forward and looking around. Passing the sleeping peasants and reaching the first reeds, Levin examined his pistols and let off his dog. One of the horses, a sleek, dark-brown three-year-old, seeing the dog, started away, switched its tail, and snorted. The other horses too were frightened: splashing through the water with their hobbled legs, and drawing their hoofs out of the thick mud with a sucking sound, they bounded out of the marsh. Laska stopped, looking ironically at the horses and inquiringly at Levin. Levin patted Laska, and whistled as a sign that she might begin.

Laska ran joyfully and anxiously through the bog, which swayed under her.

Running into the marsh among the familiar scents of roots, marsh plants, and slime, and the unfamiliar smell of horse dung, Laska detected at once a smell that pervaded the whole marsh, the scent of that strong-smelling bird that always excited her more than any other. Here and there among the moss and marsh plants this scent was very strong, but it was impossible to determine in which direction it grew stronger or fainter. To find the direction, she had to go further to the lee of the wind. Not feeling the motion of her legs, Laska bounded with a stiff gallop, so that at each bound she could stop short, to the right, away from the morning wind that blew from the east, and turned facing the wind. Sniffing in the air with dilated nostrils, she felt at once that not only their tracks but also the birds themselves were here before her, and not one, but many. Laska slackened her speed. They were here, but where precisely she could not yet determine. To find the very spot, she began to make a circle, when suddenly her master's voice drew her off. "Laska! Here?" he asked, pointing her to a different direction. She stopped, asking him if she had better not go on doing as she had begun. But he repeated his command in an angry voice, pointing to a spot covered with water, where there could not be anything. She obeyed him, pretending she was looking so as to please him, went around it, and went back to her former position, and was at once aware of the scent again. Now when he was not hindering her, she knew what to do, and without looking at what was under her feet, and to her vexation stumbling over a high stump into the water but righting herself with her strong, supple legs, she began making the circle that was to make all clear to her. The scent of them reached her, stronger and stronger, and more and more defined, and all at once it became perfectly clear to her that one of them was here, behind this tuft of reeds, five paces in front of her; she stopped, and her whole body was still and rigid. On her short legs she could see nothing in front of her, but by the scent she knew it was sitting not more than five paces off. She stood still, feeling more and more conscious of it, and enjoying it in anticipation. Her tail was stretched straight and tense, and wagging only at the extreme end. Her mouth was slightly open, her ears raised. One ear had been turned wrong side out as she ran up, and she breathed heavily but warily, and still more warily looked around, but more with her eyes than her head, to her master. He was coming along with the face she knew so well, though the eyes were always terrible to her. He stumbled over the stump as he came, and moved, as she thought, extraordinarily slowly. She thought he came slowly, but he was running.

Noticing Laska's peculiar posture as she crouched on the ground, as if dragging her hind legs along the ground, and with her mouth half open, Levin knew she was pointing at grouse, and with an inward prayer for luck, especially with the first bird, he ran up to her. Coming quite close to her, he could from his height look beyond her, and he saw with his eyes what she was seeing with her nose. In a space between two little thickets he could see a snipe. Turning its head, it was listening. Then lightly preening and folding its wings, it disappeared around a corner with a clumsy wag of its tail.

"Fetch it, fetch it!" shouted Levin, giving Laska a shove from behind.

"But I can't go," thought Laska. "Where am I to go? From here I feel them, but if I move forward I shall know nothing of where they are or who they are." But then he shoved her with his knee, and, in an excited whisper, said, "Fetch it, Laska."

"Well, if that's what he wishes, I'll do it, but I can't answer for myself now," she thought, and darted forward as fast as her legs would carry her between the hummocks. She scented nothing now; she could only see and hear, without understanding anything.

Ten paces from her former place a snipe rose with a guttural cry and the peculiar whirring sound of its wings. And immediately after the shot it splashed heavily with its white breast on the wet mire. Another bird did not linger, but rose behind Levin without the dog. When Levin turned toward it, it was already some way off. But his shot caught it. Flying twenty paces further, it rose upward, and turning over and over like a ball, it dropped heavily on a dry place.

"Now we're in business!" thought Levin, packing the warm, fat snipe into his game bag. "Eh, Laska, will it be good?"

When Levin, after loading his gun, moved on, the sun had fully risen, though invisible behind the clouds. The moon had lost all of its luster, and was like a white cloud in the sky. Not a single star could be seen. The sedge, silvery with dew before, now shone like gold.

The stagnant pools were all like amber. The blue of the grass had changed to yellow-green. The marsh birds twittered and swarmed about the brook and upon the bushes that glittered with dew and cast long shadows. A hawk woke up and settled on a haycock, turning its head from side to side and looking discontentedly at the marsh. Crows were flying about the field, and a bare-legged boy was driving the horses to an old man who had got up from under his long coat and was combing his hair. The smoke from the gun was white as milk over the green of the grass.

One of the boys ran up to Levin.

"Uncle, there were ducks here yesterday!" he shouted to him, and he walked a little way off behind him.

And Levin was doubly pleased, in sight of the boy, who expressed his approval, at killing three snipe, one after another.

CHAPTER THIRTEEN

The huntsman's saying, that if the first beast or the first bird is not missed, the day will be lucky, turned out to be true.

At ten o'clock Levin, weary, hungry, and happy after tramping twenty miles, returned to his night's lodging with nineteen head of fine game and one duck, which he tied to his belt, as it would not go into the game bag, His companions had long been awake, and had had time to get hungry and have breakfast.

"Wait a while, wait a while, I know there are nineteen," said Levin, counting again the snipe and double snipe that looked so much less handsome now, bent and dry and bloodstained, with heads crooked aside, than they did when they were flying.

The number was verified, and Stepan Arkadyevich's envy pleased Levin. He was pleased, too, on returning, to find that the man Kitty sent with a note was already there.

"I am perfectly well and happy. If you were uneasy about me, you can feel easier than ever. I've a new bodyguard, Marya Vlasyevna"— this was the midwife, a new and important person in Levin's domestic life. "She has come to have a look at me. She found me perfectly well, and we have kept her till you are back. All are happy and well, and please, don't be in a hurry to come back, but if the sport is good, stay another day."

These two pleasures, his lucky shooting and the letter from his wife, were so great that two slightly disagreeable incidents passed lightly over Levin. One was that the chestnut trace-horse was off his feed and out of sorts. The coachman said, "He was overdriven yesterday, Konstantin Dmitrievich. Yes, absolutely! Seven miles like that, without sense!"

The other unpleasant incident, which for the first minute destroyed his good humor, though later he laughed at it a great deal, was to find that of all the provisions Kitty had provided in such abundance that one would have thought there was enough for a week, nothing was left. On his way back, tired and hungry, from shooting, Levin had so distinct a vision of meat pies that as he approached the hut he seemed to smell and taste them, as Laska had smelled the game, and he immediately told Filipp to give him some. It appeared that there were no pies left, not even any chicken.

"Well, this fellow's appetite!" said Stepan Arkadyevich, laughing and pointing at Vasenka Veslovsky. "I never suffer from loss of appetite, but he's really marvelous!"

"Well, it can't be helped," said Levin, looking gloomily at Veslovsky. "Well, Filipp, give me some beef, then."

"The beef's been eaten, and the bones given to the dogs," answered Filipp.

Levin was so hurt that he said, in a tone of vexation, "You might have left me something!" and he felt ready to cry.

"Then put away the game," he said in a shaking voice to Filipp, trying not to look at Vasenka, "and cover them with some nettles. And you might at least ask for some milk for me."

But when he had drunk some milk and appeased his hunger thus, he felt ashamed of having shown his annoyance to a stranger, and he began to laugh at his hungry hostility.

In the evening they went shooting again, and Veslovsky had several successful shots and at night they drove home.

Their homeward journey was as lively as their drive out had been. Veslovsky sang songs and related with enjoyment his adventures with the peasants, who had regaled him with vodka, and said to him, "No offense meant," and his night's adventures, the games, and the servant girl and the peasant who had asked him was he married, and on learning that he was not, said to him, "Well, mind you don't run after other men's wives—you'd better get one of your own." These words had particularly amused Veslovsky.

"Altogether, I've enjoyed our outing very much. And you, Levin?"

"I have, very much," Levin said quite sincerely. It was particularly delightful to him to have got rid of the hostility he had been feeling toward Vasenka Veslovsky at home, and to feel instead the most friendly disposition toward him.

CHAPTER FOURTEEN

The next morning at ten o'clock Levin, who had already made the rounds of the estate, knocked at the room where Vasenka had been put for the night.

"*Entrez!*" Veslovsky called to him. "Excuse me, I've only just finished my ablutions," he said, smiling, standing before him in his underclothes only.

"Don't mind me, please." Levin sat down on the window sill. "Have you slept well?"

"Like the dead. What sort of day is it for shooting?"

"What will you take, tea or coffee?"

"Neither. I'll wait till lunch. I'm really ashamed. I suppose the ladies are up? A walk now would be nice. Show me your horses."

After walking about the garden, visiting the stable, and even doing some gymnastic exercises together on the parallel bars, Levin returned to the house with his guest, and went with him into the drawing room.

"We had splendid shooting and so many delightful experiences!" said Veslovsky, going up to Kitty, who was sitting at the samovar. "What a pity ladies are cut off from these delights!"

"Well, I suppose he must say something to the lady of the house," Levin said to himself. Again it seemed to him that there was something in the smile, in the all-conquering air with which their guest addressed Kitty.

The princess, sitting on the other side of the table with Marya Vlasyevna and Stepan Arkadyevich, called Levin to her side, and began to talk to him about moving to Moscow for Kitty's confinement, and getting rooms ready for them. Just as Levin had disliked all the trivial preparations for his wedding, as detracting from the grandeur of the event, now he felt still more offensive the preparations for the approaching birth, the date of which they decided, it seemed, on their fingers. For a long time he tried to turn a deaf ear to these discussions on the best methods of swaddling the new baby; tried to turn away and avoid seeing the mysterious, endless strips of knitting, the triangular pieces of linen, and so on, to which Dolly attached special importance. The birth of a son (he was certain it would be a son) which was promised him, but which he still could not believe in—so marvelous did it seem—presented itself to his mind, on one hand as a happiness so immense and therefore so incredible, on the other as an event so mysterious that this assumption of a definite knowledge of what would be, and consequent preparation for it—as for something ordinary that did happen to people—seemed shocking and degrading to him.

But the princess did not understand his feelings, and put down his reluctance to think and talk about it to carelessness and indifference, and so she gave him no peace. She had commissioned Stepan Arkadyevich to look for an apartment, and now she called Levin to her.

"I know nothing about it, Princess. Do as you think fit," he said.

"You must decide when you will move."

"I really don't know. I know millions of children are born away from Moscow, and doctors . . . why . . . "

"But if so . . . "

"Oh, no, as Kitty wishes."

"We can't talk to Kitty about it! Do you want me to frighten her? Why, this spring Natalia Golitsyna died from having an ignorant doctor."

"I will do just what you say," he said gloomily.

The princess began talking to him, but he did not hear her.

Though the conversation with the princess had indeed disturbed him, he was gloomy, not on account of that conversation, but from what he saw at the samovar.

"No, it's impossible," he thought, glancing now and then at Vasenka bending over Kitty, telling her something with his charming smile, and at her, flushed and agitated.

There was something indecent in Vasenka's attitude, in his eyes, in his smile. Levin even saw something indecent in Kitty's attitude and look. And again the light died away in his eyes. Again, as before, all of a sudden, without the slightest transition, he felt cast down from a pinnacle of happiness, peace, and dignity into an abyss of despair, rage, and humiliation. Again everything and everyone had become hateful to him.

"You do just as you think best, Princess," he said again, looking around.

" 'O heavy art thou, cap of Monomach,' "[1] Stepan Arkadyevich said playfully, hinting, evidently, not simply at the princess's conversation, but at the cause of Levin's agitation, which he had noticed.

"How late you are today, Dolly!"

Everyone got up to greet Darya Aleksandrovna. Vasenka rose only for an instant, and with the lack of courtesy to ladies characteristic of the modern young man, he scarcely bowed, and resumed his conversation again, laughing at something.

"I've been worn out by Masha. She did not sleep well, and is dreadfully petulant this morning," said Dolly.

The conversation Vasenka had started with Kitty was running on the same lines as on the previous evening, discussing Anna, and whether love is to be put higher than worldly considerations. Kitty disliked the conversation, and she was disturbed both by the subject and the tone in which it was conducted, and also by the knowledge of the effect it would have on her husband. But she was too simple and innocent to know how to cut short this conversation, or even to conceal the superficial pleasure afforded her by the young man's very obvious admiration. She wanted to stop it, but she did not know what to do. Whatever she did she knew would be observed by her hus-

[1]From Pushkin's *Boris Godunov*.

band, and the worst interpretation put on it. And, in fact, when she asked Dolly what was wrong with Masha, and Vasenka, waiting till this uninteresting conversation was over, began to gaze indifferently at Dolly, the question struck Levin as an unnatural and disgusting piece of hypocrisy.

"What do you say, shall we go and look for mushrooms today?" said Dolly.

"By all means, please, and I shall come too," said Kitty, and she blushed. She wanted from politeness to ask Vasenka whether he would come, and she did not ask him. "Where are you going, Kostya?" she asked her husband with a guilty face, as he passed by her with a resolute step. This guilty air confirmed all his suspicions.

"The mechanic came when I was away; I haven't seen him yet," he said, not looking at her.

He went downstairs, but before he had time to leave his study he heard his wife's familiar footsteps running with reckless speed to him.

"What do you want?" he said to her shortly. "We are busy."

"I beg your pardon," she said to the German mechanic; "I want a few words with my husband."

The German got up to go, but Levin said to him:

"Don't bother."

"The train is at three?" the German asked. "I mustn't be late."

Levin, not answering him, walked out with his wife.

"Well, what have you to say to me?" he said to her in French.

He did not look her in the face, for he had no wish to see that she was trembling all over, and had a piteous, crushed look.

"I . . . I want to say that we can't go on like this; that this is misery . . ." she said.

"The servants are there in the pantry," he said angrily; "don't make a scene."

"Well, let's go in here!"

They were standing in the passage. Kitty would have gone into the next room, but the English governess was giving Tanya a lesson there.

"Well, come into the garden."

In the garden they came upon a peasant weeding the path. And no longer considering that the peasant could see her tear-stained and his agitated face, that they looked like people fleeing from some disaster, they went on with rapid steps, feeling that they must talk out and clear up misunderstandings, must be alone together, and so get rid of the misery they were both feeling.

"We can't go on like this! It's misery! I am wretched; you are wretched. What for?" she said, when they had at last reached a secluded garden seat at a turn in the lime-tree avenue.

"But tell me one thing: wasn't there in his tone something improper, indecent, horribly humiliating?" he said, standing before her again in the same position, with his fists pressing his chest, as he had stood before her that night.

"Yes," she said in a shaking voice; "but, Kostya, surely you see I'm not to blame? All morning I've been trying to adopt a tone . . . but such people . . . Why did he come? How happy we were!" she said, breathless with the sobs that shook her.

Although nothing had been pursuing them, and there was nothing to run away from, and they could not possibly have found anything very delightful on that garden seat, the gardener saw with astonishment that they passed him on their way home with comforted and radiant faces.

CHAPTER FIFTEEN

After escorting his wife upstairs, Levin went to Dolly's part of the house. Darya Aleksandrovna, for her part, was in great distress too that day. She was walking about the room, talking angrily to a little girl who stood in the corner howling.

"And you shall stand all day in the corner, and have your dinner all alone, and not see one of your dolls, and I won't make you a new frock," she said, not knowing how to punish her.

"Oh, she is a disgusting child!" She turned to Levin. "Where does she get such wicked propensities?"

"Why, what has she done?" Levin said without much interest, for he had wanted to ask her advice, and so was annoyed that he had come at an unlucky moment.

"Grisha and she went into the raspberries, and there . . . I can't tell you what she did. It's a thousand pities Miss Elliot's not with us. This one notices nothing—she's an automaton . . . *Figurez-vous que la petite . . .* "[1]

And Darya Aleksandrovna described Masha's crime.

"That proves nothing; it's not a question of evil propensities at all, it's simply mischief," Levin assured her.

"But you are upset about something? What have you come for?" asked Dolly. "What's going on there?"

And in the tone of her question Levin heard that it would be easy for him to say what he had meant to say.

"I've not been in there, I've been alone in the garden with Kitty. We've had a quarrel for the second time since . . . Stiva came."

Dolly looked at him with her shrewd, comprehending eyes.

"Come, tell me, honestly, has there been . . . not in Kitty, but in that gentleman's behavior, a tone which might be unpleasant—not unpleasant, but horrible, offensive to a husband?"

"You mean, how shall I say . . . Stay, stay in the corner!" she said to Masha, who, detecting a faint smile on her mother's face, had been turning around. "The opinion of the world would be that he is behaving as young men do behave. *Il fait la cour à une jeune et jolie femme,*[2] and a husband who's a man of the world should only be flattered by it."

"Yes, yes," said Levin gloomily; "but you noticed it?"

"Not only I, but Stiva noticed it. Just after breakfast he said to me in so many words, *Je crois que Veslovsky fait un petit brin de cour à Kitty.*"[3]

"Well, that's all right, then; now I'm satisfied. I'll tell him to leave," said Levin.

"What do you mean! Are you crazy?" Dolly cried in horror. "Nonsense, Kostya, only think!" she said, laughing. "You can go now to Fanny," she said to Masha. "No, if you wish it, I'll speak to Stiva. He'll take him away. He can say you're expecting visitors. I don't think he fits into the house anyway."

"No, no, I'll do it myself."

[1]"Just imagine, the child."
[2]"He pays court to a young and pretty woman."
[3]"I believe Veslovsky is courting Kitty a tiny bit."

"But you'll quarrel with him?"

"Not at all. I'll enjoy it," Levin said, his eyes flashing with real enjoyment. "Come, forgive her, Dolly, she won't do it again," he said of the little sinner, who had not gone to Fanny, but was standing irresolutely before her mother, waiting and looking up from under her brows to catch her mother's eye.

The mother glanced at her. The child broke into sobs, hid her face on her mother's lap, and Dolly laid her thin, tender hand on her head.

"And what is there in common between us and him?" thought Levin, and he went off to look for Veslovsky.

As he passed through the passage he gave orders for the carriage to be made ready for the drive to the station.

"The spring was broken yesterday," said the footman.

"Well, the covered trap, then, and hurry up. Where's the visitor?"

"The gentleman's gone to his room."

Levin came upon Veslovsky at the moment when the latter, having unpacked his things from his trunk and laid out some new songs, was trying on leather gaiters to get ready to go riding.

Whether there was something exceptional in Levin's face, or that Vasenka was himself conscious that *ce petit brin de cour* he was making was out of place in this family, he was somewhat (as much as a young man in society can be) disconcerted at Levin's entrance.

"You ride in gaiters?"

"Yes, it's much cleaner," said Vasenka, putting his fat leg on a chair, fastening the bottom hook, and smiling with simple-hearted good humor.

He was undoubtedly a good-natured fellow, and Levin felt sorry for him and ashamed of himself, as his host, when he saw the shy look on Vasenka's face.

On the table lay a piece of stick which they had broken together that morning, trying their strength. Levin took the fragment in his hands and began smashing it up, breaking bits off the stick, not knowing how to begin.

"I wanted . . . " He paused, but suddenly, remembering Kitty and everything that had happened, he said, looking him resolutely in the face: "I have ordered the carriage for you."

"How so?" Vasenka began in surprise. "To drive where?"

"For you to drive to the station," Levin said gloomily.

"Are you going away, or has something happened?"

"It happens that I expect visitors," said Levin, his strong fingers more and more rapidly breaking off the ends of the split stick. "And I'm not expecting visitors, and nothing has happened, but I beg you to go away. You can explain my rudeness as you like."

Vasenka drew himself up.

"I beg you to explain . . . " he said with dignity, understanding at last.

"I can't explain," Levin said softly and deliberately, trying to control the trembling of his jaw; "and you'd better not ask."

And as the split ends were all broken off, Levin clutched the thick ends in his fingers, broke the stick in two, and carefully caught the end as it fell.

Probably the sight of those tense arms, of the muscles he had proved that morning at gymnastics, of the glittering eyes, the soft voice, and the quivering jaw, convinced Vasenka better than any words. He bowed, shrugging his shoulders and smiling contemptuously.

"Can I not see Oblonsky?"

The shrug and the smile did not irritate Levin. "What else was there for him to do?" he thought.

"I'll send him to you at once."

"What madness is this?" Stepan Arkadyevich said when, after hearing from his friend that he was being turned out of the house, he found Levin in the garden, where he was walking about waiting for his guest's departure. *"Mais c'est ridicule!* What fly has stung you? *Mais c'est du dernier ridicule!*[*] What did you think, if a young man . . . "

But the place where Levin had been stung was evidently still sore, for he turned pale again when Stepan Arkadyevich began to enlarge on his argument, and he cut him short.

"Please don't go into it! I can't help it. I feel ashamed of how I'm treating you and him. But it won't, I imagine, grieve him greatly to go, and his presence was distasteful to me and to my wife."

[*]"But it's ridiculous . . . But it's most ridiculous."

"But it's insulting to him! *Et plus c'est ridicule.*"[5]

"And to me it's both insulting and distressing. And I'm not to blame in any way, so there's no need for me to suffer."

"Well, this I didn't expect of you! *On peut-être jaloux, mais à ce point, c'est du dernier ridicule!*"[6]

Levin turned quickly and walked away from him to the far end of the avenue, and he went on walking up and down alone. Soon he heard the rumble of the trap, and from behind the trees, he could see Vasenka, sitting in the hay (unluckily there was no seat in the trap) in his Scotch cap, being driven along the avenue, jolting up and down over the ruts.

"What's this?" Levin thought, when a footman ran out of the house and stopped the trap. It was the mechanic, whom Levin had totally forgotten. The mechanic, bowing low, said something to Veslovsky, then clambered into the trap, and they drove off together.

Stepan Arkadyevich and the princess were much upset by Levin's action. And he himself felt not only in the highest degree *ridicule*, but also utterly guilty and disgraced. But remembering what misery he and his wife had been through, when he asked himself how he would act another time, he answered that he would do the same again.

In spite of all this, toward the end of that day, everyone except the princess, who could not pardon Levin's action, became extraordinarily lively and good-humored, like children after a punishment or grownups after a dreary, ceremonious reception, so that by evening Vasenka's dismissal was spoken of, in the absence of the princess, as though it were some remote event. And Dolly, who had inherited her father's gift of humorous story-telling, made Varenka helpless with laughter as she related for the third and fourth time, always with fresh humorous additions, how she had only just put on her new bows for the benefit of the visitor, when, on going into the drawing room, she suddenly heard the rumble of the wagon. And who should be in the wagon but Vasenka himself, with his Scotch cap, and his songs and his gaiters and all, sitting in the hay.

[5]"Besides, it's ridiculous."
[6]"One may be jealous, but to such a point is most ridiculous."

"If only you'd ordered out the carriage! But no! And then I hear: 'Stop!' 'Oh,' I thought, 'they've relented.' I look out, and there I see a fat German sit down beside him, and they drive off together . . . And my new bows were all for nothing! . . . "

CHAPTER SIXTEEN

Darya Aleksandrovna carried out her intention and went to see Anna. She was sorry to annoy her sister and to do anything Levin disliked. She quite understood how right the Levins were in not wishing to have anything to do with Vronsky. But she felt she must go and see Anna, and show her that her feelings could not be changed, in spite of the change in her position. That she might be independent of the Levins in this expedition, Darya Aleksandrovna sent to the village to hire horses for the drive; but Levin, learning of it, went to her to protest.

"What makes you suppose that I dislike your going? But, even if I did dislike it, I would still more dislike your not taking my horses," he said. "You never told me that you were going for certain. Hiring horses in the village is distasteful to me, and, what's more important, they'll undertake the job and never get you there. I have horses. And if you don't want to hurt me, you'll take mine."

Darya Aleksandrovna had to consent, and on the day fixed, Levin had ready for his sister-in-law a set of four horses and a change of horses waiting at the post station, getting them together from the farm and saddle horses—not at all a smart-looking set, but capable of taking Darya Aleksandrovna the whole distance in a single day. At that moment, when horses were needed for both the princess and the midwife, it was a difficult matter for Levin to decide on the number, but the duties of hospitality would not let him allow Darya Aleksandrovna to hire horses when staying in his house. Moreover, he was well aware that the twenty rubles that would be asked for the journey was a serious matter for her; Darya Aleksandrovna's financial affairs, which were in a very unsatisfactory state, were taken to heart by the Levins as if they were their own.

Darya Aleksandrovna, on Levin's advice, started before daybreak.

The road was good, the carriage comfortable, the horses trotted along merrily, and on the box, besides the coachman, sat the office clerk, whom Levin was sending instead of a groom for greater security. Darya Aleksandrovna dozed and waked only on reaching the inn where the horses were to be changed.

After drinking tea at the same well-to-do peasant's with whom Levin had stayed on the way to Sviazhsky's, and chatting with the women about their children and with the old man about Count Vronsky, whom the latter praised very highly, Darya Aleksandrovna, at ten o'clock, went on again. At home, looking after her children, she had no time to think. So now, after this journey of four hours, all the thoughts she had suppressed before rushed swarming into her brain, and she thought over her whole life as she never had before, and from the most different points of view. Her thoughts seemed strange even to herself. At first she thought about the children, about whom she was uneasy, although the princess and Kitty (she counted more upon her) had promised to look after them. "If only Masha does not start up with her naughty tricks, if Grisha isn't kicked by a horse, and Lily's stomach isn't upset again!" she thought. But these questions of the present were replaced by questions of the immediate future. She began thinking about how she had to get a new apartment in Moscow for the coming winter, reupholster the drawing-room furniture, and make her elder girl a cloak. Then questions of the more remote future occurred to her: how she was to place her children in the world. "The girls are all right," she thought; "but the boys?"

"It's very well that I'm teaching Grisha, but of course that's only because I am free myself now, I'm not with child. Stiva, of course, there's no counting on. And with the help of kind friends I can bring them up; but if there's another baby coming? . . . " And the thought struck her how untruly it was said that the curse laid on woman was that in sorrow she should bring forth children.

"The birth itself, that's nothing; but the months of carrying the child—that's what's so intolerable," she thought, picturing to herself her last pregnancy, and the death of the last baby. And she recalled the conversation she had just had with the young woman at the inn. On being asked whether she had any children, the handsome young woman had answered cheerfully:

"I had a girl baby, but God set me free; I buried her last Lent."

"Well, did you grieve very much for her?" asked Darya Aleksandrovna.

"Why grieve? The old man has grandchildren enough as it is. It was only trouble. No working, no anything. Only tied hand and foot."

This answer had struck Darya Aleksandrovna as revolting in spite of the good-natured and pleasing face of the young woman; but now she could not help recalling those words. In those cynical words there was indeed a grain of truth.

"Yes, altogether," thought Darya Aleksandrovna, looking back over her whole existence during those fifteen years of her married life, "pregnancy, sickness, dullness of mind, indifference to everything, and most of all—disfigurement. Kitty, young and pretty as she is, even Kitty has lost her looks; and I when I'm with child become hideous, I know it. The birth, the agony, the hideous agonies, that last moment . . . then the nursing, the sleepless nights, the fearful pains . . . "

Darya Aleksandrovna shuddered at the mere recollection of the pain from sore nipples which she had suffered with almost every child. "Then the children's illness, that everlasting apprehension; then bringing them up; evil propensities" (she thought of little Masha's crime among the raspberries), "education, Latin—it's all so incomprehensible and difficult. And on top of it all, the death of these children." And there rose again before her imagination the cruel memory, which always tore her mother's heart, of the death of her last little baby, who had died of croup; his funeral, the callous indifference of all at the little pink coffin, and her own torn heart, and her lonely anguish at the sight of the pale little brow fringed with curls, and the open, surprised little mouth seen in the coffin at the moment when it was being covered with the little pink lid with a cross braided on it.

"And all this, what's it for? What is to come of it all? That I'm wasting my life, never having a moment's peace, either with child, or nursing a child, forever irritable, peevish, wretched myself and worrying others, repulsive to my husband, while the children are growing up unhappy, badly educated and utterly poor. Even now, if it weren't for spending the summer at the Levins', I don't know how we would be managing to live. Of course Kostya and Kitty have so much tact that we don't feel it; but it can't go on. They'll have children, they won't be able to keep us; it's a drag on them as it is. How is Papa, who has hardly anything left for himself, to help us? So that I can't even bring the children up by myself, and may find it hard with the help of other people, at the cost of humiliation. Why, even if we suppose the greatest good luck, that the children don't die, and I bring them up somehow, at the very best they'll simply be decent people. That's all I can hope for. And to gain simply that—what agonies, what toil! . . . One's whole life ruined!" Again she recalled what the young peasant woman had said, and again she was revolted at the thought; but she could not help admitting that there was a grain of brutal truth in the words

"Is it far now, Mikhail?" Darya Aleksandrovna asked the office clerk, to turn her mind from thoughts that were frightening her.

"From this village, they say, it's five miles." The carriage drove along the village street and onto a bridge. On the bridge was a crowd of peasant women with ready-twisted sheaf binders on their shoulders, gaily and noisily chattering. They stood still on the bridge, staring inquisitively at the carriage. All the faces turned to Darya Aleksandrovna looked to her healthy and happy, making her envious of their enjoyment of life. "They're all living, they're all enjoying life," Darya Aleksandrovna still mused when she had passed the peasant women and was driving uphill again at a trot, seated comfortably on the soft springs of the old carriage, "while I, let out, as it were, from prison, from the world of worries that fret me to death, am only looking about me now for an instant. They all live; those peasant women and my sister Natalie and Varenka and Anna, whom I am going to see—all, but not I.

"And they attack Anna. What for? Am I any better? I have, anyway, a husband I love—not as I would like to love him, still I do love him, while Anna never loved hers. How is she to blame? She wants to live. God has put that in our hearts. Very likely I should have done the same. Even to this day I don't feel sure I did right in listening to her at that terrible time when she came to me in Moscow. I ought then to have cast off my husband and have been loved the real way.

And is it any better as it is? I don't respect him. He's necessary to me," she thought about her husband, "and I put up with him. Is that any better? At that time I could still have been admired, I had beauty left me," Darya Aleksandrovna pursued her thoughts, and felt a sudden desire to look at herself in a mirror. She had a traveling mirror in her hand bag, and she wanted to take it out; but looking at the backs of the coachman and the swaying office clerk, she felt that she would be ashamed if either of them were to look around, and she did not take out the mirror.

But without looking in the mirror, she thought that even now it was not too late; and she thought of Sergey Ivanovich, who was always particularly attentive to her, of Stiva's good-hearted friend Turovtsyn, who had helped her nurse her children through scarlet fever, and was in love with her. And there was someone else, a quiet young man who—her husband had told her as a joke—thought her more beautiful than either of her sisters. And the most passionate and impossible romances rose before Darya Aleksandrovna's imagination. "Anna did quite right, and certainly I shall never reproach her for it. She is happy, she makes another person happy, and she's not broken down as I am, but most likely just as she always was—bright, clever, open to every impression," thought Darya Aleksandrovna, and a sly smile curved her lips, for, as she pondered on Anna's love affair, Darya Aleksandrovna constructed on parallel lines an almost identical love affair for herself, with an imaginary composite figure, the ideal man who was in love with her. She, like Anna, confessed the whole affair to her husband. And the amazement and perplexity of Stepan Arkadyevich at this avowal made her smile.

Wrapped in such daydreams, she reached the turning leading from the highroad to Vozdvizhenskoe.

CHAPTER SEVENTEEN

The coachman pulled up his four horses and looked around to the right, to a field of rye, where some peasants were sitting on a cart. The office clerk was just going to jump down, but on second thought he shouted peremptorily to the peasants instead, and beckoned them to come up. The wind, which seemed to blow as they drove, dropped when the carriage stood still; gadflies settled on the steaming horses, which angrily tried to shake them off. The metallic clank of a whetstone against a scythe which came to them from the cart ceased. One of the peasants got up and came toward the carriage.

"Well, get a move on!" the clerk shouted angrily to the peasant who was stepping slowly with his bare feet over the ruts of the rough, dry road. "Hurry up, hurry!"

A curly-headed old man with a bit of bast tied around his hair, and his bent back dark with perspiration, came toward the carriage, quickening his steps, and put his sunburned arm on the mudguard.

"Vozdvizhenskoe? The manor house? The count's?" he repeated. "Go on to the end of this track. Then turn to the left. Straight along the avenue and you'll come right upon it. But whom do you want? The count himself?"

"Well, are they at home, my good man?" Darya Aleksandrovna said vaguely, not knowing how to ask about Anna, even of this peasant.

"At home for sure," said the peasant, shifting from one bare foot to the other, and leaving a distinct print of five toes and a heel in the dust. "Sure to be at home," he repeated, evidently eager to talk. "Yesterday more visitors arrived. There's a lot of visitors come. What do you want?" He turned around and called to a boy who was shouting something to him from the cart. "Oh! They all rode by here not long since, to look at the reaper. They'll be home by now. And who may you be?"

"We've come a long way," said the coachman, climbing onto the box. "So it's not far?"

"I tell you, it's just here. As soon as you get out . . . " he said, keeping hold all the while of the carriage.

A healthy-looking broad-shouldered young fellow came up too.

"Isn't there some work for the harvest?" he asked.

"I wouldn't know, my boy."

"So you keep to the left, and you'll come right on it," said the peasant, unmistakably loath to let the travelers go, and eager to converse.

The coachman started the horses, but they were only just turning when the peasant shouted: "Stop! Hey, friend! Stop!" called the two voices. The coachman stopped.

"They're coming! They're yonder!" shouted the peasant. "See what a turnout!" he said, pointing to four persons on horseback and two in a char-à-banc coming along the road.

They were Vronsky with a jockey, Veslovsky and Anna on horseback, and Princess Varvara and Sviazhsky in the char-à-banc. They had gone out to look at the operation of newly arrived reapers.

When the carriage stopped, the party on horseback were coming at a walking pace. Anna was in front beside Veslovsky, Anna quietly riding her horse, a sturdy English cob with cropped mane and short tail. Anna's beautiful head, with her black curls straying from under her top hat, her full shoulders, her slender waist in her black riding habit, and all the ease and grace of her deportment, struck Dolly.

For the first minute it seemed to her unsuitable for Anna to be on horseback. The conception of riding on horseback for a lady was, in Darya Aleksandrovna's mind, associated with ideas of youthful flirtation and frivolity, which, in her opinion, was unbecoming in Anna's position. But when she had scrutinized her, seeing her closer, she was at once reconciled to her riding. In spite of her elegance, everything was so simple, quiet, and dignified in the attitude, the dress, and the movements of Anna that nothing could have been more natural.

Beside Anna, on a steaming gray cavalry horse, was Vasenka Veslovsky in his Scotch cap with floating ribbons, his stout legs stretched out in front, obviously pleased with his own appearance. Darya Aleksandrovna could not suppress a good-humored smile as she recognized him. Behind rode Vronsky on a dark bay mare, obviously heated from galloping. He was holding her in, pulling at the reins.

After him rode a little man in the costume of a jockey. Sviazhsky and Princess Varvara, in a new char-à-banc with a big, raven-black trotter, overtook the party on horseback.

Anna's face suddenly beamed with a joyful smile at the instant when, in the little figure huddled in a corner of the old carriage, she recognized Dolly. She uttered a cry, started in the saddle, and set her horse into a gallop. On reaching the carriage, she jumped off without assistance, and holding up her riding habit, she ran up to greet Dolly.

"I thought it was you and dared not think it. How delightful! You can't imagine how glad I am!" she said, at one moment pressing her face against Dolly and kissing her, and at the next holding her off and examining her with a smile.

"Here's a delightful surprise, Aleksey!" she said, looking round at Vronsky, who had dismounted and was walking toward them.

Vronsky, taking off his gray top hat, went up to Dolly.

"You wouldn't believe how glad we are to see you," he said, giving peculiar significance to the words, and showing his strong white teeth in a smile.

Vasenka Veslovsky, without getting off his horse, took off his cap and greeted the visitor by gleefully waving the ribbons over his head.

"That's Princess Varvara," Anna said in reply to a glance of inquiry from Dolly as the char-à-banc drove up.

"Ah!" said Darya Aleksandrovna, and unconsciously her face betrayed her dissatisfaction.

Princess Varvara was her husband's aunt, and she had long known her and did not respect her. She knew that Princess Varvara had passed her whole life toadying on her rich relations, but that she should now be sponging on Vronsky, a man who was nothing to her, mortified Dolly on account of her kinship with her husband. Anna noticed Dolly's expression, and was disconcerted by it. She blushed, dropped her riding habit, and stumbled over it.

Darya Aleksandrovna went up to the char-à-banc and coldly greeted Princess Varvara. Sviazhsky too she knew. He inquired how his strange friend with the young wife was, and, running his eyes over the ill-matched horses and the carriage with its patched mudguards, proposed to the ladies that they should get into the char-à-banc.

"And I'll get into this vehicle," he said. "The horse is quiet, and the princess drives very well."

"No, stay as you were," said Anna, coming up, "and we'll go in the carriage," and taking Dolly's arm, she drew her away.

Darya Aleksandrovna's eyes were fairly dazzled by the elegant carriage of a kind she had never seen before, the splendid horses, and the elegant and gorgeous people surrounding her. But what struck her most of all was the change that had taken place in Anna, whom she knew so well and loved. Any other woman, a less close observer, not knowing Anna before, or not having thought as Darya Aleksandrovna had been thinking on the road, would not have noticed anything special in Anna. But now Dolly was struck by the temporary beauty which is found in women only during the moments of love, and which she saw now in Anna's face. Everything in her face, the clearly marked dimples in her cheeks and chin, the line of her lips, the smile which, as it were, fluttered about her face, the brilliance of her eyes, the grace and rapidity of her movements, the fullness of the notes of her voice, even the manner in which, with a sort of angry friendliness, she answered Veslovsky when he asked permission to get on her cob, so as to teach it to gallop with the right leg foremost—it was all peculiarly fascinating, and it seemed as if she were herself aware of it, and rejoicing it.

When both the women were seated in the carriage, a sudden embarrassment came over both of them. Anna was disconcerted by the intent look of inquiry Dolly fixed upon her. Dolly was embarrassed because after Sviazhsky's phrase about "this vehicle," she could not help feeling ashamed of the dirty old carriage in which Anna was sitting with her. The coachman Filipp and the office clerk was experiencing the same sensation. The clerk, to conceal his confusion, busied himself settling the ladies, but Filipp the coachman became sullen, and was bracing himself not to be overawed in the future by this show of superiority. He smiled ironically, looking at the raven horse, and was already deciding in his own mind that this smart trotter in the char-à-banc was good only for *promenage*, and wouldn't do thirty miles in a stretch in the heat.

The peasants had all got up from the cart and were inquisitively and mirthfully staring at the meeting of the friends, making their comments on it.

"They're pleased, too; haven't seen each other for a long while," said the curly-headed old man with the bast around his hair.

"Hey, Uncle Gerasim, if we could take that raven horse now, to cart the corn, that'ud be quick work!"

"Look-ee! Is that a woman in breeches?" said one of them pointing to Vasenka Veslovsky sitting sidesaddle.

"Nay, a man! See how easily he jumped up!"

"Eh, lads! seems we're not going to sleep, then?"

"What chance of sleep today!" said the old man, with a sidelong look at the sun. "Midday's past, look-ee! Get your hooks and come along!"

CHAPTER EIGHTEEN

Anna looked at Dolly's thin, careworn face, with its wrinkles filled with dust from the road, and she was on the point of saying what she was thinking, that is, that Dolly had got thinner. But, conscious that her looks had improved, and that Dolly's eyes were telling her so, she sighed and began to speak about herself.

"You are looking at me," she said, "and wondering how I can be happy in my position? Well, it's shameful to confess, but I . . . I'm inexcusably happy! Something magical has happened to me, like a dream, when you wake up and all the horrors are no more. I have waked up. I have lived through the misery, the dread, and now for a long while past, especially since we've been here, I've been so happy! . . . "

"How glad I am!" said Dolly, smiling, involuntarily speaking more coldly than she wanted to. "I'm very glad for you. Why haven't you written to me?"

"Why? . . . Because I hadn't the courage . . . You forget my position . . . "

"To me? Hadn't the courage? If you knew how I . . . I look at . . . "

Darya Aleksandrovna wanted to express her thoughts of the morning, but for some reason it seemed to her now out of place to do so.

"But of that we'll talk later. What's this, what are all these buildings?" she asked, wanting to change the conversation and pointing to the red and green roofs that came into view behind the green hedges of acacia and lilac. "Quite a little town."

But Anna did not answer.

"No, no! How do you look at my position, what do you think of it?" she asked.

"I think . . . " Darya Aleksandrovna was beginning, but at that instant Vasenka Veslovsky, having brought the cob to gallop with the

right leg foremost, galloped past them in his short jacket, bumping
heavily up and down on the chamois leather of the side saddle. "He's
doing it, Anna Arkadyevna!" he shouted.

Anna did not even glance at him; but again it seemed to Darya
Aleksandrovna out of place to enter upon such a long conversation in
the carriage, and so she cut short her thought.

"I don't think anything," she said, "but I always loved you, and if
one loves anyone, one loves the whole person just as they are and not
as one would like them to be . . . "

Anna, taking her eyes off her friend's face and lowering her eyelids
(a new habit with her), pondered, trying to penetrate the full significance of the words. And obviously interpreting them as she would
have wished, she glanced at Dolly.

"If you have any sins," she said, "they would all be forgiven you for
your coming to see me and for these words."

And Dolly saw that the tears stood in her eyes. She pressed Anna's
hand in silence.

"Well, what are these buildings? How many there are of them!"
After a moment's silence she repeated her question.

"These are the servants' houses, barns, and stables," answered
Anna. "And there the park begins. It had all gone to ruin, but Aleksey had everything renewed. He is very fond of this place, and, what
I never expected, he has become intensely interested in looking after
it. But his is such an endowed nature! Whatever he takes up, he does
splendidly. He is not only not bored, but he works with passionate
interest. He—with his temperament as I know it—he has become
careful and businesslike, a first-rate landlord, he absolutely counts
every kopek in his management of the land. But only in that. When
it's a question of tens of thousands, he doesn't think of money." She
spoke with that gleefully sly smile with which women often talk of the
secret characteristics known only to them—of those they love. "Do
you see that big building? That's the new hospital. I believe it will cost
over a hundred thousand; that's his hobby just now. And do you know
how it all came about? The peasants asked him for some meadowland,
I think it was, at a cheaper rate, and he refused, and I accused him of
being miserly. Of course it was not really because of that, but everything together, he began this hospital to prove, do you see, that he was

not miserly about money. *C'est une petitesse*,[1] if you like, but I love him all the more for it. And now you'll see the house in a moment. It was his grandfather's house, and he has had nothing altered outside."

"How beautiful!" said Dolly, looking with involuntary admiration at the handsome house with columns, standing out among the different-colored greens of the old trees in the garden.

"Isn't it fine? And from the house, from the top, the view is wonderful."

They drove into a courtyard strewn with gravel and bright with flowers, in which two laborers were at work putting a border of stones around the light mold of a flower bed, and drew up in a covered entry.

"Ah, they're here already!" said Anna, looking at the horses, which were just being led away from the steps. "It is a nice horse, isn't it? It's my cob, my favorite. Lead him here and bring me some sugar. Where is the count?" she inquired of two footmen, in impeccable livery, who darted out. "Ah, there he is!" she said, seeing Vronsky coming to meet her with Veslovsky.

"Where are you going to put the princess?" said Vronsky in French, addressing Anna, and without waiting for a reply, he once more greeted Darya Aleksandrovna, and this time he kissed her hand. "I think the large balcony room."

"Oh, no, that's too far off! Better in the corner room, we shall see each other more. Come, let's go up," said Anna, as she gave her favorite horse the sugar the footman had brought her.

"*Et vous oubliez votre devoir,*"[2] she said to Veslovsky, who also came out on the steps.

"*Pardon, j'en ai tout plein les poches,*"[3] he answered, smiling, putting his fingers in his vest pocket.

"*Mais vous venez trop tard,*"[4] she said, rubbing her handkerchief on her hand, which the horse had made wet in taking the sugar.

Anna turned to Dolly. "You can stay some time? For one day only? That's impossible!"

[1]"It's pettiness."
[2]"And you forget your duty."
[3]"Excuse me, my pockets are full of it."
[4]"But you've come too late."

"I promised to be back, and the children . . . " said Dolly, feeling embarrassed both because she had to get her bag out of the carriage, and because she knew her face must be covered with dust.

"No, Dolly, darling! Well, we'll see. Come along, come along!" and Anna led Dolly to her room.

The room was not the grand guest room Vronsky had suggested, but the one for which Anna apologized to Dolly. And this room for which apology seemed necessary was more luxurious than any in which Dolly had ever stayed, so luxurious that it reminded her of the best hotels abroad.

"Well, darling, how happy I am!" Anna said, sitting down in her riding habit for a moment beside Dolly. "Tell me about all of you. Stiva I had only a glimpse of, and he cannot tell one about the children. How is my favorite, Tanya? Quite a big girl, I expect?"

"Yes, she's very tall," Darya Aleksandrovna answered shortly, surprised herself that she should respond so coldly about her children. "We are having a delightful stay at the Levins'," she added.

"Oh, if I had known," said Anna, "that you do not despise me! . . . You might have all come to us. Stiva's an old friend and a great friend of Aleksey's, you know," she added, and suddenly she blushed.

"Yes, but we are all . . . " Dolly answered in confusion.

"But in my delight I'm talking nonsense. The one thing, darling, is that I am so glad to have you!" said Anna, kissing her again. "You haven't told me yet how and what you think about me, and I keep wanting to know. But I'm glad you will see me as I am. Above all, I wouldn't want people to think that I want to prove anything. I don't want to prove anything; I merely want to live, to do no one harm but myself. I have the right to do that, haven't I? But it is a big subject, and we'll talk over everything properly later. Now I'll go and dress and send a maid to you."

CHAPTER NINETEEN

Left alone, Darya Aleksandrovna, with an experienced housewife's eye, surveyed her room. All she had seen in entering the house and walking through it, and all she saw now in her room, gave her an impression of wealth and sumptuousness and of that modern European luxury of which she had only read in English novels, but had never seen in Russia and in the country. Everything was new, from the new French wallpaper to the carpet that covered the whole floor. The bed had a spring mattress, and a special sort of bolster and silk covers were on the little pillows. The marble washstand, the dressing table, the little sofa, the tables, the bronze clock on the mantelpiece, the window curtains and the door hangings were all new and expensive.

The smartly dressed maid, who came in to offer her services, with her hair done up more stylishly than Dolly's, and more fashionably dressed, was as new and expensive as the whole room. Darya Aleksandrovna liked her neatness, her deferential and obliging manners, but she felt ill at ease with her. She felt ashamed of her seeing the patched bed jacket that had unfortunately been packed by mistake for her. She was ashamed of the very patches and darns of which she had been so proud at home. At home it had been so clear that six bed jackets required eighteen yards of nainsook at sixty-five kopeks a yard, which was a matter of more than fifteen rubles besides the trimmings, and the work and this money had been saved. But before the maid she felt, if not exactly ashamed, at least uncomfortable.

Darya Aleksandrovna had a great sense of relief when Annushka, whom she had known for years, walked in. The smartly dressed maid was sent for to go to her mistress, and Annushka remained with Darya Aleksandrovna.

Annushka was obviously much pleased at that lady's arrival, and began to chatter away without a pause. Dolly observed that she was longing to express her opinion in regard to her mistress's position, especially as to the love and devotion of the count to Anna Arkadyevna, but Dolly carefully interrupted her whenever she began to speak about this.

"I grew up with Anna Arkadyevna; my lady's dearer to me than anything. Well, it's not for us to judge. And, to be sure, there seems so much love—"

"Kindly pour out the water for me to wash now, please," Darya Aleksandrovna cut her short.

"Certainly. We've two women kept specially for washing small things, but most of the linen's done by machinery. The count goes into everything himself. Ah, what a husband! . . . "

Dolly was glad when Anna came in and by her entrance put a stop to Annushka's gossip.

Anna had put on a very simple batiste dress. Dolly scrutinized that simple dress attentively. She knew what it meant, and the price at which such simplicity was obtained.

"An old friend," said Anna of Annushka.

Anna was not embarrassed now. She was perfectly composed and at ease. Dolly saw that she had now completely recovered from the embarrassment her arrival had caused her, and had assumed that superficial, careless tone which, as it were, closed the door on that compartment in which her deeper feelings and ideas were kept.

"Well, Anna, and how is your little girl?" asked Dolly.

"Annie?" (This was what she called her little daughter Anna.) "Very well. She's done wonderfully. Would you like to see her? Come, I'll show her to you. We had a great deal of trouble," she began telling her, "over nurses. We had an Italian wet nurse. A good creature, but so stupid! We wanted to get rid of her, but the baby is so used to her that we've gone on keeping her."

"But how have you managed? . . . " Dolly was about to ask what name the little girl would have, but noticing a sudden frown on Anna's face, she changed the drift of her question.

"How did you manage? Have you weaned her yet?"

But Anna had understood.

"You didn't mean to ask that. You meant to ask about her surname. Yes? That worries Aleksey. She has no name—that is, she's a Karenina," said Anna, lowering her eyelids till nothing could be seen but the eyelashes meeting. "But we'll talk about all that later," she said, her face suddenly brightening. "Come see her. *Elle est très gentille.*[1] She crawls now."

In the nursery the luxury which had impressed Dolly in the whole house struck her still more. There were little carts ordered from England, and appliances for teaching babies to walk, and a sofa after the fashion of a billiard table, purposely constructed for crawling,

---

[1] "She is very sweet."

and swings and baths, all of special pattern, and modern. They were all English, solid, and of good make, and obviously very expensive. The room was large, and very light and airy.

When they went in, the baby, with nothing on but her little smock, was sitting in a little armchair at the table, having her dinner of broth, which she was spilling all over her little chest. The baby was being fed, and the Russian nursemaid was evidently sharing her meal. Neither the wet nurse nor the head nurse were there; they were in the next room, from which came the sound of their conversation in the peculiar French that was their only means of communication.

Hearing Anna's voice, a tall, smartly dressed English nurse with a disagreeable face and a coarse expression walked in at the door, hurriedly shaking her fair curls, and immediately began to defend herself though Anna had not found fault with her. At every word Anna said, the English nurse said hurriedly several times, "Yes, my lady."

The rosy-faced baby, with her black eyebrows and hair, her sturdy red little body covered with gooseflesh, delighted Darya Aleksandrovna in spite of the cross expression with which she stared at the stranger. She positively envied the baby's healthy appearance. She was delighted, too, at the baby's crawling. Not one of her own children had crawled like that. When the baby was put on the carpet and its little dress tucked up behind, it was wonderfully charming. Looking around like some wild little animal at the grown-up people with her bright black eyes, she smiled, unmistakably pleased at their admiring her, and holding her legs sideways, she pressed vigorously on her arms, and rapidly drew her whole back up after, and then made another step forward with her little arms.

But the whole atmosphere of the nursery, and especially the English nurse, Darya Aleksandrovna did not like at all. It was only on the supposition that no good nurse would have entered so irregular a household as Anna's that Darya Aleksandrovna could explain to herself how Anna, with her insight into people, could take such an unprepossessing, disreputable-looking woman as nurse to her child.

Besides, from a few words that were dropped, Darya Aleksandrovna saw at once that Anna, the two nurses, and the child had no common existence, and that the mother's visit was something exceptional. Anna wanted to get the baby one of her toys, but could not find it.

Most amazing of all was the fact that on being asked how many teeth the baby had, Anna answered incorrectly, and knew nothing about the two last teeth.

"I sometimes feel sorry I'm so superfluous here," said Anna, going out of the nursery and holding up her skirt so as to escape the playthings standing in the doorway. "It was very different with my first child."

"I expected it to be the other way," said Darya Aleksandrovna shyly.

"Oh, no! By the way, do you know I saw Seryozha?" said Anna, screwing up her eyes as though looking at something far away. "But we'll talk about that later. You wouldn't believe it, I'm like a hungry beggar-woman when a full dinner is set before her and she does not know what to begin with first. The dinner is you and the talks we're going to have together, which I could never have with anyone else; and I don't know which subject to begin with first. *Mais je ne vous ferai grâce de rien.*[2] I must have everything out with you. Oh, I ought to give you an idea of the company you will meet with us," she began. "I'll begin with the ladies. Princess Varvara—you know her, and I know your opinion and Stiva's about her. Stiva says the whole aim of her existence is to prove her superiority over Auntie Katerina Pavlovna: that's all true; but she's a good-natured woman, and I am so grateful to her. In Petersburg there was a moment when a chaperon was absolutely essential for me. Then she turned up. But really she is good-natured. She did a great deal to alleviate my situation. I can see you don't understand all the difficulty of my position . . . there in Petersburg," she added. "Here I'm perfectly at ease and happy. Well, all about that later on. Then Sviazhsky—he's the marshal of the district,[3] and he's a very good sort of man, but he wants to get something out of Aleksey. You understand, with his property, now that we are settled in the country, Aleksey can exercise great influence. Then there's Tushkevich—you have seen him, you know—

[2]"But I'm not letting you off with anything."
[3]I.e., marshal of nobility. See note on page 233.

Betsy's admirer. Now he's been thrown over and he's come to see us. As Aleksey says, he's one of those people who are very pleasant if one accepts them for what they try to appear to be, *et puis il est comme il faut*,[4] as Princess Varvara says. Then Veslovsky—you know him. A very nice boy," she said, and a sly smile curved her lips. "What's this wild story about him and the Levins? Veslovsky told Aleksey about it, and we don't believe it. *Il est très gentil et naif*,"[5] she said again with the same smile. "Men need recreation, and Aleksey needs an audience, so I value all these people. We have to have the house lively and gay, so that Aleksey may not long for any novelty. Then you'll see this steward—a German, a very good fellow, and he understands his work. Aleksey has a very high opinion of him. Then the doctor, a young man, not quite a nihilist, perhaps, but you know, eats with his knife . . . but a very good doctor. Then the architect . . . *Une petite cour.*[6]

CHAPTER TWENTY

"Here's Dolly for you, Princess; you were so anxious to see her," said Anna, coming out with Darya Aleksandrovna onto the stone terrace, where Princess Varvara was sitting in the shade at an embroidery frame, working at a cover for Count Aleksey Kirillovich's easy chair. "She says she doesn't want anything before dinner, but please order some lunch for her, and I'll go and look for Aleksey and bring them all in."

Princess Varvara gave Dolly a cordial and rather patronizing reception, and began at once explaining to her that she was living with Anna because she had always cared more for her than for her sister Katerina Pavlovna, the aunt that had brought Anna up, and that now, when everyone had abandoned Anna, she thought it her duty to help her in this most difficult period of transition.

"Her husband will give her a divorce, and then I shall go back to my solitude; but now I can be of use, and I am doing my duty, how-

---

[4]"And then, he is a gentleman."
[5]"He is very sweet and naïve."
[6]"A little court."

ever difficult it may be for me—not like some other people. And how sweet it is of you, how right of you to have come! They live like the best of married couples; it's for God to judge them, not for us. And didn't Biryuzovsky and Madame Avenyeva . . . and even Nikandrov, and Vasilyev and Madame Mamonova, and Liza Neptunova . . . No one said a thing against them, and it ended by their being received by everyone. And then, *c'est un intérieur si joli, si comme il faut. Tout-à-fait a l'anglaise. On se réunit le matin au breakfast, et puis on se sépare.*[1] Everyone does as he pleases till dinner. Dinner at seven o'clock. Stiva did very well to send you. He needs their support. You know that through his mother and brother he can do anything. And then they do so much good. He didn't tell you about his hospital? *Ce sera admirable*[2]—everything from Paris."

Their conversation was interrupted by Anna, who had found the men of the party in the billiard room and returned with them to the terrace. There was still a long time before the dinner hour, it was exquisite weather, and so several different methods of spending the next two hours were proposed. There were very many methods of passing the time at Vozdvizhenskoe, and these were all unlike those in use at Pokrovskoe.

"*Une partie de lawn-tennis,*"[3] Veslovsky proposed, with his handsome smile. "We'll be partners again, Anna Arkadyevna."

"No, it's too hot; better stroll about the garden and have a row in the boat, show Darya Aleksandrovna the riverbanks," Vronsky proposed.

"I agree to anything," said Sviazhsky.

"I imagine that what Dolly would like best would be a stroll—wouldn't you? And then the boat, perhaps," said Anna.

So it was decided. Veslovsky and Tushkevich went off to the bathing place, promising to get the boat ready and to wait there for them.

They walked along the path in two pairs, Anna with Sviazhsky, and Dolly with Vronsky. Dolly was a little embarrassed and anxious

[1]"It is such a pretty, such a decent home. Everything is the English style. We meet for breakfast and then we separate."
[2]"It will be admirable."
[3]"A game of tennis."

in the new surroundings in which she found herself. Abstractly, theoretically, she did not merely justify, she positively approved of Anna's conduct. As is indeed not infrequent with women of unimpeachable virtue weary of the monotony of respectable existence, at a distance she not only excused illicit love, she positively envied it. Besides, she loved Anna with all her heart. But seeing Anna in actual life among these strangers, with this fashionable tone that was so new to Darya Aleksandrovna, she felt ill at ease. What she disliked particularly was seeing Princess Varvara ready to overlook everything for the sake of the comforts she enjoyed.

As a general principle, abstractly, Dolly approved of Anna's action; but to see the man for whose sake her action had been taken was distasteful to her. Moreover, she had never liked Vronsky. She thought him very proud, and saw nothing in him of which he could be proud except his wealth. But against her own will, here in his own house, he overawed her more than ever, and she could not be at ease with him. She felt with him the same feeling she had had with the maid about her bed jacket. Just as with the maid she had felt not exactly ashamed but embarrassed at her patches, so she felt with him not exactly ashamed but embarrassed.

Dolly was ill at ease, and tried to find a subject of conversation. Even though she supposed that, through his pride, praise of his house and garden would be sure to be disagreeable to him, she did all the same tell him how much she liked his house.

"Yes, it's a very fine building, and in the good old-fashioned style," he said.

"I so like the court in front of the steps. Was that always so?"

"Oh, no!" he said, and his face beamed with pleasure. "If you could only have seen that court last spring!"

And he began, at first rather diffidently, but more and more carried away by the subject as he went on, to draw her attention to the various details of the decoration of his house and garden. It was evident that, having devoted a great deal of trouble to improve and beautify his home, Vronsky felt a need to show off the improvements to a new person, and was genuinely delighted at Darya Aleksandrovna's praise.

"If you would care to look at the hospital and are not tired, it's not far. Shall we go?" he said, glancing into her face to convince himself that she was not bored. "Are you coming, Anna?" He turned to her.

"We will come, won't we?" she said, addressing Sviazhsky. *"Mais il ne faut pas laisser le pauvre Veslovsky et Tushkevich se morfondre là dans le bateau.*[4] We must send and tell them."

"Yes, this is a monument he will leave behind him," said Anna, turning to Dolly with that sly smile of comprehension with which she had previously talked about the hospital.

"Oh, it's a work of real importance!" said Sviazhsky. But to show he was not trying to ingratiate himself with Vronsky, he promptly added some slightly critical remarks.

"I wonder, though, Count," he said, "that while you do so much for the health of the peasants, you take so little interest in the schools."

"C'est devenu tellement commun les écoles,"[5] said Vronsky. "You understand that's not the reason. I just got carried away. This way, then, to the hospital," he said to Darya Aleksandrovna, pointing to a side path leading out of the avenue.

The ladies put up their parasols and turned into the side path. After going down several turnings, and going through a little gate, Darya Aleksandrovna saw standing on rising ground before her a large, fancy-looking red building, almost finished. The iron roof, which was not yet painted, shone with dazzling brightness in the sunshine. Beside the finished building another had been begun, surrounded by scaffolding. Workmen in aprons, standing on scaffolds, were laying bricks, pouring mortar out of vats, and smoothing it with trowels.

"How quickly work gets done with you!" said Sviazhsky. "When I was here last time the roof was not on."

"By autumn it will all be ready. Inside almost everything is done," said Anna.

"And what's this new building?"

"That's the house for the doctor and the dispensary," answered

---

[4]"But we must not leave poor Veslovsky and Tushkevich in the boat in despair."
[5]"Schools have become so common."

Vronsky, seeing the architect in a short jacket coming toward him; and excusing himself to the ladies, he went to meet him.

Going round a hole where the workmen were slaking lime, he stood still with the architect and began talking heatedly.

"The front is still too low," he said to Anna, who had asked what was the matter.

"I said the foundation ought to be raised," said Anna.

"Yes, of course it would have been much better, Anna Arkadyevna," said the architect, "but now it's too late."

"Yes, I take a great interest in it," Anna answered Sviazhsky who was expressing his surprise at her knowledge of architecture. "This new building should have been in harmony with the hospital. It was an afterthought, and was begun without a plan."

Vronsky, having finished his talk with the architect, joined the ladies and led them inside the hospital.

Although they were still at work on the cornices outside and were painting on the ground floor, upstairs almost all the rooms were finished. Going up the broad iron staircase to the landing, they walked into the first large room. The walls were stuccoed to look like marble, the huge plate-glass windows were already in, only the parquet floor was not yet finished, and the carpenters, who were planing a square of it, left their work, taking off the bands that fastened their hair, to greet the gentry.

"This is the reception room," said Vronsky. "Here there will be a desk, tables, and benches, and nothing more."

"This way; let us go in here. Don't go near the window," said Anna, trying the paint to see if it was dry. "Aleksey, the paint's dry already," she added.

From the reception room they went into the corridor. Here Vronsky showed them the new system of ventilation he had put in. Then he showed them marble baths, and beds with extraordinary spring mattresses. Then he showed them the wards one after another, the storeroom, the linen room, then the modern stoves, then the trolleys, which would make no noise as they carried everything needed along the corridors, and many other things. Sviazhsky, as a connoisseur in the latest mechanical improvements, appreciated everything fully. Dolly simply wondered at all she had not seen before, and, anxious to understand it all, made minute inquiries about everything, which gave Vronsky great satisfaction.

"Yes, I imagine that this will be the solitary example of a properly fitted hospital in Russia," said Sviazhsky.

"And won't you have a maternity ward?" asked Dolly. "That's so much needed in the country. I have often—"

In spite of his usual courtesy, Vronsky interrupted her.

"This is not a maternity home but a hospital for the sick, and is intended for all diseases except infectious complaints," he said. "Ah! Look at this," and he rolled up to Darya Aleksandrovna a wheelchair that had just been ordered for convalescents. "Look." He sat down in the chair and began moving it. "The patient can't walk—still too weak, perhaps, or something wrong with his legs, but he must have air, and he moves, rolls himself along . . . "

Darya Aleksandrovna was interested in everything. She liked everything very much, but most of all she liked Vronsky himself with his natural, simple-hearted eagerness. "Yes, he's a very nice, good man," she thought several times, not hearing what he said, but looking at him and penetrating into his expression, while she mentally put herself in Anna's place. She liked him so much just now with his eager interest that she saw how Anna could be in love with him.

CHAPTER TWENTY-ONE

"No, I think the princess is tired, and horses don't interest her," Vronsky said to Anna, who wanted to go on to the stables, where Sviazhsky wished to see the new stallion. "You go on, while I escort the princess home, and we'll have a little talk," he said, "if you would like that?" he added, turning to her.

"I know nothing about horses, and I shall be delighted," answered Darya Aleksandrovna, rather astonished.

She saw by Vronsky's face that he wanted something from her. She was not mistaken. As soon as they had passed through the little gate back into the garden, he looked in the direction Anna had taken, and having made sure that she could neither hear nor see them, he began:

"You guess that I have something I want to say to you," he said, looking at her with laughing eyes. "I am not wrong in believing you to be a friend of Anna's." He took off his hat, and taking out his handkerchief, he wiped his head, which was growing bald.

Darya Aleksandrovna made no answer, and merely stared at him with dismay. When she was left alone with him, she suddenly felt afraid; his laughing eyes and stern expression scared her.

The most diverse suppositions as to what he was about to speak of to her flashed into her brain. "He is going to beg me to come to stay with them with the children, and I shall have to refuse; or to organize a group that will receive Anna in Moscow . . . Or isn't it Veslovsky and his relations with Anna? Or perhaps about Kitty, that he feels he was to blame?" All her conjectures were unpleasant, but she did not guess what he really wanted to talk about to her.

"You have so much influence with Anna, she is so fond of you," he said; "do help me."

Darya Aleksandrovna looked with timid inquiry into his energetic face, which under the lime trees was continually being lighted up in patches by the sunshine, and then passing into complete shadow again. She waited for him to say more, but he walked in silence beside her, scratching with his stick in the gravel.

"You have come to see us, you, the only woman of Anna's former friends—I don't count Princess Varvara—but I know that you have done this not because you regard our position as normal but because, understanding all the difficulty of the position, you still love her and want to be a help to her. Have I understood you rightly?" he asked, looking round at her.

"Oh, yes," answered Darya Aleksandrovna, shutting her parasol, "but—"

"No," he broke in, and unconsciously, oblivious of the awkward position in which he was putting his companion, he stopped abruptly, so that she had to stop short too. "No one feels more deeply and intensely than I do the difficulty of Anna's position; and that you may well understand, if you do me the honor of supposing I have any heart. I am to blame for that position, and that is why I feel it."

"I understand," said Darya Aleksandrovna, involuntarily admiring the sincerity and firmness with which he said this. "But just because you feel yourself responsible, you exaggerate it, I am afraid," she said. "Her position in the world is difficult, I can well understand."

"In the world it is hell!" he brought out quickly, frowning darkly. "You can't imagine moral sufferings greater than what she went through in Petersburg those two weeks . . . and I beg you to believe it."

"Yes, but here, so long as neither Anna . . . nor you miss society . . . "

"Society!" he said contemptuously. "How could I miss society?"

"So far—and it may always be so—you are happy and at peace. I see in Anna that she is happy, perfectly happy, she has had time to tell me so much already," said Darya Aleksandrovna, smiling; even so, as she said this, at the same moment a doubt entered her mind whether Anna really was happy.

But Vronsky, it appeared, had no doubts on that score.

"Yes, yes," he said, "I know that she has revived after all her sufferings; she is happy. She is happy in the present. But I? . . . I am afraid of what is before us . . . I beg your pardon, you would like to walk on?"

"No, I don't mind."

"Well, then, let us sit here."

Darya Aleksandrovna sat down on a garden seat in a corner of the avenue. He stood up facing her.

"I see that she is happy," he repeated, and the doubt whether she was happy sank more deeply into Darya Aleksandrovna's mind. "But can it last? Whether we have acted rightly or wrongly is another question, but the die is cast," he said, passing from Russian to French, "and we are bound together for life. We are united by all the ties of love that we hold most sacred. We have a child, we may have other children. But the law and all the conditions of our position are such that thousands of complications arise which she does not see and does not want to see. And that one can well understand. But I can't help seeing them. My daughter is by law not my daughter but Karenin's. I cannot bear this deception!" he said, with a vigorous gesture of refusal, and he looked with gloomy inquiry toward Darya Aleksandrovna.

She made no answer, but simply gazed at him. He went on:

"One day a son may be born, my son, and he will be legally a Karenin; he will not be the heir of my name or of my property, and however happy we may be in our home life and however many children we may have, there will be no real tie between us. They will be Karenins. You can understand the bitterness and horror of this position! I have tried to speak of this to Anna. It irritates her. She does not understand, and to her I cannot speak plainly of all this. Now look at another side. I am happy, happy in her love, but I must have occupation. I have found occupation, and am proud of what I am doing and consider it nobler than the pursuits of my former companions at court and in the army. And most certainly I would not change the work I am doing for theirs. I am working here, settled in my own place, and I am happy and contented, and we need nothing more to make us happy. I love my work here. *Ce n'est pas un pis-aller,*[1] on the contrary . . . "

Darya Aleksandrovna noticed that at this point in his explanation he grew confused, and she did not quite understand this digression, but she felt that having once begun to speak of matters near his heart, of which he could not speak to Anna, he was now making a clean breast of everything, and that the question of his pursuits in the country fell into the same category of matters near his heart, as the question of his relations with Anna.

"Well, I will go on," he said, collecting himself. "The important thing is that as I work I want to have a conviction that what I am doing will not die with me, that I shall have heirs to come after me— and this I have not. Conceive the position of a man who knows that his children, the children of the woman he loves, will not be his, but will belong to someone who hates them and cares nothing about them! It is terrible!"

He paused, evidently much moved.

"Yes, indeed, I see that. But what can Anna do?" queried Darya Aleksandrovna.

"Yes, that brings me to the object of my conversation," he said, calming himself with an effort. "Anna can, it depends on her . . . Even to petition the Tsar for legitimization, a divorce is essential. And that depends on Anna. Her husband agreed to a divorce—at that

---

[1] "It is not a last resort."

time your husband had arranged it completely. And now, I know, he would not refuse it. It is only a matter of writing to him. He said plainly at that time that if she expressed the desire, he would not refuse. Of course," he said gloomily, "it is one of those Pharisaical cruelties of which only such heartless men are capable. He knows what agony any recollection of him must give her, and knowing her, he must have a letter from her. I can understand that it is agony to her. But the matter is of such importance, that one must *passer par-dessus toutes ces finesses de sentiment. Il y va du bonheur et de l'existence d'Anne et de ses enfants.*[2] I won't speak of myself, though it's hard for me, very hard," he said, with an expression as though he were threatening someone for its being hard for him. "And so it is, Princess, that I am shamelessly clutching at you as an anchor of salvation. Help me to persuade her to write to him and ask for a divorce."

"Yes, of course," Darya Aleksandrovna said, pensively, as she vividly recalled her last interview with Aleksey Aleksandrovich. "Yes, of course," she repeated with decision, thinking of Anna.

"Use your influence with her, make her write. I don't like—I'm almost unable to speak about this to her."

"Very well, I will talk to her. But how is it she does not think of it herself?" said Darya Aleksandrovna, and for some reason she suddenly at that point recalled Anna's strange new habit of half-closing her eyes. And she remembered that Anna drooped her eyelids just when the deeper questions of life were touched upon. "Just as though she half-shut her eyes to her own life, so as not to see everything," thought Dolly. "Yes, indeed, for my own sake and for hers I will talk to her," Dolly said in reply to his look of gratitude.

They got up and walked to the house.

[2]". . . get over all those refinements of feeling. The happiness and existence of Anna and her children depend on it."

CHAPTER TWENTY-TWO

When Anna found Dolly at home before her, she looked intently into her eyes, as though questioning her about the talk she had had with Vronsky, but she made no inquiry in words.

"I believe it's nearly dinnertime," she said. "We've not seen each other at all yet. I am counting on the evening. Now I want to go and dress. I expect you do too; we all got dirty in the new building."

Dolly went to her room and she felt amused. To change her dress was impossible, for she had already put on her best dress. But in order to signify in some way her preparation for dinner, she asked the maid to brush her dress, changed her cuffs and ribbon, and put some lace on her head.

"This is all I can do," she said with a smile to Anna, who came in to her in a third dress, again of extreme simplicity.

"Yes, we are too formal here," she said, as it were apologizing for her magnificence. "Aleksey is delighted at your visit, as he rarely is at anything. He has completely lost his heart to you," she added. "You're not tired?"

There was no time for talking about anything before dinner. Going into the drawing room, they found Princess Varvara already there, and the gentlemen of the party in black frock coats. The architect wore a swallow-tail coat. Vronsky presented the doctor and the steward to his guest. The architect he had already introduced to her at the hospital.

A stout butler, resplendent with a smoothly shaven round chin and a starched white cravat, announced that dinner was ready, and the ladies got up. Vronsky asked Sviazhsky to take in Anna Arkadyevna, and himself offered his arm to Dolly. Veslovsky was before Tushkevich in offering his arm to Princess Varvara, so that Tushkevich with the steward and the doctor walked in alone.

The dinner, the dining room, the service, the waiting at table, the wine, and the food were not simply in keeping with the general tone of modern luxury throughout the house, but seemed even more sumptuous and modern. Darya Aleksandrovna watched this luxury which was novel to her, and, as a good housekeeper used to managing a household—though she never dreamed of adapting anything she saw to her own household, as it was all in a style of luxury far above her own manner of living—she could not help scrutinizing every detail, and wondering how and by whom it was all done. Vasenka Veslovsky, her husband, and even Sviazhsky, and many other people she knew, would never have considered this question, and would have readily believed what every well-bred host tries to make his guests feel, that is, that all that is well ordered in his house has cost him, the host, no trouble whatever, but comes automatically. Darya Aleksandrovna was well aware that even porridge for the children's breakfast does not come automatically, and that therefore, where so complicated and magnificent a style of luxury was maintained, someone must give earnest attention to its organization. And from the glance with which Aleksey Kirillovich scanned the table, from the way he nodded to the butler, and offered Darya Aleksandrovna her choice between cold soup and hot soup, she saw that it was all organized and maintained by the care of the master of the house himself. It was evident that it all rested no more upon Anna than Veslovsky. She, Sviazhsky, the princess, and Veslovsky were equally guests, with light hearts enjoying what had been arranged for them.

Anna was the hostess only in conducting the conversation. The conversation was a difficult one for the lady of the house at a small table with persons present, like the steward and the architect, belonging to a completely different world, struggling not to be overawed by an elegance to which they were unaccustomed, and unable to sustain a large share in the general conversation. But this difficult conversation Anna directed with her usual tact and naturalness, and indeed she did so with actual enjoyment, as Darya Aleksandrovna observed. The conversation began about the row Tushkevich and Veslovsky had taken alone together in the boat, and Tushkevich began describing the last boat races in Petersburg at the Yacht Club. But Anna, seizing the first pause, at once turned to the architect to draw him out of his silence.

"Nikolai Ivanych was struck," she said, meaning Sviazhsky, "at the progress the new building had made since he was here last; but I am there every day, and every day I wonder at the rate at which it grows."

"It's first rate, working with His Excellency," said the architect with a smile (he was respectful and composed, though with a sense of his own dignity). "It's a very different matter to have to do with the district authorities. Where one would have to write out sheaves of papers, here I call upon the count, and in three words we settle the business."

"The American way of doing business," said Sviazhsky with a smile.

"Yes, there they build in a rational fashion . . . "

The conversation passed to the misuse of political power in the United States, but Anna quickly brought it round to another topic so as to draw the steward into talk.

"Have you ever seen a reaping machine?" she said, addressing Darya Aleksandrovna. "We had just ridden over to look at one when we met. It's the first time I ever saw one."

"How do they work?" asked Dolly.

"Exactly like little scissors. A plank and a lot of little scissors. Like this."

Anna took a knife and fork in her beautiful white hands, covered with rings, and began showing how the machine worked. It was clear that she saw nothing would be understood from her explanation, but aware that her talk was pleasant and her hands beautiful, she went on explaining.

"More like little penknives," Veslovsky said playfully, never taking his eyes off her.

Anna gave a just perceptible smile, but made no answer. "Isn't it true, Karl Fedorych, that it's just like little scissors?" she said to the steward.

"*Oh, ja,*" answered the German. "*Es ist ein ganz einfaches Ding,*"[1] and he began to explain the construction of the machine.

"It's a pity it doesn't bind too. I saw one at the Vienna exhibition which binds with a wire," said Sviazhsky. "They would be more profitable in use."

"*Es kommt drauf an . . . Der Preis vom Draht muss ausgerechnet werden.*"[2] And the German, roused from his taciturnity, turned to Vronsky. "*Das lässt sich ausrechnen, Erlaucht.*"[3] The German was just

[1] "It's a very simple thing."
[2] "It depends . . . the price of wire must be figured in."
[3] "It can be calculated, Excellency."

feeling in the pocket where his pencil and the notebook he always wrote in were, but recollecting that he was at a dinner, and observing Vronsky's chilly glance, he checked himself. *"Zu compliziert, macht zu viel Klopot,"*[4] he concluded.

"Wünscht man Dochots, so hat man auch Klopots,"[5] said Vasenka Veslovsky, mimicking the German. *"J'adore l'allemand,"*[6] he addressed Anna again with the same smile.

"Cessez,"[7] she said with playful severity.

"We expected to find you in the fields, Vasily Semyonych," she said to the doctor, a sickly-looking man; "have you been there?"

"I went there, but I disappeared," the doctor answered with gloomy jocoseness.

"Then you've taken a good constitutional?"

"Splendid!"

"Well, and how was the old woman? I hope it's not typhus?"

"Typhus it is not, but it's taking a bad turn."

"What a pity!" said Anna, and having thus paid the dues of civility to her domestic circle, she turned to her own friends.

"It would be a hard task, though, to construct a machine from your description, Anna Arkadyevna," Sviazhsky said jestingly.

"Oh, no, why so?" said Anna with a smile that betrayed that she knew there was something charming in her disquisitions upon the machine that had been noticed by Sviazhsky. This new trait of girlish coquettishness made an unpleasant impression on Dolly.

"But Anna Arkadyevna's knowledge of architecture is marvelous," said Tushkevich.

"To be sure, I heard Anna Arkadyevna talking yesterday about plinths and damp-courses," said Veslovsky. "Have I got it right?"

"There's nothing marvelous about it, when one sees and hears so much of it," said Anna. "But, I suppose you don't even know what houses are made of?"

---

[4] "Too complicated, too much trouble."
[5] "If one wants profit, one must also have trouble." (He converts the Russian singular *dokhod* into "German.")
[6] "I adore German."
[7] "Stop."

Darya Aleksandrovna saw that Anna disliked the tone of raillery that existed between her and Veslovsky, but fell in with it against her will.

Vronsky acted in this matter quite differently from Levin. He obviously attached no significance to Veslovsky's chattering; on the contrary, he encouraged his jests.

"Come now, tell us, Veslovsky, how are the bricks held together?"

"By cement, of course."

"Bravo! And what is cement?"

"Oh, some sort of paste . . . no, putty," said Veslovsky, raising a general laugh.

The company at dinner, with the exception of the doctor, the architect, and the steward, who remained plunged in gloomy silence, kept up a conversation that never paused, glancing off one subject, fastening on another, and at times stinging one or the other to the quick. Once Darya Aleksandrovna felt wounded, and got so excited that she positively flushed, and wondered afterward whether she had said anything extreme or unpleasant. Sviazhsky began talking of Levin, describing his strange view that machinery is simply pernicious in its effects on Russian agriculture.

"I have not the pleasure of knowing this M. Levin," Vronsky said, smiling, "but most likely he has never seen the machines he condemns; or if he has seen and tried any, it must have been some Russian imitation, not a machine from abroad. What sort of views can anyone have on such a subject?"

"Turkish views, in general," Veslovsky said, turning to Anna with a smile.

"I can't defend his opinions," Darya Aleksandrovna said, flushing; "but I can say that he's a highly cultivated man, and if he were here he would know very well how to answer you, though I am not capable of doing so."

"I like him extremely, and we are great friends," Sviazhsky said, smiling good-naturedly. *"Mais pardon, il est un petit peu touqé,"*[8] he

---

[8]"But excuse me, he's slightly cracked."

maintains, for instance, that district councils and arbitration boards are all of no use, and he is unwilling to take part in anything."

"It's our Russian apathy," said Vronsky, pouring water from an iced decanter into a delicate glass on a high stem; "we've no sense of the duties our privileges impose upon us, and so we refuse to recognize these duties."

"I know no man more strict in the performance of his duties," said Darya Aleksandrovna, irritated by Vronsky's tone of superiority.

"For my part," pursued Vronsky, who was evidently for some reason or other keenly affected by this conversation, "such as I am, I am, on the contrary, extremely grateful for the honor they have done me, thanks to Nikolai Ivanych" (he indicated Sviazhsky), "in electing me a justice of the peace. I consider that for me the duty of being present at the session, of judging some peasants' quarrel about a horse, is as important as anything I can do. And I shall regard it as an honor if they elect me for the district council. It's only in that way I can pay for the advantages I enjoy as a landowner. Unfortunately they don't understand the weight that the big landowners ought to have in the state."

It was strange to Darya Aleksandrovna to hear how serenely confident he was of being right at his own table. She thought how Levin, who believed the opposite, was just as positive in his opinion at his own table. But she loved Levin, and so she was on his side.

"So we can count on you, Count, for the coming elections?" said Sviazhsky. "But you must come a little beforehand, so as to be on the spot by the eighth. If you would do me the honor of staying with me."

"I rather agree with your *beau-frère*," said Anna, "though not quite on the same ground as he," she added with a smile. "I'm afraid that we have too many of these public duties in these latter days. Just as in old days there were so many government functionaries that one had to call in a functionary for every single thing, so now everyone's doing some sort of public duty. Aleksey has been here six months now, and he's a member, I do believe, of five or six different public bodies. He is a justice of the peace, a trustee, a member of the town council, a juror, and something connected with horses. *Du train que cela va,*[9] the whole time will be wasted on it. And I'm afraid that with such a multiplicity of these bodies, they'll end in being a mere form. How many are you a member of, Nikolai Ivanych?" She turned to Sviazhsky. "Over twenty, isn't it?"

Anna spoke lightly, but irritation could be discerned in her tone. Darya Aleksandrovna, watching Anna and Vronsky attentively, detected it instantly. She noticed, too, that as she spoke, Vronsky's face had immediately taken a serious and obstinate expression. Noticing this, and that Princess Varvara at once made haste to change the conversation by talking of Petersburg acquaintances, and remembering what Vronsky had without apparent connection said in the garden of his work in the country, Dolly surmised that this question of public activity was connected with some deep private disagreement between Anna and Vronsky.

The dinner, the wine, the decoration of the table were all very good; but it was like what Darya Aleksandrovna had seen at formal dinners and balls which of late years had become quite unfamiliar to her; it all had the same impersonal and constrained character, and so on an ordinary day and in a little circle of friends it made a disagreeable impression on her.

After dinner they sat on the terrace; then they proceeded to play lawn tennis. The players, divided into two parties, stood on opposite sides of a tightly drawn net with gilt poles on the carefully leveled and rolled croquet lawn. Darya Aleksandrovna made an attempt to play, but it was a long time before she could understand the game, and by the time she did understand it, she was so tired that she sat down with Princess Varvara and simply looked on at the players. Her partner, Tushkevich, gave up playing too, but the others kept the game up for a long time. Sviazhsky and Vronsky both played very well and seriously. They kept a sharp lookout on the balls served to them, and without haste or getting in each other's way, they ran adroitly up to them, waited for the rebound, and neatly and accurately returned them over the net. Veslovsky played worse than the others. He was too eager, but he kept the players lively with his high

---

[9] "At the rate at which it is going . . . "

spirits. His laughter and outcries never paused. Like the other men of the party, with the ladies' permission, he took off his coat, and his large, handsome figure in his white shirt sleeves, with his red perspiring face and his impulsive movements, made a picture that imprinted itself vividly on the memory.

When Darya Aleksandrovna lay in bed that night, as soon as she closed her eyes she saw Vasenka Veslovsky flying about the croquet lawn.

During the game Darya Aleksandrovna was not enjoying herself. She did not like the light tone of raillery that was kept up all the time between Vasenka Veslovsky and Anna, and the unnaturalness altogether of grownups, all alone without children, playing at a child's game. But to avoid breaking up the party and to get through the time somehow, after a rest she joined the game again, and pretended to be enjoying it. All that day it seemed to her as though she was acting in a theater with actors cleverer than she, and that her bad acting was spoiling the whole performance. She had come with the intention of staying two days if all went well. But in the evening, during the game, she made up her mind that she would go home the next day. The maternal cares and worries which she had so hated on the way, now, after a day spent without them, struck her in quite another light, and tempted her back to them.

When, after evening tea and a row by night in the boat, Darya Aleksandrovna went alone to her room, took off her dress, and began arranging her thin hair for the night, she had a great sense of relief. She did not even like thinking that Anna was coming to see her immediately. She longed to be alone with her own thoughts.

CHAPTER TWENTY-THREE

Dolly was ready to go to bed when Anna came in in her dressing gown. In the course of the day Anna had several times begun to speak of matters near her heart, and every time after a few words she had stopped: "Afterwards, by ourselves, we'll talk about everything. I've got so much I want to tell you," she said.

Now they were by themselves, and Anna did not know what to

talk about. She sat on the window sill looking at Dolly and going over in her own mind all these stores of intimate talk which had seemed so inexhaustible before, and she found nothing. At that moment it seemed to her that everything had been said already.

"Well, what of Kitty?" she said with a heavy sigh, looking penitently at Dolly. "Tell me the truth, Dolly: isn't she angry with me?"

"Angry? Oh, no!" said Darya Aleksandrovna, smiling.

"But she hates me, despises me?"

"Oh, no! But you know that sort of thing isn't forgiven."

"Yes, yes," said Anna, turning away and looking out of the open window. "But I was not to blame. And who is to blame? What's the meaning of being to blame? Could it have been otherwise? What do you think? Could it possibly have happened that you didn't become the wife of Stiva?"

"Really, I don't know. But this is what I want you to tell me . . . "

"Yes, yes, but we've not finished about Kitty. Is she happy? He's a very nice man, they say."

"He's much more than very nice. I don't know a better man."

"Ah, how glad I am! I'm so glad! Much more than very nice," she repeated.

Dolly smiled.

"But tell me about yourself. We've a great deal to talk about. And I've had a talk with . . . " Dolly did not know what to call him. She felt it awkward to call him Count or Aleksey Kirillovich.

"With Aleksey," said Anna, "I know what you talked about. But I wanted to ask you frankly what you think of me, of my life."

"How am I to say like that straight off? I really don't know."

"No, tell me all the same . . . You see my life. But you mustn't forget that you're seeing us in the summer, when you have come to us and we are not alone . . . But we came here early in the spring, lived quite alone, and shall be alone again, and I desire nothing better. But imagine me living alone without him, alone, and that will be . . . I see by everything that it will often be repeated, that he will be half the time away from home," she said, getting up and sitting down close by Dolly.

"Of course," she interrupted Dolly, who would have answered, "of course I won't try to keep him by force. I don't hold him back now.

The races are just coming, his horses are running, he will go. I'm very glad. But think of me, imagine my position . . . But what's the use of talking about it?" She smiled. "Well, what did he talk about with you?"

"He spoke of what I want to speak to you about myself, so it's easy for me to be his advocate; of whether there is not a possibility . . . whether you could not . . . "(Darya Aleksandrovna hesitated) "correct, improve your position . . . You know how I look at it . . . But all the same, if possible, you should get married . . . "

"Divorce, you mean?" said Anna. "Do you know, the only woman who came to see me in Petersburg was Betsy Tverskaya? You know her, of course? *Au fond, c'est la femme la plus dépravée qui existe.*[1] She was Tushkevich's mistress, deceiving her husband in the basest way. And she told me that she did not care to know me so long as my position was irregular. Don't imagine I would compare . . . I know you, darling. But I could not help remembering . . . Well, so what did he say to you?" she repeated.

"He said that he was unhappy on your account and his own. Perhaps you will say that it's egoism, but what a legitimate and noble egoism. He wants first of all to legitimize his daughter, and to be your husband, to have a legal right to you."

"What wife, what slave can be so utterly a slave as I, in my position?" she put in gloomily.

"The chief thing he desires . . . he desires that you should not suffer."

"That's impossible. Well?"

"Well, and the most legitimate desire—he wishes that your children should have a name."

"What children?" Anna said, not looking at Dolly and half closing her eyes.

"Annie and those to come . . . "

"He need not trouble on that score; I shall have no more children."

"How can you tell that you won't?"

"I shall not because I don't wish it." And, in spite of all her emo-

[1]"Basically, she's the most depraved woman in existence."

tion, Anna smiled as she caught the naïve expression of curiosity, wonder, and horror on Dolly's face.

"The doctor told me after my illness . . . "

"Impossible!" said Dolly, opening her eyes wide.

For her this was one of those discoveries the consequences and deductions of which are so immense that all that one feels for the first instant is that it is impossible to take it in, and that one will have to reflect a great, great deal upon it.

This discovery, suddenly throwing light on all those families of one or two children, which had hitherto been so incomprehensible to her, aroused so many ideas, reflections, and contradictory emotions that she had nothing to say, and simply gazed with wide-open eyes of wonder at Anna. This was the very thing she had been dreaming of, but now learning that it was possible, she was horrified. She felt that it was too simple a solution of too complicated a problem.

"*N'est-ce pas immoral?*"[2] was all she said, after a brief pause.

"Why so? Think, I have a choice between two alternatives: either to be pregnant, this is, an invalid, or to be the friend and companion of my husband—practically my husband," Anna said in a tone intentionally superficial and frivolous.

"Yes, yes," said Darya Aleksandrovna, hearing the very arguments she had used to herself, and not finding the same force in them as before.

"For you, for other people," said Anna, as though divining her thoughts, "there may be reason to hesitate; but for me . . . You must consider, I am not his wife; he loves me as long as he loves me. And how am I to keep his love? Not like this?"

She moved her white hands in a curve before her belly with extraordinary rapidity, as happens during moments of excitement; ideas and memories rushed into Darya Aleksandrovna's head. "I," she thought, "did not keep my attraction for Stiva; he left me for oth-

[2]"Isn't it immoral?"

ers, and the first woman for whom he betrayed me did not keep him by being always pretty and lively. He deserted her and took another. And can Anna attract and keep Count Vronsky in that way? If that is what he looks for, he will find dresses and manners still more attractive and charming. And however white and beautiful her bare arms are, however beautiful her full figure and her eager face under her black curls, he will find something better still, just as my disgusting, pitiful, and charming husband does."

Dolly made no answer, she merely sighed. Anna noticed this sigh, indicating dissent, and she went on. In her armory she had other arguments so strong that no answer could be made to them.

"Do you say that it's not right? But you must consider," she went on; "you forget my position. How can I desire children? I'm not speaking of the suffering, I'm not afraid of that. Think only, what are my children to be? Ill-fated children, who will have to bear a stranger's name. For the very fact of their birth they will be forced to be ashamed of their mother, their father, their birth."

"But that is just why a divorce is necessary." But Anna did not hear her. She longed to give utterance to all the arguments with which she had so many times convinced herself.

"What is reason given me for if I am not to use it to avoid bringing unhappy beings into the world!" She looked at Dolly, but without waiting for a reply she went on:

"I should always feel I had wronged these unhappy children," she said. "If they are not, at any rate they are not unhappy; while if they are unhappy, I alone should be to blame for it."

These were the very arguments Darya Aleksandrovna had used in her own reflections; but she heard them without understanding them. "How can one wrong creatures that don't exist?" she thought. And all at once the idea struck her: could it possibly, under any circumstances, have been better for her favourite Grisha if he had never existed? And this seemed to her so wild, so strange, that she shook her head to drive away this tangle of whirling, mad ideas.

"No, I don't know; it's not right," was all she said, with an expression of disgust on her face.

"Yes, but you mustn't forget that you and I . . . And besides that," added Anna, in spite of the wealth of her arguments and the poverty of Dolly's objections, seeming still to admit that it was not right, "don't forget the chief point, that I am not now in the same position as you. For you the question is: do you desire not to have any more children; while for me it is: do I desire to have them? And that's a great difference. You must see that I can't desire it in my situation."

Darya Aleksandrovna made no reply. She suddenly felt that she had got far away from Anna; that here lay between them a barrier of questions on which they could never agree, and about which it was better not to speak.

CHAPTER TWENTY-FOUR

"Then there is all the more reason for you to legalize your position if possible," said Dolly.

"Yes, if possible," said Anna, speaking all at once in an utterly different tone, subdued and mournful.

"Surely you don't mean a divorce is impossible? I was told your husband had consented to it."

"Dolly, I don't want to talk about that."

"Oh, we won't then," Darya Aleksandrovna hastened to say, noticing the expression of suffering on Anna's face. "All I see is that you take too gloomy a view of things."

"I? Not at all! I'm always bright and happy. Did you see, *je fais des passions.*[1] Veslovsky—"

"Yes, to tell the truth, I don't like Veslovsky's tone," said Darya Aleksandrovna, anxious to change the subject.

"Oh, that's nonsense! It amuses Aleksey, and that's all; but he's a boy, and quite under my control. You know, I turn him as I please. It's just as it might be with your Grisha . . . Dolly!"—she suddenly changed the subject—"you say I take too gloomy a view of things. You can't understand. It's too awful! I try not to take any view of it at all."

"But I think you ought to. You ought to do all you can."

"But what can I do? Nothing. You tell me to marry Aleksey, and

[1]"I inspire passions."

say I don't think about it. I don't think about it!" she repeated, and a flush rose into her face. She got up, straightening her chest, and sighed heavily. With her light step she began pacing up and down the room, stopping now and then. "I don't think of it? Not a day, not an hour passes that I don't think of it, and blame myself for thinking of it . . . because thinking of that may drive me mad. Drive me mad!" she repeated. "When I think of it, I can't sleep without morphine. But never mind. Let us talk quietly. They tell me, divorce. In the first place, he won't give me a divorce. He's under the influence of Countess Lydia Ivanovna now."

Darya Aleksandrovna, sitting erect on a chair, turned her head, following Anna with a face of sympathetic suffering.

"You ought to make the attempt," she said softly.

"Suppose I make the attempt. What does it mean?" she said, evidently giving utterance to a thought a thousand times thought over and learned by heart. "It means that I, hating him, but still recognizing that I have wronged him—and I consider him magnanimous— that I humiliate myself to write to him . . . Well, suppose I make the effort; I do it. Either I receive a humiliating refusal or consent . . . Well, I have received his consent, say . . . " Anna was at that moment at the furthest end of the room, and she stopped there doing something to the curtain at the window . . . " I receive his consent, but my . . . my son? They won't give him up to me. He will grow up despising me, with his father, whom I've abandoned. Do you see, I love . . . equally, I think, but both more than myself—two beings, Seryozha and Aleksey."

She came out into the middle of the room and stood facing Dolly, with her arms pressed tightly across her chest. In her white dressing gown her figure seemed more than usually grand and broad. She bent her head and, with shining, wet eyes, looked from under her brows at Dolly, a thin little pitiful figure in her patched bed jacket and nightcap, shaking all over with emotion.

"It is only those two beings that I love, and one excludes the other. I can't have them together, and that's the only thing I want. And since I can't have that, I don't care about the rest. I don't care about anything, anything. And it will end one way or another, and so I can't, I don't like to talk of it. So don't blame me, don't judge me for anything. You can't with your pure heart understand all that I'm suffering." She went up, sat down beside Dolly, and, with a guilty look, peered into her face and took her hand.

"What are you thinking? What are you thinking about me? Don't despise me. I don't deserve contempt. I'm simply unhappy. If anyone is unhappy, I am," she articulated, and turning away, she burst into tears.

Left alone, Darya Aleksandrovna said her prayers and went to bed. She had felt for Anna with all her heart while she was speaking to her, but now she could not force herself to think of her. The memories of home and of her children rose up in her imagination with a peculiar charm quite new to her, with a sort of new brilliance. That world of her own seemed to her now so sweet and precious that she would not on any account spend an extra day outside it, and she made up her mind that she would certainly go back the next day.

Anna meantime went back to her boudoir, took a wine glass, and poured into it several drops of a medicine largely composed of morphine. After drinking it and sitting still a little while, she went into her bedroom in a calmer and more cheerful frame of mind.

When she went into the bedroom, Vronsky looked intently at her. He was looking for traces of the conversation which he knew that, staying so long in Dolly's room, she must have had with her. But in her expression of restrained excitement, and of a sort of reserve, he could find nothing but the beauty that always bewitched him afresh though he was used to it, the consciousness of it, and the desire that it should affect him. He did not want to ask her what they had been talking of, but he hoped that she would tell him something of her own accord. But she only said:

"I am so glad you like Dolly. You do, don't you?"

"Oh, I've known her a long while, you know. She's very good-hearted, I suppose, *mais excessivement terre-à-terre.*[2] Still, I'm very glad to see her."

He took Anna's hand and looked inquiringly into her eyes. Misinterpreting the look, she smiled at him . . .

*   *   *

[2]"Excessively commonplace."

The next morning, in spite of the protest of her hosts, Darya Aleksandrovna prepared for her homeward journey. Levin's coachman, in his by no means new coat and shabby hat, with his ill-matched horses and his coach with the patched mudguards, drove with gloomy determination into the covered gravel approach.

Darya Aleksandrovna disliked taking leave of Princess Varvara and the gentlemen of the party. After a day spent together, both she and her hosts were distinctly aware that they did not get on together, and that it was better for them not to meet. Only Anna was sad. She knew that now, from Dolly's departure, no one again would stir up within her soul the feeling that had been roused by their conversation. It hurt her to stir up these feelings, but yet she knew that that was the best part of her soul, and that that part of her soul would quickly be smothered in the life she was leading.

As she drove out into the open country, Darya Aleksandrovna had a delightful sense of relief, and she felt tempted to ask the two men how they had liked being at Vronsky's, when suddenly the coachman, Filipp, expressed himself unasked:

"Rolling in wealth they may be, but three bushels of oats was all they gave us. Everything cleared up till there wasn't a grain left by cockcrow. What are three bushels? A mere mouthful! And oats now down to forty-five kopeks. At our place, no fear, all comers may have as much as they can eat."

"The master's close-fisted," put in the office clerk.

"Well, did you like their horses?" asked Dolly.

"The horses!—there's no two opinions about them. And the food was good. But it seemed to me sort of dreary there, Darya Aleksandrovna. I don't know what you thought," he said, turning his handsome, good-natured face to her.

"I thought so too. Well, shall we get home by evening?"

"Eh, we must!"

On reaching home and finding everyone entirely satisfactory and particularly charming, Darya Aleksandrovna began with great liveliness telling them how she had arrived, how warmly they had received her, of the luxury and good taste in which the Vronskys lived, and of their recreations, and she would not allow a word to be said against them.

"One had to know Anna and Vronsky—I have got to know him better now—to see how nice they are, and how touching," she said, speaking now with perfect sincerity, and forgetting the ineffable feeling of dissatisfaction and awkwardness she had experienced there.

CHAPTER TWENTY-FIVE

Vronsky and Anna spent the whole summer and part of the winter in the country, living in just the same way, and still taking no steps to obtain a divorce.It was an understood thing between them that they should not go away anywhere; but both felt that the longer they lived alone, especially in the autumn, without guest in the house, they could not stand this existence, and would have to alter it.

Their life was such, it would seem, that nothing better could be desired. They had ample means, good health, a child, occupations of their own. Anna devoted just as much care to her appearance when they had no visitors, and she did a great deal of reading, both of novels and of what serious literature was in fashion. She ordered all the books that were praised in the foreign papers and reviews she received, and read them with that concentrated attention which is given only to what is read in seclusion. Moreover, every subject that was of interest to Vronsky she studied in books and technical journals, so that he often went straight to her with questions relating to agriculture or architecture, sometimes even with questions relating to horse breeding or sport. He was amazed at her knowledge, her memory, and at first was disposed to doubt it, to ask for confirmation of her facts; and she would find what he asked for in some book and show it to him.

The building of the hospital, too, interested her. She did not merely assist, but planned and suggested a great deal herself. But her chief thought was still of herself—how far she was dear to Vronsky, how far she could make up to him for all he had given up. Vronsky appreciated this desire not only to please but to serve him, which had become the sole aim of her existence, but at the same time he wearied of the loving snares in which she tried to hold him fast. As time went on, and he saw himself more and more often entangled in these meshes, he had an ever-growing desire, not so much to escape from them, as to try whether they hindered his freedom. Had it not been for this growing desire to be free, not to have scenes every time he wanted to go to the town for a meeting or a race, Vronsky would have been perfectly satisfied with his life. The role he had chosen, the role of wealthy landowner, one of that class which is the very heart of the Russian aristocracy, was entirely to his taste; and now, after spending six months in that character, he derived even greater satisfaction from it. And his management of his estate, which occupied and absorbed him more and more, was most successful. In spite of the immense sums cost him by the hospital, by machinery, by cows ordered from Switzerland, and many other things, he was convinced that he was not wasting but increasing his fortune. In all matters affecting income, the sales of timber, wheat, and wool, the leasing of land, Vronsky was hard as a rock, and knew well how to keep up prices. In all operations on a large scale on this and his other estates, he kept to the simplest methods involving no risk, and in trifling details he was careful and exacting to an extreme degree. In spite of all the cunning and ingenuity of the German steward, who tried to tempt him into purchases by making his original estimate always far larger than really required, and then representing to Vronsky that he might get the thing cheaper and so make a profit, Vronsky did not give in. He listened to his steward, questioned him, and agreed to his suggestions only when the implement to be ordered or constructed was the very newest, not yet known in Russia, and likely to excite wonder. Apart from such exceptions, he resolved upon an increased outlay only where there was a surplus, and in making such an outlay, he went into the minutest details, and insisted on getting the very best for his money; so that by the method on which he managed his affairs, it was clear that he was not wasting but increasing his fortune.

In October there were the nobility elections in Kashin province, where the estates of Vronsky, Sviazhsky, Koznyshev, and Oblonsky were, as well as a small part of Levin's.

These elections were attracting public attention from several circumstances connected with them, and also from the people taking part in them. There had been a great deal of talk about them, and great preparations were being made for them. Persons who never attended the elections were coming from Moscow, from Petersburg, and from abroad to attend these. Vronsky had long before promised Sviazhsky to go to them. Before the elections Sviazhsky, who often visited Vozdvizhenskoe, drove over to fetch Vronsky. On the day before, there had been almost a quarrel between Vronsky and Anna over this proposed expedition. It was the very dullest autumn weather, which is so dreary in the country, and so, preparing himself for a struggle, Vronsky, with a hard and cold expression, informed Anna of his departure as he had never spoken to her before. But, to his surprise, Anna accepted the information with great composure, and merely asked when he would be back. He looked intently at her, at a loss to explain this composure. She smiled at his look. He knew that way she had of withdrawing into herself, and knew that it happened only when she had determined upon something without letting him know her plans. He was afraid of this; but he was so anxious to avoid a scene that he kept up appearances, and half sincerely believed in what he longed to believe in—her reasonableness.

"I hope you won't be bored!"

"I hope not," said Anna. "I got a box of books yesterday from Gautier's.[1] No, I shan't be bored."

"She wants to adopt that tone, and so much the better," he thought, "or else it would be that same thing over and over again."

And he set off for the elections without appealing to her for a candid explanation. It was the first time since the beginning of their intimacy that he had parted from her without a full explanation. From one point of view this troubled him, but on the other hand he felt that it was better so. "At first there will be, as this time, something undefined kept back, and then she will get used to it. In any case, I can give up anything for her, but not my independence," he thought.

CHAPTER TWENTY-SIX

In September, Levin moved to Moscow for Kitty's confinement. He had spent a whole month in Moscow with nothing to do, when

[1]A well-known Moscow bookstore.

Sergey Ivanovich, who had property in Kashin province and took great interest in the question of the approaching elections, made ready to set off to the elections. He invited his brother, who had a vote in Seleznev district, to come with him. Levin had, moreover, to transact in Kashin some extremely important business relating to a trusteeship and to the receiving of certain mortgage money for his sister, who was abroad.

Levin still hesitated, but Kitty, who saw that he was bored in Moscow and urged him to go, on her own authority ordered him the proper nobleman's uniform, costing eighty rubles. And the eighty rubles paid for the uniform was the chief reason that finally decided Levin to go. He went to Kashin. . . .

Levin had been in Kashin six days, visiting the assembly each day, and busily engaged about his sister's business, which still dragged on. The district marshals of nobility were all occupied with the elections, and it was impossible to get even the simple matter of the trusteeship settled. The other matter, the payment from the mortgage, was met too by difficulties. After long negotiations over the legal details, the money was at last ready to be paid; but the notary, a most obliging person, could not hand over the voucher, because it required the signature of the president, and the president, though he had not given his duties to a deputy, was at the elections. All these worrying negotiations, this endless going from place to place and talking with pleasant and excellent people who quite saw the unpleasantness of the petitioner's position but were powerless to assist him—all these efforts that yielded no result led to a feeling of misery in Levin akin to the mortifying helplessness one experiences in dreams when one tries to use physical force. He felt this frequently as he talked to his most good-natured legal adviser. This adviser did, it seemed, everything possible, and strained every nerve, to get him out of his difficulties. "I tell you what you might try," he said more than once; "go to so-and-so and so-and-so," and he drew up a whole plan for circumventing the fatal obstacle that hindered everything. But he would add immediately, "It'll mean some delay, anyway, but you might try it." And Levin did try, and did go. Everyone was kind and polite, but the point evaded seemed to crop up again in the end, and again to bar the way. What was particularly trying was that Levin could not make out with whom he was struggling, to whose interest it was that his business should not be done. That no one seemed to know; the adviser certainly did not know. If Levin could have understood why, just as he understood why one can approach the ticket office of a railway station only in a single file, it would not have been so frustrating and tiresome to him. But with the obstacles that confronted him in his business, no one could explain why they existed.

But Levin had changed a good deal since his marriage; he was patient, and if he could not see why it was all arranged like this, he told himself that he could not judge without knowing all about it, and that most likely it must be so, and he tried not to fret.

In attending the elections, too, and taking part in them, he tried now not to judge, not to argue, but to comprehend as fully as he could the question that was so earnestly and ardently absorbing honest and excellent men whom he respected. Since his marriage there had been revealed to Levin so many new and serious aspects of life that had previously, through his frivolous attitude toward them, seemed of no importance, that in the question of the elections too he assumed and tried to find some serious significance.

Sergey Ivanovich explained to him the meaning and object of the proposed revolution at the elections. The marshal of the province in whose hands the law had placed the control of so many important public functions—like trusteeships (the very department which was giving Levin so much trouble just now), the disposal of large sums subscribed by the nobility of the province, high schools for boys and girls, military schools, elementary education along the new lines, and finally the district council—the marshal of nobility, Snetkov, was a nobleman of the old school—dissipating an immense fortune, a good-hearted man, honest after his own fashion, but utterly without any comprehension of the needs of modern days. He always took, in every question, the side of the nobility; he was positively antagonistic to the spread of popular education, and he succeeded in giving a purely party character to the district council which ought by rights to be of such immense importance. What was needed was to put in his place a fresh, capable, perfectly modern man, of contemporary ideas, and to frame their policy so as from the rights conferred upon the nobles, not as the nobility, but as an element of the district council, to extract all the powers of self-government that could possibly be derived from them. In wealthy Kashin province, which always took the lead of other provinces in everything, there was now such a preponderance of forces that this policy once carried through properly there might serve as a model for the other provinces for all Russia. And hence the whole question was of the greatest importance. It was proposed to elect as marshal in place of Snetkov either Sviazhsky, or, better still, Nevedovsky, a former university professor, a man of remarkable intelligence and a great friend of Sergey Ivanovich.

The meeting was opened by the governor, who made a speech to the nobles, urging them to elect the public functionaries, not from regard for persons, but for the service and welfare of their fatherland, and hoping that the honorable nobility of Kashin province would, as at all former elections, hold their duty as sacred, and vindicate the exalted confidence of the Emperor.

When he had finished his speech, the governor walked out of the hall, and the nobleman noisily and eagerly—some even enthusiastically—followed him and thronged around him while he put on his fur coat and conversed amicably with the marshal of the province. Levin, anxious to see into everything and not to miss anything, stood there too in the crowd, and heard the governor say: "Please tell Marya Ivanovna my wife is very sorry she had to go to the orphanage." And thereupon the nobles in high good humor sorted out their fur coats and all drove off to the cathedral.

In the cathedral Levin, lifting his hand like the rest and repeating the words of the archdeacon, swore with the most solemn oaths to do all the governor had hoped they would do. Church services always affected Levin, and as he uttered the words "I kiss the cross," and glanced around at the crowd of young and old men repeating the same, he felt touched.

On the second and the third days there was business relating to the finances of the nobility and the girl's high school, of no importance whatever, as Sergey Ivanovich explained, and Levin, busy seeing after his own affairs, did not attend the meetings. On the fourth day the auditing of the provincial funds took place at the high table of the marshal of the province. And then there occurred the first skirmish between the new party and the old. The committee entrusted to verify the accounts reported to the meeting that all was in order. The marshal of the province got up, thanked the nobility for their confidence, and shed tears. The nobles gave him a loud welcome, and shook hands with him. But at that instant a nobleman of Sergey Ivanovich's party said that he had heard that the committee had not verified the accounts, considering such a verification an insult to the marshal of the province. One of the members of the committee incautiously admitted this. Then a small gentleman, very young-looking but very venomous, began to say that it would probably be agreeable to the marshal of the province to give an account of his expenditures of the public moneys, and that the misplaced delicacy of the members of the committee was depriving him of this moral satisfaction. Then the members of the committee tried to withdraw their admission, and Sergey Ivanovich began to prove that they must logically admit either that they had verified the accounts or that they had not, and he developed this dilemma in detail. Sergey Ivanovich was answered by the spokesman of the opposite party. Then Sviazhsky spoke, and then the venomous gentleman again. The discussion lasted a long time and ended in nothing. Levin was surprised that they should dispute upon this subject so long, especially as, when he asked Sergey Ivanovich whether he supposed that money had been misappropriated, Sergey Ivanovich answered:

"Oh, no! He's an honest man. But those old-fashioned methods of paternal family arrangements in the management of provincial affairs must be broken down."

On the fifth day came the elections of the district marshals. It was rather a stormy day in several districts. In the Seleznev district Sviazhsky was elected unanimously without a ballot, and he gave a dinner party that evening.

CHAPTER TWENTY-SEVEN

The sixth day was fixed for the election of the marshal of the province. The rooms, large and small, were full of noblemen in all sorts of uniforms. Many had come only for that day. Men who had not seen each other for years, some from the Crimea, some from

Petersburg, some from abroad, met in the rooms of the Hall of Nobility. There was much discussion around the governor's table under the portrait of the Tsar.

The nobles, both in the large and the smaller rooms, grouped themselves in camps, and from their hostile and suspicious glances, from the silence that fell upon them when outsiders approached a group, and from the way that some, whispering together, retreated to the further corridor, it was evident that each side had secrets from the other. In appearance the noblemen were divided into two classes: the old and the new. The old were for the most part either in old uniforms of the nobility, buttoned up tight, with swords and hats, or in their naval, cavalry, infantry, or official uniforms, which they were entitled to wear. The uniforms of the older men were embroidered in the old-fashioned way with pleats and puffs on their shoulders; they were unmistakably tight and short in the waists, as though their wearers had grown out of them. The younger men wore the uniform of the nobility with long waists and broad shoulders, unbuttoned over white vests, or uniforms with black collars with embroidered laurel leaves, the emblem of the Ministry of Justice. To the younger men belonged the court uniforms that here and there brightened up the crowd.

But the division into young and old did not correspond with the division of parties. Some of the young men, as Levin observed, belonged to the old party; and some of the very oldest noblemen, on the contrary, were whispering with Sviazhsky, and were evidently ardent partisans of the new party.

Levin stood in the smaller room, where they were smoking and taking light refreshments, close to his own friends, and listening to what they were saying, he conscientiously exerted all his intelligence trying to understand what was said. Sergey Ivanovich was the center around which the others grouped themselves. He was listening at that moment to Sviazhsky and Khlyustov, the marshal of another district, who belonged to their party. Khlyustov would not agree to go with his district to ask Snetkov to stand, while Sviazhsky was trying to persuade him to do so, and Sergey Ivanovich was approving of the plan. Levin could not make out why the opposition was to ask the marshal to stand whom they wanted to supersede.

Stepan Arkadyevich, who had just been drinking and taking some lunch, came up to them in his chamberlain's uniform, wiping his lips with a perfumed handkerchief of bordered batiste.

"We are placing our forces," he said, smoothing his whiskers, "Sergey Ivanovich!"

And listening to the conversation, he supported Sviazhsky's contention.

"One district's enough, and Sviazhsky's obviously of the opposition," he said, words evidently intelligible to all except Levin.

"Why, Kostya, you here too! I suppose you're converted, eh?" he added, turning to Levin and drawing his arm through his. Levin would have been glad indeed to be converted, but could not make out what the point was, and retreating a few steps from the speakers, he explained to Stepan Arkadyevich his inability to understand why the marshal of the province should be asked to stand.

"*O sancta simplicitas!*"[1] said Stepan Arkadyevich, and briefly and clearly he explained it to Levin. If, as at previous elections, all the districts asked the marshal of the province to stand, then he would be elected without a ballot. That must not be. Now eight districts had agreed to call upon him: if two refused to do so, Snetkov might decline to stand at all; and then the old party might choose another of their party, which would throw off their calculations. But if only one district, Sviazhsky's, did not call upon him to stand, Snetkov would let himself be balloted for. They were even, some of them, going to vote for him and purposely let him get a good many votes, so that the enemy might be thrown off the scent, and when a candidate of the other side was put up, they too might give him some votes. Levin understood to some extent, but not fully, and would have put a few more questions, when suddenly everyone began talking and making a noise and they moved toward the big room.

"What is it? Eh? Whom?" "No power of attorney? Whose? What?" "They won't pass him?" "No power of attorney?" "They won't let Flerov in?" "Eh, because of the charge against him?" "Why, at this rate, they won't admit anyone. It's a swindle!" "The law!"

---

[1]"Blessed simplicity!" Said by Jan Hus (1369?-1415), Czech religious reformer, as he was burned as a heretic.

Levin heard exclamations of all sides, and he moved into the big room together with the others, all hurrying somewhere and afraid of missing something. Squeezed by the crowding noblemen, he drew near the high table where the marshal of the province, Sviazhsky, and the other leaders were hotly disputing about something.

CHAPTER TWENTY-EIGHT

Levin was standing rather far off. A nobleman breathing heavily and hoarsely at his side, and another, whose thick-soled boots were creaking, prevented him from hearing distinctly. He could hear only the soft voice of the marshal faintly, then the shrill voice of the venomous gentleman, and then the voice of Sviazhsky. They were disputing, as far as he could make out, as to the interpretation to be put on the act and the exact meaning of the words "against whom proceedings are pending."

The crowd parted to make way for Sergey Ivanovich approaching the table. Sergey Ivanovich, waiting till the venomous gentleman had finished speaking, said that he thought the best solution would be to refer to the wording of the Act itself, and asked the secretary to find the Act. The Act said that in case of difference of opinion, there must be a ballot.

Sergey Ivanovich read the Act and began to explain its meaning, but at that point a tall, stout, round-shouldered landowner, with a dyed mustache, in a tight uniform that cut the back of his neck, interrupted him. He went up to the table, and striking it with the ring on his finger, he shouted loudly: "A ballot! Put it to the vote! No need for more talking!" Then several voices began to talk all at once, and the tall nobleman with the ring, getting more and more exasperated, shouted more and more loudly. But it was impossible to make out what he said.

He was shouting for the very course Sergey Ivanovich had proposed; but it was evident that he hated him and all his party, and this feeling of hatred spread through the whole party and roused in opposition to it the same vindictiveness, though in a more decent form, on the other side. Shouts were raised, and for a moment all was confusion, so that the marshal of the province had to call for order.

"A ballot! A ballot! Every nobleman will understand! We shed our blood for our country! . . ." "The confidence of the Emperor . . . No checking the accounts of the marshal; he's not a shop assistant! . . . But that's not the point . . . Votes, please! Disgusting! . . ." shouted furious and violent voices on all sides. Looks and faces were even more violent and furious than their words. They expressed the most implacable hatred. Levin did not in the least understand what was the matter, and he marveled at the passion with which it was disputed whether or not the decision about Flerov should be put to the vote. He forgot, as Sergey Ivanovich explained to him afterward, this syllogism: that it was necessary for the public good to get rid of the marshal of the province; that to get rid of the marshal it was necessary to have a majority of votes; that to get a majority it was necessary to secure Flerov's right to vote; that to secure the recognition of Flerov's right to vote they must decide on the interpretation to be put on the Act.

"And one vote may decide the whole question and one must be serious and consistent if one wants to be of use in public life," concluded Sergey Ivanovich. But Levin forgot all that, and it was painful to him to see all these excellent persons for whom he had a respect, in such an unpleasant and vicious state of excitement. To escape from this painful feeling he went away into the other room, where there was nobody except the waiters at the buffet. Seeing the waiters busy washing up the crockery and setting in order their plates and wine glasses, seeing their calm and cheerful faces, Levin felt an unexpected sense of relief, as though he had come out of a stuffy room into the fresh air. He began walking up and down, looking with pleasure at the waiters. He particularly liked the way one gray-whiskered waiter, who showed his scorn for the other younger ones and was jeered at by them, was teaching them how to fold napkins properly. Levin was just about to enter into conversation with the old waiter, when the secretary of the court of trusteeship, a little old man whose specialty it was to know all the noblemen of the province by name and patronymic, drew him away.

"Please come, Konstantin Dmitrievich," he said, "your brother's looking for you. They are voting on the legal point."

Levin walked into the room, received a white ball, and followed his brother, Sergey Ivanovich, to the table where Sviazhsky was standing with a significant and ironical face, holding his beard in his fist and sniffing at it. Sergey Ivanovich put his hand into the box, put the ball somewhere, and, making room for Levin, stopped. Levin advanced, but utterly forgetting what he was to do, and much embarrassed, he turned to Sergey Ivanovich with the question, "Where am I to put it?" He asked this softly, at a moment when there was talking going on near, so that he hoped his question would not be overheard. But the persons speaking paused, and his improper question was overheard. Sergey Ivanovich frowned.

"That is a matter for each man's own decision," he said severely.

Several people smiled. Levin crimsoned, hurriedly thrust his hand under the cloth, and put the ball to the right because it was in his right hand. Having put it in, he recollected that he ought to have thrust his left hand in too, and so he thrust it in though too late, and, still more overcome with confusion, he beat a hasty retreat into the background.

"A hundred and twenty-six for admission! Ninety-eight against!" sang out the voice of the secretary, who could not pronounce the letter *r*. Then there was a laugh; a button and two nuts were found in the box. The nobleman was allowed the right to vote, and the new party had won.

But the old party did not consider themselves conquered. Levin heard that they were asking Snetkov to stand, and he saw that a crowd of noblemen was surrounding the marshal, who was saying something. Levin went nearer. In reply, Snetkov spoke of the trust the noblemen of the province had placed in him, the affection they had shown him which he did not deserve, as his only merit had been his attachment to the nobility, to whom he had devoted twelve years of service. Several times he repeated the words: "I have served to the best of my powers with truth and good faith, I value your goodness and thank you," and suddenly he stopped short from the tears that choked him, and went out of the room. Whether these tears came from a sense of the injustice being done him, from his love for the nobility, or from the strain of the position he was placed in, feeling himself surrounded by enemies, his emotion infected the assembly, the majority were touched, and Levin felt a tenderness for Snetkov.

In the doorway the marshal of the province jostled against Levin.

"Beg pardon, excuse me, please," he said as to a stranger, but recognizing Levin, he smiled timidly. It seemed to Levin that he would have liked to say something, but could not speak for emotion. His face and his whole figure in his uniform with the crosses, and white trousers trimmed with gold braid, as he moved hurriedly along reminded Levin of some hunted beast who sees that he is doomed. This expression in the marshal's face was particularly touching to Levin, because only the day before he had been at his house about the trusteeship business and had seen him in all his grandeur, a kindly, fatherly man. The big house with the old family furniture; the rather dirty, far from stylish, but respectful footmen, unmistakably old house serfs who had stuck to their master; the stout, good-natured wife in a cap with lace and a Turkish shawl, petting her pretty grandchild, her daughter's daughter; the young son, a boy in his junior year in high school, coming home from school and greeting his father, kissing his big hand; the genuine, cordial words and gestures of the old man—all this had the day before roused an instinctive feeling of respect and sympathy in Levin. This old man was a touching and pathetic figure to Levin now, and he longed to say something pleasant to him.

"So you're sure to be our marshal again," he said.

"It's not likely," said the marshal, looking around nervously. "I'm worn out, I'm old. If there are men younger and more deserving than I, let them serve."

And the marshal disappeared through a side door.

The most solemn moment was at hand. They were to proceed immediately to the election. The leaders of both parties were calculating on their fingers the white and black balls they might get.

The debate about Flerov had not only given the new party Flerov's vote, but had also gained time for them, so that they could send out for three noblemen who had been rendered unable to take part in the elections by the wiles of the other party. Two noble gentlemen who had a weakness for strong drink had been made drunk by the partisans of Snetkov, and a third had been robbed of his uniform.

On learning this, the new party had made haste, during the dispute about Flerov, to send some of their men in a sleigh to clothe the stripped gentleman, and to bring along one of the intoxicated to the meeting.

"I've brought one, drenched him with water," said the landowner who had gone on this errand to Sviazhsky. "He's all right. He'll do."

"Not too drunk, he won't fall down?" said Sviazhsky, shaking his head.

"No, he's fine. If only they don't give him any more to drink . . . I've told the waiter not to give him anything on any account."

CHAPTER TWENTY-NINE

The narrow room, in which they were smoking and taking refreshments, was full of noblemen. The excitement grew more intense, and every face betrayed some uneasiness. The excitement was specially keen for the leaders of each party, who knew every detail, and had counted up every vote. They were the generals organizing the approaching battle. The rest, like the rank and file before a battle, though they were getting ready for the fight, sought for other distractions in the interval. Some were lunching, standing at the bar, or sitting at the table; others were walking up and down the long room, smoking cigarettes and talking with friends they had not seen for a long while.

Levin did not care to eat, and he was not smoking; he did not want to join his own friends, that is, Sergey Ivanovich, Stepan Arkadyevich, Sviazhsky, and the rest, because Vronsky in his equerry's uniform was standing with them in animated conversation. Levin had seen him already at the meeting on the previous day, and he had studiously avoided him, not caring to greet him. He went to the window and sat down, scanning the groups, and listening to what was being said around him. He felt depressed, especially because everyone else was, as he saw, animated, anxious, and interested, and he alone, with an old, toothless little man with mumbling lips wearing a naval uniform, sitting beside him, had no interest in it and nothing to do.

"He's such a scoundrel! I have told him so, but it makes no difference. Just think of it! He couldn't collect it in three years!" he heard vigorously uttered by a round-shouldered short country gentleman, who had pomaded hair hanging on his embroidered collar, and new boots obviously put on for the occasion, with heels that tapped vigorously as he spoke. Casting a displeased glance at Levin, this gentleman sharply turned his back.

"Yes, it's dirty business, there's no denying," a small gentleman assented in a high voice.

Next a whole crowd of country gentlemen, surrounding a stout general, hurriedly came near Levin. These persons were unmistakably seeking a place where they could talk without being overheard.

"How dare he say I had his breeches stolen! Pawned them for drink, I expect. Damn the fellow and his princely title! He'd better not say it, the swine!"

"But excuse me! They take their stand on the Act," was being said in another group; "the wife should have been registered as noble."

"Oh, damn the Act! I speak from my heart. We're all gentlemen, aren't we? Above suspicion."

"Shall we go on, Your Excellency, *fine champagne?*"

Another group was following a nobleman who was shouting something in a loud voice; it was one of the three intoxicated gentlemen.

"I always advised Marya Semyonovna to let for a fair rent, because she can never show a profit," he heard a pleasant voice say. The speaker was a country gentleman with gray whiskers, wearing the regimental uniform of an old general staff officer. It was the very landowner Levin had met at Sviazhsky's. He knew him at once. The landowner too stared at Levin, and they exchanged greetings.

"Very glad to see you! To be sure! I remember you very well. Last year at Nikolai Ivanovich's."

"Well, and how is your land doing?" asked Levin.

"Oh, still just the same, always at a loss," the landowner answered with a resigned smile, but with an expression of serenity and conviction that so it must be. "And how do you come to be in our province?" he asked. "Come to take part in our *coup d'état*?" he said, confidently pronouncing the French words with a bad accent. "All Russia's here—chamberlains, and everything short of ministers." He pointed to the imposing figure of Stepan Arkadyevich in white trousers and his court uniform, walking by with a general.

"I must confess that I don't very well understand the drift of the provincial elections," said Levin.

The landowner looked at him.

"Why, what is there to understand? There's no meaning in it at all. It's a decaying institution that goes on running only by the force of inertia. Just look, the very uniforms tell you that it's an assembly of justices of the peace, permanent officials, and so on, but not of noblemen."

"Then why do you come?" asked Levin.

"From habit, nothing else. Then, too, one must keep up connections. It's a moral obligation of a sort. And then, to tell the truth, there's one's own interests. My son-in-law wants to stand as a permanent member; they're not rich people, and I must give him a push. These gentlemen, now, what do they come for?" he said, pointing to the venomous gentleman, who was talking at the high table.

"That's the new generation of nobility."

"New it may be, but nobility it isn't. They're proprietors of a sort, but we're the landowners. As noblemen, they're cutting their own throats."

"But you say it's an institution that's served its time."

"That it may be, but still it ought to be treated a little more respectfully. Snetkov, now . . . We may be of use, or we may not, but we're the growth of a thousand years. If we're laying out a garden, planning one before the house, you know, and there you've a tree that's stood for centuries in the very spot . . . Old and gnarled it may be, and yet you don't cut down the old fellow to make room for the flower beds, but lay out your beds so as to take advantage of the tree. You won't grow him again in a year," he said cautiously, and he immediately changed the conversation. "Well, and how is your land doing?"

"Oh, not very well. I make five per cent."

"Yes, but you don't count your own work. Aren't you worth something too? I'll tell you my own case. Before I took to seeing after the land, I had a salary of three thousand yearly from the service. Now I do more work than I did in the service, and like you I get five per cent on the land, and thank God for that. But one's work is thrown in for nothing."

"Then why do you do it, if it's a clear loss?"

"Oh, well, one does it! What would you have? It's habit, and one knows it's how it should be. And what's more," the landowner went on, leaning his elbows on the window and chatting on, "my son, I must tell you, has no taste for it. There's no doubt he'll be a scholar. So there'll be no one to keep it up. And yet one does it. Here this year I've planted an orchard."

"Yes, yes," said Levin, "that's perfectly true. I always feel there's no real balance of gain in my work on the land, and yet one does it . . . It's sort of duty one feels to the land."

"But I tell you what," the landowner pursued; "a neighbor of mine, a merchant, was at my place. We walked about the fields and the garden. 'No,' said he, 'Stepan Vasilievich, everything's well looked after, but your garden's neglected.' (But, as a matter of fact, it's well kept up.) 'To my thinking,' my neighbor went on, 'I'd cut down that lime tree. Here you've about a thousand lime trees and each would make two good bundles of bast. And nowadays that's worth something. I'd cut down the lot.'

"And with what he made he'd buy cattle, or get some land dirt cheap, and let it out in lots to the peasants," Levin added, smiling. He had evidently more than once come across those commercial calculations. "And he'd make his fortune. But you and I must thank God if we keep what we've got and leave it to our children."

"You're married, I've heard?" said the landowner.

"Yes," Levin answered, with proud satisfaction. "Yes, it's rather strange," he went on. "so we live without making anything, as though we were ancient vestals set to keep some sacred fire going."

The landowner chuckled under his white mustache.

"There are some among us, too, like our friend Nikolai Ivanovich, or Count Vronsky, who's settled here lately, who try to carry on their husbandry as though it were a factory; but so far it leads to nothing but eating away their capital."

"But why is it we don't do like the merchants? Why don't we cut down our parks for timber?" said Levin, returning to a thought that had struck him.

"Why, as you said, we must protect the sacred flame. Besides, that's not work for a nobleman. And our work as noblemen isn't done here at the elections, but yonder, each in our corner. There's a class instinct, too, of what one ought and oughtn't do. I see it in the peasants too. It's the same with them; any good peasant tries to take all the land he can. However bad the land is, he'll work it. Without a return, too. At a simple loss."

"Just as we do," said Levin. "Very, very glad to have met you," he added, seeing Sviazhsky approaching him.

"And here we've met for the first time since we met at your place," said the landowner to Sviazhsky, "and we've had a good talk too."

"Well, have you been attacking the new order of things?" said Sviazhsky with a smile.

"Of course."

"Got it off our chests."

CHAPTER THIRTY

Sviazhsky took Levin's arm, and went with him to his own friends.

This time there was no avoiding Vronsky. He was standing with Stepan Arkadyevich and Sergey Ivanovich, and looking straight at Levin as he drew near.

"Delighted! I believe I've had the pleasure of meeting you . . . at Princess Shcherbatskaya's," he said, giving Levin his hand.

"Yes, I quite remember our meeting," said Levin, and blushing crimson, he turned away immediately, and began talking to his brother.

With a slight smile Vronsky went on talking to Sviazhsky, obviously without the slightest inclination to enter into conversation with Levin. But Levin, as he talked to his brother, was continually looking round at Vronsky, trying to think of something to say to him to gloss over his rudeness.

"What are we waiting for now?" asked Levin, looking at Sviazhsky and Vronsky.

"For Snetkov. He has to refuse or to consent to stand," answered Sviazhsky.

"Well, and what has he done, consented or not?"

"That's the point, that he's done neither," said Vronsky.

"And if he refuses, who will stand then?" asked Levin, looking at Vronsky.

"Whoever chooses to," said Sviazhsky.

"Will you?" asked Levin.

"Certainly not I," said Sviazhsky, looking confused, and turning an alarmed glance at the venomous gentleman, who was standing beside Sergey Ivanovich.

"Who then? Nevedovsky?" said Levin, feeling he was putting his foot into it.

But this was worse still. Nevedovsky and Sviazhsky were the two candidates.

"I certainly shall not, under any circumstances," answered the venomous gentleman.

This was Nevedovsky himself. Sviazhsky introduced him to Levin.

"Well, you find it exciting too?" said Stepan Arkadyevich, winking at Vronsky. "It's something like a race. One might bet on it."

"Yes, it is keenly exciting," said Vronsky. "And once taking the thing up, one's eager to see it through. It's a fight!" he said, scowling and setting his powerful jaws.

"What a capable fellow Sviazhsky is! Sees it all so clearly."

"Oh, yes!" Vronsky assented indifferently.

A silence followed, during which Vronsky—since he had to look at something—looked at Levin, at his feet, at his uniform, then at his face, and noticing his gloomy eyes fixed upon him, he said, in order to say something:

"How is it that you, living constantly in the country, are not a justice of the peace? You are not in the uniform of one."

"It's because I consider that the justice of the peace is a silly institution," Levin answered gloomily. He had been all the time looking for an opportunity to enter into conversation with Vronsky so as to smooth over his rudeness at their first meeting.

"I don't think so, quite the contrary," Vronsky said, with quiet surprise.

"It's a plaything," Levin cut him short. "We don't want justices of the peace. I've never had a single thing to do with them during eight years. And what I have had was decided wrongly by them. The justice of the peace is over thirty miles from me. For some matter of two rubles I should have to send a lawyer, who costs me fifteen."

And he related how a peasant had stolen some flour from the miller, and when the miller told him of it, had lodged a complaint for slander. All this was utterly uncalled for and stupid, and Levin felt it himself as he said it.

"Oh, he's such an oddball!' said Stepan Arkadyevich with his most soothing, almond-oil smile. "But come along; I think they're voting . . ."

And they separated.

"I can't understand," said Sergey Ivanovich, who had observed his brother's clumsiness, "I can't understand how anyone can be so absolutely devoid of political tact. That's where we Russians are so deficient. The marshal of the province is our opponent, and with him you're *ami cochon*,[1] and you beg him to stand. Count Vronsky, now . . . I'm not making a friend of him; he's asked me to dinner, and I'm not going; but he's one of our side—why make an enemy of him? Then you ask Nevedovsky if he's going to stand. That's not a thing to do."

"Oh, I don't understand it at all! And it's all such nonsense," Levin answered gloomily.

"You say it's all such nonsense, but as soon as you have anything to do with it, you make a muddle."

Levin did not answer, and they walked together into the big room.

The marshal of the province, though he was vaguely conscious of some trap being prepared for him, and though he had not been called upon by all to stand, had still made up his mind to stand. All was silence in the room. The secretary announced in a loud voice that the captain of the guards, Mikhail Stepanovich Snetkov, would now be balloted for as marshal of the province.

---

[1]"Very thick."

The district marshals walked carrying little plates, on which were balls, from their tables to the high table, and the election began.

"Put it in the right side," whispered Stepan Arkadyevich, as he and his brother-in-law followed the marshal of his district to the table. But Levin had forgotten by now the calculations that had been explained to him, and was afraid Stepan Arkadyevich might be mistaken in saying, "the right side." Surely Snetkov was the enemy. As he went up, he held the ball in his right hand, but thinking he was wrong, just at the box he changed to the left hand, and undoubtedly put the ball to the left. An expert in the business, standing at the box and seeing by the mere action of the elbow where each put his ball, scowled with annoyance. There was no need for him to exercise his sagacity this time.

Everything was still, and the counting of the balls was heard. Then a single voice rose and proclaimed the numbers for and against. The marshal had been voted for by a considerable majority. All was noise and there was a headlong rush toward the doors. Snetkov came in, and the nobles thronged around him, congratulating him.

"Well, now is it over?" Levin asked Sergey Ivanovich.

"It's only just beginning," Sviazhsky said, replying for Sergey Ivanovich with a smile. "Some other candidate may receive more votes than the marshal."

Levin had quite forgotten about that. Now he could only remember that there was some sort of subtle point in it, but he was too bored to think what it was exactly. He felt depressed, and longed to get out of the crowd.

As no one was paying any attention to him, and no one apparently needed him, he quietly slipped away into the little room where the refreshments were, and again had a great sense of comfort when he saw the waiters. The little old waiter pressed him to have something, and Levin agreed. After eating a cutlet with beans and talking to the waiters of their former masters, Levin, not wishing to go back to the hall, where it was all so distasteful to him, proceeded to walk through the galleries. The galleries were full of fashionably dressed ladies, leaning over the balustrade and trying not to lose a single word of what was being said below. With the ladies were sitting and standing smartly dressed lawyers, high school teachers in spectacles, and officers. Everywhere they were talking of the election, and of how worried the marshal was, and how splendid the discussions had been. In one group Levin heard his brother's praises. One lady was telling a lawyer:

"How glad I am I heard Koznyshev! It's worth missing one's dinner. He's wonderful! So clear and distinct all of it! There's not one of you in the law courts that speaks like that. The only one is Meidel, and he's not so eloquent by a long shot."

Finding a free place, Levin leaned over the balustrade and began looking and listening.

All the noblemen were sitting railed off behind barriers according to their districts. In the middle of the room stood a man in a uniform, who shouted in a loud, high voice:

"As a candidate for the marshalship of the nobility of the province we call upon staff-captain Yevgeny Ivanovich Apukhtin!" A dead silence followed, and then a weak old voice was heard: "Declined!"

"We call upon the privy councilor Piotr Petrovich Bohl," the voice began again.

"Declined!" a boyish voice replied.

Again it began and again "Declined." And so it went on for about an hour. Levin, with his elbows on the balustrade, looked and listened. At first he wondered and wanted to know what it meant; then, feeling sure that he could not make it out, he began to be bored. Then, recalling all the excitement and vindictiveness he had seen on all the faces, he felt sad; he made up his mind to go, and went downstairs. As he passed through the entry to the galleries he met a gloomy high school boy walking up and down with swollen eyes. On the stairs he met a couple—a lady running quickly on her high heels, and the jaunty deputy prosecutor.

"I told you you weren't late," the deputy prosecutor was saying at the moment when Levin moved aside to let the lady pass.

Levin was on the stairs to the way out, and was just feeling in his vest pocket for the number of his overcoat, when the secretary overtook him.

"This way, please, Konstantin Dmitrievich; they are voting."

The candidate who was being voted on was Nevedovsky, who had so stoutly denied the idea of standing. Levin went up to the door of the room; it was locked. The secretary knocked, the door opened, and Levin was met by two red-faced gentlemen, who darted out.

"I can't stand any more of it," said one red-faced gentleman.

After them the face of the marshal of the province was poked out. His face was dreadful-looking from exhaustion and dismay.

"I told you not to let anyone out!" he cried to the doorkeeper.

"I let someone in, Your Excellency!"

"Oh, Lord!" and with a heavy sigh the marshal of the province walked with downcast head to the high table in the middle of the room, his weary legs dragging in his white trousers.

Nevedovsky was elected by a majority, as they had planned, and he was the new marshal of the province. Many people were amused, many were pleased and happy, many were in ecstasies, many were disgusted and unhappy. The former marshal of the province was in a state of despair which he could not conceal. When Nevedovsky went out of the room, the crowd thronged around him and followed him enthusiastically, just as they had followed the governor who had opened the meetings, and just as they had followed Snetkov when he was elected.

CHAPTER THIRTY-ONE

The newly elected marshal and many of the successful party dined that day with Vronsky.

Vronsky had come to the elections partly because he was bored in the country and wanted to show Anna his right to independence, and also to repay Sviazhsky by his support at the election for all the trouble he had taken for Vronsky at the district council election, but chiefly in order strictly to perform all those duties of a nobleman and landowner which he had taken upon himself. But he had not in the least expected that the election would so interest him, so keenly excite him, and that he would be so good at this kind of thing. He was quite a new man in the circle of the nobility of the province, but his success was unmistakable, and he was not wrong in supposing that he had already obtained a certain influence. This influence was due to his wealth and reputation; the fine house in town lent him by his old friend Shirkov, who had a post in the department of finances and was director of a flourishing bank in Kashin; the excellent cook Vronsky had brought from the country; and his friendship with the governor, who had been a schoolmate and even his protégé. But what contributed more than all to his success was his direct, equable manner with everyone, which very quickly made the majority of the noblemen reverse the current opinion of his supposed haughtiness. He was himself conscious that, except for that whimsical gentleman married to Kitty Shcherbatskaya, who had *à propos de bottes*[1] poured out a stream of pointless absurdities with such spiteful fury, every nobleman with whom he had made acquaintance had become his adherent. He saw clearly, and other people recognized it, too, that he had done a great deal to secure the success of Nevedovsky. And now at his own table, celebrating Nevedovsky's election, he was experiencing an agreeable sense of triumph over the success of his candidate. The election itself had so fascinated him that, if he could succeed in getting married during the next three years, he began to think of standing himself—much as after winning a race ridden by a jockey, he had longed to ride a race himself.

Today he was celebrating the success of his jockey. Vronsky sat at the head of the table, and on his right sat the young governor, a general of high rank. To all the rest he was the chief man in the province, who had solemnly opened the elections with his speech, and aroused a feeling of respect and even of awe in many people, as Vronsky saw; to Vronsky he was little Katka Maslov—that had been his nickname in the Corps of Pages—whom he felt to be shy and tried to *mettre à son aise*.[2] On his left sat Nevedovsky with his youthful, stubborn, and venomous face. With him Vronsky was simple and deferential.

Sviazhsky took his failure very light-heartedly. It was indeed no failure in his eyes, as he said himself, turning, glass in hand, to Nevedovsky; they could not have found a better representative of the new movement, which the nobility ought to follow. And so every honest

---

[1]"Quite irrelevantly."
[2]"Put at his ease."

person, as he said, was on the side of today's success and was rejoicing over it.

Stepan Arkadyevich was glad, too, that he was having a good time, and that everyone was pleased. The episode of the elections served as a good occasion for a marvelous dinner. Sviazhsky comically imitated the tearful discourse of the marshal, and observed, addressing Nevedovsky, that His Excellency would have to select another more complicated method of auditing the accounts than tears. Another nobleman jocosely described how footmen in knee breeches and stockings had been ordered for the marshal's ball, and how now they would have to be sent back unless the new marshal would give a ball with footmen in knee breeches and stockings.

Continually during dinner they said of Nevedovsky: "Our marshal," and "Your Excellency."

This was said with the same pleasure with which a bride is called "Madame" and her husband's name. Nevedovsky affected to be not merely indifferent but scornful of this appellation, but it was obvious that he was highly delighted, and had to keep a curb on himself not to betray the triumph which was unsuitable to their new liberal tone.

After dinner several telegrams were sent to people interested in the result of the election. And Stepan Arkadyevich, who was in high good-humor, sent Darya Aleksandrovna a telegram: "Nevedovsky elected by twenty votes. Congratulations. Tell people." He dictated it aloud, saying: "We must let them share our rejoicing." Darya Aleksandrovna, getting the message, simply sighed over the ruble wasted on it, and understood that it was sent after dinner. She knew Stiva had a weakness after dining for *faire jouer le télégraphe*.[3]

Everything, together with the excellent dinner and the wine, not from Russian merchants, but imported direct from abroad, was extremely dignified, simple, and enjoyable. The party—some twenty—had been selected by Sviazhsky from among the more active new liberals, all of the same way of thinking, who were at once clever and well bred. They drank, also half in jest, to the health of the new marshal of the province, of the governor, of the bank director, and of "our amiable host."

[3]"Setting the telegraph going."

Vronsky was satisfied. He had never expected to find so pleasant a tone in the provinces.

Toward the end of dinner it was still more lively. The governor asked Vronsky to come to a concert for the benefit of "our Serbian brothers" which his wife, who was anxious to make his acquaintance, had arranged.

"There'll be a ball, and you'll see the belle of the province. Worth seeing, really."

"Not in my line," Vronsky answered. He liked that English phrase. But he smiled, and promised to come.

Before they rose from the table, when all of them were smoking, Vronsky's valet went up to him with a letter on a tray.

"From Vozdvizhenskoe by special messenger," he said with a significant expression.

"Astonishing! How much he resembles the deputy prosecutor Sventitsky," said one of the guests in French of the valet, while Vronsky, frowning, read the letter.

The letter was from Anna. Before he read the letter, he knew its contents. Expecting the elections to be over in five days, he had promised to be back on Friday. Today was Saturday, and he knew that the letter contained reproaches for not being back at the time fixed. The letter he had sent the previous evening had probably not reached her yet.

The letter was what he had expected, but the form of it was unexpected, and particularly disagreeable to him:

> Annie is very ill, the doctor says it may be pneumonia. I am losing my mind all alone. Princess Varvara is no help but a hindrance. I expected you the day before yesterday, and yesterday, and now I am sending to find out where you are and what you are doing. I wanted to come myself, but thought better of it, knowing you would dislike it. Send some answer, that I may know what to do.

The child ill, yet she had thought of coming herself. Their daughter ill, and this hostile tone.

The innocent festivities over the election, and this gloomy, burdensome love to which he had to return struck Vronsky by their contrast. But he had to go, and by the first train that night he set off for home.

CHAPTER THIRTY-TWO

Before Vronsky's departure for the elections, Anna had reflected that the scenes constantly repeated between them each time he left home might only make him cold to her instead of attaching him to her, and resolved to do all she could to control herself so as to bear the parting with composure. But the cold, severe glance with which he had looked at her when he came to tell her he was going had hurt her, and before he had started, her peace of mind was destroyed.

In solitude afterward, thinking over that glance which had expressed his right to freedom, she came, as she always did, to the same point—the sense of her own humiliation. "He has the right to go away when and where he chooses. Not simply to go away, but to leave me. He has every right, and I have none. But knowing that, he ought not to do it. What has he done, though? . . . He looked at me with a cold, severe expression. Of course that is something indefinable, impalpable, but it has never been so before, and that glance means a great deal," she thought. "That glance shows the beginning of indifference."

And though she felt sure that his love for her was waning, there was nothing she could do, she could not in any way alter her relations to him. Just as before, only by love and by charm could she keep him. And so, just as before, only by occupation in the day, by morphine at night, could she stifle the fearful thought of what would be if he ceased to love her. It is true there was still one means; not to keep him—for that she wanted nothing more than his love—but to be nearer to him, to be in such a position that he would not leave her. That means was divorce and marriage. And she began to long for that, and made up her mind to agree to it the first time he or Stiva approached her on the subject.

Absorbed in such thoughts, she passed five days without him, the five days that he was to be at the elections.

Walks, conversation with Princess Varvara, visits to the hospital, and, most of all, reading—reading of one book after another—filled up her time. But on the sixth day, when the coachman came back without him, she felt that now she was utterly incapable of stifling the thought of him and of what he was doing there, and just at that time her little girl was taken ill. Anna began to look after her, but even that did not distract her mind, especially as the illness was not serious. However hard she tried, she could not love this little child, and to feign love was beyond her powers. Toward the evening of that day, still alone, Anna was in such a panic about him that she decided to start for the town, but on second thought she wrote him the contradictory letter that Vronsky received and, without reading it through, sent it off by a special messenger. The next morning she received his letter and regretted her own. She dreaded a repetition of the severe look he had flung at her at parting, especially when he knew that the baby was not dangerously ill. But still she was glad she had written to him. At this moment Anna was positively admitting to herself that she was a burden to him, that he would relinquish his freedom regretfully to return to her, and in spite of that she was glad he was coming. Let him weary of her, but he would be here with her so that she would see him, would know of every action he took.

She was siting in the drawing room near a lamp, reading a new volume of Taine,[1] listening to the sound of the wind outside and every minute expecting the carriage to arrive. Several times she thought she heard the sound of wheels, but she was mistaken. At last she heard not the sound of wheels but the coachman's shout and the dull rumble in the covered entry. Even Princess Varvara, playing patience, confirmed this, and Anna, flushing hotly, got up; but instead of going down, as she had done twice before, she stood still. She suddenly felt ashamed of her duplicity, but even more she dreaded how he might meet her. All feeling of wounded pride had passed now; she was only afraid of the expression of his displeasure. She remembered that her child had been perfectly well again for the last two days. She felt positively vexed with her for getting better from the very moment her letter was sent off. Then she thought of

[1]Hippolyte Taine (1828-93), French critic and historian.

him, that he was here, all of him, with his hands, his eyes. She heard his voice. And forgetting everything, she ran joyfully to meet him.

"Well, how is Annie?" he said timidly from below, looking up to Anna as she ran down to him.

He was sitting on a chair, and a footman was pulling off his warm overboots.

"Oh, she is better."

"And you?" he said, shaking himself.

She took his hand in both of hers, and drew it to her waist, never taking her eyes off him.

"Well, I'm glad," he said, coldly scanning her, her hair, her dress, which he knew she had put on for him. All was charming, but how many times it had charmed him! And the stern, stony expression that she so dreaded settled upon his face.

"Well, I'm glad. And are you well?" he said, wiping his damp beard with his handkerchief and kissing her hand.

"Never mind," she thought, "only let him be here, and so long as he's here he cannot, he dare not, cease to love me."

The evening was spent happily and gaily in the presence of Princess Varvara, who complained to him that Anna had been taking morphine in his absence.

"What am I to do? I couldn't sleep . . . My thoughts prevented me. When he's here I never take it—hardly ever."

He told her about the election, and Anna knew how by adroit questions to bring him to what gave him most pleasure—his own success. She told him of everything that interested him at home; and all that she told him was of the most cheerful description.

But late in the evening, when they were alone, Anna, seeing that she had regained complete possession of him, wanted to erase the painful impression of the glance he had given her for her letter. She said:

"Tell me frankly, you were vexed at getting my letter, and you didn't believe me?"

As soon as she had said it, she felt that however warm his feelings were now, he had not forgiven her for that.

"Yes," he said, "the letter was so strange. First, Annie ill, and then you thought of coming yourself."

"It was all the truth."

"Oh, I don't doubt it."

"Yes, you do doubt it. You are vexed, I see."

"Not for one moment. I'm only vexed, that's true, that you seem somehow unwilling to admit that there are duties . . ."

"The duty of going to a concert . . ."

"But we won't talk about it," he said.

"Why not talk about it?" she said.

"I only meant to say that matters of real importance may turn up. Now, for instance, I shall have to go to Moscow to arrange about the house . . . Oh, Anna, why are you so irritable? Don't you know that I can't live without you?"

"If so," said Anna, her voice suddenly changing, "it means that you are sick of this life . . . Yes, you will come for a day and go away, as men do . . ."

"Anna, that's cruel. I am ready to give up my whole life."

But she did not hear him.

"If you go to Moscow, I will go too. I will not stay here. Either we must separate or else live together."

"Why, you know, that's my one desire. But for that—"

"We must get a divorce. I will write to him. I see I cannot go on like this . . . But I will come with you to Moscow."

"You talk as if you were threatening me. But I desire nothing so much as never to be parted from you," said Vronsky, smiling.

But as he said these words there gleamed in his eyes not merely a cold look but the vindictive look of a man persecuted and made cruel.

She saw the look and correctly divined its meaning.

"If so, it's a calamity!" that glance told her. It was a moment's impression, but she never forgot it.

Anna wrote to her husband asking him about a divorce, and toward the end of November, taking leave of Princess Varvara, who wanted to go to Petersburg, she went with Vronsky to Moscow. Expecting every day an answer from Aleksey Aleksandrovich, and after that the divorce, they now established themselves together like married people.

PART SEVEN

CHAPTER ONE

The Levins had been in Moscow for more than two months. The date had long passed on which, according to the most trustworthy calculations of people learned in such matters, Kitty should have been confined. But she was still about, and there was nothing to show that her time was any nearer than it was two months before. The doctor, the midwife, and Dolly and her mother, and most of all Levin, who could not think of the approaching event without terror, began to be impatient and uneasy. Kitty was the only person who felt perfectly calm and happy.

She was distinctly conscious now of the birth of a new feeling of love for the future child, for her to some extent actually existing already, and she surrendered blissfully to this feeling. The child was no longer only a part of her, but sometimes lived his own life independently of her. Often this gave her pain, but at the same time her strange new joy made her wish to laugh.

All the people she loved were with her, and all were so good to her, so attentively caring for her, so entirely pleasant was everything presented to her, that if she had not known and felt that it must all soon be over, she could not have wished for a better and pleasanter life. The only thing that spoiled the charm of this manner of life was that her husband was not here as she loved him to be and as he was in the country.

She liked his serene, friendly, and hospitable manner in the country. In town he seemed continually uneasy and on his guard, as though he was afraid someone would be rude to him, and still more to her. At home in the country, knowing himself distinctly to be in his right place, he was never in haste to be off elsewhere. He was never unoccupied. Here in town he was in a continual hurry, as though afraid of missing something, and yet he had nothing to do.

And she felt sorry for him. To others, she knew, he did not appear an object of pity. On the contrary, when Kitty looked at him in society, as one sometimes looks at those one loves, trying to see him as if he were a stranger so as to catch the impression he made on others, she saw with a panic even of jealous fear that he was far from being a pitiable figure, that he was very attractive with his fine breeding, his rather old-fashioned, reserved courtesy with women, his powerful figure, and striking, as she thought, and expressive face. But she saw him not from without but from within; she saw that here he was not himself; that was the only way she could define his condition to herself. Sometimes she inwardly reproached him for his inability to live in town; sometimes she recognized that it was really hard for him to order his life here so that he could be satisfied with it.

What, indeed, had he to do? He did not care for cards; he did not go to a club. Spending time with jovial gentlemen of Oblonsky's type—she knew now what that meant: drinking and going somewhere after drinking. She could not think without horror of where men went on such occasions. Was he to go into society? But she knew he could find satisfaction in that only if he took pleasure in the closeness of young women, and that she could not wish for. Should he stay at home with her, her mother, and her sisters? But much as she liked and enjoyed their conversations forever on the same subjects—"Aline-Nadine," as the old prince called the sisters' talks—she knew it must bore him. What was there left for him to do? To go on writing his book he had indeed attempted, and at first he used to go to the library and make extracts and look up references. But, as he told her, the more he did nothing, the less time he had to do anything. And besides, he complained that he had talked too much about his book here, and that consequently all his ideas about it were muddled and had lost their interest for him.

One advantage in this town life was that quarrels hardly ever happened between them. Whether it was that their situations were different, or that they had both become more careful and sensible in that respect, they had no quarrels in Moscow from jealousy, which they had so dreaded when they moved from the country.

One event, an event of great importance to both from that point of view, did indeed happen—that was Kitty's meeting with Vronsky.

The old Princess Marya Borisovna, Kitty's godmother, who had always been very fond of her, had insisted on seeing her. Kitty, though she did not go into society at all on account of her condition, went with her father to see the venerable old lady, and there met Vronsky.

The only thing Kitty could reproach herself for at this meeting was that at the instant when she recognized in his civilian dress the features once so familiar to her, her breath failed her, the blood rushed to her heart, and a vivid blush—she felt it—overspread her face. But this lasted only a few seconds. Before her father, who purposely began talking in a loud voice to Vronsky, had finished, she was perfectly ready to look at Vronsky, to speak to him, if necessary, exactly as she spoke to Princess Marya Borisovna, and more than that, to do so in such a way that everything to the faintest intonation and smile would have been approved by her husband, whose unseen presence she seemed to feel about her at that instant.

She said a few words to him, even smiled serenely at his joke about the elections, which he called "our parliament." (She had to smile to show she understood the joke.) But she turned away immediately to Princess Marya Borisovna, and did not once glance at him till he got up to go; then she looked at him, but evidently only because it would be impolite not to look at a man when he is saying good-by.

She was grateful to her father for saying nothing to her about their meeting Vronsky, but she saw by his special warmth to her after the visit during their usual walk that he was pleased with her. She was pleased with herself. She had not expected she would have had the power, while keeping somewhere in the bottom of her heart all the memories of her old feeling for Vronsky, not only to seem but to be perfectly indifferent and composed with him.

Levin flushed a great deal more than she when she told him she had met Vronsky at Princess Marya Borisovna's. It was very hard for her to tell him this, but still harder to go on speaking of the details of the meeting, as he did not question her but simply gazed at her with a frown.

"I am very sorry you weren't there," she said. "Not that you weren't in the room . . . I couldn't have been so natural in your presence . . . I am blushing now much more, much more," she said, blushing till the tears came into her eyes. "But I'm sorry you could not have observed through a crack."

The truthful eyes told Levin that she was satisfied with herself, and in spite of her blushing he was quickly reassured and began questioning her, which was all she wanted. When he had heard everything, even to the detail that for the first second she could not help flushing, but that afterward she was just as natural and as much at her ease as with any chance acquaintance, Levin was quite happy again and said he was glad of it, and would not now behave as stupidly as he had done at the election, but would try the first time he met Vronsky to be as friendly as possible.

"It's so wretched to think that there's a man who is almost an enemy, whom it's painful to meet," said Levin. "I'm very, very glad."

CHAPTER TWO

"Please, go then and call on the Bohls," Kitty said to her husband when he came in to see her at eleven o'clock before going out. "I know you are dining at the club; Papa put down your name. But what are you going to do in the morning?"

"I am only going to Katavasov," Levin answered.

"Why so early?"

"He promised to introduce me to Metrov. I wanted to talk to him about my work. He's a distinguished scientific man from Petersburg," said Levin.

"Yes; wasn't it his article you were praising so? Well, and after that?" said Kitty.

"I shall go to the court, perhaps, about my sister's business."

"And the concert?" she queried.

"Why should I go there alone!"

"Oh yes, do go; there are going to be some new things there . . . You used to be interested. I would certainly go."

"Well, anyway, I shall come home before dinner," he said, looking at his watch.

"Put on your frock coat, so that you can go straight to call on Countess Bohl."

"But is it absolutely necessary?"

"Oh, absolutely! He has been to see us. Come, what is it? You go in, sit down, talk for five minutes of the weather, get up and go away."

"Oh, you wouldn't believe it! I've got so out of touch with all this that it makes me feel positively ashamed. It's such a horrible thing to do! A complete outsider walks in, sits down, stays on with nothing to do, wastes their time and worries himself, and walks away!"

Kitty laughed.

"Why, I suppose you used to pay calls before you were married, didn't you?"

"Yes, I did, but I always felt ashamed, and now I'm so out of touch with it that, by God, I'd sooner go two days running without my dinner than pay this call! One's so ashamed! I feel all the while that they're annoyed, that they're saying, 'What has he come for?' "

"No, they won't. I'll answer for that," said Kitty, looking into his face with a laugh. She took his hand. "Well, good-by . . . Do go, please."

He was just going out after kissing his wife's hand, when she stopped him.

"Kostya, do you know I've only fifty rubles left?"

"Oh, all right, I'll go to the bank and get some. How much?" he said with the expression of dissatisfaction she knew so well.

"No, wait a minute." She held his hand. "Let's talk about it, it worries me. I seem to spend nothing unnecessary, but money seems to fly away simply. We don't manage well, somehow."

"Oh, it's all right," he said with a little cough, looking at her from under his brows.

That cough she knew well. It was a sign of intense dissatisfaction, not with her, but with himself. He certainly was displeased, not at so much money being spent, but at being reminded of what he, knowing something was unsatisfactory, wanted to forget.

"I have told Sokolov to sell the wheat, and to borrow an advance on the mill. We shall have money enough in any case."

"Yes, but I'm afraid that altogether—"

"Oh, it's all right, all right," he repeated. "Well, good-by, darling."

"No, I'm really sorry sometimes that I listened to Mama. How nice it would have been in the country! As it is, I'm worrying you all, and we're wasting our money."

"Not at all, not at all. Not once since I've been married have I said that things could have been better than they are . . ."

"Truly?" she said, looking into his eyes.

He had said it without thinking, simply to console her. But when he glanced at her and saw those sweet truthful eyes fastened questioningly on him, he repeated it with his whole heart. "I am positively forgetting her," he thought. And he remembered what was before them, so soon to come.

"Will it be soon? How do you feel?" he whispered, taking her two hands.

"I have so often thought about it that now I don't think about it or know anything about it."

"And you're not frightened?"

She smiled contemptuously.

"Not the least little bit," she said.

"Well, if anything happens, I shall be at Katavasov's."

"No, nothing will happen, and don't think about it. I'm going for a walk on the boulevard with Papa. We're going to see Dolly. I shall expect you before dinner. Oh, yes! Do you know that Dolly's situation is becoming utterly impossible? She's in debt all around; she hasn't a kopek. We were talking yesterday with Mama and Arseny" (this was her sister's husband Lvov), "and we determined to send you with him to talk to Stiva. It's really unbearable. One can't speak to Papa about it . . . But if you and he—"

"Why, what can we do?" said Levin.

"You'll be at Arseny's anyway; talk to him, he will tell you what we decided."

"Oh, I agree to everything Arseny thinks beforehand. I'll go and see him. By the way, if I do go to the concert, I'll go with Natalie. Well, good-by."

On the steps Levin was stopped by his old servant Kuzma, who had been with him before his marriage and now looked after their household in town.

"Beauty" (that was the left shaft horse brought from the country) "has been badly shod and is quite lame," he said. "What does Your Honor wish to be done?"

During the first part of their stay in Moscow, Levin had used his own horses brought from the country. He had tried to arrange this part of their expenses in the best and cheapest way possible; but it appeared that their own horses came dearer than hired horses, and they still had to hire anyway.

"Send for the veterinary, there may be an abrasion."

"And for Katerina Aleksandrovna?" asked Kuzma.

Levin was no longer struck as he had been at first in Moscow by the fact that to get from Vozdvizhenskoe to Sivtsev-Vrazhek, you had to have two powerful horses harnessed to a heavy carriage to take the carriage less than a quarter of a mile through the snowy slush and to keep it standing there four hours, paying five rubles for this.

Now it seemed quite natural.

"Hire a pair for our carriage," he said.

"Yes, sir."

And so, simply and easily, thanks to the facilities of town life, Levin settled a question which, in the country, would have called for much personal trouble and exertion, and going out onto the steps, he called a sleigh, sat down, and drove to Nikitsky Street. On the way he thought no more of money, but mused on the introduction that awaited him to the Petersburg savant, a writer on sociology, and what he would say to him about his book.

Only during the first days of his stay in Moscow had Levin been struck by the expenditure, strange to one living in the country, unproductive but inevitable, that was expected of him on every side. But by now he had grown used to it. That had happened to him in this matter which is said to happen to drunkards—the first glass sticks in the throat, the second flies down like a hawk, but after the third they're like tiny little birds. When Levin had changed his first hundred-ruble note to pay for liveries for his footmen and hall porter, he could not help reflecting that these liveries were of no use to anyone—but they were indubitably necessary, to judge by the amazement of the princess and Kitty when he suggested that they might do without liveries— that these liveries would cost the wages of two laborers for the summer, that is, would pay for about three hundred workings days from

Easter to Advent, and each a day of hard work from early morning to late evening—and that hundred-ruble note did stick in his throat. But the next note, changed to pay for providing a dinner for their relations, which cost twenty-eight rubles, though it did excite in Levin the reflection that twenty-eight rubles meant about seventy-two bushels of oats, which men would with groans and sweat have reaped and bound and thrashed and winnowed and sifted and sown— this next one he parted with more easily. And now the notes he changed no longer aroused such reflections, and they flew off like little birds. Whether the labor devoted to obtaining the money corresponded to the pleasure given by what was bought with it, was a consideration he had long ago dismissed. His business calculation that there was a certain price below which he could not sell certain grain was forgotten too. The rye, for the price of which he had so long held out, had been sold for fifty kopeks a measure cheaper than it had been fetching a month ago. Even the consideration that with such an expenditure he could not go on living for a year without debt, even that had no force. Only one thing was essential: to have money in the bank, without inquiring where it came from, so as to know that one had the wherewithal to buy meat for tomorrow. And this condition had hitherto been fulfilled; he had always had the money in the bank. But now the money in the bank had gone, and he could not quite tell where to get the next installment. And this it was that, at the moment when Kitty had mentioned money, had disturbed him; but he had no time to think about it. He drove off, thinking of Katavasov and the meeting with Metrov that was before him.

CHAPTER THREE

Levin had on this visit to town seen a great deal of his old friend at the university, Professor Katavasov, whom he had not seen since his marriage. He liked in Katavasov the clarity and simplicity of his conception of life. Levin thought that the clarity of Katavasov's conception of life was due to the poverty of his nature; Katavasov thought that the disconnectedness of Levin's ideas was due to his lack of intellectual discipline; but Levin enjoyed Katavasov's clarity, and

Katavasov enjoyed the abundance of Levin's untrained ideas, and they liked to meet and to discuss.

Levin had read Katavasov some parts of his book, and he had liked them. On the previous day Katavasov had met Levin at a public lecture and told him that the celebrated Metrov, whose article Levin had so much liked, was in Moscow, that he had been much interested by what Katavasov had told him about Levin's work, and that he was coming to see him tomorrow at eleven, and would be very glad to make Levin's acquaintance.

"You're positively a reformed character, I'm glad to see," said Katavasov, meeting Levin in the little drawing room. "I heard the bell and thought: 'Impossible that it can be he at the exact time!' . . . Well, what do you say to the Montenegrins now? Born fighters."

"Why, what's happened?" asked Levin.

Katavasov in a few words told him the last piece of news from the war, and going into his study, he introduced Levin to a short, thickset man of pleasant appearance. This was Metrov. The conversation touched for a brief space on politics and on how recent events were looked at in the higher spheres in Petersburg. Metrov repeated a saying that had reached him through a most trustworthy source, reported as having been uttered on this subject by the Tsar and one of the ministers. Katavasov had heard on excellent authority that the Tsar had said something quite different. Levin tried to imagine circumstances in which both sayings might have been uttered, and the conversation on that topic dropped.

"Yes, here he's almost finished a book on the natural conditions of the laborer in relation to the land," said Katavasov; "I'm not a specialist, but I, as a natural science man, was pleased at his not taking mankind as something outside biological laws; but, on the contrary, seeing his dependence on his surroundings, and in that dependence seeking the laws of his development."

"That's very interesting," said Metrov.

"What I began precisely was to write a book on agriculture; but studying the chief instrument of agriculture, the laborer," said Levin, reddening, "I could not help coming to quite unexpected results."

And Levin began carefully, as it were, feeling his ground, to expound his views. He knew Metrov had written an article against the generally accepted theory of political economy, but to what extent he could count on his sympathy with his own new views he did not know and could not guess from the clever and serene face of the learned man.

"But in what do you see the special characteristics of the Russian laborer?" said Metrov; "in his biological characteristics, so to speak, or in the condition in which he is placed?"

Levin saw that there was an idea underlying this question with which he did not agree. But he went on explaining his own idea that the Russian laborer has a quite special view of the land, different from that of other people; and to support this proposition he made haste to add that in his opinion this attitude of the Russian peasant was due to the consciousness of his predicament in peopling vast unoccupied expanses in the East.

"One may easily be led into error in basing any conclusion on the general vocation of a people," said Metrov, interrupting Levin. "The condition of the laborer will always depend on his relation to the land and to capital."

And without letting Levin finish explaining his idea, Metrov began expounding to him the special point of his own theory.

In what the point of his theory lay, Levin did not understand, because he did not take the trouble to understand. He saw that Metrov, like other people, in spite of his own article, in which he had attacked the current theory of political economy, looked at the position of the Russian peasant simply from the point of view of capital, wages, and rent. He would indeed have been obliged to admit that in the eastern—much the larger—part of Russia rent was yet nil, that for nine tenths of the eighty million Russian peasants wages took the form simply of food provided for themselves, and that capital does not so far exist except in the form of the most primitive tools. Yet it was only from that point of view that he considered every laborer, though in many points he differed from the economists and had his own new theory of wages which he expounded to Levin.

Levin listened reluctantly, and at first made objections. He would have liked to interrupt Metrov, to explain his own thought, which in his opinion would have rendered further exposition of Metrov's theories superfluous. But later on, feeling convinced that they looked at the matter so differently that they could never understand one another, he did not even oppose his statements, but simply listened. Although what Metrov was saying was by now utterly devoid of interest for him, he yet experienced a certain satisfaction in listening to him. It flattered his vanity that such a learned man should explain his ideas to him so eagerly, so painstakingly, and with such confidence in Levin's understanding of the subject, sometimes with a mere hint referring him to a whole aspect of the subject. He put this down to his own credit, unaware that Metrov, who had already discussed his theory over and over again with all his intimate friends was eager to talk to anyone on any subject that interested him, even if still obscure to himself.

"We are late, though," said Katavasov, looking at his watch as soon as Metrov had finished his discourse.

"Yes, there's a meeting of the Society of Amateurs today in commemoration of the jubilee of Svintich," said Katavasov in answer to Levin's inquiry. "Piotr Ivanovich and I were going. I've promised to deliver an address on his works in zoölogy. Come along with us, it's very interesting."

"Yes, and indeed it's time to start," said Metrov. "Come with us, and from there, if you care to, come to my place. I should be very glad to go to the meeting."

"I say, friends, have you heard? He has handed in his resolution," Katavasov called from the other room, where he was putting on his frock coat.

And a conversation sprang up about a university problem.

That university problem was a very important event that winter in Moscow. Three old professors in the council had not accepted the opinion of the younger professors. The young ones had registered a separate resolution. This, in the judgment of some people, was monstrous; in the judgment of others, it was the simplest and most just thing to do, and the professors were split up into two parties.

One party, to which Katavasov belonged, saw in the opposite party a betrayal and gross treachery, while the opposite party saw in them youthful impudence and lack of respect for the authorities. Levin, though he did not belong to the university, had several times already during his stay in Moscow heard and talked about this matter, and had his own opinion on the subject. He took part in the conversation that was continued in the street, as they all three walked to the buildings of the old university.

The meeting had already begun. Around the cloth-covered table, at which Katavasov and Metrov seated themselves, there were six persons, and one of these was bending close over a manuscript, reading something aloud. Levin sat down in one of the empty chairs that were standing around the table, and in a whisper asked a student sitting near what was being read. The student, eying Levin with displeasure, said: "Biography."

Though Levin was not interested in the biography, he could not help listening, and learned some new and interesting facts about the life of the distinguished man of science.

When the reader had finished, the chairman thanked him and read some verses the poet Ment had written in honor of the jubilee, and said a few words by way of thanks to the poet. Then Katavasov, in his loud, ringing voice, read his address on the scientific works of the man whose jubilee it was.

When Katavasov had finished, Levin looked at his watch, saw it was past one, and thought that there would not be time before the concert to read Metrov his book, and indeed, he did not now care to do so. During the reading he had thought over their conversation. He saw distinctly now that though Metrov's ideas might perhaps have value, his own ideas had value too, and their ideas could be made clear and lead to something only if each worked separately in his chosen path, and that nothing would be gained by putting their ideas together. And having made up his mind to refuse Metrov's invitation, Levin went up to him at the end of the meeting. Metrov introduced Levin to the chairman, with whom he was talking of the political news. Metrov told the chairman what he had already told Levin, and Levin made the same remarks that he had already made that morning, but for the sake of variety he expressed also a new opinion which had only just struck him. After that the conversation turned again on the university question. As Levin had already heard it all, he made haste to tell Metrov that he was sorry he could not take advantage of his invitation, took leave, and drove to Lvov's.

CHAPTER FOUR

Lvov, the husband of Natalie, Kitty's sister, had spent all his life in foreign capitals, where he had been educated, and had been in the diplomatic service.

During the previous year he had left the diplomatic service, not owing to any "unpleasantness" (he never had any "unpleasantness" with anyone), and took a position in the ministry of the court in Moscow, in order to give his two boys the best education possible.

In spite of the striking contrast in their habits and views and the fact that Lvov was older than Levin, they had seen a great deal of one another that winter, and had taken a great liking to each other.

Lvov was at home, and Levin went in to him unannounced.

Lvov, wearing an indoor jacket with a belt, and chamois leather slippers, was sitting in an armchair, and with a pince-nez with blue lenses he was reading a book that stood on a reading-desk, while in his shapely hand he held a half-burned cigar daintily away from him.

His handsome, delicate, and still youthful-looking face, to which his wavy, glistening silvery hair gave a still more aristocratic air, lighted up with a smile when he saw Levin.

"Marvelous! I was meaning to send to you. How's Kitty? Sit here, it's more comfortable." He got up and pushed forward a rocking-chair. "Have you read the last circular in the *Journal de St.Péters-bourg*?[1] I think it's excellent," he said with a slight French accent.

Levin told him that what he had heard from Katavasov was being said in Petersburg, and after talking a little about politics, he told him of his interview with Metrov, and the learned society's meeting. To Lvov it was very interesting.

"That's what I envy you, that you are able to mix in these interesting scientific circles," he said. And as he talked, he passed as usual into French, which was easier for him. "It's true I haven't the time for it. My official work and the children leave me no time; and then I'm not ashamed to admit that my education has been too defective."

"That I don't believe," said Levin with a smile, feeling, as he always did, touched at Lvov's low opinion of himself, which was not

---

[1] A French daily published in St. Petersburg.

in the least put on from a desire to seem or to be modest, but was absolutely sincere.

"Oh, yes, absolutely! I feel now how badly educated I am. To educate my children I positively have to look up a great deal, and in fact simply to study myself. For it's not enough to have teachers, there must be someone to look after them, just as on your land you want laborers and an overseer. See what I'm reading"—he pointed to Buslayev's[2] *Grammar* on the desk—"it's expected of Misha, and it's so difficult . . . Come, explain to me . . . Here he says . . ."

Levin tried to explain to him that it couldn't be understood but that it had to be taught; but Lvov would not agree with him.

"Oh, you're laughing at me!"

"On the contrary, you can't imagine how, when I look at you, I'm always learning the task that lies before me, that is, the education of one's children."

"Well, there's nothing for you to learn," said Lvov.

"All I know," said Levin, "is that I have never seen better brought-up children than yours, and I wouldn't wish for children better than yours."

Lvov visibly tried to restrain the expression of his delight, but he was positively radiant with smiles.

"If only they're better than me! That's all I desire. You don't know yet all the work," he said, "with boys who've been left like mine to run wild abroad."

"They'll catch up. They're such clever children. The great thing is moral training. That's what I learn when I look at your children."

"You talk of moral training. You can't imagine how difficult that is! You have hardly succeeded in combating one tendency when others crop up, and the struggle begins again. If one had not a support in religion—you remember we talked about that—no father could bring children up relying on his own strength alone without that help."

This subject, which always interested Levin, was cut short by the entrance of the beautiful Natalie Aleksandrovna, dressed to go out.

"I didn't know you were here," she said, obviously feeling no

---

[2]Fyodor Buslayev (1818-97), professor in Moscow University.

regret but a positive pleasure in interrupting this conversation on a topic she had heard so much of that she was by now weary of it. "Well, how is Kitty? I am dining with you today. I tell you what, Arseny"—she turned to her husband—"you take the carriage."

And the husband and wife began to discuss their arrangements for the day. As the husband had to drive to meet someone on official business, while the wife had to go to the concert and some public meeting of the South-Eastern Committee, there was a great deal to consider and settle. Levin had to take part in their plans as one of them. It was settled that Levin should go with Natalie to the concert and the meeting, and that from there they should send the carriage to the office for Arseny, and he should call for her and take her to Kitty's; or that, if he had not finished his work, he should send the carriage back and Levin would go with her.

"He's spoiling me," Lvov said to his wife.

"Arseny goes to extremes," said his wife. "He assures me that our children are perfect, when I know that they have many defects. If you look for perfection, you will never be satisfied. And it's true, as Papa says, that when we were brought up, there was one extreme—we were kept in the attic while our parents lived in the best rooms; now it's just the other way—the parents are in the storeroom, while the children are on the first floor. Parents now are not expected to live at all, but to exist altogether for their children."

"Well, what if they like it better?" Lvov said, with his beautiful smile, touching her hand. "Anyone who didn't know you would think you were a stepmother, not a true mother."

"No, extremes are not good in anything," Natalie said serenely, putting his paper knife straight in its proper place on the table.

"Well, come here, you perfect children," Lvov said to the two handsome boys who came in and, after bowing to Levin, went up to their father, obviously wishing to ask him about something.

Levin would have liked to talk to them, to hear what they would say to their father, but Natalie began talking to him, and then Lvov's colleague in the service, Makhotin, walked in, wearing his court uniform, to go with him to meet someone, and a conversation was kept up without a break upon Herzegovina, Princess Korzinskaya, the town council, and the sudden death of Madame Apraksina.

Levin even forgot the commission entrusted to him. He recollected it as he was going into the hall.

"Oh, Kitty told me to talk to you about Oblonsky," he said, as Lvov was standing on the stairs, seeing his wife and Levin off.

"Yes, yes, *Maman* wants us, *les beaux-frères*, to attack him," he said blushing. "But why should I?"

"Well, then, I will attack him," said Madame Lvova, with a smile, standing in her white fur cape, waiting till they had finished speaking. "Come, let us go."

CHAPTER FIVE

At the concert in the afternoon two very interesting works were performed. One was a fantasia, *King Lear in the Steppe*;[1] the other was a quartet dedicated to the memory of Bach. Both were new and in the modern style, and Levin was eager to form an opinion of them. After escorting his sister-in-law to her stall, he stood against a column and tried to listen as attentively and conscientiously as possible. He tried not to let his attention be distracted, and not to spoil his impression by looking at the conductor in a white tie, waving his arms, which always disturbed his enjoyment of music so much, or the ladies in bonnets, with strings carefully tied over their ears, and all these people either thinking nothing at all or thinking of all sorts of things except the music. He tried to avoid meeting music connoisseurs or talkative acquaintances, and stood looking at the floor straight before him, listening.

But the more he listened to the *King Lear* fantasia, the further he felt from forming any definite opinion on it. There seemed to be a continual beginning, a preparation for the musical expression of some feeling, but it fell to pieces again immediately, breaking into new expressions of emotions, or simply into nothing but the whims of the composer, exceedingly complex but disconnected sounds. And these fragmentary musical expressions, though sometimes beautiful, were unpleasant, because they were utterly unexpected and not pre-

[1] By Mily Balakirev (1836-1910).

pared for by anything. Gaiety and grief and despair and tenderness and triumph followed one another without any connection, like the emotions of a madman. And those emotions, like a madman's, sprang up quite unexpectedly.

During the whole of the performance Levin felt like a deaf man watching people dancing, and was in a state of complete bewilderment when the fantasia was over, and felt a great weariness from the fruitless strain on his attention. Loud applause resounded on all sides. Everyone got up, moved about, and began talking. Anxious to throw some light on his own perplexity from the impressions of others, Levin began to walk about, looking for connoisseurs, and was glad to see a well-known connoisseur in conversation with Pestsov, whom he knew.

"Marvelous!" Pestsov was saying in his mellow bass. "How are you, Konstantin Dmitrievich? Particularly graphic and sculpturesque, so to say, and richly colored is that passage where you feel Cordelia's approach, where woman, *das ewig Weibliche*,[2] enters into conflict with fate. Isn't it?"

"You mean . . . What had Cordelia to do with it?" Levin asked timidly, forgetting that the fantasia was supposed to represent King Lear.

"Cordelia comes in . . . see here!" said Pestsov, tapping his finger on the satiny surface of the program he held in his hand and passing it to Levin.

Only then did Levin recollect the title of the fantasia, and made haste to read in the Russian translation the lines from Shakespeare that were printed on the back of the program.

"You can't follow it without that," said Pestsov, addressing Levin, because the person he had been speaking to had gone away and he had no one to talk to.

In the *entr'acte* Levin and Pestsov fell into an argument upon the merits and defects of the Wagner school of music. Levin maintained that the mistake of Wagner and all his followers lay in their trying to take music into the sphere of another art, just as poetry goes wrong when it tries to paint a face, which is what should be left to

[2]"The eternal feminine."

painting, and as an instance of this mistake he cited the sculptor who carved in marble certain shadows of poetical images flitting around the figure of the poet on the pedestal. "These shadows were so far from being shadows that they were positively clinging to the ladder," said Levin. The comparison pleased him, but he could not remember whether or not he had used the same phrase before, and to Pestsov, too, and as he said it he felt embarrassed.

Pestsov maintained that art is one, and that it can attain its highest manifestations only in conjunction with all kinds of art.

The second piece that was performed Levin could not hear. Pestsov, who was standing beside him, was talking to him almost all the time, condemning the music for its excessive affected assumption of simplicity, and comparing it with the simplicity of the Pre-Raphaelites in painting. As he went out, Levin met many more acquaintances, with whom he talked of politics, of music, and of common acquaintances. Among others he met Count Bohl, whom he had utterly forgotten to call upon.

"Well, go at once, then," Madame Lvova said when he told her; "perhaps they'll not be at home, and then you can come to the meeting to fetch me. You'll find me still there."

CHAPTER SIX

"Perhaps they're not at home?" said Levin, as he went into the hall of Countess Bohl's house.

"Yes they are," said the porter, resolutely removing his overcoat.

"How annoying!" thought Levin with a sigh, taking off one glove and smoothing his hat. "What did I come for? What have I to say to them?"

As he passed through the first drawing room, Levin met Countess Bohl in the doorway; she was giving some order to a servant with a careworn and severe face. On seeing Levin, she smiled and asked him to come into the little drawing room, where he heard voices. In this room, sitting in armchairs, were the two daughters of the countess, and a Moscow colonel, whom Levin knew. Levin went up, greeted them, and sat down beside the sofa with his hat on his knees.

"How is your wife? Have you been at the concert? We couldn't go. Mama had to be at the funeral service."

"Yes, I heard . . . What a sudden death!" said Levin.

The countess came in, sat down on the sofa, and she too asked after his wife and inquired about the concert.

Levin answered, and repeated an inquiry about Madame Apraksina's sudden death.

"But she was always in weak health."

"Were you at the opera yesterday?"

"Yes, I was."

"Lucca[1] was very good."

"Yes, very good," he said, and as it was utterly of no consequence to him what they thought of him, he began repeating what they had heard a hundred times about the characteristics of the singer's talent. Countess Bohl pretended to be listening. Then, when he had said enough and paused, the colonel, who had been silent till then, began to talk. The colonel too talked of the opera, and about culture. At last, after speaking of the proposed *folle journée*[2] at Tiurin's, the colonel laughed, got up noisily, and went away. Levin too rose, but he saw by the face of the countess that it was not yet time for him to go. He must stay two minutes longer. He sat down.

But as he was thinking all the while how stupid it was, he could not find a subject for conversation, and sat silent.

"You are not going to the public meeting? They say it will be very interesting," the countess began.

"No, I promised my *belle-soeur* to fetch her there," said Levin.

A silence followed. The mother once more exchanged glances with a daughter.

"Well, now I think the time has come," thought Levin, and he got up. The ladies shook hands with him, and begged him to say *mille choses*[3] to his wife for them.

The porter asked him, as he gave him his fur coat, "Where is Your Honor staying?" and immediately wrote down his address in a big handsomely bound book.

[1]Famous Italian soprano.
[2]"Mad party."
[3]"Lots of things."

"Of course I don't care, but still I feel ashamed and awfully stupid," thought Levin, consoling himself with the reflections that everyone does it. He drove to the public meeting, where he was to find his sister-in-law so as to drive home with her.

At the public meeting of the committee there were a great many people, and almost all the highest society. Levin was in time for the report which, as everyone said, was very interesting. When the reading of the report was over, people moved about, and Levin met Sviazhsky, who invited him very pressingly to come that evening to a meeting of the Society of Agriculture, where a celebrated lecture was to be delivered, and Stepan Arkadyevich, who had only just come from the races, and many other acquaintances; and Levin heard and uttered various criticisms on the meeting, on the new fantasia, and on a public trial. But, probably from the mental fatigue he was beginning to feel, he made a blunder in speaking of the trial, and this blunder he recalled several times with vexation. Speaking of the sentence upon a foreigner who had been condemned in Russia, and of how unfair it would be to punish him by exile abroad, Levin repeated what he had heard the day before in conversation with an acquaintance.

"I think sending him abroad is much the same as punishing a pike by throwing it into the water," said Levin. Then he recollected that this idea, which he had heard from an acquaintance and uttered as his own, came from a fable of Krylov's,[4] and that the acquaintance had picked it up from a newspaper article.

After driving home with his sister-in-law, and finding Kitty in good spirits and quite well, Levin drove to the club.

CHAPTER SEVEN

Levin reached the club just at the right time. Members and visitors were driving up as he arrived. Levin had not been at the club for a very long while— not since he lived in Moscow, when he was leaving the university and going into society. He remembered the club, the external details of its arrangement, but he had completely forgotten

[4]Ivan Andreevich Krylov (1769-1844), leading Russian writer of fables.

the impression it had made on him in the old days. But as soon as, driving into the wide semicircular court and getting out of the sleigh, he mounted the steps, and the hall porter, wearing a shoulder belt, noiselessly opened the door to him with a bow; as soon as he saw in the porter's room the cloaks and galoshes of members who thought it less trouble to take them off downstairs; as soon as he heard the mysterious ringing bell that preceded him as he ascended the shallow, carpeted staircase, and saw the statue on the landing, and the third porter at the top doors, a familiar figure grown older, in the club livery, opening the door without haste or delay, and scanning the visitors as they passed in—Levin felt the old impression of the club come back in a rush, an impression of repose, comfort, and propriety.

"Your hat, please," the porter said to Levin, who forgot the club rule to leave his hat in the porter's room. "Long time since you've been. The prince put your name down yesterday. Prince Stepan Arkadyevich is not here yet."

The porter did not only know Levin, but also all his ties and relationships, and so immediately mentioned his intimate friends.

Passing through the outer hall, divided up by screens, and the room partitioned on the right where there was a fruit buffet, Levin overtook an old man walking slowly in, and entered the dining room full of noise and people.

He walked past the tables, almost all full, and looked at the visitors. He saw people of all sorts, old and young; some he knew a little, some were intimate friends. There was not a single cross or worried-looking face. All seemed to have left their cares and anxieties in the porter's room with their hats, and were all deliberately getting ready to enjoy the material blessings of life. Sviazhsky was here and Shcherbatsky, Nevedovsky and the old prince, and Vronsky and Sergey Ivanovich.

"Ah! Why are you late?" the prince said, smiling and giving him his hand over his own shoulder. "How's Kitty?" he added, smoothing out the napkin he had tucked behind a vest button.

"All right; they are dining at home, all three of them."

"Ah, 'Aline-Nadine,' to be sure! There's no room with us. Go to that table and hurry up and take a seat," said the prince, and turning away, he carefully took a plate of turbot soup.

"Levin, this way!" a good-natured voice shouted a little further on. It was Turovtsyn. He was sitting with a young officer, and beside them were two chairs turned upside down. Levin gladly went up to them. He had always liked the good-hearted rake Turovtsyn—he was associated in his mind with memories of his courtship—and at that moment, after the strain of intellectual conversation, the sight of Turovtsyn's good-natured face was particularly welcome.

"For you and Oblonsky. He'll be here directly."

The young man, holding himself very erect, with eyes forever twinkling with enjoyment, was an officer from Petersburg, Gagin. Turovtsyn introduced them.

"Oblonsky's always late."

"Ah, here he is!"

"Have you only just come?" said Oblonsky, coming quickly toward them. "Hello. Had some vodka? Well, come along, then."

Levin got up and went with him to the big table spread with vodkas and appetizers of the most various kinds. One would have thought that out of two dozen delicacies one might find something to one's taste, but Stepan Arkadyevich asked for something special, and one of the liveried waiters standing by immediately brought what was required. They drank a glassful and returned to their table.

At once, while they were still on their soup, Gagin was served with champagne, and told the waiter to fill four glasses. Levin did not refuse the wine, and asked for a second bottle. He was very hungry, and ate and drank with great enjoyment, and with still greater enjoyment he took part in the lively and simple conversation of his companions. Gagin, dropping his voice, told the last good story from Petersburg, and the story, though indecent and stupid, was so funny that Levin broke into roars of laughter so loud that those near looked around.

"That's the same as a 'that's-just-what-I-can't-bear' story! You know the story?" said Stepan Arkadyevich. "Ah, that's exquisite! Another bottle," he said to the waiter, and he began to relate his good story.

"Piotr Ilyich Vinovsky invites you to drink with him," a little old waiter interrupted Stepan Arkadyevich, bringing two delicate glasses of sparkling champagne, and addressing Stepan Arkadyevich and

Levin. Stepan Arkadyevich took the glass and, looking toward a bald man with red mustaches at the other end of the table, nodded to him, smiling.

"Who's that?" asked Levin.

"You met him once at my place, don't you remember? A good-natured fellow."

Levin did the same as Stepan Arkadyevich and took the glass.

Stepan Arkadyevich's anecdote too was very amusing. Levin told his story, and that too was successful. Then they talked of horses, of the races, of what they had been doing that day, and of how skillfully Vronsky's Atlas had won the first prize. Levin did not notice how the time passed at dinner.

"Ah! And here they are!" Stepan Arkadyevich said toward the end of dinner, leaning over the back of his chair and holding out his hand to Vronsky, who came up with a tall officer of the Guards. Vronsky's face too beamed with the look of good-humored enjoyment that was general in the club. He propped his elbow playfully on Stepan Arkadyevich's shoulder, whispering something to him, and he held out his hand to Levin with the same good-humored smile.

"Very glad to meet you," he said. "I looked for you at the elections, but I was told you had gone away."

"Yes, I left the same day. We've just been talking of your horse. I congratulate you," said Levin. "It was very well run."

"You've race horses too, haven't you?"

"No, my father had; but I remember and know something about it."

"Where have you dined?" asked Stepan Arkadyevich.

"We were at the second table, behind the columns."

"We've been celebrating his success," said the tall colonel. "It's his second Imperial prize. I wish I might have the luck at cards he has with horses. Well, why waste the precious time? I'm going to the 'infernal regions,' " added the colonel, and he walked away.

"That's Yashvin," Vronsky said in answer to Turovtsyn, and he sat down in the vacated seat beside them. He drank the glass offered him, and ordered a bottle of wine. Under the influence of the club atmosphere or the wine he had drunk, Levin chatted away to Vronsky of the best breeds of cattle, and was very glad not to feel the slightest hostility to this man. He even told him, among other things, that he had heard from his wife that she had met him at Princess Marya Borisovna's.

"Ah, Princess Marya Borisovna, she's exquisite!" said Stepan Arkadyevich, and he told an anecdote about her which set them all laughing. Vronsky particularly laughed with such simple-hearted amusement that Levin felt quite reconciled to him.

"Well, have we finished?" said Stepan Arkadyevich, getting up with a smile. "Let us go."

CHAPTER EIGHT

Getting up from the table, Levin walked with Gagin through the lofty room to the billiard room, feeling his arms swing as he walked with a peculiar lightness and ease. As he crossed the big room, he came upon his father-in-law.

"Well, how do you like our Temple of Indolence?" said the prince, taking his arm. "Come along, come along!"

"Yes, I wanted to walk about and look at everything. It's interesting."

"Yes, it's interesting for you. But its interest for me is quite different. You look at those little old men now," he said, pointing to a club member with bent back and projecting lip, shuffling toward them in his soft boots, "and imagine that they were *shlupiks* like that from their birth up."

"How *shlupiks*?"

"I see you don't know that name. That's our club designation. You know the game of rolling eggs: when one's rolled a long while it becomes a *shlupik*. So it is with us; one goes on coming and coming to the club, and ends by becoming a *shlupik*. Ah, you laugh! but we look out, for fear of dropping into it ourselves. You know Prince Chechensky?" inquired the prince; and Levin saw by his face that he was just going to relate something funny.

"No, I don't know him."

"You don't say so! Well, Prince Chechensky is a well-known figure. No matter, though. He's always playing billiards here. Only three years ago he was not a *shlupik* and kept up his spirits and even used to call other people *shlupiks*. But one day he turns up, and our porter . . . you know Vasily? Why, that fat one; he's famous for his *bon mots*. And so Prince Chechensky asks him, 'Come, Vasily, who's here? Any *shlupiks* here yet?' And he says, 'You're the third.' Yes, my dear boy, that he did!"

Talking and greeting the friends they met, Levin and the prince walked through all the rooms: the great room where tables had already been set and the usual partners were playing for small stakes; the divan room, where they were playing chess and Sergey Ivanovich was sitting talking to somebody; the billiard room, where, about a sofa in a recess, there was a lively party drinking champagne—Gagin was one of them. They peeped into the "infernal regions," where a good many men were crowding around one table, at which Yashvin was sitting. Trying not to make any noise, they walked into the dimly lighted reading room, where under the shaded lamps there sat a young man with a wrathful countenance, turning over one journal after another, and a bald general buried in a book. They went, too, into what the prince called the "intellectual room," where three gentlemen were engaged in a heated discussion of the latest political news.

"Prince, please come, we're ready," said one of his card party, who had come to look for him, and the prince went off. Levin sat down and listened, but recalling the conversation of the morning, all of a sudden he felt terribly bored. He got up hurriedly and went to look for Oblonsky and Turovtsyn, with whom it had been so pleasant.

Turovtsyn was one of the circle drinking in the billiard room, and Stepan Arkadyevich was talking with Vronsky near the door at the farther corner of the room.

"It's not that she's bored; but this undefined, this unsettled situation," Levin caught, and he was hurrying away, but Stepan Arkadyevich called to him.

"Levin!" said Stepan Arkadyevich; and Levin noticed that his eyes were not full of tears exactly, but moist, which always happened when he had been drinking, or when he was touched. Just now it was due to both causes. "Levin, don't go," he said, and he warmly squeezed his arm above the elbow, obviously not at all wishing to let him go.

"This is a true friend of mine—almost my greatest friend," he said to Vronsky. "You have become even closer and dearer to me. And I want you to, and I know you should be friends, and great friends, because you're both splendid fellows."

"Well, there's nothing for us now but to kiss and be friends," Vronsky said, with good-natured playfulness, holding out his hand.

Levin quickly took the offered hand, and pressed it warmly.

"I'm very, very glad," said Levin.

"Waiter, a bottle of champagne," said Stepan Arkadyevich.

"And I'm very glad," said Vronsky.

But in spite of Stepan Arkadyevich's desire, and their own desire, they had nothing to talk about, and both felt it.

"Do you know, he has never met Anna?" Stepan Arkadyevich said to Vronsky. "And I want more than anything to take him to see her. Let us go, Levin!"

"Really?" said Vronsky. "She will be very glad to see you. I should be going home at once," he added, "but I'm worried about Yashvin, and I want to stay till he finishes."

"Why, is he losing?"

"He keeps losing, and I'm the only friend that can restrain him."

"Well, what do you say to a pyramid? Levin, will you play? Fine!" said Stepan Arkadyevich. "Get the pyramid ready," he said to the marker.

"It has been a long time," answered the marker, who had already set the balls in a triangle and was knocking the red one about for his own diversion.

"Well, let us begin."

After the game Vronsky and Levin sat down at Gagin's table, and at Stepan Arkadyevich's suggestion Levin took a hand in the game.

Vronsky sat down at the table, surrounded by friends, who were incessantly coming up to him. Every now and then he went to the "infernal" to keep an eye on Yashvin. Levin was enjoying a delightful sense of repose after the mental fatigue of the morning. He was glad that all hostility was at an end with Vronsky, and the sense of peace, decorum, and comfort never left him.

When the game was over, Stepan Arkadyevich took Levin's arm. "Well, let us go to Anna's, then. At once? Eh? She is at home. I promised her long ago to bring you. Where were you meaning to spend the evening?"

"Oh, nowhere specially. I promised Sviazhsky to go to the Society of Agriculture. By all means, let us go," said Levin.

"Very good; come along. Find out if my carriage is here," Stepan Arkadyevich said to the waiter.

Levin went up to the table, paid the forty rubles he had lost, paid his bill, the amount of which was in some mysterious way ascertained by the little old waiter who stood at the counter, and swinging his arms, he walked through all the rooms to the way out.

CHAPTER NINE

"The Oblonsky carriage!" the porter shouted in a loud bass. The carriage drove up and both got in. It was only for the first few moments, while the carriage was still in the courtyard, that Levin was still under the influence of the club atmosphere of repose, comfort, and unimpeachable good form. But as soon as the carriage drove out into the street, and he felt it jolting over the uneven cobbled road, heard the angry shout of a sleigh driver coming toward them, saw in the uncertain light the red signboard of a tavern and the shops, this impression was dissipated, and he began to think over his actions, and to wonder whether he was doing the right thing in going to see Anna. What would Kitty say? But Stepan Arkadyevich gave him no time or reflection, and, as though divining his doubts, he scattered them.

"How glad I am," he said, "that you should know her! You know Dolly has long wished for it. And Lvov's been to see her, and often goes. Even though she is my sister," Stepan Arkadyevich pursued, "I don't hesitate to say that she's a remarkable woman. But you will see. Her position is very painful, especially now."

"Why especially now?"

"We are carrying on negotiations with her husband about a divorce. And he's agreed; but there are difficulties in regard to the son, and the business, which ought to have been arranged long ago, has been dragging on for three months now. As soon as the divorce is over, she will marry Vronsky. How stupid that old ceremony is, walking round and round and singing *Rejoice, O Isaiah*! that no one believes in and that stands in the way of the happiness of people," Stepan Arkadyevich put in. "Well, then their situation will be as regular as mine, as yours."

"What is the difficulty?" said Levin.

"Oh, it's a long and tedious story! The whole business is in such an anomaly in this country. But the point is she has been in Moscow for three months, where everyone knows her, waiting for the divorce; she goes out nowhere, sees no woman except Dolly, because, you understand, she doesn't care to have people come as a favor. That fool Princess Varvara, even she has left her, considering this a breach of propriety. Well, you see, in such a position any other woman would not have found resources in herself. But you'll see how she has arranged her life—how calm, how dignified she is. To the left, in the lane opposite the church!" shouted Stepan Arkadyevich, leaning out of the window. "Phew! How hot it is!" he said, in spite of the twenty-seven-degree temperature, flinging his unbuttoned overcoat still wider open.

"But she has a daughter: no doubt she's busy looking after her?" said Levin.

"I believe you picture every woman simply as a female, *une couveuse*,"[1] said Stepan Arkadyevich. "If she's occupied, it must be with her children. No, she brings her up very well, I believe, but one doesn't hear about her. She's busy, in the first place, with what she writes. I see you're smiling ironically, but you're wrong. She's writing a children's book, and doesn't talk about it to anyone, but she read it to me and I gave the manuscript to Vorkuyev . . . you know the publisher . . . and he's an author himself too, I think. He understands those things, and he says it's a remarkable piece of work. But are you imagining she's an authoress? Not at all. Above all, she's a woman with a heart, but you'll see. Now she has a little English girl with her, and a whole family she's looking after."

"Oh, something in a philanthropic way?"

"Why, you will look at everything in the worst light. It's not from

---

[1] "A brooding hen."

philanthropy, it's from the heart. They—that is, Vronsky—had a trainer, an Englishman, first-rate in his own line, but a drunkard. He's completely given up to drink—delirium tremens—and the family was cast on the world. She saw them, helped them, got more and more interested in them, and now the whole family is on her hands. But not by way of patronage, you know, helping with money; she's herself preparing the boys in Russian for the high school, and she's taken the little girl to live with her. But you'll see her for yourself."

The carriage drove into the courtyard, and Stepan Arkadyevich rang loudly at the entrance where sleighs were standing.

And without asking the servant who opened the door whether the lady was at home, Stepan Arkadyevich walked into the hall. Levin followed him, more and more doubtful whether he was doing right or wrong.

Looking at himself in the mirror, Levin noticed that he was red in the face, but he felt certain that he was not drunk, and he followed Stepan Arkadyevich up the carpeted stairs. At the top Stepan Arkadyevich inquired of the footman, who bowed to him as to an intimate friend, who was with Anna Arkadyevna, and received the answer that it was M. Vorkuyev.

"Where are they?"

"In the study."

Passing through the dining room, a room not very large, with dark paneled walls, Stepan Arkadyevich and Levin walked over the soft carpet to the half-dark study, lighted up by a single lamp with a big dark shade. Another lamp with a reflector was hanging on the wall, lighting up a big full-length portrait of a woman, which Levin could not help looking at. It was the portrait of Anna painted in Italy by Mikhailov. While Stepan Arkadyevich went behind the *treillage*[2] and the voice of the man who had been speaking paused, Levin gazed at the portrait, which stood out from the frame in the brilliant light thrown on it, and he could not tear himself away from it. He positively forgot where he was, and not even hearing what was said, he could not take his eyes off the marvelous portrait. It was not a picture but a living, charming woman, with black curling hair, with bare

[2]"Trellis."

arms and shoulders, with a pensive smile on lips covered with soft down; triumphantly and softly she looked at him with eyes that baffled him. She was not alive only because she was more beautiful than a living woman could be.

"I am delighted!" He suddenly heard a voice near him unmistakably addressing him, the voice of the very woman he had been admiring in the portrait. Anna had come from behind the *treillage* to meet him, and Levin saw in the dim light of the study the very woman of the portrait, in a dark dress of various shades of blue, not in the same position or with the same expression, but with the same perfection of beauty which the artist had caught in the portrait. She was less dazzling in reality, but, on the other hand, there was something fresh and seductive in the living woman which was not in the portrait.

CHAPTER TEN

She had risen to meet him, not concealing her pleasure at seeing him; and in the quiet ease with which she held out her little energetic hand, introduced him to Vorkuyev, and indicated a red-haired pretty little girl who was sitting at work, calling her her pupil, Levin recognized and liked the manners of a woman of the world, always self-possessed and natural.

"I am delighted, delighted," she repeated, and on her lips these simple words held for Levin's ears a special significance. "I have known you and liked you for a long while, both from your friendship with Stiva and for your wife's sake. I knew her for a very short time, but she left on me the impression of an exquisite flower, simply a flower. And to think, she will soon be a mother!"

She spoke easily and without haste, looking now and then from Levin to her brother, and Levin felt that the impression he was making was good, and he felt immediately at home, simple and happy with her, as though he had known her from childhood.

"Ivan Petrovich and I settled in Aleksey's study," she said in answer to Stepan Arkadyevich's question whether he might smoke, "just so as to be able to smoke"—and glancing at Levin, instead of asking whether he would care to smoke, she pulled closer a tortoiseshell cigarette case and took a cigarette.

"How are you feeling today?" her brother asked her.

"Oh, nothing. Nerves, as usual."

"Yes, isn't it extraordinarily fine?" said Stepan Arkadyevich, noticing that Levin was scrutinizing the picture.

"I have never seen a better portrait."

"An extraordinary likeness, isn't it?" said Vorkuyev.

Levin looked from the portrait to the original. A peculiar brilliance lighted up Anna's face when she felt his eyes on her. Levin flushed, and, to cover his embarrassment, was about to ask whether she had seen Darya Aleksandrovna lately; but at that moment Anna spoke. "We were just talking, Ivan Petrovich and I, of Vashchenkov's last pictures. Have you seen them?"

"Yes, I have seen them," Levin answered.

"But, I beg your pardon, I interrupted you . . . you were saying? . . ."

Levin asked if she had seen Dolly lately.

"She was here yesterday. She was very indignant with the high school people on Grisha's account. The Latin teacher, it seems, had been unfair to him."

"Yes, I have seen his pictures. I didn't care for them very much," Levin said, going back to the subject she had started.

Levin talked now not at all with that purely businesslike attitude toward the subject with which he had been talking all morning. Every word in his conversation with her had a special significance. And talking to her was pleasant; still pleasanter it was to listen to her.

Anna talked not merely naturally and cleverly, but cleverly and casually, attaching no value to her own ideas and giving great weight to the ideas of the persons she was talking to.

The conversation turned on the new movement in art, on the new illustrations of the Bible by a French artist.[1] Vorkuyev attacked the artist for a realism carried to the point of coarseness.

Levin said that the French had carried conventionality in art fur-

---

[1] Gustave Doré (1833-83), French artist, whose illustrations of the Bible appeared in 1865.

ther than anyone, and that consequently they see a great merit in the return to realism. In the very fact that they do not lie they see poetry.

Never had anything clever said by Levin given him so much pleasure as this remark. Anna's face lighted up at once, as at once she appreciated the thought. She laughed.

"I laugh," she said, "as one laughs when one sees a very striking likeness. What you said so perfectly describes French art now, painting and literature too, indeed—Zola,[2] Daudet.[3] But perhaps it is always so, that men form their conceptions from imaginary, conventional types, and then—all the combinations made—they are tired of the imaginary figures and begin to invent more natural, true figures."

"That's perfectly true," said Vorkuyev.

"So you've been at the club?" she said to her brother.

"Yes, yes, this is a woman!" Levin thought, forgetting himself and staring persistently at her lovely, mobile face, which at that moment was all at once completely transformed. Levin did not hear what she was talking of as she leaned over to her brother, but he was struck by the change of her expression. Her face—so beautiful a moment before in its repose—suddenly wore a look of strange curiosity, anger, and pride. But this lasted only an instant. She lowered her eyelids, as though recollecting something.

"Oh, well, but that's of no interest to anyone," she said and she turned to the English girl.

"Please order tea in the drawing room," she said in English.

The girl got up and went out.

"Well, how did she get through her examination?" asked Stepan Arkadyevich.

"Splendidly! She's a very gifted child and has a sweet disposition."

"It will end in your loving her more than your own."

"There a man speaks. In love there's no more nor less. I love my daughter with one love, and her with another."

"I was just telling Anna Arkadyevna," said Vorkuyev, "that if she were to put a hundredth part of the energy she devotes to this En-

---

[2]Émile Zola (1840-1902), French novelist, leading exponent of naturalism.
[3]Alphonse Daudet (1840-97), French author of novels of social criticism and satire.

glish girl to the public question of the education of Russian children, she would be doing a great and useful work."

"Yes, but I can't help it; I couldn't do it. Count Aleksey Kirillovich urged me very much" (as she uttered the words "Count Aleksey Kirillovich" she glanced with appealing timidity at Levin, and he unconsciously responded with a respectful and reassuring look), "he urged me to take up the school in the village. I visited it several times. The children were very nice, but I could not feel drawn to the work. You speak of energy. Energy rests upon love; and comes as it will, there's no forcing it. I took to this child—I could not myself say why."

And she glanced again at Levin. And her smile and her glance—all told him it was only to him that she was addressing her words, valuing his good opinion, and at the same time sure beforehand that they understood each other.

"I quite understand that," Levin answered. "It's impossible to give one's heart to a school or such institutions in general, and I believe that that's just why philanthropic institutions always give such poor results."

She was silent for a while; then she smiled.

"Yes, yes," she agreed; "I never could. *Je n'ai pas le coeur assez large*[4] to love a whole asylum of horrid little girls. *Cela ne m'a jamais réussi.*[5] There are so many women who have made themselves a *position sociale*[6] in that way. And now more than ever," she said with a mournful, confiding expression, ostensibly addressing her brother, but unmistakably intending her words only for Levin, "now when I have such need of some occupation, I cannot." And suddenly frowning (Levin saw that she was frowning at herself for talking about herself), she changed the subject. "I know about you," she said to Levin; "that you're not a public-spirited citizen, and I have defended you to the best of my ability."

"How have you defended me?"

"Oh, according to the attacks made on you. But won't you have some tea?" She rose and took up a book bound in morocco.

[4] "My heart is not big enough."
[5] "I never could succeed with that."
[6] "A social position."

"Give it to me, Anna Arkadyevna," said Vorkuyev, indicating the book. "It's well worth doing."

"Oh, no, it's all so sketchy."

"I told him about it," Stepan Arkadyevich said to his sister, nodding at Levin.

"You shouldn't have. My writing is something after the fashion of those fretwork baskets the prisoners made which Liza Merkalova used to sell me. She was chairman of the prison department in some society"—she turned to Levin— "and they were miracles of patience, the work of those poor wretches."

And Levin saw a new trait in this woman who attracted him so extraordinarily. Besides wit, grace, and beauty, she had sincerity. She had no wish to hide from him all the bitterness of her position. As she said that she sighed, and her face, suddenly taking a hard expression, looked as if it were turned to stone. With that expression on her face she was more beautiful than ever; but the expression was new; it was utterly unlike that expression, radiant with happiness and creating happiness, which had been caught by the painter in her portrait. Levin looked more than once at the portrait and at her figure, when, taking her brother's arm, she walked with him through the lofty doors, and he felt for her a tenderness and pity which surprised him.

She asked Levin and Vorkuyev to go into the drawing room while she stayed behind to say a few words to her brother. "About her divorce, about Vronsky and what he's doing at the club, about me?" Levin wondered. And he was so keenly interested in what she was saying to Stepan Arkadyevich that he scarcely heard what Vorkuyev was telling him of the virtues of the children's story Anna Arkadyevna had written.

At tea the same pleasant sort of talk, full of interesting matter, continued. There was not a single instant when they had to look for a subject for conversation; on the contrary, one hardly had time to say what one had to say, and eagerly held back to hear what the others were saying. And all that was said, not only by her, but by Vorkuyev and Stepan Arkadyevich—all, so it seemed to Levin, gained peculiar significance from her appreciation and her observations. While he followed this interesting conversation, Levin was all the time admiring her—her beauty, her intelligence, her culture, and at the same time her directness and innate ability to convey her warmth. He listened and talked, and all the while he was thinking of her inner life, trying to divine her feelings. And though he had judged her so severely hitherto, now by some strange chain of reasoning he was justifying her and also sorry for her, and afraid that Vronsky did not fully understand her. At eleven o'clock, when Stepan Arkadyevich got up to go (Vorkuyev had left earlier), it seemed to Levin that he had only just come. Levin, regretfully, got up too.

"Good-by," she said, holding his hand and glancing into his face with a look that drew him to her. "I am very glad *que la glace est rompue.*"[7]

She dropped his hand, and screwed up her eyes.

"Tell your wife that I love her as before, and that if she cannot pardon me my position, then my wish for her is that she may never pardon it. To pardon it, one must go through what I have gone through, and may God spare her that."

"Certainly, yes, I will tell her . . ." Levin said, blushing.

CHAPTER ELEVEN

"What a marvelous, sweet, and pathetic woman!" he was thinking as he stepped out into the frosty air with Stepan Arkadyevich.

"Well, didn't I tell you?" said Stepan Arkadyevich, seeing that Levin had been completely won over.

"Yes," said Levin dreamily, "an extraordinary woman! It's not her cleverness, but she has such wonderful depth of feeling. I'm awfully sorry for her!"

"Now, please God, everything will soon be settled. Well, well, don't be hard on people in the future," said Stepan Arkadyevich, opening the carriage door. "Good-by; we don't go the same way."

Still thinking of Anna, of everything, even the simplest phrase in their conversation with her, and recalling the minutest changes in her expression, sympathizing more and more with her position, Levin reached home.

---

[7]"That the ice is broken."

At home Kuzma told Levin that Katerina Aleksandrovna was quite well, and that her sisters had not long been gone, and he handed him two letters. Levin read them at once in the hall, that he might not overlook them later. One was from Sokolov, his bailiff. Sokolov wrote that the corn could not be sold, that it was bringing only five and a half rubles, and that there was no other way to raise more money. The other letter was from his sister. She scolded him for not having settled her business as yet.

"Well, we must sell it at five and a half if we can't get more," Levin decided the first question, which had always before seemed such a weighty one, with extraordinary facility on the spot. "It's amazing how all one's time is taken up here," he thought, considering the second letter. He felt himself to blame for not having got done what his sister had asked him to do for her. "Today, again, I've not been to the court, but today I've certainly not had time." And resolving that he would not fail to do it the next day, he went to his wife. As he went in, Levin rapidly ran through the day he had spent. All the events of the day consisted of conversations, conversations he had heard and taken part in. All the conversations were upon subjects which, if he had been alone at home, he would never have taken up, but here they were very interesting. And all these conversations were good; only in two places was something not quite right. One was what he had said about the pike, the other was something not quite right in the tender sympathy he was feeling for Anna.

Levin found his wife low-spirited and depressed. The dinner of the three sisters had gone off very well, but then they had waited and waited for him, all of them had felt bored, the sisters had departed, and she had been left alone.

"Well, and what have you been doing?" she asked him, looking straight into his eyes, which shone with rather a suspicious brightness. But that she might not prevent his telling her everything, she concealed her close scrutiny of him, and, with an approving smile, listened to his account of how he had spent the evening.

"Well, I'm very glad I met Vronsky. I felt quite at ease and natural with him. You understand, I shall try not to see him, but I'm glad that this awkwardness is all over," he said, and remembering that by way of trying not to see him, he had immediately gone to call on Anna, he blushed. "We talked about the peasants drinking; I don't know which drinks most, the peasantry or our own class; the peasants do on holidays, but . . ."

But Kitty took not the slightest interest in discussing the drinking habits of the peasants. She saw that he blushed, and she wanted to know why.

"Well, and then where did you go?"

"Stiva strongly urged me to go and see Anna Arkadyevna."

And as he said this, Levin blushed even more, and his doubts as to whether he had done the right thing in going to see Anna were settled once and for all. He knew now that he should not have done so.

Kitty's eyes opened in a curious way and gleamed at Anna's name, but controlling herself with an effort, she concealed her emotion and deceived him.

"Oh!" was all she said.

"I'm sure you won't be angry at my going. Stiva begged me to, and Dolly wished it," Levin went on.

"Oh, no!" she said, but he saw in her eyes a constraint that boded him no good.

"She is a very charming, very, very unhappy, good woman," he said, telling her about Anna, her occupations, and what she had told him to say to her.

"Yes, of course, she is very much to be pitied," said Kitty when he had finished. "Whom was your letter from?"

He told her, and believing in her calm tone, he went to undress.

Coming back, he found Kitty in the same chair. When he went up to her, she glanced at him and broke into sobs.

"What? What is it?" he asked, knowing beforehand what it was.

"You're in love with that hateful woman; she has bewitched you! I saw it in your eyes. Yes, yes! What can it all lead to? You were drinking at the club, drinking and gambling, and then you went . . . to her of all people! No, we must go away . . . I shall go away tomorrow."

It was a long while before Levin could soothe his wife. At last he succeeded in calming her, only by confessing that a feeling of pity, in conjunction with the wine he had drunk, had been too much for him, that he had succumbed to Anna's artful influence, and that he would avoid her. One thing he did with more sincerity confess to was that living so long in Moscow, a life of nothing but conversation, eating, and drinking, he was degenerating. They talked till three o'clock in the morning. Only at three o'clock were they sufficiently reconciled to be able to go to sleep.

CHAPTER TWELVE

After taking leave of her guests, Anna did not sit down, but began walking up and down the room. She had unconsciously the whole evening done her utmost to arouse in Levin a feeling of love—as of late she had fallen into doing with all young men—and she knew she had attained her aim, as far as was possible in one evening, with a married and honorable man. She liked him very much, and, in spite of the striking difference, from the masculine point of view, between Vronsky and Levin, as a woman she saw something they had in common, which had made Kitty able to love both. Yet as soon as he was out of the room, she ceased to think of him.

One thought, and one only, pursued her in different forms, and refused to be shaken off. "If I have so much effect on others, on this man who loves his home and his wife, why is it he is so cold to me? Not cold exactly, he loves me, I know that! But something new is drawing us apart now. Why wasn't he here all evening? He told Stiva to say he could not leave Yashvin and must watch over his play. Is Yashvin a child? But supposing it's true. He is glad of an opportunity of showing me that he has other obligations; I know that, I submit to that. But why prove that to me? He wants to show me that his love for me is not to interfere with his freedom. But I need no proofs, I need love. He ought to understand all the bitterness of this life for me here in Moscow. Is this life? I am not living but waiting for an event which is continually put off and put off. No answer again! And Stiva says he cannot go to Aleksey Aleksandrovich. And I can't write again. I can do nothing, can begin nothing, can alter nothing; I hold myself in, I wait, inventing amusements for myself—the English family, writing, reading—but it's all nothing but a sham; it's all the same as morphine. He ought to feel for me," she said, feeling tears of self-pity coming into her eyes.

She heard Vronsky's impetuous ring and hurriedly dried her tears—not only dried her tears, but sat down by a lamp and opened a book, affecting composure. She wanted to show him that she was displeased that he had not come home as he had promised—displeased only, and not on any account to let him see her distress, least of all, her self-pity. She might pity herself, but he must not pity her. She did not want a quarrel, she blamed him for wanting to quarrel, but, despite herself, the attitude she assumed was one of truculence.

"Well, you've not been bored?" he said eagerly and good-humoredly, going up to her. "What a terrible passion gambling is!"

"No, I've not been bored; I've learned long ago not to be bored. Stiva has been here and Levin."

"Yes, they meant to come and see you. Well, how did you like Levin?" he said, sitting down beside her.

"Very much. They have not long been gone. What was Yashvin doing?"

"He was winning—seventeen thousand. I got him away. He had really started home, but he went back again, and now he's losing."

"Then what did you stay for?" she asked, suddenly lifting her eyes to him. The expression of her face was cold and hostile. "You told Stiva you were staying on to get Yashvin away. And you have left him there."

The same expression of cold readiness for a fight appeared on his face too.

"In the first place, I did not ask him to give you any message; and secondly, I never tell lies. But the chief point is that I wanted to stay, and I stayed," he said, frowning. "Anna, why are you doing this?" he said after a moment's silence, bending over toward her, and he opened his hand, hoping she would lay hers in it.

She was glad of this appeal for tenderness. But some strange force of evil would not let her give herself up to her feelings, as though the rules of warfare would not permit her to surrender.

"Of course you wanted to stay, and you stayed. You do everything you want to. But what do you tell me that for? With what object?"

she said, getting more and more excited. "Does anyone contest your rights? But you want to be right, and you're welcome to be right."

His hand closed, he turned away, and his face wore a still more obstinate expression.

"For you it's a matter of obstinacy," she said, watching him intently and suddenly finding the right word for that expression that irritated her, "simple obstinacy. For you it's a question of whether you keep the upper hand, while for me . . ." Again she felt sorry for herself, and she almost burst into tears. "If you knew what it is for me! When I feel as I do now that you are hostile, yes, hostile to me, if you knew what this means to me! If you knew how I feel on the brink of calamity at this instant, how afraid I am of myself!" And she turned away, hiding her sobs.

"But what are you talking about?" he said, horrified at her expression of despair, and again bending over her, he took her hand and kissed it. "What is it for? Do I seek amusements outside our home? Don't I avoid the society of women?"

"Well, yes! If that were all!" she said.

"Come, tell me what I ought to do to give you peace of mind. I am ready to do anything to make you happy," he said, touched by her expression of despair. "What wouldn't I do to save you from distress of any sort, as now, Anna!" he said.

"It's nothing, nothing!" she said. "I don't know myself whether it's this lonely life, my nerves . . . Come, don't let us talk of it. What about the race? You haven't told me," she inquired, trying to conceal her triumph at the victory, which had, after all, been hers.

He asked for supper, and began telling her about the races; but in his tone, in his eyes, which became more and more cold, she saw that he did not forgive her for her victory, that the feeling of obstinacy with which she had been struggling had asserted itself again in him. He was colder to her than before, as though he were regretting his surrender. And she, remembering the words that had given her the victory, "how I feel on the brink of calamity, how afraid I am of myself," saw that this weapon was a dangerous one, and that it could not be used a second time. And she felt that beside the love that bound them together there had grown up between them some evil spirit of strife which she could not exorcise from his and still less from her own heart.

CHAPTER THIRTEEN

There are no conditions to which a man cannot become accustomed, especially if he sees that all around him are living in the same way. Levin could not have believed three months before that he could have gone quietly to sleep in the condition in which he was that day, that leading an aimless, senseless life, living beyond his means, after drinking to excess (he could not call what happened at the club anything else), forming inappropriately friendly relations with a man with whom his wife had once been in love, and a still more inappropriate call upon a woman who could only be called a fallen woman, after being fascinated by that woman and causing his wife distress—he could still go quietly to sleep. But under the influence of fatigue, a sleepless night, and the wine he had drunk, his sleep was sound and untroubled.

At five o'clock the creak of a door opening waked him. He jumped up and looked around. Kitty was not in bed beside him. But there was a light moving behind the screen, and he heard her steps.

"What is it? . . . What is it?" he said, half asleep. "Kitty! What is it?"

"Nothing," she said, coming from behind the screen with a candle in her hand. "I don't feel well," she said, smiling a particularly sweet and meaningful smile.

"What? Has it begun?" he said in terror. "We ought to send . . ." and hurriedly he reached for his clothes.

"No, no," she said, smiling and holding his hand. "It's sure to be nothing. I was unwell, only a little. It's all over now."

And getting into bed, she blew out the candle, lay down, and was still. Though he thought her stillness suspicious, as though she were holding her breath, and still more suspicious the expression of peculiar tenderness and excitement with which, as she came from behind the screen, she said "nothing," he was so sleepy that he fell asleep at once. Only later he remembered the stillness of her breathing, and understood all that must have been passing in her sweet, precious heart while she lay beside him, not stirring, in anticipation of the greatest event in a woman's life. At seven o'clock he was waked by the touch of her hand on his shoulder, and a gentle whisper. She seemed struggling between regret at waking him and the desire to talk to him.

"Kostya, don't be frightened. It's all right. But I think . . . we ought to send for Lizaveta Petrovna."

The candle was lighted again. She was sitting up in bed, holding some knitting which she had been busy with during the last few days.

"Please, don't be frightened, it's all right. I'm not a bit afraid," she said, seeing his frightened face, and she pressed his hand to her bosom and then to her lips.

He hurriedly jumped up, hardly awake, and kept his eyes fixed on her as he put on his dressing gown; then he stopped, still looking at her. He had to go, but he could not tear himself from her eyes. He thought he loved her face, knew her expression; her eyes, but never had he seen it like this. How hateful and horrible he seemed to himself, thinking of the distress he had caused her yesterday. Her flushed face, fringed with soft curling hair escaping from under her nightcap, was radiant with joy and courage.

Though there was so little that was conventional or artificial in Kitty's character in general, Levin was struck by what was revealed now, when suddenly all disguises were thrown off and the very kernel of her soul shone in her eyes. And in this simplicity and nakedness of her soul, she, the very woman he loved in her, was more manifest than ever. She looked at him, smiling; but all at once her brows twitched, she threw up her head, and going quickly up to him, she clutched his hand and pressed close against him, breathing her hot breath upon him. She was in pain and was, as it were, complaining to him of her suffering. And for the first minute, from habit, it seemed to him that he was to blame. But in her eyes there was a tenderness that told him that she was far from reproaching him, that she loved him for her sufferings. "If not I, who is to blame for it?" he thought unconsciously, seeking someone responsible for this suffering for him to punish; but there was no one responsible. She was suffering, complaining, and glorying in her sufferings, and rejoicing in them, and loving them. He saw that something sublime was being accomplished in her soul, but what? He could not make it out. It was beyond his understanding.

"I have sent to Mama. You go quickly to fetch Lizaveta Petrovna . . . Kostya! . . . Nothing, it's passed."

She moved away from him and rang the bell.

"Well, go now; Pasha's coming. I am all right."

And Levin saw with astonishment that she had taken up the knitting she had brought in in the night and had begun working at it again.

As Levin was going out of one door, he heard the maid come in at the other. He stood at the door and heard Kitty giving exact directions to the maid and beginning to help her move the bed.

He dressed, and while they were preparing the horses, as a hired sleigh was not to be seen yet, he ran again up to the bedroom, not on tiptoe, it seemed to him, but on wings. Two maids were busy moving something in the bedroom.

Kitty was walking about knitting rapidly and giving directions.

"I'm going for the doctor. They have sent for Lizaveta Petrovna, but I'll go on there too. Isn't there anything wanted? Yes, shall I go to Dolly's?"

She looked at him, obviously not hearing what he was saying.

"Yes, yes. Do go," she said quickly, frowning and waving her hand to him.

He had just gone into the drawing room, when suddenly a pitiful moan sounded from the bedroom, smothered instantly. He stood still, and for a long while he could not understand.

"Yes, that is she," he said to himself, and clutching at his head he ran downstairs.

"Lord have mercy on us! Pardon us! Aid us!" he repeated the words that for some reason came suddenly, to his lips. And he, an unbeliever, repeated these words not only with his lips. At that instant he knew that all his doubts, even the impossibility of believing with his reason, of which he was aware in himself, did not in the least hinder his turning to God. All of that now floated out of his soul like dust. To whom was he to turn if not to Him in whose hands he felt himself, his soul, and his love?

The horse was not yet ready, but feeling a peculiar concentration of his physical forces and his intellect on what he had to do, he started off on foot without waiting for the horse, and told Kuzma to overtake him.

At the corner he met a night cabman driving hurriedly. In the little sleigh, wrapped in a velvet cloak, sat Lizaveta Petrovna with a shawl around her head. "Thank God! Thank God!" he said, overjoyed to recognize her pale little face, which wore a peculiarly serious, even stern expression. Telling the driver not to stop, he ran along beside her.

"For two hours, then? Not more?" she inquired. "You should let Piotr Dmitrievich know, but don't hurry him. And get some opium at the chemist's."

"So you think that it will go well? Lord have mercy on us and help us!" Levin said, seeing his own horse driving out of the gate. Jumping into the sleigh beside Kuzma, he told him to drive to the doctor's.

CHAPTER FOURTEEN

The doctor was not yet up, and the footman said that "he had been up late, and had given orders not to be waked, but would get up soon." The footman was cleaning the lamp glasses and seemed very engrossed in his work. This concentration of the footman upon his lamps, and his indifference to Levin's agitated state, at first astounded him, but immediately on considering the question, he realized that no one knew or was bound to know his feelings, and that it was all the more necessary to act calmly, sensibly, and resolutely to get through this wall of indifference and attain his aim.

"Don't be in a hurry or let anything slip," Levin said to himself, feeling a greater and greater flow of physical energy and attention to all that lay before him.

Having ascertained that the doctor was not getting up, Levin considered various plans, and decided on the following one; that Kuzma should go for another doctor, while he himself should go to the pharmacy for opium, and if when he came back the doctor had not yet begun to get up, he would either by tipping the footman, or by force, wake the doctor at all costs.

At the pharmacy a lanky assistant sealed up a package of powders for a coachman who stood waiting, and refused him opium with the same callousness with which the doctor's footman had cleaned his lamp glasses. Trying not to get flurried or out of temper, Levin mentioned the names of the doctor and the midwife, and, explaining what the opium was needed for, tried to persuade him. The assistant inquired in German whether he should give it, and receiving an affirmative reply from behind the partition, he took out a bottle and a funnel, deliberately poured the opium from a bigger bottle into a little one, stuck on a label, sealed it up, in spite of Levin's request that he not do so, and was about to wrap it up, too. This was more than Levin could stand; he took the bottle firmly out of his hands, and ran to the big glass doors. The doctor was still not awake, and the footman, busy putting down a rug, refused to wake him. Levin deliberately took out a ten-ruble note, and careful to speak slowly, though losing no time over the business, he handed him the note and explained that Piotr Dmitrievich (what a great and important personage he seemed to Levin now, this Piotr Dmitrievich, who had been of so little consequence in his eyes before!) had promised to come at any time; that he would certainly not be angry, and that he must therefore wake him at once.

The footman agreed, and went upstairs, taking Levin into the waiting room.

Levin could hear through the door the doctor coughing, moving about, washing, and saying something. Three minutes passed; it seemed to Levin that more than an hour had gone by. He could not wait any longer.

"Piotr Dmitrievich, Piotr Dmitrievich!" he said in an imploring voice at the open door. "For God's sake, forgive me! See me as you are. It's been going on more than two hours already."

"In a minute; in a minute!" answered a voice, and to his amazement Levin heard that the doctor was smiling as he spoke.

"For one instant."

"In a minute."

Two minutes more passed while the doctor was putting on his

boots, and two minutes more while the doctor put on his coat and combed his hair.

"Piotr Dmitrievich!" Levin was beginning again in a plaintive voice just as the doctor came in dressed and ready. "These people have no conscience," thought Levin. "Combing his hair while we're dying!"

"Good morning!" the doctor said to him, shaking hands, and, as it were, teasing him with his composure. "There's no hurry. Well now?"

Trying to be as accurate as possible, Levin began to tell him every unnecessary detail of his wife's condition, interrupting his account repeatedly with entreaties that the doctor come with him at once.

"Oh, you needn't be in any hurry. You don't understand, you know. I'm certain I'm not wanted, still I've promised, and if you like, I'll come. But there's no hurry. Please sit down; won't you have some coffee?"

Levin stared at him with eyes that asked whether he was laughing at him; but the doctor had no notion of making fun of him.

"I know, I know," the doctor said, smiling; "I'm a married man myself, and at these moments we husbands are very much to be pitied. I've a patient whose husband always takes refuge in the stables on such occasions."

"But what do you think, Piotr Dmitrievich? Do you suppose it will go all right?"

"Everything points to a favorable issue."

"So you'll come immediately?" said Levin, looking wrathfully at the servant who was bringing in the coffee.

"In an hour's time."

"Oh, for heaven's sake!"

"Well, let me drink my coffee, anyway."

The doctor started upon his coffee. Both were silent.

"The Turks are really getting beaten, though. Did you read yesterday's dispatches?" said the doctor, munching a roll.

"No, I can't stand it!" said Levin, jumping up. "So you'll be with us in a quarter of an hour."

"In half an hour."

"On your honor?"

When Levin got home, he drove up at the same time as the princess, and they went up to the bedroom door together. The princess had tears in her eyes, and her hands were shaking. Seeing Levin, she embraced him and burst into tears.

"Well, my dear Lizaveta Petrovna?" she queried, clasping the hand of the midwife, who came out to meet them with a beaming and anxious face.

"She's doing well," she said. "Persuade her to lie down. It would be easier for her."

From the moment he had wakened and understood what was going on, Levin had prepared his mind to bear resolutely what was before him, and without considering or anticipating anything, to avoid upsetting his wife, and on the contrary to soothe her and keep up her courage. Without allowing himself even to think of what was to come, of how it would end, judging from his inquiries as to the usual duration of these ordeals, Levin had in his imagination braced himself to bear up and to keep a tight rein on his feelings for five hours, and it had seemed to him he could do this. But when he came back from the doctor's and saw her sufferings again, he fell to repeating more and more frequently: "Lord, have mercy on us, and succor us!" He sighed, and flung his head back, and began to feel afraid he could not bear it, that he would burst into tears or run away. Such agony was it for him. And only one hour had passed.

But after that hour there passed another hour, two hours, three, the full five hours he had fixed as the furthest limit of his sufferings, and the situation was still unchanged; and he was still bearing it because there was nothing to be done but bear it, every instant feeling that he had reached the utmost limits of his endurance, and that his heart would break with sympathy and pain.

But still the minutes passed by and the hours, and still more hours, and his misery and horror grew and were more and more intense.

All the ordinary conditions of life, without which one can form no conception of anything, had ceased to exist for Levin. He lost all sense of time. Minutes—those minutes when she sent for him and he held her moist hand that would squeeze his hand with extraordinary violence and then push it away—seemed to him hours, and hours seemed to him minutes. He was surprised when Lizaveta Petrovna asked him to light a candle behind a screen, and he found that it was five o'clock in the afternoon. If he had been told it was only ten o'clock in the morning he would not have been more surprised. Where he was all this time, he knew as little as he knew what was going on, anything. He saw her swollen face, sometimes bewildered and in agony, sometimes smiling and trying to reassure him. He saw the old princess too, flushed and overwrought, with her gray curls in disorder, forcing herself to gulp down her tears, biting her lips; he saw Dolly too and the doctor, smoking thick cigarettes, and Liza-veta Petrovna with a firm, resolute, reassuring face, and the old prince walking up and down the hall with a frowning face. But why they came in and went out, where they were, he did not know. The princess was with the doctor in the bedroom, then in the study, where a table set for dinner suddenly appeared; then she was not there, but Dolly was. Then Levin remembered he had been sent somewhere. Once he had been sent to move a table and a sofa. He had done this eagerly, thinking it had to be done for her sake, and only later on did he discover it was his own bed he had been getting ready. Then he had been sent to the study to ask the doctor some-thing. The doctor had answered and then had said something about the irregularities in the municipal council. Then he had been sent to the bedroom to help the old princess move the icon in its silver-gilt case, and with the princess's old maid he had clambered on a shelf to reach it and had broken the little lamp, and the old servant had tried to reassure him about the lamp and about his wife, and he car-ried the icon and set it at Kitty's head, carefully tucking it in behind the pillow. But where, when, and why all this had happened, he could not tell. He did not understand why the old princess took his hand and, looking compassionately at him, begged him not to worry him-self, and Dolly persuaded him to eat something and led him out of the room, and even the doctor looked seriously and with commiser-ation at him and offered him a drop of something.

All he knew and felt was that what was happening was what had happened nearly a year before in the hotel of the country town at the deathbed of his brother Nikolai. But that had been grief—this was joy. Yet that grief and this joy were alike beyond the ordinary condi-tions of life; they were openings, as it were, in that ordinary life through which there came glimpses of something sublime. And in the contemplation of this sublime something the soul was exalted to inconceivable heights of which it had before had no conception, while reason lagged behind, unable to keep up with it.

"Lord have mercy on us, and succor us!" he repeated to himself incessantly, feeling, in spite of his long and, as it seemed, complete alienation from religion, that he turned to God just as trustfully and simply as he had in his childhood and first youth.

All this time he was in two conflicting moods. One was away from her, with the doctor, who kept smoking one fat cigarette after another and extinguishing them on the edge of a full ashtray, with Dolly, and with the old prince, where there was talk about dinner, about politics, about Marya Petrovna's illness, and where Levin suddenly forgot for a minute what was happening, and left as though he had awakened from sleep; the other was in her presence, at her pillow, where his heart seemed breaking and still did not break from sympathetic suffering, and he prayed to God without ceasing. And every time he was brought back from a moment of oblivion by a scream reaching him from the bedroom, he fell into the same strange terror that had come upon him the first minute. Every time he heard a shriek, he jumped up, ran to justify himself, remembered on the way that he was not to blame, and he longed to defend her, to help her. But as he looked at her, he saw again that help was impossible, and he was filled with terror and prayed: "Lord have mercy on us, and help us!" And as time went on, both these conditions became more intense; the calmer he became away from her, completely forgetting her, the more agonizing became both her sufferings and his feeling of helplessness before them. He jumped up, would have liked to run away, but ran to her.

Sometimes, when again and again she called him, he reproached her; but seeing her patient, smiling face, and hearing the words "I am worrying you," he threw the blame on God; but thinking of God, at once he fell to beseeching God to forgive him and have mercy.

CHAPTER FIFTEEN

He did not know whether it was late or early. The candles had all burned out. Dolly had just been in the study and had suggested to the doctor that he should lie down. Levin sat listening to the doctor's stories of a quack mesmerizer and looking at the ashes of his cigarette. There had been a period of repose, and he had sunk into oblivion. He had completely forgotten what was going on now. He heard the doctor's chat and understood it. Suddenly there came an unearthly shriek. The shriek was so awful that Levin did not even jump up, but, holding his breath, gazed in terrified inquiry at the doctor. The doctor put his head on one side, listened, and smiled approvingly. Everything was so extraordinary that nothing could strike Levin as strange. "I suppose it must be so," he thought, and still sat where he was. Whose scream was it? He jumped up, ran on tiptoe to the bedroom, edged around Lizaveta Petrovna and the princess, and took up his position at Kitty's pillow. The scream had subsided, but there was some change now. What it was he did not see and did not comprehend, and he had no wish to see or comprehend. But he saw it by the face of Lizaveta Petrovna. Lizaveta Petrovna's face was stern and pale and still as resolute, though her jaws were twitching and her eyes were fixed intently on Kitty. Kitty's swollen and agonized face, a tress of hair clinging to her moist brow, was turned to him and sought his eyes. Her lifted hands asked for his hands. Clutching his chill hands in her moist ones, she began squeezing them to her face.

"Don't go, don't go! I'm not afraid, I'm not afraid!" she said rapidly. "Mama, take my earrings. They're in the way. You're not afraid, are you? Quick, quick, Lizaveta Petrovna . . ."

She spoke quickly, very quickly, and tried to smile. But suddenly her face was drawn, and she pushed him away.

"Oh, this is terrible! I'm dying, I'm dying! go away!" she shrieked, and again he heard that unearthly scream.

Levin clutched at his head and ran out of the room.

"It's nothing, it's nothing, it's all right," Dolly called after him.

But they might say what they liked, he knew now that all was over. He stood in the next room, his head leaning against the doorpost, and heard shrieks, howls such as he had never heard before, and he knew that what had been Kitty was uttering these shrieks. He had long ago ceased to wish for the child. By now he loathed this child. He did not even wish for her life now, all he longed for was the end of this awful anguish.

"Doctor! What is it? What is it? By God!" he said, snatching at the doctor's hand as he came up.

"It's the end," said the doctor. And the doctor's face was so grave as he said it that Levin took "the end" as meaning her death.

Beside himself, he ran into the bedroom. The first thing he saw was the face of Lizaveta Petrovna. It was even more frowning and stern. Kitty's face he did not know. In the place where it had been was something that was fearful in its strained distortion and in the sounds that came from it. He fell down with his head on the wooden framework of the bed, feeling that his heart was bursting. The awful scream never paused, it became still more awful, and as though it had reached the utmost limit of terror, suddenly it ceased. Levin could not believe his ears, but there could be no doubt; the scream had ceased and he heard a subdued stir and bustle, and hurried breathing, and her voice, gasping, alive, tender, and blissful, uttered softly, "It's over!"

He lifted his head. With her hands hanging exhausted on the quilt, looking extraordinarily lovely and serene, she looked at him in silence and tried to smile, and could not.

And suddenly, from the mysterious and awful faraway world in which he had been living for the last twenty-two hours, Levin felt himself all in an instant borne back to the old everyday world, glorified though now by such a radiance of happiness that he could not bear it. The strained chords snapped, sobs and tears of joy which he had never foreseen rose up with such violence that his whole body shook, that for long they prevented him from speaking.

Falling on his knees before the bed, he held his wife's hand before his lips and kissed it, and the hand, with a weak movement of the fingers, responded to his kiss. And meanwhile, there at the foot of the bed, in the deft hands of Lizaveta Petrovna, like a flickering light in a lamp, lay the life of a human creature which had never existed before, and which would now with the same right, with the same importance to itself, live and create in its own image.

"Alive! Alive! And a boy, too! Set your mind at rest!" Levin heard Lizaveta Petrovna saying as she slapped the baby's back with a shaking hand.

"Mama, is it true?" said Kitty's voice.

The princess's sobs were all the answer she could make. And in the midst of the silence there came in unmistakable reply to the mother's question, a voice quite unlike the subdued voices speaking in the room. It was the bold, clamorous, self-assertive squall of the new human being who had so incomprehensibly appeared.

If Levin had been told before that Kitty was dead, and that he had died with her, and that their children were angels, and that God was standing before him, he would have been surprised at nothing. But now, coming back to the world of reality, he had to make great mental efforts to realize that she was alive and well, and that the creature squalling so desperately was his son. Kitty was alive, her agony was over. And he was unutterably happy. That he understood; he was completely happy in it. But the baby? Whence, why, who was he?... He could not get used to the idea. It seemed to him something extraneous, superfluous, to which he could not accustom himself.

CHAPTER SIXTEEN

At ten o'clock the old prince, Sergey Ivanovich, and Stepan Arkadyevich were sitting at Levin's. Having inquired after Kitty, they had dropped into conversation upon other subjects. Levin heard them, and unconsciously, as they talked, going over the past, over what had been up to that morning, he thought of himself as he had been yesterday till that point. It was as though a hundred years had passed since then. He felt himself exalted to unattainable heights, from which he studiously lowered himself so as not to hurt the people he was talking to. He talked, and was all the time thinking of his wife, of her condition now, of his son, in whose existence he tried to school himself into believing. The whole world of woman, which had taken for him since his marriage a new value he had never suspected before, was now so exalted that he could not take it in in his imagination. He heard them talk of yesterday's dinner at the club, and thought: "What is happening with her now? Is she asleep? How is she? What is she thinking of? Is he crying, my son Dmitri?" And in the middle of the conversation, in the middle of a sentence, he jumped up and left the room.

"Send me word if I can see her," said the prince.

"Very well, in a minute," answered Levin, and without stopping, he went to her room.

She was not asleep, she was talking gently with her mother, making plans about the christening.

Tidied, with her hair well brushed, in a smart little cap with some blue in it, her arms out on the quilt, she was lying on her back. Meeting his eyes, her eyes drew him to her. Her face, bright before, brightened still more as he drew near her. There was the same change in it from earthly to unearthly that is seen in the face of the dead. But then it means farewell, here it meant welcome. Again a rush of emotion such as he had felt at the moment of the child's birth flooded his heart. She took his hand and asked him if he had slept. He could not answer, and turned away, struggling with his weakness.

"I have had a nap, Kostya!" she said to him. "And I am so comfortable now."

She looked at him, but suddenly her expression changed.

"Give him to me," she said, hearing the baby's cry. "Give him to me, Lizaveta Petrovna, and he will look at him."

"To be sure, his papa shall look at him," said Lizaveta Petrovna, getting up and bringing something red, and strange, and wriggling. "Wait a minute, we'll make him tidy first," and Lizaveta Petrovna laid the red wobbling thing on the bed, began untrussing and trussing up the baby, lifting him up and turning him over with one finger and powdering him with something.

Levin, looking at the tiny, pitiful creature, made strenuous efforts to discover in his heart some traces of fatherly feeling. He felt nothing but disgust. But when the baby was undressed and he caught a glimpse of wee, wee, little hands, little feet, saffron-colored, with little toes, too; and positively with a little big toe different from the rest, and when he saw Lizaveta Petrovna bending the little sticking-up arms as though they were soft springs and putting them into linen garments, such pity for the little creature came upon him, and such terror that she would hurt it, that he held her hand back.

Lizaveta Petrovna laughed.

"Don't be frightened, don't be frightened!"

When the baby had been put to rights and transformed into a firm doll, Lizaveta Petrovna dandled him as though proud of her handiwork, and stood a little away so that Levin might see his son in all his glory.

Kitty looked sideways in the same direction, never taking her eyes off the baby. "Give him to me! Give him to me!" she said, and was even going to sit up.

"What are you doing, Katerina Aleksandrovna! You mustn't move like that! Wait a minute. I'll give him to you. Here we're showing papa what a fine fellow we are!"

And Lizaveta Petrovna, with one hand supporting the wobbling head, lifted up on her other arm the strange, limp, red creature, whose head was lost in the swaddling clothes. But there was a nose, too, and slanting eyes and sucking lips.

"A splendid baby!" said Lizaveta Petrovna.

Levin sighed with mortification. This splendid baby excited in him no feeling but disgust and compassion. It was not at all the feeling he had looked forward to.

He turned away while Lizaveta Petrovna put the baby to the unaccustomed breast.

Suddenly laughter made him look around. Kitty was laughing. The baby had taken the breast.

"Come, that's enough, that's enough!" said Lizaveta Petrovna, but Kitty would not let the baby go. He fell asleep in her arms.

"Look, now," said Kitty, turning the baby so that he could see. The aged-looking little face suddenly puckered up still more and the baby sneezed.

Smiling, hardly able to restrain his tears, Levin kissed his wife and went out of the dark room. What he felt toward this little creature was utterly unlike what he had expected. There was nothing cheerful and joyous in the feeling; on the contrary, it was a new torture of apprehension. It was the consciousness of a new sphere of liability to pain. And this sense was so painful at first, the apprehension lest this helpless creature should suffer was so intense, that it prevented him from noticing the strange thrill of senseless joy and even pride that he had felt when the baby sneezed.

CHAPTER SEVENTEEN

Stepan Arkadyevich Oblonsky's affairs were in a very bad way.

Two thirds of the money for the forest had been spent already, and he had borrowed from the merchant in advance, at ten percent discount, almost all the remaining third. The merchant would not give more, especially as Darya Aleksandrovna, for the first time that winter insisting on her right to her own property, had refused to sign the receipt for the payment of the last third of the forest. All his salary went on household expenses and in payment of petty debts that could not be put off. There was positively no money.

This was unpleasant and awkward, and in Stepan Arkadyevich's opinion, things could not go on like this. The explanation of the position was, in his view, to be found in the fact that his salary was too small. The post he filled had been unmistakably very good five years ago, but it was so no longer.

Petrov, the bank director, made twelve thousand; Sventitsky, a company director, made seventeen thousand; Mitin, who had founded a bank, received fifty thousand.

"Clearly I've been napping, and they've overlooked me," Stepan Arkadyevich thought about himself. And he began keeping his eyes and ears open, and toward the end of the winter he had discovered a very good berth and had formed a plan of attack upon it, at first from Moscow through aunts, uncles, and friends, and then, when the matter was well advanced, in the spring, he went himself to Petersburg. It was one of those snug, lucrative berths of which there are so many more nowadays than there used to be, with incomes ranging from one thousand to fifty thousand rubles. It was the post of secretary of the committee of the amalgamated agency of Southern Railways and certain banking companies. This position, like all such appointments, called for such immense energy and such varied qualifications that it was difficult for them to be found united in any one man. And since a man combining all the qualifications was not to be found, it was at least better that the post be filled by an honest than by a dishonest man. And Stepan Arkadyevich was not merely an honest man in the ordinary sense of the word, he was an honest man—emphatically—in that special sense the word has in Moscow, when they talk of an "honest" politician, an "honest" writer, an "honest" newspaper, an "honest" institution, an "honest" tendency, meaning not simply that the man or the institution is not dishonest, but that they are capable on occasion of taking a line of their own in opposition to the authorities.

Stepan Arkadyevich moved in those circles in Moscow in which that expression had come into use, was regarded there as an honest man, and so had more right to this appointment than others.

The appointment yielded an income of from seven to ten thousand a year, and Oblonsky could fill it without giving up his government position. It was in the hands of two ministers, one lady, and two Jews, and all these people, though the way had been paved already with them, Stepan Arkadyevich had to see in Petersburg. Besides this business, Stepan Arkadyevich had promised his sister Anna to obtain from Karenin a definite answer on the question of divorce. And borrowing fifty rubles from Dolly, he set off for Petersburg.

Stepan Arkadyevich sat in Karenin's study listening to his report on the causes of the unsatisfactory position of Russian finance, and only waiting for the moment when he would finish to speak about his own business or about Anna.

"Yes, that's very true," he said, when Aleksey Aleksandrovich took off his pince-nez, without which he could not read now, and looked inquiringly at his former brother-in-law, "that's very true in particular cases, but still the principle of our day is freedom."

"Yes, but I lay down another principle, embracing the principle of freedom," said Aleksey Aleksandrovich, with emphasis on the word "embracing," and he put on his pince-nez again so as to read the passage in which this statement was made. And turning over the beautifully written wide-margined manuscript, Aleksey Aleksandrovich read aloud again the conclusive passage.

"I don't advocate protection for the sake of private interests but for the public weal, and for the lower and upper classes equally," he said, looking over his pince-nez at Oblonsky. "But *they* cannot grasp that, *they* are taken up now with personal interests and carried away by phrases."

Stepan Arkadyevich knew that when Karenin began to talk of what *they* were doing and thinking, the persons who would not accept his report and were the cause of everything wrong in Russia, it was coming near the end. And so now he eagerly abandoned the principle of freedom and fully agreed. Aleksey Aleksandrovich paused, thoughtfully turning over the pages of his manuscript.

"Oh, by the way," said Stepan Arkadyevich, "I wanted to ask you, some time when you see Pomorsky, to drop him a hint that I would be very glad to get that new appointment of secretary of the committee of the amalgamated agency of the Southern Railways and banking companies." Stepan Arkadyevich was familiar by now with the title of the post he coveted, and he brought it out rapidly without mistake.

Aleksey Aleksandrovich questioned him as to the duties of this new committee, and pondered. He was considering whether the new committee would not be acting in some way contrary to the views he had been advocating. But as the influence of the new committee was of a very complex nature, and his views were of very wide application, he could not decide this immediately, and taking off his pince-nez, he said:

"Of course, I can mention it to him; but what is your reason precisely for wishing to obtain the appointment?"

"It's a good salary, up to nine thousand, and my means—"

"Nine thousand!" Aleksey Aleksandrovich repeated and he frowned. The high figure made him reflect that on that side Stepan Arkadyevich's proposed position ran counter to the main tendency of his own projects of reform, which always leaned toward economy.

"I consider, and I have embodied my views in a note on the subject, that in our day these immense salaries are evidence of the unsound economic policy of our administration."

"But what's to be done?" said Stepan Arkadyevich. "Suppose a bank director gets ten thousand—well, he's worth it; or an engineer gets twenty thousand—after all, it's a growing business, you know!"

"I assume that a salary is the price paid for a commodity, and it ought to conform with the law of supply and demand. If the salary is fixed without any regard for that law, as, for instance, when I see two engineers leaving college together, both equally well trained and efficient, and one getting forty thousand while the other is satisfied with two; or when I see lawyers and hussars, having no special qualifications, appointed directors of banking companies with immense salaries, I conclude that the salary is not fixed in accordance with the law of supply and demand, but simply through personal interest. And this is an abuse of great gravity in itself, and one that reacts injuriously on the government service. I consider—"

Stepan Arkadyevich made haste to interrupt his brother-in-law.

"Yes; but you must agree that it's a new institution of undoubted utility that's being started. After all, you know, it's a growing business! What they lay particular stress on is the thing being carried on *honestly*," said Stepan Arkadyevich with emphasis.

But the Moscow significance of the word "honest" was lost on Aleksey Aleksandrovich.

"Honesty is only a negative qualification," he said.

"Well, you'll do me a great service, anyway," said Stepan Arkadyevich, "by putting in a word to Pomorsky—just in the way of conversation . . ."

"But I imagine it's more in Bolgarinov's hands," said Aleksey Aleksandrovich.

"Bolgarinov has fully assented, as far as he's concerned," said Stepan Arkadyevich, turning red. Stepan Arkadyevich reddened at the mention of that name because he had called that morning on the Jew, and the visit had left an unpleasant impression.

Stepan Arkadyevich believed most positively that the committee in which he was trying to get an appointment was a new, genuine, and honest public body, but that morning when Bolgarinov had— intentionally, beyond a doubt—kept him two hours waiting with other petitioners in his waiting room, he had suddenly felt uneasy.

Whether he was uncomfortable that he, a descendant of Rurik, Prince Oblonsky, had been kept waiting two hours to see a Jew, or that for the first time in his life he was not following the example of his ancestors in serving the government, but was turning off into a new career, anyway he was very uncomfortable. During those two hours in Bolgarinov's waiting room, Stepan Arkadyevich, stepping jauntily about the room, pulling his whiskers, entering into conversation with the other petitioners, attempting to invent a pun he would repeat afterwards—how he was *jewing* his cud at the Jew's—tried very hard to hide from others and even from himself the feeling he was experiencing.

But all the time he was uncomfortable and angry, he could not have said why—whether because he could not get his pun just right, or for some other reason. When at last Bolgarinov had received him with exaggerated politeness and unmistakable triumph at his humiliation, and had all but refused the favor asked him, Stepan Arkadyevich had made haste to forget it all as soon as possible. And now, at the mere recollection, he blushed.

CHAPTER EIGHTEEN

"Now, there is something I want to talk about, and you know what it is. About Anna," Stepan Arkadyevich said, pausing for a brief space and shaking off the unpleasant impression.

As soon as Oblonsky uttered Anna's name, the face of Aleksey Aleksandrovich was completely transformed; all the life went out of it, and it looked very weary and dead.

"What is it exactly that you want from me?" he said, moving in his chair and snapping his pince-nez.

"A decision, Aleksey Aleksandrovich, some sort of decision. I'm appealing to you" ("not as to an injured husband," Stepan Arkadyevich was going to say, but afraid of wrecking his negotiation by this, he changed the words) "not as a statesman" (which did not sound *à propos*) "but simply as a man, and a good-hearted man and a Christian. You must have pity on her," he said.

"That is, in what way precisely?" Karenin said softly.

"Yes, pity on her. If you had seen her as I have!—I have been spending all winter with her—you would have pity on her. Her position is awful, simply awful!"

"I had imagined," answered Aleksey Aleksandrovich in a higher, almost shrill voice, "that Anna Arkadyevna had everything she had desired for herself."

"Oh, Aleksey Aleksandrovich, for heaven's sake, don't let us indulge in recriminations! What is past is past, and you know what she wants and is waiting for—divorce."

"But I believe Anna Arkadyevna refuses a divorce if I make it a condition to leave me my son. I replied to that effect, and supposed that the matter was ended. I consider it at an end," shrieked Aleksey Aleksandrovich.

"But, for heaven's sake, don't get excited!" said Stepan Arkadyevich, touching his brother-in-law's knee. "The matter is not ended. If you will allow me to recapitulate, it was like this: when you parted, you were as magnanimous as could possibly be; you were ready to give her everything—freedom, divorce even. She appreciated that. No, don't think that. She did appreciate it—to such a degree that at the first moment, feeling how she had wronged you, she did not consider and could not consider everything. She gave up everything. But experience, time, have shown that her position is unbearable, impossible."

"The life of Anna Arkadyevna can have no interest for me," Aleksey Aleksandrovich put in, lifting his eyebrows.

"Allow me to disbelieve that," Stepan Arkadyevich replied gently. "Her position is intolerable for her, and of no benefit to anyone whatever. She has deserved it, you will say. She knows that and asks you for nothing; she says plainly that she dare not ask you. But I, all of us, her relatives, all who love her beg you, entreat you. Why should she suffer? Who is any better for it?"

"Excuse me, you seem to put me in the position of the guilty party," observed Aleksey Aleksandrovich.

"Oh, no, oh, no, not at all! Please understand me," said Stepan Arkadyevich, touching his hand again, as though feeling sure this physical contact would soften his brother-in-law. "All I say is this: her position is intolerable, and it might be alleviated by you, and you will lose nothing by it. I will arrange it all for you, so that you'll not notice it. You did promise it, you know."

"The promise was given before. And I had supposed that the question of my son had settled the matter. Besides, I had hoped that Anna Arkadyevna had enough generosity . . ." Aleksey Aleksandrovich articulated with difficulty, his lips twitching and his face white.

"She leaves it all to your generosity. She begs, she implores one thing of you—to extricate her from the impossible position in which she is placed. She does not ask for her son now. Aleksey Aleksandrovich, you are a good man. Put yourself in her position for a minute. The question of divorce for her in her position is a question of life and death. If you had not promised it once, she would have reconciled herself to her position, she would have gone on living in the country. But you promised it, and she wrote to you, and moved to Moscow. And here she's been for six months in Moscow, where every chance meeting cuts her to the heart, every day expecting an answer. Why, it's like keeping a condemned criminal for six months with the rope around his neck, promising him perhaps death, perhaps mercy. Have pity on her, and I will undertake to arrange everything. *Vos scruples . . .*[1]

"I am not talking about that, about that . . ." Aleksey Aleksandrovich interrupted with disgust. "But, perhaps, I promised what I had no right to promise."

"So you go back on your promise?"

"I have never refused to do all that is possible, but I want time to consider how much of what I promised is possible."

"No, Aleksey Aleksandrovich!" cried Oblonsky, jumping up, "I won't believe that! She's unhappy as only an unhappy woman can be, and you cannot refuse in such—"

"As much of what I promised as is possible. *Vous professez d'être libre penseur.*[2] But I as a believer cannot, in a matter of such gravity, act in opposition to the Christian law."

"But in Christian societies and among us, as far as I'm aware, divorce is allowed," said Stepan Arkadyevich. "Divorce is sanctioned even by our church. And we see—"

"It is allowed, but not in the sense—"

"Aleksey Aleksandrovich, you are not like yourself," said Oblonsky, after a brief pause. "Wasn't it you (and didn't we all appreciate it in you?) who forgave everything, and moved simply by Christian feeling, were ready to make any sacrifice? You said yourself: 'If a man take thy coat, give him thy cloak also,' and now—"

"I beg," said Aleksey Aleksandrovich shrilly, getting suddenly onto

[1]"Your scruples . . ."
[2]"You profess to be a freethinker."

his feet, his face white and his jaws twitching, "I beg you to drop this . . . to drop . . . this subject!"

"Oh, no! Oh, forgive me, forgive me if I have hurt you," said Stepan Arkadyevich, holding out his hand with a smile of embarrassment; "but like a messenger I have simply performed the commission given me."

Aleksey Aleksandrovich gave him his hand, pondered a little, and said:

"I must think it over and seek for guidance. The day after tomorrow I will give you a final answer," he said, after considering a moment.

CHAPTER NINETEEN

Stepan Arkadyevich was about to go away, when Korney came in to announce:

"Sergey Alekseevich!"

"Who's Sergey Alekseevich?" Stepan Arkadyevich was about to say, but he remembered immediately.

"Ah, Seryozha!" he said aloud. "Sergey Alekseevich! I thought it was the director of a department. Anna asked me to see him too," he thought.

And he recalled the timid, piteous expression with which Anna had said to him at parting: "Anyway, you will see him. Find out exactly where he is, who is looking after him. And Stiva . . . if it were possible! Could it be possible?" Stepan Arkadyevich knew what was meant by that "if it were possible"—if it were possible to arrange the divorce so as to let her have her son . . . Stepan Arkadyevich saw now that it was no good to dream of that, but still he was glad to see his nephew.

Aleksey Aleksandrovich reminded his brother-in-law that they never spoke to the boy of his mother, and he begged him not to mention a single word about her.

"He was very ill after that interview with his mother, which we had not foreseen," said Aleksey Aleksandrovich. "Indeed, we feared for his life. But with sensible treatment, and sea bathing in the summer, he regained his strength, and now, on the doctor's advice, I have let him go to school. And certainly the companionship at school has had a good effect on him, and he is perfectly well and making good progress."

"What a fine fellow he's grown! He's not little Seryozha now, but big Sergey Alekseevich!" said Stepan Arkadyevich, smiling as he looked at the handsome, broad-shouldered lad, in blue coat and long trousers, who walked in alertly and confidently. The boy looked healthy and happy. He bowed to his uncle as to a stranger, but recognizing him, he blushed and turned hurriedly away from him, as though offended and irritated at something. The boy went up to his father and handed him his report card.

"Well, that's rather good," said his father, "you can go."

"He's thinner and taller, and has grown from a child into a boy; I like that," said Stepan Arkadyevich. "Do you remember me?"

The boy looked back quickly at his uncle.

"Yes, *mon oncle*," he answered, glancing at his father, and again he looked downcast.

His uncle called him to him, and took his hand.

"Well, and how are you getting on?" he said, wanting to talk to him and not knowing what to say.

The boy, blushing and making no answer, cautiously drew his hand away. As soon as Stepan Arkadyevich let go his hand, he glanced doubtfully at his father, and, like a bird set free, darted out of the room.

A year had passed since the last time Seryozha had seen his mother. Since then he had heard nothing more of her. And in the course of that year he had gone to school and made friends among his schoolmates. The dreams and memories of his mother, which had made him ill after seeing her, did not occupy his thoughts now. When they came back to him, he studiously drove them away, regarding them as shameful and girlish, below the dignity of a boy and a schoolboy. He knew that his father and mother were separated by some quarrel, he knew that he had to remain with his father, and he tried to get used to that idea.

He disliked seeing his uncle, so like his mother, for it called up those memories of which he was ashamed. He disliked it all the more as from some words he had caught as he waited at the study door, and still more from the faces of his father and uncle, he guessed that they must have been talking of his mother. And to avoid condemning the father with whom he lived and on whom he was dependent, and, above all, to avoid giving way to sentimentality, which he considered so degrading, Seryozha tried not to look at his uncle who had come to disturb his peace of mind, and not to think of what he recalled to him.

But when Stepan Arkadyevich, going out after him, saw him on the stairs and, calling to him, asked him how he spent his playtime at school Seryozha talked more freely to him away from his father's presence.

"We play railways now," he said in answer to his uncle's question. "It's like this, do you see: two sit on a bench—they're the passengers; and one stands up straight on the belts, and they run through all the rooms—the doors are left open beforehand. Well, and it's pretty hard work being the conductor!"

"That's the one that stands?" Stepan Arkadyevich inquired, smiling.

"Yes, you need courage and must be quick too, especially when they stop all of a sudden, or someone falls down."

"Yes, that must be a serious matter," said Stepan Arkadyevich, watching with mournful interest the eager eyes, like his mother's; not childish now—no longer fully innocent. And though he had promised Aleksey Aleksandrovich not to speak of Anna, he could not restrain himself.

"Do you remember your mother?" he asked suddenly.

"No, I don't," Seryozha said quickly. He blushed crimson, and his face clouded over. And his uncle could get nothing more out of him. His tutor found his pupil on the staircase half an hour later, and for a long while he could not make out whether he was ill-tempered or crying.

"What is it? I expect you hurt yourself when you fell down?" said the tutor. "I told you it was a dangerous game. And we shall have to speak to the director."

"If I had hurt myself, nobody would have found out, I assure you."

"Well, what is it, then?"

"Leave me alone! If I remember, or if I don't remember?. . .What business is it of his? Why should I remember? Leave me in peace!" he said, addressing not his tutor but the whole world.

CHAPTER TWENTY

Stepan Arkadyevich, as usual, did not waste his time in Petersburg. In Petersburg, besides business, his sister's divorce, and his coveted appointment, he wanted, as he always did, to freshen himself up, as he said, after the mustiness of Moscow.

In spite of its *cafés chantants*[1] and its omnibuses, Moscow was still a stagnant swamp. Stepan Arkadyevich always felt it. After living for some time in Moscow, especially in close relations with his family, he was conscious of a depression of spirits. And after being there so long without a change, he reached a point when he positively began to be worrying himself over his wife's ill-humor and reproaches, over his children's health and education, and the petty details of his official work; even the fact of being in debt worried him. But he had only to go and stay a little while in Petersburg, in the circle there in which he moved, where people lived—really lived—instead of vegetating as in Moscow, and all such ideas vanished and melted away at once, like wax before the fire. His wife? . . . Only that day he had been talking to Prince Chechensky. Prince Chechensky had a wife and family, grown-up pages in the Corps . . . and he had an illegitimate family of children also. Though the first family was very nice, Prince Chechensky felt happier in his second family; and he used to take his eldest son with him to his second family, and told Stepan Arkadyevich that he thought it good for his son, broadening his ideas. What would have been said to that in Moscow?

His children? In Petersburg children did not prevent their parents from enjoying life. The children were brought up in boarding schools, and there was no trace of the wild notions that prevailed in Moscow, in Lvov's household, for instance, that all the luxuries of life were for the children, while the parents were to have nothing but

[1]"Night clubs."

work and anxiety. Here people understood that a man is in duty bound to live for himself, as every man of culture should live.

The service? Here it was not the stiff, hopeless drudgery that it was in Moscow. Here there was some interest in official life. A chance meeting, a service rendered, a happy phrase, a knack of facetious mimicry, and, in a flash, a man's career might be made. So it had been with Bryantsev, whom Stepan Arkadyevich had met the previous day, and who was one of the highest functionaries in government now. There was some interest in official work like that.

The Petersburg attitude on pecuniary matters had an especially soothing effect on Stepan Arkadyevich. Bartnyansky, who spent at least fifty thousand, to judge by the style in which he lived, had made an interesting comment the day before on that subject.

As they were talking before dinner, Stepan Arkadyevich said to Bartnyansky:

"You're friendly, I think, with Mordvinsky; you might do me a favor: say a word to him, please, for me. There's an appointment I would like to get—secretary of the agency . . . "

"Oh, I shan't remember all that, if you tell it to me . . . But what possesses you to get mixed up with railways and Jews? . . . Any way you look at it, it's a stinking business."

Stepan Arkadyevich did not say to Bartnyansky that it was a "growing business"—Bartnyansky would not have understood that.

"I want the money, I've nothing to live on."

"You're living, aren't you?"

"Yes, but in debt."

"Are you really? Heavily?" said Bartnyansky sympathetically.

"Very heavily: twenty thousand."

Bartnyansky broke into good-humored laughter.

"Oh, lucky fellow!" said he. "My debts mount up to a million and a half, and I've nothing, and still I can live, as you see!"

And Stepan Arkadyevich saw the truth of this view not in words only but in actual fact. Zhivakhov owed three hundred thousand, and hadn't a kopek to bless himself with, and he lived, and in style too! Count Krivtsov was considered a hopeless case by everyone, and yet he kept two mistresses. Petrovsky had run through five million, and still lived in just the same style, and was even a manager in the financial department with a salary of twenty thousand. But besides this, Petersburg had physically a pleasant effect on Stepan Arkadyevich. It made him younger. In Moscow he sometimes found a gray hair in his head, dropped asleep after dinner, stretched, walked slowly upstairs, breathing heavily, was bored by the society of young women, and did not dance at balls. In Petersburg he always felt ten years younger.

His experience in Petersburg was exactly what had been described to him on the previous day by Prince Piotr Oblonsky, a man of sixty, who had just come back from abroad:

"We don't know the way to live here," said Piotr Oblonsky. "I spent the summer in Baden, and you wouldn't believe it, I felt quite a young man. At a glimpse of a pretty woman, my thoughts . . . One dines and drinks a glass of wine, and feels strong and ready for anything. I came home to Russia—had to see my wife, and, what's more, go to my country place; and there, you'd hardly believe it, in two weeks I'd got into a dressing gown and given up dressing for dinner. Needless to say, I had no thoughts left for pretty women. I became quite an old gentleman. There was nothing left for me but to think of my eternal salvation. I went off to Paris—I was as right as could be at once."

Stepan Arkadyevich felt exactly the difference that Piotr Oblonsky described. In Moscow he degenerated so much that if he had had to be there much longer, he might in earnest have come to considering his salvation; in Petersburg he felt himself a man of the world again.

Between Princess Betsy Tverskaya and Stepan Arkadyevich there had long existed rather curious relations. Stepan Arkadyevich always flirted with her in jest, and used to say to her, also in jest, the most improper things, knowing that nothing delighted her so much. The day after his conversation with Karenin, Stepan Arkadyevich went to see her, and felt so youthful that in this jesting flirtation and nonsense he recklessly went so far that he did not know how to extricate himself, as unfortunately he was so far from being attracted by her that he thought her positively repulsive. What made it hard to change the conversation was the fact that he was very attractive to her. So that he was considerably relieved at the arrival of Princess Myahkaya, which cut short their tête-à-tête.

"Ah, so you're here!" she said when she saw him. "Well, and what news of your poor sister? You needn't look at me like that," she added. "Ever since they've all turned against her, all those who're a thousand times worse than she, I've thought she did a very fine thing. I can't forgive Vronsky for not letting me know when she was in Petersburg. I'd have gone to see her and gone about with her everywhere. Please give her my love. Come, tell me about her."

"Yes, her position is very difficult; she—." Stepan Arkadyevich began, in the simplicity of his heart accepting her words at face value, "tell me about her." Princess Myahkaya interrupted him immediately, as she always did, and began talking herself.

"She's done what they all do, except me—only they hide it. But she wouldn't be deceitful, and she did a fine thing. And she did better still in throwing up that crazy brother-in-law of yours. You must excuse me. Everybody used to say he was so clever, so very clever; I was the only one who said he was a fool. Now that he's so thick with Lydia Ivanovna and Landau, they all say he's crazy, and I would prefer not to agree with everybody, but this time I can't help it."

"Oh, do please explain," said Stepan Arkadyevich; "what does it mean? Yesterday I saw him on my sister's behalf, and I asked him to give me a final answer. He gave me no answer, and said he would think it over. But this morning, instead of an answer, I received an invitation from Countess Lydia Ivanovna for this evening."

"Ah, so that's it, that's it!" said Princess Myahkaya gleefully. "They're going to ask Landau what he's to say."

"Ask Landau? What for? Who or what's Landau?"

"What! You don't know Jules Landau, *le fameux Jules Landau, le clairvoyant?*[1] He's crazy too, but on him your sister's fate depends. See what comes of living in the provinces—you know nothing about anything. Landau, you see, was a *commis*[2] in Paris, and he went to a doctor's; and in the doctor's waiting room he fell asleep, and in his sleep he began giving advice to all the patients. And wonderful advice it was! Then the wife of Yury Meledinsky—you know, the invalid?— heard of this Landau, and had him see her husband. And he cured

[1]"The famous Jules Landau, the clairvoyant."
[2]"Shop assistant."

her husband, though I can't say that I see he did him much good, for he's just as feeble a creature as he ever was, but they believed in him, and took him along with them and brought him to Russia. Here there's been a general rush to him, and he's begun doctoring everyone. He cured Countess Bezzubova, and she took such a fancy to him that she adopted him."

"Adopted him?"

"Yes, as her son. He's not Landau any more now, but Count Bezzubov. That's neither here nor there, though. But Lydia—I'm very fond of her, but she has a screw loose somewhere—has lost her heart to this Landau now, and nothing is settled in her house or Aleksey Aleksandrovich's without him, and so your sister's fate is now in the hands of Landau, alias Count Bezzubov."

CHAPTER TWENTY-ONE

After an excellent dinner and a great deal of cognac drunk at Bartnyansky's, Stepan Arkadyevich, only a little later than the appointed time, went in to the Countess Lydia Ivanovna's.

"Who else is with the Countess—a Frenchman?" Stepan Arkadyevich asked the hall porter as he glanced at the familiar overcoat of Aleksey Aleksandrovich and a strange, rather artless-looking overcoat with clasps.

"Aleksey Aleksandrovich Karenin and Count Bezzubov," the porter answered severely.

"Princess Myahkaya guessed right," thought Stepan Arkadyevich as he went upstairs. "Curious! It would be quite as well, though, to get on friendly terms with her. She has immense influence. If she would say a word to Pomorsky, the thing would be a certainty."

It was still quite light outside, but in Countess Lydia Ivanovna's little drawing room the blinds were drawn and the lamps lighted. At a round table under a lamp sat the Countess and Aleksey Aleksandrovich, taking softly. A short, thinnish man, very pale and handsome, with feminine hips, knock-kneed, with fine brilliant eyes and long hair lying on the collar of his coat, was standing at the other end of the room gazing at the portraits on the wall. After greeting the lady of the house and Aleksey Aleksandrovich, Stepan Arkadyevich could not resist glancing once more at the unknown man.

"Monsieur Landau!" The Countess addressed him with a softness and caution that impressed Oblonsky, and she introduced them.

Landau looked around hurriedly, came up, and, smiling, laid his moist, lifeless hand in Stepan Arkadyevich's outstretched hand and immediately walked away and began gazing at the portraits again. The Countess and Aleksey Aleksandrovich looked at each other meaningfully.

"I am very glad to see you, particularly today," said Countess Lydia Ivanovna, pointing Stepan Arkadyevich to a seat beside Karenin.

"I introduced you to him as Landau," she said in a soft voice, glancing at the Frenchman and again immediately after at Aleksey Aleksandrovich, "but he is really Count Bezzubov, as you're probably aware. Only he does not like the title."

"Yes, I heard so," answered Stepan Arkadyevich; "they say he completely cured Countess Bezzubova."

"She was here today, poor thing!" the Countess said, turning to Aleksey Aleksandrovich. "This separation is awful for her. It's such a blow to her!"

"And he's definitely going?" queried Aleksey Aleksandrovich.

"Yes, he's going to Paris. He heard a voice yesterday," said Countess Lydia Ivanovna, looking at Stepan Arkadyevich.

"Ah, a voice!" repeated Oblonsky, feeling that he must be as circumspect as he possibly could in this society, where something peculiar was going on, or was to go on, to which he had not the key.

A moment's silence followed, after which Countess Lydia Ivanovna, as though approaching the main topic of conversation, said with a fine smile to Oblonsky:

"I've known you for a long while, and am very glad to make a closer acquaintance with you. *Les amis de nos amis sont nos amis*.[1] But to be a true friend, one must enter into the spiritual state of one's friend, and I fear that you are not doing so in the case of Aleksey Aleksandrovich. You understand what I mean?" she said, lifting her fine pensive eyes.

---

[1] "The friends of our friends are our friends."

"In part, Countess, I understand the position of Aleksey Aleksandrovich . . ." said Oblonsky. Having no clear idea what they were talking about, he wanted to confine himself to generalities.

"The change is not in his external position," Countess Lydia Ivanovna said sternly, following with eyes of love the figure of Aleksey Aleksandrovich as he got up and crossed over to Landau; "his heart is changed, a new heart has been vouchsafed him, and I fear you don't fully apprehend the change that has taken place in him."

"Oh, well, in a general way I can conceive the change. We have always been friendly, and now . . ." said Stepan Arkadyevich, responding with a sympathetic glance to the expression of the Countess, and mentally balancing the question which of the two ministers she was closer to, so as to know which one he should ask her to influence.

"The change that has taken place in him cannot lessen his love for his neighbors; on the contrary, that change can only intensify love in his heart. But I am afraid you do not understand me. Won't you have some tea?" she said, with her eyes indicating the footman, who was handing round tea on tray.

"Not altogether, Countess. Of course, his misfortune—"

"Yes, a misfortune which has proved the highest happiness, when his heart was made new, was filled full of it," she said, gazing with eyes full of love at Stepan Arkadyevich.

"I do believe I might ask her to speak to both of them," thought Stepan Arkadyevich.

"Oh, of course, Countess," he said; "but I imagine such changes are a matter so private that no one, even the most intimate friend, would care to speak of them."

"On the contrary! We ought to speak freely and help one another."

"Yes, undoubtedly so, but there is such a difference of convictions, and besides . . . " said Oblonsky with a soft smile.

"There can be no difference where it is a question of holy truth."

"Oh, no, of course; but . . . " and Stepan Arkadyevich paused in confusion. He understood at last that they were talking of religion.

"I think he will fall asleep immediately," said Aleksey Aleksandrovich in a whisper full of meaning, going up to Lydia Ivanovna.

Stepan Arkadyevich looked around. Landau was sitting at the win-

dow, leaning on his elbow and the back of his chair, his head drooping. Noticing that all eyes were turned on him, he raised his head and
smiled a smile of childlike artlessness.

"Don't take any notice," said Lydia Ivanovna, and she lightly
moved a chair up for Aleksey Aleksandrovich. "I have observed . . ."
she was beginning, when a footman came into the room with a letter. Lydia Ivanovna rapidly ran her eyes over the note, and, excusing
herself, wrote an answer with extraordinary rapidity, handed it to the
man, and came back to the table. "I have observed," she went on,
"that Moscow people, especially the men, are more indifferent to religion than anyone."

"Oh, no, Countess, I thought Moscow people had the reputation
of being the firmest in the faith," answered Stepan Arkadyevich.

"But as far as I can make out, you are unfortunately one of the
indifferent ones," said Aleksey Aleksandrovich, turning to him with a
weary smile.

"How anyone can be indifferent!" said Lydia Ivanovna.

"I am not so much indifferent on that subject as I am waiting in
suspense," said Stepan Arkadyevich, with his most deprecating smile.
"I hardly think that the time for such questions has come yet for me."

Aleksey Aleksandrovich and Lydia Ivanovna looked at each other.

"We can never tell whether the time has come for us or not," said
Aleksey Aleksandrovich severely. "We ought not to think whether we
are ready or not ready. God's grace is not guided by human considerations: sometimes it comes not to those that strive for it but to
those that are unprepared, like Saul."

"No, I believe it won't be just yet," said Lydia Ivanovna, who had
been meanwhile watching the movements of the Frenchman. Landau got up and went over to them.

"Am I allowed to listen?" he asked.

"Oh, yes; I did not want to disturb you," said Lydia Ivanovna, gazing tenderly at him. "Sit here with us."

"One has only not to close one's eyes to shut out the light," Aleksey Aleksandrovich went on.

"Ah, if you knew the happiness we know, feeling His presence ever
in our hearts!" said Countess Lydia Ivanovna with a rapturous smile.

"But a man may feel himself unworthy sometimes to rise to that height," said Stepan Arkadyevich, conscious of hypocrisy in admitting this religious height, but at the same time unable to bring himself to acknowledge his freethinking views before a person who, by a single word to Pomorsky, might procure him the coveted appointment.

"That is, you mean that sin keeps him back?" said Lydia Ivanovna. "But that is a false notion. There is no sin for believers, their sin has been atoned for. *Pardon*," she added, looking at the footman, who came in again with another letter. She read it and gave a verbal answer: "Tomorrow at the Grand Duchess's, say . . . For the believer, sin is not," she went on.

"Yes, but faith without works is dead," said Stepan Arkadyevich, recalling the phrase from the catechism, and only by his smile clinging to his independence.

"There you have it—from the Epistle of St. James," said Aleksey Aleksandrovich, addressing Lydia Ivanovna with a certain reproachfulness is his tone. It was unmistakably a subject they had discussed more than once before. "What harm has been done by the false interpretation of that passage! Nothing holds men back from belief like that misinterpretation. 'I have no works, so I cannot believe,' yet that is not said anywhere. It's just the opposite."

"Striving for God, saving the soul by fasting," said Countess Lydia Ivanovna, with absolute contempt, "those are the crude ideas of our monks . . . Yet that is nowhere said. It is far simpler and easier," she added, looking at Oblonsky with the same encouraging smile with which at court she encouraged youthful maids of honor, disconcerted by the new surroundings of the court.

"We are saved by Christ who suffered for us. We are saved by faith," Aleksey Aleksandrovich chimed in, with a glance of approval at her words.

"*Vous comprenez l'anglais*?" asked Lydia Ivanovna, and receiving a reply in the affirmative, she got up and began looking through a shelf of books.

"I want to read him *Safe and Happy*, or *Under the Wing*,"[2] she said, looking inquiringly at Karenin. And finding the book, and sitting down again in her place, she opened it. "It's very short. In it is

[2]Distributed by the American Sunday School Union in 1866.

described the way by which faith can be reached, and the happiness, above all earthly bliss, with which it fills the soul. The believer cannot be unhappy, because he is not alone. But you will see." She was just settling herself to read, when the footman came in again. "Madame Borozdina? Tell her, tomorrow at two o'clock. Yes," she said, putting her finger in the place in the book and gazing before her with her fine pensive eyes, "that is how true faith acts. You know Marie Sanina? You know about her trouble? She lost her only child. She was in despair. And what happened? She found this comforter, and she thanks God now for the death of her child. Such is the happiness faith brings!"

"Oh, yes, that is most . . . " said Stepan Arkadyevich, glad they were going to read and let him have a chance to collect his faculties. "No, I see I'd better not ask her about anything today," he thought. "If only I can get out of this without putting my foot in it!"

"It will be boring for you," said Countess Lydia Ivanovna, addressing Landau: "you don't know English, but it's short."

"Oh, I shall understand," said Landau, with the same smile, and he closed his eyes. Aleksey Aleksandrovich and Lydia Ivanovna exchanged meaningful glances, and the reading began.

CHAPTER TWENTY-TWO

Stepan Arkadyevich felt completely baffled by the strange talk that he was hearing for the first time. The complexity of Petersburg, as a rule, had a stimulating effect on him, rousing him out of his Moscow stagnation. He liked complications, but understood them only in the circles he knew and was at home in. In these unfamiliar surroundings he was puzzled and disconcerted, and could not get his bearings. As he listened to Countess Lydia Ivanovna, aware of the beautiful, artless—or perhaps artful, he could not decide which—eyes of Landau fixed upon him, Stepan Arkadyevich began to be conscious of a peculiar heaviness in his head.

The most incongruous ideas were running through his mind. "Marie Sanina is glad her child's dead . . . How good a smoke would be now! . . . To be saved, one need only believe, and the monks don't know how the thing's to be done, but Countess Lydia Ivanovna does know . . . And why is my head so heavy? Is it the cognac, or all this being so strange? Anyway, I think I've done nothing objectionable so far. But, even so, it won't do to ask her now. They say they make one say one's prayers. I only hope they won't make me! That'll be too absurd. And what nonsense she's reading! But she has a good accent. Landau—Bezzubov—what's he Bezzubov for?" All at once Stepan Arkadyevich became aware that his lower jaw was uncontrollably forming a yawn. He smoothed his whiskers to mask the yawn, and shook himself. But soon after he became aware that he was falling asleep and on the very point of snoring. He recovered himself at the very moment when the voice of Countess Lydia Ivanovna was saying "he's asleep." Stepan Arkadyevich started with dismay, feeling guilty and caught. But he was reassured at once by seeing that they were referring not to him but to Landau. The Frenchman, as well as Stepan Arkadyevich, was asleep. But Stepan Arkadyevich's being asleep would have offended them, he thought (though even this might not be so, as everything seemed so strange), while Landau's being asleep delighted them very much, especially Countess Lydia Ivanovna.

"*Mon ami*," said Lydia Ivanovna, carefully holding the folds of her silk dress so as not to rustle, and in her excitement calling Karenin not Aleksey Aleksandrovich but "*mon ami*," "*donnez-lui la main. Vous voyez?*[1] Sh!" she hissed at the footman as he came in again. "Not at home."

The Frenchman was asleep, or pretending to be asleep, with his head on the back of his chair; and his moist hand, as it lay on his knee, made faint movements, as though trying to catch something. Aleksey Aleksandrovich got up, tried to move carefully, but stumbled against the table, went up and laid his hand in the Frenchman's hand. Stepan Arkadyevich got up too, and opening his eyes wide, trying to force himself awake, he looked first at one and then at the other. It was all real. Stepan Arkadyevich felt that his head was getting worse and worse.

"*Que la personne qui est arrivée la dernière, celle qui demande, qu'elle*

---

[1]"My friend, give him your hand. You see?"

sorte! Qu'elle sorte!"[2] articulated the Frenchman, without opening his
eyes.

"*Vous m'excuserez, mais vous voyez . . . Revenez vers dix heures, encore
mieux demain.*"[3]

"*Qu'elle sorte!*" repeated the Frenchman impatiently.

"*C'est moi, n'est-ce pas?*"[4] And receiving an answer in the affirmative, Stepan Arkadyevich, forgetting the favor he had meant to ask
of Lydia Ivanovna, and forgetting his sister's affairs, caring for nothing, but filled with the sole desire to get away as soon as possible,
went out on tiptoe and ran out into the street as though from a
plague-stricken house. For a long while he chatted and joked with his
cab driver, trying to regain his senses as quickly as possible.

At the French theater where he arrived for the last act, and afterwards at the Tartar restaurant after his champagne, Stepan Arkadyevich felt a little refreshed in the atmosphere he was used to. But still
he felt quite unlike himself all that evening.

On getting home to Piotr Oblonsky's, where he was staying,
Stepan Arkadyevich found a note from Betsy. She wrote that she was
very anxious to finish their interrupted conversation, and begged him
to come the next day. He had scarcely read this note, and frowned
at its contents, when he heard below the ponderous tramp of the servants, carrying something heavy.

Stepan Arkadyevich went out to look. It was the rejuvenated Piotr
Oblonsky. He was so drunk that he could not walk upstairs; but he
told them to set him on his legs when he saw Stepan Arkadyevich,
and clinging to him, he walked with him into his room and there
began telling him how he had spent the evening, and fell asleep
doing so.

Stepan Arkadyevich was in very low spirits, which happened rarely
with him, and for a long while he could not go to sleep. Everything
he could recall to his mind, everything was disgusting; but most disgusting of all, as if it were something shameful, was the memory of
the evening he had spent at Countess Lydia Ivanovna's.

The next day he received from Aleksey Aleksandrovich a final

[2]"Let the person who came in last, the one who questions, go out! Let him go out!"
[3]"You must excuse me, but you see . . . come back at ten, or better still, tomorrow."
[4]"It's me, isn't it?"

answer, refusing to grant Anna's divorce, and he understood that this decision was based on what the Frenchman had said in his real or pretended trance the evening before.

CHAPTER TWENTY-THREE

In order to carry through any undertaking in family life, there must necessarily be either complete division between the husband and wife, or loving agreement. When the relations of a couple are vacillating and neither one thing nor the other, no sort of enterprise can be undertaken.

Many families remain for years in the same place, though both husband and wife were sick of it, simply because there is neither complete division nor agreement between them.

Both Vronsky and Anna felt life in Moscow unbearable in the heat and dust, when the spring sunshine was followed by the glare of summer, and all the trees in the boulevards had long since been in full leaf, and the leaves were covered with dust. But they did not go back to Vozdvizhenskoe, as they had arranged to do long before; they continued their stay in Moscow, though they both loathed it, because of late there had been no agreement between them.

The irritability that kept them apart had no external cause, and all efforts to come to an understanding intensified it instead of removing it. It was an inner irritation, grounded in her mind on the conviction that his love had diminished; in his, on regret that he had put himself for her sake in a difficult position, which she, instead of lightening, made still more difficult. Neither of them gave full utterance to their sense of grievance, but they considered each other in the wrong, and tried on every pretext to prove this to one another.

In her eyes the whole of him, with all his habits, ideas, desires, with all his spiritual and physical temperament, was one thing—love for women, and that love, she felt, ought to be entirely concentrated on her alone. Yet that love was diminishing; consequently, as she reasoned, he must have transferred part of his love to other women or to another woman—and she was jealous. She was jealous not of any particular woman but of the decrease of his love. Not having an object for her jealousy, she was on the lookout for it. At the slightest hint she transferred her jealousy from one object to another. At one time she was jealous of those coarse women with whom he might so easily renew his old bachelor ties; then she was jealous of the society women he might meet; then she was jealous of the imaginary girl whom he might want to marry, for whose sake he would break with her. And this last form of jealousy tortured her most of all, especially as he had unwarily told her, in a moment of frankness, that his mother knew him so little that she had had the audacity to try and persuade him to marry the young Princess Sorokina.

And being jealous of him, Anna was indignant against him and found grounds for indignation in everything. For everything that was difficult in her position she blamed him. The agonizing suspense she had suffered at Moscow, the tardiness and indecision of Aleksey Aleksandrovich, her solitude—she put it all down to him. If he had loved her he would have seen all the bitterness of her position, and would have rescued her from it. For her being in Moscow and not in the country, he was to blame too. He could not live buried in the country as she would have liked to do. He had to have society, and he had put her in this awful position, the bitterness of which he would not see. And again, it was his fault that she was forever separated from her son.

Even the rare moments of tenderness that came from time to time did not soothe her; in his tenderness now she saw a shade of complacency, of self-confidence, which had not been of old and which exasperated her.

It was dusk. Anna was alone, and waiting for him to come back from a bachelor dinner. She walked up and down in his study (the room where the noise from the street was least heard), and thought over every detail of yesterday's quarrel. Going back from the well-remembered, offensive words of the quarrel to what had been the reason for it, she arrived at last at its origin. For a long while she could hardly believe that their dissension had arisen from a conversation so inoffensive, of so little moment to either. But so it actually had been. It all arose from his laughing at the girls' high schools, declaring they were useless, while she defended them. He had spoken deprecatingly of women's education in general, and had said that

Hannah, Anna's English protégée, had not the slightest need to know anything of physics.

This irritated Anna. She saw in this a contemptuous reference to her occupations. And she thought of something that would pay him back for the pain he had given her. "I don't expect you to understand me, my feelings, as anyone who loved me might, but simple delicacy I did expect," she said.

And he had actually flushed with vexation, and had said something unpleasant. She could not recall her answer, but at that point, with an unmistakable desire to hurt her too, he had said:

"I feel no interest in your infatuation over this girl, because I see it's unnatural."

The cruelty with which he shattered the world she had built up for herself so laboriously to enable her to endure her hard life, the injustice with which he had accused her of affectation, of artificiality, aroused her.

"I am very sorry that nothing but what's coarse and material is comprehensible and natural to you," she said, and walked out of the room.

When he had come in to her yesterday evening, they had not referred to the quarrel; both felt that the quarrel had been smoothed over, but was not at an end.

Today he had not been at home all day, and she felt so lonely and wretched in being on bad terms with him that she wanted to forget it all, to forgive him and to be reconciled with him; she wanted to throw the blame on herself and to justify him.

"I myself am to blame. I'm irritable, I'm insanely jealous. I will make it up with him, and we'll go away to the country. There I shall be more at peace."

"Unnatural!" She suddenly recalled the word that had stung her most of all, not so much the word itself as the intent to hurt her with which it was said. "I know what he meant; he meant—unnatural, not loving my own daughter, to love another person's child. What does he know of love for children, of my love for Seryozha, whom I've sacrificed for him? But that wish to hurt me! No, he loves another woman, it must be so."

And perceiving that, while trying to regain her peace of mind, she had gone round the same circle that she had been round so often before, and had come back to her former state of exasperation, she was horrified at herself. "Can it be impossible? Can it be beyond me to control myself?" she said to herself, and began again, from the beginning. "He's truthful, he's honest, he loves me. I love him, and in a few days the divorce will come. What more do I want? I want peace of mind and trust, and I will take the blame on myself. Yes, now when he comes in, I will tell him I was wrong, though I was not wrong, and we will go away tomorrow."

And to escape thinking any more, and being overcome by irritability, she rang, and ordered the trunks to be brought for packing their things for the country.

At ten o'clock Vronsky came in.

CHAPTER TWENTY-FOUR

"Well, was it nice?" she asked, coming out to meet him with a penitent and meek expression.

"Just as usual," he answered, seeing at a glance that she was in one of her good moods. He was used by now to these transitions, and he was particularly glad to see it today, as he was in a specially good humor himself.

"What do I see? Ah, that's right!" he said, pointing to the trunks in the passage.

"Yes, we must go. I went out for a drive, and it was so fine I longed to be in the country. There's nothing to keep you, is there?"

"It's the one thing I desire. I'll be back in a moment, and we'll talk it over; I only want to change. Order some tea."

And he went into his room.

There was something mortifying in the way he had said "Ah, that's right!" as one says to a child when it stops being naughty, and still more mortifying was the contrast between her penitent and his self-confident tone; and for one instant she felt the desire for a fight rising up in her again, but making an effort, she conquered it, and met Vronsky as good-humoredly as before.

When he came in she told him, partly repeating phrases she had prepared beforehand, how she had spent the day, and her plans for going away.

"You know, it came to me almost like an inspiration," she said. "Why wait here for the divorce? Won't it be just the same in the country? I can't wait any longer! I don't want to go on hoping, I don't want to hear anything about the divorce. I have made up my mind it shall not have any more influence on my life. Do you agree?"

"Oh, yes!" he said, glancing uneasily at her excited face.

"What did you do? Who was there?" she said, after a pause.

Vronsky mentioned the names of the guests. "The dinner was first-rate, and the boat race, and it was all pleasant enough, but in Moscow they can never do anything without something ridiculous. Some woman turned up, teacher of swimming to the Queen of Sweden, and gave us an exhibition of her skill."

"How? Did she swim?" asked Anna, frowning.

"In an absurd red *costume de natation*[1] she was old and hideous too. So when shall we go?"

"What an absurd idea! Why, did she swim in some special way, then?" said Anna, not answering.

"There was absolutely nothing in it. That's just what I'm saying, it was awfully stupid. Well, then, when do you think of going?"

Anna shook her head as though trying to drive away some unpleasant idea.

"When? Why, the sooner the better! By tomorrow we can't be ready. The day after tomorrow."

"Yes . . . oh, no, wait a minute! The day after tomorrow's Sunday, I have to see *Maman*," said Vronsky, embarrassed, because as soon as he uttered his mother's name he was aware of her intent, suspicious eyes. His embarrassment confirmed her suspicion. She flushed hotly and drew away from him. It was now not the Queen of Sweden's swimming instructor who filled Anna's imagination, but the young Princess Sorokina. She was staying in a village near Moscow with Countess Vronskaya.

[1]"Bathing suit."

"Can't you go tomorrow?" she said.

"Well, no! The power of attorney and money for the business I'm going there for, I can't get by tomorrow," he answered.

"If so, we won't go at all."

"But why not?"

"I shall not go later. Monday or never!"

"Why?" said Vronsky, looking shocked. "Why, there's no sense in it!"

"There's no sense in it to you, because you care nothing for me. You don't care to understand my life. The one thing that I cared for here was Hannah. You say it's affectation. Why, you said yesterday that I don't love my daughter, that I love this English girl, that it's unnatural. I should like to know what life there is for me that could be natural!"

For an instant she had a clear vision of what she was doing, and was horrified at how she had fallen away from her resolution. But even though she knew it was her own ruin, she could not restrain herself, could not keep herself from proving to him that he was wrong, could not give way to him.

"I never said that; I said I did not sympathize with this sudden passion."

"How is it, though you boast of your straightforwardness, you don't tell the truth?"

"I never boast, and I never tell lies," he said slowly, restraining his rising anger. "It's a great pity if you can't respect—"

"Respect was invented to cover the empty place where love should be. And if you don't love me any more, it would be better and more honest to say so."

"No, this is becoming unbearable!" cried Vronsky, getting up from his chair; and stopping short, facing her, he said, speaking deliberately: "Why do you try my patience?" looking as though he might have said much more, but was restraining himself. "It has limits."

"What do you mean by that?" she cried, looking with terror at the undisguised hatred in his whole face, and especially in his cruel, menacing eyes.

"I mean to say . . ." he was beginning, but he checked himself. "I must ask what it is you want of me."

"What can I want? All I can want is that you should not desert me, as you think of doing," she said, understanding all he had not uttered. "But that I don't want; that's secondary. I want love, and there is none. So then all is over."

She turned toward the door.

"Wait! Wa-it!" said Vronsky, with no change in the gloomy lines of his brows, though he held her by the hand. "What is it all about? I said that we must put off going for three days, and on that you told me I was lying, that I was not an honorable man."

"Yes, and I repeat that the man who reproaches me with having sacrificed everything for me," she said, recalling the words of a still earlier quarrel, "that he's worse than a dishonorable man—he's a heartless man."

"Oh, there are limits to endurance!" he cried, and hastily let go of her hand.

"He hates me, that's clear," she thought, and in silence, without looking around, she walked with faltering steps out of the room. "He loves another woman, that's even clearer," she said to herself as she went into her own room. "I want love, and there is none. So, then, all is over." She repeated the words she had said, "and it must be ended."

"But how?" she asked herself, and she sat down in a low chair before the mirror.

Thoughts of where she would go now, whether to the aunt who had brought her up, to Dolly, or simply alone abroad, and of what *he* was doing now alone in his study; whether this was the final quarrel, or whether reconciliation was still possible; and of what all her old friends at Petersburg would say of her now; and of how Aleksey Aleksandrovich would look at it, and many other ideas of what would happen now after the break, came into her head; but she did not give herself up to them with all her heart. At the bottom of her heart was some obscure idea that alone interested her, but she could not get clear sight of it. Thinking once more of Aleksey Aleksandrovich, she recalled the time of her illness after her confinement, and the feeling which never left her at that time. "Why didn't I die?" and the words and the feeling of that time came back to her. And all at once she knew what was in her soul. Yes, it was that idea which alone solved all. "Yes, to die! . . . And the shame and disgrace of Aleksey Aleksandrovich and of Seryozha, and my terrible shame, it will all be saved by death. To die! And he will feel remorse; will be sorry; will love me; he will suffer on my account." With the trace of a smile of self-pity for herself she sat down in the armchair, taking off and putting on the rings on her left hand, vividly picturing from different sides his feelings after her death.

Approaching footsteps—his steps—distracted her attention. As though absorbed in the arrangement of her rings, she did not even turn to him.

He went up to her, and taking her by the hand, he said softly:

"Anna, we'll go the day after tomorrow, if you like. I agree to everything."

She did not speak.

"What is it?" he urged.

"You know," she said, and at the same instant, unable to restrain herself any longer, she burst into sobs.

"Abandon me, abandon me!" she articulated between her sobs. "I'll go away tomorrow . . . I'll do more. What am I? An immoral woman! A stone around your neck. I don't want to make you wretched; I don't want to! I'll set you free. You don't love me; you love someone else!"

Vronsky besought her to be calm, and declared that there was not the slightest foundation for her jealousy; that he had never ceased, and would never cease, to love her; that he loved her more than ever.

"Anna, why distress yourself and me so?" he said to her, kissing her hands. There was tenderness now in his face, and she thought she caught the sound of tears in his voice, and she felt them wet on her hand. And instantly Anna's despairing jealousy changed to a despairing passion of tenderness. She put her arms around him, and covered with kisses his head, his neck, his hands.

CHAPTER TWENTY-FIVE

Feeling that the reconciliation was complete, Anna eagerly set to work in the morning preparing for their departure. Though it was not settled whether they should go on Monday or Tuesday, as they had each given way to the other, Anna packed busily, feeling absolutely indifferent whether they went a day earlier or later. She was standing in her room over an open trunk, taking things out of it, when he came in to see her earlier than usual, dressed to go out.

"I'm going off at once to see *Maman;* she can send me the money by Yegorov. And I shall be ready to go tomorrow," he said.

Though she was in such a good mood, the thought of his visit to his mother's stung her.

"No, I shan't be ready by then myself," she said, and at once reflected, "so then it was possible to arrange to do as I wished." "No, do as you meant to do. Go into the dining room, I'll come just as soon as I've sorted out these things that aren't needed," she said, putting something more on the heap of frippery that lay in Annushka's arms.

Vronsky was eating his beefsteak when she came into the dining room.

"You wouldn't believe how distasteful these rooms have become to me," she said, sitting down beside him to her coffee. "There's nothing more awful than these *chambres garnies*.[1] There's no individuality in them, no soul. These clocks, and curtains, and, worst of all, the wallpaper—they're a nightmare. I think of Vozdvizhenskoe as the promised land. You're not sending the horses off yet?"

"No, they will come after us. Where are you going?"

"I wanted to go to Wilson's to take some dresses to her. So it's really to be tomorrow?" she said in a cheerful voice; but suddenly her face changed.

Vronsky's valet came in to ask him to sign a receipt for a telegram from Petersburg. There was nothing unusual in Vronsky's getting a telegram, but he said, as though anxious to conceal something from her, that the receipt was in his study, and he turned hurriedly to her.

[1]"Furnished rooms."

"By tomorrow, without fail, I will finish it all."

"From whom is the telegram?" she asked, not hearing him.

"From Stiva," he answered reluctantly.

"Why didn't you show it to me? What secret can there be between Stiva and you?"

Vronsky called the valet back, and told him to bring the telegram.

"I didn't want to show it to you because Stiva has such a passion for telegraphing: why telegraph when nothing is settled?"

"About the divorce?"

"Yes; but he says he has not been able to arrive at anything yet. He has promised a decisive answer in a day or two. But here it is; read it."

With trembling hands Anna took the telegram, and read what Vronsky had told her. At the end was added: "little hope; but I will do everything possible and impossible."

"I said yesterday that it's absolutely nothing to me when I get, or whether I never get, a divorce," she said, flushing crimson. "There was not the slightest necessity to hide it from me." "So he may hide and does hide his correspondence with women from me," she thought.

"Yashvin meant to come this morning with Voytov," said Vronsky. "I believe he's won from Pestsov all and more than he can pay, about sixty thousand."

"No," she said, irritated by his so obviously showing by this change of subject that he was irritated, "why did you suppose that this news would affect me so, that you must even try to hide it? I said I don't want to consider it, and I would have liked you to care as little about it as I do."

"I care about it because I like definiteness," he said.

"Definiteness is not in the form but the love," she said, more and more irritated, not by his words, but by the tone of cool composure in which he spoke. "What do you want it for?"

"My God! Love again," he thought, frowning.

"Oh, you know what for; for your sake and your children's in the future."

"There won't be children in the future."

"That's a great pity," he said.

"You want it for the children's sake, but you don't think of me?"

she said, quite forgetting or not having heard that he had said, "*For your sake* and the children's."

The question of the possibility of having children had long been a subject of dispute and irritation to her. His desire to have children she interpreted as a proof he did not prize her beauty.

"Oh, I said *for your sake*. Above all, for your sake," he repeated, wincing as though in pain, "because I am certain that the greater part of your irritability comes from the uncertainty of your position."

"Yes, now he has laid aside all pretense, and all his cold hatred for me is apparent," she thought, not hearing his words, but watching with terror the cold, cruel judge who looked mockingly at her out of his eyes.

"The cause is not that," she said, "and, indeed, I don't see how the cause of my irritability, as you call it, can be that I am completely in your power. What uncertainty is there in the position? On the contrary—"

"I am very sorry that you don't care to understand," he interrupted, obstinately anxious to give utterance to his thought. "The uncertainty consists in your imagining that I am free."

"On that score you can set your mind quite at rest," she said, and turning away from him, she began drinking her coffee.

She lifted her cup, with her little finger stuck out, and put it to her lips. After drinking a few sips she glanced at him, and by his expression, she saw clearly that he was repelled by her hand, and her gesture, and the sound made by her lips.

"I don't care in the least what your mother thinks, and what match she wants to make for you," she said, putting the cup down with a shaking hand.

"But we are not talking about that."

"Yes, that's just what we are talking about. And let me tell you that a heartless woman, whether she's old or not old, your mother or anyone else, is of no consequence to me, and I would not consent to know her."

"Anna, I beg you not to speak disrespectfully of my mother."

"A woman whose heart does not tell her where her son's happiness and honor lie has no heart."

"I repeat my request that you do not speak disrespectfully of my mother, whom I respect," he said, raising his voice and looking sternly at her.

She did not answer. Looking intently at him, at his face, his hands, she recalled all the details of their reconciliation the previous day, and his passionate caresses. "There, just such caresses he has lavished, and will lavish, and longs to lavish on other women!" she thought.

"You don't love your mother. That's all talk, and talk, and talk!" she said, looking at him with hatred in her eyes.

"Even if so, you must—"

"Must decide, and I have decided," she said, and she would have gone away, but at that moment Yashvin walked into the room. Anna greeted him and remained.

Why, when there was a tempest in her soul, and she felt she was standing at a turning-point in her life which might have fearful consequences—why, at that minute, she had to keep up appearances before an outsider, who sooner or later must know it all, she did not know. But at once quelling the storm within her, she sat down and began talking to their guest.

"Well, how are you getting on? Has your debt been paid you?" she asked Yashvin.

"Oh, pretty fair; I don't think I'll get it all, but I shall get a good half. And when are you off?" said Yashvin, looking at Vronsky and unmistakably guessing at a quarrel.

"The day after tomorrow, I think," said Vronsky.

"You've been meaning to go so long, though."

"But now it's quite decided," said Anna, looking Vronsky straight in the face with a look that told him not to dream of the possibility of reconciliation.

"Don't you feel sorry for that unlucky Pestsov?" she went on, talking to Yashvin.

"I've never asked myself the question, Anna Arkadyevna, whether I'm sorry for him or not. You see, all my fortune's here"—he touched his breast pocket—"and just now I'm a wealthy man. But today I'm going to the club, and I may come out a beggar. You see, whoever sits down to play with me, he wants to leave me without a shirt on my back, and so do I him. And so we fight it out, and that's the pleasure of it."

"Well, but suppose you were married," said Anna, "how would it be for your wife?"

Yashvin laughed.

"That's why I'm not married, and never mean to be."

"And Helsingfors?" said Vronsky, entering into the conversation and glancing at Anna's smiling face. Meeting his eyes, Anna's face instantly took on a coldly severe expression as though she were saying to him: "It's not forgotten. Nothing's changed."

"Were you really in love?" she said to Yashvin.

"Oh, heavens! Very many times! But you see, some men can play cards and yet always be ready to lay down their cards when the hour comes for a rendezvous, while I can have an affair and yet never be late for my cards in the evening. That's how I manage things."

"No, I didn't mean that, but the real thing." She would have said "Helsingfors," but would not repeat the word used by Vronsky.

Voytov, who was buying a horse from Vronsky, came in. Anna got up and went out of the room.

Before leaving the house, Vronsky went into her room. She thought of pretending to look for something on the table, but ashamed of making a pretense, she looked straight into his face with cold eyes.

"What do you want?" she asked in French.

"Gambetta's pedigree, I've sold him," he said, in a tone that said more clearly than words, "I've no time for discussing things, and it would lead to nothing."

"I'm not to blame in any way," he thought. "If she will punish herself, *tant pis pour elle*."[2] But as he was going, he thought that she said something, and his heart suddenly ached with pity for her.

"Eh, Anna?" he queried.

"I said nothing," she answered, just as coldly and calmly.

"Oh, nothing, *tant pis*, then," he thought, feeling indifferent again, and he turned and went out. As he was going out he caught a glimpse of her face in the mirror, white, with quivering lips. He wanted to stop and say some comforting word to her, but his legs carried him out of the room before he could think of what to say. The whole of

[2] "So much the worse for her."

that day he spent away from home, and when he came in late in the evening the maid told him that Anna Arkadyevna had a headache and begged him not to go in to her.

CHAPTER TWENTY-SIX

Never before had a whole day been passed in quarrel. Today was the first time. And it was not a quarrel. It was the open acknowledgment of complete estrangement. Was it possible for him to have looked at her as he had when he came into the room for the pedigree if it were otherwise? Look at her, see her heart was breaking with despair, and go out without a word with that face of callous indifference? He was not merely cold to her, he hated her because he loved another woman—that was clear.

And remembering all the cruel words he had said, Anna supplied as well the words that he had unmistakably wished to say and could have said to her, and she grew more and more exasperated.

"I'm not holding you," he might have said. "You can go where you like. You were unwilling to be divorced from your husband, no doubt so that you might go back to him. Go back to him. If you want money, I'll give it to you. How many rubles do you want?"

All the cruelest words that a brutal man could say, he said to her in her imagination, and she could not forgive him for them, as though he had actually said them.

"But didn't he only yesterday swear he loved me, he, a truthful and sincere man? Haven't I despaired for nothing many times already?" she said to herself afterwards.

All that day, except for the visit to Wilson's, which occupied two hours, Anna spent in doubts whether everything was over or whether there was still hope of reconciliation, whether she should go away at once or see him once more. She was expecting him the whole day, and in the evening, as she went to her own room, leaving a message for him that her head ached, she said to herself, "If he comes in spite of what the maid says, it means that he loves me still. If not, it means that all is over, and then I will decide what I'm to do! . . ."

In the evening she heard the rumbling of his carriage stop at the entrance, his ring, his steps, and his conversation with the servant; he believed what was told him, did not care to find out more, and went to his own room. So then everything was over.

And death rose clearly and vividly before her mind as the sole means of bringing back love for her in his heart, of punishing him and of gaining the victory in that strife which the evil spirit in possession of her heart was waging with him.

Now nothing mattered: going or not going to Vozdvizhenskoe, getting or not getting a divorce from her husband—all that did not matter. The one thing that mattered was punishing him. When she poured out her usual dose of opium, and thought that she had only to drink off the whole bottle to die, it seemed to her so simple and easy that she began musing with enjoyment on how he would suffer, and repent and love her memory when it would be too late. She lay in bed with open eyes, by the light of a single burned-down candle, gazing at the carved cornice of the ceiling and at the shadow of the screen that covered part of it, while she vividly pictured to herself how he would feel when she would be no more, when she would be only a memory to him. "How could I say such cruel things to her?" he would say. "How could I go out of the room without saying anything to her? But now she is no more. She has gone away from us forever. She is . . ." Suddenly the shadow of the screen wavered, pounced on the whole cornice, the whole ceiling; other shadows from the other side swooped to meet it, for an instant the shadows flitted back, but then with fresh swiftness they darted forward, wavered, mingled, and all was darkness. "Death!" she thought. And such horror came upon her that for a long while she could not realize where she was, and for a long while her trembling hands could not find the matches and light another candle, instead of the one that had burned down and gone out. "No, anything—only to live! Why, I love him! Why, he loves me! This has been before and will pass," she said, feeling that tears of joy at the return to life were trickling down her cheeks. And to escape from her panic she went hurriedly to his room.

He was asleep there, and sleeping soundly. She went up to him, and holding the light above his face, she gazed a long while at him. Now when he was asleep, she loved him so much that at the sight of him she could not keep back tears of tenderness. But she knew that if he awakened he would look at her with cold eyes, convinced that he was right, and that before telling him of her love, she would have to prove to him that he had been wrong in his treatment of her. Without waking him, she went back, and after a second dose of opium toward morning she fell into a heavy, incomplete sleep, during which she never quite lost consciousness.

In the morning she was awakened by a horrible nightmare, which had recurred several times in her dreams, even before her liaison with Vronsky. A little old man with unkempt beard was doing something bent down over some iron, muttering meaningless French words, and she, as she always did in this nightmare (it was what made it so horrible), felt that this peasant was taking no notice of her, but was doing something horrible with the iron—over her. And she awoke in a cold sweat.

When she got up, the previous day came back to her as though veiled in mist.

"There was a quarrel. Just what has happened several times. I said I had a headache, and he did not come in to see me. Tomorrow we're going away; I must see him and get ready for the journey," she said to herself. And learning that he was in his study, she went down to him. As she passed through the drawing room she heard a carriage stop at the entrance, and looking out of the window she saw the carriage; a young girl in a lilac hat was leaning out giving some direction to the footman ringing the bell. After a parley in the hall, someone came upstairs, and Vronsky's steps could be heard passing the drawing room. He went rapidly downstairs. Anna went again to the window. She saw him come out onto the steps without his hat and go up to the carriage. The young girl in the lilac hat handed him a parcel. Vronsky, smiling, said something to her. The carriage drove away, and he ran rapidly upstairs again.

The mists that had shrouded everything in her soul parted suddenly. The feelings of yesterday pierced the sick heart with a fresh pang. She could not understand now how she could have lowered herself by spending a whole day with him in his house. She went into his room to announce her determination.

"That was Madame Sorokina and her daughter. They came and brought me the money and the documents from *Maman*. I couldn't get them yesterday. How is your head, better?" he said quietly, not wishing to see and to understand the gloomy and solemn expression of her face.

She looked silently, intently at him, standing in the middle of the room. He glanced at her, frowned for a moment, and went on reading a letter. She turned, and went deliberately out of the room. He still could have called her back, but she had reached the door, he was still silent, and the only sound audible was the rustling of the paper as he turned it over.

"Oh, by the way," he said at the very moment she was in the doorway, "we're going tomorrow for certain, aren't we?"

"You, but not I," she said, turning around.

"Anna, we can't go on like this . . ."

"You, but not I," she repeated.

"This is getting unbearable!"

"You . . . you will be sorry for this," she said, and went out.

Frightened by the desperate expression with which these words were uttered, he jumped up with the intention of running after her, but on second thoughts he sat down and scowled, clenching his teeth. This vulgar—as he thought it—threat of something vague exasperated him. "I've tried everything," he thought; "the only thing left is not to pay attention," and he began to get ready to drive into town, and again to his mother's to get her signature to the power of attorney.

She heard the sound of his steps about the study and the dining room. At the drawing room he stood still. But he did not come in to see her; he merely gave an order that the horse should be given to Voytov if he came while he was away. Then she heard the carriage brought round, the door opened, and he came out again. But he went back into the porch again, and someone was running upstairs. It was the valet running up for his gloves that had been forgotten. She went to the window and saw him take the gloves without looking, and touching the coachman on the back, he said something to him. Then, without looking up at the window, he settled himself in his usual attitude in the carriage, with his legs crossed, and, pulling on a glove, he vanished around the corner.

CHAPTER TWENTY-SEVEN

"He's gone! It is over!" Anna said to herself, standing at the window; and in response to this thought, the impression of the darkness when the candle had flickered out and of her fearful nightmare merged into one, filling her heart with cold terror.

"No, that cannot be!" she cried, and crossing the room, she rang the bell. She was so afraid now of being alone that without waiting for the servant to come in, she went out to meet him.

"Inquire where the count has gone," she said. The servant answered that the count had gone to the stable.

"His Honor left word that if you cared to drive out, the carriage would be back immediately."

"Very good. Wait a minute. I'll write a note at once. Send Mikhail with the note to the stables. Hurry."

She sat down and wrote:

"I was wrong. Come back home; I must explain. For God's sake, come! I'm afraid."

She sealed it up and gave it to the servant.

She was afraid of being left alone now; she followed the servant out of the room, and went to the nursery.

"Why, this is wrong—this isn't he! Where are his blue eyes, his sweet, shy smile?" was her first thought when she saw her chubby, rosy-cheeked little girl with her black, curly hair instead of Seryozha, whom, in the confusion of her mind, she had expected to see in the nursery. The little girl sitting at the table was obstinately and violently battering it with a bottle stopper, and staring aimlessly at her mother with her two black, currant-like eyes. Answering the English nurse that she was quite well, and that she was going to the country tomorrow, Anna sat down by the little girl and began spinning the stopper in front of her. But the child's loud, ringing laugh and the motion of her eyebrows recalled Vronsky so vividly that she got up hurriedly, restraining her sobs, and went away. "Can it be all over? No, it cannot be!" she thought. "He will come back. But how can he explain that smile, that excitement after he had been talking to her? But even if he doesn't explain, I will believe. If I don't believe, there's only one thing left for me, and I can't."

She looked at her watch. Twenty minutes had passed. "By now he has received the note and is coming back. Not long, ten minutes more . . . But what if he doesn't come? No, that cannot be. He mustn't see me with tear-stained eyes. I'll go and wash. Yes, yes; did I do my hair or not?" she asked herself. And she could not remember. She felt her head with her hand. "Yes, my hair has been done, but when I did it, I can't in the least remember." She could not believe the evidence of her hand, and went up to the mirror to see whether she really had done her hair. She certainly had, but she could not remember when she had done it. "Who's that?" she thought, looking in the mirror at the swollen face with strangely glittering eyes that looked in a frightened way at her. "Why, it's me!" she suddenly understood, and looking around, she seemed all at once to feel his kisses on her, and twitched her shoulders, shuddering. Then she lifted her hand to her lips and kissed it.

"What is it? Why, I'm going out of my mind!" and she went into her bedroom, where Annushka was tidying the room.

"Annushka," she said, coming to a standstill before her, and she stared at the maid, not knowing what to say to her.

"You meant to go and see Darya Aleksandrovna," said the maid, as though she understood.

"Darya Aleksandrovna? Yes, I'll go."

"Fifteen minutes there, fifteen minutes back. He's coming, he'll be here soon." She took out her watch and looked at it. "But how could he go away leaving me in such a state? How can he live without making up with me?" She went to the window and began looking into the street. Judging by the time, he should be back now. But her calculations might be wrong, and she began once more to recall when he had started and to count the minutes.

At the moment when she had moved away to the big clock to compare it with her watch, someone drove up. Glancing out of the window, she saw his carriage. But no one came upstairs, and voices could be heard below. It was the messenger who had come back in the carriage. She went down to him.

"We didn't catch the count. The count had driven off to Nizhegorodsky station."

"What do you say? What! . . ." she said to the rosy-faced, cheerful Mikhail as he handed her back her note.

"Why, then, he didn't receive it!" she thought.

"Go with this note to Countess Vronskaya's place, you know it? And bring an answer back immediately," she said to the messenger.

"And I, what am I going to do?" she thought. "Yes, I'm going to Dolly's, that's right, or else I shall go out of my mind. Yes, and I can telegraph, too." And she wrote a telegram: "*I absolutely must talk to you; come at once.*" After sending off the telegram, she went to dress. When she was dressed and in her hat, she glanced again into the eyes of the plump, comfortable-looking Annushka. There was unmistakable sympathy in those good-natured little gray eyes.

"Annushka, dear, what am I to do?" said Anna, sobbing and sinking helplessly into a chair.

"Why upset yourself so, Anna Arkadyevna? Why, there's nothing unusual. Go out; it'll cheer you up," said the maid.

"Yes, I'm going," said Anna, rousing herself and getting up. "And if there's a telegram while I'm away, send it on to Darya Aleksandrovna's . . . but no, I shall be back myself."

"Yes, I mustn't think, I must do something, drive somewhere, and most of all, get out of this house," she said, feeling with terror the strange turmoil going on in her own heart, and she made haste to go out and get into the carriage.

"Where to?" asked Pyotr before getting onto the box.

"To Znamenka, the Oblonskys'."

CHAPTER TWENTY-EIGHT

The weather was bright. A fine rain had been falling all morning, but it had lately cleared up. The iron roofs, the flagstones of the pavement, the cobbled roadway, the wheels and leather, the brass and the metalwork of the carriages—all glistened brightly in the May sunshine. It was three o'clock, and the very liveliest time in the streets.

As she sat in a corner of the comfortable carriage that hardly swayed on its supple springs while the grays trotted swiftly, in the midst of the unceasing rattle of wheels and the changing impressions in the pure air, Anna ran over the events of the last days, and she saw her position quite differently from how it had seemed at home. Now the thought of death seemed no longer so frightening and so clear to her, and death itself no longer seemed so inevitable. Now she blamed herself for the humiliation to which she had lowered herself. "I entreat him to forgive me. I have given in to him. I have confessed myself at fault. What for? Can't I live without him?" And leaving unanswered the question how she was going to live without him, she began reading the signs on the shops. "Office and warehouse. Dental surgeon . . . Yes, I'll tell Dolly all about it. She doesn't like Vronsky. I shall be sick and ashamed, but I'll tell her. She loves me, and I'll follow her advice. I won't give in to him; I won't let him train me as he pleases, bakery, Filippov . . . They say they send their pastry to Petersburg. The Moscow water is so good for it. Ah, the springs at Mytishchi and the pancakes!" And she remembered how, long, long ago, when she was a girl of seventeen, she had gone with her aunt to Troitsa.[1] "Riding, too. Was that really me, with red hands? How much that seemed to me then splendid and out of reach has become worthless, while what I had then has gone out of my reach forever! Could I ever have believed then that I could come to such humiliation? How conceited and self-satisfied he will be when he gets my note! But I will show him . . . How horrid that paint smells! Why is it they're always painting and building? '*Modes et robes,*' "[2] she read. A man bowed to her. It was Annushka's husband. "Our parasites"; she remembered how Vronsky had said that. " 'Our'? Why 'our'? What's so awful is that one can't tear up the past by its roots. One can't tear it out, but one can hide one's memory of it. And I'll hide it." And then she thought of her past with Aleksey Aleksandrovich, of how she had blotted the memory of it out of her life. "Dolly will think I'm leaving my second husband, and so I certainly must be in the wrong. As if I cared to be right! I can't help it!" she said, and she wanted to cry. But at once she started wondering what those two girls could be smiling about. "Love, most likely. They don't know how dreary it is, how degrading . . . The boulevard and the children. Three boys running, playing at horses. Seryozha! And I'm losing everything and not getting him back. Yes, I'm losing everything if he doesn't return. Perhaps he was

[1] A monastery near Moscow.
[2] "Dressing and millinery."

late for the train and has come back by now. Longing for humiliation again!" she said to herself. "No, I'll go to Dolly, and say straight out to her, 'I'm unhappy, I deserve this, I'm to blame, but still I'm unhappy, help me.' These horses, this carriage—how loathsome I am to myself in this carriage—all his; but I won't see them again."

Thinking over the words in which she would tell Dolly, and mentally working her heart up to great bitterness, Anna went upstairs.

"Is there anyone with her?" she asked in the hall.

"Katerina Aleksandrovna Levina," answered the footman.

"Kitty! Kitty, whom Vronsky was in love with!" thought Anna, "the girl he thinks of with love. He's sorry he didn't marry her. But me he thinks of with hatred, and is sorry he had anything to do with me."

The sisters were having a consultation about nursing when Anna called. Dolly went down alone to see the visitor who had interrupted their conversation.

"Well, so you've not gone away yet? I meant to have come to you," she said; "I had a letter from Stiva today."

"We had a telegram too," answered Anna, looking round for Kitty.

"He writes that he can't make out quite what Aleksey Aleksandrovich wants, but he won't go away without a decisive answer."

"I thought you had someone with you. Can I see the letter?"

"Yes, Kitty," said Dolly, embarrassed. "She stayed in the nursery. She has been very ill."

"So I heard. May I see the letter?"

"I'll get it at once. But he doesn't refuse; on the contrary, Stiva has hopes," said Dolly, stopping in the doorway.

"I haven't, and indeed I don't wish it," said Anna.

"What's this? Does Kitty consider it degrading to meet me?" thought Anna when she was alone. "Perhaps she's right, too. But it's not for her, the girl who was in love with Vronsky, it's not for her to show me that, even if it is true. I know that in my position I can't be received by any decent woman. I knew that from the first moment I sacrificed everything for him. And this is my reward! Oh, how I hate him! And what did I come here for? I'm worse here, more miserable." She heard from the next room the sisters' voices in consultation. "And what am I going to say to Dolly now? Amuse Kitty by the sight of my wretchedness, submit to her patronizing? No; and besides, Dolly wouldn't understand. And it would be no good my telling her. It would only be interesting to see Kitty, to show her how I despise everyone and everything, how nothing matters to me now."

Dolly came in with the letter. Anna read it and handed it back in silence.

"I knew all that," she said, "and it doesn't interest me in the least."

"Oh, why so? On the contrary, I have hopes," said Dolly, looking inquisitively at Anna. She had never seen her in such a strangely irritable condition. "When are you going away?" she asked.

Anna, half closing her eyes, looked straight before her and did not answer.

"Why does Kitty shrink from me?" she said, looking at the door and flushing red.

"Oh, what nonsense! She's nursing, and things aren't going right with her, and I've been advising her . . . She's delighted. She'll be here in a minute," said Dolly awkwardly, not clever at lying. "Yes, here she is."

Hearing that Anna had called, Kitty had wanted not to appear, but Dolly persuaded her. Gathering her courage, Kitty went in, walked up to her, blushing, and shook hands.

"I am so glad to see you," she said with a trembling voice.

Kitty had been thrown into confusion by the inward conflict between her antagonism to this bad woman and her desire to be nice to her. But as soon as she saw Anna's lovely and attractive face, all feeling of antagonism disappeared.

"I should not have been surprised if you had not cared to meet me. I'm used to everything. You have been ill? Yes, you are changed," said Anna.

Kitty felt that Anna was looking at her with hostile eyes. She ascribed this hostility to the awkward position in which Anna, who had once patronized her, must feel toward her now, and she felt sorry for her.

They talked of Kitty's illness, of the baby, of Stiva, but it was obvious that nothing interested Anna.

"I came to say good-by to you," she said, getting up.

"Oh, when are you going?"

But again not answering, Anna turned to Kitty.

"Yes, I am very glad to have seen you," she said with a smile. "I have heard so much of you from everyone, even from your husband. He came to see me, and I liked him very much," she said, unmistakably with malicious intent. "Where is he?"

"He has gone back to the country," said Kitty, blushing.

"Remember me to him, be sure you do."

"I'll be sure to!" Kitty said naïvely, looking compassionately into her eyes.

"So, good-by, Dolly." And kissing Dolly and shaking hands with Kitty, Anna went out hurriedly.

"She's just the same and just as charming! She's very lovely!" said Kitty when she was alone with her sister. "But there's something pitiful about her. Terribly pitiful!"

"Yes, there's something unusual about her today," said Dolly. "When I went with her into the hall, I thought she was almost crying."

CHAPTER TWENTY-NINE

Anna got into the carriage again in an even worse frame of mind than when she had set out from home. To her previous tortures was added now that sense of mortification and of being an outcast which she had felt so distinctly on meeting Kitty.

"Where to? Home?" asked Piotr.

"Yes, home," she said, not even thinking now where she was going.

"How they looked at me as something dreadful, incomprehensible, and curious! What can he be telling the other with such warmth?" she thought, starting at two men who walked by. "Can one ever tell anyone what one is feeling? I meant to tell Dolly, and it's a good thing I didn't tell her. How pleased she would have been at my misery! She would have concealed it, but her chief feeling would have been delight at my being punished for the happiness she envied me for. Kitty, she would have been even more pleased. How I can see through her! She knows I was more than usually nice to her husband. And she's jealous and hates me. And she despises me. In her eyes I'm an immoral

woman. If I were an immoral woman I could have made her husband
fall in love with me . . . if I'd cared to. And, indeed, I did care to.
There's someone who's pleased with himself," she thought, as she saw
a fat, rubicund gentleman coming toward her. He took her for an
acquaintance, and lifted his glossy hat above his bald, glossy head, and
then perceived his mistake. "He thought he knew me. Well, he knows
me as well as anyone in the world knows me. I don't know myself. I
know my appetites, as the French say. Those two boys want some of
that filthy ice cream, that they do know for certain," she thought,
looking at two boys stopping an ice cream vendor, who took a tub off
his head and began wiping his perspiring face with a towel. "We all
want what is sweet and nice. If not sweets, then dirty ice cream. And
Kitty's the same—if not Vronsky, then Levin. And she envies me, and
hates me. And we all hate each other. I Kitty, Kitty me. Yes, that's the
truth. '*Tiutkin, coiffeur.' Je me fais coiffer par Tiutkin* . . .[1] I'll tell him
that when he comes," she thought, and smiled. But the same instant
she remembered that she had no one now to tell anything amusing to.
"And there's nothing amusing, nothing mirthful, really. It's all hateful.
They're ringing the bells for vespers, and how carefully that merchant
crosses himself! As if he were afraid of dropping something. Why
these churches and this ringing and this humbug? Simply to conceal
that we all hate each other, like these cab drivers who are abusing each
other so angrily. Yashvin says, 'He wants to strip me of my shirt, and
I him of his.' Yes that's the truth!"

She was plunged in these thoughts, which so engrossed her that
she ceased thinking of her own position, when the carriage drew up
at the steps of her house. It was only when she saw the porter running out to meet her that she remembered she had sent the note and
the telegram.

"Is there an answer?" she inquired.

"I'll see this minute," answered the porter, and glancing into his
room, he took out and gave her the thin, square envelope of a
telegram. "I can't come before ten o'clock—Vronsky," she read.

"And hasn't the messenger come back?"

"No," answered the porter.

---

[1] " 'Tiutkin, hairdresser,' I have my hair done by Tiutkin."

"Then, since it's so, I know what I must do," she said, and feeling a vague fury and craving for revenge rising up within her, she ran upstairs. "I'll go to him myself. Before going away forever, I'll tell him all. Never have I hated anyone as I hate that man!" she thought. Seeing his hat on the rack, she shuddered with aversion. She did not consider that his telegram was an answer to her telegram and that he had not yet received her note. She pictured him to herself as talking calmly to his mother and Princess Sorokina and rejoicing at her sufferings. "Yes, I must go quickly," she said, not knowing yet where she was going. She longed to get away as quickly as possible from the feelings she had gone through in that awful house. The servants, the walls, the things in that house—all aroused revulsion and hatred in her and lay like a weight upon her.

"Yes, I must go to the railway station, and if he's not there, then go there and catch him." Anna looked at the timetable in the newspapers. An evening train went at two minutes past eight. "Yes, I shall be in time." She gave orders for the other horses to be harnessed, and packed in a valise the things needed for a few days. She knew she would never come back here again.

Among the plans that came into her head she vaguely determined that after what would happen at the station or at the countess's house, she would go as far as the first town on the Nizhegorodsky railway and stop there.

Dinner was on the table; she went up, but the smell of the bread and cheese was enough to make her feel that all food was disgusting. She ordered the carriage and went out. The house threw a shadow now right across the street, but it was a bright evening and still warm in the sunshine. Annushka, who came down with her things, and Piotr, who put the things in the carriage, and the coachman, evidently out of humor, were all hateful to her, and irritated her by their words and actions.

"I don't want you, Piotr."

"But how about the ticket?"

"Well, as you like, it doesn't matter," she said crossly.

Piotr jumped on the box, and putting his arms akimbo, he told the coachman to drive to the station.

CHAPTER THIRTY

"There, again it's that girl! Again I understand it all!" Anna said to herself as soon as the carriage had started and, swaying lightly, rumbled over the tiny cobbles of the road, and again one impression followed rapidly upon another.

"Yes; what was the last thing I thought of so clearly?" She tried to recall it. " *'Tiutkin, coiffeur'*?—no, not that. Yes, of what Yashvin says, the struggle for existence and hatred is the one thing that holds men together. No, it's a useless journey you're making," she said, mentally addressing a party in a coach and four, evidently making an excursion into the country. "And the dog you're taking with you will be no help to you. You can't get away from yourselves." Turning her eyes in the direction Piotr had turned to look, she saw a workman almost dead drunk, with hanging head, being led away by a policeman. "Ah, he's found a quicker way," she thought. "Count Vronsky and I did not find that happiness either, though we expected so much from it." And now for the first time Anna turned that glaring light in which she was seeing everything on to her relations with him, which she had hitherto avoided thinking about. "What was it he sought in me? Not love so much as the satisfaction of vanity." She remembered his words, the expression of his face, which recalled an abject setter-dog, in the early days of their love affair. And everything now confirmed this. "Yes, there was the triumph of success in him. Of course there was love too, but the chief element was the pride of success. He boasted of me. Now that's over. There's nothing to be proud of. Nothing to be proud of, only to be ashamed of. He has taken from me all he could, and now I am no use to him. He is weary of me and is trying not to be dishonorable in his behavior toward me. He let that out yesterday—he wants divorce and marriage so as to burn his ship. He loves me, but how? The zest is gone, as the English say. That fellow wants everyone to admire him and is very much pleased with himself," she thought, looking at a red-cheeked clerk riding on a hired horse. "Yes, there's not the same flavor about me for him now. If I go away from him, at the bottom of his heart he will be glad."

This was not mere supposition, she saw it distinctly in the piercing light which revealed to her now the meaning of life and human relations.

"My love keeps growing more passionate and selfish, while his is dying, and that's why we're drifting apart," she went on musing. "And there's nothing I can do. He is everything to me, and I want him more and more to give himself up to me entirely. And he wants more and more to get away from me. We were irresistibly drawn together up to the time of our love, and now we have been irresistibly drifting apart. And there's no altering that. He tells me I'm insanely jealous; but it's not true. I'm not jealous, but I'm unsatisfied. But . . . " She opened her lips, and shifted her place in the carriage in the excitement aroused by the thoughts which suddenly struck her. "If I could be anything but a mistress, passionately caring for nothing but his caresses; but I can't and I don't care to be anything else. And by that desire I rouse aversion in him, and he rouses fury in me, and it cannot be different. Don't I know that he wouldn't deceive me, that he has no schemes about Princess Sorokina, that he's not in love with Kitty, that he won't desert me! I know all that, but it makes it no easier for me. If without loving me, from *duty* he'll be good and kind to me, without what I want, that's a thousand times worse than unkindness! That's—hell! And that's just how it is. For a long while now he hasn't loved me. And where love ends, hate begins. I don't know these streets at all. Hills it seems, and still houses, and houses . . . And in the houses always people and people. How many of them, no end, and all hating each other! Well, let me try and think what I want to make me happy. Well? Suppose I am divorced, and Aleksey Aleksandrovich lets me have Seryozha, and I marry Vronsky." Thinking of Aleksey Aleksandrovich, she at once pictured him with extraordinary vividness as though he were alive before her, with his mild, lifeless, dull eyes, the blue veins in his white hands, his intonations and the cracking of his knuckles, and remembering the feeling that had existed between them, and that was also called love, she shuddered with loathing. "Well, I'm divorced, and become Vronsky's wife. Well, will Kitty cease looking at me as she looked at me today? No. And will Seryozha stop asking and wondering about my two husbands? And is there any new feeling I can awaken between Vronsky and me? Is there possible, if not happiness, some sort of ease from misery? No, no!" she answered now without the slightest hesitation. "Impossible! We are drawn apart by life, and I make his unhappiness and he mine, and there's no changing him or me. Every attempt has been made, but the screw has lost its thread. Oh, a beggar-woman with a baby. She thinks I'm sorry for her. Aren't we all flung into the world only to hate each other, and so to torture ourselves and each other? Schoolboys coming—laughing—Seryozha?" she thought. "I thought, too, that I loved him, and used to be touched by my own tenderness. But I have lived without him, I gave him up for another love and did not regret the exchange as long as that other love satisfied me." And with loathing she thought of what she meant by that "other love." And the clearness with which she saw life now, her own and everyone's, afforded her pleasure. "It's so with me and Piotr, and the coachman, Fyodor, and that merchant, and all the people living along the Volga, where those advertisements invite one to go, and everywhere and always," she thought when she had driven up to the low building of the Nizhegorodsky station, and the porters ran to meet her.

"A ticket to Obiralovka?" said Piotr.

She had utterly forgotten where and why she was going, and only by a great effort did she understand the question.

"Yes," she said, handing him her purse, and taking a little red bag on her arm, she got out of the carriage.

Making her way through the crowd to the first-class waiting room, she gradually recollected all the details of her situation, and the plans between which she was hesitating. And again at the old sore spots, hope and then despair poisoned the wounds of her tortured, fearfully throbbing heart. As she sat on the star-shaped sofa waiting for the train, she gazed with aversion at the people coming and going (they were all hateful to her), and thought how she would arrive at the station, would write him a note, and what she would write to him, and how he was at this moment complaining to his mother of his position, not understanding her sufferings, and how she would go into the room, and what she would say to him. Then she thought that life might still be happy, and how miserably she loved and hated him, and how fearfully her heart was beating.

CHAPTER THIRTY-ONE

A bell rang; some young men, ugly and impudent, and at the same time mindful of the impression they were making, hurried by. Piotr, too, crossed the room in his livery and gaiters, with his dull, animal face, and came up to her to take her to the train. Some noisy men were quiet as she passed them on the platform, and one whispered something about her to another—something vile, no doubt. She climbed up the high step of the railway carriage and sat down in an empty compartment on a dirty seat that had been white. Her bag bounced on the springy seat and then was still. With a foolish smile Piotr raised his hat, with its colored band, at the window in token of farewell, an impudent conductor slammed the door and the latch. A grotesque-looking lady wearing a bustle (Anna mentally undressed the woman, and was appalled at her hideousness), and a little girl laughing affectedly ran down the platform.

"Katerina Andreevna, she's got everything, *ma tante!*"[1] cried the girl.

"Even the child's hideous and affected," thought Anna." To avoid seeing anyone, she got up quickly and seated herself at the opposite window of the empty carriage. A deformed peasant covered with dirt, in a cap from which his tousled hair stuck out, passed by that window, stooping down to the carriage wheels. "There's something familiar about that hideous peasant," thought Anna. And remembering her dream, she moved away to the opposite door, shaking with terror. The conductor opened the door and let in a man and his wife.

"Do you wish to get out?"

Anna made no answer. The conductor and the two fellow passengers did not notice her panic-stricken face under her veil. She went back to her corner and sat down. The couple seated themselves on the opposite side, and intently but surreptitiously scrutinized her clothes. Both husband and wife seemed repulsive to Anna. The husband asked if she would allow him to smoke, obviously not with a view to smoking but to getting into conversation with her. Receiving her assent, he said to his wife in French something about caring

[1]"My aunt!"

864

less to smoke than to talk. They made inane and affected remarks to one another, entirely for her benefit. Anna saw clearly that they were sick of each other, and hated each other. And no one could have helped hating such miserable monstrosities.

A second bell sounded, and was followed by the moving of luggage, noise, shouting, and laughter. It was so clear to Anna that there was nothing for anyone to be glad of, that this laughter irritated her agonizingly, and she would have liked to stop up her ears not to hear it. At last the third bell rang, there was a whistle and a hiss of steam, and the coupling chains jerked, and the man in her carriage crossed himself. "It would be interesting to ask him what meaning he attaches to that," thought Anna, looking angrily at him. She looked past the lady out of the window at the people who seemed whirling by as they ran beside the train or stood on the platform. The train, jerking at regular intervals at the points of the rails, rolled by the platform, past a stone wall, a signal box, past other trains, the wheels, moving more smoothly and evenly, making a slight ringing sound. The window was lighted up by the bright evening sun, and a slight breeze played against the blind. Anna forgot her fellow passengers, and to the light swaying of the train she started thinking again, as she inhaled the fresh air.

"Where did I leave off? On the thought that I couldn't conceive a position in which life would not be misery, that we are all created to be miserable, and that we all know it, and all invent means of deceiving each other. And when one sees the truth, what is one to do?"

"That's what reason is given man for, to escape from what worries him," said the lady in French, lisping affectedly, and obviously pleased with her phrase.

The words seemed an answer to Anna's thoughts.

"To escape from what worries him," repeated Anna. And glancing at the red-cheeked husband and the thin wife, she saw that the sickly wife considered herself misunderstood, and the husband deceived her and encouraged her in that idea of herself. Directing her searchlight on them, Anna seemed to see their entire history and all the crannies of their souls. But there was nothing interesting in them, and she pursued her thoughts.

"Yes, I'm very much worried, and that's what reason was given me for, to escape; so then one must escape. Why not put out the light when there's nothing more to look at, when it's sickening to look at it all? But how? Why did the conductor run along the footboard, why are they shrieking, those young men in that train? Why are they talking, why are they laughing? It's all falsehood, all lying, all humbug, all evil! . . ."

When the train came into the station, Anna got out into the crowd of passengers, and moving apart from them as if they were lepers, she stood on the platform, trying to think what she had come here for and what she meant to do. Everything that had seemed to her possible before was not so difficult to consider, especially in this noisy crowd of hideous people who would not leave her alone. At one moment porters ran up to her proffering their services, then young men, clacking their heels on the planks of the platform and talking loudly, stared at her, then people meeting her dodged past on the wrong side. Remembering that she had meant to go on if there was no answer, she stopped a porter and asked if her coachman was here with a note from Count Vronsky.

"Count Vronsky? Someone from there was just here to meet Princess Sorokina and her daughter. And what is the coachman like?"

Just as she was talking to the porter, the coachman Mikhail, red-faced and cheerful in his smart blue coat and with a watch-chain, evidently proud of having so successfully performed his commission, came up to her and gave her a letter. She broke it open, and her heart ached even before she read it.

"I am very sorry your note did not reach me. I will be home at ten," Vronsky had written in a careless hand. . . .

"Yes, that's what I expected!" she said to herself with a malicious smile.

"Very good, you can go home, then," she said softly, addressing Mikhail. She spoke softly because the rapidity of her heart's beating hindered her breathing. "No, I won't let you make me miserable," she thought menacingly, addressing not him, not herself, but the power that made her suffer, and she walked along the platform past the station buildings.

Two servant girls walking along the platform turned their heads, staring at her and making some remarks about her dress. "Real," they said of the lace she was wearing. The young men would not leave her in peace. Again they passed by, peering into her face and, with a laugh, shouting something in an unnatural voice. The stationmaster coming up asked her whether she was going by train. A boy selling kvas never took his eyes off her. "My God! Where am I to go?" she thought, going farther and farther along the platform. At the end she stopped. Some ladies and children, who had come to meet a gentleman in spectacles, paused in their loud laughter and talking and stared at her as she reached them. She quickened her pace and walked away from them to the edge of the platform. A goods train was coming in. The platform began to sway, and she imagined that she was in the train again.

And all at once she thought of the man crushed by the train the day she had first met Vronsky, and she knew what she had to do. With a rapid, light step she went down the steps that led from the water tank to the rails and stopped close to the approaching train.

She looked at the lower part of the trucks, at the bolts and chains, and the tall iron wheels of the first truck slowly moving up, and trying to measure the midpoint between the front and back wheels, and the very moment when that point would be opposite her.

"There," she said to herself, looking in the shadow of the truck at the mixture of sand and coal dust which covered the ties. "There, in the very middle, and I shall punish him and escape from everyone and from myself."

She wanted to fall halfway between the wheels of the front car, which was drawing level with her. But the red bag which she began to take from her arm delayed her, and she was too late; the car had passed. She had to wait for the next. A feeling such as she had known when about to take the first plunge in bathing came upon her, and she crossed herself. That familiar gesture brought back into her soul a whole series of memories of her childhood and girlhood, and suddenly the darkness that had covered everything for her was torn apart, and life rose up before her for an instant with all its bright past joys. But she did not take her eyes from the wheels of the second car. And exactly at the moment when the midpoint between the wheels drew level with her, she threw away the red bag, and drawing her head back into her shoulders, fell on her hands under the car, and, with a light movement, as though she would rise immediately, dropped on her knees. And at the instant she was terror-stricken at what she was doing. "Where am I? What am I doing? What for?" She tried to get up, to throw herself back; but something huge and merciless struck her on the head and dragged her down on her back. "Lord, forgive me everything!" she said, feeling it impossible to struggle. A peasant muttering something was working above the iron. And the light of the candle by which she had read the book filled with troubles, falsehoods, sorrow, and evil flared up more brightly than ever before, lighted up for her all that had been shrouded in darkness, flickered, began to grow dim, and was quenched forever.

PART EIGHT

CHAPTER ONE

Almost two months had passed. The hot summer was half over, but Sergey Ivanovich Koznyshev was only just preparing to leave Moscow.

Sergey Ivanovich's life had not been uneventful during this time. A year ago he had finished his book, the fruit of six years' labor, *Sketch of a Survey of the Principles and Forms of Government in Europe and Russia*. Several sections of this book and its introduction had appeared in periodicals, and other parts had been read by Sergey Ivanovich to persons of his circle, so that the major ideas of the work could not be completely novel to the public. But still Sergey Ivanovich had expected that on its appearance his book would be sure to make a serious impression on society, and if it did not cause a revolution in social science it would, at any rate, make a great stir in the scientific world.

After the most conscientious revision the book had last year been published, and had been distributed among the booksellers.

Though he asked no one about it, reluctantly and with feigned indifference answered his friends' inquiries as to how the book was going, and did not even inquire of the booksellers how the book was selling, Sergey Ivanovich watched eagerly, with strained attention, for the first impression his book would make in the world and in literature.

But a week passed, a second, a third, and in society no impression whatever could be detected. His friends who were specialists and scholars occasionally—unmistakably from politeness—alluded to it. The rest of his acquaintances, not interested in a book on a learned subject, did not talk of it at all. And society generally—just now especially absorbed in other things—was absolutely indifferent. In the press, too, for a whole month there was not a word about his book.

Sergey Ivanovich had calculated to a nicety the time necessary for writing a review, but a month passed, and a second, and still there was silence.

Only in the *Northern Beetle*, in a comic article on the singer Drabanti, who had lost his voice, was there a contemptuous allusion to Koznyshev's book, suggesting that the book had been long ago seen through by everyone, and was a subject of general ridicule.

At last in the third month a critical article appeared in a serious review. Sergey Ivanovich knew the author of the article. He had met him once at Golubtsov's.

The author of the article was a young, sickly man, very bold as a writer but extremely deficient in breeding and shy in personal relations.

In spite of his absolute contempt for the author, it was with complete respect that Sergey Ivanovich set about reading the article. The article was terrible.

The critic had undoubtedly put an interpretation upon the book which could not possibly be put on it. But he had selected quotations so adroitly that for people who had not read the book (and obviously scarcely anyone had read it) it seemed absolutely clear that the whole book was nothing but a medley of high-flown phrases, not even—as suggested by marks of interrogation—used appropriately, and that the author of the book was a person absolutely without knowledge of the subject. And all this was so wittily done that Sergey Ivanovich would not have disowned such wit himself. But that was just what was so terrible.

In spite of the scrupulous conscientiousness with which Sergey Ivanovich verified the correctness of the critic's arguments, he did not for a minute stop to ponder over the faults and mistakes that were ridiculed; but unconsciously he began immediately trying to recall every detail of his meeting and conversation with the author of the article.

"Didn't I offend him in some way?" Sergey Ivanovich wondered.

And remembering that when they met he had corrected the young man about something he had said that betrayed ignorance, Sergey Ivanovich found the clue to explain the article.

This article was followed by a deadly silence about the book both in the press and in conversation, and Sergey Ivanovich saw that his six years' task, toiled at with such love and labor, had gone, leaving no trace.

Sergey Ivanovich's position was still more difficult owing to the fact that, since he had finished his book, he had had no more literary work to do such as had hitherto occupied the greater part of his time.

Sergey Ivanovich was clever, cultivated, healthy, and energetic, and he did not know what use to make of his energy. Conversations in drawing rooms, in meetings, assemblies, and committees—everywhere where talk was possible—took up part of his time. But being used to town life for years, he did not waste all his energies in talk, as his less experienced younger brother did, when he was in Moscow. He had a great deal of leisure and intellectual energy still to dispose of.

Fortunately for him at this difficult period following the failure of his book, the various public questions of the dissenting sects,[1] of the American alliance,[2] of the Samara famine,[3] of exhibitions, and of spiritualism were definitely replaced in public interest by the Slavonic question, which had hitherto rather languidly interested society, and Sergey Ivanovich, who had been one of the first to raise this subject, threw himself into it heart and soul.

In the circle to which Sergey Ivanovich belonged, nothing was talked of or written about just now but the Serbian War. Everything that the idle crowd usually does to kill time was done now for the benefit of the Slavic States. Balls, concerts, dinners, speeches, fashion, beer, restaurants—everything testified to sympathy with the Slavic peoples.

From much of what was spoken and written on the subject, Sergey Ivanovich differed on various points. He saw that the Slavic question had become one of those fashionable distractions which succeed one another in providing society with an object and an occupation. He

---

[1] I.e., the Uniats of Polish provinces who, in 1875, were pressured to convert to Russian Orthodoxy.

[2] During the American Civil War, Aleksandr II, as a token of friendship, sent a squadron of soldiers to help the North. In 1866, after an attempt to kill the Tsar had failed, the United States sent a friendly mission (headed by a certain Captain Fox) to St. Petersburg.

[3] The famine that struck the Samara province in 1873.

saw, too, that a great many people were taking up the subject from motives of self-interest and self-advertisement. He recognized that the newspapers published a great deal that was superfluous and exaggerated, with the sole aim of attracting attention and outcrying one another. He saw that in this general movement those who thrust themselves forward the most and shouted the loudest were men who had failed and were smarting under a sense of injury—generals without armies, ministers not in the ministry, journalists not on any paper, party leaders without followers. He saw that there was a great deal in it that was frivolous and absurd. But he also recognized an unmistakable growing enthusiasm, uniting all classes, with which it was impossible not to sympathize. The massacre of Slavs who were fellow Christians, and Slav brethren, excited sympathy for the sufferers and indignation against the oppressors. And the heroism of the Serbians and Montenegrins, struggling for a great cause, begot in the whole people a longing to help their brothers not in word but in deed.

But in this there was another aspect that rejoiced Sergey Ivanovich. That was the manifestation of public opinion. The public had definitely expressed its desire. The soul of the people had, as Sergey Ivanovich said, found expression. And the more he worked in this cause, the more incontestable it seemed to him that it was a cause destined to assume vast dimensions, to create an epoch in Russian history.

He threw himself heart and soul into the service of this great cause, and forgot to think about his book. His whole time now was engrossed by it, so that he could scarcely manage to answer all the letters and appeals addressed to him. He worked the whole spring and part of the summer, and it was only in July that he prepared to go away to his brother's in the country.

He was going both to rest for two weeks and, in the sacred heart of the nation, in the farthest depths of the country, to enjoy the sight of that uprising of the natural spirit of which, like all residents in the capital and large cities, he was fully convinced. Katavasov had long been meaning to carry out his promise to stay with Levin, and so he was going with him.

Sergey Ivanovich and Katavasov had only just reached the Kurski station, which was particularly busy and full of people that day, when, looking round for the footman who was following with their things, they saw a party of volunteers driving up in four cabs. Ladies met them with bouquets of flowers, and followed by the rushing crowd, they went into the station.

One of the ladies who had met the volunteers came out of the hall and addressed Sergey Ivanovich.

"You too come to see them off?" she asked in French.

"No, I'm going away myself, Princess. To my brother's for a holiday. Do you always see them off?" said Sergey Ivanovich with a hardly perceptible smile.

"Oh, that would be impossible!" answered the princess. "Is it true that eight hundred have been sent from us already? Malvinsky wouldn't believe me."

"More than eight hundred. If you count those who have been sent not directly from Moscow, over a thousand," answered Sergey Ivanovich.

"There! That's just what I said!" exclaimed the lady. "And it's true too, I suppose, that more than a million has been subscribed?"

"Yes, Princess."

"What do you say to today's telegram? Beaten the Turks again."

"Yes, so I saw," Sergey Ivanovich answered. They were speaking of the last telegram stating that the Turks had been beaten for three days in succession at all points and put to flight, and that tomorrow a decisive engagement was expected.

"Ah, by the way, a splendid young fellow has asked leave to go, and they've made some difficulty, I don't know why. I meant to ask you; I know him; please write a note about his case. He's being sent by Countess Lydia Ivanovna."

Sergey Ivanovich asked for all the details the princess knew about the young man, and going into the first-class waiting room, he wrote a note to the proper authorities and handed it to the princess.

"You know Count Vronsky, the notorious . . . is going by this train?" said the princess with a smile full of triumph and meaning, when he found her again and gave her the letter.

"I had heard he was going, but I did not know when. By this train?"

"I've seen him. He's here: there's only his mother seeing him off. It's the best thing, anyway, that he could do."

"Oh, yes, of course."

While they were talking the crowd streamed by them into the restaurant. They went forward too, and heard a gentleman with a glass in his hand delivering a loud discourse to the volunteers. "In the service of religion, humanity, and our brothers," the gentleman said, his voice growing louder and louder; "to this great cause, mother Moscow dedicates you with her blessing. Zhivio!"[1] he concluded, loudly and tearfully.

Everyone shouted "Zhivio!" and a fresh crowd dashed into the hall, almost carrying the princess off her legs.

"Ah, Princess! That was something!" said Stepan Arkadyevich, suddenly appearing in the middle of the crowd and beaming upon them with a delighted smile. "Wonderfully, warmly said, wasn't it? Bravo! And Sergey Ivanovich! Why, you ought to have said something—just a few words, you know, to encourage them; you do that so well," he added with a soft, respectful, and discreet smile, moving Sergey Ivanovich forward a little by the arm.

"No, I'm just off."

"Where to?"

"To the country, to my brother's," answered Sergey Ivanovich.

"Then you'll see my wife. I've written to her, but you'll see her first. Please tell her that you've seen me and that it's 'all right,' as the English say. She'll understand. Oh, and be so good as to tell her I'm appointed secretary of the committee . . . But she'll understand! You know, *les petites misères de la vie humaine*,"[2] he said, as if apologizing, to the princess. "And Princess Myahkaya—not Liza, but Bibiche— is sending a thousand rifles and twelve nurses. Did I tell you?"

"Yes, I heard," Koznyshev answered indifferently.

[1]Serbian cheer: "Hurrah!" "Hail."
[2]"The small miseries of human life"

"It's a pity you're going away," said Stepan Arkadyevich. "Tomorrow we're giving a dinner to two who're setting off—Dimer-Bartnyansky from Petersburg and our Veslovsky, Grisha. They're both going. Veslovsky's only lately married. There's a fine fellow for you! Eh, Princess?" he said, turning to the lady.

The princess looked at Koznyshev without replying. But the fact that Sergey Ivanovich and the princess seemed anxious to get rid of him did not in the least disconcert Stepan Arkadyevich. Smiling, he stared at the feather in the princess's hat and then about him, as though he was going to pick something up. Seeing a lady approaching with a collection box, he beckoned to her and put in a five-ruble note.

"I can never see these collection boxes unmoved while I've money in my pocket," he said. "And how about today's telegram? Fine fellows those Montenegrins!"

"You don't say so!" he cried when the princess told him that Vronsky was going by this train. For an instant Stepan Arkadyevich's face looked sad, but a minute later, when, smoothing his whiskers and with a spring in his walk, he went into the hall where Vronsky was, he had completely forgotten his own despairing sobs over his sister's corpse, and he saw in Vronsky only a hero and an old friend.

"With all his faults, one can't refuse to do him justice," said the princess to Sergey Ivanovich as soon as Stepan Arkadyevich had left them. "What a typically Russian, Slav nature! Only, I'm afraid it won't be pleasant for Vronsky to see him. Say what you will, I'm touched by that man's fate. Do talk to him a little on the way," said the princess.

"Yes, perhaps, if it happens so."

"I never liked him. But this atones for a great deal. He's not merely going himself, he's taking a squadron at his own expense."

"Yes, so I heard."

A bell sounded. Everyone crowded to the doors. "Here he is!" said the princess, indicating Vronsky, who, with his mother on his arm, walked by, wearing a long overcoat and wide-brimmed black hat. Oblonsky was walking beside him, talking eagerly of something.

Vronsky was frowning and looking straight before him, as though he did not hear what Stepan Arkadyevich was saying.

Probably on Oblonsky's pointing them out, he looked around in the direction where the princess and Sergey Ivanovich were standing, and without speaking, he lifted his hat. His face, aged and worn by suffering, looked stony.

Going to the platform, Vronsky left his mother and disappeared into a compartment.

On the platform there rang out "God save the Tsar," then shouts of "Hurrah!" and "Zhivio!" One of the volunteers, a tall, very young man with a hollow chest, was particularly conspicuous, bowing and waving his felt hat and a bouquet over his head. From behind him two officers emerged, and an elderly man with a big beard, wearing a greasy cap, and they bowed.

CHAPTER THREE

Saying good-by to the princess, Sergey Ivanovich was joined by Katavasov; together they got into a carriage full to overflowing, and the train started.

At Tsaritsyno station the train was met by a chorus of young men singing "*Slavsya!*"[1] Again the volunteers bowed and poked their heads out, but Sergey Ivanovich paid no attention to them. He had had so much to do with the volunteers that the type was familiar to him and did not interest him. Katavasov, whose scientific work had prevented his having a chance of observing them hitherto, was very much interested in them and questioned Sergey Ivanovich.

Sergey Ivanovich advised him to go into the second-class carriage and talk to them himself. At the next station Katavasov acted on this suggestion.

At the first stop he moved into the second-class and made the acquaintance of the volunteers. They were sitting in a corner of the carriage, talking loudly and obviously aware that the attention of the passengers and Katavasov as he got in was concentrated upon them. More loudly than all talked the tall, hollow-chested young man. He was unmistakably tipsy, and was relating some story that had occurred at his school. Facing him sat a middle-aged officer

---

[1]"Hail to Thee!" from the opera *A Life for the Tsar* by Mikhail Glinka (1803-57).

wearing the military jacket of the Austrian Guards. He was listening with a smile to the hollow-chested youth, and tried to stop him. The third, in an artillery uniform, was sitting on a trunk beside them. A fourth was asleep.

Entering into conversation with the youth, Katavasov learned that he was a wealthy Moscow merchant who had run through a large fortune before he was twenty-two. Katavasov did not like him, because he was effeminate and spoiled and sickly. He was obviously convinced, especially now after drinking, that he was performing a heroic action, and he bragged of it in the most unpleasant way.

The second, the retired officer, made an unpleasant impression too upon Katavasov. He was, it seemed, a man who had tried everything. He had been on a railway, had been a steward on an estate, and had started factories, and he talked, quite without necessity, of all he had done, and used learned expressions quite inappropriately.

The third, the artilleryman, on the contrary, struck Katavasov very favorably. He was a quiet, modest fellow, unmistakably impressed by the knowledge of the officer and the heroic self-sacrifice of the merchant and saying nothing about himself. When Katavasov asked him what had impelled him to go to Serbia, he answered modestly:

"Oh, well, everyone's going. The Serbians need help, too. I'm sorry for them."

"Yes, you artillerymen especially are scarce there," said Katavasov.

"Oh, I wasn't in the artillery long; maybe they'll put me into the infantry or the cavalry."

"Into the infantry when they need artillery more than anything?" said Katavasov, concluding from the artilleryman's apparent age that he must have reached a fairly high grade.

"I wasn't in the artillery long; I'm a retired cadet," he said, and he began to explain how he had failed in his examination.[2]

All of this together made a disagreeable impression on Katavasov, and when the volunteers got out at a station for a drink, Katavasov would have liked to compare his unfavorable impression in conversation with someone. There was an old man in the carriage, wearing a military overcoat, who had been listening all the while to

---

[2]For a commission.

Katavasov's conversation with the volunteers. When they were left alone, Katavasov addressed him.

"What different positions they come from, all those fellows who are going off there," Katavasov said vaguely, not wishing to express his own opinion and at the same time anxious to find out the old man's views.

The old man was an officer who had served in two campaigns. He knew what makes a soldier, and judging by the appearance and the talk of those persons, by the swagger with which they had recourse to the bottle on the journey, he considered them poor soldiers. More-over, he lived in a district town, and he was longing to tell how one soldier had volunteered from his town, a drunkard and a thief whom no one would employ as a laborer. But knowing from experience that in the present condition of the public temper it was dangerous to express an opinion opposed to the general one, and especially to crit-icize the volunteers unfavorably, he watched Katavasov without com-mitting himself.

"Well, men are needed there," he said, laughing with his eyes. And they began talking of the latest war news, and each concealed from the other his perplexity as to the engagement expected the next day, since the Turks had been beaten, according to the latest news, at all points. And so they parted, neither giving expression to his opinion.

Katavasov went back to his own carriage and, with reluctant pre-varication, reported to Sergey Ivanovich his observation of the vol-unteers, from which it would appear that they were excellent fellows.

At the next big station the volunteers were again greeted with shouts and singing, again men and women with collection boxes appeared, and provincial ladies brought bouquets to the volunteers and followed them into the refreshment room; but all this was on a much smaller and feebler scale than in Moscow.

CHAPTER FOUR

While the train was stopping at the provincial town, Sergey Ivanovich did not go to the refreshment room, but walked up and down the platform.

The first time he passed Vronsky's compartment he noticed that the curtain was drawn over the window, but as he passed it the second time he saw the old countess at the window. She beckoned to Koznyshev.

"I'm going, you see, taking him as far as Kursk," she said.

"Yes, so I heard," said Sergey Ivanovich, standing at her window and looking in. "What a noble act on his part!" he added, noticing that Vronsky was not in the compartment.

"Yes, after his misfortune, what was there for him to do?"

"What a terrible thing it was!" said Sergey Ivanovich.

"Ah, what I have been through! But do get in . . . Ah, what I have been through!" she repeated, when Sergey Ivanovich had got in and sat down beside her. "You can't conceive it! For six weeks he did not speak to anyone, and would not touch food except when I implored him. And not for one minute could we leave him alone. We took away everything he could have used against himself. We lived on the ground floor, but there was no counting on anything. You know, of course, that he had shot himself once already on her account," she said, and the old lady's eyelashes twitched at the recollection. "Yes, hers was the fitting end for such a woman. Even the death she chose was coarse and vulgar."

"It's not for us to judge, Countess," said Sergey Ivanovich; "but I can understand that it has been very hard for you."

"Ah, don't speak of it! I was staying on my estate, and he was with me. A note was brought him. He wrote an answer and sent it off. We hadn't an idea that she was close by at the station. In the evening I had only just gone to my room, when my Marya told me a lady had thrown herself under the train. Something seemed to strike me at once. I knew it was she. The first thing I said was he was not to be told. But they'd told him already. His coachman was there and saw it all. When I ran into his room, he was beside himself—it was fearful to see him. He didn't say a word, but galloped off to the station. I don't know to this day what happened there, but he was brought back at death's door. I wouldn't have known him. *Prostration complète*,[1] the doctor said. And that was followed almost by madness. Oh, why

[1] "Complete prostration."

talk of it!" said the countess with a wave of her hand. "It was an awful time! No, say what you will, she was a bad woman. Why, what is the meaning of such desperate passion? It was all to prove something extraordinary. Well, and that she did do. She brought herself to ruin and two good men—her husband and my unhappy son."

"And what did her husband do?" asked Sergey Ivanovich.

"He took her daughter. Alyosha was ready to agree to anything at first. Now it worries him terribly that he should have given his own child away to another man. But he can't take back his word. Karenin came to the funeral. But we tried to prevent his meeting Alyosha. For him, for her husband, it was easier, anyway. She had set him free. But my poor son was utterly given up to her. He had thrown up everything, his career, me . . . and even then she had no mercy on him, but deliberately made his ruin complete. No, say what you will, her very death was the death of a vile woman of no religious feeling. God forgive me, but I can't help hating the memory of her, when I look at my son's misery!"

"But how is he now?"

"It was a blessing from Providence for us—this Serbian war. I'm old, and I don't understand the rights and wrongs of it, but it's come as a providential blessing to him. Of course for me, as his mother, it's terrible; and what's worse, they say, *ce n'est pas très bien vu à Péters-bourg*[2]. But it can't be helped! It was the one thing that could rouse him. Yashvin—a friend of his—he had lost all he had at cards and he was going to Serbia. He came to see him and persuaded him to go. Now it's an interest for him. Do please talk to him a little. I want to distract his mind. He's so miserable. And as bad luck would have it, he has a toothache too. But he'll be delighted to see you. Please do talk to him; he's walking up and down on that side."

Sergey Ivanovich said he would be very glad to, and crossed over to the other side of the station.

[2]"It is not favorably regarded in Petersburg."

CHAPTER FIVE

In the slanting evening shadows cast by sacks piled up on the platform, Vronsky in his long overcoat and slouch hat, with his hands in his pockets, strode up and down like a wild beast in a cage, turning sharply after twenty paces. Sergey Ivanovich thought, as he approached him, that Vronsky saw him but was pretending not to. This did not affect Sergey Ivanovich in the slightest. He was above all personal considerations with Vronsky.

At that moment Sergey Ivanovich looked upon Vronsky as a man taking an important part in a great cause, and thought it his duty to encourage him and express his approval. He went up to him.

Vronsky stood still, looked intently at him, recognized him, and, going a few steps forward to meet him, shook hands with him very warmly.

"Possibly you didn't wish to see me," said Sergey Ivanovich, "but couldn't I be of use to you?"

"There's no one I would less dislike seeing than you," said Vronsky. "Forgive me, but there's nothing in life for me to like."

"I quite understand, and I merely meant to offer you my services," said Sergey Ivanovich, scanning Vronsky's face, full of unmistakable suffering. "Wouldn't it be of use to you to have a letter to Ristich—to Milan?"

"Oh, no!" Vronsky said, seeming to understand him with difficulty. "If you don't mind, let's walk on. It's so stuffy among the carriages. A letter? No, thank you; to meet death, one needs no letters of introduction. Nor for the Turks . . . " he said, with a smile that was merely of the lips. His eyes still kept their look of angry suffering.

"Yes; but you might find it easier to establish connections, which are, after all, essential, with anyone previously prepared. But, as you like. I was very glad to hear of your intention. There have been so many attacks made on the volunteers, and a man like you raises them in the public esteem."

"My use as a man," said Vronsky, "is that life's worth nothing to me. And that I've enough physical energy to hack my way into their ranks, and to trample on them or fall—I know that. I'm glad there's something to give my life for, for it's not merely useless but loathsome to me. Anyone's welcome to it." And his jaw twitched impatiently from the incessant gnawing toothache, which prevented him from even speaking with natural expression.

"You will become a new man, I predict," said Sergey Ivanovich, feeling touched. "To deliver one's brothers from bondage is an aim worth death and life. God grant you success outwardly—and inwardly peace," he added, and he held out his hand. Vronsky warmly pressed his outstretched hand.

"Yes, as a weapon I may be of some use. But as a man, I'm a wreck," he said, hesitating between words.

He could hardly speak because of the throbbing ache in his strong teeth, which flooded his mouth with saliva. He was silent, and his eyes rested on the wheels of the tender, slowly and smoothly rolling along the rails.

And all at once a different pain, not an ache, but a tormenting inner disquiet that set his whole being in anguish, made him for an instant forget his toothache. As he glanced at the tender and the rails, stirred by the conversation he had just had with a friend he had not met since his misfortune, he suddenly recalled *her*—that is, what was left of her when he had run like one mad into the shed of the railway station—on the table, shamelessly sprawled out among strangers, the blood-stained body so recently full of life; the head unhurt, thrown back with its weight of hair, and the curling tresses about the temples, and the exquisite face, with red, half-opened mouth, the strange, frozen expression, piteous on the lips and awful in the fixed open eyes, that seemed to utter that fearful phrase she had used when they last quarreled—that he would be sorry for it.

And he tried to think of her as she was when he met her the first time, at a railway station too, mysterious, exquisite, loving, seeking and giving happiness, and not cruelly vengeful as he remembered her that last moment. He tried to recall his best moments with her, but those moments were poisoned forever. He could think of her only as triumphant in having carried out her threat to inflict him with a wholly useless but wholly ineffaceable remorse. He lost all consciousness of toothache, and his face was distorted with sobs.

Passing twice up and down beside the sacks in silence and regaining his self-possession, he addressed Sergey Ivanovich calmly:

"You don't know of any dispatch since yesterday's? Yes, driven back for a third time, but a decisive engagement is expected for tomorrow."

And after talking a little more of the proclamation of Milan as king, and the immense effect it might have, they parted, going to their carriages on hearing the second bell.

CHAPTER SIX

Sergey Ivanovich had not telegraphed his brother to send to meet him, as he did not know when he would be able to leave Moscow. Levin was not at home when Katavasov and Sergey Ivanovich, in a fly hired at the station, drove up to the steps of the Pokrovskoe house, as black as Moors from the dust of the road. Kitty, sitting on the balcony with her father and sister, recognized her brother-in-law, and ran down to meet him.

"What a shame not to have let us know," she said, giving her hand to Sergey Ivanovich and putting her forehead up for him to kiss.

"We got here easily, and have not put you out," answered Sergey Ivanovich. "I'm so dirty. I'm afraid to touch you. I've been so busy, I didn't know when I would be able to tear myself away. And so you're still as ever enjoying your peaceful, quiet happiness," he said, smiling, "out of reach of the current in your peaceful backwater. Here's our friend. Fyodor Vasilievich[1] has succeeded in getting here at last."

"But I'm not a Moor, I shall look like a human being when I wash," said Katavasov in his jesting fashion, and he shook hands and smiled, his teeth flashing white in his black face.

"Kostya will be delighted. He has gone to the farm. It's time he should be home."

"Busy as ever with his farming. It really is a peaceful backwater," said Katavasov; "while we in town think of nothing but the Serbian war. Well, how does our friend look at it? He's sure not to think like other people."

---

[1]On page 504, Katavasov is called Mikhail Semyonvich. The Academy Edition does not resolve this inconsistency.

"Oh, I don't know, like everybody else," Kitty answered, a little embarrassed, looking round at Sergey Ivanovich. "I'll send to fetch him. Papa's staying with us. He's only just come home from abroad."

And making arrangements to send for Levin and for the guests to wash, one in his room and the other in what had been Dolly's, and giving orders for their luncheon, Kitty ran out onto the balcony, enjoying the freedom and rapidity of movement, of which she had been deprived during the months of her pregnancy.

"It's Sergey Ivanovich and Katavasov, a professor," she said.

"Oh, that's too much in this heat," said the prince.

"No, Papa, he's very nice, and Kostya's very fond of him," Kitty said, with a deprecating smile, noticing the irony on her father's face.

"Oh, I didn't say anything."

"You go to them, darling," said Kitty to her sister, "and entertain them. They saw Stiva at the station; he was quite well. And I must run to Mitya. I'm afraid I haven't fed him since breakfast. He's awake now, and sure to be screaming." And feeling the flow of milk, she hurried to the nursery.

This was not a mere guess; her bond with the child was still so close that she could gauge by the flow of her milk his need for food, and knew for certain he was hungry.

She knew he was crying before she reached the nursery. And he was indeed crying. She heard him and hastened. But the faster she went, the louder he screamed. It was a fine healthy scream, hungry and impatient.

"Has he been screaming long, nurse, very long?" said Kitty hurriedly, seating herself on a chair and preparing to give the baby the breast. "But give him to me quickly. Oh, nurse, how tiresome you are! There, tie the cap afterwards!"

The baby was convulsed with hungry yells.

"But you can't manage so, ma'am," said Agafya Mikhailovna, who was almost always to be found in the nursery. "He must be put straight. A-oo! a-oo!" she cooed over him, paying no attention to the mother.

The nurse brought the baby to his mother. Agafya Mikhailovna followed him with a face dissolving with tenderness.

"He knows me, he knows me. In God's faith, Katerina Aleksandrovna, ma'am, he knew me!" Agafya Mikhailovna cried above the baby's screams.

But Kitty did not hear her words. Her impatience kept growing, like the baby's.

Their impatience hindered things for a while. The baby could not get hold of the breast right, and was furious.

At last, after despairing, breathless screaming and vain sucking things went right, and mother and child felt simultaneously soothed, and both subsided in calm.

"But poor darling, he's all sweaty!" said Kitty in a whisper, touching the baby.

"What makes you think he knows you?" she added, with a sidelong glance at the baby's eyes, which peered roguishly, it seemed to her, from under his cap, at his rhythmically puffing cheeks, and at the little rosy palm with which he made circular movements.

"Impossible! If he knew anyone, he would have known me," said Kitty, in response to Agafya Mikhailovna's statement, and she smiled.

She smiled because, though she said he could not know her, in her heart she was sure that he knew not merely Agafya Mikhailovna, but knew and understood everything, and knew and understood a great deal too that no one else knew, and that she, his mother, had learned and come to understand only through him. To Agafya Mikhailovna, to the nurse, to his grandfather, to his father even, Mitya was a living being, requiring only material care, but for his mother he had long been a mortal being, with whom there had been a whole series of spiritual relations already.

"When he wakes up, please God, you shall see for yourself. Then when I do like this, he simply beams on me, the darling! Simply beams like a sunny day!" said Agafya Mikhailovna.

"Well, well; then we shall see," whispered Kitty. "But now go away, he's going to sleep."

CHAPTER SEVEN

Agafya Mikhailovna went out on tiptoe; the nurse let down the blind, chased a fly out from under the muslin canopy of the crib, and a bumblebee struggling against the windowpane, and sat down waving a withered branch of birch over the mother and the baby.

"How hot it is! If God would only send a drop of rain," she said.

"Yes, yes, sh—sh—sh—" was all Kitty answered, rocking a little, and tenderly squeezing the plump little arm, with rolls of fat at the wrist, which Mitya still waved feebly as he opened and shut his eyes. That hand worried Kitty; she longed to kiss it but was afraid to for fear of waking him. At last the little hand ceased waving, and the eyes closed. Only from time to time, as he went on sucking, the baby raised his long, curly eyelashes and peeped at his mother with wet eyes that looked black in the twilight. The nurse had stopped fanning, and was dozing. From above came the peals of the old prince's voice, and the chuckle of Katavasov.

"They got into conversation without me," thought Kitty, "but still it's vexing that Kostya's out. He's sure to have gone to the apiary again. Though it's a pity he's there so often, still I'm glad. It distracts his mind. He's become altogether happier and better now than in the spring. He used to be so gloomy and worried, I felt frightened for him. And how funny he is!" she whispered, smiling.

She knew what tormented her husband. It was his lack of faith. Although, had she been asked whether she supposed that in the future life, if he did not believe, he would be damned, she would have had to admit that he would be damned, his lack of faith did not cause her unhappiness. And she, confessing that for an unbeliever there can be no salvation, and loving her husband's soul more than anything in the world, thought with a smile of his skepticism, and told herself that he was funny.

"Why does he keep reading philosophy of some sort all this year?" she wondered. "If it's all written in those books, he can understand them. If it's all wrong, why does he read them? He says himself that he would like to believe. Then why is it he doesn't believe? Because he thinks so much? And he thinks so much from being solitary. He's always alone, alone. He can't talk about it to us. I imagine he'll be glad of these visitors, especially Katavasov. He likes discussions with them," she thought, and passed instantly to the consideration of where it would be more convenient to put Katavasov, to sleep alone or to share Sergey Ivanovich's room. And then an idea suddenly struck her which made her shudder and even disturb Mitya, who glanced severely at her. "I do believe the laundress hasn't sent the washing yet, and all the best sheets are in use. If I don't see to it, Agafya Mikhailovna will give Sergey Ivanovich the wrong sheets," and at the very idea of this the blood rushed to Kitty's face.

"Yes, I will arrange it," she decided, and going back to her former thoughts, she remembered that some spiritual question of importance had been interrupted, and she began to recall what. "Yes, Kostya, an unbeliever," she thought again with a smile.

"Well, an unbeliever, then! Better let him always be one than like Madame Stahl, or what I tried to be in those days abroad. No, he won't ever pretend."

And a recent instance of his goodness rose vividly to her mind. Two weeks before a penitent letter had come from Stepan Arkadyevich to Dolly. He besought her to save his honor, to sell her estate to pay his debts. Dolly was in despair, she detested her husband, despised him, pitied him, resolved on a separation, resolved to refuse, but ended by agreeing to sell part of her property. After that, with an irrepressible smile of tenderness, Kitty recalled her husband's shame-faced embarrassment, his repeated awkward efforts to approach the subject, and how at last, having thought of the one means of helping Dolly without wounding her pride, he had suggested to Kitty—what had not occurred to her before—that she should give up her share of the property.

"He an unbeliever indeed! With his heart, his dread of offending anyone, even a child! Everything for others, nothing for himself. Sergey Ivanovich simply considers it Kostya's duty to be his steward. And it's the same with his sister. Now Dolly and her children are under his guardianship; all these peasants who come to him every day, as though he were bound to be at their service."

"Yes, only be like your father, only like him," she said, handing Mitya over to the nurse and putting her lips to his cheek.

CHAPTER EIGHT

Ever since, by his beloved brother's deathbed, Levin had first glanced into the questions of life and death in the light of these new convictions, as he called them, which had during the period from his twentieth to his thirty-fourth year imperceptibly replaced his childish and youthful beliefs—he had been stricken with horror, not so much of death, as of life, without any knowledge of whence, and why, and how, and what it was. The organism, its decay, the indestructibility of matter, the law of the conservation of energy, evolution, were the words that usurped the place of his old belief. These words and the ideas associated with them were very useful for intellectual purposes. But for life they yielded nothing, and Levin felt suddenly like a man who has changed his warm fur cloak for a muslin garment, and, going for the first time into the frost, is immediately convinced, not by reason, but by his whole nature that he is as good as naked, and that he must inevitably perish miserably.

From that moment, though he did not distinctly face it and still went on living as before, Levin had never lost this sense of terror at his lack of knowledge.

He vaguely felt, too, that what he called his new convictions were not merely lack of knowledge but were part of a whole order of ideas in which no knowledge of what he needed was possible.

At first, marriage, with the new joys and duties bound up with it, had completely crowded out these thoughts. But of late, while he was staying in Moscow after his wife's confinement, with nothing to do, the question that clamored for solution had more and more often, more and more insistently, haunted Levin's mind.

The question was summed up for him thus: "If I do not accept the answers Christianity gives to the problems of my life, what answers do I accept?" And in the whole arsenal of his convictions, far from finding any satisfactory answers, he was utterly unable to find anything at all like an answer.

He was in the position of a man seeking food in a toy shop or at a gunsmith's.

Instinctively, unconsciously with every book, with every conversation, with every man he met, he was on the lookout for light on these questions and their solution.

What puzzled and distracted him above everything was that the majority of men of his age and circle had, like him, exchanged their old beliefs for the same new convictions, and yet saw nothing to lament in this, and were perfectly satisfied and serene. So that, apart from the principal question, Levin was tortured by other questions too. Were these people sincere? he asked himself, or were they playing a part? Or was it that they understood the answers science gave to these problems in some different, clearer sense than he did? And he assiduously studied both these men's opinions and the books that treated these scientific explanations.

One fact he had found out since these questions had engrossed his mind: he had been quite wrong in supposing, from the recollections of the circle of his young days at college, that religion had outlived its day, and that it was now practically non-existent. All the people near to him, who lived good lives, were believers. The old prince, and Lvov, whom he liked so much, and Sergey Ivanovich, and all the women believed, and his wife believed as simply as he had believed in his earliest childhood, and ninety-nine hundredths of the Russian people, all the working people for whose life he felt the deepest respect, believed.

Another fact of which he became convinced, after reading many scientific books, was that the men who shared his views did not surmise anything in those convictions, and that they gave no explanation of the questions which he felt he could not live without answering, but simply ignored their existence and attempted to explain other questions of no possible interest to him, such as the evolution of organisms, a mechanistic explanation of the soul, and so on.

Moreover, during his wife's confinement, something had happened that seemed extraordinary to him. He, an unbeliever, had fallen into praying, and at the moment he prayed be believed. But that moment had passed, and he could not make his state of mind at that moment fit into the rest of his life.

He could not admit that at that moment he knew the truth, and that now he was wrong; for as soon as he began thinking calmly about it, it all fell to pieces. He could not admit that he was mistaken then, for his spiritual condition then was precious to him, and to admit that it was proof of weakness would have been to desecrate those moments. He was miserably divided against himself, and strained all his spiritual forces to the utmost to escape from this condition.

CHAPTER NINE

These doubts oppressed and tortured him, growing weaker or stronger from time to time, but never leaving him. He read and thought, and the more he read and the more he thought, the further he felt from the aim he was pursuing.

Of late in Moscow and in the country, since he had become convinced that he would find no solution in the materialists, he had read and reread thoroughly Plato, Spinoza, Kant, Schelling, Hegel, and Schopenhauer, the philosophers who gave a non-materialistic explanation of life.

Their ideas seemed to him fruitful when he was reading or was himself seeking arguments to refute other theories, especially those of the materialists; but as soon as he began to read or sought for himself a solution of problems, the same thing always happened. As long as he followed the fixed definition of obscure words such as "spirit," "will," "freedom," "substance," purposely letting himself enter the verbal trap set by the philosophers or himself, he seemed to comprehend something. But he had only to forget the artificial train of reasoning, and to turn from life itself to what had satisfied him while thinking in accordance with the fixed definitions, and this artificial edifice fell to pieces at once like a house of cards, and it became clear that the edifice had been built up out of those transposed words, apart from anything in life more important than reason.

At one time, reading Schopenhauer, he put in place of his "will" the word "love," and for a couple of days this new philosophy charmed him, till he moved a little away from it. But then, when he turned from life itself to glance at it again, it fell away too, and proved to be the same muslin garment with no warmth in it.

Sergey Ivanovich advised him to read the theological works of Khomyakov.[1] Levin read the second volume of Khomyakov's works, and in spite of the elegant, epigrammatic, argumentative style which at first repelled him, he was impressed by the doctrine of the church he found in them. He was struck at first by the idea that the apprehension of divine truths had not been vouchsafed to man but to a corporation of men bound together by love—to the church. What delighted him was the thought of how much easier it was to believe in a still existing living church, embracing all the beliefs of men, and having God at its head, and therefore holy and infallible, and from it to accept the faith in God, in the creation, the fall, the redemption, than to begin with God, a mysterious, faraway God, the creation, etc. But afterwards, on reading a Catholic writer's history of the church, and then a Greek Orthodox writer's history of the church, and seeing that the two churches, in their very conception infallible, each deny the authority of the other, Khomyakov's doctrine of the church lost all its charm for him, and this edifice crumbled into dust like the philosophers' edifices.

All that spring he was not himself, and went through fearful moments of horror.

"Without knowing what I am and why I am here, life's impossible; and that I can't know, and so I can't live," Levin said to himself.

"In infinite time, in infinite matter, in infinite space, is formed a bubble-organism, and that bubble lasts a while and bursts, and that bubble is I."

It was an agonizing fallacy, but it was the sole logical result of ages of human thought in that direction.

This was the ultimate belief on which all the systems elaborated by human thought in almost all their ramifications rested. It was the prevalent conviction, and of all other explanations Levin had unconsciously, not knowing when or how, chosen it as, at any rate, the clearest, and made it his own.

But it was not merely a fallacy, it was the cruel jest of some wicked power, some evil, hateful power, to whom one could not submit.

He must escape from this power. And the means of escape every

[1]Aleksey Khomyakov (1804-60), Slavophile philosopher.

man had in his own hands. He had but to cut short this dependence on evil. And there was one means—death.

And Levin, a happy father and husband, in perfect health, was several times so near suicide that he hid a rope so that he might not be tempted to hang himself, and was afraid to go out with his gun for fear of shooting himself.

But Levin did not shoot himself, and did not hang himself; he went on living.

CHAPTER TEN

When Levin thought about what he was and what he was living for, he could find no answer to the questions and was reduced to despair, but when he ceased questioning himself about it, it seemed as though he knew both what he was and why he was living, for he acted and lived resolutely and without hesitation. Indeed, in these latter days he was far more decided and unhesitating than he had ever been in his life.

When he went back to the country at the beginning of June, he went back also to his usual pursuits. The management of the estate, his relations with the peasants and the neighbors, the care of his household, the management of his sister's and brother's property, of which he had the direction, his relations with his wife and kindred, the care of his child, and the new beekeeping hobby he had taken up that spring, filled all his time.

These things occupied him now, not because he justified them to himself by any sort of general principles, as he had done in former days; on the contrary, disappointed by the failure of his former efforts for the general welfare, and too much occupied with his own thought and the mass of business with which he was burdened from all sides, he had completely given up thinking of the general good, and he busied himself with all this work simply because it seemed to him that he must do what he was doing—that he could not do otherwise. In former days—almost from childhood, and increasingly up to full manhood—when he had tried to do anything that would be good for all, for humanity, for Russia, for his own village, he had noticed that the idea of it had been pleasant, but the work itself had always been clumsy, that then he had never been fully convinced of its absolute necessity, and that the work that had begun by seeming so great had grown less and less, till it vanished into nothing. But now, since his marriage, when he had begun to confine himself more and more to living for himself, though he experienced no delight at all at the thought of the work he was doing, he felt absolutely convinced of its necessity, saw that it succeeded far better than in the past, and that it kept on growing more and more.

Now—involuntarily, it seemed—he cut more and more deeply into the soil like a plow, so that he could not be drawn out without turning aside the furrow.

To live the same family life as his father and forefathers—that is, in the same condition of culture—and so bring up his children, was incontestably necessary. It was as necessary as eating when one was hungry. And to do this, just as it was necessary to cook dinner, it was necessary to keep the Pokrovskoe farmed in such a manner that it would yield profit. Just as incontestably as it was necessary to repay a debt was it necessary to keep the property in such condition that his son, when he received it as a heritage, would say thank you to his father as Levin had said thank you to his grandfather for all he'd built and planted. And to do this, it was necessary to look after land himself, not to lease it, and to breed cattle, manure the fields, and plant timber.

It was impossible not to look after the affairs of Sergey Ivanovich, of his sister, of the peasants who came to him for advice and were accustomed to do so—as impossible as to fling down a child one is carrying in one's arms. It was necessary to look after the comfort of his sister-in-law and her children, and his wife and baby, and it was impossible not to spend with them at least a short time each day.

And all this, together with shooting and his new beekeeping, filled up the whole of Levin's life, which had no meaning at all for him, when he began to think.

But besides knowing thoroughly what he had to do, Levin knew in just the same way how he had to do it all, and what was more important than the rest.

He knew he must hire laborers as cheaply as possible; but to hire men in bond, paying them in advance less than the current rate of wages, was what he must not do, even though it was very profitable. Selling straw to the peasants in times of scarcity was what he might do, even though he felt sorry of them; but the tavern and the inn must be ignored, though they were a source of income. Stealing timber must be punished as severely as possible, but he could not exact fines for cattle being driven onto his fields; and though it annoyed the keeper and made the peasants unafraid to graze their cattle on his land, he could not keep their cattle as punishment.

To Piotr, who was paying a moneylender ten per cent a month, he must lend a sum of money to set him free. But he could not let off peasants who did not pay their rent, or let them fall into arrears. It was impossible to overlook the bailiff's not having mown the meadows and letting the hay spoil; and it was equally impossible to mow those acres where a young copse had been planted. It was impossible to excuse a laborer who had gone home in the busy season because his father was dying, however sorry he might feel for him, and he must subtract from his pay those costly months of idleness. But it was impossible not to allow monthly rations to the old servants who were of no use for anything.

Levin knew that when he got home he must first of all go to his wife, who was not well, and that the peasants who had been waiting for three hours to see him could wait a little longer. He knew too that, regardless of all the pleasure he felt in hiving a swarm, he must forego that pleasure, and leave the old man to tend to the bees alone, while he talked to the peasants who had come after him to the apiary.

Whether he was acting rightly or wrongly he did not know, and not only would he not try to prove anything nowadays, but he avoided all thought or talk about it.

Deliberation had brought him to doubt, and prevented him from seeing what he ought to do and what he ought not. When he did not think, but simply lived, he was continually aware of the presence of an infallible judge in his soul, determining which of two possible courses of action was the better and which was the worse, and as soon as he did not act rightly, he was at once aware of it.

So he lived, not knowing and not seeing any chance of knowing what he was and what he was living for, harassed at this lack of knowledge to such a point that he was afraid of suicide, and yet firmly laying down his own individual and definite path in life.

CHAPTER ELEVEN

The day on which Sergey Ivanovich came to Pokrovskoe was one of Levin's most painful days. It was the very busiest season, when all the peasantry show an extraordinary intensity of self-sacrifice in labor, such as is never known in other conditions of life and would be highly esteemed if the men who showed these qualities themselves thought highly of them, and if it were not repeated every year, and if the results of this intense labor were not so simple.

To reap and bind the rye and oats and to carry it, to mow the meadows, turn over the fallows, thresh the seed and sow the winter corn—all this seems so simple and ordinary; but to succeed in getting through it all, everyone in the village, from the old man to the young child, must toil incessantly for three or four weeks, three times as hard as usual, living on kvas, onions, and black bread, threshing and carrying the sheaves at night, not giving more than two or three hours in the twenty-four to sleep. And every year this is done all over Russia.

Having lived the greater part of his life in the country and in the closest relations with the peasants, Levin always felt in this busy time that he was infected by this general quickening of energy in the people.

In the early morning he rode over to the first sowing of the rye, and to the oats, which were being carted and stacked, and returning home at the time his wife and sister-in-law were getting up, he drank coffee with them and walked to the farm, where a new threshing machine was to be set working to thresh the seed corn.

He was standing in the cool granary, which was still fragrant with the leaves of the hazel branches interlaced on the freshly peeled aspen beams of the new thatch roof. He gazed through the open door in which the dry, bitter dust of the threshing whirled and played, at the grass of the threshing floor in the sunlight and the fresh straw that had been brought in from the barn, then at the speckle-headed, white-breasted swallows that flew chirping in under the roof and, fluttering their wings, settled in the crevices of the doorway, then at the peasants bustling in the dark, dusty barn, and he thought strange thoughts.

"Why is it all being done?" he thought. "Why am I standing here, making them work? What are they all so busy for, trying to show their zeal before me? What is it that old Matryona, my old friend, is toiling for? (I doctored her when the beam fell on her in the fire)," he thought, looking at a thin old woman who was raking up the grain, moving painfully with her bare, sun-blackened feet over the uneven, rough floor. "Then she recovered, but today or tomorrow or in ten years she won't; they'll bury her and nothing will be left either of her or of that pretty girl in the red skirt, who with that skillfull, soft action shakes the ears out of their husks. They'll bury her and this piebald gelding, and very soon too," he thought, gazing at the horse heavily breathing through dilated nostrils, its belly rising and falling as it trod the slanting wheel that turned under it. "And they will bury her and Fyodor, who feeds the machine, with his curly beard full of chaff and his shirt torn on his white shoulders—they will bury him. He's untying the sheaves, and giving order, and shouting to the women, and quickly setting straight the strap on the moving wheel. And what's more, it's not them alone—me they'll bury too, and nothing will be left. What is it all for?"

He thought this, and at the same time looked at his watch to calculate how much they threshed in an hour. He wanted to know this so as to judge by it the task to set for the day.

"It'll soon be one, and they're only beginning the third sheaf," thought Levin. He went up to the man who was feeding the machine, and shouting over the roar of the machine, he told him to put it in more slowly. "You put in too much at a time, Fyodor. Do you see—it gets choked, that's why it isn't working well. Feed it evenly."

Fyodor, black with the dust that clung to his moist face, shouted something in response, but still went on doing it as Levin did not want him to.

Levin, going up to the machine, moved Fyodor aside and began feeding the corn in himself. Working on till the peasants' dinner hour, which was not long in coming, he went out of the barn with

Fyodor and started to talk with him, stopping beside a neat yellow sheaf of rye laid on the threshing floor for seed.

Fyodor came from a village some distance from the one in which Levin had once allotted land to his co-operative association. Now it had been let to a former janitor.

Levin talked to Fyodor about this land and asked whether Platon, a well-to-do peasant of good character belonging to the same village, would not take the land for the coming year.

"It's a high rent; it wouldn't pay Platon, Konstantin Dmitrievich," answered the peasant, picking the ears off his sweat-drenched shirt.

"But how does Kirillov make it pay?"

"Mitiukh!" (so the peasant called the janitor, in a tone of contempt), "you may be sure he'll make it pay, Konstantin Dmitrievich! He'll get his share, however he has to squeeze to get it! He's no mercy on a Christian. But Uncle Fokanych" (so he called the old peasant Platon), "do you suppose he'd flay the skin off a man? Where there's debt, he'll let anyone off. And he'll not wring the last kopek out. He's that kind of a man."

"But why will he let anyone off?"

"Oh, well, of course, folks are different. One man lives for his own wants and nothing else, like Mitiukh, he only thinks of filling his belly, but Fokanych is a righteous man. He lives for his soul. He remembers God."

"How does he remember? How does he live for his soul?" Levin almost shouted.

"Why, to be sure, in truth, in God's way. Folks are different. Take you, now, you wouldn't wrong a man . . ."

"Yes, yes, good-by!" said Levin, breathless with excitement, and turning around, he took his stick and walked quickly away toward home. At the peasant's words that Fokanych lived for his soul, in truth, in God's way, undefined but significant ideas seemed to burst out as though they had been locked up, and all striving toward one goal, they thronged whirling through his head, blinding him with their light.

CHAPTER TWELVE

Levin strode along the highroad, absorbed not so much in his thoughts (he could not yet disentangle them) as in his spiritual condition, unlike anything he had experienced before.

The words uttered by the peasant had acted on his soul like an electric shock, suddenly transforming and combining into a single whole the whole swarm of disjointed, impotent, separate thoughts that incessantly occupied his mind. These thoughts had unconsciously been in his mind even when he was talking about the land.

He was aware of something new in his soul, and joyfully tested this new thing, not yet knowing what it was.

"Not living for his own wants, but for God? For what God? And could one say anything more senseless than what he said? He said that one must not live for one's own wants, that is, that one must not live for what we understand, what we are attracted by, what we desire, but must live for something incomprehensible, for God, whom no one can understand or even define. What of it? Didn't I understand those senseless words of Fyodor's? And understanding them, did I doubt their truth? Did I think them stupid, obscure, inexact? No, I understood him, and exactly as he understands the words. I understood them more fully and clearly than I understand anything in life, and never in my life have I doubted nor can I doubt about it. And not only I, but everyone, the whole world understands nothing fully but this, and about this only they have no doubt and are always agreed.

"Fyodor says that Kirillov lives for his belly. That's comprehensible and rational. All of us as rational beings can't do anything else but live for our belly. And all of a sudden the same Fyodor says that one mustn't live for one's belly but must live for truth, for God, and at a hint I understand him! And I and millions of men, men who lived ages ago and men living now—peasants, the poor in sprit and the learned who have thought and written about it, in their obscure words saying the same thing—we are all agreed about this one thing: what we must live for and what is good. I and all men have only one firm, incontestable clear knowledge, and that knowledge cannot be explained by reason—it is outside it, and has no causes and can have no effects.

"If goodness has causes, it is not goodness; if it has effects, a reward, it is not goodness either. So goodness is outside the chain of cause and effect.

"And yet I know it, and we all know it.

"And I watched for miracles, complained that I did not see a miracle that would convince me. A material miracle would have persuaded me. And here is a miracle, the sole miracle possible, continually existing, surrounding me on all sides, and I never noticed it!

"What could be a greater miracle than that?

"Can I have found the solution of it all? Can my sufferings be over?" thought Levin, striding along the dusty road, not noticing the heat or his weariness, and experiencing a sense of relief from prolonged suffering. This feeling was so delicious that it seemed to him incredible. He was breathless with emotion and incapable of going farther; he turned off the road into the forest and lay down in the shade of an aspen on the uncut grass. He took his hat off his hot head and lay propped on his elbow in the lush, feathery woodland grass.

"Yes, I must think it through and clear things up," he thought, looking intently at the untrampled grass before him, and following the movements of a green beetle advancing along a blade of couch grass and hindered in its progress by a leaf of goutwort. "Let's start over again," he said to himself, bending the leaf of goutwort out of the beetle's way and twisting another blade of grass for the beetle to cross over onto it. "What is it makes me glad? What have I discovered?

"I used to say that in my body, that in the body of this grass and of this beetle (there, she didn't care for the grass, she's opened her wings and flown away), a transformation of matter was going on in accordance with physical, chemical, and physiological laws. And in all of us, as well as in the aspens and the clouds and the nebulae, there was a process of evolution. Evolution from what? Into what? Eternal evolution and struggle . . . As though there could be any sort of tendency and struggle in the infinite. And I was astonished that in spite of the utmost effort of thought along that road I could not discover the meaning of life, the meaning of my impulses and yearnings. Whereas the meaning of my impulses is so clear to me that I lived according to them, and I am astonished and overjoyed when a peasant expressed it to me: 'To live for God, and for the Soul.'

"I have discovered nothing. I have found out only what I knew. I understand the force that in the past gave me life, and now too gives me life. I have been set free from falsity, I have found the Master."

And he briefly went through, mentally, the whole course of his ideas during the last two years, the beginning of which was the clear confronting of death at the sight of his dear brother hopelessly ill.

Then, for the first time, grasping that for every man, and himself too, there was nothing in store but suffering, death, and eternal oblivion, he had made up his mind that life was impossible like that, and that he must either interpret life so that it would not present itself to him as the evil mockery of some devil, or shoot himself.

But he had not done either; he had gone on living, thinking, and feeling, and had even at that very time married, and had had many joys and had been happy, when he was not thinking of the meaning of his life.

What did this mean? It meant that he had been living rightly but thinking wrongly.

He had lived (without being aware of it) on those spiritual truths that he had sucked in with his mother's milk, but he had thought, not merely without recognition of these truths, but studiously ignoring them.

Now it was clear to him that he could live only by virtue of the beliefs in which he had been brought up.

"What would I have been, and how would I have spent my life, if I had not had these beliefs, if I had not known that I must live for God and not for my own desires? I would have robbed and lied and killed. Nothing of what makes the chief happiness of my life would have existed for me." And not in the furthest reaches of his imagination could he conceive the brutal creature he would have been had he not known what he was living for.

"I looked for an answer to my question. And thought could not give an answer to my question—it is incommensurable with my question. The answer has been given me by life itself, in my knowledge of what is right and what is wrong. And that knowledge I did not arrive at in any way, it was given to me as to all men, given, because I could not have got it from anywhere.

"Where could I have got it? By reason could I have arrived at knowing that I must love my neighbor and not oppress him? I was told that in my childhood, and I believed it gladly, for they told me what was already in my soul. But who discovered it? Not reason. Reason discovered the struggle for existence, and the law that requires us to oppress all who hinder the satisfaction of our desires. That is the deduction of reason. But loving one's neighbour, reason could never discover, because it's unreasonable.

"Yes, pride," he said to himself, turning over on his stomach and beginning to tie a noose of blades of grass, trying not to break them.

"And not merely pride of intellect, but the stupidity of intellect. And most of all, the deceitfulness; yes, the deceitfulness of intellect. The cheating and deception of intellect, that's it," he said to himself.

CHAPTER THIRTEEN

And Levin remembered a scene he had lately witnessed between Dolly and her children. The children, left to themselves, had begun cooking raspberries over the candles and pouring jets of milk into each other's mouths. Their mother, catching them at these pranks, began impressing upon them, in Levin's presence, how much trouble what they were wasting cost grownups, and that this trouble was all for their sake, and that if they smashed the cups, they would have nothing to drink their tea out of, and that if they wasted the milk, they would have nothing to eat, and die of hunger.

And Levin had been struck by the passive, weary incredulity with which the children heard what their mother said to them. They were simply annoyed that their amusing play had been interrupted, and did not believe a word of what their mother was saying. They could not believe it, for they could not take in the immensity of all they habitually enjoyed, and so could not conceive that what they were destroying was the very thing they lived by.

"That all comes of itself," they thought, "and there's nothing interesting or important about it because it has always been so, and always will be so. And it's all always the same. We've no need to think about that, it's all ready. But we want to invent something of our own, and new. So we thought of putting raspberries in a cup, and cooking them over a candle, and squirting milk straight into each other's mouths. That's fun, and something new, and not a bit worse than drinking out of cups.

"Isn't it just the same that we do, that I did, searching by the aid of reason for the significance of the forces of nature and the meaning of the life of man?" he thought.

"And don't all the theories of philosophy do the same, trying by the path of thought, which is strange and not natural to man, to bring him to a knowledge of what he has known long ago, and knows so certainly that he could not live at all without it? Isn't it distinctly to be seen in the development of each philosopher's theory that he knows what the chief significance of life is beforehand, just as positively as the peasant Fyodor and not a bit more clearly than he, and is simply trying but a dubious intellectual path to come back to what everyone knows?

"Now, then, leave the children to themselves to get things and to make their crockery, get the milk from the cows, and so on. Would they be naughty then? Why, they'd die of hunger! Well, then, leave us with our passions and thoughts, without any idea of the one God, of the Creator, or without any idea of what is right, without any explanation of moral evil.

"Just try and build up anything without those ideas!

"We destroy them only because we're spiritually satiated. Exactly like the children!

"Whence have I that joyful knowledge, shared with the peasant, that alone gives peace to my soul? Whence did I get it?

"Brought up with an idea of God, a Christian, my whole life filled with the spiritual blessings Christianity has given me, full of them, and living on these blessings, like the children I did not understand them, and destroy, want to destroy, what I live by. And as soon as an important moment of life comes, like children when they are cold and hungry, I turn to Him, and even less than children when their mother scolds them for their childish mischief, do I feel that my childish efforts at wanton madness are counted against me.

"Yes, what I know, I know not by reason, but it has been given to me, revealed to me, and I know it with my heart, by faith in the chief thing taught by the church.

"The church! The church!" Levin repeated to himself. He turned over on the other side, and leaning on his elbow, he began gazing into the distance at a herd of cattle crossing over to the river.

"But can I believe in all the church teaches?" he thought, trying himself, and thinking of everything that could destroy his present peace of mind. Intentionally he recalled all those doctrines of the church which had always seemed most strange and had always been a stumbling block to him.

"The Creation? But how did I explain existence? By existence? By nothing? The devil and sin. But how do I explain evil? . . . The Atonement? . . ."

"But I know nothing, nothing, and I can know nothing but what has been told to me and all men."

And it seemed to him that there was not a single article of faith of the church which could destroy the chief thing—faith in God, in goodness, as the one goal of man's destiny.

Under every article of faith of the church could be put the faith in the service of truth instead of one's desires. And each doctrine did not simply leave that faith unshaken, each doctrine seemed essential to complete that great miracle, continually manifest upon earth, that made it possible for each man and millions of different sorts of men, wise men and imbeciles, old men and children—all men, peasants, Lvov, Kitty, beggars and kings—to understand perfectly the same one thing, and to build up thereby that life of the soul which alone is worth living, and which alone is precious to us.

Lying on his back, he gazed up now into the high, cloudless sky. "Do I not know that that is infinite space, and that it is not a rounded vault? But, however I screw up my eyes and strain my sight, I cannot see it but as round and finite, and in spite of my knowing about infinite space, I am incontestably right when I see a firm blue vault, far more right than when I strain my eyes to see beyond it."

Levin ceased thinking, and only, as it were, listened to mysterious voices that seemed talking joyfully and earnestly within him.

"Can this be faith?" he thought, afraid to believe in his happiness. "My God, I thank Thee!" he said, gulping down his sobs and with both hands brushing away the tears that filled his eyes.

CHAPTER FOURTEEN

Levin looked before him and saw a herd of cattle, then he caught sight of his trap with Raven in the shafts, and the coachman, who, driving up to the herd, said something to the herdsman. Then he heard the rattle of the wheels and the snort of the sleek horse close to him. But he was so buried in his thoughts that he did not even wonder why the coachman had come for him.

He thought of that only when the coachman had driven close to him and shouted to him: "The mistress sent me. Your brother has come, and some gentleman with him."

Levin got into the trap and took the reins. As though just roused out of sleep, he could not collect his faculties for a long while. He stared at the sleek horse flecked with lather between its haunches and on its neck where the harness rubbed, stared at Ivan the coachman sitting beside him, and remembered that he was expecting his brother, thought that his wife was most likely uneasy at his long absence, and tried to guess who was the visitor who had come with his brother. And his brother and his wife and the unknown guest seemed to him now quite different from before. He thought that now his relations with all men would be different.

"With my brother there will be none of that aloofness there always used to be between us, there will be no disputes; with Kitty there shall never be quarrels; with the visitor, whoever he may be, I will be friendly and nice; with the servants, with Ivan, it will all be different."

With difficulty holding in the good horse that snorted with impatience and seemed begging to be let go, Levin looked around at Ivan sitting beside him, not knowing what to do with his unoccupied hand, continually pressing down his shirt as it puffed out, and he tried to think of something to say to him. He would have said that Ivan had pulled the saddle girth up too high, but that was like reproof, and he longed for friendly, warm talk. Nothing else occurred to him

"Your Honor must keep to the right and mind that stump," said the coachman, pulling the rein Levin held.

"Please don't touch and don't teach me!" said Levin, angered by this interference. Now, as always, interference made him angry, and he felt sorrowfully at once how mistaken had been his supposition that his spiritual condition could immediately change him in contact with reality.

He was a quarter of a mile from home when he saw Grisha and Tanya running to meet him.

"Uncle Kostya! Mama's coming, and Granddad, and Sergey Ivanovich, and someone else," they said, clambering up into the trap.

"Who is he?"

"An awfully terrible person! And he does like this with his arms," said Tanya, getting up in the trap and mimicking Katavasov.

"Old or young?" asked Levin, laughing, reminded of someone, he did not know whom, by Tanya's performance.

"Oh, I hope it's not a tiresome person!" thought Levin.

As soon as he turned at a bend in the road, and saw the party coming, Levin recognized Katavasov in a straw hat, walking along swinging his arms just as Tanya had shown him. Katavasov was very fond of discussing metaphysics, having derived his notions from natural science writers who had never studied metaphysics, and in Moscow Levin had had many arguments with him of late.

And one of these arguments, in which Katavasov had obviously considered that he came off victorious, was the first thing Levin thought of as he recognized him.

"No, whatever I do, I won't argue and give utterance to my ideas lightly," he thought.

Getting out of the trap and greeting his brother and Katavasov, Levin asked about his wife.

"She has taken Mitya to Kolok" (a wood near the house). "She wanted to have him out there because it's so hot indoors," said Dolly. Levin had always advised his wife not to take the baby to the wood, thinking it unsafe, and he was not pleased to hear this.

"She rushes about from place to place with him," said the prince, smiling. "I advised her to try putting him in the ice cellar."

"She meant to come to the apiary. She thought you would be there. We are going there," said Dolly.

"Well, and what are you doing?" said Sergey Ivanovich, falling back from the rest and walking beside him.

"Oh, nothing special. Busy as usual with the land," answered Levin. "Well, and what about you? Come for long? We have been expecting you for such a long time."

"Only for two weeks. I've a great deal to do in Moscow."

At these words the brothers' eyes met, and Levin, in spite of the desire he always had, stronger than ever just now, to be on affectionate and still more open terms with his brother, felt an awkwardness in looking at him. He lowered his eyes and did not know what to say.

Casting over the subjects of conversation that would be pleasant to Sergey Ivanovich, and would keep him off the subject of the Serbian war and the Slavic question, at which he had hinted by the allusion to what he had to do in Moscow, Levin began to talk of Sergey Ivanovich's book.

"Well, have there been reviews of your book?" he asked.

Sergey Ivanovich smiled at the premeditation of the question.

"No one is interested in that now, and I less than anyone," he said. "Just look, Darya Aleksandrovna, we shall have a shower," he added, pointing with his umbrella at the white clouds that showed above the aspen tops.

And these words were enough to re-establish again between the brothers that tone—not hostile, but chilly—which Levin had been so longing to avoid.

Levin went up to Katavasov.

"It was good of you to make up your mind to come," he said to him.

"I've been meaning to a long while. Now we shall have some discussion, we'll see to that. Have you been reading Spencer?"

"No, I've not finished reading him," said Levin. "But I don't need him now."

"How's that? That's interesting. Why so?"

"I mean that I'm fully convinced that the solution of the problems that interest me I shall never find in him and in his like. Now . . . "

But Katavasov's serene and good-humored expression suddenly struck him, and he felt such tenderness for his own happy mood, which he was unmistakably disturbing by this conversation, that he remembered his resolution and stopped short.

"But we'll talk later," he added. "If we're going to the apiary, it's this way, along this little path," he said, addressing them all.

Going along the narrow path to a little uncut meadow covered on one side with thick clusters of wild pansies, among which tall, dark-green tufts of hellebore stood up here and there, Levin settled his guests in the dense, cool shade of the young aspens on a bench and some stumps purposely put there for visitors to the apiary who might be afraid of the bees, and he went off himself to the hut to get bread, cucumbers, and fresh honey for everyone.

Trying to make his movements as deliberate as possible, and listening to the bees that buzzed more and more frequently past him, he walked along the little path to the hut. In the very entry one bee hummed angrily, caught in his beard, but he carefully extricated it. Going into the shady outer room, he took down from the wall his veil, which hung on a peg, and putting it on, and thrusting his hands into his pockets, he went into the fenced-in apiary, where there stood in the midst of a closely mown space in regular rows, fastened with bast on posts, all the hives he knew so well, the old hives, each with its own history, and along the fences the younger swarms hived that year. In front of the openings of the hives, it made his eyes giddy to watch the bees and drones whirling round and round about the same spot, while among them the working bees flew in and out with spoils or in search of them, always in the same direction into the wood to the flowering lime trees and back to the hives.

His ears were filled with the incessant hum in various notes, now the busy hum of the working bee flying quickly off, then the blaring of the lazy drone, and the excited buzz of the bees on guard protecting their property from the enemy and preparing to sting. On the farther side of the fence the old beekeeper was planing a hoop for a cask, and he did not see Levin. Levin stood still in the midst of the beehives and did not call him.

He was glad of a chance to be alone to recover from the influence of ordinary reality, which had already depressed his happy mood. He thought that he had already had time to lose his temper with Ivan, to show coolness to his brother, and to talk flippantly with Katavasov.

"Can it have been only a momentary mood, and will it pass and leave no trace?" he thought. But the same instant, going back to his mood, he felt with delight that something new and important had happened to him. Real life had only for a time overcast the spiritual peace he had found, but it was still untouched within him.

Just as the bees, whirling round him, now menacing him and distracting his attention, prevented him from enjoying complete physical peace, forced him to restrain his movements to avoid them, so had the petty cares that had swarmed about him from the moment he got into the trap restricted his spiritual freedom; but that lasted only so long as he was among them. Just as his bodily strength was still unaffected in spite of the bees, so too was the spiritual strength that he had just become aware of.

CHAPTER FIFTEEN

"Do you know, Kostya, with whom Sergey Ivanovich traveled on his way here?" said Dolly, doling out cucumbers and honey to the children. "With Vronsky! He's going to Serbia."

"And not alone; he's taking a squadron out with him at his own expense," said Katavasov.

"That's the right thing for him," said Levin. "Are volunteers still going out, then?" he added, glancing at Sergey Ivanovich.

Sergey Ivanovich did not answer. He was carefully trying to free with a blunt knife a live bee that was stuck fast in the honey from a bowl in which there was a wedge of white honeycomb.

"I should think so! You should have seen what was going on at the station yesterday!" said Katavasov, biting with a juicy sound into a cucumber.

"Well, what is one to make of it? For mercy's sake, do explain to me, Sergey Ivanovich, where are all those volunteers going, whom are they fighting with," asked the old prince, obviously resuming a conversation that had sprung up in Levin's absence.

"With the Turks," Sergey Ivanovich answered, smiling serenely as he extricated the bee, dark with honey and helplessly kicking, and put it with the knife on a stout aspen leaf.

"But who has declared war on the Turks?—Ivan Ivanovich Ragozov and Countess Lydia Ivanovna, assisted by Madame Stahl?"

"No one has declared war, but people sympathizing with their neighbors' sufferings are eager to help them," said Sergey Ivanovich.

"But the prince is not speaking of help," said Levin, coming to the assistance of his father-in-law, "but of war. The prince says that private persons cannot take part in war without the permission of the government."

"Kostya, careful, that's a bee! Really, they'll sting us!" said Dolly, waving away a wasp.

"But that's not a bee, it's a wasp," said Levin.

"Well now, well, what's your own theory?" Katavasov said to Levin with a smile, distinctly challenging him to a discussion. "Why have not private persons the right to do so?"

"Oh, my theory's this: war is on one side such a beastly, cruel, and awful thing that no one man, not to speak of a Christian, can individually take upon himself the responsibility of beginning wars; that can be done only by a government, which is called upon to do this, and is driven inevitably into war. On the other hand, both political science and common sense teach us that in matters of state, and especially in the matter of war, private citizens must forego their personal individual will."

Sergey Ivanovich and Katavasov had their replies ready, and both began speaking at the same time.

"But the point is, my dear fellow, that there may be cases when the government does not carry out the will of the citizens and then the public asserts its will," said Katavasov.

But evidently Sergey Ivanovich did not approve of this answer. His brows contracted at Katavasov's words and he said something else.

"You don't put the matter in its true light. There is no question here of a declaration of war, but simply the expression of a human Christian feeling. Our brothers, one with us in religion and in race, are being massacred. Even supposing they were not our brothers or fellow Christians, but simply children, women, old people, feeling is aroused and Russians go eagerly to help in stopping these atrocities. Imagine if you were going along the street and saw drunken men beating a woman or a child—I think you would not stop to inquire whether war had been declared on the men, but would throw yourself on them, and protect the victim."

"But I would not kill them," said Levin.

"Yes, you would kill them."

"I don't know. If I saw that, I might give way to my impulse of the moment, but I can't say beforehand. And such a momentary impulse there is not, and there cannot be, in the case of the oppression of the Slavic peoples."

"Possibly for you there is not; but for others there is," said Sergey Ivanovich, frowning with displeasure. "There are traditions still alive among the people of Orthodox Christians suffering under the yoke of the 'impious sons of Hagar.' The people have heard of the sufferings of their brethren and have spoken."

"Perhaps so," said Levin evasively; "but I don't see it. I am of the people myself, and I don't feel it."

"Here am I too," said the old prince. "I've been staying abroad and reading the papers, and I must confess, up to the time of the Bulgarian atrocities,[1] I couldn't understand why it was that the Russians were all of a sudden so fond of their Slavic brethren, while I didn't feel the slightest affection for them. I was very much upset, thought I was a monster, or that it was the influence of the Carlsbad waters on me. But since I have been here, my mind's been set at rest. I see that there are people besides me who're only interested in Russia, and not in their Slavic brethren. Konstantin is one of those."

"Personal opinions mean nothing in such a case," said Sergey Ivanovich. "It's not a matter of personal opinions when all Russia—the whole people—has expressed its will."

[1] See note 2 on page 582.

"But excuse me, I don't see that. The people don't know anything about it, if you come to that," said the old prince.

"Oh, Papa! How can you say that? And last Sunday in church?" said Dolly, listening to the conversation. "Please give me a towel," she said to the old man, who was looking at the children with a smile. "Why, it's not possible that all—"

"But what was it in church on Sunday? The priest had been told to read that. He read it. They didn't understand a word of it. Then they were told that there was to be a collection for a charitable cause; well, they pulled out a kopek and gave it, but why they couldn't say."

"The people cannot help knowing; the sense of their own destinies is always in the people, and at such moments as the present that sense finds utterance," said Sergey Ivanovich with conviction, glancing at the old beekeeper.

The handsome old man, with black grizzled beard and thick silvery hair, stood motionless, holding a jar of honey, looking down from the height of his tall figure with friendly serenity at the gentlefolk, obviously understanding nothing of their conversation and not caring to understand it.

"That's so, no doubt," he said, with a significant shake of his head at Sergey Ivanovich's words.

"Here, then, ask him. He knows nothing about it and thinks nothing," said Levin. "Have you heard about the war, Mikhailych?" he said, turning to him. "What they read in the church? What do you think about it? Should we fight for the Christians?"

"What should we think? Alexandr Nikolaevich our Emperor has thought for us; he thinks for us in all things. He knows best. Shall I bring a bit more bread? Give the little lad some more?" he said, addressing Darya Aleksandrovna and pointing to Grisha, who had finished his crust.

"I don't need to ask," said Sergey Ivanovich. "We have seen and are seeing hundreds and hundreds of people who give up everything to serve a just cause, come from every part of Russia, and directly and clearly express their thought and aim. They bring their kopek or go themselves and say directly what for. What does that mean?"

"It means, to my thinking," said Levin, who was beginning to get excited, "that among eighty million people there can always be found not hundreds, as now, but tens of thousands of people who have lost caste, happy-go-lucky people who are always ready to go anywhere— to Pugachov's bands,[2] to Khiva,[3] to Serbia . . . "

"I tell you that it's not a case of hundreds or of happy-go-lucky people, but the best representatives of the people!" said Sergey Ivanovich, with as much irritation as if he were defending the last kopek of his fortune. "And what of the subscriptions? In this case it is a whole people directly expressing its will."

"That word 'people' is so vague," said Levin. "Parish clerks, teachers, and one in a thousand of the peasants, maybe, know what it's all about. The rest of the eighty million, like Mikhailych, far from expressing their will, haven't the faintest idea what there is for them to express their will about. What right have we to say that this is the people's will?"

CHAPTER SIXTEEN

Sergey Ivanovich, being practiced in dialectics, did not reply, but at once turned the conversation to another aspect of the subject.

"Oh, if you want to learn the spirit of the people by arithmetical computation, of course it's very difficult to arrive at it. And voting has not been introduced among us and cannot be introduced, for it does not express the will of the people; but there are other ways of reaching that. It is felt in the air, it is felt by the heart. I won't speak of those deep currents which are astir in the still ocean of the people, and which are evident to every unprejudiced person; let us look at society in the narrow sense. All the most diverse sections of the educated public, hostile before, are merged into one. Every division is at an end, all the public organs say the same thing over and over again, all feel the mighty torrent that has overtaken them and is carrying them in one direction."

"Yes, all the newspapers do say the same thing," said the prince.

[2](1742-75), Don Cossack who led an important peasant uprising in 1773-75.
[3]Medieval Moslem city that became a Russian protectorate in 1873.

"That's true. But so is it the same thing that all the frogs croak before a storm. One can hear nothing because of the croaking."

"Frogs or no frogs, I'm not the editor of a paper and I don't need to defend them; but I am speaking of the unanimity in the intellectual world," said Sergey Ivanovich, addressing his brother. Levin would have answered, but the old prince interrupted him.

"Well, about that unanimity, that's another thing, one may say," said the prince. "There's my son-in-law, Stepan Arkadyevich, you know him. He's got a place now on the committee of a commission and something or other, I don't remember. Only there's nothing to do in it—why, Dolly, it's no secret!—and a salary of eight thousand. You try asking him whether his post is of use, he'll prove to you that it's most necessary. And he's a truthful man too, but there's no refusing to believe in the utility of eight thousand rubles."

"Yes, he asked me to give a message to Darya Aleksandrovna that he's got the post," said Sergey Ivanovich reluctantly, feeling the prince's remark to be irrelevant.

"So it is with the unanimity of the press. That's been explained to me: as soon as there's war their incomes are doubled. How can they help believing in the destinies of the people and the Slavic races . . . and all that?"

"I don't care for many of the papers, but that's unjust," said Sergey Ivanovich.

"I would only make one condition," pursued the old prince. "Alphonse Karr[1] put it very well before the war with Prussia: 'You consider war to be inevitable? Very good. Let everyone who advocates war be enrolled in a special regiment of advance guards, for the front of every assault, of every attack, to lead them all!' "

"A nice bunch the editors would make!" said Katavasov, with a loud roar, as he pictured the editors he knew in this chosen legion.

"But they'd run," said Dolly, "they'd only be in the way."

"Oh, if they ran away, then we'd have grapeshot or Cossacks with whips behind them," said the prince.

---

[1](1808-90), French author, editor of *Figaro* who started the issue of the bitterly satirical *Les Guêpes* ("The Wasps").

"But that's a joke, and a poor one too, if you'll excuse my saying so, Prince," said Sergey Ivanovich.

"I don't see that it was a joke, that—" Levin was beginning, but Sergey Ivanovich interrupted him.

"Every member of society is called upon to do his own special work," said he. "And men of thought are doing their work when they express public opinion. And the single-hearted and full expression of public opinion is the service of the press and a phenomenon to rejoice us at the same time. Twenty years ago we would have been silent, but now we have heard the voice of the Russian people, which is ready to rise as one man and ready to sacrifice itself for its oppressed brethren; that is a great step and a proof of strength."

"But it's not only making a sacrifice, but killing Turks," said Levin timidly. "The people make sacrifices and are ready to make sacrifices for their soul, but not for murder," he added, instinctively connecting the conversation with the ideas that had been absorbing his mind.

"For their soul? That's a most puzzling expression for a naturalist, you know. What sort of thing is a soul?" said Katavasov, smiling.

"Oh, you know that!"

"No, by God, I haven't the faintest idea!" said Katavasov with a loud roar of laughter.

" 'I came not to send peace, but a sword,' says Christ," Sergey Ivanovich rejoined for his part, quoting as simply as though it was the easiest thing to understand the very passage that had always puzzled Levin most.

"That's so, no doubt," the old man repeated again. He was standing near them and responded to a chance glance turned in his direction.

"Ah, my dear fellow, you're defeated, utterly defeated!" cried Katavasov good-humoredly.

Levin reddened with vexation, not at being defeated, but at having failed to control himself and being drawn into argument.

"No, I can't argue with them," he thought; "they wear impenetrable armor, while I'm naked."

He saw that it was impossible to convince his brother and Katavasov, and he saw even less the possibility of himself agreeing with them. What they advocated was the very pride of intellect that had almost been his ruin. He could not admit that some dozens of men, among them his brother, had the right, on the ground of what they were told by some hundreds of glib volunteers swarming to the capital, to say that they and the newspapers were expressing the will and feeling of the people, and a feeling which was expressed in vengeance and murder. He could not admit this, because he neither saw the expression of such feelings in the people among whom he was living, nor found them in himself (and he could not but consider himself one of the persons making up the Russian people), and most of all because he, like the people, did not know and could not know what is for the general good, though he knew beyond a doubt that this general good could be attained only by the strict observance of that law of right and wrong which has been revealed to every man, and therefore he could not wish for war or advocate war for any general objects whatever. He said as Mikhailych did and the people, who had expressed their feeling in the traditional invitations of the Varangians:[2] "Come and rule over us. Gladly we promise complete submission. All the labor, all humiliations, all sacrifices we take upon ourselves; but we will not judge and decide." And now, according to Sergey Ivanovich's account, the people had foregone this privilege they had bought at such a costly price.

He wanted to say too that if public opinion was an infallible guide, then why were not revolutions and the commune as lawful as the movement in favor of the Slavic peoples? But these were merely thoughts that could settle nothing. One thing could be seen beyond doubt—that at the actual moment the discussion was irritating Sergey Ivanovich, and so it was wrong to continue it. And Levin ceased speaking and then called the attention of his guests to the fact that the clouds were gathering, and that they had better be going home before it rained.

[2]See note on page 10.

CHAPTER SEVENTEEN

The old prince and Sergey Ivanovich got into the trap and drove off; the rest of the party hastened homeward on foot.

But the clouds, turning white and then black, moved down so quickly that they had to quicken their pace to get home before the rain. The foremost clouds, lowering and black as soot-laden smoke, rushed with extraordinary swiftness over the sky. They were still two hundred paces from home and a gust of wind had already blown up, and every second the downpour might be expected.

The children ran ahead with frightened and gleeful shrieks. Darya Aleksandrovna, struggling painfully with her skirts that clung round her legs, was not walking but running, her eyes fixed on the children. The men of the party, holding their hats on, strode with long steps beside her. They were just at the steps when a big drop fell splashing on the edge of the iron gutter. The children and their elders after them ran into the shelter of the house, talking merrily.

"Katerina Aleksandrovna?" Levin asked of Agafya Mikhailovna, who met them with shawls and comforters in the hall.

"We thought she was with you," she said.

"And Mitya?"

"In the woods, he must be, and the nurse with him."

Levin snatched up the comforters and ran toward the woods.

In that brief interval of time the storm clouds had moved on, covering the sun so completely that it was dark as an eclipse. Stubbornly, as though insisting on its rights, the wind stopped Levin, and tearing the leaves and flowers off the lime trees and stripping the white birch branches into strange hideous nakedness, it twisted everything to one side—acacias, flowers, burdocks, grass, and tall tree-tops. The peasant girls working in the garden ran shrieking into shelter in the servants' quarters. The streaming rain had already flung its white veil over the distant forest and half the fields close by, and was rapidly swooping down upon the woods. The moisture of the rain, spattered into tiny drops, could be felt in the air.

Holding his head bent down before him, and struggling with the wind that strove to tear the wraps away from him, Levin was moving up to the copse and had just caught sight of something white behind the oak tree, when there was a sudden flash, the whole earth seemed on fire, and the vault of heaven cracked overhead. Opening his blinded eyes, Levin gazed through the thick veil of rain that separated him now from the copse, and to his horror the first thing he saw was the green crest of the familiar oak tree in the middle of the copse uncannily changing its position. "Can it have been struck?" Levin hardly had time to think when, moving more and more rapidly, the oak tree vanished behind the other trees, and he heard the crash of the great tree falling upon the others.

The flash of lighting, the crash of thunder, and the instantaneous chill that ran through him were all merged for Levin in one sense of terror.

"My God! My God! Not on them!" he said.

And though he thought at once how senseless was his prayer that they should not have been killed by the oak that had fallen now, he repeated it, knowing that he could do nothing better than utter this senseless prayer.

Running up to the place where they usually went, he did not find them there.

They were at the other end of the copse under an old lime tree; they were calling him. Two figures in dark dresses (they had been light summer dresses when they started out) were standing bending over something. It was Kitty with the nurse. The rain was already ceasing, and it was beginning to get light when Levin reached them. The nurse was not wet on the lower part of her dress, but Kitty was drenched through, and her soaked clothes clung to her. Though the rain was over, they still stood in the same position in which they had been standing when the storm broke. Both stood bending over a baby carriage with a green umbrella.

"Alive? Unhurt? Thank God!" he said, splashing with his soaked boots through the puddles and running up to them.

Kitty's rosy wet face was turned toward him, and she smiled timidly under her shapeless sopped hat.

"Aren't you ashamed of yourself? I can't think how you can be so reckless!" he said angrily to his wife.

"It wasn't my fault, really. We were just meaning to go, when he made such a to-do that we had to change him. We were just . . . " Kitty began defending herself.

Mitya was unharmed, dry, and still fast asleep.

"Well, thank God! I don't know what I'm saying!"

They gathered up the baby's wet diapers; the nurse picked up the baby and carried him. Levin walked beside his wife, and, penitent for having been angry, he squeezed her hand when the nurse was not looking.

CHAPTER EIGHTEEN

During the whole of that day, in the extremely different conversations in which he took part, only, as it were, with the top layer of his mind, in spite of the disappointment of not finding the change he expected in himself, Levin had been all the while joyfully conscious of the fullness of his heart.

After the rain it was too wet to go for a walk; besides, the storm clouds still hung about the horizon, and gathered here and there, black and thundery, on the room of the sky. The whole party spent the rest of the day in the house.

No more discussions sprang up; on the contrary, after dinner everyone was in the most amiable frame of mind.

At first Katavasov amused the ladies by his original jokes, which always pleased people on their first acquaintance with him. Then Sergey Ivanovich induced him to tell them about the very interesting observations he had made on the habits and characteristics of common house flies, and their life. Sergey Ivanovich, too, was in good spirits, and at tea his brother drew him on to explain his views of the future of the Eastern question, and he spoke so simply and so well that everyone listened eagerly.

Kitty was the only one who did not hear it all—she was summoned to give Mitya his bath.

A few minutes after Kitty had left the room she sent for Levin to come to the nursery.

Although he had been much interested by Sergey Ivanovich's

views of the new epoch in history that could be created by the emancipation of forty million men of Slavic race acting with Russia, a conception quite new to him, and although he was disturbed by uneasy
wonder at being sent for by Kitty, as soon as he came out of the
drawing room and was alone, his mind reverted at once to the
thoughts of the morning. And all the theories of the significance of
the Slav element in the history of the world seemed to him so trivial
compared with what was passing in his own soul, that he instantly
forgot it all and dropped back into the same frame of mind that he
had been in that morning.

He did not, as he had done at other times, recall the whole train of
thought—that he did not need. He fell back at once into the feeling
which had guided him, which was connected with those thoughts,
and he found that feeling in his soul even stronger and more definite than before. He did not, as he had had to do with previous
attempts to find comforting arguments, need to revive a whole chain
of thought to find the feeling. Now, on the contrary, the feeling of
joy and peace was more vivid than ever, and thought could not keep
pace with feeling.

He walked across the terrace and looked at two stars that had
come out in the darkening sky, and suddenly he remembered. "Yes,
looking at the sky, I thought that the dome I see is not a deception,
and then I thought something, I shirked facing something," he
mused. "But whatever it was, there can be no disproving it! I have but
to think, and all will come clear!"

Just as he was going into the nursery he remembered what it was
he had shirked facing. It was that if the chief proof of the Divinity
was His revelation of what is right, how is it this revelation is confined to the Christian church alone? What relation to this revelation have the beliefs of the Buddhists, Mohammedans, who preached
and did good too?

It seemed to him that he had an answer to this question; but he
had not time to formulate it to himself before he went into the nursery.

Kitty was standing, with her sleeves tucked up, over the baby in
the bath. Hearing her husband's footstep, she turned toward him,
summoning him to her with her smile. With one hand she was sup-

porting the fat baby who lay floating and sprawling on his back, while with the other she squeezed the sponge over him.

"Come, look, look!" she said, when her husband came up to her. "Agafya Mikhailovna's right. He knows us!"

Mitya had on that day given unmistakable, incontestable signs of recognizing all his own people.

As soon as Levin approached the bath, the experiment was tried, and it was completely successful. The cook, sent for with this object, bent over the baby. He frowned and shook his head disapprovingly. Kitty bent down to him, he gave her a beaming smile, propped his little hands on the sponge, and chirruped, making such a strange little contented sound with his lips that Kitty and the nurse were not alone in their admiration. Levin, too, was surprised and delighted.

The baby was taken out of the bath, drenched with water, wrapped in towels, dried, and after a piercing scream, handed to his mother.

"Well, I am glad you are beginning to love him," said Kitty to her husband when she had settled herself comfortably in her usual place, with the baby at her breast. "I am so glad! It had begun to distress me. You said you had no feeling for him."

"No; did I say that? I only said I was disappointed."

"What! Disappointed in him?"

"Not disappointed in him, but in my own feeling; I had expected more. I had expected a rush of new delightful emotion to come as a surprise. And then instead of that—disgust, pity . . . "

She listened attentively, looking at him over the baby, while she put back on her slender fingers the rings she had taken off while giving Mitya his bath.

"And most of all, at there being far more apprehension and pity than pleasure. Today, after that fright during the storm, I understand how I love him."

Kitty's smile was radiant.

"Were you very much frightened?" she said. "So was I, but I feel it more now that it's over. I'm going to look at the oak. How nice Katavasov is! And what a happy day we've had altogether. And you're so nice with Sergey Ivanovich, when you care to be . . . Well, go back to them. It's always so hot and steamy here after the bath.

CHAPTER NINETEEN

Going out of the nursery and being again alone, Levin went back at once to the thought, in which there was something not clear.

Instead of going into the drawing room, where he heard voices, he stopped on the terrace, and leaning his elbows on the parapet, he gazed up at the sky.

It was quite dark now, and in the south, where he was looking, there were no clouds. The storm had drifted on to the opposite side of the sky, and there were flashes of lightning and distant thunder from that quarter. Levin listened to the monotonous drip from the lime trees in the garden, and looked at the triangle of stars he knew so well, and the Milky Way with its ramifications that ran through its midst. At each flash of lightning the Milky Way, and even the bright stars, vanished, but as soon as the lightning died away, they reappeared in their places as though some hand had flung them back with careful aim.

"Well, what is it perplexes me?" Levin said to himself, feeling beforehand that the solution of his difficulties was ready in his soul, though he did not know it yet. "Yes, the one unmistakable, incontestable manifestation of the Divinity is the law of good and evil, which has come into the world by revelation, and which I feel in myself, and in the recognition of which I don't so much unite myself as am united, whether I will or not, with other men in one body of believers, which is called the church. Well, but the Jews, the Mohammedans, the Confucians, the Buddhists—what of them?" he thought, asking himself the question he had feared to face. "Can these hundreds of millions of men be deprived of that highest blessing without which life has no meaning?" He pondered a moment, but immediately corrected himself. "But what am I questioning?" he said to himself. "I am questioning the relation to Divinity of all the different religions of all mankind. I am questioning the universal manifestation of God to all the world with all those misty blurs. What am I about? To me individually, to my heart has been revealed a knowledge beyond all doubt, and unattainable by reason, and here I am obstinately trying to express that knowledge in reason and words.

"Don't I know that the stars don't move?" he asked himself, gazing at the bright planet which had shifted its position up to the topmost twig of the birch tree. "But looking at the movements of the stars, I can't picture to myself the rotation of the earth, and I'm right in saying that the stars move.

"And could the astronomers have understood and calculated anything if they had taken into account all the complicated and varied motions of the earth? All the marvelous conclusions they have reached about the distances, weights, movements, and deflections of the heavenly bodies are founded only on the apparent motions of the heavenly bodies about a stationary earth, on that very motion I see before me now, which has been so for millions of men during the long ages, and was and always will be alike, and can always be trusted. And just as the conclusions of the astronomers would have been vain and uncertain if not founded on observations of the seen heavens, in relation to a single meridian and a single horizon, so would my conclusions be vain and uncertain if not founded on that conception of right, which has been and will be always alike for all men, which has been revealed to me as a Christian, and which can always be trusted in my soul. The question of other religions and their relations to Divinity I have no right to decide, and no possibility of deciding."

"Oh, you haven't gone in, then?" he heard Kitty's voice all at once, as she came by the same way to the drawing room.

"What is it? You're not worried about anything?" she said, looking intently at his face in the starlight.

But she could not have seen his face if a flash of lightning had not hidden the stars and revealed it. In that flash she saw his face distinctly, and seeing him calm and happy, she smiled at him.

"She understands," he thought; "she knows what I'm thinking about. Shall I tell her or not? Yes, I'll tell her." But at the moment he was about to speak, she began speaking.

"Kostya! Do something for me," she said; "go into the corner room and see if they've made it all right for Sergey Ivanovich. I can't very well. See if they've put the new washstand in it."

"Very well, I'll go at once," said Levin, standing up and kissing her.

"No, I'd better not speak of it," he thought, when she had gone in before him. "It is a secret for me alone, of vital importance for me, and not to be put into words.

"This new feeling has not changed me, has not made me happy and enlightened all of a sudden, as I had dreamed, just like the feeling for my child. There was no surprise in this either. Faith—or not faith—I don't know what it is—but this feeling has come just as imperceptibly through suffering, and has taken firm root in my soul.

"I shall go on in the same way, losing my temper with Ivan the coachman, falling into angry discussions, expressing my opinions tactlessly; there will still be the same wall between the holy of holies of my soul and other people, even my wife; I shall still go on blaming her for my own terror, and being sorry for it; I shall still be as unable to understand with my reason why I pray, and I shall still go on praying; but my life now, my whole life apart from anything that can happen to me, every minute of it is no longer meaningless, as it was before, but it has an unquestionable meaning of the goodness which I have the power to put into it."

COMMENTARY

LEO TOLSTOY

FYODOR M. DOSTOEVSKY

THE NATION

WILLIAM DEAN HOWELLS

MATTHEW ARNOLD

THOMAS MANN

VLADIMIR NABOKOV

LEO TOLSTOY

[If] I were to try to say in words everything that I intended to express in my novel, I would have to write the same novel I wrote from the beginning. And if short-sighted critics think that I only wanted to describe the things that I like, what Oblonsky has for dinner or what Karenina's shoulders are like, they are mistaken. In everything, or nearly everything I have written, I have been guided by the need to gather together ideas which for the purpose of self-expression were interconnected; but every idea expressed separately in words loses its meaning and is terribly impoverished when taken by itself out of the connection in which it occurs. The connection itself is made up, I think, not by the idea, but by something else, and it is impossible to express the basis of this connection directly in words. It can only be expressed indirectly—by words describing characters, actions and situations.

You know all this better than I do, but it has been occupying my attention recently. For me, one of the most manifest proofs of this was Vronsky's suicide which you liked. This had never been so clear to me before. The chapter about how Vronsky accepted his role after meeting the husband had been written by me a long time ago. I began to correct it, and quite unexpectedly for me, but unmistakably, Vronsky went and shot himself. And now it turns out that this was organically necessary for what comes afterwards.

It's true that if there were no criticism at all, then . . . you who understand art would be redundant. But now indeed when 9/10 of everything printed is criticism, people are needed for the criticism of art who can show the pointlessness of looking for ideas in a work of art and can steadfastly guide readers through that endless labyrinth of connections which is the essence of art, and towards those laws that serve as the basis of these connections.

And if critics already understand and can express in a newspaper article what I wanted to say, I congratulate them and can boldly assure them *qu'ils en savent plus long que moi* ["that they know more about it than I do"].

From a letter to N. N. Strakhov, April 23, 1876

FYODOR M. DOSTOEVSKY

Anna Karenina, as an artistic production, is perfect. It has appeared at an opportune moment, and in our epoch no work in European belles-lettres can compare with it. Secondly, by its idea, the novel is something inherently ours, our *own*, specifically something constituting our Russian peculiarity as distinguished from the European world, our national "new word," or, at least, its beginning—precisely such a word as one doesn't hear in Europe, which, however, she needs so badly, despite all her haughtiness.

I am unable to embark here upon literary criticism, and will merely say a few words.

In *Anna Karenina* is expressed a view of human guilt and criminality. People are portrayed in abnormal circumstances. Evil existed before them. Caught in the whirl of deceit, people commit crime and fatally perish. It will be perceived that this is a thought dealing with the most beloved and antiquated European themes. However, how is this problem solved in Europe? Everywhere in Europe it is solved in a twofold manner. First solution: The law has been laid down, framed, formulated and conceived during millennia. Evil and good are defined, weighed, measured, and their degrees have been historically ascertained by the sages of mankind by means of uninterrupted training of the human soul and highly scientific elaboration of the extent of the cohesive force of human intercourse. It is ordered to abide blindly by this enacted code. He who fails to abide by it, he who violates it, pays for it with his freedom, his property, his life, pays literally and inhumanly. "I know"—says their own civilization—"that this is blind, cruel, impossible, since a final formula of behavior cannot be elaborated while mankind is still in the middle of the road; however, since there is no other solution, one has to abide by the written code,—abide literally and inhumanly; without this it would be worse. At the same time, despite all the abnormality and absurdity of the organization which we call the great European civilization, let the forces of the human spirit be healthy and intact; let it not dare to think that the ideal of the beautiful and the lofty has been dimmed; that the conceptions of good and evil are being distorted and twisted; that normality is continually replaced by conventionality; that simplicity and naturalness are perishing, being continually suppressed by accumulating deceit!"

The second solution is the reverse: "Inasmuch as society is abnormally organized, it is impossible to make the human entity responsible for its consequences. Therefore, the criminal is irresponsible, and at present crime does not exist. To overcome crime and human guilt, it is necessary to overcome the abnormality of society and its structure. Since it takes long to cure the existing order of things, and besides, inasmuch as no medicine has been discovered, it is necessary to destroy society *in toto* and to sweep away the old order, as it were with a broom. After that everything has to be started anew, upon different foundations, which are still unknown, but which nevertheless cannot be worse than the existing order and which, contrariwise, comprise many chances for success. The main hope is in science."

Such, then, is the second solution: people are looking forward to the future ant-hill, and meanwhile the world will be stained with blood. No other solutions of guilt and human delinquency are being offered by the Western European world.

However, in the Russian author's approach to culpability and human delinquency it is clearly revealed that no ant-hill, no triumph of "the fourth estate," no elimination of poverty, no organization of labor will save mankind from abnormality, and therefore,—from guilt and criminality. This is expressed in an immense psychological analysis of the human soul, with tremendous depth and potency, with a realism of artistic portrayal hitherto unknown in Russia. It is clear and intelligible to the point of obviousness that evil in mankind is concealed deeper than the physician-socialists suppose; that in no organization of society can evil be eliminated; that the human soul will remain identical; that abnormality and sin emanate from the soul itself, and finally, that the laws of the human spirit are so unknown to science, so obscure, so indeterminate and mysterious, that, as yet, there can neither be physicians nor *final* judges, but that there is only He who saith: "Vengeance belongeth unto me; I will recompense." He alone knows the *whole* mystery of the world and man's ultimate destiny. And man, as yet, with the pride of infallibility, should not venture to solve anything—the times and the seasons have not yet come. The human judge himself must know that he *is* not the final judge; that he himself is a sinner; that in his hands—scales and measures will be an absurdity, *if* holding the scales and the measures he fails to submit to the law of the still insoluble mystery and to resort to the only solution—to Mercy and Love. And that man should not perish in despair of the ignorance of his paths and destinies, of the conviction of the mysterious and fatal inevitability of evil, he has been given a solution. It is cleverly traced by the poet in the ingenious scene of the penultimate part of the novel,—in the scene of the mortal illness of the heroine, when criminals and enemies are suddenly transformed into superior beings, into brothers, who have forgiven each other everything; beings who by mutual all-forgiveness, have removed from themselves deceit, guilt and crime, and thereby at once acquitted themselves with full cognizance of the fact that they have become entitled to acquittal.

But later, at the end of the novel, in a dark and dreadful picture of the degradation of the human spirit, traced step by step, in the delineation of that fatal condition when evil, having taken possession of man binds his every move, paralyzes every desire of resistance, every thought, every wish to combat darkness, invading the soul, which deliberately, with delight, with a passion for vengeance, is conceived by the soul as light,—in that picture there is so much edification for the human judge, for him who holds the scales and the measures that, of course, he will exclaim with fear and perplexity: "Nay, it is not always that vengeance belongeth unto me, and not always I who shall recompense." And he will not cruelly accuse the gloomily fallen criminal of having neglected the light of the solution,—always pointed out to him—and of having *deliberately* rejected it. At least, the human judge will not cling to the letter of the law.

If we possess literary works of such power of thought and execution, why couldn't we *later* have *our own* science, our economic and social solutions? Why does Europe deny us independence, *our own* word?—These questions arise of their own accord. Indeed, one cannot presume the ridiculous thought that nature has bestowed upon us merely literary gifts. All the rest is a matter of history, of circumstances and of conditions of time. Thus, at least, our Europeans should be reasoning in anticipation of the judgment of the European Europeans.

From *The Diary of a Writer*,
translated and annotated by Boris Brasol, 1949

THE NATION

'Anna Karénine' is purely a novel, and a Russian novel. But it is not a novel in the ordinary sense of the word; there is, so to speak, no story. It is not the development of a certain plot, with a beginning, a middle, and an end; it is rather a succession of pictures, of scenes, some of which seem hardly to have any connection with the principal scenes. Such is Tolstoi's manner, so far as he has a manner. He paints life such as it is, sometimes solemn and sometimes dull; tragical and commonplace—light and shadow constantly intermingled. His actors are numerous, their name is legion. The heroes and heroines are not always alone on the stage: they are constantly drawn among people who care nothing or who care little for their passions, their preoccupations. They move in a real atmosphere of dullness, of banality, of vulgarity, of levity, of indifference. It would seem as if the interest we took in them would be diminished by this juxtaposition or interposition; it is not so. On the contrary, the contrast between the tragical elements of life and the comical or dull elements increases our interest. Tolstoi shows us life as it really is, with its complexities, its necessary tedium, its frivolities. He does not deceive us: his finest characters have their weak points; he knows that perfection is not human. It would be an impossible task to give a suitable account of 'Anna Karénine,' considered as a novel. We must go a little beneath the surface, and try to find out if Tolstoi had an object in this extraordinary delineation of human life. He does not belong to the school of writers who let you know at once what their aim is, and where they are leading you; still, it seems as if he had been thinking of contrasting love, considered in its domestic aspects—legal love, if I may say so—observed in the family life, under common, ordinary, provincial circumstances; and love, as an uncontrollable passion— wild, lawless, destructive of the family affections and ties, of all social rules.

From "Tolstoi's New Novel," August 6, 1885

WILLIAM DEAN HOWELLS

I read *Anna Karenina* with a deepening sense of the author's unrivaled greatness. I thought that I saw through his eyes a human affair of that most sorrowful sort as it must appear to the Infinite Compassion; the book is a sort of revelation of human nature in circumstances that have been so perpetually lied about that we have almost lost the faculty of perceiving the truth concerning an illicit love. When you have once read *Anna Karenina* you know how fatally miserable and essentially unhappy such a love must be. But the character of Karenin himself is quite as important as the intrigue of Anna and Vronsky. It is wonderful how such a man, cold, Philistine and even mean in certain ways, towers into a sublimity unknown (to me, at least,) in fiction when he forgives, and yet knows that he cannot forgive with dignity. There is something crucial, and something triumphant, not beyond the power, but hitherto beyond the imagination of men in this effect, which is not solicited, not forced, not in the least romantic, but comes naturally, almost inevitably from the make of man.

From "Tolstoy" in *My Literary Passions*, 1895

MATTHEW ARNOLD

We are not to take *Anna Karénine* as a work of art; we are to take it as a piece of life. A piece of life it is. The author has not invented and combined it, he has seen it; it has all happened before his inward eye, and it was in this wise that it happened. Levine's shirts were packed up, and he was late for his wedding in consequence; Warinka and Serge Ivanitch met at Levine's countryhouse and went out walking together; Serge was very near proposing, but did not. The author saw it all happening so—saw it, and therefore relates it; and what his novel in this way loses in art it gains in reality.

For this is the result which, by his extraordinary fineness of perception, and by his sincere fidelity to it, the author achieves; he works in us a sense of the absolute reality of his personages and their doings. Anna's shoulders, and masses of hair, and half-shut eyes; Alexis Karénine's updrawn eyebrows, and tired smile, and cracking finger-joints; Stiva's eyes suffused with facile moisture—these are as real to us as any of those outward peculiarities which in our own circle of acquaintance we are noticing daily, while the inner man of our own circle of acquaintance, happily or unhappily, lies a great deal less clearly revealed to us than that of Count Tolstoi's creations.

From "Count Leo Tolstoy," published in *The Fortnightly Review*, December 1887

THOMAS MANN

Tolstoy's judgements were those of a great man, arbitrary, objective, and uncompromisingly literal. One need not go back to his unfavourable comparison of Shakespeare, as immoral, with *Uncle Tom's Cabin*. But has he dealt more "justly" with his own work? Certainly not when he discarded his Titanic masterpieces as irrelevant and harmful beguilements. Earlier, indeed, while writing *Anna Karenina*, that very greatest novel of society, he threw the manuscript aside as rubbish, again and again; and had no higher regard for it later. This is hardly to be looked upon as mere morbid self-depreciation. He would not have tolerated such criticism from another. His standard of measurement was one he had found in himself. And such impatient disparagement of his own work is contradictorily an artist's acknowledgement of a self transcending his work. It may be a case of having to be more than the thing one creates; of greatness having its origin in something still greater. Apocalyptic wonders such as Leonardo, Goethe, Tolstoy, support the supposition. But why had

Tolstoy never the apologetic attitude to his prophesyings and sectarian doctrine, his ideas of moral improvement, that he has shown towards his artistic creations? Why has he never once held them up to ridicule? One is justified perhaps in this inference: since he is greater than his art, he would, naturally, be greater than his ideas.

Ah, yes—Tolstoy's opinions! Regarded as revelations, for that was their true character, autocratic pronunciamentos of what we call "personality" receiving authority from the workings of that natural magic which turned the manor-house in the Province of Tula into a shrine for distressed humanity, a world-centre radiating vitality and healing. Vitality and greatness, greatness and power, in what degree are they synonymous? It is the problem of the "great man." . . .

What modesty, what moral contagion lie in the endeavour to subdue inherent creative power—under no exterior compulsion—to "the search of truth alone" and to dedicate one's vital momentum to the service of humanity and the spirit! Though Tolstoy's genius may have miscarried a hundred times and his thought stumbled into childish, benighted, unbecoming digressions, his laborious anguish will always be "beautiful and great." It had its source in the perception of a very profound truth. Tolstoy realized that a new era was at hand, an age which would not be satisfied with an art serving merely to enhance life, but which would put socially significant virtues—leadership, decisiveness, and clear thought—above individual genius; and value morality and intelligence more than irresponsible beauty; and he never sinned against his innate greatness, never claimed a "great man's" licence to work confusion, atavism, and evil, but to the best of his understanding, in complete humility, laboured for that which is divinely reasonable.

From "Tolstoy" in *The Dial*, December 1928

VLADIMIR NABOKOV

Though one of the greatest love stories in world literature, *Anna Karenin* is of course not just a novel of adventure. Being deeply concerned with moral matters, Tolstoy was eternally preoccupied with issues of importance to all mankind at all times. Now, there is a moral issue in *Anna Karenin*, though not the one that a casual reader might read into it. This moral is certainly not that having committed adultery, Anna had to pay for it (which in a certain vague sense can be said to be the moral at the bottom of the barrel in *Madame Bovary*). Certainly not this, and for obvious reasons: had Anna remained with Karenin and skillfully concealed from the world her affair, she would not have paid for it first with her happiness and then with her life. Anna was not punished for her sin (she might have got away with that) nor for violating the conventions of a society, very temporal as all conventions are and having nothing to do with the eternal demands of morality. What was then the moral "message" Tolstoy has conveyed in his novel?

We can understand it better if we look at the rest of the book and draw a comparison between the Lyovin-Kitty story and the Vronski-Anna story. Lyovin's marriage is based on a metaphysical, not only physical, concept of love, on willingness for self-sacrifice, on mutual respect. The Anna-Vronski alliance was founded only in carnal love and therein lay its doom.

It might seem, at first blush, that Anna was punished by society for falling in love with a man who was not her husband. Now such a "moral" would be of course completely "immoral," and completely inartistic, incidentally, since other ladies of fashion, in that same society, were having as many love-affairs as they liked but having them in secrecy, under a dark veil. (Remember Emma's blue veil on her ride with Rodolphe and her dark veil in her rendezvous at Rouen with Leon.) But frank unfortunate Anna does not wear this veil of deceit. The decrees of society are temporary ones; what Tolstoy is interested in are the eternal demands of morality. And now comes the real moral point that he makes: Love cannot be exclusively carnal because then it is egotistic, and being egotistic it destroys instead of creating. It is thus sinful. And in order to make his point as artistically clear as possible, Tolstoy in a flow of extraordinary imagery depicts and places side by side, in vivid contrast, two loves: the carnal love of the Vronski-Anna couple (struggling amid their richly sensual but fateful and spiritually sterile emotions) and on the other hand the authentic, Christian love, as Tolstoy termed it, of the Lyovin-Kitty couple with the riches of sensual nature still there but balanced and harmonious in the pure atmosphere of responsibility, tenderness, truth, and family joys.

A biblical epigraph: Vengeance is *mine; I* will repay (saith the Lord) (*Romans* XII, verse 19). What are the implications? First, Society had no right to judge Anna; second, Anna had no right to punish Vronski by her revengeful suicide.

Joseph Conrad, a British novelist of Polish descent, writing to Edward Garnett, a writer of sorts, in a letter dated the 10th of June, 1902, said: "Remember me affectionately to your wife whose translation of Karenina is splendid. Of the thing itself I think but little, so that her merit shines with the greater lustre." I shall never forgive Conrad this crack.

From "Leo Tolstoy," *Lectures on Russian Literature*, 1981

READING GROUP GUIDE

1. When *Anna Karenina* was published, critics accused Tolstoy of writing a novel with too many characters, too complex a story line, and too many details. Henry James called Tolstoy's works "baggy monsters." In response, Tolstoy wrote of *Anna Karenina* "I am very proud of its architecture—its vaults are joined so that one cannot even notice where the keystone is." What do you make of Tolstoy's use of detail? Does it make for a more "realistic" novel?

2. The first line of *Anna Karenina*, "Happy families are all alike; every unhappy family is unhappy in its own way," can be interpreted a number of ways. What do you think Tolstoy means by this?

3. In your opinion, how well does Tolstoy, as a male writer, capture the perspectives of his female characters? Do you think *Anna Karenina* is the most appropriate title for the book? Is Tolstoy more critical of Anna for her adultery than he is of Oblonsky or of Vronsky?

4. What role does religion play in the novel? Compare Levin's spiritual state of mind at the beginning and the end of the novel. What parallels can you draw between Levin's search for happiness and Anna's descent into despair?

5. Why is it significant that Karenin lives in St. Petersburg, Oblonsky in Moscow, and Levin in the country? How are Moscow and St. Petersburg described by Tolstoy? What conclusions can you draw about the value assigned to *place* in the novel?

6. What are the different kinds of love that Anna, Vronsky, Levin, Kitty, Stiva, and Dolly seek? How do their desires change throughout the novel?

7. How do the ideals of love and marriage come into conflict in *Anna Karenina*? Using examples from the novel, what qualities do you think seem to make for a successful marriage? According to Tolstoy, is it more important to find love at all costs or to uphold the sanctity of marriage, even if it is a loveless one?

8. Ultimately, do you think *Anna Karenina* is a tragic novel or a hopeful one?